NOVELS

The Cleric Quintet

Canticle

In Sylvan Shadows

Night Masks

The Fallen Fortress

The Chaos Curse

R.A. Salvatore

FORGOTTEN REALMS

THE CLERIC QUINTET

Distributed to the book trade in the United States by Random House, Inc. and in Canada by Random House of Canada Ltd.

Distributed to the toy and hobby trade by regional distributors.

Distributed worldwide by Wizards of the Coast, Inc. and regional distributors.

Cover art by Daniel Horne

FORGOTTEN REALMS and the TSR logo are registered trademarks owned by TSR, Inc.

All TSR characters, character names, and the distinctive likenesses thereof are trademarks owned by TSR, Inc.

TSR, Inc. is a subsidiary of Wizards of the Coast, Inc.

First Printing: January 1999
Printed in the United States of America.
Library of Congress Catalog Card Number: 98-85777

9 8 7 6 5 4 3 2 1

21313XXX1501

ISBN: 0-7869-1313-4

U.S., CANADA, ASIA,
PACIFIC, & LATIN AMERICA
Wizards of the Coast, Inc.
P.O. Box 707
Renton, WA 98057-0707
+1-800-324-6496

EUROPEAN HEADQUARTERS
Wizards of the Coast, Belgium
P.B. 34
2300 Turnhout
Belgium
+32-14-44-30-44

Visit our website at **www.tsr.com**

DEDICATIONS

Canticle
To anyone who can honestly call himself a friend of the Earth.
And a special thanks to Brian Newton—he knows why.

In Sylvan Shadows
To Bryan, Geno, and Caitlin,
my three little motivation pills.

Night Masks
To Aunt Terry, who'll never know how much
her support has meant to me.

The Fallen Fortress
To Nancy,
for showing true courage.

The Chaos Curse
To Ann and Bruce,
for showing me a different way
of looking at the world.

Foreword

R.A. Salvatore

We were done with Drizzt.

Or at least, we thought we were. After the Dark Elf Trilogy (bringing the number of novels featuring Drizzt and his friends to six), the editors at TSR and I agreed we had seen enough of the drow ranger. But we wanted to keep working together, since the combination had proven so successful (I actually had finished the last of the Dark Elf Trilogy, *Sojourn*, soon after *The Halfling's Gem* became my first *New York Times* best-seller).

Mary Kirchoff, TSR Books' executive editor, and my editor, Eric Severson, got together on a conference call and tried to figure out what might be next for me. They suggested I come up with a synopsis for a four-book series. Seeing an opportunity because of the scheduling (they were scheduling for the two years after *Sojourn's* release, and *Sojourn* was slated to come out early in the year), and being a fan of David Eddings's Belgariad five-book set, I suggested that I outline a series of not four, but five new novels, and that I place the heroes in a new (for me, at least) part of the FORGOTTEN REALMS® setting.

Of course, this being TSR, I didn't have a lot of time to put those outlines together. I wasn't worried, though, because I had a main character clearly defined. I subscribe to the school of writing that believes that characters are more important than plot, so with my hero in mind, I figured the rest would just fall into place.

It did. My favorite AD&D® player characters are First Edition monks. I love monks, mostly because they improve in so many ways as they acquire levels in the game. I didn't have any player characters in mind for the lead of my next series—I never (with the exception of Oliver deBurrows from my Crimson Shadow

v

Trilogy) use characters I have roleplayed as characters in my novels—but I envisioned a man like David Carradine in the old *Kung Fu* television shows: a good and just man, trying to find the truth about himself, traveling the Realms and helping out where he could. I had recently finished the Bloodstone Lands sourcebook, and that area includes the Monastery of the Yellow Rose, which I had fleshed out quite a bit in the game product, so I figured I had a built-in home base.

The other reason a monk character appealed to me was the combat style. I had already gotten a reputation for choreographing pretty good battle scenes, and I thought that going from the twin-scimitar-wielding drow and the warhammer-wielding barbarian to a character with an open-hand style would create a new level of intimacy in the fighting scenes and a new battle choreography that, having been a nightclub bouncer for six years, I knew well.

By the time I called Mary and Eric back the following week, I was raring to go.

Two problems immediately arose. First, by TSR's estimation the Bloodstone Lands had been the setting for too many products, so my planned monastery was out. Second, we had entered Second Edition, in which monks had gone the way of demons and devils. While Mary and Eric liked the concept, they couldn't do a major five-book series featuring a class of character no longer part of the game. I wasn't happy, but such are the trials of professional writing.

I became even more unhappy when Mary told me that what they really wanted was a series about a cleric.

"A cleric?" I echoed incredulously.

"It'll be great."

"Yeah, right. Face it, the cleric is usually the guy who shows up last to the gaming table, a big, stupid smile on his face, saying, 'Hey, guys, I want to play. What's the party need?' To which everyone replies, 'We need healing. You're the priest. Shut up and sit down.'" (My apologies to any of you cleric-philes out there—actually, I've started running clerics almost every time I play.)

But still, the cleric back then (remember, this was pre-*Faiths and Avatars* and other such wonderful products) was not the most popular of AD&D classes.

I got off the phone, muttering more curses than an embarrassed dwarf and already missing my dear monk. Being a professional writer, though (whatever the heck that means), I took up my AD&D books and began studying the character class and the options the various gods left open to me. I found Deneir, a god of the Realms who gave great latitude for questioning to his followers. On a purely basic level, don't we all question our faith repeatedly throughoutour lives?

Now it was beginning to click. Those little writer lights were going on in my head. Instead of worrying about a character class for a lead hero in the books, I began to consider a spiritual journey this guy might take. Thus Cadderly was born, a man who grows increasingly powerful within the church of Deneir but who believes that clerical magic is just another variation of wizardly magic, not some gift of a pantheon of gods. He's a priest who, throughout the first two, and most of the third, books in the series, is actually an agnostic.

He's a priest of Deneir, a priest of a god who allows, even favors, questioning.

I remember receiving a letter shortly after the series came out, which began, "I am a born-again Christian. . . ." I braced for the storm, not because I have anything against born-again Christians—certainly not!—but because DUNGEONS AND DRAGONS® has often been misunderstood by many fundamentalist religious groups. This letter, however, went on to explain to me that the writer completely identified with Cadderly's discovery of Deneir because his own spiritual journey had been exactly like that: a series of small discoveries leading to an overwhelming epiphany. I consider that among the highest compliments I've ever received as a writer, because that is exactly the type of journey I had envisioned for Cadderly, the type of journey that I, like so many others, have been taking for most of my adult life.

Looking back, I really loved writing this series, not only because of the profound spiritual side, but because of the humor of Ivan and Pikel Bouldershoulder (Chapter 11 of the second book, In *Sylvan Shadows*, remains my all-time favorite), the relationship of Cadderly and Danica, more mature than anything I had tried with Drizzt, and several intriguing villains: the battered and confused Kierkan Rufo, and my favorite of the series—one I believes rivals Artemis Entreri—Ghost.

Do I have regrets about the series? Of course—a writer always does. I still would have liked to write the Monk Quintet. My biggest regret, though, was that shortly after beginning the series, the call for more Drizzt, to TSR and to me, became overwhelming, and so I agreed to do another Drizzt book, *The Legacy*, and then another, *Starless Night*, and so on and so on. . . .

I'm not complaining about those books, not at all! *The Legacy* was my first hardcover, and my first *New York Times* best-selling hardcover at that, and it truly changed my life. Shortly after *The Legacy* came out, I began getting letters from readers who liked the early Cleric books but complained that *Canticle*, first of the series, was a bit slow. I knew what was going on, and there was nothing I could do about it. These readers, in picking up an R.A. Salvatore book, wanted to immediately find the level of familiarity with the new characters that they already enjoyed with the Companions of the Hall (Drizzt and company).

It's not fair to compare *Canticle* to the six novels with Drizzt that came before it. You have to compare it one-on-one to *The Crystal Shard*, ignoring the other Drizzt books. In that context, I believe it holds up quite well. Perhaps going back to Drizzt in the middle of the Cleric Quintet prevented the new story from getting the attention it deserved.

Almost all of those people I know who read the series through, who took the time to get to know Cadderly and Danica, Percival and the Bouldershoulders, were quite pleased with the result and consider this group friends. So maybe I'll deviate from Drizzt and his friends again in the Realms. Maybe I'll write that monk series I once planned.

Or maybe, with Danica, I already did.

The Cleric Quintet · Book One

Canticle

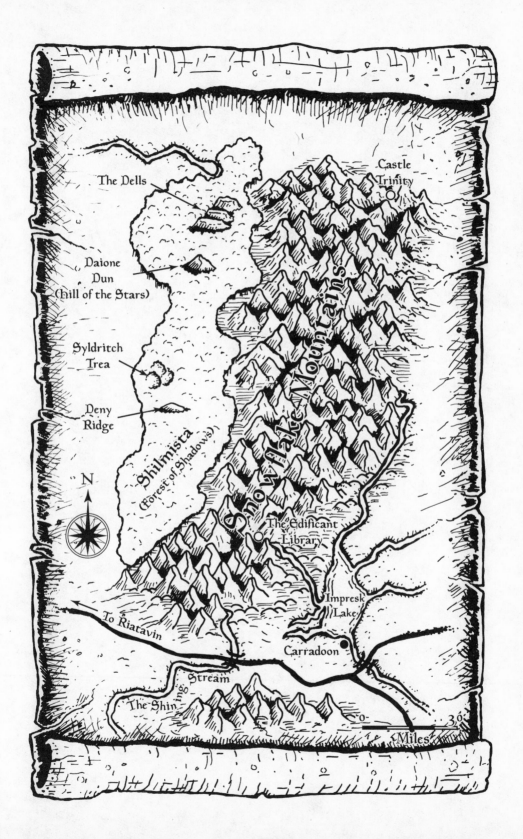

The Dells

Castle
Trinity

Daione
Dun
(hill of the Stars)

Syldritch
Trea

Deny
Ridge

Shilmista
(Forest of Shadows)

N

Snowflake Mountains

The Edificant
Library

To Riatavin

Impresk
Lake

Carradoon

The Shin-ing Stream

0   30

Miles

Prologue

Aballister Bonaduce looked long and hard at the shimmering image in his mirror. Mountains of wind-driven snow and ice lay endlessly before him, the most forbidding place in all the Realms. All he had to do was step through the mirror, onto the Great Glacier.

"Are you coming, Druzil?" the wizard said to his bat-winged imp.

Druzil folded his leathery wings around him as if to privately consider the question. "I am not so fond of the cold," he said, obviously not wanting to partake of this particular hunt. "Nor am I," Aballister said, slipping onto his finger an enchanted ring that would protect him from the killing cold. "But only on the Great Glacier does the *yote* grow." Aballister looked back to the scene in the magical mirror, one final barrier to the completion of his quest and the beginning of his conquests. The snowy region was quiet now, though dark clouds hung ominously overhead and promised an impending storm that would delay the hunt, perhaps for many days.

"There we must go," Aballister continued, talking more to himself than to the imp. His voice trailed away as he sank within his memories, to the turning point in his life more than two years before, in the Time of Troubles. He had been powerful even then, but directionless.

The avatar of the goddess Talona had shown him the way.

Aballister's grin became an open chuckle as he turned back to regard Druzil, the imp who had delivered to him the method to best please the Lady of Poison. "Come, dear Druzil," Aballister said. "You brought the recipe for the chaos curse. You must come along and help to find its last ingredient."

The imp straightened and unfolded his wings at the mention of the chaos curse. This time he offered no arguments. A lazy flap brought him to Aballister's

1

shoulder and together they walked through the magical mirror and into the blowing wind.

* * * * *

The hunched and hairy creature, resembling a more primitive form of human, grunted and growled and threw its crude spear, though Aballister and Druzil were surely far out of range. It howled again anyway, triumphantly, as though its throw had served some symbolic victory, and scooted back to the large gathering of its shaggy white kin.

"I believe they do not wish to bargain," Druzil said, shuffling about from clawed foot to clawed foot on Aballister's shoulder.

The wizard understood his familiar's excitement. Druzil was a creature of the lower planes, a creature of chaos, and he wanted desperately to see his wizard master deal with the impudent fools—just an added pleasure to this long-awaited, victorious day.

"They are taer," Aballister explained, recognizing the tribe, "crude and fierce. You are quite correct. They'll not bargain."

Aballister's eyes flashed suddenly and Druzil hopped again and clapped his hands together.

"They know not the might before them!" Aballister cried, his voice rising with his ire. All the terrible trials of two long and brutal years rolled through the wizard's thoughts in the span of a few seconds. A hundred men had died in search of the elusive ingredients for the chaos curse; a hundred men had given their lives so that Talona would be pleased. Aballister, too, had not escaped unscathed. Completing the curse had become his obsession, the driving force in his life, and he had aged with every step, had torn out clumps of his own hair every time the curse seemed to be slipping beyond his reach.

Now he was close, so close that he could see the dark patch of yote just beyond the small ridge that held the taer cave complexes. So close, but these wretched, idiotic creatures stood in his way.

Aballister's words had stirred the taer. They grumbled and hopped about in the shadow of the jagged mountain, shoving each other forward as if trying to select a leader to start their charge.

"Do something quickly," Druzil suggested from his perch.

Aballister looked up at him and nearly laughed. "They will attack," Druzil explained, trying to sound unconcerned, "and, worse, this cold stiffens my wings."

Aballister nodded at the imp's rationale. Any delay could cost him, especially if the dark clouds broke into a blinding blizzard, one that would hide both the *yote* and the shimmering doorway back to Aballister's comfortable room. He pulled out a tiny ball, a mixture of bat guano and sulphur, crushed it in his fist, and pointed one finger at the group of taer. His chant echoed off the mountain face and back across the empty glacier ice, and he smiled, thinking it wonderfully ironic that the stupid taer had no idea of what he was doing.

A moment later, they found out.

Just before his spell discharged, Aballister had a cruel thought and lifted the angle of his pointing finger. The fireball exploded above the heads of the startled taer, disintegrating the frozen bindings of the ice mountain. Huge blocks rained down, and a great rush of water swallowed those who had not been crushed. Several of the band floundered about in the ice and liquid morass, too stunned and overwhelmed to gain their footing as the pool quickly solidified around them.

One pitiful creature did manage to struggle free, but Druzil hopped off Aballister's shoulder and swooped down upon him.

The imp's claw-tipped tail whipped out as he passed by the stumbling creature, and Aballister applauded heartily.

The taer clutched at its stung shoulder, looked curiously at the departing imp, then fell dead to the ice.

"What of the rest?" Druzil asked, landing back on his perch.

Aballister considered the remaining taer, most dead, but some struggling futilely against the tightening grip of ice.

"Leave them to their slow deaths," he replied, and he laughed evilly again.

Druzil gave him an incredulous look. "The Lady of Poison would not approve," the imp said, wagging his wicked tail before him with one hand.

"Very well," Aballister replied, though he realized that Druzil was more interested in pleasing himself than Talona. Still, the reasoning was sound; poison was always the accepted method for completing Talona's work. "Go and finish the task," Aballister instructed the imp. "I will get the yote."

A short while later, Aballister plucked the last gray-brown mushroom from its stubborn grasp on the glacier and dropped it into his bag. He called over to Druzil, who was toying with the last whining taer, snapping his tail back and forth around the terrified creature's frantically jerking head—the only part of the taer that was free of the ice trap.

"Enough," Aballister said firmly.

Druzil sighed and looked mournfully at the approaching wizard. Aballister's visage did not soften. "Enough," he said again.

Druzil bent over and kissed the taer on the nose. The creature stopped whimpering and looked at him curiously, but Druzil only shrugged and drove his poison-tipped stinger straight into the taer's weepy eye.

The imp eagerly accepted the offered perch on Aballister's shoulder. Aballister let him hold the bag of *yote*, just to remind the somewhat distracted imp that more important matters awaited them beyond the shimmering door.

One
The White Squirrel's Pet

The green-robed druid issued a series of chit-chits and clucks, but the white-furred squirrel seemed oblivious to it all, sitting on a branch in the towering oak tree high above the three men.

"Well, you seem to have lost your voice," remarked another of the men, a bearded woodland priest with gentle-looking features and thick blond hair hanging well below his shoulders.

"Can you call the beast any better than I?" the green-robed druid asked indignantly. "I fear that this creature is strange in more ways than its coat."

The other two laughed at their companion's attempt to explain his ineptitude.

"I grant you," said the third of the group, the highest ranking initiate, "the squirrel's color is beyond the usual, but speaking to animals is among the easiest of our abilities. Surely by now—"

"With all respect," the frustrated druid interrupted, "I have made contact with the creature. It just refuses to reply. Try yourself, I invite you."

"A squirrel refusing to speak?" asked the second of the group with a chuckle. "Surely they are among the chattiest—"

"Not that one," came a reply from behind. The three druids turned to see a priest coming down the wide dirt road from the ivy-streaked building, the skip of youth evident in his steps.

He was of average height and build, though perhaps more muscular than most, with gray eyes that turned up at their corners when he smiled and curly brown locks that bounced under the wide brim of his hat. His tan-white tunic and trousers showed him to be a priest of Deneir, god of one of the host sects of the Edificant Library. Unlike most within his order, though, this young man also wore a decorative light blue silken cape and a wide-brimmed hat, also blue and banded in red,

4

with a plume on the right-hand side. Set in the band's center was a porcelain-and-gold pendant depicting a candle burning above an eye, the symbol of Deneir.

"That squirrel is tight-lipped, except when he chooses not to be," the young priest went on. The normally unflappable druids' stunned expressions amused him, so he decided to startle them a bit more. "Well met, Arcite, Newander, and Cleo. I congratulate you, Cleo, on your ascension to the status of initiate."

"How do you know of us?" asked Arcite, the druid leader.

"We have not yet reported to the library and have told no one of our coming." Arcite and Newander, the blond-haired priest, exchanged suspicious glances, and Arcite's voice became stem. "Have your masters been scrying, looking for us with magical means?"

"No, no, nothing like that," the young priest replied immediately, knowing the secretive druids' aversion to such tactics. "I remember you, all three, from your last visit to the library."

"Preposterous!" piped in Cleo. "That was fourteen years ago. You could not have been more than . . ."

"A boy," answered the young priest. "So I was, seven years old. You had a fourth to your party, as I recall, an aging lady of great powers. Shannon, I believe was her name!"

"Incredible," muttered Arcite. "You are correct, young priest." Again the druids exchanged concerned looks, suspecting trickery here. Druids were not overly fond of anyone not of their order; they rarely came to the renowned Edificant Library, sitting high in the secluded Snowflake Mountains, and then only when they had word of a discovery of particular interest, a rare tome of herbs or animals, or a new recipe for potions to heal wounds or better grow their gardens. As a group, they began to turn away, rudely, but then Newander, on a sudden impulse, spun back around to face the young priest, who now leaned casually on a fine walking stick, its silver handle sculpted masterfully into the image of a ram's head.

"Cadderly?" Newander asked through a widening grin. Arcite, too, recognized the young man and remembered the unusual story of the most unusual child. Cadderly had come to live at the library before his fifth birthday—rarely were any accepted before the age of ten. His mother had died several months before that, and his father, too immersed in studies of his own, had neglected the child. Thobicus, the dean of the Edificant Library, had heard of the promising boy and had generously taken him in.

"Cadderly," Arcite echoed. "Is that really you?"

"At your service," Cadderly replied, bowing low, "and well met. I am honored that you remember me, good Newander and venerable Arcite."

"Who?" Cleo whispered, looking curiously to Newander.

Cleo's face, too, brightened in recognition a few moments later.

"Yes, you were just a boy," said Newander, "an overly curious little boy, as I recall!"

"Forgive me," said Cadderly, bowing again. "One does not often find the opportunity to converse with a troupe of druids!"

"Few would care to," remarked Arcite, "but you . . . are among that few, so it would appear."

Cadderly nodded, but his smile suddenly disappeared. "I pray that nothing has happened to Shannon," he said, truly concerned. The druid had treated him well on that long-ago occasion. She had shown him beneficial plants, tasty roots, and had made flowers bloom before his eyes. To Cadderly's astonishment, Shannon had transformed herself, an ability of the most powerful druids, into a graceful swan and had flown high into the morning sky. Cadderly had dearly wished to join her—he remembered that longing most vividly—but the druid had no power to similarly transform him.

"Nothing terrible, if that is what you mean," replied Arcite.

"She died several years back, peacefully."

Cadderly nodded. He was about to offer his condolences, but he prudently remembered that druids neither feared nor lamented death, seeing it as the natural conclusion to life and a rather unimportant event in the overall scheme of universal order.

"Do you know this squirrel?" asked Cleo suddenly, determined to restore his reputation.

"Percival," Cadderly replied, "a friend of mine."

"A pet?" Newander asked, his bright eyes narrowing suspiciously. Druids did not approve of people keeping pets.

Cadderly laughed heartily. "If any is the pet in our relationship, I fear it is I," he said honestly. "Percival accepts my strokes—sometimes—and my food—rather eagerly—but as I am more interested in him than he in me, he is the one who decides when and where."

The druids shared Cadderly's laugh. "A most excellent beast," said Arcite, then with a series of clicks and chits, he congratulated Percival.

"Wonderful," came Cadderly's sarcastic response, "encourage him." The druids' laughter increased and Percival, watching it all from his high branch, shot Cadderly a supercilious look.

"Well, come down here and say hello!" Cadderly called, banging the lowest tree branch with his walking stick. "Be polite, at least."

Percival did not look up from the acorn he was munching. "He does not understand, I fear," said Cleo. "Perhaps if I translate . . ."

"He understands," Cadderly insisted, "as well as you or I. He is just a stubborn one, and I can prove it!" He looked back up to the squirrel. "When you find the time, Percival," he said slyly, "I left a plate of cacasa-nut and butter out for you in my room . . ." Before Cadderly even finished, the squirrel whipped off along a branch, hopped to another, and then to the next tree in line along the road. In a few short moments, the squirrel had leaped to a gutter along the library's roof and, not slowing a bit, zipped across a trail of thick ivy and in through an open window on the northern side of the large structure's third floor.

"Percival does have such a weakness for cacasa-nut and butter," Cadderly remarked when the druids' laughter had subsided.

"A most excellent beast!" Arcite said again. "And yourself, Cadderly, it is good to see that you have remained with your studies. Your masters spoke highly of your potential fourteen years ago, but I had no idea that your memory would be so very sharp or, perhaps, that we druids had left such a strong and favorable impression upon you."

"It is," Cadderly replied quietly, "and you did! I am glad that you have returned—for the recently uncovered treatise on woodland mosses, I would assume. I have not seen it yet. The headmasters have kept it secured until those more knowledgeable in such matters could come and appraise its value. You see, a band of druids was not wholly unexpected, though we knew not who, how many, or when you would arrive."

The three druids nodded, admiring the ivy-veiled stone structure. The Edificant Library had stood for six hundred years, and in all that time its doors had never been closed to scholars of any but the evil religions. The building was huge, a self-contained town—it had to be, in the rough and secluded Snowflakes—more than four hundred feet across and half as deep through all four of its above-ground levels. Well staffed and well stocked—rumors spoke of miles of storage tunnels and catacombs beneath—it had survived orc attacks, giant-hurled boulders, and the most brutal mountain winters, and had remained unscathed through the centuries.

The library's collection of books, parchments, and artifacts was considerable, filling nearly the entire first floor, the library proper, and many smaller study chambers on the second floor, and the complex contained many unique and ancient works.

While not as large as the great libraries of the Realms, such as the treasured collections of Silverymoon to the north and the artifact museums of Calimport to the south, the Edificant Library was convenient to the west-central Realms and the Cormyr region and was open to all who wished to learn, on the condition that they did not plan to use their knowledge for baneful purposes.

The building housed other important research tools, such as alchemy and herbalist shops, and was set in an inspiring atmosphere with breathtaking mountain views and manicured grounds that included a small topiary garden. The Edificant Library had been designed as more than a storage house for old books; it was a place for poetry reading, painting, and sculpting, a place for discussions of the profound and often unanswerable questions common to the intelligent races. Indeed, the library was a fitting tribute to Deneir and Oghma, the allied gods of knowledge, literature, and art.

"The treatise is a large work, so I have been told," said Arcite. "Much time will be expended in examining it properly. I pray that the boarding rates are not excessive. We are men of little material means."

"Dean Thobicus will take you in without cost, I would expect," answered Cadderly. "Your service cannot be underestimated in this matter." He shot a wink at Arcite. "If not, come to me. I recently inscribed a tome for a nearby wizard, a spellbook he lost in a fire. The man was generous. You see, I had originally inscribed the spellbook, and the wizard, forgetful as most wizards seem to be, never had made a copy."

"The work was unique?" Cleo asked, shaking his head in disbelief that a wizard could be so foolish with his most prized possession.

"It was," Cadderly replied, tapping his temple, "except for in here."

"You remembered the intricacies of a wizard's spellbook enough to recreate it from memory?" Cleo asked, stunned.

Cadderly shrugged his shoulders. "The wizard was generous."

"Truly you are a remarkable one, young Cadderly," said Arcite.

"A most excellent beast?" the young priest asked hopefully, drawing wide smiles from all three.

"Indeed!" said Arcite. "Do look in on us in the days ahead."

Given the druids' reputation for seclusion, Cadderly understood how great a compliment he had just been paid. He bowed low, and the druids did likewise, then they bid Cadderly farewell and moved up the road to the library.

Cadderly watched them, then looked up to his open window.

Percival sat on the sill, determinedly licking the remains of his cacasa-nut and butter lunch from his tiny paws.

* * * * *

A tiny drop slipped off the end of the coil, touching a saturated cloth that led down into a small beaker. Cadderly shook his head and put a hand on the spigot controlling the flow.

"Remove your hand from that!" cried the frantic alchemist from a workbench across his shop. He jumped up and stormed over to the too-curious young priest.

"It is terribly slow," Cadderly remarked.

"It has to be," Vicero Belago explained for perhaps the hundredth time. "You are no fool, Cadderly. You know better than to be impatient. This is *Oil of Impact*, remember? A most volatile substance. A stronger drip could cause a cataclysm in a shop so filled with unstable potions!"

Cadderly sighed and accepted the scolding with a conceding nod. "How much do you have for me?" he asked, reaching into one of the many pouches on his belt and producing a tiny vial.

"You are so very impatient," remarked Belago, but Cadderly knew that he was not really angry. Cadderly was a prime customer and had many times provided important translations of archaic alchemical notes. "Only what is in the beaker, I fear. I had to wait for some ingredients—hill giant fingernails and crushed oxen horn."

Cadderly gently lifted the soaked cloth and tilted the beaker.

It contained just a few drops, enough to fill only one of his tiny vials. "That makes six," he said, using the cloth to coax the liquid into the vial. "Forty-four to go."

"Are you confident that you want that many?" Belago asked him, not for the first time.

"Fifty," Cadderly declared.

"The price . . ."

"Well worth it!" Cadderly laughed as he secured his vial and skipped out of the shop. His spirits did not diminish as he moved down the hall to the southern wing of the third floor and the chambers of Histra, a visiting priestess of Sune, Goddess of Love.

"Dear Cadderly," greeted the priestess, who was twenty years Cadderly's senior but quite alluring. She wore a deep crimson habit, cut low in the front and high on the sides, revealing most of her curvy figure. Cadderly had to remind himself to keep his manners proper and his gaze on her eyes.

"Do come in," Histra purred. She grabbed the front of Cadderly's tunic and yanked him into the room, pointedly shutting the door behind him.

He managed to glance away from Histra long enough to see a brightly glowing object shining through a heavy blanket.

"Is it finished?" Cadderly asked squeakily. He cleared his throat, embarrassed.

Histra ran a finger lightly down his arm and smiled at his involuntary shudder. "The dweomer is cast," she replied. "All that remains is payment."

"Two hundred . . . gold pieces," Cadderly stammered, "as we agreed." He reached for a pouch, but Histra's hand intercepted his.

"It was a difficult spell," she said, "a variation of the norm."

She paused and gave a coy smile. "But I do so love variations," Histra declared teasingly. "The price could be less, you know, for you."

Cadderly did not doubt that his gulp was heard out in the hallway. He was a disciplined scholar and had come here for a specific purpose. He had much work to do, but Histra's allure was undeniable and her fine perfume overpowering. Cadderly reminded himself to breathe.

"We could forget the gold payment altogether," Histra offered, her fingers smoothly tracing the outline of Cadderly's ear. The young scholar wondered if he might fall over.

In the end, though, an image of spirited Danica sitting on Histra's back, casually rubbing the priestess's face across the floor, brought Cadderly under control. Danica's room was not far away, just across the hall and a few doors down. He firmly removed Histra's hand from his ear, handed her the pouch as payment, and scooped up the shrouded, glowing object.

For all his practicality, though, when Cadderly exited the chambers two hundred gold pieces poorer, he feared that his face was shining as brightly as the disk Histra had enchanted for him.

Cadderly had other business—he always did—but, not wanting to arouse suspicions by roaming about the library with an eerily glowing pouch, he made straight for the north wing and his own room. Percival was still on the windowsill when he entered, basking in the late morning sun.

"I have it!" Cadderly said excitedly, taking out the disk. The room immediately brightened, as if in full sunlight, and the startled squirrel darted for the shadows under Cadderly's bed.

Cadderly didn't take time to reassure Percival. He rushed to his desk and, from the jumbled and overfilled side drawer, produced a cylinder a foot long and two inches in diameter.

With a slight twist, Cadderly removed the casing from the back end, revealing a slot just large enough for the disk. He eagerly dropped the disk in and replaced the casing, shielding the light.

"I know you are under there," Cadderly teased, and he popped the metal cap off the front end of the tube, loosing a focused beam of light.

Percival didn't particularly enjoy the spectacle. He darted back and forth under the bed, and Cadderly, laughing that he had finally gotten the best of the sneaky squirrel, followed him diligently with the light. This went on for a few moments, until Percival dashed out from under the bed and hopped out the open window. The squirrel returned a second later, though, just long enough to snatch up the cacasa-nut and butter bowl and chatter a few uncomplimentary remarks to Cadderly.

Still laughing, the young priest capped his new toy and hung it on his belt, then moved to his oaken wardrobe. Most of the library's host priests kept their closets stocked with extra vestments, wanting always to look their best for the continual stream of visiting scholars. In Cadderly's wardrobe, however, the packed clothing took up just a small fraction of the space.

Piles of notes and even larger piles of various inventions cluttered the floor, and custom-designed leather belts and straps took up most of the hanging bar. Also, hanging inside one of the doors was a large mirror, an extravagance far beyond the meager purses of most other priests at the library, particularly the younger, lower-ranking ones such as Cadderly.

Cadderly took out a wide bandoleer and moved to the bed.

The leather shoulder harness contained fifty specially made darts and, with the vial he had taken from the alchemist's shop, Cadderly was about to complete the sixth. The darts were small and narrow and made of iron, except for silver tips, and their centers were hollowed to the exact size of the vials.

Cadderly flinched as he eased the vial into the dart, trying to exert enough pressure to snap it into place without breaking it.

"*Oil of Impact*," he reminded himself, conjuring images of blackened fingertips.

The young scholar breathed easier when the volatile potion was properly set. He removed his silken cape, meaning to put on the bandoleer and go to the mirror to see how it fit, as he always did after completing another dart, but a sharp rap on his door gave him just enough time to place the leather belt behind him before Headmaster Avery Schell, a rotund and redfaced man, burst in.

"What are these calls for payment?" the priest cried, waving a stack of parchments at Cadderly. He began peeling them off and tossing them to the floor as he read their banners. "Leatherworker, silversmith, weaponsmith . . . You are squandering your gold!"

Over Avery's shoulder, Cadderly noticed the toothy smile of Kierkan Rufo and knew where the headmaster had gained his information and the fuel for his ire. The tall and sharp-featured Rufo was only a year older than Cadderly, and the two, while friends, were principal rivals in their ascent through the ranks of their order, and possibly in other pursuits as well, considering a few longing stares Cadderly had seen Rufo toss Danica's way. Getting each other into trouble had become a game between them, a most tiresome game as far as the headmasters, particularly the beleaguered Avery, were concerned.

"The money was well spent, Headmaster," Cadderly began tentatively, well aware that his and Avery's interpretations of "well spent" differed widely. "In pursuit of knowledge."

"In pursuit of toys," Rufo remarked with a snicker from the doorway, and Cadderly noted the tall man's satisfied expression. Cadderly had earned the headmaster's highest praise for his work on the lost spellbook, to his rival's obvious dismay, and Rufo was obviously enjoying bringing Cadderly back down.

"You are too irresponsible to be allowed to keep such sums!" Avery roared, heaving the rest of the parchments into the air. "You have not the wisdom."

"I kept only a portion of the profits," Cadderly reminded him, "and spent that in accord with Deneir's—"

"No!" Avery interrupted. "Do not hide behind a name that you obviously do not understand. Deneir. What do you know of Deneir, young inventor? You have spent all but your earliest years here in the Edificant Library, but you display so little understanding of our tenets and mores. Go south to Lantan with your toys, if that would please you, and play with the priests of Gond!"

"I do not understand."

"Indeed you do not," Avery answered, his tone becoming almost resigned. He paused for a long moment, and Cadderly recognized that he was choosing his words very carefully.

"We are a center of learning," the headmaster began. "We impose few restrictions upon those who wish to come here—even Gondsmen have ventured through our doors. You have seen them, but have you noticed that they were never warmly received?"

Cadderly thought for a moment, then nodded. Indeed, he remembered clearly that Avery had gone out of his way to keep him from meeting the Gondish priests every time they visited the library. "You are correct, and I do not understand," Cadderly replied. "I should think that priests of Deneir and Gond, dedicated to knowledge, would act as partners."

Avery shook his head slowly and very determinedly. "There you err," he said. "We put a condition on knowledge that the Gondsmen do not follow." He paused and shook his head again, a simple action that stung Cadderly more than any wild screaming fit Avery had ever launched at him.

"Why are you here?" Avery asked quietly, in controlled tones. "Have you ever asked yourself that question? You frustrate me, boy. You are perhaps the most intelligent person I have ever known—and I have known quite a few scholars—but you possess the impulses and emotions of a child. I knew it would be like this. When Thobicus said we would take you in . . ." Avery stopped abruptly, as if reconsidering his words, then finished with a sigh.

It seemed to Cadderly that the headmaster always stopped short of finishing this same, beleaguered point about morality, stopped short of preaching, as though he expected Cadderly to come to conclusions of his own. Cadderly was not surprised a moment later when Avery abruptly changed the subject.

"What of your duties while you sit here in your 'pursuit of knowledge'?" the headmaster asked, his voice filling with anger once again. "Did you bother to light the candles in the study chambers this morning?"

Cadderly flinched. He knew he had forgotten something.

"I did not think so," Avery said. "You are a valuable asset to our order, Cadderly, and undeniably gifted as both a scholar and scribe, but, I warn you, your behavior is far from acceptable." Avery's face flushed bright red as Cadderly, still not properly sorting through the headmaster's concerns for him, met his unblinking stare.

Cadderly was almost used to these scoldings; it was Avery who always came rushing to investigate Rufo's claims. Cadderly did not think that a bad thing; Avery, for all his fuming, was surely more lenient than some of the other, older, headmasters.

Avery turned suddenly, nearly knocking Rufo over, and stormed down the hallway, sweeping the angular man up in his wake.

Cadderly shrugged and tried to dismiss the whole incident as another of Headmaster Avery's misplaced explosions. Avery obviously just didn't understand him. The young priest wasn't overly worried; his scribing skills brought in huge amounts of money, which he split evenly with the library. Admittedly, he was not the most dutiful follower of Deneir. He was lax concerning the rituals of his station and it often got him into trouble. But Cadderly knew that most of the headmasters understood that his indiscretions came not from any disrespect for the order, but simply because he was so busy learning and creating, two very high priorities in the teachings of Deneir—and two often profitable priorities for the expensive-to-maintain library. By Cadderly's figuring, the priests of Deneir, like most religious orders, could find it in their hearts to overlook minor indiscretions, especially considering the greater gain.

"Oh, Rufo," Cadderly called, reaching to his belt.

Rufo's angular face poked back around the jamb of the open door, his little black eyes sparkling with victorious glee.

"Yes?" the tall man purred.

"You won that one."

Rufo's grin widened.

Cadderly shone a beam of light in his face, and the stunned Rufo recoiled in terror, bumping heavily against the wall across the corridor.

"Keep your eyes open," Cadderly said through a wide smile. "The next attack is mine." He gave a wink, but Rufo, realizing the relatively inoffensive nature of Cadderly's newest invention, only sneered back, brushed his matted black hair aside, and rushed away, his hard black boots clomping on the tiled floor as loudly as a shoed horse on cobblestones.

* * * * *

The three druids were granted a room in a remote corner of the fourth floor, far from the bustle of the library, as Arcite had requested. They settled in easily, not having much gear, and Arcite suggested they set off at once to study the newly found moss tome.

"I shall remain behind," Newander replied. "It was a long road, and I am truly weary. I would be no help to you with my eyes falling closed."

"As you wish," Arcite said. "We shall not be gone too long. Perhaps you can go down and pick up on the work when we have ended."

Newander moved to the room's window when his friends had gone and stared out across the majestic Snowflake Mountains. He had been to the Edificant Library only once before, when he had first met Cadderly. Newander had been but a young man then, about the same age as Cadderly was now, and the library, with its bustle of humanity, crafted items, and penned tomes, had affected him deeply. Before he had come, Newander had known only the quiet woodlands, where the animals ruled and men were few.

After he had left, Newander had questioned his calling. He preferred the woodlands, that much he knew, but he could not deny the attraction he felt for civilization, the curiosity about advances in architecture and knowledge.

Newander had remained a druid, though, a servant of Silvanus, the Oak Father, and had done well in his studies. The natural order was of primary importance, by his sincere measure, but still . . .

It was not without concern that Newander had returned to the Edificant Library. He looked out at majestic mountains and wished he were out there, where the world was simple and safe.

Two
Agent of Talona

From a distance, the rocky spur at the northeastern edge of the Snowflake Mountains seemed quite unremarkable: piles of strewn boulders covering tightly packed slopes of smaller stones. But so, too, to those who did not know better, might a wolverine seem an innocuous thing. A dozen separate tunnels led under that rocky slope, and each of them promised only death to wayward adventurers seeking shelter from the night.

This particular mountain spur, which was far from natural, housed Castle Trinity, a castle-in-mountain's-clothing, a fortress for an evil brotherhood determined to gain in power.

Wary must wanderers be in the Realms, for civilization often ends at a city wall.

"Will it work?" Aballister whispered nervously, tentatively fingering the precious parchment. Rationally, he held faith in the recipe—Talona had led him to it—but after so much pain and trouble, and with the moment of victory so close at hand, he could not prevent a bit of apprehension. He looked up from the scroll and out a small window in the fortified complex. The Shining Plains lay flat and dark to the east, and the setting sun lit reflected fires on the Snowflake Mountains' snow-capped peaks to the west.

The small imp folded his leathery wings around in front of himself and crossed his arms over them, impatiently tapping one clawed foot. "*Quiesta bene tellemara,*" he mumbled under his breath.

"What was that?" Aballister replied, turning sharply and cocking one thin eyebrow at his often impertinent familiar. "Did you say something, Druzil?"

"It will work, I said. It will work," Druzil lied in his raspy, breathless voice. "Would you doubt the Lady Talona? Would you doubt her wisdom in bringing us together?"

Aballister muttered suspiciously, accepting the suspected insult as an unfortunate but unavoidable consequence of having so wise and wicked a familiar. The lean wizard knew that Druzil's translation was less than accurate, and that "quiesta bene tellemara" was undoubtedly something uncomplimentary. He didn't doubt Druzil's appraisal of the powerful potion, though, and that somehow unnerved him most of all. If Druzil's claims for the chaos curse proved true, Aballister and his evil companions would soon realize more power than even the ambitious wizard had ever hoped for. For many years Castle Trinity had aspired to conquer the Snowflake Mountain region, the elven wood of Shilmista, and the human settlement of Carradoon. Now, with the chaos curse, that process might soon begin.

Aballister looked beside the small window to the golden brazier, supported by a tripod, that always burned in his room. This was his gate to the lower planes, the same gate that had delivered Druzil. The wizard remembered that time vividly, a day of tingling anticipation. The avatar of the goddess Talona had instructed him to use his powers of sorcery and had given him Druzil's name, promising him that the imp would deliver a most delicious recipe for entropy. Little did he know then that the imp's precious scheme would involve two years of painstaking and costly effort, tax the wizard to the limits of his endurance, and destroy so many others in the process.

Druzil's recipe, the chaos curse, was worth it, Aballister decided. He had taken its creation as his personal quest for Talona, as the great task of his life, and as the gift to his goddess that would elevate him above her priests.

The interplanar gate was closed now; Aballister had powders that could open and shut it as readily as if he were turning a knob. The powders sat in small, carefully marked pouches, half for opening, half for closing, lined up alternately on a nearby table. Only Druzil knew about them besides Aballister, and the imp had never gone against the wizard's demands and tampered with the gate. Druzil could be impertinent and was often a tremendous nuisance, but he was reliable enough concerning important matters.

Aballister continued his scan and saw his reflection in a mirror across the room. Once he had been a handsome man, with inquisitive eyes and a bright smile. The change had been dramatic. Aballister was hollowed and worn now, all the dabbling in dark magic, worshiping a demanding goddess, and controlling chaotic creatures such as Druzil having taken their toll.

Many years before, the wizard had given up everything—his family and friends, and all the joys he once had held dear—in his hunger for knowledge and power, and that obsession had only multiplied when he had met Talona.

More than once, though, both before and after that meeting, Aballister had wondered if it had been worth it. Druzil offered him the attainment of his lifelong quest, power beyond his grandest imaginings, but the reality hadn't lived up to Aballister's expectations. At this point in his wretched life, the power seemed as hollow as his own face.

"But these ingredients!" Aballister went on, trying, perhaps hoping, that he could find a weakness in the imp's seemingly solid designs. "Eyes of an umber hulk? Blood of a druid? And what is the purpose of this, tentacles of a displacer beast?"

"Chaos curse," Druzil replied, as if the words alone should dispell the wizard's doubts. "It is a mighty potion you plan to brew, my master." Druzil's toothy smile sent a shudder of revulsion along Aballister's backbone. The wizard had never become overly comfortable around the cruel imp.

"*Del quiniera cas ciem-pa,*" Druzil said through his long and pointy teeth. "A powerful potion indeed!" he translated falsely. In truth, Druzil had said, "Even considering your limitations," but Aballister didn't need to know that.

"Yes," Aballister muttered again, tapping a bony finger on the end of his hawkish nose. "I really must take the time to learn your language, my dear Druzil."

"Yes," Druzil echoed, wiggling his elongated ears. "*Iye quiesta pas tellemara,*" he said, which meant, "If you weren't so stupid." Druzil dropped into a low bow to cover his deceptions, but the act only convinced Aballister further that the imp was making fun of him.

"The expense of these ingredients has been considerable," Aballister said, getting back to the subject.

"And the brewing is not exact," added Druzil with obvious sarcasm. "And we could find, my master, a hundred more problems if we searched, but the gains, I remind you. The gains! Your brotherhood is not so strong, not so. It shan't survive, I say! Not without the brew."

"God-stuff?" mused Aballister.

"Call it so," replied Druzil. "Since it was Talona who led you to it, that her designs be furthered, perhaps it truly is. A fitting title, for the sake of Barjin and his wretched priests. They will be more devout and attentive if they understand that they are fabricating a true agent of Talona, a power in itself to lavish their worship upon, and their devotion will help keep orc-faced Ragnor and his brutish warriors in line."

Aballister laughed aloud as he thought of the three clerics, the second order of the evil triumvirate, kneeling and praying before a simple magical device.

"Name it *Tuanta Miancay*, the Fatal Horror," Druzil offered, his snickers purely sarcastic. "Barjin will like that." Druzil contemplated the suggestion for a moment, then added, "No, not the Fatal Horror. *Tuanta Quiro Miancay*, the Most Fatal Horror."

Aballister's laughter trebled, with just a hint of uneasiness in it. "Most Fatal Horror" was a title associated with Talona's highest-ranking and most devout priests. Barjin, Castle Trinity's clerical leader, had not yet attained that honor, being referred to only as a Most Debilitating Holiness. That this chaos curse would outstrip him in title would sting the arrogant cleric, and Aballister would enjoy that spectacle. Barjin and his band had been at the castle for only a year. The priest had traveled all the way from Damara, homeless and broken and with no god to call his own since a new order of paladin kings had banished his vile deity back to the lower planes. Like Aballister, Barjin claimed to have encountered the avatar of Talona and that it was she who had shown him the way to Castle Trinity.

Barjin's dynamism and powers were considerable, and his followers had carried uncounted treasures along with them on their journey. When they first had arrived, the ruling triumvirate, particularly Aballister, had welcomed them with open arms, thinking it grand that Talona had brought together so powerful a union, a marriage that would strengthen the castle and provide the resources to complete Druzil's recipe. Now, months later, Aballister had begun to foster reservations about the union, particularly about the priest. Barjin was a charismatic man, something frowned upon in an order dedicated to disease and poison. Many of Talona's priests scarred themselves or covered their skin with grotesque tattoos. Barjin had done none of that, had sacrificed nothing to his new goddess, but, because of his wealth and his uncanny persuasive powers, he quickly had risen to the leadership of the castle's clerics.

Aballister had allowed the ascent, thinking it Talona's will, and had gone out of his way to appease Barjin—in retrospect, he was not so certain of his choice. Now, however, he needed Barjin's support to hold Castle Trinity together, and Barjin's riches to fund the continuing creation of the chaos curse.

"I must see about the brewing of our ingredients for the god-stuff," the wizard said with that thought in mind. "When we find a quiet time, though, Druzil, I would like to learn a bit of that full-flavored language you so often toss about."

"As you please, my master," replied the imp, bowing as Aballister left the small room and closed the door behind him.

Druzil spoke his next words in his private tongue, the language of the lower planes, fearing that Aballister might be listening at the door, "Quiesta bene tellemara, Aballister!" The mischievous imp couldn't help himself as he whispered, "But you are too stupid," aloud, for no better reason than to hear the words spoken in both tongues.

For all of the insults he so casually threw his master's way, though, Druzil appreciated the wizard. Aballister was marvelously intelligent for a human, and the most powerful of his order of three, and by Druzil's estimation those three wizards were the strongest leg of the triumvirate. Aballister would complete the cursing potion and supply the device to deliver it, and for that, Druzil, who had craved this day for decades, would be undyingly grateful. Druzil was smarter than most imps, smarter than most people, and when he had come upon the ancient recipe in an obscure manuscript a century before, he wisely had kept it hidden from his former master, another human. That wizard hadn't the resources or the wisdom to carry through the plan and properly spread the cause of chaos, but Aballister did.

* * * * *

Aballister felt a mixture of hope and trepidation as he stared hard at the reddish glow emanating from within the clear bottle. This was the first test of the chaos curse, and all of the wizard's expectations were tempered by the huge expense of putting this small amount together.

"One more ingredient," whispered the anxious imp, sharing none of his master's doubts. "Add the yote, then we may release the smoke."

"It is not to be imbibed?" Aballister asked.

Druzil paled noticeably. "No, master, not that," he rasped. "The consequences are too grave. Too grave!"

Aballister spent a long moment studying the imp. In the two years Druzil had been beside him, he could not recall ever seeing the imp so badly shaken. The wizard walked across the room to a cabinet and produced a second bottle, smaller than the plain one holding the potion, but intricately decorated with countless magical runes. When Aballister pulled off the stopper, a steady stream of smoke issued forth.

"It is ever-smoking," the wizard explained. "A minor item of magical . . ."

"I know," Druzil interrupted. "And I have already come to know that the flask will mate correctly with our potion."

Aballister started to ask how Druzil could possibly know that, how Druzil could even know about his ever-smoking bottle, but he held his questions, remembering that the mischievous imp had contacts on other planes that could answer many things.

"Could you create more of those?" Druzil asked, indicating the wondrous bottle.

Aballister gritted his teeth at yet another added expense, and his expression alone answered the question.

"The chaos curse is best served in mist, and with its magical properties, the bottle will continue to spew it forth for many years, though its range will be limited," Druzil explained. "Another container will be necessary if we mean to spread the intoxicant properly."

"Intoxicant?" Aballister balked, on the verge of rage. Druzil gave a quick flap of his leathery wings, putting him farther across the room from Aballister—not that distance mattered much where the powerful wizard was concerned.

"Intoxicant?" Aballister said again. "My dear, dear Druzil, do you mean to tell me that we have spent a fortune in gold, that I have groveled before Barjin and those utterly wretched priests, just to mix a batch of elvish wine?"

"*Bene tellemara*," came the imp's exasperated reply. "You still do not understand what we have created? Elvish wine?"

"Dwarvish mead, then?" Aballister snarled sarcastically. He took up his staff and advanced a threatening step.

"You do not understand what will happen when it is loosed," Druzil barked derisively.

"Do tell me."

Druzil snapped his wings over his face, then back behind him again, a movement that plainly revealed his frustration. "It will invade the hearts of our targets," the imp explained, "and exaggerate their desires. Simple impulses will become god-given commands. None will be affected in quite the same way, nor will the effects remain consistent to any one victim. Purely chaotic! Those affected will . . ."

Aballister raised a hand to stop him, needing no further explanation.

"I have given you power beyond your greatest hopes!" the imp growled forcefully. "Have you forgotten Talona's promise? "

"The avatar only suggested that I summon you," Aballister countered, "and only hinted that you might possess something of value."

"You cannot begin to understand the potency of the chaos curse," Druzil replied smugly. "All the races of the region will be yours to control when their own inner controls have been destroyed. Chaos is a beautiful thing, mortal master, a force of destruction and conquest, the ultimate disease, the Most Fatal Horror. Orchestrating chaos brings power to he who remains beyond its crippling grip!"

Aballister leaned on his staff and looked away. He had to believe Druzil, and yet he feared to believe. He had given so much to this unknown recipe.

"You must learn," the imp said, seeing that Aballister was not impressed. "If we are to succeed, then you must believe."

He folded his leathery wings over his head for a moment, burying himself in thought. "That young fighter, the arrogant one?" he asked suddenly.

"Haverly," Aballister answered.

"He thinks himself Ragnor's better," Druzil said, a wicked, toothy smile spreading over his face. "He desires Ragnor's death so that he might assume captainship of the fighters."

Aballister did not argue. On several occasions, young Haverly, drunken with ale, had indicated those very desires, though he had never gone so far as to threaten the ogrillon.

Even arrogant Haverly was not that stupid.

"Call him to us," Druzil begged. "Let him complete our test. Tell him that this potion could strengthen his position in the triumvirate. Tell him that it could make him even stronger than Ragnor."

Aballister stood quietly for a few moments to consider his options. Barjin had expressed grave doubts about the whole project, despite Aballister's claims that it would serve Talona beyond anything else in all the world. The priest had only funded Aballister's treasure hunt on the wizard's promise, made before a dozen witnesses, that every copper piece would be repaid if the priest was not overjoyed with the results. Barjin had lost much in his flight from the northern kingdom of Damara: his prestige, his army, and many valuable and powerful items, some enchanted. His retained wealth alone had played the major role in preserving a measure of his former power.

Now, as the weeks dragged on with rising expenses and no measurable results, Barjin grew increasingly impatient.

"I will get Haverly at once," Aballister replied, suddenly intrigued. Neither the wizard nor Barjin held any love for either Ragnor, whom they considered too dangerous to be trusted, or Haverly, whom they considered too foolish, and any havoc that the test wreaked on that pair could help to diminish Barjin's doubts.

Besides, Aballister thought, it might be fun to watch.

* * * * *

Druzil sat motionless on Aballister's great desk, watching the events across the room with great interest. The imp wished he could play a larger role in this part of the test, but only the other wizards knew of his position as Aballister's familiar, or that he was alive at all. The fighters of the triumvirate, even the clerics, thought the imp merely a garish statue, for on the few occasions that any of them had entered Aballister's private quarters, Druzil had sat perfectly motionless on the desk.

"Bend low over the beaker as you add the final drop," Aballister bade Haverly, looking back to Druzil for confirmation.

The imp nodded imperceptibly and flared his nostrils in anticipation.

"That is correct!" Aballister said to Haverly. "Breathe deeply as you pour."

Haverly stood straight and cast a suspicious gaze at the wizard. He obviously didn't trust Aballister—certainly the wizard had shown him no friendship before now. "I have great plans," he said threateningly, "and being turned into a newt or some other strange creature is not part of them."

"You doubt?" Aballister roared suddenly, knowing that he must scare off the young fighter's doubts without hesitation. "Then go away! Anyone can complete the brewing. I thought that one as ambitious as you . . ."

"Enough," Haverly interrupted, and Aballister knew his words had hit home. Haverly's suspicion was no match for his hunger for power. "I will trust you, wizard, though you have never given me cause to trust you," Haverly finished.

"Nor have I ever given you cause not to trust me," Aballister reminded him.

Haverly stared a moment longer at Aballister, his grimace not softening, then bent low over the beaker and poured the final drops. As soon as the liquids touched, the red-glowing elixir belched a puff of red smoke right in Haverly's face. The fighter jumped back, his hand going straight to his sword.

"What have you done to me?" he demanded.

"Done?" Aballister echoed innocently. "Nothing. The smoke was harmless enough, if a bit startling."

Haverly took a moment to inspect himself to be sure that he had suffered no ill effects, then he relaxed and nodded at the wizard. "What will happen next?" he asked sharply. "Where is the power you promised me?"

"In time, dear Haverly, in time," replied Aballister. "The brewing of the elixir is only the first process!"

"How long?" demanded the eager fighter.

"I could have invited Ragnor instead of you," Aballister pointedly reminded him.

Haverly's transformation at the mention of Ragnor forced the wizard back several steps: The young fighter's eyes widened grotesquely; he bit his lip so hard that blood dripped down his chin. "Ragnor!" he growled through gritted teeth. "Ragnor the imposter! Ragnor the pretender! You would not invite him, for I am his better!"

"Of course you are, dear Haverly," the wizard cooed, trying to soothe the wild-eyed man, recognizing that Haverly was on the verge of explosion. "That is why . . ." Aballister never finished, for Haverly, muttering under his breath, drew his sword and charged out of the room, nearly destroying the door as he passed. Aballister stared into the hallway, blinking in disbelief.

"Intoxicant?" came a sarcastic query from across the room.

Drawn away by the screams of "Ragnor!" Aballister didn't bother to answer the imp. The wizard rushed out, not wanting to miss the coming spectacle, and soon found his two colleagues as they made their way through the halls.

"It is Haverly, the young fighter," said Dorigen, the only female wizard in the castle. Aballister's evil smile stopped her and her companion in their tracks.

"The potion is completed?" Dorigen asked hopefully, her amber eyes sparkling as she tossed her long black hair back over her shoulder.

"Chaos curse," Aballister confirmed as he led them on.

When they arrived at the complex's large dining hall, they found that the fighting had already begun. Several tables had been flung about and a hundred startled men and orcs, and even a few giants, lined the room's perimeter, watching in amazement. Ragnor and Haverly stood facing each other in the center of the room, swords drawn.

"The fighters will need a new third in their ruling council," Dorigen remarked. "Surely either Ragnor or Haverly will fall this day, leaving only two."

"Ragnor!" Haverly proclaimed loudly. "Today I take my place as leader of the fighters!"

The other warrior, a powerfully built ogrillon, having ancestors both ogre and orc, and carrying the scars of a thousand battles, hardly seemed impressed. "Today you take your place among your ancestors," he chided.

Haverly charged, his foolishly straightforward attack costing him so deep a gash on one shoulder that his arm was nearly severed. The crazed fighter didn't even grimace, didn't even notice the wound or the pain.

Though plainly amazed that the vicious wound had not slowed his opponent, Ragnor still managed to deflect Haverly's sword and get in close to the man. He caught Haverly's sword arm with his free hand and tried to position his own weapon for a strike.

Gasps of astonishment arose throughout the gathering as Haverly somehow managed to lift his brutally torn arm and similarly block Ragnor's strike.

Haverly was almost as tall as Ragnor, but many pounds lighter and not nearly as strong. Still, and despite the wicked wound, he held Ragnor at bay for many moments.

"You are stronger than you seem," Ragnor admitted, somewhat impressed, but showing no concern; on the few occasions that his incredible strength had failed him, the ogrillon had always found a way to improvise. He pressed a disguised button on his sword hilt, and a second blade, a long, slender dirk, appeared, protruding straight down from the sword hilt, right in line with Haverly's unhelmeted head.

Haverly was too engrossed to even notice. "Ragnor!" he screamed again, hysterically, his face contorted. He slammed his forehead into Ragnor's face, squashing the ogrillon's nose.

Haverly's head came crashing in again, but Ragnor managed to ignore the pain and keep his concentration on the more lethal attack. Haverly's head came back in line a third time. Ragnor, tasting his own blood, savagely twisted his sword arm free and plunged straight down, impaling the dirk deeply into Haverly's skull.

* * * * *

The three priests of the ruling triumvirate entered the room then, led by Barjin, who was obviously not pleased by the combat.

"What is the meaning of this?" he demanded of Aballister, understanding that the wizard had played a role here.

"A matter for the fighters to explain, it would seem," Aballister replied with a shrug. Seeing that the priest was about to intervene in the continuing battle, Aballister bent over and whispered, "The chaos curse," in Barjin's ear.

Barjin's face brightened immediately and he watched the bloody battle with sudden enthusiasm.

* * * * *

Ragnor could hardly believe that Haverly still struggled. His foot-long dirk was bloodied right to the pommel, but his opponent stubbornly backed away, thrashing to free himself of the blade.

Ragnor let him go, thinking Haverly in his death throes. But, to the continuing gasps of the onlookers—Barjin's heard most loudly—Haverly did not topple.

"Ragnor!" he growled, slurring badly and spitting thick blood with every syllable. Blood filled one of his eyes and poured from his head wound, matting his brown hair, but he raised his sword and stumbled in.

Ragnor, terrified, struck first, taking advantage of Haverly's partial blindness and hacking at his already wounded arm. The force of the blow severed the arm completely, just below the shoulder, and knocked Haverly several feet to the side.

"Ragnor!" Haverly sputtered again, barely keeping his balance. Again he came in, and again Ragnor beat him back, this time slicing through Haverly's exposed ribs, digging at his heart and lungs.

Haverly's cries became unintelligible wheezes as he continued his advance. Ragnor frantically rushed out to meet him, locking him in a tight embrace that rendered both long swords useless. Haverly had no defenses against Ragnor's free hand, now holding a dirk, and the weapon dug repeatedly, viciously, at his back. Still, many minutes passed before Haverly finally tumbled dead to the floor.

"A worthy adversary," one bold orc remarked, coming over to inspect the body.

Covered in Haverly's blood, and with his own nose broken, Ragnor was in no mood to hear any praises for Haverly. "A stubborn fool!" he corrected, and he lopped off the orc's head with a single strike.

Barjin nodded at Aballister. "Talona watches with pleasure. Perhaps your chaos curse will prove worth the expense."

"Chaos curse?" Aballister replied as though a notion had struck him. "That is not a fitting title for such a powerful agent of Talona. *Tuanta Miancay*, perhaps . . . no, *Tuanta Quiro Miancay*."

One of Barjin's associates, understanding the language and the implications of the title, gasped aloud. His companions stared at him, and he translated, "The Most Fatal Horror!"

Barjin snapped his gaze back on Aballister, realizing the wizard's ploy. Aballister had played the most important role in the brewing and, with a few simple words, had ranked the potion above Barjin. Already the other two clerics, fanatic followers of Talona, were nodding eagerly and whispering their praises for Aballister's creation.

"*Tuanta Quiro Miancay*," the cornered priest echoed, forcing a smile. "Yes, that will do properly."

Three
Danica

The obese wrestler rubbed a pudgy hand over his newest bruise, trying to ignore the growing taunts of his colleagues. "I have been too relaxed against you," he said to the young woman, "my being thrice your weight and you being a girl."

Danica brushed her hair out of her almond-shaped brown eyes and tried to hide her smile. She didn't want to humiliate the proud cleric, a disciple of Oghma. She knew his boasts were ridiculous. He had fought with all his fury, but it hadn't done him any good.

Danica looked like a wisp of a thing, barely five feet tall, with a floppy mop of curly strawberry-blond hair hanging just below her shoulders and a smile to steal a paladin's heart. Those who looked more closely found much more than "girlish" dressing, though. Years of meditation and training had honed Danica's reflexes and muscles to a fine fighting edge, as the clerics of Oghma, fancying themselves great wrestlers in the image of their god figure, were painfully discovering one after another.

Every time Danica needed information in the great Edificant Library, she found it offered only in exchange for a wrestling match. For the gain of a single scroll penned by a long-dead monk, Danica now found herself faced off against this latest adversary, a sweaty and smelly behemoth. She didn't really mind the play; she knew she could defeat this one as easily as she had dispatched all the others.

The fat man straightened his black-and-gold vest, lowered his round head, and charged.

Danica waited until he was right in front of her, and to the onlookers it looked as if the woman would be buried beneath mounds of flesh. At the last moment, she dipped her head under the fat man's lunging arm, caught his hand, and casually stepped behind him as he lumbered past. A subtle twist of her wrist stopped him dead in his tracks and, before he even realized what was happening, Danica kicked the back of both his knees, dropping him to a kneel.

While the big man went down, his arm, bent backward and held firmly in Danica's amazingly strong grasp, did not. Sympathetic groans and derisive laughter erupted from those gathered to watch.

"Eastern corner!" the big man cried. "Third row, third shelf from the top in a silver tube!"

"My thanks," Danica said, releasing her hold. She looked around, flashing that innocent smile. "Perhaps the next time I require information, you can fight me two against one."

The clerics of Oghma, fearing that their god was not pleased, grumbled and turned away.

Danica offered her hand to the downed priest, but he proudly refused. He struggled to his feet, nearly falling again for lack of breath, and rushed to catch up with the others.

Danica shook her head helplessly and retrieved her two daggers from a nearby bench. She took a moment to examine them, as she always did before putting them back into their respective boot sheaths. One had a hilt of gold, twisted into a tiger's head, while the other had one of silver, bearing an image of a dragon. Both sported transparent crystal blades and were enhanced by a wizard's spell to give them the strength of steel and perfect balance. They had been a very valuable and treasured gift from Danica's master, a man whom Danica dearly missed. She had been with Master Turkel since her parents had died, and the wizened old man had become all the family she had. Danica thought of him as she resheathed the weapons, vowing for the millionth time to visit him when she had completed her studies.

Danica Maupoissant had been raised amid the bustle of the Westgate marketplace, five hundred miles to the northeast of the Edificant Library, on the neck between the Lake of Dragons and the Sea of Fallen Stars. Her father, Pavel, was a craftsman, reputably the finest wagonmaker in the region, who, like many people of Westgate, possessed a stubborn and fierce independence and no small amount of pride. Theirs was a life of simple pleasures and unconditional love.

Danica was twelve when she left her parents to serve as an apprentice to the aged, white-bearded potter named Turkel Bastan. Only months later did Danica come to understand her parents' reasoning in sending her to him: they had foreseen what was to come.

She spent a year shuffling back and forth across the city, splitting her time between her extensive duties with Master Turkel and those rare opportunities she found to go home.

Then, suddenly, there was nowhere to go. The raid had come in the dark of night, and when the assassins had gone, so, too, were Danica's parents, the house she had grown up in, and the wagon shop that had been her father's lifelong toil.

Master Turkel showed little emotion when he told Danica the terrible news, but the young girl heard him crying later, in the solitude of his small room. Only then did Danica come to realize that Turkel and her parents had orchestrated her apprenticeship. She had assumed it an accidental thing, and had feared that perhaps her parents had simply shuffled her away for their own convenience. She knew that Turkel was from the far-off eastern land of Tabot, the mountainous region of some of her mother's ancestors, and she wondered if Turkel might be a distant relative. Whatever their relationship, Danica's apprenticeship with the master soon had taken on a different light. He had helped her through her grieving, then had begun her true instruction, lessons that had little to do with making pottery. Turkel was a Tabotan monk, a disciple of Grandmaster Penpahg D'Ahn, whose religion combined mental discipline with physical training to achieve harmony of the soul. Danica guessed Turkel to be no less than eighty years old, but he could move with the grace of a hunting cat and strike with his bare hands with the force of iron weapons. His displays more than amazed Danica; they consumed her. Quiet and unassuming, Turkel was as peaceful and contented a man as Danica had ever known, yet underneath that outward guise was a fighting tiger that could be brought roaring forth in times of need.

So, too, grew the tiger in Danica. She learned and practiced; nothing else mattered to her. She used her constant work as a litany against her memories, a barricade against the pain with which she could not yet come to terms. Turkel understood, Danica later realized, and he chose carefully when he would tell her more of her parents' demise.

The craftsmen and merchants of Westgate, along with, or perhaps because of, their fierce independence, were often bitter rivals, and Pavel had not escaped this fact of Westgate life.

There were several other wagonmakers—Turkel would not tell Danica their names—who were jealous of Pavel's continuing prosperity. They went to Pavel on a few occasions, threatening him with severe consequences if he would not share with them his long backlog of orders.

"If they had come as friends and fellow craftsmen, Pavel would have shared the wealth," Turkel had said, as though he and Danica's father had been much more than the slight acquaintances they pretended to be in public. "But your father was a proud man. He would not give in to threats, no matter how real the danger behind them."

Danica had never pressed Turkel for the identity of the men who had killed her parents—or, rather, had hired the dreaded Night Masks, the usual means of assassination in Westgate, and to this day, she did not know who they were. She trusted that the master would tell her when he felt she was prepared to know, prepared to take revenge, if that was her choice, or when he believed she was willing to let go of the past and build on the future. Turkel had always indicated that to be his preference.

The image of the aged master came clearly to Danica's mind as she stood there, holding the magnificent daggers. "You have outgrown me," he had said to her, and there was no remorse, only pride, in his tone. "Your skills surpass my own in so many areas."

Danica remembered vividly that she had thought the time of revelation at hand, that Turkel would tell her the names of the conspirators who had killed her parents and tell her to go out and seek revenge.

Turkel had other ideas.

"There remains only one master who can continue to instruct you," Turkel had said, and as soon as he mentioned the Edificant Library, Danica knew what was to come. The library was home to many of Grandmaster Penpahg D'Ahn's rare and priceless scrolls; Turkel wanted her to learn directly from the records of the long-dead grandmaster. It was then that Turkel had given her the two magnificent daggers.

So she had left Westgate, barely more than a child, to build on her future, to attain new heights of self-discipline. Once again, Master Turkel had shown his love and respect for her, placing her needs above his own obvious despair at her departure.

Danica believed that she had accomplished much in her first year at the library, both in her studies and in her understanding of other people, of the world that suddenly seemed so very large. She thought it ironic that her education of the wide world would come in a place of almost monastic seclusion, but she couldn't deny that her views had matured considerably in the year she had spent at the library. Before she had lived in the private desire for revenge; now Westgate and the hired assassins seemed so very far away, and so many other, more positive, opportunities were opened to her.

She dismissed those dark memories now, left them with a final image of her father's calm smile, her mother's almond eyes, and the many wrinkles of Master Turkel's wizened old face. Then even those pleasing images dissipated, buried beneath Danica's many responsibilities to her craft.

The library was a massive room supported by dozens and dozens of arched pillars, which were even more confusing because of the thousands of distracting bas-reliefs carved into each one. It took Danica many minutes to determine which was the eastern corner. When she finally got there, moving down a narrow isle of tightly packed books, she found someone waiting for her.

Cadderly couldn't hide his smile; he never could when he looked upon Danica, since the very first time he had seen her.

He knew she had come from Westgate, several hundred miles to the northeast. That alone made her worldly by his standards, and there were so many other things about her that piqued his imagination. Although Danica's features and mannerisms were mostly Western and not so different from the norm in the central realms, the shape of her eyes revealed some ancestry in the far and exotic East.

Cadderly often wondered if that was what had initially attracted him to Danica. Those almond eyes had promised adventure to him, and he was a man sorely in need of adventure.

He had passed his twenty-first birthday and had been off the grounds of the Edificant Library only a few dozen times—and on those occasions, he had always been accompanied by at least one of the headmasters, usually Avery, and several other priests. Sometimes Cadderly thought himself pitifully bereft of any real experiences. To him, adventures and battles were events to be read about. He had never even seen a living orc, or monster of any kind.

Enter mysterious Danica and those alluring promises.

"It took you long enough," Cadderly remarked slyly.

"I have been at the library just a year," Danica retorted, "but you have lived here since before your fifth birthday."

"I had the library figured out in a week, even at that age," Cadderly assured her with a snap of his fingers. He fell into step beside her as she walked briskly toward the corner.

Danica glanced up at him, then bit back her sarcastic reply, not certain if the amazing Cadderly was teasing her or not.

"So you are fighting the big ones now?" Cadderly asked. "Should I be concerned?"

Danica stopped suddenly, pulled Cadderly's face down to her own, and kissed him eagerly. She moved back from him just a few inches, her almond eyes, striking and exotic, boring into him.

Cadderly silently thanked Deneir that neither he nor Danica were of a celibate order, but, as always when they kissed, the contact made both of them nervous. "Fighting excites you," Cadderly remarked coyly, stealing the romance and relieving the tension. "Now I am concerned."

Danica pushed him back but did not let go of his tunic.

"You should be careful, you know," Cadderly went on, suddenly serious. "If any of the headmasters caught you wrestling . . ."

"The proud young loremasters do not leave me much choice," Danica replied, casually tossing her hair and pulling it back from her face. She hadn't really worked up much of a sweat against her latest opponent. "In this maze you call a library, I could not find half of what I need in a hundred years!" She rolled her eyes about to emphasize the vastness of the pillared room.

"Not a problem," Cadderly assured her. "I had the library figured out . . ."

"When you were five!" Danica finished for him and she pulled him close again. This time Cadderly decided that her attention might bring some added benefits. He prudently moved around to Danica's right side—he scribed left-handed, and the last time he had attempted this with his left hand, he had not been able to work for several days. Cadderly had been thrilled by what Danica called her "Withering Touch" for many months, considering it the most effective nonlethal attack form he had ever witnessed. He had begged Danica to teach it to him, but the skilled monk carefully guarded her fighting secrets, explaining to Cadderly that her fighting methods were but a small part of her religion, as much a discipline of the mind as of the body. She would not allow others to copy simple techniques without first achieving the mental preparation and philosophical attitudes that accompanied them.

In the middle of the kiss, Cadderly rubbed his hand across Danica's belly, under the bottom of her short vest. As always, the young priest was amazed by the hard, rolling muscles of her stomach. A moment later, Cadderly started moving his hand slowly upward.

Danica's reaction came in the blink of an eye. Her hand, one finger extended, snapped out across Cadderly's chest and drove into his shoulder.

Under the vest, Cadderly's hand stopped immediately, then fell lifeless to hang by his side. He grimaced for a moment as the burning pain became a general numbness the length of his arm.

"You are such a . . ." Danica stammered, "a . . . a boy!"

At first, Cadderly thought her anger just the expected reaction to his bold advance, then Danica stunned him completely.

"Can you never forget your studies?"

"She knows!" a horrified Cadderly muttered to himself as Danica stormed away. Expecting the attack, he had carefully watched out of the corner of his eye and believed he knew precisely where Danica's finger had struck. Until that moment, he had considered this attempt a success, despite the continuing pain. But now Danica knew!

The young scholar paused a moment to consider the implications, then was relieved when he heard Danica's soft laughter from just beyond the next bookshelf. He took a step toward her, meaning to amend things, but Danica spun as soon as he rounded the corner, her finger poised to strike.

"The touch will work on your head as well," the young woman promised, her light brown eyes sparkling eagerly.

Cadderly didn't doubt that for a moment, and he surely didn't want Danica to prove her words. It always amazed him that Danica, barely half his weight, could so easily take him down. He looked upon her with sincere admiration, even envy, for Cadderly dearly wished that he possessed Danica's direction and dedication, her passion for her studies. While Cadderly went through his life busy but distracted, Danica's vision of the world remained narrowly focused, based in a rigid and philosophical religion little-known in the western realms. That passion, too, enhanced the enchantment Danica had cast over Cadderly. He wanted to open her mind and her heart and look into both, knowing that only there would he find answers to fill the missing elements of his own life.

Danica embodied his dreams and his hopes; he didn't even try to remember how sorely empty his life had been before he had met her. He backed away slowly, lifting his palms and holding them open and out wide to show that he wanted no part of any further displays.

"Stand!" Danica commanded as sharply as her melodious voice allowed. "Have you nothing to say to me?"

Cadderly thought for a moment, wondering what she wanted to hear. "I love you?" he asked as much as declared.

Danica nodded and smiled disarmingly, then dropped her hand. Cadderly's gray eyes returned the smile tenfold and he took a step toward her.

The dangerous finger shot up and waved about, resembling some hellish viper.

Cadderly shook his head and ran from the room, pausing only to grab a scrap of parchment and dip the quill he kept stuck under his hat band into an open inkwell. He had witnessed the Withering Touch perfectly, and he wanted to sketch the image while it was fresh in his mind.

This time, Danica's laughter was not so soft.

Four
Canticle

T hey are singing to it!" Druzil cried in amazement, not certain of whether that was a good thing or not.

The religious fanatics of Castle Trinity had taken the potion to heart; even the not-so-faithful, such as Ragnor and, by Aballister's estimation, Barjin, had been swept up in the zealous flow. "Though not very well, I fear." The imp put his wings over his ears to lessen the sound.

Aballister, too, did not enjoy the discordant wails that resounded throughout the castle complex with a zeal that walls and doors could not diminish, but he tolerated the clerics better than his worrisome imp. The wizard, too, was not without his reservations, though. Ever since the battle in the dining hall four weeks before, Barjin had forcefully taken the project as his own and had led the chorus of chants to the Most Fatal Horror.

"Barjin has the wealth," Druzil reminded the wizard, as though the imp had sensed Aballister's thoughts.

Aballister replied with a grim nod. "I fear that my insult has been turned back on me," he explained, moving slowly to the window and looking out over the Shining Plains. "By naming the chaos curse the Most Fatal Horror, I sought to demean Barjin, to weaken his position, but he has weathered the torment and resisted his prideful urging better than I had expected. All the followers believe his sincerity, to Talona and to the chaos curse." Aballister sighed. On the one hand, he was disappointed that his ploy had not stung Barjin, at least not outwardly, but on the other hand, the priest leader, sincere or not, was surely preparing Castle Trinity for the coming trials and thus was furthering Talona's will.

"If the followers believe our mixture is a simple magical concoction, no matter how potent, they will not so readily give their lives to the cause," Aballister

31

reasoned, turning back on Druzil. "There is nothing like religion to rouse the rabble."

"You do not believe the elixir is an agent of Talona?" Druzil asked, though he already knew the answer.

"I know the difference between a magical concoction and a sentient shield man," Aballister replied dryly. "The elixir will indeed serve the Lady of Poison's cause, and so its title is a fitting one."

"Barjin has put all the forces of Castle Trinity behind him," Druzil quickly responded, his tone ominous. "Even Ragnor does not dare go against him."

"Why would he, or anyone else, want to?" Aballister replied. "The chaos curse soon will be put to proper use, and Barjin has played a major role in that."

"At what price?" the imp demanded. "I gave the recipe for the chaos curse to you, my master, not the priest. Yet it is the priest who controls its fate and uses you and the other wizards to serve his own designs."

"We are a brotherhood, sworn to loyalty."

"You are a gathering of thieves," Druzil retorted. "Be not so swift in presuming the existence of honor. If Ragnor did not fear you, and did not see profit in keeping you, he would cut you down. Barjin—" Druzil rolled his bulbous eyes "—Barjin cares for nothing except Barjin. Where are his scars? His tattoos? He does not deserve his title, nor the leadership of the priests. He falls to his knees for the goddess only because doing so makes those around him praise him for his holiness. There is nothing religious—"

"Enough, dear Druzil," soothed the wizard, waving one hand calmly.

"Do you deny that Barjin controls the chaos curse?" Druzil retorted. "Do you believe that Barjin would show any loyalty to Aballister if he did not need Aballister?"

The wizard walked away from the small window and fell back into his wooden chair, unable to argue those points. But even if he admitted that he had miscalculated, he could do little now to stop events from following their course. Barjin had the elixir and the money, and if Aballister meant to recapture control of the potion for himself, he might have to fight a war within the triumvirate. Aballister and his wizard comrades were powerful, but they were only three. With Barjin whipping the hundreds of Castle Trinity soldiers into religious fervor, the wizards had become somewhat secluded within the complex.

"They have added rituals and conditions," the imp went on, spitting every word with distaste. "Did you know that Barjin has placed warding glyphs on the flask, so that it might be opened only by an innocent?"

"That is a typical priestly ploy," Aballister replied casually, trying to alleviate Druzil's worries.

"He does not understand the power under his control," Druzil retorted. "The chaos curse needs no 'priestly ploys.' "

Aballister gave an unconcerned shrug, but he, too, had not agreed with Barjin's decision concerning those glyphs. Barjin thought that allowing an innocent

to serve as an unintentional catalyst was fitting for the agent of the chaotic goddess, but Aballister feared that the cleric was simply adding conditions to an
already complicated process.

"*Barjin quiesta pas tellemara*," Druzil muttered.

Aballister narrowed his eyes. He had heard that obviously unflattering phrase
in many different contexts these last few weeks, most often aimed at him. He
kept his suspicions to himself, though, realizing that many of Druzil's complaints
were valid.

"Perhaps it is time for the Most Fatal Horror to go out and perform Talona's
will beyond this pile of rocks," Aballister said. "Perhaps we have spent too long
in preparation."

"Barjin's power is too consolidated," Druzil said. "Do not underestimate him."

Aballister nodded, then rose and walked across the room.

"You should not underestimate," he pointed out to the imp, "the advantages in
convincing people that there is a higher purpose to their actions, a higher authority guiding their leaders' decisions." The wizard opened the heavy door, and the
unholy canticle drowned out his next words. More than Barjin's handful of clerics were singing; the canticle was a hundred screaming voices strong, echoing
off the stone walls with frantic urgency. Aballister shook his head in disbelief as
he exited.

Druzil could not deny Barjin's effectiveness in preparing the force for the
tasks ahead, but the imp still held reservations about the Most Fatal Horror and
all the complications that title implied. The imp knew, if the wizard did not, that
Aballister would not have an easy time of walking away with the elixir bottle.

* * * * *

"More like this one," Cadderly said to Ivan Bouldershoulder, a square-shouldered dwarf with a yellow beard hanging low enough to trip him if he didn't
watch his step. The two were beside Cadderly's bed—Cadderly kneeling and
Ivan standing—examining a tapestry depicting the legendary war wherein the
elvish race had been split into surface and drow. Only half unrolled, the huge
woven cloth still covered the bed. "The design is right, but its shaft might be a
little tight for my darts."

Ivan pulled out a small-stick, notched at regular intervals, and took some
measurements of the hand-held crossbow Cadderly had indicated, then of the
arm of the drow elf holding it.

"They'll fit," the dwarf replied, confident of his work. He looked across the
room to his brother, Pikel, who busied himself with several models Cadderly had
constructed. "You got the bow?"

Engrossed in his play, Pikel didn't even hear him. He was older than Ivan by
several years, but he was by far the less serious of the two. They were about the
same size, though Pikel was a bit more round-shouldered, an attribute exagger-

ated by his loose-fitting, drooping robes. His beard was green this week, for he had dyed it in honor of the visiting druids.

Pikel liked druids, a fact that made his brother roll his eyes and blush. It wasn't usual that a dwarf would get on well with woodland folk, but Pikel was far from usual. Rather than let his beard hang loose to his toes, as did Ivan, he parted it in the middle and pulled it back over his huge ears, braiding it together with his hair to hang halfway down his back. It looked rather silly to Ivan, but Pikel, the library's cook, thought it practical for keeping his beard out of the soup. Besides, Pikel didn't wear the boots common to his race; he wore sandals—a gift from the druids—and his long beard tickled his free-wiggling, gnarly toes.

"Oo oi," Pikel chuckled, rearranging the models. One was remarkably similar to the Edificant Library, a squat, square, four-storied structure with rows of tiny windows. Another model was a displaced wall like those in the library, supported by huge, heavily blocked arches. It was the third and tallest model that intrigued Pikel. It, too, was of a wall, but unlike anything the dwarf, no novice to masonry, had ever seen. The model stood straight to half the dwarf's four-foot height but was not nearly as wide or bulky as the other, shorter, wall.

Slender and graceful, it was really two structures: the wall and a supporting pillar, connected by two bridges, one halfway up and the other at the very top.

Pikel pushed down hard on the model, but, fragile though it appeared, it did not bend under his considerable strength.

"Oo oi!" the delighted dwarf squealed.

"The crossbow?" demanded Ivan, now standing behind Pikel. Pikel fumbled about the many pockets in his cook's apron, finally handing over a small wooden coffer.

Pikel squeaked at Cadderly, pointed to the strange wall, and gave an inquisitive look.

"Just something I investigated a few months ago," Cadderly explained. He tried to sound nonchalant, but a clear trace of excitement rang in his voice. With all that had been going on lately, he had almost forgotten the models, though the new design had shown remarkable promise. The Edificant Library was far from a mundane structure. Elaborate sculptures, enhanced by the ivy, covered its walls, and some of the most wondrous gargoyles in all the Realms completed its intricate and effective gutter system. Many of the finest minds in the region had designed and constructed the place, but whenever Cadderly looked upon it, all that he could see were its limitations. For all its detail, the library was square and squat, and its windows were small and unremarkable.

"An idea for expanding the library," he explained to Pikel.

He gathered up a nearby blanket and slipped it under the model of the library, folding its sides to resemble the rough surrounding mountain terrain.

Ivan shook his head and walked back to the bed, knowing that Cadderly and Pikel could continue their outlandish conversations for hours on end.

"Centuries ago, when the library was built," Cadderly began, "no one had any idea it would grow so large. The founders wanted a secluded spot where they could study in private, so they chose the high passes of the Snowflake Mountains.

"Most of the northern and eastern wings, as well as the third and fourth stories were added much later, but we have run out of room. To the front and both sides, the ground slopes too steeply to allow further expansion without supports, and to the west, behind us, the mountain stone is too tough to be properly cleared away."

"Oh?" muttered Pikel, not so sure of that. The Bouldershoulder brothers had come from the forbidding Galena Mountains, far to the north beyond Vaasa, where the ground was ever frozen and the stones were as tough as any in the Realms. But not too tough for a determined dwarf! Pikel kept his thoughts private, though, not wanting to halt Cadderly's mounting momentum.

"I think we should go up," Cadderly said casually. "Add a fifth, and possibly sixth level."

"It'd never hold," grumbled Ivan from the bed, not so intrigued and wanting to get back to the business of the crossbow.

"Aha!" said Cadderly, pointing a finger straight up in the air.

Ivan knew by the look on Cadderly's face that he had played right into the young man's hopes. Cadderly did so love doubters where his inventions were concerned.

"The aerial buttress!" the young priest proclaimed, holding his hands out to the strange, two-structured wall.

"Oo oi!" agreed Pikel, who had already tested the wall's strength.

"There's one for the faeries," grumbled a doubting Ivan.

"Look at it, Ivan," Cadderly said reverently. "One for the faeries, indeed, if that phrase implies grace. The strength of the design cannot be underestimated. The bridges displace stress so that the walls, with minimal stonework, can hold much more than you might believe, leaving incredible possibilities for window designs."

"Sure, from the top," the dwarf replied gruffly, "but how might it take a giant's ram on the side? And what about the wind? There are mighty cross-breezes up here, and mightier still if you go building higher!"

Cadderly spent a long moment considering the aerial buttress. Every time he looked upon the model, he was filled with hope. He thought that a library should be an enlightening place, physically and mentally, and while the Edificant Library was surrounded by impressive grounds and mountain views, it remained a dark and thick-stoned place. The popular architecture of the time required massive stone foundations and did not allow for large windows. In the world of the Edificant Library, sunlight was something to be enjoyed outside.

"Scholars should not sit squinting by candlelight, even at midday, to read their tomes," Cadderly argued.

"The greatest weapons in all the world were forged in deep holes by my ancestors," Ivan countered.

"It was just the beginnings of an idea," mumbled Cadderly defensively, suddenly agreeing with Ivan that they should get back to the crossbow. Cadderly did not doubt his design's potential, but he realized that he would have a hard time convincing a dwarf, who had lived a century in tight tunnels, of the value of sunlight.

Ever sympathetic, Pikel put a hand on Cadderly's shoulder.

"Now for the bow," Ivan said, opening the wooden coffer.

The dwarf gently lifted a small, nearly completed crossbow, beautifully constructed and resembling the bow depicted on the tapestry. "The work's making me thirsty!"

"The scroll is nearly translated," Cadderly assured him, not missing the reference to the ancient dwarven mead recipe he had promised in return for the crossbow. Cadderly had actually translated the recipe many weeks before but had held it back, knowing that Ivan would complete the bow more quickly with such a prize dangling just out of his reach.

"That's good, boy," Ivan replied, smacking his lips. "You get your bow in a week, but I'll need the picture to finish it. You got something smaller showing it?"

Cadderly shook his head. "All I have is the tapestry," he admitted.

"You want me to walk through the halls with a stolen tapestry under me arm?" Ivan roared.

"Borrowed," Cadderly corrected.

"With Headmistress Pertelope's blessings?" Ivan asked sarcastically.

"Uh oh," added Pikel.

"She will never miss it," Cadderly replied, unconvincingly. "If she does, I will tell her that I needed it to confirm some passages in the drow tome I am translating."

"Pertelope knows more of drow than does yerself," Ivan reminded him. "She's the one who gave you the book!"

"Uh oh," Pikel said again.

"The mead is blacker than midnight," Cadderly said offhandedly, "so the recipe says. It would kill a fair-sized tree if you poured only a pint of it along the roots."

"Get the other end," Ivan said to Pikel. Pikel pulled his mushroom-shaped cook's cap over the tangle of green hair, which made his ears stick out even farther, then helped Ivan roll the tapestry up tight. They hoisted it together while Cadderly cracked open the door and made sure that the hall was empty. Cadderly glanced over his shoulder at the diminishing angle of the shining sun through his window. His floor was marked in measured intervals to serve as a morning clock. "A few minutes to noon," he said to the dwarves. "Brother Chauncticleer will begin the midday canticle soon. All the host priests are required to attend and most of the others usually go. The way should be clear."

Ivan gave Cadderly a sour look.

"Tut-tut," muttered Pikel, shaking his furry face and wagging a finger at Cadderly.

"I will get there!" Cadderly growled at them. "No one notices if I am just a few moments late."

The melody began then, Brother Chaunticleer's perfect soprano wafting gently through the corridors of the ancient library. Every noon, Chaunticleer ascended to his place at the podium of the library's great hall to sing two songs, the respective legends of Deneir and Oghma. Many scholars came to the library to study, it was true, but many others came to hear the renowned Chaunticleer. He sang a cappella but could fill the great hall and the rooms beyond with his amazing four-octave voice so fully that listeners had to look at him often just to make sure that no choir stood behind him.

Oghma's song was first this day, and under the cover of that energetic and rousing tune, the brothers Bouldershoulder bounced and stumbled their way down two curving stairways and through a dozen too-tight doorways to their quarters beside the library's kitchen.

Cadderly entered the great hall at about the same time, slipping quietly through the high oaken double doors and moving to the side, behind a large arch support.

"Aerial buttress," he couldn't help but mutter, shaking his head in dismay at the bulky pillar. He realized then that he had not entered unnoticed. Kierkan Rufo smiled at him from the shadows of the next nearest arch.

Cadderly knew that the conniving Rufo had waited for him, seeking new fuel for Headmaster Avery's ire, and he knew that Avery would not excuse his tardiness. Cadderly pretended not to care, not wanting to give Rufo the satisfaction. He pointedly looked away and pulled out his spindle-disks, an archaic weapon used by ancient halfling tribesmen of southern Luiren. The device consisted of two circular rock crystal disks, each a finger's breadth wide and a finger's length in diameter, joined in their centers by a small bar on which was wrapped a string. Cadderly had discovered the weapon in an obscure tome and had actually improved on the design, using a metal connecting bar with a small hole through which the string could be threaded and knotted rather than tied.

Cadderly slipped his finger through the loop on the string's loose end. With a flick of his wrist, he sent the spindle-disks rolling down the length of the string, then brought them spinning back to his hand with a slight jerk of his finger.

Cadderly sneaked a look out of the corner of his eye. Knowing that he had Rufo's attention, he sent the disks down again, quickly looped the string over the fingers of his free hand to form a triangle, and held the still-spinning disks in the middle, rocking them back and forth like a baby's cradle. Rufo was leaning forward now, mesmerized by the game, and Cadderly didn't miss the opportunity.

He released the string from his cradling hand, gathering the spindle-disks too suddenly for the eye to follow, then flicked them out straight at his rival. The string brought the flying device back to Cadderly's hand before it got halfway to Rufo, but the startled man stumbled backward and toppled. Cadderly congratulated himself for his timing, for Rufo's noisy descent coincided with the most dramatic pause in Brother Chaunticleer's song.

"Ssshhh!" came the angry hisses from every direction, and Cadderly's was not the least among them. It seemed that Headmaster Avery would have two students to discipline that night.

Five

To Know Your Allies

The meeting chamber at Castle Trinity was quite different from the great and ornate hall of the Edificant Library. Its ceiling was low and its door squat and barred and heavily guarded. A single triangular table dominated the room, with three chairs on each side, one group for the wizards, one for the fighters, and one for the clerics.

Scan the room, Druzil suggested telepathically to Aballister, who was in the room. The imp surveyed through the wizard's eyes, using their telepathic link to view whatever Aballister was looking at. Aballister did as he was bidden, moving his gaze around the triangular table, first to Ragnor and the other two fighters, then to Barjin and his two cleric companions.

Druzil broke the mental connection suddenly and hissed a wicked laugh, knowing that he had left Aballister in complete confusion. He could feel the wizard trying to reestablish the mental link, could hear Aballister's thoughts calling to him.

But Aballister was not in command of their telepathy; the imp had used this mental form of communication for more decades than Aballister had been alive and it was he who decided when and where he and the wizard would link. For now, Druzil had no reason to continue contact; he had seen all that he needed to see. Barjin was in the meeting hall and would be busy there for some time. Druzil found his center of magic, his otherworldly essence, which allowed him to transcend the physical rules governing creatures of this host plane. A few seconds later, the imp faded from sight, becoming transparent, then he was off, flapping down the hallways to a wing of Castle Trinity to which he rarely traveled.

It was risky business, Druzil knew, but if the chaos curse was to be in the priest's hands, then Druzil needed to know more about him.

Druzil knew that Barjin's door would be locked and heavily warded against intrusion, but he considered that a minor problem with one of Barjin's bodyguards standing rigid in the hall just outside it. Druzil entered the man's thoughts just long enough to plant a suggestion, a magical request.

"There is an intruder in Barjin's room," came Druzil's silent beckon.

The guard glanced about nervously for a moment, as if seeking the source of the call. He stared long at Barjin's door looking right through the invisible imp—then hastily fumbled with some keys, spoke a command word to prevent the warding glyphs from exploding, and entered.

Druzil quietly mouthed the same command word and walked in behind.

After a few minutes of inspecting the apparently empty room, the guard shook his head and left, locking the door behind him.

Druzil snickered at how easily some humans could be controlled. The imp didn't have the time or inclination to gloat, though, not with all of the mysterious Barjin's secrets open for his inspection.

The room was ordinary enough for one of Barjin's stature. A large canopy bed dominated the wall opposite the door, with a night table beside it. Druzil rubbed his hands together eagerly as he headed for the table. Atop it, next to the lamp, was a black-bound book and, next to that, several quills and an inkwell.

"How thoughtful of you to keep a journal," Druzil rasped, carefully opening the work. He read through the first entries, dated two years earlier. They were mostly lamentations by Barjin, accounts of his exploits in the northern kingdoms of Vaasa, Damara, and Narfell, to the north. Druzil's already considerable respect for the priest grew as he devoured the words. Barjin once had commanded an army and had served a powerful master—he gave no direct references to the man, if it was a man—not as a cleric, but as a wizard!

Druzil paused to consider this revelation, then hissed and read on. Although formidable, Barjin admitted that he had not been the most powerful of the wizards in his master's service—again a vague reference to the mysterious master, giving Druzil the impression that perhaps Barjin, even years later, feared to speak the creature's name aloud or write it down. Barjin's rise to power had come later, when the army had taken on a religious zeal and his master apparently had assumed godlike proportions.

Druzil couldn't contain a snicker at the striking parallels between the priest's ascent and the chaos curse's transformation into a goddess's direct agent.

Barjin had become a priest and headed an army to fulfill his evil master's desire to conquer the whole of the northland. The plans had fallen through, though, when an order of paladins—Druzil hissed aloud when he read that cursed word—arose in Damara and organized an army of its own. Barjin's master and most of his cohorts had been thrown down, but Barjin had barely escaped with his life and a portion of the evil army's accumulated wealth.

Barjin had fled south, alone but for a few lackeys. Since his proclaimed "god" had been dispatched, his clerical powers had greatly diminished. Druzil spent a while musing over this revelation; nowhere did Barjin mention his claimed meeting with Talona's avatar. The journal went on to tell of Barjin's joining the triumvirate at Castle Trinity—again with no mention of the avatar. Druzil snickered aloud at Barjin's opportunism. Even a year ago, coming in as a pitiful refugee, Barjin had duped Castle Trinity's leaders, had used their fanaticism against them.

After only a month in the castle, Barjin had ascended to the third rank in the priestly hierarchy, and after only a few more weeks, Barjin had taken over undisputed command as Talona's chief representative. And yet, Druzil realized as he flipped quickly through the pages, Barjin thought not enough about his goddess to give her more than a few passing references in his journal.

Aballister was correct: Barjin was a hypocrite, a fact that hardly seemed to matter. Again Druzil snickered aloud at the irony, at the pure chaos.

Druzil knew the rest of Barjin's story well enough; he had been present long before Barjin ever arrived. The journal, sadly, did not offer any further revelations, but the imp was not disappointed when he closed the book; there were too many other items to be investigated.

Barjin's new vestments, a conical cap and expensive purple robes embroidered in red with the new insignia of the triumvirate, hung beside the bed. An offspring of Talona's symbol, the three teardrops inside a triangle's points, this one sported a trident, its three prongs tipped by teardrop-shaped bottles, much like the one carrying the chaos curse. Barjin had designed it personally, and only Ragnor had offered any resistance.

"So you do plan to spread the word of your god," Druzil muttered a few moments later when he discovered Barjin's bedroll, folded tent, and stuffed backpack under the bed. He reached for the items, then jumped back suddenly, sensing a presence in that pile. He felt the beginnings of a telepathic communication, but not from Aballister. Eagerly, the imp reached under the bed and pulled the items out, recognizing the telepathic source immediately as Barjin's magical mace.

"Screaming Maiden," Druzil said, echoing the item's telepathic declaration and examining the crafted item. Its obsidian head was that of a pretty young girl, strangely innocuous and appealing. Druzil saw through the grotesque facade. He knew this was not a weapon of the material plane, but one that had been forged in the Abyss, or in the Nine Hells, or in Tarterus, or in one of the other lower planes. It was sentient, obviously, and hungry. More than anything else, Druzil could feel its hunger, its blood-lust. He watched in joyful amazement as the mace enhanced that point, its obsidian head twisting into a leering visage, a fanged maw opening wide.

Druzil clapped his padded hands together and smiled wickedly. His respect for Barjin continued to mount, for any mortal capable of wielding such a weapon must be powerful indeed.

Rumors around the fortress expressed disdain that Barjin did not favor the poisoned dagger, the usual weapon of Talona's clerics, but, seeing this mace up close and sensing its terrible power, Druzil agreed with the priest's choice.

Inside the rolled tent Druzil found a brazier and tripod nearly as intricate and rune-covered as Aballister's. "You are a sorcerer, too, Barjin," the imp whispered, wondering what future events that might imply. Already Druzil imagined what his life might be like if he had stepped through the brazier to Barjin's call instead of Aballister's.

The thick backpack held other wondrous items. Druzil found a deep, gem-encrusted bowl of beaten platinum, no doubt worth a king's fortune. Druzil placed it carefully on the floor and reached back into the pack, as exuberant as a hungry orc shoving its arm down a rat hole.

He pulled out a solid and heavy object, fist-sized and wrapped in black cloth. Whatever was inside clearly emanated magical energies, and Druzil took care to lift only one corner of the cloth to peek in. He beheld a huge black sapphire, recognized it as a necromancer's stone, and quickly rewrapped it in the shielding cloth. If exposed, such a stone could send out a call to the dead, summoning ghosts or ghouls, or any other netherworld monsters in the area.

Of similar magical properties was the small ceramic flask that Druzil inspected next. He unstoppered it and sniffed, sneezing as some ashes came into his ample nose.

"Ashes?" the imp whispered curiously, peering in. Under the black cloth, the necromancer's stone pulsed, and Druzil understood. "Long dead spirit," he muttered, quickly closing the flask.

Nothing else showed to be of any particular interest, so Druzil carefully rewrapped and replaced everything as he had found it. He hopped up on the comfortable bed, secure with his invisibility, and relaxed, pondering all that he had learned. This Barjin was a diversified human-priest, wizard, general, dabbling in sorcery, necromancy, and who could guess what else.

"Yes, a very resourceful human," Druzil decided. He felt better about Barjin's involvement in the chaos curse. He checked in telepathically with Aballister for just a moment, to make certain that the meeting was in full swing, then congratulated himself on his cunning and folded his plump hands behind his head.

Soon he was fast asleep.

* * * * *

"We have only the one suitable bottle," said Aballister, representing the wizards. "The ever-smoking devices are difficult to create, requiring rare gems and metals, and we all know how costly it was to brew even a small amount of the elixir." He felt Barjin's stare boring into him at the reference to the cost.

"Do not speak of the Most Fatal Horror as an elixir," the clerical leader commanded. "Once it may have been just a magical potion, but now it is much more."

"*Tuanta Quiro Miancay*," chanted the other two priests, scarred and ugly men with blotchy tattoos covering nearly every inch of their exposed skin.

Aballister returned Barjin's glare. He wanted to scream at Barjin's hypocrisy, to shake the other clerics into action against him, but Aballister wisely checked his outburst. He knew that any accusations against Barjin would produce the opposite results and that he would become the target of the faithful. Druzil's estimation of Barjin had been correct, Aballister had to admit. The priest had indeed consolidated his power.

"Brewing the Most Fatal Horror," conceded Aballister, "has depleted our resources. To begin again and create more, and also acquire another bottle, could well prove beyond our limits."

"Why do we need these stupid bottles?" interrupted Ragnor. "If the stuff's a god as you say, then . . ."

Barjin was quick to answer. "The Most Fatal Horror is merely an agent of Talona," the priest explained calmly. "In itself, it is not a god, but it will aid us to comply with Talona's edicts."

Ragnor's eyes narrowed dangerously. It was obvious that the volatile ogrillon's patience had just about expired.

"All of your followers embrace *Tuanta Quiro Miancay*," Barjin reminded Ragnor, "embrace it with all their hearts." Ragnor eased back in his seat, flinching at the threatening implications.

Aballister studied Barjin curiously for a long while, awed by how easily the priest had calmed the ogrillon. Barjin was tall, vigorous, and imposing, but he was no match physically for Ragnor. Usually, physical strength was all that mattered to the powerful fighter; Ragnor normally showed the clerics and wizards less respect than he gave to even his lowliest soldiers.

Barjin seemed to be the exception, though; especially of late, Ragnor had not openly opposed him on any issue.

Aballister, while concerned, was not surprised. He knew that Barjin's powers went far beyond the priest's physical abilities. Barjin was a charmer and a hypnotist, a careful strategist who weighed his opponent's mind-set above all else and used spells as often for simple enhancement of a favorable situation as to affect those he meant to destroy. Just a few weeks earlier, a conspiracy had been discovered within the evil triumvirate. The single prisoner had resisted Ragnor's interrogations, at the price of incredible pain and several toes, but Barjin had the wretch talking within an hour, willingly divulging all that he knew about his fellow conspirators. Whispers said that the tortured man actually believed Barjin was an ally, right up until the priest casually bashed in his skull.

Aballister did not doubt those whispers and was not surprised. That was how Barjin worked; few could resist the priest's hypnotic charisma. Aballister did not know much of Barjin's former deity, lost in the wastelands of Vaasa, but what he had seen of the refugee priest's spell repertoire was beyond the norm that he would expect of clerics. Again Aballister referred to the whispers for his answers, rumors that indicated Barjin dabbled in wizardry as well as clerical magic.

Barjin was still speaking reverently of the elixir when Aballister turned his attention back to the meeting. The priest's preaching held the other clerics, and

Ragnor's two fighter companions, awestruck. Aballister shook his head and dared not interrupt. He considered again the course that his life had taken, how the avatar had led him to Druzil, and Druzil had delivered the recipe. Then the avatar had led Barjin to Castle Trinity. That was the part of the puzzle that did not fit in Aballister's reasoning. After a year of watching the priest, Aballister remained convinced that Barjin was no true disciple of Talona, but again he reminded himself that Barjin, sincere or not, was furthering the cause, and that because of Barjin's purse and influence, all the region might soon be claimed in the goddess's name.

Aballister let out a profound sigh; such were the paradoxes of chaos.

"Aballister?" Barjin asked. The wizard cleared his throat nervously and glanced around, realizing he had missed much of the conversation.

"Ragnor was inquiring about the necessity of the bottles," Barjin politely explained.

"The bottles, yes," Aballister stuttered. "The elix— . . . the Most Fatal Horror is potent with or without them. Minute amounts are all that are required for the chaos curse to take effect, but it will last only a short while. With the ever-smoking bottles, the god-stuff is released continually. We have created just a few drops, but I believe there is enough liquid to fuel the ever-smoking bottle for months, perhaps years, if the mixture within the bottle is correct."

Barjin looked around and exchanged nods with his clerical companions. "We have decided that Talona's agent is ready," he declared.

"You have . . ." the wizard Dorigen stammered in disbelief.

Aballister stared long and hard at Barjin. He had meant to take command of the meeting and suggest just what the priest was getting at; again Barjin had thought one step ahead of him, had stolen his thunder.

"We are the representatives of Talona," Barjin coolly replied to Dorigen's outrage. His companions bobbed their heads stupidly.

Aballister's clenched fingers nearly tore a chunk out of his oaken chair.

"The goddess has spoken to us, has revealed her wishes," Barjin continued smugly. "Our conquests will soon begin!"

Ragnor beat a fist on the table in excited agreement; now the priest was speaking in terms the ogrillon warrior could understand. "Who are you planning for carrying the bottle?" Ragnor asked bluntly.

"I will carry it," Aballister quickly put in. He knew as soon as he heard his own words that his claim sounded desperate, a last attempt to salvage his own position of power.

Barjin shot him an incredulous look.

"It was I who met Talona's avatar," Aballister insisted, "and I who discovered the recipe for the Most Fatal Horror."

"For that, we thank you," remarked the priest in a condescending tone. Aballister started to protest, but sank back in his chair as a magical message was whispered into his ear. *Do not fight with me over this, wizard*, Barjin quietly warned.

Aballister knew that the critical moment was upon him. If he gave in now, he felt he might never recover his standing in Castle Trinity, but if he argued against Barjin, against the religious fury that the priest had inspired, he would surely split the order and might find himself badly outnumbered.

"The priests of Talona will carry the bottle, of course," Barjin answered Ragnor. "We are the true disciples."

"You are one leg of a ruling triumvirate," Aballister dared to remind him. "Do not claim the Most Fatal Horror solely as your own."

Ragnor did not see things quite the same way. "Leave it to the priests," the ogrillon demanded.

Aballister's surprise disappeared as soon as he realized that the brutish fighter, suspicious of magic, was simply relieved that he would not have to carry the bottle.

"Agreed," Barjin quickly put in. Aballister started to speak out, but Dorigen put a hand over his arm and gave him a look that begged him to let it go.

"You have something to say, good wizard?" Barjin asked.

Aballister shook his head and sank even deeper into his chair—and even deeper into despair.

"Then it is settled," said Barjin. "The Most Fatal Horror will descend upon our enemies, carried by my second—" he nodded to the priests on his right and on his left "—and my third."

"No!" Aballister blurted, seeing a way to salvage something of this disaster. All gazes descended upon him; he saw Ragnor put a hand to his sword hilt. "Your second?" the wizard asked, and now it was he who feigned an incredulous tone. "Your third?" Aballister rose from his chair and held his arms outstretched.

"Is this not the direct agent of our goddess?" he preached. "Is this not the beginning of our greatest ambitions? No, only Barjin is fit to carry such a precious artifact. Only Barjin can properly begin the reign of chaos." The gathering turned as one to Barjin, and Aballister returned to his seat, thinking that he had at last outmaneuvered the clever priest. If he could get Barjin out of Castle Trinity for a time, he could reestablish his claim as the chief speaker for the brotherhood.

Unexpectedly, the priest didn't argue. "I will carry it," he said. He looked to the other, startled clerics and added, "and I will go alone."

"All the fun for you?" Ragnor complained.

"Merely the first battle of the war," Barjin responded.

"My warriors desire battle," Ragnor pressed. "They hunger for blood!"

"They will have all that they can drink and more!" Barjin snapped. "But I will go first and cripple our enemies. When I return, Ragnor can lead the second assault."

This seemed to satisfy the ogrillon, and now Aballister understood Barjin's salvaging ploy. By going alone, the priest would not only leave his clerical cohorts to keep an eye on things, but he would leave Ragnor and his soldiers. Always vying for power, the ogrillon, with the prodding of the remaining clerics, would not allow Aballister and the wizards to regain a firm foothold.

"Where will you loose it?" Aballister asked. "And when?"

"There are preparations to be made before I leave," Barjin answered, "things that only a priest, a true disciple, would understand. As to where, let it be of no concern to you."

"But—" Aballister started, only to be interrupted sharply.

"Talona alone will tell me," Barjin growled with finality.

Aballister glared in outrage but did not respond. Barjin was a slippery opponent; every time Aballister had him cornered, he merely invoked the name of the goddess, as if that answered everything.

"It is decided," Barjin continued, seeing no response forthcoming. "This meeting is at an end."

* * * * *

"Oh, go away," Druzil slurred, both audibly and telepathically. Aballister was looking for him, trying to get into his thoughts. Druzil smiled at his superiority in keeping the wizard out and lazily rolled over.

Then the imp realized what Aballister's call might signify. He sat up with a start and looked into Aballister's mind just long enough to see that the wizard had returned to his own room.

Druzil hadn't meant to sleep this long, had wanted to be far from this place before the meeting adjourned.

Druzil held very still when the door opened and Barjin entered the room.

If he had been more attentive, the priest might have sensed the invisible presence. Barjin had other things on his mind, though. He rushed for the bed and Druzil recoiled, thinking Barjin meant to attack him. But Barjin dropped to his knees and reached eagerly for his pack and his enchanted mace.

"You and I," Barjin said to the weapon, holding it out before him, "will spread the word of their goddess and reap the rewards of chaos. It has been too long since you feasted on the blood of humans, my pet, far too long." The mace couldn't audibly reply, of course, but Druzil thought he saw a smile widen on the pretty girl's sculpted face.

"And you," Barjin said into the backpack, to the ceramic, ash-filled flask as far as Druzil could tell. "Prince Khalif. Could it be the time for you to walk the earth again?" Barjin snapped the backpack shut and roared with such sincere and exuberant laughter that Druzil almost joined in.

The imp promptly reminded himself that he and Barjin were not, as yet, formally allied, and that Barjin would most definitely prove a dangerous enemy. Fortunately for the imp, Barjin, in his haste, had not closed the door behind him. Druzil crawled off the bed, using Barjin's laughter as cover, and slipped out the door, wisely uttering the password for the warding glyph as he crossed the threshold.

* * * * *

Barjin left Castle Trinity five days later, bearing the ever-smoking bottle. He traveled with a small entourage of Ragnor's fighters, but they would only serve as escorts as far as the human settlement of Carradoon, near Impresk Lake on the southeastern edge of the Snowflake Mountains. Barjin would go alone from there to his final destination, which he and his clerical conspirators would still not reveal to the other leaders of Castle Trinity.

Back at the fortress, Aballister and the wizards waited as patiently as possible, confident that their turn would come.

Ragnor's force was not so patient, though. The ogrillon wanted battle, wanted to begin the offensive right away. Ragnor was not a stupid creature, though. He knew that his small force, only a few hundred strong unless he managed to entice the neighboring goblinoid tribes to join in, would not have an easy time of conquering the lake, the mountains, and the forest.

Still, and despite all his reasoning, Ragnor was hungry.

Since his very first day at Castle Trinity, nearly five years before, the ogrillon had vowed revenge on Shilmista Forest, on the elves who had defeated his tribe and driven him and the other refugees far from the wood.

Every member of Castle Trinity, from lowly soldier to wizard to priest, had spoken often of the day they would rise from their disguised holes and blacken the region. All now held their breath, awaiting Barjin's return, awaiting confirmation that the conquest had begun.

Six

Water and Dust

The cloaked figure moved slowly toward Danica.

Thinking it a monk of some obscure and eccentric sect—and such monks were usually hostile and dangerous, determined to prove their fighting prowess against any other monks they encountered—the woman gathered up the pile of parchments she had been studying and quickly moved to another table.

The tall figure, cowl pulled low to hide its face, turned to pursue, its feet making unrecognizable scuffling noises on the stone floor.

Danica looked around. It was late; this study hall, on the second floor above the library, was nearly empty and Danica decided that it might be time for her to retire, too. She realized that she was exhausted, and she wondered if she might be imagining things.

The figure came on, slowly, menacingly, and Danica thought that perhaps it was not some other monk. What horrors might that low cowl be hiding? she wondered. She gathered the parchments again and started boldly for the main aisle, though that course meant passing right by the figure.

A hand shot out and caught her shoulder. Danica stifled a startled cry and spun about—to face the shadowy cowl, losing many of her scrolls in the action. As she collected her wits, though, Danica realized that it was no skeletal apparition holding her in an icy, undead grip. It was a human hand, warm and gentle, and showing signs of ink near the fingernails.

The hand of a scribe.

"Fear not!" the specter rasped.

Danica knew that voice too well to be deceived by the breathless mask. She scowled and crossed her arms over her chest.

Understanding that the joke was ended, Cadderly removed his hand from Danica's shoulder and quickly pulled back the cowl. "Greetings!" he said, smiling widely into Danica's frown as though he hoped his mirth to be a contagious thing. "I thought I might find you here."

Danica's silence did not promise reciprocal warmth.

"Do you like my disguise?" Cadderly went on. "It had to be convincing for me to get past Avery's spies. They are everywhere, and Rufo watches my every move even more closely now, though he shared equal punishment."

"You both deserved it!" Danica snapped back. "After your behavior in the great hall."

"So now we clean," Cadderly agreed with a resigned shrug. "Everywhere, every day. It has been a long two weeks, with a longer two still to come."

"More than that if Headmaster Avery catches you here," Danica warned.

Cadderly shook his head and threw up his hands. "I was cleaning the kitchen," he explained. "Ivan and Pikel threw me out. 'It's me kitchen, boy!' " Cadderly said in his best dwarven voice, slamming his fists on his hips and puffing out his chest. " 'If there's any cleanin' to be done, it'll be done by meself! I'm not needing a . . .' "

Danica reminded him where he was to quiet him and pulled him to the side, behind the cover of some book racks.

"That was Ivan," Cadderly said. "Pikel did not say much. So the kitchen will be cleaned by the dwarves if it is to be cleaned at all, and a good thing, I say. An hour in there could put an end to my appetite for some time to come!"

"That does not excuse you from your work," Danica protested.

"I am working," Cadderly retorted. He pulled aside the front of his heavy woolen cloak and lifted a foot, revealing a sandal that was half shoe and half scrubbing brush. "Every step I take cleans the library a little bit more."

Danica couldn't argue with Cadderly's unending stream of personalized logic. In truth, she was glad that Cadderly had come to visit her. She hadn't seen much of him in the last two weeks and found that she missed him dearly. Also, on a more practical level, Danica was having trouble deciphering some important parchments and Cadderly was just the person to help her.

"Could you look at these?" she asked, retrieving the fallen scrolls.

"Master Penpahg D'Ahn?" Cadderly replied, hardly surprised. He knew that Danica had come to the Edificant Library more than a year before to study the collected notes of Penpahg D'Ahn of Ashanath, the grandmaster monk who had died five hundred years before. Danica's order was small and secretive, and few in this part of the Realms had ever heard of Penpahg D'Ahn, but those who studied the grandmaster's fighting and concentration techniques gave their lives over to his philosophies wholeheartedly. Cadderly had only seen a fraction of Danica's notes, but those had intrigued him, and he certainly could not dispute Danica's fighting prowess. More than half of the proud Oghman clerics had been walking around rubbing numerous bruises since the fiery young woman had come to the library.

"I am not quite certain of this interpretation," Danica explained, spreading a parchment over a table.

Cadderly moved to her side and examined the scroll. It began with a picture of crossed fists, which indicated that it was a battle technique, but then showed the single open eye indicating a concentration technique. Cadderly read on. "Gigel Nugel," he said aloud, then he thought that over for a moment.

"Iron Skull. The maneuver is called Iron Skull."

Danica banged a fist onto the table. "As I believed!" she said.

Cadderly was almost afraid to ask. "What is it?"

Danica held the parchment up over the table's lamp, emphasizing a small, nearly lost sketch in the lower corner. Cadderly eyed it closely. It appeared to be a large rock sitting atop a man's head. "Is that supposed to be a representation of Penpahg D'Ahn?" he asked.

Danica nodded.

"So now we know how he died," Cadderly snickered.

Danica snapped the parchment away, not appreciating the humor. Sometimes Cadderly's irreverence crossed the boundaries of her considerable tolerance.

"I am sorry," Cadderly apologized with a low bow. "Truly Penpahg D'Ahn was an amazing person, but are you saying he could break stone with his head?"

"It is a test of discipline," Danica replied, her voice edged with mounting excitement. "As are all of Grandmaster Penpahg D'Ahn's teachings. The grandmaster was in control of his body, of his very being."

"I am quite certain that you would forget my very name if Master Penpahg D'Ahn returned from the grave," Cadderly said mournfully.

"Forget who's name?" Danica replied calmly, not playing into his game.

Cadderly cast a hard glare at her but smiled as she smiled, unable to resist her charms. The young scholar grew suddenly serious, though, and looked back to the parchment. "Promise me that you are not intending to smash your face into a stone," he said.

Danica crossed her arms over her chest and tilted her head in an obstinate way, silently telling Cadderly to mind his own business.

"Danica," Cadderly said firmly.

In reply, Danica extended one finger and placed it down on the table. Her thoughts turned inward; her concentration had to be complete. She lifted herself by that single extended digit, bending at the waist and bringing her legs up even with the table top. She held the pose for some time, glad for Cadderly's amazed gape.

"The powers of the body are beyond our comprehension and expectations," Danica remarked, shifting to a sitting position on the table and wiggling her finger to show Cadderly that it had suffered no damage. "Grandmaster Penpahg D'Ahn understood them and learned to channel them to fit his needs. I will not go out this night, nor any night soon, and attempt the Iron Skull, that much I can promise you. You must understand that Iron Skull is but a minor test compared to what I came here to achieve."

"Physical suspension," Cadderly muttered with obvious distaste.

Danica's face brightened. "Think of it!" she said. "The grandmaster was able to stop his heart, to suspend his very breathing."

"There are priests who can do the very same thing," Cadderly reminded her, "and wizards, too. I saw the spell in the book I inscribed . . ."

"This is not a spell," Danica retorted. "Wizards and priests call upon powers beyond their own minds and bodies. Think, though, of the control necessary to do as Grandmaster Penpahg D'Ahn did. He could stop his heart from beating at any time, using only his own understanding of his physical being. You above all should appreciate that."

"I do," Cadderly replied sincerely. His visage softened and he ran the back of his hand gently across Danica's soft cheek. "But you scare me, Danica. You are relying on tomes a half millennium old for techniques that could be tragic. I do not remember with fondness how my life was before I met you, and I do not want to think of what it would be without you."

"I cannot change who I am," Danica replied quietly, but without compromise, "nor will I surrender the goals I have chosen for my life."

Cadderly considered her words for a few moments, weighing them against his own feelings. He respected everything about Danica, and above all else it was her fire, her willingness to accept and defeat all challenges, that he most loved. To tame her, to put out that fire, Cadderly knew, would be to kill this Danica, his Danica, more surely than any of Penpahg D'Ahn's seemingly impossible tests ever could.

"I cannot change," Danica said again.

Cadderly's reply came straight from his heart. "I would not want you to."

* * * * *

Barjin knew that he could not enter the ivy-streaked building through any of its windows or doors. While the Edificant Library was always open to scholars of all nonevil sects, warding glyphs had been placed over every known entrance to protect against those not invited—persons, such as Barjin, dedicated to the spread of chaos and misery.

The Edificant Library was an ancient building, and Barjin knew that ancient buildings usually held secrets, even from their present inhabitants.

The priest held the red-glowing bottle aloft before his eyes.

"We have come to our destination," he said, speaking as if the bottle could hear him, "to where I will secure my position of rulership over Castle Trinity, and over all the region once our conquest is completed." Barjin wanted to rush in, find his catalyst, and set the events in motion. He really didn't believe the elixir was an agent of Talona, but then, Barjin didn't consider himself an agent of Talona, though he had joined her clerical order. He had adopted the goddess for convenience, for mutual benefit, and knew that as long as his actions furthered the Lady of Poison's evil designs, she would be content.

Barjin spent the rest of the day, which was drizzly and dreary for late spring, in the shadows behind the trees lining the wide road. He heard the midday canticle, then watched many priests and other scholars exit alone or in groups for an early afternoon stroll.

The evil priest took a few precautionary measures, casting simple spells that would help him blend into his background and remain undetected. He listened to the casual banter of the passing groups, wondering with amusement how their words might change when he loosed the Most Fatal Horror in their midst.

The figure that soon caught Barjin's attention, though, was neither priest nor scholar. Disheveled and gray haired, with a dirty and stubbly face and skin wrinkled and browned from many years in the sun, Mullivy, the groundskeeper, went about his routines as he had for four decades, sweeping the road and the stairs to the front doors, heedless of the drizzle.

Barjin's wicked grin spread wide. If there was a secret way into the Edificant Library, this old man would know of it.

* * * * *

The clouds had broken by sunset, and a beautiful crimson patina lined the mountains west of the library. Mullivy hardly noticed it, though, having seen too many sunsets to be impressed anymore. He stretched the aches out of his old bones and strolled to his small workshed off to the side of the library's huge main building.

"You're getting old, too," the groundskeeper said to the shack as the door opened with a loud creak. He reached inside, meaning to replace his broom, then stopped abruptly, frozen in place by some power he did not understand.

A hand reached around him, prying the broom from his stubborn grasp. Mullivy's mind shouted warnings, but he could not bring his body to react, could not shout or spin to face the person guiding that unexpected hand. He then was pushed into the shed—fell face down, not able to lift an arm to break the fall—and the door closed behind him. He knew he was not alone.

* * * * *

"You will tell me," the sinister voice promised from the darkness.

Mullivy hung by his wrists, as he had for several hours. The room was totally black, but the groundskeeper sensed the awful presence all too near.

"I could kill you and ask your corpse," Barjin said with a chuckle. "Dead men talk, I assure you, and they do not lie."

"There's no other way in," Mullivy said for perhaps the hundredth time.

Barjin knew the old man was lying. At the beginning of the interrogation, the priest had cast spells to distinguish truth from falsehood and Mullivy had failed that test completely.

Barjin reached out and gently grabbed the groundskeeper's stomach in one hand.

"No! No!" he begged, thrashing and trying to wiggle out of that grip. Barjin held tight and began a soft chant, and soon Mullivy's insides felt as if they were on fire, his stomach ripped by agony that no man could endure. His screams, primal, hopeless, and helpless, emanated from that pained area.

"Do cry out," Barjin chided him. "All about the shed is a spell of silence, old fool. You will not disturb the slumber of those within the library. But then, why would you care for their sleep?" Barjin asked quietly, his voice filled with feigned sympathy. He released his grip and softly stroked Mullivy's wounded belly.

Mullivy stopped thrashing and screaming, though the pain of the sinister spell lingered.

"To them you are insignificant," Barjin purred, and his suggestion carried the weight of magical influences. "The priests think themselves your betters. They allow you to sweep for them and keep the rain gutters clean, but do they care for your pain? You are out here suffering terribly, but do any of them rush to your aid?"

Mullivy's heaving breaths settled into a calmer rhythm.

"Still you defend them so stubbornly," Barjin purred, knowing that his torture was beginning to wear the groundskeeper down. "They would not defend you, and still you will not show me your secret, at the cost of your life."

Even in his most lucid state, Mullivy was not a powerful thinker. His best friend most often was a bottle of stolen wine, and now, in his agony-racked jumble of thoughts, this unseen assailant's words rang loudly of truth. Why shouldn't he show this man his secret, the damp, moss-and-spider-filled dirt tunnel that led to the lowest level of the library complex, the ancient and unused catacombs below the wine cellar and the upper dungeon level? Suddenly, as Barjin had planned, Mullivy's imagined appearance of the unseen assailant softened. In his desperation, the groundskeeper needed to believe that his tormentor could actually be his ally.

"You won't tell them?" Mullivy asked.

"They will be the last to know," Barjin promised hopefully.

"You won't stop me from getting at the wine?"

Barjin backed off a step, surprised. He understood the old man's initial hesitance. The groundskeeper's secret way into the library led to the wine cellar, a stash that the wretch would not easily part with. "Dear man," Barjin purred, "you may have all the wine you desire—and much more, so much more."

* * * * *

They had barely entered the tunnel when Mullivy, carrying the torch, turned and waved it threateningly at Barjin.

Barjin's laughter mocked him, but Mullivy's voice remained Canticle firm. "I showed you the way," the groundskeeper declared. "Now I'm leaving."

"No," Barjin replied evenly. A shrug sent the priest's traveling cloak to the floor, revealing him in all his splendor. He wore his new vestments, the purple silken robes depicting a trident capped by three red flasks. On his belt was his peculiar mace, its head a sculpture of a young girl. "You have joined me now," Barjin explained. "You will never be leaving."

Terror drove Mullivy's movements. He slapped the burning torch against Barjin's shoulder and tried to push by, but the priest had prepared himself well before handing the torch to the groundskeeper. The flames did not touch Barjin, did not even singe his magnificent vestments, for they were defeated by a protection spell.

Mullivy tried a different tactic, slamming the torch like a club, but the vestments carried a magical armor as solid as metal plate mail and the wooden torch bounced off Barjin's shoulder without so much as causing the priest to flinch.

"Come now, dear Mullivy," Barjin cajoled, taking no offense. "You do not want me as an enemy."

Mullivy fell back and nearly dropped the torch. It took him a long moment to get past his terror, to even find his breath.

"Lead on," Barjin bade him. "You know this tunnel and the passages beyond. Show them to me."

Barjin liked the catacombs—dusty and private and filled with the remains of long-dead priests, some embalmed and others only cobweb-covered skeletons. He would have use for them.

Mullivy led him through a tour of the level, including the rickety stairwell that led up to the library's wine cellar and a medium-sized chamber that once had been used as a study for the original library. Barjin thought this room an excellent place to set up his unholy altar, but first he had to see exactly how useful the groundskeeper might prove.

They lit several torches and set them in wall sconces, then Barjin led Mullivy to an ancient table, one of many furnishings in the room, and produced his precious baggage. The bottle had been heavily warded back at Castle Trinity; only disciples of Talona or someone of pure heart could even touch it, and only the latter could open it. Like Aballister, Barjin knew this to be an obstacle, but unlike the wizard, the priest believed it a fitting one. What better irony than to have one of pure heart loose the chaos curse?

"Open it, I pray you," Barjin said.

The groundskeeper studied the flask for a moment, then looked curiously at the priest.

Barjin knew Mullivy's weak spot. "It is ambrosia," the priest lied. "The drink of the gods. One taste of it and forever after wines will taste to you ten times as sweet, for the lingering effects of ambrosia will never diminish. Drink, I pray you. You have certainly earned your reward."

Mullivy licked his lips eagerly, took one final look at Barjin, then reached for the glowing bottle. A jolt of electricity shot into him as he touched it, blackening his fingers and throwing him across the room to where he slammed into a wall. Barjin went over and dropped one arm under Mullivy's shoulder to help him stand.

"I thought not," the priest muttered to himself.

Still twitching from the blast, his hair dancing wildly with lingering static, Mullivy could not find his voice to reply.

"Fear not," Barjin assured him. "You will serve me in other ways." Mullivy noticed then that the priest held his girl's-head mace in his other hand.

Mullivy fell back against the wall and put his arms up defensively, but they were hardly protection from Barjin's foul weapon. The innocent looking head swung in at the doomed groundskeeper, transforming as it went. The weapon's image became angular, evil, the Screaming Maiden, her mouth opening impossibly wide, to reveal long, venom-tipped fangs.

She bit hungrily through the bone in Mullivy's forearm and plowed on, crushing and tearing into the man's chest. He twitched wildly for several agonizing moments, then he slid down the wall and died.

Barjin, with many preparations still to make, paid him no heed.

* * * * *

Aballister leaned back in his chair, breaking his concentration from his magical mirror but not breaking the connection he had made. He had located Barjin and had recognized the priest's surroundings: the Edificant Library. Aballister rubbed his hands through his thinning hair and considered the revelation, news that he found more than a little disturbing.

The wizard had mixed emotions concerning the library, unresolved feelings that he did not care to examine at this important time. Aballister had actually studied there once, many years before, but his curiosity with denizens of the lower planes had ended that relationship. The host priests thought it a pity that one of Aballister's potential had to be asked to leave, but they expressed their concerns that Aballister had some trouble distinguishing between good and evil, between proper studies and dangerous practices.

The expulsion did not end Aballister's relationship with the Edificant Library, though. Other events over the ensuing years had served to increase the wizard's ambiguous feelings toward the place. Now, in the overall plan of regional conquest, Aballister would have greatly preferred to leave the library for last, with him personally directing the attack. He never would have guessed that Barjin would be so daring as to go after the place in the initial assault, believing that the priest would venture to Shilmista, or to some vital spot in Carradoon.

"Well?" came a question from across the room.

"He is in the Edificant Library," Aballister answered grimly. "The priest has chosen to begin our campaign against our most powerful enemies."

Aballister anticipated Druzil's reply well enough to mouth "*bene tellemara*" along with the imp.

"Find him," Druzil demanded. "What is he thinking?"

Aballister put a curious gaze the imp's way, but if he had any notion to reprimand Druzil, it was lost in his agreement with the demand. He leaned forward again toward the large mirror and scried deeper, into the library's lower levels, through the cobweb-covered tunnels to the room where Barjin had built his altar.

Barjin glanced around nervously for a moment, then apparently recognized the source of the mental connection. "Well met, Aballister," the priest said smugly.

"You take great chances," the wizard remarked.

"Do you doubt the power of *Tuanta Quiro Miancay*?" Barjin asked. "The agent of Talona?"

Aballister had no intentions of reopening that unresolvable debate. Before he could respond, another figure moved into the picture, pallid and unblinking, with one broken arm hanging grotesquely and blood covering the left side of its chest.

"My first soldier," Barjin explained, pulling Mullivy's body close to his side. "I have a hundred more awaiting my call."

Aballister recognized the "soldier" as an animated corpse, a zombie, and, knowing that Barjin was in catacombs no doubt laced with burial vaults, the wizard did not have to ask where he intended to find his army. Suddenly Barjin's choice to assault the library did not seem so foolhardy; Aballister had to wonder just how powerful his conniving rival might be, or might become. Again the wizard's mixed feelings about the Edificant Library flooded over him. Aballister wanted to order Barjin out of the place at once, but of course, he had not the power to enforce the demand.

"Do not underestimate me," Barjin said, as though he had read the wizard's mind. "Once the library is defeated, all the region will be opened to us. Now be gone from here; I have duties to attend that a simple wizard cannot understand."

Aballister wanted to voice his protest at Barjin's demeaning tone, but again, he knew that words would carry no real weight. He broke the connection immediately and fell back in his chair, memories welling inside him.

"*Bene tellemara*," Druzil said again.

Aballister looked over to the imp. "Barjin may bring us a great victory much earlier than we expected," the wizard said, but there was little excitement in his voice.

"It is an unnecessary risk," Druzil spat back. "With Ragnor's forces ready to march, Barjin could have found a better target. He could have gone to the elves and loosed the curse there—Ragnor certainly hates them and intends to make them his first target. If we took Shilmista Forest, we could march south around the mountains to isolate the priests, surround the powerful library before they ever even realized that trouble had come to their land."

Aballister did not argue and wondered again if he had been wise in so easily relinquishing control of the elixir to Barjin. He had justified each action, each failing, but he knew in his heart that his cowardice had betrayed him.

"I must go to him," Druzil remarked unexpectedly.

After taking a moment to consider the request, Aballister decided not to contest it. Sending Druzil would be a risk, the wizard knew, but he realized, too, that if he had found the strength to take more risks in his earlier meetings with Barjin, he might not now be in so awkward a position.

"Dorigen informed me that Barjin carried an enchanted brazier with him," the wizard said, rising and taking up his staff. "She is the best with sorcery. She will know if Barjin opens a gate to the lower planes in search of allies. When Dorigen confirms the opening, I will open a gate here. Your journey will be a short one. Barjin will not know you as my emissary and will think that he freely summoned you and that it is he who controls you."

Druzil snapped his batlike wings around him and wisely held his tongue until Aballister had exited the room.

"Your emissary?" the imp snarled at the closed door.

Aballister had a lot to learn.

Seven
Sunlight and Darkness

Newander felt invigorated as soon as he walked out the building's front doors, into the morning sunshine. He had just completed his turn at translating the ancient moss tome, hours huddled over the book with walls closing in all about him. For all his doubts concerning his own views about civilization, Newander knew with certainty that he preferred the open sky to any ceiling.

He was supposed to be in the small chamber, resting now, while Cleo worked at the book and Arcite performed the daily druidic rituals. Newander didn't often go against Arcite's orders, but he could justify this transgression; he was much more at rest walking along the mountain trails than in any room, no matter how comfortable its bed.

The druid found Percival skipping through the branches along the tree-lined lane. "Will you come and talk with me, white one?" he called.

The squirrel looked Newander's way, then glanced back to a different tree. Following the gaze, Newander saw another squirrel, this one a normal gray female, sitting very still and watching him.

"A thousand pardons," Newander piped to Percival. "I did not know that you were engaged, so to speak." He gave a low bow and went on his merry way down the mountain road.

Percival chattered at the departing druid for a few moments, then hopped back toward his mate.

The morning turned into afternoon and still the druid walked, away from the Edificant Library. He had broken off the main road some time ago, following a deer trail deep into the wilderness. Here he was at home and at peace, and he was confident that no animal would rise against him.

Clouds gathered over distant ridges, promising another of the common spring thunderstorms. As with the animals, the druid did not fear the weather. He would walk in a downpour and call it a bath, skip and slide along snow-covered trails and call it play. While the gathering storm clouds did not deter the druid, they did remind him that he still had duties back at the library and that Arcite and Cleo soon would realize that he was gone. "Just a little bit farther," he promised himself.

He meant to turn back a short while later but caught sight of an eagle, soaring high on the warm updrafts. The eagle spotted him, too, and swooped down low at him, cawing angrily. At first, Newander thought the bird meant to attack, but then he sorted through enough of its excited chatter to realize that it had recognized him as a friend.

"What is your trouble?" Newander asked the bird. He was fairly adept at understanding bird calls, but the eagle was too agitated and spoke too rapidly for Newander to hear anything but a clear warning of danger.

"Show me," the druid replied, and he whistled and cawed to ensure that the eagle understood. The great bird rushed off, climbing high into the sky so that Newander would not lose sight of it as it soared ever deeper, and ever higher, into the mountains.

When he came out on a high and treeless ridge, the wind buffeted his green cloak fiercely and the druid realized the cause of the eagle's distress. Across a deep ravine, three filthy gray, monkeylike creatures scrambled up the side of a tall, sheer cliff, using their prehensile tails and four clawed paws to gain a secure hold on even the tiniest juts and cracks.

On a shallow ledge near the top of the cliff sat a great pile of twigs and sticks, an eagle aerie. Newander could guess what was inside that nest.

The infuriated eagle dove at the intruders repeatedly, but the monsters only spat at it as it helplessly passed, or swiped at it with their formidable claws.

Newander recognized these creatures as su-monsters, but he had no direct knowledge of them and had never encountered them before. It was widely agreed that they were vicious and bloodthirsty, but the druids had taken no formal stance concerning them. Were they an intelligent, evil group, or just a superbly adapted predator, feared because of their prowess? Animal or monster?

To many, the distinction would mean nothing, but to a druid, that question concerned the very tenets of his or her religion.

If the su-monsters were animal, then terms such as "evil" did not apply to them and Newander could play no role in aiding the pitiful eagle. Watching their eager climb, saliva dripping from their toothy maws, Newander knew that he must do something. He called out a few of the more common natural warning cries, and the su-monsters stopped suddenly and looked at him, apparently noticing him for the first time. They hooted and spat and waved their claws threateningly, then resumed their climb.

Newander called out again. The su-monsters ignored him.

"Guide me, Silvanus," Newander begged, closing his eyes.

He knew that the greatest druids of his order had held council about these rare but nightmarish creatures, and that they had come to no definite conclusions. Thus, the common practice among the order, though no edict had been issued, was to interfere with su-monsters only if threatened directly.

In his heart, though, Newander knew that the scene before him was unnatural.

He called again to Silvanus, the Oak Father, and, to his utter amazement, he believed that he was answered. He looked to the nearest thunderhead, gauging the distance, then back to the su-monsters.

"Halt!" Newander cried out. "Go no farther!"

The su-monsters turned at once, startled perhaps by the urgency, the power, in the druid's voice. One found a loose stone and heaved it Newander's way, but the ravine was wide as well as deep and the missile fell harmlessly.

"I warn you again," the druid cried, sincerely desiring no battle. "I have no fight with you, but you'll not get to the aerie."

The monsters spat again and clawed ferociously at the empty air.

"Be gone from here!" Newander cried. Their reply came in the form of spittle and they turned and started up again.

Newander had seen enough; the su-monsters were too close to the aerie for him to waste any more time screaming warnings. He closed his eyes, clutched the oak leaf holy symbol hanging on a leather cord about his neck, and called out to the thunderstorm.

The su-monsters paid him no heed, intent on the egg-filled nest just a few dozen yards above them.

Druids considered themselves the guardians of nature and the natural order. Unlike wizards and priests of many other sects, druids accepted that they were the watchdogs of the world and that the powers they brought were more a call for help to nature than any manifestation of their own internal power. So it was as Newander called again to the heavy black cloud, directing its fury.

The thunderstroke shook the mountains for many miles around, sent the surprised eagle spinning away blindly, and nearly knocked Newander from his feet. When his sight returned, the druid saw that the cliff face was clear, the aerie was safe. The su-monsters were nowhere to be seen, and the only evidence that they had ever been there was a long scorch mark, a dripping crimson stain along the mountain wall, and a small tuft of fur, a severed tail perhaps, burning on a shallow ledge.

The eagle flew to its nest, squawked happily, and soared down to thank the druid.

"You are very welcome," the druid assured the bird. In conversing with the eagle, he felt much better about his own destructive actions. Like most druids, Newander was a gentle sort, and he was always uncomfortable when called to battle.

The fact that the cloud had answered his summons, a calling power that he believed came from Silvanus, also gave him confidence that he had acted correctly, that the su-monsters were indeed monsters and no natural predators.

Newander interpreted the next series of the eagle's caws as an invitation to join the bird at its aerie. The druid would have loved that, but the cliff across the way was too formidable a barrier with night fast approaching.

"Another day," he replied.

The eagle cackled a few more thanks, then, explaining that many preparations were still needed for the coming brood, bade the druid farewell and soared off. Newander watched the bird fly away with sincere lament. He wished that he was more skilled at his religion; druids of higher rank, including both Arcite and Cleo, could actually assume the form of animals. If Newander were as skilled as either of them, he could simply shed his light robes and transform himself into an eagle, joining his new friend on the high, shallow ledge. Even more enticing, as an eagle Newander could explore these majestic mountains from a much improved viewpoint, with the wind breaking over his wings and eyes sharp enough to sort out the movements of a field mouse from a mile up.

He shook his head and shook away, too, his laments for what could not be. It was a beautiful day, with a cleansing shower close at hand, full of new-blossoming flowers, chattering birds, fresh air on a chill breeze, and clear and cold mountain spring water around every bend—all the things that the druid loved best.

He stripped off his robes and put them under a thick bush, then sat cross-legged out on a high and open perch, awaiting the rain. It came in a torrential downpour, and Newander considered its patter on the stones the sweetest of nature's many songs.

The storm broke in time for a wondrous sunset, scarlet fading to pink, and filling every break in the towering mountain peaks to the west.

"I fear that I am late in returning," Newander said to himself. He gave a resigned shrug and could not prevent a boyish grin from spreading over his face. "The library will still be there on the morrow," he rationalized as he retrieved his robes, found a comfortable spot, and settled in for the night.

* * * * *

Barjin hung the brazier pot in place on the tripod and put in the special mixture of wood chips and incense blocks. He did not light the brazier at this time, though, uncertain of how long it would take him to find a proper catalyst for the chaos curse.

Denizens of lower planes could be powerful allies, but they were usually a wearisome lot, demanding more of their summoner's time and energy than Barjin now had to give.

Similarly, Barjin kept his necromancer's stone tightly wrapped in the shielding cloth. As with lower-plane creatures, some types of undead could prove difficult to control, and, like the gate created by the enchanted brazier, the necromancer's stone could summon an assortment of monsters, anything from the lowliest, unthinking skeletons and zombies to cunning ghosts.

Still, for all his glyphs and wards, Barjin felt insecure about leaving the altar room, and the precious bottle, with nothing more intelligent and powerful than Mullivy to stand guard. He needed an ally, and he knew where to find it.

"Khalif," the evil priest muttered, retrieving the ceramic flask. He had carried it for years, even before his days in Vaasa and before he had turned to Talona. He had found the ash urn among some ancient ruins while working as an apprentice to a now dead wizard. Barjin, by the terms of his apprenticeship, was not supposed to claim any discoveries as his own, but then, Barjin had never played by any rules but his own. He had kept the ceramic urn, filled with the ashes of Prince Khalif, a noble of some ancient civilization according to the accompanying parchment, private and safe through many years.

Barjin hadn't fully come to appreciate the potential value of such a find until after he began his training in clerical magic. Now he understood what he could do with the ashes; all he needed was a proper receptacle.

He led Mullivy out into the passageway beyond the altar room's door, a wide corridor lined with alcoves, burial vaults of the highest-ranking founders of the Edificant Library. Unlike the other vaults Barjin had seen down here, these were not open chairs, but elaborately designed caskets, sarcophagi, gem-studded and extravagant. Barjin could only hope, as he instructed Mullivy to open the closest sarcophagus, that the early scholars had spared no expenses on the contents within the casket as well, that they had used some embalming techniques.

Mullivy, for all his strength, could not begin to open the first sarcophagus, its lock and hinges rusted fast. The zombie had better luck with the second, for its cover simply fell away under Mullivy's heavy tug. As soon as the door opened, a long tentacle shot out at Mullivy, followed by a second and a third. They did no real damage, but Barjin was glad that the zombie, and not he, had opened the lid.

Inside was a carrion crawler, a monstrous wormlike beast with eight tentacles tipped with paralyzing poison. Undead Mullivy could not be affected by such an attack and, beyond the tentacles, the carrion crawler was virtually defenseless.

"Kill it!" Barjin instructed. Mullivy pounded away with his one good arm. The carrion crawler was no more than a lifeless lump at the bottom of the casket when Mullivy at last backed away.

"This one will not do," Barjin mumbled, inspecting the empty husk inside the sarcophagus. There was no dismay in his voice, though, for the body, ruined by the carrion crawler, had been carefully wrapped in thick linen, a sure sign that the ancient scholars had used some embalming techniques. Barjin also found a small hole at the back of the sarcophagus, and he correctly assumed that the carrion crawler had come in there, gorged itself for months, perhaps even years, on the full corpse, then had grown too large to crawl back out.

Barjin pulled Mullivy along eagerly, seeking another sarcophagus, one with no obvious external holes. The third time paid for all, as the saying goes, for, with help from the Screaming Maiden, Barjin and Mullivy were able to break through the locks of the next casket. Inside, wrapped in linen, lay a well-preserved corpse, the receptacle that Barjin needed.

Barjin instructed Mullivy to carry the corpse gently into the altar room—he did not want to touch the scabrous thing himself—then to rearrange the sarcophagi so that this one's would be closest to the altar room door.

Barjin shut the door behind his zombie, not wanting to be distracted by the noises outside. He took out his clerical spellbook, turned to the section on necromantic practices, and took out his necromancer's stone, thinking its summoning powers to be helpful in calling back the spirit of Prince Khalif.

The priest's chanting went on for more than an hour, and all the while he dropped pinches of the ash onto the wrapped corpse. When the ceramic urn was emptied, the priest broke it apart, rubbing it clean on the receptacle body's linen. Khalif's spirit had been contained in the whole of the ash; the absence of the slightest motes could prove disastrous.

Barjin became distracted by the necromancer's stone, for it began to glow with an eerie, purple-black light. The priest snapped his gaze back to the mummy, his attention caught by the sudden red glow as two dots of light appeared behind the linen wrappings that covered the corpse's eyes. Barjin covered his hand in clean cloth and carefully pulled away the linen.

He fell back with a start. The mummy rose before him.

It looked upon the priest with utter hatred, its eyes burning as bright red dots. Barjin knew that mummies, like most monsters of the netherworld, hated all living things, and Barjin, for the moment anyway, was a living thing.

"Back, Khalif!" Barjin commanded as forcefully as he could manage. The mummy took another stiff-legged step forward.

"Back, I say!" Barjin snarled, replacing his fear with determined anger. "It was I who retrieved your spirit, and here in my service you shall stay until I, Barjin, release you to your eternal rest!"

He thought his words pitifully inept, but the mummy responded, sliding back to its original position.

"Turn away!" Barjin cried, and the mummy did.

A smile spread wide over the evil priest's face. He had dealt with denizens of the lower planes many times before and had animated simple undead monsters, like Mullivy, but this was a new and higher step for him. He had called to a powerful spirit, torn it from the grave and forced it under his control.

Barjin moved back to the door. "Come in, Mullivy," he ordered in a mirthful tone. "Come and meet your new brother."

Eight
Catalyst

P ikel just shook his hairy head and continued stirring the cauldron's contents with his huge wooden spoon as Cadderly considered Ivan's grim news.

"Can you finish the crossbow?" Cadderly asked.

"I can," Ivan replied, "but me thinkin's that you should be more worried about yer own fate, boy. The headmistress was not smiling much when she found her tapestry in my kitchen—not smiling a bit when she saw that Pikel had spilled gravy on one corner."

Cadderly flinched at that remark. Headmistress Pertelope was a tolerant woman, especially of Cadderly and his inventions, but she prized her art collection above all else. The tapestry depicting the elven war was one of her favorites.

"I am sorry if I have caused you two any problems," Cadderly said sincerely, though the honest lament did not stop him from dipping his fingers into a bowl that Ivan had recently used for cake baking. "I did not believe . . ."

Ivan waved his concerns away. "Not a problem," the dwarf grunted. "We just blamed everything on yerself."

"Just finish the crossbow," Cadderly instructed with a halfhearted chuckle. "I will go to Headmistress Pertelope and set things right."

"Perhaps Headmistress Pertelope will come to you," came a woman's voice from the kitchen's doorway, behind Cadderly.

The young scholar turned slowly and winced even more when he saw that Headmaster Avery stood beside Pertelope.

"So you have elevated your mischief to theft," Avery remarked. "I fear that your time in the library may be drawing to an end, Brother Cadderly, though that unfortunate conclusion was not altogether unexpected, given your heri—"

"You must be given the opportunity to explain," Pertelope interrupted, flashing a sudden dark glare Avery's way. "I am not pleased, whatever excuse you might offer."

"I had . . ." Cadderly stuttered. "I meant to . . ."

"Enough!" Avery commanded, glowering at both Cadderly and the headmistress. "You may explain about Headmistress Pertelope's tapestry later," he said to Cadderly. "First, do tell me why are you here. Have you no work to do? I thought that I had given you enough to keep you busy, but if I thought wrong, I can surely correct the situation!"

"I am busy," Cadderly insisted. "I only wanted to check on the kitchen, to make certain that I had not missed anything in my cleaning." As soon as Cadderly glanced around, he realized how ludicrous his claim sounded. Ivan and Pikel never kept an overly neat shop. Half the floor was covered with spilled flour, the other half with assorted herbs and sauces. Fungus-lined bowls, some empty and some half full of last week's meals some from meals even older than that—sat on every available space, counter, or table.

Avery's brow crinkled as he recognized the lie for what it was. "Do make certain that the task was done correctly, Brother Cadderly," the headmaster crooned with dripping sarcasm. "Then you may join Brother Rufo in his inventory of the wine cellar. You will be informed of how Dean Thobicus will proceed concerning your greater transgression." Avery turned and stalked away, but Pertelope did not immediately follow.

"I know that you meant to return the tapestry," the stately older woman said. "Might I know why you saw the need to appropriate it at all? You might have asked."

"We only needed it for a few days," Cadderly replied. He looked to Ivan and indicated the drawer, and the dwarf reached into it and produced the nearly completed crossbow. "For this."

Pertelope's hazel eyes sparkled at the sight. She moved across the room and tentatively took the small weapon from the dwarf. "Exquisite," she muttered, truly awed by the reproduction.

"My thanks," Ivan replied proudly.

"Oo oi!" Pikel added in a triumphant tone.

"I would have shown it to you," Cadderly explained, "but I thought the surprise would prove more pleasurable when it was completed."

Pertelope smiled warmly at Cadderly. "Can you complete it without the tapestry?"

Cadderly nodded.

"I will want to see it then, when it is done," said the headmistress, suddenly businesslike. "You should have asked for the tapestry," she scolded, then she glanced around and added under her breath, "Do not fear too much for Headmaster Avery. He is excitable, but he forgets quickly. He likes you, whatever his bluster. Go, now, to your duties."

* * * * *

Barjin crept from cask to cask, studying the angular man at work sorting wine bottles. The evil priest had suspected that his victim, the catalyst for the chaos curse, would come from the cellar, but he was no less delighted when he found this man unexpectedly at work here on his very first trip up the rickety stairway. The door to the lower dungeons was cleverly concealed—no doubt by the thirsty groundskeeper—in a thickly packed and remote corner of the huge chamber. The portal probably had been long forgotten by the priests of the library, allowing Barjin easy and secret access.

Barjin's delight diminished considerably when he worked his way far enough around the room to cast some detection spells on the man. The same spells had been ambiguous on the groundskeeper—Barjin had not known for certain whether the old wretch would suffice until the warding glyphs had blown him back from the bottle, but the spells were not so ambiguous concerning Kierkan Rufo. This man was not possessed of innocence and would have no more luck with the magic bottle than did the groundskeeper.

"Hypocrite," Barjin grumbled silently. He rested back in the shadows and wondered how he might still find some use for the angular man. Certainly visitors to the wine cellar were not commonplace and Barjin could not allow anyone to pass through without extracting some benefit.

He was still contemplating things when a second priest unexpectedly came skipping down the stairwell. Barjin watched curiously as this smiling young man, hair bouncing about his shoulders under a wide-brimmed hat, moved to confer with the angular worker. Barjin's detection spells had not yet expired and when he focused on this newest arrival, his curiosity turned to delight.

Here was his catalyst.

He watched a bit longer—long enough to discern that there was some tension between the two—then sneaked back to the concealed door. He knew that his next critical moves must be planned carefully.

* * * * *

"Should we work together?" Cadderly offered in an exaggerated, bubbly voice.

Kierkan Rufo glared at him. "Have you any tricks planned for me now?" he asked. "Any new baubles to show off at my expense?"

"Are you saying that you did not deserve it?" Cadderly asked. "You started the battle when you brought Avery to my room."

"Pity the mighty scribe," came the sarcastic reply.

Cadderly started to respond, but held his tongue. He sympathized with Rufo, truly an attentive priest. Cadderly knew that the headmasters had pushed Rufo aside after Cadderly's success with the wizard's spellbook. The wound was too fresh to mend it here, Cadderly knew, and neither he nor Rufo had any desire to work together.

Rufo explained his logging system for the inventory so that their lists might be compatible. Cadderly saw several possibilities for improvement but again said nothing. "Do you understand?" Rufo asked, handing Cadderly a counting chart.

Cadderly nodded. "A good system," he offered.

Rufo bruskly waved him away, then continued his inventory, working his way slowly around the long and shadowy racks.

A flash of light in a distant corner caught the angular man's attention, but it was gone as fast as it had appeared. Rufo cocked his head, took up his torch, and inched his way over. A wall of casks confronted him, but he noticed an opening around to the side.

"Is anyone there?" Rufo asked, a bit nervously. Torch leading the way, he peeked into the opening and saw the ancient portal. "What is it?" came a voice behind him. Rufo jumped in surprise, dropped his torch at his feet, and upset a cask as he danced away from the flames. He was not comforted when the crashing had ended and he looked back into Cadderly's grinning face.

"It is a door," Rufo replied through gritted teeth.

Cadderly picked up the torch and peered in. "Now where might that lead?" he asked rhetorically.

"It is none of our concern," Rufo said firmly.

"Of course it is," Cadderly retorted. "It is part of the library and the library is our concern."

"We must tell a headmaster and let him decide the proper way to investigate it," Rufo offered. "Now give me the torch."

Cadderly ignored him and advanced to the small wooden portal. It opened easily, revealing a descending stairway, and Cadderly was surprised and delighted once more.

"You surely will get us into even more trouble!" Rufo complained at his back. "Do you wish to count and clean until your hundredth birthday?"

"To the lowest levels?" Cadderly said excitedly, ignoring the warning. He looked back at Rufo, his face glowing brightly in the near torchlight.

The nervous Rufo backed away from the weirdly shadowed specter. He seemed not to understand his companion's excitement.

"The lowest levels," Cadderly repeated as though those words should hold some significance. "When the library was originally built, most of it was below ground. The Snowflakes were wilder back then, and the founders thought an underground complex more easily defended. The lowest catacombs were abandoned as the mountains were tamed and the building expanded, and eventually it was believed that all the exits had been sealed." He looked back to the enticing stair. "Apparently that was not the case."

"Then we must tell a headmaster," Rufo declared nervously. "It is not our place to investigate hidden doorways."

Cadderly shot him an incredulous stare, hardly believing the man to be so childish. "We will tell them," the young scholar agreed, poking his head through the dusty opening. "In time."

* * * * *

A short distance away, Barjin watched the two men with nervous anticipation, one hand holding tight to the security of his cruel mace. The evil priest knew that he had taken quite a chance in calling up the magical light signaling the portal's location. If the two men decided to go and tell their masters, Barjin would have to intercept them—forcefully. But Barjin had never been patient, which was why he had come directly to the Edificant Library in the first place. There was a degree of danger in his gamble, both in coming here and in revealing the door, but the potential gains of both actions could not be ignored. If these two decided to explore, then Barjin would be one giant step closer to realizing his desires.

They disappeared from sight around the barricading casks, so Barjin crept closer. "The stairs are fairly solid, though they are ancient," he heard Cadderly call back, "and they go down a long, long way."

Appearing skeptical, even afraid, the angular priest slowly backed out of the concealed area. "The headmaster," he muttered softly and turned abruptly for the stairs.

Barjin stepped out before him.

Before Rufo could even cry out, the evil priest's spell fell over him. Rufo's gaze locked fast to the evil priest's dark eyes, held in place by Barjin's hypnotic stare. In his studies of wizardry, charms had always been the charismatic Barjin's strength. His adoption of Talona had not diminished that touch, though the Lady of Poison's clerics were not normally adept at such magic, and Kierkan Rufo was not a difficult opponent.

Nor were Barjin's magically enhanced suggestions to the enthralled Rufo contrary to the angular man's deepest desires.

* * * * *

Cadderly creeped slowly toward the open door, never taking his gaze from the enticing blackness beyond the meager limits of his torchlight. What wonders remained down there in the oldest rooms of the Edificant Library? he wondered. What secrets long forgotten about the founders and initial scholars?

"We should investigate—we'll be working down here for many days," Cadderly said, leaning forward and peering over the stairs. "No one would have to know until we decided to tell them."

Despite his consuming curiosity for the mysteries before him, Cadderly kept enough wits about him to realize that he had been betrayed as soon as he felt a boot against his lower back. He grabbed the flimsy railing, but the wood broke away in his hand. He managed to look back for just an instant and saw Rufo crouched in the low doorway, a weird, emotionless expression on his dark and hollowed face.

Cadderly's torch flew away, and he tumbled into the blackness, bouncing down the stairs and coming to rest heavily on the stone floor below. All the world fell into blackness; he did not hear the door close above him.

* * * * *

Kierkan Rufo went right from the wine cellar to his room that night, wanting to confront no one and respond to no questions. The recent events were but a blur to the charmed man.

He vaguely remembered what he had done to Cadderly, though he couldn't be certain if it had been real or a dream. He remembered, too, closing and blocking off the hidden door.

There was something else, or someone else, though, in the picture, hovering off to the side in the shadows just out of reach of Rufo's consciousness.

Try as he may, poor Rufo could not remember anything about Barjin, as a result of the enchanting priest's devious instructions. In the back of his mind, Rufo retained the strange sensation that he had made a friend this night, one who understood his frustrations and who agreed that Cadderly was an unworthy man.

Nine

Barjin's World

Cadderly awoke in utter darkness; he could not see his hand if he waved his fingers just an inch in front of his face. His other senses told him much, though. He could smell the thick dust and feel the sticky lines of cobwebs hanging all about.

"Rufo!" he called, but his voice carried nowhere in the dead air, just reminded him that he was alone in the dark. He crawled to his knees and found that he was sore in a dozen places, particularly on the side of his head, and that his tunic was crusted as if with dried blood. His torch lay beside him, but in pawing about it, Cadderly realized that it had expired many hours before.

Cadderly snapped his fingers, then reached down to his belt.

A moment later, he popped the cap from a cylindrical tube and a ray of light cut through the darkness. Even to Cadderly, the light seemed an intruder in these corridors, which had known only darkness for centuries uncounted. A dozen small creatures scuttled away on the edges of Cadderly's vision, just out of the light. Better to have them scurry away, Cadderly thought, than to have them lay in wait in the darkness for him to pass.

Cadderly examined his immediate surroundings with the light tube's aperture wide open, mostly focusing on the shattered stairway beside him. Several stairs remained attached at the top, near the closed door, but most of the boards lay scattered about, apparently shattered by Cadderly's heavy descent. No easy path back that way, he told himself, and he narrowed the beam to see down the greater distances. He was in a corridor, one of many crisscrossing and weaving together to form a honeycomb-type maze, judging from the many passages lining both walls. The supporting arches were similar to those of the library above, but, being an earlier architectural design, they were even thicker and lower, and seemed lower still covered with layers of dust, hanging webs, and promises of crawly things.

When Cadderly took the time to examine himself, he saw that his tunic was, as he expected, crusted with his own blood.

He noticed a broken board lying next to him, sharply splintered and darkly stained. Tentatively, the young priest unbuttoned his tunic and pulled it aside, expecting a garish wound.

What he found instead was a scab and a bruise. Although the more dutiful priests of Deneir, even those Cadderly's age, were accomplished healers, Cadderly was hardly practiced in the medicinal arts. He could tell, though, by the stains on the splintered board that his wound had been deep and it was obvious from his soaked shirt alone that he had lost quite a bit of blood. The wound was undeniably on the mend, though, and if it once had been serious, it was not now.

"Rufo?" Cadderly called again, wondering if his companion had come down behind him and healed him. There was no answer, not a sound in the dusty corridor. "If not Rufo, then who?" Cadderly asked himself softly. He shrugged his shoulders a moment later; the riddle was quite beyond him.

"Young and strong," Cadderly congratulated himself, having no other answer. He stretched the rest of his aches out and finished his survey of the area, wondering if there might be some way to reconstruct enough of the stairway to get back near the door. He set his light tube on the floor and pieced together some boards. The wood was terribly deteriorated and smashed beyond repair—too much so, Cadderly thought, to have been caused just by his fall. Several pieces were no more than splinters, as though they had been battered repeatedly.

After a short while, Cadderly gave up the idea of going back through the wine cellar. The old, rotted wood would never support his weight even if he could find some way to piece it back together. "It could be worse," he whispered aloud, picking up his light tube and taking his spindle-disks from a pouch.

He took a deep breath to steady himself and started off—any way seemed as good as another.

Crawling things darted to dark holes on the perimeter of the light beam, and a shudder coursed along Cadderly's spine as he imagined again what this journey might be like in darkness.

The walls were of brickwork in most of the passages, crushed under uncountable tonnage and cracked in many places. Bas-reliefs had worn away, the lines of an artist's chisel filled in by the dust of centuries, the fine detail of sculptures replaced by the artwork of spiderwebs. Somewhere in the dark distance, Cadderly heard the drip of water, a dull and dead *thump-thump*. "The heartbeat of the catacombs," Cadderly muttered grimly, and the thought did not comfort him.

He wandered for many minutes, trying to formulate some logical scheme for conquering the tunnel layout. While the builders of the original library had been an orderly group and had carefully thought out the catacomb design, the initial purposes, and courses, of the various tunnels had been adapted over the decades to fit the changing needs of the structure above.

Every time Cadderly thought he had some sense of where he might be, the next corner showed him differently. He moved along one low and wide corridor, taking care to keep away from the rotting crates lining the walls. If this was the storage area, he reasoned, there might be an outside exit nearby, a tunnel large enough for wagons, perhaps.

The corridor ended at a wide arch that fanned out diagonally under two smaller arches to the left and the right. These were congested by webs so thick that Cadderly had to retrieve a plank from the crates just to poke his way through.

The passages beyond the arched intersection were identical, layered stonework and only half as wide as the corridor he had just traveled. His instinct told him to go left, but it was just a guess, for in the winding ways Cadderly really had little idea of where he was in relation to the buildings above him.

He kept his pace swift, following the narrow beam faithfully and trying to ignore the rat squeaks and imagined perils to the sides and behind him. His fears were persistent, though, and each step came with more effort. He shifted the beam from side to side and saw that this passage's walls were lined with dark holes, alcoves. Hiding places, Cadderly imagined, for crouched monsters.

Cadderly turned slowly, bringing his light to bear, and realized that in his narrow focus on the path ahead, he had crossed the first few sets of these alcoves. A shudder ran through his spine, for he figured out the purpose of the alcoves before his light ever angled properly for him to see inside one.

Cadderly jumped back. The distant *thump-thump* of the catacomb heartbeat remained steady, but the young scholar's own heart missed a few beats, for the beam of light fell upon a seated skeleton just a few feet to Cadderly's side. If this passage had been intended for storage, its goods were macabre indeed! Where once may have been stored crates of food, now there was only food for the carrion eaters. Cadderly had entered the crypts, he knew, the burial vaults for the earliest scholars of the Edificant Library.

The skeleton sat impassive and oblivious in its tattered shroud, hand bones crossed over its lap. Webs extended from a dozen angles in the small alcove, seeming to support the skeleton in its upright posture.

Cadderly sublimated his mounting terror, reminded himself that these were simply natural remains, the remains of great men, good-hearted and thinking men, and that he, too, one day would resemble the skeleton seated before him. He looked back and counted four alcoves on either side of the corridor behind him and considered whether he should turn back.

Stubbornly, Cadderly dismissed all his fears as irrational and focused again on the path before him. He kept his light in the middle of the passage, not wanting to look into any more of the alcoves, not wanting to test his determination any further. But his eyes inevitably glanced to the side, to the hushed darkness. He imagined skeletal heads turning slowly to watch him pass.

Some fears were not so easily conquered.

A scuffle behind and to his left spun Cadderly about, his spindle-disks at the ready. His defensive reflexes launched the weapon before his mind could register the source of the noise: a small rat crawling across a wobbling skull.

The rodent flew away into webs and darkness when the disks struck full on the skull's forehead. The wobbly skull flew, too, rebounding off the alcove's back wall, rolling down the front of its former possessor, and coming to a rattling stop between the seated skeleton's legs.

A chuckle burst from Cadderly's mouth, relieved laughter at his own cowardice. The sound died away quickly as the dusty stillness reclaimed the ancient passage, and Cadderly relaxed . . . until the skeleton reached down between its legs and retrieved its fallen head.

Cadderly stumbled backward against the opposite wall—and promptly felt a bony grip on his elbow. He tore away, snapped his spindle-disks at this newest foe, and turned to flee, not pausing to note the damage his weapon had exacted. As his light swung about, though, Cadderly saw that the skeletons he had passed had risen and congregated in the corridor, and were now advancing, their faces locked in lipless grins, their arms outstretched as though they desired to pull Cadderly fully into their dark realm.

He had only one path open and he went with all speed, trying to keep his eyes ahead, trying to ignore the rattling of still more skeletons rising from every alcove he passed. He could only hope that no monstrous spiders were nearby as he charged right through another heavily webbed archway, tasting webs and spitting them out in disgust. He stumbled and fell more than once but always scrambled back to his feet, running blindly, knowing not where he should run, only what he must keep behind him.

More passages. More crypts. The rattling mounted behind him and he heard again, startlingly clear, the *thump-thump* water-drop heartbeat of the catacombs. He burst through another webbed archway, and then another, then came to a three-way intersection. He turned to the left but saw that the skeletons down that passage had already risen to block his way.

To the right he ran, too afraid to sort out any patterns, too distracted to realize that he was being herded.

He came to another low archway, noted that this one had no webs, but hadn't the time to pause and consider the implications. He was in a wider, higher passage, a grander hall, and saw that the alcoves here were filled not by raggedly shrouded skeletons, but by standing sarcophagi, exquisitely detailed and gilded in precious metals and gemstones.

Cadderly only noticed them for a moment, for down at the end of the long hallway he saw light—not daylight, which he would have welcomed with open arms, but light nonetheless peeking out at him from the cracks and loosened seals of an ancient door.

The rattling intensified, booming all about him. An eerie red mist appeared at

Cadderly's feet, following his progress, adding a surreal and dreamlike quality. Reality and nightmare battled in his rushing thoughts, reason fighting fear. The resolution to that battle lay in the light, Cadderly knew.

The young scholar staggered forward, his feet dragging as though the mist itself weighed heavily upon them. He lowered his shoulder, meaning to push right through the door, to charge right into the light.

The door squeaked open just before he collided, and he stumbled in, sinking down to his knees on the clean floor within. Then the door swung closed of its own accord, leaving the red mist and the macabre rattle out in the darkness. Cadderly remained very still for a long moment, confused and trying to slow his racing heart.

After a moment, Cadderly rose shakily to survey the room, hardly even registering that the door had closed behind him.

He was struck by the cleanliness of this room, so out of place in the rest of the dungeons. He recognized the place as a former study hall; it was similar in design and contained similar furniture to those studies still in use in the library proper. Several small cabinets, worktables, and free-standing two-sided bookcases sat at regular intervals about the room, and a brazier rested on a tripod along the right-hand wall. Torches burned in two sconces, and the walls were lined with bookshelves, empty except for a few scattered parchments, yellow with age, and an occasional small sculpture, once a book end, perhaps.

Cadderly's gaze went to the brazier first, thinking it oddly out of place, but it was the display in the center that ultimately commanded his attention.

A long and narrow table had been placed there, with a purple and crimson blanket spread over it and hanging down the front and sides. Atop the table was a podium, and on this sat a clear bottle sealed with a large cork and filled with some red glowing substance. In front of the bottle was a silvery bowl, platinum perhaps, intricately designed and covered with strange runes.

Cadderly was hardly surprised, or alarmed, at the blue mist he noted covering the floors and swirling about his legs. This entire adventure had taken on a blurry feeling of unreality to him. Rationally, he could tell himself that he was wide awake, but the dull ache on the side of his skull made him wonder just how badly he had banged his head. Whatever this was, though, Cadderly was now more intrigued than afraid, so, with great effort, he forced himself to his feet and took a cautious step toward the central table.

There were designs, tridents capped by three bottles, woven into the blanket. He noticed that the bottles of the designs were similar to the real one atop the table. Cadderly thought he knew most of the major holy symbols and alliance crests of the central Realms, but this was totally foreign. He wished he had prepared some spells that might reveal more of the strange altar, if it was an altar. Cadderly smiled at his own ineptitude. He rarely prepared any spells at all, and even when he took the time, his accomplishments with clerical magic were far from highly regarded. Cadderly was more scholar than priest, and he viewed his vows to Deneir more as an agreement of attitude and priorities than a pledge of devotion.

As he approached the table, he saw that the silvery bowl was filled with a clear liquid—probably water, though Cadderly did not dare dip his fingers into it. More intrigued by the glowing bottle behind it, Cadderly meant to pay it little heed at all, but the reflection of the flask in that strange rune-covered bowl captured his attention suddenly and for some reason would not let go.

Cadderly felt himself drawn toward that reflected image. He moved right up to the bowl and bent low, his face nearly touching the liquid. Then, as if a tiny pebble had fallen into the bowl, little circular ripples rolled out from the exact center. Far from breaking Cadderly's concentration on the reflection, the watery dance only enhanced it. The light bounced and rolled around the tiny waves and the image of the bottle elongated and bent, side to side.

Cadderly knew somehow that the water was pleasantly warm. He wanted to immerse himself in the bowl, to silence all the noises of the world around him in watery stillness and feel nothing but the warmth.

Still there was the image, swaying enticingly, capturing Cadderly's thoughts.

Cadderly looked up from the bowl to the bottle. Somewhere deep inside him he knew that something was amiss and that he should resist the strangely comforting sensations. Inanimate objects were not supposed to offer suggestions.

Open the bottle, came a call within his head. He did not recognize the soothing voice, but it promised only pleasure. *Open the bottle.*

Before he realized what he was doing, Cadderly had the bottle in his hands. He had no idea what the bottle truly was, or how and why this unknown altar had been set up. There was a danger here—Cadderly sensed it—but he could not sort it out clearly; the ripples in the silvery bowl had been so enthralling.

Open the bottle, came the quiet suggestion a third time.

Cadderly simply could not determine whether or not he should resist and that indecision weakened his resolve. The cork stopper was stubborn, but not overly so, and it came out with a loud *foomp*!

That pop cut through the smoky confusion in the young scholar's brain, rang out like a clarion call of reality, warning him of the risk he had taken, but it was too late.

Red smoke poured out of the flask, engulfing Cadderly and spreading to fill the room. Cadderly realized his error at once and he moved to replace the cork, but watching from behind the cabinet, an unseen enemy was already at work.

"Hold!" came an undeniable command from the side of the room.

Cadderly had the cork almost back to the bottle when his hands stopped moving. Still the smoke poured out. Cadderly could not react, could not move at all, could not even make his eyes look away. His whole body grew weirdly numb, tingled in the grasp of a magical grip. A moment later, Cadderly saw a hand reach around him but did not even feel the bottle being pried from his grasp. He then was forcefully turned about to face a man he did not know.

The man was waving and chanting, though Cadderly could not hear the words. He recognized the movements as some sort of spellcasting and knew that he was in dire peril. His mind struggled against the paralysis that had overcome him.

It was a futile effort.

Cadderly felt his eyes drooping. The sensations suddenly came rushing back to his limbs, but all the world grew dark around him and he felt himself falling, forever falling.

* * * * *

"Come, groundskeeper," Barjin called. From out of the same cabinet in which Barjin had hidden came Mullivy's pallid corpse.

Barjin spent a moment inspecting his latest victim. Cadderly's light tube and spindle-disks, along with a dozen other curiosities, intrigued the priest, but Barjin quickly dismissed the idea of taking anything. He had used the same spell of forgetfulness on this man as he had on the tall, angular man back in the wine cellar. Barjin knew that this man, unlike the other, was strong of mind and will, and would unconsciously battle such a spell. Missing items might aid his fight to regain the blocked parts of his memory, and for the priest, alone and beneath a virtual army of enemies, that could prove disastrous.

Barjin dropped a hand to his hungry mace. Perhaps he should kill this one now, add this young priest to his undead army so that he would bring Barjin no trouble in the future.

The evil priest dismissed the idea as quickly as it had come to him; his goddess, a deity of chaos, would not approve of eliminating the excruciating irony. This man had served as catalyst for the curse; let him see the destruction wrought of his own hands!

"Bring him," Barjin instructed, dropping Cadderly to his zombie. With one stiff arm and little effort, Mullivy lifted Cadderly from the floor.

"And bring the old ladder," Barjin added. "We must get back up to the wine cellar. We have much work to do before the dawn."

Barjin wrung his hands with mounting excitement. The primary component of the ritual had been executed easily; all that remained to complete the curse, to fully loose the Most Fatal Horror upon the Edificant Library, were a few minor ceremonies.

Ten

The Puzzle

Danica knew by the approaching headmaster's expression, and by the fact that Kierkan Rufo shuffled along at Avery's heels, that Cadderly had done something wrong again. She pushed away the book she was reading and folded her arms on the table in front of her.

Avery, normally polite to guests of the library, came quickly and bluntly to his point. "Where is he?" the headmaster demanded.

"He?" Danica replied. She knew perfectly well that Avery was referring to Cadderly, but she didn't appreciate the headmaster's tone.

"You know . . ." Avery began loudly, but then he realized Danica's objections and caught himself, looked around, and blushed with embarrassment.

"I am sorry, Lady Danica," he apologized sincerely. "I had only thought . . . I mean, you and . . ." He stomped hard with one foot to steady himself and proclaimed, "That Cadderly frustrates me so!"

Danica accepted the apology with a grin and a nod, understanding, even sympathizing, with Avery's feelings. Cadderly was an easily distracted free spirit, and, like most formal religious organizations, the Order of Deneir was firmly based on discipline. It was not a difficult task for Danica to remember just a few of the many times she had waited for Cadderly at an appointed place and time, only to eventually give up and go back to her chambers alone, cursing the day she ever saw his boyish smile and inquisitive eyes.

For all her frustrations, though, the young woman could not deny the pangs in her heart whenever she looked upon Cadderly. Her smile only widened as she thought of him now, flying in the face of Avery's bubbling anger. As soon as Danica turned her attention back to the present and looked over Avery's shoulder, though, her grin disappeared. There stood Kierkan Rufo, leaning slightly to one side, as always, but wearing a mask of concern rather than the normally smug expression he displayed whenever he had one-upped his rival.

Danica locked stares with the man, her unconscious grimace revealing her true feelings toward him. She knew that he was Cadderly's friend—sort of—and she never spoke out against him to Cadderly, but in her heart she didn't trust the man, not at all.

Rufo had made many advances on Danica, beginning on her very first day at the Edificant Library, the first time the two had ever met. Danica was young and pretty and not unused to such advances, but Rufo had unnerved her on that occasion. When she had politely turned Rufo down, he just stood towering over her, tilting his head and staring, for many minutes with that same frozen, unblinking stare on his face. Danica didn't know exactly what it was that had caused her to rebuff Rufo way back then, but she suspected it was his dark, deepset eyes. They showed the same inner light of intelligence as Cadderly's, but if Cadderly's were inquisitive, then Rufo's were conniving. Cadderly's eyes sparkled joyfully as if in search of answers to the uncounted mysteries of the world; Rufo's, too, collected information, but his, Danica believed, searched for advantage.

Rufo had never given up on Danica, even after her budding relationship with Cadderly had become common talk in the library. Rufo still approached her often, and still she sent him away, but sometimes she saw him, out of the corner of her eye, sitting across the room and staring at her, studying her as though she were some amusing book.

"Do you know where he is?" Avery asked her, his tone more controlled.

"Who?" Danica answered, hardly hearing the question.

"Cadderly!" cried the flustered headmaster.

Danica looked at him, surprised by the sudden outburst.

"Cadderly," Avery said again, regaining his composure. "Do you know where Cadderly might be found?"

Danica paused and considered the question and the look on Rufo's face, wondering if she should be worried. As far as she knew, Avery was the one directing Cadderly's movements.

"I have not seen him this morning," she answered honestly. "I thought that you had put him to work—in the wine cellar, by the words of the dwarven brothers."

Avery nodded. "So, too, did I believe, but it seems as if our dear Cadderly has had enough of his labors. He did not report to me this morning, as he had been instructed, nor was he in his room when I went to find him."

"Had he been in his room at all this morning?" Danica asked. She found her gaze again drawn to Kierkan Rufo, fearing for Cadderly and somehow guessing that if trouble had befallen him, Rufo was involved.

Rufo's reaction did not diminish her suspicions. He blinked—one of the few times Danica had ever seen him blink—and tried hard to appear unconcerned as he looked away.

"I cannot say," Avery replied and he, too, turned to Rufo for some answers.

The angular man only shrugged. "I left him in the wine cellar," he said. "I was down there working long before he arrived. I thought it fitting that I retire earlier than he."

Before Avery could even suggest that they go search the wine cellar, Danica had pushed past him and started on her way.

* * * * *

The darkness and the weight. Those were the two facts of Cadderly's predicament: the darkness and the weight. And the pain. There was pain, too. He didn't know where he was or how he had gotten to this dark place or why he could not move. He was lying face down on the stone floor, buried by something. He tried calling out several times but found little breath.

Images of walking skeletons and thick spiderwebs flitted about his consciousness as he lay there, but they had no real definition, nor any solid place in his memory. Somewhere—in a dream?—he had seen them, but whether that place had anything to do with this place, he could not guess.

Then he saw the flicker of torchlight, far away but coming down toward him, and as the shadows revealed tall and open racks, he at last recognized his surroundings.

"The wine cellar," Cadderly grunted, though the effort sorely hurt. "Rufo?" It was all a blur. He remembered coming down from the kitchen to join Rufo in his inventory, and remembered beginning his work, away from the angular man, but that was all. Something obviously had happened subsequent to that, but Cadderly had no recollection of it, or of how he might possibly have gotten in his current predicament.

"Cadderly?" came a call, Danica's voice. Not one, but three torches had entered the large wine cellar.

"Here!" Cadderly gasped with all his breath, though the wheeze was not nearly loud enough to be heard. The torches fanned out in different directions, sometimes disappearing from Cadderly's sight, other times flickering at regular intervals as they moved behind the open, bottle-filled racks. All three bearers— Avery, Rufo, and Danica, Cadderly realized, called out now.

"Here!" he gasped as often as he could. Still, the cellar was wide and sectioned by dozens of tall wine racks, and it was many minutes before Cadderly's call was heard.

Kierkan Rufo found him. The tall man seemed more ghastly than ever to Cadderly as he looked up at the shadows splayed across Rufo's angular features. Rufo appeared surprised to find Cadderly, then he glanced all about, as if undecided as to how to react.

"Could you . . ." Cadderly began, and he paused to catch his breath. "Please get . . . me . . . get this off me."

Still Rufo hesitated, confusion and concern crossing his face.

"Over here," he called out finally. "I have found him."

Cadderly didn't note much relief in Rufo's tone.

Rufo laid his torch down and began removing the pile of casks that were pinning Cadderly. Over his shoulder, Cadderly noticed Rufo tipping one heavy cask over him, and the thought came to him for just an instant that the angular man had tilted it purposely and meant to drop it on his head. Then Danica came running up, and she helped Rufo push it away.

All the casks were cleared before Headmaster Avery ever got there, and Cadderly started to rise.

Danica held him down. "Do not move!" she instructed firmly. Her expression was grave, her brown almond eyes intense and uncompromising. "Not until I have inspected your wounds."

"I am all right," Cadderly tried to insist, but he knew his words fell on deaf ears. Danica had been scared, and the stubborn woman rarely bothered to argue when she was scared.

Cadderly tried halfheartedly to rise again, but this time Danica's strong hand stopped him, pressing on a particularly vulnerable area on the back of his neck.

"I have ways of stopping you from struggling," Danica promised, and Cadderly didn't doubt her. He put his cheek down on folded arms and let Danica have her way.

"How did this happen?" demanded the chubby, red-faced Avery, huffing up to join them.

"He was counting bottles when I left," Rufo offered nervously.

Cadderly's face crinkled in confusion as he tried again to sort through the blur of his memories. He got the uncomfortable feeling that Rufo expected his explanation to sound like an accusation, and Cadderly himself wondered what part Rufo might have had in his troubles. A feeling of something hard—a boot?—against his back slipped past him too quickly to make any sense.

"I know not," Cadderly answered honestly. "I just cannot remember. I was counting . . ." He stopped there and shook his head in frustration. Cadderly's existence depended on knowledge; he didn't like illogical puzzles.

"And you wandered away," Avery finished for him. "You went exploring when you should have been working."

"The wounds are not too severe," Danica cut in suddenly.

Cadderly knew that she had purposely deflected the headmaster's rising agitation, and he smiled his thanks as Danica helped him to his feet. It felt good to be standing again, though Cadderly had to lean on Danica for support for several minutes.

Somehow Avery's supposition didn't fit into Cadderly's memories—whatever they might be. He did not believe that he had just "wandered away" to fall into trouble. "No," he declared. "Not like that. There was something here." He looked at Danica, then to Rufo. "A light?"

Hearing the word triggered another memory for Cadderly.

"The door!" he cried suddenly.

If the torchlight had been stronger, they all would have noticed the blood drain from Kierkan Rufo's face.

"The door," Cadderly said again. "Behind the wall of casks."

"What door?" Avery demanded.

Cadderly paused and thought for a moment but had no answers. His considerable willpower subconsciously battled Barjin's memory blocking spell, but all he could remember was the door, some door, somewhere. And wherever that portal might have led, Cadderly could only guess. He resolved to find out again, as soon as he rounded the casks and opened it.

It was gone.

Cadderly stood for a long while, staring at the dusty bricks of the solid wall.

"What door?" the impatient headmaster asked again.

"It was here," Cadderly insisted with as much conviction as he could muster. He moved closer to the wall and felt it. That, too, proved futile. "I remember . . ." Cadderly started to protest. He felt an arm reach under his shoulder.

"You have been hurt in the head," Danica said quietly. "Confusion is not unexpected after such a blow, nor usually lasting," she added quickly to comfort him.

"No, no," Cadderly protested, but he let Danica lead him out.

"What door?" the flustered Avery asked a third time.

"He has hurt his head," Danica interjected.

"I thought . . ." Cadderly began. "It must have been a dream—" he looked at Avery directly "—but what a strange dream."

Rufo's sigh was audible. "He is not hurt too badly?" the tall man asked embarrassedly when curious expressions turned toward him.

"Not too badly," replied Danica, the tone of her voice indicating her suspicions.

Cadderly hardly noticed, too engrossed was he with trying to remember. "What would be below here?" he asked on impulse.

"Nothing to concern you," Avery replied sharply.

Skeletons walked intangibly through Cadderly's subconscious again. "Crypts?" he asked.

"Nothing to concern you!" Avery answered sternly. "I grow tired of your curiosity, brother."

Cadderly, too, was annoyed, not enjoying the puzzles within his own mind. Avery's glare was uncompromising, but Cadderly was too upset to be scared off. "Sssh!" he hissed sarcastically, putting a finger to his pursed lips. "You would not want Deneir, whose edict is the seeking of knowledge, to hear you say that."

Avery's face turned so red that Cadderly almost expected it to burst. "Go and see the healers," the headmaster growled at Cadderly, "then come back to see me. I have a thousand tasks prepared for you." He spun about and stormed away, Rufo close on his heels, though all the way to the stairs, Rufo kept glancing back over his shoulder.

Danica gave Cadderly a forceful nudge—and a painful one against his sorely bruised ribs. "You never know when to hold your tongue," she scolded. "If you keep talking so to Headmaster Avery, we will never find the opportunity to see each other!" With her torch in one hand and her other wrapped about Cadderly's back, she pulled him roughly toward the distant stairs.

Cadderly looked down at her, thinking that he owed her an apology, but he saw that Danica was biting back laughter and he realized that she hadn't truly disapproved of his sarcasm.

* * * * *

Barjin watched the steady stream of reddish smoke rise from the opened flask and slip into cracks in the ceiling, making its way up into the library above. The evil priest still had several ceremonies to perform to complete the formal ritual, as agreed upon back in Castle Trinity, but these were merely a formality. The Most Fatal Horror had been released, and the chaos curse was under way.

It would take longer to exact a toll here, Barjin knew, than it had with Haverly back at Castle Trinity. According to Aballister, Haverly had taken a concentrated dose right in the face.

Producing the elixir was far too expensive to duplicate those effects on enemy after enemy, thus the mixture in the ever-smoking bottle had been greatly diluted. The priests here would absorb the elixir gradually, each hour bringing them closer to the edge of doom. Barjin held no reservations, though. He believed in the powers of the elixir, in the powers of his goddess—particularly with himself serving as her agent.

"Let us see how these pious fools behave when their truest emotions are revealed," he snickered to Mullivy. The zombie did not respond, of course. He just stood very still, unblinking and unmoving. Barjin gave him a sour look and turned his gaze back to the ever-smoking bottle.

"The next day will be the most dangerous," he whispered to himself. "Beyond that, the priests will have no power to stand against me." He looked back to Mullivy and grinned wickedly.

"We will be ready," Barjin promised. He already had animated dozens of skeletons and had enacted further spells upon Mullivy's corpse to strengthen it. And, of course, there was Khalif, Barjin's prized soldier, awaiting the priest's command from the sarcophagus just outside the altar room door.

Barjin meant to add new and more horrible monsters to his growing army. First, he would uncover the necromancer's stone and see what undead allies it might bring in. Then, taking Aballister's advice, he would open a gate to the least of the lower planes, summoning minor monsters to serve as advisers and scouts for his expanding evil network.

"Let the foolish priests come after us," Barjin said, taking an ancient and evil tome, a book of sorcery and necromancy, out of the folds of his robes. "Let them see the horror that has befallen them!"

Eleven
Oddities

Cadderly sat before his open window, watching the dawn and feeding Percival cacasa-nut-and-butter biscuits. The Shining Plains lived up to their name this morning, with dew-speckled grass catching the morning sunlight and throwing it back to the sky in a dazzling dance. The sun climbed higher and the line of brightness moved up into the foothills of the Snowflake Mountains. Pockets of darkness, valleys, dotted the region and a wispy mist rose to the south, from the valley of the Impresk River, feeding the wide lake to the east.

"Ow!" Cadderly cried, pulling his hand away from the hungry squirrel. Percival had gotten a bit too eager, nipping through the biscuit and into Cadderly's palm. Cadderly pinched the wound between his thumb and forefinger to stem the blood flow.

Busily licking the last of the cacasa-nut from his paws, Percival hardly seemed to notice Cadderly's discomfort.

"It is my own fault, I suppose," Cadderly admitted. "I cannot expect you to behave rationally when there is cacasa-nut and butter to be won!"

Percival's tail twitched excitedly, but that was the only indication Cadderly had that the squirrel was even listening. The young man turned his attention again to the world outside.

The daylight had reached the library, and though Cadderly had to squint against its fresh brightness, it felt warm and wonderful upon his face.

"It will be another beautiful day," he remarked, and even as he spoke the words, he realized that he probably would spend the whole of it in the dark and dreary wine cellar, or in some other hole that Headmaster Avery found for him.

"Perhaps I can trick him into letting me tend the grounds this morning," Cadderly said to the squirrel. "I could help old Mullivy."

Percival chittered excitedly at the mention of the groundskeeper.

"I know," Cadderly offered comfortingly. "You do not like Mullivy." Cadderly shrugged and smiled, remembering the time he had seen the crooked old groundskeeper waving a rake and spitting threats at the tree that Percival and other squirrels were sitting in, complaining about the mess of acorn husks all over his freshly raked ground.

"Here you go, Percival," Cadderly said, pushing the rest of the biscuit to the windowsill. "I have many things to attend to before Avery catches up with me." He left Percival sitting on the sill, and the squirrel went on munching and crunching and licking his paws, and basking in the warm daylight, apparently having already dismissed any uneasiness at the mention of Mullivy.

* * * * *

"Ye're bats!" Ivan yelled. "Ye can't be one of them!"

"Doo-dad!" Pikel replied indignantly.

"Ye think they'd have ye?" Ivan roared. "Tell him, boy!" he cried at Cadderly, who had just entered the kitchen. "Tell the fool that dwarves can't be druids!"

"You want to be a druid?" Cadderly asked with interest.

"Oo oi!" piped a happy Pikel. "Doo-dad!"

Ivan had heard enough. He hoisted a frying pan—dumping its half-cooked eggs on the floor—and heaved it at his brother.

Pikel wasn't quick enough to get out of the way of the missile, but he managed to bow into it, taking the blow on the top of his head and suffering no serious damage.

Still fuming, Ivan reached for another pan, but Cadderly grabbed his arm to stop him. "Wait!" Cadderly pleaded.

Ivan paused for just a moment, even whistled to show his patience, then cried, "Long enough!" and pushed Cadderly to the floor. The dwarf hoisted the pan and charged, but Pikel, now similarly armed, was ready for him.

Cadderly had read many tales of valor describing the ring of iron on iron, but he had never imagined the sound attributed to two dwarves sparring with frying pans.

Ivan got the first strike in, a wicked smash to Pikel's forearm. Pikel grunted and retaliated, slamming his pan straight down on top of Ivan's head.

Ivan backed up a step, trying to stop his eyes from spinning. He looked to the side, to a littered table, and was struck with a sudden inspiration, no doubt from the head blow. Pikel returned his smile. "Pots?" Ivan asked.

Pikel nodded eagerly and the two rushed to the table to find one that fit properly. Food went flying everywhere, followed by pots that had proven too small or too big. Then Ivan and Pikel faced off again, wielding their trusty pans and helmeted in the cookware of last night's stew.

Cadderly watched it all in blank amazement, not quite certain of how to take the actions. It seemed a comedy at times, but the growing welts and bruises on

Ivan and Pikel's arms and faces told a different tale. Cadderly had seen the brothers argue before, and certainly he had come to expect all sorts of strange things from dwarves, but this was too wild, even for Ivan and Pikel.

"Stop it!" Cadderly yelled at them. Pikel's answer came in the form of a hurled cleaver that narrowly missed Cadderly's head and buried itself an inch deep in the oaken door beside him. Cadderly stared in disbelief at the deadly instrument, still shuddering from the force of Pikel's throw, and knew that something was terribly wrong here, and terribly dangerous.

The young priest didn't give up, though. He just redirected his efforts. "I know a better way to fight!" he cried, moving cautiously toward the dwarves.

"Eh?" asked Pikel.

"Better way?" Ivan added. "For fighting?"

Ivan seemed already convinced—Pikel was winning the cookware battle— but Pikel only used Ivan's ensuing hesitation to press him even harder. Pikel's pan hummed as it dove in at a wide arc, smashing Ivan's elbow and knocking the yellow bearded dwarf off balance. Pikel recognized his clear advantage. His wicked pan went up high again for a follow-up strike.

"Druids do not fight with metal weapons!" Cadderly yelled.

"Oo," Pikel said, halting in midswing. The brothers looked at each other, shrugged once, and tossed their pots and pans to the ground.

Cadderly had to think quickly. He brushed off a section of the long table. "Sit here," he instructed Ivan, pulling up a stool.

"And you over here," he said to Pikel, indicating a second seat across from Ivan.

"Put the elbows of your right arms on the table," Cadderly explained.

"Arm-pulling?" Ivan scoffed incredulously. "Get me back me pan!"

"No!" Cadderly shouted. "No. This is a better way, a true test of strength."

"Bah!" snorted Ivan. "I'll clobber him!"

"Oh?" said Pikel.

They clasped hands roughly and started pulling before Cadderly could give any signal, or even line them up. He considered them for a moment, wanting to stay and see things through to conclusion, but the brothers were evenly matched, Cadderly realized, and their contest might last a while. Cadderly heard other priests shuffling by outside the open kitchen door; it was time for the midday canticle. Whatever the emergency, Cadderly simply could not be late for the required ceremony again. He watched the struggle a moment longer, to ensure that the dwarves were fully engaged, then shook his head in confusion and walked away. He had known Ivan and Pikel for more than a decade, since his childhood days, and had never seen either one of them lift a fist at the other. If that had not been bad enough, the cleaver, still wobbling in the door, vividly proved that something was terribly out of sorts.

* * * * *

Brother Chaunticleer's voice rang out with its usual quality, filling the great hall with perfect notes and filling the gathering of priests and scholars with sincere pleasure, but those most observant among the group, Cadderly included, glanced around at the crowd's reaction, as if they noticed something missing in Chaunticleer's delivery. The key was perfect and the words correct, but there seemed to be a lacking in the strength of the song.

Chaunticleer didn't notice them. He performed as always, the same songs he had sung at midday for several years. This time, though, unlike any of the others, Chaunticleer was indeed distracted. His thoughts drifted down to the rivers in the mountain foothills, still swollen from the winter melt and teeming with trout and silver perch. It had always been said that fishing was second only to singing in Brother Chaunticleer's heart. The priest was learning now that the perceived order of his desires might not be so correct.

Then it happened.

Brother Chaunticleer forgot the words.

He stood at the podium of the great hall, perplexed, as undeniable images of rushing water and leaping fish added to his confusion and put the song farther from his thoughts.

Whispers sprang up throughout the hall; mouths dropped open in disbelief. Dean Thobicus, never an excitable man, calmly moved up toward the podium. "Do go on, Brother Chaunticleer," he said softly, soothingly.

Chaunticleer could not continue. The song of Deneir was no match for the joyful sound of leaping trout.

The whispers turned to quiet giggles. Dean Thobicus waited a few moments, then whispered into Headmaster Avery's ear, and Avery, obviously more shaken than his superior, dismissed the gathering. He turned back to question Chaunticleer, but the singing priest was already gone, running for his hook and line.

* * * * *

Cadderly used the confusion in the great hall to get out from under Avery's watchful eye. He had spent a dreary morning scrubbing floors, but had completed the tasks and was free, at least until Avery found him idle and issued new orders. Avery was busy now, trying to figure out what had happened to Brother Chaunticleer. If Cadderly correctly understood the gravity of Chaunticleer's misfortunes, the headmaster would be busy with him for some time. Chaunticleer was considered among the most devout priests in the order of Deneir, and his highest duty, his only real priority, was the midday canticle.

Cadderly, too, was concerned by the events at the ceremony, especially after his visit with the dwarves that morning.

More disturbing than Chaunticleer's problems with the songs, Danica had not been at the canticle. She was not associated with either the Oghman or

Deneir sects and therefore not required to attend, but she rarely missed the event, and never before without telling Cadderly that she would not attend.

Even more disquieting, Kierkan Rufo had not been in attendance.

Since the main library was on the first floor and not far from the great hall, Cadderly decided to begin his search there. He skipped along briskly, his pace quickening as his suspicions continued to gnaw at him. A moaning sound from a side corridor stopped him abruptly.

Cadderly peeked around the corner to see Kierkan Rufo coming down the stairs, leaning heavily on the wall. Rufo seemed barely coherent; his face was covered in blood and he nearly toppled with each step.

"What happened?" Cadderly asked, rushing to help the man.

A wild light came into Rufo's eyes and he slapped Cadderly's reaching hands away. The action cost the disoriented man his balance and he tumbled down the last few steps to the floor.

The manner in which Rufo fell revealed much to Cadderly. Rufo had reached out to catch himself with one arm, the same arm he had used to slap at Cadderly, but his other arm remained limp at his side, useless.

"Where is she?" Cadderly demanded, suddenly very afraid.

He grabbed Rufo by the collar, despite the man's protests, and pulled him to his feet, viewing up close the damage to his face. Blood continued to flow from Rufo's obviously broken nose, and one of his eyes was swollen and purple and nearly closed. The man had numerous other bruises, and the way he flinched when Cadderly straightened him indicated other wounds in his abdomen or just a little bit lower.

"Where is she?" Cadderly said again.

Rufo gritted his teeth and turned away.

Cadderly forcibly turned him back. "What is wrong with you?" he demanded.

Rufo spat in his face.

Cadderly resisted the urge to strike out. There had always been tension in his friendship with Rufo, an element of rivalry that had only heightened when Danica came to the library.

Cadderly, usually getting the upper hand with Danica and the headmasters, realized that he often upset Rufo, but never before had the tall man shown him any open hostility.

"If you hurt Danica, I will come back to find you," Cadderly warned, though he thought that highly improbable. He let go of Rufo's wet tunic and ran up the stairs.

Rufo's blood trail led him to the south wing of the third floor, the library's guest quarters. Despite his urgency, Cadderly stopped his tracking as he neared Histra's room, for he heard cries emanating from within. At first Cadderly thought the priestess of Sune to be in peril, but as he reached for the door handle, he recognized the sounds as something other than pain.

Down the hall he rushed, too worried to be embarrassed.

The blood trail led to Danica's door, as he had feared it would.

He knocked loudly on the door and called out, "Danica?"

No answer.

Cadderly banged more urgently. "Danica?" he yelled. "Are you in there?"

Still no answer.

Cadderly lowered his shoulder and easily plowed through the unlocked door.

Danica stood perfectly still in the middle of the small room on the thick carpet she used for exercising. She held her open hands out in front of her, a meditative pose, and she did not even acknowledge that someone had entered the room. Her concentration was straight ahead, on a solid block of stone supported between two sawhorses.

"Danica?" Cadderly asked again. "Are you all right?" He moved over to her tentatively.

Danica turned her head, and her blank stare fell over him.

"Of course," she said. "Why would I not be?"

Her blond locks were matted with sweat and her hands were caked in drying blood.

"I just saw Kierkan Rufo," Cadderly remarked.

"As did I," Danica said calmly.

"What happened to him?"

"He tried to put his hands where they did not belong," Danica said casually, turning to stare back at the stone block. "I stopped him."

None of it made any sense to Cadderly; Rufo had leered and stared, but had never been foolish enough to make a move toward Danica. "Rufo attacked you?" he asked.

Danica laughed hysterically, and that, too, unnerved the young priest. "He tried to touch me, I said."

Cadderly scratched his head and looked around the room for some further clues as to what had transpired. He still couldn't believe that Rufo would make an open advance toward Danica, but even more remarkable had been Danica's response. She was a controlled and disciplined warrior. Cadderly would never expect such overkill as the beating she had apparently given Rufo.

"You hurt him badly," Cadderly said, needing to hear Danica's explanation.

"He will recover," was all that the woman replied.

Cadderly grabbed her arm, meaning to turn her about to face him. Danica was too quick. Her arm flicked back and forth, breaking the hold, then she snapped her hand onto Cadderly's thumb and bent it backward, nearly driving him to his knees. Her ensuing glare alone would have backed Cadderly away, and he honestly believed that she would break his finger.

Then Danica's look softened, as if she suddenly recognized the man at her side. She released her grip on his thumb and grabbed around his head instead, pulling him close. "Oh Cadderly!" she cried between kisses. "Did I hurt you?"

Cadderly pushed her back to arm's length and stared at her for a long while.

She appeared fine, except for Rufo's blood on her hands and a curious, urgent look in her eyes.

"Have you been drinking any wine?" Cadderly asked.

"Of course not," Danica replied, surprised by the question. "You know that I am allowed only one glass . . ." Her voice trailed off as the hard glare returned. "Are you doubting my loyalty to oath?" she asked sharply.

Cadderly's face crinkled in confusion.

"Let go of me."

Her tone was serious, and when the stunned Cadderly did not immediately respond, she accentuated her point. She and Cadderly were only standing about two feet apart, but the limber monk kicked with her foot, up between them, and waved it threateningly in Cadderly's face.

Cadderly released her and fell back. "What is wrong with you?" he demanded.

Danica's visage softened again.

"You beat Rufo badly," Cadderly said. "If he made inappropriate advances—"

"He interrupted me!" Danica cut him off. "He . . ." she looked to the block of stone, then back to Cadderly, again glowering. "And now you are interrupting me."

Cadderly wisely backed away. "I will go," he promised, studying the block, "if you tell me what I am interrupting."

"I am a true disciple of Grandmaster Penpahg D'Ahn!" Danica cried as though that answered everything.

"Of course you are," said Cadderly.

His agreement calmed Danica. "The time has come for Gigel Nugel," she said, "Iron Skull, but I must not be interrupted in my concentration!"

Cadderly regarded the solid block for a moment—a block far larger than the one in the sketch of Penpahg D'Ahn—then eyed Danica's delicate face, trying unsuccessfully to digest the news. "You plan to smash that block with your head?"

"I am a true disciple," Danica reiterated.

Cadderly nearly swooned. "Do not," he begged, reaching for Danica.

Seeing her impending reaction, Cadderly pulled his arms back and qualified his statement. "Not yet," he pleaded. "This is a great event in the history of the library. Dean Thobicus should be informed. We could make it a public showing."

"This is a private matter," Danica replied. "It is not a curiosity show for the pleasures of unbelievers!"

"Unbelievers?" Cadderly whispered, and at this strange moment he knew that the label fit him, but for more reasons than his and Danica's differing faiths. He had to think quickly.

"But," he improvised, "surely the event must be properly witnessed and recorded."

Danica looked at him curiously.

"For future disciples," Cadderly explained. "Who will come to study Grandmaster Penpahg D'Ahn in a hundred years? Would that disciple not also benefit from the practices and successes of Grandmistress Danica? You cannot be selfish with this achievement. Surely that would not be in accord with Penpahg D'Ahn's teachings."

Danica mulled over his words. "It would be selfish," she admitted.

Even her acquiescence reinforced Cadderly's fears that something was terribly wrong. Danica was sharp thinking and never before so easily manipulated.

"I will wait for you to make the arrangements," she agreed, "but not for long! The time has come for Iron Skull. This I know is true. I am a true disciple of Grandmaster Penpahg D'Ahn."

Cadderly did not know how to proceed. He sensed that if he left Danica, she would go right back to her attempt. He looked all around, his gaze finally settling on Danica's bed. "It would be well for you to rest," he offered.

Danica looked to the bed, then back to Cadderly, a sly look on her face. "I know something better than rest," she purred, moving much closer. The urgency of her unexpected kiss weakened Cadderly in the knees and promised him many wonderful things.

But not like this. He reminded himself that something was wrong with Danica, that something was apparently wrong with almost everything around him.

"I have to go," he said, pulling away. "To Dean Thobicus, to make the arrangements. You rest now. Surely you will need your strength."

Danica reluctantly let him go, honestly torn between her perception of duty and the needs of love.

* * * * *

Cadderly stumbled back down to the first level. The hallways were unnervingly empty and quiet, and Cadderly wasn't certain of where he should turn. He had few close friends in the library—he wasn't about to go to Kierkan Rufo with this problem, and he wanted to keep far away from the living and working quarters of Dean Thobicus and the headmasters, fearing an encounter with Avery.

In the end, he went back to the kitchen and found Pikel and Ivan, nearly collapsed with exhaustion, still stubbornly arm wrestling at the table. Cadderly knew that the dwarves were headstrong, but more than an hour had passed since they had begun their match.

When Cadderly approached, shaking his head in disbelief, he saw just how headstrong the Bouldershoulder brothers could be. Purplish bruises from popped veins lined their arms and their entire bodies trembled violently under the continuing strain, but their visages were unyieldingly locked.

"I'll put ye down!" Ivan snarled.

Pikel growled back and strained harder at the pull.

"Stop it!" Cadderly demanded. Both dwarves looked up from the match, realizing only then that someone had entered the kitchen.

"I can take him," Ivan assured Cadderly.

"Why are you fighting?" Cadderly asked, guessing that the dwarves would not remember.

"Yerself was here," Ivan replied. "Ye saw he was the one what started it."

"Oh?" Pikel piped in sarcastically.

"What did he start?" Cadderly asked.

"The fight!" growled an exasperated Ivan.

"How?"

Ivan had run out of answers. He looked at Pikel, who only shrugged in reply.

"Then why are you fighting?" Cadderly asked again with no answer forthcoming.

Both dwarves stopped at the same time and sat looking across the table at each other.

"Me brother!" Ivan cried suddenly, springing over the table. Pikel caught him in midflight and their hugs and pats on the back were nearly as vicious as the arm wrestling had been.

Ivan turned happily on Cadderly. "He's me brother!" the dwarf announced.

Cadderly strained a smile and figured that it might be best to divert the dwarves as he had diverted Danica. "It is not so far from suppertime," was all he had to say.

"Supper?" Ivan bellowed.

"Oo oi!" added Pikel, and they were off, whirling like little bearded tornados, sweeping the kitchen into order in preparation of the evening meal. Cadderly waited just a few minutes, to make sure that the dwarves wouldn't get back to their fighting, then he slipped out and headed back to check on Danica.

He found her in her room, sleeping contentedly. He pulled her blankets up over her, then went to the stone to see if he could find some way to remove it.

"How did you ever get this up here?" he asked, staring at the heavy block. It would take at least two strong men to move it, and even then, or even with three men, the stairs would not be easily negotiated. For now, Cadderly figured that he could just drop the block down from the sawhorses, put it on the floor to stop Danica from making her Iron Skull attempt. He went back to the bed and took the heaviest blankets. He tied them together and wrapped them about the block, then threw both ends over a rafter in the low room.

Cadderly grabbed the dangling ends and hoisted himself right off the floor to kick at the block. The sawhorses leaned, then toppled and the rafter creaked in protest, but Cadderly's counterbalancing weight brought the blanketed block down slowly and quietly.

Using the sawhorse legs as levers, he managed to wiggle the blankets out from under the stone. Then he tucked Danica back in and headed away, his mind racing to find some logical reason for all the illogical events of the day.

* * * * *

It was a wondrous oak, a most excellent tree indeed, and Newander gently stroked each of its spreading branches as he made his way higher. The view from the uppermost branches was splendid, a scene that sent shivers of delight along the druid's spine.

When he turned about to regard the mountains to the southwest, though, Newander's smile disappeared.

There sat the Edificant Library, a barely seen square block far in the distance. Newander hadn't meant to be gone this long; for all the freedom and individuality their order offered, he knew that Arcite would not be pleased.

A bird flitted down and landed not far from the druid's head.

"I should be getting back," the druid said to it, though he wanted to remain out here in the wilderness, away from the temptations of civilization.

Newander started reluctantly down the tree. With the distant library removed from sight, he nearly headed off again in the opposite direction. He didn't, though. Chastising himself for his fears and weaknesses, he grudgingly started back toward the library, back to his duties.

* * * * *

Cadderly meant to lie down and rest for only a short while when he returned to his room. The afternoon was barely half over, but it already had been an exhausting day. Soon the young priest was snoring loudly.

But not contentedly. From the depths of his mist-filled dreams came the walking dead, skeletons and gruesome ghouls, reaching for him with sharp, bony hands and rotting fingers.

He sat up in pitch blackness. Cold trails of sweat lined his face, and his blankets were moist and clammy. He heard a noise to the side of the bed. He hadn't undressed when he lay down, and he fumbled about, finding his spindle-disks and then his light tube.

Something was close.

The end cap popped off and the light streamed out. Cadderly nearly flicked his spindle-disks out of sheer terror, but he managed to forego his attack when he recognized the white fur of a friend.

As startled as Cadderly, Percival rushed across the room, upsetting all sorts of things, and darted under the bed. The squirrel came up tentatively a moment later at Cadderly's feet and slowly moved up to nestle in the pit of the man's arm.

Cadderly was glad for the company. He recapped his light, but kept it in his hand, and soon was fast asleep.

The walking dead were waiting for him.

Twelve

The Time to Act

Barjin is preparing to open the gate," Dorigen told Aballister. "My contacts on the lower planes sense the beginnings of the portal."

"How long?" the wizard asked grimly. Aballister was glad that Druzil soon would be close to Barjin, keeping an eye on the dangerous man, but he was not pleased that Barjin had so quickly advanced to this level of preparedness. If Barjin meant to open a gate, then his plans were probably in full swing.

Dorigen shrugged. "An hour or two," she replied. "I cannot know which methods of sorcery the priest will employ." She looked over to Druzil, sitting comfortably atop Aballister's desk, appearing impassive, though both wizards knew better than to think that. "Do you really believe it's necessary to send the imp?"

"Do you trust Barjin" Aballister answered.

"Talona would not have allowed him to take the elixir if he was not loyal to our cause," Dorigen replied.

"Do not presume that the goddess is so directly interested in our cause," warned Aballister, rising from and walking nervously about his oaken chair. "The Time of Troubles has passed and much has changed. Talona's avatar was pleased to bring me into her dark fold, but I am not her only concern, and I do not presume to be her chief concern. She directed me to Druzil, and he provided the chaos curse. Its fate is in my . . . in our hands now."

"But if Barjin was not of Talona's clergy . . ." Dorigen argued, shifting tentatively from foot to foot and letting her companion complete the warning for himself.

Aballister considered Dorigen for a long moment, surprised that she was as fearful as he about Barjin. She was a middle-aged wizard, thin and drawn, with darting eyes and a tangle of graying black hair that she never bothered to brush.

"Perhaps he is of Talona's clergy," Aballister replied. "I believe that he is." Aballister had played these possible scenarios through his thoughts a hundred times over the last few days. "Do not let that fact comfort you. If Barjin stuck a poisoned dagger into my heart, Talona would not be pleased, but neither would she seek vengeance on the priest. That is the price of serving a goddess such as ours."

Dorigen considered those words for a few moments, then nodded her agreement.

"We vie for power with the priests," Aballister went on. "It has been that way since the beginning of Castle Trinity, and that contest intensified with Barjin's arrival. He gained control of the elixir from me. I admit my own failure in not anticipating his cunning, but I have not conceded defeat, I promise you. Now, go back to your chambers and converse with your contacts. Inform me at once if there is any change in Barjin's gate."

Aballister looked over to his magical mirror and considered whether he should scry into Barjin's altar room to confirm what Dorigen had told him. He decided against it, though, knowing that Barjin would easily sense the scrying and recognize its source. Aballister did not want Barjin to know how concerned he was, did not want the priest to understand how great an advantage he was gaining in their competition.

The wizard looked over his shoulder and nodded to Druzil.

"The priest is a daring one," Druzil remarked, "to open a gate right below so many enemies of magical power. *Bene tellemara*. If the priests of the library discover the gate . . ."

"It was not unexpected," Aballister retorted defensively. "We knew that Barjin was taking materials for sorcery."

"If he is opening the gate already," Druzil put in, "then perhaps the curse has begun!" The imp rubbed his pudgy, leathery hands eagerly at that prospect.

"Or perhaps Barjin's situation has become desperate," Aballister quickly replied.

Druzil wisely disguised his excitement.

"We must get the brazier prepared," Aballister said, "and quickly. We must be ready before Barjin begins his summoning." He moved over to his own burning brazier and picked up the closest bag, checking to ensure that the powder inside was blue.

"I will provide you with two powders," the wizard explained. "One to close Barjin's gate behind you as you pass through to join him, another to reopen it so that you may return to me."

"To ensure that I am his only catch?" Druzil asked, cocking his dog-faced head curiously.

"I am not as confident of Barjin's powers as he appears to be," Aballister replied. "If he summons too many denizens, even minor creatures, of the lower planes through to serve him, his control will be sorely taxed. No doubt he is bringing in undead to serve him as well. That type of an army could be beyond him when the priests of the Edificant Library strike back. I fear Barjin may be reaching too far. It all could crumble around him."

"Fear?" Druzil asked slyly. "Or hope?"

Aballister's hollowed eyes narrowed dangerously. "Examine the situation from another point of view, my dear Druzil," he purred. "From your own. Do you wish to find competitors from your filthy home at Barjin's side? Might not another imp, or a midge perhaps, know you and know that you have been in service to me?"

The wizard enjoyed the way the imp's features suddenly seemed to droop.

"Barjin would know you as my agent then," Aballister went on. "If you were fortunate, he would only banish you."

Druzil looked over to Aballister's brazier and nodded his agreement.

"Get through as soon as Barjin opens his gate," Aballister instructed, dumping the blue powder into the burning brazier.

The flames roared and shifted through the colors of the spectrum. Druzil walked by the wizard, taking the two tiny bags and looping them over the foreclaws on his wing.

"Close Barjin's gate as you step out of the flames," Aballister continued. "He will not understand the sudden shift in his fire's hue. He will think it is the result of your passing."

Again Druzil nodded and then, eager to be away from Aballister, and even more eager to see exactly what was going on at the library, he jumped into the brazier and was gone.

"Aballister's plans serve everyone," Druzil muttered to himself a few minutes later, as he floated in the black void at the edge of the material plane, just waiting for Barjin's gate to open. The imp realized, too, that other things—jealousy and fear—guided the wizard's actions. Barjin had shown no signs of weakness throughout and Aballister knew as well as Druzil did that a gate to the lower planes would not seriously threaten the priest's successes. Still, Druzil was more than happy when he looked down at the magical powders Aballister had provided. The imp remained intrigued by Barjin's brashness and confidence. The priest's preliminary victories, both at Castle Trinity, against Aballister, and possibly in the dungeons of the library, could not easily be dismissed. While Aballister might fear for his own position, Druzil's only concern was the chaos curse, the recipe he had waited so very long to exploit.

Where the chaos curse was concerned, Barjin deserved some serious attention.

* * * * *

The terrible, clawed hand grabbed at Cadderly's heart. He dove to the side wildly, his arms flailing in futile defense.

He woke up when he hit the floor and spent several long moments trying to orient himself. It was morning, and Cadderly's nightmares faded fast under the sun's enlightening rays. Cadderly tried to hold on to them so that he might better decipher any hidden meaning, but they could not withstand the light of day.

With a resigned shrug, Cadderly focused his thoughts back to the previous afternoon, remembering the events before he had come for some rest.

Some rest! How much time had passed? he wondered frantically, looking at his clocking measurements on the floor. Fifteen hours?

Percival was still in the room but apparently had been up and about for some time. The squirrel sat on Cadderly's desk just inside the window, contentedly munching on an acorn. Below him lay the discarded husks of a dozen appetizers.

Cadderly sat up beside the bed and tried again to recover the fading blur of his dreams, seeking some clue to the confusion that had so suddenly come into his life. His light tube, opened and glowing faintly, lay under the thick jumble of bed covers.

"There is something here," Cadderly remarked to Percival, absently grabbing and recapping the tube. "Something I cannot yet understand." There was more confusion than determination in Cadderly's voice. Yesterday seemed a long time ago, and he seriously wondered where his memories ended and his dreams began. How unusual had yesterday's events really been? How much of the apparent strangeness was no more than Cadderly's own fear? Danica could be a stubborn one, after all, he reminded himself, and who could predict the actions of dwarves?

Unconsciously, Cadderly rubbed the deep bruise on the side of his head. The daylight streaming into his room made everything seem in order. They made all of his fears that something had gone awry in the secure library seem almost childish.

A moment later, he realized a new fear, one based surely in reality. There came a knock on his door and the call of a familiar voice. "Cadderly? Cadderly, boy, are you in there?"

Headmaster Avery.

Percival popped the acorn into a chubby cheek and skittered out the window. Cadderly hadn't gotten to his feet when the headmaster entered.

"Cadderly!" Avery cried, rushing to him. "Are you all right, my boy?"

"It is nothing," Cadderly replied tentatively, keeping out of Avery's reaching hands. "I just fell out of bed."

Avery's distress did not diminish. "That is terrible!" the headmaster cried. "We cannot have that, oh, no!" Avery's eyes darted about frantically, then he snapped his fingers and smiled widely. "We will get the dwarves to put up a railing. Yes, that is it! We cannot have you falling out of bed and injuring yourself. You are much too valuable an asset to the Order of Deneir for us to allow such potential tragedy!"

The young scholar looked at him blankly, uncertain whether this was sarcasm or strange reality.

"It is nothing," Cadderly replied timidly.

"Oh, yes," Avery spouted, "you would say that. Such a fine lad! Never concerned for your own safety!" Avery's exuberant pat on the back hurt Cadderly more than the fall.

"You have come to give me my list of duties," Cadderly reasoned, eager to change the subject. Somehow he liked Avery better when the headmaster was screaming at him. At least then he could be certain of Avery's intent.

"Duties?" Avery asked, seeming sincerely confused. "Why, I do not believe that you have any this day. Or, if you do, ignore them. We cannot have one of your potential busied by menial tasks. Make your own routines. Certainly you know better than any where you might be of greatest value."

Cadderly didn't believe a word of it. Or if he did allow himself to believe Avery's sincerity, he couldn't quite comprehend it anyway. "Then why are you here?" he asked.

"Do I need a reason to look in on my most-prized acolyte?" Avery answered, giving Cadderly a second rough pat. "No, no reason. I just came to say good morning, and I say it now. Good morning!" He started away, then stopped abruptly, spun about and wrapped a bear hug on Cadderly. "Good morning indeed!"

Avery, his eyes suddenly misted, put him out at arm's length. "I knew that you would grow to be a fine lad when first you came to us," he said.

Cadderly expected him to abruptly change the subject, as he always did when speaking of Cadderly's early days at the Edificant Library, but Avery rambled on.

"We feared that you would become just like your father—he was an intelligent one, just like you! But he had no guidance, you see." Avery's laughter erupted straight from his belly. "I called him a Gondsman!" the priest roared, slapping Cadderly's shoulder.

Cadderly failed to see the humor, but he was truly intrigued to hear about his father. That subject had always been avoided at the library, and Cadderly, with no recollections at all before his arrival, had never pressed it seriously.

"And indeed he was," Avery continued, becoming calm and grim. "Or worse, I fear. He could not remain here, you see. We could not allow him to take our knowledge and put it to destructive practice."

"Where did he go?" Cadderly asked.

"I know not. That was twenty years ago!" Avery replied. "We saw him only once after that, the day he presented Dean Thobicus with his son. Do you understand, then, my boy, why I am always chasing after you, why I fear that your course might lead you astray?"

Cadderly didn't even try to find a voice to respond with, though he would have liked to learn more while he had the headmaster in so talkative a mood. He quickly reminded himself that these actions were out of sorts for Avery, and just further confirmation that something was going wrong.

"Well, then," the headmaster said. He slammed Cadderly with one more hug, then pushed the young man away, spinning briskly for the door. "Do not waste too much of this glorious day!" he roared as he entered the hall.

Percival came back to the window, working on a new acorn.

"Do not even ask," Cadderly warned him, but if the squirrel cared at all, he did not show it.

"So much for dreams," Cadderly remarked grimly. If ever he doubted his memories of the previous day, he did not now, not in light of Avery's outburst. Cadderly dressed quickly. He would have to check on Ivan and Pikel, to make sure they were not back at their fighting, and on Kierkan Rufo, to make sure the man had no designs against Danica.

The hallway was strangely quiet, though the morning was in full swing. Cadderly started for the kitchen but changed his direction suddenly when he got to the spiral stairway. The only change in the daily routines, the only unusual occurrence at the library before this inexplicable weirdness, had been the arrival of the druids.

They had been housed on the fourth floor. Normally that level was reserved for the novice priests of the host sects, the servants, and for storage, but the druids had expressed a desire to be away from the rest of the gathered scholars. Not without reservations, for he did not want to disturb the xenophobic group, Cadderly started up the stairs instead of down.

He didn't really believe that Arcite, Newander, and Cleo were the source of the problems, but they were wise and experienced and might have some insight about what was going on.

The first sign Cadderly noticed that something up here, too, was amiss, was a growl and a scraping noise. He stood outside the door to the druids' quarters in a remote corner of the north wing, uncertain of whether to continue, wondering whether the woodland priests might be engaged in some private ritual.

Memories of Danica and Avery and Brother Chaunticleer spurred him on. He knocked lightly on the door.

No answer.

Cadderly turned the handle and opened the door a crack.

The room was a mess, the work of an obviously agitated brown bear. The creature squatted on the bed, which had broken under its great weight, and was now casually tearing apart a down-filled pillow. Shuffling slowly across the floor in front of it was a huge tortoise.

The bear seemed to pay little attention to him, so Cadderly boldly opened the door a bit wider. Newander sat on the windowsill, staring despairingly out at the wide mountains, his blond hair hanging limply about his shoulders.

"Arcite and Cleo," the druid remarked offhandedly. "Arcite is the bear."

"A ritual?" Cadderly asked. He remembered when the druid named Shannon had enacted such physical changes before his eyes years ago, and he knew that the shape-changing ability was common for the most powerful druids. Actually witnessing it again amazed him nonetheless.

Newander shrugged, not really knowing the answer. He looked at Cadderly, a saddened expression on his face.

Cadderly started to go to him, but Arcite, the bear, didn't seem to like that idea. He stood high and issued a growl that turned Cadderly right around.

"Keep yourself safely back from him," Newander explained. "I am not yet certain of his intentions."

"Have you asked?"

"He does not answer," Newander replied.

"Then can you be sure it is really Arcite?" Cadderly asked.

Shannon had explained that the druidic shape change was purely physical, with retention of the woodland priest's mental facilities. Shape-changed druids could even converse in the common tongue.

"It was," Newander replied, "and is. I recognize the animal. Perhaps it is Arcite now, more truly Arcite than Arcite ever was."

Cadderly could not exactly decipher those words, but he thought he understood the druid's basic meaning. "The turtle, then, is Cleo?" he asked. "Or is Cleo really the turtle?"

"Yes," Newander answered. "Both ways, as far as I can discern."

"Why is Newander still Newander?" Cadderly pressed, guessing the source of Newander's despair.

He saw that his question greatly wounded the still-human druid, and he figured that he had his answers. He bowed quickly, exited, and closed the door. He started to walk away, but changed his mind and ran instead.

Newander sat back against the windowsill and looked at his animal companions. Something had happened here, while he was gone, though he still wasn't certain whether it had been a good or a bad thing. Newander feared for his comrades, but he envied them, too. Had they found some secret while he was away, some measure by which they could slip fully into the natural order? He had seen Arcite in bear form before, and clearly recognized the druid, but never had it been like this.

This bear resisted Newander's every attempt to communicate; Arcite was fully a bear, in body and mind. The same held true of Cleo, the turtle.

Newander remained a human, alone now in a house of tempting civilization. He hoped that his friends would return soon; he feared he would lose his way without their guidance.

Newander looked back out the window, back to the mountains majestic and the world that he so loved. For all of that love, though, the druid still did not know where he fit in.

* * * * *

When he arrived at the kitchen, Cadderly found that the dwarves had resumed their fighting. Pots, pans, and kitchen knives hummed about the room, smashing ceramic items, clanging against iron ones, and knocking holes in the walls.

"Ivan!" Cadderly screamed, and the desperation in his voice actually stopped the barrage.

Ivan looked at Cadderly blankly and, from across the room, Pikel added, "Oo."

"What are you fighting about now?" Cadderly asked.

"That one's fault!" Ivan growled. "He spoiled me soup. Put in roots and leaves and grass and things. Says it's druidlike that way. Bah! A dwarven druid!"

"Put your desires on hold, Pikel," Cadderly advised solemnly. "Now is not the time to be thinking of joining a druidic order."

Pikel's big, round eyes narrowed dangerously.

"The druids are not in the mood for visitors," Cadderly explained, "even for aspiring druids. I just came from them." Cadderly shook his head. "Something very wrong is going on," he said to Ivan. "Look at you two, fighting. Never have you done that in all the years I have known you."

"Never before did me stupid brother claim that he's a druid!" Ivan replied.

"Doo-dad," Pikel pointedly added.

"Granted," said Cadderly, glancing curiously at Pikel, "but look around at the destruction in this kitchen. Do you not believe this is a bit out of hand?"

Tears flooded both Ivan and Pikel's eyes when they took a moment to survey their prized kitchen. Every pot had been upset; the spice rack was thoroughly smashed and all spices lost; their oven, Pikel's own design, was damaged so brutally that it could not possibly be repaired.

Cadderly was glad that his appeal had not gone unnoticed, but the dwarven tears made him shake his head in continued disbelief. "Everyone has gone mad," he said. "The druids are up in their room, pretending to be animals. Headmaster Avery acts as if I am his favorite protégé. Even Danica is out of sorts. She nearly crippled Rufo yesterday and has it in her mind to try this Iron Skull maneuver."

"That'd explain the block," remarked Ivan.

"You know about that?" Cadderly asked.

"Brought it up yesterday," Ivan explained. "Solid and heavy, that one! Yer lady was here this morning, needing to put the thing back up on the sawhorses."

"You didn't . . ."

"'Course we did," Ivan replied, puffing out his barrellike chest. "Who else'd be able to lift the thing . . .?" The dwarf stopped abruptly. Cadderly was already gone.

The renewed clamor from Histra's room haunted Cadderly when he got back to the third level. The priestess of Sune's cries had only intensified, taking on a primordial urgency that truly frightened Cadderly and made every running stride toward Danica's room seem a futile, dream-weighted step.

He burst through Danica's door, not even slowing to knock.

He knew in his heart what he would find.

Danica lay on her back in the center of the floor, her forehead covered in blood. The stone block was not broken, but her pounding had moved the sawhorses back a few feet. Like Danica, the block was caked in blood in several places, indicating that the monk had slammed it repeatedly, even after splitting open her head.

"Danica," Cadderly breathed, moving to her. He tilted her head back and stroked her face, still delicate beneath her swollen and battered forehead.

Danica stirred just a bit, managing to drape one arm weakly over Cadderly's shoulder. One of her almond eyes cracked open, but Cadderly did not think she saw anything.

"What have you done to her?" came a cry from the doorway. Cadderly turned to see Newander glaring at him, quarterstaff leveled at the ready.

"I did nothing," Cadderly retorted. "Danica did it to herself. Against that block." He pointed to the bloodied stone, and the druid relaxed his grip on the staff. "What is happening?" Cadderly demanded. "With your friends, with Danica? With everyone, Newander? Something is wrong!"

Newander shook his head helplessly. "This is a cursed place," he agreed, dropping his gaze to the floor. "I have sensed it since my return."

"It?" Cadderly asked, wondering what Newander knew that he did not.

"A perversion," the druid tried to explain, though he stuttered over the words, as though he, himself, had not yet come to understand his fears. "Something out of the natural order, something . . ."

"Yes," Cadderly agreed. "Something not as it should be."

"A cursed place," Newander said again.

"We must figure out how it is cursed," reasoned Cadderly, "and why."

"Not we," Newander corrected. "I am a failure, good lad. You must find your own answers."

Cadderly wasn't even surprised anymore at the unexpected and uncharacteristic response, nor did he try to argue. He gently lifted Danica in his arms and carried her over to the bed, where Newander joined them.

"Her wounds are not too serious," the druid announced after a quick inspection. "I have some healing herbs." He reached into a belt pouch.

Cadderly grabbed his wrist. "What is happening?" he asked again, quietly. "Have all the priests gone mad?"

Newander pulled away and sniffled. "I care nothing for your priests," he said. "It is for my own order that I fear, and for myself!"

"Arcite and Cleo," Cadderly remarked grimly. "Can you help them?"

"Help them?" Newander replied. "Surely it is not they who need help. It is me. They are of the order. Their hearts lie with the animals. Pity Newander, I say. He has found his voice and it is not the bay nor the growl, nor even the cackle of a bird!"

Cadderly's face crinkled at the absurd words. The druid considered himself a failure because he had not changed into some beast and crawled about on the floor!

"Newander, the druid," Newander went on, fully absorbed in self-pity. "Not so, I say. Not a druid by my own measure."

Cadderly had a definite feeling that time was running out for all of them. He had awakened that morning full of hope, but things certainly had not improved.

He looked closely at Newander. The druid considered himself a failure, but by Cadderly's observation, he remained the most rational person at the library. Cadderly needed some help now, desperately. "Then be Newander, the healer" he said. "Tend to Danica—on your word."

Newander nodded.

"Heal her, and do not let her back to that block!" As if in response to his own words, Cadderly rushed across the room and pushed the stone over, not even caring about the resounding crash or the damage to the floor.

"Do not let her do anything," Cadderly went on firmly.

"Would you put your trust in a failure?" the pitiful Newander asked.

Cadderly did not hesitate. "Self-pity does not become you," he scolded. He grabbed the druid roughly by the front of his green cloak. "Danica is the most important person in all the world to me," he said sincerely, "but I have some things I must do, though I fear I do not yet understand what they might be. Newander will care for Danica—there is no one else—on his word and with my trust."

Newander nodded gravely and put his hand back into his pouch.

Cadderly moved swiftly to the door, paused, and looked back at the druid. He didn't feel comfortable leaving Danica, even with Newander, whom he trusted despite the druid's self-doubts. Cadderly dismissed his protective urges. If he really wanted to help Danica, to help everyone in the library, he would have to find out what was going on, find the source of the infection that had apparently come over the place, and not merely bandage its symptoms. It was up to him, he decided.

He nodded to Newander and headed for his room.

Thirteen

Cryptic

The tunnel was fiery and swirling, but not so long for the imp. These were summoning flames and did not burn a creature of Druzil's otherworldly constitution. Barjin had opened his interplanar gate, exactly as Dorigen had predicted, and Druzil was quick to rush to the cleric's call.

A puff of red smoke—Druzil dropping the powder to effectively shut the gate behind him—signaled Barjin that his first summoned ally had arrived. He stared deeply into the brazier's orange flames at the grotesque face taking definite form.

A batlike wing extended from the side of the brazier, then another, and a moment later Druzil hopped through.

"Who has dared to call me?" the imp snorted, playing the part of an unwitting lower-planar creature caught by Barjin's magical call.

"An imp?" the priest retorted derisively. "I have extended all my efforts for the sake of summoning a mere imp?"

Druzil folded his wings around him and snarled, not appreciating Barjin's tone.

If Barjin exhibited sarcastic disdain, Druzil knew that that, too, was part of the summoning game. As with the summoned creature, if the summoner accepted the situation without grumbles, he would be giving a definite advantage to his counterpart. Sorcery, the magic of conjuring creatures from other planes, was a contest of wills, where perceived strength was often more important than actual strength.

Druzil knew that the priest was thrilled that his first call had been answered at all, and an imp, resourceful and clever, was no small catch. But Barjin had to seem disappointed, had to make Druzil believe he was capable of calling and controlling much larger and stronger denizens.

Druzil didn't appear impressed. "I may go?" he replied as he turned back to the brazier.

104

"Hold!" Barjin shouted at him. "Do not assume anything, I warn you. I have not dismissed you, nor shall I for many days to come. What is your name?"

"*Cueltar qui tellermar gwi*," Druzil replied.

"Lackey of the stupid one?" Barjin translated, laughing, though he did not fully understand the connotations of Druzil's words. "Surely you can concoct a better title than that for yourself!"

Druzil rocked back on his clawed feet, hardly believing that Barjin could understand the common language of the lower planes. This priest was full of surprises.

"Druzil," the imp replied suddenly, though he didn't quite understand why he had revealed his true name. Barjin's quiet chuckle told him that the priest might have mentally compelled such a truthful response.

Yes, Druzil thought again, this priest was full of surprises.

"Druzil," Barjin muttered, as though he had heard the name before, a fact that did not please the imp. "Welcome, Druzil," Barjin said sincerely, "and be glad that I have called you to my side. You are a creature of chaos, and you will not be disappointed by what you witness in your short stay here."

"I have seen the Abyss," Druzil reminded him. "You cannot imagine the wonders there."

Barjin conceded the point with a nod. No matter how completely the Most Fatal Horror engulfed the priests of the Edificant Library, it could not, of course, rival the unending hellish chaos of the Abyss.

"We are in the dungeons of a bastion dedicated to order and goodness," Barjin explained.

Druzil crinkled his bulbous nose sourly, acting as though Barjin had revealed something he did not already know.

"That is about to change," Barjin assured him. "A curse has befallen this place, one that will bring the goodly priests to their knees. Even an imp who has witnessed the Abyss should enjoy that spectacle."

The glimmer in Druzil's black eyes was genuine. This was the whole purpose in giving Aballister the recipe for the chaos curse. Aballister had expressed concerns, even distress over Barjin's choice of target and Barjin's apparent successes, but Druzil was not Aballister's stooge. If Barjin could indeed take down the Edificant Library, then Druzil would be much closer to realizing his hopes of throwing an entire region of the Realms into absolute disarray.

He looked around at the altar room, impressed by Barjin's work, particularly by the setup around the precious bottle. His gaze then went to the door, and he was truly amazed.

There stood Barjin's newest bodyguard, wrapped head to toe in graying linen. Some of the cloth had slipped, revealing part of the mummy's face, dried and hollowed skin on bone with several lesions where the skilled preservation techniques had not held up to the test of centuries.

"Do you like him?" Barjin asked.

Druzil did not know how to respond. A mummy! Mummies were among the most powerful of the undead, strong and disease ridden, hateful of all living things and nearly invulnerable to most attacks. Few could animate such a monster; fewer still would dare to, fearing that they could not begin to keep the monster under control.

"The priests and scholars above soon will be helpless, lost in their own confusion," Barjin explained, "then they will meet my army. Look at him, my new friend, Druzil," the priest said triumphantly, moving over to Khalif. He started to drape an arm over the scabrous thing, then apparently reconsidered the act and prudently pulled back. "Is he not beautiful? He does love me so." To illustrate his power, Barjin turned to the mummy and commanded, "Khalif, kneel!"

The monster stiffly dropped to its knees.

"There are other preserved corpses that offer similar promise," Barjin bluffed. He had no other ashes, and any attempts to animate a mummified corpse without such aid would prove futile or produce nothing more powerful than a simple zombie.

Druzil's growing admiration for Barjin did not diminish when the priest led him out on a tour of the catacombs. Cunning, explosive glyphs, both fiery and electrical, had been placed at strategic positions, and a virtual army of animated skeletons sat patiently in their open tombs, awaiting Barjin's commands or the predetermined conditions for action the priest had set upon them.

Druzil did not need to be reminded that all of these precautions could well be unnecessary. If the chaos curse continued to work effectively in the library above, no enemies would be likely to find their way down to bother Barjin.

"Caution," Barjin muttered as though he had read Druzil's thoughts when the two had returned to the altar room. "I always assume the worst, thus am I pleasantly surprised if anything better occurs."

Druzil could not hide his agreement or his excitement. Barjin's thinking had been complete; the priest had taken no chances.

"This library soon will be mine," Barjin assured the imp, and Druzil did not doubt his boasts. "With the Edificant Library, the very cornerstone of the Impresk region, defeated, all the area from Shilmista Forest to Impresk Lake will fall before me."

Druzil liked what he heard, but Barjin's reference to "me" and not to the triumvirate was a bit unnerving. Druzil did not want any open warfare among the ruling factions of Castle Trinity, but if it did come, the imp had to make certain that he chose the winning side. He was even more glad now that Aballister had chosen to send him to Barjin, glad that he could view both sides of the coming storm.

"It is almost done," Barjin reiterated. "The curse grabs at the sensibilities of the priests above and the library soon will fall."

"How can you know what happens above?" Druzil asked him, for the tour had not included any windows or passages up into the library. The one stairway Barjin had shown him had been smashed into pieces, and the door it once had led to had been recently bricked off. The only apparent weakness in Barjin's setup was isolation, not knowing the exact sequence of events in the library above.

"I have only indications," Barjin admitted. "Behind the new wall I showed you lies the library's wine cellar. I have heard many priests passing through there for more than a day now, grabbing bottles at random—some of which are extraordinarily expensive—and apparently guzzling them down. Their talk and actions speak loudly of the growing chaos, for this certainly is not within the rules of behavior in the disciplined library. Yet you are correct in your observations, friend imp. I do indeed require more details to the events above."

"So you have summoned me," said Druzil.

"So I have opened the gate," Barjin corrected, flashing a sly look Druzil's way. "I had hoped for a more powerful ally."

More of the summoner's façade, Druzil thought, but he did not question Barjin's claims. Anxious to see for himself what effects the curse was having, Druzil was more than willing to serve Barjin in a scouting capacity. "Please, my master," the imp whined. "Let me go and see for you. Please, oh, please!"

"Yes, yes," Barjin chuckled condescendingly. "You may go above while I bring more allies through the gate."

"Does a path remain through the wine cellar?" the imp asked.

"No," Barjin explained, grabbing Mullivy by the arm. "My good groundskeeper has sealed that door well. Take my imp out the western tunnel," Barjin instructed the zombie. "Then return to me!" Mullivy's stinking, bloated corpse shuffled, stiff-legged, out of its guard position and through the altar room door. Not revolted in the least by the disgusting thing, Druzil flapped over and found a perch on Mullivy's shoulder.

"Take care, for it is daylight above," Barjin called after him.

In response, Druzil chuckled, whispered an arcane phrase, and became invisible.

Barjin moved excitedly back to the gate, hoping for continued good fortune in his summoning. An imp was a prized catch for so small a gate, though if Barjin had known the identity of this particular imp and his wizard master, or that Druzil had sealed the gate behind his entry, he would not have been so thrilled.

He tried for more than an hour, calling out general spells of summoning and the names of every minor denizen he knew.

Flames leaped and danced, but no forms appeared within their orange glow. Barjin wasn't too concerned. The brazier would burn for many days, and the necromancer's stone, though it had not yet produced results, continued to send out its call for undead. The priest would find many opportunities to add to his force.

* * * * *

Cadderly wandered the hallways of the building, stunned by the emptiness, the brooding quiet. Many priests, both visitors and those of the host sects, such as Brother Chaunticleer, had left the library without explanation, and many of those who had remained apparently preferred the solitude of their rooms.

Cadderly did find Ivan and Pikel, in the kitchen, busily cooking a variety of dishes.

"Your fights have ended?" Cadderly asked, grabbing a biscuit as he entered. He realized then that he hadn't eaten much in nearly a day, and that Danica and Newander no doubt would be hungry also.

"Fights?" Ivan balked. "No time for fighting, boy! Been cooking since the eve. Not a many for supper, but them that's there won't go away."

A terrible, sick feeling washed over Cadderly. He moved through the kitchen to peek out the other door, which led to the library's large dining hall. A score of people were in there, Headmaster Avery among them, stuffing themselves hand over hand. Several had fallen to the floor, so full that they could hardly move, but still trying to shove more food into their eager mouths.

"You are killing them, you know," Cadderly remarked to the dwarves, his tone resigned. The young scholar was beginning to get an idea of what was going on. He thought of Histra and her unending passion, of Danica's sudden obsession with lessons that were beyond her level of achievement, and of the druids, Arcite and Cleo, so fanatic to their tenets that they had lost their very identities.

"They will eat as long as you put food before them," Cadderly explained. "They will gorge themselves until they die."

Both Ivan and Pikel stopped their stirring and stared long and hard at the young priest.

"Slow the meals down," Cadderly instructed them.

For the first time in a while, Cadderly noted some measure of comprehension. Both dwarves seemed almost repulsed by their own participation in the food orgy. Together they backed away from their respective pots.

"Slow the meals down," Cadderly asked again.

Ivan nodded gravely.

"Oo," added Pikel.

Cadderly studied the brothers for a long moment, sensing that they had regained their sanity, that he could trust them as he had trusted Newander.

"I will be back as soon as I can," he promised, then he took a couple of plates, packed a meal, and took his leave.

Anyone watching would have noticed a profound difference in the strides of the young scholar as he left the kitchen. Cadderly had come down tentatively, afraid of something he could not understand. He still had not figured out the curse or its cause, nor could he remember his trials in the lower catacombs, but, more and more, it was becoming evident to Cadderly that fate had placed a great burden upon him, and the price of his success or failure was terrifying indeed.

To his relief, Newander had the situation in Danica's room under control.

Danica was still in her bed, conscious but unable to move, for the druid had compelled long vines of ivy to come in through the window and wrap the woman where she lay. Newander, too, seemed in better spirits, and his face brightened even more when Cadderly handed him the supper plate.

"You have done well," Cadderly remarked.

"Minor magic," the druid answered. "Her wounds were not so bad. What have you learned?"

Cadderly shrugged. "Little," he answered. "Whatever is wrong in this place grows worse by the moment. I have an idea, though, a way that I might learn what is happening."

Newander perked up, expecting some revelation.

"I am going to go to sleep."

The druid's fair face crinkled in confusion, but Cadderly's confident smile deflected any forthcoming questions. Newander took the plate and began eating, mumbling to himself with every bite.

Cadderly knelt beside Danica. She seemed barely coherent, but she managed to whisper, "Iron Skull."

"Forget Iron Skull," Cadderly replied quietly. "You must rest and heal. Something is wrong here, Danica, wrong with you and with all the library. I do not know why, but I seem to have not been affected." He paused, searching for the words.

"I think I did something," he said. Newander shuffled uneasily behind him. "I cannot explain. . . . I do not understand, but I have this feeling, this vagrant thought, that I somehow caused all of this."

"Surely you cannot blame yourself," Newander said.

Cadderly turned on him. "I am not looking to place any blame at all," he replied evenly, "but I believe I played a part in this growing catastrophe, whatever it might be. If I did, then I must accept that fact and search, not for blame, but for a solution."

"How do you mean to search?" the druid asked. His tone turned sarcastic. "By going to sleep?"

"It is hard to explain," Cadderly replied to the druid's stare. "I have been dreaming—vivid dreams. I feel there is a connection. I cannot explain."

Newander's visage softened. "You need not explain," he said, no longer doubting. "Dreams sometimes do have the power of prophecy, and we have no clearer trail to follow. Take your rest, then. I will watch over you."

Cadderly kissed Danica's pale cheek.

"Iron Skull," the woman whispered.

More determined than ever, Cadderly pulled a blanket to the corner of the room and lay down, placing an inkwell, quill, and parchments beside him. He threw an arm across his eyes and filled his thoughts with skeletons and ghouls, beckoning the nightmare.

* * * * *

The skeletons were waiting for him. Cadderly could smell the rot and the thick dust, and hear the scuffle of fleshless feet on the hard stone. He ran in a red fog, his legs heavy, too heavy. He saw a door down a long hallway, and there was light peeking through its cracks. His legs were too heavy; he could not get there.

Cold beads of sweat caked Cadderly's clothing and streaked his face. His eyes popped open and there, hovering over him, stood the druid.

"What have you seen, boy?" Newander asked. The druid quickly handed him the writing materials.

Cadderly tried to articulate the gruesome scene, but it was fast fading from his thoughts. He snatched up the quill and began writing and sketching, capturing as many of the images as he could, forcing his thoughts back into the dimming recesses of his nightmare.

Then it was daytime again, midafternoon, and the dream was no more. Cadderly remembered the skeletons and the smell of dust, but the details were foggy and indistinct. He looked down to the parchment and was surprised by what he saw, as if someone else had done the writing. At the top of the scroll were the words, "slow . . . red fog . . . reaching for me . . . too close!" and below these was a sketch of a long hallway, its sides lined by sarcophagi-filled alcoves and with a cracked door at its end.

"I know this place," Cadderly began tentatively, then he stopped abruptly, his elation and train of thought disrupted by Barjin's insidious and incessant memory-blocking spell.

Before Cadderly could fight back against the sudden lapse, a scream from the hallway froze him where he sat. He looked at Newander, who was equally disturbed.

"That was not the priestess of Sune," the druid remarked.

They rushed through the door and into the hallway.

There stood a gray-capped priest, holding his entrails in his hands, an eerie, almost ecstatic expression on his face. His tunic, too, was gray, though most of it now was blood-stained, and still more blood poured out of the man's opened belly with each passing second.

Cadderly and Newander could not immediately find the strength to go to him, knew the futility of it anyway. They watched in blank horror as the priest fell face down, a pool of blood widening around him.

Fourteen
Disturbing Answers

Mulivy was not a swift walker, and Druzil used this time away from Barjin to reestablish contact with his master. He sent his thoughts out across the miles to Castle Trinity and found an eager recipient awaiting them.

Greetings, my master, the imp communicated.

You have found Barjin?

In the catacombs, as you believed, Druzil replied.

The fool.

Druzil wasn't certain that he shared Aballister's appraisal, but the wizard didn't need to know that.

He has other allies, the imp imparted. *Undead allies, including a mummy.*

Druzil smiled widely as he sensed Aballister's reaction to that bit of news. The wizard didn't mean to communicate his next thoughts, but Druzil was deeply enough into his mind to hear them anyway.

I never would have believed that Barjin could achieve that.

Many emotions accompanied those words, Druzil knew, and fear was not the least among them.

The mighty Edificant Library is in peril, Druzil added, just to prod the wizard. *If Barjin succeeds, then the Most Fatal Horror will have put us on the path toward a great victory. All the region will fall without the guidance of the library's clerics.*

Aballister was wondering if the price was too high, Druzil realized, and the imp decided that he had told the wizard enough for this day. Besides, he could see the daylight up ahead as his zombie chauffeur neared the tunnel exit. He broke off direct communication, though he let the wizard remain in his mind and view through the imp's eyes. Druzil wanted Aballister to get a good look at the glory of the chaos curse.

* * * * *

The white squirrel kept high in the branches, unsure of what its keen senses were telling it. Mullivy came to the edge of the earthen tunnel, then immediately turned around and disappeared back into it. Another scent, an unfamiliar scent, lingered. Percival saw nothing, but like other foraging animals, low on the food chain, the squirrel had learned quickly to trust more than just its eyes.

Percival followed the scent—it was moving—to the treelined lane. The road was quiet, as it had been for the last two days, though the sun shone bright and warm in a clear blue sky. The squirrel's ears perked up and twitched nervously as the library's door opened, seemingly of its own accord, and the strange scent moved inside.

The unusualness of it all kept the squirrel sitting nervously still for many moments, but the sun was warm and the nuts and berries in the trees and shrubs were abundant, just waiting to be plucked. Percival rarely kept any thought for any length of time, and when he spotted a pile of acorns lying unattended on the ground, he was too relieved that the groundskeeper had stayed in the tunnel to worry about anything else.

* * * * *

Druzil's perceptions of the state of the Edificant Library were far different from Cadderly's. Unlike the young scholar, the imp thought the rising, paralyzing chaos a marvelous thing.

He found just a few priests in the study halls, sitting unmoving in front of open books, so riveted by their studies that they barely remembered to draw breath. Druzil understood the hold of the chaos curse better than any; if Barjin entered the hall with a host of skeletons at his back, these priests would offer no resistance, would probably not even notice.

Druzil enjoyed the spectacle in the dining hall most of all, where gluttonous priests sat on chairs set back from the table to accommodate their swelling bellies, and other priests lay semiconscious on the floor. At one end of the table, three priests were engaged in mortal combat over a single remaining turkey leg.

Arguments, particularly between priests of differing faiths, were general throughout the building, often becoming more serious encounters. The least faithful or studious simply wandered away from the library altogether, and few had a care to stop them. Those most faithful were so absorbed in their rituals that they seemed to notice nothing else. In another of the second-floor study chambers, Druzil found a pile of Oghman priests heaped together in a great ball, having wrestled until they were too exhausted even to move.

When Druzil left an hour later to report to Barjin, he was quite satisfied that the chaos curse had done its work to unpredictable perfection.

He felt the first insistent demands of his master when he rounded the northern side of the building, approaching the tunnel.

You have seen? his thoughts asked Aballister. He knew that if Aballister had been paying attention, the wizard would know the state of the library as well as Druzil did.

The Most Fatal Horror, Aballister remarked somewhat sourly.

Barjin has brought us a great victory, Druzil promptly reminded the ever-skeptical wizard.

Aballister was quick to reply. *The library is not yet won. Do not count our victory until Barjin is actually in control of the structure.*

Druzil replied by shutting the wizard completely out of his thoughts in mid-conversation. *"Tellemara,"* the imp muttered to himself. The curse was working. Already the few score priests remaining at the library probably would not be able to fend off Barjin's undead forces, and their potential for resistance lessened with each passing moment. Soon, many of them likely would kill each other and many others simply would wander away. How much more control did the wizard require before claiming victory?

Druzil paid no heed to Aballister's final warning. Barjin would win here, the imp decided, and he was thinking, too, that maybe he could find extra gains in his mission from Aballister, in spying on the powerful priest. Ever since the magical elixir had been dubbed an agent of Talona, the priests of Castle Trinity had enjoyed a more prominent role in the evil triumvirate. With the Edificant Library in Barjin's hands, and with Barjin controlling a strong undead army, that domination would only increase.

Aballister was an acceptable "master," as masters went, but Druzil was an imp from the domain of chaos, and imps owed no loyalty to anyone except themselves.

It was too early to make a definitive judgment, of course, but already Druzil was beginning to suspect that he would find more pleasure and more chaos at Barjin's side than at Aballister's.

* * * * *

"Do something for him!" Cadderly pleaded, but Newander only shook his head helplessly.

"Ilmater!" gasped the dying priest. "The . . . pain," he stammered. "It is so won—" He shuddered one final time and fell limp in Cadderly's arms.

"Who could have done this?" Cadderly asked, though he feared he knew the answer.

"Is not Ilmater the Crying God, a deity dedicated to suffering?" the druid asked, leading Cadderly to a clear conclusion.

Cadderly nodded gravely. "Priests of Ilmater often engage in self-flagellation, but it is usually a minor ritual of no serious consequence."

"Until now," Newander remarked dryly.

"Come on," Cadderly said, laying the dead priest onto the floor. The blood trail was easily followed, and both Cadderly and Newander could have guessed where it led anyway.

Cadderly didn't even bother knocking on the partly opened door. He pushed it in, then turned away, too horrified to enter.

In the middle of the floor lay the remaining five priests of the Ilmater delegation, torn and bloodied.

Newander rushed in to check on them but returned in only a few moments, shaking his head grimly.

"Priests of Ilmater never carry it this far," Cadderly said, as much to himself as to the druid, "and druids never go so far as to become, heart and body, their favored animals." He looked up at the druid, his gray eyes revealing that he thought his words important. "Danica was never so obsessed as to slam her face into a stone block repeatedly."

Newander was beginning to catch on.

"Why were we not affected?" Cadderly asked.

"I fear that I have been," replied the sullen druid.

When Cadderly looked more closely at Newander, he understood. The druid continued to fear not for his animal transformed friends, but for himself.

"I have not the true heart for my chosen calling," explained the druid.

"You make too many judgments," Cadderly scolded. "We know that something is wrong—" he waved toward the room of carnage "—terribly wrong. You have heard the priestess of Sune. You have seen these priests, and your own druid brothers. For some reason, we two have been spared—and perhaps I know of two others who have not been so badly affected—and that is not cause to lament. Whatever has happened threatens the whole library."

"You are wise for one so young," admitted Newander, "but what are we to do? Surely my druid brothers and the girl will be of no help."

"We will go to Dean Thobicus," Cadderly said hopefully. "He has overseen the library for many years. Perhaps he will know what to do." Cadderly didn't have to speak his hopes that Dean Thobicus, aged and wise, had not fallen under the curse also.

The journey down to the second floor only increased the companions' apprehension. The halls were quiet and empty, until a group of drunken rowdies appeared down at the other end of a long hallway. As soon as the mob spotted Cadderly and Newander, they set out after them. Cadderly and the druid did not know if the men meant to attack them or coerce them into joining the party, but neither of them had any intentions of finding out.

Newander turned back after rounding one corner and cast a simple spell. The group came in fast pursuit, but the druid had laid a magical trip-wire and the intoxicated mob had no defense against such a subtle attack. They tumbled in a twisting and squirming heap and came up too busily wrestling with each other to remember that they had been chasing somebody.

Cadderly considered the headmasters' area his best hope until he and Newander crossed through the large double doors at the southern end of the second level. The area was eerily quiet, with no one to be seen. Dean Thobicus's office door was among the few that were not open. Cadderly moved up slowly and knocked.

He knew in his heart that he would get no response.

Dean Thobicus was never an excitable man. His love was introspection, spending hours on end staring at the night sky, or at nothing at all. Thobicus's loves were in his own mind, and when Cadderly and Newander entered his office, that was exactly where they found him. He sat very still behind his large oaken desk and apparently hadn't moved for quite a while. He had soiled himself, and his lips were dry and parched, though a beaker full of water sat only inches away on his desk.

Cadderly called to him several times and shook him roughly, but the dean showed no sign of having heard him. Cadderly gave him one last shake, and Thobicus fell right over and remained where he dropped, as if he hadn't noticed.

Newander bent to examine the man. "We'll get no answers from this one," he announced.

"We are running out of places to look," Cadderly replied.

"Let us get back to the girl," said the druid. "No good in staying here, and I am afraid for Danica with the drunken mob roaming the halls."

They were relieved to find no sign of the drunken men as they exited the headmasters' area, and their return trip through the quiet and empty hallways was uneventful.

Their sighs of relief upon entering Danica's room would have been lessened considerably if either of them had noticed the dark figure lurking in the shadows, eyeing Cadderly with utter hatred.

* * * * *

Danica was awake but unblinking when the two men returned to her. Newander started toward her, concerned and thinking that she had fallen into the same catatonic state as the dean, but Cadderly recognized the difference.

"She is meditating," Cadderly explained, and even as he spoke the words, he realized what Danica had in mind. "She is fighting whatever it is that compels her."

"You cannot know that," reasoned Newander.

Cadderly refused to yield his assumptions. "Look at her closely," he observed, "at her concentration. She is fighting, I say."

The claim was beyond Newander's experience, either to agree or refute, so he accepted Cadderly's logic without further argument.

"You said you know of others who might have escaped?" he said, wanting to get back to the business at hand.

"The dwarven cooks," replied Cadderly, "Ivan and Pikel Bouldershoulder.

They have been acting strangely, I admit, but each time I have been able to bring them to reason."

Newander thought for a few minutes, chuckling quietly when he remembered Pikel, the green-bearded dwarf that so badly wanted to join the druidical order. The notion was absurd, of course, but Pikel was an appealing chap—for a dwarf.

Newander snapped his fingers and allowed himself a smile of hope as he found a clue in Cadderly's report. "Magical," he said, looking back to Cadderly. "It is said by all who know that dwarves are a tough lot against magical enchantments. Might it be that the cooks can resist where men cannot?"

Cadderly nodded and looked to the vine-covered bed. "And Danica will resist in time, I know," he said and turned back to Newander immediately. "But what about us? Why have we been spared?"

"As I told you," replied Newander, "it might well be that I have not been spared. I was gone all of yesterday, out walking in the sunshine and feeling the mountain breezes. I found Arcite and Cleo, bear and tortoise, upon my return, but since I came back, I must admit that I, too, have felt compulsions."

"But you have resisted them," said Cadderly.

"Perhaps," Newander corrected. "I cannot be sure. My heart of late has not been for the animals, as seemingly were the hearts of my druid kin."

"And so you doubt your calling," Cadderly remarked.

Newander nodded. "It is a difficult thing. I so badly wish to join Arcite and Cleo, to join the search they have begun for the natural order, but I want, too . . ."

"Go on," Cadderly prompted as though he believed the revelations were vital.

"I want to learn of Deneir and the other gods," Newander admitted. "I want to watch the progress of the world, the rise of cities. I want to . . . I want," Newander shook his head suddenly. "I do not know what I want!"

Cadderly's gray eyes lit up. "Even in your own heart you do not know what is in your own heart," he said. "That is a rare thing, and it has saved you, unless I miss my guess. That, and the fact that you have not been here for very long since this all began."

"What do you know?" Newander asked, a sharp edge on his voice. He softened quickly, though, wondering how much truth was in the young scholar's words.

Cadderly only shrugged in response. "It is only a theory."

"What of you?" Newander asked. "Why are you not affected?"

Cadderly nearly laughed for lack of a suitable answer. "I cannot say," he honestly admitted. He looked to Danica again.

"But I know now how I might find out."

Newander followed the young scholar's gaze to the meditating woman. "Are you going back to sleep?"

Cadderly gave him a sly wink. "Sort of."

Newander did not argue. He wanted the time alone anyway to consider his own predicament. He could not accept Cadderly's reasoning concerning his exclusion from whatever was cursing the library, though he hoped it was as simple as that.

Newander suspected that something else was going on, something he could not begin to understand, something wonderful or terrible—he could not be sure. For all of his thinking, though, the druid could not rid himself of the image of Arcite and Cleo, contented and natural, and could not dismiss his fears that his ambivalence had caused him to fail Silvanus in a time of dire need.

* * * * *

Cadderly sat crosslegged with his eyes closed for a long time, relaxing each part of his body in turn, causing his mind to sink within his physical self. He had learned these techniques from Danica—one of the few things she had revealed about her religion—and had found them quite useful, restful, and enjoyable.

Now, though, the meditation had taken on a more important role.

Cadderly opened his eyes slowly and viewed the room, seeing it in surreal tones. He focused first on the block of stone, stained with his dear Danica's blood. It sat between the downed sawhorses, and then it was gone, removed to blackness. Behind it was Danica's cabinet and wardrobe, and then they, too, were gone.

He glanced left, to the door and Newander keeping a watchful guard. The druid watched him curiously, but Cadderly hardly noticed. A moment later, both druid and door were holes of blackness.

His visual sweep eliminated the rest of the room: Danica's desk and her weapons, two crystalline daggers, in their boot sheaths against the wall; the window, bright with late morning light; and, lastly, Danica herself, still deep in her own meditation on the vine-wrapped bed.

"Dear Danica," Cadderly muttered, though even he didn't hear the words. Then Danica, too, and everything else, was out of his thoughts.

Again he returned to relaxation—toes, then feet, then legs; fingers, then hands, then arms—until he had achieved a sedated state. His breathing came slowly and easily. His eyes were open, but they saw nothing.

There was only quiet blackness, calm.

Cadderly could not summon thoughts in this state. He had to hope that answers would flow to him, that his subconscious would give him images and clues. He had no concept of time passing, but it seemed a long while of emptiness, of simple, uncluttered existence.

The walking dead were alongside him then in the blackness.

Unlike his dreams, he saw the skeletal figures as no threat now, as though he were an unattached observer instead of an active participant. They scuffled along on his mental journey, falling behind him, leaving him in a hallway. There was the familiar door, cracked and showing lines of light, always the ending image of his nightmare.

The picture faded, as if some unseen force were trying to stop him from proceeding, a mental barrier that he now, for some reason unknown to him, believed to be a magical spell.

The images became a gray blur for just a moment, then focused again, and he was at the door, then through the door.

The altar room!

Cadderly watched, hopeful and afraid, as the room darkened, leaving only a single, red-glowing object, a bottle, visible before him. He saw the bottle up close then, and he saw hands, his own hands, twisting off the stopper.

Red smoke exploded all about him, stole every other image.

Cadderly looked again on Danica's room, the image identical to the one he had blocked out—even Newander remained at his position near the door—except that now there hung in the air an almost imperceptible pink haze.

Cadderly felt his heart quicken as the purpose of that haze became all too clear. His gaze fell over Danica, still deep in her own meditation. Cadderly's thoughts reached out to Danica and were answered. She was battling, as he had suspected, fighting back against that permeating pink haze, trying to recover her sensibilities against its debilitating effects.

"Fight, Danica!" he heard himself say, and the words broke his trance. He looked over to Newander, his expression desperate.

"I was the cause," he said, holding up his hands as though they were covered in blood. "I opened it!"

Newander rushed over and knelt beside Cadderly, trying to calm him. "Opened?"

"The bottle," Cadderly stammered. "The bottle! The red glowing bottle. The mist—do you see the mist?"

Newander glanced around, then shook his head.

"It is there . . . here," Cadderly said, grabbing the druid's arm and using it to help him to his feet. "We have to close that bottle!"

"Where?" the druid asked.

Cadderly stopped suddenly, considering the question. He remembered the skeletons, the dusty smell, the corridors lined with alcoves. "There really was a door in the wine cellar," he said at length, "a door to the lowest catacombs, those dungeons no longer used in the library."

"We must go there?" asked Newander, rising beside Cadderly.

"No," Cadderly cautioned, "not yet. The catacombs are not empty. We have to prepare." He looked to Danica again, seeing her in a new light now that he understood her mental struggles.

"Will she be fighting beside us?" Newander asked, noticing Cadderly's focus.

"Danica is fighting now," Cadderly assured him, "but the mist hangs all about us, and it is insistent." He gave Newander a confused look. "I still do not know why I have been spared its effects."

"If you were indeed the cause, as you believe," replied the druid, who had lengthy experience with magical practices, "then that fact alone might have spared you."

Cadderly considered the words for a moment, but they hardly seemed to matter. "Whatever the reason" he said determinedly, "we—I—have to close that bottle." He spent a few minutes trying to recall the obstacles before him and imagining even more frightening monsters that might be lurking just outside his nightmarish visions. Cadderly knew that he would need allies in this fight, powerful allies to help him get back to the altar room.

"Ivan and Pikel," he said to Newander. "The dwarves are more resistant, as you said. They will help us."

"Go to them," Newander bade him.

"You stay with Danica," Cadderly replied. "Let no one, except for me and the dwarven brothers, into the room."

"I have ways of keeping the world out," Newander assured him.

As soon as he entered the hallway, Cadderly heard the druid chanting softly. Danica's wooden door, suddenly brought to life by Newander's spell, warped and expanded, wedging tightly, immovably, into its frame.

* * * * *

Ivan and Pikel were not fighting when Cadderly entered the kitchen this time, but neither were they cooking. They sat quietly, somberly, at the room's main table opposite each other.

As soon as he noticed Cadderly, Ivan absently handed him the one-handed crossbow, finished to perfection. "Had an urge," the dwarf explained, not giving the magnificent item a second look.

Cadderly was not surprised. It seemed that many people in the Edificant Library were having "urges" these days.

"What's it about?" Ivan asked suddenly.

Cadderly did not understand. Pikel, a grim expression on his normally carefree features, pointed to the door leading into the dining room. Cadderly crossed the kitchen tentatively and when he looked into the adjoining room, he came to realize the reason for the dwarves' somber mood. Half the gluttonous priests, Avery included, remained at the table, hardly able to move. The other half were worse yet, lying on the floor in their own vomit. Cadderly knew without going to them that several were dead, and his face, too, was ashen when he turned back into the kitchen.

"So what's it about?" Ivan asked again.

Cadderly looked at him long and hard, unsure of how he could begin to explain the bottle and his own, still unclear actions. Finally, he said only, "I am not certain what has happened, but I believe I know now how to stop it."

He thought his proclamation would excite the dwarves, but they hardly stirred at the news.

"Will you help me?" Cadderly asked. "I cannot do it alone."

"What do ye need?" Ivan asked offhandedly.

"You," Cadderly replied, "and your brother. The curse—and it is a curse—

comes from below the cellars. I have to go down there to end it, but I fear that the place is guarded."

"Guarded?" Ivan balked. "How can ye guess that?"

"Just trust me, I beg," replied Cadderly. "I am not so skilled with weapons, but I have witnessed you two at your fighting and could use your strong arms. Will you come with me?"

The dwarves exchanged bored looks and shrugs. "I'd rather be cooking," Ivan remarked. "Gave up me adventuring pack long ago. Pikel'd rather be . . ." He stopped and eyed his brother intently.

Pikel fixed a smug look on his face, reached up, and waggled one side of his green beard.

"A druid!" Ivan yelled, hopping to his feet and grabbing a nearby pan. "Ye stupid bird-loving, oak-kissin' . . .!"

"Oo oi!" Pikel exclaimed, arming himself with a rolling pin.

Cadderly was between them in an instant. "It is all part of the curse!" he cried. "Can you not see that? It makes you argue and fight!"

Both dwarves jumped back a step and lowered their utensil weapons.

"Oo," muttered Pikel curiously.

"If you want to fight a true enemy," Cadderly began, "then come to my room and help me prepare. There is something below the cellars, something horrible and evil. If we do not stop it, then all the library is doomed."

Ivan leaned to the side and looked around the young scholar to his similarly leaning brother. They shared a shrug and simultaneously heaved their cookware weapons across to the other side of the room.

"Let us go to the gluttons first," Cadderly instructed. "We should leave them as comfortable as we may."

The dwarves nodded. "Then I'll get me axe," Ivan declared, "and me brother'll get his tree!"

"Tree?" Cadderly echoed quietly at the departing dwarves' backs. One look at Pikel's green-dyed braid bouncing halfway down the dwarfs back and his huge, gnarly, and smelly feet flopping out every which way from his delicate sandals told Cadderly not even to bother pressing the question.

Fifteen
Blood on His Hands

Cadderly sorted through the many leather straps hanging in his wardrobe, finally pulling out a belt with a strangely shaped, wide and shallow leather sheath on one side. The fit of the small crossbow was perfect—there was even a place for the loading pin. As usual, Ivan and Pikel had crafted the metal to exact specifications.

Cadderly drew the crossbow out again as soon as he had put it in. He tested the pin next, cranking the bow and firing several times. The action was smooth and easy; Cadderly even managed, without too much difficulty, to manipulate the weapon enough to crank it with one hand.

Next Cadderly took out a bandoleer and slung it over his shoulder, carefully lining up the sixteen loaded darts in front of him, within easy reach. He winced when he wondered what damage a blow to his chest might cause, but he held faith that the darts and the bandoleer had been properly constructed. He felt better when he saw himself in the mirror, as if wearing his latest inventions had returned to him some control over his surroundings. Any smile he felt welling was quickly sublimated, though, when he remembered the dangerous task ahead. This was no game, he reminded himself. Already, and because of his own actions, several men had died and all the library was threatened.

Cadderly moved across the room, behind the door, to a closed and sealed iron box. He fitted a key into the lock, then paused for a long moment, considering carefully the precise steps he had to follow once the box was opened. He had practiced this maneuver many times, but never before had he believed he would need it.

As soon as the box lid was opened, all the area around Cadderly fell into a globe of absolute darkness. It was not a surprise to the young scholar; Cadderly

121

had paid Histra handsomely for placing this reversed form of her light spell within the box. It was inconvenient—and Cadderly did not enjoy dealing with Histra—but necessary to protect one of Cadderly's most prized possessions. In an ancient tome, Cadderly had stumbled upon the formula for the very potent sleep poison used by the drow elves. The exotic ingredients had not been found easily—one fungus in particular could only be gained in deep tunnels far below Toril's surface—and the arrangements to mix them—which the alchemist, Belago, had done deep underground also—had been even more difficult to secure, but Cadderly had persevered. With the blessings and backing of Dean Thobicus, his efforts had produced five tiny vials of the poison.

At least, Cadderly hoped it was the poison—one does not often find the opportunity to test such things.

Even with the apparent success of the brewing, though, there remained one severe limitation. The potion was a drow mix, brewed in the strange magical emanations found only in the Underdark, the lightless world beneath Toril's surface. It was a well-known fact that if drow poison was exposed to the sun, even for a moment, it would become useless in a very short while. The open air alone could destroy the expensive mixture, so Cadderly had taken great steps, like the spell of darkness, to protect his investment.

He closed his eyes and worked from memory. First he unscrewed the tiny compartment of his feathered ring and laid the top in a predetermined place to the side, then he removed one of the vials from the box, carefully popping its cork. He poured the gooey contents into his opened ring, then found and replaced the feathered top.

Cadderly breathed easier. If he had slipped at all, he would have wasted perhaps a thousand gold pieces' worth of ingredients and many weeks of labor. Also, if he had spilled even a drop of the poison onto his hand, and if it had found its way into a tiny scratch or nick, he no doubt would be snoozing soundly right beside the box.

None of that had happened. Cadderly was precise and disciplined when he needed to be, and his many practice sessions with vials of water had paid off.

The darkness disappeared within the confines of the sealed box when Cadderly closed the lid. Ivan and Pikel were already in the room, surrounding the young scholar, weapons ready and faces grim at the sight of the unexpected darkness.

"Just yourself, then," Ivan grumbled, relaxing his grip on his heavy, two-headed axe.

Cadderly could not immediately find his breath to reply. He just sat and stared at the dwarven brothers. Both wore armor of interlocking rings, dusty from decades of idleness and rusted in several spots. Ivan wore a helm fashioned with deer antlers—an eight-pointer—while Pikel wore a cooking pot! For all his precautionary armor, Pikel still wore his open-toed sandals.

Most amazing of all, though, was Pikel's weapon. Looking upon it, Cadderly understood Ivan's earlier reference. It was indeed a "tree," the polished trunk of some black and smoothbarked variety that Cadderly did not recognize. The club was fully four feet long, nearly as tall as Pikel, a foot in diameter on the wide end, and less than half that on the narrow, gripping end. Looped leather hand-grips were spiked on at various intervals to aid the wielder, but still it seemed an awkward and cumbersome thing.

As if he sensed Cadderly's private doubts, Pikel whipped the club about through several attack and defense routines with obvious ease.

Cadderly nodded his appreciation, sincerely relieved that he had not been on the receiving end of any of Pikel's mock strikes.

"Are ye set to go?" Ivan asked, adjusting his armor.

"Almost," Cadderly answered. "I have just a few more minor preparations, and I want to look in on Danica before we go."

"How can we help ye?" offered Ivan.

Cadderly could see that the dwarves were both anxious to get on with it. He knew that it had been many years since the Bouldershoulder brothers had walked into adventure, many years spent cooking meals in the haven that was the Edificant Library. It wasn't a bad life by anyone's measure, but the thought of imminent danger and adventure obviously had worked an enchantment over the dwarves. There was an unmistakable luster to their dark eyes and their movements were agitated and nervous.

"Go to Belago's alchemy shop," Cadderly replied, thinking it best to keep the dwarves busy. He described the distillation equipment and the potion that Belago was brewing for him. "If he has any more for me, bring it back," Cadderly instructed, thinking the task simple enough.

The dwarves already had hopped off down the hallway when Cadderly realized that he hadn't seen Belago about lately, not since before the curse had taken hold of the library. What had happened to the alchemist? Cadderly wondered. Was the shop still operational? Were the proper mixtures for blending his *Oil of Impact* still slipping in the precise amounts through the hoppers? Cadderly shrugged away his worries, trusting in Ivan and Pikel to use their best judgment.

Percival was at the window again, chittering with his customary excitement. Cadderly went over and leaned on the sill, bending to put his face close to his little friend's and listening intently. Cadderly could not understand the squirrel's talk, of course, no more than a child could understand a pet dog's, but he and Percival had developed quite an emotive rapport, and he knew well enough that Percival comprehended some simple words or phrases, mostly those pertaining to food.

"I will be gone for a while," Cadderly said. The squirrel probably wouldn't understand so complex a message, he realized, but talking to Percival often helped Cadderly sort through his own confusion. Percival never really provided any answers, but Cadderly often found them hidden within his own words.

Percival sat up on his hind legs, licking his forepaws and running them quickly over his face.

"Something bad has happened," Cadderly tried to explain, "something that I caused. Now I am going to fix it."

His somber tone, if not his words, had a calming effect on the rodent. Percival stopped licking and sat very still.

"So I will be gone," Cadderly continued, "down below the library, in the deep tunnels that are no longer used."

Something he had said apparently struck the squirrel profoundly. Percival ran in tight circles, chattering and clicking, and it was a very long while before Cadderly could calm the beast down. He knew that Percival had something important—by Percival's standards—to tell him, but he had no time for the squirrel's distractions.

"Do not worry," Cadderly said, as much to himself as to Percival. "I will return soon, and then all will be as it was."

The words sounded hollow to him. Things would not be as they had been. Even if he managed to close the smoking bottle, and even if that simple act removed the curse, it wouldn't bring back the priests of Ilmater or the dead gluttons in the dining room.

Cadderly shook those dark thoughts away. He could not hope to succeed if he began his quest in despair.

"Do not worry!" he said again, firmly.

Again the squirrel went crazy, and this time, Cadderly realized, from the direction of Percival's gaze, the source of the excitement. Cadderly looked back over his shoulder, expecting to see that Ivan and Pikel had returned.

He saw instead Kierkan Rufo, and more pointedly, the dagger in Rufo's hand.

"What is it?" Cadderly asked weakly, but he needed no verbal answer to decipher the man's intent. Rufo's left eye was still bruised and closed, and his nose pointed as much toward his cheek as straight ahead. His ugly wounds only accentuated the look of sheer hatred in his cold, dark eyes.

"Where is your light now?" the tall man sneered. "But then, it would not do you much good, would it?" He limped noticeably, but his approach was steady.

"What are you doing?" Cadderly asked him.

"Is not the mighty Cadderly smart enough to figure that out?" Rufo mocked him.

"You do not want to do this," Cadderly said as calmly as he could. "There are consequences . . ."

"Want?" Rufo cried wildly. "Oh, but I do indeed want to do this. I want to hold your heart in my hands. I want to bring it to your dear Danica and show her who was the stronger."

Cadderly looked for some retort. He thought of mentioning the obvious weakness in Rufo's plan—if he did bring Cadderly's heart to Danica, she would kill him—but even that, Cadderly guessed, would not stop Kierkan Rufo. Rufo was under the curse fully, following its devious call with no regard for consequences. Reluctantly, but with no apparent options, Cadderly slipped one finger inside the loop of his spindle-disk cord and moved right up against the side of his bed.

Rufo came straight in, dagger leading, and Cadderly rolled sideways across the bed, just getting out of the angular man's long reach.

Rufo jumped back quickly, faster than Cadderly expected he could move, to cut off Cadderly's angle for the door. He rushed around the bottom of the bed, launching a wide, arcing swing at Cadderly's belly.

Cadderly easily kept back beyond the dagger, then he retaliated, snapping his spindle-disks above Rufo's swinging arm.

Rufo's already broken nose crackled under the impact and a new stream of blood flowed thickly over the dried stains on his lip. Rufo, obsessed with utter hatred, shook away the minor hit and came on.

Though the blow had not been very solid, it still had almost broken the rhythm of Cadderly's working wrist. He managed to coax the disks back to his hand, but the cord was now loosely wound and he couldn't immediately strike again effectively.

Rufo seemed to sense his weakness. He grinned wickedly and came in again.

Percival saved Cadderly's life, leaping from the window to land squarely on Rufo's face. With a single swipe, Rufo sent the squirrel flying across the room, and Percival had done no real damage, but Cadderly had not wasted the time.

With Rufo distracted, he had snapped the spindle-disks straight down and back up several times to realign and tighten the cord.

Rufo seemed not to even notice the twin lines of blood running down his face from his newest wound, a small bite on his cheek from Percival. "I will hold your heart in my hands!" he promised again, laughing insanely.

Cadderly jerked his arm once, and then again, feigning a throw to keep Rufo off guard. Between dodges, Rufo managed a few weak thrusts that did not come near to hitting the mark.

Cadderly launched the disks finally, in a long and wide throw that brought them to the very end of their reach. He flicked his wrist, bringing the disks back to his grasp, but not with the usual suddenness.

Rufo measured the pace of the throws and bided his time.

The disks came on again, and Rufo leaned back, then rushed toward Cadderly right behind them as they retracted.

Cadderly's bait had worked. On this throw, he had shortened up on the cord, bringing the spindle-disks smacking back into his palm much more quickly than Rufo had anticipated.

Rufo had barely taken his first step when the young scholar's weapon shot out again, deliberately low. Rufo squealed in shock and pain and grasped at his smashed kneecap, his leg nearly buckling. He was under the influences of the chaos curse, though, and nearly impervious to pain. His squeal became a growl and he plowed ahead, slashing wildly.

Again Cadderly had to dive across the bed to avoid the blade, but when he came up this time, Kierkan Rufo had already circled the bottom of the bed and stood facing him. Cadderly knew that he was in trouble. He could not trade hits, dagger against spindle-disks. Normally, the disks might have proven effective, but in Rufo's state of mind, nothing short of a perfect and powerful strike would slow him. That type of attack would be risky indeed for Cadderly, and he doubted that he could even get one through his wild opponent's defenses.

They traded feints and teasing lunges for a few moments, Rufo grinning and Cadderly wondering if he had a better chance by diving out the window.

Then the whole building shook suddenly as if it had been hit by lightning. The explosion roiled on for several seconds and Cadderly understood its source when he heard a single word from the corridor. "Oo!"

Rufo hesitated and glanced over his shoulder, toward the open door. Cadderly realized that his sudden advantage wasn't really fair, but decided immediately to worry about that later. He cocked his arm and let go with all his strength. Rufo turned back just in time to catch the soaring disks right between the eyes.

Rufo's head snapped straight back, and when he righted himself again, he was no longer grinning. A startled, stupefied look came over him and his eyes crossed, as if they were both straining to see the newest bruise.

Cadderly, too transfixed to take his gaze from Rufo's contorted features, heard the dagger hit the floor. A moment later, Rufo followed it down with a crash. Still Cadderly did not react. He just stood there, his spindle-disks hanging by his side at the end of their cord, spinning end-around-end.

When Cadderly finally reached down to wind his weapon, his stomach turned over. The spindle-disks were covered in blood and one had a piece of Rufo's eyebrow glued onto it by the thick, drying red fluid. Cadderly slipped down to the bed and let the disks fall to the floor. He felt betrayed, by himself and by his toy.

All priests of the library were required to train with some weapon, usually a more conventional instrument of destruction, such as the quarterstaff, mace, or club. Cadderly had begun with the staff, and could use his ram-headed walking stick fairly well if the occasion arose, but he was never really comfortable with carrying any weapon. He lived in a dangerous world, so he was told, but he had spent the majority of his life in the secure confines of the Edificant Library. He had never even seen a goblin, except for a dead one once, that being one of the library's most wretched servants, who was said to be a half-breed. The headmasters had not allowed him to bend the rule of preparedness, though; every priest was required to train.

Cadderly had come across the spindle-disks in an archaic halfling treatise, and had quickly constructed his own. Some of the headmasters balked at his new choice, calling it more a toy than a weapon, but it fit all of the requirements set out in the ethical codes of Deneir. The vocal opposition, particularly Headmaster Avery's, only strengthened Cadderly's resolve to use the ancient weapon.

For Cadderly, the spindle-disks had replaced hours of savage fighting with hours of enjoyable playing. He learned a dozen tricks, tests of skill that didn't hurt anybody, with his new toy, for a toy he, too, secretly considered it. Now, though, covered in Rufo's blood, the spindle-disks did not seem so amusing.

Rufo groaned and shifted slightly, and Cadderly was glad that he was still alive. He took a deep breath and reached down for the disks, determinedly reminding himself of the gravity of the task ahead, and that he would have to be brave and thick-skinned to see it through.

Percival was on the bed at his side, lending further support.

Cadderly rubbed a finger down the white squirrel's smooth coat, then nodded gravely and rewound his weapon.

"He dead?" asked Ivan, entering the room with a smoldering Pikel at his heels. Percival darted out the open window, and Cadderly, when he looked upon the brothers, nearly joined him. Ivan's antlers, face, and beard, which stuck out wildly in several directions, were blackened with soot, and one of his heavy boots was now as open-toed as his brother's sandals.

Pikel wasn't much better off. Flecks of ceramics dotted his sooty face, his smile showed a missing tooth, and a shard of glass had actually embedded itself right into his iron pot helmet.

"Belago was not in?" Cadderly asked evenly.

Ivan shrugged. "Not a sight of that one," he replied, "but me brother found yer potion—what little there was of it."

He held up the small catch basin. "We figured ye'd be wanting more, so we . . ."

"Turned up the spigot," Cadderly finished for him.

"Boom!" added Pikel.

"He dead?" Ivan asked again, and the casual tone of the question sent a shudder through Cadderly.

Both dwarves noted the young scholar's discomfort. They glanced at each other and shook their heads. "Ye'd best get the belly for it," Ivan said. "If ye mean to go adventuring, ye'd best get the belly for things that are likely to be falling yer way." He led Cadderly's gaze back to Kierkan Rufo. "Or at yer feet!"

"I never meant to go adventuring," Cadderly replied, somewhat sourly.

"And I never meant to be a cook," retorted Ivan, "but that's what I got, ain't it? Ye said we got a job to do, and so we do. Let's get doing what needs doing, and if some try to get in our way, well . . ."

"He is not dead," Cadderly interjected. "Put him on the bed and tie him there."

Again Ivan and Pikel exchanged glances, but this time, they nodded in favor of Cadderly's determined tone.

"Oo," remarked Pikel, obviously impressed.

Cadderly wiped his spindle-disks clean, picked up his ram-headed walking stick and a waterskin, and headed down the hall. He was relieved to see Danica's door still warped and tightly wedged, and even more relieved to hear Newander's calm voice answering his knock.

"How is she?" Cadderly asked immediately.

"She is still deep within her meditation," Newander replied, "but she appears comfortable enough."

Cadderly conjured his meditative image of Danica, fighting back the insidious red haze.

"I can reverse the spell and let you in," the druid offered.

"No," Cadderly replied, though he truly wanted to see Danica again. His last image of Danica was a comforting one; he could not take the chance that something she did now would worry him and steal his heart from his coming trials. On a more practical level, Cadderly thought it best to let Newander preserve his magical energies. "When I return, perhaps your spell will no longer be needed," he said.

"Then you want me to stay with Danica?"

"I have the dwarves with me," Cadderly explained. "They are better suited to the underground tunnels than a druid would be. Stay with her and keep her safe."

Ivan and Pikel came up then, and by the eager gleam in their eyes, Cadderly knew that the time had come to set off. Cadderly glanced back at Danica's door several times as they walked away, emotionally torn. A large part of him argued against his journey, reasoned that his best course would be to go with his armed friends, sit by Danica's side, and ride this whole nightmare to its conclusion.

Cadderly did not find it difficult to argue against that irrational notion. Men were dying all around him. How many more Kierkan Rufos lurked in the shadows, murder in their hearts?

"Dear Cadderly," came a purring voice that only reinforced the young scholar's determination. Histra stood behind her chamber's door, opened just a crack, but that was enough to show Cadderly and the dwarves that she wore no more than a filmy, transparent negligee. "Do come in and sit with me."

"Oo!" said Pikel.

"She's wanting more than sitting, boy," chuckled Ivan.

Cadderly ignored them all and ran right by the door. He felt Histra grab at him as he passed and heard her door creak open wider.

"Come back here!" the priestess of Sune screamed, jumping into the middle of the hall.

"Oo!" an admiring Pikel remarked again.

Histra concentrated deeply, meaning to utter a magical command for her would-be lover to "Return!" But Pikel, for all his obvious enchantment, kept a pragmatic attitude about the situation. As Histra began her spell, he clamped a sooty hand onto her rump and casually tossed her back into her room.

"Oo," Pikel uttered a third time when he moved into the room to close the door, and Ivan, standing right behind his brother, whole-heartedly agreed. A dozen young men lay sprawled about the room, exhausted by their exploits.

"Are you so certain that you want to leave?" Histra purred at the dirty brothers.

By the time the blushing dwarves caught up to Cadderly, he was down to the first floor, dipping his waterskin into a font in the great hall.

"Wretched stuff," Ivan whispered to Pikel. "Oils and water. Tried drinking it once." He hung his floppy tongue out in disgust.

Cadderly smiled at the dwarf's remarks. He had better uses than drinking in mind for the holy water. When the skin was full, he took out a narrow tube, fitted on one end with a rubbery ball of some gooey substance. He popped this onto the open tip of his water skin and capped it with a smaller ball of the same goo.

"You will understand in time," was all the explanation he offered to the curious dwarves.

The Bouldershoulder brothers grew alarmed when the group entered the kitchen and found the place full of priests.

Headmaster Avery led the impromptu chefs, though their progress was limited since each of them spent more time stuffing food into his mouth than actually cooking anything.

More alarming to Cadderly than the eating frenzy was his companions' reactions. Both seemed on the verge of abandoning the quest, as though some greater compulsions now pulled at them.

"Fight it," Cadderly said to them, recognizing their growing desires as curse-induced. Ivan and Pikel were protective of their kitchen, and both took extreme satisfaction in keeping the hungriest priests of the library fed to contentment.

They looked around at the messy kitchen and the gluttonous priests, and for a moment, Cadderly feared that he would be traveling down to the lower catacombs alone. But Newander's claims of dwarven resistance to magical enchantment held true this time, for the Bouldershoulders shrugged unhappily at the disaster that had befallen their space, then pushed Cadderly on, prodding him toward the door to the wine cellar.

The musty stairs were dark and quiet; the torches lining the wall had not been tended. Cadderly opened his light tube and moved down a few steps, waiting there for the brothers to strike torches. Ivan came in last and closed and bolted the iron-bound door, even taking the trouble to slide an iron locking bar into place.

"We've as much trouble behind as ahead," the dwarf explained to Cadderly's questioning look. "If that group gets as thirsty as they are hungry, they'll only bring trouble along with them!"

The reasoning seemed sound enough, so Cadderly turned and started down. Pikel grabbed him, though, and took up the lead, tapping his heavy club to his pot helmet.

"Keep yerself between us," Ivan explained. "We've been on this road before!"

His confidence comforted Cadderly, but the clamor as the bulky dwarves thumped and rattled down the stairs did not.

Their lights intruded into absolute darkness as they came down, but all three sensed that they were not alone. Beside the first wine rack, they found their first clues that someone else had come this way. Broken glass covered the floor and many bottles—bottles that Cadderly had inventoried only a few days before— were missing. The trail led to yet another dead priest. His stomach grossly distended, he lay curled on the floor, surrounded by emptied bottles.

They heard a shuffle to the side and Cadderly put a narrow beam of light down between the wine racks. Another priest was in there, trying futilely to stand. He was too drunk to even notice the light, and his stomach, too, bulged and sloshed. Despite his stupor, he still held a bottle to his lips, stubbornly forcing more liquid down his throat.

Cadderly started toward the drunk, but Ivan held him back.

"Show me yer door," Ivan said to him, then the dwarf nodded to Pikel. As Cadderly and Ivan headed deeper into the cellar, Pikel moved the other way, between the racks. Cadderly soon heard a thump, a groan, and a bottle breaking on the stone floor.

"For his own good," Ivan explained.

They came to the casks where Cadderly had been found and, once again, the young scholar grew confused and frustrated that there was no door to be found. Ivan and Pikel shoved all the casks far away, and the three of them searched every inch of the wall.

Cadderly stuttered an apology; perhaps his entire theory was misguided. Ivan and Pikel stubbornly continued their search, though, keeping faith in their friend. They found their answers not on the unremarkable wall, but on a series of scratches in the floor.

"The casks were dragged," Ivan asserted. He bent low to study the dust, the absence of dust, in the marks. "Not too long ago."

Cadderly's focused beam made the tracking easy and as they moved across the room, he began to get more excited.

"How could I have missed this?" he said. He turned the light back to the wine racks. "We—Rufo and I—came from over there, so the door could not have been back where we found the piled casks. It was a purposeful deception. I should have known."

"Ye took a hit on the head," Ivan reminded him. "And it's a clever trick."

The trail led to yet another cask, tight up against the wall.

The companions knew before Ivan even kicked it aside that the mysterious door would indeed be found behind it. Ivan nodding and smiling, moved right up to the door and pulled it, but it did not budge.

"Locked," the dwarf grunted, examining a keyhole above the pull ring. He looked to his brother, who nodded eagerly.

"Pikel's one for unlocking doors," Ivan explained to Cadderly, and Cadderly got the point when Pikel leveled his tree trunk like a battering ram and lined himself up with the door.

"Hold!" Cadderly said. "I have a better way."

"Ye're a lockpick, too?" Ivan asked.

"Oh," groaned a disappointed Pikel.

"You could say that," Cadderly replied smugly, but instead of instruments for picking locks, he produced the hand-held crossbow. Cadderly had been hoping that he would get to try out his newest invention, and he was hardly able to keep from shaking as he cranked the bow and loaded a dart.

"Stand back," he warned, taking aim at the keyhole. The crossbow clicked and the dart plunked in. A split second later, the momentum of the dart collapsed its weak middle section, crushing the vial of *Oil of Impact*, and the ensuing explosion left a blackened and blasted hole where the lock had been. The door creaked open only an inch but hung there loosely.

"Oh, I'm wanting one of those!" Ivan cried happily.

"Oo oi!" agreed Pikel.

Their glee was short-lived, for behind the open door they found, not the top of the broken stairway, as Cadderly had predicted, but a brick wall.

"New work," Ivan muttered after a quick inspection. He cast a sly glance Cadderly's way. "Ye got a dart for this one, boy?"

Ivan didn't wait to hear an answer. He ran his hands over the wall, pushing at certain points as though he was testing its strength. "Pikel's got the key," he declared and he moved out of the way.

Cadderly started to protest, but Pikel paid him no heed. The dwarf began a curious whining sound and his stubby legs churned up and down, running in place, as though he were winding himself up like a spring. Then, with a grunt, Pikel charged, his battering ram tight against his side.

Bricks and mortar flew wildly. Several fiery explosions indicated that warding glyphs had been placed on the other side of the wall, but Pikel's furious charge was not slowed, by either the flimsy wall or the magical wards. Neither was Pikel able to halt his momentum. As Cadderly had told them before, and as he had tried to warn them again, the stairway beyond the short landing was down.

"Ooooooooo!" came Pikel's diminishing wail, followed by a dull *thump*.

"Me brother!" Ivan cried, and before Cadderly could stop him, he, too, charged through the opening. His torch flared in the dust cloud for just a moment, then both the light and the dwarf dropped from sight.

Cadderly winced and shuddered at Ivan's final words: "I can see the grou—!"

Sixteen

The Walking Dead

Cadderly came down the rope slowly and in control, using a technique he had seen illustrated in a manuscript. He held the rope both in front of and behind him, looping it under one thigh and using his legs to control his descent. He had heard the dwarven brothers grumbling while he was tying off the rope, so he knew that they had survived the fall. That fact offered some comfort, at least. As he neared the stone floor, within the area of torchlight, he saw Pikel running about in circles, with Ivan close on his heels, smacking out the last wisps of smoke from his brother's smoldering behind.

"Oo, oo, oo, oo!" Pikel cried, slapping at his own rump whenever he got the chance.

"Hold still, ye stinking oak kisser!" Ivan bellowed, whacking wildly.

"Quiet," Cadderly cautioned them as he dropped down to the tunnel.

"Oo," Pikel replied, giving one last brisk rub. The dwarf then noticed the stonework in the walls and forgot all about the sting. He wandered off happily to investigate.

"Somebody wanted to keep us outa here," Ivan reasoned. "His fire-wards got me brother good, right on the backside!"

Cadderly agreed with the dwarf's conclusion and sensed that he should know who had set out the glyphs, that he had seen someone in the same room as the bottle. . . .

He couldn't remember, though, and he had no time now to meditate and explore his suspicions. More importantly, neither dwarf had suffered any real damage; Ivan's antler-topped helmet had even been cleaned a bit by the jolt.

"How far to yer cursed flask?" Ivan asked. "Do ye think we'll be seeing more of the magical barriers?" Ivan's face lit up at the notion. "You gotta let a dwarf walk first if you think so, ye know." He pounded a fist onto his breastplate. "A dwarf can take it. A dwarf can eat it up and spit it back at the one who set it! Do ye think we'll be meeting that one? The one who put the fire-ward up there? I've a word to speak with that one. He burned me brother! No, I'm not for letting one go and burn me brother!"

The look in Ivan's eyes grew ever more distant as he spoke, and Cadderly realized that the dwarf was walking a tentative line of control. Off to the side, Pikel, too, had become overly consumed. He was down on his hands and knees, sniffing at the cracks in the wall and uttering an excited "Oo!" every so often. A dozen frantic spiders scurried to get free of their own webs, hopelessly entangled in Pikel's tough beard.

Cadderly set his rock crystal spindle-disks spinning end-around-end in front of Ivan's face and used his light tube to focus a narrow beam on them. The dwarf's talking faded away as he fell more and more into the mesmerizing dance of the light on the disks' many facets.

"Remember why we are here," Cadderly prompted the dwarf. "Concentrate, Ivan Bouldershoulder. If we do not remove the curse, then all the library, the Edificant Library, will be lost." Cadderly couldn't be certain whether his words or the dancing light on the disks had reminded Ivan to resist the stubborn curse, but whatever the cause, the dwarf's eyes popped wide, as if he had just come from a deep slumber, and he shook his head so wildly that he had to lean on his doublebladed axe to keep from falling over.

"Which way, lad?" the now lucid dwarf asked.

"That's more to the point," Cadderly remarked under his breath. He glanced over at Pikel and wondered if the same technique would be needed on him. It didn't matter, Cadderly decided at once. Pikel wasn't really wide awake even when he was wide awake.

Cadderly looked down at the floor, searching for some sign of his previous passing, but found nothing. He sent his light down to either side of the bricked corridor, but both ways seemed identical and jogged no memories for him.

"This way," he decided simply to get them moving, and he stepped past Ivan. "Do bring your brother." Cadderly heard a clang over his shoulder—axe on cooking pot, he supposed—and Ivan and Pikel came hustling up to his side a moment later.

After many dead ends and many circular treks that brought them right back to where they had started, they came to an ancient storage area of wide corridors lined with rotted crates.

"I was here," Cadderly insisted, speaking the words aloud in an attempt to jog his memory.

Ivan dropped to the floor, seeking to confirm Cadderly's declaration. As with all the corridors, though, no clear tracks were discernable. Clearly the dust had been recently disturbed, but either someone had deliberately brushed away any sure signs or simply too many had passed by this point for the dwarf to track.

Cadderly closed his eyes and tried to envision his previous passage. Many images of his wanderings in the tunnels flooded through him, scenes of skeletons and corridors lined with sinister-looking alcoves, but they wouldn't connect in any logical pattern. They had no focal point, no starting ground where Cadderly could begin to sort them out.

Then he heard the heartbeat.

Somewhere in the unseen distance, water was dripping, steadily, rhythmically. That sound had been here with him, Cadderly knew. It came from no particular direction, and he had not used it as any sort of a guiding beacon his first time through, but now, he realized, it could guide his memory. For, though its interval was constant, its volume became louder and more insistent at some bends in the passages, softer and more distant at others. Too engaged with other pressing problems his first time through, Cadderly had only noticed it on a subconscious level, but that had left an imprint on his memory.

Now Cadderly trusted his instincts. Instead of cluttering his consciousness with futile worries, he moved along and let his subconscious memories guide his steps.

Ivan and Pikel didn't question him; they had nothing better to suggest. It wasn't until they came to a three-way arch, and Cadderly's face brightened noticeably, that even Cadderly really believed he knew where he was going.

"To the left," Cadderly insisted, and indeed, the left archway was less thick with cobwebs than the right, as if someone had passed through there. Cadderly turned back to the dwarves just as he started under the archway, a look of trepidation, even outright dread, on his face.

"What've ye seen?" Ivan demanded, and he pushed his way past Cadderly, under the arches.

"The skeletons," Cadderly started to explain.

Pikel hopped to his guard, and Ivan held his torch far out in front, peering into the dusty gloom. "I see no skeletons!" Ivan remarked after a short pause.

The encounter with the walking dead remained a nightmarish blur for Cadderly. He couldn't quite remember where he had encountered the skeletons, and he didn't know why the thought had suddenly come to him now. "They might be in this area," he offered in a whisper. "Something makes me believe they are nearby."

Ivan and Pikel relaxed visibly and leaned to the side in unison to glance at each other around the young scholar. "Come on, then," Ivan huffed, following his torch's clearing fire into the left passage.

"The skeletons," Cadderly announced again as soon as he came through the archway. He knew this place, a crate-lined corridor wide enough for ten to walk abreast. A bit farther, alcoves lined the corridor's walls on both sides.

"Ye going to start that again?" asked Ivan.

Cadderly waved his light beam in the direction of the alcoves. "In there," he explained.

His warning seemed ominous, at least to him, but the dwarves reacted to it as though it was an invitation. Rather than dim the lights and creep along, they both leaped out in front and strode defiantly down the center of the corridor, stopping in front of the first alcove.

"Oo oi," remarked Pikel.

"Ye're right, lad," agreed Ivan. "It's a skeleton." He propped his axe up on one shoulder, put his other hand on his hip, and walked right up to the alcove.

"Well?" he cried at the bones. "Are ye going to just sit there and rot, or are you going to come out and block me way?"

Cadderly came up tentatively, despite the dwarves' bravado.

"Just as ye said," Ivan said to him when he arrived, "but not moving about much, as I see it."

"They were moving," Cadderly insisted, "chasing me."

The brothers leaned to the side—they were getting used to this maneuver—and glanced at each other around Cadderly.

"I did not dream it!" Cadderly snarled at them, taking a step to the side to block their exchanged stares. "Look!" He started for the skeleton, then had second thoughts about that course and put his light beam into the alcove instead. "See the cobwebs hanging freely in there? And the bits of web on the bones? They were attached, but now the webs hang free. Either this skeleton has been out of the alcove recently, or someone came down here and cut the strands from it, to make it look as though it has been out of the alcove."

"Yerself was the only one down here," Ivan blurted before he even realized the accusatory connotations of his statement.

"Do you believe I cut the strands?" Cadderly cried. "I would not want to go near the thing. Why would I waste the time and effort to do that?"

Again came the dwarven lean-and-look maneuver, but when Ivan came up straight this time, his expression was less doubting. "Then why are they sitting tight?" he asked. "If they want a fight, why . . .?"

"Because we did not attack them!" Cadderly interrupted suddenly. "Of course," he continued, the revelation coming clearer. "The skeletons did not rise against me until I attacked one of them."

"Why'd ye hit a pile of bones?" Ivan had to ask.

"I did not," Cadderly stuttered. "I mean . . . I thought I saw it move."

"Aha!" cried Pikel.

Ivan elaborated on his excited brother's conclusion. "Then the skeleton moved before ye hit it, and ye're wrong now in yer thinking."

"No, it did not move!" Cadderly shot back. "I thought it had, but it was only a rat or a mouse, or something like that."

"Mouses don't look like bones," Ivan said dryly. Cadderly expected the remark.

Pikel squeaked and crinkled his nose, putting on his best rodent face.

"If we just leave them alone, they might let us pass," Cadderly reasoned.

"Whoever animated them probably gave them instructions to defend themselves."

Ivan thought about it for a moment, then nodded. The reasoning seemed sound enough. He motioned to his brother, and Pikel understood the silent request. The green-bearded dwarf pushed Cadderly out of the way, lowered his club like a battering ram, and, before the startled young scholar could move to stop him, charged full speed into the alcove. The terrific impact reduced the skull to a pile of flecks and dust and Pikel's continuing momentum scattered the rest of the bones in every direction.

"That one won't be getting up to fight us," remarked a satisfied Ivan, brushing a rib off his brother's shoulder as Pikel came back out.

Cadderly stood perfectly still, his mouth hanging open in absolute disbelief.

"We had to check it," Ivan insisted. "Ye want to be leaving walking skeletons behind us?"

"Uh oh," groaned Pikel. Cadderly and Ivan turned at the call, Cadderly's light beam showing the source of Pikel's dismay. This skeleton would not rise to fight them, as Ivan had said, but dozens of others were already up and moving.

Ivan clapped Cadderly hard on the back. "Good thinking, lad!" the dwarf congratulated him. "Ye were right! It took a hit to rouse them!"

"That is a good thing?" Cadderly asked. Images of his last trip through here came rushing back to him, particularly when he had backed away from the first skeleton he had struck, into the waiting grasp of another. Cadderly spun to the side. The skeleton from across the corridor was nearly upon him.

Pikel had seen it, too. Undaunted, the dwarf grasped his club with both hands down low on the handle and stepped in with a mighty roundhouse swing, catching the monster on the side of the head and sending the skull soaring down the corridor behind them. The remaining bones just stood shakily for the moment it took Pikel to smash them down.

Cadderly watched the batted skull until it disappeared into the darkness, then he shouted, "Run!"

"Run!" Ivan echoed, dropping his torch, and he and Pikel charged down the corridor, straight at the advancing host.

That wasn't exactly what Cadderly had in mind, but when he realized that there was no way he was going to turn the wild brothers around, he shrugged his shoulders, took out his spindle-disks, and followed, seriously pondering the value of friendship when weighed against the burdens.

The closest skeletons did not react quickly enough to the dwarven charge. Ivan sliced one cleanly in half with a great cut of his axe, but then, on his back swing, snagged the weapon's other head in the rib cage of his next intended victim. Never one to quibble over finesse, the dwarf heaved mightily, pulling his weapon and the entangled skeleton into the air around him and then slamming the whole jumble into the next nearest monster. The two skeletons were hopelessly hooked together, but so was Ivan's axe.

"I need ye, me brother!" Ivan cried as yet another skeleton moved in on him, reaching for his face with dirty, sharp finger bones.

Pikel had fared better initially, plowing into the first ranks like a boulder bouncing down a mountainside, breaking three skeletons apart and pushing the rest back several feet. The rush had not been without consequences, though, for Pikel stumbled down to one knee before he could halt his momentum. The fearless undead came in all around the dwarf, advancing from every angle. Pikel grasped his club down low, held it out to arm's length, and began turning fast circles.

The skeletons were mindless creatures, not thinking fighters. Their outstretched arms leading, they came right in fearlessly, stupidly, and Pikel's whirling club whittled them down, fingers, hands, and arms. The dwarf laughed wildly as each bone went humming away, thinking he could keep this up forever.

Then Pikel heard his brother's call. He stopped his spin and tried to discern the right direction, then sent his stubby legs pumping in place, building momentum.

"Oooo!" the dwarf roared, and off he sprang, bursting out the side of the skeletal ring. Unfortunately, his dizziness had deceived him, and as soon as he broke clear of the ring, he slammed headfirst into the corridor's brick wall.

"Oo," came a hollow echo from under the pot helmet of the now seated Pikel.

Only a single skeleton had slipped between the dwarves to face Cadderly, odds that the young scholar thought he could handle. He danced about, up on the balls of his feet as Danica once had shown him, flicking out a few warning shots with his spindle-disks.

The skeleton paid no heed to his dancing feints, or the harmless throws, and continued straight in for Cadderly's mass.

The spindle-disks smacked into its cheekbone and spun its head right around so that is was looking behind itself. Still the skeleton came on, and Cadderly fired again, this time trying to break the thing's body. As soon as he threw, he realized his error.

The disks slipped through the skeleton's rib cage, but got tangled when Cadderly tried to retract them. To make matters worse, the sudden tug of the snag tightened the loop on Cadderly's finger, binding him to the skeleton.

Blindly, the monster swiped out at him. Cadderly dove straight for the floor, took up his walking stick, and shoved it through the rib cage, hoping to dislodge his spindle-disks. As soon as the tip of the stick wedged into the skeleton's backbone, the crafty young scholar changed his tactics. An image of a fulcrum and lever popped into his mind and he let go of his walking stick, then slammed its head with all his might.

The rib fulcrum held firm and the shock of Cadderly's downward blow shot up along the skeleton's backbone and sent its head straight into the air, where it ricocheted off the corridor ceiling. The shattering jolt broke apart the rest of the undead thing.

Cadderly congratulated himself many times as he worked both his weapons free, but his relief lasted only until he looked farther down the corridor, into the flickering light of Ivan's dropped torch. Both dwarves were down, Ivan unarmed and trying to keep out of one skeleton's reach, and Pikel, sitting near the other wall, his pot down to his shoulders, with a whole host of skeletons advancing on him.

.* * * * *

Druzil peered suspiciously from between his folded bat wings at the dark and quiet altar room. The brazier fire was down to embers now—Barjin would not leave an interplanar gate burning while he slept—and there was no other light source. That hardly hindered the imp, who had spent eons wandering about the swirling gray mists of the lower planes.

All seemed as it should. To the side of the room, Barjin slept peacefully, confident that his victory was at hand. Mullivy and Khalif flanked the doorway, as still as death and instructed not to move unless one of the conditions set by Barjin had been met.

To Druzil's uneasy relief, none of those conditions apparently had. No intruders had entered the room, the door remained shut fast, and Druzil sensed no probing wizard eyes nor any distant call from Aballister.

The altar room's serenity did not diminish the imp's sense that something was amiss, though. Something had disturbed Druzil's slumber; he had thought it another call from that persistent Aballister. Druzil tightened his wings and sank within himself, turning from his physical senses to the more subtle inner feelings, empathic sensations, that served an imp as well as eyes might serve a human. He pictured the area beyond the closed door, mentally probing the maze of twisting corridors.

The imp's bat wings popped open suddenly. The skeletons were up!

Druzil reached into his magical energies and faded to invisibility. A single flap of his wings carried him between Mullivy and the mummy, and he quickly uttered the key word to prevent Barjin's series of warding glyphs from exploding as he slipped out of the room. Then he was off, flying sometimes, creeping on clawed toes at others, picking his way carefully toward the outermost burial chambers. Already his physical hearing had confirmed what he had sensed, for a battle was in full swing.

The imp paused and considered the options before him. The skeletons were fighting, there could be no doubt, and that could only mean that intruders had come down to this level.

Perhaps they had simply wandered down here in their curse-induced stupor, vagabond priests soon to be dispatched by the undead force, but Druzil could not dismiss the possibility that whoever it was had come with a more definite purpose in mind.

Druzil glanced over his shoulder, down the corridors that would take him back to Barjin. He was torn. If he sent his thoughts to Barjin, established that personal familiar-master telepathic link, he would be bringing his relationship with the priest to a level of which Aballister certainly would not approve. If the wizard back at Castle Trinity ever found out, he might well banish Druzil back to his home plane—a fate that the imp, with the chaos curse finally unleashed on the world, certainly did not desire.

Yet it was Barjin, the imp reminded himself, not Aballister, who had taken the forefront in this battle. Resourceful Barjin, the powerful priest, was the one who had struck boldly and effectively against the heart of law in the Snowflake region.

Druzil sent his thoughts careening down the corridors, into the altar room, and into the sleeping priest's mind. Barjin was awake in a second, and a moment later, he understood that danger had come to his domain.

I will divert them if they get past the skeletons, Druzil assured the priest, *but prepare your defenses!*

* * * * *

Ivan knew he was running out of room. One hand raked at his shoulder, and all that he got for his retaliatory punch was a torn fingernail. The experienced dwarf decided to use his head. He tucked his powerful little legs under him, and the next time the pursuing skeleton lunged for him, he sprang forward.

Ivan's helmet was fitted with the antlers of an eight-point deer, a trophy Ivan had bagged with a "dwarven bow"—that being a hammer balanced for long-range throwing—in a challenge hunt against a visiting elf from Shilmista Forest. In mounting the horns on his helmet, clever Ivan had used an old lacquering trick involving several different metals, and he only prayed that they would prove strong enough now.

He drove into the skeleton's chest, knowing that his horns would likely be entangled, then he stood up and straightened his neck, hoisting the skeleton overhead. Ivan wasn't certain how much his maneuver had gained him, though, for the skeleton, suspended perpendicularly across the dwarf's shoulders, continued its raking attacks.

Ivan whipped his head back and forth, but the skeleton's sharp fingers found a hold on the side of his neck and dug a deep cut. Others were advancing.

Ivan found his answer along the side of the corridor, in an alcove. He could slip in there easily enough, but could the skeleton fit through, laid out sideways? Ivan lowered his head and charged, nearly bursting with laughter. The impact as the skeleton's head and legs connected with the arch surrounding the alcove slowed the dwarf only a step. Bones, dust, and webs flew, and Ivan's helmet nearly tore free of his head as the dwarf tumbled in headlong. He came back out into the corridor a moment later with half a rib cage and several web strands hanging loosely from his horns. He had defeated the immediate threat, but a whole corridor of enemies still remained.

Cadderly saved Pikel. The dazed dwarf sat near the wall, with a ringing in his ears that would last for a long time, and with a host of skeletons swiftly closing.

"Druid, Pikel!" Cadderly yelled, trying to find something that would shake the dwarf back to reality. "Think like a druid. Envision the animals! Become an animal!"

Pikel lifted the front of his pot helmet and glanced absently toward Cadderly. "Eh?"

"Animals!" Cadderly screamed. "Druids and animals. An animal could get up and away! Spring . . . snake, Pikel. Spring like a coiled snake!"

The pot helmet went back down over the dwarf's eyes, but Cadderly was not dismayed, for he heard a hissing sound coming from under it and he noticed the slight movement as Pikel tensed the muscles in his arms and legs.

A dozen skeletons reached for him.

And the coiled snake snapped.

Pikel came up in a wild rush, batting with both arms, kicking with both legs, even gnawing on one skeleton's forearm. As soon as he regained his footing, the dwarf scooped up his club and began the most vicious and frantic assault Cadderly had ever witnessed. He took a dozen hits but didn't care. Only one thought, the memory that his brother had called for him, rang clear in the would-be druid's mind.

He saw Ivan coming out of the alcove and spotted Ivan's axe, caught fast in the tangle of two skeletons making their unsteady way toward Ivan. Pikel caught up to them long before they reached his brother.

The tree trunk club smashed again and again, beating the skeletons, punishing them for stealing Ivan's weapon.

"That'll be enough, brother," Ivan cried happily, scooping his axe from the bone pile. "There are walking foes still to smash!"

Cadderly outmaneuvered the slow-moving skeletons to rejoin the dwarves. "Which way?" he gasped.

"Forward," Ivan replied without hesitation.

"Oo oi!" Pikel agreed.

"Just get between us," growled Ivan, blasting the skull from a skeleton who had ventured too near.

As they worked their way down the corridor, Cadderly's tactics improved. He kept his spindle-disks flying for skulls only—less chance of getting them hooked that way—and used his walking stick to ward off the reaching monsters.

Much more devastating to the skeletons were the two fighters flanking the young scholar. Pikel growled like a bear, barked like a dog, hooted like an owl, and hissed like a snake, but whatever sound came from his mouth did not alter his crushing attack routines with his tree trunk club.

Ivan was no less furious. The dwarf accepted a hit for every hit he gave out, but while the skeletons managed to inflict sometimes painful scratches, each of Ivan's strikes shattered another of their ranks into scattered and useless bones.

The trio worked its way through one archway, around several sharp corners, and through yet another archway. Soon more of the skeletal host was behind them than in front, and the gap only widened as less and less resistance stood to hinder their way. The dwarves seemed to enjoy the now lopsided fight and Cadderly had to continually remind them of their more important mission in order to prevent them from turning back to find more skeletons to whack.

Finally they came clear of the threat and Cadderly had a moment to pause and try to get his bearings. He knew that the door, the critical door with the light shining through, could not be too far from here, but the crisscrossing corridors offered few landmarks to jog his memory.

* * * * *

Druzil concluded from the sheer quantity of smashed skeletons that these invaders were not stupefied victims of the chaos curse. He quickly closed in behind the fleeing intruders, taking care, even though he was invisible, to keep to the safety of sheltered shadows. Never allowing Cadderly and the dwarves to get out of his sight, the imp used his telepathy to contact Barjin again, and this time he asked the cleric for direct help.

Give me the commands for the skeletons, Druzil demanded.

Barjin hesitated, his own evil methods forcing him to consider if the imp might be attempting to wrest control.

Give the words to me or prepare to face a formidable band, Druzil warned. *I can serve you well now, my master, but only if you choose wisely.*

Barjin had come out of his sleep to find danger suddenly close, and he meant to take no chances of losing what he had so painstakingly achieved. He still didn't trust the imp—no wise master ever would—but he figured that he could handle Druzil if it came down to that. Besides, if the imp tried to turn the skeletons against him, he could merely exert his own will and wrest back control of them.

Destroy the intruders! came Barjin's telepathic command, and he followed it with a careful recounting of all the command words and phrases recognizable by his skeletal force.

Druzil needed no prodding from Barjin; protecting the flask of his precious chaos curse was more important to him than it ever could be to the priest. He memorized all the proper phrases and inflections for handling the skeletons, then, seeing that Cadderly and the dwarves had stopped to rest in an out-of-the-way and empty passage, went back to retrieve the remaining undead forces.

The next time the intruders met them, the skeletons would not be a disorganized and directionless band. "We will surround and strike in unison," Druzil vowed to the skeletons, though the words meant nothing to the unthinking monsters.

Druzil had to hear them, though. "We will tear apart the dwarves and the human," the imp went on, growing more excited. The chaotic imp couldn't immediately contain his hopes there, pondering the possibilities of taking the skeletal host against Barjin. Druzil dismissed the absurd notion as soon as he had thought of it. Barjin served him well for now, as Aballister had done.

But who could guess what the future might hold?

Seventeen
Danica's Battle

S he found herself in the throes of repeated urges, building to overwhelming crescendos and then dying away to be replaced by other insistent impulses. Surely this was Danica's definition of Hell, the discipline and strict codes of her beloved religion swept away by waves of sheer chaos. She tried to staunch those waves, to beat back the images of Iron Skull, the urges she had felt when Cadderly had touched her, and the many others, but she found no secure footholds in her violently shifting thoughts.

Danica touched upon something that even the chaos could not disrupt. To fight the battle of the present, the young woman sent her thoughts into the simpler past.

She saw her father, Pavel, again, his small but powerful frame and blond hair turning to white on the temples. Mostly, Danica saw his gray eyes, always tender when they looked upon his little girl. There, too, was her mother and namesake, solid, immovable, and wildly in love with her father. Danica was the exact image of that woman, except that her mother's hair was raven black, not blond, showing closer resemblance to the woman's partially eastern background. She was petite and fair like her daughter, with the same clear brown, almond eyes, not dark but almost tan, that could sparkle with innocence or turn fast to unbreakable determination.

Danica's images of her parents faded and were replaced by the wrinkled, wizened image of mysterious Master Turkel.

His skin was thick, leathery, from uncounted hours spent sitting in the sun and meditating atop a mountain, high above the lines of shading trees. Truly he was a man of extremes, of explosive fighting abilities buried under seemingly limitless serenity. His ferocity during sparring matches often scared Danica, made her think the man was out of control.

143

But Danica had learned better than to believe that; Master Turkel was never out of control. Discipline was at the core of his, their, religion, the same discipline that Danica needed now.

She had labored beside her dear master for six years, until that day when Turkel honestly admitted that he could give no more to her. Despite her anticipation at studying the actual works of Penpahg D'Ahn, it had been a sad day for Danica when she left Westgate and started down the long road to the Edificant Library.

Then she had found Cadderly.

Cadderly! She had loved him from the first moment she had ever seen him, chasing a white squirrel along the groves lining the winding road to the library's front door. Cadderly hadn't noticed Danica right away, not until he tumbled headlong into a bush of clinging burrs. That first look struck Danica profoundly both then and now, as she battled to reclaim her identity. Cadderly had been embarrassed, to be sure, but the sudden flash of light in his eyes, eyes even purer gray than Danica's father's, and the way his mouth dropped open just a hint, then widened in a sheepish, boyish smile, had sent a curious warm sensation through Danica's whole body.

The courtship had been equally thrilling and unpredictable; Danica never knew what ingenious event Cadderly would spring on her next. But entrenched beside Cadderly's unpredictability was a rock-solid foundation that Danica could depend upon. Cadderly gave her friendship, an ear for her problems and excitement alike, and, most of all, respect for her and her studies, never competing against Grandmaster Penpahg D'Ahn for her time.

Cadderly?

Danica heard an echo deep in her mind, a soothing but determined call from Cadderly, urging her to "fight."

Fight?

Danica looked inward, to those overwhelming urges and deeper, to their source, then she saw the manifestation, as had Cadderly. It was within her and not in the open room around her. She envisioned a red mist permeating her thoughts, an ungraspable force compelling her to its will and not her own. It was a fleeting vision, gone an instant after she glimpsed it, but Danica had always been a stubborn one. She summoned back the vision with all her will and this time she held onto it. Now she had an identified enemy, something tangible to battle.

"Fight, Danica," Cadderly had said. She knew that; she heard the echoes. Danica formulated her thoughts in direct opposition to the mist's urging. She denied whatever her impulses told her to do and to think. If her heart told her that something was correct, she called her heart a liar.

"Iron Skull," compelled a voice inside her.

Danica countered with a memory of pain and warm blood running down her face, a memory that revealed to her how stupid she had been in attempting to smash the stone.

* * * * *

It was not a call heard by physical ears; it needed neither the wind nor open air to carry it. The energy emanating from Barjin's necromancer's stone called to a specific group only, to monsters of the negative plane, the land of the dead.

A few short miles from the Edificant Library, where once there had been a small mining town, the call was heard.

A ghoulish hand, withered and filthy, tore up through the sod, reaching into the world of the living. Another followed, and another, just a short distance away. Soon the gruesome pack of ghouls was up out of their holes, drooling tongues hanging between yellow fangs.

Running low, knuckles to the ground, the ghoul pack made for the stone's call, for the Edificant Library.

* * * * *

Newander could only guess what inner turmoil racked the young woman. Sweat soaked Danica's clothes and she squirmed and groaned under the tightly binding vines. At first, the druid had thought her in pain, and he quickly prepared a sedating spell to calm her. Fortunately, it occurred to Newander that Danica's nightmare might be self-inflicted, that she might have found, as Cadderly had promised, some way to fight back the curse.

Newander sat beside the bed and placed his hands gently but firmly on Danica's arms. While he did not call to her, or do anything else that might hinder her concentration, he watched her closely, fearful lest his guess be wrong.

Danica opened her eyes. "Cadderly?" she asked. Then she saw that the man over her was not Cadderly, and she realized, too, that she was tightly strapped down. She flexed her muscles and twisted as much as the vines would allow, testing their play.

"Calm, dear lass," Newander said softly, sensing her growing distress. "Your Cadderly was here, but he could not stay. He set me to watch over you."

Danica stopped her struggling, recognizing the man's accent. She didn't know his name, but his dialect, and the presence of the vines, told her his profession. "You are one of the druids?" she asked.

"I am Newander," the druid replied, bowing low, "friend of your Cadderly."

Danica accepted his words without question and spent a moment reorienting herself to her surroundings. She was in her own room, she knew, the room she had lived in for a year, but something seemed terribly out of place. It wasn't Newander, or even the vines. Something in this room, in Danica's most secure of places, burned on the edges of the young woman's consciousness, tortured her soul. Danica's gaze settled on the fallen block of stone, stained darkly on one side. The ache in her forehead told her that her dreams had been correct, that her own lifeblood had made that stain.

"How could I have been so foolish?" Danica groaned.

"You were not foolish," Newander assured her. "There has been a curse about this place, a curse that Cadderly has set out to remove."

Again Danica knew instinctively that the druid spoke truthfully. She envisioned her mental struggle against the insinuating red mist, a battle that had been won temporarily but was far from over. Even as she lay there, Danica knew that the red mist continued its assault on her mind.

"Where is he?" Danica asked, near panic.

"He went below," Newander replied, seeing no need to hide the facts from the bound woman. "He spoke of a smoking bottle, deep in the cellars."

"The smoke," Danica echoed mysteriously. "Red mist. It is all about us, Newander."

The druid nodded. "That is what Cadderly claimed. It was he who opened the bottle, and he that means to close it."

"Alone?"

"No, no," Newander assured her. "The two dwarves went with him. They have not been as affected by the curse as the rest."

"The rest?" Danica gasped. Danica knew that her own resistance to such mind-affecting spells was greater than the average person's and she suddenly feared for the other priests. If she had been driven to slam her head into a block of stone, then what tragedies might have befallen less disciplined priests?

"Aye, the rest," Newander replied grimly. "The curse is general on the library. Few, if any, have escaped it, Cadderly excepted. Dwarves are tougher than most against magic, and the brother cooks seemed in good sorts."

Danica could hardly digest what she was hearing. The last thing she could remember was finding Cadderly unconscious under the casks in the wine cellar. Everything after that seemed just a strange dream to her, fleeting images of irrational moments. Now, in concentrating with all her willpower, she remembered Kierkan Rufo's advances and her punishing him severely for them. Danica remembered even more vividly the block of stone, the exploding flashes of pain, and her own refusal to admit the futility of her attempt.

Danica did not dare to let her imagination conjure images of the state of the library if the druid's words were true, if this same curse was general throughout the place. She focused her thoughts instead on a more personal level, on Cadderly and his quest down in the dusty, dangerous cellars.

"We must go and help him," she, declared, renewing her struggles against the stubborn vines.

"No," said Newander. "We are to stay here, by Cadderly's own bidding."

"No," Danica stated flatly, shaking her head. "Of course Cadderly would say that, trying to protect me—and it seems I needed protecting, until a few moments ago. Cadderly and the dwarves might need us, and I'll not lie here under your vines while he walks into danger."

Newander was about to question her on why she thought there might be danger in the cellars, when he recalled Cadderly's own morbid descriptions of the haunted place.

"Have your plants let me go, Newander, I beg," Danica appealed to the druid. "You can remain here if you choose, but I must go to Cadderly's side quickly, before this cursing mist regains its hold on me!"

Her last statement, that the curse might fall back over her, only reinforced Newander's logical conclusion that she should be kept under tight control, that her reprieve from the curse, if that was what this was, might be a temporary thing. But the druid could not ignore the determination in the young woman's voice. He had heard stories of the remarkable Danica from many sources since his arrival at the library and he did not doubt that she would be a powerful ally to Cadderly if she could remain clear-headed. Still, the druid could not underestimate the curse's power—the evidence was too clear all about him, and the choice to release her seemed a great risk.

"What have you to gain by keeping me here?" Danica asked, as though she had read the druid's thoughts. "If Cadderly is not in danger, then he will find and defeat the curse before I . . . we, can get to him. But if he and the dwarves have found danger, then they could surely use our help."

Newander waved his hands and whistled shrilly to the vines.

They jumped to his call, releasing their hold on Danica and the bed, rolling back out the open window.

Danica stretched her arms and legs for many moments before she could bring herself to stand, and even then she got up quite unsteadily, needing Newander's support.

"Are you so certain that you are fit for walking?" the druid asked. "You suffered some serious wounds to the head."

Danica pulled roughly from his grasp and staggered to the middle of the room. There she began an exercise routine, falling more and more easily into the familiar movements. Her arms waved and darted in perfect harmony, each guiding the other to its next maneuver. Every now and again, one of her feet came whistling up in front of her, arcing high over her head.

Newander watched her tentatively at first, then smiled and nodded his agreement that the young woman had fully regained control of her movements, movements that seemed ever so graceful and appealing, almost animal-like, to the druid.

"We should be going, then," Newander offered, taking up his oaken staff and moving to the door.

Renewed sounds from Histra's room greeted them as they entered the hall. Danica glanced anxiously at Newander, then started for the priestess's door. Newander's hand clasped her shoulder and stopped her.

"The curse," the druid explained.

"But we must go to help," Danica started to retort, but she stopped suddenly as she recognized the connotations of those cries.

Danica's blush became a deep red, and she giggled in spite of the seriousness of the situation. Newander tried to hurry her down the corridor and she did not resist. Indeed, it was Danica pulling the druid by the time they passed Histra's closed door.

Their first stop was Cadderly's room, and they entered just as Kierkan Rufo was pulling himself free from the last of Ivan's stubborn bindings.

Danica's eyes lit up at the sight. Vivid memories of Rufo prodding her and grabbing at her assaulted her thoughts, and a wave of sheer hatred, augmented by the red mist, nearly overwhelmed her.

"Where is Cadderly?" Danica demanded through clenched teeth.

Newander knew nothing of Rufo, of course, but the druid recognized immediately that Danica's feelings for the angular man were not positive.

Rufo twisted his wrist free and tore away from the bed. He averted his gaze, obviously not wanting to face Danica, or anyone else at that moment. Thoroughly wretched, the beaten man wanted only to crawl under his own bed in his own dark room. He had the misfortune, though, or the poor judgment, to walk near Danica on his way out of the room.

"Where is Cadderly?" Danica insisted again, stepping in Rufo's way.

Rufo sneered at her and swung a backhand that never got close. Before Newander could begin to intervene, Danica had caught Rufo's wrist and used its own momentum, with a slight twist, to send the angular man lurching to the side. Newander heard the dull thud, though Danica's next movement had been too subtle to follow. The druid wasn't sure where Danica had hit the man, but from the curious way Rufo squealed and hopped up onto his toes, Newander could make a guess.

"Danica!" the druid cried, wrapping himself around Danica's arms and pulling her back from the tiptoeing man. "Danica," he whispered in Danica's ear. "It is the curse. Remember the curse? You must fight it, girl!"

Danica relaxed immediately and let Rufo slip by. The stubborn man couldn't resist the temptation to turn back as he passed and put one more sneer in Danica's face.

Danica's foot caught him on the side of the head and sent him tumbling out into the hall.

"I meant to do that," Danica assured Newander, making no struggles against his continuing hold, "curse or no curse!"

The druid nodded resignedly; Rufo had asked for that one.

He let Danica go as soon as he heard Rufo scramble away down the corridor.

"He is stubborn, that one," Newander remarked.

"Too true," said Danica. "He must have come in on Cadderly and the dwarves."

"Did you notice the bruises on his face?" said the druid. "It would seem that he did not fare too well in that fight."

Danica agreed quietly, thinking it best not to tell Newander that she was the one who had put most of those bruises on Rufo's face. "So Rufo did not slow them," Danica reasoned. "They have made their way to the cellars, and we must be quick to follow."

The druid hesitated.

"What is it?"

"I am afraid for you," Newander admitted, "and of you. How free are you of the mist? Less than I was believing, by the look on your face when we came upon that one."

"I admit that, for all my efforts, the mist remains," replied Danica, "but your words brought me back under control, I assure you, even against Kierkan Rufo. My argument with him goes beyond this curse. I'll not forget the way he has stared at me, or what he tried to do to me." A suspicious look came into Danica's brown eyes, and she cautiously backed away from Newander. "Why is Newander, the druid, not affected by this thing? And what does Cadderly possess that frees him from the influences of the red mist?"

"As for myself, I know not," Newander replied immediately. "Your Cadderly believes I am free because there are no hidden desires in my heart, and because I came into the library after the curse had started. I knew that something was amiss here as soon as I went to my friends—perhaps that warning has allowed me to fend off the cursing effects."

Danica didn't seem convinced. "I am a disciplined warrior," she replied, "but the curse found its way into my thoughts easily enough, even just now, though I understand the dangers of it."

Newander shrugged, having no explanation. "That was your Cadderly's theory, not my own," he reminded her.

"What does Newander believe?"

Again the druid merely shrugged. "For Cadderly," he said a moment later, "it was he who opened the bottle, and that alone might have saved him. Often in magical curses, the bringer of the curse does not feel its sting."

Danica didn't really appreciate the value of anything the druid had said, but the sincerity in Newander's voice was undeniable. She lowered her guard and walked out beside the man.

The kitchen still belonged to the gluttons. Several more had fallen in an overstuffed stupor, but others continued to wander about, pillaging the dwarves' well-organized cupboards.

Newander and Danica tried to keep their distance as they made their way toward the cellar door, but one fat priest took more than a passing interest in the beautiful young woman.

"Here's a tasty bit still to be tried," he slobbered between several thunderous belches. Rubbing his greasy fingers on his greasier robes, he started straight for Danica.

He had nearly reached her—and Danica thought she would have to clobber the man—when a pudgy hand grabbed him on the shoulder and roughly spun him about.

"Hold!" shouted Headmaster Avery. "What do you think you are about?"

The priest eyed Avery with sincere confusion, as did Danica, standing behind him.

"Danica," Avery explained to the man. "Danica and Cadderly! You keep away from her." Before the man could make any apologies, before Danica could try to calm Avery, the pudgy headmaster swung across with his other arm, holding a hefty leg of mutton, and cracked the offending priest on the side of the head. The man dropped in a heap and did not move.

"But, Headmaster . . ." Danica began.

Avery cut her off. "No need to thank me," he said. "I watch out for my dear friend, Cadderly. And for his friends, too, of course. No need to thank me!" He wandered off without waiting for any reply, gorging on his mutton and searching for new stores to raid.

Danica and Newander started for the fallen man, but the priest awoke with a start and shook his head briskly. He wiped a hand across the mutton-wetted side of his head, smelled his fingers curiously for a moment when he realized the wetness was not his own blood, then began licking them wildly.

The two companions' relief when they reached the heavy, iron-bound cellar door dissipated as soon as they found the portal barred. Danica worked at the jam for a few moments, trying to discover the source of the lock, while the druid prepared a spell.

Newander spoke a few words—they sounded elvish to Danica—and the door groaned, as if in answer. Wood planks warped and loosened and the whole door rattled to Danica's slightest touch.

When the druid's spell was completed, Danica went at the door more forcefully. It no longer fit neatly on any side, though the locking bar remained firmly in place behind it.

Danica spent a long moment in deep concentration, then lashed out with her open palm. Her blow would have dropped any man, but the door was very old, of ancient oak, and very thick, and the punch had little effect. This portal had been constructed for defense in the earliest days of the library. If a goblin raid ever overpowered the outside defenses, the priests could retreat to the cellars. It had only happened twice in the history of the library, and both times, the oaken door had stopped the intruders. Neither the flames of goblin torches, nor the weight of their crude battering rams had broken through, and now, Danica, for all her power and training, was simply overmatched.

"It appears that Cadderly and the dwarves will have to get the task finished without our help," Newander remarked grimly, though there was a hint of relief in his voice.

Danica was not so willing to surrender. "Outside," she ordered, starting back across the kitchen. "There may be a window, or some other way down."

Newander did not think her hopes likely, but Danica hadn't asked for, or even waited to hear, his opinion. Reluctantly, the druid shrugged and ran to catch up with her.

They split up just outside the double doors, Danica searching along the base of the wall to the south, Newander going north. Danica had gone only a few steps when she was joined by a welcomed friend.

"Percival," the woman said happily, glad for the distraction as the white squirrel peered over the edge of the roof right above her, chattering excitedly. Danica knew immediately that something was bothering the squirrel, but while she could sometimes figure out the connotations of a few of Percival's basic cries, she could not begin to follow his wild stream of chatter.

"Oh, Percival!" she scolded loudly, interrupting the squirrel's banter. "I do not understand."

"Surely I do," said Newander, coming up quickly behind Danica. To the squirrel, he said, "Do continue," and he uttered a series of squeaks and clicks.

Percival began again at once, at such a pace that Newander was hard pressed to keep up.

"We may have found our way in," the druid announced to Danica when Percival had finished. "That is, if we can trust the beast."

Danica studied the squirrel for a brief moment, then vouched for him.

The first place Percival led them was the old work shed to the side of the library. As soon as they entered, they understood the squirrel's noisy introduction to the place, for the chains still hung from the ceiling near to the back wall and droplets of blood had spattered the floor beneath them.

"Mullivy?" Danica asked to no one in particular. Her question set Percival off on a new stream of gossip. Danica waited patiently for the squirrel to finish, then turned to Newander for a translation.

"This Mullivy," the druid asked, looking about with even more concern, "might he be the caretaker?"

Danica nodded. "He has been groundskeeper of the library for decades."

"Percival claims he was brought here by another man," the druid explained, "then they both went off to the hole."

"The hole?"

"Tunnel, he means, as best as I can figure," explained Newander. "All this happened several days ago, perhaps. Percival's grasp of time is weak. Still, it is remarkable that the squirrel can recall the incident at all. They are not known for long memories, you know."

Percival hopped down from the shelf and raced out the door as though he had taken exception to the druid's last remark.

Danica and Newander rushed to follow, Danica pausing to collect a couple of torches that Mullivy had conveniently stocked in the work shed.

It seemed as if Percival was almost playing a deliberate game with them as they tried to follow his darting movements along the broken ground and rough underbrush south of the library. At last, after many wrong turns, they caught up to the squirrel along a ridge. Below them, under an overhang thick with brush, they saw the ancient tunnel, heading into the mountain in the general direction of the library.

"This might not get us anywhere near the cellars we are seeking," Newander offered.

"How long will it take us to get through the door in the kitchen?" Danica asked, mostly to remind the druid of their lack of options. To accentuate her point, she led Newander's gaze to the west, where the sun was already disappearing behind the high peaks of the Snowflakes.

Newander took a torch from her, uttered a few words, and produced a flame in his open palm. The fire did not burn the druid, but it lit the torch, and then lit Danica's torch, easily enough before Newander extinguished it.

They walked in side by side, taking note that there were indeed prints in the dust on the tunnel floor—boot prints, possibly, though most were scraped away in a manner that neither of them could explain.

Neither of them realized that zombies dragged their feet when they walked.

Eighteen

General Druzil

Ivan wiped a line of blood from his brother's neck.

"Druid?" Ivan asked, and there now remained little sarcasm in his tone. Pikel's wild fighting obviously had impressed Ivan, and the dwarf had no way of knowing how much more there was to being a druid than barking animal noises during a fight. "Maybe that'd not be so bad."

Pikel nodded gratefully, his smile wide under his low hanging helmet.

"Where do we go from here?" Ivan asked Cadderly, who was leaning quietly against the wall.

Cadderly opened his eyes. This passage was new to him and the fight had agitated him. Even concentrating on the dripping water did little to help him get his bearings. "We went mostly west," he offered tentatively. "We have to come back around . . ."

"North," Ivan corrected, then he whispered to Pikel, "Never met a human who could tell his way underground," which brought a chuckle from both dwarves.

"Whatever the direction," Cadderly went on, "we have to get back to the original area. We were close to our goal before the attack. I am certain of that."

"The best way back is the way we ran," reasoned Ivan.

"Uh oh," muttered Pikel, peeking around the corner to the passage behind them.

Cadderly and Ivan didn't miss the dwarf's point, and they understood even more clearly a second later, when the now familiar scraping-scuffing sound of approaching bony feet came from beyond the bend.

Ivan and Pikel clasped their weapons and nodded eagerly, too eagerly, by the young scholar's estimation. Cadderly moved quickly to quench the battle-fires burning in their eyes.

"We go the other way," he ordered. "This passage must have another exit, just like all the others, and no doubt it connects to tunnels that will allow us to get behind our pursuers."

"Ye fearing a fight?" balked Ivan, narrowing his eyes with contempt.

The dwarf's suddenly gruff tone alarmed Cadderly. "The bottle," he reminded Ivan. "That is our first and most important target. Once we close it, you can go back after all the skeletons you desire." The answer seemed to appease Ivan, but Cadderly was hoping that once they had closed the bottle and defeated whoever or whatever was behind this whole curse, no further fighting would be necessary.

The corridor went on for a long way with no side passages, and no alcoves, though some areas were lined by rotted crates.

When they at last did see a turn up ahead, a bend that went back the same way as the one they had left behind, they were greeted once again by the scraping-scuffling sound. All three glanced at each other with concern; Ivan's glare at Cadderly was not complimentary.

"We left the others far behind," the dwarf reasoned. "This must be a new group. Now they're on both sides! I told ye we should've fought them when we could!"

"Turn back," Cadderly said, thinking that perhaps the dwarf's reasoning was not correct.

Ivan didn't seem to like the idea. "There are more behind us," he huffed. "Ye want to be fighting both groups at once?"

Cadderly wanted to argue that perhaps there were not skeletons behind them, that perhaps this unseen group in front of them was the same as those they had left behind. He saw clearly that he wouldn't convince the grumbling dwarves, so he didn't waste the time in trying. "We have wood," he said. "Let us at least build some defenses."

The brothers had no problem with that suggestion, and they quickly followed Cadderly a short way back down the passage, to the last grouping of rotted crates. Ivan and Pikel conferred in a private huddle for a moment, then swept into action. Several of the boxes, weakened by the decades, fell apart at the touch, but soon the dwarves had two shoulder-high-to-a-man and fairly solid lines running out from one wall, forming a corridor too narrow for more than one or two skeletons to come through at a time.

"Just get yerself behind me and me brother," Ivan instructed Cadderly. "We're better for smashing walking bones than that toy ye carry!"

By then, the scuffling was quite loud in front of them and Cadderly could detect some movement just at the end of his narrow light beam. The skeletons did not advance any farther, though.

"Have they lost the trail?" Cadderly whispered.

Ivan shook his head. "They know we're here," he insisted.

"Why do they hold back?"

"Uh oh," moaned Pikel.

"Ye're right," Ivan said to his brother. He looked up at Cadderly. "Ye should've left the fighting to us," he said. "Be keeping that thought in yer head in the future. Now they're waiting for the other group, the one we shouldn't have left behind us, to catch up."

Cadderly rocked back on his heels. Skeletons were not thinking creatures. If Ivan's appraisal was correct, then someone, or something, else was in the area, directing the attack.

Shuffling noises proved the dwarves' guess right only a few moments later and Cadderly nodded grimly. Perhaps he should have left the fighting decisions to his more seasoned companions. He took up his appointed position behind the dwarven brothers, not sounding his concerns that the undead seemed to have some organization.

The skeletons came at them in a rush, a score from one side and at least that many from the other, and when they found the single opening to get at their living enemies, they banged against each other trying to get in.

A single chop from Ivan's axe dispatched the first one that made its way down. Several more followed in a tight group, and Ivan backed away and nodded to his brother. Pikel lowered his club like a battering ram and started pumping his legs frantically, building momentum. Cadderly grabbed the dwarf's shoulder, hoping to keep their defensive posture intact, and it was Ivan, not Pikel, who knocked his hand away.

"Tactics, boy, tactics," Ivan grumbled, shaking his head incredulously. "I told ye to leave the fighting to us."

Cadderly nodded again and pulled back.

Pikel sprang away, battering into the advancing skeletons like some animated ballista missile. With the general jumble of bones, it was hard to determine how many skeletons the dwarf actually had destroyed. The important factor was that many more still remained. Pikel wheeled about quickly and came rushing back, one skeleton right behind him.

"Down!" Ivan yelled and Pikel dove to the ground just as Ivan's great axe swiped about, bashing Pikel's pursuer into little pieces.

Cadderly vowed then to let the dwarves handle any future battle arrangements, humbling himself to the fact that the dwarves understood tactics far better than he ever could.

Another small group of skeletons came on, and Ivan and Pikel used alternating attack routines, each playing off his brother's feints and charges, to easily defeat them. Cadderly rested back against the wall in sincere admiration, believing that the brothers could keep this up for a long, long time.

Then, suddenly, the skeletons stopped advancing. They milled about by the entrance to the crate run for a moment, then systematically began dismantling the piles.

"When did those things learn to think?" asked a disbelieving Ivan.

"Something is guiding them," Cadderly replied, shifting his light beam all about the passage in search of the undead leader.

* * * * *

No light could reveal Druzil's invisibility. The imp watched impatiently and with growing concern. Counting the skeletons back in the earlier passages, these three adventurers had destroyed more than half the undead force.

Druzil was not normally a gambling creature, not when his own safety was concerned, but this was not a normal situation.

If these three were not stopped, they eventually would get into the altar room. Who could guess what kind of damage the two wild dwarves might cause in there?

Yet, it was something about the human that bothered Druzil most of all. His eyes, the imp thought, and the careful and calculating way he swept his light beam, reminded Druzil pointedly of another powerful and dangerous human. Druzil had heard of dwarven resistance to all magic, even potent ones such as the chaos curse, so he could understand how the two had found their way down, but this human seemed even more clear-headed, more focused, than his companions.

There could be only one answer: this one had been Barjin's catalyst in opening the bottle. Barjin had assured Druzil that he had put spells on the catalyst that would keep the man from remembering anything and from posing any threat. Had Barjin, perhaps, underestimated his foe? That possibility only increased Druzil's respect for Cadderly.

Yes, the imp decided, this human was the true threat. Druzil rubbed his hands together eagerly and stretched his wings. It was time to end that threat.

* * * * *

"We've got to charge them before they rip it all down!" Ivan declared, but before he and Pikel could move, there came a sudden rush of wind.

"Oo!" Pikel yelled, instinctively recognizing the sound as an attack. He grabbed the front of Cadderly's tunic and pulled him to the ground. A split second later, Pikel yelped out in pain and grabbed at his neck.

The attacker became visible as it struck, and Cadderly, though he didn't recognize the creature precisely, knew it was a denizen of the lower planes, some sort of imp. The batwinged thing flew off, its barbed tail trailing behind, dripping Pikel's blood.

"Me brother!" shouted Ivan, but, though Pikel seemed a bit dazed, he warded off Ivan's attempts to see to his wound.

"That was an imp," Cadderly explained, keeping the light beam in the direction the creature had flown. "Its sting is—" he stopped when he looked at the concerned brothers "—poisoned," Cadderly said softly.

As if on cue, Pikel began to tremble violently and both Cadderly and Ivan thought he surely would go down. Dwarves, though, were a tough lot, and Pikel was a tough dwarf. A moment later, he growled loudly and threw off the trembling in a sudden violent jolt. Straightening, he smiled at his brother, hoisted his tree trunk, and nodded toward the skeletal host, still at work taking apart the crate defenses.

"So it was poisoned," Ivan explained, looking pointedly at Cadderly. "Might've killed a man."

"My thanks," Cadderly said to Pikel, and he would have gone on, except that other things demanded his attention at the moment. The imp had targeted him, he realized, and it most probably would be back.

Cadderly released a latch on his walking stick and tilted the ram's head backward on cleverly hidden hinges. He then popped off the stick's bottom cap, leaving him a hollow tube.

"Eh?" asked Pikel, wording Ivan's thoughts exactly.

Cadderly only smiled in reply and continued his preparations. He unscrewed his feathered ring, the one filled with drow-style sleep poison, and showed the dwarves the tiny feather, its other end a cat's claw dripping with the potent black solution. Cadderly winked and fitted the dart into the end of his walking stick, then grabbed a nearby plank and waited.

The fluttering sound of bat wings returned a moment later and both dwarves hoisted their weapons to defend. Cadderly had anticipated that the imp would be invisible again. He determined the general direction of the attack and, when the flapping grew near, tossed out the plank.

The agile imp dodged the heavy board, just nicking it with one wing tip as he passed. While the hit hadn't done any real damage, it did cost Druzil dearly.

With his walking stick blow-gun held to pursed lips, Cadderly registered the sound of the nick, aimed, and puffed. A slight thud told him that the dart had struck home.

"Oo oi!" Pikel squealed in glee as the invisible imp, stuck with a quite visible dart, fluttered overhead. "Oo oi!"

* * * * *

Druzil wasn't sure if he or the corridor was spinning. Whichever it was, he knew, somewhere in the back of his dreamy thoughts, that it was not a good thing. Normally poisons would not affect an imp, especially on a plane of existence other than its own. But the cat's-claw dart that had struck Druzil was coated in drow sleep poison, which was among the most potent concoctions in all the world.

"My skeletons," the imp whispered, remembering his command, and feeling that he was somehow needed in some distant battle. Druzil couldn't sort it out; all he wanted to do was sleep.

He should have landed first.

He hit the wall before he realized that he was flying, and fell with a heavy groan. The concussion shook a bit of the slumber from him and he remembered suddenly that the battle was not so distant and that he was indeed needed . . . but the thought of sleep felt so much better.

Druzil kept enough of his wits about him to get out of the open corridor. His bones crackled in transformation, leathery skin ripped and reshaped. Soon he was a large centipede, invisible still, and he slipped in through a crack in the wall and let the slumber overtake him.

* * * * *

When Druzil fell, so did any semblance of organization in the skeleton forces. Now the imp's intrusions into the undead creatures' predetermined commands worked against the skeletons, for they were not thinking creatures and their original course had been seriously interrupted.

Some skeletons wandered aimlessly away, others hung their bony arms down by their sides and stood perfectly still, while others continued their methodical dismantling of the crate barricades, though they no longer followed any purpose in their actions. Only one group remained hostile, rushing down the narrow channel at Cadderly and the dwarves, their arms reaching out eagerly.

Ivan and Pikel met them squarely with powerful chops and straightforward thrusts. Even Cadderly managed to get in a few hits. He stood behind Pikel, knowing that Ivan's antlers probably would foul his spindle-disks. Pikel was only about four feet tall, with another few inches added for the pot helmet, and Cadderly, standing at six feet, snapped off shots whenever the dwarf's clubbing maneuvers allowed him an opening.

At Cadderly's suggestion, they worked their way down the channel, leaving piles of bones in their wake. The imp had been controlling the skeletons, Cadderly realized, and with the imp down—Cadderly had heard it hit the wall—Cadderly suspected that the monsters would take little initiative in the fight.

With the one attacking group dispatched, Ivan and Pikel moved cautiously toward those breaking down the barricades.

The skeletons offered no resistance, didn't even look up from their work, as the dwarves smashed them into bits. Similarly, those skeletons still remaining in the area, those standing still and showing no signs that they had even been animated, fell easy prey to the dwarves.

"That's the lot," Ivan announced, blasting the skull from the last standing skeleton, "except for those that are running away. We can catch them!"

"Let them wander," Cadderly offered.

Ivan glared at him.

"We have more important business," Cadderly replied, his words more a suggestion than a command. He moved slowly toward where the imp had crashed, the dwarves at his side, but found no sign of Druzil, not even the feathered dart.

"Which way then?" asked an impatient Ivan.

"Back the way we came," Cadderly replied. "I will have an easier time finding the altar room if we return to tunnels I know. Now that the skeletons have been defeated . . ."

"Oo!" chirped Pikel suddenly. Cadderly and Ivan looked around anxiously, thinking another attack imminent.

"What do ye see?" asked Ivan, staring into the empty distance.

"Oo!" Pikel said again, and when his brother and Cadderly looked back at him, they understood that he was responding to no outside threat.

He was trembling again.

"Oo!" Pikel clutched at his chest and went into a series of short hops.

"Poison!" Cadderly cried to Ivan. "The excitement of battle allowed him to fight it off, but only temporarily!"

"Oo!" Pikel agreed, scratching furiously at his breastplate, as if he were trying to get at his heart.

Ivan ran over and grabbed him to hold him steady. "Ye're a dwarf!" he yowled. "Ye don't go falling to poison!"

Cadderly knew better. In the same book he had found the drow recipe, he had read of many of the Realms' known poisons. Near the top of the potency list, beside the deadly sting of a wyvern's tail and the bite of the dreaded two-headed amphisbaena snake, were listed several poisons of lower plane denizens, among them one from the tail stingers of imps.

Dwarves were as resistant to poison as to magic, but if the imp had hit Pikel solidly . . .

"Oo!" Pikel cried one final time. His trembling mocked Ivan's desperate efforts to hold him steady and, with a sudden burst of power, he threw his brother aside and stood staring blankly ahead for just a moment. Then he fell, and both Ivan and Cadderly knew he was dead before they ever got to him.

Nineteen
Ghouls

They had heard the call of the necromancer's stone; they had sensed the dead walking and knew that a crypt had been disturbed. They were hungry now—they were always hungry—and the promises of carrion, ancient and new, brought them running, hunched low on legs that once had been human. Long tongues wagged between pointy teeth, dripping lines of dirty saliva along chins and necks.

They didn't care; they were hungry.

They came up along the road, darting in and out of the deepening afternoon shadows as they made their way toward the large building. One man, a tall human in long gray robes, was up there milling about the great doors. The lead ghoul bent low over its bowed legs and charged, arms hanging low, knuckles dragging on the ground, and fingers twitching excitedly.

Long and filthy fingernails, as sharp and tough as a wild animal's claws, caught the unsuspecting priest on the shoulder.

His agonized cries only increased the frenzy. He tried to fight back, but the chill of the diseased, ghoulish touch deadened his limbs. His features locked in a horror-filled, paralyzed contortion, and the pack fell over him, tearing him apart in seconds.

One by one, the ghouls drifted away from the devoured corpse, toward the great doors and the promise of more food.

But each of them veered away, shielding its eyes with raised arms as it approached, for the doors were blessed and heavily warded against intrusions by undead creatures. The ghouls wandered about for a moment, hungry and frustrated, then one of them heard the call of the stone again, to the south of the structure, and the pack swept off to find it.

* * * * *

It was a damp place, with pools of muddy water dotting the earthen floor and mossy vines, covered by crawling things, hanging from the evenly spaced support beams. Danica moved cautiously, the torch far out in front of her, and she kept as far from the sinister-looking moss as possible.

Newander was less concerned with the hanging strands, for they were a natural growth, as were the insects crawling over them, and so were within the druid's realm of understanding.

Still, though, Newander seemed even more anxious than Danica. He stopped several times and looked around, as if he was trying to locate something.

Finally his fears infected Danica. She moved beside him, studying him closely in the torchlight.

"What do you seek?" she asked bluntly.

"I sense a wrongness," Newander replied cryptically.

"An evil?"

"Your Cadderly told me of undead monsters walking the crypts," Newander explained. "Now I know he was telling me true. They are the greatest perversion of nature's order, a wrong upon the earth itself."

Danica could understand why a druid, whose entire life was based on natural order, might be sensitive to the presence of undead monsters, but she was amazed that Newander could actually sense they were nearby. "The walking dead have passed this place?" she asked, fully trusting that his answer would be correct.

Newander shrugged and looked around nervously again.

"They are close about," he replied, "too close."

"How can you know?" Danica pressed.

Newander looked at her curiously, confusedly. "I . . . I cannot," he stammered, "and yet I do."

"The curse?" Danica wondered aloud.

"My senses do not lie to me," Newander insisted. He spun about suddenly, back toward the tunnel entrance, as if he had heard something.

Just an instant later, Danica jumped in surprise as a screech sounded from the tunnel entrance, now no more than a gray blur far behind. She recognized the cry as Percival's, but that fact did not calm her, for even then the hunched forms appeared at the entrance, the sound of their hungry slobbers carrying all the way down to the woman and the druid.

"Run, Danica!" Newander cried and turned to go.

Danica did not move, unafraid of any enemy. She saw eight man-sized shapes distinctly, though she had no idea if they were priests from the library or monsters. Either way, Danica saw no advantage in stumbling down the tunnel, perhaps running into a waiting enemy and having to fight both foes at the same time. Also, Danica could not ignore Percival. She would fight for the white squirrel as surely as she would fight for any friend.

"They are undead," the druid tried to explain and, even as he spoke the words, the rotted ghoul stench filled their nostrils. The odor told Newander much about their enemy, and his desire to flee only increased. It was too late, though. "Do not let them scratch you," Newander advised. "Their touch will freeze the marrow of your bones."

Danica crouched low, feeling the balance of the torch and tuning all her senses to her surroundings. Above her, Percival skittered along a wooden beam; behind her, Newander had begun a low chant, a spell preparation; and before her, the pack came on, hissing and sputtering, but slower now, out of respect for the blazing torch.

The pack came to within a dozen running strides of Danica and halted. Danica saw their yellow, sickly eyes, but unlike those of a corpse, these shone with inner, hungry fires. She heard their breathless gasps and saw their long and pointy tongues, flicking like a reptile's might. Danica crouched even lower, sensing their mounting excitement.

As a group, they charged, but it was Newander who struck first. As the ghouls passed under a crossbeam, the moss came to life. Like the vines that had held Danica to her bed, the moss strands grabbed at the passing ghouls. Three of the creatures were fully entangled; two others scrambled and spat in horrifying rage, their ankles hooked, but three came right through.

The lead ghoul bore down on Danica, who stood poised and unafraid. She held her unthreatening posture until the very last moment, luring the ghoul right in on her, so close that even Newander let out an alarmed cry.

Danica was in perfect control of the situation. Her torch shot out suddenly, its fiery end slamming the ghoul right in the eye.

The creature recoiled and let out a shriek that sent tingling shivers along Danica's spine.

She popped the ghoul in the other eye for good measure, but the move put her torch out of line for a continuing defense. A second foe appeared beside the first, its tongue hanging low and its wretched hands reaching for Danica.

Danica moved to punch it but remembered Newander's warning and knew that her own arm's reach could not match the taller ghoul's. Danica possessed other weapons. She threw her head backward suddenly, so far that it seemed she would tumble to the ground. Her continued balance caught the still-advancing ghoul by surprise and brought an astounded gasp from Newander behind her, for Danica did not fall. She pivoted her body on one leg, her other leg shooting up before her and her foot catching the charging ghoul right under the chin. The monster's jaw smacked shut, its severed tongue dropped to the floor, and it stopped abruptly, hideous red-green blood and mucus pouring from its mouth.

Danica wasn't nearly finished with it. She dropped her torch and leaped straight up, catching the crossbeam support, and snap-kicked one foot into the ghoul's face, sending gore flying.

Again and again Danica's kicks pounded it.

The third advancing ghoul had met equal punishment.

Newander held his open palm out before him and uttered a few words to produce another ball of magical flame, similar to the one he had used to light the torch back at the tunnel entrance.

As the ghoul came hobbling in, Newander launched the fiery missile. It hit the advancing monster squarely in the chest and suddenly the ghoul was more concerned with patting out the flames than attacking the druid. It had nearly put out the first fire when another ball came in, this one taking it in the shoulder. Then came the third missile, bursting into a shower of sparks as it hit the ghoul in the face.

Danica held her position on the crossbeam and kicked one final time. She knew that she had snapped the ghoul's neck, but the doomed creature managed to get a claw on the side of her leg. As it fell, its dirty nail dug a deep line down Danica's calf. Danica looked upon the wound in horror, feeling the paralyzing touch taking hold of her. "No!" she growled, and she used all her years of training, all her mental discipline, to fight back, to force the chill from her bones.

She dropped from the beam and scooped up the torch, glad to learn that her leg could still support her. Her anger controlled her now; part of Danica's discipline involved the knowledge of when to let go, of when to let sheer anger guide her actions. The ghoul with the burned eyes spun about wildly, slashing blindly with its claws in its search for something to hit.

Its mouth opened impossibly wide in a hungry, vicious scream.

Danica grasped the torch in both hands and rammed it with an overhead chop down the ghoul's throat. The creature thrashed wildly, scoring several hits on Danica's arms, but the furious woman did not relent. She drove the torch deeper down the ghoul's gullet, twisting and grinding until the ghoul stopped thrashing.

Hardly slowing, Danica tightened one hand and spun about, catching the ghoul battling Newander's fires with a left hook.

The blow lifted the monster from its feet and sent it crashing into the tunnel wall. Newander came on it in an instant, pounding with his oaken staff.

The fight was far from over. Five ghouls remained, though three were still helplessly entangled by the moss strands. The other two had worked their way free and charged, paying no concern to their dead companions.

Danica dropped into a low crouch, pulled her daggers from their boot sheaths, and struck before the monsters ever got close. To the lead ghoul, the coming dagger probably seemed no more than a sliver, flickering as it spun in the dim torchlight.

Then the creature got the point, as the dagger buried itself to the hilt in its eye. The ghoul shrieked and teetered to the side, clutching its face. Danica's second shot followed with equal precision, thudding into the creature's chest, again burying to the hilt, and the ghoul tumbled, writhing in the throes of death.

The second charging ghoul, not a fortunate creature, now had a clear path at Danica. The monk waited again until the very last moment, then sprang to grab the beam and her deadly foot flashed out. The powerful kick caught the ghoul on the forehead, stopping it cold and snapping its head backward. As the head came back, Danica's foot met it again, then a third and a fourth time.

Danica dropped from the beam, letting the momentum of her fall take her down into a low squat. Like a coiled spring, she came back up, spinning as she rose and letting one foot fly out behind her. The circle-kick maneuver caught the stunned and battered ghoul on the side of the jaw and snapped its head to the side so brutally that the ghoul was sent into an airborne somersault. It landed in a kneeling position, weirdly contorted, with its legs straight out to either side, its lifeless body hunched heavily and its head lolling about, looking over one shoulder.

Danica's rage was not appeased. She charged down the passage, issuing a single-toned scream all the way. She put her right hand in a partial list, extending her index and little fingers rigidly. The closest moss-wrapped ghoul, not Danica's target, managed to free one arm to lash at the woman. Danica easily dove under the awkward attack, went into a roll right past the attacker, and came up a few feet in front of the next ghoul without breaking her momentum in the least. She leaped into the air and struck viciously as she descended. Eagle Talon, this attack was named, according to the scrolls of Grandmaster Penpahg D'Ahn, and Danica worked it to perfection as her extending fingers drove right through the ghoul's eyes, exploding into its rotted brain. It took Danica nearly a minute to extract her hand from the creature's shattered head, but it didn't matter, she knew. This ghoul offered no further threat.

Newander, finished with his ghoul, started toward the young woman. He stopped, though, seeing that Danica had things well under control, and went instead to retrieve the low-burning torch.

Finally free, Danica went back at the ghoul that had swung at her. Her fist thudded grotesquely against the rotted flesh of the creature's chest; Danica knew that its ribs had collapsed under the blow, but the ghoul, nearly free before the attack, fell clear of the moss with the weight of the punch. It came up screaming horribly, wailing away like a thing gone insane.

Danica matched its intensity, hitting it three times for each hit she suffered. Again she felt the paralyzing chill of a ghoul's touch and again she growled it away. Still, she could not ignore the lines of blood on her arms, and her pain and weariness were mounting. She feigned another straightforward punch, then dropped into a squat under the ghoul's lurching swings.

Her foot flashed straight out, catching the ghoul inside its knee and sending it face-first to the ground. In an instant, Danica was back up. She clutched her hands together in a double fist, reached back over her head and dropped to her knees, using the momentum of her fall to add to the power of her chop. She caught the rising ghoul on the back of the head, slamming it back to the ground. The creature bounced under the terrific impact and then lay very still.

Danica didn't wait to see if it would move again. She grabbed a handful of its scraggly hair, reached under to cup its chin in her other hand, and twisted its head so violently that before the crackling of neck bones had finished, the ghoul's dead eyes were staring straight up over its back.

Danica came up with an enraged scream and advanced steadily on the one remaining ghoul. The moss had lifted this one clear of the ground and it hung there still, barely struggling against the impossible bonds. Danica punched it on the side of the head, sending it into a spin. As the face came around in a full circle, Danica, too, spun a circuit and circle-kicked, reversing the creature's spin. And so it went, punch, kick, around one way and then the other.

"It is dead," Newander started to say, but he didn't bother to press the point, understanding that Danica needed to work through her rage. Still she kicked and punched, and still the limply hanging ghoul spun.

Finally, the exhausted monk dropped to her knees before the latest kill and put her head in her blood-soaked hands.

* * * * *

"Druzil?" Barjin didn't know why he had spoken the word aloud; perhaps he had thought that the sound would help him reestablish the suddenly broken telepathic link with his imp familiar. "Druzil?"

There was no reply, no hint that the imp kept any link at all opened to the cleric. Barjin waited a moment longer, still trying to send his thoughts along the outer passageways, still hoping that Druzil would answer.

Soon, the priest had to admit that his outer eyes had somehow been closed. Perhaps Druzil had been slain, or perhaps an enemy priest had banished the imp back to his own plane. With that uncomfortable thought in mind, Barjin moved to his low-burning brazier. He spoke a few command words, ordering the flames higher and trying to reopen his mysteriously unproductive interplanar gate. He called to midges and manes and lesser denizens; he called to Druzil, hoping that if the imp had been banished, he might bring him back. But the flames crackled unimpeded by any otherworldly presence. Barjin did not know, of course, of the magical powder Druzil had sprinkled to close the gate.

The priest continued his calling for a short while, then realized the futility of it and realized, too, that if Druzil had indeed been defeated, he might have some serious problems brewing. Another thought came to him then, the image of the imp returning to the altar room at the head of the skeletal force with ideas of overthrowing the priest's leadership. Imps had never been known for their undying loyalty.

In either case, Barjin needed to strengthen his own position.

He moved to Mullivy first and spent a long moment considering how he might further strengthen the zombie. He already had given Mullivy a patchwork armor plating and had magically increased the zombie's strength, but now he had something more devious in mind. He took out a tiny vial and poured a drop of mercury over Mullivy, uttering an arcane chant. The spell completed, Barjin retrieved several flasks of volatile oil and soaked Mullivy's clothes.

Barjin turned to his most powerful ally, Khalif, the mummy.

There was little the priest could do to enhance the already monstrous creation, so he issued a new set of unambiguous commands to it and set it in a more strategic position outside the altar room.

All that remained for Barjin was his personal preparations.

He donned his clerical vestments, enchanted cloth as armored as a knight's suit of mail, and uttered a prayer to enhance this protection even more. He took up the Screaming Maiden, his devilish woman-headed mace, and rechecked the wards at the room's single door. Let his enemies come; whether it was a traitor imp or a host of priests from above, Barjin was confident that the attackers soon would wish they had remained in the outer passages.

* * * * *

Newander moved to comfort Danica, but Percival got there first, dropping from a crossbeam to the woman's shoulder. Danica's smile returned when she looked upon the white squirrel, a reminder of better times, to be sure.

"They sense the raising of the dead," Newander explained, indicating the ghouls. "The meat of their table is the meat of a corpse."

Danica shot him an incredulous look.

"Even if they must create the corpse on their own," Newander replied. "But it is the raising of the dead that brings them." Newander seemed to doubt his own words, but he knew nothing of the necromancer's stone and had no other explanation. "Ghouls will flock to undead from anywhere near, though where these wretches have come from, I cannot guess."

Danica struggled unsteadily to her feet. "It does not matter where they came from," she said. "Only that they are dead and will stay dead this time. Let us go on. Cadderly and the dwarves might have met troubles farther in."

Newander grabbed her arm and held her back. "You cannot go," he insisted.

Danica glared at him.

"My spells are nearly exhausted," the druid explained, "but I have some salves that might help your wounds and a curative spell that can defeat any poison you might have suffered."

"We have no time," Danica argued, pulling free. "Save that poison cure. My wounds are not so serious, but we might need that before this is ended."

"Only a minute for treating your wounds then," Newander argued back, conceding the point concerning the spell but adamant that Danica's scratches at least should be cleaned. He took out a small pouch. "You might be needing me, Lady Danica, but I'll not go in with you if you do not let me tend to your wounds."

Danica wanted no delays, but she didn't doubt the stubborn druid's resolve. She kneeled before Newander and held her torn forearms out to him, and, despite her own stubbornness, she had to admit that the gashes felt much better the instant the druid applied his salves.

They set off again, Newander bearing the torch and his staff, Danica holding her daggers, stained darkly with ghoul gore, and the newest member of the party, Percival, wrapped nervously about Danica's neck and shoulders.

Twenty

Oh, Brother, Me Brother

M e brother!" Ivan wailed, bowing over Pikel's prostrate form. "Oh, me brother!" The dwarf sniffled and wept openly, cradling Pikel's head in his hands.

Cadderly had no words to comfort Ivan. Indeed, the young scholar was nearly as overcome as the dwarf. Pikel had been a dear friend, always ready to listen to Cadderly's latest wild idea, and always adding an emphatic "Oo oi!" just to make Cadderly feel good.

Cadderly had never known the pangs of a friend's death. His mother had died when he was very young, but he didn't remember that. He saw the priests of Ilmater and the dead gluttons in the kitchen, but they were only faces to him, distant and unknown. Now, looking at dear Pikel, he didn't know how he should feel, didn't know what he could do. It seemed a macabre game, and for the very first time in his life, Cadderly understood that some things were beyond his power to control or change, that all his rationale, his intelligence, in the final estimation seemed just a minor thing.

"Ye should've been a druid," Ivan said quietly. "Ye always were better under the sky than the stone." Ivan let out a great cry and buried his head in Pikel's chest, his shoulders shuddering uncontrollably.

Cadderly could understand the dwarf's pain, but he was shocked nonetheless that Ivan was so openly emotional. The priest wondered if something was wrong with him for not falling over Pikel as Ivan had done, or if Ivan's love for his brother was so much greater than his own feelings for the dwarf. Cadderly kept his wits about him; no matter how agonizing Pikel's death was, if they did not move on and close the bottle, many others would share a similar fate.

"We must go," Cadderly said softly to Ivan.

"Shut yer mouth!" Ivan roared, on the verge of an explosion, never taking his gaze from his brother.

The response caught Cadderly by surprise, but again he did not understand the nature of grief, did not know if it was Ivan who was acting out of sorts or if he was. When the dwarf finally did look back at him, tears streaked his contorted face and Cadderly feared that he knew what was going on.

"The curse," he muttered breathlessly. As far as he could tell, this red mist worked to exaggerate one's emotions. Apparently the curse had found a hold in Ivan's sincere grief, a chink in the tough dwarf's magic-resistant constitution.

Cadderly feared that it was taking hold of Ivan. The dwarf's blubbering increased with each passing moment; he could hardly draw breath, so violent was his weeping.

"Ivan," he said quietly, moving over to put a hand on the dwarf's shoulder. "We can do no more for Pikel. Come away now. We have other business to attend."

Ivan snapped an angry glare on Cadderly and smacked his hands away. "Ye're wanting me to leave him?" the dwarf cried. "Me brother! Me dead brother! No, I'm not going, never going. I'll stay by me brother's side. Stay here and keep me Pikel druid warm!"

"He is dead, Ivan," Cadderly said through his own budding sniffles. "Gone. You cannot keep the warmth in his body. You cannot do anything for him."

"Shut yer mouth!" Ivan roared again, reaching for his axe.

Cadderly thought the dwarf meant to chop him down, feared that Ivan blamed him for what had happened to Pikel, but Ivan never even found the strength to lift the heavy weapon and instead tumbled back down over Pikel.

Cadderly realized that he would get nowhere reasoning with the grieving dwarf, but Ivan's outburst incited other ideas in the young scholar. There was one emotion that could overrule even grief, and Ivan seemed all too willing to let that emotion take charge.

"You can do nothing," Cadderly said again, "but repay the one who did this to Pikel."

Suddenly Cadderly had Ivan's full attention.

"He is down here, Ivan," Cadderly prodded, though he didn't like leading the dwarf on like this. "Pikel's killer is down here."

"The imp!" Ivan roared, looking around wildly for the creature.

"No," Cadderly replied, "not the imp, but the imp's master."

"The imp's what poisoned me brother!" Ivan protested.

"Yes, but the imp's master brought the imp, and the curse, and all the evil that led to Pikel's demise," replied Cadderly. He knew he was taking license in drawing such conclusions, but if he could get Ivan moving, then it would be worth the deceit. "If we can defeat the master, then the imp and all the evil will follow. The master, Ivan," Cadderly said again, "he who brought the curse."

"Ye brought the curse," Ivan snarled, fingering his two-headed axe again and eyeing Cadderly suspiciously.

"No," Cadderly quickly corrected, seeing his conniving tactics taking an entirely different light. "I played an unfortunate role in its release, but I did not bring it. There is one down here—there must be—who brought the curse and sent the skeletons and the imp down here after us, down here to kill your brother!"

"Where is he?" Ivan cried, springing up from Pikel and clasping his heavy axe in both hands. "Where's me brother's killer?" The dwarf's eyes darted all about wildly, as if he expected some new monster to appear at any moment.

"We must find him," Cadderly prodded. "We can go back the way we came, back into the tunnels I remember."

"Go back?" The idea didn't seem to please Ivan.

"Just until I remember the way, Ivan," Cadderly explained, "then we'll go forward, to the room with the cursed bottle, to where we shall find your brother's killer." He could only hope his words were true and that Ivan would relax by the time they found the room.

"Forward!" Ivan yelled, and he scooped up one of the barely glowing torches, whipped it about frantically to refuel the flame, and stormed off back the way they had come. Cadderly checked to make certain that he had all of his belongings, said a final good-bye to Pikel, and ran to catch up.

They had not gone far when they came upon the first group of skeletons, five monsters wandering down a side passage. The disoriented skeletons, refugees from Druzil's disastrous battle, made no move to attack, but Ivan, blind with rage, turned on them with a fury that Cadderly had never before imagined.

"Ivan, no," Cadderly pleaded, seeing the dwarf's intent. "Let them alone. We have more important . . ."

Ivan never heard him. The dwarf let out a roar and a snarl and rushed at the skeletons. The two closest turned to meet the charge, but Ivan overwhelmed them. He launched a mighty side cut with his axe that cleaved one in half, then shifted the weapon's momentum as it whirled behind him and drove it straight over his head, coming down on top of the second skeleton with enough force to shatter the monster.

Ivan let go of the weapon, entangled once more in bones, and caught the third skeleton with his deer-horned helmet, lifting the monster clear of the ground, shaking it wildly for a moment, then slamming it into the wall. The attack damaged the skeleton, but it also dislodged Ivan's helmet. The clawing fingers of the fourth skeleton found an opening in the dwarf's defenses and dug into the back of his neck.

Cadderly came running down to help, readying his walking stick for a swing at Ivan's newest attacker. Before he could get into the fray, though, Ivan took things into his own hands. He reached around and caught the skeleton by its bony wrist, then pulled and spun for all his life.

Cadderly dove for the ground, nearly sliced by the flying skeleton's legs and feet. Ivan picked up momentum in his twirl and soon had the skeleton spinning straight out at arms' length. He let the momentum build for a moment, then shuffled a step closer to a wall and let the bricks do his work. The skeleton slammed against them and broke apart and Ivan was left holding an unattached bone.

The last of the skeletons was on the dwarf then, and Ivan, dizzy and a bit disoriented, took the monster's first clawing hand squarely in the face. Again Cadderly started to help his friend, but one of the other skeletons was back up and closing, still bearing Ivan's helmet entangled in its ribs.

Ivan slammed a forearm into his attacker's ribs. The dwarf's stubby legs pumped wildly, driving the monster back toward a wall. When it pressed in, Ivan did not stop. His every muscle tensed and then snapped, launching him forward and bringing the only weapon he had available, his forehead, to bear.

He slammed the skeleton in the face, and the creature's skull exploded in the crush between the rock wall and the dwarf's equally tough head. Bits of bone popped out to the sides, other pieces were ground into dust, and Ivan bounced back, his head badly gashed.

Cadderly smacked at the remaining monster with his walking stick and snapped his spindle-disks into its face once and then again. The stubborn creature came on, slashing its bony fingers and forcing Cadderly into retreat. Soon, though, Cadderly felt the wall at his back and had nowhere left to run.

One hand had latched firmly onto Cadderly's shoulder. The other slashed at his face. He got his own hand up to block but found himself helplessly pinned with the bony fingers digging deeper into his flesh. He tried desperately to hook the skeleton's arm under his own, to twist it around and break the monster's grasp, but Cadderly's attack was designed to twist muscles and tendons and inflict such pain on an attacker as to disable him. Skeletons had no muscles or tendons and felt no pain. Cadderly put his one free hand against the skeleton's face and tried to push it away—and got a wicked bite on the wrist for his efforts.

Then the skeleton's head disappeared in an instant, went flying away. Cadderly didn't understand until Ivan's second axe chop, a downward cut, destroyed the skeletal body.

Cadderly leaned back against the wall and clutched at his bloodied wrist. He simply dismissed his own pain a moment later, thinking his wounds minor indeed when he looked upon Ivan.

Pieces of skull bone were embedded in the dwarf's forehead. Blood ran freely down Ivan's face, along the sides of his neck, and from numerous cuts on his gnarly hands. Even more horrifying, a skeleton's broken rib bone stuck out from the side of the dwarf's abdomen. Cadderly could not tell how deeply the bone had gone, but the wound seemed wicked indeed and he was truly amazed that the dwarf was still standing.

He reached for Ivan, meaning to support his friend, fearing that Ivan would topple. Ivan roughly slapped his hand away. "No time for coddling," the dwarf barked. "Where's the one that killed me brother?"

"You need help," Cadderly replied, horrified by his friend's condition. "Your wounds . . ."

"Forget them," Ivan retorted. "Get me to the one that killed me brother!"

"But Ivan," Cadderly continued to protest. He pointed to the skeletal rib.

Ivan's eyes did widen when he noticed the ghastly wound, but he only shrugged his shoulders, reached down to grasp the bone, and pulled it free, casually tossing it aside as though he hadn't even noticed the several inches of bloodstains upon it.

Ivan's attitude was similarly uncaring when he tried to put his helmet back on, only to find that the embedded bones blocked him from seating it correctly on his head. He plucked a few chips from his forehead, then, with a grunt, forced the helmet into place.

Cadderly could only assume that the cursing mist had increased the dwarf's rage to a point where Ivan simply did not acknowledge pain. He knew that dwarves were a tough lot, Ivan more than most, but this was beyond belief.

"Ye said ye'd take me to him!" Ivan roared, and his words rang like a threat in Cadderly's ears. "Ye said ye'd find the way!" In a move of concession, Ivan reached up and tore off Cadderly's cloak and used it to quickly tie off his wound.

Cadderly had to be satisfied with that. He knew that the best he could do for everybody, Ivan included, was to find and close the smoking bottle as quickly as he could. Only then would the enraged dwarf allow Cadderly or anyone else to tend to his injuries.

Only then, but Cadderly was not so certain that Ivan would make it that far.

They soon came back to the original areas where they had encountered the undead monsters. All was quiet now, deathly still, giving Cadderly the opportunity to carefully reconstruct his first passage through. He thought that he was making some progress, leading Ivan down several adjoining passages, when he noticed some movement far down one hall, at the very edge of his narrow light beam.

Ivan noticed it, too, and he set off at once, his grief for his dead brother transferred again into uncontrollable battle lust.

Cadderly fumbled with his bandoleer and tried futilely to keep up with the dwarf, pleading with Ivan to let this enemy go.

It was a single skeleton this time, wandering aimlessly at first, but then coming straight in at the charging dwarf.

Cadderly came to a very important decision at that moment.

He held his light beam in one hand and his loaded crossbow in the other, lining both up between the horns of the dwarf's helmet at the skeletal face beyond. Cadderly had never intended his custom-designed crossbow to be used as a weapon, especially not while firing the exploding darts. He had designed the bow for opening locked doors, or blasting away troublesome tree branches that scraped against his window, or a variety of other nonviolent purposes. Also, he had to admit, he had designed the crossbow and the bolts in part for the simple challenge of designing them. But Cadderly had vowed to himself, as much as an excuse as anything else, never to use the darts or the bow as a weapon, never to unleash the concentrated violence of the explosive darts against a living target.

The arguments in this instance were many, of course. Ivan could ill afford another fight, even against a single skeleton, and the skeleton, after all, was not really a living creature.

Still, Cadderly's guilt hovered over him as he took aim. He knew that he was breaking the spirit of his vow.

He fired. The bolt arced over Ivan's head and crashed into the charging skeleton's face. The initial impact wasn't so great, but then the dart collapsed, setting off the *Oil of Impact*.

When the dust cleared a moment later, the skeleton's head and neck were gone. The headless bones stood a moment longer, then dropped with a rattle.

Ivan, just a few strides away, stopped abruptly and stared in amazement, his jaw hanging open and his dark eyes wide. He turned slowly back to Cadderly, who only shrugged apologetically and looked away.

"It had to be done," Cadderly remarked, more to himself than to Ivan.

"And ye did it well!" Ivan replied, coming back down the passage. He clapped Cadderly on the back, though Cadderly did not feel heroic in the least.

"Let us go on," Cadderly said quietly, slipping the crossbow back into its wide and shallow sheath.

They crossed under another low archway, Cadderly beginning to believe that they were again on the right path, and then came to a fork in the dusty passage. Two tunnels ran out from the one, parallel and very near together. Cadderly thought for a moment, then started down the right side. He went only a few steps, though, before he recognized his location more clearly. He backtracked, ignoring Ivan's grumbling, and moved at a determined pace down the left passage. This corridor went on for just a short distance, then angled farther to the left and opened into a wider passage.

Standing sarcophagi filled the alcove in this passage, confirmation to Cadderly that he had chosen the right path. A few steps in and beyond a slight bend, he knew beyond doubt. Far in front of them, at the end of the passage, loomed a door, cracked open and with light shining through.

"That the place?" Ivan demanded, though he had already guessed the answer. He started off before Cadderly nodded in reply.

Again Cadderly tried futilely to slow the dwarf's charge, desiring a more cautious approach. He was just a couple of steps behind Ivan when the last sarcophagus swung open and a mummy stepped out to block the way. Too enraged to care, Ivan continued on undaunted, but Cadderly no longer followed. The young scholar was frozen with fear, stricken by the sheer evilness of the powerful undead presence. The skeletons had been terrifying, but they seemed only minor inconveniences next to this monster.

"Irrational," Cadderly tried to tell himself. It was acceptable to be afraid, but ridiculous to let that fear paralyze him in so urgent a situation.

"Outta me way!" Ivan roared, bearing in. He chopped viciously with his axe, scoring a hit, but, unlike the battle against the skeletons, the weapon met stiff resistance this time. The mummy's thick wraps deflected much of the blow's force, and pieces of the linen came unraveled, snarling the axe-head and preventing Ivan from following through.

The hit hardly hindered the mummy. It clubbed with its arm, catching Ivan on the shoulder and sending him spinning into the nearest alcove. He crashed heavily and nearly swooned but stubbornly, unsteadily, forced himself back to his feet.

The mummy was waiting for him. A second hit knocked the dwarf down to his back.

That would have been the end of Ivan Bouldershoulder had it not been for Cadderly. His first attack was almost inadvertent, for the mummy, in going after Ivan, crossed the direct, narrow beam of Cadderly's light tube. A creature of the night, of a dark and lightless world, Khalif was neither accustomed to, nor tolerant of, brightness of any kind.

Seeing the mummy recoil and lift its scabrous arm to block the beam restored a bit of composure in Cadderly. He kept the light focused on the monster, forcing it back from Ivan, while he nimbly loaded another dart with his free hand. Cadderly held no reservations about using his crossbow on this monster; the mummy was simply too hideous for his conscience to argue.

Still shielding its eyes, the mummy advanced on Cadderly, slapping at the beam of light with every sliding step.

The first dart buried itself deeply into the mummy's chest before exploding, and the blast sent the monster back a couple of steps and left scorch marks both front and back on the creature's linen wrappings. If it had suffered any serious damage, though, the mummy didn't show it, for it came on again.

Cadderly scrambled to reload the crossbow. His design had been good, fortunately, and the crank was not difficult to execute. A second dart joined the first, again driving the monster backward.

The mummy came on again, and again after Cadderly had shot it a third time, and each time its stubborn advance brought it a step or two closer to the frantic young man. The fourth shot proved disastrous to Cadderly, for the dart's initial momentum drove it right through the mummy without ever igniting the magical oil. The mummy hardly slowed and Cadderly nearly held the crossbow right against its filthy wrappings when he fired his fifth shot.

This time the dart had more effect, but again it only slowed, and did not stop, the monster. Cadderly had no time to load another dart.

"Coming!" slurred Ivan as he crawled from the alcove.

Cadderly doubted that the dwarf could help him, even if Ivan could reach the monster in time, which he obviously couldn't. The young scholar knew, too, that neither of his conventional weapons, spindle-disks or walking stick, could hurt this monster.

He had just one weapon to use. He stuck the light tube out in front of him, slowing the mummy further, causing it to shield its eyes and half turn away from him, then he dropped his crossbow and reached with his free hand for the waterskin hanging at his side. He grabbed it by the extended nozzle, tucked it tight under his arm, and used his thumb to pop off its gooey cap. Cadderly squeezed with his arm, slowly and steadily sending a stream of the blessed water into his attacker's face.

The holy water sizzled as it struck the evilly enchanted monster and, for the first time in the battle, the mummy revealed its agony. It let out an unearthly, spine-chilling wail that filled Cadderly with fear and even stopped Ivan temporarily. It was the proverbial bark with no bite, for while the mummy continued to advance, it purposely shied away from the man with the light beam and the stinging water. Soon it had passed Cadderly altogether, but it continued down the passage, roaring with pain and frustration, clubbing with its powerful arms against the walls, the sarcophagi, and anything else that got in its way.

Ivan came rushing past Cadderly, intent on resuming the battle.

"The man who killed your brother is behind the door!" Cadderly cried as quickly as he could, desperate to stop the dwarf this time. He couldn't know the truth of his claim, of course, but at that critical moment, he would have said anything to turn Ivan around.

Predictably, Ivan did wheel about. He let out a growl and charged back past Cadderly, forgetting all about the fleeing mummy, his unblinking eyes glued instead on the door at the end of the passage.

Cadderly saw disaster coming. He recalled the newly constructed wall in the wine cellar and the blasts that had followed Pikel's battering-ram charge. He had to believe that this door might also be magically warded, and he saw that the door was heavy, iron-bound. If Ivan didn't get right through, but was held in the area of exploding glyphs . . .

Cadderly dove to the ground, pulling a dart and grabbing for his crossbow. In a single motion, he cocked it, fitted the bolt, and spun about, using his light beam to show him the target.

The dart passed Ivan just a stride from the door. It didn't hit the lock area directly but exploded with enough force to weaken the jam.

Surprised by the sudden blast, but unable to stop even if he chose to, Ivan - barreled in.

Twenty-One
A Well-Placed Blow

N o!" she heard the druid say at her back, but it was a distant call, as if Newander's voice were no more than a memory of some other time and some other place. All that mattered to Danica was the wall, made of stonework now and not like the natural dirt tunnel that had led them in. The wall, inviting her, enticing her, to emulate her long-dead hero.

That distant voice spoke again, but in clicks and chatter that Danica could not understand.

A furry tail fell down over Danica's eyes, breaking her concentration on the stone. She moved one hand merely by reflex to push aside the distraction.

Following the druid's instructions, Percival promptly bit her.

Danica dipped her shoulder and came across with an instinctive chop that would have killed the squirrel. She recognized Percival before she struck, though, and that led her again out of the red mist and back to reality.

"The wall," she stammered. "I meant to . . ."

"It is not your fault," Newander said to her. "The curse affected you again. It would seem to be an endless fight."

Danica slumped back against the stone, weary and ashamed. She had put every effort into resisting the intrusive mist, had seen it for what it was and planted deeply in her own thinking the logical conclusion that such destructive impulses must be avoided. Yet here she was, near the heart of danger, abandoning their entire hopes for success for the sake of her curse-enhanced desires.

"Do not accept the guilt," Newander said to her. "You are braving the curse better than any of the priests above us. You have come this far against it, and that alone is more than most others can say."

"The dwarves walk with Cadderly," Danica reminded him.

"Do not hold yourself against that measure," Newander warned. "You are no dwarf. The bearded folk have a natural resistance to magic that no human can match. Theirs is not a question of self-discipline, Lady Danica, but of physical differences."

Danica realized that the druid spoke the truth, but the knowledge that Pikel and Ivan had an advantage over her in resisting the curse did little to diminish her sense of guilt. For all of the druid's talk, Danica considered the intrusive mist a mental challenge, a test of discipline.

"What of Newander?" she asked suddenly, more sarcastically than she had intended. "Does the blood of the bearded folk run in your veins? You are no dwarf. Why, then, are you not affected?"

The druid looked away; it was his turn to feel the weight of guilt. "I do not know," he admitted, "but you must believe that I feel the curse keenly with my every step. "Cadderly guessed that the mist pushes a person to what is in his heart. The gluttons eat themselves to death. The suffering priests cut each other apart in religious frenzy. My own druid brothers revert to animal form, losing themselves in altered states of being. Why, then, is Newander not running with the animals?"

Danica recognized that the druid's last question was a source of great and sincere anguish. They had discussed this once before, but Newander had offered little explanation for himself, focusing his responses on why Cadderly might have escaped the curse.

"My guess is that the curse has found no hold on my heart, that my own desires are not known to me," the druid went on. "Have I failed at my calling?"

Tears rolled openly down Newander's face and he appeared on the verge of a breakdown, a clear sign to Danica that he was indeed being affected by the red mist. "Have I no calling?" Newander wailed. He crumbled to the floor, head in hands, his shoulders shuddering with heavy sobs.

"You are mistaken," Danica said with enough force to command the druid's attention. "If you have failed in your calling, or if you have no calling, then why do you retain the magical spells that are a gift of your god, Silvanus? You brought the vines in my window, and the moss to life against the ghouls."

Newander composed himself, intrigued by Danica's words.

He found the strength to stand and this time did not look away from her.

"Perhaps it is the truth in your heart that has led you to defeat the curse," Danica reasoned. "When did you first feel the curse acting upon you?"

Newander thought back a couple of days, to when he had returned to the library to find Arcite and Cleo already in the throes of their shape change. "I felt it soon after I returned," he explained. "I had been out in the mountains, watching over an eagle aerie." Newander recalled that time clearly, remembered his own insight concerning the su-monsters. "I knew that something was out of sorts as soon as I came back in the library's doors. I went to find my druid brothers, but, alas, they were deep into their animal forms by then, and I could not reach them."

"There is your answer," Danica said after a moment of thought. "You are a priest of natural order, and this curse is certainly a perversion of that order. You said that you can sense the presence of undead—so, I believe, did you sense the presence of the curse."

How had he known that the ghouls were coming? Newander wondered. There were spells to detect the presence of such undead, but he had not enacted any and still knew that they were there, just as he had known that the su-monsters were evil creatures and not just predatory animals. The implications of his insight nearly overwhelmed the druid.

"You give me more credit than I deserve," he said somberly to Danica.

"You are a priest of the natural order," Danica said again. "I do not think you alone have resisted this curse, but you were not, are not, alone. You walk with your faith, and it is that sincere calling that has given you the strength to resist. Arcite and Cleo had no warning. The curse was upon them before they knew anything was wrong, but their failure forewarned you of the danger, and with that warning, you have been able to keep true to your calling."

Newander shook his head, not convinced, not daring to believe that he possessed such inner strength. He had no rebuttals against Danica's reasoning, though, and he would not deny anything where Silvanus, the Oak Father, was concerned. He had given his heart to Silvanus long ago, and there his heart remained, despite any curiosities Newander might hold for the ways of progress and civilization. Was it possible that he was so true a disciple of the Oak Father? Was it possible that what he had perceived as failure, in not transforming into animal form, as Arcite and Cleo had done, might actually reflect strength?

"We lose time in asking questions we cannot answer," he said at length, his voice more steady. "Whatever the cause, both you and I found the way clear."

Danica looked back to the stone wall with concern. "For now at least," she added. "Let us be off again, before my will wanes."

They crossed under several archways, Danica holding the torch far out in front of her to burn the unrelenting cobwebs from their path. Neither of them had much experience with travel underground, or with the common designs of catacombs, and their course was a wandering one; they chose tunnels more or less at random. Danica was thoughtful enough to scratch directional marks at the more confusing turns, in case they had to retrace their steps, but still she feared that she and the druid would become lost in the surprisingly intricate complex.

They saw some signs of previous passage—torn webbing hanging in loose strands, an upset crate in one corner—but whether these had been caused by Cadderly, by other monsters such as the ghouls, or simply by some animal that had made its home in the catacombs, neither could say.

Their torch burned low as they entered one long passage. Several side corridors ran off this one, mostly along the righthand wall, and Danica and Newander agreed that they would stay the course this time and not continue to wander in circles.

They passed by the first few passages, Danica entering just a few feet with the torch to get a quick glimpse of what lay down each, but stayed in the main tunnel and meant to until they reached its end.

Finally they came to a passage they could not ignore. Danica went in, again for a quick perusal. "They have been here!" she cried out, the realization drawing her farther down the tunnel. The sights there confirmed Danica's suspicions. A battle had been fought here; dozens of bone piles lay strewn about the floor and several skulls, forcibly removed from their skeletal bodies, greeted them with sightless eye sockets. Two lines of piled crates formed a defensive run farther in, a place where Danica soon reasoned that Cadderly and the dwarves had made their stand.

"The bones agree with my sensing of the undead," Newander said grimly, "but we cannot be certain that it was our friends who fought them here."

The confirmation came even as he spoke, as Danica moved her torch slowly about for a wider view of the battle-torn area.

"Pikel!" the woman cried, running to the fallen dwarf. Pikel lay cold and still just as Ivan had left him, his burly arms crossed over his chest and his tree-trunk club lying at his side.

Danica fell to her knees to examine the dwarf but had no doubts that he was dead. She shook her head as she studied his wounds, for none of them seemed serious enough to fell one of Pikel's toughness.

Newander understood her confusion. He knelt beside her and uttered a few words as he waved his hand slowly over the body. "There is a poison in this one," the druid announced grimly. "A wicked brew indeed, gone straight to his heart."

Danica cupped her hands under Pikel's head and gently lifted his face to hers. He had been a dear friend, possibly the most likable person Danica ever had known. It occurred to her, holding him, that he had not been dead for very long. His lips had gone blue, but there was no swelling at all and there remained warmth in his body.

Danica's eyes widened and she turned on Newander. "After we fought the ghouls, you told me that you had a spell to counter any poisons I might have contracted," she said.

"And so I do," Newander replied, understanding her intent, "but the poison has done its work on this one. My spell cannot undo the dwarf's death."

"Use the spell," Danica insisted. She moved quickly, propping Pikel under the neck with one arm and tilting his head backward.

"But it will not—"

"Use it, Newander!" Danica snapped at him. The druid backed off a step, fearing that the mist had again taken hold of his companion.

"Trust me, I beg," Danica continued, softening her tone, for she recognized the druid's sudden caution.

Newander didn't understand what Danica might have in mind, but after all they had been through, he did trust her. He paused a moment to consider the spell, then took an oak leaf from his pocket and crumbled it on top of the dwarf, uttering the proper chant.

Danica opened Pikel's cloak and unbuckled the breastplates of his heavy armor. She looked to Newander for confirmation that his spell was complete.

"If there is any poison left in this one, it has been neutralized," the druid assured her.

It was Danica's turn. She closed her eyes and thought of Grandmaster Penpahg D'Ahn's most prized scroll, the notes of physical suspension. Penpahg D'Ahn had stopped his breathing, even his heart, for several hours. One day Danica meant to do the same. She was not yet ready for such a demanding trial, she knew, but there were aspects of Penpahg D'Ahn's writings, particularly those involved with coming out of the physical suspension, that she knew would be of help to her now.

Danica thought of the steps required to restart the suspended heart. In the writings, these were internal, of course, but their principles might be duplicated by an outside force.

Danica laid Pikel back down flat, unbuttoned his vest, and pulled his nightshirt up high. She could hardly see the details of his chest through the virtual sweater of hair, but she persisted, feeling his ribs and hoping that a dwarf's anatomy was not so different from a human's.

She had found the spot—she thought. She looked back to Newander for support, then, to the druid's obvious surprise, turned back suddenly and rapped her free hand sharply into the hollow of the dwarf's breast. She waited just a moment, then rapped again. Danica's intensity multiplied; all her heart went into her work on Pikel, and that only encouraged the cursing mist to creep back in.

"Lady Danica!" Newander cried, grabbing the frantic woman's shoulder. "You should show more respect to the dead!"

Danica whipped her arm around and back, hooking the druid behind the knees. A sudden jerk sent Newander to the floor, then Danica resumed her work, furiously pounding away. She heard a rib crack but wound up for yet another blow.

Newander was back at her, grabbing her more forcefully this time and tearing her from the corpse. They wrestled for a moment, Danica easily gaining an advantage. She put Newander flat on his back and scrambled atop him, her fist coming up dangerously over the druid's face.

"Oo oi!"

The call froze both Danica and Newander.

"What have you done?" Newander gasped.

Danica, as surprised as the druid, shook her head and slowly turned about. There sat Pikel, looking sore and confused but very much alive. He smiled when he gazed upon Danica.

The woman rushed off Newander and tackled the dwarf, wrapping him in a tight hug. Newander came over, too, patting both of them heartily on the shoulders.

"A miracle," the druid muttered.

Danica knew better, knew that reviving Pikel had involved some very logical and well-documented principles in the teachings of Grandmaster Penpahg D'Ahn. Nonetheless, Danica, too amazed by what she had done and too relieved to see Pikel again drawing breath, did not find the resolve to answer.

"This is a fortunate meeting," Danica reasoned after the hugging had ended.

"Oo oi!" Pikel was quick to agree.

"More than for you," Danica started to explain.

Newander cast her a curious look.

"This is our first proof that the tunnel we entered connects to the area that Cadderly went into," said Danica. "Until we found Pikel, we were lost."

"Now we know," added Newander, "and we know, too, that we have crossed Cadderly's path. Perhaps now we shall find a clearer trail to follow." He bent low with the torch, studying the floor for some signs, but came up a moment later shaking his head. "It is a tiny path if it is one at all," he lamented.

A smile widened on Danica's face. "Tiny for us, perhaps," she said. "But maybe clear enough for Percival."

Pikel sat confused, but Newander's smile surpassed Danica's. The druid uttered a few sounds to Percival, asking the squirrel to lead them to Cadderly. Percival hopped about for a few moments, scratching at the ground and searching for some pattern, either in the scuff marks or the scent.

He caught the trail and set off down the passage, Newander right behind. Danica helped Pikel to his feet. He was still unsteady, and still thoroughly confused, but he called upon the two most prominent dwarven traits, toughness and stubbornness, and made his way beside the young woman.

* * * * *

Sleep had been such a pleasant thing, but somewhere deep in his thoughts Druzil realized that he was dangerously vulnerable lying in a crack in the wall of a deserted corridor. The imp pulled himself out of the cubby and shape-changed back to his more customary, batwinged form. Somewhere in his slumber, he had lost the concentration necessary for invisibility and could not sort through the fog that remained in his mind enough to recover it. That sleepy fog was heavy, but the imp kept one thought clear: He must get back to Barjin, back to the safety of his magical gate connection to Castle Trinity. He knew that someone recently had exited this passage and, having no desire to meet any enemies, he took a roundabout, meandering course.

He stopped and held very still a short while later when the crazed mummy came storming by, smashing anything and everything in its path. Druzil realized that something had gone terribly wrong, recognized that the mummy, scorched and blasted in many places, had gone out of control.

The monster was gone then, slamming down a side corridor, growling and bashing things with its heavy arms with every step.

Druzil's wings flapped slowly as he half-walked and half-flew back toward the altar room.

Yes, Barjin would help him, and if not Barjin, then surely Aballister. With that thought in mind, the imp sent out a weak, sleepy message to his master back at Castle Trinity.

Twenty-Two

Face to Face

Ivan hit the loose-swinging door with a terrific impact, jolting it free of one of its hinges. Cadderly's fears were proved true, for several fiery explosions went off in rapid succession as Ivan crossed the threshold. If the door had stopped, or even delayed his charge, he would have been roasted.

As it was, Cadderly was not certain if the dwarf had survived. Ivan skidded into the room on his face, wisps of smoke rising from several points on his body. Cadderly rushed in right behind to get to his friend; he could only hope that no glyphs remained.

The young scholar didn't quite make it to Ivan, though. As soon as he entered the room, squinting in the brightness of the several torches and blazing brazier, he saw that he and Ivan were not alone.

"You have done well to come so far," Barjin said calmly, standing halfway across the room, beside the altar that held the ever-smoking bottle. Torches lined the wall to either side of the priest, but the brighter light came from a brazier along the wall to Cadderly's right, which Cadderly correctly guessed was an interplanar gate.

"I applaud your resilience," Barjin continued, his tone teasing, "futile though it will prove."

Every memory came rushing back to Cadderly in clear order and focus when he saw Barjin. The first thought that crossed his mind was that he would go back up and have a few nasty words with Kierkan Rufo, the man who had, he believed, kicked him down the stairway from the wine cellar in the first place. His resolve to scold Rufo did not take firm hold, though, not when Cadderly considered the dangers before him. His eyes did not linger on the priest, but rather on the man standing next to Barjin.

"Mullivy?" he asked, though he knew by Mullivy's posture and the grotesque bend of his wrecked arm that this was not the groundskeeper he once had known.

The dead man did not reply.

"A friend of yours?" Barjin teased, draping an arm over his zombie. "Now he is my friend, too. I could have him kill you quite easily," Barjin went on.

"But, you see, I believe I shall reserve that pleasure for myself." He removed the obsidian-headed mace from his belt, its sculpted visage that of a pretty young girl. Next, Barjin pulled on the conical hood hanging in back of his clerical robes. This fit over his head as a helmet might, with holes cut for Barjin's eyes. Cadderly had heard about enchanted, protecting vestments and he knew that his nemesis was armored.

"For all your valiant efforts, young priest, you remain a minuscule thorn in my side," Barjin remarked. He took a step toward Cadderly but stopped suddenly when Ivan hopped back to his feet.

The dwarf shook his head vigorously, then looked about, as if seeing the room for the first time. He glanced at Cadderly, then focused on Barjin. "Tell me, lad," Ivan asked, swinging his double-bladed axe up to a ready position on his shoulder, "is he the one who killed me brother?"

* * * * *

Aballister wiped a cloth over his sweaty brow. He could not bear to continue peering through his magical mirror, but he had not the strength to turn his eyes away. He had felt Barjin's urgency when first he sent his thoughts to the distant altar room, unable to bear his inability to contact his imp. Aballister worried for Druzil and for the cleric, though his fears for and of Barjin were double-sided indeed. For all of his ambiguity, though, for all of his fears of Barjin and the power gains his rival would enjoy, Aballister honestly believed he did not want to see *Tuanta Quiro Miancay*, the Most Fatal Horror, fail.

Then the enemies had revealed themselves—himself, for Aballister hardly took note of the stumbling dwarf. It was the young scholar who held the wizard's thoughts, the tall and straight lad, twenty years old perhaps, with the familiar, inquisitive eyes.

Aballister sensed Barjin's mounting confidence and knew that the evil priest was back in control, that Barjin and *Tuanta Quiro Miancay* would not be defeated.

Somehow that notion seemed even more disturbing to the wizard. He stared hard and long at the young scholar, a boy really, who had come in bravely and foolishly to face his doom.

* * * * *

Cadderly nodded at Ivan. The dwarf's eyes narrowed dangerously as he glared back at the evil priest. "Ye shouldn't have done that," Ivan growled in a low and death-promising tone. He held his axe high and began a steady advance. "Ye shouldn't have—"

Waves of mental energy stopped Ivan in midsentence and midstep. Barjin's spell broke the dwarf's thought patterns, holding him firmly in place. Ivan struggled with all his mental strength and all the resistance a dwarf could muster, but Barjin was no minor spellcaster and this was his evilly blessed altar room, where his clerical magic was at its highest. Ivan managed a few indecipherable sounds, then stopped talking and moving altogether.

"Ivan?" Cadderly asked, his voice shaky as he suspected his companion's fate.

"Do keep talking," Barjin taunted. "The dwarf can hear your every word, though I assure you that he'll not respond."

Barjin's ensuing laughter sent shivers through Cadderly's bones. They had come so far and through so much. Pikel had died to get them here, and Ivan had taken a terrible beating.

And now to fail. Looking at this evil priest, with gruesome Mullivy standing obediently at his side, Cadderly knew that he was overmatched.

"You battled through my outer defenses, and for that you deserve my applause," Barjin continued, "but if you believed my true power would be revealed to you out in the empty and meaningless corridors, then know your folly! Look upon me, foolish young priest—" he waved a hand to the ever-smoking bottle"—and look upon the agent of Talona that you yourself brought to life. *Tuanta Quiro Miancay*, the Most Fatal Horror! You should feel blessed, young priest, for your pitiful library is the first to feel the awesome power of the chaos that will dominate the region for centuries to come!"

At that awful moment, the threat did not sound so hollow in Cadderly's ears. Talona—he knew the name: the Lady of Poison, of disease.

"Did you expect to find the bottle unguarded?" Barjin laughed. "Did you think to stroll in here after defeating a few minor monsters and simply close the flask that you yourself—" again the priest emphasized those painful words "—opened?"

Cadderly hardly heard the banter. His attention had gone to the bottle and the steady stream of pinkish mist that issued from it. He thought of loading his crossbow and putting an explosive dart into the bottle. Where would this Talona's agent be then? Cadderly wondered. But Cadderly feared that action, feared that to destroy the bottle would only release the evil agent, or whatever it was, in full.

His attention was stolen from the bottle suddenly, and he realized that the choice, if ever he had one, had passed. The evil priest strode casually toward him, his arm uplifted and holding a curious black mace, its head the image of a pretty young girl, an innocent face so very out of place atop a weapon, a face that strangely reminded Cadderly of Danica.

* * * * *

Aballister did not pause to consider his actions. His thoughts focused on the dwarf, standing rigid a few steps ahead of the young man. The wizard summoned all of his powers, sent a spell into the magic mirror and across the miles, tried to use the scrying device as a magical gate for his focused magical energies.

The mirror's own dweomer, not designed for such uses, resisted the attempt. It could be used to see distant places, to converse with viewed creatures, even to transport Aballister to those places viewed, but Aballister tried to carry that ability farther now, to send not only his thoughts or physical being but his magical energy flowing to the rigid dwarf.

It would have been a difficult enough task, even for a wizard as powerful as Aballister, if the attempt had been made on a human, but Ivan, though fully in the throes of Barjin's paralyzing spell, fought back with typical dwarven stubbornness against the wizard's intrusions.

Aballister gritted his teeth and focused his concentration.

Veins stood out on his forehead; he thought the toll of the attempt would destroy him, but Barjin was close to the young man now—too close!—the awful mace held high.

Aballister put his lips right up against the mirror and whispered, hoping that the dwarf alone would hear, "Let me in, you fool!"

* * * * *

Barjin came on, smiling wickedly, victoriously. Cadderly gave him every reason for confidence, offering no outward sign of resistance. The young scholar did have his ram's head walking stick in one hand, but he hadn't even lifted it yet.

In truth, Cadderly had decided on another defense, the only one he believed could slow this imposing priest. His free hand clenched and unclenched at his side, tightening the muscles, straightening a single finger for the coming strike. He had seen, and keenly felt, Danica do this a dozen times.

Barjin was only a step away, moving cautiously now for fear that Cadderly would take a swipe at him with the walking stick.

Cadderly kept its butt end firmly to the ground. Barjin maneuvered to the side, away from the weapon, and swung his mace in a teasing cut. Cadderly easily stepped back, though his concentration nearly faltered when he saw the mace's head transform into the leering, open-mouthed visage of some unearthly monster, fanged and hungry.

He kept his wits enough to retaliate, though, and with Barjin expecting him to strike with the walking stick, his hand got through the cleric's defenses.

Cadderly drove his finger powerfully into Barjin's shoulder.

He knew that he had hit the precise spot, just as Danica had so often done to him. A look of sincere confusion crossed the evil priest's face, and Cadderly nearly squealed in glee.

"Withering Touch!" he proclaimed.

While Barjin was indeed confused, his arm, and the cruel mace at the end of it, did not fall limply to his side.

Cadderly was confused as well, and he barely reacted, at the very last instant, as Barjin's mace whipped in with more determination. Cadderly turned and dove, but the weapon clipped his shoulder, the evilly contorted face biting a deep gash. Cadderly had intended to roll back to his feet a short distance away, but the hit put him off balance and he crashed heavily instead into one of the room's many bookcases.

The wound itself was not too severe, but the frozen waves of agony rolling through the young scholar's body most certainly were. Cadderly shuddered and trembled, hardly able to comprehend, hardly able to focus through the dizzy blur. He knew that he was doomed, knew that he could never recover in time to parry or dodge the priest's next attack.

"—killed me brother!" he heard Ivan roar, right where the dwarf had left off, and then he heard Barjin yelp in surprise.

Ivan's axe pounded into the priest's back, a blow that would have felled any man, but Barjin was protected. His magical vestments absorbed the brunt of the hit; the priest didn't even lose his breath. He wheeled about, swiping with his mace in response.

Skilled and seasoned, Ivan Bouldershoulder was ready.

From just his single attack, he realized that the priest was somehow powerfully armored. Barjin's blow cut harmlessly short, and Ivan stepped in behind it, hooked one head of his weapon under Barjin's shoulder, and heaved with all his strength, sending Barjin tumbling head over heels back toward the altar in the center of the room.

Ivan dropped his weapon's head to the ground and clasped his legs about its handle so that he could spit into his hands before continuing. The priest had a wicked weapon and nearly invulnerable armor, but the fiery dwarf had no doubts as to how this fight would end. "You shouldn't have killed me brother," Ivan muttered one more time, then he grabbed his axe and moved in to finish the work.

Barjin had other ideas. He had no time to ponder how the dwarf might have broken free from his binding spell, and it didn't really matter anyway. Barjin understood the fury in this formidable foe, a curse-enhanced rage that more than evened the odds, but Barjin didn't play with even odds.

He scrambled over to the wall behind Mullivy. "Kill the dwarf!" he instructed his zombie, and he pulled a burning torch from its sconce and touched it to Mullivy's shoulder. The zombie's oil-soaked clothing ignited immediately, but Barjin's protective spell did not fail. While the flames consumed the oil and Mullivy's clothes, the zombie's body was quite unharmed.

Ivan's startled response as the flaming zombie bore down on him would have made Pikel proud: "Oo oi!"

Cadderly started to rise, but the continuing, debilitating chilling bite of his wound sent him spiraling back to the floor. He tried to shake away the pain, tried to find some focus.

He saw Ivan swiping wildly but sorely missing his mark as the dwarf steadily backed away from the fiery zombie. Mullivy's advance showed no concern for the dwarf's meager attacks. Cadderly heard the evil priest laughing, somewhere back by the altar, by the cursing bottle. The priest would get Ivan, even if the flaming zombie did not, Cadderly knew. Then the priest would get him, and then this Most Fatal Horror, this evil agent of an evil goddess, would win over the Edificant Library fully and destroy everything the young scholar valued.

"No!" Cadderly managed to cry, multiplying his concentration tenfold.

The devilish mace had done its work well, even in a glancing blow on Cadderly's shoulder. The mace had a life of its own, an inner and foul energy spawned somewhere in the lowest pits of hell.

Cadderly continued to battle against its stunning touch, tried to realign his physical control with his mental determination, but his body didn't heed to his commands; there remained a long road to travel.

* * * * *

Nothing rose to hinder the three companions' progress, and Percival appeared quite adept at following Cadderly's trail. They came through several passageways, always slowing to peer into the nearest alcoves and ensure that no monsters waited to spring out.

Pikel grew steadier with each passing step but seemed distracted, introspective. Danica could appreciate his somber mood; he had just passed through death and returned. What tales might the enlightened dwarf tell? Danica wondered.

When she questioned him about the experience, though, he said only, "Oo," and would not elaborate.

At many places, they could confirm that Percival was leading them correctly. Three-way alcoves, thick with webbing on one side, had been burned clear on the other.

Soon the party came to a fork in the tunnel. Hardly hesitating, Percival scampered off down the right hand side.

Sounds of battle, not far off, echoed in their ears.

The squirrel stopped suddenly and chattered excitedly, but his squeaks and chirps were lost in the sudden commotion.

Pikel, Danica, and Newander heard the fighting, and none of them stopped to listen to the squirrel's banter. The noise came from farther down the tunnel; that was all they needed to know. Off they charged, the dwarf no longer introspective, but head down and running to his brother's aid, and Danica and the druid no less determined to help their friends.

When they came to the altar room wall, they heard Ivan growling about some "flaming hunk of walking kindling," and understood their error. While the words were clear, the path certainly was not. No doors lined this section of the passage, just blank wall.

Percival came up chattering and scolding.

"We have come the wrong way, so says the squirrel!" Newander told them. "The path tracks back to the left!"

Danica nodded. "Run, then!" she cried.

She and Newander started away, but both stopped abruptly to regard Pikel, who was not following.

The agitated dwarf hopped up and down, stubby legs pumping rapidly, his whole body building into a tremendous tremble.

"Me brudder!" Pikel cried, and he lowered both his head and his tree trunk and burst forward into the brick wall.

Twenty-Three

In the Druid's Heart

The wall was made only of brick and mortar and was no match for the rage of Pikel Bouldershoulder. The dwarf battered through into the altar room, sending up a cloud of dust and a shower of bricks.

Pikel stood in the new doorway for a moment, his eyes darting about to take in the scene. Several bricks came straight down, bouncing off his pot helmet with dull clangs, but Pikel seemed not to notice. He was looking for Ivan, his "brudder," and it would take a lot more than a few chunks of stone, however heavy, to deter him.

Then he saw Ivan, far to his left, near the room's original door and backing away from a flaming humanoid creature. Repelled by the intense heat, Ivan's defensive chops were falling short and, fast approaching a corner, Ivan soon would be out of running room.

"Oo oi!" Pikel cried, and he bounded off, pot-covered head and tree trunk leading the way.

Danica started in right behind, but Newander stopped her.

She turned and saw a look of sudden revelation on the druid's face, an expression that quickly changed to one of sincere joy.

"You spoke the truth, dear lady," Newander said. "It was not ambivalence, but a sense of order that kept me free of the cursing mist. Now I know how I was spared, why I was spared, and, in truth, it was a power far beyond my own will."

Danica consider the profound changes that had come over the man. No longer did Newander stoop in despair. His back was straight and his visage proud.

"I hear the call of Silvanus himself!" the druid declared. "His own voice, I tell you."

Truly intrigued, Danica would have liked to stay and hear Newander's explanation, but the situation wouldn't allow it.

She nodded quickly and pulled away from the druid's grasp, taking only the split second it took her to come through the wall to survey the room and determine her course. Her heart told her to go to Cadderly, still dazed and struggling by the door, but her warrior instincts told her that the best she could do for her beloved, and for all her friends, was to stop the imposing priest who stood by the altar.

She took two running strides at Barjin, dove into a roll just in case he had some spell or dart aimed her way, then came back to her feet and pounded in. She enacted her moves too quickly for Barjin to block, and she got her fist through his defenses, slamming him solidly on the chest.

Danica bounced back, stunned, her hand sore, as if she had struck an iron wall. Barjin hadn't even moved.

Danica kept her wits enough to dodge Barjin's first attack, and to take note of the contorting, biting movement of the enchanted mace's sculpted head. She circled to the priest's right, away from the altar, wondering if perhaps her daggers would have more effect. By all appearances, the priest wasn't wearing any armor, but Danica trusted her sore hand more than her eyes. She knew that magic could deceive, and she understood already that her tactics against the priest would have to be akin to those she might use against an armored knight.

Barjin waved the Screaming Maiden again easily, attacks designed to keep Danica at bay and to test her reflexes. She realized that again the priest had underestimated her quickness.

She stepped in right behind the swing and snapped off two jabs at her opponent's weapon arm. There, too, the magical vestments repelled the blow.

Her understanding of the extent of the priest's armor growing, Danica realized that she would find few openings for strikes. The priest was covered head to toe, and the kind of power Danica expected she would need to get through the enchanted vestments, a blow that required long concentration, would leave her vulnerable to a preemptive hit. She took a different path then, one designed to get that awful mace away from her adversary.

Danica came in low, feigning a strike at Barjin's groin. The priest whipped the Screaming Maiden straight down at the stooping woman, just as Danica had expected. She brought her forearm up to block the blow. Her next move would have been to reach under with her free hand, grabbing the priest's wrist. Pulling with this hand and pushing with her locked forearm would then tear the mace from his grasp. But, while Danica had correctly anticipated Barjin's overhand strike, she had not foreseen the reaction of his vile, sentient, weapon.

The Screaming Maiden twisted, its maw snapping futilely at the out-of-reach blocking forearm. The ugly visage opened its mouth wide and hissed, loosing a cone of frost over Danica.

Danica began her dodge at the instant the chill emanated from the mouth, but the cone encompassed too wide an area for her to get fully out of harm's way. Chilling ice descended on her, so cold that it burned at her skin and so evil, the chill of death, that it found its way deeper, into Danica's heart and bones. Her lungs ached with her next gasp and it was all she could do to break away from the encounter and stagger back toward the broken wall.

Newander watched it all through a dull haze. He wisely registered the important facts—Barjin's vestment armor and the mace, in particular—but the druid's thoughts were turned primarily inward now, heeding, he believed, the personal summons of Silvanus, the Oak Father. The sight of this room, of the cursing bottle, had put many things into perspective for Newander. Gone now were his fears that he, unlike his transformed druid companions, was somehow not true to his calling. Gone was his fear that he had only avoided the brunt of the curse because of some inner ambivalence. Perhaps that had been the case, but it hardly mattered now to the druid. His gaze locked upon the evil priest, the one who had raised the dead, the bringer of perversion, and he heard the commands of nature's god.

He remembered the su-monsters and how clearly he had sensed the approach of ghouls, and Newander knew his purpose. Druids were dedicated to preserving the natural order, the natural harmony, and his faith demanded that the evil priest be stopped, here and now.

Newander let his thoughts slip to the woodland, to the home of druidic power. He felt the beginning twinges in his body the first time he had ever achieved this level of druidic concentration. Though a bit afraid, he encouraged the engulfing power fully, focusing his own energies to push it along. There was a sensation of distant pain as his bones cracked and reconfigured, a tickle as hair sprouted across his body.

As had Cleo and Arcite, Newander let himself go to his urging, let his body follow his thoughts. Unlike his companions, though, Newander did not relinquish his thinking to the instincts of the animal. His focus did not change with his body.

He saw the evil priest's eyes widen as he pawed toward the altar, past the recoiling Danica.

* * * * *

Ivan saw Pikel's storming approach, but the flaming zombie never turned to witness the attack. At the last moment, Ivan dodged to the side and Pikel slammed in, his tree trunk connecting squarely on Mullivy's rump. His stubby legs pumping wildly, Pikel brutally drove the zombie into the wall. Still Pikel's legs did not stop thrashing; he ignored the intense heat and kept the zombie pinned.

Mullivy swung his good arm about wildly, but his back was to the attacker and he could not reach beyond Pikel's pinning club. He wriggled and squirmed, trying to get out the side of the pin. Every time he made some progress, though, Ivan rushed over and smacked him hard with the axe.

This went on for several moments, then luck turned against the dwarves. Mullivy started out the side; Ivan waded in and hit him. The powerful blow drove deep into Mullivy's arm, but sent a gout of flame flying back in Ivan's direction, instantly igniting the dwarf's beard.

Ivan dove away, slapping at the flames, and Pikel, distracted by his brother's sudden distress, unconsciously loosened his hold.

Mullivy slipped free of his captor and advanced on the rolling Ivan.

Pikel overbalanced and stumbled forward into the wall. He came back up in an instant, but again he saw Ivan in dire need and again the sight sent him on a ferocious charge. This time Pikel held his club perpendicularly in front of him, one hand on either end. Mullivy was just reaching down at Ivan when Pikel hit him. Again the dwarf drove on, pushing the zombie before him. They passed the open door—Pikel thought he saw a batwinged impish form hovering outside—and barreled headlong into an empty bookcase. The ancient wooden shelves fell apart under their weight, and dwarf, zombie, and kindling crashed down in a fiery heap.

* * * * *

Long and pointy teeth bared, the giant wolverine that Newander had become charged the evil priest. The druid had a surprise in mind, an attack that the priest's cloth vestments, however strengthened, might not be able to withstand. Just before he reached the mark, Newander spun over suddenly and loosed a cloud of vile musk.

The disgusting spray rolled over Barjin, stinging his eyes, permeating his clothing, and nearly overwhelming him. He fell back as quickly as he could, trying to escape the cloud, gagging and gasping.

Newander's pursuit was furious. He hooked his claws around the backpeddling priest's knees and bore Barjin to the ground. Barjin kicked and scrambled, but the wolverine was too quick and strong to be easily dislodged. Newander bit into Barjin's thigh, tearing and gnawing. Still the magical vestments repelled the attacks, but they seemed not so invulnerable now. The stinking musk clung to them as would an acid, already wearing at their integrity.

Barjin twisted and screamed. He couldn't see through the burn in his eyes; he couldn't think straight against the suddenness of the attack. He felt the gnawing bites grow sharper and knew that he was in trouble. Very soon, the wolverine would be through his vestments and those wicked teeth would be tearing at his exposed thigh.

The Screaming Maiden reached out empathically to Barjin, calmed him and let him see through its eyes. Barjin stopped his struggling and followed the mace's lead. Newander burrowed in, but the Screaming Maiden bit back.

Barjin hit the wolverine perhaps a dozen times; each strike put more blood and more fur into the hungry mace's gaping mouth. The burrowing stopped, but Barjin kept pounding.

* * * * *

"Ow! Ow! Ow! Ow! Ow!" Pikel grunted, rolling out of the burning pile. His clothes had caught in several places; his beard no longer appeared green, but the thick-skinned dwarf had taken no real damage in his tumble with the flaming zombie, and he rolled about the floor, suffocating the last stubborn embers.

Ivan started toward his brother but changed direction suddenly, seeing that Mullivy, too, had begun to rise. Ivan had seen enough of that one. He crept over, using the crackle of the fire to cover his footsteps, and took up a position just to the side of the rising zombie.

Mullivy was no longer burning. Barjin's protection spell kept the flames from his rotting flesh, and now all the oil and clothing, the fuel for his fires, had been consumed. He came up and inadvertently focused on Pikel, taking no notice of the dwarf winding up just behind his shoulder.

Ivan quickly put a finger across each side of his doublebladed axe, testing to see which edge was the sharper. He shrugged then—both seemed equally capable—and whipped the blade across at his own eye level. It sliced just above the zombie's shoulder, as Ivan had planned, and hit the creature squarely on the side of the neck. More than the weakened flesh of a zombie's thin neck would be needed to slow the blow of an enraged Ivan Bouldershoulder.

Ivan smiled with grim satisfaction as the zombie tumbled to the side, its head spinning through the air far from its body.

"Oo!" remarked an appreciative and admiring Pikel.

"Had it coming," Ivan snorted back, sharing a smile with the brother he had thought dead.

Their mirth was short-lived. Mullivy's corpse stood up between them, deaf and blind but flailing wildly with both arms. One connected on the side of Pikel's head, knocking off his pot helmet.

"Oo!" Pikel squeaked again, and he slipped one step to the side and smacked the headless zombie with his club. He leaned and glanced at Ivan and both brothers understood the proper tactics.

They worked in unison, two dwarves who knew each other's moves as well as his own. They surrounded the zombie, one on either side, and moved synchronously in circles. Ivan prodded Mullivy's shoulder, then jumped back. The zombie shifted and waved its arms futilely at the empty air. Pikel, behind the monster, waded in with a heavy blow.

Mullivy spun to get at the newest attacker, and Ivan came in behind, launching an overhead chop into the zombie's shoulder with enough force to take off one arm.

It went on for a long while, though both dwarves actually would have preferred to make this fun last a bit longer. Finally, though, Mullivy's dismembered corpse fell to the floor and did not try to rise.

* * * * *

Still dazed and disoriented, Cadderly witnessed the horrors at the altar from across the room. He knew that Newander was probably dead, and he knew, too, that the evil priest would advance next toward Danica.

He saw his love, climbing up from the floor, trembling violently from the chilling frost and gasping and squinting on the edges of Newander's musk cloud.

Blood stained one of Barjin's legs, and he limped noticeably as he struggled away from the still wolverine's stubborn clutch, but the priest's expression showed only rage, and he waved his mace with sure and easy swings.

"Newander," Cadderly called hopelessly, desperately, wanting someone to intervene and stop this madness. He knew that the druid, his head and back a bloody pulp, would never answer.

Danica moved next, drawing her crystalline daggers and launching them in rapid succession. The first hit the priest in the shoulder, drawing just a tiny line of blood. The second had even less success. It managed to cut through the priest's conical cap, but the angle of the hat deflected it above Barjin's head, where it hung weirdly and harmlessly.

Barjin rubbed his eyes, stepped over the druid, and bore down on Danica. She fell into a low, defensive posture as though she would spring into him, but then dove straight backward.

Cadderly understood Danica's reaction; she feared another blast from that awful mace. And even as Cadderly watched, the priest brought the weapon in line.

Cadderly watched Danica move back beside the altar, steadily backpedaling from the advancing priest. All of Cadderly's pain, so overwhelming just a moment ago, suddenly seemed insignificant next to Danica's troubles. He shook the dizziness away, denied the weakness in his limbs, and forced himself to his knees, drawing his crossbow and fitting another dart.

He nearly swooned from the permeating cold and bit his lip right through in fighting against it, understanding the price of failure. He leveled the crossbow Barjin's way, had the evil priest in line, and knew that those vestments would not stop the enchanted dart.

He hesitated. A voice screamed in protest inside Cadderly's head, a distant echo of the vow he had made when he had first decided to construct the bow and darts. "Not as a weapon!" he growled under his breath, but as the bow began to slip toward the floor, Cadderly looked back at Danica, growled in defiance, and tightened his grip. Struggling with his conscience through every inch, he stubbornly brought the crossbow up level again.

Cadderly nearly cried out a moment later, believing his hesitation might have cost Danica dearly. Barjin launched a series of mighty blows at the young woman, who somehow managed to stagger out of the biting mace's grasp.

Cadderly saw an out.

"Feel the cold," he heard Barjin snarl, distantly, as though he were viewing it all through a crystal ball. The priest held the cruel mace out in front of him, its mouth opened wide.

Danica, agile despite her wounds, desperately leaped to the side.

"No!" Cadderly cried, and his dart found its way right between the evil weapon's fangs.

There was a sharp crack, and Barjin barely managed to keep his grip on the jolted mace. For an interminable moment, nothing at all seemed to happen, but Cadderly could tell from the priest's shocked expression that something was indeed going on within Barjin's prized weapon.

Without warning, the top of the Screaming Maiden's head blew off. Barjin still held the broken weapon by the handle; he seemed as if he could not let go. Multicolored sparks flared as the magical energy burst forth unbridled, showering the entire center region of the room.

"Oo!" Pikel and Ivan squealed together.

The sparks caught on Barjin's vestments, burning little holes. The priest screamed in agony as a spark slipped through the cap's view hole and sizzled into his eye.

Danica fell away, diving and rolling and shielding her own eyes with a raised arm.

The spark shower went on unabated. Blue sparks erupted right into Barjin's head, catching the side of his conical hood as he desperately lurched. Red sparks flew out in a sudden circular explosion, spinning and rising and then falling over Danica, Barjin, and the evil altar. A small fireball popped straight up from the broken mace, exploding into the ceiling. Lighted specks of dust descended, only to be devoured by the continuing shower.

Across the room, Cadderly squinted and wondered if he had inadvertently set something into motion that would destroy them all.

Then it ended. The base of the Screaming Maiden dropped to the floor and sputtered to a smoldering death.

Off came Barjin's conical hood, and then off, too, came the fast-burning vestments. They fell apart, destroyed by both the wolverine musk and the sparks, as Barjin clawed at them, frantically trying to get the hot embers away from his skin.

He cursed and spat at his own foolishness for putting the spell of fire protection on his zombie instead of on himself. The priest's eyes darted wildly. Cadderly was still kneeling.

To his side, the triumphant dwarves stood over the gruesome remains of the zombie. Then his gaze settled on Danica, apparently unarmed and unarmored, who seemed the easiest target. Wiping the musk and sparks from her face, she wasn't even looking at him.

Barjin had made many mistakes in his life, but none were more complete than his assumption that Danica would be an easy catch. He reached out for her, meaning to hook her around the neck with his strong arm and bring her in, choking, against his chest.

His arm had almost reached her shoulder when Danica reacted. She spun fully and used her momentum to drive her finger hard against Barjin's shoulder.

"I already tried that!" Cadderly warned, but he fell silent, and Barjin's arm fell dead.

The priest looked down in amazement at his numbed right arm. He started to strike out with his left, but Danica was simply too quick for him. She caught his punch in midswing, hooked her fingers over his hand, and jerked his thumb back so forcefully that, with a crack of bones that sounded as loudly as one of Pikel's tree trunk hits, Barjin's thumbnail touched his wrist.

Danica wasn't finished. With a slight twist, she cupped her fingers around Barjin's, curling her fingertips over the top of the priest's hand. Looking Barjin straight in the eye, Danica squeezed, her grip forcing Barjin's top knuckles back in on themselves and sending waves of excruciating pain rolling up his arm. He tried to resist, mentally telling his arm to pull away, but Danica's assault blocked out his determined call; the unrelenting pain prevented him from taking any actions against her, or any actions at all. Even if his other arm had not been "killed," he could not have responded.

He gurgled indecipherably; all the world became a blur.

Danica sneered and pulled down on the trapped hand, driving Barjin to his knees. She tightened her free hand into a ball and lined up Barjin's face.

"Danica . . ." breathed a horrified Cadderly.

"Here, now, don't we get a piece of him?" came a gruff call from the side. "He's the one who killed me brother."

Pikel turned incredulously on Ivan. "Oh?"

"Well, he tried to kill me brother," Ivan corrected, grinning from ear to ear.

Danica uncurled her fist. Her anger was lost in sadness and concern as she looked at Cadderly. The pitiful image stopped her cold. Cadderly was still kneeling, staring at Danica, his hands outstretched in a silent plea and his gray eyes unconsciously judging her.

Danica twisted Barjin's arm around, cupped her other arm under his shoulder and sent him rolling toward the dwarves.

Ivan scooped him up roughly and half-rolled and half-bounced him to Pikel, crying, "Ye killed me brother!"

"Me brudder!" Pikel echoed, spinning the dizzy priest about and launching him back at Ivan.

Ivan caught him and sent him bounding back.

Cadderly realized that the dwarf's game could easily get out of hand. Both were injured, and angry, and with the cursing bottle spewing smoke so very close, their pain and rage could bring them to new heights of violence.

"Do not kill him!" Cadderly screamed at them. Pikel looked at him incredulously and Ivan caught Barjin, slammed the priest to the ground, and held him by the hair.

"Not kill him?" Ivan asked. "What're ye thinking to do with this one?"

"Do not kill him!" Cadderly demanded again. He suspected that he'd need more than the protests of his own conscience to convince the agitated dwarves, so he played a pragmatic game. "We need to question him, to learn if he has allies and where they might be."

"Yeah!" roared Ivan. "What about it?" He jerked Barjin's head back so violently that Cadderly thought the dwarf had broken the man's neck.

"Not now, Ivan," Cadderly explained. "Later, in the library, where we will find maps and writings to aid us in our interrogation."

"Ye're a lucky one, ye are," Ivan said, putting his considerable nose right against Barjin's, pushing the priest's smaller proboscis flat against his cheek. "I'd get ye talking, don't ye doubt!"

Indeed Barjin didn't doubt Ivan's words, but he hardly felt lucky, especially when Ivan hoisted him back up and bounced him over to Pikel once again.

Cadderly walked over and draped his arm across Danica's shoulders. She stood quietly, looking down at the druid who had sacrificed everything for their cause. Newander's bones continued to crackle, as his body tried to revert to its natural form in death. He got about halfway there. His calm and wise face once more became recognizable, and most of the wolverine hair disappeared, but then the transition stopped. Death had stolen the magic, the energy.

"He was a good friend," Cadderly whispered, but he thought his words incredibly lame. Words could not carry the sense of grief that he felt, both for the druid and for the many others who had perished under the curse—the curse that he had loosed.

That thought inevitably led Cadderly's gaze to the altar and the bottle, still pouring smoke, oblivious to the defeat of its guiding priest.

"It is for me to do," Cadderly surmised, hoping he was right. He took the stopper from the altar and gingerly reached out, his mind rushing through a hundred different scenarios of what would happen if he were unable to close the bottle.

He was not. He placed the stopper over the bottle and patted it down, ending the smoky stream.

Cadderly felt a bump on his shoulder and thought that Danica had put her head on him for support. He turned to acknowledge her apparent relief, but she limply fell past him, face down to the floor.

Back by the door, the others went down, too. Barjin tumbled heavily over Ivan, and for a moment, not a thing moved.

Only Barjin got back up, snarling and cursing.

"You," he said accusingly at Cadderly. The evil priest grabbed Ivan's axe in his one working arm and headed Cadderly's way.

Twenty-Four
The Most Fatal Horror

The shock brought Druzil abruptly from his sleepy state. The bottle had been closed! The chaos curse, which Druzil had waited decades to witness, had been defeated! The imp still could recognize the misty magic in the air, but already it was beginning to diminish.

Druzil reached out with his thoughts toward Barjin but found telepathic communication to the priest blocked by a wall of rage. He didn't really want to go into the altar room; he had seen the formidable dwarves tear apart Barjin's zombie and feared another dart from the young priest. When Druzil glanced around at the empty corridors, he realized that he had no other way to go. He reached down to the small pouch hanging on the base of one wing and pulled it free, clutching it in his taloned hands.

He crept up to the door. Beyond Mullivy's chopped up remains lay the two unconscious dwarves, and farther in, by the altar, a young woman. Druzil's surprise at the unexpected scene lasted only as long as it took the imp to consider what had transpired. The sudden shock of the chaos curse's end, the termination of the magic that had permeated these peoples' thoughts so fully, had overcome them.

Druzil saw Barjin advance on the young priest—and now the imp knew that this young man had been the catalyst, the one who had opened the bottle. Apparently, he also had been the one to close it.

The great evil priest seemed not so powerful in Druzil's eyes anymore. Barjin's vestments and weapon were gone, one arm hung limply at his side, and, most important, he had allowed the bottle to be closed.

There it rested, powerless, atop the altar. Druzil had an impulse to go and get it, to whisk it away through the fire gate back to Castle Trinity. The imp quickly dismissed that notion.

Not only would he have to get within striking distance of the young man who earlier had brought him down, but if he took the bottle and Barjin somehow survived the day, the priest's continuing mission at the library would be futile. And the priest would not be happy.

No, Druzil decided, right now the bottle was not worth the many risks. If Barjin survived, perhaps the priest would find another catalyst to rejuvenate the curse. Druzil could get back here if that came to pass.

The imp opened the small pouch he held and looked away from the impending battle, to the brazier that, fortunately, still burned.

* * * * *

Cadderly started to reach for another dart but realized that the evil priest would get to him before he could load it. Even if he did get his crossbow readied, Cadderly doubted that he could find the courage to use it against a living man.

Barjin sensed his ambivalence. "You should have let the dwarves kill me," he snickered.

"No!" Cadderly replied firmly. He dropped his crossbow and slipped one finger into his pocket, into the loop of his spindle-disks.

"Did you really believe that I would provide information, that keeping me alive would prove beneficial?" Barjin asked.

Cadderly shook his head. Barjin had missed the point. Cadderly had only made that claim to convince Ivan and Pikel not to kill him. His true motives in keeping Barjin alive had nothing to do with information, but with his own desire not to kill a man he did not have to kill. "We had no reason to kill you," he said evenly. "The fight was already won."

"So you believed," snarled Barjin. He skipped across the remaining distance to Cadderly and whipped Ivan's axe across as viciously as his wounded hand would allow.

Anticipating the attack, Cadderly easily dodged aside. He pulled his hand from his pocket and sent his spindle-disks flying out at Barjin. They connected with a thud on Barjin's chest, but the mighty priest was more startled than injured.

He looked at Cadderly—or more pointedly, at Cadderly's coiled weapon hand—for a moment, then laughed aloud.

Cadderly nearly threw himself at the mocking priest, but he realized that was exactly what his opponent wanted him to do. His only chance in this fight was to play defensively, the same way he had defeated Kierkan Rufo back in his room. He grinned widely against the continuing laughter and tried to appear as confident as possible.

Barjin was not Kierkan Rufo. The evil priest had seen countless battles, had defeated seasoned warriors in single combat, and had directed armies marching across the Vaasan plains.

After just a single viewing, this veteran's confident smile revealed that he had surmised the limitations of Cadderly's strange weapon, and he knew as well as Cadderly that he would have to make a huge mistake if the young priest was to have any chance.

"You should not have returned to this place," Barjin said, calmly. "You should have left the Edificant Library altogether and given up what was already lost."

Cadderly paused to consider the unexpected words, and the even more unexpected, almost resigned, tone. "I erred," he replied, "when first I came down here. I returned only to correct the wrong." He glanced over at the bottle to emphasize his point. "And now I have done that."

"Have you?" Barjin teased. "Your friends are down, young fool. All those in the library are down, I would guess. When you closed the bottle, you weakened your allies more than your enemies."

Cadderly could not deny the priest's taunt, but he still believed that he had done the right thing in closing the bottle. He would find a way to revive his friends, and all the others. Perhaps they were only sleeping.

"Do you truly believe that, once loosed, *Tuanta Quiro Miancay*, the Most Fatal Horror, could be defeated simply by placing the stopper back in the flask?" Barjin smiled widely. "Look," he said, pointing over at the altar. "Even now the agent of my goddess Talona battles its way back through your pitiful barrier, back into the air it has claimed as Talona's domain."

Cadderly should have seen the trick coming, but his own insecurity concerning the unknown bottle and curse caused him to glance to the side again. Still, he was not caught completely off his guard when Barjin waded straight in, growling and swinging.

Cadderly ducked under one cut, then rolled to the side as Barjin reversed his swing and came with a wicked overhead chop. Cadderly tried to scramble back to his feet, but Barjin was too quick. Before he could rise, he was rolling again, back the other way, to avoid another dipping slice.

Cadderly knew that he couldn't keep this up for long, nor could he launch any effective counters from a position on the floor. Barjin, relentless with the taste of victory on his drooling lips, kept the two-headed axe under perfect control and readied yet another strike. The issue seemed decided.

It became an eerie, almost slow-motion sequence for Cadderly as he watched Barjin maneuvering into position. Was this the moment of his death? What then of Danica and Ivan and Pikel?

The flap of wings sounded by the door. Cadderly, too engrossed with his own dilemma, hardly took note, but Barjin did glance around.

Seeing his opening, Cadderly rolled away as fast as he could.

Barjin easily could have caught up to him, but the priest seemed more concerned with the unexpected appearance of his missing imp.

"Where have you been?" Barjin demanded. Stripped of his vestments and weapon, ragged and beaten, the priest's words did not carry much authority.

Druzil didn't even answer. He floated across to the brazier, pausing only to scoop up Barjin's necromancer's stone.

"Put it back!" Barjin roared. "You play a dangerous game, imp."

Druzil considered the stone, then the priest, then moved to the brazier. His gaze again drifted back to the closed bottle, but if he was considering a try for it, he quickly thought better of it. The enraged Barjin, if not the young priest, surely would strike him down if he went within reach.

"I will protect it," Druzil offered, holding up the stone. "And the bottle?"

"You will run and hide!" Barjin retorted sharply. "You think me beaten?"

Druzil shrugged, his wings nearly burying his head with the action.

"Stay and watch, cowardly imp," Barjin proclaimed. "Watch as I regain my victory and finish off this pitiful library."

Druzil hesitated for a long moment, considering the offer. "I prefer a safer haven," he announced. "I will return when things are under your control."

"Leave the stone!" Barjin commanded.

Druzil's smile revealed much to the priest. The imp clutched the powerful necromancer's stone all the tighter and dropped his powder into the burning brazier. The magical fire flashed and burned with a bluish hue, and Druzil casually stepped through the reopened gate.

"Coward!" Barjin cried. "I will win this day. I will loose *Tuanta Quiro Miancay* again, and you, cowardly imp, will no longer be treated as an ally!"

His threats were lost in the crackle of the brazier's flames.

Barjin spun back on Cadderly, now standing around on the other side of the altar, opposite the priest. "You can still save yourself and your friends," Barjin purred, suddenly friendly. "Join me. Open the bottle once more. The power you will realize . . ."

Cadderly saw through the lie and cut the priest short, though Barjin's sudden charm was effective enough to be shocking. "You need me to open it because you cannot, because it must be opened by one who is not allied with your god," he reasoned.

Barjin's coercive smile did not diminish.

"How can I agree, then? Cadderly asked him. "To do so would be to join with you, but would that not ally me with your designs and with your god? Would that not break the conditions?" Cadderly thought himself quite clever, thought that his logic had cornered the priest, as Barjin mulled the words over.

When Barjin looked back at him, his eyes shining fiercely, Cadderly knew that he had thought wrong.

"Not if you open the bottle for a better reason," Barjin said, turning to view Danica and the dwarves, "to save the woman perhaps." Barjin took a step away.

All fear flew from Cadderly at that moment. He jumped out from behind the altar, meaning to intercept Barjin, determined to stop the priest at any cost. He stopped suddenly, eyes widening in horror.

Another being had entered the room, one that Cadderly had seen before.

Barjin's reaction was just the opposite of Cadderly's. He swung the axe high above his head victoriously, feeling that his base of power was returning, that his fortunes had turned back for the better. "I had thought you destroyed," he said to the scorched mummy.

Khalif, the less than complete spirit, savaged and removed from all sense of sanity, did not respond.

"What are you doing?" the evil priest demanded as the mummy stalked in. Barjin swiped with the axe, hoping to keep the monster at bay, but the mummy simply slapped the weapon from his hand.

"Halt!" Barjin cried. "You must obey me!"

Khalif had other ideas. Before Barjin could say anything else, a heavy arm slammed into the side of his head and sent him tumbling to the wall by the brazier.

Barjin knew his doom. The mummy was out of control, crazed with pain and rage. It hated all life, hated Barjin for bringing it back from its rest. With all that had happened, both to Barjin and to the mummy, the priest's domination was no more.

Barjin looked desperately to the table where he had left the necromancer's stone, the one item that might aid him now against this undead foe. Then he remembered, and he cursed Druzil's abrupt departure.

He propped himself up against the wall and looked about desperately. To his right loomed the burning brazier, the gate reopened but not an escape route for a being of the material plane. To Barjin's left, though, was Pikel's impromptu doorway, an exit to the tunnels beyond the room.

He tried to rise, but a throbbing pain in his head dropped him back to his knees. Undaunted, Barjin began to crawl. Before he could get to the hole, though, the mummy cut him off and slammed him again into the wall. Barjin had no defense against the ensuing onslaught. He raised his one functioning arm, but the mummy's heavy blows snapped it aside.

Cadderly stood very still beside the altar, consciously telling himself to take some action. The fear gripped him, but he at last overcame it by conjuring an image of the mummy's next move after finishing off Barjin. Danica was the next closest target.

He took his crossbow in hand and loaded it, seeking some way to get the monster off the priest. Cadderly had no love for the man, and he held no hopes that helping Barjin might bring some mutually beneficial compromise, but despite the fact that Barjin was his enemy, he could not let the human be killed by this undead monster.

Another problem presented itself as Cadderly leveled his bow for a shot. The imp's passage had reopened the interplanar gate, and now some lower plane denizen had found its way in. A hideous face appeared in the flames, obscure, but huge, and growing more tangible with each passing second.

Cadderly instinctively lined his crossbow up with this newest intruder, but then swung it back at the mummy, realizing that it was his most pressing problem.

Another scorch mark appeared on the mummy's rotted linen; another jolt shook the monster, but the scabrous thing did not turn away from Barjin. The priest managed once to stand up, only to be immediately pounded back to the floor.

A huge black wing tip came out the side of the brazier fire.

Cadderly nearly lost his breath; the creature forming in the flames was monstrous, much larger than the imp.

Cadderly loaded and fired again at the mummy. Another hit, and now, with Barjin offering no resistance, the mummy wheeled about.

Cadderly felt that paralyzing fear welling in him again, but he did not let it slow his practiced movements. He had used more than half his darts and had no idea if he had enough remaining to finally defeat this undead thing, had no idea if his attacks were even causing any real damage to the monster.

Again, he refused to let his fears slow him. Another dart whistled out at the mummy. This one did not explode, but dove through a hole created by a previous dart and cut right through the tattered linen bindings.

At first Cadderly was more concerned with getting another dart fitted; he knew that his miss would allow the monster to close, but then he heard Barjin grunt.

The dart thudded into the chest of the sitting priest. The next interminable second ended with the noise that Cadderly now dreaded, for the dart had enough remaining momentum to collapse and explode.

The mummy took a step out, giving Cadderly a view of the priest. Barjin lay nearly flat. Only his head and shoulders remained propped against the wall. He gasped and clutched the hole in his chest, his eyes unblinking, though he seemed not to see anything, not to be aware of anything beyond his own demise. He gasped again, a gout of blood bursting from his mouth, and then he lay still.

Cadderly did not even think of his movements. His mind seemed to disengage from his body, to give way to his own instincts for survival and his own boiling rage at what he had done. He took up his waterskin under his free arm, popped off the cap, and drove the mummy back toward the wall with a steady stream of blessed water.

The liquid hissed as it struck the evilly enchanted linen, etching blackened scars. The mummy issued a loud, outraged roar and tried to cover up, but it had no way to block the small but painful stream.

In the brazier, a hideous face was clear now, leering hungrily at Cadderly. Cadderly thought to defeat both foes with a single attack. He angled his waterskin, seeking to drive the mummy into the flames, perhaps to topple the brazier and close the gate.

The mummy did indeed recoil from the spray, but if it feared the blessed water, it feared the open flames even more. Try as he might, Cadderly could not force it too near the burning gate.

He apparently was doing some damage, but Cadderly could not afford this stalemate. He was running out of water; then what might he use to finish off the mummy? And if that monster came through the gate . . .

Helplessly, Cadderly fumbled to keep up the stream and to load another dart. He lifted his crossbow toward the mummy, trying to find a vital area beyond its blocking arms. What area, he wondered helplessly, might be the most vulnerable? The eyes? The heart?

The waterskin was empty. The mummy stood straight.

"Last shot," Cadderly muttered resignedly. He started to pull on the trigger, then, as he had with Barjin earlier in the fight, he noticed another possibility.

Pikel's charge through the wall had caused tremendous structural damage. The hole in the brickwork was fully four feet wide and half that again high, nearly reaching the beamed ceiling. One crossbeam, directly above the hole, balanced precariously on a cracked support. Cadderly moved his arm in that direction and fired.

The dart smacked into the wood at the joint between crossbeam and support, exploding into a small fireball, sending splinters everywhere. The crossbeam slipped, but, still attached at its other end, it swung down like a pendulum.

The mummy took only one short step from the wall before the beam slammed into it, driving it sidelong. It pitched into the brazier, taking the fiery tripod and bowl right over with it.

The hideous image of the otherworldly denizen disappeared in a huge fireball. Flames engulfed the mummy, eagerly devouring its layered cloth wrappings. It managed to stagger to its feet—Cadderly wondered with horror if it might survive even this—but then it crumpled and was consumed.

Without the enchanted brazier, the gate was closed, and gone, too, was Barjin's greatest undead monster. The flames flared a couple of times, then burned very low, leaving the room smoky in the dimness of low-burning torches.

Cadderly understood that victory was within his grasp, but he hardly felt in the mood for rejoicing. Newander lay dead at his feet, others had died upstairs, and, perhaps most disconcerting of all to the young scholar, no longer an innocent, he had killed a man.

Barjin remained propped against the wall, his lifeless eyes staring out at Cadderly, holding the defenseless young priest in an accusing gaze.

Cadderly's arm drooped to his side and the crossbow fell to the floor.

Twenty-Five
Out of the Mist

Cadderly so desperately wanted to close those eyes! He willed himself to go over to the dead priest and turn his head away, get that accusing stare off him, but it was an impotent command, and Cadderly knew it. He had not the strength to go anywhere near Barjin. He moved a few short steps to the side, to get to Danica, but looked back and imagined that the dead priest's eyes followed him still.

Cadderly wondered if they would forever.

He slammed his fist on the floor, trying to shake free of the guilt, to accept the priest's stare as a necessary price that he must pay. Events had dictated his actions, he reminded himself, and he determinedly told himself to foster no regrets.

He jumped defensively when a small form suddenly darted in through the opening beside the priest, then managed a weak smile as Percival climbed up him and sat atop his shoulder, chittering and complaining as always. Cadderly patted the squirrel between the ears with a single finger—he needed to do that—then went to his friends.

Danica seemed to be sleeping quite peacefully. She would not wake, though, to Cadderly's call or shake. He found both dwarves in similar states, their thunderous snores complimenting each other in strange, rock-grating harmony. Pikel's snores, in particular, sounded contented.

Cadderly grew worried. He had believed the battle won finally—but why couldn't he wake his friends? How long would they sleep? Cadderly had heard of curses that caused slumber for a thousand years, or until certain conditions had been met, however long that might take.

Perhaps the battle wasn't yet won. He went back to the altar and examined the bottle. It seemed harmless enough now, to the naked eye, so Cadderly decided to look deeper. He moved his thoughts through a series of relaxation exercises that slipped him into a semimeditative trance. The mist was fast dissipating, that much he could tell, and no more was emanating from the stoppered bottle. That gave Cadderly hope; perhaps the slumber would last until the mist was gone.

The bottle itself, though, did not appear completely neutralized. Cadderly sensed a life, an energy, within it, a pulsating evil, contained but not destroyed. It might have been only his imagination, or perhaps what he thought was a life-force was merely a manifestation of his own fears. Cadderly honestly wondered if the remaining flickers within that bottle were playing some role in the lingering mist. The evil priest had called the mist the Most Fatal Horror, an agent of Talona. Cadderly recognized the name of the vile goddess, and the title, normally reserved for Talona's highest-ranking clerics. If this mist was indeed some sort of god-stuff, a simple stopper would not suffice.

Cadderly came out of his trance and sat down to consider the situation. The key, he decided, was to accept the evil priest's description of the bottle and not think of it simply as some secular, though potent, magic.

"Battle gods with gods," Cadderly mumbled a moment later. He stood again before the altar, studying not the bottle, but the reflective, gem-studded bowl in front of it. Cadderly feared what magic this item might contain, but he chanced it without delay, tipping the bowl to the side and dumping out the water stained by the evil priest's foul hands.

He retrieved a piece of cloth, a piece of Barjin's own vestments, and wiped the bowl thoroughly, then found Newander's waterskin, full as usual, out in the hallway beyond Pikel's impromptu door. Cadderly consciously avoided looking at Newander as he reentered the room, meaning to go straight to the altar, but Percival delayed him. The squirrel sat atop the dead druid, still in his semitransformed state.

"Get away from there," Cadderly scolded, but Percival only sat up higher, clicking excitedly and displaying some small item.

"What have you got?" Cadderly asked, moving slowly back so as not to startle the excitable squirrel.

Percival displayed an oak leaf pendant, the holy symbol of Silvanus, dangling from a fine leather thong.

"Do not take that!" Cadderly started to scold, but then he realized that Percival had something in mind.

Cadderly bent low, studying Percival more closely and seeking guidance in the wise druid's face. Newander's visage, so peaceful and accepting of his fate, held him fully.

Percival shrieked in Cadderly's ear, demanding his attention. The squirrel held out the pendant and seemed to motion toward the altar.

Confusion twisted Cadderly's face. "Percival?" he asked.

The squirrel danced an agitated circle, then shook his little head briskly. Cadderly blanched.

"Newander?" he asked meekly.

The squirrel held out the holy symbol.

Cadderly considered it for a moment, then, remembering the druids' creed concerning death as a natural extension of life, he accepted the oak leaf and started back toward the altar.

The squirrel shook suddenly, then leaped back up to Cadderly's shoulder.

"Newander?" Cadderly asked again. The squirrel did not answer. "Percival?" The squirrel perked up its ears.

Cadderly paused and wondered what had just transpired.

His instincts told him that Newander's departing spirit somehow had used Percival's body to get a message to him, but his stubborn sense of reality told him that he probably had imagined the whole episode. Whatever it was, he now had the druid's holy symbol in his hand and he knew that the aid of Silvanus could be only a good thing.

Cadderly wished he had been more attentive in his mundane duties, the simple ceremonies required of the lesser priests of the Edificant Library. His hands trembling, he poured the water from Newander's waterskin into the gem-studded bowl, and added to it, with a silent call to Newander's god, the holy symbol.

Cadderly figured that two gods would be better than one in containing this evil, and also that Newander's god, dedicated to natural order, might be the most effective in battling the curse. He closed his eyes and recited the ceremony to purify the water, stumbling a few times over the words he had not spoken very often.

Then it was completed and Cadderly was left with only his hopes. He lifted the evil bottle and gently immersed it in the bowl. The water went cold and took on the same red hue as that within the bottle, and Cadderly feared that he had not accomplished anything positive.

A moment later, though, the red hue disappeared altogether, from the water and the bottle. Cadderly studied it closely, somehow sensing that the pulsating evil was no more.

Behind him, Pikel's snore was replaced by a questioning, "Oo oi?"

Cadderly scooped up the bowl carefully and looked around.

Danica and both dwarves were stirring, though they were not yet coherent. Cadderly moved across the room to a small cabinet and placed the bowl inside, closing the door as he turned away.

Danica groaned and sat up, holding her head in both hands.

"Me head," Ivan said in a sluggish voice. "Me head."

They exited the tunnel to the south side of the great library half an hour later, Ivan and Pikel bearing Newander's rigid body and both dwarves and Danica sporting tremendous headaches. The dawn, just breaking, looked so good to Cadderly that he considered it a sign that all had been put right and that the nightmare had ended. His three companions groaned loudly and shielded their eyes when they came out into the brightness.

Cadderly would have laughed at them, but when he turned, the sight of Newander stole his mirth.

* * * * *

"Ah, there you are, Rufo," Headmaster Avery said upon entering the angular man's room. Kierkan Rufo lay on his bed and groaned weakly, pained by the many wounds he had received in the last couple of days and by a pounding headache that would not relent.

Avery waddled over toward him, pausing to belch several times. Avery's head ached, too, but it was nothing compared to the agony in his bloated stomach. "Get up, then," the headmaster said, reaching for Rufo's limp wrist. "Where is Cadderly?"

Rufo did not reply, did not even allow himself to blink. The curse was no more, but Rufo had not forgotten all that he had suffered in the past couple of days, at the hands of both Cadderly and the monk, Danica. He had not forgotten his own actions, either, and he feared the accusations that might be brought against him in the coming days.

"We have so very much to do," Avery went on, "so very much. I do not know what has befallen our library, but it is a very wicked business indeed. There are dead, Rufo, many dead, and many more are wandering confused."

Rufo at last forced himself to a sitting position. His face was bruised and caked in several places with dried blood, and his wrists and ankles were still sore from the dwarves' bindings.

He hardly thought of the pain at that moment, however. What had happened to him? What had caused him to so foolishly go after Danica? What had caused him to reveal his jealousy, in the form of outright hostility, so clearly to Cadderly?

"Cadderly," he breathed quietly. He had almost killed Cadderly; he feared that memory nearly as much as the potential consequences. His memories came to him as if from a dark mirror in his heart, and Rufo was not certain that he liked what he saw.

* * * * *

"We have been five days with no further incidents," Dean Thobicus said to the gathering in his audience hall a few days later. All the surviving headmasters, of both the Oghman and Deneiran sects, were present, as well as Cadderly, Kierkan Rufo, and the two remaining druids.

Thobicus shuffled through a pile of reports, then declared, "The Edificant Library will recover."

There was a chorus of somewhat subdued cheers and nods.

The future might have looked bright again, but the recent past, particularly the wholesale slaughter of the visiting Ilmater sect and the death of the heroic druid, Newander, could not be so easily dismissed.

"We have you to thank for it," Thobicus said to Cadderly.

"You and your nonsectarian friends—" he nodded an acknowledgment to the druids"—displayed great bravery and ingenuity in defeating the evil infection that came into our midst."

Kierkan Rufo subtly nudged Headmaster Avery.

"Yes?" Dean Thobicus inquired.

"I have been requested to remind us all that Cadderly, brave though he was, is not without responsibility for this catastrophe," Avery began. He cast a look at Cadderly that showed he was not angered by the young scholar, but that he indeed held Cadderly's actions against the invading priest in high regard.

Cadderly took no offense; after seeing the headmaster under the influences of the curse, he suspected he knew how Avery really felt about him. He almost wished that he could get the headmaster back under the influence of the curse and talking again about Cadderly's father and the young scholar's first days at the library.

It was an absurd notion, but one that Cadderly enjoyed imagining nonetheless. He looked past Avery to the tall and angular man leering over the headmaster's shoulder. Cadderly could point a finger at Rufo, concerning the man's actions against Danica and himself, and including Cadderly's firm belief that Rufo was the one who had knocked him into the catacombs in the first place, but many of Rufo's actions already had been reported and it was unlikely that, given the extraordinary circumstances, any action would be taken against him, or against any of the others caught in the curse. Cadderly, still not fully understanding what the cursing mist had done, was not sure if any reprimands would be appropriate.

As to the most serious charge, Cadderly believed that Rufo had kicked him down the stairs, but he really hadn't seen the blow. Perhaps the evil priest had been in the wine cellar with him and Rufo. Perhaps the priest had immobilized Rufo, as he had Ivan later on, then crept up past the man to knock Cadderly down.

Cadderly shook his head and nearly laughed aloud. It didn't matter, he believed. Now was a time of forgiveness, when all the remaining priests must band together to restore the library.

"Do you find something amusing?" Dean Thobicus asked, somewhat sternly. Cadderly remembered the accusation against him then and realized that his introspection might not have been so timely.

"If I may speak," Arcite interjected.

Thobicus nodded.

"The lad cannot be blamed for opening the bottle," the druid explained. "He is a brave one just for admitting such a thing. Let us all remember the foe he battled, one who beat us all, except for a handful. Were it not for Cadderly, and for my friend and god, the evil one would have proved strong enough to win the day."

"True enough," admitted Dean Thobicus, "and true enough, too, that Cadderly must bear some responsibility for what has transpired. Therefore, I declare that young Cadderly's duties in this incident are not at an end. Who would be better than he to study the works we possess concerning such curses, to learn more of the origin of both the priest and this Most Fatal Horror that he described as an agent of Talona?"

"A year quest?" Cadderly dared to ask, though it was not his place to speak.

"A year quest," Dean Thobicus echoed. "At the end of which you are to deliver a full report to this office. Do not take this responsibility lightly, as you seem to take so many of your responsibilities." He went on with his warnings, reminders of the gravity of the situation, but Cadderly didn't even hear him.

He had been given a year quest, an honor normally bestowed exclusively upon the top-ranking Deneiran priests, and one most often given only to the headmasters themselves!

When Cadderly glanced back to Avery, and to Rufo behind him, he saw that they, too, understood the honor he had been given. Avery tried unsuccessfully to hide his widening smile, and Rufo, even more unsuccessfully, to hide his frustration. Indeed, Rufo, surely out of order and surely to be punished for it, turned about and stormed out of the audience chamber.

The meeting was adjourned soon after that, and Cadderly came out flanked by the two druids.

"I thank you," Cadderly said to Arcite.

"It is we who should be grateful," Arcite reminded him. "When the curse befell us all, it was Arcite and Cleo who could not fight against it and who would have been beaten."

Cadderly couldn't hide a chuckle. The druids, and Danica and the dwarves, who had come over to join the group, looked at him curiously.

"It is ironic indeed," Cadderly explained. "Newander thought he had failed because he could not find it in his heart to become as you had, to revert to an animal form in mind and body."

"Newander did not fail," Arcite declared.

"Silvanus held him close," Cleo added.

Cadderly nodded and smiled again, remembering the sincere peace on the departed druid's face. He looked up at Arcite suddenly and thought about the squirrel incident, and whether the druids would know if Newander's departing spirit had communicated through Percival's body. He stopped himself, though, before the question was asked. Maybe some things were better left to the imagination.

"I'll be needing that crossbow of yours, and a dart or two," Ivan said after the druids took their leave. "Figuring to make one for meself!"

Cadderly instinctively reached for the weapon belted on his hip, then recoiled suddenly and shook his head. "No more," he said gravely.

"It's a fine weapon," Ivan protested.

"Too fine," Cadderly replied. He had heard recently of smoke powder, of cannons hurling huge projectiles at opposing armies, elsewhere in the Realms. Avery's scolding, calling Cadderly a "Gondsman," echoed in the young scholar's mind, for rumors claimed it was the Gondish priests who had loosed this new and terrible weapon on the world.

For all that it had aided him, Cadderly did not look upon his crossbow with admiration. The thought of copies being constructed horrified him. Truly, the crossbow's power was meager compared to a wizard's fireball or the summoned lightning of a druid, but it was a power that could fall into the hands of the untrained. Warriors and magic-users alike spent years training both their minds and their bodies to attain such proficiency. Weapons such as smoke powder, and Cadderly's crossbow-and-dart design, circumvented that need of any sacrifice or self-discipline. Cadderly understood that it was that very discipline that held the powers in check.

Ivan started to protest again, but Danica reached around him and covered his mouth with her hand. Ivan pulled away and grumbled a few curses, but he let the matter drop.

Cadderly looked over to Danica, knowing that she understood. For the same reasons that Danica would not show him the Withering Touch, he could not let his design become commonplace.

* * * * *

Druzil waited for a very long time in the smoking stench of the lower planes. He knew that Barjin's gate had been closed again shortly after he left, though he had no way of knowing if the priest had done it intentionally or not. Had Barjin survived? If so, had he found another victim to reopen the cursing flask?

The questions nagged at the imp. Even if Barjin had not succeeded or survived, even if the precious bottle had been destroyed, he knew now the potential for his recipe and vowed that one day the chaos curse would again descend on the Realms.

"Do hurry, Aballister," the imp groaned nervously. The wizard had not summoned him back to the material plane, a fact that the nervous imp could not ignore, particularly since the wizard still possessed the recipe. If Aballister somehow had learned of Druzil's mental connection with Barjin, the wizard might never trust Druzil enough to bring him back.

The imp knew not how many days had passed—time was measured differently in the lower planes—but finally he heard a distant call, a familiar voice. He saw the distant flicker of a fiery gate and heard the call again, more demanding this time.

Off he soared, through the planar tunnel, and soon he crawled out of Aballister's brazier to stand in a familiar room in Castle Trinity.

"Too long," the imp snorted derisively, trying to gain an upper hand. "Why did you delay?"

Aballister cast a foul look at him. "I did not know that you had returned to the lower planes. My contact with Barjin was broken."

Druzil's long and pointy ears perked up at the mention of the priest, a fact that brought a sneer to Aballister's lips. Across the room, the magical mirror sat broken, a wide crack running its length.

"What happened?" Druzil asked, leading Aballister's gaze to the mirror.

"I overextended its powers," the wizard replied. "Trying to aid Barjin."

"And?"

"Barjin is dead," Aballister said. "He has failed utterly."

Druzil ran a clawed hand along the wall and snarled in distress.

Aballister was more pragmatic. "The priest was too reckless," he declared. "He should have taken more care, should have set his goals on a more vulnerable target. The Edificant Library! It is the most defended structure in all the region, a fortress teeming with mighty priests who would seek our destruction if they learned of our plans! Barjin was a fool, do you hear? A fool!"

Druzil, ever the practical familiar, thought it prudent not to disagree. Besides, Aballister's observations apparently were correct.

"But fear not, my leathery friend," Aballister went on, his attitude becoming more friendly toward his imp. "It is but a minor setback to our cause."

Druzil thought Aballister might be enjoying this just a bit too much. Barjin may have been a potential rival, but he was also, after all, an ally.

"Ragnor and his charges march for Shilmista," Aballister went on. "The ogrillon will win against the elves and sweep south around the mountains. The region will fall to more conventional methods."

Druzil allowed himself a bit of optimism, though he preferred a more insidious attack method, like the chaos curse. "But he was so close, my master," the imp whined. "Barjin had brought the library to its knees. It was his to finish, and then the cornerstone of any resistance we might face would have been gone before the rest of the region even knew the danger in its midst." Druzil clenched a clawed hand before him. "He had victory in his grasp!"

"His grasp was not as strong as he believed," Aballister sharply pointed out.

"Perhaps," Druzil conceded, "but it was that one human, the young man who had first opened the bottle, who came back to defeat him. Barjin should have killed that one right away."

Aballister nodded, remembering the last image he had seen of Barjin's altar room, and could not help but smile.

"Surprisingly resourceful, that one," Druzil sputtered.

"Not so surprising," Aballister replied casually. "He is my son."

Epilogue

He huddled between towering piles of huge tomes, immersed in his important year quest. The security of the Edificant Library was at stake, Cadderly believed, and his ability to discern the source of the chaos curse and the background of the powerful priest would be a critical factor in re-establishing that security.

Cadderly knew that the implications of what had happened might go far beyond the library itself. Carradoon, on the lake to the east, was not a large and well-fortified town, and the elves of Shilmista were neither numerous nor particularly interested in affairs beyond their own borders. If the appearance of the evil priest foreshadowed things to come, then Cadderly's headmasters desperately needed information.

The young scholar alternated his time researching known curses and known symbols. He pored through dozens of tomes and ancient, yellowed scrolls, and interviewed every scholar, host or visitor, who had any knowledge of either field.

The evil priest had proclaimed Talona as his goddess, and the trident symbol was somewhat similar to the Lady of Poison's triangle-and-teardrop insignia, but what particular organization that trident represented, Cadderly could not discover.

Danica watched Cadderly from a distance, not wanting to disturb his vital work. She understood the discipline that Cadderly now needed, the focused determination that excluded everything else, including her, from his days. The young woman was not concerned; she knew that as soon as time permitted, she and Cadderly would continue their relationship.

For Ivan and Pikel, the days passed with wonderful boredom. Both dwarves had been beaten badly in the catacombs, but both were soon well on the way to recovery. Pikel held fast to his resolve to become a druid, and Ivan, after witnessing Newander's heroics, no longer chided him about his choice.

"I'm not thinking a dwarf would make a druid," Ivan huffed whenever anyone asked him about it, "but it's me brother's choice to be making."

So life gradually returned to normal at the proud and ancient library. Summer came on in full and the sunshine seemed like deliverance from the nightmare. Those who came to the library's front doors that season often noticed, basking high in the branches of a tree along the road, a plump white squirrel, usually licking casasa-nut and butter from its paws.

* * * * *

To the elf prince Elbereth, the sun did not seem so marvelous. Rather, it revealed him, leaving him open and vulnerable.

It was a strange feeling for the skilled warrior, who could put four arrows in the air before the first ever hit its mark, and who could cut down an enraged giant with his finely crafted sword.

It was that same warrior training that told Elbereth to be afraid now. A week before, he had led a contingent of elves against a small party of huge and hairy bugbears. His troops had won the encounter quickly, but, unlike the expected rabble filtering down from the wild mountains, these bugbears were well disciplined and well armed, and each wore a glove bearing a similar insignia.

Elbereth had fought in several wars. He knew an advance scouting party when he encountered one.

The determined elf plodded on through the broken mountain passes, leading his weary horse. The multitude of bells on the shining white steed did not ring cheerily in Elbereth's ears, nor did the sun seem so warm. The magic of Shilmista had long been on the wane; Elbereth's proud people were not so numerous anymore. If a major attack did come, Shilmista would be sorely pressed.

Elbereth had left the forest, bearing one of the gloves, to discover what his people might be up against, to the only place in the region where he might learn of his enemies: the Edificant Library.

He looked again at the curious trident-and-bottle design on the glove, then high and far in the distance, to the ivy-strewn structure just coming into view.

The Cleric Quintet • Book Two

In Sylvan Shadows

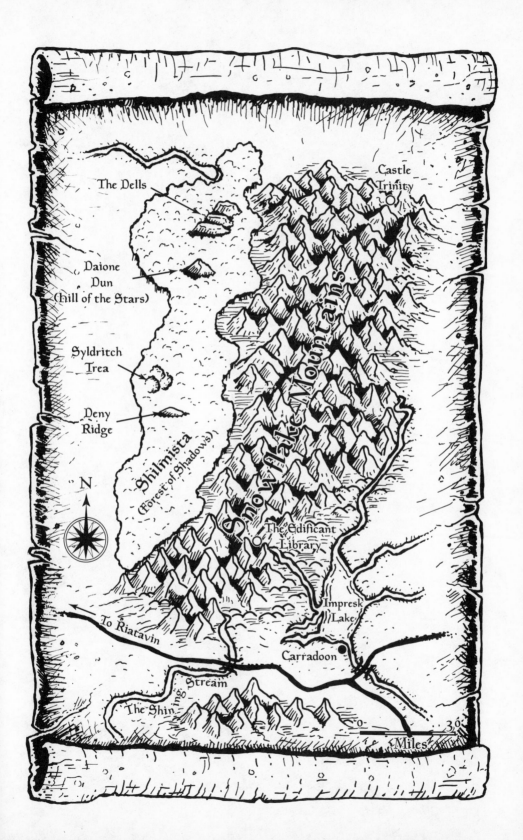

The Dells

Daione
Dun
(hill of the Stars)

Syldritch
Trea

Deny
Ridge

Shilmista
(Forest of Shadows)

N

Castle
Trinity

Snowflake Mountains

The Edificant
Library

Impresk
Lake

To Riatavin

Carradoon

Shining Stream

The Shin

0   30

Miles

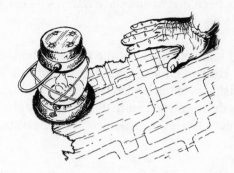

Prologue

C adderly moved his quill out toward the inkwell, then changed his mind and put the instrument down on his desk. He looked out the window at the foliage surrounding the Edificant Library, and at Percival, the white squirrel, tangling with acorns along the rain gutter of the lower level. It was the month of Eleasias, Highsun, the height of summer, and the season had been unusually bright and warm so high in the Snowflake Mountains.

Everything was as it always had been for Cadderly—at least, that's what the young scholar tried to convince himself. Percival was at play in the sunshine; the library was secure and peaceful once more; the lazy remainder of summer promised leisure and quiet walks.

As it always had been.

Cadderly dropped his chin into his palm, then ran his hand back through his sandy brown hair. He tried to concentrate on the peaceful images before him, on the quiet summer world of the Snowflake Mountains, but eyes looked back at him from the depths of his mind: the eyes of a man he had killed.

Nothing would ever be the same. Cadderly's gray eyes were no longer so quick to turn up in that boyish, full-faced smile.

Determinedly this time, the young scholar poked the quill into the ink and smoothed the parchment before him.

Entry Number Seventeen
by Cadderly of Carradoon
Appointed Scholar, Order of Deneir

Fourth Day of Eleasias, 1361 (Year of the Maidens)

> It has been five weeks since Barjin's defeat,
> yet I see his dead eyes.

Cadderly stopped and scribbled out the thought, both from the parchment and from his mind. He looked again out the window, dropped his quill, and rubbed his hands briskly over his boyish face. This was important, he reminded himself. He hadn't made an entry in more than a week, and if he failed at this year quest, the consequences to all the region could be devastating. Again the quill went into the inkwell.

> It has been five weeks since we defeated the curse
> that befell the Edificant Library. The most distressing
> news since then: Ivan and Pikel Bouldershoulder
> have left the library, in pursuit of Pikel's aspirations to
> druidhood. I wish Pikel well, though I doubt that the
> woodland priests will welcome a dwarf into their
> order. The dwarves would not say where they were
> going (I do not believe they themselves knew). I miss
> them terribly, for they, Danica, and Newander were
> the true heroes in the fight against the evil priest
> named Barjin—if that was his name.

Cadderly paused for a few moments. Assigning a name to the man he had killed did not make things easier for the innocent young scholar. It took him some time before he could concentrate on the information necessary to his entry, the interview he had done with the interrogating priests.

> The clerics who called back the dead man's spirit
> warned me to take their findings as probable rather
> than exact. Witnesses from beyond the grave are
> often elusive, they explained, and Barjin's stubborn
> spirit proved to be as difficult an opponent as the
> priest had been in life. Little real information was gar-
> nered, but the clerics came away believing that the
> evil priest was part of a conspiracy—one of conquest
> that still threatens the region, I must assume. That
> only increases the importance of my task.

Again, many moments passed before Cadderly was able to continue. He looked at the sunshine, at the white squirrel, and pushed away those staring eyes.

> Barjin uttered another name, Talona, and that

bodes ill indeed for the library and the region. The Lady of Poison, Talona is called, a vile deity of chaos, restricted by no moral code whatsoever. I am hard-pressed to explain one discrepancy: Barjin hardly fit the description of a Talona disciple; he had not scarred himself in any visible way, as priests worshiping the Lady of Poison typically do. The holy symbol he wore, though, the trident with small vials atop each point, does resemble the triangular, three-teardrop design of Talona.

But with this, too, we have been led down a trail that leads only to assumption and reasonable guesses. More exact information must be gained, and gained soon, I fear.

This day, my quest has taken a different turn. Prince Elbereth of Shilmista, a most respected elf lord, has come to the library, bearing gloves taken from a band of marauding bugbears in the elven wood. The insignia on these gloves match Barjin's symbol exactly—there can be little doubt that the bugbears and the evil priest were allied.

The headmasters have made no decisions yet, beyond agreeing that someone should accompany Prince Elbereth back to the forest. It seems only logical that I will be their choice. My quest can go no further here; already I have perused every source of information on Talona in our possession—our knowledge is not vast on this subject. And, concerning the magical elixir that Barjin used, I have looked through every major alchemical and elixir tome and have consulted extensively with Vicero Belago, the library's resident alchemist. Further study will be required as time permits, but my inquiries have hit against dead ends. Belago believes that he would learn more of the elixir if he had the bottle in his possession, but the headmasters have flatly refused that request. The lower catacombs have been sealed—no one is to be allowed down there, and the bottle is to remain where I put it, immersed in a font of blessed water in the room that Barjin used for his vile altar.

The only clues remaining, then, lead to Shilmista.
Always have I wanted to visit the enchanted forest, to
witness the elves' dance and hear their melancholy
song. But not like this.

Cadderly set the quill down and blew lightly on the parchment to help dry the
ink. His entry seemed terribly short, considering that he had not recorded anything for many days and there was so much to catch up on. It would have to do,
though, for Cadderly's thoughts were too jumbled for him to make sense of them
in writing.

Orphaned at a very young age, Cadderly had lived at the Edificant Library
since his earliest recollections. The library was a fortress, never threatened in
modern times until Barjin had come, and, to Cadderly, orcs and goblins, undead
monsters, and evil wizards had been the stuff of tales in dusty books.

It had suddenly become all too real and Cadderly had been thrust into the
midst of it. The other priests, even Headmaster Avery, called him "hero" for his
actions in defeating Barjin. Cadderly saw things differently, though. Confusion
and chaos and blind fate had facilitated his every move. Even killing Barjin had
been an accident—a fortunate accident?

Cadderly honestly didn't know, didn't understand what Deneir wanted or
expected of him. Accident or not, the act of killing Barjin haunted the young
scholar. He saw Barjin's dead eyes in his thoughts and in his dreams, staring at
him, accusing him.

The scholar-priest had to wear the mantle of hero, because others had placed
it there, but he felt certain the mantle's weight would bow his shoulders until he
broke.

Outside the window, Percival danced and played along the rain gutter as
warm sunshine filtered through the thick leaves of the huge oaks and maples
common to the mountainside. Far, far below, Impresk Lake glittered, quiet and
serene, in the gentle rays of the summer light.

To Cadderly, the "hero," it all seemed a horrible facade.

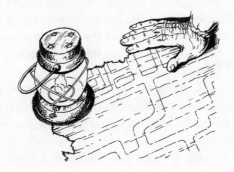

One

By Surprise

Twilight.

Fifty elven archers lay concealed across the first ridge; fifty more waited behind them, atop the second in this rolling, up-and-down region of Shilmista known as the Dells.

The flicker of torches came into view far away through the trees.

"That is not the leading edge," the elf maiden Shayleigh warned, and indeed, lines of goblins were soon spotted much closer than the torches, traveling swiftly and silently through the darkness. Shayleigh's violet eyes glittered eagerly in the starlight; she kept the cowl of her cloak up high, fearing that the luster of her golden hair, undiminished by the quiet colors of night, would betray her position.

The advancing goblins came on. Great long bows bent back; long arrows poised to strike.

The skilled elves held their bows steady, not one of them trembling under the great pull of their powerful weapons. They looked around somewhat nervously, though, awaiting Shayleigh's command, their discipline severely tested as orcs and goblins and larger, more ominous forms came almost to the base of the ridge.

Shayleigh moved down the line quickly. "Two arrows away and retreat," she instructed, using a silent code of hand signals and hushed whispers. "On my call."

Orcs were on the hillock, climbing steadily toward the ridge. Still Shayleigh held the elven volley, trusting in the erupting chaos to keep her enemies at bay.

A large orc, just ten paces from the ridge, stopped suddenly and sniffed the air. Those in line behind the beast similarly stopped, glancing about in an effort to discern what their companion had sensed. The pig-faced creature tilted its head back, trying to bring some focus to the unusual form lying just a few feet ahead of it.

"Now!" came Shayleigh's cry.

The lead orc never managed to squeal a warning before the arrow dove into its face, the force of the blow lifting the creature from the ground and sending it tumbling back down the slope. All across the northern face of the hillock, the invading monsters screamed out and fell, some hit by two or three arrows in just a split second.

Then the ground shook under the monstrous charge as the invading army's second rank learned of the enemy concealed atop the ridge. Almost every arrow of the elves' ensuing volley hit the mark, but it hardly slowed the sudden press of drooling, monstrous forms.

According to plan, Shayleigh and her troops took flight, with goblins, orcs, and many ogres on their heels.

Galladel, the elf king of Shilmista, commanding the second line, turned his archers loose as soon as the monsters appeared over the lip of the first ridge. Arrow after arrow hit home; four elves together concentrated their fire on single targets—huge ogres—and the great monsters were brought crashing down.

Shayleigh's group crossed the second ridge and fell into place beside their elven companions, then turned their long bows and joined in the massacre. With horrifying speed, the valley between the ridges filled with corpses and blood.

One ogre slipped through the throng and nearly got to the elven line—even had its club raised high for a strike but a dozen arrows burrowed into its chest, staggering it. Shayleigh, fearless and grim, leaped over the closest archer and drove her fine sword into the stunned monster's heart.

* * * * *

As soon as he heard the fighting in the Dells, the wizard Tintagel knew that he and his three magic-using associates would soon be hard-pressed by monstrous invaders. Only a dozen archers had been spared to go with the wizards, and these, Tintagel knew, would spend more time scouting to the east and keeping communication open with the main host in the west than in fighting. The four elven magic-users had mapped out their defenses carefully, and they trusted in their craft. If the ambush at the Dells was to succeed, then Tintagel and his companions would have to hold the line in the east. They could not fail.

A scout rushed by Tintagel, and the wizard brushed aside his thick, dark locks and squinted with blue eyes toward the north.

"Mixed group," the young elf explained, looking back. "Goblins, mostly, but with a fair number of orcs beside them."

Tintagel rubbed his hands together and motioned to his three wizard comrades. All four began their spells at about the same time and soon the air north of their position became filled with sticky filaments, drifting down to form thick webs between the trees. The scout's warning had come at the last moment, for even as the webs began to take shape, several goblins rushed into them, becoming helplessly stuck.

Cries went up from several areas to the north. The press of goblins and orcs, though considerable, could not break through the wizard's spells, and many monsters were crushed into the webs, to gag on the sticky substance and die slowly of suffocation. The few archers accompanying the wizards picked their shots carefully, protecting their precious few arrows, firing only if it appeared that a monster was about to break loose of the sticky bonds.

Many more fiends were still free beyond the webbing, Tintagel knew. Many, many more, but at least the spells had bought the elves in the Dells some time.

* * * * *

The second ridge was given up, but not before scores of dead invaders lay piled across the small valley. The elven retreat was swift, down one hill, over the piled leaves at its base, and up another hill, then falling into familiar positions atop the third ridge.

Screams to the east told Shayleigh that many monsters had approached from that way, and hundreds of torches had sprung up in the night far to the north.

"How many are you?" the elf maiden whispered breathlessly.

As if in answer, the black tide rolled down the southern side of the second ridge.

The invaders found a surprise waiting for them at the bottom of the small valley. The elves had leaped over the piled leaves, for they knew of the spike-filled pits hidden beneath.

With the charge stalled, showers of arrows had even more devastating effects. Goblin after goblin died; tough ogres growled away a dozen arrow hits, only to be hit a dozen more times.

The elves cried out in savage fury, raining death on the evil intruders, but no smile found Shayleigh's face. She knew that the main host, coming in steadily behind these advance lines of fodder, would be more organized and more controlled.

"Death to enemies of Shilmista!" one exuberant elf screamed, leaping to his feet and hurling his fist into the air. In answer, a huge rock sailed through the darkness and caught the foolish young elf squarely in the face, nearly decapitating him.

"Giant!" came the cry from several positions all at once.

Another rock whipped past, narrowly missing Shayleigh's cowled head.

* * * * *

The wizards couldn't possibly conjure enough webbing to block the entire eastern region. They had known that from the beginning and had selected specific trees on which to anchor their webs, creating a maze to slow the enemy's approach. Tintagel and his three cohorts nodded grimly to each other, took up predetermined positions at the mouths of the web tunnels, and prepared their next spells.

"They have entered the second channel!" called a scout.

Tintagel mentally counted to five, then clapped his hands. At the sound of the signal, the four wizards began their identical chants. They saw the forms, shadowy and blurred by the web veils, slipping through the maze, apparently having solved the riddle. On came the charging goblins, hungry for elven blood. The wizards kept their composure, though, concentrating on their spells and trusting that they had timed the approach through the maze correctly.

Groups of goblins came straight at each of them, all in a line between the channeling webs.

One after another, the elven wizards pointed out to the enemy and uttered final, triggering syllables. Bolts of lightning split the darkness, shot down each of the channels with killing fury.

The goblins didn't even have time to cry out before they fell, scorched corpses in a sylvan grave.

* * * * *

"It is time to leave," Galladel told Shayleigh, and the maiden, for once, didn't argue. The woods beyond the second ridge were lit by so many torches that it seemed as though the sun had come up—and still more were coming in.

Shayleigh couldn't tell how many giants had taken positions beyond the ridge, but judging from the numbers of boulders sailing the elves' way, there were several at least.

"Five more arrows!" the fiery elf maiden cried to her troops.

But many of the elves couldn't follow that command. They had to drop their bows suddenly and take up swords, for a host of bugbears, stealthy despite their great size, had slipped in from the west.

Shayleigh raced over to join the melee; if the bugbears delayed the retreat even for a short while, the elves would be overwhelmed. By the time she got there, though, the competent elves had dispatched most of the bugbears, with only a single loss. Three elves had one of the remaining monsters surrounded; another group was in pursuit of two bugbears, heading back to the west. To the side, though, another bugbear appeared, and only one elf, a young maiden, stood before it.

Shayleigh veered straight in, recognizing the elf as Cellanie and knowing that she was too inexperienced to handle the likes of a bugbear.

The young elf fell before Shayleigh got there, her skull crushed by the bugbear's heavy club. The seven-foot, hairy goblinoid stood there, grinning evilly with its yellow teeth.

Shayleigh dipped her head and growled loudly, as though to charge. The bugbear braced itself and clenched its wicked club tightly, but the elf maiden stopped suddenly and used her forward momentum to hurl her sword.

The bugbear stood dumbfounded. Swords were not designed for such attacks! But if the creature doubted Shayleigh's intelligence in throwing the weapon, or her prowess with such a trick, all it had to do was look to its chest, to the elf's sword hilt, vibrating horribly just five inches out of the bugbear's hairy ribs. The creature's blood spurted across the sword hilt and stained the ground.

The bugbear looked down, glanced up at Shayleigh, then it fell dead.

"To the west!" Shayleigh cried, rushing over to retrieve her sword. "As we planned! To the west!" She grabbed the bloodied hilt and tugged, but the weapon would not slip free. Shayleigh remained more concerned with the progress of her troops than her own vulnerable position. Still looking back to oversee the retreat, she braced her foot on the dead bugbear's chest and gripped her sword hilt tightly in both hands.

When she heard the snort above her, she knew her folly. Both her hands were on a weapon she could not use, either to strike or to parry.

Defenseless, Shayleigh looked up to see another bugbear and its huge, spiked club.

* * * * *

The wizards, coming in to join their allies, concentrated their magical attacks on the torches of the enemy host beyond the second ridge. Enchanted flames roared to life under the pyrotechnical magic. Sparks flew wildly, burning into any monsters standing too close. Other torches poured heavy smoke, filling the area, blinding and choking, forcing the monsters to drop back or fall to the ground.

With that magical cover holding back their foes, the elves soon cleared the third ridge.

* * * * *

A flash emanated from beside Shayleigh's face, burned her and blinded her. At first, she thought it was the impact from the bugbear's club, but when the elf maiden's wits and vision returned, she still stood over the bugbear she had killed, clutching her impaled sword.

She finally sorted out the other bugbear, its back against a tree, a smoldering hole burned right through its belly. The creature's hair danced wildly, charged, Shayleigh realized, from a wizard's lightning bolt.

Tintagel was beside her.

"Come," he said, helping her tear her sword from the dead monster. "We have slowed the enemy charge, but the great, dark force will not be stopped. Already, our lead runners have encountered resistance in the west."

Shayleigh tried to respond, but found that her jaw would not easily move.

The wizard looked to the two archers covering his rear. "Gather up poor Cellanie," he said grimly. "We must leave no dead for our cruel enemies to toy with!" Tintagel took Shayleigh's arm and led her off after the rest of the fleeing elven host.

Cries and monstrous shouts erupted from all about them, but the elves did not panic. They stayed with their carefully designed plan and executed it to perfection.

They met pockets of resistance in the west, but the broken ground worked in their favor against the slower, less agile monsters, especially since the elves could shoot their bows with deadly accuracy, even on the run. Every group of monsters was overwhelmed and the elves continued on their way without taking another loss.

The eastern sky had become pink with the budding dawn before they regrouped and found some rest. Shayleigh had seen no more fighting during the night, fortunately, for her head ached so badly that she could not even keep her bearings without Tintagel's aid. The wizard stayed beside her through it all, would have willingly died beside her if the enemy had caught them.

"I must beg your pardon," Tintagel said to her after the new camp had been set, south of the Dells. "The bugbear was too close—I had to begin the bolt too near you."

"You apologize for saving my life?" Shayleigh asked. Every word she spoke pained the valiant maiden.

"Your face shines with the redness of a burn," Tintagel said, touching her glowing cheek lightly and wincing with sympathy as he did.

"It will heal," Shayleigh replied, managing a weak smile. "Better than would my head if that bugbear had clubbed me!" She couldn't even manage a smile at her statement, though, and not for the pain, but for the memory of Cellanie, falling dead to the ground.

"How many did we lose?" Shayleigh asked somberly.

"Three," replied Tintagel in equally grim tones.

"Only three," came the voice of King Galladel, moving to them from the side. "Only three! And the blood of hundreds of goblins and their allies stains the ground. By some accounts, even a giant was felled last night." Galladel winced when he noticed Shayleigh's red face.

"It is nothing," the elf maiden said into his wide-eyed stare, waving her hand his way.

Galladel broke his concentrated stare, embarrassed. "We are in your debt," he said, his smile returning. "Because of your fine planning, we scored a great victory this night." The elf king nodded, patted Shayleigh on the shoulder, and took his leave, having many other matters to attend.

Shayleigh's grimace told Tintagel that she did not share Galladel's good feelings for the battle.

"We did win," the wizard reminded her. "The outcome could have been much, much worse."

From his somber tone, Shayleigh knew that she did not have to explain her fears. They had hit their enemy by surprise, on a battlefield that they had prepared and that their enemy had not seen before. They had lost only three, it was true, but it seemed to Shayleigh that those three dead elves held more value for the elven cause than the hundreds of dead goblinoids held for the seemingly countless masses invading Shilmista's northern border.

And for all their surprise and all the slaughter, it was the elves and not the invaders who had been forced into flight.

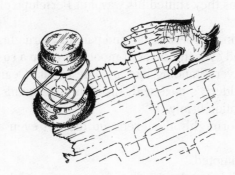

Two

A Book Worth Reading

Y ou have met Prince Elbereth?" Headmaster Avery Schell asked Cadderly
as soon as the young scholar entered Dean Thobicus's office. The large
headmaster rubbed a kerchief across his blotchy face, huffing and puffing
almost continually as his bloated body tried to pull in enough air. Even before the
advent of the chaos curse, Avery had been a rotund man. Now he was obese, having gone on a gluttonous spree along with several other of the Edificant Library's
most prominent eaters. In the throes of the chaos curse, some of those priests
had literally eaten themselves to death.

"You must take longer walks each morning," offered Headmistress Pertelope, a neatly groomed, graying woman with hazel eyes that still showed the
inquisitive luster more common to a much younger person. Cadderly carefully
considered the woman, standing easily by Avery's side. Pertelope was the
young scholar's favorite instructor, a wistful, often irreverent woman more concerned with common sense than steadfast rules. He noted her long-sleeved,
ankle-length gown, bound tightly about the collar, and the gloves that she had
been wearing every time Cadderly had seen her since the chaos curse. Never
before had Pertelope been so modest, if it was indeed modesty that kept her so
covered. She wouldn't talk about it, though, to Cadderly or to anyone else; she
wouldn't talk about anything that had occurred during the time of the curse.
Cadderly wasn't overly concerned, for even with the new wrappings, Pertelope
seemed her old mischievous self. Even as Cadderly watched, she grabbed a
handful of Avery's blubber and gave a playful shake, to the incredulous stares
of both Avery and Dean Thobicus, the skinny and wrinkled leader of the
library.

A chuckle erupted from Cadderly's lips faster than he could bite it back. The stares turned grave as they shifted his way, but Pertelope offered him a playful wink to comfort him.

Through it all, Prince Elbereth, tall and painfully straight, with hair the color of a raven's wings and eyes the silver of moonbeams on a rushing river, showed no emotion whatsoever. Standing like a statue beside Dean Thobicus's oaken desk, he caught Cadderly's gaze with his own penetrating stare and held the young scholar's attention firmly.

Cadderly was thoroughly flustered and did not even notice the seconds passing by.

"Well?" Avery prompted.

Cadderly at first didn't understand, so Avery motioned the elven prince's way.

"No," Cadderly answered quickly, "I have not had the honor of a formal intro-duction, though I have heard much of Prince Elbereth since his arrival three days ago." Cadderly flashed his boyish smile, the corners of his gray eyes turn-ing up to match his grin. He pushed his unkempt, sandy brown locks from his face and moved toward Elbereth, a hand extended. "Well met!"

Elbereth regarded the offered hand for some time before extending his own in response. He nodded gravely, making Cadderly more than a little bit embar-rassed and uncomfortable about the easy smile splayed across his face. Yet again, Cadderly felt out of his element, beyond his experiences. Elbereth had come with potentially catastrophic news and Cadderly, sheltered for all of his life, sim-ply did not know how to respond in such a situation.

"This is the scholar I have told you about," Avery explained to the elf. "Cad-derly of Carradoon, a most remarkable young man."

Elbereth's handshake was incredibly strong for so slender a being, and when the elf turned Cadderly's hand over suddenly, the young scholar offered only token resistance.

Elbereth examined Cadderly's palm, rubbing his thumb across the base of Cad-derly's fingers. "These are not the hands of a warrior," the elf said, unimpressed.

"I never claimed to be a warrior," Cadderly retorted before Avery or Thobicus could explain. The dean and headmaster put accusing glares back on Cadderly and, this time, even easygoing Pertelope did not offer any escape.

Again, seconds slipped past.

Headmaster Avery cleared his throat loudly to break the tension.

"Cadderly is indeed a warrior," the robust headmaster explained. "It was he who defeated both the evil priest Barjin and Barjin's most awful undead soldiers. Even a mummy rose up against the lad and was summarily put down!"

The recounting did not make Cadderly swell with pride. The mere mention of the dead priest made Cadderly see him again, slumped against the wall in the makeshift altar room in the catacombs, a blasted hole in his chest and his dead eyes staring accusingly at his killer.

"But more than that," Avery continued, moving over to drape a heavy, sweaty arm over the young scholar, "Cadderly is a warrior whose greatest weapon is knowledge. We have a riddle here, Prince Elbereth, a most dangerous riddle, I fear. And Cadderly, I tell you now, is the man who will solve it."

Avery's proclamation added more weight to Cadderly's shoulder than the headmaster's considerable arm. The young scholar wasn't absolutely certain, but he believed he liked Avery better before the events of the chaos curse. Back then, the headmaster often went out of his way to make Cadderly's life miserable. Under the influences of the intoxicating curse, Avery had admitted his almost fatherly love for the young scholar, and now the headmaster's friendship was proving even more miserable to Cadderly than his former, too-strict actions.

"Enough of this banter," said Dean Thobicus in his shaky voice, his speech more often sounding like a whine than normal words. "We have chosen Cadderly as our representative in this matter. The decision was ours alone to make. Prince Elbereth will treat him accordingly."

The elf turned to the seated dean and dipped a curt and precise bow.

Thobicus nodded in reply. "Tell Cadderly of the gloves, and of how you came to possess them," he bade.

Elbereth reached into the pocket of his traveling cloak—an action that pushed the garment open and gave Cadderly a quick glance at the elf prince's magnificent armor, links of golden and silvery chain finely meshed—and produced several gloves, each clearly marked with stitching that showed the same trident-and-bottle design that Barjin had displayed on his clerical vestments. Elbereth sorted through the tangle to free one glove, and handed it to Cadderly.

"Evil vermin does not often find its way into Shilmista," the proud elf began, "but we are ever alert for its encroachment. A party of bugbears wandered into the forest. None of them escaped with their lives."

None of this was news to Cadderly, of course; rumors had been circulating throughout the Edificant Library since the elf prince's arrival. Cadderly nodded and examined the gauntlet. "It is the same as Barjin's," he declared at once, indicating the three-bottle-over-trident design.

"But what does it mean?" asked an impatient Avery.

"An adaptation of Talona's symbol," Cadderly explained, shrugging to let them know that he was not absolutely certain of his reasoning.

"The bugbears carried poisoned daggers," Elbereth remarked. "That would be in accord with the Lady of Poison's edicts."

"You know of Talona?" Cadderly asked.

Elbereth's silvery eyes flashed, a moonbeam sparkling off a cresting wave, and he gave Cadderly a derisive, sidelong glance. "I have seen the birth and death of three centuries, young human. I will still be young at the time of your ·death, though you might live more years than all others of your race."

Cadderly bit back his retort, knowing that he would find little support in antagonizing the elf.

"Do not underestimate that which I, Prince of Shilmista, might know,"

Elbereth continued haughtily. "We are not a simple folk wasting our years dancing under the stars, as so many would choose to believe."

Cadderly did start to reply, sharply again, but Pertelope, ever the calming influence, moved in front of him and took the glove, shooting him another wink and subtly stepping on the young scholar's toe.

"We would never think so of our friends in Shilmista," the headmistress offered. "Often has the Edificant Library sought the wisdom of ancient Galladel, your father and king."

Apparently appeased, Elbereth gave a quick nod.

"If it is indeed a sect of Talona, then what might we conclude?" Dean Thobicus asked.

Cadderly shrugged helplessly. "Little," he replied. "Since the Time of Troubles, so much has changed. We do not yet know the intentions and methods of the various sects, but I doubt that coincidence brought Barjin to us and the bugbears to Shilmista, especially since each carried not the normal symbol of Talona, but an adapted design. A renegade sect, it would seem, but undeniably coordinated in its attacks."

"You will come to Shilmista," Elbereth said to Cadderly. The scholar thought for a moment that the elf was asking him, but then he realized from Elbereth's unblinking, uncompromising stare, that it had been a command and not a request. Helplessly, the young scholar looked to his headmasters and to the dean, but they, even Pertelope, nodded in accord.

"When?" Cadderly asked Dean Thobicus, pointedly looking past Elbereth's ensnaring gaze.

"A few days," Thobicus replied. "There are many preparations to be made."

"A few days may be too long for my people," Elbereth remarked evenly, his eyes still boring into Cadderly.

"We will move as fast as we can," was the best that Thobicus could offer. "We have suffered grave injuries, elf prince. An emissary from the Church of Ilmater is on the way, to make an inquiry concerning a group of his priests who were found slaughtered in their room. He will demand a thorough investigation and that will require an audience with Cadderly."

"Then Cadderly will leave him a statement," Elbereth replied. "Or the emissary will wait until Cadderly returns from Shilmista. I am concerned for the living, Dean Thobicus, not the dead."

To Cadderly's amazement, Thobicus did not argue.

They adjourned the meeting then, on Headmaster Avery's suggestion, for there was an event scheduled in the Edificant Library that day that many wished to witness—and which Cadderly flatly refused to miss for any reason.

"Come with us, Prince Elbereth," the portly headmaster offered, moving by Cadderly's side. Cadderly gave Avery a somewhat sour look, not so certain that he wanted the haughty elf along. "One of the visiting priestesses, Danica Maupoissant, of Westgate, will perform a most unusual feat."

Elbereth gave a quick glance at Cadderly—it was obvious that Cadderly did not want him along—smiled, and agreed. Cadderly knew, to his further dismay, that Elbereth honestly enjoyed the fact that accepting Avery's invitation would bother the young scholar.

They came into the great hall on the library's first floor, a huge and ornate, thick-pillared room lined by grand tapestries depicting the glories of Deneir and Oghma, deities of the building's host religions. Most of the library's priests, of both orders, had turned out, nearly a hundred men and women, gathered in a wide circle around a block of stone supported on cross-legged sawhorses.

Danica kneeled motionlessly on a mat a few feet from the stone, her almond eyes closed and her arms held out before her and crossed at the wrists. She was a tiny woman, barely five feet tall, and seemed tinier still when kneeling before the formidable solid block. Cadderly resisted the urge to go to her, realizing that she was deep in meditation.

"Is that the priestess?" Elbereth asked, a tinge of excitement in his voice. Cadderly snapped his head about and regarded the elf curiously, noting the sparkle in Elbereth's silvery eyes.

"That is Danica," Avery replied. "She is beautiful, is she not?" Indeed Danica was, with perfect, delicate features and a thick mop of strawberry blond hair dancing about her shoulders. "Do not allow that beauty to deceive you, elf prince," Avery went on proudly, as though Danica was his own child. "Danica is among the finest fighters I have ever seen. Deadly are her bare hands, and boundless is her discipline and dedication."

The sparkle in Elbereth's admiring eyes did not diminish; those shining dots of light shot out like tiny spears at Cadderly's heart.

Preparation or no preparation, Cadderly figured it was time to go and see his Danica. He crossed through the onlookers' circle and knelt before her, gently reaching out to lightly touch her long hair.

She did not stir.

"Danica," Cadderly called softly, taking her deceptively soft hand in his own.

Danica opened her eyes, those exotic brown orbs that sent shivers up Cadderly's spine every time he gazed into them. Her wide smile told Cadderly that she was not angry about the interruption.

"I feared that you would not be here," she whispered.

"A thousand ogres could not have held me from this place," he replied, "not today." Cadderly glanced back over his shoulder at the stone block. It seemed so huge and so solid, and Danica so very delicate. "Are you certain?" he asked.

"I am ready," Danica replied grimly. "Do you doubt me?"

Cadderly thought back a few weeks, to the horrible day when he had entered Danica's room and found her barely conscious on the floor, after having slammed her head repeatedly against a similar stone. Her wounds were long gone now, healed by salves and the magic of the library's mightiest clerics, but Cadderly would never forget how close Danica had come to death, nor would he forget his own terrible feelings of emptiness when he feared that he might lose her.

"I was under the curse's influence then," Danica explained, easily reading his thoughts. "The mist prevented me from attaining the proper concentration. I have studied Grandmaster Penpahg D'Ahn's scrolls . . ."

"I know," Cadderly assured her, stroking her delicate hand. "And I know you are ready. Forgive me my fears. They do not come from any doubts about you or your dedication or your wisdom." His smile was sincere, if strained. He moved near, as if to kiss her, but backed away suddenly and glanced around.

"I would not want to disturb your concentration," he stammered.

Danica knew better, knew that Cadderly had remembered the gathering about him and that his embarrassment alone had pulled him away from her. She laughed aloud, charmed as always by his innocence. "Do you not find this alluring?" she asked with mock sarcasm to comfort the nervous young man.

"Oh, yes," the young scholar answered. "I have always wanted to be in love with one who could put her head through solid stone." This time, they shared a laugh.

Then Danica noticed Elbereth and abruptly stopped laughing. The elf prince stared at her with his penetrating gaze, looked right through her, it seemed. She pulled her loose robes tighter about her, feeling naked under that stare, but she did not look away.

"That is Prince Elbereth?" she asked with what little breath she could find.

Cadderly considered her for a long moment, then turned to regard Elbereth. The gathering be damned, he thought, and he bent back in and kissed Danica hard, forcing her attention away from the elf.

This time, Danica, not Cadderly, was the flustered one, and Cadderly couldn't be certain if her embarrassment came from the kiss or from her own realization that she had been caught staring a bit too intently at the visiting elf.

"Go back to your meditation," Cadderly offered, afraid of what the growing number of distractions might do to Danica's attempt. He felt childish indeed that he had let his own emotions take precedence at such an important moment. He kissed her again, a light peck on the cheek. "I know you will succeed," he offered, and he took his leave.

Danica took several deep breaths to steady herself and cleanse her mind. She looked to the stone first, the obstacle that stood in the way of her progress as one of the leading disciples of Penpahg D'Ahn. She grew angry at that stone, putting it in the light of an enemy. Then she left it with a final mental threat, turned her attention to the wide room around her, the distractions she had to be rid of.

Danica focused on Elbereth first. She saw the elf prince, his strange eyes still staring her way, and then he was gone, a black hole where he had been standing. Avery went away next, and then those standing beside the portly headmaster. Danica's gaze shifted and locked on one of the many huge archways supporting the great hall. It, too, disappeared into the darkness.

"Phien denifi ca," Danica whispered as another group of people disappeared. "They are only images." All the room was fast replaced by blackness. Only the block remained, and Cadderly. Danica had saved Cadderly for last. He was her greatest supporter; he was as much her strength as her own inner discipline.

But then he, too, was gone.

Danica rose and slowly approached the enemy stone.

You cannot resist, her thoughts called out to the block. *I am the stronger.*

Her arms waved slowly before her, weaving in an intricate dance, and she continued her mental assault on the stone, treating it as some sentient thing, assuring herself that she was convincing it that it could not win. This was the technique of Penpahg D'Ahn, and Penpahg D'Ahn had broken the stone.

Danica looked beyond the block, imagined her head crashing through the stone and exiting the other side. She studied the depth of the block, then mentally reduced it to a parchment's width.

You are parchment, and I am the stronger, she mentally told the stone.

It went on for many minutes, the arm dance, Danica's feet shifting, always in perfect balance, and then she was chanting softly in a melodic and rhythmical way, seeking complete harmony of body and spirit.

It came so suddenly that the crowd barely had time to gasp. Danica fell forward into two quick steps. Every muscle in her small, finely toned frame seemed to snap forward and down, driving her forehead into the stone.

Danica heard nothing and saw nothing for a long moment. Then there was the blackness of the meditation-dispatched room, gradually fading back into images that the young monk recognized. She looked around her, surprised to see the block lying on the floor in two nearly equal-sized pieces.

An arm was around her; she knew it was Cadderly's.

"You are now the highest-ranking disciple of Grandmaster Penpahg D'Ahn!" Cadderly whispered into her ear, and she heard him clearly, though the gathering had erupted into a wild burst of cheering.

Danica turned and hugged Cadderly close, but couldn't help looking over his shoulder to regard Elbereth. The serious elf prince was not cheering, but clapping his graceful hands and staring at Danica with clear approval in his sparkling silver eyes.

* * * * *

Headmistress Pertelope heard the cheering from her room above the great hall and knew that Danica had successfully broken the stone. Pertelope was not surprised; she had seen the event in a dream that she knew was prophetic. She was glad of Danica's continuing success and growing power, and glad, too, that Danica would remain by Cadderly's side in the coming days.

Pertelope feared for the young scholar, for she alone among all the priests at the library understood the personal trials Cadderly would soon face.

He was of the chosen, Pertelope knew.

"Will it be enough?" the headmistress asked quietly, hugging the *Tome of Universal Harmony*, the most holy book of Deneir. "Will you survive, dear Cadderly, as I have survived, or will the callings of Deneir devour you and leave you an empty thing?"

Almost to mock her own claims of survival, the headmistress noticed then that her sharp-edged skin had again sliced several lines in the long sleeve of her gown.

Pertelope shook her head and hugged the book tightly to her fully covered body. The potential for insight and knowledge was virtually unlimited, but so, too, was the potential for disaster.

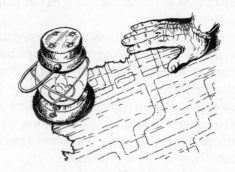

Three
Intrigue

The wizard Dorigen reached out tentatively for the door handle to the chambers of Aballister, her leader. Surprised by her own hesitancy to go to the man she considered her mentor and had formerly called her lover, Dorigen angrily grabbed the handle and walked in.

Aballister sat in his comfortable chair, gazing out a small window at the distant Shining Plains and at the new construction he had ordered begun at Castle Trinity. He seemed a wretched thing to Dorigen now, not nearly the vital, powerful wizard who had so captivated her and fanned her passions. Aballister was still powerful, but his strength lay in his magic and not in his body. His black hair lay matted to his head; his eyes, dark before, seemed like empty holes now, sunken deeply into his sharply featured face. Dorigen wondered how she ever could have found him alluring, could have lain beside the loose-skinned bag of bones she saw before her.

She shook the thoughts away and reminded herself that Aballister's tutoring had brought her considerable power, and that it had been worth it after all.

Aballister's impish familiar, a bat-winged creature named Druzil, perched on the desk behind the wizard, posing as a gargoylelike statue. A nervous-looking orc soldier stood before the desk, unaware that the creature just a few inches away was alive.

Dorigen hardly looked at the orc, focusing more on Druzil, a sneaky character whom Dorigen did not trust in the least. Druzil had been with Barjin when the priest had been defeated at the Edificant Library. The only reason that everyone in Castle Trinity wasn't muttering about the imp's role in bringing Barjin down was that few other than Aballister, Dorigen, and the castle's third wizard, Bogo Rath, even knew that Druzil existed. Aballister had declared that he would introduce Druzil to the castle's garrison, but Dorigen had managed to change his mind—at least for the time being.

Dorigen looked back to the wizard's hollowed face and nearly sneered at the notion of his sudden and dangerous arrogance. Always before, Aballister had carefully guarded Druzil as his personal secret, and Dorigen wasn't certain she trusted so drastic a change in the man.

Aballister, this hollowed man who had somehow traded physical strength for magical power, had grown quite confident in the last few weeks. Barjin, as head of Castle Trinity's clerical order, had been Aballister's principal rival for control of the ruling triumvirate. Now Barjin was no more.

Druzil managed to slip a sly wink at Dorigen without alerting the oblivious orc.

Dorigen replied with a private scowl, then turned to Aballister. "You requested my presence?" she asked, sharp and to the point.

"I did," the wizard answered offhandedly, not bothering to look Dorigen's way. "Aballister," he mumbled to himself, then, "Bonaduce." He considered each word for a moment, then turned to Dorigen, his smile wide. "Or Aballister Bonaduce, perhaps? Do you have a preference, or should I use both names when I claim rule over the region?"

"That claim would be premature," Dorigen reminded him. "Our only expedition so far has failed utterly." She studied the orc soldier, no doubt one of Ragnor's personal attendants, then turned to stare back at Aballister, amazed that the wizard would be so brash with his new rival's henchman standing before him.

"Patience," Aballister said, waving his hand derisively. "Ragnor is on Shilmista's border. When he chooses to march, the elves will be no more."

"The elves comprise but one part of our enemy," said Dorigen, again looking toward the trembling orc. Aballister waited a few moments, seeming to enjoy Dorigen's discomfort, then dismissed the wretched creature.

"Get word back to Ragnor that he has our blessings and the blessings of Talona," Aballister said. "And good fighting!" The orc spun and rushed from the room, slamming the door behind it.

Aballister clapped his hands with glee.

"Greetings, Mistress Magic," Druzil slurred his customary title for the female wizard. He unwrapped his leathery wings and stretched wide now that the orc was gone. "And how is your nose today?"

Dorigen winced at the remark. She was a handsome woman—a bit too round for her liking, perhaps—with fair, if a bit plain, features and small but remarkably lustrous eyes the color of pure amber. Her nose was her one disfigurement, though, the one weak spot of the wizard's vanity. In her earliest days practicing magic, Dorigen had executed a magically enhanced jump in the air. Her landing had been less than perfect, though, for she had overbalanced on her descent, slammed face first into the stone floor, and bent her nose halfway over her cheek. It had never grown straight since.

"Greetings to yourself, imp," Dorigen replied. She moved right to the desk and began drumming her hand atop it, prominently displaying an onyx ring. Druzil knew what that ring could do, and he retreated into his leathery wings as though he expected Dorigen to loose its fiery magic at him then and there.

"I need no fights between my allies," Aballister said, seemingly amused by it all. "I have important decisions before me—such as what to call myself when I have claimed my title."

Dorigen did not appreciate Aballister's overconfidence. "There remains Carradoon and the Edificant Library," she said grimly. She thought she saw Aballister flinch at the library's mention, but she couldn't be sure, for the wizard hid his emotions well in the hollowed features of his drained face.

"The men of Carradoon will surrender without a fight," Aballister reasoned. "They are fishermen and farmers, not warriors. You see, dear Dorigen, we must begin our preparations for what is to come after the conquest. Riatavin is not so far away, nor Westgate. We must establish our appearance as orderly and lawful rulers if we are to become accepted by the surrounding kingdoms."

"Aballister the diplomat?" Dorigen asked. "Orderly and lawful? Talona will not be pleased."

"It was I who met the goddess's avatar," Aballister reminded her sharply.

Dorigen hardly needed the reminder. It was that very meeting that had so changed Aballister, had turned his simple ambitions to excel at his craft into something more dire, more consuming. It was no coincidence that Dorigen had broken off her relationship with Aballister not long after that time of Arrival.

"Barjin is dead, and our clerics are in disarray," Aballister went on. "We cannot know how weakened Ragnor will become in his march. Would you have us begin a larger war with our surrounding kingdoms so soon after the first conquest is completed?"

"The first conquest has not yet begun," Dorigen dared to say.

Aballister seemed on the verge of an explosion, but he calmed quickly. "Of course," he agreed, seeming in that instant more his old, patient self. "Ragnor is on the edge of Shilmista, though, even now making forays into the elven wood."

"Have you considered the implications of his eventual march?" Dorigen asked. On the desk, Druzil sighed and nodded in agreement, as if the imp had been hoping that someone would point out the potential problems to the increasingly arrogant wizard.

"Ragnor is powerful," Dorigen began, "and the ogrillon holds little respect for magic-users."

"We could defeat him," Aballister reasoned.

Dorigen nodded her agreement. "Perhaps," she said, "but what would such a conflict cost Castle Trinity? I know you have shed no tears for Barjin—and rightly so," she added, seeing Aballister's scowl. "But the priest's defeat has cost us dearly. If he and the curse had taken down the Edificant Library, then we could march on Carradoon even as Ragnor begins his assault on Shilmista. We cannot, though, not with the library's priests looking over the town. If Ragnor wins in the elven wood without incurring heavy losses, he will gain in prestige among the rabble. He might now be wondering how the neighboring kingdoms might deal with an ogrillon king."

The blunt words slapped Aballister as if Dorigen had hit him with a mace. He sat very still in his chair, staring ahead for a very long time.

He has known of this threat all along, came an unexpected message to Dorigen's mind. The woman glanced over to Druzil, who peeked at her from above his bat wings.

He has refused to accept it, the imp added, *for he is too immersed in his debate over whether to call himself 'Aballister the Beneficent' or 'Bonaduce the Conqueror.'*

Dorigen held no doubts that the imp was sincere in his sarcasm, but she could hardly believe that the familiar could be so bold with his master sitting right before him. Wisely, Dorigen did not reply. She pointedly looked away from the imp and back to the seated wizard.

"There can be no doubt that you are in control of Castle Trinity," Dorigen offered, "but we must continue with caution, for the seat has been a precarious one. What new cleric will rise in Barjin's place to lead the order? How strong will Ragnor become?"

"And what of Boygo Rath?" Aballister asked slyly, referring to the third and least adept wizard of Castle Trinity, whom both Aballister and Dorigen considered an upstart child. The wizard's real name was Bogo Rath, but Aballister and Dorigen referred to him as Boygo, even to his face. "And what of you?" Aballister added.

"Do not doubt my loyalty," Dorigen assured him. "In your absence, I would indeed have designs on ruling the triumvirate, but I know my betters and have more patience than you believe. As for Boygo . . ." She let the thought hang and gave an amused look, as though the notion of the young upstart challenging the likes of Aballister Bonaduce was simply too ridiculous to consider.

Aballister's laughter showed that he wholeheartedly agreed. "The clerics and Ragnor, then," the wizard said, "and neither should pose too serious a threat if we are cautious and attentive."

"Ragnor is a long way from here," Dorigen reminded him, prompting an invitation.

Aballister looked at her carefully for a moment, as though trying to discern her agenda. "Ragnor will not easily accept your presence in his camp," the wizard remarked.

"I do not fear him," replied Dorigen. She clapped her hands sharply three times. Aballister's door opened again, and in strode a man nearly seven feet tall, with corded muscles obvious under his fine silken clothes. His hair hung, thick and blond, braided down over his shoulders, and his pale blue eyes stared ahead with incredible intensity. Aballister hardly recognized him, except for his bronze skin and the curious tattoo, a polar worm, he wore upon his forehead.

"Surely this cannot be . . ." the wizard began.

"Tiennek," Dorigen confirmed, "the barbarian I plucked from the shadows of the Great Glacier in far away Vaasa."

"Dear Dorigen," cried the wizard, his tone revealing sincere amazement, but also disdain, "you have civilized him!"

Tiennek growled.

"Perhaps a bit," Dorigen replied, "but I would not destroy Tiennek's spirit. That would serve neither my purpose nor my pleasure in keeping him at my side."

Aballister's jaw tightened at the remark. The image of his former lover in this huge man's arms did not sit well with him, not well at all. "Impressive," he admitted, "but be warned if you think him a match for Ragnor."

Again Tiennek growled softly.

"Take no offense," Aballister quickly added. The wizard had never been comfortable around Dorigen's dangerous pet. Under the lip of his great desk, he fingered a wand that would blast the barbarian apart if Tiennek even hinted at charging.

"Your barbarian companion is powerful beyond doubt, possibly the strongest human I have ever seen," the wizard continued, looking to Dorigen once more, "but I do doubt that any human could defeat Ragnor in combat. The ogrillon would kill him, and then you would have to go all the way back to the Great Glacier to catch yourself another one."

"I, too, have never seen mighty Ragnor bested," Dorigen admitted. "Perhaps you are correct in your assessment, but Tiennek would not prove an easy opponent. Within his breast beats the heart of a warrior of the White Worm, and I have given him much more than just that. I have disciplined him so that he might better use those savage powers. Ragnor would find himself hard-pressed to defeat this one, and even more so with me standing behind Tiennek." Again she drummed her fingers, displaying her deadly ring.

Aballister spent a long time considering Dorigen's claims, and Dorigen could see the doubts plainly upon his pale, wrinkled face. In truth, she doubted that Tiennek could stand up to Ragnor as well as she had proclaimed—or that she, for all her magical prowess, could offer much help if Ragnor decided to do away with both of them—but going to Shilmista was simply too important for the success of this campaign for Dorigen to accept such possibilities.

"Ragnor could become too powerful to control," she remarked. "By one count, he has five thousand at his command."

"We have three thousand," Aballister retorted, "a strong defensive position, and the services of three wizards!"

"Do you desire such a war?" Dorigen asked. "What title would you gain in fighting Ragnor and his soldiers?"

Aballister nodded grimly and put his sharp chin in his skinny hand. "Go to him, then," the wizard said at length. "Go to Shilmista and help our dear Ragnor. He should have a wizard at his side anyway, if he hopes to deal with the elves. I will watch the clerics and prepare for the next step in our conquest."

Dorigen didn't wait around to see if Aballister might reconsider. She bowed and started from the room.

"Dorigen," Aballister called after her. She stopped and clenched her fist at her side, somehow knowing that the wily wizard would throw a new complication her way.

"Take Druzil along with you," Aballister said as she turned back around. "With the imp beside you, you and I can communicate from time to time. I do not like to be left out of so important a matter as Ragnor's progress."

Suspicions concerning Druzil's role in Barjin's death hovered about Dorigen's thoughts, and she did not doubt for a moment that Aballister was sending the imp along to watch over her as much as Ragnor. But how could she argue? The hierarchy at Castle Trinity was specific, and Aballister ruled the wizard's leg of the triumvirate.

"A wise decision," she said.

More than you believe, came another of Druzil's intrusions.

Dorigen hid well her surprise.

Aballister turned back to the small window and alternately muttered his names to see which would best serve him as king.

Less than an hour later, Dorigen walked out of Castle Trinity, Tiennek at her side and the bat-winged imp flapping lazily behind them, invisible through his own innate magic. Dorigen tried to hide her disdain as she passed the soldiers building the castle's new walls, fearing that Druzil might already be reporting back to his master.

Dorigen was not pleased by the construction and thought Aballister a fool for ordering it begun. Because of the enclave's secrecy—it resembled no more than a natural outcropping of stone—Castle Trinity had survived unmolested in the otherwise civilized region for several years. Travelers had walked right past the hidden castle on the northern slopes of the Snowflake Mountains without beginning to guess that a wondrous tunnel-and-chamber complex lay beneath their feet.

But, as with his nearly revealed secret of Druzil to the castle's common soldiers, Aballister was apparently feeling invulnerable. They would need the new walls, he had argued, if the final battles reached their gates. Dorigen favored secrecy, preferred that the fight never got this far north. She guessed, too, Aballister's real motivations. Again the senior wizard was thinking ahead, beyond the conquest. He did not really expect to be attacked at the castle, but knew that an impressive stronghold might help him in his diplomatic dealings with neighboring realms.

I share your thoughts, came Druzil's not-so-unexpected call. Dorigen turned abruptly on the imp, and frantic flaps revealed that he had darted to the side in a wild flurry.

"Apparently you do," the female wizard snarled, "for I was thinking of blasting you from the sky!"

"A thousand pardons," the imp said aloud, landing on the ground before

Dorigen, becoming visible, and falling immediately into a low bow. "Forgive my intrusion, but your feelings were obvious. You like neither Aballister's plans nor the way he has behaved since Barjin's demise."

Dorigen did not reply, but purposely kept her features locked in an unforgiving grimace.

"You will come to learn that I am no enemy," the imp promised.

Dorigen hoped he spoke the truth, but she didn't believe him for a minute.

* * * * *

Cadderly knew that his time was up as soon as Elbereth and Headmaster Avery entered his room, neither smiling.

"We leave today for Shilmista," Elbereth said.

"Farewell," Cadderly quipped.

Elbereth was not amused. "You will pack for the road," the elf prince ordered. "Carry little. Our pace will be swift and the mountain trails are not easy."

Cadderly frowned. He started to reply, but Avery, seeing the mounting tension between the two, cut him off. "A grand adventure for you, my young lad!" The portly headmaster beamed as he walked over and dropped his heavy hands on Cadderly's shoulders. "Time for you to see some of the land beyond our library doors."

"And what are you packing?" Cadderly asked, his sarcasm unrelenting.

His words stung Avery more than he had intended. "I wished to go," the headmaster replied sharply, rubbing a kerchief over his blotchy face. "I pleaded with Dean Thobicus to let me accompany you."

"Dean Thobicus refused?" Cadderly could not believe the placid dean would refuse any request from one of his headmasters.

"*I* refused," Elbereth explained.

Cadderly, incredulous, stared at him over Avery's shoulder.

"I am Prince of Shilmista," the elf reminded him. "None may enter my domain without my leave."

"Why would you refuse Headmaster Avery?" Cadderly dared to ask, right in the face of Avery's silent, and rather frantic, signals for him to let the matter drop.

"As I have told you," the elf replied, "our pace will be swift. Horses cannot carry us through all of the mountain passes, and I fear that the headmaster would not keep up. I'll not delay my return, and I do not wish to leave an exhausted man in the wild to die."

Cadderly had no rebuttal, and Avery's embarrassed expression pleaded with him not to press on.

"Just you and I?" Cadderly asked the elf, his tone revealing that he wasn't pleased by that thought.

"No," Avery answered. "Another has agreed to go along, at Prince Elbereth's request."

"Headmistress Pertelope?"

"Lady Maupoissant."

Danica! The name came like a mule's kick into Cadderly's face. He straightened, eyes wide, and tried to figure out when Elbereth had found the chance to invite Danica along. His Danica! And she had accepted! Cadderly had to wonder if Danica had known that he, too, would be venturing to the wood before she had agreed to go.

"Why does that so surprise you?" Elbereth asked, a slight trace of sarcasm in his melodic voice. "Do you doubt—"

"I doubt nothing where Danica is concerned," Cadderly was quick to reply. His scowl turned to an expression of confusion as he realized the many implications of his claim.

"Easy, lad," Avery said, holding him steady. "Danica agreed to go along only when she learned that you would be accompanying Prince Elbereth."

"As you wish," Elbereth added slyly, and Avery joined Cadderly in scowling at the elf, both knowing that Elbereth had made that last remark to throw some doubts at Cadderly.

"We shall depart in an hour," Elbereth said, standing impassively, fully composed. His black hair and silver eyes shone in the morning light, which streamed through Cadderly's window. "You will come then with whatever you have packed and silently endure any hardships resulting from what you have neglected to take along." The tall, proud elf turned and walked away without another word.

"I am starting to dislike him," Cadderly admitted, easing away from Avery's grip.

"He fears for his homeland," the headmaster explained.

"He is arrogant."

"Most elves are," said Avery. "It comes from living so long. Makes them believe they have experienced so much more than anyone else, and, thus, that they are wiser than anyone else."

"Have they, and are they?" Cadderly asked, his shoulders slumping a bit. He hadn't considered that fact about Prince Elbereth, that the elf had seen more in his life than Cadderly ever would, and probably would live on long after Cadderly's body was no more than a pile of dust.

"Some have, and they are indeed wise, I would presume," replied Avery, "but not most. The elves have become increasingly untrusting and xenophobic. They keep to their own, and to their own lands, and know little beyond their borders. I first met Prince Elbereth three decades ago and would guess that I have learned much more than he in that time. He seems much the same as he did then, in body and attitude.

"Well," Avery continued, turning for the door, "I will leave you to your packing. Elbereth said an hour, and I would not expect him to wait one moment longer!"

"I would not care to live through centuries, "Cadderly remarked just before the headmaster exited the room. "But, then," the young scholar continued when Avery turned back to him, "I am not certain that I have begun to live at all."

Avery studied Cadderly for a long while, caught off guard by the unexpected words. He had noticed a change in Cadderly since the incident with Barjin, but this was the most dramatic evidence that something deeply troubled the young scholar. Avery waited a few moments longer, then, seeing that Cadderly had nothing further to offer, shrugged and closed the door.

Cadderly sat unblinking on his bed. The world was going too fast for him. Why had Elbereth asked Danica along? Why had it fallen upon him to kill Barjin? The world was going too fast.

And he was going too slow, he soon realized. He would find enough time on the road for contemplations; right now he had to prepare himself for the journey, before Elbereth pulled him out of the library with only the clothes on his back.

He stuffed a pack with extra clothing and his writing kit, then placed in his magical light tube, a narrow, cylindrical device which, when uncapped, issued a beam of light that Cadderly could widen or narrow with a turn of the wrist.

Satisfied with the pack, the young scholar donned his blue silk traveling cloak and wide-brimmed hat, banded in red and set with the eye-over-candle holy symbol of Deneir in its center. He took up his ram's-head walking stick and headed for the hall.

At the doorway, he turned back, stopped by the cries of his conscience.

Cadderly looked down to his feathered ring, as if that might offer him some relief from what he knew he must do. The ring's base was circular and hollow, holding a tiny vial of drow-style sleep poison, which Cadderly had brewed. The point of the tiny dart was a cat's claw and, once fitted into the hollow shaft of Cadderly's walking stick, it became a potent weapon indeed.

But Cadderly couldn't count on that. Using the blowgun required time to set the dart, and he wasn't even certain of its potency anymore. Drow poison did not last long on the surface world, and though Cadderly had taken great pains to protect his investment, placing the sealed vials into a strong box enchanted with a darkness spell, many weeks had passed since its creation.

Reluctantly the young scholar walked back to the wardrobe and put his hand on the door handle. He looked around helplessly, as if searching for some way out of this trap.

He must not fail in his year quest.

Cadderly opened the wardrobe door, picked a wide strap from among dozens of hanging leather ties, and belted it around his waist. It sported a wide, shallow holster on one side, which held a single-hand crossbow of dark elf design. Cadderly took out a bandoleer next, and found some comfort in the fact that only three explosive darts remained. Nearly two score other darts were in the bandoleer—it was designed to hold as many as fifty—but their centers were hollow and empty, not yet fitted with the tiny vials of *Oil of Impact* that gave the loaded three their wicked punch.

Despite his ambivalent feelings, Cadderly couldn't resist undoing the small leather tie and taking out the crossbow. It was an instrument of beauty, perfectly tooled by Ivan and Pikel. That beauty paled beside Barjin's dead eyes, though, for this was the same weapon that Cadderly had used on that fateful day. He had fired at a mummy, trying to destroy the undead monster as it tried to destroy Barjin. One shot had slipped through the mummy's meager wrappings, though, thudding into helpless Barjin's chest as he lay propped against a wall.

Cadderly distinctly remembered the sound as that dart collapsed on the magical vial and exploded, a sharp echo that had followed him every day and every night.

"Belago asked me to give you this," came a voice from the doorway. Cadderly turned and was surprised to see Kierkan Rufo, tall and angular and tilting, standing in the doorway. Although they had once been friends, Rufo had pretty much avoided Cadderly in the last few weeks.

Cadderly winced as Rufo held out a small ceramic container, for he knew what was inside. Belago's alchemy shop had been blown up during the confusion of the chaos curse, and the alchemist had thought the formula for the Oil of Impact lost in the flames. Not lamenting the loss, Cadderly had lied and told Belago that he did not remember where he had found the formula, but the alchemist, determined to reward Cadderly for his heroics against the evil priest, had vowed to recover it.

The same trapped, resigned expression he had worn when retrieving the crossbow crossed Cadderly's face as he took the flask. The container was heavy; Cadderly guessed that he could fill perhaps twenty more darts with this amount. He searched for some way out; he thought of letting the flask slip to the floor, feigning an accident, but reconsidered that course immediately, knowing the potentially catastrophic consequences.

"You are surprised to see me," Kierkan Rufo said in his monotone voice. His dark hair clung tightly to his head; his dark eyes sparkled like little points of shimmering blackness.

"You have not been around lately," Cadderly replied, turning his head up to look the taller man in the face. "Are you angry with me?"

"I . . ." Rufo stammered, his angular features contorting uncomfortably. He ran a hand through his matted black hair. "The curse affected me deeply," he explained.

"Forget the curse," Cadderly advised him, feeling some sympathy, but not too much, for Rufo's actions during the curse had not been above suspicion. The tall man had even made advances toward Danica, which the young woman had promptly discouraged—by beating Rufo severely.

"We shall talk more when I return," Cadderly said. "I have no time—"

"It was I who pushed you down the stairs," Rufo announced unexpectedly. Cadderly's reply caught in his throat, and his mouth hung open. He had suspected Rufo, but never expected an admission.

"Many acted unwisely during the curse," Cadderly managed to say after a long silence.

"It was before the curse," Rufo reminded him. In fact, that action had set in motion the events leading to the curse.

"Why are you telling me this?" Cadderly demanded, his gray eyes narrowing angrily. "And why did you do it?"

Rufo shrugged and looked away. "The evil priest, I suppose," he whispered. "He caught me in the wine cellar while you were looking down the secret stairway to the lower levels."

"Then forget the incident," said Cadderly with as little anger as he could, "and accept no blame. Barjin was a powerful adversary, with tricks and charms beyond our comprehension."

"I cannot forget it," Rufo replied.

"Then why do you come to me?" Cadderly snapped. "Am I to forgive you? All right, then, I do. You are forgiven. Your conscience is cleared." Cadderly pushed by, heading for the hall.

Rufo grabbed him by the shoulder and turned him about. "I cannot ask your forgiveness until I have forgiven myself," he explained, and his wounded expression touched Cadderly.

"We all have cause to forgive ourselves," Cadderly remarked, glancing down to the flask in his hands. His gaze betrayed his haunting thoughts of Barjin's death.

"I wish to come with you," Rufo said.

Cadderly could not reply for many moments; Rufo was full of surprises this day!

"I must regain my dignity," the angular man explained. "As with you, I must see this threat, or whatever it may be, through to its conclusion. Only then will I forgive my actions of five weeks ago." Cadderly started to drift toward the hall, but Rufo determinedly pulled him back.

"The dwarven brothers are gone," Rufo reminded him. "And the druid Newander is dead. You may need help."

"You are asking the wrong person," Cadderly replied. "Dean Thobicus—"

"Dean Thobicus left the choice to Headmaster Avery," Rufo interrupted, "and Avery left it to you. I may go with your permission, so say they, and Prince Elbereth has agreed as well."

Cadderly hesitated and thought it over for just a few moments. After all that had happened, he wasn't certain he trusted Rufo, but he couldn't ignore the pleading look in the angular man's dark eyes.

"You have less than half an hour to prepare your gear," he said. Rufo's dark face brightened.

"I am already packed."

Somehow, Cadderly wasn't surprised.

Elbereth and Danica were waiting for Cadderly outside the library's ornate double doors. There, too, were Avery, Pertelope, and two spare horses— apparently the headmasters had expected Cadderly to allow Rufo along.

Danica flashed a wide smile Cadderly's way, but it dissipated immediately and her full lips turned down into a scowl when she saw Rufo coming out the doors on Cadderly's heels.

Cadderly offered only a shrug for an explanation as he mounted the horse next to Danica's.

The monk's visage softened as she watched Rufo fumble with his horse. The man was so awkward, and Danica was not without pity. She nodded Cadderly's way; she too determined that she would put the past behind her and concentrate on the road ahead.

"You will see many sights along the road and in the elven wood," Pertelope said to Cadderly as she moved beside his horse. Cadderly tried not to notice the carefree headmistress's prudish dress, but her long gloves seemed out of place, especially in a summer day's warmth.

"Wondrous sights," Pertelope continued. "I know you will learn more in your short time away from the library than in all the years you have been here."

Cadderly looked at her curiously, not certain of how to take her strange words.

"You will see," Pertelope explained, and she tried hard to hide a chuckle, not wanting to mock the young scholar. "There is more to life than the adventures of others, dear Cadderly, and more to living than reading books.

"But, when you find some empty time out there . . ." she continued, and she produced a large tome from under her robes. Cadderly knew the book as soon as she handed it to him, for he, like all priests of his order, had studied the work since his first days in the library: the *Tome of Universal Harmony*, the most holy book of Deneir.

"For good fortunes?" he asked, still confused.

"For reading," Pertelope replied sharply.

"But—"

"I am sure you have the work memorized," Pertelope interrupted, "but I doubt that you have ever truly read it."

Cadderly wondered if he looked as stupid as he felt. He consciously forced himself to close his hanging jaw.

"Words can be read in many ways," Pertelope said, and she pulled herself up enough to peck Cadderly on the cheek. "That was for good fortunes," the headmistress explained, throwing a wink Danica's way.

"I wish I were going with you!" Headmaster Avery cried suddenly. "Oh, to see Shilmista again!" He wiped a kerchief over his eyes and then over his chubby face.

"You may not," Elbereth said coldly, tiring of the lengthy farewell. He touched the reigns of Temmerisa, his shining white stallion, and the mighty horse kicked off, a thousand bells jingling with each step. Kierkan Rufo fell in behind the elf and Danica, too, started away.

Cadderly looked from the *Tome of Universal Harmony* to Headmistress Pertelope and smiled.

"Your perceptions of the world will change often as you grow," Pertelope said quietly, so that the others would not hear. "And while the words in the book remain the same, your reading of them will not. Deneir's heart is a poet's heart, and a poet's heart drifts with the shadows of the clouds."

Cadderly held the thick book in both hands. His perceptions of the world, of morality, had indeed changed. He had killed a man, and had somehow found his first adventure beyond the thousands he had read about in books of legend.

"Read it," Pertelope told him gravely. She turned back to the library, hooked Avery by the arm, and dragged him along.

Cadderly's mount took its first step, and the young priest was on his way.

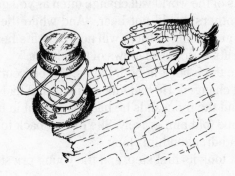

Four

Indecision

Felkin looked around at his eight companions, feeling terribly insecure despite the company. They had come probing deep into Shilmista on orders from Ragnor, the brutish, unmerciful ogrillon. Felkin hadn't questioned the orders at all, not even to his fellow goblins, thinking that whatever dangers awaited them in the elven wood could not match the sure doom of Ragnor's wrath!

Now Felkin wasn't so sure. They had seen nothing, heard nothing, but every member of the nine-goblin scouting party sensed that they were not alone.

They crossed one sandy ridge and came into a deep patch of tall green ferns growing in the shadows of wide-spreading elms.

"What was that?" one goblin croaked, dipping into a defensive crouch and trying to visually follow an elusive, darting figure through the deepening shadows. All in the group danced about nervously, sensing they were vulnerable.

"Quiets!" Felkin scolded, fearing the noise more than any suspected spies.

"What was—?" the goblin tried to ask again, but its words were cut short as an arrow pierced its throat.

The eight remaining goblins scrambled for cover, dropping under the ferns and crawling for the elms. Felkin heard a noise like a snapping stick, and the goblin closest to him soared into the air, kicking and gasping, as a vine noose tightened about its neck.

That proved too much for two of the others. They jumped up and broke into a run for the trees. Neither got more than a few short strides before arrows took them down.

"Where was they?" Felkin called to his companions.

"Left!" cried one goblin.

"Right!" screamed another.

There came a flurry of bow shots, arrows slicing through the ferns and knocking into trees, then all went quiet. The goblin in the air stopped its thrashing and began turning slowly with the wind.

Felkin crept over to one of his companions, lying still in the ferns. "Five of usses left," Felkin reasoned. When the other didn't answer, Felkin roughly turned him about.

A green arrow shaft protruded from one of the goblin's eyes. The other eye stared ahead blankly.

Felkin dropped the corpse and scrambled wildly away, drawing several bow shots in his noisy wake. Somewhere to the side, another goblin tried to run and was cut down with brutal efficiency.

"There remain no more than four of you," said a melodic voice in the goblin tongue, but with the unmistakable accent of a female elf. "Perhaps only three. Do you wish to come out and fight me fairly?"

"Me?" Felkin echoed quietly, confused. "Only one elf?" His entire party had been trimmed by a single elf? Boldly, the goblin poked his head above the ferns and saw the elven warrior, sword in hand, standing beside an elm, with her bow leaning against the tree, within easy reach.

Felkin looked to his own crude spear, wondering if he could make the shot. One of his companions apparently entertained the same notion, for the goblin leaped from the ferns and hurled its spear.

The elf, not caught unaware, dropped to her knees, and the spear flew harmlessly high. Faster than Felkin could follow, she took up her bow and put two shots into the air. The foolish goblin hadn't even the chance to drop back into the fern cover. The first arrow thudded into its chest and the second caught the goblin in the throat.

Felkin looked at his spear again, glad that one of the others had shown him his folly. By his count, only he and one other remained—still two against one if they could get close to the elf warrior.

"Felkin!" He heard a call, and he recognized the voice of Rake, a fine fighter. "How many of usses?"

"Two!" he replied, then he called to the elf. "Two of usses, elf. Will you puts your nasty bow down and fights us fair-like?"

The elf leaned her bow back against the tree and took up her sword. "Come on, then," she said. "The day grows long and my supper awaits!"

"Yous is ready, Rake?" Felkin cried.

"Ready!" the other goblin replied eagerly.

Felkin licked his cracked lips and set his floppy feet for a good start. He'd send Rake into action against the elf and use the diversion to run away into the forest. "Ready?" he called again.

"Ready!" Rake assured him.

"Charge!" came Felkin's cry, and he heard the rustle as Rake, far to his right, leaped from the ferns. Felkin, too, leaped up, but ran off to the left, away from the elf. He looked back once, thinking himself clever, and saw that Rake had similarly retreated to the right. The elf, now wearing an amused smile, took up her bow.

Felkin put his head down and sprinted into the shadows, running as fast as his spindly goblin legs would carry him. There came a distant twang of a bowstring and Rake's steady stream of curses. Felkin's hopes returned with the knowledge that the elf had gone after his companion.

There came an agonized scream, and Felkin knew he was alone. He ran on, not daring to slow. Only a few minutes later, Felkin thought he heard a rustle behind him.

"Don't kills me! Don't kills me!" Felkin cried pitifully and breathlessly over and over. Panicking, he looked behind him once again—and turned back just in time to see that he had veered straight into an oak tree.

Felkin went down in a heap, folding neatly into a leafy crook between the huge roots at the great tree's base. He didn't hear the footsteps pass him by, a few strides to the side, didn't hear anything at all.

* * * * *

"Are you in contact with Aballister?" Dorigen asked Druzil, seeing the imp in a contemplative stance.

Druzil laughed at her. "Why?" he asked innocently. "I have nothing to tell him."

Dorigen closed her eyes and muttered a short chant, casting a simple spell that might allow her to confirm Druzil's claim. When she looked at the imp again, she seemed satisfied.

"That is good," she muttered. "You are not a familiar in the accepted sense of the word, are you, dear Druzil?"

Again the imp laughed in his raspy, breathless voice.

"You do not seem so tied to Aballister," Dorigen explained. "You do not treat him as master."

"Truly you err, Mistress Magic," Druzil replied, wondering if Aballister had arranged a little test of fealty. "I am loyal to my master, he who summoned me from the torment of the Abyss."

Dorigen didn't seem impressed, and Druzil didn't push it. Rumors had said that he had helped kill Barjin, but, in truth, the imp had considered joining the cleric and abandoning Aballister altogether. Then Barjin's grand designs had come crashing down. The rumors worked in Druzil's favor, though. They made upstarts such as Dorigen treat him with a bit of respect and kept Aballister off track in figuring what had really transpired in the Edificant Library's catacombs.

"We work for a single cause," Dorigen said, "a cause given to us by Talona. This entire region will fall to Castle Trinity, do not doubt, and those who stand beside us shall profit greatly—but those who stand against us shall suffer even more!"

"You make a threat?" The imp's simple question nearly knocked Dorigen over.

Dorigen took a moment to collect her thoughts, then replied, "If you believe so. Should it be?" She seemed more unsure of herself than Druzil had ever seen her.

"I am loyal to my master," Druzil said again, firmly, "and now to you, the wizard my master has bade me to travel beside."

Dorigen relaxed a bit. "Then let us travel," she said. "The sun is rising, and we are still several days from Shilmista. I do not like the prospects of having Ragnor running about uncontrolled." She called Tiennek, who was gathering water from a nearby stream, back to her and took up her walking stick.

Druzil wholeheartedly agreed. He gave a lazy flap and landed on Dorigen's shoulder, then folded the leathery wings about him to shield him from the sun. He liked his position now. In journeying with Mistress Magic, he could see the progress of Castle Trinity's conquest, and, even more importantly, in Shilmista he would be out of Aballister's reach.

Druzil knew that Cadderly, the young priest who had defeated Barjin, was Aballister's deserted son, and Aballister knew that he knew. The web of intrigue seemed to tighten around Aballister, and the imp did not want to get choked by its strands.

*****

"One of them got away," Shayleigh reported to Tintagel when she returned to the new elven camp, "but eight others are dead."

The elf wizard nodded, having heard similar reports all day. The enemy had backed off after the slaughter in the Dells, and now sent small probing groups— mostly goblins—deeper into Shilmista. "Perhaps it is good that one escaped," the elf wizard offered, the corners of his blue eyes turning up in a smile. "Let it return to its foul brethren and tell them that only death awaits them under Shilmista's boughs!"

Shayleigh, too, managed a smile, but there was worry reflected in the elf maiden's violet orbs. The enemy scouting parties were being slaughtered, but the fact that their leader apparently accepted the losses only heightened Shayleigh's belief that a huge force indeed had found its way into Shilmista's northern reaches.

"Come," Tintagel said. "Let us go to the king and see what plans he has formulated."

They found Galladel alone in a clearing beyond a shielding wall of thick pines, pacing nervously. The elf king motioned for them to join him, then brought his slender hand up to stroke his raven-black hair, still vibrant and thick, though Galladel had lived many centuries. He stopped his movement when he saw that the hand was trembling, and dropped it back to his side. He glanced at Shayleigh and Tintagel to make sure that they had not seen.

"The slaughter continues," Tintagel announced, trying to calm the nervous king.

"For how long?" Galladel retorted. "The reports, sightings—so many sightings of monstrous scum in our fair wood!—have continued to come in."

"We will beat them back," Shayleigh pronounced.

Galladel appreciated his fine young commander's confidence, but in the face of the emerging force against him, it seemed only a minor thing.

"For how long?" he asked again, less sharply. "This black tide has rolled over the northern reaches. Our enemy is cunning."

"He sends his troops to be massacred," Tintagel argued.

"He bides his time," the elf king countered. "He sacrifices his weakest fodder to keep us busy. Damn this waiting game."

"Something will happen soon," Shayleigh said. "I can feel the tension. Our enemy will reveal himself in full."

Galladel looked at her curiously, but knew better than to dismiss the elf maiden's intuition. Shayleigh had been the one to argue for, and to organize, the ambush in the Dells, having read the enemy's initial probing actions perfectly. Certainly the king was glad to have her at his side, especially with Elbereth, his son and closest advisor, in the east, trying to gain some insight from the priests of the Edificant Library. Galladel had ordered Elbereth not to go, but lately his commands carried little weight with his headstrong son.

"Soon," Shayleigh said again, seeing that the tension was near to breaking Galladel.

"They are marching now," came a chirping voice from the side. Both Galladel and Shayleigh turned and curiously eyed a large oak tree.

They heard a tittering laughter. Thinking to defend her king, Shayleigh drew her slender sword and advanced boldly. Tintagel took up a position to the side, producing a spell component from his pocket and ready to strike at a moment's warning.

"Oh, do not tell me you have not heard the warnings of the trees!" came the voice, followed by a movement around the back of the tree. A pixie-featured woman, her skin as tan as the oak's bark and her hair as green as the great tree's dark leaves, peeked out from around the thick trunk.

Shayleigh's sword went back into its scabbard. "We have heard nothing but the dying gasps of intruders," the elf maiden said coldly.

"Who is it?" demanded Galladel.

"A dryad," Shayleigh replied. "Hammadeen, I believe."

"Oh, you remember me!" chirped Hammadeen, and she clapped her delicate hands together. "But you just said you can feel it!"

The dryad's abrupt changes of subject left the elf maiden bewildered. "I feel what?" she asked.

"The excitement in the air!" cried Hammadeen. "It is the talk of the trees that you hear. They are afraid, and so they should be."

"What nonsense is this?" growled Galladel, moving to join Shayleigh.

"Oh, no, not nonsense!" replied Hammadeen, suddenly sounding distressed.

"They are marching in force, too many for the trees to count. And they have fire and axes! Oh, the elves must stop them—you must."

Shayleigh and Galladel exchanged confused looks.

"Listen!" cried the dryad. "You must listen."

"We are listening!" roared a frustrated Galladel.

"To the trees . . ." Hammadeen explained. Her voice diminished—and her body seemed to, as well—as she blended into the oak. Shayleigh rushed over, trying to catch the dryad or to follow, but the elf maiden's reaching hands found only the rough bark of the wide oak.

"Dryads," Shayleigh remarked, her tone less than complimentary.

"Listen to the trees," spat Galladel. He kicked dirt at the base of the oak and spun away.

Shayleigh was surprised by the intensity of the king's disdain. It was said that the trees of Shilmista had often spoken with the forest elves, that once the trees had even uprooted and walked to fight beside Dellanil Quil'quien, an elven hero and king in times long past. That was only legend to young Shayleigh, but surely aged Galladel, a direct descendent of Dellanil's, had lived in those times.

"We know now that our enemy is on the move again," Shayleigh offered, "in great numbers. And we know from where they will come. I will arrange another surprise—"

"We know only what a dryad has told us!" yelled Galladel. "You would risk our entire defense on the fleeting words of a dryad, by nature a creature of half-truths and insidious charms?"

Again the elf maiden was taken aback by Galladel's unwarranted anger. The dryads most certainly were not the elven host's enemies, and could well prove valuable allies.

Galladel took a deep breath and seemed to calm himself, as though he, too, realized his misplaced wrath.

"We have only the word of Hammadeen," Shayleigh offered tentatively, "but I do not doubt that our enemy is on the march. There are many defensible ridges between here and the northern reaches. It would seem prudent to begin preparations even without the dryad's warning."

"No," Galladel said firmly. "We'll not go out to meet the enemy again. We will not catch him so unaware, and the result might be disastrous.

"Our powers are greater near the center of the forest," Galladel continued, "and there we may more easily elude this great force, if indeed it is coming."

Shayleigh was livid and adamant. "If we run, we give them miles of the forest to destroy," she growled. "Shilmista is our home, from the southernmost to the northernmost tree!"

"Daoine Dun is not so far," Tintagel offered as a compromise location. "The caves there offer us shelter, and certainly the hill figures prominently in our power."

Shayleigh considered the suggestion for a moment. She would have preferred taking the offensive again, but she knew well that Galladel would not give in to her reasoning. Daoine Dun, the Hill of the Stars, seemed a reasonable compromise. She nodded to Galladel.

The elf king didn't seem convinced. "There are better choices more to the south," he said.

Shayleigh and Tintagel exchanged fearful glances. Both wished that Elbereth had not gone away, for the elf prince was more attuned to their way of thinking, more determined to preserve what little remained of Shilmista's glory. Perhaps Galladel had lived too long; the burdens of rulership over the centuries could not be underestimated.

"Our enemy numbers in the thousands, by every report," Galladel snapped at them, apparently sensing their heartfelt disapproval—for his decision and for him. "We number barely seven score and hope that our courage alone will turn aside that black tide. Do not confuse courage with foolishness, I say, and I am still your king!"

The younger elves would have lost the argument then, except that cries rang out in the elven camp beyond the pine grove. "Fire!" the shouts proclaimed.

One elf rushed in through the trees to report to his king. "Fire!" he cried. "Our enemy burns the forest. In the north! In the north!" The elf turned and fled then, back through the natural barrier.

Galladel turned away from Shayleigh and Tintagel, ran his hand nervously through his raven-black hair, and muttered several silent curses at Elbereth for going away.

"Daoine Dun?" Tintagel asked tentatively and hopefully.

Galladel waved a resigned hand the wizard's way. "As you will," he offered listlessly. "As you will."

* * * * *

When Felkin opened his eyes again, he had to squint against the morning sunlight. The forest around him was deathly quiet, and a long time passed before the goblin mustered the nerve to crawl out of the leaves. He considered going back to check on his companions, then snorted the thought away and made off with all speed for Ragnor's camp on the forest's northern borders.

Felkin felt a bit relieved a short while later, when he heard the hacking of axes. The sky lightened in front of him, the thick canopy thinned, and he came out of the trees suddenly, only to find himself immediately surrounded by Ragnor's elite guard, a contingent of eight huge and hairy bugbears.

They looked down at poor, shivering Felkin from their seven-foot height, evil, yellow-eyed gazes boring into the goblin.

"Who are you?" one of the creatures demanded, poking a trident against the goblin's shoulder.

Felkin winced from the pain and fear, nearly as terrified of bugbears as of the elf he had left behind. "Felkin," he squeaked, bowing his head submissively. "Scout."

The bugbears murmured something in their own guttural tongue, then one of them prodded Felkin even harder. "Where are the others?"

Felkin bit his lip to prevent crying out in pain; revealing weakness would only inspire the cruel monsters to greater acts of torture. "In the forest," he whispered.

"Dead?"

Felkin nodded meekly, then he felt as if he were flying as one bugbear grabbed him by the scraggly hair and hoisted him high off the ground. Felkin's skinny arms flapped as he tried to secure a supporting hold on the bugbear's sinewy arm. The merciless creature carried him by just the hair all the way across the large encampment. Felkin continued to gnaw on his lip and fought back tears as best he could.

He determined their destination to be a large, hide-covered tent. Ragnor! The world seemed to spin about to the quivering goblin; he knew that he was fainting and hoped he would never wake up.

He did awaken, and then he wished that he had stayed in the forest and taken his chances with the elf.

Ragnor did not seem so imposing at first, sitting behind a large oaken table across the tent. Then the ogrillon stood, and Felkin whined and crawled backward across the ground. A prod from a trident forced him back to his place.

Ragnor was as tall as the bugbears and twice as wide. His features were orcish, mostly, with a snout resembling a pig's nose and one tusklike tooth protruding from his bottom jaw, up over his upper lip. His eyes were large and bloodshot, and his brow heavy, always crinkled in an ominous glare. While his features were orcish, his body more resembled his ogre ancestors, with thick, powerful limbs, corded muscles, and a barrel-like torso that could stop a charging horse dead in its tracks.

The ogrillon took three heavy strides to stand before Felkin, reached down, and easily—too easily!—lifted the goblin to his feet.

"The others are dead?" Ragnor asked in his throaty, commanding voice.

"Elveses!" Felkin cried. "Elveses killed them!"

"How many?"

"Lots and lots!" Felkin answered, but the ogrillon didn't seem impressed. Ragnor put a single large finger under Felkin's chin and lifted the goblin to his tiptoes. The ugly orc face with evil-smelling breath moved just an inch from the goblin, and Felkin thought he would faint again—though he realized that Ragnor would skin him if he did.

"How many?" Ragnor asked again, slowly and deliberately.

"One," squeaked Felkin, thinking the better of adding that it was a female. Ragnor dropped him to the floor.

"An entire patrol cut down by a single elf!" the ogrillon roared at the bugbears. The hairy monsters looked around to each other, but did not seem overly concerned.

"You send goblins and orcs," one of them remarked.

"I first sent bugbears!" Ragnor reminded them. "How many of your kin returned?"

The embarrassed bugbears mumbled excuses in their own tongue. "Send bigger scouting groups?" the bugbear spokesman offered a few moments later.

Ragnor thought it over, then shook his huge head. "We cannot match the elves with such tactics in the woods. We have the advantage of numbers and strength, but that is all in this cursed forest."

"They know the region well," agreed the bugbear.

"And I do not doubt that they have many spies about," added Ragnor. "Even the trees I do not trust!"

"Then how do we proceed?"

"We continue our march!" the frustrated ogrillon growled. He grabbed Felkin tightly about the throat and pulled him off the ground, again close to Ragnor's ugly face.

"The elves know their forest, so we will destroy their forest!" the ogrillon growled. "We will force them out in the open ground and crush them!" Too excited by his own words, Ragnor's hand jerked suddenly. There came a loud crack, and Felkin twitched violently, then was still.

The bugbears looked on in amazement. One of them chuckled, but bit it back quickly. Too late; the other bugbears burst out in laughter, and their mirth increased tenfold when Ragnor joined in, giving the goblin a shake to make sure it was dead.

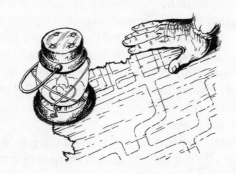

Five

First Contact

Cadderly sat in the dim light of the dying campfire, a line of tiny vials on the ground before him, paralleling a line of empty crossbow darts. One by one, he took the vials and very carefully dripped in a few drops from the flask that Kierkan Rufo had delivered to him.

"What is he doing?" Elbereth asked Rufo as they stood on the edge of the firelight.

"Making darts for his crossbow," the tall man explained. His face seemed even more angular, almost inhuman, in the flickering shadows.

Elbereth studied the diminutive weapon, resting on the ground at Cadderly's side. The elf's expression was not complimentary.

"That is a drow device," he spat, loudly enough for Cadderly to hear. Cadderly looked up and knew that the elf prince was about to put him on trial.

"Do you consort with dark elves?" Elbereth asked bluntly.

"I have never met one," Cadderly answered simply, thinking, but not adding, that if Elbereth's arrogance exemplified the good side of the elven nation, he most certainly would have no desire to meet one of the bad side!

"Where did you acquire the crossbow then?" Elbereth pressed, as though he was just looking for a reason to begin an argument with Cadderly. "And why would you wish to carry the weapon of such an evil race?"

Cadderly picked up the crossbow, somehow comforted in the fact that it had brought Elbereth some grief. He understood that Elbereth provoked him now simply out of general frustration, and he certainly sympathized with the elf's worries for Shilmista. Still, Cadderly had his own concerns and was in no mood for Elbereth's continued insults. "Dwarf-made, actually," he corrected.

"Nearly as bad," the elf snipped without hesitation.

Cadderly's gray eyes were not as striking as Elbereth's silvery orbs, but his glare more than equaled the elf's in intensity. In a fight of weapons, of course, Elbereth could easily cut him down, but if the elf prince launched more insults Ivan and Pikel's way, Cadderly had every intention of pummeling him with fists. Cadderly was a fine wrestler, having grown up among the clerics of Oghma, whose principal rituals involved weaponless combat. While Elbereth was nearly as tall as the six-foot-high scholar, Cadderly figured that he outweighed the slender elf by at least seventy pounds.

Apparently understanding that he had pushed the young scholar as far as he could without starting a fight, Elbereth did not immediately continue, but neither did he blink his silver eyes.

"The perimeter is clear," said Danica as she came back into camp. She looked from Elbereth to Cadderly and saw the obvious tension. "What has happened?"

Elbereth turned to her and smiled warmly, which bothered Cadderly more than the uncompromising glare the elf had given him.

"A discussion of the crossbow, nothing more," Elbereth assured Danica. "I do not understand the value of such a puny weapon—nor the honor."

Danica put a sympathetic look Cadderly's way. If the young scholar was vulnerable about anything in the world, it was the crossbow and the memories it inevitably conjured. Unexpectedly, Cadderly launched himself in the face of those memories.

"I killed a man with this," he growled dangerously. Danica's look turned to one of horror, and Cadderly realized how stupid that proclamation had been. What a ridiculous and disgusting thing to brag about! He knew he had laid himself open to the elf now, that Elbereth could easily destroy him in this argument, for Cadderly would find no courage to back up his bravado.

But the elf, looking from Cadderly to Danica, chose to discontinue the discussion. "It is my watch," he said simply and disappeared into the darkness.

Cadderly looked to Danica and shrugged apologetically. The young woman just sat across the fire from him, wrapped herself in a heavy blanket, and lay down to sleep.

Cadderly considered the crossbow, feeling that it had betrayed him once again. He wished he had been more attentive in his combat studies at the library; then, perhaps, he would not need to carry the unconventional weapon. But while the other clerics had practiced with the mace, quarterstaff, or club, Cadderly had concentrated on his spindle-disks—twin disks joined by a connecting bar, on which was tied a slender cord—a useful enough weapon for felling small game and an enjoyable toy to put through a variety of mesmerizing tricks, but hardly a match for a sword.

Cadderly's hand went unconsciously to the disks, which were looped on his belt. He had used them in battle a couple of times, had dropped Kierkan Rufo when the angular man, under the chaos curse's influence, had come after Cadderly with a knife. Even against the tiny blade that Rufo had carried, Cadderly had won only because his opponent had become distracted. A single lucky throw had saved him.

Cadderly considered his walking stick as well, with its sculpted ram's-head handle and smooth-bored interior. It was an expensive item and well balanced, and Cadderly had used it, too, in battle. Danica had told him that such a small staff—she called it a bo stick—was a favorite among monks in her mother's ancient homeland of Tabot. Cadderly was barely skilled with it. He could twirl it and thrust it, even parry basic attacks, but he wouldn't want to test his talents against a seasoned fighter like Elbereth, or any monster, for that matter.

Resigned, the young scholar filled another vial and carefully snapped it into place in the hollow of a dart. He slipped the loaded dart into a loop on his bandoleer; that made twelve.

In the first few fights at least, Cadderly might show as well as Elbereth. The young scholar hated that that fact mattered to him, but he couldn't deny that it did.

The eastern fringes of Shilmista were not too far from the Edificant Library, and, even crossing the rough mountain trails, the travelers could have seen the forest on their second day out. Shilmista was a long wood, though, running one hundred and fifty miles from north to south, and Elbereth wanted to come out of the mountains nearer the forest's center, where the elves made their primary homes.

For several more days, the four companions walked up, down, and around high peaks and through steep valleys. It was summer, even in the mountains, and the air was warm and the sky blue. Each turn in the trail promised a new majestic view, but even mountain scenery became somewhat dull to Cadderly after several straight days.

Often during this quiet time, Cadderly took the *Tome of Universal Harmony* from his horse's pack. He did not begin reading it, though, for he was too agitated by the potential trials ahead and Elbereth's growing relationship with Danica— the two got on famously, swapping tales of places Cadderly had never seen—to concentrate enough for a proper read.

On the fifth day, they came at last to the western ridges. Looking down, they could see the dark canopy of Shilmista, a peaceful and quiet cover for the mounting tumult beneath the thick boughs.

"That is my home," Elbereth announced to Danica. "There is no place in all the world to match Shilmista's beauty."

Cadderly wanted to rebuff him. The young scholar had read of many wondrous lands, magical lands, and by all accounts, Shilmista, though a fitting wood for elven folk, was nothing extraordinary. Cadderly had the foresight, though, to understand how pitiful he would sound in making such a claim, and the common sense to anticipate Elbereth's angry reaction. He wisely kept his thoughts to himself and resolved to point out Shilmista's weak points to Danica later.

Although the path had become clear and smooth enough for riding, the steep decline and winding turns forced the party to continue walking the horses. As they came to the lower foothills, mountain stone gave way to earthen ground, and here walking their mounts proved a fortunate thing, for on the back of Temmerisa, his great stallion, Elbereth would not have noticed the tracks.

He stooped low to examine them and said nothing for a long while.

Cadderly and the others could guess from the elf's grim expression the source of those markings.

"Goblins?" Danica asked finally.

"Some, perhaps," Elbereth replied, his gaze drifting back toward his precious forest, "but most are too big to have been made by goblins." The elf took out his longbow and handed the reigns of his horse to Kierkan Rufo. He then motioned for Danica to give her mount over to Cadderly.

The young scholar wasn't thrilled with acting the part of a page, but he couldn't argue against the value of having Danica and Elbereth with their hands free, ready to meet any sudden attacks.

Elbereth took up the lead, pausing often to study new tracks, and Danica fell into line at the rear of the party, watching all directions.

They came back into the tree line and grew even more cautious, for shadows loomed all about them, possible hiding spots for monsters setting an ambush. For an hour they crossed in and out of the gloom, moving under thick trees one moment and coming suddenly into the open sunlight the next as the trail wound across wide stones.

Temmerisa's thousand bells tinkled suddenly with the steed's nervous movement. Elbereth immediately went on his guard, crouching low and looking all about. He moved across the trail, slipped into concealment amid a tumble of boulders, and peered down at the mountainsides below.

Danica and Cadderly joined him immediately, but Rufo stayed back with the horses, seeming ready to spring upon his roan mount in an instant and fly away.

"The trail doubles back on itself down below," the elf explained in a whisper. His observations were evident to Cadderly and Danica, for the trees and brush were not thick below them and the looping road was clearly visible. Elbereth seemed intent on one huge maple tree, its thick branches overhanging the road.

"There!" Danica whispered, pointing to the very same tree. "On the lowest branch above the road." Elbereth nodded gravely, and Danica blew a quiet whistle.

Cadderly watched them in confusion. He, too, peered intently at the tree, but all he saw were thick, overlapping leaves.

"The limb bends under their weight," Elbereth remarked.

"Whose weight?" Cadderly had to ask. Elbereth scowled, but Danica took pity on Cadderly and continued to point out what she had noticed until he, at last, nodded in recognition. Several dark forms were crouched together on that low branch, high above the road.

"Orcs?" Danica asked.

"Too big for orcs," reasoned Elbereth. "Orogs."

Danica's delicate features crinkled with confusion.

"Orogs are kin to orcs," cut in Cadderly, beating the elf to the explanation. Orogs were not a common monster, but one that Cadderly had read about in many books. "Larger and stronger than their pig-faced cousins. It is believed that they originated—"

"What do you think they are waiting for?" Danica interrupted before Cadderly could make a complete fool of himself.

"Us," Elbereth said grimly. "They have heard our horses, perhaps seen us on the open expanses of the higher trails."

"Is there another way around?" Cadderly knew the question sounded ridiculous even as he asked it. Danica, and especially Elbereth, had no intention of going around the monsters.

Elbereth considered the terrain straight from his position. "If I pick my way down the mountainside while you continue along the trail," he reasoned, "I may be able to take a few of them down with my bow." The elf prince nodded in affirmation of his own plan. "Come, then," he said, "we must get the horses moving again before the orogs grow suspicious."

Danica turned and started back to Rufo, but Cadderly was struck with an idea. "Let me go," he offered, a smile widening across his face.

Elbereth regarded him curiously, and even more so when Cadderly took out his tiny crossbow.

"You believe you can inflict more damage with that than I with my longbow?" the elf prince asked.

"Wouldn't you prefer to fight them on the ground?" Cadderly replied, grinning Danica's way. Elbereth, too, looked to the woman, and she nodded and smiled, trusting in Cadderly and knowing that playing a role in the fight was important to the young scholar.

"Go along the trail," Cadderly told them. "I shall meet you at the tree."

Elbereth, still not convinced, turned back to study the young scholar. "Your hat and cape," the elf said, holding out his hands.

Cadderly's pause displayed his confusion.

"Blue is not a forest color," Elbereth explained. "It shows as clearly as a fire in the dark of night. We will be fortunate if the orogs have not already spotted you."

"They have not," Danica insisted, realizing that Elbereth had made that last statement only to belittle Cadderly.

The scholar untied his short cape and handed it and the hat to Elbereth. "I will see you at the tree," he said finally, trying to appear confident.

His firm jaw weakened as soon as the others moved out of sight. What had he gotten himself into? Even if he managed to get down the steep slope without breaking his neck and causing enough noise for all the orogs in the Snowflake Mountains to hear, what would he do if they noticed him? What defense could Cadderly present against even a single opponent?

He shook the dark thoughts away and started down, having no other choice, he believed, if he wished to hold any honor at all in Danica's almond eyes. He stumbled and tripped, stubbed his toes a dozen times, and set several stones skipping down, but somehow managed to get level with the giant maple apparently without disturbing the ambush-intent monsters. He crawled into a crevice between two sharp-edged rocks a short distance from the side of the trail. He could see the orogs clearly then; nearly a dozen crouched side by side on the low branch. They held nets and spears and crude swords, and it wasn't difficult for Cadderly to discern their tactics.

The monsters went quiet. At first, Cadderly feared he had been discovered, but he soon realized that the orogs continued looking up the trail. He knew that his friends would arrive soon.

He loaded the crossbow, taking care to move the small crank slowly and smoothly so that it wouldn't make any noise. Then he leveled the weapon—but where to shoot? He could probably knock an orog out of the tree, maybe even kill one if his aim or his luck was good enough. His earlier boasts seemed so foolish now, with the danger so very close and the responsibility fully on his shoulders.

He had to go with his original plan; Elbereth and Danica were counting on him to get the monsters out of the tree. He took aim, not at any of the monsters, but at where the thick branch joined the trunk. It was not a difficult shot with the accurate crossbow, but would the explosive suffice? Cadderly took out a second dart, just in case.

The orogs shifted nervously; Cadderly could hear the plodding hoofbeats down the trail.

"Deneir be with me," the young scholar mumbled, and he squeezed the crossbow's trigger. The dart floated in, struck the branch, and collapsed on the vial, and the ensuing explosion shook the tree violently. Orogs grabbed on—one tumbled from the branch—and Cadderly, to his relief, heard a loud cracking noise. The young scholar sent another dart looping in.

The branch blew apart. An orog screamed as its ankle got hooked on the jagged break, the skin tearing off the side of its leg as it fell.

Danica and Elbereth, upon their horses, were barely thirty feet from the tree when the orogs tumbled out. Elbereth, concerned, glanced sidelong at the young woman, for only one of the monsters seemed injured and the others were well armed.

"There are only ten of them!" Danica cried, reaching down to pull a crystalline-bladed dagger from a boot sheath. She laughed wildly and spurred her horse ahead. Temmerisa, bearing the elf, charged right behind.

Danica came in hard and fast on the closest three monsters. Just before she reached them, she rolled off the side of her horse, caught a handhold on the saddle's cinch, and pulled herself under the horse, straight through the beast's legs. The horse blasted through the stunned orogs, all of them expecting Danica on the wrong side.

Danica hit the ground running, used her momentum to leap into a spin, and connected on the closest orog with a circle kick that snapped the creature's neck and sent it tumbling away.

Her wrist flicked as soon as she got her bearings, launching the dagger, point over hilt. It spun several times, a glittering sliver in the sunlight, before burying itself hilt-deep in the second orog's face.

The third monster heaved its spear and drew out a crude sword. Its aim had been perfect, but Danica was too quick to be taken by such a clumsy weapon. She side-stepped and threw out a forearm parry that sent the spear flying harmlessly wide.

The orog came in unconcerned, and Danica nearly laughed at how defense-less she must have appeared to the six-and-a-half-foot, two-hundred-pound monster. Slender and pretty, she barely topped five feet, with unkempt locks flying wildly about her shoulders and eyes that sparkled, to the unknowing observer, with childish innocence.

Blood quickly replaced drool on the orog's hungry lips. It stepped in and reached for Danica with its free hand. She caught it with a lightning-quick jab that took out two of its front teeth. Danica jumped back, bouncing on the balls of her feet and feeling good about the beginning of this battle. It had taken just a few seconds, but two monsters lay dead or dying and the third stood teetering and trying to shake the stars out of its vision.

Elbereth's charge was even more straightforward and more brutal. He led with a single bow shot, catching a monster in the shoulder. Then, drawing his sword and slipping his arm through the leather straps of his shield, the elf trusted in his disciplined steed and crashed right into the main group of orogs. His magical blade glowed a bluish flame as he hacked at the monstrous throng. He took several quick hits from the monsters' crude weapons, but his fine shield and finer armor deflected the blows.

More deadly were Elbereth's thrusts; the unarmored orogs simply couldn't afford to swap blows with the elf, as the closest monster, the one with the arrow in its shoulder, learned when Elbereth responded to its spear thrust by lopping off its head.

Temmerisa reared and danced about, keeping in perfect balance and har-mony with its familiar rider. One orog slipped behind the shining white horse, its spear held high for a throw that would have taken Elbereth squarely in the back. Temmerisa kicked with both hind feet, connecting on the orog's chest and launching it many yards away. The broken monster crumpled to the ground, gasping futilely with lungs that had collapsed.

Elbereth's battle would have been a rout then, for only two monsters remained (and one of these could barely stand, leaning against the huge tree with one of its legs torn apart). But when the limb had broken, a single orog had managed to keep a handhold in the tree. Grasping a net in its free hand, the mon-ster swung out on the higher branch and timed its leap perfectly, coming down on the slender elf's back and bearing Elbereth to the ground under it and under the net.

A deceptively swift sword cut forced Danica to hop and throw her head backward. She knew that a monster as powerful as an orog could not be taken lightly, but she found herself distracted, for off to the side, Elbereth had gone down, and Kierkan Rufo had not yet entered the fray. Just as unnerving to the young woman, two of the orogs had fled toward Cadderly.

Another slice made Danica drop almost to the ground; a third sent her rolling to the side. The orog, confident again, advanced steadily.

It swung again, but this time Danica, instead of backing away, charged straight ahead. She caught the orog's sword hand in her own and stepped toward it, hooking her free forearm so forcefully around the orog's extended arm that she heard the monster's elbow snap. Fierce Danica barely gave the monster time to cry in pain. Still holding fast to its sword hand, she whipped her other arm back, free of the monster's, and threw her elbow up and out, slamming the creature in the nose.

Danica's elbow came back tight to her side and her backhand went snapping out, scoring another solid hit. When the arm recoiled, still before the orog had time to react, Danica straightened her hand tightly and chopped across the orog's throat.

She dipped under the monster's trapped arm. Her grip turned the muscled limb half a circuit as she passed under it, and Danica turned about to face the creature.

The orog reached for her weakly, but Danica paid the lame attempt no heed. Her foot shot up under the orog's reach and slammed the monster in the chin, then again, and a third time, in rapid succession.

"Cadderly," the monk breathed, looking down the trail, for the two fleeing monsters were close to her beloved.

Cadderly, acting on pure instinct, didn't hesitate to consider the moral consequences in the least as the first orog bore down on him, pointedly shifting its course when it noticed him lying between the stones.

An exploding dart abruptly halted its charge.

The monster's surprised roar came out as a wheeze, for the dart had put a hole cleanly through one lung. Stubbornly the monster came on, and Cadderly shot it again, this time in the belly.

The orog doubled over, growling in agony.

"Die, damn you," Cadderly moaned when it straightened and came on again. This time his shot blew off the top of the orog's head.

Cadderly himself was having trouble finding his breath, and his revulsion turned to stark horror when he looked up to see the second orog towering over him, straddling the stones with its very big sword angled to split Cadderly in half. There was no time for another dart, the young scholar knew, so he grabbed his walking stick and tossed it up toward the monster.

The orog's face contorted in confusion as it batted the walking stick aside, but Cadderly's ruse was not without purpose. In the split second the orog's attention was stolen, Cadderly turned himself about and rolled to his back, looking up to the orog's backside. He curled up in a ball, hooking his calves behind the orog's knees and then straightened and pulled with all his might.

For a long moment, nothing happened, and Cadderly thought that he must look ridiculous indeed, as though he were straining against an immovable object. Then the orog did fall forward, but not heavily, and with no damage done. Cadderly scrambled forward, over the orog's back, and he hooked one arm about the orog's thick neck and pulled for all his life.

Undaunted, the creature stood back up, taking Cadderly with it. It casually looked around for its sword, dropped in the fall, then spotted the weapon and made for it.

Cadderly realized that the monster could easily jab the weapon behind it, right into his vulnerable torso. Frantic now, the young scholar considered letting go and making a run for cover. He knew that he would never get out of the monster's reach in time.

"Fall, damn you!" Cadderly growled, tightening and twisting his arm.

The orog, to Cadderly's astonishment, dropped its sword back to the ground. As though it had noticed the choke hold for the first time, the monster's thick hands came up to grab at Cadderly's arm, but by that time, there remained little strength in them.

Eyes closed, Cadderly desperately held on, still pulling with all his might.

Finally, the orog tumbled face down.

The last orog, near the tree, could not put its right foot on the ground. It wanted to go with its two companions, one lying atop the netted elf and the other waving a sword menacingly and looking for an opening, but the creature winced whenever its toe came near the ground. The beast looked up and saw the flesh from its leg hanging grotesquely from the jag on the broken tree branch.

Cursing its luck and ignoring the burning agony, the stubborn creature hopped on its good foot out from the maple's wide trunk.

Right in Kierkan Rufo's path.

Rufo rode one horse and held the other beside it, and his charge came powerfully, if a bit late. The angular man hadn't meant to run the orog down with his own horse—he had purposely placed the riderless steed closer to the tree—but the orog's unexpected movement had put it right between both horses.

The monster got tangled in the worst possible way and was stepped on several times, but when the horses passed, it was still alive, lying helplessly on its back. Its spine was crushed, leaving it staring straight up at the dripping meat of its own ripped leg.

The riderless horse crossed the broken branch without trouble, but Rufo's horse, stumbling from the tangled orog, flipped headlong, sending the angular man on a long, bouncing roll. Rufo spat dirt, shifted about, and sat looking back on the battle. His attack did much to aid Elbereth's cause, for one of the three orogs moving to engage the elf was down and a second had broken away from the fray.

It was little comfort to poor Rufo, though, for the orog had only run because it had spotted an easier target—Rufo. It charged down the trail, its huge sword waving and its tongue hanging hungrily between broken yellow teeth.

Rufo saw Danica, over to the side, react. She snapped off one more kick, which sent her orog's head jerking backward, then broke free of the monster. She hesitated, glanced at Elbereth, but apparently figured that the elf had the situation under control, and ran after the orog approaching Rufo.

Elbereth squirmed around to face the heavy orog. He worked his hand to his belt, using his other arm to keep the ugly monster's snapping mouth from biting at his face.

Elbereth's arm moved in three rapid jolts, the orog heaving with each. The fourth time, Elbereth held his arm tight against the monster and began twisting his wrist back and forth.

The monster rolled off the elf's slender stiletto and thrashed in the road, trying to hold its entrails inside its opened belly.

In a single movement, the agile Elbereth slipped out from under the crude net and came up to his knees. Merciless and grim-faced, he whipped his dagger into the squirming orog's leg so that it couldn't run while he retrieved his sword.

Danica was swift, as fast as anyone Rufo had ever seen, but the orog's lead was too great. Reluctantly, the angular man pulled his mace from his belt and tried to stand. He was less skilled with weapons than even Cadderly and could not hope to hold out for long. Even worse, Rufo's ankle, twisted in the fall, would not support him, and he fell back to the seat of his pants. The orog was almost upon him; he knew he was about to die.

The orog's head jerked suddenly to the side, then half of its face blew off, showering Rufo and Danica, as she rushed in, with blood and gore.

Rufo and Danica stared at each other in disbelief for a moment, then turned in unison to the side, to see Cadderly standing between the rocks, crossbow in hand and a horrified expression splayed across his face.

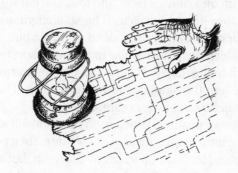

Six
The Quality of Mercy

Cadderly stood perfectly still for a few moments, too immersed to even notice his two friends' approach. All of his thoughts were focused on what had just occurred, on what he had just done. Three orogs lay dead by his actions, and, worse yet, he had killed one of them with his bare hands.

It had been so easy. Cadderly hadn't even thought about his actions, had moved solely on instincts—killing instincts—that had even urged him to destroy the orog running down the road toward Rufo, nowhere near Cadderly. The orog was there, in his crossbow sights, then it was dead.

It was too easy.

Not for the first time in the last few weeks, Cadderly questioned his purpose in life, the sincerity of his calling to the god Deneir. Headmaster Avery had once called Cadderly a Gondsman, referring to a sect of inventive priests who showed little moral guidance in forming their dangerous constructions. That word, "Gondsman," hovered about the young scholar now, like the dead eyes of a man he had killed.

Cadderly came out of his trance to see Danica standing beside him, wiping her face, and Kierkan Rufo holding Cadderly's wide-brimmed hat and nodding appreciatively. Cadderly shuddered as Danica wiped blood from her fair cheek. Could she really clean it? he wondered. And could he cleanse his hands? The image of beautiful Danica covered in gore seemed horribly symbolic; Cadderly felt as if the world had been turned upside down, as if the lines of good and evil had flip-flopped and blurred together to become a gray area based purely on savage and primal instincts for survival.

The simple truth was that the companions could have bypassed this tree, could have avoided the slaughter altogether.

Sympathy was plain on Danica's face. She took the hat from Rufo and offered it to Cadderly, then she offered her arm. The shaken young scholar took both without hesitation. Kierkan Rufo again nodded grimly at him, a gesture of thanks, and it seemed to Cadderly as if the angular man, too, respected his inner turmoil.

They headed back to the maple, Danica and Cadderly arm in arm, just in time to see Elbereth smash in the skull of the writhing orog. The elf prince unceremoniously tore his stiletto out of the creature's leg.

Cadderly looked away, pushed Danica from him, and felt sure he would vomit. He eyed the elf prince for a moment with a grave stare, then pointedly turned and walked from the scene. He moved parallel to Elbereth, but did not look at him.

"What would you have me do?" he heard an angry Elbereth call out. Danica mumbled something to the elf that Cadderly could not hear, but Elbereth was not finished with his tirade.

"If it were *his* home . . ." Cadderly heard clearly, and he knew that Elbereth, though talking to Danica, was directing the remark his way. He looked back to see Danica nodding at Elbereth, the two exchanging grim smiles, then clasping hands warmly.

The world had turned upside down.

A sound by the maple caught his attention. He saw the lone living orog, lying still and staring upward. Cadderly followed its gaze up to the broken tree limb, to the piece of dripping flesh. Horrified, the young scholar rushed to the wounded creature. It took him a moment to discern that the creature was alive, that it actually still drew breath, for its chest moved so slowly, its breathing shallow and uneven. Cadderly pulled the eye-above-candle emblem, his holy symbol, from the front of his hat and fumbled with a pouch on his belt. He heard the others moving behind him, but paid them no heed.

"What are you doing?" Elbereth asked him.

"He is still alive," Cadderly replied. "I have spells . . ."

"No!"

The sharpness of the retort did not strike Cadderly as profoundly as the fact that it had been Danica, not Elbereth, who snapped at him. He turned about slowly, as if he expected to see a horrid monster looming over him.

It was just Danica and Elbereth and Rufo; Cadderly hoped there remained a difference.

"The creature is too far gone," Danica said, her voice suddenly quiet.

"You shall not waste your spells on the likes of an orog!" Elbereth added, and there was nothing at all quiet about his sharp tones.

"We cannot leave it here to die," Cadderly shot back, fumbling again with his pouch. "Surely its lifeblood will spill out into the mud."

"A fitting end for an orog," Elbereth replied evenly.

Cadderly looked at him, still surprised by the grim elf's lack of mercy.

"Go if you will," Cadderly growled. "I am a cleric of a merciful god and I'll not leave a wounded creature like this!"

Danica pulled Elbereth away then. They had much to do before they could leave, in any case. A lot of their equipment lay scattered, weapons buried in orog flesh, and one horse, the one that had stumbled over the broken branch, needed tending.

Elbereth understood and honored the young woman's feelings. Cadderly had fought well—the elf couldn't deny that—and they could prepare to leave without his assistance.

Back up the trail, Elbereth retrieved his dropped bow. As he began to sling it over his shoulder, he heard a gasp from Danica, picking up her pack just a few feet from him.

Elbereth spun to her, then turned immediately to where she was looking.

Black smoke rose over Shilmista's northwestern edge.

Oblivious to the distant spectacle, Cadderly worked furiously to stem the blood flow from the orog's torn leg. Where to begin? All the flesh of the outside half of the leg, from ankle to midthigh, had been ripped away. Furthermore, the creature had suffered a dozen other severe wounds, including broken bones, from being run down by Rufo's horse. Cadderly had never been overly proficient at his priestly studies, and clerical magic was not easy for him. Even if he was the finest healer of the Edificant Library, though, he doubted he could do much for this broken creature.

Every so often, a drop of blood plopped beside him from the hanging skin. A pointed reminder, Cadderly believed, falling rhythmically, like a heartbeat. Then it stopped. Cadderly took great pains not to look up.

The least he could do was comfort the doomed creature, though that hardly seemed sufficient in the face of his actions. He pulled in a piece of the broken branch and propped it under the orog's head. Then he went back to work, refusing to consider the beast's nature, refusing to remember that the orogs had planned to kill him and the others. He wrapped and tied, plugged holes with his fingers and was not disgusted by the newest blood on his hands.

"Young scholar!" he heard Elbereth say. Cadderly looked to the side, then fell back and cried out, seeing a drawn bow leveled his way.

The arrow cut right by his chest—he felt the windy wake of its rushing flight—and dove into the wounded orog, catching the monster under the chin and driving up into its brain. The creature gave one violent jerk, then lay still.

"We have no time for your folly," Elbereth snarled, and he stormed past the stunned man, not taking his glare off Cadderly until he reached the wounded horse.

Cadderly wanted to cry out in protest, wanted to run over and punch Elbereth in the face, but Danica was beside him, calming him and helping him to his feet.

"Let the matter drop," the young woman offered. Cadderly turned on her fiercely, but saw only tenderness in her clear brown eyes and pursed lips.

"We must leave at once," Danica said. "The forest is burning."

With his already bloodied sword, Elbereth mercifully finished off the doomed horse. Cadderly noted the elf's sad expression and the gentle way he completed the grim task, noted that the elf cared more for the horse than for the orogs.

It had been Cadderly's mount, and when they left, Cadderly was the one walking, refusing offers from Danica and Rufo to share their steeds, and not even answering Elbereth's offer that the elf prince would walk and Cadderly ride.

Cadderly looked straight ahead, every step, refusing to acknowledge his companions. In his silent vigil, though, the battle replayed, and Barjin's dead eyes stared at them all from above the mental battlefield, forever judging.

They entered the thick boughs of Shilmista at twilight, and Elbereth, despite his desire to find his people, quickly moved to set up camp. "We will leave long before dawn," the elf explained sternly. "If you wish to sleep, do so now. The night will not be a long one."

"Can you sleep?" Cadderly snarled at him. Elbereth's silver eyes narrowed as the young scholar boldly approached.

"Can you?" Cadderly asked again, his voice growing dangerously loud. "Does your heart cry at the deeds of your bow and sword? Do you even care?"

Danica and Rufo looked on with alarm, almost expecting Elbereth to kill Cadderly where he stood.

"They were orogs, orc kin," Elbereth calmly reminded him.

"Without mercy, how much better are we?" Cadderly growled in frustration. "Do our veins run thick with the same blood as orcs?"

"It is not your home," the elf replied evenly. His voice filled with sarcasm. "Have you ever had a home?"

Cadderly did not reply, but he did not, could not, ignore the question. He really didn't know the answer. He had lived in Carradoon, the town on Impresk Lake, before going to the library, but he remembered nothing of that distant time. Perhaps the library was his home; he could not be certain, for he had nothing to compare it against.

"If your home was in danger, you would fight for it, do not doubt," Elbereth continued as he maintained control. "You would kill whatever threatened your home without mercy, and would hold no laments for its death." The elf stared into Cadderly's gray eyes for a few moments longer, awaiting a reply.

Then Elbereth was gone, disappeared into the forest gloom to scout out the region.

Cadderly heard Danica's relieved sigh behind him.

Exhausted, Kierkan Rufo tumbled down and was snoring almost immediately. Danica had the same idea, but Cadderly sat before the low-burning fire, wrapped in a heavy blanket. Its thickness did little to warm the chill in his heart.

He hardly noticed when Danica came over to sit beside him.

"You should not be so troubled," she offered after a long silence.

"Was I to let the orog die?" Cadderly asked sharply.

Danica shrugged and nodded. "Orogs are vicious, evil things," she said. "They live to destroy, further no causes beyond their own vile desires. I do not lament their deaths." She glanced sidelong at Cadderly. "Nor do you.

"It is Barjin, is it not?" Danica asked him, her voice full of pity.

The words stung. Incredulous, Cadderly turned on Danica.

"It was never about the orog," Danica continued, undaunted. "The fury of your movements as you tended the creature was not befitting any kin of orcs. It was guilt that drove you, memories of the dead priest."

Cadderly's expression did not change, though he found it difficult to dispute Danica's claims. Why had he cared so deeply for the orog, a notorious villain that would have torn the heart from his chest if given the chance? Why had that wounded orog evoked so much pity?

"You acted, you fought, as the situation demanded," Danica said quietly. "Against the orogs and against the priest. It was Barjin, not Cadderly, who caused Barjin's death. Lament that it had to happen at all. Do not accept guilt for that which you could not control."

"What is the difference?" Cadderly asked sincerely.

Danica draped an arm about his shoulders and moved close. Cadderly could feel her breath, hear her heartbeat, and see the moisture on her full lips.

"You must judge yourself as fairly as you judge others," Danica whispered. "I, too, battled Barjin and would have killed him if given the opportunity. How would you look upon me if that had come to pass?"

Cadderly had no answers.

Danica leaned closer and kissed him, then hugged him tightly, though he had not the strength to respond. Without another word, she moved back to her blanket and lay down, offering him a parting smile before she closed her eyes and gave in to her weariness.

Cadderly sat for a while longer, watching the young woman. She understood him so well, better than he understood himself. Or was it just that Danica understood the wide world as sheltered Cadderly could not? For all of his short life, Cadderly had found his answers in books, while Danica, worldly wise, had searched out her answers through experience.

Some things, it seemed, could not be learned simply by reading about them.

Elbereth came back into camp a short while later. Cadderly was down, but not asleep, and he watched the elf. Elbereth rested his bow against a log, and unbelted his sword, and place it beside his bedroll. Then, to Cadderly's surprise, Elbereth went over to Danica and gently tucked her blankets up tightly about her shoulders. He stroked Danica's thick hair, then walked back to his own bedroll and lay under the myriad stars.

For the second time that day, Cadderly didn't know what to think or how to feel.

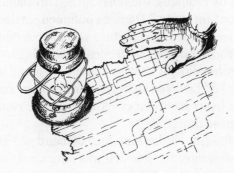

Seven
Pragmatic Magic

"What have you learned?" Tintagel asked Shayleigh when he found her atop Daoine Dun, the Hill of the Stars. Another day neared its end in Shilmista, another day of hit-and-run battles against the overwhelming force of invaders.

"Fifty goblins were killed in one fight," Shayleigh replied, but there was no smile on her face, fair and undeniably beautiful even though one side remained bright red from Tintagel's lightning bolt of a few days earlier. "And a giant was brought down in another. We suffered a few wounded, but none too seriously."

"That is good news," the elf wizard said, his smile intentionally wide in an effort to cheer the young maiden. It was a meager attempt, though, for Tintagel knew as well as Shayleigh that victory or defeat could not be measured by counting dead bodies. The enemy forces had indeed, as Hammadeen had told them, taken to the march, and for all the devastation the elves were handing them, they slowly but steadily progressed through beautiful Shilmista, scarring the land as they passed.

"They have taken a hundred square miles," Shayleigh said grimly. "They are burning the wood in the northwest."

Tintagel, for all his strained optimism, understood that Shayleigh was not alone among the elves in despair. "The night will be clear and dark, for the moon is new," the elf wizard offered hopefully, lifting his light blue eyes heavenward. "Might King Galladel call for Daoine Teague Feer?"

"The Star Enchantment?" Shayleigh echoed softly in the Common tongue. Without even considering the motion, she ran her slender fingers through her hair—and her face crinkled in obvious disgust, for her golden locks were matted with blood and grime. Shayleigh felt dirty, as did many of Shilmista's elves. The woodland folk had a way of countering those negative thoughts, though, with a cleansing of body and soul, an ancient ritual of rejuvenation.

Daoine Teague Feer.

"Let us go to Galladel," Shayleigh said, hope and excitement in her melodic voice for the first time in many days.

They found the aged king in one of the caves along the side of the hill that had become the elves' sanctuary. From this cave, Galladel directed the scouting missions, coordinating patrol times and designating group members. It was a heroic task, surely, for the elf king had to keep in mind which of his people were experienced fighters and which were novices, and ensure a proper blend in each party. Even more complicated, many of the elves had been injured and required rest.

As soon as they entered the torchlit cave, both Shayleigh and Tintagel recognized how heavy Galladel's burden had become. His once-straight shoulders sagged and circles lined his eyes.

"What do you want?" the elf king snapped. He threw his hands out to the side, unintentionally knocking several parchments from the chamber's main table. Obviously embarrassed, Galladel's visage softened immediately and he reiterated his question in a quieter tone.

"The moon is new," Shayleigh said, hoping that the hint would be enough. Galladel just stared at her blankly, though, and he seemed to grow angry, as if the two were wasting his precious time.

"The sky is clear," added Tintagel. "A million stars will show themselves to us, lend us their strength for the morrow's fight."

"Daoine Teague Feer?" Galladel asked. "You wish to dance and play?"

"It is more than play," Shayleigh reminded him.

"The millions of stars will not complete my million tasks!" cried the frustrated elf king.

Shayleigh had to bite her lip to keep from responding. She and a dozen others had offered to assist the king in his planning when they were not out on patrol, but Galladel had taken it all on himself, called it his duty despite the obvious fact that he could not carry the burden alone.

"Forgive me," the king said quietly, seeing Shayleigh's wounded expression. "I have not the time for Daoine Teague Feer. Perform the celebration in my absence," he offered graciously.

Shayleigh was not ungrateful, but the king's request was impossible. "Only one of the ruling line may perform Daoine Teague Feer," she reminded Galladel. The look on the elf king's face explained much to Shayleigh and Tintagel. Galladel was old and tired and made no secret of the fact that he no longer held much faith for Shilmista's ancient magic. Daoine Teague Feer was indeed just play to him, a dance with little value beyond its immediate enjoyment. If taken from the king's disbelieving perspective, then, what did it matter who led the celebration?

Still, Shayleigh could not hide her frown. Her king had grown pragmatic, even humanlike, and she could not find the courage to blame him. When she was but

a child, only a short two centuries before, a thousand elves had danced in
Shilmista. The whole forest, from north to south, echoed with their unending
song. Those days seemed far removed now. How many of Shilmista's children
had passed to Evermeet, never to return?

Tintagel tapped the maiden on the elbow and nodded to the exit. "You are due
on patrol," the elf wizard whispered to prompt the maiden along.

Shayleigh had the presence of mind to dip a bow as she left, but Galladel,
already back to poring over the many parchments, did not even notice.

* * * * *

A mood of similar frustration gripped the invaders' camp as twilight
descended over Shilmista. Ragnor's march was making gains, but they came
painfully slow and at incredible expense. The elves were fighting better than the
ogrilion had expected; he thought he would be more than halfway through
Shilmista by this time, but his forces had put only ten to fifteen of the hundred-
and-fifty-mile expanse behind them—and they hadn't even secured those miles
they had covered! Ragnor feared that his troops were looking more to the sides
for fear of concealed archers than ahead to the trails of conquest.

Better news came from the flanks, where resistance had been minimal. Orogs
and orcs, running in the foothills of the Snowflake Mountains, had passed the forest's halfway point, and a tribe of goblins out on the plains to the west had nearly
entered the southwestern pass around the forest, where they would set up camp
and discourage any reinforcements from the city of Riatavin.

But Ragnor knew he did not have the numbers to surround the forest, and if
the elves continued to hold him off at the present rate, they would surely find
allies before the ogrillon claimed Shilmista for Castle Trinity. And what of the
coming winter? Even cocky Ragnor did not believe he could hold the goblinoid
rabble at his side when the first snows fell on the forest. Time worked against
him, and the brutal elves intended to fight him every step of the way.

If the ogrillon had any doubts of the elves' intent, he had the proof right
before him. Looking out across a steep valley and a rushing river, Ragnor
watched the latest skirmish. A mixed group of goblins, orcs, and a few ogres had
been surprised by a band of elves. Ragnor's troops had been crossing a field,
approaching a thick grove, when a hail of arrows had sent them scrambling for
cover. From this far back, the ogrillon had no idea how many enemies his forces
faced, but he suspected that the elves were not numerous. Still, they were undeniably effective, for the orcs and goblins had not come out of hiding, and those
few brave and stupid ogres who had rushed the tree line had gone crashing down
with a score of arrows in their bodies.

"Have you sent the giant and a band of bugbears?" the ogrillon snapped at his
closest lieutenant, a weak but cunning goblin.

"Yesses, my general," the goblin replied, cowering, and with good reason.

Ragnor's first few "closest advisors" now numbered among the dead, though none of them had gotten anywhere near any elves.

Ragnor glared at the goblin, and it cowered even lower, nearly rubbing its belly on the turf. Fortunately for the pitiful creature, the ogrillon had other business on his mind. Ragnor looked back out to the distant battle scene, trying to figure how long it would take his giant to get across the river and within boulder-throwing range.

Another anguished cry split the morning air as yet another monstrous soldier caught an elven arrow. Ragnor reflexively swung his hand out to the side, catching his advisor with a backhand slap that sent the goblin tumbling away.

"That should inspire loyalty," came a woman's voice from behind. The ogrillon spun about to see the wizard Dorigen, a bat-winged imp on her shoulder and a huge human at her flank.

"What are you doing here, wizard?" the ogrillon spat. "This is not your place, nor the place of your favored boy!" He eyed Tiennek dangerously and Dorigen feared she might already have to intervene between the two.

"Well met, to you as well," the wizard replied. She hadn't expected a warm reception from Ragnor; he was smart enough to understand that Aballister had sent her to spy on his progress and his ambitions.

Ragnor took a threatening step Tiennek's way, and Dorigen wondered honestly if she had anything in her magical repertoire that could stop the monstrous general. She fingered her magical onyx ring, considering the time it would take for her to loose its fiery fury, and the potential for that fury to stop the brutish ogrillon.

"I am here because I was commanded to be here," she said sternly, hiding her concerns. "You have been out of Castle Trinity for many days, Ragnor, but you seem to be stumbling about the northern woods with few clear gains to show for our considerable expense." Ragnor backed off a bit and Dorigen hid her smile, amazed at how easily she had put the powerful beast on the defensive. Her conclusions had been no more than an educated guess—she had no way of knowing how Ragnor's battle plan was progressing—but the ogrillon's reaction had confirmed that she wasn't far from the mark.

"We are concerned," Dorigen continued, mellow and nonthreatening. "The summer is nearly past, and Aballister wants to take Carradoon before the first snow."

"So he sent you," huffed Ragnor, "thinking that you might help poor Ragnor."

"Perhaps," Dorigen purred noncommittally.

"You need the help," Druzil added, then he dropped back under his bat wings to escape the ogrillon's glare.

"I need no weakling wizards in my camp!" Ragnor growled. "Be gone, and take Aballister's bat and your boy with you." He turned back to the valley and the river and tried to look busy.

"Then all goes well?" Dorigen asked, using the most innocent tones she could muster, cocking her head coyly.

When Ragnor didn't react, Dorigen got more direct after selecting the components for a defensive spell from one of her deep pockets, in case Ragnor seriously objected. "You are stopped, Ragnor," she declared. "Admit it before you fall like Barjin did." The ogrillon spun on her, but she did not relent.

Did you have to make that reference? Druzil asked telepathically, for the imp most certainly did not like the way Ragnor was now looking at him.

"And have you come to bring that about?" Ragnor spat.

"I have come as an agent of Talona," Dorigen insisted, "to aid an ally, even one too foolish to accept the help he needs!"

Dorigen looked past the ogrillon then, to the distant valley and the battle that was not going Ragnor's way. She waved her hand and chanted, and a block of shimmering, flickering blue light appeared before her.

Ragnor took a tentative step backward. Dorigen handed Druzil over to Tiennek, took one step forward, into the light, and was gone.

After a split second to consider his new position, Druzil dove into the portal behind her.

Ragnor instinctively spun about and saw a similar field of blue flickering beyond the river. It diminished as soon as Dorigen stepped through, Druzil again on her shoulder.

"I do not like elves," Druzil whispered, and he faded into invisibility. "Nasty creatures!"

Dorigen paid him no heed, except to offer a scowl to let him know that she had wanted him to remain with Tiennek. Dorigen had no time to worry about the bothersome imp, though. She studied the battle, trying to get a perspective on what was happening around her. She saw orcs and goblins far ahead of her, crouched behind fallen logs, small ridges, anything they could find to shelter them from the tree line. Other monsters lay dead or dying, some of the ogres covered with arrows. Dorigen followed Druzil's lead and became invisible, not trusting the range of fine elven bows.

Even with the masking spell, Dorigen dared not approach the trees. Elves, being magically inclined, had a natural sense for such magic. Dorigen considered her options for a moment, then fumbled about in the many pockets of her robes.

"Damn!" she growled, then, with sudden insight, she reached up, felt for Druzil, and tore a bit of fur from the joint at the base of the imp's wing. The movement, offensive in nature, forced the wizard back to visibility.

"What are you doing?" Druzil demanded, shifting about and digging his claws into Dorigen's shoulder. He, too, became visible, only to fade away a moment later.

"Sit still!" Dorigen commanded. She felt the tuft for a moment, hoping it would suffice. The spell called for bat fur, but the wizard couldn't seem to find any among her components at the moment, and she had no time to go hunting bats. Dorigen found some natural cover behind a tree and prepared herself.

For several minutes, for this spell was not a quick and easy one to cast, the wizard went through the designated motions, chanting softly. Another goblin died in that time, but Dorigen considered it a minor loss in light of the coming gains.

Then it was done and an eyeball hovered in the air a few feet ahead of Dorigen. It became translucent almost immediately and, following Dorigen's mental commands, floated off toward the tree line.

Dorigen closed her own eyes and saw through the detached orb. It made the trees and flitted about, looking this way and that, floating the length of the elven line. Dorigen kept it moving swiftly, but even so, several elves stiffened and looked about nervously as it passed.

Dorigen soon came to the conclusion that all of the elves—not a substantial number—were above the ground in the trees. The greatest factor working against the orcs and goblins was their own fear, for a bold charge would dislodge the few elves from their tenuous positions.

"I must begin the charge," the wizard whispered.

She chose as her target a large elm in the center of the elven line. The detached eyeball floated in so that the wizard could make a count of her intended victims. One maiden, golden haired and with striking violet eyes, turned abruptly, following the floating orb's path.

Dorigen released her thoughts from the eyeball, pulled a different component from her robe, and began another spell.

"Down! Down!" she heard the distant elven maiden cry. "Wizard! They have a wizard! Get down!"

Dorigen moved her next spell along with all the speed she could muster. She saw a slender form drop from the distant tree, then another, but she hardly cared, for her spell was done and the rest would not escape.

A tiny ball of fire flew from Dorigen's fingers, making great speed for the tree. Dorigen had to stand partly in the open to direct its course, but she knew the elves would be too busy to bother with her.

The ball disappeared into the elm's boughs. In the blink of a magical eye, the great tree became a fiery torch.

The savage flames quickly consumed all the fuel that the elm, and the elves in its boughs, could offer. Branches crackled and tumbled down beside the charred bodies and blackened suits of fine mesh armor.

Dorigen aimed her next spell at her own troops.

Do not hesitate! she roared in a magically enhanced, thunderous voice. *Charge them! Kill them!*

The sheer power of her command, a voice as great as a dragon's roar, sent the orcs and goblins scrambling toward the tree line. A few died from random bow shots, but most tore right into the brush. They found only one living elf to hack, a pitifully wounded creature at the base of the ruined elm. Near death even before the goblins arrived, he offered only minor resistance. With wicked glee, the goblins took him apart.

Just as satisfying, the monsters recovered bodies, the first enemy bodies they had seen since the start of the campaign: charred and blackened elves.

Gratified by their whoops of joy, Dorigen turned about, conjured another extradimensional door of shimmering light, and stepped through, back to the high ground beyond the river.

"I believe they killed one wounded elf," the wizard said calmly, walking by the stunned ogrillon. "Foolish. He might have made a valuable prisoner. You should better control your bloodthirsty troops, General Ragnor."

Ragnor's sudden burst of laughter turned her about.

"Have I welcomed you to Shilmista?" the ogrillon offered, his tusk-adorned smile stretching from ear to ear.

Dorigen was glad she had improved the surly monster's mood.

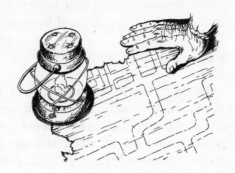

Eight

Quietly

T he forest was eerily still. No birdcalls greeted the dawn. No animals scurried through the thick branches overhead.

Elbereth glanced back to the others every few steps, a look of dread clear on his face.

"At least there are no battles in the area," Danica offered, her voice a whisper, but still seeming loud in the quiet wood.

Elbereth moved back to join them. "The paths are clear, but I fear to ride," he said softly. "Even leading the horses at so slow a pace, their hoofbeats can be heard many yards away."

Cadderly snapped his fingers, then cringed at the sharp sound. Ignoring the surprised looks, and a scowl from Elbereth, the young scholar pulled his pack from Temmerisa, the horse he had been leading. The bells had been removed and muffled with clothing, then packed away in saddlebags.

"Wrap them," Cadderly said, producing a thick woolen blanket. The others didn't seem to understand.

"The hooves," Cadderly explained. "Rip the blanket into strips . . ." His voice trailed off as he locked gazes with the stern elf. Elbereth eyed him curiously—Cadderly thought he noted a flash of admiration in Elbereth's silver eyes.

Without another word, Elbereth pulled out his knife and took the blanket from Cadderly. In a few minutes, they were moving again, the hoofbeats still audible but somewhat muffled. When Elbereth looked back again and nodded his approval, Danica nudged Cadderly and smiled.

They stopped for a short rest late that morning, far from the wood's eastern edge. Still the forest was quiet; they had found no sign of anyone, friend or foe.

"My people will fight in quick skirmishes," Elbereth explained. "They are not numerous enough to afford the losses of any large battles. They will move swiftly and silently, striking at the enemy from afar and being gone when he moves against them."

"Then our chances of finding them are not promising," said Danica. "More likely, they will find us."

"Not so," the elf explained. "They have horses to tend, and undoubtedly—" the next words came hard to him, "—wounded who will need to rest in a secure place. Shilmista was not caught without plans for defense, no matter how sudden the attack was. We are not many, and not allied with any great powers. We of Shilmista have rehearsed our home's defense since the first elf walked into this wood many centuries ago."

"Predetermined camps," Cadderly reasoned.

Elbereth nodded. He picked up a twig and drew a rough map of the forest on the ground. "By the location of the rising smoke, the fight is up here," he said, pointing to the northern section.

"Then we need not muffle the horses," Rufo put in, "and we might ride instead of walk." The angular man's suggestion met with only tentative acceptance.

"We are near the center of the wood." Elbereth went on, leaving Rufo's thoughts hanging unanswered for the moment. "The first camp would have been here, just south of a defensible region known as the Dells." Again the elf seemed to fight past a lump in his throat. "I would presume that camp has been deserted by now."

"And the next?" Cadderly asked, simply because he thought Elbereth needed a moment to recover.

"Here," the elf said, indicating an area not too far from their present position. He looked up to find a break in the trees, then pointed out a fair-sized hill, poking out of the green canopy several miles to the north.

"Daoine Dun, Hill of the Stars," the elf prince explained. "Its sides are thick with pine and blocked by tangled birch to the north and west. There are many caves, easily concealed, and some large enough to house the horses."

"How long to get there?" Danica asked.

"Faster if we ride," said Rufo.

"Before we decide to ride," Cadderly cut in, drawing Elbereth's attention before the elf had time to answer the angular man, "explain to me why the wood is so quiet?"

"It hangs thick with dread," Danica agreed.

Elbereth nodded. "I think it better that we walk. Even so, we can make Daoine Dun soon after sunset. I will go first, far in front."

"And I will go to the side of the trail," offered Danica, "concealed in the brush." She looked to Cadderly. "You can lead two mounts."

Cadderly's nod set them off again, plodding slowly and as quietly as possible through the forest. Rufo, pausing to rub his feet every so often, was not happy to be walking again, but he didn't complain with anything more than occasional sour looks toward Cadderly.

Three hours later, with the sun beginning its western descent in earnest, Danica whispered for Cadderly and Rufo to hold the horses still. Both were amazed at how close the woman actually was to them, for though the brush beside the path was thick and tangled, they had not heard a sound of her passing.

Elbereth came rushing back then, motioning for the two men to lead the horses from the open path.

"Goblins," the elf explained when they were all under the thick cover. "Many goblins, spread out east and west. Their eyes are on Daoine Dun, but they have guards, archers, posted along the way."

"Can we go around them?" Cadderly asked.

"I do not know," the elf answered honestly. "Their line is long, I believe, and to pass beyond them we will have to go far from the road, among tangles that our mounts may not be able to cross."

Danica was shaking her head. "If their line is long," she reasoned, "then likely it is not deep. We could charge right through them."

"And the archers?" Rufo reminded her.

"How many are along the road?" Danica asked Elbereth.

"I saw two," the elf replied, "but I believe there were others, at least a few, hidden in the brush."

"I can get them," the woman promised.

Elbereth started to protest, but Cadderly grabbed his elbow. The young scholar's nod took the bite from the elf's argument.

Danica drew a rough sketch of the road in the dirt. "You take a position here," she explained. She gave Elbereth a wink. "Be ready with your bow!" she offered, pointedly including the elf in her plans.

She remained cryptic, though, completing the plans by merely stating, "When you hear the jay, charge on." With no reply forthcoming, and not wanting to waste a moment, Danica started quietly off along the bushes.

"I will catch you as I pass," Cadderly promised at her back. Danica didn't doubt that for a minute.

Elbereth and Cadderly took up positions near a bend in the road that allowed them to watch the distant goblins, while Rufo stayed back with the three horses, ready to spring ahead at the elf's call. Elbereth, keen-eyed and attuned to the forest, pointed out Danica's progress as the young woman made her silent way through the bushes on the right side of the road. Barely visible even though she had just set out, Danica soon disappeared altogether, not a shaking twig to mark her movement.

There came a sudden rustle beside the goblins. Elbereth leveled his bow, but Cadderly put a hand on the elf's arm, reminding him to keep patient. Apparently the movement had been more obvious to Cadderly and Elbereth than to the two goblin sentries on the road, for the monsters did not even turn toward it.

All was quiet again for seconds that seemed like hours to the nervous companions.

"Where are you?" Cadderly whispered to the empty path ahead, trusting in

Danica's skills but fearful nonetheless. He held his small crossbow, cranked and ready, and had to remind himself several times, as he had reminded Elbereth, to have patience and trust in Danica. "Where are you?"

As if in reply, Danica shot up suddenly behind one of the goblin guards. Her arm flicked, then she reached around the goblin's head, put her hand over its mouth, and pulled it down into the bushes.

The other guard slumped to its knees, clutching at the dagger embedded deeply into its chest.

The cry of a jay sounded almost immediately, and Elbereth echoed it back to Rufo. In seconds, they were up and riding, with powerful Temmerisa easily outpacing the lesser mounts.

To the left of the road, an archer popped up, but Elbereth was quicker on the draw and the goblin went down in a heap.

Two other archers appeared from the brush farther down the road. Danica noticed them and rushed ahead. She spun to the side, dodging one arrow, and stopped her spin perfectly to continue her charge, then dove flat to her belly to avoid another arrow. She never slowed through the evasive movements, and the goblins never had the time to ready their bows again before Danica leaped at them, turning flat out and horizontal in midair to knock both of them to the ground.

His blue silk cape flying behind him, Cadderly put his head down, held on to his wide-brimmed hat, and spurred his horse on, desperate to get beside Danica. He could see the bushes shaking with the struggle. A goblin arm shot up, holding a sword, then chopped down wickedly.

"No!" Cadderly cried. Then the same sword reappeared above the brush, this time in Danica's hand. When it descended, a goblin squealed in agony.

Elbereth's mount reared as it passed the wounded guard on the road. The elf finished the monster off with his sword, then bent low in his saddle to retrieve Danica's valuable dagger. A goblin rushed out from the brush on the other side, intent on the elf.

Using his now favorite tactic, Kierkan Rufo—or, more accurately, Kierkan Rufo's horse—promptly ran the creature down.

Danica was back to the edge of the road, crouching low and waiting for Cadderly to get to her. Another goblin appeared, rushing toward her with sword drawn.

Cadderly's wide-brimmed hat flew off, bouncing behind his neck at the end of its tie and flying with his silken cape. He drew his loaded crossbow and tried to get a shot at the creature. Frustrated by the bounce of the horse's gallop, he spurred his mount on, thundering right up behind the goblin. The goblin turned, growled, and waved its sword about.

It never got the chance to use it. Just a couple of feet away, Cadderly let the dart fly. Another long horse stride took him right by the goblin, within the creature's sword reach, but the goblin was in the air, flying away into the brush, already dead.

Cadderly hadn't escaped unscathed, though. So close to his target, the flash of the exploding dart burned and blinded him, and he nearly lost his seat. Then Danica was up behind him, guiding the horse back to the center of the path and holding Cadderly steady.

Elbereth and Rufo were right behind; hoots and calls went up all about them.

"Ride on!" the elf prince cried, rearing and spinning Temmerisa about. His great bow twanged again, then again, each shot sending another enemy to the grave.

Rufo's horse, with just one rider, got a few paces ahead of Cadderly's, making Cadderly and Danica the prime targets for those goblins springing from the brush along the road. A few clumsily thrown spears bounced harmlessly short, one arrow whistled by, and another came in, straight for Cadderly's back.

Danica noticed it at the last instant and threw her arm up to block.

"What?" came Cadderly's alarmed cry.

"It is nothing!" Danica replied. "Ride on!" She figured that now was not the time to show Cadderly the arrow sticking right through her forearm.

A few more strides, and they were running free. Then came Temmerisa, as fast as an arrow. In mere seconds, Elbereth was beside them again, grim-faced but unhurt.

When they had put half a mile behind them, they slowed their pace and dismounted. It was then that they noticed Danica's wound.

Cadderly nearly fell over, seeing the bloody arrow shaft protruding from both sides of Danica's delicate arm. Elbereth rushed over to her, spurring the young scholar to do the same.

"It is not serious," Danica said to calm them.

"How can you say that?" came Cadderly's retort. He went back to the horse to retrieve his pack and returned bearing bandages and a jar of salve. By the time he was back beside her, Danica had pulled the arrow all the way through and was deep in concentration, using her meditative powers to gather the strength she would need to battle the pain.

Cadderly tried not to disturb her concentration as he gently wrapped the wound. Danica's mental powers were truly amazing; Cadderly had once seen her force a two-inch sliver from her leg without even touching it with her hands, using nothing but sheer concentration and muscle control. He did the best he could in wrapping the arm, then hesitated, a trapped expression clouding his face.

"What is it?" Elbereth demanded.

Cadderly ignored him and summoned the courage to call upon Deneir. He muttered the chants of minor healing spells, one after another (though he wasn't well-versed in the art and didn't know how much good he was doing).

Reluctantly, for he had hoped to save his curative spells for himself, Kierkan Rufo came over to join him.

Before Rufo could begin to work on the arm, though, Danica opened her eyes. "That will not be necessary," she said calmly to the sharp-featured priest, her eyes glazed and a look of sincere contentment on her smooth face. Elbereth and Cadderly both started to protest, but then Cadderly looked more closely at the wrapping and realized that the wound had already stopped bleeding. He couldn't be sure if his spells or Danica's own concentration had stemmed the flow, and he honestly didn't care either way.

"We must continue," Danica said, her voice almost sleepy, "as before, with Elbereth in front and me to the side."

Elbereth protested. "I will take the lead," he agreed, "but you will stay with the others and the horses. We are not so far from Daoine Dun. If that is my people's camp, I do not believe we will encounter any more enemies between here and there."

Cadderly was surprised when Danica did not argue. He knew then that her wound was much more serious and painful than she had let on.

They walked on into the twilight, when all the wood, shrouded in deepening gloom, took on an even more ominous appearance to Cadderly. He grew alarmed as Elbereth disappeared from sight, slipping suddenly into the trees. Soon, though, the elf was back on the path and approaching, two other tall and grim-faced elves beside him. He introduced them as his cousins and was glad to report that his people had indeed set camp on the Hill of the Stars, just a mile north.

One of the elves accompanied them the rest of the way; the other went back to his watch.

Their escort told Elbereth of the battles; Cadderly saw the elf prince grimace as the other elf described the last skirmish, wherein a wizard had appeared and turned a tree to flames.

"Ralmarith is dead," the elf said grimly, "and Shayleigh . . ."

Elbereth spun on him and grabbed him by the shoulders.

"She lives," the elf said immediately, "though she is sorely wounded, and sorely wounded, too, is her heart. She was the last to leave Ralmarith and had to be pulled away."

Elbereth was not surprised. "She is a loyal friend," he agreed solemnly.

Elbereth went first to find Shayleigh when they reached Daoine Dun, though word was quickly (and often) passed to him that his father, the king, wished to speak with him.

Cadderly was amazed at how easily the elf prince seemed to ignore that request and follow his own agenda. It reminded the young scholar somewhat of himself on one of the many occasions he had avoided a summons from Head-master Avery. Cadderly dismissed the thought quickly, not yet comfortable with any comparisons between himself and the arrogant, unmerciful Elbereth.

They found the wounded maiden on a cot in a small cave that had been set up to care for the injured. She was heavily bandaged in several places but did not seem so bad to Cadderly—until he looked into her eyes. There loomed a sadness the young scholar thought would never diminish.

"We left Ralmarith," the maiden whispered, her voice choked, as soon as Elbereth moved beside her. "They killed him, hacked his body . . ."

"Shhhh." Elbereth tried to calm her. "Ralmarith lies with the gods now. Do not fear for him."

Shayleigh nodded but had to look away.

They sat in silence for many minutes. Another elf entered and immediately moved to tend Danica's injured arm. The stubborn monk politely refused, but Cadderly nudged her hard and reminded her that the dressing had to be changed. With a defeated sigh, Danica moved off with the elf.

"When will you be back in the fighting?" Elbereth asked Shayleigh at length. Both looked the attendant's way.

"Tomorrow!" the maiden said firmly. The attendant just shrugged and nodded helplessly.

"That is good," said Elbereth. "Rest well this night. Tomorrow we shall fight together, and together avenge Ralmarith!" He took a step toward the entrance.

"You are leaving?" Shayleigh asked, alarmed.

"There are goblins to the south," Elbereth explained. "They intend to surround the hill, I would guess. We cannot allow that." He looked over to Danica. "She will remain beside you," he said to Shayleigh. "A fine warrior and ally for our struggle."

"Are you going after the goblins tonight?" Cadderly asked, behind Elbereth. "The day would seem more favorable," he explained when Elbereth turned to him. "Goblins do not fight well in sunlight."

"This is Shilmista," Elbereth reminded him, as though that fact alone explained everything. The elf prince stood tall and straight, his jaw firm, his silver eyes narrowed and stern. "The goblins shall die, day or night."

"I will go with you," Cadderly offered.

"I will not have you," Elbereth replied, turning back to Shayleigh. "You are not elven and will not see through the darkness." To the maiden he asked, "Where is Tintagel?"

"With your father," Shayleigh replied. "We have called for Daoine Teague Feer, but Galladel has refused thus far."

Elbereth considered that news for a few moments but had no time to worry about it. He swept out of the tent, telling Cadderly and Rufo to rest easily and find a fine meal.

Ten minutes later, fifty elves set out on the goblin hunt, Elbereth leading upon Temmerisa, and the wizard Tintagel at his side. They returned at midnight, reporting a hundred goblins slain and scores more sent running. Not a single elf had been wounded.

* * * * *

Cadderly was too excited to sleep, weary though he was. He had read much about elves over the years, but had met only a few—and those only at the library. Something about being in Shilmista, on a hill under the stars, surrounded by elves, transcended the experience of reading about the people. There was a flavor here, an eldritch aura, that mere words, however well constructed, could not hope to capture.

He wandered about the camp, greeted by smiles on otherwise grim faces at every turn, noting the rich colors, even in the quiet darkness, of elven hair and eyes. All those stirring in the camp were too busy to be disturbed, he figured, so he didn't bother to introduce himself, just tipped his wide-brimmed hat and wandered past.

He had known from the moment he had left the Edificant Library that this journey would change his life, and he had feared that. He feared it still, for already the world seemed a wider place—more dangerous and more wonderful all at once.

What of Elbereth? Cadderly didn't like the elf or the way the elf treated him, but instincts told him differently, told him of the elf's honor and loyalty.

When his thoughts inevitably turned to Danica, he found a rocky seat on the north side of the hill and dropped his chin into his hands. Danica, it seemed, held no reservations concerning Elbereth; she had accepted the elf fully, as friend and companion. That fact bothered Cadderly more than he cared to admit.

Cadderly sat for a long while, long after the elven war party had returned. In the end, he resolved nothing.

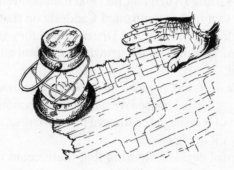

Nine
Daoine Teague Feer

Many elven eyes had opened wide when Elbereth had entered the encampment escorted by three humans, for few visitors came to Shilmista, and, with the battle raging, none had been expected. Another set of eyes opened even wider, though, evil yellow eyes sown with tiny red arteries.

Druzil nearly fell out of his perch, high in a thin beech overlooking the camp, when he saw Rufo, Danica, and especially Cadderly. The imp recognized the young scholar at once and instinctively rubbed the remnants of a bruise on his flank where Cadderly had once popped him with a poisoned dart.

Druzil felt suddenly vulnerable, despite the fact that he was invisible and in a tree too weak-limbed for even the lithe elves to climb. He hadn't approached the camp too closely, fearing that the elves would discover him, but now, with this devilish young man in the area, the imp wondered what distance might be safe.

Immediately Druzil sent his thoughts back to Dorigen, who awaited his return a mile to the north. Druzil let the wizard fully into his mind, allowing her to see through his eyes as he followed Cadderly's progress through the camp.

What is he doing here? Druzil demanded, as though he expected Dorigen to know.

He? came her incredulous thoughts. *Who is he?*

The young priest! the imp shot back. His thoughts almost screamed that Cadderly was Aballister's son, but Druzil deflected that notion, preferring to hold that bit of news until he could watch Dorigen's facial response.

He is from the Edificant Library, the one who defeated Barjin! the imp continued. From the long pause, Druzil could tell that Dorigen had caught on to his sense of urgency. The imp recalled the battle in which Cadderly had brought him down with a dart coated in sleep poison. Druzil thought he sensed Dorigen's amusement at the mental recounting, and he sent a stream of curses her way.

Another thought struck Druzil and he looked all about the camp, searching for the two dwarves that had accompanied Cadderly on that previous occasion. They were not to be found, though, and Druzil hoped they were dead.

Who are the others? Dorigen asked, growing impatient after many uneventful moments had passed.

The girl was beside the priest, though I do not know what role she played, the imp explained. *The other . . .* Druzil paused, recalling the description Barjin had given him of the fool who had initially aided the evil priest's cause: angular and tall, and walking with a slight tilt to his stance.

Kierkan Rufo, Druzil decided, figuring that there could not be two priests at the library who so accurately fit Barjin's description. Dorigen didn't immediately press him further, and Druzil decided to be blunt with the wizard.

I wish to be gone from here, the imp communicated clearly. Around him, the camp seemed to come alive with activity, elves running about and shouting that Prince Elbereth had returned.

Come to me, Druzil, Dorigen bade, apparently seeing the imp's wisdom. She didn't have to ask twice.

* * * * *

"I requested your presence some hours ago," Galladel said coldly when Elbereth finally walked into his chamber. "In times of peace, I can overlook your irrespon—"

"A force of goblins had set up to the south of Daoine Dun," Elbereth interrupted. "Would you rather I had allowed them to fortify and entrench? They are gone now, and the way is clear if we are forced to flee—as I suspect we might if rumors of the approaching northern force are true."

The news took the momentum from the aged king's ire. He abruptly turned to the many parchments strewn across the wide stone table.

"I will need your assistance," he said sharply. "The patrols need to be coordinated. We must keep count of weapons and food." He roughed the papers around a bit, just to show his obvious displeasure.

Elbereth watched his father with growing concern. There was something too restrictive about Galladel's movements and tactics, something too humanlike for the younger elf's liking.

"The forest is our home," Elbereth said, as though that remark alone explained his disrespect.

Galladel glared at him, suspecting he had just been insulted.

"We must be out fighting," Elbereth continued, "freely, as our instincts and the trees guide us."

"Our attacks must be planned," the older elf argued. "Our enemy is many times stronger than we, and well organized."

"Then awaken the wood," Elbereth said matter-of-factly.

Galladel's silver eyes, so similar to his son's, widened in disbelief.

"Awaken the trees," Elbereth said again, more firmly. "Call up the allies of our past, that together we might destroy those who have come to conquer Shilmista!"

Galladel's soft laughter mocked him. "You know nothing of what you speak," he said. "You talk of the task as though it were a foregone event, easily manifested. Even in the older days, when I, Galladel, was a young elf, the trees would no longer come to the elf king's call."

Elbereth had only made the remark to draw a response from his weary father. When he saw the sadness creep into Galladel's eyes, he came to doubt his own wisdom.

"The ancient magic is gone, my son," Galladel continued, his voice subdued, "as faded as the days when the world belonged to the older races. Legends for fireside tales and no more. We will win this war, but we will win it through blood and arrows."

"You have sent emissaries to the Edificant Library, begging aid?" Elbereth asked.

Galladel paled noticeably. "I sent you," he replied defensively.

"I was sent to gather information. I knew nothing of the start of a war," Elbereth argued calmly, for he knew that he was in the right, but knew, too, that his father's patience had worn thin. "The library must be asked for aid, and the legion of Carradoon raised."

"Send the emissary," Galladel replied absently, seeming very tired. "Go now. I have much to prepare."

"There is one other matter," Elbereth pressed.

The king gave him a sour look, as though he understood what was coming.

"Some of the people have requested Daoine Teague Feer," Elbereth said.

"We have no time—" Galladel started to protest.

"We could not spend our time in any better manner," the younger elf insisted. "Our people carry many wounds. They wear the blood of enemies and friends alike. They see the smoke of their burning forest and find goblins and orogs in every direction. Blood and arrows, yes, but battles are fought with emotion, my father. They are won by those willing to die if that must be, and by those eager to kill. Our spirits will carry us where your parchments—" he waved a hand derisively at the stone table "—cannot!"

Galladel neither blinked nor made any move to reply.

"Daoine Teague Feer will lift those spirits," Elbereth said quietly, trying to bring the conversation back to a reasonable level.

"You are of noble blood," answered Galladel, an unmistakable edge of anger and disappointment to his voice. "You perform the ceremony." He looked back to his parchments then, taking particular interest in one and purposely avoiding lifting his eyes his son's way.

Elbereth waited a few moments torn between what he knew was the right course and the fact that his course would wound his father. Galladel's invitation to perform Daoine Teague Feer was wrought of sarcasm, and if Elbereth went through with the ritual, his father certainly would not be pleased. But Elbereth,

for all his loyalty to Galladel, had to follow his heart. He left the small cave to find
his ceremonial robes and tell all the others to find theirs.

* * * * *

"Aballister's son?" Dorigen could hardly believe the news. This young priest,
Cadderly by name, was the estranged son of Aballister Bonaduce!

"I battled him in the library," Druzil rasped, not liking the taste of the bitter
words, "as I showed you when we communicated from afar. He is a trickster—
take heed! And he surrounds himself with powerful friends."

"Does Aballister know of him?" Dorigen asked, wondering what intrigue
might be going on about her. Was Aballister perhaps in contact with this young
priest in those fateful moments of Barjin's demise? she wondered. Could it be
possible that the wizard had aided his son in defeating Barjin?

Druzil nodded, his tall, doglike ears flipping forward. "Aballister learned of
Cadderly when the priest battled Barjin," he explained. "Aballister was not
pleased to find Cadderly in the library. He will be most upset to learn that the
trickster aids the elves!"

A hundred possibilities whirled through Dorigen's mind then, of how she
might gain the uppermost hand in this conflict against the elves, and in her own
struggles within the hierarchy of Castle Trinity.

"You are sure that this Rufo is the fool Barjin spoke of?" she asked eagerly.

"I am," Druzil lied, hoping that his guess was correct, but not daring to disappoint Dorigen when she was so excited. He studied her amber eyes, sparkling
dots straddling the bridge of her disfigured nose.

"Go back to the elves," Dorigen commanded. She had to lift her voice over
Druzil's whine to complete her orders. "Arrange a meeting with this Kierkan
Rufo. If he was Barjin's fool, then he will be mine as well."

Druzil groaned but flapped his wings and obediently started off.

"And Druzil," Dorigen called, "I trust that you will make no contact with Aballister, or that, if you do, nothing of this will be mentioned."

Druzil nodded. "What would be my gain?" he asked innocently, then continued on his way.

Dorigen considered the question carefully, and she knew that the best way to
trust the imp was to keep him well advised. Indeed, what would be Druzil's gain
in telling Aballister of these latest events? Dorigen clapped her hands. Unlike
the imp, she was not sorry that the young scholar and his friends had come to
help the elves. With Ragnor and his huge force finding a foothold in the forest,
and with her beside them, Dorigen believed Shilmista's fate sealed anyway, and
she resolved then to add to her personal gains, at the expense of Aballister's son.

* * * * *

"Tonight," Elbereth whispered into the wounded maiden's ear.

Shayleigh stirred and opened a sleepy eye.

Cadderly and Danica watched from across the cave, Cadderly still thinking that Shayleigh would have been better off left asleep. He had protested that the wounded elf needed her sleep, but Elbereth had waved his doubts away, assuring Cadderly that Daoine Teague Feer would do much more to improve Shayleigh's health and strength than any amount of rest.

"Tonight?" Shayleigh echoed, her voice melodic even through her drowsiness and pain.

"Tonight we gather strength from the stars," Elbereth replied.

Shayleigh was up in a moment, to Cadderly's surprise. Just the mention of Daoine Teague Feer seemed to pump new vitality into the elven maiden. Elbereth bade Danica to help Shayleigh dress, and he and Cadderly exited the cave.

"Do we get to watch this celebration?" Cadderly asked. "Or would you prefer privacy?"

Elbereth's answer surprised him.

"You have become a part of our struggle," the elf prince replied. "You have earned the right to partake of this ritual. The choice is yours."

Cadderly understood the honor that had just been given him and his companions, and he was truly overwhelmed and amazed. "Forgive my arguments against waking Shayleigh," he said.

Elbereth nodded. "Your concern for my friend did not escape me." Elbereth glanced back toward the cave, his expression grim. "Our enemies have found a powerful ally," he said. "This wizard must not be allowed to appear on any other battlefield."

Cadderly understood the proud elf's meaning and intentions and he was not the least bit surprised by Elbereth's ensuing vow.

"When the celebration is complete and my people are prepared to take up the fight, I will hunt the wizard, whose head shall avenge Ralmarith's death and Shayleigh's wounds.

"Go now and find your remaining companion," Elbereth instructed. "Daoine Teague Feer will begin atop the hill as soon as the others are gathered."

* * * * *

Cadderly, Danica, and Rufo sat to the side of the gathered elves, talking quietly among themselves. Cadderly told them of Elbereth's vow to go after the wizard, and again was not surprised when Danica vowed that she would hunt beside the elf.

More and more elves gathered atop the hill; nearly all the camp was there—the guards had decided to rotate their watch so that all might enjoy the celebration for at least a while—with the notable exception of King Galladel. Elbereth gave apologies for his father, explaining that the king had many duties to attend to and would come out later if he found the time. Whispers around Cadderly and

Danica told them the elves doubted the truth of that explanation and hinted that the king hadn't come out because he thought the whole thing a waste of time.

As soon as the ceremony began, any doubts those whispers had placed in the young scholar's mind washed away.

All the elves rose up and formed a circle atop the hill. Hands were offered to the visitors. Rufo declined immediately, seeming uncomfortable. Danica looked to Cadderly with a wishful smile, and he nodded for her to go, but said that he would rather watch the beginning, at least, from the side. He took out his writing kit and his light tube, smoothed a parchment in front of him, determined to prepare a firsthand account of the rarely watched ritual. He took care, though, to shield the light. Somehow it did not seem fitting, magical though it was, in the starlight of the enchanted forest.

The elven song began slowly, almost as a spoken chant. The elves, and Danica, lifted bowls to the sky and began to walk the circle. Their walk became a dance, their chant a melodic song. Though he couldn't understand all of the words, the emotions evoked by the song affected Cadderly as much as any of the elves. Sad and sweet at the same time, and edged by the experiences of centuries long past, the Song of Shilmista offered the elven experience more fully than any book ever could. Cadderly came to understand then that the elves were a people of feeling, a race of aesthetics, spiritual and at one with their natural surroundings, even more so than the humans who dedicated their lives as woodland priests. Cadderly thought of the three druids who had come to the Edificant Library not so long ago, particularly Newander, who had died at Barjin's hands.

He thought of Pikel, who longed to be a druid, and knew then, with a touch of sadness that the dwarf, however unlike his gruff and pragmatic kin, could never achieve this level of spirituality.

The song went on for more than an hour and ended, not suddenly, but gently, becoming a walk and a chant and fading away as subtly as the setting moon. The elves and Danica still stood holding their bowls to the sky, and Cadderly wished then that he had joined them from the start. He diligently kept to his recording, though when he looked to the parchment he wondered honestly whether his god would have preferred him to write about Daoine Teague Feer or experience it.

Elbereth, splendid in his purple robes, moved to the closest elf and took the bowl. He began a quiet chant to the heavens, to the millions of stars that dotted the night sky, then he reached into the bowl and threw its contents heavenward.

The glitter of stardust filled the air, descending over the targeted elf. His eyes sparkled, his rich golden hair seemed to shine more brightly, and when the stardust had settled, he stood perfectly still, glowing with inner contentment.

Cadderly could hardly find the words to express this transformation. He sat dumbfounded as Elbereth moved about the ring, repeating the ceremony. Most dramatic was the change that came over Shayleigh. Before the stardust descended over her, she had hardly been able to stand and had seemed more concerned with keeping her balance than in any precise movements of the dance.

But after the stardust! Cadderly had seen many healers at work in the Edificant Library, powerful clerics with powerful spells, but none of them could compare to the healing that took place in Shayleigh. Her smile returned, dazzling, the
blood washed from her hair. Even her burned face took on the tanned, creamy
complexion of her elven kin.

Elbereth went to Danica last, and though the stardust did not affect her as it
had affected the elves, the woman seemed much comforted and much pleased.
She stared at the elf prince with sincere admiration unblinking.

A twinge of jealousy shot through Cadderly, but he found that he could not
sustain it. Unexpectedly, Elbereth took a bowl from another elf and came over to
him. Cadderly looked to where Rufo had been seated, excited, but the angular
man was gone.

"You wished to record the ceremony," the elf prince said, towering over Cadderly, "and watch from afar, that you might better understand it."

"That was my mistake," Cadderly admitted.

"Stand, friend," Elbereth bade, and Cadderly slowly rose to his feet. Elbereth
looked around to his people, all nodding, and to Danica, who smiled with anticipation. The prince began the chant and sprinkled the stardust.

From inside the shower, the view was even more glorious. Cadderly saw a million stars reflected a million times. They reached out to him, communicated to him
a sense of universal harmony, a rightness of nature. He thought that, for that too
short moment, he saw the world as an elf saw the world, and when it was over, he
found himself looking at Elbereth in the same appreciative way that Danica had.

Never again would Cadderly feel jealousy toward his wonderful new friend,
he vowed, and his sudden determination to save Shilmista was no less than that
of any elf in the forest.

* * * * *

Kierkan Rufo wandered down the side of Daoine Dun, secure that no goblins
would stray too near the enchanted mound that night. The elven celebration had
meant little to the angular man; like King Galladel, he considered it a waste of
time. All Rufo wanted was to be out of the forest and back to the security of the
Edificant Library. He was never a warrior by choice and had no intention of dying
to save someone else's homeland.

He thought himself incredibly stupid then, for giving in to his guilt and offering, begging, to go along with Cadderly.

"Greetings, Kierkan Rufo," said a raspy voice behind him. Rufo spun about to
see a grotesque, dog-faced and bat-winged imp staring at him from a perch on a
branch just a few feet away. Instinctively, the tall man backed away and looked for
an escape route, but the imp stopped him short.

"If you try to flee or call out, I will kill you," Druzil promised. He looped his
barbed tail, dripping venom, over his shoulder in prominent display.

Rufo steadied himself and tried to appear unafraid. "Who are you?" he demanded. "And how do you know my name?"

"A mutual friend once told me," Druzil replied cryptically, hiding his relief that this man was indeed the priest Barjin had so easily charmed. "I never forget names, you see. They are so important in choosing future allies."

"Enough of your riddles!" snapped Rufo.

"As you wish," said the imp. "My mistress wishes to meet with you—to the benefit of both."

"The wizard?" Rufo reasoned. "If she wishes to parley with an emissary—"

"She wishes to meet with you," Druzil interrupted, "only you. And if you do not agree, I am instructed to kill you.

"But you shall agree, shan't you?" Druzil went on. "What have you to lose? My mistress will not harm you in any way, but the gains . . ." He let the implication hang, a teasing glimmer in his rodentlike black eyes.

"How do you know my name?" Rufo asked again, intrigued, but not yet convinced of anything.

"Meet with my mistress and find out," the imp replied. "Tomorrow night, soon after sunset, I will come for you. You need not pack anything, for you will be returned to the elven camp long before dawn. Are we agreed?"

Rufo hesitated, looking at the poison-tipped tail. To his horror, Druzil gave a flap of leathery wings and, before Rufo could even react, landed upon his shoulder. Rufo nodded weakly, having little choice but to agree with the poisonous stinger so close to his exposed neck.

Druzil eyed him for a while, then grabbed him by the front of his tunic and tossed out a threatening snarl. The imp locked Rufo's stare with his own, purposely keeping the man's gaze high so that Rufo would not notice Druzil's hand movements.

"If you do not come along tomorrow, or if you tell anyone of this meeting, then you will become my mistress's marked target," Druzil warned. "Do not doubt that she will see to your death before your friends can find her, Kierkan Rufo!" The imp laughed its wicked, rasping laugh, then was gone, fading away to invisibility.

Rufo stood there, alone on the trail, for some time. He considered going immediately to tell Elbereth and the others, to surround himself with the elven host, but Rufo feared magic-users and had no desire to cross an imp, a creature that no doubt had allies in the dreaded lower planes. The angular priest went to his cave instead of to the elves and tried to lose himself in sleep.

He twisted and turned on his blankets, never noticing the tiny amulet that Druzil had pinned to an inside fold of his tan tunic.

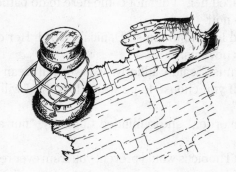

Ten

Betrayed

The elven camp was astir the next morning, the revitalized elves eager to find enemies to battle. Cadderly, Danica, and Rufo tried their best to keep out of the way as the fair folk rushed about, resupplying their patrol groups with rope and arrows.

"I am going with Elbereth in his hunt," Danica insisted to her two friends. "Wizards are not such a threat to one of my training."

"You do not even know if Elbereth is going at all," Cadderly retorted. Indeed, in the central cave before them, the elf prince and his father were engaged in a terrible argument.

"Elbereth will go as he promised," remarked Shayleigh, who, looking much better than she had before Daoine Teague Feer, approached the friends. "Just as he went in to King Galladel this day to argue the value of last night's celebration. The whispers say the king was not pleased that Elbereth presided over Daoine Teague Feer." As if to accentuate the maiden's point, several loud shouts echoed out of the cave.

Shayleigh shook her head and walked away. She could not go out on patrol this day, but those tending her agreed that she would not be much longer in healing.

Cadderly considered the noise from the cave in light of Shayleigh's words. He knew that Danica would not listen to him; the monk was as headstrong as he. "If you are going, then so am I," the young scholar said.

Danica scowled at him. "You are not trained in stealth," she said. "You may hinder us and endanger us."

"Priests have measures to counter a wizard's powers," Kierkan Rufo reminded her.

Danica balked. "You intend to go as well?"

301

"Not I," Rufo assured her. "I did not come here to do battle, and the elves will be better for it if I do not!"

His admission did little to diminish Danica's scowl. Her continued dislike of the angular man was obvious.

"I will do what I must," said Cadderly. "By word of Dean Thobicus, I am the leader of our party. If you choose to go with Elbereth, I will not stop you, but I must go beside you."

"I am not of your order," she reminded Cadderly, "nor am I bound to your library."

"To disobey Dean Thobicus would prevent you from ever returning there," Cadderly warned, "would prevent you from resuming your studies of Penpahg D'ahn."

Danica's glower intensified, but she gave no retort.

Elbereth came out of Galladel's chambers then, his face flushed with anger. He mellowed when he saw Danica and the others, and came straight over to join them.

"Your father is not pleased with you," Danica remarked.

"He never is," said Elbereth, managing a weak smile, "but we share respect, and do not doubt our love."

Cadderly did not doubt, and that left him with a hollow, empty feeling. He would have liked to have had a father, if only to argue with the man!

"Are you to join any patrols this day?" Danica asked.

"I will scout alone," the elf prince replied, looking to the dark forest spread below them. "I must find and destroy the wizard before more harm is done."

"You will not be alone," said Danica. Elbereth understood her intent as soon as he looked into her brown, almond-shaped eyes. He did not appear pleased.

"Danica and I wish to go with you," Cadderly explained. Many expressions crossed Elbereth's face as he considered the unexpected request.

"I will not be riding," he said at length, "and I expect to pass far beyond the closest lines of goblins."

"More the reason to have companions," said Cadderly.

"Perhaps," the elf admitted, eyeing Danica more carefully. Elbereth certainly couldn't deny the young woman's value if it came to battle. "And none of my own people might be spared," he said, "but I can offer no guaran—"

"We need no guarantees," Cadderly assured him. "We understand the dangers." The young scholar flashed his boyish smile at Elbereth, and then to Danica. "Consider it repayment for Daoine Teague Feer."

That thought touched Elbereth, and he soon agreed that the two could accompany him. He told them that an elven warrior would also leave for the Edificant Library, an emissary asking for aid, and that they or Rufo were welcome to go along with that elf if they so chose.

"You have heard our choice," Danica insisted.

"And I cannot go," Kierkan Rufo stammered, coming back over when he heard his name. "Back to the library, I mean."

Danica looked at the angular man curiously, thinking it would be more to Rufo's character to simply run away. Cadderly congratulated his fellow priest on his brave decision to remain in Shilmista. Danica was too suspicious to agree.

In truth, Rufo would have liked nothing better than to go back with the elven emissary, but he dared not miss a certain meeting he had arranged the previous night.

* * * * *

"A wise decision," the imp said, again from behind, when Rufo came down from the hill shortly after sunset.

Rufo spun on him angrily. "You left me with little choice," he growled, his volume causing Druzil to look around nervously.

"Follow!" the imp commanded, thinking it prudent that they get as far from the enchanted hill as possible. He led Rufo through the dark trees to the appointed meeting place with Dorigen. Rufo was surprised to find a woman before him, a not-unattractive woman, though she was older than he and sported a severely crooked nose.

The wizard and Rufo stared at each other for a long while, neither moving to begin the conversation. Finally, Rufo could bear the suspense no longer.

"You called me out here," he protested.

Dorigen let her stare linger a bit longer, let Rufo shift uncomfortably from one foot to the other several times before offering any explanation. "I need information," she eventually replied.

"You would ask me to betray my companions?" Rufo asked, trying to sound incredulous. "Perhaps I should go back. . . ."

"Do not sound so surprised," Dorigen scolded. "You understood the purpose of this meeting before you ever agreed to it."

"I only agreed because I was left with no choice," Rufo argued.

"You are left with no choice again," Dorigen said coldly. "Consider yourself my prisoner, if that might ease your pitiful conscience. I need information, Kierkan Rufo, he who aided Barjin. . . ." Rufo's eyes widened in disbelief.

"Yes, I know who you are," Dorigen continued, thinking she had gained the upper hand. "You were Barjin's pawn, and so you shall be mine!"

"No!" Rufo roared, but when he turned to leave, he found himself facing Druzil's poison-tipped tail. The angular priest's bluster flew away in the blink of an eye.

"Do not be angry, dear man," Dorigen purred. "I have done you a favor, though you do not yet understand that. The forest is doomed, and so, too, are all who fight beside the elves."

"Then why do you need me?" Rufo asked.

"That does not concern the war," Dorigen replied. She paused for a moment to discern how she might explain without giving away too much. "Consider it a personal matter, between me and those who accompanied you to Shilmista."

"The elf prince?" Rufo asked.

"Perhaps," Dorigen answered slyly, thinking it best that Rufo be kept guessing. Not wanting to lose momentum, she pressed on again, her amber eyes flickering with growing delight. "It does not matter. I offer you survival, Kierkan Rufo. When I claim victory, your life will be spared. You might even find a place among my ranks of advisors."

Rufo appeared intrigued, but not convinced.

"And if the elves should somehow escape, and your friends along with them," Dorigen added, "then none will know of your deceit and still you will emerge with nothing lost."

"And if I refuse?"

"Must I go into the unpleasant details?" Dorigen replied, her voice so calm and even-toned that it sent shivers up Rufo's spine. "Oh, I might not kill you now," Dorigen continued. "No, it would be a sweeter thing to see you dishonored for your actions beside Barjin, to lay public those deeds you committed in the library's cellar." Dorigen enjoyed the way Rufo squirmed, and she gave Druzil an approving nod for supplying her with such valuable information.

"How do you know about that?" Rufo asked, as though he had read her thoughts.

"I am not without my sources," Dorigen stated the obvious. "And do not think that your torment shall end with disgrace," she went on, her voice taking a distinctly evil edge. "After your humiliation has ebbed, I will have you killed—in time. Consider the life you will lead if you disappoint me now, Kierkan Rufo. Consider years of looking over your shoulder for assassins."

Rufo again shifted from foot to foot.

"And know that your grave will not be sanctified by the Edificant Library, for certainly your indiscretions with Barjin shall come out in full—I will see to it that they are not easily forgotten—to dishonor you even in death."

The weight of the threat lay heavy on the angular man, both because of the deadly imp just a few feet behind him and the fact that he was indeed vulnerable to the wizard's accusations.

"But let us not focus on such unpleasantness," Dorigen offered. "I require very little of you, and then you may go on your way, secure that whatever the outcome of this war, you will be safe."

Rufo could hardly believe the words as they escaped his thin lips. "What do you wish to know?"

* * * * *

Cadderly felt clumsy, crunching through the brush beside the stealthy Danica and Elbereth. He did not regret his decision to accompany the two, though, and neither of them gave more than a slight frown at the young scholar's loudest crackles.

They had passed several goblin and orc encampments, the creatures sleeping under the light of day, with the exception of a few bleary-eyed and hardly alert guards. Elbereth's planned destination was the same grove in which the wizard had appeared, where Ralmarith had been killed. The elf prince hoped he could pick up the trail from there.

He never would have imagined that finding Dorigen could be so easy.

They had believed their progress exceptional, for they had moved unhindered long after dusk. The forest grew quiet around them as they rested.

Too quiet.

Elbereth sat regarding his sword. "I had thought to bloody it before now," he whispered to the others. "I did not expect that the resistance would be so meager. Perhaps our enemies are not as many as we have been led to believe."

Cadderly had a sickening thought. "Or perhaps . . ." he began, but he never got the chance to finish the sentence, for Elbereth, detecting movement in the thick brush to the west of their hasty camp, motioned for silence and crept away.

Danica, too, went on the alert, only she crouched low and turned toward the snap of a twig in the shadows to the east.

"I have a bad feeling," Cadderly remarked. He quickly loaded a dart on his crossbow and took up his spindle-disks in his other hand.

"Ogres!" cried Elbereth. Cadderly spun about to see the elf engaged with two of the gigantic creatures. Danica disappeared into the brush back to the east, forcing Cadderly's attention.

He turned again just in time to see an ogre bearing down on him, a net held wide in its long arms. Ten ogre strides away, the monster lurched suddenly, as Danica burst out of the brush and rammed her shoulder against the inside of the monster's knee.

Cadderly heard the crack of the huge bone, but the ogre remained standing, though dazed—until Danica came charging back in, leaped high in the air, and double-kicked it in the chest. It flew down into a patch of brambles.

Danica had no time to finish it off; a group of orogs appeared, and orcs beside them. Danica went into a fighting fury, spinning and kicking as the creatures flowed around her.

An orc was the first to get to Cadderly. The young scholar leveled his crossbow to blast it away, but wisely decided to hold that shot until sheer desperation forced it. As the orc came in, slowly now, measuring its enemy, Cadderly set his spindle-disks spinning down to the length of their string.

Cadderly was not well-versed in the orcish tongue, but he had picked up a few words and phrases from his readings.

"Watch!" he said to the orc, trying to sound excited, and he sent the disks into a wide, looping circuit.

The orc did watch, almost mesmerized.

Cadderly snapped the disks back into his hand, continued his arm's circular motion to confuse the stupid monster, and waded ahead a long stride.

The orc's head went back up, expecting the disks to go flying up into the air.

Cadderly snapped them straight out instead, where they slammed under the orc's raised chin and into the creature's exposed throat. It went down on its back, clutching at its crushed windpipe.

Cadderly had barely registered that the orc was down when he heard a rush behind him. He spun and fired his crossbow point blank into an orog that had charged in to tackle him. The dart hit the mark and exploded, but the heavy creature slammed into Cadderly anyway and bore him to the ground.

Cadderly struggled and thrashed for many moments before he realized that the orog's chest was blown wide open and that the creature was quite dead.

Elbereth spent a long time parrying, keeping out of the huge ogres' tremendous reach and the paths of their monstrous clubs. For some reason, the monsters seemed to be only half-swinging, as though they didn't want to crush the elf completely.

Elbereth wasn't about to let them hit him in any case.

An orc sprang up from a bush to the side, just a couple of feet from Elbereth, and readied to throw a net. Elbereth was quicker, though, and his side-cut opened a gash in the monster's face and sent it tumbling.

The battle had begun in full behind the elf—he heard one of Cadderly's darts go off—and he knew that he could afford no more delays. He waited for the exact moment, then charged between the ogres, slashing and sticking as he passed.

More harmful to the beasts, though, were their own clubs. They turned to swipe at the elf, but could not match his quickness and wound up slamming each other instead. One of the unfortunate ogres caught its companion's club in the head as it bent low to grab the elf. It spun two full circles before winding down to the ground.

Elbereth was back on the other before it could recover from the force of the clubbing and the shock of downing its companion. The elf leaped right up the creature's chest and drove his sword hard into its neck. The magical blade bent as it slipped into the thick hide, but its steel proved stronger than ogre flesh.

The doomed monster did manage to slap Elbereth from it before it died, sending the elf flying into the brush between two wide elms. Elbereth was not badly hurt, but he knew he was in trouble. He looked up to see the tree full of waiting orcs. He scrambled desperately as the first of the monsters dropped on him.

Danica met the monstrous charge head-on, though she feared straying too far from Cadderly, still back in the original camp, and Elbereth, all the way over to the other side. She kicked one orc in the throat and took another down with three quick punches to the face.

There were too many targets. Danica blocked one orog club between crossed arms and quickly snapped her arms back out wide, tearing the weapon from the monster's grip. Her foot came straight up, catching the orog under the chin and launching it head-over-heels backward. Another orc rushed in from the side, and Danica, frantically turning, sent her foot flying out to meet it.

A club smashed into her back, blasting her breath away. Danica resisted the urge to fall and stubbornly turned to meet this newest orc attacker, but an ogre crashed out of the brush suddenly and locked its huge hand on her head, twisting her neck dangerously to the side.

Danica started to counter, but the orc's club hit her again, then orogs grabbed her arms and pressed against her.

She thought her head would burst as the ogre's great hand clenched and twisted some more.

Back near the camp's center, warm blood dripped over Cadderly's face and neck. By the time he was able to push his way out from under the dead orog, he was drenched with the gruesome stuff. He scrambled to his feet and loaded another dart.

A large group of orogs, orcs, and a single ogre approached from the east; desperate, Cadderly didn't know who to shoot first, then he saw the ogre's cargo: Danica, held firmly by the head, with two orogs loosely holding her arms. The ogre eyed Cadderly and gave a quick twist, and Danica's face contorted in pain.

"Enough!" roared an orc from behind the lead rank. The creature moved cautiously around its ogre companion. "Surrender or me ogre breakses the girl's neck!"

Cadderly wanted to swing his bow around and destroy the arrogant orc, but he couldn't deny Danica's predicament. He looked to his love helplessly. He thought of his ring and poisoned dart but dismissed the notion. He didn't even have his walking stick and doubted that the dosage on the tiny cat's claw would even affect the large ogre.

Then another thought came to him.

Danica eyed him curiously, then flashed him a wistful smile, and Cadderly knew she understood.

Slowly, Cadderly lowered the crossbow toward the ground. It swung back up suddenly and the young scholar fired the dart into the ogre's shoulder. The ogre hardly flinched at the explosion, but Cadderly knew he had hurt the creature badly.

Danica knew it, too, could tell from the way the monster's grip suddenly loosened. She dipped free, snapping her arms from her orog captors as she continued to drop. Her crouch brought her right to the ground before she reversed her momentum and leaped straight up.

The stunned orogs stared dumbfounded as the powerful monk soared into the air, rising above them. They had only barely begun to react when Danica kicked out to the sides, each foot smashing an orog in the face and sending it flying away.

Danica hit the ground and whirled about, punching straight out at her shoulder level, which was the same level as the wounded ogre's groin. The monster bellowed and went back on its heels, and ferocious Danica pounded it again.

"Stop them!" the orc to her side screeched. Another explosion sounded and the monster fell silent—several feet from where it had been standing.

Cadderly wondered if their last ploy had been worth it as he watched Danica batter the ogre's midsection. Would death be preferable to capture at the hands of such vile monsters?

Orogs came at the young scholar slowly, fearing his deadly crossbow. Cadderly knew he was doomed, though he didn't even realize that Elbereth was no longer fighting and a host of orcs was rushing in from behind.

He felt a hot explosion as a club slammed against the back of his neck. His last sensation was the taste of dirt in his mouth.

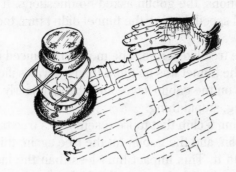

Eleven

The Trouble With Traps

The goblin kept its back pressed against the tree for a very long time, not even daring to breathe. A dozen of its companions lay dead, their lives snuffed out in the blink of an eye, it seemed. The frightened goblin heard the steadily diminishing screams of its only living companion, the terrified creature putting more and more distance between itself and the massacre site.

Finally, the remaining goblin mustered the courage to slip out from the tree. It peeked around the trunk's huge girth, looked to its hacked and battered companions.

No sign of the murderous monsters.

The goblin crept out a bit farther and glanced all about.

Still nothing.

Hugging the trunk, it moved around one more step.

"I knowed ye was there!" cried a yellow-bearded dwarf.

The goblin fell back and looked up to see a swiftly descending double-bladed axe.

That business finished, the dwarf turned about to see how his brother was doing.

"Aiyeegh!" the last living goblin screamed, running full speed, knowing that the dwarf with the nasty club was just a few steps behind.

"Oo oi!" the dwarf answered happily.

"Aiyeegh!" The goblin made straight for a row of enormous beech trees, thinking it might find an escape route through the massive trunks and thick roots. It saw, then, a beautiful human female, tan-skinned and with green hair, beckoning it her way. The woman pointed to the side, revealing a tunnel leading right into one tree.

With no other options, the goblin asked no questions. It bent its gruesome head low and ran full speed, hoping the tunnel didn't turn too sharply a few feet into the blackness.

The goblin hit the tree like a ram. The monster bounced back two steps, not understanding that the tunnel was no more than a dryad's illusion. Blood flowed from a dozen gashes on the goblin's face and chest; it nearly swooned, but stubbornly held its footing, stupid thing.

The dwarf, lowering a club that more resembled a tree trunk, never slowed. The club hit the goblin, and the goblin hit the tree again, this time with considerable weight behind it. This impact hurt less than the last, though, for the wretched creature was dead before it realized what had happened.

Pikel Bouldershoulder spent a moment considering the squashed object between his club and the great beech, honestly wondering how it once might have resembled a living goblin. Then the dwarf looked over to Hammadeen and gave a resounding "Oo oi!"

The dryad blushed in response and disappeared into the grove.

"Ye hit him hard," Pikel's brother, Ivan, remarked a bit later as he came up behind. The yellow-bearded dwarf held his great axe over his shoulder with an impaled goblin still stuck to one blade.

Pikel regarded it curiously and scratched at his green-dyed hair and beard. Unlike his brother, who tucked his long beard into his belt, Pikel pulled his back over his ears and braided it along with his top hair down his back.

Ivan heaved the impaled goblin over his shoulder and let it fall in front of him. "Hit mine hard, too," he explained. He put one foot on the dead monster's shoulder, spat in both his gnarly, calloused hands, and clenched the axe handle tightly.

Bone crackled as the dwarf stubbornly tugged. "Didn't want to wait and do this back there," he explained between grunts. "Thought ye might be needing me help."

"Uh-uh," Pikel replied, shaking his head and looking to the splattered goblin still stuck against the tree.

Ivan finally wrenched his axe free. "Messy things," he remarked.

"Another battle mars the forest just a few miles west," came the melodic voice of Hammadeen.

Ivan shook his head in disbelief. "Always another battle!" he growled at the dryad, then he looked incredulously at Pikel. "Bloody life, this druid thing."

"Doo-dad!" Pikel howled enthusiastically.

"We ain't found a day's quiet since we came to this stinking—" he glanced at Hammadeen and winced "—this pretty forest."

Pikel shrugged, having no explanation. Indeed, the dwarven brothers had discovered one fight after another since their arrival in Shilmista more than a week before. Not that they minded, given the nature of their opponents, but even Ivan was beginning to worry about the sheer number of goblinoids and giant-kin in the supposedly peaceful wood.

The dryad put her ear and gentle hands against the oak's rough bark, as though listening to the tree. "The fight is just ended," she announced.

"Elves win?" asked Ivan. "Not that I'm caring!" he quickly clarified. Ivan was not fond of elves; they were too fanciful and scatterbrained for his dwarven sensibilities.

"Eh?" Pikel prodded, nudging his brother hard in the arm as though he had just caught Ivan in a rare moment of compassion.

"They're a better lot than orcs," Ivan admitted, "but I've no heart for sharing a meal with either breed!" Pikel joined in with his gruff chuckle, then they both turned on Hammadeen.

"Well, did they win?" Ivan asked again.

The dryad drew a blank and somewhat worried look, having no answers.

"Me guess's that we should go and see what we can do," Ivan said grudgingly. "We got the one body away from them under the burned tree—even an elf deserves better than to be served up on a goblin's dinner table!"

They reached the battlefield about an hour later. Pikel was the first to spot a victim, a slashed orc lying in a thick bush.

"Oo!" the dwarf squealed with delight when he got to the body and found four other orcs in similar states.

"Oo!" he howled even more enthusiastically when he spotted two dead ogres a few paces away, one with its throat pierced and the other with its head caved in.

"Someone did some fine fighting," Ivan agreed, circling wide about the area. He saw a dead orc and orog lying beside what looked to be a small campsite, but continued on around the camp to an area that apparently had seen even more action.

Two orogs lay dead, their heads twisted almost all the way around to the back, and several orcs and orogs were strewn about the ground a short distance from them. Ivan spent a while inspecting the creatures and their curious wounds. None had been slashed by sword or pierced by spear or arrow, and even the killing, crushing blows did not resemble any mace or hammer marks the dwarf had ever seen. Also, the way the two orogs had died, their necks snapped in strikingly similar manners, did not seem the work of any elf.

Pikel's call turned the dwarf about. Ivan's brother was in the campsite then, holding high the head and chest of the dead orog and pointing to the creature's scorched wound. Only one weapon Ivan had ever seen could have caused that mark. He glanced back at the two dead orogs, an image of Danica suddenly coming to his mind.

"Wizard's work," Ivan offered hopefully, moving to join his brother. "Or . . ."

That last thought was answered soon enough as Pikel dropped the orog suddenly, leaped over to some brush, and produced a familiar ram's-head walking stick.

"Uh-oh," said Pikel.

"Dryad!" Ivan bellowed.

"Quiet would serve better in the dangerous forest," Hammadeen offered as she appeared from a tree behind the dwarf. She gave Ivan a wink and a wistful smile.

"None o' yer charming stuff!" the dwarf yelled at her, but even gruff Ivan mellowed when Hammadeen's disarming smile became a frown. "This is too important," Ivan explained. "Who fought the fight?"

The dryad shrugged.

"Well, ask yer trees!" roared the dwarf. "Was it elves or humans?"

Hammadeen turned about for just a moment, then announced, "Both."

"Where'd they go?" Ivan asked, looking all around.

Hammadeen pointed to the northeast. Ivan and Pikel ran off at once, Ivan begging the dryad to lead them.

They were relieved when they caught up to the capture party, to find Cadderly and Danica still alive, though badly beaten. Danica was held suspended from the ground by two ogres holding a large stick tied across her shoulders and along the back of her neck. The giant monsters showed the woman plenty of respect, keeping far from her, even though her arms and legs were securely bound. One of them limped badly; the other was all scratched and bruised. The dwarves could easily guess that the ogres had found the misfortune of tangling with Danica back in the camp.

Cadderly came next, walking with his hands tied behind his back, a hood over his head, and four orogs surrounding him and prodding him every step. Last in line was an elf, being dragged by a host of orcs, his ankles bound to a plank.

"Too many," Ivan muttered, and indeed, no fewer than twenty formidable monsters surrounded their helpless friends. He looked to his brother and smiled. "We need to set us a trap."

"Oo oi," Pikel agreed, and they ran off, circling far ahead of the caravan. Some time later, they stopped in a small clearing. Ivan glanced all about and scratched at his beard.

He looked up a thick-limbed elm, to a tumble of boulders a short distance away, and then back down the path to where the caravan would make its approach.

"If we can get a few of them rocks up the tree," the dwarf mused. His dark eyes sparkled, and he slammed his hands together twice in rapid succession. "*Thump! Thump!* And two less ogres to fight!"

"Uh-oh," Pikel whispered ominously, rolling his eyes about. A chuckle from the boughs showed that the dryad saw the same disastrous possibilities as the doubting dwarf.

Ivan had no time to hear any protests. He pulled his brother along and together they managed to roll one large rock under the overhanging limb. Ivan scratched his yellow beard and considered how they might get the boulder up the tree, for at its lowest point, the branch was still eight or nine feet from the ground—and it was the lowest branch in the elm.

"Ye pick up the stone and get on me shoulders," Ivan said. "Stick it in the crook and we'll climb up and sort it out later."

Pikel eyed the stone and the branch and shook his head doubtfully.

"Do it!" Ivan commanded. "Ye want to see Cadderly and Danica served up for ogre snacks?"

Grunting and groaning every inch, Pikel managed to heave the two-hundred-pound rock up to his chest. Ivan dropped his deer-horned helmet to the side, stepped up behind Pikel, and dipped his head between his brother's legs. The mighty dwarf heaved with all his might, finally bringing Pikel unsteadily into the air.

"Put it up! Put it up!" Ivan begged between grunts. In the wavering seat, Pikel couldn't hope to get the stone far enough from his body to clear the thick branch.

"I'll take a run at it," Ivan offered, seeing his brother's dilemma. He swerved back a few steps from the tree, then charged ahead, hoping his momentum would aid Pikel.

Pikel heaved mightily, pushing the stone out to arm's length, then slammed into the branch. Oblivious to his brother's sudden dilemma, Ivan continued on, stretching poor Pikel to his limit. The rock went atop the branch and rolled over, dropping straight at Ivan's head.

"Oops!" came Pikel's warning. Ivan managed to get his arms up to deflect the bomb, but he went sprawling anyway, leaving Pikel hanging from the branch by his fingertips.

"Ooooooo!" Pikel wailed, and he fell, his landing cushioned by Ivan's chest.

Unseen but not unheard, Hammadeen's titters didn't do much to improve Ivan's mood.

When they had recovered a few minutes later, they next tried using their ropes to coax the boulder up. It slipped out of their noose a few times—until they got the hang of properly tying it—and bounced once off Ivan's foot. They nearly had it to the branch, when the rope snapped.

Pikel wagged his head and looked nervously back down the path, thinking that their time was just about up.

"Ye're the druid!" Ivan growled at him. "Tell yer tree to bend down and pick the damned thing up!"

Pikel threw his hands on hips and scowled fiercely.

Ivan put his fist in Pikel's eye; Pikel grabbed the hand and bit Ivan's knuckle. They rolled about the dirt, pinching, biting, kicking—whatever worked in the close quarters until Ivan broke off, a grin of inspiration spread across his thick-skinned face.

"I get ye up the tree and toss ye the rock!" he beamed.

Pikel looked about, then grinned similarly.

Putting Pikel up was no problem, but the stubborn rock proved a different matter. As strong as he was, Ivan couldn't hope to heave the boulder high enough for Pikel to catch it. Growing as frustrated as his brother, Pikel turned around, hooked his stubby legs at the knees over the branch and reached down as far as he could.

The rock hit him square in the face and chest, but he managed to hold his precarious perch, though he had no idea of how he was going to right himself with the heavy stone.

Ivan called out support, urging his brother on. He realized—too late—that he had wandered directly under his brother.

Pikel had just about turned upright when his legs let go. Ivan managed a single desperate step before his brother and the boulder buried him.

Hammadeen's laughter echoed louder.

"That did it!" Ivan bellowed, hopping to his feet. He grabbed the stone and tried to pry it away from Pikel, who just lay there, saying "Oo," over and over and clutching the rock like it was some dwarf baby—and, in truth, it somewhat resembled one.

Then Ivan had the stone. He charged the tree and hurled it at where the limb met the trunk. It bounced off, but Ivan scooped it back up and heaved it again, and then again, and again after that.

Pikel just sat in the dirt, watching his brother in disbelief.

Then, amazingly, the stone wedged into the crook and held, and Ivan turned about triumphantly.

"They'll get here soon," he observed, gathering the rope. "No time for another rock."

"Phew," Pikel remarked under his breath.

They looped the rope over the branch and started up, one on either side. Pikel, less armored and less laden than his brother, gained a quick advantage, then put his sandal on Ivan's shoulder (waggling his smelly toes in his brother's face), and pushed off. His momentum carried him the rest of the way, and he pulled himself over and sat up, forgetting to keep his weight on the rope. He watched, mesmerized, as it flew by, and Ivan plummeted back to the dirt.

The yellow-bearded dwarf sat up, spitting twigs and pebbles and scolding himself for not knowing better.

"Oops," Pikel offered apologetically.

"Tie off the rope!" Ivan growled. Pikel considered the task and the consequences of letting his angry brother get near him, then shook his head.

"Tie it off!" Ivan roared. "Or I'll cut the tree down!" He picked up his axe and took a stride toward the thick trunk before Hammadeen appeared between him and his target.

"Do not do that," the dryad warned. Of more concern to Ivan was his brother, the would-be druid, who had slid down the branch near the crook and the heavy rock's precarious perch. Ivan had no doubts that if he went to chop at the tree, Pikel would drop the stone on his head.

Ivan crossed his burly arms in front of his chest and stood staring up at Pikel. Finally, the seated dwarf relented and tied off the rope, motioning for his brother to climb up. Soon then they sat together on the branch, Ivan impatient and uncomfortable, but Pikel, thinking his perch very druidlike, quite content.

"What are ye laughing about now?" Ivan demanded of the pesky dryad some time later. Hammadeen appeared on a branch above them, pointing to the north.

"The ogres did not come this way," she said. Sure enough, peering through the trees, Ivan and Pikel could just make out the distant commotion of the prisoner caravan, some distance north and moving away.

Pikel looked to Ivan, then to the rock, then back to Ivan, a sour expression on his cherubic face.

"Shut—" Ivan started, but he stopped abruptly, noticing some movement in the not-too-distant brush. A moment later, he made out an orc, foraging through the trees, cutting pieces of kindling with a long knife. Ivan considered the creature's path and realized it would pass not too far from the trap.

"Get it over here," he whispered to Pikel.

His brother squeaked and poked a finger into his own chest.

"Yeah, yerself!" Ivan whispered harshly, and he slapped Pikel on the back of his head, dislodging him from the branch.

"Oooooo!" Pikel wailed before hitting the ground with a thud.

Ivan paid his brother no heed. He was more concerned with the orc, who had noticed the noise. The creature crept in slowly, knife held ready.

Pikel rolled about for a moment, then glared up at Ivan, but kept enough wits to move to the clearing's far side. He turned his back to the approaching orc, put his hands in his pockets, and began to whistle nonchalantly.

The orc slipped up to the tree trunk, oblivious of Ivan, holding the rock above its head. One step out, then two, then it broke into a run.

Then it was dead.

Ivan looped the rope and swung down. He slammed a heavy boot atop his squashed victim, pounding a hand triumphantly against his barrellike chest. "I telled ye it would work!" he proclaimed.

Pikel looked to the crushed orc and up the branch, an amused expression splayed across his face. Ivan knew what his brother was thinking: that it would have been much easier just to walk over and put an axe through the orc's thick head.

"Don't ye say a word!" Ivan growled ominously. Fortunately, Pikel never had trouble following that particular command.

"I think we can get the rock back in place," Ivan started, looking back to the crook. "If I can . . ."

Pikel ran him down, and the fight was on. Quite unknown to the battling dwarves, another orc was nearby, collecting wood. It came to the clearing, noticed its squashed companion, and considered the titanic struggle. It looked discomfitedly at its meager knife.

The orc shrugged and moved along, thinking that some sights were better forgotten.

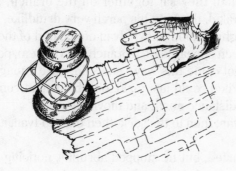

Twelve
Under Guard

"C adderly." The word came from a great distance, from beyond the edge of the young scholar's consciousness. "Cadderly," it came again, more insistent.

Cadderly strained to open his eyes. He recognized the voice, and he recognized the caring eyes he found himself looking into, rich brown and exotic. Still, it took him a while to remember the woman's name.

"Danica?"

"I feared you would never awaken," Danica replied. "The bruise on your lower neck is wicked indeed." Cadderly didn't doubt that; even the slightest shift of his head hurt him.

He gradually came back to consciousness. He and she were in a tent of animal skins, Cadderly's hands tightly bound behind his back and Danica's behind hers. Danica sat with Cadderly's head and shoulders gently propped on her lap. No guards were in sight, but Cadderly heard the guttural grunts of orcs and orogs outside, and that noise inevitably led him to recall the battle, and the last desperate act in which he had blasted the ogre's shoulder.

"They did not kill us?" he asked, confused. He wriggled his hands about and could feel that he still wore his feathered ring.

Danica shook her head. "They were under orders not to, I must assume—strict orders," she replied. "The orc that struck you was punished by the orogs for hitting you so hard. They all feared you would die."

Cadderly considered the news for a moment, but found no solution to this puzzle. "Elbereth?" he asked, panic obvious in his voice.

Danica looked beyond the young scholar, to the back of the skin tent. With some effort, Cadderly managed to shift around for a glance as well. Elbereth, the elf prince, seemed far removed from royalty at that moment. Dirty and blood-stained, he sat with his head down, his arms tied to his knees, with one eye bruised so badly that it would not open.

He sensed the stares and looked up.

"I caused our capture," he admitted, his choked voice barely more than a whisper. "It was I they sought, an elf prince to ransom."

"You cannot know that," Danica offered, trying to comfort the distraught elf. There was little conviction in the young woman's voice—Elbereth's guess seemed logical. The elf put his head back down and did not answer.

"Orogs," Cadderly muttered, trying to jog his memory. He had read several passages concerning the brutes and searched now for some answers to the situation. Had he and his companions, perhaps, been taken prisoner to become sacrifices in some horrible ritual? Were they to be the meat of an orog's dinner? Neither explanation offered much solace, and Cadderly nearly jumped upright when the flap of the tent was thrown aside.

It was no orog that walked in from the dusky light, but a man, great and tall, bronze-skinned and golden-haired. A tattoo of some strange creature was centered in his forehead, between his ice-blue, piercing eyes.

Cadderly studied him intently, thinking that the tattoo—Cadderly recognized it as a remorhaz, a polar worm—should tell him something.

The huge man walked over to Danica and gave a leer that sent shivers through her spine and evoked silent rage in Cadderly. Then, casually, with the slightest flick of his muscled arm, he tossed the young woman aside. With one hand and similar ease, he grabbed the front of Cadderly's tunic and hoisted the young scholar to his feet.

"White Worm," Cadderly muttered, unconsciously thinking aloud, the words brought on by the man's sheer size. He was nearly a foot taller than Cadderly's six feet, and easily a hundred pounds heavier, though there wasn't a bit of softness on his mighty frame.

The bronze-skinned giant's frown quickly became a threatening scowl aimed at Cadderly. "What do you know of the White Worm?" he demanded, his voice edged by the hint of an accent from a distant land.

It was Cadderly's turn to frown. The big man's command of the language seemed too smooth and unaccented for the young scholar's budding theory to be correct. Also, the man's clothes were richly made, of silk and other fine materials, cut as a king might wear them, or a servant of a king's court. The man seemed quite comfortable in them—too comfortable, Cadderly noted, for a barbarian.

"What do you know?" the man demanded, and he lifted Cadderly from the floor again with one gigantic hand.

"The painting on your forehead," Cadderly gasped. "It is a remorhaz, a white worm, an uncommon beast, even in the northern reaches, and known not at all among the Snowflake Mountains and the Shining Plains."

The large man's scowl did not relent. He eyed Cadderly for some time, as if waiting for the young priest to elaborate on his explanation.

There came a rustle from the door, and the giant promptly lowered Cadderly to the floor. In walked a black-haired woman, a wizard, judging from the robes she wore. She reminded Cadderly somewhat of a younger Pertelope, except that her eyes were dots of amber, not hazel, and she wore her hair longer and less tended than the neatly groomed Pertelope. And while Pertelope's nose was arrow straight, the wizard's had obviously been broken and forever bent to the side.

"Welcome, dear Cadderly," the wizard said, her words drawing surprised looks from both Cadderly and Danica. Even Elbereth looked up. "Have you enjoyed your visit to Shilmista? I know Kierkan Rufo longs for home."

Danica sucked in her breath at the mention of Rufo. Cadderly turned to her, anticipating her anger and trying to diffuse it for the time being.

"Yes, I know your name, young priest of the Edificant Library," the woman continued, reveling in her superior position. "You will come to understand that I know many things."

"Then you are at an advantage," Cadderly dared to remark, "for I know nothing of you."

"Nothing?" The woman chuckled. "If you knew nothing of me, then surely you would not have come out to kill me." This time, Cadderly and Danica could not even manage to stifle gasps, their astonishment plain on their faces.

Cadderly heard Danica mutter, "Rufo."

"I do not wish to die, you must understand," the wizard said sarcastically.

Not as Barjin died, rang a voice inside Cadderly's head. He glanced around at Danica, then realized that the words had been telepathic, not audible communication. The unexpected connection to the slain priest brought a thousand questions rushing through Cadderly's thoughts. He settled them quickly, though, asking himself if someone, or something, had actually communicated with him, or if that inner voice had been his own, reasonably placing this wizard in the same conspiracy as the slain priest.

Cadderly looked the wizard over, up and down. Her dress was unremarkable enough, certainly not as ornamented as Barjin's clerical robes had been. The young scholar strained his neck, trying to get a better view of the wizard's rings. She wore three, and one of them appeared to hold an insignia.

The wizard smiled at him, drawing his eyes to hers, then pointedly slipped her hands into her pockets.

"Always curious," she mumbled, but loud enough so that Cadderly could hear. "So similar to that other one."

The way she spoke that reference surprised Cadderly.

"Yes, young priest," the woman continued, "you will prove a valuable well of information."

Cadderly wanted to spit on her foot—he knew that his dwarven friend Ivan would have without a second thought—but he couldn't muster the courage. His sour expression revealed his feelings, though.

That disdainful, uncompromising expression gave way to despair when the wizard took her hand back out of her deep pocket. She held something, something terrible by Cadderly's estimation.

Dorigen leveled Cadderly's deadly crossbow, cocked and loaded with an explosive dart, at Danica. Cadderly didn't breathe for what seemed like minutes.

"You will do as I command you," the wizard said, glaring at Cadderly, her visage suddenly icy and removed. "Say it!"

Cadderly couldn't say anything past the lump in his throat.

"Say it!" the wizard cried, jerking the crossbow Danica's way. For a split second, Cadderly thought she had pulled the trigger, and he nearly fainted away.

"I will do as you command!" he cried desperately as soon as he realized that the bow hadn't fired.

"No!" Danica shouted at him.

"A well of information," the wizard said again, her lips turning up in a comfortable smile. She turned to her bronze-skinned soldier. "Take him."

Stubborn Danica was up in a second, cutting between Cadderly and the huge man. She tugged at her ropes, but was unable to get her hands free and settled instead for kicking at the large man.

His agility and quick reactions surprised the young woman. He was down in a crouch even as Danica's foot flew up, and he caught her leg cleanly. A subtle twist of his powerful arms sent Danica off balance, gritting her teeth in pain. The huge man tossed her aside, again with no more than a casual flick of his hands.

"Enough!" the wizard commanded. "Do not kill her." She gave Cadderly an awful smile. "Fear not, young priest, I will not kill those who allow me to control you like a marionette! Ah, to have my prize, and an elf prince thrown into the package by sheer chance! Yes, I know of you, too, Elbereth, and do not doubt that you shall be reunited with your people soon. You are much too dangerous a prisoner for me to keep." Dorigen snickered again. "Or at least, your head will soon be reunited with your father."

Her words renewed Elbereth's futile struggling with his tight bonds. The wizard laughed aloud, mocking him. "Take him!" she said again to the warrior, indicating Cadderly.

The huge man grabbed Cadderly quickly, before Danica could react, and wrapped him in a tight headlock, the great man's other hand waving ready in case the fiery woman decided to come back for more.

"Stay back!" Cadderly called out meekly, and Danica did, for she saw that the warrior could snap Cadderly's neck with ease.

"Stay back," the huge man echoed. "Come only when you are summoned." The manner in which he spoke, through a lascivious grin, renewed the shivers along the young woman's spine.

Behind the huge man, the wizard frowned, and Danica was quick to understand the jealousy behind that look.

At the wizard's snapping command, two orogs took up positions inside the tent as she and her giant lackey departed with Cadderly in tow.

The camp itself struck Cadderly as out of place, as wrong, from the moment he was half-dragged, half-carried outside. Even in the fading daylight he could see that beautiful Shilmista had been scarred and torn, with trees that had lived a hundred years ripped down and broken apart. It was an odd feeling for the young scholar, something he hadn't expected. He himself had used firewood back at the Edificant Library, had plucked a flower from the roadside to give to Danica without a second thought. But there was a majesty about Shilmista that Cadderly had never known, a raw and natural beauty that even the print of a boot seemed to mar.

Watching filthy orogs and orcs milling about the forest pained Cadderly's heart profoundly. He recognized many of the creatures, mostly from wounds—such as the limp one ogre exhibited and the heavy bandage on its shoulder. The monster noticed Cadderly, too, and its scowl promised death if the thing ever got its hands on the young scholar.

The wizard's tent was on the far side of the camp. While on the outside it seemed a normal skin canopy, the inside revealed that this wizard enjoyed her niceties. Plush cloth covered the one table and the four chairs around it; the bed was thick and soft—no blanket on the ground for this woman; and a silver serving set was perched upon a cart off to the side.

The bronze giant roughly placed Cadderly in one of the chairs.

"You may leave us, Tiennek," the wizard said, taking a seat opposite the young scholar.

Tiennek didn't seem overly pleased by that idea. He scowled at Cadderly and made no move toward the flap.

"Oh, be gone!" his mistress scolded, waving her hand. "Do you believe I cannot protect myself from the likes of this one?"

Tiennek bent close to Cadderly and issued a threatening growl, then bowed low to his lady and departed.

Cadderly shifted in his seat, letting the wizard know that his bindings were uncomfortable. Now was the time for him to take command, he decided, to let his enemy understand that he was not some coward she could do with as she pleased. Cadderly wasn't certain he could hold up that facade, especially not with Danica and Elbereth's lives hanging so tenuously before him. But that facade, he realized, might be the only thing that kept them all alive.

The wizard considered him for a long while, then muttered some words under her breath. Cadderly felt the ties about his wrists being undone, and soon his aching arms were free.

His first thoughts centered on his feathered ring. If he could manage to get the cat's claw out and stick the wizard . . .

Cadderly dismissed that notion. He didn't even know if the drow sleep poison was still active. If he made his attempt and failed, he did not doubt that the wizard would punish him severely—or, more likely, punish his helpless friends.

"He is cultured beyond what one would expect from a barbarian," the young scholar said, thinking to catch the wizard off her guard.

The wizard's chuckle mocked him. "Deductive, as I expected," she said, more to herself than to Cadderly. Again her tone gave Cadderly pause.

"The marking on his forehead, I mean," Cadderly stammered, trying to regain his composure. "Tiennek is of the White Worm, the barbarian tribe living under the shadows of the Great Glacier."

"Is he?" the wizard purred, leaning forward in her chair, as if to better hear Cadderly's startling revelations.

Cadderly realized that it was useless to continue.

The wizard fell back comfortably in her seat. "You are correct, young priest," she said sincerely. "Amazingly so. Few from the region would recognize the remorhaz at all, let alone connect the marking to an obscure barbarian tribe that never ventures south of the Galena Mountains. I congratulate you as you have congratulated me."

Cadderly's eyebrows rolled up with curiosity.

"Tiennek's mannerisms are indeed an aberration," the wizard explained, "far from what one would expect from the savage warriors of the White Worm."

"You taught him that culture," Cadderly added.

"It was necessary if he was to properly serve me," the wizard explained.

The casual conversation put Cadderly at ease enough to offer a prompt. "Does he properly serve his lady . . .?"

"Dorigen," the wizard said. "I am Dorigen Kel Lamond."

"Of?"

Again came that mocking chuckle. "Yes, you are inquisitive," she said, her excitement mounting. "I have dealt far too long with one too much like you for your words to entangle me." She calmed immediately, putting the conversation back into a casual mode. "So many things have happened so quickly, and Cadderly Bo—" Dorigen paused and smiled, seeing his reaction. It was true, Dorigen realized, the young priest did not know his heritage, or even his family name.

"You will pardon me," Dorigen went on. "For all my knowledge, I fear I know not your surname."

Cadderly slumped back, understanding that Dorigen had lied to him. What was the significance of that single syllable the wizard had uttered? he wondered. Did Dorigen know of his parentage? Determinedly, Cadderly resolved not to play this mocking game with the wizard. To do so would put Dorigen in an even higher position of authority, something he and his friends could not afford.

"Cadderly of Carradoon," he answered curtly. "That is all."

"Is it?" Dorigen teased, and Cadderly had to concentrate hard to hide his interest.

Dorigen broke the ensuing silence with a heartfelt laugh. "Let me answer some of your questions, young priest," she said, and she tapped her shoulder, or rather, she tapped something invisible that was perched upon her shoulder.

Druzil, the imp, faded into view.

So they were connected! Cadderly realized, recognizing the imp, the same imp who had poisoned Pikel back in the library's catacombs. There could be no doubt. Barjin and this wizard had come from the same source. Cadderly understood then the silent voice he had heard back in the other tent. He looked immediately to Dorigen's delicate hand and the signet ring, recognizing it now that he realized what should be upon it. The trident and bottle design, the variation of Talona's holy symbol that had so quickly become a mark of disaster to the region.

"Greetings again, young priest," the imp said in his raspy voice. Druzil's forked tongue flicked, lizardlike, between his pointed yellow teeth, and he leered at Cadderly as an ogre might stare at a piece of roasting mutton. "You have been well, I presume?"

Cadderly didn't blink, refused to show any weakness. "And you have recovered from your flight into a wall?" he replied evenly.

Druzil growled and disappeared from view.

Dorigen laughed again. "Very fine," she congratulated Cadderly. "Druzil usually is not so easily intimidated."

Still Cadderly did not blink. He felt an intrusion in his mind, an empathic bond he knew was coming from the imp.

"Let him in," Dorigen instructed. "He challenges you. Do you fear to learn who is the stronger?"

Cadderly didn't understand, but, still determined not to reveal any weakness, he closed his eyes and lowered his mental defenses.

He heard Dorigen chanting softly, heard Druzil snicker, then felt the energy of a magical spell fall over him. His mind became a tangible blackness, as though he had been mentally transported to an empty place. Then a light, a glowing and sparkling orb, appeared in the distance, floating toward Cadderly.

His mind watched the orb curiously as it neared, not understanding the danger. Then it was upon him, a part of his thoughts, burning him like a flame! A thousand fiery explosions went off inside his brain, a thousand searing blasts of agony.

Cadderly grimaced, thrashed about in his seat, and opened his eyes. Through a dark cloud he saw the wizard, and the imp, seated, smiling, on her shoulder. The pain intensified; Cadderly cried out and feared he would fall unconscious—or dead, and he almost wished that he would.

He closed his eyes again, tried to concentrate and find some way to relieve the agony.

"Push it away," came a distant voice that Cadderly recognized as Dorigen's. "Use your will, young priest, and push the fire away."

Cadderly heard her and understood her words, but he could hardly find his focus through the pain. He took a deep breath and slammed his fists on the table before him, determined to distract himself from the ball of fiery light.

Still it burned. He heard Druzil snicker.

Cadderly mentally reached for his meditation techniques, tried to blot out the light as he could blot out the material world, bit by bit.

It would not go away. Druzil snickered again.

Anger replaced the vacuum of meditation, destroyed any serenity the young scholar had managed to create. The light became his enemy; he convinced himself that it would turn on Danica after it devoured him.

"No!" Cadderly growled, and suddenly the ball was moving away, out of the void he had entered. It wavered for many moments, then slipped beyond Cadderly's mentality. The pain was no more, and no more were Druzil's snickers.

Cadderly realized another void, another hole of blackness beyond his own, and he knew instinctively that it belonged to the imp, to the one who had forced the pain upon him. His anger did not relent; the ball of sparkling light moved toward the other blackness.

"Enough," he heard Druzil cry, to which Dorigen merely laughed.

Cadderly forced the orb into Druzil's thoughts. The imp squealed out, and that only prompted Cadderly on. He would show no mercy; he would hold the fire in Druzil's mind until it burned the imp away to nothing!

Then it was over, abruptly, and Cadderly found himself seated at a table opposite Dorigen and Druzil, the imp reeling, his bulbous eyes promising death to the young scholar.

"Excellent!" Dorigen cried, clapping her hands together. "You are powerful indeed if you can defeat Druzil, who is practiced in the game. Perhaps even more powerful than your—" She stopped and tossed Cadderly a teasing stare. "You will do well beside me."

Again the young scholar would not play along. "I do not serve Talona," he announced, and it was Dorigen's turn to try to hide her surprise. "I never shall, whatever the price."

"We shall see," Dorigen replied after a short pause. "Tiennek!"

The barbarian was upon Cadderly in an instant, fiercely tugging his arms behind his back and retying his hands so tightly that the cords cut into his wrists. The young scholar was hoisted into the air and briskly carried away.

Cadderly struggled to sit up when the barbarian dropped him back in his tent. Tiennek offered one more leer Danica's way before he departed.

"What happened to you?" Danica asked when the barbarian was gone. She shuffled over to Cadderly, resting her head against his.

Cadderly, still overwhelmed and with too many questions whirling about in his thoughts, did not answer.

Danica gave a concerned look Elbereth's way.

"Alas for my studies," the woman lamented.

Cadderly looked at her in disbelief.

"Physical suspension," Danica explained. "If I could achieve that state, slow my heart so that its beating could not be detected . . ."

Cadderly's incredulous stare did not diminish.

"But I cannot," Danica said, lowering her eyes. "That feat is beyond me." Her declaration rang ominously for the prisoners, a general sound of doom. Cadderly, too, allowed his head to bow.

"I shall kill that wizard," Cadderly heard the elf vow.

"And I, her giant lackey," Danica added, a ring of determination returning to her voice. That thought did little to comfort Cadderly, though, given his new insight concerning Tiennek.

"He is of the White Worm," Cadderly said, turning to Danica.

She shrugged; the words meant nothing to her.

"A barbarian tribe of the north," Cadderly explained. "Savage, living—surviving—in brutal conditions. And Tiennek—that is his name—is of Kura-winther, the elite warriors, unless I am mistaken."

Danica looked at him curiously, and he realized that his words still meant little to her.

"Fear him," Cadderly said grimly. "Do not underestimate his prowess. Kura-winther," he said again, closing his eyes to recall all he had read of the White Worm. "To get the marking upon his forehead, Tiennek would have had to kill a polar worm, a remorhaz, single-handedly. He is an elite warrior of a tribe of warriors." Cadderly's expression, sincerely terrified, unnerved Danica more than any words ever could.

"Fear him," Cadderly said again.

*　*　*　*　*

"There's the camp," Ivan whispered to Pikel, "though I'm not fond of fighting orc-types in a dark forest night."

Pikel wagged his head in agreement; dwarves were more accustomed to the blackness of a deep cave, a much different situation than the starlit forest.

"We could get after them just afore the dawn," Ivan offered, talking as much to himself as to his brother. "Yeah, that'd do fine. But there's too many. We can't just go walking into them. We're needing a plan."

"Uh-oh."

Ivan glared at his doubting brother, but his expression lightened considerably when a thought came to him. He pulled his deer-antler helm from his head, fished a small hammer from one impossibly deep pocket, and began chipping away at the lacquer holding one of the antlers firmly in place.

Pikel wagged his head fearfully and tried not to watch.

Ivan had done well in making the helmet, and it was a long time before he had the lacquer cleared enough to unscrew the antler, and even then, he had to fight with the firm hold of his setting. He got it free, finally, and handed it to Pikel, putting the now-lopsided helmet back in place on his hairy head.

"When we go, ye hold it up atop ye and keep close by me," Ivan instructed.

Pikel prudently waited for Ivan to take up a more distant spying position before uttering "Uh-oh" again. Somewhere unseen in the shadows of the trees behind him, Hammadeen tittered.

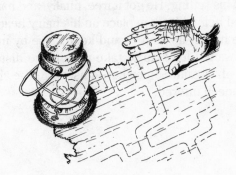

Thirteen

Ooooo, Said the Deer

It was a dreamless sleep, where sheer exhaustion overruled the tumult of Cadderly's emotions. That deep slumber made it all the more shocking to the young scholar when Danica's cry shattered his serenity.

Cadderly jerked to a sitting position and made out a hulking form bending over Danica. He knew at once that it was Tiennek who'd come calling; he prayed that the barbarian hadn't been in the tent very long.

Cadderly started toward his love, but found his wrists roughly grabbed and jerked painfully high behind him.

"If she fights, break the priest's arms," Tiennek said, and Danica, with one look Cadderly's way, stopped her struggling. Tiennek heaved the young woman over his shoulder and started out, flanked by two orogs. The third beast, giving one final, painful tug on Cadderly's arms, soon moved to follow. Cadderly stubbornly stood up behind the orog, but the beast spun about and smacked him to the floor.

The world became a blur of pain and unresolvable confusion. Cadderly noticed Elbereth, still seated at the back of the tent, struggling fiercely but futilely. The elf's wrists were bound so tightly about his knees that he could not even begin to stand.

Growling, on the very edge of control, Cadderly started up, but the orog kicked him in the ribs and sent him crashing down again. He looked all about, to his feathered ring, to a cask on the side of the room, to Elbereth, but had no recourse. Danica was gone and in peril, and Cadderly had no way to fight back.

"No!" he snarled, drawing another kick from the orog. "No! No!" Like a man gone mad, Cadderly repeated the word, ignoring the outraged orog's kicks.

"No! No! No!" But for all Cadderly's stubbornness and anger, his words rang hollow, a puny retaliation.

* * * * *

Danica did not struggle atop Tiennek's huge shoulder. She would bide her time, she decided, wait for an opportunity when she would have the bronze-skinned man alone. Or at least she hoped that she would have Tiennek alone.

Tiennek's obvious intentions revolted her, but the thought that orogs would be present was too much for her to bear.

Tiennek's tent was the third largest in the encampment, centered at the back side of the camp and doubling as a warehouse for the enemy troupe. The blond-haired barbarian, to Danica's profound relief, told his flanking orogs to remain on guard outside, then pushed his way past stacked barrels and boxes to a pile of blankets and furs in the center of the room.

An oil lamp burned low in one corner; the smell of meat was strong in the air. Tiennek lowered Danica to her feet, more gently than the young woman expected. He stared into her almond eyes and stroked her strawberry blond hair.

Play along, Danica told herself, against every instinct in her body. "Untie me," she whispered to her huge captor. "It will be better for the both of us." Tiennek's huge hand slid over Danica's smooth cheek, barely touching her and sending shivers through her in spite of her revulsion.

"Untie me," she whispered again.

Tiennek laughed at her. His gentle touch became an iron grasp on her face, nearly snapping her jaw apart. Danica jerked back from him, got free for an instant, but was then pulled back, this time with the barbarian tugging at a clump of her thick hair.

"You think me a foo—" He stopped abruptly as Danica's knee slammed into his groin; she had to hop off the ground to even reach her target.

Tiennek grimaced for just a moment, then flung Danica backward. She managed to keep her balance, and snapped a kick into the man's rock-hard belly as he stalked her.

Tiennek, his face locked in a murderous stare, didn't seemed to notice the kick, but Danica could tell from his slight limp that her first attack had done some damage.

This time Danica went for his knee, but she had to stop in midkick and dodge instead as Tiennek launched a heavy punch for her face. She was able to duck aside, awkwardly, but the agile barbarian's second hand came in more quickly, clipping her on the cheek.

The tent spun about, and Danica was down to her knees. Tiennek had her and could do as he pleased with her, she knew; there was nothing she could do against such a mighty warrior with her hands bound behind her back. Danica tugged at her cords, ignoring the burn of rough rope on her wrists, and savagely fought to free herself.

Many moments passed. Danica could feel warm blood on her hands. Why hadn't Tiennek continued his assault?

Danica dared to look over her shoulder, to see the giant limping away. That initial knee strike she had launched against him had apparently changed his lewd intentions, for the time being, at least.

The barbarian called a huge orog into the tent and gave it orders to watch Danica, but not to touch her unless she tried to escape. If she did, Tiennek explained, looking pointedly at Danica as he spoke, the orog could do whatever it wanted with the prisoner.

Tiennek eyed Danica slyly. "Give me your weapons," he commanded the orog. The creature balked and put a hand defensively over its sword.

"Give them!" Tiennek growled. "That one will take them from you and kill you with them, do not doubt." The orog continued to snarl, but it handed over the sword and the long dagger from its boot.

Then the bronze-skinned man was gone, and the orog cautiously stalked over to stand beside Danica, its breathing coming in short, hopeful gasps. "Make a break, pretty one," it whispered under its stinking breath, thinking that this duty might turn out to be a bit of fun.

"Could you help me to my feet?" Danica asked innocently after some time. She suspected that Tiennek would return before dawn, before Dorigen realized what had happened, and knew that sunrise was not too far away.

The orog reached down and grabbed her by the hair, pulling her roughly to a standing position. "Ye likes that better?" it growled, again putting its stinking breath in Danica's face.

Danica nodded and told herself that she must act now, or never. She hoped she had loosened her bindings enough, prayed that she had, for the consequences of failure were too wretched for her to even imagine.

The young woman called upon all her discipline in that critical moment, mustering her courage. She dropped toward the floor, feigned that she was falling. The orog instinctively started down to catch her, but Danica's legs coiled under her and she sprang past the surprised beast. She bent her knees up to her chest and whipped her bound hands down under her feet. Even as she descended, she launched her first attack, snapping one leg out straight to drive her foot under the orog's chin.

The creature gasped and fell back. Danica was standing again, still bound, but with her hands now in front of her. The orog, stunned but barely hurt, whooped and charged back in. Danica slowed it considerably with a straight kick to the chest and another to the knee. She clenched her hands together and smacked the monster across the face, once and then again. Growling with every movement, her motions became a blur, kicking, kneeing, punching, and the orog could only hold its arms across its face and try to cover up.

The vicious attack abruptly ceased and the orog moved, just as Danica had expected, to the offensive. The creature lunged awkwardly for her, but caught only air as Danica took a quick step back. Before the overbalanced monster could recover, Danica attacked. She dove right over the orog's shoulder, turning a somersault as she went and hooking her bindings around the monster's thick neck.

The orog bent backward under the brutal pull; a man's neck would have snapped under the great strain. Danica realized quickly that she could not hope to hold on long enough to choke such a thick-skinned and thick-muscled monster. Already the orog had begun to recover and had grabbed at Danica's wrists, tugging and loosening the choking cords from about its neck.

Danica saw her chance was slipping away. She scanned the orog, but found no visible weapons. She scanned the room, but nothing presented itself as a club or knife. A desperate plan came to her. She reversed her grip suddenly, going along with the orog's pull and turning about to face the creature as it tugged. Predictably, the orog swung about.

Danica caught its lumbering swing and yanked it along, then dropped and twisted, flipping the orog over her. Danica dove with it, guiding its descent, plopping it head down in an open water barrel. The monster disappeared up to its waist and Danica jumped atop it, threw one leg between its flailing legs and hung on for all her life.

The creature was much stronger than she, but Danica called upon powers that the orog couldn't begin to understand. She locked her legs inside the rim of the barrel and clamped her hands vicelike on its rim for further support. The orog's hands came up over the lip and it pulled mightily, but Danica held her position, using her stiffened legs as a wedge to prevent her from being dislodged.

The monster's thrashing battered her and bruised her, but she reminded herself that it would not last for long.

Still, it seemed like hours to the weary, beaten woman as the orog fought wildly, trying to get its head up above the water. A knee bloodied her nose, a foot scraped across the side of her head so wickedly that Danica had to wonder if her ear had been torn off.

Then it stopped, suddenly. Almost surprised, Danica held her seat for many seconds longer, just to make sure. She realized that Tiennek might soon return, and she crawled off the barrel. Soaking wet, tears in her eyes, and blood running freely from her nose, she discerned which side of the tent would provide the best exit and rushed over, biting at her bindings as she went.

* * * * *

The orc rubbed its bleary eyes and looked to the east, hoping the dawn would come quickly and end its tedious watch. South of the monster, in its watch direction, was a field of tall grass, sparsely dotted by occasional trees.

The dawn's light was not nearly in full, and the orc heard a distant rustle before it noticed the antlers moving steadily through the grass. At first, the creature lifted its spear, thinking a fine venison dinner had walked right up. Then the orc blinked and rubbed its eyes again, wondering how any deer with such a large rack could be small enough to be concealed by grass no more than three feet high.

The antlers came gliding on, still a fair distance away. They neared the trunk of a twisted apple tree, then the orc blinked again as the antlers passed by the barrier, one on either side.

"Molargro," the orc called to its orog watch chief. The large and ugly orog, warming its gnarly toes by the campfire, cast the sentry an indifferent look, then turned away.

"Molargro!" the orc called again, more insistently. The orog reluctantly rose and came over, not even bothering to put on its worn and tattered boots.

"Deer," the orc explained when the orog arrived, pointing to the approaching antlers, now not so distant.

"Deer?" Molargro questioned, scratching its huge head. "Bah, ye're a stupid one," the orog said a moment later. "What kinda deer says 'ooooo'?"

Both the orog and the orc crinkled their faces in confusion. They glanced back toward the approaching antlers and asked in unison, "Ooooo?"

They got their answer a split second later, at the end of Ivan's great axe and Pikel's tree-trunk club.

* * * * *

Crawling along the brush on the camp's perimeter, Danica had nearly reached the prisoners' tent when the cries of alarm rang out. At first she assumed that Tiennek had found the dead orog, but then she heard, "Oo oi!" above the commotion, followed by a heavy thud and the grunt of a wounded ogre.

"How?" Danica wondered, but, having no time to figure things out at that moment, she stood and ran the rest of the way, carefully slipping in under the loosely tied skins of the tent sides. She stopped halfway in and scrambled to the side, behind some piled crates, as Tiennek and an orc rushed in through the tent flap.

"Take the human to Dorigen!" the barbarian commanded, indicating Cadderly. Tiennek drew Elbereth's finely crafted sword from his belt and grinned evilly. "I will deal with the elf."

Danica's first reaction, as Cadderly was whisked away, was to slip back out, encircle the tent, and go to his aid. She had to resist those urges, though, for Tiennek's intentions concerning Elbereth were painfully obvious. The barbarian took a long stride toward the elf, but then, in the blink of an eye, Danica was between them.

"Flee!" she heard Elbereth say at her back. "I accept my doom. Do not die for me."

Tiennek's shock disappeared in the second it took him to conjure his mocking smile. "The orog is dead?" he asked, showing little concern. He nodded his handsome head as though he was not the least bit surprised.

Danica's visage did not soften, nor did she move from her defensive crouch. Tiennek brought the sword her way.

"A great loss, I fear," he said slyly. "My dear lady, I could have shown you pleasures you cannot imagine."

"I am not your lady!" Danica growled, and she kicked him in the chest, driving him back a step.

"A great loss," the barbarian said again, a bit breathless but otherwise appearing unshaken. He pulled a small net from his belt, holding it wrapped about his free hand.

Danica circled cautiously, understanding the potentially disastrous consequences of getting a kicking leg entangled in that net. She looked for openings, weaknesses, but saw none. The giant barbarian held the elf's slender sword as though it had been designed for him; his balance remained perfect as he executed the circles to keep in step with the young woman.

Danica rushed forward and started to kick, then dropped to the floor suddenly and swept both legs across Tiennek's ankles. The barbarian got one foot clear of the move, but did stumble as Danica's flying feet clipped his other foot. He caught his balance quickly and leaned back in, meaning to hack at the prone woman while waving the net to keep her kicks away.

Danica was not so foolish as to continue her offensive move, though. She was back up and balanced before Tiennek took his first chop.

"I am the stronger," the barbarian teased. "Better armed and equally skilled. You cannot hope to survive."

Danica had trouble convincing herself that the big man was not speaking the truth. She had hit him with several solid shots, but he had barely flinched. She saw his obvious comfort in handling a sword and had already felt his iron grip.

He came straight at her then, in a vicious flurry, thrusting and chopping, weaving the net deftly around his flying blade.

Danica dodged and dove, deflected one thrust aside, though she gashed her arm in the process, and finally wound up in full retreat.

"Flee!" Elbereth cried, struggling futilely with his tight bonds. He rolled and kicked, pulled his arms until they bled, but the stubborn ropes would not relax their painful grip.

Danica was glad that Tiennek continued his pursuit of her. The barbarian could have turned about and easily finished Elbereth before she ever got close enough to interfere.

"He will die after I have defeated you," Tiennek explained, as if he had read her thoughts. "After he has watched. After I have taken you!" Elbereth's groan brought another smile to the cruel barbarian's lips.

Tiennek charged again, but Danica was not caught off her guard. She lifted a foot, as if to kick straight out at her attacker, but kicked to the side instead, snapping the large tent's center support. The roof drooped in around them, defeating Tiennek's attack.

The barbarian thrashed about to get the drooping skins high enough in case Danica charged him, but the young woman was not to be seen.

"A worthy chase!" Tiennek howled, refusing to be intimidated. "And a prize worth catching." He stalked off, pushing the skin roof from his path.

Danica easily could have slipped away and out of the collapsed tent, but that would have left Elbereth helpless. The barbarian, fearless and thinking this fight no contest, was making no secret of his whereabouts. And Danica, desperate for something to equalize this lopsided contest, determined to use that against him.

* * * * *

"Ye got that one!" Ivan bellowed, pointing to a fleeing orc.

Pikel stepped out from behind a tree, right in the orc's path. Holding his club in both hands by its slender, tapered end, the dwarf leaned into a swing that blasted right through the miserable creature's blocking arm and hit its head with enough force to snap its scrawny neck.

"Oo oi!" the happy dwarf squealed to his brother.

"Behind ye," Ivan replied, and Pikel spun about, this time crunching an orc's head between his flying club and the tree. The orc's skull cracked apart with a sickening sound.

Bellowing advice to his brother did nothing to hinder Ivan's own ferocious attacks. He stood atop the felled ogre's back, chopping at the orogs and orcs encircling him. The ogre wasn't quite dead yet, and every time it groaned or stirred a bit, Ivan made a point of stomping hard on the back of the monster's fat head.

Sheer viciousness replaced finesse as the dwarf held several monsters at bay with deadly chops of his mighty axe. One orc managed to get upon the ogre behind Ivan, clubbing the dwarf solidly on the back of his head.

Ivan laughed at it, then sent it flying away with a cut that drove one side of his double-bladed axe halfway through the creature's rib cage.

* * * * *

Tiennek stopped his thrashing and shouting and stalked about slowly, easing the fallen roof out of his way. "I am not a weakling fighter of civilized lands," he said calmly. "I am Kura-winther!"

He sensed a bit of movement, a shift in the fallen tent roof, off to the side, and he took one small step that way. He raised one hand up high so that the roof would not sag, and bent as low as he could.

He saw Danica's legs, under the low skins a few feet away. The game was over, Tiennek decided, knowing that he was needed in the battle outside.

"I know your tricks!" he cried, and he heaved at the roof and charged Danica's way, sword leading. Tiennek grinned with the knowledge that his long reach would give the woman no opportunity to parry or counter.

What confident Tiennek didn't know was that Danica had grabbed the broken bottom half of the center pole, a crude spear that was longer than his sword.

Tiennek's eyes widened in disbelief as he impaled himself on Danica's set weapon. "Some of my tricks, perhaps," the woman said icily, showing no remorse for the man's demise. She drove the pole deeper and twisted it about.

Elbereth's sword fell from Tiennek's outstretched arm; the net in his other hand hung loosely. He dropped to his knees, and Danica released her grip.

The spear propped Tiennek up, supported him in that kneeling position, and the tent roof descended over him, a fitting death shroud.

Danica didn't hesitate. Poor Elbereth, sitting blindly in the back of the collapsed tent, would simply have to wait. The young woman got her bearings and crawled and scrambled her way into the open air.

The dawn's light was full now, early morning. Orogs and orcs were scattering and howling in chaos, with the exception of one group putting up a fair fight against the Bouldershoulder brothers, now standing back-to-back atop the felled ogre. Cadderly was off to the other side, still being pulled along by the orc.

Danica ran after her love, then skidded to a stop as the wizard appeared suddenly beside the tent Tiennek had used. Dorigen made several gestures, held something Danica could not discern in one outstretched hand, and uttered a triggering incantation.

Danica's instincts sent her diving between two trees just as the wizard's lightning bolt went off. The blast split one of the small trees and rebounded into the other, scorching it just above the sprawled woman's head. Danica was up and running in an instant, but soon, too, came Dorigen's second spell.

Sticky filaments filled the air, descending all around Danica and catching hold of the trees, the shrubs, anything at all, to form a thick web. Danica scrambled every which way, used her speed and agility to stay one step ahead of the forming trap.

Then she was clear of the tangle, though a bit to the side of her original course, and Dorigen was not so far away. She heard a flap of wings, but saw nothing. Suddenly, Druzil became visible right in her path, and the imp's barbed tail shot at her shoulder.

The wound was minor, just a scratch, but the sudden tingling numbness and the burn in Danica's arm told her that the imp had indeed poisoned her. She slumped back against a tree, Druzil hovering in front of her, smiling evilly and wagging his tail as though he meant to lash at her again.

* * * * *

Cadderly's thrill at seeing Ivan and Pikel unexpectedly rushing to his aid was tempered by the fact that the dwarves were fully engaged and would not have the opportunity to prevent the orc from getting him to Dorigen. The creature's grip on Cadderly's arm was unrelenting, though the monster was looking more at its comrades' fight than to its prisoner.

"No one but me," Cadderly muttered under his breath. He saw an opportunity to pull away as the orc released its grasp for just an instant.

But it passed without Cadderly mustering the courage to make the attempt. He heard a blast to the side and saw Dorigen loosing some thunderous wizardry, though at what target he could not discern.

Another chance presented itself when they neared the fire, and this time, Cadderly was up to the test. He stumbled and dropped at the orc's feet, groaning and feigning injury. When the startled creature reached for him, he swung his legs inside the creature's, hooked the orc behind the knees, and heaved with all his strength. The startled orc tumbled headlong past him. Not a pretty maneuver, perhaps, but effective—and even more so since the campfire burned low just a few feet away. Sparks flew all about when the orc hit the embers. It came up shrieking and screaming and smacking at the sparks that had caught hold on its clothing.

Cadderly struggled to his feet and dove against the creature's back, knocking it into the fire once again. This time the orc came up on the other side, running away and paying no more heed to the young scholar.

"Well done, lad!" Cadderly heard Ivan cry, and he turned about just in time to see the dwarf cleave an orog nearly in half with a mighty overhead chop. Cadderly was feeling good about his trickery, but for all he had accomplished, he still found himself in the middle of a battlefield unarmed indeed, with his wrists bound behind his back! He scooted off to the quietest side and fell for cover behind a water trough.

* * * * *

Danica turned her thoughts inward, personified the poison as a tiny, devilish thing biting her shoulder. Her muscles became her tools, flexing and tightening, turning about to drive the insinuating intruder back toward the wound.

The poison devil was a stubborn one, gnawing and burning, but Danica, too, possessed determination far beyond that of an ordinary human. Her muscles worked intricately, shifting the poison to one side, then back an inch. She pictured the open wound as a doorway and, working relentlessly, finally drove the fiend through.

Waves of dizziness rolled over her when she opened her eyes. She saw Druzil again, still wagging his deadly tail, but wearing an expression that was considerably less cocksure. Danica followed the imp's surprised gaze to her own shoulder, to the black liquid that had poured from her wound to roll down her arm.

Druzil's tail whipped back and then shot forward, but Danica's attack, a straight-ahead punch, came quicker, sending the hovering imp spinning head over heels.

Danica moved to give chase, but had to brace herself against a tree for a moment to stop from falling over. She saw the wizard scoop up the stunned imp and begin casting yet another spell, this time holding her closed fist out toward the monk, an onyx ring clearly visible.

Danica forced herself forward, ignored the dizziness, and focused on reaching Dorigen.

Dorigen abruptly changed her plans and uttered a few quick incantations instead. A shimmering blue light appeared in front of the wizard, and she and Druzil stepped through and were gone.

* * * * *

The six remaining orogs had no desire to continue their combat with the brutal dwarves. They took flight together, Ivan and Pikel right on their heels. The monsters took to the trees as soon as they crossed the clearing, figuring that the armored dwarves would have a harder time climbing.

Ivan and Pikel stopped at the trunk. Pikel hopped about, trying to reach a branch to pull himself up. Ivan had another course in mind. He dropped the head of his great axe between his feet, spit in both hands, then took up the weapon and stalked in for the trunk.

"Uh-uh," Pikel, the would-be druid, growled, wagging his head and throwing his short arms wide about the precious trunk.

"What? Have ye gone bats?" Ivan cried. "There's damned big orcs up there, me brother. Damned big!"

"Uh-uh." There was no compromise in Pikel's tone.

The discussion was resolved a second later, when Cadderly spotted a shimmering field of blue in the distance and saw Dorigen step out and begin casting a spell toward the camp.

" 'Ware the wizard!" the young scholar cried. Pikel just managed to reply, "Eh?" before the spell went off, engulfing the tree, and the dwarves, in a ball of flame.

Cadderly leaped up from the trough and rushed over.

Pikel emerged from the carnage first, his clothes and face blackened with soot and his beard singed and sticking wildly every which way. Ivan came behind, in a state of similar dishevelment. Worse off were the orogs, toasted in the branches of the leafless, charred tree.

"Boom!" the druid-minded dwarf said. Ivan toppled face down in the dirt.

Cadderly started for him, but Pikel stopped the young scholar with an outstretched hand, pointing back toward the large tent at the rear of the compound, and to Danica, stumbling out of the brush.

Cadderly ran to her side while Pikel saw to his brother.

Danica's face seemed too pale, too delicate, and Cadderly nearly screamed in rage. Danica assured him that she was all right—or that she would be—but then she collapsed against him and seemed on the verge of losing consciousness.

Riddled with guilt, the young scholar wondered how in the Nine Hells he had gotten her into this awful setting, into the middle of a war.

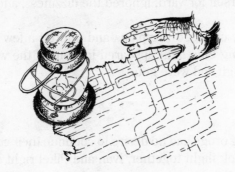

Fourteen

Revelations and Reluctant Allies

Cadderly saw the black liquid oozing from Danica's wound and grew doubly concerned. He had seen the imp's sting fell Pikel, and the dwarf would have died if it hadn't been for a druid's healing magic. How could a human survive a poison potent enough to overpower a dwarf?

Danica's arm continued to twitch, and still more of the evil substance flowed out, mixing with her blood. Her breathing came slower, alarming Cadderly until he realized she was using a technique to keep herself calm. Then she opened her eyes and smiled at him, and he knew, though did not understand how, that she would be all right.

"A wicked sting," she whispered. "And the burn . . ."

"I know," Cadderly replied gently. "Rest easily. The battle is won."

Danica's eyes looked past Cadderly and she couldn't suppress a chuckle. Cadderly turned and understood, for Ivan and Pikel, both covered head to toe in soot, rushed about the camp, searching the bodies of dead monsters.

Danica sat up, took a deep breath, and shook her head vigorously. "The poison is no more," she announced, her voice suddenly solid again. "I have defeated it, forced it from my body."

Cadderly could not begin to express his amazement. He shook his head slowly and made a mental note to question Danica on how she had overcome the deadly substance. But that would wait for another, more peaceful time. Now Cadderly had other concerns.

"Dorigen got away," he said. Danica nodded and began working at the bindings on his wrists.

"You do not understand," Cadderly continued, building himself into a minor fit of frenzy. "She has my crossbow. The weapon has fallen into the hands of an enemy!"

Danica didn't seem overly concerned. "We are alive and free again," she said. "That is all that matters. If you get into a fight again, you'll find a way to win without that weapon."

Danica's confidence in his ingenuity touched Cadderly, but she had missed his point. It wasn't for himself that he was frightened, it was for all the region. "She has the crossbow," he said again. "And the explosive darts."

"How many?"

Cadderly thought for a moment, trying to recall all those he had used and all the ones he had continued to make during his stay in Shilmista. "Six, I believe," he said, then he sighed with relief as he remembered another important point. "But she does not have the flask containing more of the potion. I left that back at the elven camp."

"Then fear not," Danica said, still not understanding his concern.

"Fear not," Cadderly echoed sarcastically, as though his worries should be plain to see. "She has it—do you not understand the implications? Dorigen could copy the design, unleash a new . . ." He stopped, unable to penetrate the frown on Danica's face. She pointed behind him and he looked again over his shoulder.

Not even the dwarves were there. Cadderly didn't understand.

"The tree," Danica explained. "Look at the tree."

Cadderly did as instructed. The proud elm, just moments before lush and vibrant in its late summer colors, remained only a charred and blackened skeleton. Small fires burned in several nooks; waves of rising heat distorted the air above and around the tree. Heaped, blackened forms of the dead orogs seemed to meld together with the dark limbs.

"Do you believe that a wizard who could wreak such sudden and terrible destruction would be impressed by your tiny crossbow?" Danica reasoned. "In Dorigen's eyes, would the bow be worth the expense?"

"She raised it against you," Cadderly argued, but he knew before Danica even scowled at him that Dorigen had threatened with the bow only to heighten the effect on Cadderly.

"Your bow is a fine weapon," Danica said softly, "but one that a wizard of Dorigen's power does not need."

Cadderly could not argue that logic, but he was not comforted. Whatever the outcome, he could not ignore the fact that a weapon he had designed might be used against an innocent, perhaps even against someone close to him.

Again the crossbow was a symbol of the insanity around him, the rushing violence that he could not control and from which he could not hide.

* * * * *

The haul was a bit meager by Ivan's standards, and the stubborn dwarf refused to yield until he had searched every inch of the camp. He sent Pikel to a

tent across the way while he moved to the collapsed one that Cadderly and Danica had exited.

He slapped at the fallen skins with his free hand and used his axe to hold
enough of the roof up so that a monster wouldn't crash into him. He came upon
Tiennek's body first, still kneeling, propped by the crude spear

"I bet that hurt," Ivan said, seeing the gruesome wound. He didn't know
whether this man had been friend or foe, so he didn't go out of his way to search
the body. Ivan did scoop up the fine sword that lay beside the dead man's hand,
though, muttering, "Ye won't be needing this," almost apologetically as he
pressed farther under the fallen canopy.

"Another one," the dwarf said in surprise, nearly stepping on poor Elbereth a
moment later. "And still alive," he added when Elbereth snarled and wriggled
away.

Ivan's expression turned sour when he saw it was an elf seated before him,
but his disdain did not outdo the antipathy plainly exhibited on the elf's face.

"You have my sword," Elbereth said grimly, staring hard into the dwarf's dark
eyes.

Ivan looked down to his belt. "So I do!" he replied, making no move toward
the sword or the elf.

Elbereth waited as patiently as he could for a long moment. "I am still bound,"
he said, his voice trembling with anger.

Ivan looked at him long and hard, finally bobbing his hairy head. "So ye are!"
the dwarf agreed, and he walked away. He nearly bumped into Cadderly and
Danica back outside the tent.

"Where is Elbereth?" Cadderly asked, surprised that Ivan had come out alone.

"What's an Elbereth?" the dwarf answered smugly.

Cadderly wasn't in the mood for bantering. "Ivan!" he shouted.

The dwarf's eyes widened, two shining orbs in the middle of his blackened
face. "That's a fine 'well met,' ye ungrateful—"

"All of our thanks!" Danica interrupted, relieved to see the dwarf but also
wanting to calm the increasingly volatile scholar. She stepped over and threw a
huge hug around the dirty dwarf, even kissing him on his hairy cheek—and leaving a clean spot in the plane of soot.

"That's better," Ivan said, an inevitable tenderness emerging in his normally
gruff voice as he looked at Danica.

"Now, where is Elbereth?" Danica asked calmly.

Ivan poked his thick thumb back over his shoulder. "In a foul mood, that one,"
he explained. Danica started for the collapsed tent, and Cadderly, too, but Ivan
stomped a boot on the young scholar's foot, holding him in place.

"I still ain't heard a word of thanks from yer mouth," the dwarf growled.

Cadderly's expression was warmly sincere. He bent over quickly and kissed
Ivan's other cheek, sending the dwarf in a sputtering tirade across the
compound. "Durned fool boy!" Ivan growled, wiping at the wet mark. "Durned

fool!" Cadderly enjoyed a much-needed smile at the spectacle.

The young man's relief was short-lived, though, as Danica pulled him under the tent and led him to Tiennek's body. She lifted the skin roof high to make sure that Cadderly had a good view of the corpse.

"Slain at my hands," Danica announced, no pride evident in her voice. "I killed him, do you understand? I did as I had to do, as the barbarian forced me to do."

Cadderly shuddered but did not seem to get Danica's point, if there was any.

"Just as you did with the evil priest," she said, putting it more bluntly.

"Why do you bring Barjin into this?" Cadderly demanded, horrified. That now-familiar image of the dead priest's eyes came at him from the depths of his subconscious.

"I do not bring Barjin into it," Danica corrected him. "You do." She went on quickly, cutting short Cadderly's forthcoming protest. "You bring Barjin with you wherever you go," she explained, "a ghost that haunts your every thought."

Cadderly's expression reflected his confusion.

"As with the wounded orogs back in the foothills," Danica said, her tone softening. "Leave dead Barjin behind. I beg you. His death was brought about by his own actions. You did only as you had to do."

"You do not care that you killed this man?" Cadderly asked, almost accusingly.

"I care," Danica snapped, "but I know that if I were given the chance to do it again, Tiennek would be dead exactly as he is now. Can you say differently about Barjin?"

Cadderly thought back to the events in the Edificant Library's catacombs. They seemed as if they had happened just that morning and had occurred a hundred years before, all at the same time. Cadderly had no answer to Danica's disturbing question, and she didn't wait for any, remembering that Elbereth, bound and probably humiliated, awaited his rescue. Cadderly followed at Danica's heels, his eyes locked on dead Tiennek until the drooping roof put the barbarian out of sight.

Elbereth didn't blink through the long moments it took Danica and Cadderly to free him. He would not show weakness openly, would not reveal the humiliation in his helplessness and capture. Only anger shone in the elf's silver eyes and showed in the set of his angular jaw. When he was free, he rushed from the collapsed tent, tearing through the skins with fury.

Ivan and Pikel stood beside the flap to Dorigen's tent. Ivan fingered Danica's crystal-bladed daggers, admiring the golden tiger hilt of one and the silver dragon hilt of the other. Pikel held a thick purple robe while trying futilely to get Cadderly's spindle-disks to spin back up into his chubby palm. At the dwarves' feet lay Cadderly's pack and walking stick.

It wasn't hard for Cadderly and Danica to guess where Elbereth was heading.

"My sword!" the elf prince shouted at the dwarf. Elbereth threw his slender hand out Ivan's way. When Ivan didn't immediately react, Elbereth grabbed the sword right from Ivan's belt.

"Skinny thing anyway," Ivan remarked to Pikel. "Probably break the first time

I hit something with it."

In the blink of an eye, Elbereth had his sword tip against Ivan's thick throat.

"And ye're welcome," came the dwarf's reply.

"Uh-oh," remarked Pikel.

"Ye keep playing like that, and ye're going to get hurt," Ivan added evenly, locking stares with the silver-eyed elf.

It went on for a long, uncomfortable while, a battle of wills that teetered on the brink of violence.

"We have no time for this," Cadderly said meekly, going to inspect his pack. The *Tome of Universal Harmony* was there, to his relief, as was his light tube. All his belongings remained, in fact, with the notable exception of his crossbow.

Danica's approach was more straightforward. She casually pushed Elbereth's sword aside and stepped between the elf and dwarf, alternately shaming each of them with her uncompromising glare.

"Haven't we enough enemies?" the woman scolded. "An army of monsters surrounds us, and you two think to do battle with each other?"

"I have never seen much difference between an orc and a dwarf," Elbereth spat.

"Oo," answered a wounded Pikel.

"Ye view yer betters in a similar light, then," Ivan fought back.

"Oo," said Pikel, regarding Ivan with admiration.

Elbereth drew in his breath. Danica could see his grip tighten on his sword.

"They saved us," Danica reminded Elbereth. "Without Ivan and Pikel, we would remain Dorigen's prisoners—or we would be dead."

Elbereth scowled at the notion. "You would have defeated the barbarian in any case," he argued, "then we would have been free."

"How many orogs and orcs would have come to Tiennek's cries if the dwarves had not held them in battle outside our tent?" Cadderly interjected.

Elbereth's scowl did not diminish, but he did slide his sword into its sheath. "When this is over . . ." he warned Ivan, letting the threat hang open-ended.

"When this is over, ye're not likely to be around," Ivan huffed back, and the smugness of his tone suggested that he knew something the others did not.

He let them wait a while before offering an explanation. "How many kinfolk ye got, elf?" he asked. "How many to fight against the army that's come to yer wood?"

"Two more now," Cadderly replied.

"If ye're talking of me and me brother, then ye're talking nonsense," Ivan said. "I'm not about to die for the likes of some elves!"

"It is not just for the elves, Ivan," Cadderly explained. He looked about to all of them to get their attention. "This battle—this war—goes beyond Shilmista, I fear."

"How can you know?" Danica asked.

"Dorigen serves Talona," Cadderly replied. "We suspected that from the gloves Elbereth took from the bugbears before we ever came here. Now the connection is undeniable." He looked to Pikel. "Do you remember the imp that stung you?"

"Oo," answered the dwarf, rubbing his shoulder.

"That very imp was with Dorigen in her tent," Cadderly explained. "She and Barjin have come from the same source, and if they have attacked the library and now the forest, then . . ."

"Then all the region is in danger," Danica finished for him, "and the headmasters' worst fears shall be realized."

"So, you and your brother will fight," Cadderly said to Ivan. "If not for the elves, then for everyone else."

Ivan's dark eyes narrowed, but he did not refute the young scholar's logic.

"This would seem the place to begin," Cadderly went on, determined to forge an alliance. "We cannot allow our enemies a hold in Shilmista, and the Boulder-shoulder brothers' help would go far in accomplishing our tasks."

"All right, elf," Ivan said after looking to Pikel for confirmation. "We'll help ye out, ungrateful though ye're sure to be."

"Do you believe I would accept . . ." Elbereth started, but Danica's glare stopped him short.

"Then fight well," Elbereth said instead. "But do not doubt, dwarf, that when this is ended, you and I will speak again about our meeting in the tent."

"Ye won't be here," Ivan said again.

"Why do you keep saying that?" Cadderly asked.

"Because I seen the enemy, lad," Ivan answered somberly. "Hundreds of them, I tell ye. Ye think the elves'll beat that number?"

Elbereth shook his head and turned away.

"There," Ivan said, pointing to a tree where he had spotted the elusive Hammadeen. "If ye don't believe me, then ask the faerie-thing!"

Elbereth did just that, and when he returned from his private conversation with Hammadeen, his face was pale.

"We cannot stay here," Danica said, trying to shake the elf from his concerns. "Do we go after the wizard?"

"No," Elbereth replied absently, his eyes looking to the distant south. "They have battled at the Hill of the Stars. I must go to my people."

"It would be a better course," Cadderly agreed. "Dorigen is too dangerous. She has spies. . . ." He stopped to consider Danica, who was mouthing their missing companion's name and pounding a fist into her hand. Cadderly didn't indicate his agreement, though. He refused to believe that Kierkan Rufo, for all his faults, willingly would have given information to the evil wizard.

But Cadderly had to admit that, lately, he simply did not know what to believe.

* * * * *

Dorigen approached Ragnor's camp tentatively, not certain of how the volatile ogrillon would act now that the battle had taken such an unexpected twist. She had been absent, away hunting Cadderly and his friends, when Ragnor had launched his attack on the elven camp. Even without her help, though, the ogrillon had routed the elves and driven them miles southward.

Dorigen cursed her own stupidity. She had supplied Ragnor with the elves' position; she should have foreseen that the cocky brute would move against them, particularly if she would not be around to share in the victory.

Now Dorigen found herself in an awkward position, for while the ogrillon's moves had met with success, Dorigen's had met with disaster. She went to see Ragnor anyway. Her magical energies were all but exhausted this day and she needed Ragnor even if he did not need her.

"Where are my soldiers?" was the first thing the burly ogrillon barked at her when she entered his tent. Ragnor looked around slyly to his elite bugbear guard, realizing that this was the first time he had seen Dorigen without her barbarian escort. "And where is that slab of flesh you keep at your side?" he asked.

"We have powerful enemies," Dorigen answered and countered all at once, raising her voice loud enough to silence the bugbear chuckles. "You should not be so smug in your temporary victory."

"Temporary?" the ogrillon roared, and Dorigen wondered if perhaps she had pushed the ogrillon too far. She half expected Ragnor to rush over and tear her apart.

"Two score of the elves fell!" the ogrillon went on. "Six I killed myself!" Ragnor displayed a gruesome necklace featuring twelve elf ears.

"At what cost?" Dorigen asked.

"It does not matter," Ragnor replied, and Dorigen knew by the way Ragnor winced that the elven camp had not been overrun easily. "The elves are few, but my troops are many," the ogrillon went on. "I will not fear even a few thousand dead when Shilmista falls under my shadow."

"*My* shadow?" Dorigen asked slyly, emphasizing Ragnor's use of the personal pronoun. For the first time since she had entered the tent, she saw a hint of trepidation in the ogrillon's eye.

"You were away on private matters," Ragnor argued, somewhat subdued. "The time had come to attack, and I did; I struck with every soldier I could muster. I led the attack myself and carry the scars of battle!"

Dorigen bowed her head respectfully to calm the volatile beast. Ragnor had told her much more than he had intended. He mentioned that she was away, but she had not told him that she would be far from camp. For some reason, Ragnor had chosen that time to attack, without Dorigen to help him. With the ogrillon so adamant in his statement that Shilmista would fall under his control, and not to Castle Trinity, Dorigen worried just how far Ragnor's newfound independence would take him.

She had no desire to be anywhere near the ogrillon when he decided he did not need Castle Trinity.

"I go to my rest," she said, bowing again. "Accept my congratulations on your great victory, mighty General." Ragnor couldn't hide his thrill at hearing those words. Figuring that was a good note on which to depart, Dorigen left the tent, thinking it strange that a merciless brute such as Ragnor could be so easy a mark for flattery.

"He got scared," Druzil remarked from his perch on Dorigen's shoulder, soon after the wizard had departed the tent. The imp materialized. "He feared that you would control the battle and that he would not be needed."

"Let us hope he still believes that I can be of some use to him," Dorigen replied. "He will not be pleased to learn how many of his soldiers I have lost."

"Do not mention them," Druzil suggested. "I do not believe Ragnor can count anyway."

Dorigen turned her head sharply to face the imp. "You will never underestimate the ogrillon again!" she growled. "Any mistakes could bring a swift end to our lives."

Druzil snarled and grumbled but did not really argue. "What are your plans?" he asked after a long enough while for Dorigen to cool down.

Dorigen stopped her march to consider the question. "I will see where I may be of use," she answered.

"Have you given up on Aballister's son?" The imp sounded surprised.

"Never!" Dorigen snapped. "This Cadderly of Carradoon is a dangerous one, as are his friends. When this fight is over, whatever path Ragnor chooses, young Cadderly will prove valuable." Her eyes narrowed as though she had reminded herself of something important.

"You can still contact Kierkan Rufo?" she asked.

Druzil chuckled, the rough laugh sounding almost like a cough in his raspy little voice. "Contact?" he echoed. "Intrude upon would be a better description. Kierkan Rufo wears the amulet. His mind is mine to explore."

"Then hear his thoughts," Dorigen instructed. "If Cadderly returns to the elven camp, I wish to know."

Druzil muttered as usual and faded away, but Dorigen, too engrossed by the intrigue unfolding around her, paid his complaints little heed.

* * * * *

"Afore ye set yer sights on going back to the hill," Ivan said gruffly, "me brother and me has got something ye should see."

Elbereth eyed the dwarf curiously, wondering what cruel surprise Ivan had in store for him this time. But when they at last arrived at the dwarves' small camp, just a mile or so out of their way, Elbereth cast a surprised look Ivan's way. Buried under a cairn of piled rocks lay a partially burned elven body, which Elbereth knew at once was Ralmarith's, his friend who had been slain in the enemy wizard's initial attack.

"How did you come by this?" the elf demanded, his voice a mix of suspicion and relief.

"Took it from the goblins," Ivan said, taking care to keep all hints of sympathy out of his gruff voice. "We figured that even an elf deserved a better resting place than a goblin's belly."

Elbereth turned back to Ralmarith's body and said no more. Danica moved and knelt beside him, putting an arm over his slender shoulders.

"Them two're a bit friendly, eh?" Ivan said to Cadderly, and the young scholar had to bite his lip to hold back his thoughts—indeed, to force them from his mind. He had to trust in Danica, and in their love, he knew, for their situation was too dangerous to allow for any rifts between him and Elbereth.

Danica nodded more than once Ivan and Pikel's way, trying to prompt the elf to offer some thanks. Elbereth did not respond, though. He just whispered his farewells to his friend and carefully repacked the cairn, leaving Ralmarith's body to the forest the slain elf had so loved.

Shilmista was strangely quiet as the five companions made their stealthy way toward Daoine Dun. They stopped once for a short break, with Elbereth heading off to scout the area and see if he might find Hammadeen or some other woodland being to gather some information.

"You must forgive Elbereth," Cadderly said to Ivan, taking the opportunity to try to play peacemaker.

"What's an Elbereth?" Ivan asked snootily, not looking up from his work resetting the antler in his helmet. The dwarf grimaced and tightened the screw as much as he could, since he had no lacquer to reinforce the fit.

"He is the prince of Shilmista," Cadderly went on, wincing at, but otherwise ignoring, the dwarf's unyielding stubbornness. "And Shilmista might prove the cornerstone to support our struggles."

"I'm not for giving much hope to our struggles," Ivan replied grimly. "Yer handful of elves won't do much against the army that's walked in."

"If you really believed that, you would not have agreed to come along," Cadderly reasoned, thinking he had found a chip in the dwarf's iron facade.

The incredulous grin Ivan gave stole that thought away. "I'm not for missing a chance to bash a few orc brains," the dwarf retorted. "And yerself and the girl needed me and me brother."

Cadderly couldn't compete with Ivan's seemingly endless surliness, so he walked away, shaking his head at Danica and Pikel as he passed them. A few moments later, Elbereth came back to the camp and announced that the path to the hill was clear.

Daoine Dun was not as Cadderly remembered it. The once beautiful Hill of the Stars lay blasted and blackened, its thick grasses trampled under the charge of monstrous feet and its lush trees broken or burned. Even worse was the stench. Flocks of carrion birds flew off at the companions' approach; for the dead—a fair number of elves among them—had been left out to rot.

Even Ivan had no comment in the face of Elbereth's shock. Indeed, Ivan called Pikel to the side, and together they began to dig a common grave.

The elf prince wandered back and forth across the battlefield, checking the bodies of his kinfolk to see if he could determine which elves had fallen. Most had been mutilated, though, and the stoic elf just shook his head sadly at Danica and Cadderly as they followed him through his silent vigil.

They buried the fallen elves, Danica offering her thanks to the dwarves, though stubborn Elbereth would not, then they searched the whole hill. Elbereth kept to the trees, seeking to learn more of what had happened and where his friends and enemies might now be. Ivan and Pikel led the search of the caves. In one they found the half-eaten bodies of several horses, though, fortunately, Temmerisa was not among them.

In another chamber, in the cave that Galladel had used as his own, they made what Cadderly considered a remarkable discovery. Several books and scrolls were strewn about the floor, as if the elf king had hurriedly departed, quickly selecting what he should take with him and what to leave behind. Most of the writings were meaningless notes, but in one corner Cadderly found an ancient tome, bound in black leather and bearing the high elven runes for the letters "D," "Q," and "q." Cadderly took up the book in trembling hands, suspecting its contents. He gingerly undid the snap and opened it.

The ink was faded and the page was filled with many symbols that Cadderly could not understand. It bore the name Cadderly expected to see, though: Dellanil Quil'quien, the long-dead king of Shilmista and one of the forest's legendary heroes.

"What have you found?" came Elbereth's call from the cave entrance. He stood beside Danica; Ivan and Pikel had moved on to the next hole.

"Your father would not have left this intentionally," Cadderly explained, turning about and displaying the black-covered tome. "It is the book of Dellanil Quil'quien, a priceless work."

"I am surprised my father brought it along at all," Elbereth replied, "but I am not surprised that he left it behind. The book holds little value for him. Its writings are arcane, using many symbols that we of Shilmista can no longer comprehend. The book holds nothing for us. Take it back to your library if you desire."

"Surely you err," Cadderly said. "Dellanil Quil'quien was among your greatest heroes. His feats, his magic, could prove critical examples at this dire time."

"As I have told you," replied Elbereth, "we can no longer even read the work. Nor can you. Many of the symbols have not been used for centuries."

"Come now," Elbereth bade the two humans. "We must move on. Even as we speak, my people may be in another battle, and I do not wish to remain at this scarred place any longer than is necessary." The elf walked out into the afternoon sunlight.

Danica waited by the entrance for Cadderly. "You are keeping the book?" she asked, seeing him placing it in his pack.

"I do not agree with Elbereth's estimation of the work," Cadderly replied. "There may be something in Dellanil's writings that will help us in our fight."

"But you cannot even read it," Danica said.

"We shall see," Cadderly replied. "I have translated many works back at the library. Now, at least, I have a task that I am prepared to handle—as you might, when you are faced with physical battle."

Danica nodded and said no more. She led Cadderly out of the cave and down to where the elf prince waited for the dwarves to complete their search.

For Cadderly, the book came as a godsend. He really didn't believe, didn't dare to hope, that he would find something important in the work, even if he could manage to translate the strange runes. But just working toward the common goal of saving the forest while using his unique skills added a bit of spring to the young scholar's steps.

Most important of all, finding and working with the book of Dellanil Quil'quien would somewhat remove Cadderly from the violence. He longed for that time past, before Barjin had come to the Edificant Library, when adventures were found only in the words of ancient books.

Perhaps this work would block the harsh realities that had so suddenly surrounded the young scholar.

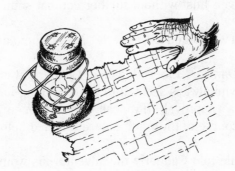

Fifteen

Aiming High

W e can get past them a mile to the east," Danica explained when she rejoined the others in the small evergreen grove they had taken as shelter. "The enemy line is not deep there. We will be beyond them before they ever realize we have passed."

The plan met with approval from Cadderly, but Ivan and Pikel did not seem too pleased to learn that they had marched this far and might not even get the chance to crunch an orog's skull. The companions had journeyed several miles from Daoine Dun without incident, though signs of the enemy's passing—hack marks and scorch marks on almost every tree—were painfully obvious. At last the companions had found the enemy along a rushing river, in a line that seemed to span the forest's width. Elbereth's people had apparently made a stand at the river and were now encamped beyond its protective banks.

Elbereth did not immediately embrace Danica's plan. He, too, had gone scouting, and while Danica had found a potential break to the east that might get them to the elven camp, the elf prince had found something that might alter the entire battle's course.

A short distance west of their position, on a high ridge above the river and overlooking the lands to the south, lay an enemy camp dotted with tents—the only tents Elbereth had seen. "I have found their leader's camp," Elbereth explained to Danica. "Or so I believe."

"Well guarded, no doubt," Cadderly had to put in, especially when he saw a gleam in Danica's almond eyes.

"Perhaps," Elbereth answered, hardly paying any heed to the worried young scholar, "but no more than any other position in the enemy's lines."

"Except the break that Danica has found," Cadderly replied, his desire to be rejoined with the elven host without further combat sounding obvious in his almost-frantic tone.

"Not to fear," Ivan whispered to Cadderly. "Me brother and me can be making our own breaks."

"What say you, Danica?" Elbereth asked. Cadderly wasn't certain he liked that the elf prince, who always seemed to value nothing but his own opinions, had asked for Danica's approval. "If we can get to the enemy leader, we may be able to change the course of the war," Elbereth added before the woman gave her answer.

Danica's wry smile told Cadderly the adventurous woman's answer before she opened her mouth to reply. "It seems a desperate course," she began, but her tone reflected no fear. "A desperate course for a desperate situation."

"Oo oi!" Pikel heartily agreed. Cadderly gave the dwarf a frown that stole his widening smile.

Elbereth quickly knelt and cleared away some pine needles. He took up a stick and drew a map of the ridge area.

"There are only five of us," Cadderly reminded them, though no one was listening.

"I have heard the leader's name is Ragnor," Elbereth began, "a monstrous beast, half-breed, my scouts believe, marked by a tusk protruding over his upper lip."

"Wonderful," Cadderly muttered grimly. This time, Ivan paid enough attention to kick him in the shin.

"If Ragnor is at the camp, then we can expect he will separate himself from us by whatever monstrous guards he can muster."

"Wonderful," Cadderly said again. Danica elbowed him hard in the ribs. The young scholar began to get the feeling that he wouldn't even make it to the enemy camp if he kept commenting.

"And what monsters did ye see?" asked Ivan, leaning toward the crude map closer than anybody.

Elbereth seemed almost surprised at the dwarf's interest. "Bugbears, mostly," the elf answered. "Actually, I would have expected more obvious guards, ogres at least and perhaps a giant or two."

Cadderly winced but held his thoughts silent. The orogs, large and powerful, had come as a shock to him; the ogres' sheer size had nearly made him swoon. What would be his reaction, he wondered, if he found himself facing a true giant?

"Can you be certain, then, that this is the leader's camp?" Danica asked.

Elbereth thought for a moment, then shook his head. "It is an assumption," he admitted. "I saw no other tents anywhere along the line, just crude lean-tos of twigs. And this particular ridge is most favorable for the enemy leader to keep a watch on the action to the south."

"Maybe it is Dorigen's camp," Cadderly put in.

"Either way," Ivan boomed, slapping his great axe against his hand, "we'll give the scum a thing or two to think about!"

Again, Elbereth was surprised by the dwarf's interest. "I do not know how we might best approach," the elf said honestly. "If we sneak in as close as we may, perhaps we will discern an appropriate attack route."

"In what order?" Ivan asked.

Elbereth looked at him blankly.

"As I thought," remarked the dwarf. "Ye're more for working on yer own than to leading a fight. Step aside, elf. I'll give ye a plan!"

Elbereth neither moved nor blinked.

"Listen, ye stubborn son of a willow tree," Ivan growled, poking a stubby finger Elbereth's way. "I know ye're doubting me friendship—and ye should be, for I'm not calling ye friend. And when the fighting's done, yerself and me have a date. Don't ye hope for a moment that I'm forgetting that! And I'm not caring a thing for yer people or yer stinking wood, neither!"

Pikel's growl slowed Ivan's budding momentum.

"Well, me brother likes yer wood," Ivan said to calm the savage would-be druid. He spun back on Elbereth. "For all yer suspicions, though, don't ye be doubting me friendship to Cadderly and Danica. If they're to go in, then me and me brother are fighting aside them, and I'm betting that me axe takes more heads than yer skinny sword!"

"We shall learn the truth of that boast," Elbereth said, his silver eyes narrowed. For all his pride, Elbereth had to admit that he was indeed more accustomed to working alone, and that Ivan might just be better suited to design the course of this attack. His grim expression did not relent, but he shifted away from the map, giving the dwarf full access.

Ivan bent low over the sketch, grunting and pulling at his still sooty beard. "How deep's the river beyond the ridge?" he asked.

"To my waist, perhaps," the elf replied.

"Hmmm," mumbled the dwarf. "And the drop's a bit high to take that course. We'll have to hit them hard and get quick to the east, to where yerself—" he pointed to Danica "—saw a way through."

"Our lives are not important," said Elbereth. "If we can kill the enemy leader, whether or not we escape is of no concern."

Cadderly's mouth dropped open.

"Yer own life's not important," Ivan agreed, "but the rest of us would prefer to keep our skin, thank ye."

Cadderly's sigh sounded clearly like a note of gratitude to Ivan.

"But if we can hit them hard and fast enough, we'll get our way back out," Ivan went on. "We'd be better off if ye had yer bow, elf, to lead our way in, but I've got a hammer or two to spin into a bugbear's eye. Here's me thinking. Yerself, elf, and Danica will lead us in. The two of ye are the fastest and should get yer chance at the boss. Cadderly will come next, watching both sides to see where he's most needed."

Cadderly realized that Ivan had politely told him to keep out of the way—not that he minded.

"Me and me brother'll take up the back end," Ivan went on. "That way ye won't need to be worrying that a bugbear will be crawling up yer backside."

Elbereth studied the drawing and found little to complain about concerning Ivan's plan. It seemed solid enough, though the elf was somewhat surprised that the dwarf had made allowances for him to personally battle Ragnor. Elbereth had presumed that Ivan would want that glory for himself.

"Suppose Dorigen is still there," Cadderly interjected, still not thrilled with the whole idea.

"Then we can do even more harm to our enemies," Elbereth replied.

"Many of my fighting styles are designed to deal with wizards," Danica added, offering Cadderly the consolation that he obviously needed. "As in my previous encounter with Dorigen, I believe the wizard will have little in her repertoire to harm me."

"Unless you are busy battling bugbears or some other monsters," Cadderly retorted. "Then you might prove an easy target for one of Dorigen's lightning blasts."

"It'll be up to yerself," Ivan decided. "Keep yer watch for the wizard. If ye see her, then knock her down with yer fancy bow."

"I do not have it," Cadderly said.

"Then use yer stick, or that toy ye dance at the string's end," said Ivan.

"Dorigen has my crossbow," Cadderly said, on the verge of panic. None of the others seemed to share his apprehension about that fact. In unison, they looked to Ivan to continue with his plotting.

"She has my crossbow and some of the magically loaded darts!" Cadderly said again, even more anxiously.

"If Dorigen is more concerned with that weapon than with her repertoire of spells, we'll be better off," Danica said, her calm tone mocking Cadderly's concern.

"We'll just hope she's not as good a shot with the thing as yerself, lad," Ivan added. Similarly unconcerned, he went back to his plan. "I'm thinking that twilight would be the best time to go, when the light's down a bit but before the darkness takes advantage from our human friends."

Elbereth looked to Danica, who nodded her accord.

"When ye're done with the brute boss, ye'll have me and Pikel to take ye back out again," Ivan explained to Elbereth. "We'll cut ye a path ye could ride yer horse through!"

"That we do not doubt," Danica said, and even Elbereth, so angry at the dwarf just a short while before, made no sarcastic comments.

"We're off then," Ivan said, taking up his great axe. He motioned with his arm for Elbereth to take up the lead.

The group moved quietly into position under the widespread boughs of a pine tree and waited while the last of the daylight faded. Cadderly sat on the western edge of the shadows, trying to get every last moment of light as he worked hard over an open book. At first, Danica thought he was still trying to translate the book of Dellanil Quil 'quien, but then she saw that he held the *Tome of Universal Harmony*, the Deneir bible.

"There are spells that might be of use," Cadderly explained at her inquisitive glance.

Danica's expression revealed her surprise; she had never seen Cadderly attempt any clerical magic beyond simple spells of healing, had never really considered him that manner of priest.

"I have spent my life in the order of Deneir!" Cadderly protested, drawing a slap from nearby Ivan and a profound "Sssshhh!" from Pikel.

Cadderly turned back to the book. "There is a spell of silence," he whispered, "which might hinder Dorigen if she appears in the battle and attempts her magic."

He saw that Danica didn't appear convinced, and he couldn't honestly find the words to argue against that look. Cadderly had performed minor ceremonies before, had once created a font of holy water (in which he had immersed the bottle containing the dreaded chaos curse), but in truth, he had never put much store in clerical magic. He was a disciple of Deneir, the god of art and literature, primarily because he had been raised among that sect at the Edificant Library and because Deneir's edicts so befit Cadderly's intelligent and kind nature. Cadderly had spent nearly as much time with the priests of Oghma, god of knowledge, and secretly considered himself a true priest of neither—to Headmaster Avery Schell's ultimate frustration.

"Time to go," Ivan whispered. Cadderly quickly perused the spell of silence one last time, hoping that if the need arose, he would find the strength to use it. Full of trepidation—should he have tried to study spells of healing instead?—he slipped the tome back into his pack beside Dellanil's book.

They started off cautiously for the sloping, grassy incline that led to the tent-covered ridge. Danica stopped them a short distance out and disappeared into the brush, returning a few moments later.

"Sentry," she explained when she came back to them.

"Bugbear?" Elbereth asked.

"Goblin."

"Dead goblin," Ivan muttered, giving Danica an appreciative wink, and Pikel added a happy, "Hee hee."

They came to a halt crouched in a line of thick brush just below the enemy camp. The grassy slope was teasingly quiet. A couple of bugbears wandered along no apparent course, and, through the open flaps of one of the side tents, the companions could see others milling about. It was the topmost tent, on the crest of the ridge, that held the companions' attention. Somewhat smaller than the other two tents, it was by far the finest and left little doubt where the enemy leader, if this was indeed Ragnor's camp, would be located.

"Now or not at all," Ivan whispered to Elbereth. The elf turned to the dwarf and gave a determined nod. Then Elbereth looked to Danica and they burst from the brush and began their wild charge up the hill.

Head low, arms and legs pumping in perfect harmony, Danica quickly outdistanced the elf. She hit the first two bugbears before they could guess that they were under attack. Knees and elbows flew wildly, then so did the bugbears, which tumbled to the grass with little desire to return to battle the frenzied woman.

Elbereth charged past Danica as the second bugbear flew away, the elf bearing down on a third monster, similarly surprised but with time enough to ready a long spear with which to meet the attackers.

The elf prince's focus went beyond the creature, to the flap of the fine tent he knew was Ragnor's. He hardly noticed the spear thrust his way.

His fine sword whipped across, snapping the bugbear's crude weapon before it got near its mark. Elbereth ran right by the stunned bugbear, sticking his sword into its knee as he passed so that it could not follow him up the hill.

The unfortunate creature, clutching at its wound, unwittingly remained in Danica's path as she followed the elf. Hardly slowing, she launched a perfectly synchronized kick with her running strides, catching the bending monster in the chin and laying it straight out on the ground.

The felled beast noticed another human running past a second later, then it felt the heavy stomps of dwarven boots. The last thing the bugbear saw was the swift descent of a huge axe.

Alarms rang out all through the encampment; the two side tents opened up, with many bugbears and several goblins spilling out onto the grassy hill.

"More than we thought!" Ivan bellowed.

Cadderly held his spindle-disks and his walking stick close, hoping he would not be forced to use them. He looked about frantically, expecting and fearing that Dorigen would make her appearance, and tried to keep the spell of silence in his thoughts through the growing tumult around him.

Danica and Elbereth widened the gap ahead of Cadderly, and suddenly Ivan and Pikel were fully engaged in combat right behind him. He turned about, then turned back, and looked all around as the bugbears—even more were pouring from the tents—began to surround the small group.

Elbereth and Danica paid no heed to the events behind them. Their goal was in plain sight, and their strides quickened when a burly, brutish monster stepped from the fine tent. Both knew at once that it was Ragnor come to meet them, huge and terrible and with that telltale single tusk sticking up over his lip.

Standing at the very top of the ridge, the ogrillon grinned evilly and beckoned them on.

Danica realized that they would not get to him, though. A group of three bugbears closed from the side, and the monsters' angle would put them between their leader and the attackers. Danica was confident that she could outdistance them if she ran full stride, but Elbereth would have no chance of getting to Ragnor.

"Run on!" she cried to the elf, and she veered to the side to meet the interceptors.

She started in high, forcing the monsters to raise their spears, then dove to the grass and slid sideways, clipping their feet and sending all three tumbling down about her.

Elbereth's first instincts were to go to her, caught in the middle, of such powerful enemies, but the elf continued his course, realizing that Danica had made the move for his benefit and reminding himself that their lives were not important when weighed against the potential gains of destroying Ragnor.

If the ogrillon was afraid, he did not show it. Elbereth came fast and hard, his sword weaving and thrusting, using his momentum to get in strikes too quickly for Ragnor to defend.

Blood oozed from the monster's shoulder. Another gash lined one cheek. Still Ragnor grinned, and Elbereth's charging advantage quickly played itself out.

It was the ogrillon's turn.

* * * * *

Cadderly had never seen such brilliant teamwork before. The dwarven brothers held the higher ground, but that still didn't bring them close to eye level with gigantic bugbears, and they were outnumbered two to one.

That hardly seemed to matter.

Ivan cut a crossing swipe with his axe, not close to hitting the mark. A bugbear waded in behind, then Cadderly understood the dwarf's attack to be no more than a feint, drawing the monster in. For Pikel suddenly broke from his own fight and followed up his brother's swing with a low thrust from his tree-trunk club.

The lunging bugbear's knee snapped backward—Cadderly thought that it resembled the gait of an exotic bird he had once read about—and the monster fell away, writhing in agony.

Ivan, meanwhile, had not been idle. He went with the momentum of his powerful cut, stepping right beside his dipping brother and taking Pikel's place with the other two monsters. The surprised bugbears hardly seemed to comprehend what had happened—the dwarves' movements were so in harmony—and they did not immediately understand the difference in this dwarf's fighting style.

They kept their arms extended, a proper style for defending against Pikel's wide-armed club swings, but thoroughly useless against Ivan's sheer ferocity. The dwarf charged inside their long reach, butting with his antlered head, biting, kicking with his heavy boots, and waggling his double-bladed axe through a series of short chops.

One of them was down, the other running away, before Cadderly had even remembered to draw breath.

"Oo!" Pikel howled appreciatively, seeing his brother make such quick work of the two, and purposely turning his back on his remaining bugbear in the process.

"Behind you!" Cadderly cried, not knowing that the dwarf was in complete control.

The bugbear raised its spear over its head and leaped, but Pikel dipped low and rushed backward, slamming his back into the monster's knees. The bugbear barely caught its balance and didn't go headlong over the dwarf, but it would have been better off if it had. Pikel dropped down to one knee, held his club on its narrow end, and drove it straight up between the bugbear's legs, heaving the creature from the ground.

By the time the bugbear came back down, still standing but quite winded, Pikel was behind the monster and had realigned his grip on the club. The dwarf stepped into his swing with all his bulky weight, slamming the bugbear in the lower back.

The breathless monster tried to howl, and when that didn't work, it settled instead for slumping to its knees, clutching its blasted back and watching the world spin.

"Wish we had the time to finish a few of these," Ivan grumbled as he and Pikel moved higher up the hill. Many more bugbears came at them from both sides, and cries of alarm sounded all about the area now, not just on the grassy slope.

Cadderly clutched his weapons and continued his scan for Dorigen, though he was beginning to understand that the missing wizard was the least of their problems.

* * * * *

Every bugbear strike seemed to be just an inch behind the scrambling woman, and whatever contorted position Danica had to put herself into to avoid the attacks, she seemed quite able to launch her own. One bugbear yelped in glee, thinking it had finally caught up to its prey, only to catch Danica's foot squarely in the face.

Danica sprang to her feet, a bugbear kneeling before her. She envisioned it immediately as a block of stone and slammed her head into the monster's chest. Ribs—a dozen, perhaps—snapped apart, but they did so with a single sickening crack.

Then there were two.

* * * * *

"One more elf head for my trophy wall!" Ragnor laughed. Elbereth got his shield up to block the ogrillon's heavy sword, but his arm went numb under the sheer weight of that incredibly powerful blow.

"You'll look fine next to your kinfolk!" Ragnor boasted, wiggling his elf-ear necklace for his adversary to see. Thinking Elbereth distracted by the gruesome sight, Ragnor stepped in. Elbereth, horrified indeed, managed to skip back from the ogrillon's strike, though he slipped on the thick grass and nearly went to one knee. He came up fast instead, stepping within Ragnor's follow-up attack and driving his sword into the ogrillon's thigh. A fine counter, except that Ragnor's free hand grabbed the elf as he passed and, with tremendous strength, hurled Elbereth backward and to the ground.

The heavy sword sliced at him but buried itself halfway to the hilt into the soft ground as Elbereth frantically rolled aside.

The elf climbed back to his feet as Ragnor withdrew his sword. Elbereth took a quick glance around and saw that all sides seemed to be caving in on his companions. If he was to gain any semblance of a victory, he would have to strike Ragnor quickly. When he took a quick survey of the ogrillon, though, that didn't seem likely. Speed and agility were on Elbereth's side, but Ragnor could take anything Elbereth could throw his way. Defeating this brute would require time, plenty of time, to wear the heavier monster down, nicking and jabbing until Ragnor's blood ran from a hundred grazing wounds.

"Damn you," Elbereth muttered, and with all his world at stake, the valiant elf launched himself at Ragnor. He hacked once with his sword, then, when he was too close to use the long blade, punched fiercely with the weapon's gem-encrusted hilt.

* * * * *

"No time!" Ivan bellowed, seeing that his plan could not succeed with so many bugbears, goblins, and now a host of orogs, appearing from all about the base of the ridge. He turned to Pikel and winked. "Second choice!"

"Oo oi!" Pikel heartily agreed.

Cadderly was about to ask what "second choice" might mean, when Pikel rushed right up to him, and right through him, barreling along up the hill with the stunned young scholar firmly in tow.

* * * * *

Ragnor and Elbereth held their deadly embrace. The elf's punches had bent the ogrillon's piglike snout every which way and lines of thick blood covered the monster's face. Still Ragnor maintained his fiendish grin.

Finally, one huge hand clamped onto the back of the elf's neck, and Elbereth was hauled out to arm's length. They were still too close for any effective sword strikes, but Ragnor's sword arm, held at the wrist by Elbereth's shield hand, hovered dangerously above the elf's head. Elbereth feared that the ogrillon would overpower him and drive his sword hilt down onto Elbereth's head.

Elbereth's fears trebled as Ragnor pushed a secret button on his weapon's crosspiece and a second blade, a gleaming stiletto, protruded from the bottom of his sword, its wicked tip just an inch from Elbereth's head.

Elbereth struggled wildly, kicked Ragnor repeatedly about the knees and groin. The ogrillon only grinned and forced his huge arm down.

Something slammed into Elbereth's side. He saw the sudden confusion on Ragnor's face, then the world went flying about him. He hit the waist-deep river hard, twisting an ankle and a knee in the process, then he understood, for he heard Ivan griping and water gurgling.

"You pulled me from my battle!" Elbereth roared as he grabbed his sword. "I could have—"

"Died," Ivan finished evenly, though that wasn't exactly what the elf had in mind. "Stop yer whining, elf," said the dwarf with a derisive chuckle. "And get me helmet, would ye?"

Elbereth blustered and growled, looking for a retort. To Ivan's surprise, the elf reached over and scooped the half-floating helmet from the water, even hopping a few steps downstream to recover one of the antlers, which had come loose.

Cadderly flew over the precipice next, backpedaling, his scrambling feet barely able to keep up at the end of Pikel's thick club. Both man and dwarf hit the river just a few feet from their companions. Cadderly came up spitting a stream of water and sputtering in shock. He kept enough wits about him to pull his precious pack above the water and fish out his short and stunned companion's head.

Pikel tried to squeak his thanks but wound up sending a stream of water into Cadderly's eye instead. The dwarf shrugged meekly and smiled.

"There she is!" they heard Ivan cry, and they looked up to the ledge to see Danica spinning over. The incredible monk half-ran, half-fell down the bank, grabbing for root-holds with one hand but holding her other arm, her wounded arm, tight against her body. Somewhere in the fight, Danica had reopened the arrow wound, and the sleeve and side of her tunic were deeply stained.

She managed her controlled descent, though, coming lightly into the water at the river's edge and easily outdistancing the two bugbears that pursued her. The monsters came on stubbornly, gingerly searching for handholds as they made their way down.

A hail of arrows whistled out of the trees beyond the far bank, every shot scoring a direct hit on the vulnerable monsters. Danica had to duck aside as the two hairy forms came crashing down.

There would be no cheers from the companions, though, for another arrow whistled from the trees, burying itself into Ivan's leg and sending the startled dwarf spinning to the ground. Before Ivan could begin to recover, fine swords landed heavily on his shoulders, one against either side of his thick, but quite vulnerable, neck.

"Uh-oh," muttered Pikel, who understood the misperceptions enough to slip behind the cover of Cadderly's body.

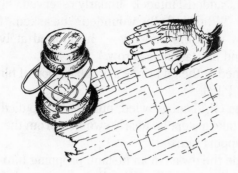

Sixteen

Ancient Wisdom

"Hold! Hold!" Elbereth cried, splashing from the river and shoving aside the two elves holding swords to Ivan's throat. "He is no enemy!"

The proclamation caught Ivan by surprise. "Thank ye, elf," he said, grimacing in pain with every word. The black-shafted arrow was nearly halfway through his thick and muscled thigh.

The two elves, thoroughly flummoxed, dipped their shoulders under Ivan's arms and hoisted the dwarf the rest of the way from the river. "Away, and quickly!" one of them said. "The enemy will cross after us if we remain in the open." None of the weary band had to be asked twice to leave, especially since they could still hear Ragnor above the din of the rushing waters, back out of sight over the ridge, wildly bellowing orders to his soldiers.

Elbereth, most of all, looked back to that ridge. Never before had the elf prince been bested in battle, yet for all his complaining at Ivan, Elbereth had to admit that if the dwarf had not torn him from the fight, Ragnor would have killed him.

The elf prince left the river with that dark thought in mind.

The elven camp wasn't formally an encampment. Rather, it was an area where the shadowy boughs of every tree seemed to hold an archer, grim-faced and ready should the enemy attempt to cross the river.

Elbereth and his companions were met in a small clearing by welcome faces, Shayleigh and Tintagel, two elves that the elf prince had feared slain at Daoine Dun. They offered no smiles as they walked over to join the companions; they even frowned at the sight and smell of the dwarves.

"It is good that you have returned," Shayleigh said, her melodic voice more somber than Elbereth ever remembered hearing it. He stared long and hard at her, just then beginning to understand the depth of the defeat at Daoine Dun.

"Many have died," added Tintagel, similarly reserved.

Elbereth nodded. "Who tends the wounded?" he asked. "Lady Maupoissant's arm requires a new dressing and my—" he looked at Ivan curiously for a moment, "—my friend has taken an arrow."

Ivan's eyes widened at the elf prince's proclamation of him as a friend.

"Wow," breathed Pikel.

"Bah! It's nothing, elf," Ivan growled, but when he pulled away from his supporters and tried to take a step, he nearly swooned from the pain and found that the leg would not support him.

Danica was beside the dwarf in an instant, propping him with her good arm. "Come," she said, straining a smile. "We will go to be tended together."

"Two old and broken travelers, eh?" chuckled Ivan.

"Not as broken as the enemies we left behind," Danica pointed out. She noticed that Shayleigh and Tintagel had not relinquished their frowns, and she nearly growled at them as she and Ivan walked past.

"The dwarves are to be treated as allies," Elbereth ordered, "for that they are, and let no elf consider them otherwise."

"By whose command?" came a voice from the side, which Elbereth recognized as his father's before he ever turned to regard the elven king.

"Have you taken command of the forces?" Galladel snarled, moving to his son. "Is it your right to choose our alliances?"

Danica and Ivan stopped and turned to watch; Cadderly and Pikel didn't blink, but Cadderly dropped a hand on Pikel's shoulder to keep the dwarf calm as the elf king walked close by them.

Elbereth wasn't convinced that his father's outburst was even worthy of an answer, but he knew that the trouble would only increase if he did not face Galladel then and there. "I did not believe we were in a favorable enough position to refuse offered help," he said.

"I never claimed to help ye, elf," barked Ivan, wanting to put the whole thing back into a perspective that his dwarven sensibilities could accept. "Me and me brother came to watch over Cadderly and Danica, not yerself!"

"Oo oi!" Pikel agreed firmly.

"Indeed," said Galladel, putting his glare upon one brother, then the other. "Do watch over Cadderly and Danica, then, and keep out of my people's way."

"Father," Elbereth began sharply.

"And I will hear no arguments from you, elf prince of Shilmista!" Galladel shouted sarcastically. "Where was Elbereth when Daoine Dun was overrun? Where was my son while his people were slaughtered?"

For the first time since he had met Elbereth, Cadderly thought that the elf prince looked very small. The young scholar looked past the elf, to Danica, and saw that a wetness rimmed her almond eyes. No jealousy came over the young scholar this time, for he shared Danica's sympathy.

"Go off again, if you so desire," growled Galladel. "Then, perhaps, you will not be forced to watch our final moments, the destruction of our home." The elf king wheeled about and disappeared into the brush.

Elbereth stood long and silent in the deepening shadows.

"They'll not attack at night," Tintagel offered to the companions, hoping to break the grim mood.

"Darkness favors goblins," Cadderly said, more to continue the conversation than to argue the point.

"Not in Shilmista!" the blue-eyed elven wizard replied, forcing a smile. "Our enemies have learned to fear the darkness. They attack only during the day. Such was the case at Daoine Dun." Tintagel's voice trailed away meekly as he mentioned the fateful battle.

Elbereth said nothing. He did not lower his face, refused to dip his proud chin, as he slowly walked away.

* * * * *

The night was extraordinarily chilly for late summer, and Cadderly was allowed a fire far back from the front lines. He took up his light tube and the book of Dellanil Quil'quien and began his task at translating, determined to do what he might to help the elven cause. He became distracted soon after, though, by a night bird's melodic cries a short distance away.

A thought came over Cadderly. He placed the ancient book down and recalled the spell of silence he had memorized earlier that day. It was not an easy spell; Cadderly had known all along that casting it would challenge him. While he was glad that Dorigen had not appeared in Ragnor's camp, he almost wished he had found the opportunity to take that challenge.

"Why not?" the young scholar mused, and he slipped away from the fire, narrowing the light tube's beam to better locate the bird.

He recited the runes exactly, not sure of his inflections, but confident that he would omit no words from the prescribed chant. Several seconds passed; Cadderly felt a strange energy building within him.

It gathered strength and urgency, called for him to let it loose. And he did so, uttering the last syllable with all the determination he could throw into his voice.

He paused a moment. The night bird was suddenly silent; all the forest was quiet.

Cadderly clenched his fist victoriously. He went back to the ancient book, feeling better about the role he might play in the coming battles.

His enthusiasm was stolen soon after, though, when Danica approached his fire. The young woman's lips moved in greeting, but no words came from her mouth. She looked about, confused.

Cadderly understood, and he dropped his face into his hands.

His sigh, too, could not be heard, nor could the crackle of the fire, he then realized. Grabbing a stick, he wrote, "It will pass," in the dirt and motioned for Danica to sit beside him.

"What has happened?" Danica asked a few minutes later, when the noise of the flames had returned.

"I have once again proved my uselessness," Cadderly replied. He kicked his pack, containing the *Tome of Universal Harmony.* "I am no priest of Deneir. I am no priest at all. Even the simplest spells roll awkwardly from my lips; only then to fall upon targets I do not desire. I tried to silence a bird and quieted myself instead. We should be glad that the wizard did not appear at the last battle. We all would have died if she had, though no one would have heard our final screams."

Despite Cadderly's grave tone, despite everything around her and the pain in her injured arm, Danica laughed aloud at that thought.

"I am afraid to call for even the simplest healing spells," Cadderly continued, "knowing that they would probably deepen a wound and not lessen it!"

Danica wanted to comfort him, to tell him that he was the most intelligent man she had ever met and the highest regarded young priest in the Edificant Library. But she found no sympathy for his minor problems, not with the weight of doom hanging heavily in Shilmista's ancient boughs.

"Self-pity does not become you," she remarked dryly.

"Self-truth," Cadderly corrected.

"So it may be," argued Danica, "but an irrelevant one now."

"All my life—" Cadderly began.

"Has not been wasted," Danica interrupted before the young scholar could sink lower into despair. "All your life? You have just begun to live it."

"I had thought to live it as a priest of Deneir," Cadderly lamented, "but that does not seem my course."

"You cannot know that," Danica scolded.

"Agreed," came a voice. They looked up and were surprised to see Kierkan Rufo approaching the fire.

Danica had nearly forgotten about the angular man, and seeing him now brought back many unpleasant thoughts. Cadderly sensed her sudden anger, and he put a hand upon her shoulder, fearing that she would spring at Rufo and throttle him.

"Some of the highest-ranking members of our order are inept at spellcasting," Rufo went on, taking a seat on a log opposite the low fire and pointedly avoiding Danica's cold stare. "Your friend, the headmistress, for example. Even the simplest spells often fail when uttered by Headmistress Pertelope."

Rufo's angular features seemed sharper in the flickering shadows, and Cadderly detected a tremor in his voice. The young scholar paid that fact little heed, though, more concerned with the revelation Rufo had given him.

"How can that be true?" Cadderly asked. "Pertelope is a leader among the order. How could she have attained such heights as headmistress at the Edificant Library if she cannot perform the simplest spells?"

"Because she is a scholar, as are you," Rufo replied, "and in Deneir's favor, do not doubt, even if that favor does not manifest itself in the form of clerical magic. Headmistress Pertelope is no pretender to her title."

"How do you know this?" Danica asked, and she had many other questions she wanted to ask of Rufo, particularly concerning his interactions with Dorigen.

"I heard Avery talking once," Rufo replied, trying to sound casual, though his monotone voice quivered with every word. "And I have been attentive since." He leaned back on his bony elbows, again trying futilely to appear calm.

Cadderly realized that a lot more was going on in this conversation, both from Danica's and Rufo's perspectives, than the casual banter implied. Passing moments did little to dissipate the tension; indeed, it seemed to Cadderly to be mounting in both his fireside companions. Still, Cadderly was relieved to hear Rufo's claims about Pertelope. He considered the words in light of his own experiences with the headmistress, and he had to agree that he had rarely seen Pertelope attempt any spellcasting at all.

Rufo stood stiffly. "I am glad that you have returned," he said, somewhat strained. From his pack he produced Cadderly's silken cape and wide-brimmed hat, the latter a bit crumpled. "I am glad," Rufo said again. He half-bowed and started away, nearly tripping over the log as he went.

"Surprised to see us, do you think?" Danica remarked when Rufo was beyond hearing distance. "Certainly our friend was a bit nervous."

"Kierkan Rufo has always been nervous," Cadderly replied, his voice sounding relaxed for the first time since he had discovered the failure of his spell of silence.

"You think it is a coincidence, then," Danica muttered. "And is it coincidence that Dorigen knew of him?"

"She may have learned of Rufo from the same source who told her of us," Cadderly reasoned.

"Indeed," the young woman agreed, and her wry tone shifted the connotation of Cadderly's own words to sound like an accusation against their angular companion. "Indeed."

* * * * *

Cadderly awakened to the sounds of battle shortly past dawn. He fumbled about his pack for his spindle-disks, grabbed his walking stick, and rushed away. The fight was over before he ever got close, with the elves successfully beating back yet another enemy probe.

Despite the success, though, neither Danica, Elbereth, nor the dwarves seemed pleased when Cadderly came upon them.

"I am sorry," the young scholar apologized, stuttering the words. "I was asleep. No one told me . . ."

"Fear not," Elbereth replied. "You would have had little role in the fight. Elven archers turned the enemy back before very many of them even got across the river."

"And them that did wished they had turned back!" added Ivan, seeming none the worse for his leg wound. He pointedly held out his bloodied axe for Cadderly to see. Pikel, meanwhile, was busily pulling a clump of goblin hair from a thin crack in his club.

Cadderly didn't miss the appreciative stare Elbereth cast the dwarves' way, though the elf obviously tried to mask the look. "Go and gather your strength now," Elbereth said to Danica, then he looked around to indicate that his words were meant for all of them. "I must attend council with my father. Our scouts will return this morning with more complete estimates of the enemy's strength." The elf bowed and was gone.

Ivan and Pikel were asleep almost immediately after they returned to Cadderly's small camp. The dwarves had been up all night, showing some of the more receptive elves how to construct a proper barricade, complete with cunning traps.

Danica, too, stretched out to rest, and Cadderly, after a quick meal of tasty biscuits, dove back into the book of Dellanil Quil'quien. His translating had gone slowly through the late hours; he thought he had discerned the meaning of just a single rune. A hundred more arcane symbols remained a mystery to him.

Elbereth came to see them later that morning, accompanied by Tintagel and Shayleigh. The elf prince's grim expression revealed much about what the returning scouts had reported.

"Our enemy is more disciplined and organized than we had believed," Elbereth admitted.

"And the enemy wizard returned this morning," added Shayleigh. "She sent a line of fire from her hand, shrouding an unfortunate scout. He is alive, but our healers do not expect him to survive the day."

Cadderly reflexively glanced over to his pack, to the *Tome of Universal Harmony*. What healing secrets might he discover there? he wondered. Could he find the strength to help the wounded elf?

He looked away, ashamed, admitting that he could not. He was no cleric of Deneir; he had established that fact the night before.

"What of allies?" Danica asked. "Has the Edificant Library responded to our call?"

"There has been no word of outside help," Elbereth replied. "It is believed that the library could not muster sufficient force anyway, even if they could arrive in time."

"Where does that leave us?" Cadderly asked.

"Galladel speaks of leaving Shilmista," Elbereth said past the welling lump in his slender throat. "He talks often of Evermeet, and says that our day in the common Realms has passed."

"And what do you say?" Danica asked, her question sounding almost like an accusation.

"It is not time to go," the proud elf answered sternly. "I'll not leave Shilmista to the goblins, but . . ."

"But our hopes here are fast fading," Shayleigh answered.

Cadderly did not miss the edge of sadness in her violet eyes, a somber look that had stolen her vigor and heart for the fight.

"We cannot defeat so large an enemy," the elven maiden admitted. "Many goblins will die, it is true, but our numbers will continue to dwindle until we are no more."

To his own surprise, Cadderly abruptly broke the ensuing silence. "I have begun the translation of Dellanil's book," he said determinedly. "We will find our answers there."

Elbereth shook his head. "You have little time," he explained, "and we do not expect as much as you from the ancient work. The magic of the forest is not as it used to be—in that regard, I fear, my father is correct."

"When will you decide our course?" Danica asked.

"Later this day," replied the elf prince, "though I believe the meeting is just a formality, for the decision has already been made."

There was no more to be said, but so much more to be done, and the three elves took their leave. Danica fell back to her blanket, squirming about in a futile attempt to find some sleep, and Cadderly went back to the ancient book.

He spent another hour, frustrated by two simple runes that appeared on nearly every page. If these two could take so much of his time, how then could he hope to complete the work in a single day?

He moved the book aside and stretched out, exhausted and defeated, filled with loathing for his own inadequacies. Cadderly the priest? Apparently not. Cadderly the fighter? Hardly. Cadderly the scholar?

Perhaps, but that talent suddenly seemed so very useless in the real and violent world. Cadderly could recount the adventures of a thousand ancient heroes, tell of long-past wars, and inscribe a wizard's lost spellbook after having seen it only once. But he couldn't turn the black tide from beautiful Shilmista, and now none of his other talents really seemed to matter.

Sleep did take him, mercifully, and in that sleep came a dream that Cadderly could not have expected.

He saw Shilmista under the light of an ancient sky, under starlight of violet and blue and crisp yellow rays, filtering softly through the thick leafy canopy. There danced the elves, ten times the number of Shilmista's present host, led in song by the greatest of Shilmista's kings.

The words were strange to Cadderly, though he fluently spoke the elvish language common to his day. Stranger still came the reaction of the forest around the elves, for the trees themselves reverberated with Dellanil's song, answering the elf king. Only a slight breeze wafted through this ancient vision of Shilmista, yet the great and thick limbs bent and swayed, synchronous to the graceful movements of the sylvan folk.

Then the vision was gone, and Cadderly sat up, awakened by Ivan and Pikel's thunderous snores. The young scholar shook his head and lay back, hoping to recapture that lost moment. His dreams were fast fading, only a blur, but he remembered the serenity, and the magic, acutely.

His eyes popped open wide and he scrambled for the black-bound book.

Those unknown runes greeted him once again, but this time Cadderly threw aside his notes and logical, practiced techniques. This time, the young scholar used his emotional revelations, felt as Dellanil had felt in his dreamy vision, and sent his soul dancing as the elves and the trees had danced, their song sounding within him.

* * * * *

"Get out!" Kierkan Rufo growled, banging his arm against a tree trunk. "I did as you demanded, now leave me alone!" The angular man glanced around nervously, fearing that he had spoken too loudly. The elves were everywhere, it seemed, and Rufo did not doubt that one of them would gladly put an arrow into him if that elf ever discovered the source of Rufo's dilemma.

He was alone in the forest, physically at least, and had been since his departure from Cadderly and Danica the previous night. Rufo could find no sleep—an impish voice in his head would not allow that. Already the angular man appeared haggard, haunted, for he could not be rid of Druzil's telepathic intrusions.

What have you to lose? purred the imp's raspy voice. *All the world will be your gain.*

"I do not know what they are planning, nor would I reveal it to you if I did," Rufo insisted.

Oh, but you would, came Druzil's confident reply. *And you shall indeed.*

"Never!"

You have once betrayed your friends, Kierkan Rufo, Druzil reminded him. *How merciful would the elf prince be if he learned of your weakness?*

Rufo's breath came in short gasps. He understood that Druzil's question was a direct threat.

But think not of such unpleasantness, Druzil continued. *Aid us now. We will prove victorious—that is obvious—and you will be well rewarded when the battle is won. Scorn us, and you will pay.*

Rufo didn't realize his own movements, was oblivious to the sharp pain. He looked down in shock to his hand, holding a clump of his matted black hair.

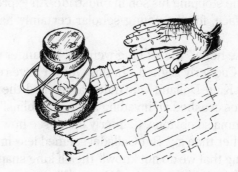

Seventeen
A Desperate Attempt

"Our sincere pardon," Danica said quietly when she and Cadderly entered the small glade beyond a thick grove of pines that blocked the outside world. Here the elven leaders gathered—Galladel and Elbereth, Shayleigh, Tintagel, and several others that Danica and Cadderly did not know. Their faces were grim indeed, and though Galladel said nothing immediately about the interruption, both friends could see that the elf king was not pleased by their appearance.

"I have translated the work," Cadderly announced, holding up the book of Dellanil Quil'quien for all to see.

"Where did you get that?" Galladel demanded.

"He found it at Daoine Dun," Elbereth explained, "and has it now with my permission."

Galladel glowered at his son, but Elbereth turned to Cadderly. "You have not had time to read the entire tome," the elf prince remarked. "How could you possibly have translated it?"

"I have not," Cadderly replied guardedly. "I mean . . ." He paused to search for the correct way to explain what he had accomplished, and also to calm himself under Galladel's imposing stare.

"I have deciphered the meanings of the connotations, of the ancient runes," Cadderly continued. "The symbols pose no more difficulties. Together we can read through the work and see what secrets it might provide."

Some of the elves, Elbereth and Shayleigh in particular, seemed intrigued. Elbereth rose and approached Cadderly, his silver eyes sparkling with a hint of renewed hope.

"What value do you expect to find within those pages?" Galladel asked sharply, his angry tone stopping his son in midstride. An expression of confusion crossed Cadderly's face, for the young scholar certainly hadn't expected that reaction.

"You bring us false hope," the elf king went on, his anger unrelenting.

"There is more," Cadderly argued. "In this work, I have read a most remarkable account of how King Dellanil Quil'quien awakened the trees of Shilmista, and of how those trees crushed an invading force of goblins!" With the parallels to their present dilemma so obvious, Cadderly didn't see how that news could be met with anything other than joy. But Galladel seemed less impressed than ever.

"You tell us nothing that we do not know!" the elf king snapped. "Do you think that none among us has read the book of Dellanil?"

"I had thought the runes ancient and lost to understanding," Cadderly stammered. Danica put her hand on his shoulder, and the young scholar appreciated the much needed support.

"Lost now," Galladel replied, "but I, too, have read the work, centuries ago when those runes were not so uncommon. I could decipher them still, if I had the mind and the time to do so."

"You did not think to awaken the trees?" Elbereth asked his father in disbelief.

Galladel's glare bored into his impertinent son. "You speak of that act as though it were some simple magical spell."

"It is not a spell," Cadderly put in, "but a summons, a calling to awaken the powers of the forest."

"Powers that are no more," Galladel added.

"How can you—" Elbereth began, but Galladel cut him short.

"This is not the first war that has come to Shilmista since I began my reign," the elf king explained. He seemed suddenly old and vulnerable, his face pale and hollow. "And I read the account of Dellanil's battle, as you have," he offered sympathetically to Cadderly. "Like you, I was filled with hope on that long ago occasion and filled with belief of the magic of Shilmista.

"But the trees did not come to my call," the elf king continued, drawing nods of recognition from two other aged elves sitting by his side. "Not a single one. Many elves died repelling the invaders, more than should have, I fear, since their king was too busy to join in their fight."

It seemed to Cadderly as if the aged elf's shoulders sagged even lower as he recalled that tragic time.

"That is a summons for another age," Galladel said, his voice resolute once more, "an age when the trees were the sentient sentinels of Shilmista Forest."

"But are they not?" Shayleigh dared to interject. "Hammadeen bade us to hear their warning song."

"Hammadeen is a dryad," Galladel explained, "much more attuned to the flora than any elf ever could be. She would hear the song of any plant anywhere in the world. Do not allow her cryptic bidding to bring you false hope."

"We have few options," Elbereth reminded his father.

"The summons will not work," Galladel insisted, his tone showing clearly that he considered the conversation at an end. "You do have our thanks, scholar Cadderly," he said, somewhat condescendingly. "Your efforts have not gone unnoticed."

"Come," Danica whispered into Cadderly's ear, pulling him by the hand back out of the glade.

"No!" Cadderly replied, twisting from her grasp. "What will you do?" he snapped at Galladel. He approached the elf king, sitting directly across the glade, pushing right by the shocked Elbereth on his way.

"I have heard many admit that the force opposing Shilmista is too great for the elves to defeat," Cadderly went on. "I have heard that no help will arrive in time or in sufficient numbers to save the forest. If all that is true, then what will you do?"

"That is what we have gathered here to discuss privately," the elf king replied sternly.

"What have you who have gathered here decided?" Cadderly shot back, not backing down in the least. "Are you to run away, leave the forest for the invaders?"

Galladel stood and met Cadderly's determined stare with one equally unyielding. Cadderly heard Danica rushing to corral him, then heard, to his surprise, Elbereth intercept her.

"Most will go," Galladel admitted. "Some—" he spoke the word callously and looked pointedly at Elbereth as he uttered it, "—wish to stay and fight, determined to hinder and punish the enemy until they have joined their elven kin in death."

"And you will go . . . to the Edificant Library?" Cadderly asked. "Then away from there, to Evermeet perhaps?"

Galladel nodded gravely. "Our time in Shilmista has passed, young priest," he admitted, and Cadderly could see that the words pained him deeply.

Cadderly was not unsympathetic, and he did not doubt the truth of Galladel's claims, but there were other ramifications to their actions that the elves apparently had not considered, most prominently the fate of the region. "As an emissary of the Edificant Library, I can assure you that you and your people will be welcomed there for as long as you wish to stay," Cadderly replied. "But as one who has seen what befell the library, and now Shilmista, I must beg you to reconsider your course. If the forest falls, then so, too, shall the men of the mountains, and of the lake region to the east, I fear. The enemy must not be allowed so easy a victory."

Galladel seemed on the verge of exploding. "You would sacrifice us?" he growled, his face only inches from Cadderly's. "You would give the lives of my people, that a few *men* might survive? We owe you nothing, I say! Do you believe it is with light hearts that we surrender our homeland? I have lived in Shilmista since before your precious library was even constructed!"

Cadderly wanted to argue that Galladel's own claims proved that Shilmista, then, was worth fighting for, and that every possibility, even the attempt to awaken the trees, should be exhausted before the elves fled their homes. The young scholar couldn't, though. He could find nothing to throw against Galladel's outrage, nothing to diminish the elf king's ire. When Danica again came to him and pulled him toward the glade entrance, he did not resist.

"I thought I could help them," he said to her, and he did not look back at Galladel.

"We all wish to help," Danica replied softly. "That is our frustration."

They said nothing more as they walked slowly away and heard an argument raging behind them within the ring of pines. When they were back at the campsite with Kierkan Rufo and the dwarven brothers, the weight of the world seemed to bow Cadderly's shoulders.

They were surprised an hour later, when Elbereth, Shayleigh, and Tintagel came to join them.

"You are certain that you have the runes deciphered?" Elbereth asked sternly, his jaw firm and eyes staring hard at Cadderly.

"I am certain," Cadderly replied, jumping to his feet, suspecting what the bold elf prince had in mind.

The expressions splayed across the faces of both Shayleigh and Tintagel revealed their discomfort with this meeting.

"What was the council's decision?" Danica asked of Elbereth. She rose beside Cadderly and looked hard at the elf prince.

Elbereth didn't retreat from his stance. "By my father's word, my people will depart the forest," he admitted. "We surrender the ground in exchange for our lives, and never shall we return."

"It was not an easy decision for Galladel to come by," Tintagel offered. "Your father has witnessed the deaths of many elves these last days."

The statement stung Elbereth, as Tintagel, obviously not pleased with Elbereth's intentions, apparently had hoped it would.

"Their deaths will have been in vain if the enemy is handed Shilmista," the elf prince declared. "We have options still, and I'll not leave until they are exhausted."

"You plan to awaken the trees," Cadderly reasoned.

"Oo oi!" piped in a happy Pikel, who dearly wanted to see such druidlike magic.

All three elves cast a disconcerting look the round-shouldered dwarf's way.

"Oo," Pikel chirped, and he lowered his eyes.

"With your help," Elbereth said to Cadderly, "we shall recapture the magic of days long past. We shall turn the forest against our enemies and drive them back to their mountain holes!"

Cadderly was excited by the thought, but he saw that he and Elbereth, and perhaps Pikel, were the only ones holding out much hope.

"You father does not believe that," Danica reminded the elf prince.

"He would not approve of your actions," added Shayleigh.

"How can we leave until we have tried?" Elbereth asked. "If we fail, then we shall go along with Galladel's plans, and what have we lost? If we succeed, if the forest comes to life, if great trees walk beside us as allies . . ."

Tintagel and Shayleigh managed somewhat hopeful smiles. Danica looked to Cadderly, doubting, but ready to support him in whatever manner he required.

"I am ready to show you the words," Cadderly said determinedly. "Together we shall find the song of Dellanil Quil'quien and implore the trees to our side!"

The three elves took their leave then, and Cadderly, visage set firm, took up the ancient book and flipped it open to the appropriate passage.

Danica wanted to tell him of the futility, wanted to warn him of the dire consequences his failure might have on the elven host's already weakened morale, but looking at her love sitting so stern and determined as he pored through the book, she could not find the words.

None of them noticed Kierkan Rufo quietly slip away.

* * * * *

The elves will depart? came the telepathic voice, revealing the imp's excitement. *What defenses will they leave behind? And what of young Cadderly? Tell me of Cadderly!*

"Leave me alone!" Rufo screamed back. "You have gained enough from me. Go and question another." The angular man could sense the imp's distant laughter.

"The elves will depart," Rufo admitted, hoping to mask the more important news with something the enemy would discern soon enough in any case.

And that is all? came the expected question.

"That is all," Rufo replied. "A few may remain, just to slow your advance, but the rest will go, never to return."

And what of Cadderly?

"He will go with them, back to his home, the library," Rufo lied, knowing that to reveal anything else would invariably lead him into the middle of another conspiracy.

Again came the reverberations of the imp's distant laughter. *You have not told me all,* came his thoughts, *but you have revealed more than you intended simply by trying to hide that which you cannot. I will be with you, Kierkan Rufo, every step. And know that your unwillingness to cooperate will be revealed once our conquest is complete, once you face my mistress. I assure you that she is not a merciful victor. Go and reconsider your course and your untruths. Think of the path that lies ahead for Kierkan Rufo.*

Rufo felt the connection break, then he was alone, stumbling through the woods, a haunted man.

* * * * *

Danica was glad of the change that came over Cadderly, whatever the out-come of their desperate attempt. She knew that Cadderly was a sensitive man, frustrated by the violence that had been forced upon him and by the destruction of so many wondrous things, both in beautiful Shilmista and back in the Edificant Library. Danica didn't doubt Cadderly's willingness to fight back however he could. They stood in the same glade that the elves had used earlier for council, wanting their attempt to be private in case it failed, as Galladel had predicted. Watching Cadderly and Elbereth in their preparations for the ceremony, the young scholar tutoring the elf on particular inflections and movements, Danica almost allowed herself to believe that the trees of Shilmista would awaken, and that the forest would be saved.

Tintagel, Shayleigh, and Pikel, beside Danica, seemed to hold similar, though unspoken hopes. Ivan merely grumbled a stream of complaints, though, thinking that they should all be out "clobbering orcs" instead of wasting their time calling to "trees that ain't got ears!"

Several other elves appeared when Elbereth began the song, an even-paced, melodic chant that sounded appropriate under the mystic evening canopy.

Pikel nearly swooned and began a dance, graceful by dwarven standards, but a bit strained in an elven wood. Still, Tintagel and Shayleigh couldn't help smiling when they saw the would-be druid, his green-dyed and braided beard bouncing about his shoulders with every twirl.

Then Galladel stepped between Shayleigh and Danica, his scowl threatening the magical aura as surely as would a goblin attack.

"Do not disturb them, I beg," Danica whispered to the elf king, and to her surprise, he nodded gravely and remained quiet. He glanced over to Pikel and frowned, then turned his attention back to his son, who was fully immersed in the ancient song.

Danica watched the elf king's eyes well with tears, and she knew that Galladel looked upon an image of himself centuries ago, that he recalled that time when he had failed to awaken the trees at the cost of many elven lives.

Elbereth's song reached out to Shilmista; Danica could not understand the words, but they seemed fitting for the forest, almost otherworldly and even more purely elven than Daoine Teague Feer had seemed. Those elves, many now, gathered around the small glade's fringes did not even whisper among them-selves—did nothing but hear their prince's enchanting call.

A wolf howled somewhere in the distance; another took up the call, and another in response to that.

Then, too suddenly it seemed, Elbereth was done. He stood in the center of the glade, Cadderly moving beside him, and they, and all those about them, waited with held breath for Shilmista to respond.

There came nothing, save the howl of the wolves and the lamenting keen of the evening wind.

"Trees ain't got ears," Ivan muttered after a long while.

"I told you it would not work," Galladel berated them, the anticipation of the moment stolen by the wide-eyed dwarf's comment. "Are you finished with your folly? Might we get along with the business of saving our people?"

The look Elbereth gave Cadderly showed only remorse. "We have tried," the elf prince offered. "We have tried." He turned and walked slowly away to rejoin his father.

Truly perplexed, Cadderly stood in the middle of the glade, moving the beam of his light tube across the words of the ancient book.

"It was worth the attempt," said Danica as she and the dwarven brothers came over to join him.

"Worthy indeed," came a tittering voice that they recognized at once. In unison, they turned and spotted Hammadeen the dryad, standing beside a pine opposite from where Galladel and the others had just departed.

"What do you know?" Cadderly demanded, heading for the dryad. "You must tell us! The trees did not respond to the call, and you know the reason."

"Oh, they did hear!" Hammadeen replied, clapping her hands happily. She moved behind the pine and was gone, reappearing a moment later behind another tree many feet from the volatile young man. "They did!"

"Have they begun their march upon our enemies?" Cadderly breathed, hardly daring to believe.

Hammadeen's laughter mocked his hopes. "Of course they have not!" the dryad chirped. "These trees are young. They have not the power of the ancients. You are in the wrong place, do you not understand?"

Cadderly's crestfallen look was matched by Danica's and Pikel's expressions. Ivan just grumbled something, huffed, and stormed away.

"But the trees in this region of the forest have heard the elven song," Hammadeen offered to brighten their mood, "and they are pleased by it."

"Lot o' good that'll do them," the departing Ivan chided.

Danica echoed the thoughts of the remaining three perfectly when she whispered, "How pleased will the trees be to hear the crack of orcish axes?"

Hammadeen stopped laughing and faded into the pine.

The four companions were on the trail south later that same night, joined by Kierkan Rufo. Many elves accompanied them, though the fair folk did not walk the straight trails, as Cadderly and his friends had been told to do. Rather, they dipped in and out of the shadows to the sides, wary though weary, and those who were not riding often kept to the trees, crossing silently among high and intertwined branches.

Shayleigh found the travelers and dropped from her horse to walk beside them, but her presence did little to comfort them, particularly when it became apparent that she could not look Cadderly in the eye.

"They are fighting again, behind us," the elf maiden said, "as it shall be all the way out of Shilmista."

R. A. Salvatore

"Stupid orcs," Ivan muttered, and that was the only response forthcoming from the group.

"This time it would seem King Galladel was correct," Shayleigh went on.

"We had nothing to lose," Cadderly replied, a bit more sharply than he had intended.

"But we did," said Shayleigh. "For word has spread of our failure. All the elves know that Shilmista would not rise beside them. Our hearts are heavy. Few will remain beside Elbereth as he continues to hinder the enemy."

Both Cadderly and Danica started to say something, but Ivan promptly diffused their stubborn enthusiasm.

"No, ye won't!" the dwarf insisted to the two of them. "Ye won't be staying, nor will me or me brother."

"Oo," said Pikel sadly.

"This ain't our place," Ivan roared on. "And there ain't a thing we can do now to slow them monsters down! Too many of the damned things!"

Shayleigh left them then, and Danica and Cadderly couldn't even muster the strength to bid her farewell.

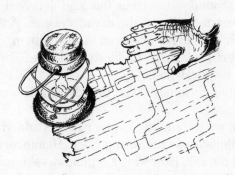

Eighteen
A Wood Worth Fighting For

D anica noticed a change in her companion during their long and dismal walk. It started with Cadderly glancing all around, staring into Shilmista's shadows, his gray eyes rimmed with wetness. But the tears never came; they were replaced by an anger so profound that the young scholar could hardly keep his breathing steady, could hardly keep his fists unclenched.

He dropped out of the retreating line and pulled his pack off his back, offering no explanation to Danica, Rufo, and the dwarven brothers as they moved beside him.

"A bit of reading for the road?" Ivan asked, seeing Cadderly take out the ancient book of Dellanil Quil'quien.

"It should have worked," Cadderly replied firmly. "The words were spoken correctly. Every syllable was as King Dellanil spoke them centuries ago."

"Of course they were," said Danica. "No one in all Shilmista doubts the sincerity of your attempt or that your heart was for the forest."

"Flattery?" Cadderly barked at her, his voice more full of anger than it ever had been toward his love.

Danica backed away a step, stunned.

"Oo," moaned Pikel.

"Ye've no right to be speaking to the lady that way," Ivan said, slapping his axe loudly against his open hand.

Cadderly nodded in agreement but would not let his embarrassment steal his mounting determination. "The summons must work," he declared. "We have nothing else—Shilmista has no other hope."

"Then we have nothing at all," Ivan replied evenly. "Ye heard the wood sprite yerself. Ye're in the wrong place, lad. Shilmista will not come to yer call."

373

Cadderly looked around at the trees that had deceived him, searching for escape from the apparent finality of the dryad's claims. A thought struck him then, one so simple that it had not occurred to any of them.

"Hammadeen did not say that," Cadderly told Ivan. The scholar turned to include the others in his revelation.

Danica's head tilted curiously. "The dryad's words were direct enough," she argued.

"Hammadeen said we were in the wrong place," Cadderly replied. "We took that to mean that Shilmista was the wrong place. Hammadeen said the trees of the region had heard the call. How wide a region was she speaking of?"

"What are ye babbling about?" Ivan demanded. "What other place might there be?"

"Think of where we were when Elbereth read the incantation," Cadderly prompted.

"The clearing," Ivan replied at once.

"But the trees around that grove!" Cadderly said. "Think of the trees."

"I'm not for telling one tree from another," Ivan protested. "Ask me brother if ye're wanting to know—"

"Not the trees' types," Cadderly explained, "but their age."

"The camp was surrounded by young growth," Danica realized. "Even the circling pines were not so tall."

"Yes, too young," Cadderly explained. "Those trees were not alive when Dellanil intoned the ancient words, not alive even when Galladel tried to awaken the wood. They did not exist when magic filled Shilmista's air."

"Would that matter?" Danica asked. "A magical—"

"This is not a magical spell," Cadderly interrupted. "It is a call to a once-sentient forest. The new trees might still speak so that a dryad would hear, but they have lost the ability to walk beside the elves. But the oldest ones, the ones from Dellanil's time, may not have."

"If any of those remain," Danica stated.

"Not likely," Kierkan Rufo had to add, fearing that Cadderly's newest revelations would keep them all in the forest longer than the angular man desired.

"Oh, but there are," came a voice from the side. An elf that none of them knew rose from the brush just a few feet away and smiled at Ivan's glower and the others' stupefied expressions.

"Pardon my eavesdropping," the elf said. "Your conversation was much too interesting for me to interrupt, and I only speak now to tell you that there are indeed trees in Shilmista from the days of King Dellanil: a grove of huge oaks, west of here. The place is called Syldritch Trea, the Most Ancient Trees."

"Did King Galladel go to Syldritch Trea when he failed in his attempt at the summoning?" Cadderly asked, already suspecting the answer but eager for confirmation.

The elf thought for a moment, then answered, "No, I do not believe he did. But neither was King Dellanil in Syldritch Trea when he called the trees."

"Bring Elbereth, I beg, and hurry," said Cadderly, ignoring the elf's last statement. "Shilmista's day may not be past."

The elf nodded curtly and was gone, disappearing into the surrounding brush in the blink of an eye.

"Ye cannot be thinking . . ." Ivan began slowly.

"Indeed I can," Cadderly replied evenly.

"He just said that Dellanil—" Danica started to protest.

"Do not presume anything about the ancient forest," Cadderly interrupted. "Perhaps, in that time, the trees called to each other after Dellanil began the enchantment. Perhaps the trees spread the summons throughout Shilmista."

Ivan's look reflected his doubts. Even Pikel, so hopeful when they had first tried to awaken the trees, frowned.

"It will work," Cadderly growled at them, so determinedly that even Ivan did not try to tell him differently.

Danica hooked his arm for support and gave him an approving wink.

* * * * *

Elbereth arrived a short while later, accompanied by Shayleigh and Galladel. The three had already heard of Cadderly's latest revelation, and Galladel in particular seemed hardly pleased.

"Syldritch Trea," Cadderly said as soon as they arrived, giving the pessimistic elf king no time to quash his momentum. "The summons will work in Syldritch Trea."

"You cannot know that," Elbereth replied, though the elf prince appeared intrigued.

"And we cannot afford to waste precious time," King Galladel added sharply. "You have seen the despair your false hopes have given us, priest. It would be better now for all concerned—if you continued on your way home."

"Home," Cadderly echoed wistfully, aiming his remark at Elbereth. "Quite a concept, that. A place to be defended, perhaps. At least, that is what I, who have never had a true home, was once told."

Danica winced and gave Cadderly's arm a jerk as Elbereth stormed over to stand before them.

"What do you know of it?" the elf prince demanded. "Do you believe it is with light hearts that we leave Shilmista?"

"I do not believe most of you wish to leave at all," Cadderly replied, not bending an inch under Elbereth's cold glare. "And perhaps you need not. Perhaps . . ."

" 'Ware his twisted tongue!" Galladel cried. "I understand you now, young priest, " the elf king roared, wagging an accusatory finger Cadderly's way. "You have come to encourage us to continue this hopeless battle, to sacrifice us, that your precious home might be saved."

"The library is not my home," Cadderly muttered, but his words were lost in the ensuing explosion of protests aimed at the elf king from Ivan and Danica, a "Hey!" from Pikel, and even a few stern words from Elbereth.

When things quieted again, Cadderly gave Galladel's accusation not another thought. He looked at Elbereth, and at Elbereth only, as he made his case. "The summons must work," he said. "I believe in it with all my heart. This is no ruse, no deception to encourage an elven sacrifice. It is a hope that your home will not fall under our monstrous enemy's shadow, that the elven dance will continue throughout my lifetime in this forest so dear."

"Syldritch Trea lies to the west and north," Elbereth replied. "To get there, I will have to cross the enemy lines once more, and far deeper this time. If the summons does not work . . ."

"You'll not go alone," Cadderly vowed, and he shot a glance Galladel's way.

"He'll not go at all!" the elf king growled.

"What say you, Elbereth?" Cadderly continued, holding the elf prince's gaze from his father's scowl. "Back on the paths of the Snowflakes you told me you would fight for Shilmista, that you would kill every invader without mercy. You were correct in your assumption—I have no home but I will go with you, fight with you and die with you if that must be, on this last chance for the forest."

"As will I," Danica asserted.

"Seems we're going for another walk, me brother," Ivan piped in. Pikel's head wagged in full approval.

Elbereth looked around to all of them, his smile growing wider with each second. "You have given me hope, friend," he said to Cadderly. "I will read the words in Syldritch Trea, then let the forest decide its fate."

"And yours," Galladel snarled. "What will you do when the trees do not awaken? You will be caught in the open and vulnerable, surrounded by our merciless enemies. I hoped I would not live to see my son perish, but never would I have imagined that his death would come from his own foolishness!"

Shayleigh, for so long biting back her increasingly bitter thoughts, broke her silence at last. "Not foolishness," she cried. "Courage. Many will go with you, Prince Elbereth, entrusting their lives to your hopes and to the forest."

"That would not be wise," Elbereth replied, but for purely practical reasons and not because of any doubts he had concerning the ancient summons. "A small band might slip through without a fight."

"Then we shall meet your return," Shayleigh promised. "With the trees of Syldritch Trea beside us, we will drive the enemy from our land!"

"I am still king of Shilmista," Galladel, standing some distance from the conspirators, reminded them.

"You wish to come along and read the summons?" Cadderly asked, for he knew well that Galladel had no desire to do any such thing. Beside him, Danica gasped at his impudence.

"I could strike you down for that remark," Galladel growled at him.

"I don't think so," Ivan remarked, his axe bouncing prominently on one shoulder.

"And you, dwarf," spat the elven king. "When this is ended . . ."

"Aw, shut yer mouth and get in line behind yer son," Ivan snapped. Galladel cast a murderous glare at all of them, turned about, and stormed away.

"How dare you speak to the king of Shilmista like that?" Danica scolded Cadderly, amazed, though obviously not as upset as her words made her sound.

Cadderly looked away from her, to Elbereth, more interested, in this instance, in what the elf might think. Elbereth said nothing, but his nod was one of approval.

"You have inspired my father's hopes as well," Elbereth said sincerely. "I do not doubt that King Galladel will be among those awaiting our return from Syldritch Trea, waiting to fight beside the forest itself to rid our land of the foul invaders." The elf prince and Shayleigh followed Galladel away then, with many plans to be made.

* * * * *

Kierkan Rufo didn't know what to make of Danica's approach, or of her grim visage. Sensing another telepathic intrusion from that wretched imp, Rufo had wandered off alone, away from Cadderly and the others.

"And so I shall return to the library alone," the angular man said meekly to the approaching woman. "To tell of your bravery, and of Cadderly's, and to hope that all goes well in this ancient grove of oaks, this Syldritch Trea that the elves speak of so reverently."

"Your hopes for our success had better be sincere," Danica replied, "for you are coming with us."

Rufo nearly toppled at the announcement. "I?" he balked. "What use could I be? I am hardly a fighter and am not knowledgeable of the woodlands in any way."

"It is not for your value that I insist you come," Danica explained. "I fear the consequences of leaving you here."

"How dare you speak such words?" Rufo groused.

"I dare not hesitate to speak them," Danica retorted. "I do not trust you, Kierkan Rufo. Know that and know that you shall accompany us."

"I will not!"

Rufo didn't even see her move, but suddenly he lay on his back, looking up at the stars with a burning pain behind his knees. Danica bent over him and scowled.

"You will not be left behind, " she said evenly. "Understand that, for the sake of your very life."

* * * * *

By the time the sun began its ascent in the east, Elbereth, Shayleigh, and two score of other elves had found their way back to Cadderly and his companions.

"It is decided," the elf prince announced. "We three—you, Danica, and I—shall go to Syldritch Trea."

"Ahem." Pikel cleared his throat.

Elbereth looked to Cadderly and Danica.

"They did save your—our—lives," Cadderly reminded the elf prince. "And I would honestly feel safer with the brothers beside me."

"Why would you wish to come along?" Elbereth asked Ivan. "This journey could prove ill-fated, and even if it is not, the gain will mean little to you."

"Me brother likes trees," Ivan answered without the slightest hesitation.

Elbereth shrugged hopelessly; Cadderly thought he saw the elf quickly dismiss an appreciative smile. "Then we five shall go—"

"Six," Danica corrected.

Even Cadderly turned on her curiously.

"Kierkan Rufo insists that he come along," Danica explained. "He fears being left alone in the forest with only the elves, whom he does not understand."

The notion seemed absurd—Rufo had already been left with the elves—but when Cadderly looked to the angular man, he was nodding his head, if somewhat gravely.

"Six, then," said Elbereth.

"None of yer own folk got the belly for it?" Ivan asked.

"Perhaps when all of this is ended, I should get in line behind Elbereth and King Galladel," Shayleigh answered sternly, before Elbereth could explain. She tried to cast a threatening glare but could not hold it in the face of Ivan's amused chuckle.

"My people will be there," Elbereth explained. "All of my people. Even my father. They'll be not far from us, unseen in the boughs. They will bring about the distractions to allow us to get through to Syldritch Trea, and they will be ready to begin the final battle when the summons is complete.

"You must understand the risks," Elbereth continued, mostly to Cadderly. "If the trees do not come to my call, then many, perhaps all, of Shilmista's elves will die. In light of that, tell me again of your confidence in the ancient words."

"If the trees do not answer, then my life, too, will be forfeit," the scholar replied in defense of his claims. "As will Danica's, which I treasure above my own."

Danica glanced sidelong at Cadderly. He didn't return the look, intent on Elbereth, but she knew he understood her approval of the change that had come over him.

They set off immediately after their morning meal, the company of six with a host of elves slipping all about them, clearing their path.

Kierkan Rufo was not pleased, though he was smart enough to keep his complaints silent. Merciless Danica had left him no choice, and so he had come along.

So, too, in Rufo's mind, had Druzil, the imp.

* * * * *

Dorigen got the news of the departure only an hour later. She sat in her tent in Ragnor's camp, trying to decide what course to take.

"They tried once before to awaken the trees," Druzil reminded her, hoping to ease her obvious torment. "Why should we believe their luck will be any better this time?"

"We would be wise to fear anything involving the young scholar and his resourceful friends," Dorigen replied.

"We can catch them," Druzil said, eagerly rubbing his plump hands together.

Dorigen shook her head. "Not again."

Druzil's bulbous eyes narrowed. "Has Dorigen lost her courage along with her barbarian lover?"

Dorigen's answering glare stole the bite from the absurd remark. "Dorigen's wisdom has grown with her failures," she corrected. "Our last defeat cost me much prestige in this camp, and in Ragnor's eyes. I doubt the ogrillon would lend me the soldiers to capture that crew—and that number, I fear, would be considerable."

"He is just a boy," Druzil remarked, "and his friends as unlikely a group of heroes as ever there was."

"He is a boy who nearly destroyed you in mental combat," Dorigen reminded him, "and whose friends include an elf prince and a woman able to dodge lightning! Must I remind you of the mighty dwarves as well? Ogres, a dozen orogs . . ."

"Enough, enough," Druzil conceded, not wanting to hear the disastrous battle recounted. "I had only hoped that we might discover some method to regain our advantage. Their course might prove dangerous to us all. I had thought to lessen—"

"You are correct," Dorigen interrupted, rising determinedly from her seat. This is too important to be concerned with the petty squabbles of Castle Trinity."

"You are going to Ragnor?" Druzil asked. "What of the young priest?"

"I am," Dorigen answered. "As for Cadderly, we two will look for a way to take him, as we had originally planned. If that way cannot be found, then he will die with the rest of them."

She left the tent in a rush, leaving Druzil to sit alone on the small table with his private thoughts. "People," the imp muttered.

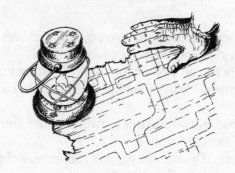

Nineteen
Through the Lines Dangerously

When you pass the birch tangle, get down to the left*, came Druzil's telepathic instructions. *The soldiers have been instructed not to harm you.*
Kierkan Rufo looked all around anxiously, fearing that the cold sweat on his forehead would give him away. The others seemed unconcerned with him. They were all nervous, even Ivan, crouching and crawling along with the undeniable knowledge that monsters were all about them. They heard the cries of battle somewhere behind them and to the north, and they knew that Shayleigh and Tintagel were hard at work, keeping the pressure off their secretive band.

Rufo pondered the reference to the birch tangle. Elbereth had mentioned the place just a short while before, saying that they would get beyond it in less than an hour. Rufo was running out of time.

* * * * *

Danica crawled along, her crystal-bladed daggers tight in her hands. She saw Elbereth to the side, similarly crawling, making for a goblin guard twenty feet from the two Danica had chosen as her targets.

It had to be done swiftly and quietly; they could smell the goblins in the woods all about them and wanted to avoid battle if at all possible. These unfortunate three were in their path, though, and the companions had no time to go around them. Skirmishes were becoming too common about the group, echoing from both sides and behind. Shayleigh, Tintagel, and the other elves soon would be hard-pressed as the enemy closed in on this section of the forest, and Elbereth's party had to get to Syldritch Trea without delay—to the misfortune of these three goblin guards.

Danica looked over to Elbereth, now in position just a few feet behind his goblin. The elf nodded for her to go first, and Danica agreed, since her task would be more difficult.

She clutched her daggers, feeling the golden tiger sculpture in one hand and the silver dragon in the other. Crouching low, she crossed her wrists in front of her at waist level, with the dagger blades pointing up and out.

The goblins, backs to her, were only two strides away, talking easily, suspecting nothing.

Danica leaped between them. They managed to gasp just once before the monk, in a single movement, snapped her arms out wide, driving the daggers up under their chins. The goblins twitched; one got its hand weakly up to grab Danica's wrist.

A cry to the side turned Danica about. Elbereth's goblin stood facing her, its weapon dropped and its arms held out wide. The creature jerked violently, its face contorted in confusion.

Danica understood when Elbereth's sword came bursting out the front of the doomed creature's chest.

Then only Danica and Elbereth stood. They nodded to each other and dropped back into the brush, holding their positions for a few moments to ensure that no other monsters were about. Together they rejoined the others and explained that the way was now clear.

"We should make the birch tangle without further delay," Elbereth explained softly. "Syldritch Trea is less than a mile to the west of that." Elbereth paused, and a curious expression crossed his face as he regarded Kierkan Rufo, who stood trembling, with sweat rolling down his face.

"What is it?" the elf asked.

"If ye've not the belly for it . . ." Ivan began, but Danica hushed him quickly.

"I cannot get him out of my thoughts," Rufo admitted frantically. The angular man looked all around, his beady, dark eyes darting desperately, as though he expected all the monsters of the Realms to descend upon him.

"He knows of our plans," Rufo explained, trying vainly to keep calm. He stuttered through a few jumbled words, then his control blew away. "He knows!" Rufo cried, and his volume sent the others into defensive crouches, looking all around. "I have doomed you all!"

"Quiet him!" Elbereth whispered, and he slipped out a few steps to ensure that no enemies were nearby.

Danica and Cadderly took Rufo's arms and eased him to a sitting position.

"Who knows?" Cadderly prompted, eyeing Danica, whose scowl gave Cadderly the distinct feeling that she would soon break Rufo's head open.

"It is not my fault," Rufo declared. "I have tried to resist him—the imp!—with all my strength."

"Uh-oh," Pikel muttered, echoing all their thoughts.

"You have tried to resist the imp, but you cannot," Cadderly prompted. "In what way? You must tell me."

"In my head!" Rufo replied, taking care now to keep his voice to a whisper. "The imp follows my thoughts, learns things from me, though I do not tell them to him."

Cadderly looked to Danica, his face twisted in confusion.

"I have never heard of such a thing," he said. "Dorigen's imp is telepathic. That much I learned." He turned back on Rufo. "But to invade your thoughts, and remain there, without your consent?"

"If you are lying . . ." Danica threatened, wagging a fist in Rufo's direction.

"Unless," Cadderly mumbled, scratching his smooth chin and thinking of any old stories that might give him an idea of what was going on. When he looked back to the others, he saw that all of them stared at him, waiting.

"Have you ever seen the imp?" Cadderly asked Rufo.

"Once," the angular man admitted, thinking that he would keep his second meeting, the one with Dorigen, secret at all costs.

"And did the imp give you something to carry?" Cadderly asked. "A personal item, perhaps? Or did he touch you, or handle any of your possessions?" He looked to Ivan and Pikel and nodded.

"What?" was all Rufo could stammer before the dwarves grabbed his ankles and laid him out on the ground. They then began systematically stripping the man, holding up each possession for Cadderly to see, and when he shook his head, the item went flying.

Pikel was about to rip Rufo's tunic open when the dwarf spotted something. "Oo oi!" Pikel squealed, realizing that his find might be important.

"What ye got there?" Ivan asked, and when his eyes widened also, Cadderly and Danica moved over for a look.

"Where did you get that amulet?" Cadderly asked. He figured that their search was at its end, for this amulet, edged in gold and centered with a fabulous emerald, was far beyond Rufo's meager means.

"What amulet?" the angular man replied, perplexed.

"This one," Cadderly explained. He unpinned the thing and held it up for Rufo to see.

Even Danica did not doubt Rufo's sincerely confused expression. Without a thought, Cadderly handed the amulet to Ivan, and the dwarf, with a wink to his brother, produced a frog from his pocket and pinned the amulet to a loose fold in the creature's skin.

"That'll keep the imp-thing guessing," the dwarf explained. " 'Course now I'll be needing to catch me a new supper!"

"This allowed the imp to invade your thoughts," Cadderly explained above the quiet chuckles of Danica and the two dwarves. The young scholar was certain of his guess and continued with some confidence. "Without it, you are free—unless you choose to let him back in."

"And you would not do that, would you?" Danica asked, suddenly grim. She grabbed Rufo by the shoulder and roughly spun him about to stare into her glowering face.

Rufo pulled free and tried to regain some measure of his dignity. "I have admitted my weakness," he said. "Surely I cannot be blamed . . ."

"No one is blaming you," Cadderly answered, speaking more to Danica than Rufo. "Now, you said you have betrayed us. What do you know?"

"The tangle of birch," Rufo said tentatively. "I was instructed to keep out of the way when the enemy attacks."

Cadderly looked to Elbereth, who, satisfied that no enemies were in the area, had come back to stand beside them. "Have you heard?" the young scholar asked.

Elbereth nodded gravely. "The forest is strangely quiet," he replied. "I had suspected that some mischief was afoot." His unyielding stare bored into Rufo. "Now I understand. How much did you tell the imp?"

Cadderly wanted to calm the elf, but he understood that Elbereth's fears went far beyond the safety of their little group. All of the elf's people had come west and would be dangerously exposed if the enemy knew their movements.

"I do not know," Rufo replied, lowering his gaze. "It is . . . was, difficult to mask . . ."

"We must assume that Druzil learned quite a lot from Rufo," Cadderly put in grimly, "about our whereabouts and the position of the elven force." Elbereth's wince made Cadderly pause a moment. "Should one of us go back and find your people and warn them of the danger?" the young scholar offered.

Elbereth thought it over for a moment, sincerely torn. "No," he answered at length. "The best we can do for my people is to finish our business quickly. We can go around the birch tangle and avoid the ambush, though that course will cost us some time."

"And time lost will surely cost more elves their lives," Danica had to add, her unblinking gaze not turning from the angular man.

"I did not wish to come along," Rufo started to protest. But he couldn't maintain his anger and turned away, then finished meekly, "I knew the imp would follow."

"Pity us if you had stayed behind," Danica spat, "for then we would never have learned of your betrayal!"

"Enough of this," Cadderly demanded. "We cannot change what has transpired, and we must not waste our time arguing."

"Agreed," said Elbereth with an approving nod. "We will turn south, then back to the west when the course is clear. And you," he said to Rufo, his eyes narrowing, "if the imp somehow finds its way back into your thoughts, speak at once!" The elf started off then, with Danica falling into line right behind. Rufo went next, flanked by the dwarves, who eyed him suspiciously with every step.

Cadderly hesitated a moment before joining them. The frog Ivan had pinned still sat on the ground at the young scholar's feet. Cadderly knew he was taking a chance as he reached down and removed the amulet, then pinned it under a fold of his own cloak, but it was a risk he decided to take. He had battled Druzil mentally once before, and had won that contest. If the imp tried to make contact with Rufo again, Cadderly would be waiting for him.

Danica and Elbereth noticed several enemy guards crouched in the brush and veered to keep out of harm's way. They wanted no more fights if they could help it, suspecting from Rufo's disclosure that the enemy had set a sizable force in the region for the ambush.

Cadderly felt the telepathic intrusions.

What is taking so long? came the thoughts that the scholar knew belonged to the familiar imp. *The soldiers are in place and grow impatient.*

In response, Cadderly conjured an image of the area they had been in when they had discovered the amulet upon Rufo, an area a short distance east of the birch tangle. He could only hope that Druzil wouldn't recognize his thought patterns as different from Rufo's, and he breathed a little easier when the imp's next communication came to him.

Good, Druzil told him. *You are near the spot. When your companions get moving again, stay close to them until you see the birch, then get low and to the side. Mistress Dorigen would like to speak with you again.*

Then, abruptly, Druzil was gone from Cadderly's thoughts. The young scholar clenched hard on the amulet.

"Cadderly?" he heard distantly. His eyes popped open—he hadn't realized that they were closed—and he saw his companions standing around him, staring curiously.

"It is nothing," he tried to explain. Elbereth grabbed his hand and forced it open.

"You should have been rid of this evil item," the elf scolded.

"I do not fear the imp," Cadderly replied. His confident smile gave the others some measure of relief. That smile disappeared suddenly when Cadderly looked upon Rufo, though, given the new revelations concerning his tall companion. So you have met Dorigen? Cadderly mused, but he kept his thoughts private, fearing that revealing what the imp had told him would cause trouble that the party could ill afford.

"Let us go on," Cadderly bade. "We have fooled our enemies. They still sit, anticipating an ambush at the birch tangle, but they grow impatient."

Elbereth took the lead immediately, Danica following on his heels, and Cadderly and the others in a pack behind.

"Ye didn't happen to bring along me frog?" Ivan asked hopefully, rubbing his belly. Cadderly only smiled and shook his head.

Elbereth turned back to the west a short while later, the elf hastening them along and slipping in and out of the shadows to the side and ahead with obvious urgency. They came down one slope into a region with less undergrowth than usual. Thick oaks dominated the area, and, though these were not much larger than the other trees of Shilmista, Cadderly could sense their age, and could sense, too, a brooding sentience; as if he were being watched from all sides and from above.

He knew they had come to Syldritch Trea. He moved over to one of the oaks and felt its rough bark, toughened by the passing years, the birth and death of many centuries. What tales these trees might tell him, and Cadderly believed that they could indeed. He believed that the oaks somehow could, and would if he had the time and patience to pause and listen.

Pikel, too, seemed caught in the sudden enchantment of this most ancient grove. The dwarf called out, "Oo!" several times as he hopped happily from oak to oak. He hugged one so tightly that, when he turned away, his hairy face was creased by imprints of the tree's bark.

"We have come to Syldritch Trea," Elbereth announced, though he could see that his companions, with the possible exceptions of Ivan and Rufo, had already realized that. Danica nodded, then scrambled up the tallest oak she could find and looked back to the east to see what storms might be brewing.

Cadderly took out the book of Dellanil Quil'quien reverently, for the tome seemed to hold much more meaning in this place. He looked to Elbereth, his jaw set firmly, and opened the book to the ancient summons. He felt again the sheer power of the trees, their inner life so different from any trees he had experienced before, and he knew beyond doubt that he had done right in convincing the elf prince to come to this place. He knew, too, the truth of his words when he again declared to those around him, "It will work."

* * * * *

Temmerisa reared and Shayleigh dropped from her saddle. Around her she saw only trees, but she knew from memory that no trees should have stood in this place.

"Tintagel?" she called softly. In response, one of the trees shifted form, becoming the elf wizard and stepping out to greet Shayleigh.

"Well met," Tintagel answered, smiling in spite of their dire situation.

Shayleigh returned the grin and looked around at the unnatural trees. "How many?" she asked.

"A score and seven," the blue-eyed wizard replied. "It is my most powerful spell and one that should catch our enemies by surprise. Do you like my work?"

Shayleigh imagined the astonishment on the passing orcs' and goblins' faces as twenty-seven illusionary trees reverted to their true forms as elven warriors! Her widening grin answered Tintagel's question.

"How go the other fronts?" the elf wizard asked.

Shayleigh's smile disappeared. "Not well," she admitted. "Our enemies have gone farther south than we believed. And those monsters in the east have learned of our movement and are sweeping back toward the west. We have scouts searching now to see if those southwest of here are moving east to join them, or if we still have an escape route open to us."

Tintagel considered the grim news. When they had formulated their plans to come out near Syldritch Trea, they had known their success likely would depend on secrecy. Now, somehow, the enemy apparently understood the scale of their movement, and that boded ill indeed.

The tension did not lessen a short time later when several elves rode up, King Galladel at the lead.

"The south is blocked," the elf king proclaimed in a superior tone. "Our folly in coming here is revealed to us in full."

Shayleigh did not turn away under the elf king's accusing stare. Only a few of Shilmista's elves, most notably Galladel, had argued against the action, but so determined were most of the people, Shayleigh included, that the elf king finally had agreed to the desperate plan.

Even with the enemy moving to surround them, Shayleigh held firm to her belief that they had done the right thing in trusting in Shilmista's magic. Shayleigh believed, too, that her dear forest was worth dying for.

"We will find the weakest point in their advancing line," Galladel reasoned. "If we move fast and hard, perhaps we might break through."

"When we came out here, we knew that our success would depend on Elbereth's call to Syldritch Trea," Tintagel reminded them. "If we had not the courage to see that through, then we should not have come out at all."

Galladel glared at him. "We are barely a hundred strong," he said, "with only a handful of horses. Our enemy's force numbers in the thousands, giants and ogres among their ranks."

"Let the battle begin then," Shayleigh added. "Let our enemies come on, every one. When it is ended, Shilmista will again belong to the elves!"

"When it is over," Galladel growled, "Shilmista will be no more."

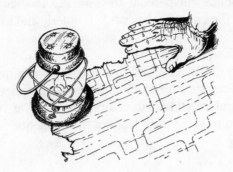

Twenty
When Magic Filled the Air

What is the delay? came a telepathic call, but Cadderly didn't have time for the imp's intrusions. He dropped the amulet to the dirt and placed his foot over it, then took up Dellanil's book and continued his scan, double-checking his translation before uttering the words to Elbereth.

Where are you? came Druzil's call again, but it was distant, and Cadderly easily pushed it far away. Still, the young scholar recognized the desperation in Druzil's thoughts and knew the clever imp would remain active.

"We must hurry," Cadderly implored Elbereth. "Our enemies will soon understand that we have traveled around them."

Elbereth rubbed his hands slowly across the bark of the nearest oak, gathering strength from the wood's solidity. He was the most nervous of the group. If the summons failed, all of them would likely lose their lives, but Elbereth stood to lose even more. The basis of his existence, the magic of Shilmista, hung in the balance. If the trees did not answer his call this time, his father's dismal beliefs— that magic no longer filled Shilmista's clear air—would be proven true, to the dismay and doom of all of Elbereth's people.

Cadderly held the book open before him. "Are you ready?" the young scholar asked.

"Flames in the east!" came Danica's call from the high boughs of a nearby tree. Her companions on the ground heard the branches rustling as Danica made a swift descent. "A force approaches swiftly."

Cadderly nodded to Elbereth, gaining the elf's attention. "*Seide plein una malabreche,*" the scholar began slowly.

Elbereth held his hands out wide to the wood and walked around the nearest oaks as he echoed the words. "*Seide plein una malabreche.*"

"Come along," Danica whispered to the dwarves and, somewhat hesitantly, to Rufo. "We shall keep the enemy at bay while Cadderly and Elbereth complete the calling."

"Oh," moaned a disappointed Pikel.

"What's an Elbereth?" Ivan asked, but his wry smile quickly diffused Danica's sudden frown. They took up positions along the perimeter of Syldritch Trea, hoping that their friends would finish before the enemy arrived.

None of them had to voice their fears of the consequences should the summons fail.

* * * * *

The great white horse carried Shayleigh effortlessly, springing over patches of brush and gliding between the tightly packed trees. Shayleigh reined in Temmerisa many times, not wanting to outdistance King Galladel and the seven other elven riders. The great horse heeded her commands, though the maiden could sense from the rippling muscles in Temmerisa's shining white neck that the horse wanted to run strong and hard.

A host of orcs trailed the elven troupe, rushing wildly, hungrily, in pursuit, hooting and howling. A hundred strong, they numbered as many as all of the elves remaining in the forest, and their evil kin, many times their number, were all around them. Soon, the orcs believed, this small elven band would be surrounded and the slaughter would begin.

So the orcs believed, and so Galladel and Shayleigh and the other elves wanted the orcs to believe.

Shayleigh led them into a wide expanse of low shrubs and young trees. The elven riders took extra care to avoid the saplings here, practically walking their mounts and taking no heed of the orc force fast closing from behind.

The elves came to the opposite edge of the expanse, where the forest darkened once more under the canopy of older growth, and urged their horses into the shadows. Just a short way in, they reared and turned about.

Oblivious to the danger, the stupid orcs charged through the open area.

Tintagel waited until all the baited monsters had come within the perimeter of his devious trap. Then the wizard stepped from his tree form and uttered a triggering rune. A score and seven other trees reverted to their true elven forms and stepped into the middle of the orcish host. They cut into the unsuspecting orcs from every angle, each elf felling several of the foul beasts before the orcs began to comprehend what had happened.

Shayleigh held Temmerisa back no longer. The mighty steed burst out of the shadows and trampled an orc, and the warrior atop it bent low in her saddle, her golden hair flying wildly behind her and her gleaming sword hacking at any monster that strayed too near.

Galladel and the others charged right behind, circling the perimeter of the open region, killing all those orcs that thought to flee. The wretched creatures dove and rolled and tried to run, but ultimately had nowhere to go.

Elven bows twanged mercilessly; elven swords bit deep into orcish flesh.

It was over in seconds; orc bodies covering the open expanse. None of the elves held any notions of victory, though, and not one of them was smiling. They knew that this battle was just beginning. Cries of another fight sprang up somewhere to the east, and farther north the enemy had started fires. The season had not been dry, and the fires did not rush through the forest, but they were fueled by the prodding of many, many monsters.

Another group of elves, flushed out by the flames, sprinted by the area, with hulking orogs in close pursuit.

"Take to the shadows!" Shayleigh cried, and most of Tintagel's contingent already moved for the trees, knowing that to get caught in the open was to die.

Shayleigh didn't look back to her king for instructions. For the fiery elven maiden, the appropriate course was easy to discern. Amid all the confusion of the expanding battle and swirling smoke, she had clearly seen a new enemy to strike.

"Come, Temmerisa!" she cried, and the spirited horse, apparently in complete agreement with its courageous rider, broke into a wild charge in pursuit of the orogs chasing the elves.

One of the other riders moved to follow Shayleigh, but Galladel held him back.

"We eight shall stay together," the elf king said sternly. "The fight will come in full, and if Elbereth's attempt does not awaken the trees, our course will be whichever way is quickest from Shilmista's bloody boughs. "The other riders could tell by Galladel's grim tone that their king did not hold out much hope for his son's attempt. And at that dark time, with the forest thick with monsters and smoke, cries of battle erupting from every direction, and hundreds, perhaps thousands, of enemy soldiers moving to surround them, not one of Galladel's cavalry companions could muster the courage to dispute the king's fears.

* * * * *

"*Teague!*" Cadderly cried.

"*Teague!*" he heard Elbereth repeat.

The young scholar inadvertently glanced over his shoulder, hearing the fighting not too far away. "Concentrate!" he growled, more to himself than to Elbereth, and he forced his gaze down into the book of Dellanil Quil'quien and looked for the next phrase in the woodland summons.

"*Teague!*" Elbereth echoed several more times, growing nearly as frantic as Cadderly. His people were dying while he danced about an oak grove; he could not ignore that his sword was needed just a few hundred feet away.

Cadderly saw that the elf prince was slipping from the trance. The young scholar dropped the book—somehow guessing that he would not need it, that the ancient words had become a part of him, or rather, that their meaning was now so crystalline clear to him that he could follow the path of their cant from his heart alone.

"What're ye doing . . . ?" he heard Ivan stammer. Kierkan Rufo added something Cadderly could not discern, and Pikel piped in with "Huh?"

Cadderly blocked them all from his mind. He rushed over to Elbereth and grabbed the elf prince's hands, tearing one's stubborn grasp from Elbereth's sword hilt.

"*Teague immen syldritch fae,*" the young scholar said firmly. Whether it was his tone or his grave expression, he could not tell, but he knew then that he had gained Elbereth's full attention, that by his demands, Elbereth had put the closing battle back out of his thoughts. Elbereth took up the chant, and Cadderly continued, keeping a few words ahead of the mesmerized elf.

The young scholar felt a power budding within him, an awakening of his soul and a strength he never suspected he possessed. His words came faster—too fast for anyone to possibly keep up.

And yet, Elbereth, pulled along by a similar inner urgency, caught in the throes of building magic, repeated with perfection each of the phrases Cadderly uttered, matched the young scholar's timbre and inflection as perfectly as a mountain echo.

Then Elbereth and Cadderly spoke as one, the words, the summons, coming from both their mouths in unison.

It was impossible, Cadderly knew. Neither of them knew the phrases well enough to recite them from memory. But the young scholar did not doubt that their words rang perfectly, that they spoke exactly as Dellanil Quil'quien had spoken on a mystical day centuries before.

They neared the end; their phrases slowed as the final runes built within. Cadderly grabbed Elbereth's hands, looking for support, unable to contain the power.

Elbereth, equally terrified, held on with all his strength.

"*A intunivial dolas quey!*" they cried together, the words torn from their hearts by a power that consumed their minds and left their bodies leaning heavily against one another. Together they slipped down to the thick grass.

Cadderly nearly swooned—in truth, he wasn't certain if he had blacked out for a moment—and when he looked to Elbereth, he saw that the elf wore the same expression of weariness and confusion. Their companions were all about them, even Kierkan Rufo, wearing a mien of concern.

"Ye all right, lad?" Cadderly heard Ivan ask, and the young scholar wasn't really certain how he should answer.

With the dwarves' help, Cadderly managed to get back to his feet, while Danica and Rufo helped Elbereth to stand. The forest was quiet, except for the continuing din of distant battle.

"It did not work," Elbereth groaned after many long moments had slipped by.

Cadderly held his hand up to stop the elf from continuing. He remembered the sounds of birds in the trees before the summoning, but now there were none. It could have been his and Elbereth's shouting that had scared them off, or perhaps they had taken flight from the approaching fight, but Cadderly thought differently. He sensed the stillness of Syldritch Trea to be a prelude, a deceptive calm.

"What do you know?" Danica asked him, moving to his side. She studied his face a moment longer, then reiterated, "What do you know?"

"Do you feel it?" Cadderly finally replied, looking all around at the great oaks. "The mounting energy?" Hardly taking note of his own actions, he bent down and picked up the dropped amulet, slipping it into a deep pocket. "Do you feel it?" he asked again, more insistently.

Danica did feel it, an awakening, a growing sentience all about her, as though she was being watched. She looked to Elbereth, and he, too, glanced about in anticipation.

"Oo," Pikel remarked, but his spoken thought fell on deaf ears.

"What is it?" Ivan growled uncomfortably. He took up his axe and hopped in circles, eyeing the trees suspiciously.

Behind Kierkan Rufo, the earth trembled. The angular man spun about to see a gigantic root tear up through the ground. There came a rustle as the branches of a huge oak began to shake, and the sound increased, multiplied, as several other trees joined in.

"What have we done?" Elbereth asked, his tone reflecting amazement and trepidation.

Cadderly was too entranced to answer. More roots came up through the ground; more branches shook and bent.

Ivan seemed on the verge of exploding, holding his axe as though to rush over and chop down the nearest tree. Next to him, Pikel hopped up and down in glee, thrilled by the growing display of druidic magic. The round-shouldered dwarf grabbed his nervous brother's weapon arm and wagged a finger back and forth in Ivan's face.

The companions didn't even notice that they were all moving closer together, back-to-back.

The first tree, the one behind Rufo, broke free of the ground and took a sliding stride toward them.

"Do something!" the terrified man said to Elbereth.

All fear had left the elf prince. He jumped out in front of Rufo and cried, "I am Elbereth, son of Galladel, son of Gil Telleman, son of Dellanil Quil'quien! War has come to Shilmista, a great force not seen since the days of my father's father's father! Thus I have summoned you, guardians of Shilmista, to march beside me and cleanse this, our home!"

Another great tree moved over to join the first, and others followed suit. Elbereth took up the lead, thinking to head straight for the battle, but Ivan patted the elf's shoulder, turning him about.

"Fine words, elf," the obviously relieved dwarf offered.

Elbereth smiled grimly and looked to Danica, who stood quietly beside

Cadderly. Both the young scholar and the woman understood the elf prince's tentative intentions from the look on his face, and, almost in unison, they smiled and nodded their agreement. Elbereth returned the smile and pulled Ivan beside him at the lead of the column. Together they started off, unlikely allies. Pikel, more interested in the continuing spectacle of the moving trees than in anything that lay ahead, came behind.

Kierkan Rufo looked about anxiously, not knowing where he fit in. As he came to trust that the great oaks would not harm him, his horror of the trees began to wane and he found his place in it all. He climbed one of the oaks, moving as high as he could—higher, he figured, than a goblin could throw its spear.

Cadderly continued to hold Danica back as the woodland column, some dozen or so ancient trees, slipped past. "Dorigen knew where we were going," he explained as the thunder of the tree walk diminished. "And for whatever reason, she wants me as her prisoner."

Danica motioned to a shadowy hollow to the side, and she and Cadderly took up a watch there, agreeing that they would set out after Elbereth and the others if the wizard did not appear in the next few minutes.

* * * * *

A group of orogs stared curiously at the spectacle, not sure of what to make of the approaching oaks. They jostled each other and scratched at their scraggly hair, pointing and lifting spears the trees' way in an almost comic threat.

They understood more—at least that these gigantic trees were not friendly things—when they saw an elf and two dwarves hop down from the closest tree's lowest branches. The orogs took up a unified hoot and one launched its spear, but they still did not seem to fathom how they should react to such a display.

Ivan, Pikel, and Elbereth charged at them, eager to begin the fight.

The lead tree's reach was longer, though, and it sent huge branches crashing down upon the beasts, battering and thrashing them. A couple of orogs slipped away, out of range, and ran straight off, not daring to look back.

"Aw, this ain't about to be much fun!" Ivan roared, for by the time he and his two companions reached the orogs, not a single one of the beasts could offer any resistance.

"Except fun to watch!" Ivan quickly added, noticing an orog high in the air, kicking futilely against the stranglehold one branch had put around its neck.

The surly dwarf grabbed Pikel by the arm. "Come, me brother!" Ivan yelled. "Let's find a goblin head to cleave!"

Pikel looked back longingly to the moving oaks, not wanting to part from them. But there were indeed many monsters about, and it didn't take Ivan long to convince his equally fierce brother that the games had just begun.

Elbereth watched them sprint off into the shadows, falling immediately over a small band of goblins. In just a few seconds, the two remaining goblins were running fast into the forest, Ivan and Pikel hot on their heels.

The elf prince managed a weak smile, and managed, too, to hope that the day might yet be won.

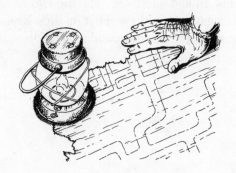

Twenty-One

Long Live the King

T he battle begins in full," Danica whispered in Cadderly's ear. "We must go."
Cadderly held her in place, pulled her lower into the shadows. He
sensed something, a presence, perhaps, and knew instinctively that danger was about. Unconsciously, the young scholar dropped a hand into a pocket of his traveling cloak and closed his fingers around the tiny amulet.

"Druzil," he whispered, surprised as he spoke the word. Danica looked at him curiously.

"The amulet works both ways," Cadderly realized. "I know the imp is nearby. And if the imp is about . . ."

As if on cue, Dorigen stepped into the clearing in the wake of the passing trees. Cadderly and Danica crouched lower, but the wizard was obviously intent on the now-distant spectacle of the marching trees.

Danica pointed to the west, then started stealthily away, circling behind the wizard. Not daring to speak a word, Cadderly held up the amulet to remind her that Dorigen's devilish henchman was probably also in the area, and probably invisible.

"What have you done?" Dorigen cried, and Cadderly nearly fainted from fear, thinking that she was addressing him. Her narrow-eyed gaze remained locked on the moving trees, though. She thrust her fist out in front of her and cried, "*Fete*," an elvish word for fire.

A jet of flame roared from Dorigen's hand—Cadderly thought that perhaps it came from a ring—a burning line that stretched across the yards to engulf the last tree in the procession.

"*Fete!*" the wizard repeated, and the flames did not relent. She moved her hand about, shifting the angle of the fire to immolate the tree. The great oak

394

turned its cumbersome bulk about, inadvertently setting small fires on the trees beside it. It reached out with a long root for Dorigen, but the wizard lowered her hand in line with the root and burned it away to nothingness.

So horrified at the sheer wickedness of Dorigen's destructive actions, Cadderly couldn't draw his breath. He looked to his right, the west, for some sign of Danica, praying that his love would come out and stop Dorigen's carnage. But while Danica was indeed concealed in the brush behind the wizard, she couldn't easily get to Dorigen. Three orogs had moved out of the shadows and taken up a defensive position behind and to either side of the wizard.

The tree crackled and split apart, falling into a flaming heap. Dorigen stopped her attack, but kept her fist clenched, trying, it appeared, to make out another target through the smoke and flames.

Cadderly knew he could not allow that to happen.

Dorigen extended her fist again and started to utter the triggering rune, but she stopped, distracted by a curious sight off to the side. A beam of light emanated through the brush and from the shadows, rocking slowly back and forth. Keeping her fist extended, the wizard slowly moved over to investigate.

Her expression turned to one of curiosity as she neared the shadowed hollow. A cylindrical tube, the source of the light beam, rocked along the inner edge of a light blue, wide-brimmed hat that had been placed on its side. Dorigen didn't recognize the hat, but she had seen the cylindrical object before, inside the pack belonging to the young priest, Cadderly.

Dorigen realized that she was vulnerable, knew that she should be wary of the young priest, but pride had always been her greatest weakness.

A short distance away, low behind the trunk of a tree, Cadderly unscrewed his feathered ring, pulled back the ram head of his walking stick, and inserted the dart. He took great care to keep it out of the sunlight, but he was less than confident as he pursed his lips against his blowgun and drew a bead on Dorigen.

"Where are you, young priest?" Dorigen called. She turned to signal to her orog guards, then flinched as something small and sharp struck her on the cheek.

"What?" she stammered, pulling free the feathered dart. She nearly laughed aloud at the puny thing.

"Damn," Cadderly groaned, seeing her still standing. Dorigen yawned then, profoundly, and wiped bleary eyes.

Cadderly knew that his chance was slipping by. He jumped from the side of the tree and rushed at his enemy.

Seeing their mistress endangered, the orogs howled and charged to intercept the young scholar. They found Danica instead, suddenly, and each tasted a foot or a fist before it realized what had happened.

Dorigen didn't seem to need them, though. Her fist, still clenched, pointed to greet Cadderly—he could see now that it was the onyx ring she wore on that hand. He couldn't possibly get to her in time, and he had no other weapons to strike with from a distance.

Dorigen began to speak—Cadderly expected the words to fall over him like the pronouncement of doom.

* * * * *

"Where will you hide, elf king?" Ragnor roared above the ring of steel and the cries of the dying.

Galladel reined in his horse and wheeled about, as did the others of his cavalry group.

"There!" one of the elves shouted, pointing to a break in a line of beech trees. There stood Ragnor in all his evil splendor, his bottom tusk sticking up grotesquely over his upper lip and his elite bugbear guards fanned out in a semicircle around him, their sharp-tipped tridents gleaming wickedly. Galladel led the charge, the seven other riders bravely at his side.

The elf king pulled up short, though, knowing that he and his troops could not get through Ragnor's defensive ring. Somehow, Galladel realized, he would have to get to the ogrillon, would have to strike a decisive blow in the lopsided battle.

"You are Ragnor?" Galladel cried in a derisive tone. "He who hides behind his minions, who cowers while others die in his name?"

The ogrillon's laughter defeated Galladel's bluster. "I am Ragnor!" the beast proclaimed. "Who claims Shilmista as his own. Come, pitiful elf king, and pass your crown to one who deserves it!" The ogrillon reached over his shoulder and pulled out his huge and heavy broadsword.

"Do not, my king," one of Galladel's escorts said to him.

"Together we can crush their ranks," offered another.

Galladel put his slender hand up to quiet them all. The elf king thought of his past failures, of the time he had failed to awaken the trees at the price of many elven lives. Truly, he was weary and wanted only to travel to Evermeet. But noble, too, was the elf king of Shilmista, and now he saw his duty clearly before him. He spurred his horse ahead a few strides, ordering his escort to stay back.

Ragnor's bugbears parted, and Galladel's charge was on. He thought to bury the ogrillon, smash straight in with his powerful steed and crush the invader. His plans came to a crashing end as a huge boulder, hurled by a giant in the shadows, caught his horse on the flank and sent the poor, doomed beast spinning to the ground.

Galladel's escort roared and charged; the bugbears and the giant moved quickly to block them. When Galladel pulled himself from the pile and regained his feet, shaken but not seriously injured, he found himself alone, faced off against mighty Ragnor.

"Now the fight is fair!" Ragnor growled, steadily advancing.

Galladel readied his own sword. How much larger the brutish ogrillon seemed to him now, with his horse lying dead at his side.

* * * * *

Cadderly fully expected to be fried long before he got to Dorigen. The wizard began to utter the triggering rune, but yawned instead as the sleep poison continued to work its insidious way inside her.

Cadderly didn't hesitate. He charged straight in, launching a roundhouse, two-handed swing with his walking stick that caught Dorigen on the side of the head and blasted her to the ground. In all his life, Cadderly had never hit anything so very hard.

Dorigen lay still at his feet, eyes closed and blood trickling from a cut the ram's head had torn along her ear.

The sight unnerved Cadderly, sent his thoughts spinning back to the tragic events of a few weeks before. Barjin's dead eyes hovered about the young scholar as he looked down at Dorigen, praying that she was not dead.

* * * * *

Danica uttered no such prayers for the first orog she had felled. She had hit the beast squarely in the throat and knew that its windpipe was crushed and that it soon would suffocate. The other two fought savagely, though, despite the wounds Danica had inflicted. Wielding finely crafted, razor-edged swords, they soon had the young woman backing steadily away.

A sword cut just above her head as she ducked. She kicked straight out, connecting on the monster's thigh, but had to back off as the other monster pressed her savagely. One, two, and three, came the monster's wicked swipes, each missing the scrambling woman by no more than an inch.

Then Danica was up again, balanced on the balls of her feet. The orog she had kicked lagged behind its companion in the pursuit, and Danica found her opening.

The single orog thrust its sword straight at her. Faster than the weapon could get to her, Danica fell into a crouch, nearly sitting upon the ground, then came up hard and angled in toward her attacker, the fingers of her right hand bent in tightly against themselves. Her left arm led the way, brushing aside the orog's sword, leaving the monster defenseless. Her deadly right arm, coiled tight against her chest, snapped in through the opening, slamming her open palm into the hollow of the orog's chest with every ounce of power the young woman could throw into it.

The beast hopped two feet from the ground and landed back to its feet, breathless, then it fell dead.

The remaining orog, moving in on the young woman, looked at its fallen companion curiously, then abruptly changed its course, howling and hooting and scrambling for the trees.

Danica started to follow, then dropped to her knees in surprise as something whistled past her, just a few feet to the side. She understood when the dart hit the orog in the back and exploded, throwing the creature face down on the ground. It gasped once for breath that would not come, and lay very still.

Danica looked back to see Cadderly, his crossbow, taken from the unconscious wizard, securely in his hand. Standing over Dorigen, he almost seemed a terrible thing to Danica, his visage stern and angry.

Danica guessed what emotions tore at poor Cadderly; she understood the guilt and confusion that had brought him to this point. But now was not the time for weakness. "Finish her," Danica instructed coldly. She glanced around quickly to ensure that there were no more enemies in the area, then ran after the departing trees, where the larger battles had been joined.

Cadderly looked down to the unconscious wizard, disgusted at what he knew he must do.

*　*　*　*　*

When he had led the procession from Syldritch Trea, Elbereth had thought to keep his forces together and cut a wedge through the enemy lines to rejoin his people. As the elf prince came upon the area of battle, though, he saw the folly of his plans.

There was no line to cut through, and no clear group of his own people to rejoin. Chaos ruled in Shilmista this day, a wild scramble of elf and goblinoid, giant trees and giantkin.

"Good fighting, elf!" were the last words Elbereth heard from Ivan, circling back out of the trees with Pikel, as the elf prince sprinted off to the side to engage a bugbear moving along a patch of brambles.

By the time Elbereth had finished the creature, the trees had moved past and split up, many going for the fires burning in the north or for the cries of battle in the east, and the dwarves were nowhere to be seen. Too busy to go in search of them, Elbereth sounded his horn, a call that he hoped would soon be answered.

Temmerisa appeared in mere seconds, flying like the wind, with Shayleigh holding tight to the steed's reins. The horse ran down one goblin, and leaped over several others as they crawled through the thicket.

"The trees!" Shayleigh cried, her words choked with hope and astonishment. She looked back over her shoulder to one oak that was pounding down a host of monsters. "Shilmista has come alive!"

Shayleigh dropped from the saddle. "Take Temmerisa," she said quickly to Elbereth.

"The horse is in fine hands," Elbereth replied, refusing the bridle. "I only called to ensure that Temmerisa and his rider were still about."

"Take him!" Shayleigh implored the elf prince. "Find your father. I have heard whispers that he battles Ragnor, and if that is true, then he will need his son beside him!"

Elbereth needed to hear nothing more to convince him. He grabbed the bridle and swung up into the saddle. "Where are they?" he cried.

"The line of beech!" Shayleigh replied. She started to warn Elbereth about the bugbear guard, but stopped, realizing that the elf prince, already flying away on his powerful mount, was too far gone to hear her.

Elbereth pounded through the forest. He saw dozens of small encounters where his sword might have been of use, but he had not the time. Galladel battling Ragnor! The thought stuck in Elbereth's throat and stuck his heart like a sharp pin. He recalled his own painful encounter with the powerful ogrillon, a fight he would have lost. Elbereth was more highly regarded in swordplay than was Galladel.

Elbereth ducked under a low branch and pulled Temmerisa in a tight turn through a narrow gap between two maples, then urged the horse into a long leap across a patch of brambles. He could feel the lather on Temmerisa's muscled neck, could hear the proud steed's lungs straining to pull in the air needed for such exertion.

Another leap, another turn, then a straight charge, and Temmerisa seemed up to the task, running hard, sensing its beloved master's urgency.

Elbereth caught sight of the giant out of the corner of his eye, saw the hurled boulder rushing in. He yanked hard on Temmerisa's reins, turning the horse aside, but not fully out of harm's way. The white stallion went down under the force of that impact, but came right back up, stubbornly, and continued on its way.

"We will pay back that beast," Elbereth promised, slapping his precious steed's neck. Temmerisa snorted, lowered its great head, and charged on.

* * * * *

Ivan and Pikel tried as best they could to stay in the vicinity of the marching trees. Every orc or goblin the dwarves encountered slowed them down, though, while the oaks walked right through, scattering horrified monsters wherever they went.

The dwarves heard elven cheers from all about, though they saw few of Elbereth's people. Not that they minded; the brothers were certainly more interested in spotting enemies than in finding allies they didn't really believe they needed.

Then the trees were far beyond them, fanning out in their steady march, and the Bouldershoulders were all alone.

"Uh-oh," Pikel remarked, suspecting what was to come. Sure enough, dozens of monsters appeared from their concealment in the wake of the passing trees, dozens of monsters with no apparent targets other than the dwarven brothers.

"Get yerself ready for some fighting," Ivan said to Pikel.

The words were hardly necessary; Pikel smashed one orc even as Ivan spoke.

Then Pikel grabbed his brother and scrambled to the side, under the low-hanging, thick boughs of some pines. Ivan understood his brother's intent, and wisdom, as soon as the monsters closed in on them, for the close quarters and low visibility favored the outnumbered dwarves.

Still, almost everywhere that Ivan swung his axe, blindly or not, he found some monster waiting to catch it and a dozen others in line behind, ready to step in.

* * * * *

Safe in his high perch, Kierkan Rufo thought himself quite clever. The angular man had no intention of playing any role in this horrific battle beyond that of observer, and in that regard, he thoroughly enjoyed watching the pitiful goblins and orcs and orogs fleeing before the incredible power of his moving oak.

He changed his mind abruptly when the oak stumbled upon a different enemy: two giants that were not so cowardly and not so small. The tree shuddered violently as a boulder slammed against its trunk. It swung a branch at the nearest monster, connecting solidly, but the giant, instead of falling dead, grabbed the limb and twisted.

Above, Rufo heard the sharp crack of living wood and thought he would faint away.

Another branch swung in to pound on the monster, but the second giant got in close to the trunk, grabbing on with frightening strength. The giant heaved and pulled, and the huge oak swayed to one side and then the other.

More branches descended over the more distant giant, battering it and lashing it. The monster caught a few and snapped them apart with its huge hands, but the beatings were taking a heavy toll. Soon the giant fell to its knees, and, soon after that, the oak pounded it to the ground.

Another thick branch, the lowest on the great tree, wrapped about the trunk, encircling the tugging giant in an unbreakable hold.

Kierkan Rufo found himself cheering the tree on as the giant fought for its breath. The angular man thought the battle won, thought that his oak could finish this foe and move on, hopefully to safer and smaller opponents.

The gasping giant slumped as low as it could get on its thick, trunklike legs, then heaved for all its life, pushing up and to the side.

One of the oak's roots bent back on itself, and the tree went down in a heap, never to rise again, clutched in a death grip with its doomed destroyer. More branches wriggled in to ensure the giant's fate.

Rufo was sure that one of his legs had been broken, though he couldn't see the leg, pinned underneath a huge tree branch. He thought of crying out, then realized the stupidity of that. Many more monsters than allies were about to hear him.

He scooped away some dirt, digging a shallow pit, then he pulled as many small, leafy branches over him as he could and lay very still.

* * * * *

Danica came into the chaos with her mouth hanging open in amazement. Never had the young woman witnessed such destruction. She saw the tree go down with the giant, then another tree went down, farther in, under a press of bugbears.

Danica looked back behind her, worried for Cadderly. She couldn't protect him this time—she didn't really believe she could protect herself. With a resigned shrug and one longing glance back to where she had left the young scholar, the young woman set off, knowing that she would not have difficulty finding an enemy to hit.

A resounding "Oo oi!" turned her head to a grove of thick pines. A bugbear rushed out desperately, followed by a flying club. The weapon took the creature in the legs, knocking it to the ground. Before it could rise, Pikel ran out, collected his club, and splattered the bugbear's head against the ground. The dwarf looked up at Danica, his white smile shining within the layer of gore that covered his face.

Despite the craziness and danger all about her, Danica returned his smile and winked at the dwarf, and both she and Pikel suspected that it would be a wink of farewell.

Pikel disappeared back into the pines, and Danica bent low and took out her twin daggers. Then the young monk went a-hunting.

* * * * *

Cadderly fumbled with the *Tome of Universal Harmony*, trying to find some answers that would offer him escape from the task Danica and the insane situation had placed upon his shoulders. Dorigen lay very still below him, groaning softly every now and then.

More important was the growing roar of the battle. Cadderly knew that he could not afford to delay much longer, that he should join in the fight beside his friends, and that even if he did not, the battle would likely come to him all too soon. He had his retrieved crossbow reloaded—only five darts remained—and lying ready atop the fallen wizard.

The pages of the great book seemed a blur to him; in his frantic state of mind, he could hardly read the words, much less discern some value in them. Then he was pulled from the pages altogether, distracted by a distinct sensation that he was not alone. He spent a brief moment concentrating on that feeling, focusing his thoughts.

Slowly, Cadderly reached down and took up the crossbow. He spun about, letting his senses guide him where his eyes could not, and fired.

The explosive dart slammed against the trunk of a sapling, blasting the tree apart. Just to the side of it Cadderly heard a sudden flap of leathery wings.

"You cannot hide from me, Druzil!" the young scholar cried. "I know where you are!"

The sound of beating wings faded away into the forest and Cadderly could not prevent a grin of superiority from crossing his face. Druzil would not bother him again.

Dorigen groaned and began to shift her weight, groggily trying to get up to her elbows. Cadderly turned the crossbow down at her and loaded another dart.

His eyes widened in shock at his actions; how could he think of killing the defenseless woman, and how could he think of using his damning weapon to commit the foul deed? His breath came in gasps; Barjin's eyes stared at him from the shadows.

He dropped the bow and took up the book, closing it and grasping it tightly in both hands.

"This is not what you had in mind when you gave this to me," he admitted, as though he were addressing Headmistress Pertelope, then he slammed the heavy tome on the back of Dorigen's head, again dropping her flat to the ground.

Cadderly worked frantically, before the wizard recovered again. He pulled three rings from Dorigen's hands: one her signet ring bearing the design of this sect of Talona; one of gold and set with a shining black onyx (this was the one that Cadderly suspected had shot the magical flames); and the last of gold and set with several small diamond chips. The wizard's robe came off next, Cadderly stuffing it into his backpack. He found a slender wand slipped under a tie in Dorigen's undergarments, and fumbled through any pouches or pockets in her remaining clothing, making certain that she had no more magical devices or spell components.

When he was done, he stood staring at the helpless woman, wondering what to do next. Some spells, he knew, required no physical components, and others used small and common items that could be found almost anywhere. If he left Dorigen like this, she might still play a role in the continuing battle, might wake up and kill any of them, kill Danica, perhaps, by uttering a few simple syllables.

Outraged by that thought, Cadderly grabbed his walking stick and laid the wizard's hands out to the side. Grimacing as he swung, he smashed Dorigen's fingers, on one hand and then the other, repeatedly, until her hands were black and blue and wickedly swollen. Through it all, the drugged and battered wizard only groaned softly and made no move to pull her hands away.

Cadderly gathered his possessions, placed the bandoleer with the remaining darts over his shoulder, and started away, not having any idea of where he should go.

* * * * *

At last Elbereth spotted his father, fighting in the small clearing with huge Ragnor. The elf prince knew it would take him some time to circumvent the many other battles in the area to get near Galladel, and he knew, too, that Ragnor was fast gaining an advantage.

He watched his father try a desperate, straightforward strike. Ragnor caught the elf king's arm and sent his sword in an overhand chop, which Galladel stopped by grabbing the ogrillon's wrist. It all seemed horribly familiar to

Elbereth. He wanted to scream a warning, wanted to destroy himself for not telling his father of the ogrillon's favorite tactic.

The stiletto popped from Ragnor's sword hilt, straight down at Galladel's vulnerable head, and Elbereth could only watch.

They continued their struggle for another moment before Ragnor freed his huge arm and plunged it down.

Suddenly, so suddenly, Elbereth was king of Shilmista.

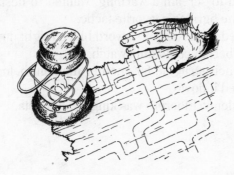

Twenty-Two

Visions of Hell

The mighty horse stormed in, bravely bearing its rider toward the enemy leader. Bugbears stepped out to intercept the ride, but Temmerisa lowered its head and plowed straight through them, scattering them like falling leaves.

Temmerisa stumbled, the great horse's forelegs tangled in one falling creature. A trident, thrown from the concealing brush, entered Temmerisa's side, finishing the proud horse's charge. Down Temmerisa went, heavily, whinnying, and thrashing from the poison that had tipped the devilish weapon.

Elbereth rolled free of the tangle and looked back in horror as his proud steed stilled.

When the elf prince looked around, he saw that his path was clear all the way to Ragnor.

"Come along, elf," the ogrillon spat, recognizing Elbereth from their earlier encounter. "I have beaten you before. This time I will kill you!" Just to spur his opponent on, Ragnor kicked the elven corpse at his feet.

For all his confidence, though, the ogrillon was shocked at the sheer wildness of Elbereth's ensuing charge. Elbereth's sword whipped and hacked furiously, cut in on Ragnor, then stubbornly came back in after the ogrillon barely managed to parry the first strike.

"I avenge my father!" Elbereth cried, slashing away.

Confident Ragnor smiled wickedly. The elf king was this one's father? What victories Ragnor would pile up this day!

Elbereth's furious assault went on and on; Ragnor's actions remained defensive. The ogrillon was a veteran of a thousand battles. He knew that this one's rage would play itself out and soon give way to exhaustion. Then it would be Ragnor's turn.

404

* * * * *

By the time Cadderly got in sight of any of those doing battle, he had passed the scarred remains of the earlier fights. Blasted trees and bodies lay all about him. The cries of the dying seemed a macabre game of ventriloquism with too many bodies about for the young man to discern the source of any single cry.

One goblin grabbed his ankle as he passed. Instinct told him to fire his crossbow at the monster, but he realized that the goblin, blinded from a sword slash and near death, had grabbed him out of fear, with no thoughts of attacking. Cadderly pulled his leg free and stumbled away, having neither the courage to finish the creature, nor the time to tend its mortal wounds.

In the distance, another of the walking trees tumbled, buried under the bulk of a hundred monsters. Most of these creatures were already dead, tangled in strangling branches, but those that weren't hacked wildly at the fallen oak. An elf rushed to the tree's defense, taking down two orogs before he was buried by the others and ripped to pieces.

Cadderly didn't know which way to run or what to do. For the young scholar, who had lived his whole life in the sheltered and secure library, this was his vision of Hell.

He heard soft weeping in a nearby tree and saw Hammadeen in its boughs, her shoulders bobbing with her sobs.

Another groan came from a goblin dying in the shadows; another shriek split the air from somewhere in the unseen distance.

Cadderly ran on, circling the monsters still hacking at the fallen tree. He wanted to find a hole and hide in it, but he knew that to stop moving meant death.

He crossed through a tight copse of birch—the birch tangle that he and the others had avoided on their way to Syldritch Trea, he assumed—and came into a small field of chest-high blueberry bushes, dotted by occasional trees. Suddenly the fight was all about Cadderly. At the tree line across this small field, a force of goblinoids tried to penetrate the stiff defense of many elven archers, and in several places combatants rolled about in the blueberry bushes, altogether hidden from Cadderly's view.

He heard them, though, and saw the bushes tremble with the vicious fighting.

Cadderly worked his way through, went down a slope, and came around to the backside of a hill. There he froze, stunned by yet another sight. "Great Deneir," the stunned young priest muttered, hardly conscious that he had spoken. Cadderly had seen ogres before, and had nearly swooned at the size of the huge monsters. Now he saw his first giant, nearly twice the height of an ogre and, Cadderly would guess, ten times an ogre's weight. That made Cadderly, standing in its shadow, puny indeed!

Fortunately, the giant's back was to Cadderly and the creature was busy gathering rocks, probably to throw at the elves in the tree line. Cadderly would have been wise to walk past, but his reactions came from his terror.

He fired a dart into the giant's backside.

"Hey!" the monster roared, rubbing its burning buttocks and turning about. Cadderly, having realized his drastic error, had already taken flight and turned about just once to fire another dart. This one caught the monster squarely in the chest, but the giant hardly flinched at the explosion.

Cadderly put his head down and sprinted for the safety of the trees, hoping that no elf would mistake him for an orc and shoot him down.

He didn't look back again at the giant, guessing correctly that it had taken up the chase.

The giant laughed stupidly, thinking this human an easy catch. Its expression changed considerably when the two dwarven brothers popped up from the bushes beside it. One sliced into the back of the monster's hamstring with an axe; the other crushed the giant's kneecap with a club.

The giant veered and tumbled down, and the Bouldershoulders were atop it before it ever stopped bouncing.

"Nice high ground to make a stand," Ivan remarked to Pikel, burying his axe into the giant's neck.

"Oo oi!" Pikel heartily agreed, striking the giant on the back of the skull with his tree-trunk club.

"Was that Cadderly that came running by?" Ivan asked. Pikel looked to the dark trees and nodded.

"Good bait, that one!" Ivan roared. The conversation ended abruptly as a group of orogs crashed through the brush and charged at the exposed dwarves.

* * * * *

A blinding flash ripped through the shadows. Cadderly heard several goblins squeal, then spotted the source of the lightning bolt, a familiar and welcome face.

"Tintagel!" he called, rushing to the elf wizard's side.

"Well met, young priest!" the blue-eyed elf replied sincerely. "Have you seen Elbereth?"

Cadderly shook his head. "I just came onto the field," he explained. "Dorigen is down." He displayed the rings he had taken from the wizard and the wand sticking from under his belt. "Might these be of—"

"Down!" Tintagel cried, pushing Cadderly aside as a spear narrowly missed them both. The elf threw out one hand and uttered a spell. Magical bolts of energy erupted from his fingertips, swerving unerringly through the trees and diving behind one large trunk. Out the other side fell a dead bugbear, its hairy body singed in several places from the magical attack.

"Elbereth," the wizard said again to Cadderly. "I must get to him, for it is said that he battles Ragnor!"

"He does," said a dryad's melodic voice to the side.

"Where are they?" Cadderly demanded, moving toward Hammadeen. The dryad shied back against the tree, and Cadderly suspected that she meant to vanish.

"Do not go, I beg," the young scholar pleaded, mellowing his voice so as not to frighten the skittish creature. "You must tell us, Hammadeen. The fate of Shilmista rests in your hands."

Hammadeen did not reply or move, and Cadderly had to look hard to sort her out from the tree bark.

"Coward!" Cadderly growled at her. "You claim to be a friend of the trees, but you will do nothing in their time of need!" He closed his eyes, then, concentrating on the tree hiding the dryad. Strange and marvelous emotions came over him as he attuned his senses to that tree, and he recognized the paths the tree had privately opened for Hammadeen's escape.

"No!" Cadderly growled, reaching for the tree with his thoughts.

To Cadderly's amazement, the dryad suddenly reappeared, looking back at the tree as though it had somehow betrayed her.

"They fight in the grove of beech, to the south and west and not so far," the dryad said to Tintagel. "Do you know the place?"

"I do," Tintagel replied, eyeing Cadderly sidelong. "What did you do?" he asked after the skittish dryad had fled.

Cadderly stood dumbfounded, having no idea of how he might reply.

The elf wizard, so very familiar with this forest, his home, conjured an image of the beech grove and recalled the words of another spell.

"Watch over me," he said to Cadderly, and the young scholar nodded, knowing that the wizard would be vulnerable while casting. Cadderly took one of the two remaining darts from his bandoleer and cocked his crossbow.

A door of shimmering light, similar to the one Cadderly had seen Dorigen step through, appeared in front of Tintagel. Cadderly heard a familiar rustle as another nearby bugbear heaved a spear.

The young scholar spun around, picked out the target, crouching in some bushes, and fired, blasting the monster right out the back side of the brush. There was no joy in Cadderly, and his satisfaction was soon lost, for when he turned back, he found Tintagel slumping, the spear buried deep in his side.

Cadderly cried out to him, grabbed the elf close, and, having nowhere else to go, leaned forward, taking them both through the shimmering door.

* * * * *

The giant groaned loudly, and Pikel broke away from his fight with an orog just long enough to smack the fallen behemoth on the back of the head. Seeing its opponent diverted, the orog tried to leap up onto the giant's back. Pikel's club caught it in midflight, dropping it back to the ground some distance away in a writhing heap.

The dwarves fought back to back, as they had atop the dead ogre in Dorigen's camp. Only now the dwarves were even higher, standing taller than the orogs they battled, and the evil creatures had a considerable climb in trying to get at their enemies. Half the orog band of ten lay dead beside the giant, and not one of the monsters had gotten close to standing beside the dwarves.

The brothers Bouldershoulder were truly enjoying themselves.

A commotion from the tree line made both dwarf and orog glance to the side. Out came Danica, running like the wind, a mixed group of orcs, goblins, and bugbears close behind. Two of the orogs broke away from their fight with the dwarves and moved to cut her off.

An arrow got one in the chest, a second arrow thudding in a split second later, just an inch from the first. The remaining orog made the mistake of looking to the side, to the elven maiden in the shadows of the tree line.

Feet first, Danica soared through the air, connecting with a double kick into the distracted orog's chest. It flew away, disappearing under the blueberry bushes, and did not reappear.

Danica was back up and running in an instant.

"I'll cut ye a path!" Ivan promised, and he leaped from the giant, right between two orogs. His axe whipped left and right, and his promise was quickly fulfilled.

"Good to see ye, Lady Danica," Ivan said, offering his gnarly hand. They went back up together, joining Pikel as he clobbered the last orog. New enemies were not far behind, but the mixed band of monsters found their ranks thinned as they charged. Arrows soared out from the tree line, scoring hit after hit.

"Shayleigh," Danica explained to the admiring dwarves.

"Glad she's on our side," Ivan remarked. Even as he spoke, another arrow soared out, hitting a goblin in the side of the head and dropping it dead on the spot.

"We cannot stay here for long," Danica told the brothers. "The area is in turmoil. Goblins and giants are everywhere, it seems!"

"How are the trees doing?" Ivan asked.

"Yeah," Pikel concurred excitedly.

"The trees have caused tremendous losses to our enemies," Danica answered. "But they are few, and fewer still since several have been brought down and several more battle the fires our enemies have started. The elves are scattered, and many, I fear, are dead."

"To the woods, then!" Ivan bellowed. He leaped down again and charged into the approaching host, swinging so ferociously that more monsters turned and fled than remained to fight him. Danica nearly laughed aloud, and she pulled out her daggers, whipped them into the nearest target, and charged down, Pikel going right beside her, to join Ivan.

They were back under the trees in minutes.

* * * * *

Cadderly loaded his last explosive dart as he came through the other side of Tintagel's shimmering gate, carefully laying the wounded elf wizard at his side,

He spotted Ragnor and Elbereth immediately, in the throes of a titanic struggle just a few yards away.

He spotted Galladel, too, dead in the dirt at their feet.

Cadderly had no doubts as to where he wanted to place this last dart, and told himself that he would feel no remorse for blowing a large hole in Ragnor's ugly face.

A charging bugbear changed Cadderly's plans.

The young scholar had no time to think of his movements, just swung about and popped the dart into the hairy monster's belly when it was only a stride away. The bugbear lurched violently and stumbled past, tumbling face down in the dirt.

Cadderly looked to Tintagel, lying helpless and writhing in agony. He wanted to tend to the elf wizard, to get the spear out of Tintagel's side at least, but he saw clearly that Elbereth could not hold out against the powerful ogrillon.

"I vowed that I would die beside you," the young scholar whispered. He thought for a moment of searching his pack, of getting out the flask of Oil of Impact and trying to load another dart, but realized that he had no time. Reluctantly, Cadderly dropped his useless crossbow and took up his walking stick and spindle-disks, thinking them ridiculous against a foe as obviously powerful as Ragnor. He reiterated his vow to Elbereth one last time and charged in beside the elf prince.

"Why are you here?" Elbereth demanded breathlessly when Cadderly rushed up. The elf ducked a quick cut of Ragnor's heavy sword, one of the few offensive strikes the ogrillon had taken.

Cadderly understood immediately the course this fight had taken. Elbereth was plainly tired, couldn't even seem to catch his breath, and Ragnor showed a dozen nicks and scratches, none of them deep or serious.

"I said I would fight beside you," Cadderly replied. He stepped ahead, motioned with his walking stick, then threw out his spindle-disks. Ragnor blocked the attack with his forearm, curiously eyeing the strange but hardly effective weapon.

"You have powerful allies, elf prince," the ogrillon laughed derisively. Cadderly struck again with the spindle-disks, and the ogrillon didn't even bother to throw up his arm, taking the blow squarely on the chest and laughing all the while.

Then Elbereth came on wickedly, his fine sword darting to and fro, and sometimes straight ahead. Ragnor showed considerable respect for this weapon, and while the ogrillon was fully engaged, Cadderly grabbed his walking stick in both hands and connected on Ragnor's elbow.

The ogrillon winced in pain. "You will die slowly for that!" he promised Cadderly, while furiously parrying Elbereth's cunning cuts and slashes. "Slowly."

Cadderly looked to his weapons as if they had deceived him. He knew he couldn't really hurt Ragnor, no matter how clean his blow, but he knew, too, for Elbereth's sake, that he must try to play some important role in the battle.

He waited and watched the fight's ebb and flow, stayed back in the hopes that Ragnor would pay him even less attention over the next few moments.

If Ragnor was at all concerned about the young scholar, the ogrillon didn't show it.

Elbereth's blade spun in circles about Ragnor's, then poked ahead, into the ogrillon's arm. Ragnor growled, but if Elbereth was the faster swordsman, Ragnor was the tougher. The ogrillon went on the offensive, repeatedly hacking with his huge broadsword. He connected on Elbereth's shield, the sheer force of the blow splitting it and throwing Elbereth to the ground.

Cadderly knew he had to act then or watch the elf prince be cut apart. He dropped his walking stick to the ground and yelled wildly, taking two steps toward Ragnor and leaping onto the ogrillon's arm. The young scholar caught hold stubbornly, his arms about the ogrillon's neck and both of his legs locked tightly around one of Ragnor's.

Cadderly was neither a small man nor a weak one, but powerful Ragnor hardly swayed from his path toward the elf. The ogrillon glanced to the side incredulously, and Cadderly hung on for all his life.

Ragnor would have finished Cadderly then, except that Elbereth jumped back to his feet and wasted no time in returning to the attack. With Cadderly clutching and tugging and generally distracting Ragnor, Elbereth's cunning maneuvers scored even more hits.

"Off!" the ogrillon howled. He drove Elbereth back with a vicious flurry, then slipped his free arm around Cadderly's, breaking the young scholar's grip. Ragnor's strength was frightening indeed, and a moment later, Cadderly found himself flying through the air.

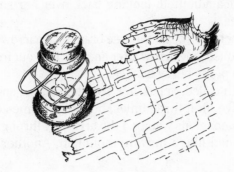

Twenty-Three

Between a Dwarf and a Hard Place

B ack in the shadows of the trees, Ivan and Pikel hardly had trouble finding enemies. Goblins and orcs popped up from the undergrowth all about them, drooling and hungry for battle.

True to their dwarven heritage, the Bouldershoulder brothers promptly went berserk, clubbing and slicing, and though they had been fighting steadily for many minutes, neither showed any signs of weariness. Goblins flew every which way, launched by Pikel's heavy club, and Ivan, with a mighty overhead chop, sliced one orc nearly in half.

Through all the fury of that initial skirmish, Danica rested back behind the brothers, gathering her energy for when she would inevitably be needed. Cadderly dominated the young woman's thoughts in that lull. Danica had found no time before this to consider where the young scholar might be and she feared that he had met a gruesome end. Her duty was clear to her, though, and she would not sway from it. This time, unlike any other, Danica had to trust in Cadderly to take care of himself, had to focus on the desperate battle.

No matter how many times Danica reminded herself of that fact, her heart longed to find Cadderly.

The last orc's head flew off into the bushes. In the respite, Ivan turned about and noticed the despair in Danica's almond eyes.

"Don't ye worry, lass," the dwarf comforted. "We'll save ye a few in the next fight."

Danica's face crinkled at the words, revealing to the dwarf that he had misjudged the source of her sadness.

"It's yer Cadderly, then," Ivan guessed, remembering the young scholar himself. "Where'd that one get himself off to, anyhow?"

411

"I left him," Danica admitted, looking back over her shoulder to the west, toward Syldritch Trea.

A boulder plummeted through the tree branches, narrowly missing the three companions. In response, one arrow after another flew out from the side, zipping back in the direction of the berry bushes.

"Giant!" Shayleigh called, appearing from her hiding spot and stringing yet another arrow. "I have hit it three times, but still it comes on!" She drew back and fired, and the companions watched the arrow fly through the leafy tangle to thud into what seemed like a moving mountain. Another huge form shifted beside the first.

"Two giants!" Ivan bellowed hopefully.

Danica grabbed him, and Pikel, as they started past her on their way to the newest foes. "No doubt with a host of escorts beside them," the fiery young woman explained. "Do not be so foolish," she scolded. "You are much to valuable to us—to me."

"Oh," Pikel replied rather sadly.

Shayleigh popped another arrow into the approaching monsters, then caught up with Danica and the dwarves.

"We must be gone quickly," Shayleigh said.

"You three go on," Danica bade them. "I will search for Cadderly."

"The priest is with Tintagel," Shayleigh replied. "Fear not, for if any can keep him safe in the fight, it is the wizard."

The news did brighten Danica's mood. Knowing that Cadderly was beside one as seasoned and wise as Tintagel eased her fears that her love had been abandoned to make his way alone in this forest of horrors. "The four of us, then," Danica offered determinedly.

"Oo oi!" was Pikel's reply.

"Woe to any monsters that cross our path!" Shayleigh vowed. She spun about and launched another arrow at the mass of approaching giants, just for good luck, and together the fighting foursome sprinted off into the shadows, formulating plans as they went.

* * * * *

Without his shield, Elbereth could only grasp his sword hilt in both hands to deflect Ragnor's mighty blows. The ogrillon was finished with his defensive tactics now, determined to end this fight and move on to new battles. He cut a two-handed swipe straight across at Elbereth's chest, stepping into the blow so that the elf could not back away and would have to use his sword to parry.

Elbereth's weapon rang loudly under the force of the blow, vibrating for many moments. Elbereth's arms went numb, and he had to struggle just to hold his grip on the sword. Ragnor launched a second strike, identical to the first.

Elbereth knew that to similarly block this blow would tear the sword from his hands. He threw himself straight back instead, tumbling to the ground.

Ragnor attacked furiously, thinking that the fight was won.

Elbereth's agility and speed crossed the ogrillon up, though, for the elf suddenly twisted about and whipped his sword across, swift and low, stinging Ragnor's shins and abruptly halting the ogrillon's charge.

Elbereth was back up again, wary and keeping his distance as Ragnor, spitting curses and limping only slightly, steadily advanced.

Cadderly groaned and forced himself up to his elbows, knowing that he, and especially Elbereth, could not afford any delays. The young scholar had landed hard from Ragnor's throw, and had lost his breath in the tumble.

He looked now at Elbereth, weary and sorely outmatched, and knew that Ragnor would soon win.

"Back to the fight," Cadderly vowed, but he didn't even manage to get to his feet before he felt the wetness along the back of his neck. Thinking it blood, Cadderly put a hand over it and scrambled to remove his pack.

He breathed a sigh of relief when he saw that the moisture came from his pack, not his own body, but then he nearly swooned when he realized the only possible source.

Slowly, carefully, the young scholar untied and opened the pack and removed the cracked flask. He shuddered to think of what might have happened if his landing had shattered, and not just cracked, the container of volatile *Oil of Impact*. He looked up to the high branches of the beech trees and imagined himself hanging up there, twisted and broken from the horrendous blast.

Cadderly glanced suddenly at Ragnor, then back to the flask. A wicked smile found its way across his face. He carefully removed the top half of the cracked container, then scooped his spindle-disks inside, cupping his hand to get as much of the remaining liquid as he could.

When Elbereth's back went against a tree, both the elf and the ogrillon realized that the running game had ended. Bravely, Elbereth launched a series of vicious thrusts, a few getting through to poke at Ragnor, but none solidly enough to keep the huge monster at bay.

Elbereth barely ducked in time as the ogrillon's sword smashed in, chopping a sizable chunk from the tree. Elbereth managed yet another hit as Ragnor tore his blade free. The ogrillon winced and swung again, this time shortening up on his stroke so that he would connect on the elf, or on nothing at all.

His blade flew freely as Elbereth dove to the ground, the overmatched elf's only retreat.

"Now it is done!" Ragnor proclaimed, and Elbereth, cornered and on the ground, could hardly argue.

Ragnor saw Cadderly coming in fast from the side, the young scholar's arm cocked and the curious (and useless) weapon readied for a throw. The ogrillon, sword high for a killing strike, paid the young scholar no heed, didn't even lower one arm to block the attack.

Cadderly growled and threw all of his weight and strength into the throw. The spindle-disks slammed against the side of Ragnor's barrel-like chest, and the force of the explosion spun the ogrillon about to face Cadderly squarely.

For a moment, Cadderly thought that Ragnor was running backward, away from him, but then the young scholar realized that Ragnor's feet, pumping helplessly, were several inches off the ground.

Ragnor's arms and legs continued to flail wildly as the ogrillon tried to slow his flight. A branch bent then cracked behind him, and he came to a sudden stop, impaled through the backbone against the tree. Ragnor hung there, a foot from the ground, a scorched hole in one side of his furry leather tunic (and in the skin underneath), and his legs lifeless below him. He felt no pain in those lower limbs, felt nothing at all. He tried to plant his feet against the tree, that he might push himself free, but alas, his legs would not heed his call.

Stunned beyond words, Cadderly looked down to his weapon hand. There hung the cord, shortened by half and its end blackened. Of the rock crystal disks, there was nothing to be found except a single scorched flake on the ground where Ragnor had been standing.

Similarly amazed, Elbereth rose to his feet. He looked at Cadderly curiously for a moment, then took up his sword and stomped over to Ragnor.

The world was a blur to the burly leader of the invading forces. Ragnor had to forcibly thrust out his chest just to draw breath. Still, the stubborn creature had held fast to his sword, and he managed to raise it in a semblance of defense against Elbereth's determined approach.

Elbereth swatted the blade once, then again, driving it aside. The elf's sword slashed across the ogrillon's eyes, blinding Ragnor. Wisely, Elbereth stepped back as Ragnor's fury played itself out in a series of vicious cuts.

Cadderly thought Ragnor a pitiful thing as the blinded ogrillon continued to slice wildly at the empty air. Ragnor began to tire, and Cadderly looked away as Elbereth stepped back in. He heard a growl, then a groan.

When he looked back, Elbereth was wiping his crimson-stained blade and Ragnor hung near death, one hand twitching pitifully at the hole Elbereth had cut through his throat.

* * * * *

"Stupid things," Ivan whispered, looking ahead across a small clearing to the group of mixed monsters. The dwarf and his three companions had easily backtracked to get behind the two giants, several orogs, and numerous goblins that had been pursuing them. One of the giant's movements appeared strained, the creature having caught several of Shayleigh's arrows.

"Bring them in," Ivan said with a wink to the elf maiden. He and Pikel slipped out of the tree line into the thick and deep grass of the lea.

Shayleigh looked to Danica. The elf was not timid by anyone's standards, but this group of monsters seemed a bit too powerful for the small band to handle.

Danica, similarly concerned but better understanding the dwarves' prowess, nodded grimly and motioned for Shayleigh to continue.

Shayleigh raised her great bow and took aim for the already wounded giant. She put a second and third arrow into the air before the first ever struck the mark.

The first hit the giant at the base of its thick neck. The monster howled and grasped at the quivering shaft, and the second arrow whipped in beside the first, pinning the giant's hand in place. By the time the third arrow hit, just below the first two, the giant was on its way down. It fell to its knees and held unsteadily there for a few moments, then dropped into the grass.

The rest of the monstrous band let out a common shout of outrage and spun about, charging wildly back across the lea. Shayleigh promptly dropped one ferocious orog, putting an arrow between its bulbous eyes.

"Take to the trees," Danica instructed her. "Shoot for the lesser monsters. Be confident that the dwarves have a plan in mind for the giant." Shayleigh looked to the grass where Ivan and Pikel had disappeared, then she smiled, surprised to learn that she, too, had come to trust a couple of dwarves. With agility befitting an elf, Shayleigh found a handhold and pulled herself into the branches of the nearest tree with remarkable ease.

With its great strides, the remaining giant came ahead of its smaller companions. It heaved a boulder Danica's way, and the nimble monk barely dodged it as the rock took down a small sapling.

An arrow from above cut down a goblin.

Danica looked up and winked her appreciation to Shayleigh. Then, to the elf maiden's amazement, Danica stormed ahead, right at the approaching giant.

As the lumbering creature raised its huge club, Danica whipped her two already bloodied daggers into its face. The giant roared in outrage, dropped its club, and grabbed at the stuck weapons. Danica veered, smiling as Ivan and Pikel popped up from the grass, hacking and bashing at the monster's thick legs.

The confused giant didn't know which way to turn. Ivan chopped at one of its legs, cutting out wedges as though he were felling a tree, but the pain in the monster's face demanded its attention. Finally, the giant mustered the courage to tear out one of the stubborn daggers, but by then it was too late for the leg, and the creature toppled to the side.

Ivan rushed past the monster toward the oncoming orogs; Pikel headed for the giant's head to finish the job. The giant got a hand on Pikel as he neared its face, and started to squeeze. Pikel wasn't overly concerned, though, for he was close enough for a strike and Danica's remaining dagger, deep in the monster's cheek, offered a positively marvelous target.

As Danica broke to the side, so, too, did a group of three orogs. Danica continued to veer, allowing the monsters to stay close enough so that they would not give up the chase. Soon, the monk had nearly completed a full circuit, heading back for the same trees she had just exited. Orog swords nipped at her heels, but Danica was confident that she could keep just ahead of the stupid things. She heard a yowl of pain and surprise behind her, and a gasp after that, and knew that Shayleigh had begun her work.

Danica dove headlong, twisting as she rolled, to come up facing the charging orogs. The closest beast, glancing back at its companion, who had taken two arrows, turned back just in time to catch Danica's fist on the chin. A sickening crack resounded above the din of battle, and the orog's jaw broke apart. When the creature at last settled on the ground, the bottom half of its jaw was aligned more with its left ear than with the upper half of its mouth.

The remaining orog immediately spun about and took flight. It managed to get a few strides away before Shayleigh's next arrow pierced its thigh, slowing it enough for Danica to rush up and bury it.

Ivan waded into the horde of goblins and orogs with typical dwarven finesse. The dwarf butted with his horned helmet, bit where he could, kicked with both feet, and generally whipped his axe to and fro with such ferocity that the entire band of monsters had to give ground steadily. Those that could not retreat, caught between the dwarf and their own companions, most often hit the ground at about the same time as their severed extremities.

The downside to Ivan's tactics, in addition to the weariness that inevitably would accompany such a wild display, was that Ivan was all but blind to the events around him. And so the dwarf was off his guard as one orog managed to slip in behind his tirade. The creature, timing its attack between axe swipes so as not to get caught in a follow-through, stepped right up to the dwarf and let loose a wicked downward cut with its heavy club that Ivan couldn't begin to dodge or deflect.

"Yuck," Pikel remarked as soon as he realized that his head-bashing had become rather redundant. The giant's grip had become quite relaxed by that point, and Pikel stepped purposely away from the gruesome thing that had once been the creature's head. The dwarf considered retrieving Danica's dagger, which was buried in giant flesh with the tip of its point poking out the other side of the huge head, but Pikel quickly decided that if Danica wanted it back, she would have to get it herself.

That business done, Pikel crawled over the giant's chest to join his brother, and let out a squeaky warning just as the orog's club descended on Ivan's head.

"Ye called?" Ivan replied, then he added, "Ouch!" almost as an afterthought. He spun about to clobber the orog, but kept on spinning, around and around, finding no bearings until his cheek came to rest on the cool grass.

The orog howled in victory, a cry of glee cut short by Shayleigh's next arrow and even more so by Pikel's fury. The dwarf imitated the orog's own tactics, but while the orog's clubbing had sent Ivan in a spin, Pikel's bash dropped the monster straight down in a heap, weirdly, with its legs straight out to the sides and its head lolling about on a useless neck.

Pikel wanted to hit the thing again, and again after that, but he had no time, for the remaining monsters had descended over helpless Ivan.

"Ooooo!" the dwarf bellowed, following yet another arrow into the throng. Goblins flew every which way—even powerful orogs prudently leaped aside— and in mere moments, Pikel straddled Ivan's prone form.

Danica hit the group from the side a moment later, with equal fury; Shayleigh dropped another orog, sinking an arrow right through its eye.

The monsters broke ranks and scattered.

Pikel remained defensively over his brother while Danica took up the pursuit, tackling an orog and rolling over it in the grass. Shayleigh fired off several shots, but realized to her dismay that she could not down all of the monsters before they found the safety of the trees.

The monsters' hoots of relief as they made the tree line were short-lived indeed, though, for out of those same shadows came a host of elves. In a few seconds, not a goblin or orog remained alive on that blood-soaked field.

* * * * *

Cadderly stood staring as Elbereth came over to join him. The world had gone crazy, Cadderly decided, and he had been fully caught up in that insanity. Just a few weeks before, the young scholar had known nothing but peace and security, had never even seen a living monster. But everything was upside down now, with Cadderly—almost by accident—playing the role of hero and with monsters, so many monsters, suddenly very real in the young scholar's life.

The world had gone crazy, and Elbereth's forthcoming congratulations, the mighty elf's thanks for a blow that had defeated a monster beyond innocent Cadderly's wildest nightmares, only confirmed the young scholar's suspicions. Imagine, Cadderly winning where Elbereth could not, where King Galladel, lying dead at their feet, could not!

There was no pride in the young scholar's thoughts, just blank amazement. What cruel trick fate had played him, to drop him so terribly unprepared into such a role, and into such chaos. Was this what Deneir had in store for him? If so, did Cadderly really want to remain his disciple?

Elbereth's startled look turned the young scholar about. Ragnor's remaining elite guard, half a dozen mighty bugbears wielding tridents dripping with a substance the two companions could only assume was poison, charged at the two, not so far away, certainly not far enough for Cadderly to escape.

"And so we die," he heard Elbereth mutter as the elf lifted his stained sword, and the young scholar, weaponless and weary, had no words to deny the proclamation.

A blast of lightning abruptly ended the threat. Four of the bugbears died on the spot; the other two rolled about in the dirt, scorched and crippled.

Cadderly looked to the side, to Tintagel, bravely propped against a tree, wearing a smile only occasionally diminished by throbs of pain. Cadderly and Elbereth ran to their friend. Elbereth started to tend the wound, but Cadderly shoved the elf aside.

"Damn you, Deneir, if you do not help me now!" the young scholar growled.

It didn't take someone knowledgeable in the healing arts to see that Tintagel's wound would soon prove fatal. Where the elf had found the strength and presence of mind to release the magical strike, Cadderly would never guess, but he knew that such courage could not be a prelude to death.

Not if he had anything to say about it.

Elbereth put a hand on his shoulder, but Cadderly muttered and slapped it away. The young scholar grasped the spear shaft, still deep in Tintagel's side. He looked up to the blue-eyed elf, who understood and nodded.

Cadderly tore the spear out.

Blood gushed from the wound—Cadderly's fingers could not begin to hold it in—and Tintagel swooned and stumbled to the side.

"Hold him steady!" Cadderly cried, and Elbereth, a helpless observer in the spectacle, did as he was told.

Cadderly futilely slapped at the pouring blood, actually held in Tintagel's spilling guts.

"Deneir!" the young priest cried, more in rage than reverence. "Deneir!"

Then something marvelous happened.

Cadderly felt the power surge through him, though he did not understand it and hardly expected it. It came on the notes of a distant, melodious song. Too surprised to react, the young priest simply hung on desperately.

He watched in amazement as Tintagel's wound began to mend. The blood flow lessened, then stopped altogether; Cadderly's hands were forced aside by the magically binding skin.

A minute passed, then another.

"Get me to the fight," a rejuvenated Tintagel bade them. Elbereth threw a hug on his elven friend; Cadderly fell to the ground.

The world had gone crazy.

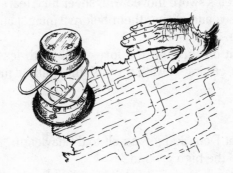

Twenty-Four

Pack of Wolves

Hammadeen's hand stroked Temmerisa's muscled flank, tenderly touching the bloodied white flesh around the garish three-holed trident wound. The great horse hardly moved in response, only snorted now and again.

"Can you do for Temmerisa what you did for me?" Tintagel asked Cadderly.

The young priest, retrieving his walking stick, shrugged helplessly, still not even certain of exactly what he had done for Tintagel.

"You must try," Elbereth bade him. Cadderly saw the sincere grief in his friend's face and wanted dearly to say that he could mend the horse's wounds.

He never got the chance to make the attempt, though, for Temmerisa gave one final snort, then lay very still. Hammadeen, tears in her dark eyes, began a soft song in a tongue that none of the companions could understand.

Cadderly's vision blurred and the forest around him took on a preternatural edge, a surrealistic, too-sharp contrast. He blinked many times, and many more when he looked at Temmerisa, for he saw the horse's spirit rise suddenly and step from its corporeal body.

Hammadeen spoke a few quiet words in the horse's ear, and both she and the spirit walked slowly away, disappearing into the trees.

Cadderly nearly fell over as his vision shifted back into the real and material world. The young scholar didn't know how he could apologize to Elbereth, didn't know what in the world he might say to the elf, now a king, whose father and prized steed lay dead at their feet.

Tintagel started to offer condolences, but Elbereth wasn't hearing any. The proud elf looked to his father and to Temmerisa, then rushed away, stained sword in hand. Cadderly propped up the injured wizard, that they might follow.

A pair of orcs were the first monsters to have the misfortune of crossing

Elbereth's path. The elf's sword moved with sheer fury, tearing through the monsters' meager defenses and slicing them before Tintagel and Cadderly had the opportunity to join in.

And so they went on through the forest, Elbereth leading, his sword, an extension of his rage, cutting a swath through the ranks of monsters in the trees.

* * * * *

"The trees fight at Deny Ridge," an elf told Shayleigh. "A great force of our enemies has taken to the high ground."

"Then we must take it back," Shayleigh replied firmly. She and the other elf looked around, counting heads. Including the dwarves and Danica, their numbers totaled twenty-three, but while the other elf held reservations, Shayleigh, with full confidence in her nonelf companions, only smiled and started away to the south.

They came within sight of the ridge twenty uneventful minutes later. A dozen more elves, one a wizard, had fallen into their ranks as they went, relieved to see some semblance of organization amid the chaos.

Deny Ridge was aptly named, Danica noted, staring at it from the tree line across a small, grassy break. From this side, the ground sloped upward at a steep pitch for a hundred feet, climbed straight up a rock face for thirty more, then sloped another hundred feet or so through thick grasses to the ridge top. According to Shayleigh, the other side, where the goblinoids battled the remaining sentient trees, was even more defensible, being a rocky and almost sheer drop from top to bottom.

The band could hear the fighting, and could tell from the sounds that the trees were having a hard time of it. Goblinoids lined the top of the ridge, using burning torches as their main weapons. Several archers were among their ranks, eagerly tying rags to their arrows, lighting them on the torches, and shooting them down into the attacking trees.

"We must get up there, and quickly," Shayleigh said, pointing to the left, to still another band of monsters making their way to join their comrades atop the ridge. "If our enemies are allowed to hold this ground, more will come beside them and they will have an unbeatable base from which to conduct their conquest."

"Two, three hundred of the things up there now," Ivan replied. "Ye might find getting to the top a bit of work. But still . . ." the dwarf mused, and he wandered off toward his brother.

"Have you any ideas?" Shayleigh asked Danica and another elf by her side. Danica looked to the dwarven brothers, now engaged in a private conversation, pointing this way and that. Ivan was doing most of the talking, with Pikel nodding eagerly, or shaking his head vehemently and piping in an "Oo," or an "Uh-uh," every now and then.

"They will find a way if there is one," Danica explained to the confused elves.

Ivan stomped over a few seconds later and announced that he and Pikel had done just that. "Get us down to the right," he said. "And we're going to be needing plenty of ropes." Ivan wet one finger and held it up. Pikel pointed behind them and Ivan nodded his confirmation that the wind was favorable.

Shayleigh and Danica understood none of it but had nothing better to go on. On the maiden's command, the entire elven band moved silently through the trees down to the right as Ivan had instructed. They managed to produce five lengths of fine cord, which Ivan declared long enough for the task.

"Set some of yer friends about, looking back to the woods," Ivan instructed. "If we get caught here by some more goblins making their way in afore we make the top, then the game's up. But put yerself and yer archer friends, and that wizard elf, too, in line for shooting to the ridge top. Me and me brother'll make it to the rocks easy enough. After we get up on them, we'll be needing yer help."

"What are we to do?" Shayleigh asked, somewhat hesitantly, for others of the elven band had expressed some concerns about being led by dwarves.

"Ye'll know," Ivan said slyly. He looked to Pikel. "Ye ready?"

Pikel hoisted the coiled lengths of cord over his shoulders, stuck a small hammer between his teeth, and responded with an enthusiastic, "Hroo hoi!"

From one of the many pouches on his wide belt Ivan produced a similar hammer and several iron spikes. His nod sent the brothers off and running, up the first grassy slope toward the rock break. Shayleigh, Danica, the elf wizard, and half a dozen archers took up positions along the tree line, their flanks and rear guarded by the remainder of the elven troops. Whispers circulated among the ranks, most in admiration for the brave, if foolish, dwarves.

Ivan and Pikel picked their careful way up the rock face, apparently still unnoticed by the monsters atop the ridge.

Just under the lip of the cliff, the dwarven hammers rang out, driving spikes to hang down the five lengths of cord.

"Are we to charge and climb?" Shayleigh asked Danica, wondering if the time to act had come. She thought that the plan was not such a good one, for the elves, though they might make the top of the rocks, would still be out in the open with more than a hundred sloping feet between them and their enemies.

Danica held her hand up to calm Shayleigh. "Ivan and Pikel are not finished," she replied with some certainty, though she, too, still had not quite figured out what the brothers had in mind.

Danica's guess soon proved correct, for Ivan and Pikel were far from finished. Pikel swung himself over the rocks first, coming onto the higher grassy slope. Immediately the goblins spotted him and let out a unified hoot. Pikel dove for the cover of a boulder, but wasn't quick enough to dodge the first arrow.

"Ow!" The dwarf grimaced and pulled the shaft from his hip—not too serious a wound. Pikel looked back to the trees, then peeked back up the slope. He smiled despite the pain when the first elven arrow took out the archer who had hit him, sending the goblin flying over the back side of the ridge.

Ivan came up over the rock face next, hollering, "Dwarven brigade, charge!" at the top of his lungs and in the goblin tongue. Pikel ignored his wound and rushed out beside his brother.

"What are they doing?" Shayleigh asked. "And why did he cry out the attack in the goblin tongue?"

Danica seemed similarly stunned for just a moment, until she noticed the goblins' reactions. The creatures atop that section of the ridge went berserk, it seemed, many of them rushing down toward Ivan and Pikel and heaving their flaming torches down the hill.

"Dwarves," Danica muttered above the din of twanging bowstrings as the elves let loose on the suddenly open targets. "In all the wide world, there is nothing a goblin hates, or fears, more than dwarves."

"Oh, fine trick!" the elf wizard cried, and he rushed from the trees to get into range and sent a volley of magical bolts from his fingertips, dropping two of the closest goblins.

Ivan and Pikel were no longer hanging around for the battle. As the flaming torches flew thick around them, the dwarves headed back for the rocks, caught two of the ropes they had hung, and swung out below the ledge.

The goblins' mirth at the apparent rout—from their viewpoint, only two of the wretched dwarves had even shown their ugly faces—lasted only as long as it took the dimwitted creatures to realize that the fires begun by their own hurled torches were swiftly making their way back up the slope!

"Follow the flames!" Ivan roared, hearing the startled screams from above. Then he added quietly to Pikel as they made their way back over the lip, "Goblins been around for a hundred, hundred years, and they ain't learned yet, when things get tough, that fire burns up!"

"Hee hee," came Pikel's reply.

With incredible agility and swiftness, Danica and the bulk of the elven force got to the hanging ropes and climbed to the top of the rock face, while Shayleigh, her archers, and the wizard remained behind to continue their distant assault.

The fires led their way to the ridge top, clearing a path in the goblin lines. Monsters fell all over each other; many were pushed over the cliff on the back side of the ridge in an effort to get away from the fast-moving blaze.

The fuel soon consumed, the fires died away as quickly as they had started, leaving the elven force holding a high spot atop the ridge. Enraged goblins came at them from both sides, outnumbering the small band ten to one, determined to recapture the lost ground.

"Forward!" Shayleigh instructed, knowing that she and her archer companions would have to get closer to provide any real aid in the desperate battle. The handful of elves sprinted up the first slope and took to the ropes.

Ivan, Pikel, and Danica centered the defensive line on the right, the short side of the ridge. The three worked with their typical harmony, complementing each other's movements and biting so fiercely into the goblin lines that many elves were freed up to join their kin on the other flank, where the bulk of the enemy force remained. It was a tenuous position indeed for the defenders, and every elf that fell left a large hole for the enemy to get through.

Danica thought the fight would be lost, especially after Shayleigh's band came up over the rock face, only to be met in close quarters and hard pressed, with their backs to the cliff, by another group of goblins.

"Should we be planning a retreat?" Danica asked Ivan.

"Never said it'd be easy," was all the dwarf replied as he chopped down a goblin that had come too near.

Then a strange cloud, greenish and thick, appeared over the ranks of goblins, just a few feet from Danica and the dwarves. The companions couldn't see under the opaque layers of that cloud, but they could hear the goblins gagging and choking. One miserable creature stumbled out, too intent on grasping at its churning belly to even realize its doom as Ivan and Pikel simultaneously smashed it down.

Most of the goblins that managed to escape the sickly vapors went out the back side of the cloud, angling down the slope, away from the fight. They found little running room, though, for there waited Elbereth, stern and mighty, and his sword worked tirelessly on the startled and weakened creatures.

Then the magical cloud dissipated suddenly, leaving more than a dozen goblins exposed and helpless on the ridge top. Ivan and Pikel started for them, but furious Elbereth got there first, hacking and slashing his way through. Without a word of greeting, the grim elf passed the dwarves, Danica, and the first rank of elves. He crashed through the faltering elven line defending the left flank and threw himself headlong into the pressing goblin throng.

No goblin sword or spear seemed to harm him; he did not sway an inch from his path. In just a few furious moments, goblins ran from his terrible blade and the elves rallied behind him.

With the right side of the ridge swiftly cleared, Ivan and Pikel led several elves down to aid Shayleigh and the archers. Danica did not accompany them, for she saw someone else, a friend she could not ignore.

Cadderly and Tintagel braced themselves for trouble as those goblins who had escaped both the cloud and Elbereth's fury rushed down at them. Tintagel muttered a quick spell, and Cadderly stood amazed as several images of himself and the wizard appeared, making their band of two seem like many. The goblins, already panicked and with the high ground fully lost, came nowhere near the unexpected throng, veering instead into the tree line to run away screaming.

Then the goblins were gone, and Danica was with Cadderly, and for both of them for just that quick moment, the world seemed right once more.

All across Deny Ridge, the battle became a rout. With Elbereth in the lead and Shayleigh and her archers freed once more, the elves and the dwarven brothers plowed the goblins away, crushed them and scattered them. Ivan and

Pikel turned one band around at the base of the ridge, drove the stupid things into the waiting branches of four enraged oak trees.

It was over in ten short minutes, and Deny Ridge belonged to Elbereth.

* * * * *

"Ye give me six hours, a dozen elves—including yer hurt wizard there—and move them trees where I tell ye, and I'll hold this place for a hundred years, and a hundred more after that if ye need me to!" Ivan boasted, and, after the dwarf's exploits in leading the charge up the hill, not an elf in the camp doubted his words.

Elbereth looked to Cadderly.

"The trees will move as we bid," the young scholar answered confidently, though he wasn't quite certain of how he knew that to be true.

"The ridge is yours to defend," Elbereth said to Ivan. "A fine base from which our hunting parties might strike out."

"And your strikes will not be blindly orchestrated," Cadderly announced, looking to the nearest of the oak trees. "Will they, Hammadeen?"

The dryad stepped out a moment later, confused as to how the young scholar had seen her. No human eyes, not even elven eyes, could normally penetrate her camouflage.

"You will guide the elves," Cadderly said to her, "to their enemies and to their wayward friends."

The dryad started to turn back to the tree, but Cadderly cried, "Halt!" so forcefully that Hammadeen froze in her tracks.

"You will do this, Hammadeen," Cadderly commanded, seeming suddenly terrible to all watching the spectacle. Amazingly, the dryad turned and nodded her compliance.

Cadderly nodded, too, and walked away, needing some time alone to try to decipher all the surprises that were meeting him at every turn. How had he seen the horse's spirit? He hadn't asked, but he knew instinctively that Elbereth and Tintagel had not seen it. And how had he known that Hammadeen was in those trees? Furthermore, how in the world had Cadderly so commanded the wild dryad?

He simply did not know.

All through that night and the next day, while Ivan and Pikel set the defenses of Deny Ridge, small bands of elves—"packs of wolves," Ivan called them—slipped out into Shilmista and, following Hammadeen's guidance, struck hard at the disorganized enemy. More elves were discovered in the woods, or found their own way to the new camp, and soon Elbereth's forces had systematically sliced holes through the encircling monsters.

Cadderly remained at the ridge beside Tintagel and the other wounded, though Danica was quick to join Shayleigh and set out on the hunt. It didn't fall upon Cadderly to strive for the level of healing power he had needed to save

Tintagel, and Cadderly thought that a good thing, for he did not believe the heal-ing powers would ever flow through him with such intensity again.

He knew that something was happening all about him, or to him, but he didn't want to depend on this unknown entity, for he certainly did not understand it.

* * * * *

The first real test of Ivan's defenses came late the next afternoon, when a band of more than two hundred monsters, ranging from skinny goblins to hill giants, set their sights on reclaiming the high ground. Only a score of elves were on the ridge beside Cadderly and the dwarves at that time, but that number included both wizards. After two hours of vicious fighting, more than half of the monsters lay dead and the rest had been scattered to the woods, easy pickings for the "packs of wolves" that roamed the forest.

Not a single elf had died in the fight, though two had been nicked by giant-hurled rocks, for the battle had never come to hand-to-hand fighting. Cunning dwarf-made traps, volleys of arrows, magical strikes, and the four towering oak trees slaughtered the enemy before they ever got past the steep rock face halfway up the ridge.

By Ivan's estimation, the most difficult part of the whole fight was in cleaning up the fallen goblinoids when it was all over.

"I'd forgotten that one," Ivan remarked to Cadderly, pointing to the tree line as darkness began to fall over the forest. Out of the trees came three elves and a companion whom Cadderly, too, had forgotten in the commotion of battle.

Kierkan Rufo leaned heavily on a staff and, even with the stick, still needed the support of one of the elves. The angular man's leg was not broken, as he had feared, but it was badly bruised and twisted and would not support his weight. He instructed his escorts to take him to Cadderly, and after several minutes of struggling to get past the natural obstacles of the ridge, Rufo plopped down in the grass beside Ivan and the young scholar.

"So nice of you to look over me," the angular man, in a foul mood, remarked.

"Bah, ye took to the trees, way up, to keep out of the fight," Ivan retorted, more amused than angered.

"High ground!" Rufo protested.

" 'Hide ground' would be a better way to name it," Ivan replied.

"Hee hee hee." Rufo didn't need to look over his shoulder to know that the laugh belonged to Pikel, walking behind him.

"Could you at least get me something to eat?" Rufo growled at Cadderly. "I have spent the last day under the limbs of a fallen oak, miserable and hungry!"

"Hee hee hee," came a distant answer.

* * * * *

Danica and Shayleigh returned a short while later. Neither of them was over-joyed to find Kierkan Rufo in the camp. The angular man defiantly pulled himself to his feet beside Danica.

"Another supposed friend," he spat. "Where was Danica Maupoissant when poor Rufo was in need? What alliances are these, I ask, when companions care nothing for each other's welfare?"

Danica looked from Cadderly to Ivan to Pikel as the angular man continued his tirade.

"You are all to blame!" Rufo fumed, his anger gaining momentum. Danica curled up her fist and gritted her teeth.

"You are all—" With that, Rufo fell to the earth and abruptly slept.

Danica's shrug was not an apology for her blow, just an admission that her behavior in slugging Rufo might have been a bit impulsive. She expected Cadderly to berate her, but the young scholar could not, not against the wave of approval coming in from all around her.

* * * * *

When the friends came upon Elbereth later that night, they found him smiling more than they had seen in many, many days.

"The news is good," the elf explained. "More than seventy of my people are known to live, and that number might increase, for nearly a score of elves are as yet unaccounted for and Hammadeen has told us that a battle was fought back in the east. And the paths farther to the east, through the Snowflake Mountains, are open once more, for a contingent of priests has arrived from the Edificant Library. Guided by the dryad, one of our hunting parties has joined the group, and even now they make their way to Deny Ridge.

"We are still badly outnumbered," Shayleigh put in, "but our enemy is disorganized and confused. With both Ragnor and Dorigen dead . . ."

Cadderly's sudden grunt stopped her and turned all eyes toward the young scholar.

"Dorigen is not dead," he admitted. The looks all about him turned sour, but the most painful retort to Cadderly, by far, was the sharpness of Danica's tone.

"You did not finish her?" the young woman cried. "You had her down and helpless!"

"I could not."

"I am doomed!" Rufo wailed. "Dorigen will see to our end, to my end! You fool!" he yelled at Cadderly.

"Are ye looking for more sleep?" Ivan asked him, and Rufo realized from Danica's scowl that he would be wise to remain silent.

But in this encounter, Kierkan Rufo did have an ally.

"Fool indeed!" roared Elbereth. "How?" he demanded of Cadderly. "Why did you let the wizard escape?"

Cadderly couldn't begin to explain, knew that his admission of compassion would not be appreciated by the new elf king. He was truly amazed at how quickly Elbereth had apparently forgotten his actions in the battle, in Syldritch Trea and against Ragnor, and in saving Tintagel.

"Dorigen cannot use her magical powers," the young scholar offered weakly. "She is sorely wounded and stripped of her magical devices." Cadderly unconsciously dropped a hand in his pocket, to feel the rings he had taken from Dorigen. He had considered giving them and Dorigen's wand to Tintagel, to learn if they might aid in the fighting, but he had dismissed the notion and resolved to check out the dangerous devices himself when he found the time.

Cadderly's claims did nothing to alleviate Elbereth's anger. "Her presence will bring unity to our enemies!" the elf growled. "That alone dooms Shilmista!" Elbereth shook his head and stalked away, Shayleigh at his side. The others, too, dispersed, Pikel sadly, leaving Cadderly and Danica alone by the campfire.

"Mercy," Cadderly remarked. He looked at his love, caught her brown eyes in a gaze that would not let go. "Mercy," he whispered again. "Does that make me weak?"

Danica spent a long moment considering the question. "I do not know," she answered honestly.

They stood quietly, watching the fire and the stars for a very long time. Cadderly slipped his hand into Danica's and she accepted the grasp, if somewhat hesitantly.

"I will remain in the forest," she said finally, dropping Cadderly's hand. Cadderly looked at her, but she did not return the stare. "To fight beside Elbereth and Shayleigh. The priests will arrive tomorrow, so it is rumored. Likely they will stay a few days to forge pacts with the elves, and then some might remain to fight on. But most, I assume, will return to the library. You should go with them."

Cadderly found no words to immediately reply. Was Danica sending him away? Had she, too, perceived his compassion as a weakness?

"This is not your place," Danica whispered.

Cadderly took a step away from her. "Was Syldritch Trea my place, then?" he grumbled coldly, as openly angry at Danica as he had ever been. "And have you heard of how mighty Ragnor met his end? Or have you forgotten Barjin?"

"I do not question your value," Danica answered honestly, turning to regard Cadderly, "in this fight, as in anything. You will find no comfort in the continuing battle for Shilmista, just more violence, more killing. I do not like what that will do to you. I do not like what it has done to me."

"What are you saying?"

"There is a coldness here," Danica replied, poking a finger to her heart. She crossed her arms in front of her, as if to ward off a wintry blast. "A numbness," she continued. "A fading of compassion. How easily I told you to kill Dorigen!" She stopped, choked by the admission, and looked away.

Cadderly's visage softened with sincere pity.

"Go away," Danica begged. "Go back to the library, to your home."

"No," Cadderly replied. "That place was never my home."

Danica turned back and eyed him curiously, expecting some revelation.

"This is not my place, that much is true," Cadderly went on, "and I have little fight left in me, I fear. I will leave with the priests when they depart, but to the library only long enough to retrieve my belongings."

"Then where?" Danica's voice hinted, just a tiny bit, of desperation.

Cadderly shrugged. He wanted desperately to beg Danica to come away with him, but he knew that he must not, and that she would refuse in any case. It struck them both then, that this was farewell, perhaps forever.

Danica hugged Cadderly suddenly and kissed him hard, then moved back and pushed him away. "I wanted to stay beside you when the fighting began in earnest," she said, "after the trees had come to life. But I knew I could not, that the situation would not allow me my wishes."

"And so it is now," Cadderly said, "for both of us." He ran his fingers through Danica's strawberry-blond hair, matted and tangled from so many days of battle.

Danica started to kiss him again, but changed her mind and walked away instead.

Cadderly remained at Deny Ridge for five more days, but he did not see her again.

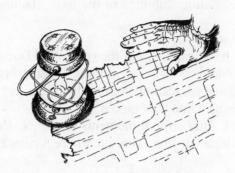

Epilogue

Y ou should have stayed in the forest," Aballister said, pacing the length of his small room at Castle Trinity.

Dorigen wisely kept her stare locked upon him. Unlike Barjin's demise, this defeat had brought a somber mood to the head of Castle Trinity, a real fear that his plans for conquest might not be so easily accomplished. He still had more than three thousand soldiers at his command, and many more might be salvaged from the tribes returning to their mountain homes, but Shilmista was lost, at least for now, and the new elf king was determined and valorous. Dorigen had heard, and recounted for Aballister, many tales concerning mighty Elbereth's exploits in the battle for the wood.

"You should have stayed!" the older wizard growled again, more forcefully.

"I would not remain among such treacherous rabble with my fingers broken," Dorigen answered, holding up her bandaged hands. "Do you really believe that I would have been safe among goblins and orcs?"

Aballister could not deny the truth of her observations. He had seen first-hand what wild goblinoids might do to a woman. "Without you to guide them, Ragnor's army is no more than scattered bands," he reasoned, "easy targets for the organized elves and this new king they hold so dear. We will be months in recovering our losses."

"The goblins will find a leader amongst them," Dorigen replied.

"One loyal to us?" Aballister asked incredulously.

"We still have time before the onset of winter to go back and set things in Shilmista to our advantage!" Dorigen snapped back at him, not conceding an inch regarding her decision to leave. "The elves are not many, no matter how well organized and how well led they might be. For all their gains now, they'll surely

429

have a long road in ridding Shilmista of the dark plague Castle Trinity has dropped upon it."

"You should have stayed."

"And you should have watched out for your son!" Dorigen rejoined before her better judgment could overrule her actions. Druzil, perched on Aballister's desk, groaned and folded his leathery wings about him, certain that his master was about to blast Dorigen into little pieces.

Nothing happened. After several moments of silence, Dorigen, also fearful, realized that she had hit a sensitive area, one where Aballister, mighty Aballister, felt vulnerable.

"Cadderly," the wizard mumbled. "Twice he has wandered into my way—and I had thought myself rid of the boy. Well, the first inconvenience could be forgotten. I wasn't so certain that I wanted Barjin to conquer the library in any case," the wizard admitted openly. "But this! No, Cadderly has become too much a threat to be tolerated."

"How do you intend to end that threat?" Dorigen asked bluntly. She could hardly believe the coldness on Aballister's face when he spoke of his long-lost son.

"Boygo Rath has some helpful connections in Westgate," Aballister answered, his thin lips curling up in a wicked smile.

Dorigen winced, suspecting what the wizard had in mind.

"You have heard of the Night Masks?" Aballister asked.

Dorigen winced again at the mention of the assassin band. Of course she had heard of them—everyone from the Dragon Reach to Waterdeep had heard of them! She nodded, her expression openly revealing her disbelief that Aballister would be wicked enough to hire such a band to kill his own son.

Aballister laughed at that incredulous expression. "Let us just say," he remarked, "that Cadderly, too, will soon hear of them."

Dorigen took the news with mixed feelings. She was angry with Cadderly, to be sure, for what he had done to her, but she could not ignore the fact that the young priest easily could have killed her. She shrugged her thoughts away and reminded herself that it was none of her affair, that what now transpired was between Aballister, Boygo, and Cadderly.

And the Night Masks.

* * * * *

"Them goblin things are to be dancing in the trees tonight when they hear that ye're a dead one," Ivan remarked, cutting an easy swipe with his great axe.

"More likely, they shall sing of the death of a dwarf," Elbereth retorted, easily backing from the lazy swing. He rushed in behind the swipe, looking for an opening, but Ivan's defenses were back in place before the elf got within reach.

"What's an Elbereth?" Ivan taunted, white teeth shining through his yellow beard.

"I shall use that phrase for your epitaph!" the elf roared, and he played his sword through a dazzling display of feints and thrusts, ending up with its point sinking through Ivan's armor, toward the dwarf's chest.

Ivan fell back and blinked stupidly.

"Oo," moaned Pikel from the side, a sentiment echoed by Shayleigh, Tintagel, and many of the other gathered elves, including even Elbereth.

"Ye killed me, elf," Ivan grunted, his breath coming hard. He stumbled backward, barely holding his balance.

Elbereth lowered his sword and rushed in, terrified at what he had done. When he got two steps from Ivan, bending low to examine the wound, he noticed Ivan's lips curl up in a smile and knew he had been deceived.

"Hee hee hee," came a knowing chuckle from the side.

Ivan turned his axe sideways and thumped Elbereth on the forehead, sending him tumbling backward. The elf threw his weight into the roll and came back to his feet some distance away. He watched curiously as two images of Ivan Bouldershoulder steadily closed.

"Ye think yer skinny blade'd get through me dwarf-made armor?" Ivan huffed. "Silly elf."

They joined in melee again, this time Ivan taking the lead. Elbereth learned his lesson well, and he used his superior speed and agility to parry Ivan's attacks and keep out of the dwarf's shorter reach. Every time the cunning elf found an opening, he slapped the side of his sword against the side of Ivan's head.

He might as well have been banging stone.

After many minutes, the only somewhat serious wound came when Ivan tripped and inadvertently dropped the head of his heavy axe on Elbereth's toes.

The call around the perimeter of the battle, where nearly the entire elven camp had by then gathered to watch, became general.

"Hee hee hee."

* * * * *

Cadderly looked out the open window, beyond the rooftops of Carradoon, toward Impresk Lake, but his thoughts were many miles away, back in the forest he had left four weeks before. The morning fog rose from the still water; a distant loon uttered its mournful cry.

Where was Danica now? Cadderly wondered. And what of Ivan and Pikel? The young scholar dearly missed his friends and lumped that emptiness into the same void he had discovered when he had realized that the Edificant Library was not his home, and never had been.

He had gone back to the library with Headmaster Avery, Kierkan Rufo, and a score of other priests after leaving Shilmista. Avery had begged him to stay and continue his studies, but Cadderly would not, could not. Nothing about the place seemed familiar to the young scholar; he could not help but view the library as a lie, a facade of serenity in a world gone crazy.

"There are too many questions," Cadderly had told the headmaster. "And here I fear that I will find too few of the answers." So young Cadderly had taken his purse and his walking stick, and all the other possessions he had considered worthwhile, and had left the library, doubting that he would ever return.

A knock on the door broke the young scholar from his contemplations. He moved across the small room and cracked open the portal just enough to retrieve the breakfast plate that had been left for him.

When he had finished his meal, he replaced the plate outside his door, leaving a silver coin as a tip for obliging Brennan, son of the innkeeper of the Dragon's Codpiece. Cadderly had asked for his privacy and the innkeeper had given it to him without question, delivering his meals and leaving him alone.

The calls in the street began again shortly after, as Cadderly expected they would. Carradoon was being roused for war; a force was quickly being mustered to organize a defense of the town. At first, the call was for soldiers to go to the aid of the elves in their noble battle for Shilmista, but the latest reports had changed that. Shilmista was secured, it seemed, with most of the scattered goblinoids fully on the run.

Still the force in Carradoon swelled, and restrictions, including a curfew, had been placed on the town.

Cadderly did not enjoy the rising level of anxiety, but he thought the town wise in making preparations. The evil that had inspired Barjin's attempt on the Edificant Library and Ragnor's invasion of Shilmista was not fully defeated, Cadderly knew, and it would no doubt soon descend over Carradoon.

Cadderly did not close his window against those calls. The wind coming off the lake was comfortably cool and gave him at least some tie to the outside world. Reverently, the young scholar took out his most valuable possession, the *Tome of Universal Harmony* opened it on his small desk, and sat down to read.

Too many questions filled his mind.

The Cleric Quintet · Book Three

Night Masks

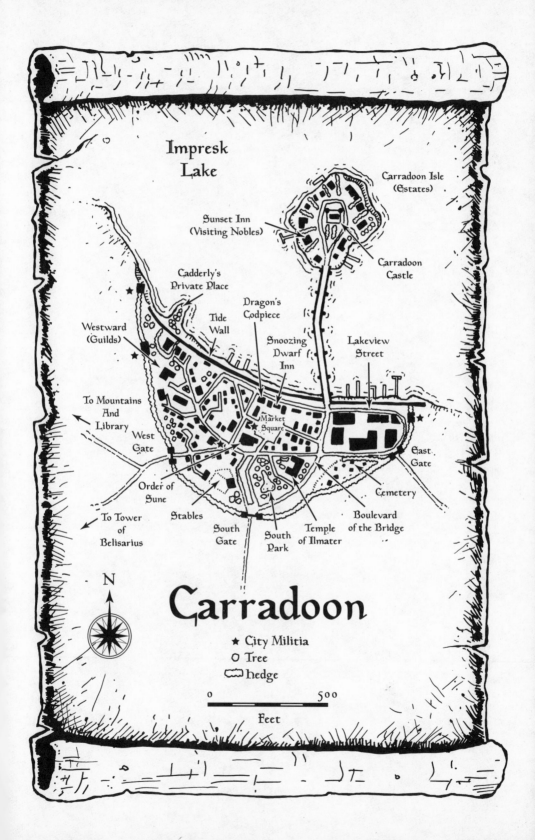

Impresk
Lake

Carradoon Isle
(Estates)

Sunset Inn
(Visiting Nobles)

Carradoon
Castle

Cadderly's
Private Place

Dragon's
Codpiece

Tide
Wall

Westward
(Guilds)

Snoozing
Dwarf
Inn

Lakeview
Street

To Mountains
And
Library

West
Gate

Market
Square

East
Gate

Order of
Sune

Cemetery

To Tower
of
Belisarius

Stables

South
Gate

South
Park

Temple
of Ilmater

Boulevard
of the Bridge

N

Carradoon

★ City Militia
O Tree
〰 hedge

0   500

Feet

Prologue

The large fighter shifted uneasily in his seat, looking all about the nearly empty tavern.

"Not so busy this night," the slender, drowsy-looking man across the table remarked. He shifted back lazily in his seat, crossed his legs in front of him, and draped a skinny arm over them.

The larger man regarded him warily as he began to understand. "And you know all in attendance," he replied.

"Of course."

The burly fighter looked back just in time to see the last of the other patrons slip out the door. "They have left by your bidding?" he asked.

"Of course."

"Mako sent you."

The weakling man curled his lips in a wicked grin, one that widened as the burly fighter regarded his skinny arms with obvious disdain.

"To kill me," the large man finished, trying to appear calm. His wringing hands, fingers moving as if seeking something to keep them occupied, revealed his nervousness.

He licked his dried lips and glanced around quickly, not taking his dark eyes from the assassin for any length of time. He noticed that the man wore gloves, one white and one black, and silently berated himself for not being more observant.

The thin man replied at length, "You knew Mako would repay you for his cousin's death."

"His own fault!" the large man retorted. "It was he who struck the first blow. I had no choi—"

"I am neither judge nor jury," the puny man reminded him.

"Just a killer," the fighter replied, "serving whoever gives you the largest sack of gold."

The assassin nodded, not the least bit insulted by the description.

The little man noticed his target's hand slipping casually into the hidden pouch, the fitchet, in the V cut of his tunic, above his right hip.

"Please, do not," the assassin said. He had been monitoring this man for many weeks, carefully, completely, and he knew of the knife concealed within.

The fighter stopped the movement and eyed him incredulously.

"Of course I know the trick," the assassin explained. "Do you not understand, dear dead Vaclav? You have no surprises left for me."

The man paused, then protested, "Why now?" The large man's ire rose with his obvious frustration.

"Now is the time," replied the assassin. "All things have their time. Should a killing be any different? Besides, I have pressing business in the west and can play the game no longer."

"You have had ample opportunity to finish this business many times before now," Vaclav argued. In fact, the little man had been hovering about him for weeks, had gained his trust somewhat, though he didn't even know the man's name. The fighter's eyes narrowed with further frustration when he contemplated that notion and realized that the man's frail frame—too frail to be viewed as any threat—had precipitated that acceptance. If this man, now revealed as an enemy, had appeared more threatening, Vaclav never would have let him get this close.

"More chances than you would believe," the assassin replied with a snicker. The large man had seen him often, but not nearly as often as the killer, in perfect and varied disguises, had seen Vaclav.

"I pride myself on my business," the assassin continued, "unlike so many of the crass killers that walk the Realms. They prefer to keep their distance until the opportunity to strike presents itself, but I —" his beady eyes flickered with pride, "—prefer to personalize things. I have been all about you. Several of your friends are dead, and I now know you so well that I can anticipate your every movement."

Vaclav's breathing came in short rasps. Several friends dead? And this weakling threatening him openly? He had defeated countless monsters ten times this one's weight, had served honorably in three wars, had even battled a dragon! He was scared now, however. Vaclav had to admit that. Something was terribly wrong about this whole set-up, terribly out of place.

"I am an artist," the slender, sleepy man rambled. "That is why I will never err, why I will survive while so many other hired murderers go to early graves."

"You are a simple killer and nothing more!" the large man cried, his frustration boiling over. He leaped from his seat and drew a huge sword.

A sharp pain slowed him, and he found himself somehow sitting again. He blinked, trying to make sense of it all, for he saw himself at the empty bar, was, in fact, staring at his own face! He stood gawking as he—as his own body!—slid the heavy sword back into its scabbard.

"So crude," Vaclav heard his own body say. He looked down to the figure he now wore, the killer's weak form.

"And so messy," the assassin continued.

"How . . . ?"

"I do not have the time to explain, I fear," the assassin replied.

"What is your name?" Vaclav cried, desperate for any diversion.

"Ghost," answered the assassin. He lurched over, confident that the seemingly androgynous form, one he knew so well, could not muster the speed to escape him or the strength to fend him off.

Vaclav felt himself being lifted from the floor, felt the huge hands slipping about his neck. "The ghost of who?" managed the out-of-control, desperate man. He kicked as hard as his new body would allow, so pitiful an attempt against the burly, powerful form his enemy now possessed. Then his breath would not come.

Vaclav heard the snap of bone, and it was the last sound he would ever hear.

"Not 'the ghost,' " the victorious assassin replied to the dead form, "just 'Ghost.' " He sat then to finish his drink. How perfect this job had been; how easily Vaclav had been coaxed into so vulnerable a position.

"An artist," Ghost said, lifting his cup in a toast to himself. His more familiar body would be magically repaired before the dawn, and he could then take it back, leaving the empty shell of Vaclav's corpse behind.

Ghost had not lied when he had mentioned pressing business in the west. A wizard had contacted the assassin's guild, promising exorbitant payments for a minor execution.

The price must have been high indeed, Ghost knew, for his superiors had requested that he take on the task. The wizard apparently wanted the best.

The wizard wanted an artist.

One
Placid Fields

Cadderly walked slowly from the single stone tower, across the fields, toward the lakeside town of Carradoon. Autumn had come to the region; the few trees along Cadderly's path, red maples mostly, shone brilliantly in their fall wardrobe. The sun was bright this day and warm, in contrast with the chilly breezes blowing down from the nearby Snowflake Mountains, gusting strong enough to float Cadderly's silken blue cape out behind him as he walked, and strong enough to bend the wide brim of his similarly blue hat.

The troubled young scholar noticed nothing.

Cadderly absently pushed his sand-brown locks from his gray eyes, then grew frustrated as the unkempt hair, much longer than he had ever worn it, defiantly dropped back down. He pushed it away again, and then again, and finally tucked it tightly under the brim of his hat.

Carradoon came within sight a short while later, on the banks of wide Impresk Lake and surrounded by hedge-lined fields of sheep and cattle and crops. The city proper was walled, as were most cities of the Realms, with many multistory structures huddled inside against ever-present perils. A long bridge connected Carradoon to a nearby island, the section of the town reserved for the more well-to-do merchants and governing officials.

As always when he came by this route, Cadderly looked at the town with mixed and uncertain feelings. He had been born in Carradoon, but did not remember that early part of his life. Cadderly's gaze drifted past the walled city, to the west and to the towering Snowflakes, to the passes that led high into the mountains, where lay the Edificant Library, a sheltered and secure bastion of learning.

That had been Cadderly's home, though he realized that now it was not, and thus he felt he could not return there. He was not a poor man. The wizard in the tower he had recently left had once paid him a huge sum for transcribing a lost spell book—and he had the means to support himself in relative comfort.

But all the gold in the world could not have produced a home for Cadderly, nor could it have released his troubled spirit from its turmoil.

Cadderly had grown up, had learned the truth of his violent, imperfect world, too suddenly. The young scholar had been thrust into situations beyond his experience, forced into the role of hero-warrior when all he really wanted was to read of adventures in books of legend. Cadderly had recently killed a man, and had fought in a war that had blasted, torn, and ultimately tainted a once-pristine sylvan forest.

Now he had no answers, only questions.

Cadderly thought of his room at the Dragon's Codpiece, where the *Tome of Universal Harmony*, the most prized book of the god named Deneir, sat open on his small table. It had been given to Cadderly by Pertelope, a high-ranking priestess of his order, with the promise that within its thick bindings Cadderly would find his answers.

Cadderly wasn't sure he believed that.

The young scholar sat on a grassy rise overlooking the town, scratched at his stubbly beard, and wondered again about his purpose and calling in this confusing life. He removed his wide-brimmed hat and stared at the porcelain insignia attached to its red band: an eye and a single candle, the holy symbol of Deneir, the deity dedicated to literature and the arts.

Cadderly had served Deneir since his earliest recollections, though he had never really been certain of what that service entailed, or of the real purpose in dedicating his life to any god. He was a scholar and an inventor and believed wholeheartedly in the powers of knowledge and creation, two very important tenets for the Deneirian sect.

Only recently had Cadderly begun to feel that the god was something more than a symbol, more than a fabricated ideal for the scholars to emulate. In the elven forest Cadderly had felt the birth of powers he could not begin to understand. He had magically healed a friend's wound that otherwise would have proved fatal. He had gained supernatural insight into the history of the elves, not just their recorded events, but the feelings, the eldritch aura, that had given the ancient race its identity. He had watched in amazement as the spirit of a noble horse rose from its broken body and walked solemnly away. He had seen a dryad disappear into a tree and had commanded the tree to push the elusive creature back out—and the tree had heeded his command!

There could be no doubt for young Cadderly: mighty magic was with him, granting him these terrifying powers. His peers called that magic Deneir and called it a good thing, but in light of what he had done, of what he had become, and the horrors he had witnessed, Cadderly was not certain that he wanted Deneir with him.

He got up from the grassy rise and continued his journey to the walled town, to the Dragon's Codpiece, and to the *Tome of Universal Harmony*, where he could only pray that he would find some answers and some peace.

* * * * *

He flipped the page, his eyes desperately trying to scan the newest material in the split second it took him to turn the page again. It was impossible; Cadderly simply could not keep up with his desire, his insatiable hunger, to turn the pages.

He was finished with the *Tome of Universal Harmony*, a work of nearly two thousand pages, in mere minutes. Cadderly slammed the book shut, frustrated and fearful, and tried to rise from his small desk, thinking that perhaps he should go for a walk, or go to find Brennan, the innkeeper's teenage son who had become a close friend.

The tome grabbed at him before he could get out of his seat. With a defiant but impotant snarl, the young scholar flipped the book back over and began his frantic scan once more. The pages flipped at a wild pace; Cadderly couldn't begin to read more than a single word or two on any one page, and yet, the *song* of the book, the special meanings behind the simple words, rang clearly in his mind. It seemed as though all the mysteries of the universe were embedded in the sweet and melancholy melody, a song of living and dying, of salvation and damnation, of eternal energy and finite matter.

He heard voices as well—ancient accents and reverent tones singing in the deepest corners of his mind, but he could not make out any of the words, like the written words on the pages of the book. Cadderly could see them as a whole, could see their connotations, if not the actual lettering.

Cadderly felt his strength quickly draining as he continued to press on. His eyes ached, but he could not close them; his mind raced in too many directions, unlocking secrets, then storing them back into his subconscious in a more organized fashion. In those brief transitions from one page to another, Cadderly managed to wonder if he would go insane, or if the work would consume him emotionally.

He understood something else, then, and the thought finally gave to him the strength to slam the book shut. Several of the higher ranking Deneirian priests at the Edificant Library had been found dead, lying across this very book. Always the deaths had been seen as by natural causes—all of those priests had been much older than Cadderly—but Cadderly's insight told him differently.

They had tried to hear the song of Deneir, the song of universal mysteries, but they had not been strong enough to control the effects of that strange and beautiful music. They had been consumed.

Cadderly frowned at the black cover of the closed tome as though it were a demonic thing. It was not, he reminded himself, and, before his fears could argue back, he opened the book once more, from the beginning, and began his frantic scan.

Melancholy assaulted him; the doors blocking revelations swung wide, their contents finding a place in the receptacle of young Cadderly's mind.

Gradually the young scholar's eyes drooped from sheer exhaustion, but still the song played on, the music of the heavenly spheres, of sunrise and sunset and all the details that played eternally in between.

It played on and on, a song without end, and Cadderly felt himself falling toward it, becoming no more than a passing note among an infinite number of passing notes.

On and on . . .

"Cadderly?" The call came from far away, as if from another world perhaps. Cadderly felt a hand grasp his shoulder, tangible and chill, and felt himself turned gently about. He opened a sleepy eye and saw young Brennan's curly black mop and beaming face.

"Are you all right?"

Cadderly managed a weak nod and rubbed his bleary eyes. He sat up in his chair, felt a dozen aches in various parts of his stiff body. How long had he been asleep?

It was not sleep, the young scholar realized then, to his mounting horror. The weariness that had taken him from consciousness was too profound to be cured by simple sleep. What, then?

It was a journey, he sensed. He felt as though he had been on a journey. But to where?

"What were you reading?" Brennan asked, leaning past him to regard the open book. The words shook Cadderly from his reflections. Suddenly terrified, he shoved Brennan aside and slammed the book.

"Do not look at it!" he answered harshly.

Brennan seemed at a loss. "I . . . I am sorry," he apologized, obviously confused, his green eyes downcast. "I did not mean—"

"No," Cadderly interrupted, forcing a disarming smile to his face. He hadn't intended to wound the young lad who had been so kind to him over the last few weeks. "You did nothing wrong. But promise me that you will never look into this book—not unless I am here to guide you."

Brennan took a step away from the desk, eyeing the closed tome with sincere fear.

"It is magical," Cadderly acknowledged, "and it could cause harm to one who does not know how to read it properly. I am not angry with you—truly. You just startled me."

Brennan nodded weakly, seeming unconvinced.

"I brought your food," he explained, pointing to a tray he had placed on the night table beside Cadderly's small bed.

Cadderly smiled at the sight. Dependable Brennan. When he had come to the

Dragon's Codpiece, Cadderly had desired solitude and had arranged with Fredegar Harriman, the innkeeper, to have his meals delivered outside his door. That arrangement had quickly changed, though, as Cadderly had come to know and like Brennan. Now the young man felt free to enter Cadderly's room and deliver the plates of food—always more than the price had called for—personally. Cadderly, for all his stubbornness and the icy demeanor he had developed after the horrors of Shilmista's war, had soon found that he could not resist the unthreatening companionship.

Cadderly eyed the plate of supper for a long while. He noticed a few specks of crumbs on the floor, some from a biscuit and some darker—the crust of the midday bread, he realized. The curtains over his small window had been drawn and his lamp had been turned down, and then turned back up.

"You could not wake me the last three times you came in here?" he asked.

Brennan stuttered, surprised that Cadderly had deduced that he had been in the room three times previously. "Three times?" he replied.

"To deliver breakfast and then lunch," Cadderly reasoned, and then he paused, realizing that he should not know what he knew. "Then once more to check on me, when you turned the lamp back up and drew the curtains."

Cadderly looked back to Brennan and was surprised again. He almost called out in alarm, but quickly realized that the images he saw dancing on the young man's shoulders—shadowy forms of scantily clad dancing girls and disembodied breasts—were of his own making, an interpretation from his own mind.

Cadderly turned away and snapped his eyes shut. An interpretation of what?

He heard the song again, distantly. The chant was specific this time, the same phrases repeated over and over, though Cadderly still could not make out the exact words, except for one: *aurora.*

"Are you all right?" Brennan asked again.

Cadderly nodded and looked back, this time not so startled by the dancing shadows. "I am," he replied sincerely. "And I have kept you here longer than you wished."

Brennan's face screwed up with curiosity.

"You be careful at the Moth Closet," Cadderly warned, referring to the seedy private club at the end of Lakeview Street, on the eastern side of Carradoon, near where Impresk Lake spilled into Shalane River. "How does a boy your age get into the place?"

"How . . ." Brennan stuttered, his pimpled face blushing to deep crimson.

Cadderly waved him away, a wide smile on his face. The dancing shadow breasts atop Brennan's shoulder disappeared in a burst of splotchy black dots. Apparently Cadderly's guesses had knocked out the teenager's hormonal urgings.

Temporarily, Cadderly realized as Brennan headed for the door, for the shadows already began to form anew. Cadderly's laugh turned Brennan back around.

"You will not tell my father?" he pleaded.

Cadderly waved him away, stifling the urge to burst out in laughter. Brennan hesitated, perplexed. He relaxed almost immediately, reminding himself that Cadderly was his friend. A smile found his face, and a dancing girl found a perch on his shoulder. He snapped his fingers and swiftly disappeared from the room.

Cadderly stared long and hard at the closed door, and at the telltale crumbs on the floor beside his night table.

Things had seemed so very obvious to him, both of what had transpired in his room while he was asleep, and of Brennan's intentions for a night of mischief. So obvious, and yet, Cadderly knew they should not have been.

"Aurora?" he whispered, searching for the significance. "The dawn?" Cadderly translated, and shook his head slowly; what could the dawn have to do with silhouettes of dancing girls on Brennan's shoulder?

The young priest looked back to the tome. Would he find his answer there?

He had to force himself to eat, to remind himself that he would need all his strength for the hours ahead. Soon after, one hunger sated and another tearing at him, Cadderly dove back into the *Tome of Universal Harmony*.

The pages began to flip, and the song played on and on.

Two
Mopping Up

Danica blew a lock of her strawberry-blond hair from in front of her exotic, almond-shaped brown eyes and peered intently down the forest path, searching for some sign of the approaching enemy. She shifted her compact, hundred-pound frame from foot to foot, always keeping perfect balance, her finely toned muscles tense in anticipation of what was to come.

"Are the dwarves in position?" Elbereth, the new king of Shilmista's elves, asked her, his strange, almost eerie, silver eyes looking more to the trees surrounding the path than to the trail itself.

Two other elves, one a golden-haired maiden, the other with black hair as striking as Elbereth's, came to join the friends.

"I would expect the dwarves to be ready in time," Danica assured the elf king. "Ivan and Pikel have never let us down."

The three elves nodded; Elbereth could not help but smile. He remembered when he had first encountered the gruff dwarves, when Ivan, the tougher of the pair, had found him bound and helpless as a prisoner of their enemy. Never would the elf have believed that he would soon come to trust so implicitly in the bearded brothers.

"The dryad has returned," the black-haired elf wizard, Tintagel, said to Elbereth. He led the elf king's gaze to a nearby tree, where Elbereth managed to make out Hammadeen, the elusive dryad, as her tan-skinned, green-haired form peeked from around the trunk.

"She brings news that the enemy will soon arrive," remarked Shayleigh, the elven maiden. The anxious tone of her voice and the sudden sparkle that came into her violet eyes reminded Danica of the fiery maiden's lust for battle. Danica had seen Shayleigh "at play" with both sword and bow, and she had to agree with

Ivan Bouldershoulder's proclamation that he was glad Shayleigh was on their side.

Tintagel motioned for the others to follow him to the rest of the gathered elves, some two score of Elbereth's people, almost half of the remaining elves in Shilmista. The wizard considered the landscape for a moment, then began positioning the elves along both sides of the path, trying to properly distribute those better in hand-to-hand combat and those better with their great bows. He called Danica to his side and began his spellcasting chant, walking along the elven lines and sprinkling white birch bark chips.

As he neared the end of the spell, Tintagel took up his own position, Danica moving to her customary spot beside him, and sprinkled chips upon himself and his human escort.

Then it was completed, and where Danica and forty elven warriors had been standing now stood rows of unremarkable birch trees.

Danica looked out from her new disguise to the forest about her, which seemed vague and foggy to her now, more like a feeling than any definite vision. She focused on the path, knowing that she and Tintagel must remain aware of their surroundings, must be ready to come out of the shape-changing spell as soon as Ivan and Pikel began the assault.

She wondered what she looked like as a tree, and thought, as she always thought when Tintagel performed this spell, that she might like to spend some quiet time in this form, viewing the forest around her, feeling its strength in her feet-become-roots.

But now there was killing to do.

* * * * *

"Oo," moaned Pikel Bouldershoulder, a round-shouldered dwarf with a green-dyed beard braided halfway down his back and open-toed sandals on his gnarly feet, as he watched the distant spectacle of Tintagel's spell. The longing gaze was plain to see, and Pikel almost toppled out of the tree in which he sat.

"No, ye don't!" his brother whispered harshly from across the way, disdaining Pikel's druidic tendencies. Ivan tucked his yellow beard into his wide belt and shifted his dwarven-hard buttocks about on the tree branch and his deer-antlered helmet about on his head, trying to find a comfortable position in this very undwarvenlike perch. In one hand he held a club made from the thick trunk of a dead tree. A heavy rope had been tied about his waist and looped up over a branch halfway across the trail.

Ivan had accepted the high seat, knowing what fun it would bring, but he drew the line at being turned into a tree—above his would-be druid brother's whining protests. Ivan had offered a compromise, enquiring of Tintagel about a variation of his mighty spell, but the elf wizard had declined, explaining that he had no power to turn people into rocks.

Across the path, in a perch opposite Ivan, Pikel seemed much more comfortable, both with his tree seat and tree-trunk club. He, too, sported a rope about his waist, the other end of Ivan's. Pikel's comfort with the perch could not defeat his frown, though, a frown brought on by his longing to be with the elves, to be a tree in Shilmista's soil.

Guttural goblin grumbling down the path alerted the dwarves of the enemy's approach.

"Sneaksters," Ivan whispered with a wide smile, trying to brighten his brother's surly mood. Ivan didn't want Pikel pouting at this critical moment.

Both dwarves tightened their grip on their clubs.

Soon the enemy band passed directly under them, spindle-armed and ugly goblins mixed in with pig-faced orcs and larger orogs. Ivan had to force himself not to spit on the wretched throng, had to remind himself that more fun would be had if he and his brother could hold their positions just a short while longer.

Then, as the dryad Hammadeen had told them it would, a giant came into view, plodding slowly down the path, seemingly oblivious to its surroundings. By the dryad's words this was the last giant remaining in Shilmista, and Ivan wasn't about to let the evil thing go crawling back to its mountain home.

"Sneaksters," Ivan whispered again, the title he had chosen for him and his brother, a title he knew that the giant, above all others, would appreciate in just another moment.

The huge head bobbed steadily closer. One goblin stopped suddenly and sniffed the air.

Too late.

Ivan and Pikel leveled their clubs and, with a nod to each other, hopped off their high perches, swinging down at the path. Their timing proved perfect and the oblivious giant stepped between them, its gaze straight ahead, its head bobbing at just the right height.

Pikel connected just a split-second before Ivan, the heavy dwarves sandwiching the monster's head in a tremendous slam. Ivan immediately dropped his bloodied club and tore out his favored double-bladed axe instead.

On the path below, the smaller monsters went into a frenzy, pushing and shoving, diving to the dirt, and running in all directions. They had lost many companions in the last few weeks, and they knew what was to come.

The wizard, Tintagel, cried out the dispelling syllable; Danica and forty elves behind her reverted to their original forms, drew back their bowstrings, and charged with gleaming swords waving high.

The dazed giant wobbled, but stubbornly, stupidly, held its balance, and Ivan and Pikel, dangling nearly twenty feet above the forest path, went to work.

Ivan's axe took off an ear; Pikel's club splattered the monster's nose all over its cheek. Again and again they smacked at the beast. They knew they were vulnerable up there, knew that if the giant managed to get even a single hit in, it would probably knock one of them halfway back to the Edificant Library. But the brothers didn't think of that grim fact at the time; they were having too much fun.

Below the hanging dwarves came the sound of elven bows loosing hail after hail of arrows deep into goblin, orc, and orog flesh.

Creatures died by the score; others cried in agony and terror, and the merciless elves came on, swords in hand, hacking at the squirming forms of these vile invaders, the monsters that had so tainted the precious elven home.

Danica spotted one group of monsters slipping away through the trees to the side. She called to Tintagel and sped off in pursuit, taking up her crystal-bladed daggers, one with a golden pommel carved into the likeness of a tiger, the other, with a hilt of silver, carved into a dragon.

* * * * *

Pikel's club knocked the giant's head backward so brutally that the dwarves heard the sharp crack of the huge monster's neck bone. The giant somehow held its balance for just a moment longer, looking dazed and confused, and then became quite dead. It rolled up on the balls of its huge feet and toppled forward like a chopped tree.

Ivan quickly surveyed the path ahead of the falling beast.

"Two!" the dwarf yelled, and the giant's body buried two unfortunate goblins as it landed.

"Ye owe me a gold piece!" Ivan roared, and Pikel nodded happily, more than willing to pay the bet.

"Ye ready for more?" Ivan cried.

"Oo oi!" Pikel replied with enthusiasm. Without a word of warning to his brother, Pikel grabbed a nearby branch and quickly pulled the loop around his waist, freeing his end of the rope.

Ivan did manage to open his eyes wide, but the inevitable curses aimed at his brother would have to wait as he took a more direct descent to the ground. To Pikel's credit, the plummeting Ivan did clobber a goblin beneath him.

The yellow-bearded dwarf hopped back to his feet, spitting dirt and curses. He casually dropped his heavy axe onto the back of the wounded goblin's head, ending its complaints, and looked back up to his brother, who was making a more conventional way down the tree.

Pikel shrugged and smiled meekly. "Oops," he offered, and Ivan silently mouthed the word at the same instant Pikel spoke it, fully expecting the all-too-common apology.

"When ye get down here . . ." Ivan began to threaten, but goblins suddenly closed in around the vulnerable dwarf. Ivan howled happily and forgot any anger harbored against Pikel. After all, how could he possibly stay mad at someone who had dropped him right in the middle of so much fun?

* * * * *

The fleeing band's lead goblin scrambled through the thick underbrush, desperate to leave the slaughter behind. The monster hooked one ankle on one of many crisscrossing roots in this overgrown region, and stubbornly pulled itself free. Then it got hooked again, and this time the grasp was not so easily broken.

The goblin squealed and pulled, then looked back to see, not a root, but a woman, smiling wickedly and holding fast to its ankle.

Danica twisted her arm in a sudden jerk and charged up and ahead from her low concealment, tripping the unfortunate creature. She was atop the thing in an instant, her free hand pushing away the frantic beast's futile slaps while her other hand, holding the golden-hilted dagger, came slashing in for a single, vicious strike.

Danica rarely needed more than one.

The young woman pulled herself up from the slain creature, openly facing its surprised comrades, who weaved in and out of the trees behind and to the sides. The band eyed her curiously and looked all about, not really knowing what to make of the woman. Where had she come from, and why was she alone? Not another leaf or bush in this area moved, though the fighting continued back on the trail.

With that thought in mind, an orog cried for a charge, eager to claim at least one victim amidst the disaster. The monstrous band came crashing in at Danica from three sides, through the bushes and brambles, gaining confidence and resolve with every step.

Elbereth dropped from a tree limb above Danica, his gleaming sword and shining armor revealing his prominent stature among the elven clan. Some of the monsters halted altogether, and the others slowed, looking back and forth curiously from the elf and woman to their less brave comrades.

A short distance to the side, Shayleigh appeared from behind a tree and set her bow immediately to work, dropping the creature closest to her companions.

The orogs cried out to run away, a command goblins were always ready to follow. Elbereth and Danica moved first, though, catching the nearest goblins in a furious rush, while Shayleigh concentrated her fire on the orogs.

Those monsters not engaged ran wildly, picking their escape routes through the thick trees and brush.

A wall of mist rolled up before them. Terrified goblins skidded to a stop. The orogs, right behind, prodded them, knowing that to halt was to die.

An arrow thudded into the back of an orog; another bolt followed its flight just a split second later, and the remaining two orogs shoved the lead goblin into the fog.

Watching from the boughs above, Tintagel quickly launched another spell, throwing his voice through a rolled-up cone of parchment into the area of the vapors. His fog wall was a harmless thing, but the cries of agony that suddenly emanated from within made the hesitant creatures think otherwise.

Three arrows took down the second orog. The remaining brute scrambled about, seeking cover behind its goblin fodder. It came out the side of the group, thinking to circle around the fog wall . . . but it found Elbereth, and Elbereth's sword, instead.

* * * * *

"It's about time ye got here!" Ivan growled when Pikel finally made his way down the towering tree to come to his side. Many yards from the host of elves, and with many monsters between him and them, Ivan had been sorely pressed. Still, the tough dwarf had managed to escape any serious injury, for the bulk of the monsters were more interested in escaping than in fighting.

And it had quickly become obvious to the goblins that any who ventured near Ivan's furious axe swipes would not long survive.

Now, back to back, the dwarven brothers elevated the battle to new heights of slaughter. They overwhelmed the nearby monsters in mere minutes, then shuffled up the path to overwhelm another group.

The elves cut in just as fiercely, swordsmen driving the monstrous throng every which way, and archers, just a short distance behind, making short work of those creatures that broke out of the pack. The goblinoids had nowhere to run and nowhere to hide. Already, more monsters lay dead than those standing to continue the fight, and that ratio came to favor the elves more and more with every passing second.

* * * * *

Tintagel watched as the first goblin that had been pushed into the wall emerged from the other side unharmed. The elf wizard resisted the urge to blast the thing down, for his role in this fight was to contain the monsters so that Elbereth, Shayleigh, and Danica could finish them. He pulled more dried peas from his pouch and tossed them to the ground, perpendicular to the mist wall. Uttering the proper chant, the wizard summoned a second fog wall to box in the monsters.

Danica followed Shayleigh's next three arrows into the confused horde. She whipped her daggers into the nearest targets, killing one goblin and dropping a second in screaming pain, and came in with a fury that her enemies could not match.

Nor could the remaining orog match Elbereth's skill. The creature parried the elf's initial, testing swing, then brought its heavy club across wickedly. Elbereth easily sidestepped the blow and waded in behind, jabbing his fine sword repeatedly into the slower beast's chest.

The creature blinked many times as though it was trying to focus through eyes that were no longer seeing clearly. Elbereth couldn't wait for it to decide its next move. He whipped his shield arm about, slamming the shield—which had belonged to his father not so long ago—against the orog's head. The monster dropped heavily, star-shaped welts from the embossed symbols of Shilmista crossing the side of its piggish face.

Shayleigh, now with a sword in hand, came up beside the elven king and together they waded confidently into the goblins.

With no options readily before them, the trapped goblins began to fight back. Three surrounded Danica, hacking wildly with their short swords. They couldn't keep up with her darting movements, dips, and dodges, though, and weren't really coming very close to connecting.

Danica bided her time. One frustrated creature whipped its sword across in a harmlessly wide arc. Before the goblin could recover from its overbalanced swing, Danica's foot snapped straight up, connected under its chin, and drove its jaw up under its nose. The goblin promptly disappeared under the brush.

A second beast rushed at the distracted woman's back.

Bolts of magical energy flashed down from the tree above, burning into its head and neck. The goblin howled and grabbed at the wound, and Danica, fully balanced at all times, spun a half-circle, one foot flying wide, and circle-kicked it across the face. Its head looking far back over one shoulder, the goblin joined its dead companion on the ground.

Danica managed to nod her thanks to Tintagel as she waded into the lone goblin facing her, her hands and feet flying in from all sides, finding opening after opening in the pitiful creature's defenses. One kick knocked its sword away and, before it could cry out a surrender, Danica's stiffened fingers rifled into its throat, tearing out its windpipe.

Suddenly, it was over, with no more monsters to hit. The four companions, three of them covered in the blood of their enemies, stood solemn and grim, surveying their necessary handiwork.

* * * * *

"Ye know, elf," Ivan said when Elbereth and the others came back to the group on the trail, "this is getting too easy." The dwarf spat in both hands and grasped his axe handle, the blade of his weapon buried deeply into an orog's thick head. With a sickening crack, Ivan pulled the mighty weapon free.

"First fight in a week," Ivan continued, "and this group seemed more keen on running than fighting!"

Elbereth couldn't deny the dwarf's observations, but he was far from upset at what the goblins' retreat indicated.

"If we are fortunate, it will be another week before we find the need to fight again," he replied.

Ivan balked, and drove his gore-stained blade into the earth to clean it. As Elbereth moved away, the dwarf muttered to his brother, "Spoken like a true elf."

Three
Heartfelt

Y ou sit here and wait while all of our dreams—all of the dreams Talona
herself gave you—fall to pieces!" Dorigen Kel Lamond, second most powerful wizard in all of Castle Trinity, sat back in her chair, somewhat surprised by her uncharacteristic outburst. Her amber eyes looked away from
Aballister, her mentor and superior.

The hollow-featured, older wizard seemed to take no offense. He rocked back
in his comfortable chair, his sticklike fingers tap-tapping in front of him and an
amused expression upon his gaunt face.

"Pieces?" he asked after a silence designed to make Dorigen uncomfortable.
"Shilmista has been, or soon will be, reclaimed by the elves, that much is true,"
he admitted. "But their insignificant number has been halved by all reports—less
than a hundred of them remain to defend the forest."

"And we lost more than a thousand soldiers," Dorigen snapped sharply.
"Thousands more have fled our dominion, gone back to their mountain holes."

"Where we might reclaim them," Aballister assured her, "when the time is
right."

Dorigen fumed but remained silent. She brushed a bead of sweat from her
crooked nose and again looked away. Sporting two broken hands, the woman
felt vulnerable with both unpredictable Aballister and upstart Bogo Rath in the
private room, to say nothing of Druzil, Aballister's pet imp. That was one of the
problems in working beside such evil men, Dorigen reminded herself. She
could never be certain when Aballister might think he would be better off without her.

"We still have three thousand soldiers—mostly human—at our immediate
disposal," Aballister went on. "The goblinoids will be brought back when we

455

need them—after the winter, perhaps, when the season is favorable for an invasion."

"How many will we need?" he asked, more to Bogo than to Dorigen. "Shilmista is but a semblance of itself, and the Edificant Library has been severely wounded. That leaves only Carradoon." The tone of Aballister's voice showed clearly how he felt about the farmers and fishermen of the small community on the banks of Impresk Lake.

"I'll not deny that the library has been wounded," Dorigen replied, "but we really do not know the extent of those wounds. You seem to have underestimated Shilmista as well. Must I remind you of our most recent defeat?"

"And must I remind you that it was you, not I, who presided over that defeat?" the older wizard growled, his dark-eyed gaze boring into Dorigen. "That it was Dorigen who fled the forest at the most critical stages of the battle?" Seeing her cowed, Aballister again rocked back in his chair and calmed.

"I sympathize with your pains," he said quietly. "You have lost Tiennek. That must have been a terrible blow."

Dorigen winced. She had expected the remark, but it stung her nonetheless. Tiennek, a barbarian warrior she had plucked from the northland and trained to serve as her consort, had replaced Aballister as her lover. Dorigen didn't doubt for a minute the older wizard's satisfaction upon hearing that the great warrior had been killed. A woman nearly two feet shorter than Tiennek and barely a third of his weight had done the deed. In reporting the incident, the imp Druzil had purposely downplayed the young woman's prowess, Dorigen knew, just to fan the flames that had come between the two wizards.

Dorigen wanted to fight back, wanted to shout in the wizard's face that he could not understand the power of that young woman, Danica, the monk escort of Cadderly, and of all the enemies she had met in Shilmista. She looked to Druzil, who had been there beside her, but the imp covered his doglike face with his leathery wings and made no move to support her.

"Wretched, cowardly creature," Dorigen muttered. Since their return to Castle Trinity, Druzil had avoided contact with Dorigen. He held no loyalty to Aballister, she knew, except that Aballister was in control here, and the prudent imp always preferred to be on the winning side.

"Enough of this bantering," Aballister said suddenly. "Our plans have been delayed by some unexpected problems."

"Like your own son," Dorigen had to put in.

Aballister's smile hinted that Dorigen might have overstepped her bounds. "My son," the wizard echoed, "dear young Cadderly. Yes, Dorigen, he has proved the most unexpected and severe of our problems. Do you agree, Boygo?"

Dorigen looked to the youngest of Castle Trinity's wizards, Bogo Rath, whom she and her mentor routinely called "Boygo."

The young man narrowed his eyes at the insult, not that he hadn't expected it. He was so very different from his two peers, and so often the butt of their jokes. He jerked his head back and forth, flipping his long, stringy brown hair over one ear, away from the side of his head that he kept shaved.

Dorigen, tiring of Bogo's outrageous actions, almost growled at his ridiculous haircut.

"Your son has indeed proved to be quite a problem," Bogo replied. "What else might we expect from the offspring of mighty Aballister? If young Cadderly must fight on the other side, then we would be wise to pay attention to him."

"Young Cadderly," Dorigen mumbled, her face locked in an expression of disgust. "Young Cadderly" had to be at least two or three years older than this upstart!

Aballister held up a small, bulging bag and shook it once to show the others that its thickness came from many coins—gold, probably. Dorigen understood the bag's significance, understood what it would buy for Aballister, and for Bogo as well. Bogo had come from Westgate, a city four hundred miles to the northeast, at the mouth of the Lake of Dragons. Westgate was notable as a bustling trading town, and it was known, too, for an assassin band called the Night Masks, who were among the cruelest killers in the Realms.

"Even your Night Masks will have a difficult time striking at our young scholar, whether he is in Shilmista or has returned to the Edificant Library," Dorigen asserted, if for no better reason than to take some of the bite out of Aballister's icy demeanor concerning his son. For all that she hated Cadderly—he had broken her hands and stolen several magical items from her—Dorigen simply could not believe Aballister's viciousness toward his own son.

"He is not in Shilmista," Bogo replied with a grin, his brown eyes flashing with excitement, "nor in the library." Dorigen stared at Bogo, and her sudden interest obviously pleased the young wizard. "He is in Carradoon."

"Rousing the garrison, no doubt," Aballister added.

"How can you be certain?" Dorigen asked Bogo.

Bogo looked to Aballister, who shook the bag of gold once more. Its tinkling coins sent a shiver along Dorigen's spine. Bogo's assassin connections with Westgate, his one claim to any prestige in Castle Trinity, were already on the trail.

Even though her hands continued to throb, Dorigen felt pity for the young scholar.

"One problem at a time, dear Dorigen," Aballister said, a thought he had iterated before, when he had first told Dorigen of his plans for his son. Again the older wizard shook the bag of gold, and again a shiver coursed along Dorigen's spine.

* * * * *

Elbereth and Danica sat atop Deny Ridge, a defensible position that the elves had taken as their base. Few of the elven folk were about this starry night, and there was no longer any danger demanding an alert garrison. Indeed, according to Hammadeen—and dryad's tree-gotten information had been accurate since Cadderly had pressed her into service weeks earlier—no monsters were within ten miles of the ridge.

It was peaceful and quiet, not the ring of swords or the cries of the dying to be heard.

"The wind grows chill," Elbereth commented, offering Danica his traveling cloak. She accepted it and lay in the thick grass beside the elf, looking up to the countless stars and the few black forms of meandering clouds.

Elbereth's soft chuckle led her to sit up once more. She followed the elf's gaze to the base of the sloping hill. Squinting, she could just make out three forms—one elven and the other two obviously dwarven—darting in and out of the shadows along the tree line.

"Shayleigh?" Danica asked.

Elbereth nodded. "She and the dwarves have become great friends in the last few weeks," he noted. "Shayleigh admires their courage and is not ungrateful that they have remained to aid in our fight."

"Is the elf king ungrateful?" Danica asked slyly.

Elbereth managed a smile at her good-natured sarcasm. He recalled his first meeting with the dwarves, and how he had come close to trading serious blows with Ivan. How long ago that seemed now! Elbereth had been just a prince then, in disfavor with his father, the king, at a time when the forest was in peril.

"I am not ungrateful," he replied softly. "I will never forget the debt I owe the dwarves . . . and you." He locked stares with Danica then, his silver eyes catching the woman's rich brown orbs in an unblinking gaze.

Their faces lingered, barely an inch apart.

Danica cleared her throat and turned away. "The fighting nears its end," she remarked, stealing the romance from the moment. Elbereth knew at once where her comment would lead, for she had hinted at her plans for several days.

"We will be ridding Shilmista of the goblin vermin for the rest of the season," the elf king said firmly. "And I fear that a new attack might begin in the spring, after the mountain trails are clear."

"Hopefully by then Carradoon and the library will be roused," Danica offered.

"Will you help that process?"

Danica looked back down the grassy slope, where the three forms were now steadily approaching.

"Never did care much for trees," they heard Ivan complaining as he rubbed at his nose.

"I would have thought that one as short as a dwarf would be able to avoid low-hanging branches," Shayleigh replied with a melodic laugh.

"Hee hee hee," added Pikel, prudently swerving out of Ivan's backhanded reach.

"The time has come for me, and Ivan and Pikel, to depart," Danica blurted, hating the words but having to say them. Elbereth's smile was gone in an instant.

He looked long and hard at the woman and did not respond.

"Perhaps we should have left with Avery and Rufo for the library," Danica went on.

"Or perhaps you should trust them to handle the affairs at the library and in Carradoon," Elbereth put in. "You could remain, all three. The invitation is open, and I assure you that Shilmista takes on an entirely new beauty under winter's white blanket."

"I do not doubt your words," Danica replied, "but I fear I must go. There is—"

"Cadderly," Elbereth interrupted, smiling despite his disappointment that his three friends would soon leave.

Danica did not reply, was not even sure of how she felt. She looked back to the slope, where Ivan and Pikel still tried to make their way to where Shayleigh waited. They almost made it this time, but apparently Ivan muttered something that offended his brother, for Pikel sprang upon him and the two rolled down once more. The elf maiden threw up her hands in surrender and sprinted the rest of the way to Danica and Elbereth.

As soon as she joined the two, her smile was replaced by a curious expression. She studied Danica's face for a moment, then commented matter-of-factly, "You are leaving."

Danica did not respond, could hardly look the elven maiden in the face.

"When?" Shayleigh asked, her tone still calm and composed.

"Soon—perhaps tomorrow," Danica replied.

Shayleigh spent a long moment considering the bittersweet news. Danica was leaving after the victory, with the forest secured. She could return, or the elves could go to her, freely, with little threat of goblins and orcs.

"I applaud your choice," Shayleigh said evenly. Danica turned to regard her, caught off guard by the elf's approval.

"The fight here is won, at least for now," the elf maiden continued, gaily spinning a turn in the clean and crisp evening air. "You have many duties to attend to, and, of course, you have studies back at the Edificant Library."

"I expect that Ivan and Pikel will accompany me," Danica replied. "They also have duties at the library."

Shayleigh nodded and looked back to the slope, where the brothers were trying a third time to get all the way up. At that angle, in the clear starlight, Danica could see the sincere admiration in the elf maiden's violet eyes. Danica understood that Shayleigh had put on her carefree attitude because she believed Danica's decision was the right one, not because she was pleased that Danica and the dwarves would soon depart.

"If the fight begins anew in the spring . . ." Shayleigh started to say.

"We will be back," Danica assured her.

"Back where?" Ivan finally came up, shook from his yellow beard the twigs and leaves that had gotten caught up in it from his two rolls down the hill, and tucked it into his wide belt.

"Back to Shilmista," Shayleigh explained. "If the fighting begins anew."

"We going somewhere?" Ivan asked Danica.

"Uh-oh," moaned Pikel, beginning to understand.

"The first blows of winter will be upon us soon," Danica replied. "The trails through the Snowflakes will become impassable."

"Uh-oh," Pikel said again.

"Ye're right," Ivan said after thinking things over for a moment. "Things're settling here—not much left to hit. Me and me brother'd get bored soon enough, and besides, them priests at the library probably ain't had a good-cooked meal since we left!"

Shayleigh slapped Ivan on the side of the head. Ivan turned to stare incredulously into her wistful smile, and even the gruff dwarf could recognize the pain hidden beneath the fair maiden's delicate features.

"You still owe me a fight," Shayleigh explained.

Ivan snorted and cleared his throat, sneakily moving his shirt sleeve high enough to wipe the moisture from his eyes as he ran his sleeve across his nose. Danica was amazed by the obvious chink in the dwarf's callous demeanor.

"Bah!" Ivan growled. "What fight? Ye're just like the other one!" He waggled an accusing finger at Elbereth, whom he had battled to a draw in a similar challenge just a few weeks before. "Ye'd dance all about and run in circles until we both fell down tired!"

"Do you think I would release you from the insult you gave my people?" Shayleigh snarled, hands on hips, and moved over to tower above the dwarf.

"Ye think I'd let ye?" Ivan retorted, poking a stubby finger into Shayleigh's belly. "Bah!" Ivan snorted, and he turned and stormed away.

"Bah!" Shayleigh mimicked, her voice too melodic to properly copy the dwarf's grating tone.

Ivan spun back and glowered at her, then motioned for Pikel to follow him away. "Well, ye got yer wood back, elf," Ivan said to Elbereth. "Ye're welcome!"

"Farewell to you, too, Ivan Bouldershoulder," Elbereth replied. "Our thanks to you and your splendid brother. Know that Shilmista will be open to either of you if you choose to pass this way again."

Ivan smiled Pikel's way. "As if that one could stop us anyhow!" he roared, and he slapped Shayleigh across the rump and darted away before she recovered enough to respond.

"I must go as well," Danica said to Elbereth. "I have many preparations to make before dawn."

Elbereth nodded but could not reply past the lump in his throat. As soon as Danica was gone, skipping down the slope to catch up with the dwarves, Shayleigh took a seat beside the silver-eyed elf king.

"You love her," the elf maiden remarked after a few silent moments.

Elbereth sat quietly for a while, then admitted, "With all my heart."

"And she loves Cadderly," said Shayleigh.

"With all her heart," Elbereth replied somberly.

Shayleigh managed a weak grin, trying to bolster her friend's resolve.

"Never would I have believed that an elf king of Shilmista would fall in love with a human!" Shayleigh spouted, nudging Elbereth in the shoulder.

The elf turned his silver-eyed gaze upon her and smiled wryly. "Nor I that an elf maiden would be enchanted by a yellow-bearded dwarf," he replied.

Shayleigh's initial reaction came out as an incredulous burst of laughter. Certainly Shayleigh had come to know Ivan and Pikel as friends, and trusted allies, but to hint at anything more than that was simply ridiculous. Still, the elven maiden quieted considerably when she looked down the now empty slope.

Empty indeed did it seem with the Bouldershoulder brothers gone from view.

Four

A Long Time to Dawn

Bogo Rath tentatively knocked on the door of the small conference room. He was never secure in his dealings with the dreaded Night Masks. A score of assassins had accompanied the two Night Mask leaders into Castle Trinity that same morning, many more trained killers than Bogo had anticipated for such a seemingly simple execution.

Black-robed sentries searched the young wizard before he was allowed entry. These two were unremarkable enough, Bogo noted, probably beginners in the dark band. They wore the customary dress of Westgate's assassin guild, nondescript yeoman's clothes and silver-edged black eye masks. One sentry's tusky grin made Bogo think his heritage might be more orc than human, something common in the underground band, and that thought sent a shudder along the young wizard's spine.

Whether these two were human or not, though, Bogo would not have been comfortable. He knew that, while the assassins openly displayed no weapons, each of them carried many and were trained to kill with their bare hands as well.

When the searching was done, the two guards led the young wizard into the room, then stepped back to the door, standing impassively on either side of the portal.

Bogo forgot about them as soon as they were behind him, for the young wizard found the two persons inside the comfortable room much more interesting. Closest to him sat a puny man—if it was a man—effeminate and obviously weak, issuing a steady stream of phlegm-filled coughs. The man showed no beard at all, not even stubble; his face was too clean and soft-looking to be an adult's. His heavy eyelids drooped lazily, and his lips, too thick and too full, seemed almost a childlike caricature.

462

Across the way sat the man's opposite, a thick-muscled, robust specimen with a full, thick beard and shock of hair, both flaming red, and arms that could snap Bogo in half with little effort. Still, this powerful man seemed even more out of place (from what Bogo knew of the Night Masks) than did the weakling. He brandished a huge sword on his girdle and bore the scars of many battles. His dress, too, was far from that preferred by assassins. Wide, studded bracers, glittering with dozens of small jewels, adorned the man's wrists, and his snow-white traveling cloak had been cut from the back of a northern bear, albeit a small one.

"You are Bogo Rath?" the large man asked in a smooth baritone, with an articulation that was sharper and more sophisticated than Bogo had expected.

The wizard nodded. "Well met, fellow Night Mask," the young wizard replied with a low bow.

The red-haired man gave him a curious look. "I was not told you retained any connection to the guild," he said. "I was informed that you left the band of mutual consent."

Bogo shifted nervously from foot to foot. He had paid a huge sum to be allowed out of the Night Masks three years earlier, and even with the bribe, if it hadn't been for the fact that his father was an influential merchant in Westgate— one with political associations and ties to the dark guild—Bogo would have been given the customary send-off for one who could not meet the Night Masks' standards: death.

"It is unusual to see a person who can claim that he once belonged to our beloved brotherhood," the red-haired man teased, his cultured voice dripping with sarcasm.

Again Bogo shifted, and he had to remind himself that this was Castle Trinity, his home, and that Aballister and Dorigen, for all their taunts, would look out for him.

"It was an unusual circumstance," the young wizard replied, revealing his nervousness with an uneasy flip of his stringy brown hair. "I had another calling, one that took me far from Westgate. As you can see, my departure has done us both some good. I have attained a level of power that you cannot comprehend, and you shall be paid well for doing me this one small task."

The huge man grinned, seeming to mock Bogo's claims of power, and looked to his puny companion, who seemed none too pleased by this whole business.

"Do sit with us," the large man bade Bogo. "I am Vander, the taskmaster for this small bit of business of which you speak. My associate is Ghost, a most unusual and talented man."

Bogo took a seat between the two, alternating his gaze to try to find clues about his untrusted associates.

"Is there a problem?" Vander asked him after studying Bogo's actions for a moment.

"No," Bogo blurted immediately. He forced himself to calm down. "I am just surprised that so many have been sent for so simple an execution," he admitted.

Vander laughed aloud, but then stopped abruptly, a curious expression cross-ing his face. His glower fell over Ghost as his body went into a series of convul-sions, and then, to Bogo's amazement, Vander and his possessions began to grow.

The sword, huge to begin with, took on gigantic proportions, and the north-ern bear that comprised the fine cloak no longer seemed a cub. Because Vander was seated, Bogo couldn't tell just exactly how large the man became—at least ten feet tall, he guessed.

"Firbolg?" he asked as much as stated, recognizing the giant for what it was. Now Bogo was at a loss. Having a huge, red-haired man, so easily distinguish-able, in the Night Masks, was stunning enough, but a firbolg?

Vander's angry glare did not relent. His dark eyes peered intently at Ghost from under his bushy brows. He regained his composure quickly, though, and rested back in his seat.

"Forgive me," he said unexpectedly to Bogo. "I am indeed of the race of giant-kin, though I do not openly reveal my more-than-human stature."

"Then why—?" Bogo began to ask.

"An indiscretion," Vander quickly interrupted, the tone of his deep voice indi-cating that he did not wish to continue.

Bogo wasn't about to argue with an eight-hundred-pound giant. He crossed his hands defensively over his lap and tried hard to appear relaxed.

"You question our number?" Vander asked, going back to the wizard's origi-nal inquiry.

"I did not expect so many," Bogo reiterated.

"The Night Masks take no chances," Vander replied evenly. "Often execu-tions appearing so simple prove the most difficult. We do not make mistakes. That is why we are so well rewarded for our efforts." He cocked his giant head to one side—a curiously ungiantlike action, Bogo thought—and looked to the pouch on Bogo's rope belt.

Taking the cue, the young wizard pulled the bag of gold from his belt and handed it to Vander. "Half payment," he explained, "as was agreed to by your superiors."

"And by yours," Vander was quick to remark, not willing to give Bogo the upper hand, "a wizard named Aballister, I believe."

Bogo did not respond, did not confirm or deny the claim.

"And you will accompany us as a representative of Castle Trinity in this mat-ter?" Vander stated as much as asked. "Another unusual circumstance."

"That, too, was agreed upon," Bogo replied firmly, though the way he contin-ually moved his fingers defeated the conviction in his tone. "By both parties," he prudently added, "most likely because I was once a member of your guild and understand your ways."

Vander stifled his urge to deflate the pretentious young man's swelling ego. The giant knew that Aballister had paid a considerable amount of extra gold to get Bogo included, and that the young wizard's assignment had nothing to do with Bogo's past employment with the assassin band.

"I will journey to Carradoon beside you," Bogo continued, "to offer a full report to my sup—associates."

Vander smiled widely, catching the slip. "Whatever role you might play in the death of Cadderly does not change the sum owed the Night Masks," he said grimly.

Bogo nodded. "My role will be as observer, nothing more, unless, of course, you, as taskmaster, decide otherwise," he agreed. "Might I enquire of your own role?" Bogo paused. He knew he might be overstepping his bounds, but he could not let Vander have such an obvious advantage in their dealings. "It seems unlikely that a firbolg could parade through the streets of Carradoon. And what of the Ghost?"

"He is called Ghost, not 'the Ghost,'" Vander snapped. "You would do well to remember that. My own role," he continued, mellowing a bit, "is none of your concern."

It struck Bogo as more than a little curious that Vander took more offense at his concerns for Ghost than for himself, particularly since Bogo had directly questioned the firbolg's value.

"Ghost will lead the way in, gather information, and prepare the target," Vander went on. "I have twenty skilled assassins at my disposal, so we will need to secure a base near, but not within, the walls of Carradoon."

Bogo nodded at the simple logic.

"We will leave in the morning, then," Vander continued. "Are you prepared?"

"Of course."

"Then our meeting is concluded," Vander stated abruptly, flatly, motioning to the door. Immediately the two black-robed sentries moved to each side of Bogo to escort him from the room.

Bogo looked back at the door many times as he made his way slowly down the corridor. A firbolg and a weakling? It seemed very unusual, but then, Bogo had been in the Night Masks only a day more than a month before he had begged to leave, and he had to admit, at least to himself, that he knew very little about the band's methods.

Bogo soon dismissed all thoughts of Vander and Ghost, concentrating instead on another meeting he had planned. At Aballister's request, Bogo would meet with Druzil to learn all he could about Cadderly and his cohorts. The imp had dealt with Cadderly on two occasions—both disastrous for Castle Trinity—and knew as much about him as anyone.

Bogo desperately wanted that knowledge. He was a bit dismayed that so many Night Masks had been assigned to this task, not because he wanted Cadderly to have a chance to escape, but because he wanted to be in on the action. More than anything else, Bogo Rath wanted to play a vital role in the kill, wanted to gain the respect of Aballister and, particularly, Dorigen.

He was tired of the taunts, of being referred to as Boygo. How would mighty Dorigen, who returned from Shilmista stripped of her valuable possessions and with her hands broken and swollen, feel when Bogo delivered the head of Aballister's troublesome son? Cadderly, after all, had been the source of Dorigen's humiliation.

Bogo dared to dream that he might ascend within Castle Trinity's hierarchy to become Aballister's second. Dorigen's hands were slow to heal; the fortress's clerics doubted that many of her fingers would ever straighten. Given that precise movements played a vital role in spell casting, who could guess the implications to Dorigen's power?

Bogo rubbed his soft hands together eagerly and sped off for the meeting room, to where Druzil, his guide to a better life, waited.

* * * * *

"How dare you do that to me!" the firbolg growled at his companion as soon as Bogo had gone. A nod from him sent the two guards scrambling from the room. The giant leaped from his seat and threateningly advanced a step.

"I did not know that my . . . that your . . . body's size would return to normal," the little man protested, trying to sink deeper into the cushions of his soft chair. "I believed the enchantment would last longer, at least through the meeting." The firbolg grabbed the little man by the collar and hoisted him into the air. "Ah, Vander," the giant purred, his features too calm, "dear Vander." The firbolg's face contorted suddenly in rage and he punched the little man in the face, destroying his nose. A backhand slap raised a welt on one cheek; a second slap did likewise on the other. Then, with an evil grin, the firbolg grabbed the little man by one forearm and snapped his bone so severely that the man's fingers brushed against his elbow.

The beating went on for many minutes, and finally the firbolg dropped the barely conscious man back to his seat.

"If you ever deceive me so again . . ." the red-haired giant warned. "If ever again you humiliate me in front of one such as Bogo Rath, I will torment you until you beg for death!"

The smaller man, the real Vander, curled up in a fetal position, cradling his shattered arm, feeling terribly vulnerable and afraid trapped inside the puny body of the weakling, Ghost.

"I want my body back," Ghost said suddenly, tugging uncomfortably at his firbolg trappings. "You are so hairy and itchy!"

Vander sat up and nodded, eager to be back in his own form.

"Not now," Ghost growled at him. "Not until the wounds heal. I would not accept my body back in less than perfect condition," he said wryly. "As it was when I gave it to you."

Vander slumped back. This game had grown quite old over the last few years, but what options lay before him? He couldn't escape Ghost's evil clutches, couldn't resist the demands of Ghost's magic. Vander wanted nothing more than to get back into his firbolg form and pound the little man, but he knew that Ghost would simply initiate a switch back, and then Vander would feel the pain of his own attacks. Ghost would continue the beating, Vander knew, for hours sometimes, until poor Vander broke and wept openly, and begged his master to stop.

The trapped firbolg put a hand to his broken human nose. Already it was on the mend; the pain was no more and the blood flow had stopped. The broken forearm had straightened again and Vander could feel tingling as the bones knitted. Just a few more minutes, he thought to comfort himself, and I will have my body back, my own strong body.

"I will be leaving this hour," Ghost said to him. He pointed a threatening finger Vander's way. "Remember that you are my spirit-mate," he warned. "I can come back for you, just for you, Vander, from any distance, at any time."

Vander averted his eyes, unable to deny the threat. Once he had tried to flee this nightmare, had gotten all the way home to the Spine of the World Mountains, but Ghost, thousands of miles away, had found him and forced a body switch. Merely to show Vander the folly of his actions, Ghost mercilessly had slaughtered several of Vander's fellow firbolgs, including his brother, on a little-used mountain trail east of Mirabar. Vander vividly remembered the terrible moment when Ghost had given him back his body, holding his oldest son's left arm in his gigantic hand.

Vander had killed Ghost when he returned to Westgate, had nearly torn the little man's head from his shoulders, but, a week later, Ghost had walked into Vander's camp, smiling.

Vander came out of his contemplations and regarded his hated companion. Ghost towered above him, a black glove on one hand, a white one on the other, and wearing a familiar golden-edged mirror hanging on a golden chain around his neck.

At the clap of the firbolg's hands, Vander felt himself floating. His noncorporeal spirit looked back to the weak, drowsy form on the floor with contempt, then looked ahead to the giant receptacle. There came a flash of burning pain as Vander entered his firbolg body. His spirit twisted about and shifted to reconfigure itself to the proper form, to reorient Vander to his new coil.

Ghost had come out of the spirit-walk faster than Vander, as always, and was sitting comfortably in a chair, watching the firbolg intently, as Vander came back to consciousness. The puny body now wore the gloves and mirror; the magic device always transferred with its master. As soon as it became obvious that Vander would not attack him, Ghost clenched his hands and closed his eyes. The gloves and mirror disappeared, but Vander knew from bitter and painful experience that they were well within immediate recall.

"You will depart as planned with the band and the young wizard," Ghost instructed.

"What of this Bogo Rath?" Vander asked. "I do not trust him."

"That is of no consequence," Ghost replied. "After all, you do not trust me, either, but I know you are enamored of my warm personality."

Vander wanted to smash the smug smile off Ghost's sleepy-eyed face.

"The wizard is to accompany us," Ghost instructed. "Aballister paid us handsomely to take Rath along, a fine cache of gold for so minor an inconvenience."

"To what purpose?" Vander had to ask, always amazed at the webs of seemingly pointless intrigue created by less than honorable people.

"Aballister believes that sending an emissary will keep him informed," Ghost replied. "The wizard has a weakness for knowledge. He cannot tolerate the occurrence of anything that affects him, directly or even indirectly, without his knowledge."

Vander did not disagree. He had met Aballister only once, and Ghost had spoken with the hollow-featured wizard no more than three times. But the firbolg didn't doubt Ghost's perceptions. The little man possessed an uncanny understanding of character, particularly of character flaws, and always found a way to use that to his advantage.

* * * * *

The young scholar blinked at the morning brightness, shining across Impresk Lake and through the windows of his room's balcony doors. Breakfast sat on the table next to Cadderly—extra portions, he noted, and he smiled. They were a bribe, Brennan's way of saying thank you for Cadderly's continued discretion. Fredegar wouldn't be happy with his son if he knew where Brennan had spent the evening.

Cadderly was indeed hungry, and the food looked good, but when the young scholar noticed the *Tome of Universal Harmony* sitting open on his desk by the window, he realized a more profound and demanding hunger. He took a single biscuit with him as he went to the desk.

Like so many times before, Cadderly devoured the pages, the blurred words, faster than his eyes could follow. He was through the tome in a matter of minutes, then turned it back over and began again, rushing, almost desperately, to keep the mysterious song flowing uninterrupted. How many times Cadderly went through the work that day, he could not know. When Brennan came in with his lunch, then his supper, he did not look up from his reading, from his listening to the song.

The daylight waned, and still Cadderly pored on. His first thought, when the room became too dark to read in, was to go and light his lamp, but he hated to waste the time that action would take. Hardly considering his actions, Cadderly recalled a page in the tome, a particular melody, and uttered a few simple words, and instantly the room was filled with light.

The stream of the song was broken. Cadderly sat blinking in amazement at what he had done. He retraced his mental steps, recalled that same page, its image clear in his mind. He uttered the chant again, changing his inflections and alternating two of the words.

The light went out.

Shaking, Cadderly slipped out of his chair and over to his bed. He threw an arm across his eyes, as though that act might hide the confusing memory of what had just occurred.

"I'll see the wizard in the morning," he whispered aloud. "He will understand."

Cadderly didn't believe a word of it, but he refused to listen to the truth.

"In the morning," he whispered again, as he sought the serenity of sleep.

The morning was many hours and many dreams away for the troubled young man.

* * * * *

Percival hopped up to the room's window—no, not the window, but the terrace doors. Cadderly considered the strange sight, for the squirrel's sheer size made the doors look more like a tiny window. It was Percival, Cadderly knew instinctively, but why was the squirrel six feet tall?

The white squirrel entered the room and came beside him. Cadderly extended his hand to pat the beast, but Percival recoiled, then rushed back in, his not-so-tiny paws ripping tears in the pouches on Cadderly's belt. Cadderly began to protest, but one of the pouches broke open, spilling a continual stream of cacasa nuts onto the floor.

Hundreds of cacasa nuts! Thousands of cacasa nuts! The gigantic squirrel eagerly stuffed them into his bulging mouth by the score and soon the floor was clear again.

"Where are you going?" Cadderly heard himself ask as the squirrel bounded away. The doors were closed again somehow, but the squirrel ran right through them, knocking them from their hinges. Then Percival hopped over the balcony railing and was gone.

Cadderly sat up in his bed—but it was not his bed, for he was not in his room. Rather, he was lying in the inn's common room. It was very late, he knew, and very quiet.

Cadderly was not alone. He felt a ghostlike presence behind him. Mustering his courage, he spun about.

Then he cried out, the scream torn from his lungs by sheer desperation. There lay Headmaster Avery, Cadderly's mentor, his surrogate father spread across one of the room's small circular tables, his chest opened wide.

Cadderly didn't have to examine the man to know he was dead and that his heart had been torn out.

* * * * *

Cadderly sat up in his bed—and now it was indeed his bed. His room was quiet, except for the occasional rattling of the balcony doors, shivering in the night wind. A full moon was up, its silvery light dancing through the window, splaying shadows across the floor.

The serenity seemed hardly enough to chase away the dreams. Cadderly tried to recall that page in the tome again, tried to remember the chant, the spell, to bathe the room in light. He was weary and troubled and had not eaten all that day, and hardly at all the day before. The image of the page would not come, so he lay still, terrified, in the dim light.

There was only the quiet light of the moon.

Dawn was a long while away.

Five

Home Again

A steady stream of shouts led the way for Danica and the Bouldershoulder brothers as they walked the halls in the southern section of the Edificant Library's second floor. All three companions knew the source of the ruckus was Headmaster Avery even before they approached his office, and they knew, too, from whispers that had greeted them on their arrival, that Kierkan Rufo bore the brunt of the verbal assault.

"It is good that you have returned," came a voice to the side. Headmistress Pertelope strode toward the three. She smiled warmly and wore, as had become her norm, a full-length, long-sleeved gown and black gloves. Not an inch of skin peeked out below her neck, and, between the dark robes and the tightly cropped salt-and-pepper hair, her face seemed almost detached, floating in an empty background. "I'd feared you had lost your hearts to Shilmista—something perfectly reasonable," the headmistress said sincerely, with no hint of judgment in her perpetually calm tone.

"Ye're bats!" Ivan snorted, shaking his head vigorously. "An elfish place, and not for me liking."

Pikel kicked him in the shin, and the brothers glared long and hard at each other.

"Shilmista was wonderful," Danica admitted. "Especially when we sent the monsters in full flight. Already it seems as if the shadows have lightened in the elven wood."

Pertelope nodded and flashed her warm smile once more. "You are going to see Avery?" she stated as much as asked.

"It is our duty," Danica replied, "but he does not seem to be in a good mood this day."

"Rufo'd spoil anyone's day, by me reckoning," Ivan put in.

Again Pertelope nodded, and she managed a somewhat strained smile. "Kierkan Rufo's actions in the forest will not be easily forgotten," she explained. "The young priest has much to prove if he wishes to regain the favor of the headmasters, particularly Headmaster Avery."

"Good enough for him!" Ivan snorted.

"Oo oi!" Pikel added.

"I've heard that Rufo has already received some punishment," Pertelope continued wryly, looking pointedly at Danica's fist.

Danica unconsciously slipped her guilty hands behind her back. She couldn't deny that she had slugged Rufo, back in the forest when he was complaining about his companions' deficiencies. She also couldn't deny how much she had enjoyed dropping the blustering fool. Her actions had been rash, though, and probably not without consequence.

Pertelope sensed the young woman's discomfort and quickly moved on to a different subject. "When you are done talking with Headmaster Avery," she said to Danica, "do come and see me. We have much to discuss."

Danica knew that Pertelope was speaking of Cadderly, and she wanted to ask a hundred questions of the headmistress then and there. She only nodded, though, and remained silent, conscientious of her duty and knowing that her desires would have to wait.

The perceptive headmistress smiled knowingly and said, "Later," then gave the young woman a wink and walked on.

Danica watched her go, a thousand thoughts of Cadderly following kind Pertelope's every step. Ivan's tapping boot reminded her that she had other considerations, and she reluctantly turned back to the dwarves. "Are you two ready to face Avery?"

Ivan chuckled wickedly. "Not to worry," the dwarf assured her, grabbing her by the arm and leading her to the portly headmaster's office. "If the fat one gets outta line with ye, I'll threaten him with smaller portions at the dinner table. There's a measure of power from being a place's cook!"

Danica couldn't disagree, but that offered little comfort as she neared the door and heard more clearly the level of Avery's rage.

"Excuses!" the headmaster roared. "Always excuses! Why do you refuse to take responsibility for your actions?"

"I did not—" they heard Rufo begin meekly, but Avery promptly cut him off.

"You did!" the headmaster cried. "You betrayed them to that wretched imp—and more than once!" There came a pause, then Avery's voice sounded again, more composed. "Your actions after that were somewhat courageous, I will admit," he said, "but they do not excuse you. Do not presume for a moment that you are forgiven. Now, go to your tasks with the knowledge that any transgression, however minor, will cost you dearly!"

The door swung open and a haggard Rufo rushed out, seeming displeased to see Danica and the dwarves.

"Surprised?" Ivan asked him with a wide grin.

The angular man, tilting slightly, ran his fingers through his matted black hair. His dark eyes darted about as if in search of escape. With nowhere to go, Rufo shoved his way between Danica and Pikel and scurried away, obviously embarrassed.

"Yer day just got better, eh?" Ivan called after him, enjoying the tall man's torment.

"It took you a while to find your way to me," came a surly call from the room, turning the companions back to Avery.

"Uh-oh," muttered Pikel, but Ivan merely snorted and strode into the room, right up to Avery's oaken desk. Danica and Pikel came in a bit more hesitantly.

Avery's bluster seemed to have played itself out. The chubby man pulled a handkerchief from his pocket and rubbed it across his sweaty, blotchy face. "I did not believe you would come back," he said, huffing with labored breath. He alternated his glance from Ivan to Pikel. "I had even suggested to Dean Thobicus that we begin to search for new cooks."

"Not to worry," Ivan assured him with a bow that swept the dwarf's yellow beard across the floor. "The masters of yer belly have returned."

Pikel piped up in hearty agreement, but Avery's renewed glare showed he did not enjoy the boisterous dwarf's smug attitude.

"We will, of course, need a full report of your time in Shilmista—a written report," he said, shuffling some papers about on his large desk.

"I don't write," Ivan teased, "but I can cook ye a goblin ear stew. That'll fairly sum up me time in the wood." Even Danica couldn't bite back a chuckle at that.

"Lady Maupoissant will help you then," Avery said, articulating each word slowly to show them he was not amused.

"When will you need this?" Danica asked, hoping he would give her the whole winter. Her thoughts were on Carradoon, on Cadderly, and she was beginning to suspect that perhaps she should have continued through the mountains and gone straight to him.

"You are scheduled to meet with Dean Thobicus in three days," Avery informed her. "That should give you ample time—"

"Impossible," Danica said to him. "I will meet with the dean this day, or in the morning, perhaps, but—"

"Three days," Avery repeated. "The dean's schedule is not for you to manipulate, Lady Maupoissant." Again he used her surname, and Danica knew it was to emphasize his anger.

Danica felt trapped. "I am not of your order," she reminded the portly man. "I am under no obligation—"

Again Avery cut her short. "You will do as you are told," he said grimly. "Do not think your actions in Shilmista have been forgotten or forgiven."

Danica fell back a step; Ivan, as angry as he was confused, hopped to his toes and glowered at Avery.

"Huh?" was all that stunned Pikel could mutter.

"As I said," Avery declared, slamming a heavy fist on the desk. "You all played the role of hero, both in Shilmista and before that, when the evil priest and his insidious curse fell over the library, but that does not excuse your actions, Lady Maupoissant."

Danica wanted to scream "What actions?" but she couldn't get a sound past the mounting rage in her throat.

"You struck him," Avery finally explained. "You attacked Rufo, a priest of Deneir, a host of the Edificant Library, without provocation?"

"He had it coming," Ivan retorted.

Avery managed a bit of a smile. "Somehow, I do not doubt that," he agreed, for a moment seeming his old, likable self. "Yet there are rules concerning such behavior." He looked straight into Danica's brown eyes. "You might well be banned from the library for life if I were to pursue Rufo's charges.

"Think of it," Avery continued after giving Danica and the dwarves a moment to absorb his meaning. "All of your texts are here, all of the known works of Grandmaster Penpahg D'Ahn. I know how dear your studies are to you."

"Then why do you threaten me like this?" Danica snapped. She flipped a lock of her unkempt hair from in front of her face and crossed her arms before her. "If I erred in striking Rufo, then so be it, but if the same situation was repeated—if, after so many trials and so much killing, I had to listen to his endless whining and berating of me and my friends—I cannot honestly say that I would not punch him again."

"Oo oi!" Pikel readily agreed.

"Had it coming," Ivan said again.

Avery waved his hand in a patting motion to try to calm the three. "Agreed," he said, "and I assure you I have no intention of letting Rufo's accusations go beyond this point. But in exchange, I demand that you give me these few things I have asked. Prepare the report and meet with Thobicus in three days, as he desires. On my word, Rufo's accusations will never again be mentioned, to you or to anyone else."

Danica blew the stubborn strand of hair away from her face, an action Avery understood as a resigned sigh.

"Cadderly is all right, by all reports," the headmaster said quietly. Danica winced. Hearing the name aloud brought fears and painful recollections.

"He stays at the Dragon's Codpiece, a fine inn," Avery went on. "Fredegar, the innkeeper, is a friend, and he has looked after Cadderly, though that has not been difficult since our man rarely leaves his room."

The portly headmaster's obvious concern for Cadderly reminded Danica that Avery was no enemy—for her or for her love. She understood, too, that most of Avery's surly behavior could be attributed to the same fact that had been gnawing away at her: Cadderly had remained at the library only as long as it took to retrieve his possessions. Cadderly had not, and might not ever, come home.

"I leave for Carradoon this afternoon," Avery announced. "There is much business to be handled between the headmasters and the town's leaders. With this threat of war hanging over us and . . . well, worry not about it. You three have earned at least a few days of relaxation."

Again Danica understood the implication of the portly headmaster's words. Certainly there was business between the library and the town, but Danica thought it unlikely that Avery, whose duties were to preside over and guide the younger priests, would be chosen as the library's representative in town matters. Avery had volunteered to go, had insisted, Danica knew, and not because of any threat to the region. His business in Carradoon was an excuse to look in on Cadderly, the young man whom he loved as dearly as he would his own son.

Danica and the dwarves took their leave, the brothers protectively flanking Danica as they exited the room.

"Not to worry," Ivan said to Danica. "Me and me brother'll have to go to town soon anyway, to stock up for the winter. Get yer business and yer meeting done and we'll set off right after. It's not a long road to Carradoon, but 'tis better, in these times, that ye don't go down it alone."

Pikel nodded his agreement, then they parted, the dwarves heading down the stairs for the kitchen and Danica toward her room. Ivan and Pikel missed Cadderly, too, the young woman realized. She gave a flip of her strawberry-blond hair, which now hung several inches below her shoulders, as though that symbolic act would allow her to put her troubles behind her for the moment. Like the stubborn hair that inevitably found its way back around to her face, though, Danica's fears did not stay away.

She desperately wanted to see Cadderly, to hold him and kiss him, but at the same time she feared that meeting. If the young scholar rejected her again, as he had in Shilmista, her life, even her dedication to her studies, would fail to have meaning.

* * * * *

"I did not see much," Danica admitted, adjusting her position on the edge of Headmistress Pertelope's cushioned bed. "I was guarding against the approaching battle. I knew Cadderly and Elbereth would be vulnerable while they cast their summons to the trees."

"But you are convinced that Cadderly played a role in that summoning?" Pertelope pressed, repeating the question for perhaps the fifth time. Pertelope sat near Danica and was clad in her usual modest garments. "It was not just the elf prince."

Danica shook her head. "I heard Cadderly's chant," she tried to explain. "There was something more to it, some underlying power . . ." She struggled to find the words, but how could she? What had happened back in Shilmista, when Cadderly and Elbereth had awakened the great oaks, had seemed almost miraculous to the young woman. And miracles, by definition, defied description.

"Cadderly told me he had played a role," a flustered Danica responded at last. "There was more to the summons than simply repeating the ancient words. He spoke of gathering energy, of a mindset that brought him into the trees' world before awakening them and coaxing them to ours."

Pertelope nodded slowly as she digested the words. She held no doubts about Danica's honesty, or about Cadderly's mysterious, budding power. "And the elf wizard's wound?" she prompted.

"By Elbereth's description, the spear had gone a foot or more into Tintagel's side," Danica replied. "So very much blood covered his clothing—I saw that much for myself—and Elbereth had not expected him to survive for more than a few moments longer. Yet when I saw him, just half an hour after he was wounded, he was nearly healed and casting spells at our enemies once more."

"You have seen spells of healing at the library," Pertelope said, trying to hide her excitement. "When the Oghman priest broke his arm in wrestling you, for example."

"Minor compared to the healing Cadderly did on Tintagel," Danica assured her. "By Elbereth's word, he held the wizard's belly in while the skin mended around his fingers!"

Pertelope nodded again and remained quiet for a long while. There was no need to go over it all again. Danica's recounting had been consistent and, Pertelope knew instinctively, honest. Her hazel eyes stared into emptiness for a time before she focused again on Danica.

The young monk sat quietly and very still, lost in her own contemplations. To Pertelope's eyes, a shadow appeared on Danica's shoulder, a silhouette of a tiny female, trembling and glancing nervously about. Extraordinary heat emanated from the young monk's body, and her breathing, steady to the casual observer, reflected her anxieties to Pertelope's knowing and probing gaze.

Danica was full of passion, yet full of fear, the headmistress knew. Merely thinking of Cadderly stirred a boiling turmoil within her.

Pertelope shook the insightful visions away, ended the distant song that played in the recesses of her mind, and put a comforting hand on Danica's shoulder. "Thank you for coming to sit with me," she said sincerely. "You have been a great help to me—and to Cadderly, do not doubt."

A confused look came over Danica. Pertelope hated that she had to be cryptic with someone so obviously attached to Cadderly, but she knew Danica would not understand the powers at work on the young priest. Those same powers had been with Pertelope for nearly a score of years, and Pertelope wasn't certain that even she understood them.

The bed creaked as Danica stood. "I have to go now," she explained, looking back to the small room's door. "If you wish, I can come back . . ."

"No need," the headmistress answered, offering a warm smile. "Unless you feel you would like to talk," she quickly added. Pertelope intensified her gaze again and bade the song begin, searching for that insightful, supernatural, level of perception. The trembling shadow remained upon Danica's shoulder, but it seemed calmer now, and the young monk's breathing had steadied.

The heat was still there, though, the vital energy of anticipated passion for this young woman, no more a girl. Even after Danica had departed, the door handle glowed softly from her touch.

Pertelope blew out a long sigh. She slipped one of her arm-length gloves off to scratch at the shark skin it hid and tried to recall her own trials when Deneir had selected her—had cursed her, she often believed.

Pertelope smiled at the dark thought. "No, not a curse," she said aloud, lifting her eyes toward the ceiling as though she were addressing a higher presence. She played the song more strongly in her mind, the universal harmony that she had heard a thousand times in the turning pages of the tome she had given to Cadderly. She fell into the song and followed its notes, gaining communion with her dearest god.

"So you have chosen Cadderly," she whispered.

She received no answer, and had expected none.

"He could not otherwise have accomplished all of those 'miracles' in the elven wood," Pertelope went on, speaking aloud her conclusions to bolster her suspicions. "I pity him, and yet I envy him, for he is young and strong, stronger than I ever was. How powerful will he become?"

Again, except for the continuing melody in Pertelope's head, there came no response.

That was why the headmistress often felt as though she had been cursed; there never were any answers granted. She had always had to discover them for herself.

And so, too, she knew, would Cadderly.

Six

A Beggar Man, A Thief

C adderly purposely avoided looking at the guardsman as he moved through the short tunnel and under the raised portcullis leading out of the lakeside town. All along his route to the western gate the young scholar had observed people of every station and every demeanor, and the variety of shadowy images he had seen leaping from their shoulders had nearly overwhelmed him. Again the song of Deneir played in his thoughts, as though he had subconsciously summoned it, and again, *aurora* remained the only identifiable term. Cadderly could not make sense of it all; he feared that this new insight would drive him mad.

He grew more at ease when he had put the bustle of Carradoon behind him and was walking along the hedge- and tree-lined roads, with nothing more to attract his attention than the chatter of birds and the overhead rustle of squirrels gathering their winter stores.

"Is mine the curse of the hermits?" he asked himself aloud. "That it is!" he proclaimed loudly, startling a nearby squirrel that had frozen in place on the camouflaging gray bark of a tree. The rising volume of Cadderly's voice sent the critter hop-skipping up the tree, where it froze again, not even its bushy tail twitching.

"Well, it is," Cadderly cried to the rodent in feigned exasperation. "All those poor, wretched, solitary souls, so frowned upon by the rest of us. They are not hermits by choice. They possess this same vision that haunts me, and it drives them mad, drives them to where they cannot bear the sight of another intelligent thing."

Cadderly moved to the base of the tree to better view the beast. "I see no shadows leaping from your shoulders, Mr. Gray," he called. "You have no hidden desires, no cravings beyond those you obviously seek to fill."

478

"Unless there be a lady squirrel about!" came a cry from down the path. Cadderly nearly leaped out of his boots. He spun about to see a large, dirty man dressed in ragged, ill-fitting clothes and boots whose toes had long ago worn away.

"A lady squirrel would get his mind from those nuts," the stubble-faced man continued, advancing easily down the road.

Cadderly unconsciously brought his ram-headed walking stick up in front of him. Thieves were common on the roads close to the town, especially in this season, with winter fast approaching.

"But, then . . ." the large man continued, putting a finger upon his lower lip in a contemplative gesture. Cadderly noted that he wore mismatched fingerless gloves, one black, one brown leather. "If the lady was about, the squirrel would still have no 'hidden desires,' since the unabashed beast would seek to fill whatever his heart deemed necessary, the call of his belly or the call of his loins.

"I'd be one to choose the loins, eh?" the dirty man said with a lascivious wink.

Cadderly blushed slightly and nearly laughed aloud, though he still hadn't figured out what to make of this well-spoken vagabond, and he still wasn't comfortable near the dirty man. He peered closer, trying to find a revealing shadow on the man's shoulders. But Cadderly's surprise had stolen the song fully, and nothing rested there, except the badly worn folds of an old woolen scarf.

"It is a fine day to be about, talking to the beasts," the man went on, seeing no response forthcoming from Cadderly. "A pity, then, that I must get myself inside the gates of Carradoon, in the realm of smells more unpleasant, where high buildings hide the panorama of beauty so easily taken for granted on this most lovely of country roads."

"You will not easily pass by the guards," Cadderly remarked, knowing how carefully the city militiamen were protecting their home, especially with rumors of war brewing.

The vagabond opened a small pouch on the side of his rope belt and produced a single silver coin.

"A bribe?" Cadderly asked.

"Admission," the beggar corrected. " 'One must spend gold'—or silver, as the case may be—'to make gold,' goes the old saying. I will accept the lore as true, since I know I will indeed secure some gold once I am within the town's wall."

Cadderly studied the man more closely. He wore no insignia of any lawful guild, showed no signs of any money-making talents whatsoever. "A thief," he stated flatly.

"Never," the man asserted.

"A beggar?" Cadderly asked, this word coming out with the same obvious venom.

The larger man clutched his chest and staggered back several steps, as though Cadderly had launched a dagger into his heart.

Now Cadderly did notice some shadows. He caught the flicker of a pained look beneath the man's sarcastic, playful facade. He saw a woman on one shoulder, holding a small child, and an older child on the man's other shoulder. The images were gone in an instant, and Cadderly noticed for the first time that the man had a slight limp and a blue-green bruise on his wrist just above the edge of the brown glove.

Waves of nausea nearly overwhelmed the young scholar; as he focused his senses, he felt the emanations of the disease clearly and knew beyond doubt why this intelligent, articulate man had sunk to his lowly station.

He was a leper.

"M-my pardon," Cadderly stammered. "I did not know . . ."

"Does anyone . . . ever?" the large man asked, in a snarling voice. "I do not appreciate your pity, young priest of Deneir, but I'll gladly accept your pittance."

Cadderly clenched his walking stick tightly, mistaking the remark as a threat.

"You know of what I speak," the beggar man said to him, "the coins you inevitably will throw my way to alleviate your guilt."

Cadderly winced at the biting remark, but couldn't deny his pity that one so intelligent had sunk so low. He was surprised, too, that the beggar had discerned his order, even though he wore his holy symbol prominently on the front of his wide-brimmed hat. The large man studied Cadderly intently as the tumult of emotions rolled through the young priest.

"Pig," the man said with a sneer, to Cadderly's surprise. "How terrible that one such as I should have sunk to the level of a street beggar!"

Cadderly bit his lip in the face of such dramatics.

"To wallow in the mud beside the wretches," the man continued, throwing one arm out wide, the other still clutching at his mock-wounded chest.

He stopped suddenly in that pose and turned a confused expression Cadderly's way. "Wretches?" he asked. "What do you know of them, arrogant priest? You, who are so intelligent—that is the weal of your order, is it not?

"Intelligence." The beggar spat with distaste. "An excuse, I say, for those such as you. It is what separates you, what elevates you." He eyed Cadderly dangerously and finished, deliberately, "It is what blinds you."

"I do not deserve this!" Cadderly declared.

The man threw his hands above his head and blurted a mocking, incredulous shout. "Deserve?" he cried. He jerked the sleeve up on one arm, revealing a row of rotting, bruised skin.

"Deserve?" he asked again. "What, pray tell me, young priest who is so wise, do those kneeling before, and crawling from, the alleys of Carradoon deserve?"

Cadderly thought he would burst apart. He felt an angry energy building within him, gathering explosive strength. He remembered when he had awakened the trees in Shilmista, and when he had healed Tintagel, had held the elf wizard's guts in while a similar energy had mended the garish wound. A page from the *Tome of Universal Harmony* flashed in Cadderly's head, as clearly as if he held the open book before him, and he knew then the object of his rage. He eyed the bruises on the large man's arm, filled his nostrils with the stench of the disease that had so tormented this undeserving man's soul.

"*Pieta pieta, dominus* . . ." Cadderly began, reciting the chant as he read the words from the clear image in his mind.

"No!" the large man cried, charging ahead. Cadderly halted the chant and tried to throw up his arms to block, but the man was surprisingly fast and balanced for one so tall, and he caught hold of Cadderly's clothing and shook the young priest thoroughly.

Cadderly saw an opening, could have jammed his walking stick up under the man's chin. He knew, though, that the frustrated beggar meant him no real harm, and he was not surprised when the man released him, shoving him back a step.

"I could cure you!" Cadderly growled.

"Could you?" the man mocked. "And could you cure them?" he cried, waggling a finger toward the distant town. "Could you cure them all? Are all the world's ills to fall before this young priest of Deneir? Call to the wretched, I say!" the beggar cried, whirling about and shouting to the four winds. "Line them up before this . . . this . . ." He searched for the word, his dirty lips moving silently. "This godsend!" he cried at last.

A nearby squirrel broke into a dead run along the branches across the path.

"I do not deserve this," Cadderly said again, calmly.

His tone seemed infectious, for the large man dropped his hands to his sides immediately and his shoulders visibly slumped.

"No," the leper agreed, "but accept it, I pray you, as but a small penance in a world filled with undeserved penance."

Cadderly blinked away the moisture that suddenly came into his gray eyes. "What are their names?" he asked quietly.

The beggar looked at him curiously for a moment, then his lips curled up in his first sincere smile. "Jhanine, my wife," he answered. "Toby, my son, and Millinea, my young daughter. None have shown signs of my infection as yet," he explained, guessing Cadderly's unspoken question. "I see them rarely—to deliver the pittance I have gained from the guilty arrogants of Carradoon."

The beggar chuckled, seeing Cadderly's blush. "My pardon," he said, dipping into a low bow. "I, too, am sometimes blind, seeing the well and fortunate in a similar light."

Cadderly nodded his acceptance of that inevitable—and excusable—fault. "What is your name?"

"Nameless," the beggar answered without hesitation. "Yes, that is a good name for one such as me. Nameless akin to all the other Namelesses huddled in the squalor between the towers of the wealthy."

"You hold such self-pity?" Cadderly asked.

"Self-truth," Nameless answered immediately.

Cadderly conceded the point. "I could cure you," the young priest said again. Nameless shrugged his shoulders. "Others have tried," he explained, "priests from your own order, and those of Oghma as well. I went to the Edificant Library—of course I went to the library—when the signs first appeared."

The mention of the Edificant Library brought an unconscious frown to Cadderly's face. "I am not like the others," he asserted more forcefully than he had intended.

The beggar smiled. "No, you're not," he agreed.

"Then you will accept my aid?"

Nameless did not relinquish his smile. "I will . . . consider it," he replied quietly. Cadderly caught an unmistakable glimmer of hope in his dark brown eyes, and saw a shadow appear atop the man's shoulder, a shadow of the beggar himself, gaily tossing a small form—Millinea, he somehow knew—into the air and catching her. The shadow fell apart quickly, dissipating in the wind.

Cadderly nodded somewhat grimly, suspecting the dangers of false hopes for one in this man's position. Suspecting the risks, but not truly understanding them, Cadderly now knew, for he was not, for all his sympathy, standing in the beggar man's holey shoes.

The young priest tore the pouch from his belt. "Then accept this," he said forcefully, tossing it to the large man.

Nameless caught it and eyed Cadderly curiously, but made no move to return the coin-filled purse. Here was an offering holding no false hopes, Cadderly understood, an offering of face value and nothing more.

"I am one of those arrogants," Cadderly explained, "guilty, as you have accused."

"And this will alleviate that guilt?" the beggar man asked, his eyes narrowing.

Cadderly couldn't hold back his chuckle. "Hardly," he replied, and he knew that if Nameless believed the purse would alleviate his guilt, then Nameless would have thrown it back at him. "Hardly a proper penance. I give it to you because you, and Jhanine, Toby, and Millinea, are more *deserving* of it than I, not for any lessening of the guilt. That guilt I must carry until I have learned better." Cadderly cocked his head to the side as a thought came to him.

"Call the gold a tutor's fee if that helps you to lessen your own guilt for waylaying one as innocent as me!" he said.

The beggar man laughed and bowed low. "Indeed, young priest, you are not like those of your order who greeted me at the library's great door, those who were more concerned with their own failings to cure me than with the consequences of my ailment."

That is why they failed, Cadderly knew, but he did not interrupt.

"It is a fine day!" Nameless went on. "And I pray you enjoy it." He held up the purse and shook it. His whole body shaking in a joyful dance, he smiled at the loud jingle of coins. "Perhaps I will as well. To the Nine Hells with Carradoon's stinking alleys this day!"

Nameless stopped his dance abruptly and stood stock-still, eyeing Cadderly gravely. Slowly, he extended his right hand, seemingly conscious, for the first time, of his dirty, fingerless glove.

Cadderly understood the action as a test, a test he was glad he could pass so easily. Without a thought for superstitious consequences, the young priest accepted the handshake.

"I pass by here often," Cadderly said quietly. "Consider my offer of healing."

The beggar man, too touched to reply verbally, nodded sincerely. He turned about and walked briskly away, his limp more pronounced, as though he no longer cared to hide it. Cadderly watched him for few moments, then turned and continued away from Carradoon. He smiled as more squirrels scrabbled overhead, but he hardly looked up to see them.

It seemed to the young priest that the day had grown finer and less fine at the same time.

* * * * *

Nameless smiled as a squirrel nearly lost its balance on a small branch, catching hold and righting itself at the last moment. The beggar man tried to use that simple, natural movement as a symbol of what had just transpired between him and the curious young priest, viewing himself as the branch and Cadderly as the creature righting its course. The thought made the leper feel good, valuable, for the first time in a long, long while.

He couldn't brood on it, though, and could hardly hope to meet enough people like this curious Cadderly, who would care to see their arrogance laid out before them. No, Nameless would have to continue as he had for more than a year, struggling daily to gain enough trinkets to keep his wife and children from starving.

He had at least a temporary reprieve. He tossed the purse into the air, caught it gingerly, and smiled again. It was indeed a fine day!

Nameless spun about, prepared to pay Jhanine and the children a long overdue visit, but his smile fast became a frown.

"So sorry to startle you, good friend," said a puny man, his drooping, thick eyelids open only enough for Nameless to make out his small, dark eyes.

Nameless instinctively moved the coin-filled pouch out of sight and kept his arms in front of him.

"I am a leper," he growled, using his disease as a threat.

The smaller man chuckled and gave a wheezing laugh that sounded more like a cough. "You think me a thief?" he asked, holding his hands out wide. Nameless blinked at the man's curious gloves, one white, the other black. "As you can see, I carry no weapons," the little man assured.

"None openly," Nameless admitted.

"I see we both wear a mixed set of gloves," Ghost remarked. "Kindred spirits, eh?"

Nameless slipped his hands under the folds of his badly fitting clothes, embarrassed for some reason he did not understand. Kindred spirits? he thought. Hardly. The fine gloves this little man wore, matched or not, must have cost more than Nameless had seen in many months, the young priest's pouch included.

"But we are," Ghost asserted, noticing the frown.

"You are a beggar, then?" Nameless dared to ask. "Carradoon is but a mile down the road. I was going there myself. The take is always good."

"But the young priest changed your mind?" the stranger asked. "Do tell me about that one."

Nameless shrugged and shook his head slightly, hardly conscious of the movement. Ghost caught it, though, and the beggar man's confusion told the wicked man much.

"Ah," Ghost said, his arms still wide, "you do not know young Cadderly."

"You do?"

"Of course," Ghost replied, motioning to the pouch Nameless tried to hide. "Shouldn't all those of our ilk know one as generous as Cadderly?"

"Then you are a beggar," Nameless reasoned, relaxing a bit. There was an unspoken code among the people of squalor, an implied brotherhood.

"Perhaps," Ghost answered cryptically. "I have been many things, but now I am a beggar man." He wheezed another chuckle. "Or soon I will be," he corrected. Nameless watched as the man unbuttoned the top of his surcoat and pulled the woolen folds aside.

"A mirror?" the beggar man muttered, then he said no more, transfixed by his own image in the silvery device.

Nameless felt the intrusion. He tried to pull away, but could not, held firmly by the strange magic. He saw nothing except for his own image, lined in black as though he had been transported to some other place, some dark, otherworldly place. Nameless tried desperately to look around at his surroundings, tried to make sense of them, find some familiarity.

He saw only his image.

He heard a clap, then he was moving, or he felt as though he was moving, even though he knew that his physical body had not stirred in the least. There came a brief, sharp pain as his spirit exited his body and floated helplessly toward the effeminate vessel that awaited it.

The pain came again.

Nameless blinked, consciously fighting against the heavy droop of his eyelids. He saw his own beggar's image again, wearing gloves, black and white. His confusion lasted only until he realized that it was no longer a reflected image he saw, but his own body.

"What have you done to me?" the beggar man cried, reaching for the stranger in his body. Every movement seemed to drag; his arms had little strength to convey his fury.

Ghost snapped his fingers, and the black and white gloves disappeared, leaving his newly acquired hands half exposed in the fingerless gloves. Halfheartedly, he pushed the weakling back. How useful that lax body had proven to Ghost. How benign and unthreatening, a body that even a young boy could defeat. With an almost resigned shrug, he advanced on the whimpering and sorely confused wretch and wrapped his dirty hands about the skinny neck.

Nameless fought desperately, as desperately as Ghost's puny form had ever battled, but there was no strength in his arms, no power to loosen the larger attacker's hold. Soon he stopped struggling, and Ghost knew the beggar's resignation was founded in grief for those he would leave behind.

The wicked man contemplated the change with amusement, thinking it curious, even humorous, that one as obviously wretched as this leprous beggar would lament the end of his life.

There was no mercy in Ghost, though. He had killed this body a hundred times, perhaps, and had killed his previous body a like number, and the body he had used before that as well.

The corpse slumped to the ground. Ghost immediately brought back his magical device and called upon its powers to watch the beggar man's spirit step out of the slain form. Ghost quickly pulled off the fine black glove and placed it on his unoccupied body. He closed his eyes and stiffened his resolve against the ensuing pain, for the simple act had transferred a part of his own spirit back into the corpse.

It was a necessary step for two reasons. The body would heal—Ghost had a powerful magical item concealed in one boot to see to that—and if the receptacle remained open, then the beggar man's spirit would find its way back in. Also, if Ghost allowed the body to die, if he allowed the item in his boot to call back a spirit, the item's regenerative powers would partially consume the form. Considering how many times Ghost had made this switch, the item would have burned up the puny form long ago.

But that wouldn't happen. Ghost knew how to use the items in conjunction; the *Ghearufu*, the glove-and-mirror device, had long ago shown him the way, and he had spent three lifetimes perfecting the act.

Ghost looked both ways along the empty road, then pulled the slender body far from the trail, into some covering brush. He felt the disease in this new form that he had taken. It was an unpleasant sensation, but Ghost took heart that he would not wear this disguise for long—just long enough to meet this young Cadderly for himself.

He hopped back out to the road and wandered along, wondering how much of the day he would have to watch pass him by before young Cadderly returned down the road.

After the thief in the beggar's body had departed, Nameless's spirit stood beside the puny corpse, confused and helpless. If Cadderly, with his new insight, had gazed upon the spirit then, he would have seen the shadows of Jhanine, Toby, and Millinea scattering to the four winds, fading like the images of hope that Nameless had never dared to sustain.

Seven
The Maze

Cadderly approached the steep-sided, round hillock and the tower of Belisarius tentatively, fully expecting that the wizard, as knowledgeable as he was, would offer him little insight into the strange things that had been happening to him. Actually, Cadderly had no idea if the wizard would grant him an audience. He had done some valuable penning for Belisarius on several occasions, but he couldn't really call the man a friend. Furthermore, Cadderly wasn't sure that Belisarius would be home.

The young scholar relaxed a bit when a wide line up the nearly seventy-degree incline transformed from unremarkable grass to a stone stairway with flat and even steps. The wizard was home and apparently had seen Cadderly coming.

Seventy-five steps brought Cadderly to the hillock's flat top and the cobblestone walkway that encircled the tower. Cadderly had to walk nearly halfway around the base, for Belisarius had placed his steps far to the side of the entrance this day. The steps never appeared on the same spot on the hillock, and Cadderly hadn't yet figured out if the wizard created new steps each time, had some way of rotating the grassy knoll under the stationary tower, or simply deceived visitors of the steps' actual location. Cadderly thought the last possibility, deception, the most likely, since Belisarius used his magic primarily for elaborate illusions.

The tower's iron-bound door swung open as Cadderly approached (or had it been open all along, only appearing to be closed? Cadderly mused). Cadderly paused as he started over the threshold, for there came the sound of grating stone and an entire section of the stone wall in the foyer shifted and swung out, blocking the inner entry door and revealing a cobwebbed stairway winding down into the blackness.

Cadderly scratched the stubble on his chin, his gray eyes flashing inquisitively at the unexpected invitation. He remembered the days when he had come to the tower with Headmaster Avery. Every time, the skilled wizard presented the duo with a new test of cunning. Cadderly was glad for the diversion, glad that Belisarius had apparently come up with something new, something that might take the young man's mind from the disturbing questions the beggar man had raised.

"This is a new path, and a new trick," Cadderly said aloud, congratulating the wizard, who was no doubt listening. Always curious, the young scholar promptly pulled a torch from its sconce on the foyer wall and started down. Twenty spiraling steps later, he came to a low corridor ending at a thick wooden door. Cadderly carefully studied the portal for a long moment, then slowly placed his hand against it, feeling the solidity of its grain. Satisfied that it was real, he pushed it open and continued on, finding another descending stairway behind it.

The next level proved a bit more confusing. The stairway ended in a three-way intersection of similar, unremarkable stone passageways. Cadderly took a step straight ahead, then changed his mind and went to the left, passing through another door (after repeating his pause and study test), then another after that. Again he had entered an intersection, this one much more confusing, since each of the ways revealed many side passages, both left and right. Cadderly nearly laughed aloud and he silently congratulated the clever wizard. With a helpless shrug, he let his walking stick fall to the floor, then followed the path determined by the unseeing gaze of the carved ram's head. Any way seemed as good as another as the young priest moved along, left, and then right, right again, and then straight ahead. Three more doors were left open behind him; one passage sloped down at a noticeable angle.

"Excellent!" Cadderly exclaimed when he passed a sharp corner, and found himself back where he had started, at the bottom of the second stairway. His torch was beginning to burn low, but the curious young priest pressed ahead once more, consciously selecting different avenues than on his first time through.

The torch burned away, leaving Cadderly in utter blackness. Calmly he closed his eyes and recalled a page in the *Tome of Universal Harmony*. He heard a few notes of Deneir's endless song and muttered the appropriate chant, pointing to the tip of his burned-out torch. He blinked many times and squinted against the glare as the magical light came on, much brighter than the flickering torch flame had been. When his eyes at last adjusted, he went on, turning corner after corner.

A scuffling, scraping sound made him pause. It was no rat, Cadderly knew; the animal, if it was an animal, that had made the sound was much larger.

An image of a bull came into Cadderly's thoughts. He recalled a day as a youngster, out with Headmaster Avery, when he had passed a pasture full of cows. At least, Avery had thought they were cows. Cadderly couldn't help but smile when he remembered the image of portly Avery huffing and puffing in full flight from an angry bull.

The scuffling came again.

Cadderly considered extinguishing his magical light, but reconsidered immediately, realizing the predicament that act would leave him in. He crept up to the next corner, took off his wide-brimmed hat, and slowly peeked around.

The scuffler was humanoid, but certainly not human. It towered seven feet tall, shoulders and chest wide and impossibly strong, and its head—no mask, Cadderly knew—resembled the bull in that long-ago field. Wearing only a wolf pelt loincloth, the creature carried no weapon, though that hardly brought a sense of relief to the minimally armed young scholar.

A minotaur! Cadderly's heart nearly failed him. Suddenly he wasn't so sure that this whole trek through the tower's catacombs was inspired by Belisarius. It occurred to Cadderly that something pernicious might have happened to the congenial mage, that some dark force might have overcome the tower's formidable defenses.

His thoughts were blown away, along with his breath, a moment later, as the bull-headed giant scraped one foot on the stone again and charged, slamming into Cadderly and launching him across the corridor. He cracked his shoulder blade as he smashed into the stone, and his torch flew away, though of course the magical light did not diminish.

The minotaur snorted and stormed in. Cadderly took up his walking stick defensively, wondering what in the Nine Hells the minuscule weapon could do against this awesome beast. The minotaur seemed none too concerned with it, striding right in to meet its foe.

Cadderly swung with all his might, but the skinny club broke apart as he connected on the brute's thick-skinned chest.

The minotaur slapped him once, then leaned its horned head in, squashing Cadderly against the stone. The young man freed one arm and punched the beast, to no avail. The beast pressed more forcefully and Cadderly could neither squirm nor breathe.

His estimate of how long he had to live shortened considerably when the minotaur opened its huge mouth, putting its formidable teeth in line with Cadderly's exposed neck.

In that split second, the young priest recognized the fields of energy floating about him. He looked down to the floor, to his unbroken walking stick.

Cadderly jammed his free arm into the gaping maw, and plunged his hand down the minotaur's throat. A moment later, he retracted the hand, holding the bull-headed monster's beating heart. The creature fell back a step, not daring to do anything at all.

"I have traveled down two stairways, which actually went up," Cadderly announced firmly. "And through six doors, two of which were illusionary. That would put me in the west wing of your library, would it not, good Belisarius?"

The illusionary minotaur disappeared, but, strangely, Cadderly still held the pumping heart. The scene reverted to its true form, the west wing, as Cadderly had guessed, and Belisarius, a confused, almost frightened look on his bushy-browed, bearded face, stood across the room, leaning heavily on a bookcase.

Cadderly winked at him, then opened his mouth and moved as though to take a bite of the thing in his hand.

"Oh, you!" the wizard cried. He turned away and put a hand to his mouth, trying to keep his stomach's contents down. "Oh, do not! I beg, do not!"

Cadderly dismissed the gruesome image, willed it away, though he was not certain how he had brought it into being in the first place.

"How?" the wizard gasped, finally composed.

"My magic has shifted recently," Cadderly tried to explain, "grown."

"That is no clerical magic I have ever heard of," Belisarius insisted. "To create such perfect illusions . . ." Just the words made the wizard picture the heart, and he gagged yet again.

Cadderly understood something that Belisarius apparently did not. "I did not create the image," the young scholar explained, as much to himself as to the wizard, "nor did I collect the magical forces necessary to create the image."

The wizard dismissed any remaining revulsion, too intrigued by what Cadderly was hinting at. He moved quietly across the room toward the young priest.

"I saw the energies gathered," Cadderly went on. "I discovered the trick for what it was and . . . perverted . . . your grand imagery."

"Couldn't you have dispelled it altogether, as most priests would have?" Belisarius asked dryly.

Cadderly shrugged. "I thought I had," he replied with a wry smile, "in a grand fashion befitting your illusions."

Belisarius tipped his floppy woolen cap to the young priest.

"But I am not sure," Cadderly admitted. "Actually, I am not sure of much where my magic is concerned, and that is why I have returned."

Belisarius led the young man to the adjoining sitting room where they both nestled into comfortable chairs. The wizard produced four items—three rings and a slender wand—that Cadderly had given him three weeks before, and laid them aside, anxious to hear Cadderly's revelations.

It took Cadderly a while to begin his many tales—so much had happened to him! Once he began, though, he went on and on, covering every minute detail. He told Belisarius about summoning Shilmista's trees, about healing Tintagel, and about watching the gallant horse Temmerisa's spirit depart. Then he spoke of the more specific and recent incidents, of creating light and then darkness in his room and in Belisarius's maze. Most disturbing of all to the young priest were the shadowy images he had seen dancing atop shoulders. Cadderly said nothing immediately about his dreams, though, not quite certain of how they fit into anything, and also a bit afraid of what they might reveal.

"The spells you speak of are not so unusual to one of priestly magic," the wizard said when the obviously exasperated young man had finished his worrisome tale. "Many can be duplicated by a wizard as well, such as the manipulation of light. As for the shadows, well, clerics have been able to determine the general weal of individuals for centuries."

"Aurora," Cadderly replied, speaking the one word he had been able to decipher from that particular chant. "I do not understand how 'the dawn' would affect such a spell."

Belisarius scratched his graying beard. "That is unusual," he said at length. "But is 'the dawn' the only meaning of the word? When was this wondrous tome penned?"

Cadderly thought for a moment, then had his answer. "Aurora," he said firmly, "aura." He looked up to the wizard and smiled widely.

"Aurora means aura," Belisarius agreed, "or at least it used to, referring to the emanation of light, of good, surrounding an individual. There you have it, then, a clerical spell to be sure. Perhaps that is what has happened to you, only you have not yet learned to interpret what you see."

Cadderly nodded, though he did not really agree. He certainly knew how to—or *felt* how to—interpret the dancing and fleeting shadows; that was not the problem.

"I have witnessed extreme examples of clerical magic," Cadderly replied, "but these powers, I fear, are different. I do not study the spells before I call on them, as do the priests at the library. I make no preparations at all—as with the illusion that I defeated before your eyes. I did not expect you to challenge me so. I was not even expecting you to know I had come to visit."

Cadderly had to pause for a long moment to compose himself, and during the silence, Belisarius mumbled almost constantly under his breath and scratched at his bushy beard.

"You know something," Cadderly declared, his words sounding like an accusation.

"I suspect something," Belisarius replied. "Since the Time of Troubles, there have been increasing reports of individuals with internal magical powers."

"Psionics," Cadderly said immediately.

"You have heard of them, then," the wizard said. He threw his wiry arms out wide in heightened resignation. "Of course you have," he muttered. "You have heard of everything. That is what is so very frustrating about dealing with you."

The dramatics pulled a smile out of Cadderly and allowed him to relax back in the comfortable leather seat.

Belisarius seemed truly intrigued, as though he desperately hoped his guess was correct. "Might you be a psionicist?" he asked.

"I know little about them," the young priest admitted. "If that is what is happening to me, then it is happening without my assistance or approval."

"The powers are not so different from those of a wizard," Belisarius explained, "except that they come from the individual's mind and not the external powers of the universe. I am well acquainted with your mental abilities." He snickered, obviously referring to his spell book, which Cadderly had replaced from memory alone. "That type of prowess is the prime element of a psionicist's power."

Cadderly considered the words and gradually began to shake his head. "The power I manipulated in this tower was external," he reasoned. "Could psionics interact so with a wizard's spell?"

Belisarius patted a knobby finger against his lower lip, his frown revealing the snag in the logic. "I do not know," he admitted. The two sat quietly, digesting the details of their conversation.

"It does not fit," Cadderly announced a moment later. "I am the receptacle of the power and the transmuter of the power to the desired effect, of that much I am sure."

"I will not argue," Belisarius replied, "but such power must have a conduit— a spell, if you will. One cannot simply tap into the external energies of the universe on a whim!"

Cadderly understood the growing excitement in the wizard's voice. If Belisarius was wrong, then the wizard's entire life, his hermitlike devotion to his magical studies, might be revealed as an exercise in futility.

"The song," Cadderly muttered, suddenly realizing the truth of it all.

"Song?"

"The *Tome of Universal Harmony*," the young priest explained. "The book of Deneir. Whenever I have used the powers, even unconsciously, as with the dancing shadows, I have heard the song of that book in the recesses of my mind. My answers are in that song."

"Song of the book?" Belisarius could not begin to understand.

"The rhythm of the words," Cadderly tried to explain, though he knew he could not, not really.

Belisarius shrugged and seemed to accept the simple explanation. "Then you have found your conduit," he said, "but I fear there is little I can tell you concerning it. This book would seem to be more a matter to take up with the headmasters at the Edificant Library."

"Or with my deity," Cadderly mumbled.

Belisarius shrugged noncommittally. "As you will," he said. "I can tell you this much, though, and I know I am right simply by looking at your haggard features."

"I have not been sleeping well," Cadderly promptly put in, fearing what the wizard would say.

"Magic, the transference of such energies," Belisarius went on, undeflected by Cadderly's announcement, "exacts a toll on the practitioner. We wizards are very careful not to exceed our limitations. Normally we could not anyway, since the memorization of any spell is when those limits are revealed.

"Likewise, a cleric's granted powers stem from his or her faith and are tempered by agents of the gods, or even by the gods themselves where the high priests are sometimes concerned," Belisarius reasoned. "I warn you, young Cadderly, I have seen foolish mages consumed when trying to cast the spells of those more powerful than they, spells beyond their abilities. If you have found a way to avoid the normal boundaries and limitations of magic use, whatever type of magic might be involved, then I pray you will find the wisdom to moderate your activities, else it will consume you."

A thousand possibilities began their progression through Cadderly's thoughts. Perhaps he should go back to the library with his dilemma. He could speak to Pertelope . . .

"Now for some items that I know more about," Belisarius said. The wizard reached for the rings and the wand. He first held up a signet ring inscribed with the trident-and-bottle design of Castle Trinity. It once had belonged to the evil mage Dorigen.

"There is no detectable magic in this, as you believed," the wizard said, tossing it to Cadderly.

"I know," Cadderly said, as he caught it and put it into his pouch.

The declaration made Belisarius pause and consider the young man. "This ring," he said slowly, holding up the gold band set with a large onyx stone, "is indeed magical, and powerful."

"It evokes a line of flame," Cadderly said, "when the possessor utters '*Fete,*' the elven word for fire. I have seen it in use," the young priest added quickly, noticing Belisarius's deepening frown.

"Indeed," muttered the wizard. "And have you ever heard of a wizard named Agannazzar?"

Belisarius smiled as Cadderly shook his head. "He is a mage of no large fame born two centuries ago," the wizard explained.

"Now dead," Cadderly reasoned.

"Perhaps," Belisarius said wryly, flashing a wink. "One can never be certain where wizards are concerned."

"And was this his ring?" Cadderly asked.

"I cannot be sure," Belisarius replied. "Either he or one of his associates created it with this specific power imbued. It is not too powerful, but you may find it useful." He tossed it to Cadderly and took up the wand. The young priest suspected that Belisarius had purposely saved the remaining ring for last.

"This is a common device," the wizard began, but Cadderly stopped him with an upraised hand. At first the wand seemed an unremarkable, slender shaft of black wood just over a foot long, but, as he looked at it, Cadderly heard the notes of a distant song playing in his mind.

Cadderly studied deeper, sensed, and then saw clearly, the magic of the item.

"Light," he said to the wizard. "The wand's power has to do with the manipulation of illumination."

Belisarius frowned again and looked at the wand, as if ensuring that there were no runes visibly etched on its smooth side. "You have seen it in use?" the wizard asked hopefully, already tired of being upstaged.

"No," Cadderly said absently, not releasing his attention from the revelations. In his mind, he saw lights forming different images and dancing about.

"*Domin illu*," he muttered. The light he pictured became constant and of the same intensity as the light he had conjured in his room and in the maze.

"*Illu*," an arcane word for light, escaped his trembling lips. The light intensified, brightened to where Cadderly squinted against the glare in his mind.

"*Mas illu*," he said, the literal translation being "great light." The image burst forth in all its splendor, a fiery green explosion of light spewing golden rays and blazing in Cadderly's mind. Cadderly cried out and looked away, nearly shouting, "*Illumas belle!*" as he fell out of his chair.

Cadderly sat up and looked at the wizard, who was still sitting, holding the unremarkable wand in his extended hand.

"What just happened?" Belisarius asked bluntly.

"I saw the powers—four distinctly," Cadderly stammered, "in my mind."

"And you repeated the triggering phrases," the perturbed wizard added, "exactly."

"But how?" Cadderly asked him, honestly perplexed.

"Go see a priest," Belisarius said with a snarl. "Why did you waste my time and effort on things you already knew?"

"I did not," Cadderly insisted.

"Go see a priest," Belisarius repeated, tossing the wand to Cadderly.

The young man accepted the item and looked to the floor beside the wizard's chair. "We have one more ring to explore," he remarked, backing away into his chair as he spoke.

Belisarius scooped up the remaining ring, a gold band lined with diamond chips, and held it out for Cadderly to see. "You tell me," the wizard insisted.

Again Cadderly heard the distant song playing, but for the sake of his valued friend's pride, he consciously pushed it away.

"It is not magical," he lied, extending his hand to accept it.

"Hah!" the wizard snapped and pulled back his hand. "This is the most potent item of all!" He held it close to his sparkling, admiring eyes. "A ring for wizards," he explained, "to heighten their powers. It would be quite useless to you."

An alarm went off in Cadderly's head. What was sneaky Belisarius up to? The young priest concentrated not on the ring, but on the wizard himself, and saw a shadow image of Belisarius perched on the wizard's shoulder, waggling its eager fingers and rubbing its hands anxiously as it peered at the ring. But Cadderly realized that the wizard's greed was indeed for a wizard's item. The bent of the shadow told him beyond any doubt that Belisarius had not lied to him, and he privately berated himself for thinking differently.

"Keep it," he offered.

The wizard nearly toppled from his chair. His smile seemed as though it would engulf his ears. "I will," he said, his voice an unintentional shriek. "What might I pay you in return?"

Cadderly waved the thought away.

"I must insist," Belisarius continued, undaunted. "This is too valuable a gift—"

"Not to me," Cadderly reminded him.

Belisarius conceded the point with a nod, but still searched for some way to give something back to the young priest.

"Your walking stick!" he proclaimed at last.

Cadderly took up the item, not understanding.

"You use it as a weapon?"

"If I must use anything at all," Cadderly answered. "It is harder than my hand." The mere mention of open-handed combat inevitably brought an image of Danica to Cadderly's mind.

"But not as sturdy as you would like?" Belisarius went on, not noticing the cloud of despair that briefly crossed Cadderly's face.

"Do not deny it," the wizard insisted. "You revealed your fears for the feebleness of the weapon in your fight with the minotaur, when you readily accepted the image of it breaking."

Cadderly didn't argue.

"Leave it with me, my boy!" Belisarius cried. "Give me a few days, and I promise you that you will never consider it a feeble weapon again."

"So you are an enchanter as well?" Cadderly remarked.

"There are many wizardly talents that a cleric would not understand," the wizard replied with an exaggerated air of superiority.

"Especially a cleric who does not understand his own talents," Cadderly replied, his simple admission stealing the wizard's bluster.

Belisarius nodded and managed a weak smile, then left Cadderly with a final thought: "Moderation."

* * * * *

Cadderly was a bit surprised to find Nameless still wandering the road between the wizard's tower and Carradoon, expecting that the beggar would either have gone to Carradoon to further his day's take, or to his wife and children to enjoy a reprieve from the unenviable lifestyle that had been forced upon him.

Cadderly grew even more surprised when the beggar looked at him and gave him an exaggerated wink, holding up and jingling the purse of gold with a lascivious smile on his dirty face.

Something about that gesture struck Cadderly as badly out of character for Nameless, an act of open greed or open thanks, neither of which applied to the proud, unfortunate man Cadderly had met earlier on the road.

Then Cadderly saw the shadows.

He could not make them out distinctly, as he had the images of Jhanine and her children. They were hunched and growling things, their forms shifting continually, but always emanating a clear and unrepentant wickedness to the young priest. One imaginary claw reached out from the beggar's shoulder and raked the air in Cadderly's direction.

Suddenly Cadderly was very afraid. His neck hair stood on end; his heart began to drum rapidly. A sickly sweet smell came to him then; he thought he heard the buzz of flies. Cadderly shook his head vigorously, feeling that he must be going insane. It seemed as if his senses had heightened, become animal-like, and the sudden intrusion of so much stimulation nearly overwhelmed the young priest.

Then he was calm again and looking at the innocent beggar man. He wished that he had his walking stick, and glanced back to the distant tower.

"Fine day!" the beggar said, seeming cheery, though Cadderly instinctively knew better.

Fete. The word came into Cadderly's head and he almost uttered it. He looked down to his hand, the onyx ring upon one finger, and saw that he had subconsciously angled it the beggar's way.

"Must you be gone so soon?" the beggar man asked, sounding innocent, almost wounded.

Cadderly saw the black shadows crouched upon the man's shoulder, saw the claws and venom-dripping fangs. He nodded briskly, pulled his cloak tightly around his shoulders, and hurried on his way.

He caught a whiff of that sickly sweet scent again and heard the flies. If he had been alone and not so unnerved, he would have stopped and sought out the source. He glanced to the side only briefly as he passed, to the bushes lining the road.

If he had looked closer, Cadderly would have discovered the body, already bloated after just a few hours in the late summer sun. And if he had found the strength to work his magical perceptions, Cadderly would have seen, too, the spirit of Nameless, helpless and hopeless and pitifully wandering until the gods came to claim it.

Eight
Unnecessary Evils

The young priest had noticed the change! Ghost cursed himself and considered the implications of the unexpected occurrence. He had never really believed that he would be able to kill Cadderly so easily—according to every piece of information he had been given, this young priest was a deadly opponent—but when he had seen Cadderly coming down the road, alone and with no obvious witnesses around, Ghost had briefly wondered if the purse might be earned quickly, if his artistry had so easily paid off.

The beggar man had gained Cadderly's confidence; that much Ghost knew from eavesdropping on their conversation. Now, posing as that man, the assassin thought he could get close, could catch Cadderly with his guard down. But the young priest had noticed the change!

Ghost replayed the brief encounter, trying to discern where his act had failed. Nothing obvious came to him; certainly nothing so blatant as to justify sending a defensively huddled Cadderly running on his way. A singular fear came to the assassin then: if Cadderly proved as formidable as the reports had indicated—and as Ghost was now beginning to suspect—then he might be strong enough to fend off the magic of the *Ghearufu*. It had been done only twice before, both times by wizards, when Ghost's attempts at possession had been mentally blocked.

"There are other options," Ghost said aloud, reminding himself of his many allies and of the fact that both of those resisting wizards had wound up as worm food. One of those times, Ghost had possessed a victim that the unsuspecting mage could not suspect—his wife. What a sweet kill that had been! On the other occasion, Ghost had served the attending Night Mask band as an infiltrator, providing them with such an enormous amount of information that the targeted wizard, as powerful as he was, had been among the society's easiest kills.

"Either way, young Cadderly," the merciless assassin whispered to the wind, "I shall paint my picture, and you shall be dead before the first of winter's snows."

With an evil snicker, the assassin in a beggar's body went to the bushes and retrieved his own form. The magical ring had nearly completed its healing work on the limp-muscled figure by then; the stench was fast fading and the flies had gone away.

"Do you wear a ring such as mine?" the evil man teased to the formless spirit he knew would still be wandering the area. Ghost willed the *Ghearufu*, white glove and mirror, back into sight and took the black-gloved hand from the hand of the corpse. He fell back into his mind, connecting with the powers of the magical device.

The eyes of the assassin's more familiar form blinked open just in time to watch the beggar's body fall stiffly to the side. Ghost spent a moment reorienting himself to his customary form, then propped himself up on his elbows.

"No magic ring?" He laughed at the beggar man's corpse. "Then you will stay dead, pitiful fool, though whoever finds your body will have no idea of how you died!"

The thought widened Ghost's smile. In his earliest days with the *Ghearufu*, more than a hundred years before, he had hacked up his unmarked victims. His confidence had quickly grown, though, and Ghost had soon changed tactics, thinking in his budding arrogance that the mysteries surrounding the demise of an apparently healthy body would serve as an appropriate calling card.

Ghost willed the *Ghearufu* away and brushed the dirt from his clothes. He started down the road immediately for the distant gates of Carradoon, for his room at the Dragon's Codpiece.

* * * * *

The firbolg noted with distaste the apparently normal situation at the farmhouse on the outskirts of Carradoon. A few hens clucked and strutted, pecking at discarded seed here and there; the three horses in the stable beside the barn showed no signs that they had been spooked in the least; and the house itself seemed perfectly secure, not a broken window or even a visible scrape mark on any door.

Vander knew better. It was always this way, always done in absolute secrecy. It all seemed so perfectly cowardly to the warrior giant.

"We could have stayed in the forest," Vander muttered, flipping his white-furred cloak back over his muscular shoulders.

The black-and-silver-outfitted assassins at the firbolg's sides looked at each other curiously. "It was by your orders . . ." one of them began to reply, but Vander's upraised hand silenced him.

Not by my orders, the firbolg thought, remembering when Ghost, in Vander's magnificent body, had set the troupe into motion, while Vander could only sit and watch helplessly from inside Ghost's weak form.

"We must get inside," offered the assassin after a few moments of uncomfortable silence. "This yard can be seen from the road."

"The light of day offends you," the firbolg remarked.

"It reveals us," the Night Mask replied obstinately.

Vander cast him a threatening scowl but did follow the two men to the door. The portal was large enough so that Vander did not have to alter his size, and he was glad, for he did not enjoy wearing a human frame, especially not around the treacherous murderers. He liked the imposing strength of his giant body, the long and muscled limbs that could reach an enemy from across a room and easily throttle him.

Vander hesitated at the threshold.

"The house is secure," one of the assassins inside assured the firbolg, misunderstanding his dismay. "Only the elder daughter remains alive, and she is held—" the lewd way the man spoke that word irritated Vander profoundly, "—in the bedroom."

Vander strode in. "Where?" he demanded, purposely redirecting his gaze from the bloodied male and female bodies in the corner of the small kitchen. The human assassin, obviously unbothered by the gruesome sight, sat at the table, casually eating breakfast. He motioned to a door at the back of the room.

Propelled by his mounting rage, Vander was across the kitchen and through the door in an instant. He nearly tripped over a smaller bloodied form just inside the second room, and that moved him along only faster, more determinedly.

This room connected to a side bedroom, its door open a crack. A whimpering sound came from within, revealing to Vander what was going on before the firbolg even shoved the door wide.

The girl lay on the bed, half-dressed and securely tied to the posts by her wrists and ankles, with the sides of her mouth pulled tightly back by a cloth gag. An assassin lay on each side of her, teasing her and taking delight at her terrified movements.

Vander had to stoop low in this room to avoid the ceiling beams, but that didn't slow him. He swept aside the three Night Masks standing in his way with a single movement, then stepped to the foot of the bed.

One of the prone assassins looked up and grinned wickedly, misconstruing the firbolg's urgency. The fool motioned for Vander to join in the fun.

Vander's great hands caught both the men by their collars and sent them flying across the room to collide heavily with the wall on each side of the door. The firbolg quickly threw a blanket over the exposed young woman and turned to face his hated associates.

The three on the side of the room looked to each other nervously; one of the men who had hit the wall lay crumpled in a heap at its base. The other, though, was up and outraged, a short sword in one hand.

Vander couldn't help but grin as he considered the situation. Might this be the long-awaited showdown? A nagging thought stole his mirth. He could kill these men, all five, and probably the other dozen or so that were in and about the house, but what about Ghost?

Always, the firbolg had to remember Ghost.

"You three," he commanded to the men on the side of the room. "Your associate has drawn a weapon on your master."

The three understood the implications immediately, as did the man holding the short sword, if his suddenly fearful expression correctly revealed his thoughts. The Night Masks were a vicious and evil band, but within the organization existed strict codes of conduct and horrible forms of discipline that even the hardiest assassin feared. The three by the wall drew their own weapons and faced the traitor.

The man with the short sword fumbled to put his weapon away. He jerked once, then again, a confused expression on his face.

His accomplice, crumpled at the base of the wall, was not as dazed as he had appeared, and he was eager to regain the taskmaster's favor. In his hand he held the last of three daggers, and this one, too, he whipped across to find a place in the traitor's side.

Anxious to show their respect and loyalty to their powerful leader, the other three promptly rushed the dying man. A club slapped the short sword from trembling hands, and all four loyal soldiers set upon the doomed man, hacking and crushing until he lay in a bloody heap on the floor.

"Put him with the other dead," Vander said to them. He looked back to the bed. "And find a proper prison for this girl."

"She is a witness and must be killed," an assassin replied. "That is our way."

"On my word alone," Vander growled back, his voice carrying tremendous influence now, considering the grim fate of the one who had dared to oppose him. "Now take her!" The same man who had questioned the decision started immediately for the bed, sheathing his weapon but not relenting his steely-eyed glare.

Vander caught him in one hand by the throat and easily lifted him from the floor.

"You are not to touch her." The firbolg snarled in his face. He noticed the man's hand inching toward his belt. "Yes," Vander purred, "do draw your little knife!"

The three remaining men seemed at a loss.

"She must be killed," one of them dared to offer in support of his threatened colleague.

The man in Vander's grasp twisted free enough to growl defiantly at the firbolg.

Vander heaved him through the nearest wall, back into the kitchen. Several assassins who had gathered in the other room stared through the hole in disbelief at the angry firbolg.

"On your word alone," the three men by the door said obediently.

"I will make my place in the barn," Vander said to them all. "It is more fitting to my size and there I will not have to deal with your impertinence. I warn you just one more time," he growled ominously. "If the girl is harmed in any way . . ."

Vander left it at that, preferring to end the threat by leading the others' gazes to the squirming and groaning Night Mask caught fast by broken, stabbing planks halfway between the bedroom and the kitchen.

* * * * *

Fredegar Harriman, proprietor of the Dragon's Codpiece, shook his thick-jowled face in disbelief at the request for yet another private room. The inn had only eight such rooms, and while the much less expensive common room was nearly empty, all of the private rooms were occupied. That alone seemed amazing enough, but what struck Fredegar as even more odd was the makeup of his guests. Five of the rooms belonged to visiting merchants, as was common. A sixth had been paid for until the end of the year by Cadderly, and a seventh had been reserved by the Edificant Library for use by a soon-to-arrive headmaster. Even more unexpectedly, the last room had been rented that very day, to a stranger nearly as curious-looking as this brown-haired lad.

"Common room won't do?" the flustered innkeeper asked. "At least for a few nights? It's on the back side of the building. Not much of a view, but quiet enough."

The young man shook his head, his stringy brown hair flopping to one side, revealing that half of his head had been shaved. "I can pay you well," Bogo offered, giving his purse a quick shake to accentuate the point.

Fredegar continued to wipe the bar and tried to find a way around the dilemma. He didn't want to put the young man out, more for the innkeeper's reputation and his sincerity than for the lost coins, but he didn't see a way around it. The hearth room was teeming this night—it had been full every night since the rumors of impending war had spread through Carradoon—mostly with locals. Fredegar peered through the throng, trying to see if any of his private guests were in attendance.

"I have just one room empty," he explained, "but it won't be for long—might even be filled this night."

"I am here now to fill it," Bogo argued. "Is my gold not as good as another's?"

"Your gold is fine," Fredegar assured him, hoping to keep the tension low. "The one open room has been reserved for more than a week by priests from the Edificant Library. I have assured them that it will be available, and, well, if you are from the area, you know that it is not wise for an honest merchant such as myself to alienate the Edificant Library."

Bogo perked his ears up at mention of the place and the notion that other priests were on their way to town.

"Headmaster Avery and Kierkan Rufo will be in soon," the talkative innkeeper went on. "I haven't seen the good, fat headmaster for almost a year now. I expect he and Rufo have come to town to meet with young Cadderly, another of my guests and another of their priests, and to prepare for this potential war that everyone seems to be talking about."

Bogo scrutinized every word, all the while trying to appear unconcerned. The news about Rufo seemed almost too good to be true. Having the two-time stooge so close at hand could aid his plans to make the kill on Cadderly.

Fredegar, as usual, rambled on in many unimportant directions, speaking mostly of the outrageous rumors that had been circulating. Bogo put in an occasional smile or grunt to make it appear that he was listening, but his mind was whirling down the many avenues the newest information had opened to him.

"I have it!" Fredegar announced suddenly, so loudly that several patrons at the nearest tables of the hearth room stopped their conversations and turned to regard the innkeeper.

"Malcolm," Fredegar called across the room. An older gentleman, a merchant by his rich and fanciful dress, looked up from his table.

"Half price if you will share a room with my Brennan," Fredegar offered.

The old gentleman smiled and turned to talk with his companions at the table, then stood and came over to the bar.

"I have only one more night in town," he answered when he arrived. "I leave for Riatavin in the morning." He winked conspiratorially, both at Fredegar and the odd-looking young man standing at the bar. "One can make fine trades with such grim news filling the air, eh?"

"A night with my Brennan?" Fredegar said hopefully.

The merchant gazed across the room to a younger woman, fine in stature and looking back at him with obvious interest. "I had hoped to be accompanied on my last night in town," he explained. Again came his wink, this time even more lecherous. "After all, back in Riatavin tomorrow night, I will be forced to spend some time with my wife."

Fredegar, blushing, joined him in his laughter.

"I could spend a single night in the common room," Bogo interjected, not at all amused by the worthless bantering, "if you will guarantee me this man's room by midday tomorrow." Bogo turned his thin lips up in a wry smile, thinking it best to play the conniving buddy game. "Free of charge this night?" he asked coyly.

Fredegar, never one to bicker (especially not when the inn was so full), readily agreed. "And an ale with my compliments, young stranger," the innkeeper offered as he filled a tankard. "And one for your intended?" Fredegar asked Malcolm.

"I will meet it at the table," the lecherous merchant replied, going back to his seat.

Bogo accepted the drink with a smile and turned about, leaning with his elbow propped on the bar. The crowd buzzed and played; it was a jovial and warm inn, its atmosphere not at all hindered (perhaps even enhanced) by the still-distant rumors of war. The perfect cover, Bogo thought as he watched the bustle, and he nearly laughed aloud as he considered how the events of the next few days might steal a bit of the mirth.

"So good that you have returned!" he heard Fredegar say a short while later. Bogo's eyes widened and he purposely shifted farther down the bar as a young man, of above average height and solid build, moved to join the innkeeper.

He wore a blue, wide-brimmed hat lined with a red sash. Set in its middle was a porcelain brooch bearing the holy symbol of Deneir. There could be little doubt as to this one's identity—Dorigen's description of Cadderly had not included the beard, but Bogo could see that it was newly grown, and the unkempt sand-brown hair and gray eyes certainly fit.

"Headmaster Avery and Kierkan Rufo are coming in," Fredegar explained, "perhaps this very night."

Bogo noticed the young man flinch at that remark, though the priest had tried to cover his reaction. "Do they know I am staying here?" he asked.

Fredegar seemed at a loss by his guest's obvious discomfort.

"Why, Cadderly," he replied slyly, "have you done something wrong?"

The young priest smiled noncommittally and started for the staircase beside the bar. Distracted, Cadderly did not even notice the odd-looking young man as he passed by.

But Bogo certainly noticed Cadderly. He watched the priest go, thinking how easy this all might be.

Nine
Evil Visions, Evil Deeds

H e stood in a lighted room, the sitting room of Belisarius's tower perhaps, holding a beating heart in his hand. The slain minotaur lay at his feet and all his closest friends, Danica and the dwarven brothers, stood by it, laughing wildly, uncontrollably.

Cadderly, too, joined in the laughter but as soon as he did, he realized that his friends were not laughing at all. Rather, they were crying, sobbing great tears that streaked their cheeks and fell in impossibly large puddles at their feet.

He did not understand.

Something was logically wrong; Cadderly sensed that something about the entire scene was out of place. He felt the warm blood running down his arm, soaking his tunic, but in his perversion of the wizard's minotaur and maze illusion, there had been no blood! Slowly, fearfully the young scholar looked down.

The minotaur was not a minotaur any longer, nor had it vanished like some insubstantial illusion, as Cadderly had expected. It was Avery—Cadderly knew it was Avery, though he could not see the face of the man who lay on his back across a table, arms and legs splayed wide and his chest savagely torn open.

Cadderly held Avery's still-beating heart.

He tried to scream but could not. There came a rapping noise, sharp but distant.

He could not scream.

* * * * *

Cadderly sat up. The rapping came again, more insistently, followed by a voice that Cadderly could not ignore. At last he dared to open his eyes and sighed

504

deeply when he learned that he was in his own room, that it had all been another terrible dream.

"Cadderly?"

The call was not a dream, and his recognition of the commanding, fatherly voice could not be wrong. He closed his eyes again, tried to pretend he was not there, or that Avery was not there.

"Cadderly?" The knocking did not diminish.

What time was it? Cadderly wondered. The moon was up, though beyond its zenith, for no direct silvery light played through the young priest's east window.

Resignedly, Cadderly pulled himself out of bed, straightened his nightshirt, and went to the closed door.

"Cadderly?"

He cracked open the portal and winced at the sight of Headmaster Avery. Kierkan Rufo, leaning as always in his customary position, leered over the headmaster's broad shoulder.

"It is late," Cadderly mumbled through the cottony sensation and the lump of revulsion in his mouth. He could not look at Avery without the gruesome dream image coming clearly to his thoughts, could not regard the man without the warm sensation of blood running along his arm. Unconsciously, he rubbed one hand against his nightshirt.

"So it is," Avery replied, somewhat embarrassed, "but I thought you would be pleased to learn that Rufo here, and I, have arrived in town. We shall be staying at the inn, just four doors down from you, across from the stairway." The portly headmaster glanced that way, his expression clearly revealing an invitation for the young priest.

Cadderly only nodded, then winced again as another drop of imaginary blood ran the length of his forearm.

Avery did not miss the sour expression. "Is something wrong, lad?" the headmaster asked with compassion.

"Nothing," Cadderly replied curtly. He mellowed immediately, guessing that his demeanor would inspire further curiosity. "I am just tired. I was sleeping . . ."

"My pardon," Avery said, straining to be lighthearted, "but you are not sleeping now." He took a step forward, as though to push his way into the room.

Cadderly shifted to block the door. "I will soon be sleeping again," he said evenly.

Avery stepped back and, for the first time since he had arrived, regarded Cadderly with a less than appreciative glint in his puffy eyes.

"Still stubborn?" Avery asked him sharply. "You tread on dangerous ground, young priest. Your absence from the library might be overlooked. Dean Thobicus has promised that he will allow you to make up your missed duties and studies."

"I do not care for his promise."

"If you continue on your wayward path," Avery went on, his voice a growl

against Cadderly's biting remark, "then you may move beyond the order altogether. I am not certain even kind Thobicus could forgive your transgressions
against Deneir. . . ."

"What do you know of Deneir?" Cadderly asked. In his mind he saw Avery
again, lying dead across the table, but he shook the evil thought away, realizing
how much he loved this man who had been a surrogate father to him. "And why
would you care for me? Did you not once call me a 'Gondsman'?" Cadderly asked
sharply, referring to the order of inventive priests who created without conscience, without regard to the implications of their creations.

His tirade exhausted, Cadderly looked at the headmaster, the father he had
just terribly wounded with his impertinence. Avery couldn't respond to his last
statement and seemed more on the verge of tears than an explosion of anger.
Behind him, Kierkan Rufo wore an almost amused expression of disbelief.

"I am sorry," Cadderly stammered. Avery put a large hand up to halt him.

"I am tired, that is all," Cadderly tried to explain. "I have had some terrible
dreams of late."

Avery's expression shifted to one of concern, and Cadderly knew his apology
had been accepted, or would be soon.

"We are but four doors down," the portly headmaster reiterated. "If you feel
the need to talk, do come and join us."

Cadderly nodded, though he knew he would not go to them, and shut the
door the second Avery had turned away. He fell back against the door heavily,
thinking how flimsy a barrier it was against the doubts and confusion of the outside world. He looked to his table by the window, to the open tome. When was
the last time that book had been closed?

Cadderly couldn't even muster the strength to go to it; he slipped over to his
bed and collapsed, hoping that he had put this night's evil dreams behind him.

* * * * *

Bogo Rath released his spell of clairaudience and cracked open the common
room's door. The common room was on the southwestern wing of the inn's second level; almost directly across from him, over the hearth room, loomed Cadderly's door, closed once more. Avery and Rufo rounded the corner diagonally
to Bogo's right, moving toward the door directly opposite the wide staircase.
The hearth room was quiet now and Bogo could hear their conversation
clearly.

"His surliness has not relented one bit since he passed through the library,"
Rufo said in an accusatory tone.

"He appeared weary," Avery answered with a resigned sigh. "Poor lad—perhaps Danica's arrival will brighten his mood."

They entered their room then, and Bogo considered using his eavesdropping
magic to hear the rest of their discussion.

"Who is Danica?" came a quiet, monotone question from behind Bogo. The young wizard froze, then slowly managed to turn about.

There stood Ghost, in the otherwise empty common room. The puny man held no weapon and made no move toward Bogo, but the wizard felt vulnerable nonetheless. How had Ghost come in so easily behind him? There was but one door to the room, and it had no outside balcony, as did the more expensive private rooms.

"How did you get in here?" Bogo asked, managing to steady his voice.

"I have been in here all along," Ghost replied. He turned and pointed to a pile of blankets. "In there, awaiting your return from the hearth room."

"You should have told me."

Ghost's wheezing laughter mocked him and showed him how ridiculous he had sounded.

"Who is Danica?" the evil little man asked again, more determinedly.

"Lady Danica Maupoissant," Bogo replied, "from Westgate. Do you know of her?"

Ghost shook his head.

"She is Cadderly's dearest friend," Bogo went on, "a beautiful wisp of a woman, by all descriptions, but formidable." Bogo's expression and tone grew grave. "This is not good news, my associate," he explained. "Lady Maupoissant has been a terrible foe to Castle Trinity in the fight thus far. If she arrives soon, then you would be well advised to finish your business with Cadderly promptly and be gone from here."

Ghost nodded, considering the warning. "From where will she come?" he asked. "The library?"

"That would seem likely," Bogo replied. He flipped his brown hair to one side and smiled slyly. "What are you thinking?"

Ghost's glare stole the wizard's mirth. "That is none of your concern," he rasped with sudden anger, pushing past Bogo to the door. "If you are thinking of making any moves against Cadderly on your own . . ." He let the implication hang in the air.

"Well, let us just say that the consequences of failure can be terrible indeed," Ghost finished, and he started away. He turned back immediately, though, his gaze directing Bogo to the pile of blankets that had hidden Ghost. "Do watch your back, young wizard," Ghost said evenly, then he coughed a wheezing laugh and went to his room, in the corner of the north wing, halfway between Cadderly's room and the room occupied by Avery and Rufo.

"From the library, from the mountains," Ghost mused, closing the door behind him. "Well, we shall see if Lady Maupoissant follows her path all the way to Carradoon." Ghost sat on his bed and summoned the *Ghearufu*. Using its powers, he sent his thoughts out of the town, to Vander, in the farmhouse.

Ghost felt the firbolg's typical revulsion and knew from its depth that Vander was angry both with the situation at the farm and with Ghost's intrusion.

Let me in, Vander, the wicked man teased, confident that the firbolg could not deny access even if he tried. Vander was Ghost's chosen victim, his special target, and with Vander alone, Ghost could make the body transfer from almost any range. He felt the sharp, burning pain as his spirit stepped out of his body, and then he was floating, flying on the winds, propelled straight for the firbolg's shell. As he entered the giant body, he knew that Vander had entered his, back in the room at the Dragon's Codpiece.

Do not leave the room, Ghost instructed telepathically through the continuing mental link. *Admit no visitors, particularly not that foolish wizard, Bogo Rath!*

Ghost willed away the *Ghearufu* and considered his surroundings. Curiously enough, he was in a barn, surrounded by stabled horses and cows. The man in the firbolg's body shook his head at Vander's continuing surprises and made his way to the large door.

The farmyard was quiet under the light of the westering moon, and the house, dark; not a single candle burned in any window. Ghost made his way across to the porch and heard a shuffle up above.

"It is only the master," he said to the unseen guards. "Gather the others and come into the barn, all of you. The time has come to tighten our noose."

Just a few minutes later, the entire band of nineteen remaining Night Masks assembled around their leader. Ghost noted that one of his henchmen was missing, but he said nothing about it, realizing that Vander probably knew what had happened to the man and that he might confuse them all by questioning the absence while wearing Vander's form.

He drew a quick map on the ground in front of him. "I have word that a woman is on her way to Carradoon from the Edificant Library," he said, indicating the location of the mountain structure. "There are only a few trails down the mountains, and they all exit in this general area. She should not be hard to find."

"How many should we send?" one of the assassins asked.

Ghost paused as much to consider the angry edge to the man's tone as to consider the question itself. Perhaps the missing Night Mask had met an unfortunate demise at Vander's impulsive hands.

"Five," Ghost said at last. "The woman is to be killed, as are any who travel beside her."

"It could be a large and formidable band," the same assassin argued.

"If so, then kill only the woman and be gone from there," Ghost snapped back, his firbolg-strength voice resounding off the barn's walls.

"Which five?" asked one of the group.

"Choose among yourselves," Ghost replied, "but do not take this woman lightly. She is, by all reports, formidable indeed.

"Another group of five is to strike within the town," Ghost went on. "Our information was correct. Cadderly stays at the Dragon's Codpiece. Here," he said, extending his map to show the lakeside section of Carradoon and indicating the lane running along the shore, "on Lakeview Street. Secure positions near the inn, where you will be at my . . . at Ghost's call. But take care to be far enough out of reach so as not to arouse suspicion."

"With five stringers to open a line of contact to the group within the city?" the same questioning assassin put in.

"That is our usual method," Ghost answered calmly.

"That will leave only four here at the farmhouse, excluding yourself," the angry assassin reasoned. Ghost did not understand the problem. "If we are forced to maintain a continual guard over the girl—"

"The girl?" Ghost didn't mean to sound so startled.

The assassin, and several others, cocked an eye curiously. "The girl that Mishalak died for," he said contemptuously. Ghost saw a problem building, and he scowled immediately to force the upstart back on the defensive.

"I do not question your decision to let her live," the assassin quickly explained. "Nor do I deny that Mishalak deserved death for drawing a weapon against you, the taskmaster. But if only four of us remain to guard the farmhouse, then the girl becomes a threat."

It all made perfect sense to the cunning impersonator. Vander's soft heart had caused problems before now. Oftentimes the firbolg was too intent on honor, placing the foolish notion above his duty. Ghost spent a moment considering how he might punish the giant, then smiled widely as a typically fiendish idea came into his head.

"You are correct," he said to the assassin. "It is time for you to end that threat." The man nodded eagerly, and Ghost's smile widened, the wicked man thinking how furious Vander would become, and how helpless, impotent, Vander would be. The proud firbolg would hate that most of all.

"End that threat this night," Ghost purred, "but, first, you and your friends might have your way with her." All about the ring, the evil assassins smiled. "We cannot survive on duty alone!"

That brought a cheer from the group.

"Go for the mountains this night as well," Ghost continued. "I do not know how many days away this Lady Maupoissant is from Carradoon, but she cannot be allowed to enter the town."

"Maupoissant?" one of the assassins, an older killer with salt and pepper hair, piped in.

"You know the name?"

"Nearly a decade ago, we killed a wainwright by that name," the man admitted, "a wagon maker and his wife. And we were paid handsomely for the task, I must say."

"The name is unusual and she is, by my informant's words, from Westgate," Ghost reasoned. "There could be a connection."

"Good," said the man, drawing a dagger and running the flat of the blade slowly along his bony cheek. "I always like to keep it in the family."

The nineteen Night Masks were pleased to see their unpredictable firbolg taskmaster joining in the laughter, the giant's heartfelt roars smothering their own. They were nervous; the time to kill was drawing near, and adding this "Lady Maupoissant" to the victim list was akin to smearing icing on an already delicious cake.

Ten

Professionals

W hat time is it?" Ivan asked, rolling out of his blankets and giving a profound stretch.

"It is hours past the dawn," Danica answered sharply, privately berating herself for being foolish enough to take the last watch.

"Ye should've woked me up," Ivan complained. He started to sit, then changed his mind and fell back into the bedroll in a heap.

"I have," Danica muttered, though the dwarf was no longer listening. "Six times!

"But not again," the fiery woman whispered. This time she was prepared. She took up two small buckets, filled with the icy cold water of a nearby mountain stream. Stealthily, she slipped up to the dwarves, their bedrolls having merged from their typically wild slumber during the night into a single large tangle. Danica sorted out the mess and moved the blankets aside enough to reveal the backs of hairy necks.

Pikel's presented the most problem, since the dwarf wore his beard pulled back over his ears and braided with his long hair (which he had recently redyed forest green) halfway down his back. Gently Danica moved the tousle aside, drawing a semiconscious "Hee hee," from the snoozing dwarf, and lifted one of the buckets.

The next thunderous roars resounding from the camp sent animals for nearly a mile around scurrying for cover. Even a fat black bear, out to catch some morning sunshine, raced through a tangle and up the side of a thick oak, sniffing the air nervously, fearfully.

The dwarves ran about in circles, crashed into each other several times, and threw their blankets into the air.

"Me weapon!" Ivan cried in distress.

"Oo oi!" Pikel wholeheartedly agreed, unable to locate his tree-trunk club.

Ivan calmed first, noticing Danica standing next to a tree, her arms folded across her chest and her grin spreading from ear to ear. The dwarf stopped his running altogether and regarded her with dart-throwing eyes.

He should have looked out for his brother instead.

Pikel hit him broadside, and the two flew away into some brambles. By the time they extricated themselves and had stomped back into the camp, their beards were thrown wildly about and their nightshirts seemed almost furry with burrs.

"Yerself did that to us!" Ivan shouted accusingly at Danica.

"I wish to be in Carradoon no later than tomorrow," the woman replied just as angrily. "I welcomed your company, but did not know it would mean holding camp until after noon each day! I thought dwarves were industrious!"

"Oooo," Pikel moaned, ashamed of his perceived laziness.

"Not our fault," Ivan muttered, also on the defensive. "It's the ground," he blurted. "Yeah, the ground. Too hard and comfortable for a dwarf to want to get himself up in the morning!"

"You have forfeited breakfast," Danica scolded.

"When halflings shave their feet!" Ivan roared, and Danica suspected—correctly—that she was overstepping her bounds. Throwing ice-cold water down the backs of sleeping dwarves was one thing, but denying them food was something altogether different, something downright dangerous.

"A quick meal then," she conceded, "then we are off."

Sixteen trout, four tankards of ale (each), half a sack of biscuits and three bowls of berries (each) later, the dwarven brothers gathered their belongings and skipped off down the mountain trails behind Danica. Impresk Lake was clearly visible whenever they came to an open ridge, and Carradoon soon came into sight as well, far below.

Despite Danica's desire for haste, the trio took all caution in their trek. The Snowflake Mountains were a dangerous place, even in their southern reaches, where the charges of the Edificant Library dominated the region. With war brewing in the north and battles continuing back to the west, in Shilmista, the companions had to assume that the trails would now be even more dangerous.

Danica led the way, bending low to inspect every track, every bent blade of grass. Ivan and Pikel bobbed along behind her, Ivan in his deer-antlered helmet and Pikel wearing a many-dented cooking pot for lack of any true headgear. Even though Danica continually searched the ground as she traveled, the speedy monk had little trouble outpacing the dwarves and forced them to scurry along just to keep up.

Danica slowed considerably; Ivan and Pikel nearly ran her down.

"Uh-oh," Pikel muttered, seeing Danica's curious expression.

"What'd ye find?" Ivan asked quietly, pulling his brother along behind him.

Danica shook her head, unsure. "Someone has passed this way," she declared.

"Avery and Rufo," Ivan replied.

"More recently," Danica said, standing straight again and taking a long, hard look at the nearby brush.

"Coming or going?" Ivan pressed.

Danica shook her head, unable to decide. She was confident that her guess had been correct, but what bothered her was the nature of the tracks, the scratching marks made over the apparent boot prints. If someone had crossed this trail earlier that morning, then they had gone to great lengths to conceal their tracks.

Ivan looked down at the unremarkable ground and, scratching confusedly at his yellow beard, produced yet another stubborn burr. "I don't see tracks," he huffed.

Danica pointed out a slight depression in the ground, barely visible, then indicated the pattern that made her believe that brush had been scraped over the ground.

Ivan snorted in disbelief. "That all ye got to go on?" he asked loudly, no longer afraid of the volume of his voice.

Danica didn't even try to hush him. She remained confident of her guess; she could hope only that some ranger, or one of Elbereth's elven kin, perhaps, was in the region. If not a ranger or an elf, then Danica felt certain that these tracks had been made by someone intent on concealing himself.

In the wilds of the mountains, that rarely boded well for travelers.

A few hundred yards down the trail, Danica found further signs of passage. This time even Ivan could not discount the obvious boot print in the soft trail, though half of it had been just as obviously brushed away.

The dwarf put his hands on his hips and looked about, focusing on the crook of a low branch hanging over the trail.

"I seen some rocks aside the trail just a dozen yards back," the dwarf began.

"Uh-oh," muttered Pikel, suspecting what his brother was getting at.

"Got some big enough trees hanging over the trail," Ivan continued, not hearing Pikel's flustered sigh. He looked at Danica, who seemed not to understand.

"Could set us a trap," Ivan spouted. "Could haul a rock up one of them trees and—"

Pikel slapped him across the back of the head.

"You've tried that before," Danica reasoned from the sour look on Pikel's face.

Pikel groaned and Ivan glared at him, but the yellow-bearded dwarf took no retribution against his brother. They had indeed tried that trap before. Although Ivan stubbornly, if with little real conviction, insisted that it had been a success (they had clobbered an orc with the rock), Pikel just as stubbornly insisted that the meager kill had hardly been worth the terrific effort of putting the rock in the tree in the first place.

Knowing that this time there would be another witness, Ivan would have conceded the point and gone along without further mention of the trap and Pikel's assault—it was only a slap, after all—but then, without explanation, Pikel whipped his club up in front of Ivan's face. To Danica, standing to the side, it seemed clear that Pikel tried to halt the weapon's momentum short of Ivan, but the club still connected with Ivan's great nose. It knocked him back several steps and sent a stream of warm blood flowing over the dwarf's hairy lip.

"What'd ye . . ." Ivan stammered, hardly believing the attack. He took up his double-bladed axe, snarled, and stepped toward his frantically squeaking brother.

Pikel couldn't explain the action to either Ivan or Danica, but he did manage to turn his fat club around in time, revealing a heavy dart buried halfway into the hard wood.

Now came Ivan's turn to do his brother a good deed. Looking to the thick bushes past Pikel, to where his warrior instincts immediately told him the dart had come from, he saw a crossbow leveled Pikel's way.

A tall form fell from a branch to land softly behind Danica.

Ivan's pointing finger made Pikel turn about.

"Uh-oh," the green-bearded dwarf squeaked, knowing he had no time to get out of harm's way.

Ivan hit him just before the quarrel, though, taking him down in a perfect tackle as the bolt flew harmlessly past. Ivan did not relent. As he rolled, he heaved Pikel right over him, and Pikel understood the tactic, likewise heaving Ivan back over him. Like a rolling boulder, the dwarven brothers barreled into the brush, forcefully enough to tangle the two men concealed there.

The Night Mask behind Danica, his sword bared and held high, had no reason to believe that the woman, intent on the spectacle of the dwarves, even knew that she was about to die. His surprise was complete when Danica snapped into a bend at her waist, her leg shooting out behind her, high enough to connect on the man's chest.

He flew back several feet, slamming into a tree trunk heavily, but managed to regain his dropped sword. More wary, he began backing away defensively, step for step with the dangerous woman's approach.

Danica broke into a run and came in hard and fast, but skidded suddenly to her knees and dipped her head as another form appeared from behind the trunk and launched a shoulder-high swipe at her with a short, slender staff. The weapon banged hard against the tree, spitting flakes of bark.

Danica slipped one foot back under her and kicked out with the other, thinking to break this second enemy's knee. He got his staff down in time to deflect the attack, though, then countered with several sharp and furious thrusts.

The young monk knew at once that she was in trouble. These were not ordinary highwaymen, though their dress seemed ordinary enough. She managed to fall out of the way as the other's sword flashed at her skull, but took a hit on the hip from the fast-flying staff.

Then she was up in a crouch a few feet away from the two men, taking careful measure of their tempered approach, looking for an opening where there seemed to be none.

* * * * *

Ivan bit down hard, and continued to bite, until he realized from the steady stream of "Oooooo's" that it was Pikel's calf, not an enemy's, in his mouth.

The dwarf scrambled to gain his footing in the tight quarters, branches and brambles grabbing at him with every move, and the nearest man landing no less than three punches on his already wounded nose.

Then Ivan was up, as was Pikel, with weapons ready. Ivan launched a vicious swipe with his axe, but his arm slipped through another thin but tough branch, shortening his reach so that he never got close to hitting the man.

Pikel yelped in terror and dove aside as his brother followed through, the wild flying axe nearly connecting. Again, albeit unintentionally, Ivan had saved his brother's life, for as Pikel leaped aside, another crossbow bolt soared in, cutting the air between the dwarves with a sizzling sound and thudding heavily into the shoulder of the man facing Ivan.

Both brothers paused long enough to look behind them to the crossbowman, who was frantically recocking the weapon. Pikel went back at his attacker, who had finally extricated himself from the brush tangle, and Ivan turned to where his closest enemy had been standing.

The man was not to be seen, and Ivan suspected from the still-shaking bushes that he had been laid out flat. Not to argue with good fortune, the dwarf howled and bolted back the other way, crunching out of the brambles to find the clear path leading to the crossbowman.

* * * * *

The swordsman was wounded; that was something at least. Danica's kick apparently had done some damage, for he winced with every circling step he took. Danica had already come to the conclusion that the staff-wielder was the more formidable of the two, though. His salt-and-pepper hair showed experience, and the perfect balance of his measured strides made her realize that this one had spent his lifetime training in the fighting arts. His staff seemed puny compared to the other's sword, but in his hands it was a deadly weapon indeed.

A sword cut sent the woman low; the staff clipped her shoulder and she had to dive over backward, rolling back to her feet just in time to prevent a killing follow-up attack.

Danica had used the roll to her advantage. Crouched in a ball on the way over, the monk had slipped one of her crystal-bladed daggers from her boot sheath.

The swordsman came on again, seeming more confident.

Danica planted her right foot out in front of her and pivoted on it, launching her left foot high and wide behind her as she twirled. She knew that her circle-kick attack would have no more effect than to force the swordsman's blade out wide, and knew, too, that she had left herself vulnerable to the other attacker. She threw her supporting leg out from under her and completed her circuit as she crashed down to the ground, hearing the whiz of the staff as it flew inches above her head.

Danica broke her fall with one arm and kept her torso high enough from the ground for her to snap her other arm underneath her, releasing the dagger. Its short flight ended in the swordsman's belly, and he fell back, eyes wide in disbelief and mouth wide in a silent scream.

The staff-wielder laughed and congratulated Danica for the cunning move, then came on relentlessly.

* * * * *

Pikel's attacker, too, wielded a club, but he faced two serious disadvantages. First, Pikel's club was much larger than his, and, second, he couldn't possibly hit the thick-skinned and thicker-headed dwarf hard enough with a blunt weapon to do any serious damage. Lightning fast, he smacked Pikel twice on the shoulder and once on the pot helmet, which rang loudly.

Pikel hardly cared, accepting the three hits for the one he returned. His tree-trunk club caught the man's exposed side and sent him flying from the brush to roll hard against the base of a tree.

The man's face could not have reflected a greater terror if he had been tied to a stake in the path of a horse stampede when Pikel came rushing out in pursuit, his pot all the way down over his face, but his club leveled perfectly to squash the man between the tree and its thick end.

The man rolled aside and Pikel slammed in, snapping the young tree down and going headlong over its broken trunk.

"Oo," the dwarf grunted as he skidded to a stop along the felled tree's rough bark. Then came that loud ring again as his stubborn attacker rushed back in and planted a two-hander on the top of his helmet.

* * * * *

Ivan realized he would not get to the crossbowman before the man had the weapon readied, so he hoisted his axe above his head in both hands and roared, "Time to die, ye thieving dog!" as he let the weapon fly.

The man dove over backward, thrusting his crossbow up in front of him as a makeshift shield. The axe took it solidly, tearing it from the man's hands and carrying it along on its flight until the whole connected with a tree, the crossbow falling in two pieces and the axe burying several inches into the trunk.

Ivan slowed his charge as the man came back up to his feet, drawing a long, thin sword, and not at all unnerved by the fine throw. In fact, the killer smiled widely at the now unarmed dwarf's approach.

"I could be wrong," Ivan admitted quietly, his ferocious charge withering to a halt.

* * * * *

Danica punched and punched again, both attacks deflected harmlessly wide by the small staff. Her attacker countered with a straight thrust and Danica threw her forearm up at the last moment to push it out of line with her face. She countered with a snapping kick, but her attacker had his staff back in place quickly enough to slow the blow so that it did no real damage.

A groan drew Danica's attention to the side. There stood the swordsman, his trembling hand at last closed around Danica's bloodied dagger. The man's face contorted in obvious agony, but also in obvious rage, and Danica suspected that he would soon be back in the fray. No matter how ineffective he might prove, she feared she could not handle both of these men at once.

Her temporary distraction cost her; the staff connected on her side. Danica rolled sidelong with the blow, diminishing its painful sting, and grabbed at her other boot as she went over and came back up to a crouch.

The staff-wielder leaped and spun in a flurry of defensive movements, anticipating another dagger throw. Danica pumped her arm several times, delicately shifting her angle with each forward movement. Each time, her intended victim placed himself in a position to block the throw or dodge aside.

The man was good.

Danica carefully aligned herself, pumped her arm once more, and threw. The staff-wielder easily slipped to the side, his expression revealing confusion that this skilled woman would have missed him so cleanly. He understood a moment later, when his companion groaned again, loudly.

The swordsman's trembling hand slipped free of the golden tiger hilt of the dagger in his belly and inched upward to the silver dragon protruding from his chest. Helplessly, he fell back against a tree and slid down to the ground.

"You and I," said the staff-wielder, and he accentuated his point with a furious rush and a blinding, dizzying series of thrusts and swipes.

* * * * *

Pikel looked mournfully at the tree he had felled, his pause for sorrowful contemplations costing him yet another ringing slam on his pot helmet.

The druidic-minded dwarf felt nothing but a most profound rage welling inside of him. Pikel had always been regarded by those who knew him as among the most even-minded of people, the slowest of the slow to anger. But now he had killed a tree.

He had killed a tree!

"Ooooooo!" the groan issued out of his trembling lips, between gnashing, gritted teeth.

"Ooooooo!" He turned around to face his attacker, who backed off a step at the sheer strength of the dwarf's bared fury.

"Ooooooo!" Pikel tripped over the tree stump as he charged, diving headlong. His attacker turned to flee, but the sprawling dwarf caught him by the ankle. The man's club came down hard on Pikel's grasping fingers repeatedly, but the enraged dwarf felt no pain.

Pikel dragged the man in, grabbed him in both hands, and hoisted him into the air. Gaining his feet, the powerful dwarf held the man above his head and looked around curiously, as though he was wondering what to do next.

The club rang again on Pikel's cooking pot helmet.

Pikel decided he had had enough. He impaled the man on the jagged edge of the broken tree stump.

* * * * *

Ivan whipped off his backpack, fumbling with the straps as his enemy rushed in. The dwarf blocked a sword thrust with the pack, tangling the sword in its straps long enough for Ivan to get out a package, six inches square and carefully wrapped.

The swordsman yanked away and tore the pack from his blade, then looked back to the dwarf curiously.

Ivan had ripped open the box and removed its contents: a toy he had been making for Cadderly ever since the young priest's heroics against the evil Barjin.

The black adamantite border of the spindle-disks contrasted mesmerizingly with the semiprecious crystal center. The swordsman paused, wondering what purpose these twin disks, joined in their center by a small rod, might possibly serve.

Ivan fumbled to get his fat finger through the loop in the string wrapping that small rod. He had seen Cadderly use this type of toy a thousand times, had marveled at how the young priest so easily let the disks roll down to the end of their cord, then casually, with a flip of his wrist, sent them spinning back to his waiting hand.

"Ye ever seen one of these?" Ivan asked the curious swordsman.

The man charged; Ivan flung the disks out at him. The man got his sword in the way to block, then eyed his weapon incredulously, regarding the ample nick the harder adamantite had caused.

Ivan had no time to gloat over the integrity of the craftsmanship, though. His throw had been strong, but, unlike Cadderly, he had no idea of how to recall the spinning disks. They hung near the end of the string, spinning sidelong.

"Ooooooo!" Pikel's rush from the side turned the swordsman about. He sidestepped the raging dwarf and regained his balance as Pikel swung about, scraping one foot on the ground for leverage to begin yet another furious charge.

This time, the green-bearded dwarf stopped short of passing the man, instead launching a series of furious blows with his heavy club. The swordsman worked hard, but managed to keep out of harm's way.

Ivan shoulder-blocked Pikel aside.

"This one's mine!" the gruff dwarf explained.

The swordsman smiled at the dwarf's apparent stupidity—together these two could have easily finished him.

His smile went away—literally—when Ivan suddenly hurled the spindle-disks again. This time, surprisingly, the small weapon was not attached to the dwarf's finger, had no encumbrance at all as it zipped past the swordsman's futile attempt to block.

The man's head snapped backward viciously and his face seemed to melt away when the adamantite disks connected squarely, removing every visible tooth, smashing apart his nose and both cheekbones, and neatly tucking his chin up under his upper jaw.

"Didn't think a dwarf could throw like that, did ye?" Ivan bellowed.

The man stood staring in disbelief; his sword fell to the ground.

"Oo," Pikel muttered as the man's head lolled freely to one side, for only then did either of the brothers realize that Ivan's powerful throw had snapped the man's neck.

Ivan reiterated Pikel's grim thought. "Oo."

* * * * *

Kick and swipe, punch and spearing thrust.

Danica and the staff-wielder moved in vicious harmony, attacking and parrying with incredible speed. For seconds that stretched into minutes, neither scored any hit at all.

But in the heightened competition, the adrenaline pumping fiercely, neither seemed to tire in the least.

"You are good, Lady . . ." the staff-wielder remarked, his voice trailing off as though he had meant to say more. "As I expected you would be."

Danica could hardly reply. Had the man just teased her, almost uttering her name? How could he know? A hundred thoughts raced through Danica's mind with the sudden suspicion that this was not a random ambush. Was Cadderly safe? she wondered frantically. And what of Avery and Rufo, who had come down this same path just a couple of days before?

Thinking her distracted, the Night Mask came in viciously.

Danica dropped straight to the ground and kicked out, connecting on the man's knee hard enough to halt his rush.

Danica stepped ahead, coming up right in the man's face. She took a painful hit on the shoulder for her efforts, but got in one of her own, a snapping chop to the man's throat. In the single instant the man was forced to pause and gulp for breath, Danica got one hand planted on his chin and the other around the back of his head to grab a clump of hair.

The man dropped his staff and clamped his hands desperately onto Danica's wrists, preventing her from twisting his head around. They held the pose for several moments, with Danica simply not strong enough to continue the intended maneuver.

The man, sensing his superiority, smiled wickedly.

Never releasing her grip, Danica leaped and rolled right over his shoulder, letting her weight do what her strength could not. They twisted and squirmed, Danica bending her knees to keep her full weight on the hold. The man wisely dropped to the ground, but Danica rolled again, under and to the side, now with her forearm locked tightly under the man's chin.

He gasped futilely for breath, scratched and clawed at Danica's arms, then shoved his own hand into Danica's face, probing for her eyes.

Danica felt the hardness of a stone under her hip and she quickly shifted again, putting the man's head in line. Frantically, brutally, the young monk realigned her grip on the man's hair, leaving the back of his head exposed, and began slamming him down to the stone.

Still, he could not breath; all the world disappeared in a darkening fog.

"He's dead!" Ivan cried, and Danica realized only then that the dwarf had been uttering the words over and over.

Horrified and sorely bruised, the young woman released her grip and rolled away from the man, fighting back her nausea.

"That one'll be gone soon, too," Ivan said calmly, indicating the man slumped against the tree, two daggers protruding from his bloody torso. "Unless we tend his wounds."

The man seemed to hear and looked pleadingly at the three companions.

"We must," Danica, composed again, explained to the dwarves. "I think this one knew my name. There may be a conspiracy here and he—" she pointed to the man against the tree, "—can tell us what it is."

Ivan shrugged his agreement and took a step toward the man, who seemed to take some comfort in the fact that his life would be spared. But there came a click from the side, and the man jerked violently a moment later, a crossbow quarrel next to the silver-hilted dagger.

* * * * *

The lone surviving Night Mask, wounded with a crossbow quarrel protruding from his shoulder, crashed through the brush, on the edge of delirium from the searing pain and the loss of blood. One thought dominated his thoughts:

he had failed in his mission. But at least he had stopped his cowardly comrade from revealing the greater mission—rule number one to the merciless band.

The man didn't know where to run. Vander would kill him when the firbolg learned that Lady Maupoissant had survived—the man regretted now that he had chosen his one remaining shot to finish the potential informant instead of trying again for Danica. Then he took heart as he reminded himself that even if he had been able to hit Danica, even if he had killed her, the dwarves would have had their informant and the more important plan to eliminate Cadderly would have been in jeopardy.

Still, the man regretted the decision, all the more when he heard the pursuit. Even wounded and weakened, he was confident that he could outrun the short-legged dwarves. When he looked back over his shoulder, though, he saw the young monk, flying effortlessly through the brush, gaining on him with every sure-footed stride.

The trees and brush opened up to more barren, rocky ground, and the desperate man smiled as he recalled his immediate terrain. He was a Night Mask to the bitter end, loyal and proud. His duty, wicked though it often was, had been his all, a dedication bordering on obsession.

The cruel monk was only a few strides behind him, he knew.

Loyal and proud, he never slowed as he came upon the edge of the hundred-foot cliff, and his scream as he leaped into the air was one of victory, not terror.

Eleven
What the Shadows Say

L ong shadows of the day's last light streaked across the barn's floor and walls. Gray webs glistened across gaps in the rafters, then went dark as the sun slipped farther away. Vander leaned against the wooden wall, glad to be back in his body again, but not so glad to learn what had transpired in the few short hours that Ghost had taken his form.

The farmer's girl was dead, and her end had been most unpleasant.

Memories of the time he had fled to his homeland, the Spine of the World, when Ghost had caught up to him and taken his body, coursed through Vander's thoughts, forcing the firbolg lower against the wall. For the proud firbolg, the defeat was complete. To Vander's warrior sensibilities, this was the ultimate humiliation. He could accept being defeated in honest battle, could kneel to a rightful king, but Ghost had dared to take that one step further; Ghost had taken Vander's valor, his honor, his very identity.

"Have they returned?" the firbolg snapped at the black-and-silver robed man as soon as he appeared at the barn door.

"The trip to the mountains would have taken them all of last night," the Night Mask replied, as if he sensed Vander's frustration. "Likely, they have not yet even encountered Lady Maupoissant."

Vander looked away.

"The line has been set up to Carradoon, and the group has taken position near the Dragon's Codpiece," the assassin went on hopefully.

Vander eyed the man for a long moment. He knew what the human was thinking, knew that the man had only blurted that information in the hopes that the news would be well received and would spare him from the firbolg's unpredictable wrath.

Unpredictable! Vander nearly laughed at the vicious irony of that thought. He waved the man away, and the Night Mask seemed more than happy to follow the silent command.

Vander sat alone once more in the deepening shadows. He took some measure of solace in the fact that the noose was apparently tightening around their latest target and that this business might soon be concluded.

Vander hardly began to smile before a frown again captured his visage. The business would be finished and another would soon begin. It would not end, Vander knew, until Ghost decided that the firbolg had outlived his usefulness.

The sun was gone, leaving Vander in the darkness.

* * * * *

"You have indicated that you wanted to be of help," Ghost said to the surprised wizard. "Now I offer you that chance."

Bogo Rath's beady green eyes seemed to grow even smaller as he studied the sleepy-eyed man. He had just moved his small pack of belongings to the private room that Fredegar had provided, only to find the mysterious assassin sitting on his bed and waiting for him.

Ghost understood the wizard's suspicion and his hesitation. Bogo did not trust Ghost (and rightly so) and Bogo's agenda was his own. Surely Bogo wanted Cadderly dead, but Ghost knew that the opportunistic and ambitious young wizard was not working with the assassin band. Rather, he was working independently, hopeful that he might use them to meet his own ends. Ghost, above all others, could understand that self-serving methodology and, above all others, the wicked man knew the dangers that might accompany such actions.

"I am to serve as sentry?" Bogo replied, incredulous.

Ghost thought it over, then nodded—that was as good a description as he could think of. "For this minor exploration only," he answered. "The time has come for us to learn a bit more about Cadderly's room and personal defenses. I can do that, do not doubt, but I would not be pleased to have the other two priests of the library return to the inn while I am otherwise engaged."

Bogo spent a long moment staring at the man. "You are so filled with riddles," he said at length. "You can get near Cadderly, hint that you can get even closer, and yet, the young priest lives. Is it caution or macabre pleasure that makes you play the game?"

Ghost smiled, congratulating Bogo for his perceptiveness. "Both," he answered honestly, more than willing to tout his own prowess. "I am an artist, young wizard, and not a common killer. The game, for that is what it is, must be played on my terms and by my rules." Ghost carefully chose his emphasis for that last sentence, letting it sound just enough like a threat to keep Bogo on edge.

"It is early for the hearth room," Bogo reasoned. "The sun is just down. Most of the patrons are still at home, finishing their dinners. And I am not yet settled into my new quarters," he added, a hint of dissatisfaction in his tone.

"Do you consider that so very important?" Ghost asked bluntly.

Bogo found no immediate reply.

"Take your dinner down in the hearth room," Ghost replied. "It is not so unusual a practice for guests of the inn."

"The priests went to the Temple of Ilmater," Bogo argued. "It is unlikely they will return within the hour you say you will need."

"But they might," Ghost said, his voice hinting of mounting anger. "Artist," he reiterated, voicing each syllable slowly and clearly. "Perfectionist."

Bogo gave up the argument and resignedly nodded in agreement. Ghost had indicated that he wouldn't yet kill Cadderly, and the young wizard had no reason to believe otherwise. Certainly, if the weakling assassin had wanted to strike against the young priest, he could have done so at almost any time over the last few days, and he would not have had to go out of his way and engage Bogo to stand watch in the hearth room.

They left Bogo's room together, Ghost stopping Bogo at the door and whispering to him, "Do inform young Brennan, the innkeeper's son, that Cadderly wishes to take his dinner now." Bogo cocked an eyebrow at him.

"It will get the door open," Ghost explained, a perfectly reasonable lie.

Ghost turned into his own room, with Bogo continuing on to the stairway. The puny assassin silently congratulated himself for so easily handling the potentially troubling wizard. He willed the *Ghearufu* into sight as he slipped behind the protection of his partly opened door.

The industrious Brennan came hopping up the stairs a short while later, carrying a dinner tray balanced easily in one hand and a long and narrow package in the other. Ghost admired the spring in the teenager's step, the vigor and boundless energy of awakening manhood for the handsome, if a bit slender, Brennan.

"Boy!" Ghost called out softly as Brennan turned the corner past Avery's room and headed past the assassin's door. Brennan stopped and turned to regard the curious man, following the waving motion of Ghost's white-gloved hand.

"Let me deliver this and then I'll get you whatever . . ." Brennan began, but Ghost cut him short with his upheld hand, this one, Brennan noted curiously, adorned with a black glove.

"My business will take only a moment," Ghost said, the significance of his wry smile lost on the unsuspecting youth.

A split second later, Brennan found himself staring back into his own face, and to the hallway beyond. At first, he thought that the strange man had put up some sort of mirror, but then the image, his image, moved independently. And he, or at least his image, was now wearing the black and white gloves!

"What?" Brennan stammered, on the verge of panic.

Ghost shoved the trapped man back into the room and waded in, closing the door behind him, dropping the narrow bundle—he knew it now to be some sort of staff or rod—and setting the tray on his own night table.

"It is just a game," Ghost purred, trying to keep the terrified victim from calling out. "How do you like your borrowed body?"

Brennan's eyes darted about in search of some escape. Gradually, his terror shifted to curiosity; the man standing before him, wearing his body, certainly did not seem so ominous.

"I feel weak," he admitted bluntly, then cringed, realizing that he might have offended the man.

"But you are!" Ghost teased. "Do you not understand? That is the point of the game."

Brennan's face crinkled in further confusion, then his eyes popped open wide as Ghost, moving with the speed of youth, clenched his borrowed fist and launched a roundhouse punch. Brennan tried to dodge, tried to block, but the weak body did not respond quickly enough. The fist slipped through the pitiful defenses, slamming Brennan between the eyes, and he was falling helplessly, with no strength to resist the waves of blackness closing over him.

Ghost regarded the body for a long while, trying to discern his next move. The prudent act, he knew, would be to strangle Brennan then and there, as he had done with the beggar on the road, and put one glove on the body to prevent the regeneration process from recalling the lad's wandering spirit.

Other sensations argued against that course. The wretched assassin felt wonderful in the youth's body, full of barely controllable energy, and with his passions fluctuating almost violently, beckoning him urgently toward base actions he had not seriously considered for decades. The impulsive notion came to Ghost to reach over and remove the boot and the magical ring, to kill Brennan in the weakling body and leave him dead. Ghost could then claim this form as his own until he had burned it out as he had nearly burned out the effeminate mantle.

He again wore the black and white gloves when his hands went around the weakling's neck.

Ghost realized that he must not do it—not yet. He berated himself for even beginning to act on such a rash notion. Moving methodically, he tied and gagged his victim securely, dragged him behind the bed, and wedged him between the bed and the wall.

The ring had already begun its work, and young Brennan's eyelids fluttered with the first signs of consciousness.

Ghost smashed him again, and again after that.

Brennan groaned through the gag and Ghost leaned in close, putting his lips to the trapped boy's ear. "You must be quiet," he purred, "or you will be punished."

Brennan groaned again, more loudly.

"Would you like me to tell you the punishments I have planned for your disobedience?" Ghost asked, putting a finger into Brennan's eye.

The terrified Brennan made no sounds and no movements at all.

"Good, wise lad," Ghost cooed. "Now let us see what you have brought." The assassin moved away and quickly unwrapped the bundle, revealing a ram-headed walking stick, finely crafted and perfectly balanced. Ghost had seen the marvelous item before, in Cadderly's hands when the priest had gone to the wizard's tower outside Carradoon. Only then did Ghost realize that the young priest had not been carrying the stick when he had returned down the road.

"How convenient!" he said, moving back over to Brennan. "I said I would tell you of the punishments, but here, let me show you instead," he said, patting the formidable club against his open palm.

Ghost's face contorted with sudden rage, and he launched a two-handed overhead chop. He felt the magic of the weapon thrumming when he slammed the ram's head down on Brennan's shoulder, and smiled even more widely when he saw the skinny limb crumble under the weapon's tremendous enchantment. Ghost had never fancied weapons, but he thought of keeping this one.

Ghost considered the wisdom of turning the walking stick over to Cadderly. The assassin was left in a quandary, for if the young priest was expecting the weapon's return, he might seek out Fredegar, or the wizard in the tower, and either would likely pose larger, more dangerous, questions.

That would be the worst of the possibilities.

The artist-killer left the room a few minutes later, bearing the tray and the retied bundle for Cadderly, and leaving the crumpled, unconscious Brennan hidden behind the bed in a pool of blood. Ghost had beaten Brennan severely, and the young man in the pitiful body would soon have died, except for the persistent healing magic of the ring concealed under the boot.

Semiconscious, Brennan almost hoped he would die. A thousand fiery explosions seemed to be going off within him; every joint ached, and the evil man with the club had paid particularly painful attention to his groin and collarbone.

He tried to move his head but could not; tried to wriggle his body out of the tight cubby, despite the pain, but found he was securely bound in place. He reflexively coughed up another gout of blood, his survival instincts barely managing to force the warm liquid past the gag so that he would not choke on it.

Broken, Brennan prayed that this torment would soon end, even if that end meant death. He did not know, of course, that he wore a magical ring, that he would soon be healed once more.

* * * * *

Cadderly wasn't thinking of dinner, wasn't thinking of anything at all beyond the alluring song playing in his mind as he turned the pages of the *Tome of Universal Harmony*. The book had offered him shelter once again, had chased away the images of Avery and Rufo—they had come back to see Cadderly that morning, and had again been abruptly turned away—and all the other troubles weighing heavily on the young priest's shoulders.

Under the protection of the sweet song of Deneir, Cadderly felt none of that weight, but sat straight and tall. He worked his arms out to the sides when they were not engaged in turning the pages, in a manner similar to the meditative techniques Danica had once shown him back at the Edificant Library. Back then, these movements had been simple exercise, but now, with the song flowing through his every movement, Cadderly felt the strength, his inner strength, coursing through his limbs.

"I have your supper!" he heard Brennan call from behind him, and he knew from the young man's volume that Brennan had probably called him several times and knocked loudly on the door before that. Embarrassed, Cadderly closed the great book and turned to meet the young man.

Brennan's eyes opened wide.

"Excuse me," Cadderly apologized, looking around helplessly for something with which to cover up. He was naked from the waist up, his well-muscled chest and shoulders glistening with sweat, and the rippling muscles of his waistline, newly trim from the meditative exercises over the tome, quivering from the recent exertion.

Brennan quickly composed himself, even flipped Cadderly a towel from the dinner tray with which he could rub down.

"It would seem that you could use the meal," Ghost offered. "I did not know that reading could be so strenuous."

Cadderly chuckled at the witticism, though he was a bit confused that Brennan had made such a remark. The young man had seen him at his reading many times before, and many times involved, as he was now, in the meditative exercises.

"What have you there?" Cadderly asked, seeing the long and narrow bundle.

Ghost fumbled with the item, still unsure if the young priest had expected it or not. "It came in just this afternoon," he explained, "from the wizard, I would assume." He unwrapped the bundle and handed the fine walking stick to Cadderly.

"Yes, Belisarius," Cadderly replied absently. He waved the walking stick about easily, testing its balance, then tossed it casually on the bed. "I had nearly forgotten about it," he remarked, and added with obvious sarcasm, "I wonder what mighty enchantments my wizard friend bestowed upon it!"

Ghost only shrugged, though secretly he was gnawing at his lower lip, angry now that he had decided to return the unlooked-for present.

Cadderly gave the young man a wink. "Not that I will ever find use for it, you understand."

"We never know when a fight might fall our way," Ghost replied, sliding the tray onto Cadderly's small table and arranging the silverware. Cadderly eyed him curiously, caught off guard by the grim tones and uncharacteristically reflective thought of the passion-driven youth.

The young man held a serrated knife in his hand for just a moment, with his hand only inches from Cadderly's bare chest. For some reason, that dangerous image suddenly mattered to Cadderly; silent alarms went off inside him. The young priest fought them away, as easily as he rubbed the sweat from his neck, rationally telling himself that he was letting his imagination run wild.

The song played in the back of Cadderly's mind. He almost turned about to see if he had left the tome open, but he had not; he could not. Shadows began to form atop Brennan's slender shoulders.

Aurora.

For some reason he could not understand, Cadderly sensed again the unfathomable possibility that Brennan was considering striking him with the knife.

Suddenly, Brennan dropped the knife to the tray and fumbled about with the small bowl and plate. Cadderly did not relax; Brennan's movements were too stiff, too edgy, as if Brennan was consciously trying to act as though nothing unusual had occurred.

Cadderly said nothing, but held the small towel around his neck with both hands, his muscles tight and ready. He did not concentrate on the man's specific actions; rather, he shifted back to the young man's shoulders, to the misshapen, growling shadows huddled there, black claws raking empty air.

Aurora.

The song played in the distant recesses of his mind, revealing the truth before him. But Cadderly, still a novice, still unsure of his power's source, did not know if he should trust in it or not.

Cadderly could not recognize the shadows any more than to equate them with the same fearsome things he had seen perched upon the shoulders of the beggar on the road. He sensed that they boded evil, both then and now, sensed that they were images resulting from vile thoughts. Considering that Brennan had just been holding a cutting knife, that a short stroke could have driven the serrated instrument into Cadderly's bare chest, those sensations did not put the young priest at ease.

"You must go," he said to the youth.

Ghost looked up at him, confused, but again, the expression did not seem right to Cadderly. "Is something wrong?" the slender youth asked innocently.

"Go," Cadderly said again, his scowl unrelenting, and this time the word held the strength of a minor magical enchantment.

Surprisingly, the young man held stubbornly to his position. The shadows on Brennan's shoulders dissipated and Cadderly had to wonder if he had misread the signals, if those shadows represented something else altogether.

Brennan gave him a curt bow—another unexpected movement from the young man that Cadderly thought he knew quite well—and then prudently slipped from the room, closing the door behind him.

Cadderly stood staring at the door for a long time, thinking that he must be going mad. He looked back to the *Tome of Universal Harmony*, wondering if it was a cursed book, a book inspiring lies and a discordant song that sounded true to the foolish victim's ear. How many priests had been found dead, lying across its open pages?

Cadderly labored for breath for a few crucial moments, at a crossroad in his life, though he did not realize it.

No, he decided at length. He had to believe in the book, wanted desperately to believe in something.

Still he remained in the same position, looking back to the door, to the tome, and lastly to his own heart. He realized that his meal was getting cold, then knew he did not care.

The emptiness within him could not be sated by food.

* * * * *

Bogo had given Ghost more than the hour the evil man had asked for, but the eager wizard decided to stay in the hearth room anyway, to see what he might learn. The talk among the growing number of patrons settled always on the rumors of war, but, to Bogo's relief, none of the gathering seemed to have any idea of the depth of the danger that hung over their heads. When Aballister decided to march, most likely in the early spring, the army of Castle Trinity would have little trouble in bringing Carradoon to its knees.

The night deepened, the warm fires and the many conversations blazed, and Bogo, despite his fears that Ghost had already dispatched Cadderly, remained in the room, listening and chatting. Every time the door to the foyer opened, the young wizard looked up, anxious to note the return of the two priests, thinking that perhaps they would provide him with better information than the misinformed townsmen.

Bogo's smile curled up when Kierkan Rufo entered a short while later, for the more formidable headmaster was not beside the angular man. Rufo headed right for the stairs, but Bogo cut him off.

"You are of the Edificant Library?" he asked, his tone sounding hopeful.

Rufo's sharp features seemed sharper still in the flickering firelight, and his dark eyes did not blink as he regarded the curious-looking young man.

"Might I buy you some ale, or fine wine perhaps?" Bogo pressed, seeing no answer forthcoming.

Rufo's answer dripped of suspicion. "Why?"

"I am not of the region," Bogo replied without the slightest hesitation. The ambitious mage had played this scene out a dozen times in his mind, along with several other potential scenarios concerning the priest who would be stooge. "All the night, I have been assailed with rumors of war," he explained. "And all the rumors hint that the one hope lies in the Edificant Library."

Again Rufo did not respond, but Bogo noticed the vain man straighten his shoulders with some pride.

"I am not without skills," Bogo went on, confident that Rufo was falling into his trap. "Perhaps I might aid in those hopes. Surely I would try."

"Let me buy you some wine, then," Bogo offered after a short pause, not wanting to break his budding momentum. "We can talk, and perhaps a wise priest can guide me to where my skills would be most helpful."

Rufo looked back to the foyer door, as though he expected, and feared, that Headmaster Avery would come pounding through at any moment. Then he nodded curtly and followed Bogo to one of the few empty tables remaining in the hearth room.

The talk remained casual for some time, with Bogo and Rufo sipping their wine, and Bogo quickly losing any hope that he would be able to get too much of the drink into the angular man. Rufo, who had been through many torments these last few weeks, remained cautious and guarded, covering his half-filled glass whenever Brennan, waiting on tables, made one of his frequent visits.

Bogo noted several times that the innkeeper's son seemed to be regarding him suspiciously, but he attributed it to the lad's natural curiosity that a stranger would have business with a priest from the library, and thought no more of it.

Bogo wasted little time in shifting the conversation to more specific topics, such as the Edificant Library and the ranking of Rufo's portly friend. Gradually, casually, the wizard led the talk to include the other priest who was a guest at the inn. Rufo, cryptic from the start, backed off even more and seemed to grow somewhat suspicious, but Bogo did not relent.

"Why are you in town?" Bogo asked, rather sharply.

Rufo seemed to note the subtle shift in the increasingly impatient wizard's tone. He rested back in his chair and regarded Bogo silently.

"I must go," the angular priest announced unexpectedly, bracing himself on the table and beginning to rise.

"Sit down, Kierkan Rufo," Bogo snarled at him. Rufo looked at him curiously for a moment, and realized he had not, in the course of the conversation, told the man his name. A small whine escaped the angular man's thin lips as he fell back into his chair, now almost expecting what was to come.

"How do you know my name?" Rufo demanded with as much courage as he could muster.

"Druzil told it to me," Bogo answered bluntly. Again came that almost imperceptible whine.

Rufo began to ask another question, but Bogo promptly silenced him.

"You will answer and obey," Bogo explained casually.

"Not again," Rufo growled with defiance that surprised even himself.

"Dorigen thinks differently," Bogo replied, "as does Druzil, who has been in your room for both nights you have been in town," Bogo lied. "The imp has been in your room since before you and Avery occupied the room. Did you think to escape so easily, Kierkan Rufo? Did you think the battle was won despite the minor setback we were given in Shilmista Forest?"

Rufo found no words with which to respond.

"There," Bogo said calmly, settling back into his chair and flipping his stringy brown hair over to one side. "Now we understand each other."

"What do you require of me this time?" Rufo asked, his voice sharp and a bit too loud for Bogo's liking (especially since Brennan was nearby again, regarding the two men with open curiosity). Rufo's visage continued to appear defiant, but Bogo was not concerned. The man was weak, he knew, else Rufo would have already left, or struck out against his revealed enemy.

"As of now, nothing," Bogo answered, not wanting to set too many things into motion until he better understood what Ghost and the Night Masks were planning. "I will be nearby, and you will remain available to me. I have some specific things planned for my visit to Carradoon, and you, Rufo, will play a role in those, do not doubt." He tipped his glass to the angular man and drained it, then rose from the table and started away, leaving Rufo lost in yet another unresolvable trap.

"Be wary, young mage," Bogo heard from the side as he took his first step up the stairs beside the hearth room's bar. He turned to see young Brennan, casually wiping down the bar and regarding him dangerously.

"Are you addressing me?" Bogo asked, trying to sound superior, though he was indeed becoming a bit unnerved by the innkeeper's son's sudden attention.

"I am warning you," Ghost, appearing as Brennan, clarified. "And know that it is the only warning you will receive. Your business here is as observer—that position determined by Aballister himself. If you interfere, you might find yourself lying in a hole beside Cadderly."

Bogo's eyes widened in shock, an expression that brought a satisfied smile to Ghost's borrowed lips.

"Who are you?" the wizard demanded. "How . . . ?"

"We are many," Ghost replied cryptically, obviously enjoying the spectacle of the squirming mage. "We are many and we are all about you. You were told that we do things properly, Bogo Rath. You were told that we take no chances." Ghost let it drop there and turned back to his work at the bar.

Bogo understood the reason behind the sudden break in the conversation when Avery, just returned to the inn, and Kierkan Rufo walked past him up the stairs, heading for their rooms.

Bogo followed them at a safe distance, no longer certain that he would have further instructions for Kierkan Rufo, no longer certain of anything.

Twelve
Mortality

T he dawn found Cadderly at his meditation, at his exercises, reaching his arms far to the side one at a time, muscle playing powerfully against muscle. He eyed the open book on the table before him as he moved, heard the song in his head, and felt in tune with it. Sweat lathered his bare chest and streaked the sides of his face, and the young priest felt it keenly, his senses heightened in this meditative state.

When at last he finished, Cadderly was thoroughly weary. He considered his bed, then changed his mind, thinking that he had been spending too much time in his room the past few days. The day would be bright and warm; outside his window, Impresk Lake glittered with a thousand sparkles in the morning sun.

Cadderly closed the *Tome of Universal Harmony*, but, looking upon the waters of that lake, so serene and inspiring, he still heard the song acutely. It was time to take the knowledge (the emotional strength, he hoped) that he had gained from the book out into the world. It was time to see how his new insights might fit into the everyday struggles of the people around him.

Cadderly feared those revelations. Could he control the shadows he would inevitably see dancing atop the shoulders of the many people of Carradoon? And could he decipher their meaning—truly? He thought back to the events of the night before, when he had turned young Brennan away, frightened at the implications of the squirming, growling manifestations he had seen.

The young priest washed and toweled off, strengthening his resolve. The choices seemed clear: go out and learn to assimilate in light of his newfound knowledge, or remain in his room, living a hermitlike existence. Cadderly thought of Belisarius, alone in his tower. The wizard would die there, alone, and, most likely, his body would not be discovered for weeks.

Cadderly did not wish to share that grim fate.

* * * * *

Still wearing the mantle of young Brennan, Ghost, absently replacing the candles on the lowered chandelier at the top of the staircase, watched the young priest leave the Dragon's Codpiece. He had heard Cadderly tell Fredegar that he would not return until late, and Ghost thought that a good thing. The Night Masks were in town and ready; Ghost had to meet with them this day. Perhaps young Cadderly would have a rather unpleasant surprise waiting for him when he returned that evening.

A patient killer, an artist, Ghost would have preferred to wait a few more days before arranging the strike, would have liked to get even closer to this curious young man, to know everything about him so that there could be no mistakes. The assassin considered this especially important in light of the potential problems arising from the arrival of the two other priests. Powerful priests had been known to resurrect the dead, and under normal circumstances, Ghost would prefer to take the time and discern exactly how much magical interference might be expected from the newcomers, particularly the priest bearing the title of headmaster. Might the Night Masks slay young Cadderly, only to have Avery locate his body and bring him back to life?

Bogo Rath presented even more complications. What might the upstart wizard be planning? the assassin wondered. Bogo had spoken with the other, lesser priest on the previous night, and that could not be a good thing.

Ghost did not like loose ends. He was a consummate professional who prided himself on being a perfect killer with never a lingering problem left behind. But while this operation seemed ragged to him, he had to believe that the problems could be circumvented—or eliminated. A new wrinkle had come into this picture, a new desire for Ghost that, in his mind at least, justified his seeming carelessness. Ghost felt the vitality coursing through his limbs, felt the powerful urges of adolescence, and remembered the pleasure those urges might bring.

He did not want to give up his new body.

But he knew, too, that he could not continue to play this charade much longer. With a single meeting, Cadderly had come to suspect that something was amiss, and Ghost did not doubt that those suspicions would only increase with time. Also, in this form, Ghost was severely restricted. His other body remained alive, and it would until the assassin fully committed himself to the idea of taking Brennan's body as his own, a dangerous action indeed until this mission was completed. And while that other, puny form drew breath, Ghost could not use the *Ghearufu* on any new victims. Even to get to Vander, his chosen victim, Ghost would have to go through his own body, and doing that would release young Brennan.

Things would become so much simpler when Cadderly lay dead, he knew. Ghost had considered trying the strike the night before, when he had held a cutting knife in his hand just inches from Cadderly's bare chest. If his aim had been good, the game would have ended then and there, and he could collect his gold, and seriously consider his immediate impulse to retain this young and vital body, to kill the trapped spirit of the young man back in his own room and remove the magical ring from the corpse's foot. In just a few days, his spirit would become acclimated to this new form, and then the *Ghearufu* would be his to use again. Vital youth would be his once more.

Hesitance had cost the assassin his chance. Before he had resolved to move, Cadderly was again intent upon him. The loose ends—his ignorance of Cadderly's powers, his ignorance of the other two priests—had held him back.

"Brennan!" Fredegar's cry startled the assassin from his contemplations.

"What are you waiting for?" the innkeeper bellowed. "Get that chandelier cranked back to its place, and soon! The hearth room needs cleaning, boy. Now get to it!"

More restrictions accompanied the pleasing young form. Ghost did not even argue. The Night Masks were not far—he had plenty of time to get to them—and in truth, he was glad for the delay so that he could better sort through the many potential problems and the many interesting questions.

About an hour later, the assassin was even more grateful for the delay that had kept him at the inn, when a young woman, strawberry-blond hair bouncing gaily about her shoulders, entered the Dragon's Codpiece, looking for Cadderly and introducing herself as Lady Danica Maupoissant.

Another wrinkle.

* * * * *

"There's the lad!" Ivan called, pointing back toward the front of the Dragon's Codpiece and roughly spinning Pikel about.

"Oo oi!" Pikel piped as soon as he spotted Cadderly, more concerned with getting Ivan's hands off him so that he might stop his spin. Dizzied, the green-bearded dwarf shuffled from foot to foot, struggling to straighten his cooking pot helmet.

Ivan started for Cadderly, who had not yet noticed them, but Danica put a hand on the dwarf's shoulder. As soon as the startled dwarf turned about and looked into Danica's pleading eyes, he understood.

"Ye want to go to him yerself," Ivan reasoned.

"Might I?" Danica asked. "I do not know how Cadderly will respond to seeing me. I would prefer . . ."

"Say no more, Lady," Ivan bellowed. "Me and me brother got more than a bit of work afore us, and it's getting late in the day already. I'll get us some rooms there." He pointed to the sign of an inn two doors down from where they stood, and two doors shy of the Dragon's Codpiece. "Ye can come and get us when ye want us.

"And ye can give him this from me and me brother," Ivan added, pulling the adamantite spindle-disks from a deep pocket. He started to give them to Danica, then pulled them back, embarrassed. As discreetly as he could, the gruff dwarf rubbed off a chunk of the weapon's first victim's face. Danica could not miss the movement. With a helpless shrug, Ivan tossed the disks to her.

Danica bent low and kissed the understanding dwarf on the forehead, drawing a deep blush from Ivan.

"Hee hee hee," Pikel chirped.

"Aw, what'd ye go and do that for?" the flustered dwarf asked Danica. He slapped his chuckling brother across the shoulder to set them both into motion, moving away from the inn and away from Cadderly. Ivan knew that if the young scholar saw them all, he would probably invite them in, thus ruining Danica's desires.

Danica stood alone in the crowded street, watching Cadderly's every step as he made his way into the Dragon's Codpiece. Across from her, the waters of Impresk Lake sparkled in late afternoon sunlight, and she almost followed their spellbinding allure and ran away from her fears. Truly, Danica did not know how Cadderly would react, did not know how final their parting in Shilmista Forest had been.

If Cadderly rebuked her now, Danica did not know where she would turn.

For the young monk, who had faced many challenges, many enemies, no moment had ever been so trying. It took every measure of courage that Danica could muster, but, finally, she skipped off toward the waiting inn.

Cadderly was on the stairs, heading up, when Danica entered. He held his familiar walking stick in the crook of one elbow and was looking at some wrinkled parchment, apparently oblivious to the world around him.

Quiet as a cat, the agile monk crossed the room and made the stairs. A boy of perhaps fifteen years eyed her curiously as she passed, she noted, and she half expected the lad to stop her, for she was not a paying guest. He did not, though, and soon Cadderly, still too busy with the parchment to notice her, loomed just two steps ahead of her.

Danica studied him a moment longer. He looked leaner than he had just a few weeks ago, but she knew it was not for lack of eating. Cadderly's boyish form had taken on the hardness of manhood; even his step seemed more sure and solid, less inclined to skip aside from his chosen path.

"You look good," Danica blurted, hardly thinking before she made the comment. Cadderly stopped abruptly, stumbling over the next step. Slowly, he lifted his gaze from the parchment. Danica heard him gulp for breath.

It seemed like many minutes had passed before the young priest finally mustered the courage to turn and face her, and when he did, Danica stared into a confused face indeed. She waited for Cadderly to reply, but, apparently, he either could not find his voice, or had nothing to say.

"You look good," Danica said again, and she thought herself incredibly inane. "I . . . we, had to come to Carradoon . . ."

She stopped, her words halted by the look in Cadderly's gray eyes. Danica had many times before stared intently into those eyes, but she saw something new there now, a sadness of bitter experiences.

Again, it seemed like many minutes slipped by.

Cadderly's walking stick fell to the stairs with an impossibly loud thud. Danica looked to it curiously, and when she looked up again, Cadderly was with her, his arms wrapped about her, nearly crushing her.

Danica was independent and strong, arguably one of the very finest fighters in all the land, but never in her life had she felt so secure and warm. Gentle tears made their way down her smooth cheeks; there was no sadness in her heart.

* * * * *

Still wearing Brennan's body as his own, Ghost watched the pair from the bottom of the stairs as he absently pushed a broom back and forth. His devious mind continued its typical whirling, formulating new plans, making subtle adjustments in the old plans. Ghost had to get things moving quickly now, he knew. The complications were undeniably piling up.

The skilled killer, the artist, was not afraid. He liked challenges, and compared to the many dead heroes he had left in his wake, this action, this victim, Cadderly, did not seem so much a problem.

* * * * *

Danica.

Cadderly had not seen her in more than five weeks, and while he had not forgotten her appearance, he was nonetheless surprised by her beauty. She stood inside the closed door of his room, her head cocked patiently to the side, strawberry hair dancing against one shoulder, and her exotic eyes, rich and brown, tender and knowing, gazing at him.

He had initiated their breakup. He had been the one who had left—had left Danica, the war, and Shilmista. He still was not certain of Danica's intentions in coming to see him, but whatever they might be, Cadderly knew it was surely his turn to speak, to explain.

"I did not expect you to come," he said, moving beside his reading table and gently closing the *Tome of Universal Harmony*. A nervous chuckle escaped his dry lips. "I feared I would receive an invitation to Shilmista Forest to witness the wedding of Danica and Elbereth."

"I do not deserve that," Danica replied, keeping her melodic voice even-toned and steady.

Cadderly threw up his hands helplessly. "I would have deserved it," he admitted.

Danica produced Ivan's gift and tossed it to him. "From the dwarves," she explained as Cadderly caught the heavy disks. "They began it long ago, a present to the one who saved the Edificant Library."

Cadderly could feel the strength of the weapon, and that horrified him as much as thrilled him. "Always weapons," he muttered resignedly and tossed the spindle-disks to the floor at the foot of his bed, where they bounced against a small clothes chest, dented the hardwood, and rolled to a stop inches from Cadderly's newly enchanted walking stick.

Cadderly regarded the fitting image and nearly laughed aloud, but he would not let Danica's obvious distraction keep him from his point. "You loved the elf prince," he said to her.

"He is now the elf king," Danica reminded him.

Cadderly did not miss the fact that she did not respond to his accusation.

"You did . . . do love Elbereth," Cadderly said again, quietly.

"As do you," Danica replied. "He is a dear friend, and among the most extraordinary and honorable people I have ever had the privilege of fighting beside. I would give my life for the elf king of Shilmista, as would you."

Her words did not come as any revelation to Cadderly. All along, beneath the veil of his fears, he had known the truth of Danica's relationship with Elbereth, had known that her love for the elf—and it was indeed love—was irrelevant to her feelings for the priest. Danica and Elbereth had bonded in a common cause, as warriors with shared values. If Cadderly loved Danica, and he did with all of his heart, then how could he not also love Elbereth?

But there remained a nagging question, a nagging doubt, and not one about Danica.

"You would give your life for him," Cadderly replied with all sincerity. "I wish I could claim equal courage."

Danica's smile was not meant to mock him, but he felt it keenly anyway.

"I ran from there," Cadderly pointedly reminded her.

"Not when you were needed," Danica replied. "Neither I nor the elves have forgotten what you did at Syldritch Trea, or in the height of the fight. Tintagel is alive because of you. Shilmista is back in the hands of Elbereth's people because of you."

"But I ran away," Cadderly argued. "Do not doubt that."

Danica's next question, tinged with innocence and honest trepidation, caught the young priest off his guard. "Why did you run?"

She dropped her traveling cloak on the small night table and moved over to sit on Cadderly's bed, and he turned about to look out of his window, over the still-glittering lake in the dying light of day. Cadderly had never asked himself that question so bluntly, had never considered the cause of his distress.

"Because," he said after a moment, then he paused again, the words still not clear in his mind. He heard the bed creak and feared for a moment that Danica was coming to him; he did not want her to see the pain on his face at that moment. The bed creaked again and he realized that she had only shifted and had not risen.

"Too much was spinning about me," he said. "The fighting, the magic, my dilemma over Dorigen's unconscious form and the fear that I did wrong in not killing her, the cries of the dying that would not leave my ears." Cadderly managed a soft chuckle. "And the way you looked at Elbereth."

"All of that would seem cause to remain beside those who love you, not to run away," Danica observed.

"This madness has been mounting for some time," Cadderly explained, "perhaps even before the evil priest began his assault on the library. Perhaps I have been troubled all of my adult life. That would not surprise me.

"I must face these troubles and get beyond them," he continued, stealing a look at Danica over his shoulder. "I know that now."

"But again . . ." Danica began, but Cadderly, facing the lake again, cut her off with an outstretched palm.

"I could not face them beside you, do you not understand?" he asked, his voice pleading, hoping that she would forgive him. "Back in the library, whenever the many questions threatened to overwhelm me, all I had to do was seek out my Danica, my love. Beside you, watching you, there were no troubles, no unanswerable questions."

He turned to face her squarely, saw the joy emanating from her beautiful face.

"You are not my answer," Cadderly admitted, and he winced as Danica's light went out, a great pain washing through her almond eyes.

"You are not my cure," Cadderly quickly tried to explain, lamenting his initial choice of words. "You are a salve, a temporary relief."

"A plaything?"

"Never!" The word was torn from Cadderly's heart, bursting forth with the sureness that Danica needed to hear.

"When I am with you, then all the world and all of my life is beautiful," Cadderly went on. "In truth, it is not, of course. Shilmista proved that beyond doubt. When I am with you, I can hide behind my love. You, my Danica, have been my mask. Wearing it, I could even hide from the horrors of that continuing battle, I am sure."

"But you could not hide from yourself," Danica put in, beginning to catch on.

Cadderly nodded. "There are troubles in here," he explained, pointing to his heart and then to his head, "that will remain beside me until I can resolve them. Or until they destroy me."

"And you could not face them while your mask was there to hide behind," Danica reasoned. There was no malice in her quiet tones. Honestly sympathetic for Cadderly, she asked softly, "Have you found your answers?"

Cadderly nearly laughed out loud. "I have found more questions," he admitted.

"The world has only become more confusing since I delved into myself." He pointed to the *Tome of Universal Harmony.*" You would hardly believe the sights that book has shown to me, though whether they are true sights or clever deceptions, I cannot tell."

By the way Danica's posture seemed to shrink back from him, Cadderly realized that he had said something revealing. He waited long moments for Danica to respond, to share the revelation with him.

"You question your faith?" she asked bluntly.

Cadderly spun away, his gaze again searching for the dying light on the lake. She had hit the mark squarely, he only then realized. How could he, as a priest of Deneir, doubt the vision and magic shown to him by the most holy book of his god?

"I do not doubt the principles espoused by the clerics of Deneir," Cadderly asserted with conviction.

"Then it is the god himself," Danica reasoned incredulously. "You question the existence of such beings?" her voice nearly broke apart with the words. "How can one who was raised among priests, and who has witnessed so much clerical magic, claim to be agnostic?"

"I claim nothing," Cadderly protested. "I am just not certain of anything!"

"You have seen the magic bestowed by the gods," Danica argued. "You felt the magic . . . in healing Tintagel."

"I believe in magic," Cadderly reasoned. "It is an undeniable fact on the soil of Faerun. And, yes, I have felt the power, but where it comes from I cannot say."

"The curse of intelligence," Danica muttered ironically. Cadderly regarded her over his shoulder once more. "You cannot believe anything you cannot prove beyond doubt," she said to him. "Must everything be tangible? Is there no room for faith in a mind that can unravel any of the lesser mysteries?"

A wind had kicked up across the lake. Ripples rolled to the shore, carrying the last daylight on their crests.

"I just do not know," Cadderly said, regarding the rolling water, trying to find some fitting symbolism in its transport of the dying light.

"Why did you run?" Danica asked him again, and he knew by her determined tone that she meant to force him through this, whatever the cost to them both.

"I was afraid," he admitted. "Afraid to kill any more. Afraid that you would be killed. That I could not bear." Cadderly paused and swallowed hard, forced to come to terms with this difficult realization. His silence went on, Danica not daring to interrupt his train of thought.

"I was afraid to die." There it was. Cadderly had just admitted his own cowardice. He tightened his arms against his sides, fearing Danica's stinging rebuttal.

"Of course you were," she said instead, and there was no sarcasm in her remark. "You question your faith, question that there is anything beyond this existence. If you believe there is nothing more, then of what worth is honor? Bravery rides the crest of a cause, Cadderly. You would die for Elbereth. You have already proven that. And if a spear were aimed for my heart, you would willingly take it in my stead. That I do not doubt."

Cadderly continued to stare out the window. He heard Danica shifting on the bed again, but was too lost in contemplations of her wisdom. He watched the last gasps of light riding the waves, riding the crest, and knew that there was truth in Danica's description. He had been afraid to die in Shilmista, but only because the justification for continuing that fight was founded in a cause of principles, and those principles were, in turn, founded in faith. And he had been so angry at Danica and Elbereth, and all the others, because he had feared for them and could not appreciate their dedication to those higher principles, their willingness to continue a course that might easily lead to their deaths.

"I would take the spear," Cadderly decided.

"I never doubted you," Danica replied. There was something in the ring of her voice, something softer and mysterious, that made Cadderly turn back to her.

She lay on her side comfortably on his bed, her clothes dropped in a pile at the bedside. If Cadderly lived a thousand years, he would never forget the sight of Danica at that moment. She rested her head against her hand, propped at the elbow, her thick strawberry-blond locks cascading down her arm to dance on the single pillow. The minimal light accentuated the curves of Danica's soft skin, the shine of her sculpted legs.

"Through all the weeks, I never doubted you," she said.

Cadderly sensed the slight tremor in her voice, but still could not believe how brave she had been. Without blinking, he unbuttoned his shirt and started to her.

A moment later, they were together. The song played again in Cadderly's mind. No, rather, he felt it, thrumming with urgency through every facet of his body, guiding him through every subtle motion, and convincing him that nothing had ever been so right.

Cadderly's mind whirled through a dizzying jumble of thoughts and emotions. He thought of Danica bearing his child, and considered the implications of mortality.

Most of all, Cadderly focused his thoughts on Danica, his soul mate, and he loved her all the more. Perhaps once she had been his shelter, but only because he had made that her role. Now, Cadderly had revealed his vulnerability, his deepest fears, and Danica had accepted them, and him, with all her heart, and with the sincere desire to help him resolve them.

Later, as Danica slept, Cadderly rose from the bed and lit a single candle on his table, beside the *Tome of Universal Harmony*. Not bothering to dress, he looked back to Danica on the bed, and felt a surge of love course through his veins. Strengthened by that security, Cadderly sat down and opened the book, hopeful that, in light of this night's revelations, he would hear the song a different way.

* * * * *

Many hours before Cadderly lit that candle, Ghost had slipped away from the young priest's door, confident from his eavesdropping that the arrival of Danica Maupoissant would do little to deflect his solidifying plans. Actually, Ghost had come to the conclusion that he might be able to use Danica—her body, at least—to substantially increase the pleasure offered by this kill.

If he could possess the body of Cadderly's lover, he might catch the young priest with his guard about as far down as it could possibly go.

But for all the eagerness reflected when Ghost rubbed his hands together, every step of the way back to his own room, he was wise enough to realize that things had become dangerously complicated.

Still bound in the cubby between bed and wall, poor, beaten Brennan looked up pleadingly.

"I will release you this night," Ghost promised. "I have decided that I cannot afford to keep your body—and a pity that is, for the body is fine!"

Brennan, desperate to hope, almost managed to smile right up until the point when Ghost's hands—Brennan's own hands—closed around his borrowed throat. There was no pain this time for the beleaguered innkeeper's son; there was only blackness.

The task completed, Ghost sat down on the bed, untying the weakling form and waiting impatiently for when he could take back his own body. He lamented that he had lost his chance at this fine young form, but reminded himself of the pressing business and pressing danger. He assured himself that he would find another suitable body soon enough, when Cadderly lay dead.

Thirteen
The Stooge's Stooge

Kierkan Rufo eyed the stocked shelves with open contempt. Shopping! For more than a dozen years, he had labored in the Edificant Library, had meticulously attended to his duties, and now Headmaster Avery had sent him shopping!

This entire trip to Carradoon had been one humiliation after another for poor Rufo. He knew his actions in Shilmista had angered Avery (though he had convinced himself by this time that none of it had really been his fault), but he never would have believed that the headmaster would degrade him so. Through all the many meetings, with the priests of Ilmater, with several of the other religious Sects in the city, and with the city officials, Rufo had been ordered to stand behind Avery and remain silent. These meetings were vital to the defense of the region, vital to the survival of the Edificant Library, yet Rufo was, for all purposes, left out of them. Not only was his input not wanted by Avery, the headmaster had outright forbidden it!

And now he was shopping. Rufo stood before the shelves for many moments, fantasizing that the other side had won in Shilmista Forest, thinking that he would have been better off if Dorigen's forces had slaughtered the elves and had taken him into their ranks as the imp had promised. Perhaps the world would be a better place for Kierkan Rufo if Cadderly had fallen in the sylvan shadows.

Cadderly! The word screamed out in Rufo's mind like the most damning of curses. Cadderly had apparently forsaken the library and the Order of Deneir, had virtually slapped Headmaster Avery and all the other priests in the face with his desertion—there could be no other word for the young priest's actions. Cadderly had never been a good priest—not by Rufo's estimation—had never attended to the many duties given the lesser clerics with any kind of dedication.

542

And yet, in Avery's eyes at least, Cadderly ranked far above Rufo, far above any except the ruling order in the library.

Rufo grabbed a sack of flour and pulled it to him so forcefully that a small white puff burst up at him, covering his face.

"Someone's not seeming a bit too happy," came a gruff, gravelly voice beside him.

"Uh-uh," agreed a voice on the other side.

The angular priest did not have to look sidelong or down to know that the Bouldershoulder brothers had flanked him, and that fact did little to improve his sour mood. He had known that the dwarves were coming to Carradoon, but he had hoped that he and Avery would be well on their way back to the library before these two ever arrived.

He turned toward Ivan and started to push past the dwarf, through the narrow aisle of the cramped store. Ivan did little to aid the angular man, and with the dwarf's considerable girth, Rufo had nowhere to go.

"Ye're in a hurry," Ivan remarked. "I thinked ye'd be glad to see me and me brother."

"Get out of my way, dwarf," Rufo said grimly.

"Dwarf?" Ivan echoed, feigning a mortal wound. "Ye saying that like it's an insult?"

"Take it for what you will," Rufo replied evenly, "but do get out of my way. I am in Carradoon on important business, something you obviously could not understand."

"I always figured flour to be important," Ivan replied sarcastically, giving the bag a rough pat that sent another white burst into Rufo's face. The angular man trembled with mounting rage, but that only spurred Ivan to further taunts.

"Ye're acting like ye're not so glad to see me and me brother," the dwarf said.

"Should I be?" Rufo asked. "When have we ever claimed friendship to one another?"

"We fought together in the wood," Ivan reminded him, "or at least, some of us fought. Others figured to hide in a tall tree, if me memory's working proper."

Rufo growled and pushed ahead, dislodging several packages in his attempt to get beyond Ivan. He had nearly made his way past when the dwarf threw out one strong arm, stopping Rufo as completely as a stone wall.

"Danica's in town, too," Ivan remarked, his other hand held high and balled into a fist.

"Boom," Pikel added grimly behind the angular man.

The reference to Danica's humiliating attack made Rufo's face flush red with rage. He growled again and shoved past Ivan, stumbling all the rest of the way down the narrow aisle and knocking many more items from the shelves.

"A fine day to ye," Ivan called behind him. Rufo dropped the sack of flour and passed right by the counter, fleeing for the street.

"Good to see him," Ivan said to Pikel. "Adds a bit of flavor to a dull trip."

"Hee hee hee," Pikel agreed.

Ivan's face went serious once more as he noticed a tall man selecting goods from a shelf behind Pikel. The man's gait and movements were easy and graceful, his eyes sharp and steady, and he hoisted a twenty-pound bag of meal easily with one hand. His tunic moved up from the back of his trousers as he moved, revealing a dagger tucked securely in the back of his belt.

That alone would not have fired off any alarms in Ivan; many people carried concealed weapons in Carradoon, and Ivan himself had a knife in one pocket.

But the dwarf was certain he'd seen this man before, in a different guise. He watched the man for a few moments longer, until the man noticed him, snarled, and headed off the other way down the aisle.

"Eh?" Pikel asked, wondering what problem so obviously bothered his brother.

Ivan did not immediately reply, for he was too busy searching his memory. Then it came to him: he had seen a man closely resembling the shopper in the alley beside the Dragon's Codpiece. The man had been more disheveled then, wearing tattered clothing and seeming like an ordinary street beggar, of which Carradoon had its share. Even then, though, Ivan had noted the grace of the beggar's movements, a skilled and measured step.

The dwarf hadn't thought much about it, and wouldn't even have given it more than a passing thought now, except for the unpleasant incident on his journey into the city. Danica was convinced that the would-be bandits were not ordinary highwaymen and had been waiting to ambush the three companions. Ivan had little proof either way, and, while he held many private doubts, he knew Danica better than to openly disagree with her reasoning. An inspection of the bodies had revealed little, though, for the men carried no obvious marks, not even the familiar trident-and-bottle insignia of the enemy, which the companions had expected to find.

By all appearances, they had been simple robbers, coincidentally stumbling into the companions' path, and that had seemed even more plausible when Ivan and the others had arrived in Carradoon to find Cadderly, Avery, and Rufo safe and secure at the Dragon's Codpiece.

But prudent, battle-tested Ivan had not let his guard down, not one bit.

"We should go find Cadderly and Danica," he said to Pikel.

"Tut tut," Pikel argued, blushing with embarrassment and waggling a stubby finger Ivan's way. Danica had not returned to her room the previous night, and the dwarves didn't have to struggle to figure out where she had stayed, and why she had stayed there.

"We won't bother them if we don't need to," Ivan growled back. "Just want to keep an eye on them, that's all." Ivan nodded to the end of the aisle, where the suspicious shopper was gathering more goods. "I'm not so sure we seen the last of the group that hit us on the road."

"Eh?" Pikel balked.

"Sure, that bunch is dead," Ivan said as Pikel finally hopped around to regard the man, "but me thinking's that they got friends, and me fear's that we were more than accidental targets."

"Uh-oh," Pikel whined. He looked back to Ivan, crestfallen and obviously worried.

"We'll just watch 'em, that's all," Ivan said comfortingly. "We'll just watch 'em close."

* * * * *

Vander paced nervously about the barn on the outskirts of town. Ghost had telepathically contacted him using the power of the *Ghearufu* that morning to set the plans into motion; the strike against Cadderly would come before the next dawn. All of the other assassins were gone from the farm, sent into position with their remaining associates in Carradoon. There had still been no word of the five who had gone into the mountains, but word of the arrival of Danica and the dwarves into the city did not bode well for the missing Night Masks.

Still, fourteen expertly trained assassins should prove an ample number for a single, unsuspecting kill. At least, that had been Ghost's reasoning when he had told Vander, the most powerful of the group, to remain at the farm, out of the way.

Truly the firbolg did not mind the specifics of the instructions; executions had always left a sour taste in the honorable giant's mouth. What bothered Vander now was Ghost's motivations in keeping him beyond the immediate action. The only times the devious little assassin ever used this method of attack was when Ghost sincerely respected the powers of his intended victim. On those occasions, Vander became no more than a secret escape route for Ghost. If the assassin got into serious trouble, he could just summon his magical item and flee to Vander's body . . . leaving Vander back in Ghost's body to suffer whatever peril the assassin had gotten himself into.

How long would it continue? the firbolg wondered for about the ten thousandth time. How long would he remain the plaything of that wicked, honorless little weakling?

For all of his pacing and all of his painstaking thought, Vander could see no end and no escape. He could find consolation only by telling himself that in the morning Cadderly would be dead, and this wretched chapter of his miserable life would be at an end.

* * * * *

"You seem in a hurry," the young wizard commented when Rufo, his face chalk white with flour, entered the Dragon's Codpiece and made his way straight for the stairs.

Rufo looked at Bogo Rath and snorted derisively, but didn't have the courage to ignore the young wizard's hand gesture that Rufo should go over and join him.

"What do you need?" Rufo snapped, angry at all the world and especially impatient in yet another situation in which he was forced to serve. Everywhere the angular man turned, he found someone more than willing to give him orders.

Bogo laughed heartily and flipped his stringy hair over to the side, out of his green eyes. "How go your meetings?" the wizard asked.

Again Rufo snorted. "You should ask Avery," he replied, venom dripping from every word. "Certainly I, the errand boy, would not know!" As evidence to his point, Rufo held up the few small sacks of purchases he had made in the first stores he had visited that day.

"You deserve better treatment than this," Bogo commented, trying to sound like an honest friend.

"From you as well," Rufo replied sharply.

Bogo nodded and did not argue. In truth, the young wizard, "Boygo" to his older associates, could sympathize with Rufo's dilemma.

"Well, have you a task for me, or are you merely wasting my time?" Rufo asked. "Not that my time is such a precious thing."

"Nothing," Bogo replied. Immediately, the angular man spun away, heading back for the stairs. "As of yet," Bogo remarked after him, stealing some of the ire-filled thunder from Rufo's determined steps. The priest looked back one final time.

"You will be informed when you are needed," Bogo said evenly, his visage stern and unyielding. The young wizard might sympathize with Rufo, but that would offer the priest little reprieve from the duties Bogo would eventually require of him.

* * * * *

"You met with the priest again this day," Ghost said to Bogo when the young wizard entered his room later that afternoon. He really wasn't surprised to find the sneaky assassin waiting for him, or by the fact that Ghost knew of his meeting with Rufo.

"I have warned you once of your meddling," Ghost went on. Bogo's face twisted curiously, and Ghost realized that he had made a mistake. He hadn't warned Bogo of any such thing; the innkeeper's son had done that, at least as far as Bogo was concerned.

"You?" Bogo questioned, his lips turning up in a smile. "I have not seen young Brennan today," he remarked cryptically. "Actually, his father is quite worried about him."

Ghost settled back on the bed and nodded silent congratulations to the observant wizard. "Let us just say that the young man outlived his usefulness," he explained. "A very dangerous thing to do."

Neither man spoke for a very long while, but there remained little tension between them. Ghost studied Bogo long and hard, and the young wizard seemed to sense that the assassin was forming some plans—plans that Bogo could only hope would include him.

"The time is close then," Bogo remarked. "The disappearance of young Brennan is a question that you cannot let hang unanswered for a very long time."

Again, Ghost nodded his silent appreciation of Bogo's reasoning powers. "The time is nearly upon us," he confirmed, "but it would seem that some things have changed."

"The arrival of the priests and Danica?" Bogo asked.

"Complications," Ghost replied.

"And what else has changed?"

"Your role," Ghost answered immediately. Bogo initially took a cautious step back, fearing that he, too, might have outlived his usefulness.

"I had said you were only an observer," the assassin explained, "and, so, by Aballister's measure, you were meant to be. But you never believed that, did you, Rath? You never planned to sit back and watch while the Night Masks had all the fun of killing this young Cadderly."

Bogo cocked his head curiously at the assassin, obviously unsure of what that plain fact might mean.

"And you have proven to me," Ghost continued, "both by your astute conclusions and your ability to get close to our enemies, that your value extends beyond your assigned role."

"I thought you did not want me talking with Rufo," Bogo replied, still a safe distance from the dangerous man.

"I just explained to you that things have changed," Ghost retorted. "We have a headmaster from the library to deal with and a formidable young woman, it would seem. I intend to handle the latter problem personally, and for that I will need to borrow your stooge."

Bogo moved over to the bed, now more curious than afraid.

"A simple matter," Ghost explained. "A simple, innocuous task for Kierkan Rufo that will allow me to get at the Lady Maupoissant."

"You will kill her?"

"In a manner," Ghost replied. "First I will use her so that when the Night Masks come for Cadderly, the one he believes is his closest ally will, in truth, be his enemy."

Bogo's smile widened, mimicking Ghost's devious expression. The assassin's plan was beautifully simple, with Bogo, and more particularly, Rufo, being the only potential trouble areas that he could foresee. To that end, the assassin then delivered a secure hook.

His smile abruptly disappeared, causing Bogo's visage to assume a similarly grim tone.

"I offer you a part in this execution," Ghost explained, "something you have craved since before we left Castle Trinity. I assure you that your role will be well received by Aballister.

"But," Ghost continued slyly, and this was the real hook, "my pay will be as originally agreed."

"Of course . . ." Bogo started, but Ghost didn't pause long enough to let him continue.

"And if Aballister does not deliver to me the full amount," Ghost went on grimly, "then you must make up the difference—to the gold piece."

Bogo nodded eagerly, more than happy to pay such a pittance in exchange for the prestige, and also beginning to understand for the first time, how very bad it might be to get on the wrong side of this wicked little man.

They spent another hour together, with Ghost detailing the plans and the role Bogo would play. To the ambitious young wizard, the plan and his part seemed safe enough (Rufo would actually be doing most of the work) and rewarding enough to satisfy him.

Just as Ghost had known it would.

Fourteen
To Capture a Soul

Cadderly and Danica had slept very late that day. Brennan did not appear with Cadderly's breakfast, and Cadderly, in his modesty, was glad of that. He suspected that the innkeeper's son had probably come to the door, then had turned away, blushing, at what he had heard inside. With a private smile, Cadderly thought no more about it.

The lovers left their room shortly after noon, taking a meal together in the hearth room. Fredegar served them himself—an unusual occurrence that Cadderly realized was out of sorts only when the innkeeper asked him if he had seen anything of Brennan that morning.

Still, Cadderly was too consumed by the presence of Danica to appreciate the implications of the missing youth. He promised to keep an eye out for Brennan when he and Danica went out walking. Fredegar nodded his thanks, but he was plainly worried.

"The mistakes of adolescence," Cadderly explained to Danica, not too concerned for the welfare of the youth. He figured that Brennan had been out late in pursuit of some young lady, and that maybe this time Brennan had made the catch. For all of Cadderly's inner turmoil, all the world seemed calm that morning, with Danica beside him again, and the young priest couldn't even begin to think dark and ominous thoughts.

They left the inn together, crossed the wide way of Lakeview Street, and moved down to Impresk Lake's sandy shore. The breeze was stiff off the water, chill but not cold, and long-winged birds zipped about at impossible angles and cut sharply in daring maneuvers all about them. The normal morning mist had long since dissipated, leaving the two with a grand view of the island that comprised the wealthier section of Carradoon, and the wide, arching stone bridge that led to it. Several multistory structures peeked up above the trees, and a fleet of boats, both pleasure and fishing, meandered around the land mass.

"I suppose I might come to accept the beard," Danica said after many minutes of quiet watching. She moved over and tugged at an exceptionally long strand. "As long as you keep it trimmed!"

"And I love you," Cadderly replied with a contented smile. "Will you stay beside me?"

"Are you certain you want me to?" Danica said in a teasing tone, but there was a subtle undercurrent of dread in her question.

"Stay with me," Cadderly said again, more forcefully.

Danica looked back to the water and did not answer. The request seemed so simple and obvious, and yet, the woman realized that many obstacles remained. She had gone to the Edificant Library to study the ancient works of Grandmaster Penpahg D'Ahn, the Most Holy One, prophet and founder of her order. Only in the library could Danica continue her work, and that work was very important to her, the culmination of all her personal goals.

As important as Cadderly?

Danica was not honestly sure, but she knew that if she gave up her goals to remain beside her lover, then she would forever look back to this time and wonder what might have been, what level of perfection she might have achieved.

And there remained, too, the war. The last few days had come as a reprieve to the battle-weary woman, despite the attack on the road, but Danica knew that this quiet time was only temporary. More fighting would break out, if not now, then in the spring, and Danica had long ago resolved to be a part of that.

Cadderly, though, had run away from it, and the woman now did not know if he would change his mind.

So Danica did not answer the question, and Cadderly, wise enough to understand her hesitancy and her fears, did not ask it again. Day by day, he decided. They would pass their time together day by day and see what changes the wind across the lake brought.

They walked quietly along the beach for some time, Cadderly leading Danica to one of his favorite places. The shoreline jutted sharply out into the water in a small, tree-covered peninsula with banks only a foot above the water level. A single path, barely a foot wide, led the way into the thick tangle, ending at a small clearing right in the center of the peninsula. Although they were barely a half-mile from the bustle of Carradoon, and barely a half-mile from the island section as well, it seemed to Cadderly and Danica that the world had disappeared beyond the shelter of those trees.

Danica looked slyly at Cadderly, suddenly suspecting the reason he had brought her out here.

But Cadderly had other ideas. He led Danica down another narrow path, to the very tip of the peninsula, beside a small pool formed by the waves whenever a large boat passed by. Cadderly, indicated a mossy stone and bade Danica to sit.

Cadderly walked the perimeter of the pool, muttering something under his breath that Danica could not make out. She soon came to understand that the young priest was chanting, a magical spell, most likely.

Cadderly halted the walk. His body swayed gently, a willow in the wind, he seemed, and his arms moved about in graceful circles. Danica's eyes settled on Cadderly's holy symbol, the single eye-and-candle design set in the center of his wide-brimmed hat. She felt a pulse of power from that emblem; it seemed to glow with some inner strength.

Cadderly's arms waved again as he reached low in front of him and swung them slowly out wide to either side.

The water reacted to his call. The center of the pool bubbled with sudden energy, then rolled outward, great ripples moving to every edge. Danica moved her feet in close to her, thinking that she was going to get splashed, but the water did not break the edges of the pool. As the waves crested, there came a great hissing sound and the water vaporized, rolling up into the air to form a grayish cloud.

More water rolled out to be consumed, and when it was done, just a few small puddles remained where the pool had been. The cloud hovered for a few moments, until the pull of the wind broke it apart to nothingness.

Danica blinked in amazement and looked to Cadderly, who stood very still, staring at the mud-and-puddle pit.

"You have become powerful," she remarked after some time had passed. "For a nonbeliever."

Cadderly glared at her but could not sustain any anger in the face of her disarming smile. Through his smile, though, Danica recognized the young man's torment.

"Perhaps it is just a variation of a wizard's magic, as you fear," she offered, "but perhaps the strength does come from Deneir. You seem too quick to deny what others of your order—"

"My order?" Cadderly was quick to interrupt, his tone both sarcastic and incredulous.

"Your holy symbol vibrated with power," Danica replied. "I witnessed it myself."

"A conduit to the energy, much like the tome on my desk," Cadderly said more sharply than Danica deserved. He seemed to understand that, and his tone softened considerably as he continued. "Whenever I call on the magic, I merely recall some of the words in that book."

"And it is a book of Deneir," Danica reasoned.

Cadderly shook his head. "Do you know of Belisarius?" he asked.

"The wizard in the tower to the south?" Danica said.

Cadderly nodded. "Belisarius has a similar book—a spell book. If he attached a god's name to it, would it then become a holy book?"

"It is not the same," Danica muttered, frustrated.

"I do not know," Cadderly said finally.

Danica looked to the lake behind her, to the gently lapping waves against the many small rocks at the peninsula's tip, determined to change the subject. Then she looked at the muddy hole, somewhat disconcertingly. "How long will it take to refill?" she asked, clearly not happy with the results of Cadderly's display. "Or must it wait for the next rain?"

Cadderly smiled and bent low, scooping a few drops of the remaining water into his cupped palms. He pulled his hand in close to his chest, again muttered some words under his breath.

"As the graceful rain must fall!" he ended, then he threw his hands out before him, threw the water to the air above the muddy pit. A tiny cloud appeared, hovering and churning in the air, and a moment later, a steady stream of water poured forth, splashing into the mud.

Before Danica ended her first burst of laughter, the pool had returned, as full as when she had first seen it.

"You find this humorous?" Cadderly asked, narrowing his gray eyes and thumping his fists against his hips so that he seemed a caricature of wounded pride.

"I find you humorous," Danica retorted, and Cadderly's expression revealed that he was truly hurt.

"You have all the proof right before you," Danica explained, "more proof than the vast majority of ordinary people will ever know, and yet you remain so filled with doubts. My poor Cadderly, so damned by the unending questions of his own intelligence!"

Cadderly looked to the pool he had magically evaporated and then refilled, and chuckled at the irony of it all. Danica took his hand then and led him back to the clearing at the center of the peninsula. Cadderly thought to keep going, down the other narrow path and back out to the wider beaches, but Danica held tight to his hand and did not continue, forcing him to turn about.

They were alone in the sun and the breeze, and all the world seemed peaceful. Danica smiled mischievously, her almond eyes telling Cadderly without the slightest doubt that it was not yet time to leave.

* * * * *

It was nearly twilight when Cadderly and Danica made their way back to the Dragon's Codpiece. Farther down Lakeview Street, fatherly Ivan watched their progress. The dwarf was much more at ease than he had been, and the safe return of Cadderly and Danica told him that his suspicions might be unfounded, that he was acting as silly as a mother hen.

But was it a coincidence, just a moment later, when a beggar came to the end of the alleyway next to the Dragon's Codpiece, and appeared to be watching the young couple as intently as Ivan?

Ivan sensed that the man meant to go after the two, and the dwarf started to make his way slowly up the street. He didn't have his great axe with him—it wasn't considered proper to stand about on one of Carradoon's streets so obviously armed—but he was wearing his deer-antlered helmet. If this beggar made a move against Cadderly, Ivan resolved to gore him good.

Cadderly and Danica turned into the inn, and the beggar leaned casually against the wall. Ivan stopped, perplexed and feeling very foolish. He looked all about, as if expecting everyone else on the street to be pointing at him and chuckling, but no one had apparently noticed anything unusual about his stalking advance.

"Stupid dwarf," he muttered under his breath. "What're ye getting so anxious about? Just a poor man, looking for a bit of coins." Ivan stopped and scratched his yellow beard curiously when he looked back toward the alleyway.

The man was gone.

* * * * *

Danica giggled, but Cadderly was not amused at the knock on his door—not at that particular moment.

"Oh, go and answer it," Danica whispered to him. "It is probably the innkeeper's son, whom you have been worried over the whole of the day!"

"I do not want to go," Cadderly replied, pouting like a child. This brought another chuckle from Danica, who pulled the bedclothes up tight about her neck.

Groaning with every move, Cadderly pulled himself out of bed and eased over to the door, wrapping himself in his discarded cloak.

"Rufo?" he asked as he cracked the door open. The hallway was dark, the candles in the great chandelier atop the stairs having long since died away. Only the glow from the hearth room's fireplace offered any light at all. Still, Cadderly could not mistake Rufo's tilting posture.

"My greetings," the angular man replied. "And my apologies for disturbing you." Cadderly blushed deeply, a sight the angular man obviously enjoyed.

"What do you want?"

"You are needed in the hearth room," Rufo explained, "as soon as you can."

"No." The answer seemed simple enough, and Cadderly moved to shut the door, but Rufo stuck his foot in the way.

"Headmaster Avery will return with a delegation from the Ilmater chapel," Rufo lied, for he knew well that Headmaster Avery was snoring contentedly back in their room.

Cadderly looked back over his shoulder to the balcony doors, to the blackness of the night. "What time is it?" he asked.

"It is very late," Rufo admitted. "The priests of Ilmater wish this done in private. They seek information about the deaths of their acolytes at the Edificant Library during the time of the chaos curse."

"I have already written my testimony—"

"Avery asks that you come," Rufo pressed. "He has not required much of you, certainly less than he asks of me." Obvious resentment rang clearly in the angular man's tone. "You can do this much for him, impudent Cadderly, after all the headmaster has done for you."

The argument seemed solid enough. Cadderly groaned again, then nodded. "Ten minutes," he said.

Danica's giggling renewed as soon as the door was closed.

"I will not be gone long," Cadderly promised as he pulled on his clothes.

"It does not matter," Danica replied coyly. "I am certain I shall fall asleep immediately." She stretched languidly and rolled to her side, and Cadderly, cursing his luck, left the room.

He, too, must have been sleepy, for he didn't even notice the weasel-like man—was it a man?—behind a slightly opened door, watching him go.

* * * * *

"Cadderly?" Danica uttered the question, but she heard it as though someone else had spoken the words. A smell of exotic flowers permeated the room.

Somewhere deep in her mind, she was surprised that she had fallen asleep so soon. Or had she? How long had Cadderly been gone? she wondered. And what was that smell?

"Cadderly?" she asked again.

"Hardly."

The word should have sounded like a warning to the woman—she knew she should open her eyes and find out what in the Nine Hells was going on . . . but she couldn't.

She felt a thumb, a gloved hand, she believed, pressed against her eyelid, and then her eye was forced open, just a crack. Danica tried to focus her thoughts—why was she so sleepy?

Through the blur, she saw herself in a small mirror. She knew that the mirror was hanging around someone's neck.

Whose neck?

"Cadderly?"

The laughter that came back at her filled her with dread, and her eyes popped open against the permeating drowsiness, suddenly alert.

She saw Ghost for just an instant, too briefly to strike out, or even to cry out. Then she fell back into her own thoughts, into the blackness that suddenly became her own mind, and she felt a burning pain throughout every inch of her body.

Danica did not understand what was happening, but she sensed that it was not good. She felt herself moving away, but knew that her body was not moving.

Another blackness loomed in the distance, across a gray expanse, and Danica felt herself pulled toward it, compelled to sink into it. The first blackness, her mortal coil, was left behind, far behind.

Few in all of Faerun would have understood, but few in all of Faerun were as well versed in meditation as Danica.

Her identity!

Someone was stealing her very identity!

"No!" Danica tried to cry out, but control of her body's voice was almost gone by then and the word came out as an indecipherable whimper.

Danica focused her will, dismissed the continuing smell that she now suspected was some sort of sleeping poison. She located that approaching blackness and pushed against it with all her mental strength, understanding that to enter it was to be lost.

A moment later, she felt another presence, similarly wandering out of body.

Her thoughts screamed a thousand protests at it, but it did not respond; it just kept making its way for the blackness that Danica had left behind.

* * * * *

"Where are they?" Cadderly asked impatiently when he came down into the hearth room. The fire burned low and the place was empty, except for him and for Rufo, sitting nervously at a table in the far corner.

"Well?" Cadderly growled as he moved over and took a seat opposite the angular man.

"Patience," Rufo replied. "It will not be long."

Cadderly leaned back and threw one arm over the back of the chair. By his estimation, it had already been too long. He looked at Rufo again, noting a subtle undercurrent of nervousness in the angular man. Cadderly dismissed the feeling and any suspicions it started to encourage, reminding himself that Kierkan Rufo was always nervous.

The young priest closed his eyes and let the minutes slip past, let his thoughts linger back to Danica and the pleasures and implications this day had brought. He would never leave her again, of that much he was sure.

Cadderly's eyes popped wide.

"What is it?" he heard Rufo ask loudly. Cadderly studied the man, saw Rufo blink.

Heard Rufo blink!

The fire crackled so powerfully that Cadderly thought the whole wall would be aflame, but when he turned to regard the hearth, the embers barely seemed to glow with their last flickers of life.

A fly buzzed by the bar. Gods! Cadderly thought, the thing must be the size of a small pony!

He saw nothing there.

And then he was aware of that song again, playing softly in the back of his mind. Instead of trying to figure all of this out, Cadderly wisely just allowed himself to feel.

Something—some danger?—had put him on his guard, and he had subconsciously replayed a page from the tome, enacted a magical spell to heighten his hearing.

"What is it?" Rufo asked him again, more urgently. Cadderly did not look at the man, just held a hand up to silence him.

Breathing.

Cadderly heard the steady inhale and exhale of breath a few tables away. He looked over but saw nothing.

But there was something, someone, there! Shifting his probe, Cadderly felt the magical energy.

"What are you saying?" he heard Rufo ask, and he realized only then that his lips were moving, forming the words from yet another page of the *Tome of Universal Harmony.*

Cadderly saw a silvery outline of a young man, recognized the stringy locks of hair hanging down to one side of the invisible intruder's head.

Rufo shoved him roughly, forcing his attention.

"What?" the angular man demanded.

Cadderly started to rebuke him, then stopped and instead locked his intent gaze on Rufo.

* * * * *

Danica calmed her thoughts; she had to beat the other presence to the void of her physical mind. She turned her spirit about, willed her mind to connect fully with the tiny part of her that she had left behind, the part that had forced her mouth to utter that pitiful sound. She sensed the other presence pushing at the blackness then, nearly entering her form.

She felt a burning sensation.

Danica saw too many things in the next instant for her to possibly sort through them. She saw, most clearly, murders, dozens of murders. She saw Night Masks.

Night Masks!

The assassin band, the scourge of Westgate, had killed her parents. She saw a clan of giants, through the eyes of a giant.

She saw the other giants die at her own giant hands.

She saw Cadderly, on the road to Carradoon, huddled at his desk over the *Tome of Universal Harmony,* crouched behind the protection of his partly opened door.

To her horror, Danica realized that she was recalling someone else's memories, had connected with the small part this other identity had left behind on its journey to take her body! And that this person, whoever it might be, had been close to Cadderly on several occasions.

Night Masks!

Let me out! her thoughts protested.

The other identity cried out to her in rage and agony and disbelief. She heard no words, but understood its meaning acutely, understood that her focused rage could push her back to where she belonged.

Let me out!

Danica pushed against the foreign blackness with all her mental strength, called upon her rage in combination with her years of mental training. The burning intensified, then abated, and Danica felt a physical presence once more—her own body.

The smell returned and Danica felt a cloth pressed against her face. Giving in to her warrior instincts, she locked her fingers into a gouging position and cocked her arm for a strike.

She fell hard against the floor, but she didn't realize it.

* * * * *

Shadows, evil, misshapen things, grumbled and growled from the angular man's shoulders, their demeanor toward Cadderly obviously hostile. Rufo reached out across the small table to touch Cadderly again, but the young priest slapped his hand away.

"Cadderly!" Rufo responded, but the young priest sensed clearly that the man's apparent concern was a facade. Before Rufo could move again, Cadderly pushed against the table, slamming its other edge into the angular man's belly.

Cadderly honestly did not know what to do, did not know whether he was being warned or misled.

"Tell Avery that he can find me in the morning," the young priest said, rising and spinning about to survey the room. He sensed that the invisible wizard was long gone.

"Avery will not like that," he heard Rufo say, but more acutely, he heard a thump from somewhere upstairs that he knew instinctively was his own room.

Danica!

Cadderly bounded across the floor to the stairs, but then he was moving slowly, as if in a dream, barely able to put one heavy foot in front of the other.

The song played in his head; he instinctively pictured a page from the great book, a page describing focused magical energies, describing how to dispel such malevolent collections of magic.

A moment later he was moving again normally, free of whatever magical bonds had been placed on him. The door to his room was closed, as he had left it, and all seemed as it should.

Cadderly burst through the door anyway, to find Danica, her breathing rapid, sprawled upon the floor, tangled in a pile of blankets next to the bed. Cadderly knew she was alive and not seriously hurt as he held her in his arms.

The young priest surveyed the room. The notes from the song seemed more distant to him now and all seemed calm, but still the young priest wondered if someone had come in during his absence.

"Cadderly," Danica breathed, suddenly coming awake.

She looked about her, confused for a moment, pulled the blankets high and brought her arms in close—actions that struck Cadderly as curious gestures.

"A terrible dream," Danica tried to explain.

Cadderly kissed her gently on the forehead and told her that everything was all right. He placed his chin atop Danica's head and rocked her in his arms, his own smile widening with growing security.

Danica was unharmed. It had been only a dream.

Fifteen
A Good Day to Die

As the night wound on toward morning, the guests in half of the eight private rooms at the Dragon's Codpiece slept soundly.

Bogo Rath was simply too agitated to think of sleeping. Knowing what was to come, and knowing that he had played a part in the prelude to the actual assassination, the young wizard thought through the potential problems facing him that morning. Would Kierkan Rufo remain loyal? And even if the priest did, would the odd and angular man be able to carry out the mission Bogo had set before him? Things could get very troublesome at the Dragon's Codpiece very quickly if a certain headmaster from the Edificant Library was not dealt with properly and efficiently.

Bogo understood the unmerciful Night Mask organization well enough to realize that Ghost would hold him responsible if Kierkan Rufo failed. The wizard paced his small room, taking care to keep his footsteps as quiet as possible. He wished that Ghost would come to him then, or that one of the approaching band would at least make contact to let him know how things progressed.

The young wizard resisted an urge to crack open his door, remembering that if he interrupted at an inopportune moment, he might well share Cadderly's grim fate.

In his own room, Ghost sat staring out his window, bitter and full of rage. He hadn't slept at all that night, after Danica's mental discipline had defeated his attempted possession. He had wanted to be close at hand when the assassin band roared in; he had even been forced to go to the band that night and change the orders. Danica must die beside her lover.

For all the unexpected twists, the assassin remained confident that Cadderly

559

would die that day, but even if the young priest fell easily now, this had been a messy execution, filled with complications and unexpected losses. Vander had killed one man; five others were missing in the foothills of the Snowflakes.

And young Cadderly was still very much alive.

And very much awake. In his room, the young priest sat at his table, dressed for the coming day and reading through the pages of the *Tome of Universal Harmony*. The hearth room had shown Cadderly many surprises earlier that night, and he searched for an entry that might help explain the sudden heightening of his senses, particularly his hearing.

Danica sat cross-legged on the floor beside the bed in quiet meditation, allowing the priest his needed privacy and taking some for herself. Hers was a life of discipline, of private challenges and trials, and though it was a bit early, she had already begun her daily morning ritual, working her inner being, stretching her limbs, and clearing her mind in preparation for the coming day.

Danica had discovered no answers for her strange experience earlier that night, and, truthfully, she hadn't sought any. To her, the encounter with the unknown other mind remained a dream; since nothing else traumatic or dangerous had occurred, the explanation seemed to satisfy.

* * * * *

"The sun has not peeked over the rim!" Headmaster Avery protested, managing with some difficulty to roll his bulky form out of bed.

"That was Cadderly's wish," Kierkan Rufo reminded him. "He desired secrecy, and I believe what he might have to say will be worth the effort."

Avery struggled to clear his throat of its nighttime phlegm and draw in a profound breath, never taking his curious stare off the angular man.

Rufo struggled even harder to remain calm under that searching gaze. He kept his breathing steady; so many things depended on his facade now. And beneath the calm front, turmoil boiled in Rufo. He honestly wondered how it had come down to this, how he had been led to such a dramatic point. He had been used by Barjin when the evil priest had invaded the library several months before; he had been the one who had kicked Cadderly down the secret stairway, nearly leading to the library's downfall.

Rufo had never quite forgiven himself—no, not forgiven himself, but rather, had never quite been able to justify the action to himself. Self-forgiveness would imply that he held guilty thoughts for that treacherous act, and by this time, the angular man held none. With every event that had come after Barjin's invasion, Cadderly had become more Rufo's rival, more his bane. In Shilmista, Cadderly had emerged a hero, while Rufo, through no fault of his own (at least, none that he would admit, even to himself), had become a scapegoat.

Bleary-eyed, Avery stumbled across the floor and pulled on his clothes. Rufo was glad to be released from the headmaster's gaze.

"Are you coming down with me?" Avery asked.

"Cadderly does not want me there," the angular man lied. "He said he would meet with you alone in the hearth room before Fredegar began his work."

"Before dawn," Avery muttered distastefully.

Rufo continued to stare at the portly headmaster's back. How had it gotten this far? Rufo didn't hate Avery—on the contrary, the headmaster had acted on Rufo's behalf many times over the last decade.

But that was behind them now, the angular man reminded himself. Shilmista had undeniably changed Rufo's life course, but now, looking at vulnerable Avery, the angular man had to pause and consider just how drastically.

"Well, I am off for the hearth room, then," Avery announced, moving to the door.

He wasn't even carrying his mace in the loop on his belt, Rufo noted. And he hadn't yet prayed and prepared any spells.

"Truly I wish Cadderly would be more conventional," Avery remarked, his obvious fondness for the young priest showing through, and that only strengthening the treacherous Rufo's resolve. "But, then, that is his charm, I suppose." Avery paused and smiled, and Rufo knew the portly man was engaged in some private recollection of Cadderly.

"Meet me in the hearth room for the morning meal," Avery instructed. "Perhaps I will be able to persuade Cadderly to dine with us."

"Just what I desire," the angular man muttered grimly. He moved to the door and watched Avery descend the sweeping stairway to the dimly lighted hearth room.

Rufo closed the door softly. His part was done. He had set events into motion, as the young wizard had instructed him to do. Avery's fate was the headmaster's own to deal with.

The angular man leaned back against the wall, desperately trying to dismiss his growing guilt. He recalled Avery's recent treatment of him, of the terrible things the headmaster had said to him and the threats to drive Rufo from the order.

For Kierkan Rufo, so consumed by resentment, guilt was not a difficult emotion to overcome.

* * * * *

Half asleep in the common room of the inn two doors down from the Dragon's Codpiece, his head resting on the ledge of the alley window, Pikel heard a distinct whistle. The dwarf's grogginess held fast only for the few moments it took Pikel to remember what his brother would do to him if Ivan caught him asleep on his watch.

Pikel stuck his head out the window and took in a deep breath of the chilly predawn air.

Another whistle sounded, from the alley on the other side of the building he was facing.

"Eh?" the dwarf questioned, his instincts telling him that the whistles were not random, more probably a signal. Pikel hopped up from his seat and ran to the front door, throwing aside the locking bar and hopping out onto the inn's front porch.

He saw shapes moving out of the alley beyond the nearest building, shapes moving onto the veranda of the Dragon's Codpiece, slipping quietly through the open door.

Pikel started forward to better investigate when a movement close beside him stole his attention. A large man rushed up to him, sword slicing wildly. The first hit bounced off the dwarf's armored shoulder, not penetrating but leaving a painful bruise.

"Oooo!" Pikel exclaimed in surprise, backpedaling the way he had come. The man kept right with him, flailing away viciously. Pikel had no weapon—he had left his club back in his room, not really believing Ivan's growing suspicions that dangers were lurking just outside.

The green-bearded dwarf believed them now, with this man hacking away at him, driving him backward with every step. Blood rolled down one of Pikel's arms; he took a glancing hit across the cheek that drew a thin red line.

The beating continued relentlessly, and Pikel, nearly across the common room, had little distance left to run.

* * * * *

The lockpick had been silent. Headmaster Avery, his heavy eyelids drooping, didn't even realize that anyone had entered the Dragon's Codpiece until the assassins were upon him.

Then they were beyond him, slipping up the stairs as quietly as shadows.

Cadderly looked up from the *Tome of Universal Harmony* and glanced over his shoulder at Danica.

"What is it?" the woman asked, her meditation interrupted by the sheer intensity of the young scholar's stare.

Cadderly lifted a finger over pursed lips, beckoning the woman to be silent. Something had called out to him, a distant song, a voice of impending danger. He took up his spindle-disks and his walking stick and started to rise, facing the closed door.

He hadn't even left his chair when the door burst open and dark shapes stormed in.

Danica was still sitting cross-legged when the first assassin, sword in hand, rushed at her. The killer came in low, gaping in disbelief as Danica's coiled legs sprang, her momentum lifting her into the air. She tucked her legs under as she rose, clearing the low strike, then descended on the bending man.

Her legs locked around his neck as she came down, clamping tightly, and she jerked herself to the side violently, dipping into a full bend and throwing her full weight right under the bending man.

The assassin saw the room spin, but his body had not turned.

* * * * *

Cadderly whipped his walking stick across in front of him and was amazed when he heard something—a crossbow quarrel, he realized—tick off it and fly harmlessly wide. He swung again in a wide, shoulder-level arc, this time offensively, as two men bore down on him. Instinctively, Cadderly dropped to one knee and snapped his spindle-disks straight out ahead of him.

The ducking Night Mask came down right in line with this second weapon, catching the adamantite disks on his forearm.

Cadderly expected the man to immediately retaliate, for the young priest had not yet learned of the power of Ivan's forging. Cadderly stared as the man's arm folded—it seemed as though he had grown a second elbow!—under the power of the blow.

But pausing to gape with a second enemy so near was not a wise choice. By the time Cadderly realized his error, realized that a spiked club was on its way down to crunch his head, he knew that his life was at its end.

* * * * *

Pikel managed to keep close enough to his pursuer so that the man hadn't been able to extend his long arms and get in a serious hit. Still, the dwarf said "Oooo!" repeatedly, feeling the sting of a dozen razorlike slashes.

Pikel's first thought was to go for the stairs, but he dismissed the idea, realizing that if he started up, he would rise to his enemy's level and lose his desperately needed advantage of being down below the man's optimum striking area. The dwarf veered to the side, backpedaling faster, nearly tumbling over in the effort.

The man stayed with him, every step.

The killer stopped suddenly, and Pikel realized that he could not do likewise, leaving the dwarf wide open for a full-force roundhouse. "Oooo!" Pikel screamed, desperately hurling himself backward through the air. He collided heavily with the wall before he had gotten very far, and the assassin's sword whipped across just under the breastplate of the dwarf's fine armor.

Pikel didn't even have the time to cry out for this newest wound. He bounced back off the wall and charged forward wildly. The assassin held his sword level in front of him, and Pikel would have impaled himself, except that he grabbed the sharp blade with his bare hand and turned it aside.

Then Pikel was up against the man. He released the sword almost immediately and wrapped the man's arms in his own, pushing with all his strength, his stubby, muscled legs pumping frantically.

Now the killer was backpedaling and Pikel driving forward, gaining speed and momentum. The dwarf could hardly see around the larger man. He aimed for the open door but missed, two feet to the left.

The inn suddenly had a second door.

* * * * *

Danica hit the floor harder than she would have liked, but she managed to scramble back under her victim fast enough so that the next closest Night Mask inadvertently sliced his sword into the back of his still-standing companion.

Out the other side, Danica ran to the foot of the bed, hooked the post in one arm, and spun right around, hopping up onto the mattress. A Night Mask came up on the bed as well, at the other end, bearing down on the apparently unarmed woman.

Danica kept low and kicked straight out. She could hardly brace herself amidst the tangle of blankets, so her kick was not fierce, but neither could the assassin brace himself, so it did not have to be. The man stumbled in the tangle and lurched over. Danica came up under him, hooking her arm under and behind his shoulder and heaved him away, using his own momentum to launch him over the foot end of the bed.

She was up, grabbing the blankets as she went, knowing the sword-wielder was too close. Instinctively she lifted the tangle of cloth out in front of her, smiling grimly as she felt it absorb the weight of the coming blow.

Caught in, and concerned with, the impromptu web, the assassin didn't even realize Danica's next attack until her foot connected solidly with his belly.

The agile monk let herself drop as the man lurched over, using the spring of the bed to lift her right back up, her forearm slamming against the stooping man's face. Danica's second arm, coiled against her chest, snapped out under the first, thumping into the man's throat, then she reversed the angle of her first arm, flying high over her head in its follow-through, and came down diagonally at her stunned victim, blasting against his collarbone. He flew to the side, and Danica, temporarily free of any immediate threat, was not pleased by what she saw beyond him.

Again using the spring of the bed, the young woman leaped out, diving between the posts at the foot of the bed. She heard a heavy thump distinctly as a crossbow quarrel hit the wall right behind her.

The man she had thrown this way was back up and turning back to the fight, but hardly prepared as Danica's shoulder-block launched him over the table and crashing into the wall.

* * * * *

"Stop!" The word came from somewhere deep inside Cadderly. He wasn't even aware of the magical strength it carried until the killer above him, already beginning his stroke, pulled his spiked club to a halt and stood perfectly still. The weapon hovered just a few inches above Cadderly's head.

The command had no lasting power, and the assassin came out of it quickly, snarling and lifting his club for another strike.

Still purely on instinct, Cadderly lashed out in two directions at once, slamming his walking stick against the side of the man's knee, and heaving his spindle-disks straight ahead, to collide with the crumbling killer's chest and send him flying backward.

"The balcony!" Danica cried, and Cadderly, seeing the group of killers—some cocking crossbows—still coming in the door, could hardly disagree.

Danica hooked his arm as she passed and threw open the door.

The song had started again in Cadderly's head, somehow passing through the confusion and the many noises.

He grabbed Danica's hair and jerked violently backward just as the woman took her first step out of the room. Fully caught by surprise, Danica fell back.

Cadderly snapped his spindle-disks across her angled torso, to meet head on with a thrusting dagger coming the other way.

Ivan's disks easily won the contest, bending the dagger blade and crushing the hand that held it.

Cadderly recoiled quickly, felt the sting as the disks snapped back into his own hand, and then whipped them straight back, this time hitting the wounded Night Mask in the chest, driving him over the railing.

The assassin reached out as he tumbled, grasping futilely at the rail. His hand hooked the balcony just enough to allow him to continue in his spin, to put his legs straight out under him so that when he fell the twenty feet to the ground, he landed flat on his back.

And he lay very still.

* * * * *

Pikel shook the splinters from his beard and hair.

"Me brother!" The call, though emphatic, sounded distant, and then was accentuated by the crash of shattering glass and splintering wood as Ivan, hearing his brother's distress, ran full speed down the inn's second story hallway and flung himself headlong through the window above the inn's front door.

He crashed down with a groan, two feet to the right of Pikel and the stunned assassin, showering the two of them with glass and shards of broken wood.

The killer, up first, his back bleeding from many gashes, turned around to discern this newest threat. He saw the lower half of Ivan—the dwarf's upper torso having plummeted right through the raised wooden decking—but he knew by the way the dwarf was flailing and cursing that Ivan would not be held captive long.

He almost got his sword up before Pikel grabbed him by the ankles and yanked his legs out from under him.

Pikel continued to pull, dragging the man away from Ivan. Rage blinded the green-bearded dwarf. "Ooooooo!" he growled, winding up, beginning his spin, and locking the man's feet under his arms.

The Night Mask twisted and turned to get at the dwarf, but Pikel's footing was sure and his spin quickly gained enough momentum to force the man out straight.

"Ooooooo!"

The man bounced and flailed, and had all that he could handle in just keeping a hold on his sword.

"Ooooooo!"

Now the only part of the Night Mask making any contact with the ground was his arms as he struggled to find a handhold, to find something to grab on to.

"Ooooooo!"

Pikel spun furiously; the man, narrowly missing porch posts and the inn's wall, heartily joined in his scream.

Ivan, back up, watched in disbelief that soon turned to amusement. The dwarf laid his brother's club aside, spat in both his hands, and took up his huge double-bladed axe.

The killer noticed Ivan's preparations and gave a half-hearted swing of his sword, not even coming close to hitting the mark. His arm still extended, he slammed his wrist against the porch support as he came around, his sword flying harmlessly out into the street.

Ivan tightened his grasp on the axe. He started to swing, but the man was by him.

"Gotta lead him," the dwarf reminded himself, taking a bead as the circling target came around again. He saw the Night Mask's face go ghastly pale, saw the most profound look of horror the tough dwarf had ever witnessed.

Slam!

Distracted by a rare onset of sympathy, Ivan's timing was not so good and he buried his axe deeply into the wooden decking.

Pikel didn't even notice his brother or the axe, didn't notice that the killer's scream had dissipated in a breathless gasp of terror, and had no idea of how he would stop this spin, or stop the world from spinning in his dizzy head.

"Ooooooo!"

The weight was gone suddenly and Pikel twirled into the wall. He looked down to the empty boots, still held tightly under his arms.

The poor assassin took out the closest supporting pole and crashed through the railing, breaking under the top rail and skidding along through the thin, carved balusters. He bounced along for several feet, then came to an abrupt halt, his hip driving onto the pointed edge of a broken beam. There he lay, half on the porch and half hanging out over the cobblestone street, groaning softly.

"Nice boots," Ivan remarked, running past Pikel and tossing his brother the tree-trunk club he had brought along. Ivan started for the fallen man, then veered away, hearing a scream as someone went toppling over a balcony—Cadderly's balcony—of the Dragon's Codpiece, two doors down.

Both dwarves breathed a sigh of relief when they rushed past the unmoving form of the fallen man, glad that it was not Cadderly or Danica who had gone for such a tumble. But the continuing sounds of battle twenty feet above them told them that their friends were not out of trouble just yet.

The door to the inn was closed again, and barred, but such had never stopped the Bouldershoulder brothers. Actually, coming into the hearth room with a dislodged door in front of them proved a good thing for the dwarves, for several crossbow quarrels greeted their entrance, thudding harmlessly into the oaken barrier.

* * * * *

A quarrel ripped past Cadderly's shoulder, drawing a line of blood along his arm. Night Masks bore down on him from behind; two others waited on the balcony, a sword and a heavy axe gleaming dully in the predawn light.

Still holding Danica by the hair, Cadderly pulled the young woman to her feet. Immediately, she became a blur of motion, snapping a burst of kicks and punches at the already wounded men who were closing from behind. She landed several solid hits, enough to force one of the assassins to back off. But the other caught Danica around the waist and his momentum carried both of them across the narrow balcony to the rail.

Danica got one hand up onto her attacker's face, her fingers seeking out the man's vulnerable eyes. One of the Night Masks on the balcony, though, forewarned of this extraordinary woman's prowess, found a devilish answer. A single swing of his huge axe broke apart the railing that was supporting both Danica and her attacker.

They pitched over the side together, Danica releasing her grasp on the man's face and swinging both her arms wildly to find a handhold.

Cadderly saw her fall away, his face locked in a stare of helpless denial.

A crossbow quarrel smacked into the back of the young priest's thigh. He turned about as he sank to the deck, sheer rage splayed clearly on his usually calm features.

Without even thinking of the movement, Cadderly lifted a clenched fist toward the bowman and uttered, "*Fete!*" the elven word for fire, the command word for his magical ring.

A line of flames shot out from Cadderly's hand, seeking his attacker, immolating the man in a burning shroud.

With a mental shriek of revulsion, Cadderly ended the fire. He spun about again, his walking stick leading, and got a solid hit on the swordsman. He didn't really care how badly he had hurt the man; all he wanted was to get the man out of his way, to clear the path to the axe-wielder who had sent Danica away.

Again, inexperience had led Cadderly to an unwise single-mindedness. Before he ever got near to the axe-wielder, strong hands grabbed at his shoulders and drove him to the side railing.

* * * * *

Ivan threw the heavy door aside, meaning to charge right to the stairs. A gruesome sight off to the side slowed him, though, for just a moment, and when he resumed his charge, his fury had heightened tenfold.

Pikel, too, thought to head straight for the stairs. "Uh-oh," he mumbled and he ran to the right, for the cover of the room's bar instead, for several dark shapes knelt in formation on and above that staircase, all holding deadly crossbows.

Pikel dove over the long bar, coming to a crashing halt along the narrow walkway behind, up against kegs of thick ale. To the dwarf's surprise, he was not alone, and he just managed to convince Fredegar Harriman that he was not an enemy a split second before the terrified innkeeper bonked him over the head with a full bottle of brandy.

A quarrel ricocheted off the blade of Ivan's axe; another struck the dwarf on the head, stunning him, though his fine helmet managed to deflect the thing up between the deer antlers. Perhaps that particular quarrel knocked some sense into the thick-headed dwarf, for Ivan wisely cut to the side, skidding in around the staircase and scrambling for cover underneath it. He slammed hard into one of the structure's supports as he rushed in, getting all tangled up with it. By the time the dwarf figured out that it was just an ordinary wooden pillar and not some lurking enemy, he had battered it to pieces.

Ivan blushed, thinking himself incredibly foolish. Then he looked around, noticing the other four supports—one more on this side, two on the opposite side and one in the middle—and a wide and wicked grin spread over his face.

* * * * *

Danica caught hold of the feeble trim along Cadderly's balcony, and her strong hands would not let go, despite the nagging weight of the Night Mask, still clutching at her waist.

The woman wriggled and squirmed, freed up one foot, and slapped it back and forth across the stubborn man's face.

Only a dozen feet from the ground, the attacker wisely let go, dropping heavily but unharmed, on the cobblestones.

Danica's thoughts of climbing back up to join Cadderly on the balcony lasted only a moment, until the trim split away on one end from the main frame, sending Danica on a swinging ride around the corner of the balcony.

Instinctively, she kicked out and leaped before the trim broke away altogether, latching on to the sill of a window near the building's corner, opposite from where she had left Cadderly. Unable to break her momentum, Danica was forced to leap out again, farther from the fight, but this time landing with a more solid handhold and foothold on a gutter running up the side of the building, just around the corner.

By the time she managed to peek around, the balcony was crowded with black-and-silver-outfitted assassins. She didn't see Cadderly at first amid that throng and could not pause long enough to sort him out, for one crossbowman put her immediately in his sights and two other assassins came over the rail, walking the ledge toward the gutter.

Danica scrambled the ten feet or so to the rooftop. Only as she pulled herself over did she realize that she had somehow badly twisted her knee, probably in the struggle over the railing.

"Cadderly," she mumbled over and over; this scenario reminded her vividly of when she had left the young priest to join the fray in Shilmista, when she had been forced to trust in Cadderly to take care of himself.

She started across the roof, thinking to go right above the balcony and leap down upon the enemy. She turned, though, hearing the gutter groan under the weight of a pursuer.

"Do come up," Danica muttered grimly, thinking to clobber the fool as soon as he poked his head over the roof's edge. It never occurred to her that this well-prepared band might already have someone planted on the roof.

She heard the crossbow click behind her.

"A valiant fight, Lady Maupoissant," said a baritone voice at her back, "but a futile effort against the skill of the Night Masks."

* * * * *

Cadderly's walking stick flew away when he collided with the railing. He hardly kept his bearings as he spun over, but did manage to loop one arm about the railing.

It seemed a wasted effort, though, for the Night Mask clubbed at that arm mercilessly, determined to drop the young priest over the side.

Cadderly's first instinct told him to just drop—the fall probably wouldn't kill him. He realized, though, that another assassin loomed below, and he would be easy prey before he ever recovered from the fall.

None of it seemed to matter when the second Night Mask, the axe-wielder, joined the first at the railing above him.

"Farewell, young priest," the man said evilly, lifting his cruel weapon to split Cadderly's head wide.

Cadderly tried to utter a magical command at that man, but he could do no more than groan as the club connected again against his already wounded shoulder.

The young priest glanced around desperately, only a brief moment left open to him. He saw a tiny ledge along the building a few feet away, behind him, and for some reason he did not understand, a memory of Percival, the white squirrel, came to him, an image of Percival skittering happily and easily along ledges at least that thin back at the Edificant Library.

There was no way that any man could make that leap to the ledge, as twisted as Cadderly was. Yet somehow, he was there, and not holding desperately. Hand over hand, foot over foot, the young priest ran along the ledge.

"Get him!" he heard one of the frustrated and astonished assassins yell from behind, and then the other called for a crossbow.

Cadderly came up fast on the corner, with no intentions of turning aside. The alley was only about eight feet wide at this point, but the only apparent handhold on the building across the way was several feet higher than his present perch. By the time Cadderly registered this fact in the still-dim morning light, though, it was too late for him to alter his course.

He leaped, soared, impossibly high and impossibly far. Hardly slowing, he found himself scrambling easily up the side of the other building, disappearing over the top before any crossbowman back on the balcony could begin to get a shot at him.

* * * * *

Pikel peeked up over the bar to see one of the assassins bearing down on him, the other two leaning over the far side of the staircase, trying to get a shot at Ivan.

The green-bearded dwarf hopped up, club in hand, ready to meet the challenge.

"Here," came Fredegar's call behind him. Pikel glanced back to see the brandy bottle, now stuffed with a burning rag, coming for him.

"Oo oi!" Pikel cried, too startled to catch it, as Fredegar had intended. The dwarf did get a hand off his club fast enough to tap the bottle over him, though, and he spun about immediately and slammed the slow-moving missile with his club, creating a small fireball and showering the approaching assassin with glass shards and flaming liquid.

"Oo oi!" Pikel squealed again, this time happily, as the man fell away to the floor and rolled about desperately to get the stubborn flames off his robes. When the assassin finally got back up, he ran screaming for the door, having no more heart for the fight.

The dwarf hopped up on the bar, then fell back again as the bowmen on the stairs took note of him.

* * * * *

Cunning Ivan's only mistake was that he saved the center support for last. Not until he knocked it out, with a single powerful swipe of his axe, did the grinning dwarf realize that he was standing directly under the heavy structure.

The stairs, and the two surprised Night Masks standing on them, came tumbling down.

Only one of the assassins had regained his feet when Ivan finally managed to burst through the pile of broken wood. The dwarf came up with a roar and tried to swing his axe, only to find its head caught fast on a random beam.

The assassin, bruised but not too hurt, grinned at him and pulled out a short sword.

Ivan tugged mightily, and the axe pulled free, coming across so swiftly that neither the dwarf nor the assassin even realized its movement as it struck the assailant, cutting cleanly through the man's belly.

"Bet that hurt," Ivan mumbled with a helpless, almost embarrassed shrug.

* * * * *

Again Pikel hopped up on the bar, and again he reconsidered, seeing a pair of dark shapes rush out of Cadderly's room into the aisle above, right to the lip of the fallen stairway.

The frustrated dwarf groaned loudly—these two also carried those wretched crossbows.

Pikel realized that he wasn't their target, but he knew, too, that Ivan, standing unsuspectingly right below the ledge, was.

Sixteen
Scramble

Night Masks.

The words stung Danica's heart as surely as could the crossbow quarrel aimed her way. Night Masks. The band that had killed her parents; the wretched, evil assassins of Westgate, the town where Danica had been raised. The questions that rushed into the young woman's mind—Had they come for her? Were they working for the same enemy that had sent Barjin and the invading army into Shilmista?—were no match for the bile, the sheer rage, that climbed up the young woman's throat.

Slowly, she turned to face her adversary, locking his gaze with her own. He was a curious sight, bleeding in several places, leaning to one side, and struggling to draw breath, with half of his face swelling in a grotesque purple bruise and wooden splinters sticking from his hair, face, and arms. And for some reason, the man was barefoot.

"I will not ask for a surrender," the assassin slurred, waving the weapon. "Not after the dwarves . . ." He shook away the frightening memory of the fight at the other inn, dropping several splinters to the roof with the effort.

"You shall be offered none," Danica assured, barely able to spit the words through gritted teeth. A growl escaped her lips as she dove to the roof and rolled.

The crossbow fired and Danica felt something thud against her side, though she was too enraged to know the seriousness of the wound or even to realize the pain. She came up near where the man had been, to find that he had taken flight.

Danica was on him in a few strides. He spun to face her, and she leaped into him, grabbing him tightly. Her knee moved repeatedly, each blow connecting on the man's groin.

She hit him a dozen times, grabbed his hair and ears and yanked his head back from her, then pulled it forward and drove her forehead in to meet it, splattering the man's nose and knocking out several teeth.

She kneed him a dozen more times and butted him again. Her fingers raked the beaten man's face; she drove one finger right through his eye.

Night Masks!

Danica jumped back from the doomed man, spinning a circle kick that snapped his head to the side violently and forced him into a series of stumbling steps. Somehow he did not fall down, though he was hardly conscious of his surroundings.

Danica leaped high behind him, lay herself flat out, planted both feet on the man's back, and sent him in a running takeoff over the roof's edge.

She pulled herself back to her feet, saw that two men had gained the roof by the gutter, though neither had summoned the courage to charge the furious woman.

Too many emotions assaulted the wounded and weary monk. The appearance of the assassin band, the knowledge that these were Night Masks, sent her mind careening down a hundred corridors of distant memories. More recent memories, too, like the strange dream of the previous night, when she had, for a moment, entered the consciousness of her mental attacker.

What had happened to Cadderly? Danica's fear multiplied when she learned the identity of the killers. Had the Night Masks again taken the love from Danica's life?

She fled, her eyes filled with tears, her arm and side throbbing. Up the sloping rooftops, across the uneven angles, leaping the small gaps, the young monk went.

The two killers followed her every step.

* * * * *

Ivan looked down, an inch to the side, to the neat hole the crossbow quarrel had drilled into the lumber pile. Slowly, the dwarf lifted his gaze to the men standing ten feet above him, one leaning over the broken ledge, smiling grimly, with a cocked crossbow pointed Ivan's way.

Sheer desperation shoved new heights of insight into the mind of Pikel Bouldershoulder. Ivan—his brother!—was about to die! Pikel's eyes darted all about, taking in a surrealistic view of the grim scene.

Bar . . . pile . . . dead man (guts, yech) . . . struggling men . . . Ivan . . . precipice . . . crossbowman . . . chandelier . . .

Chandelier? Chandelier above the leaning man.

They had to bring the thing down to light the candles, Pikel reasoned. The dwarf whipped his head about, his gaze coming to rest on the crank, conveniently located at the back of the bar.

The assassin standing over Ivan paused long enough to wave good-bye to the helpless dwarf.

Pikel could have just pulled the pin out of the crank to set the spindle spinning, but now was not the time for finesse. With a "Whoop!" to try to distract the crossbowman a moment longer, the green-bearded dwarf hopped from the bar to the shelving along the wall, crashing aside scores of mugs and bottles, the shelves breaking away under his weight.

"Ooooooo!" he wailed as he slammed his club against the crank. Spindle and all broke out from the wall, hanging stubbornly by a single peg. Pikel, on his knees beside Fredegar, looked at it as though it had tricked him, but then, with a loud popping noise, the last peg gave and the whole assembly rocketed up into the air.

"What?" the confused crossbowman asked.

His companion behind him gasped.

The chandelier took the crossbowman on the shoulder, spinning him over the precipice.

He crashed into the wood pile beside Ivan, the stunned dwarf nodding, stupefied. As though the gods had decided to play some macabre joke, Ivan heard the distinctive click a moment later as the crushed man's crossbow, pressed harmlessly between the man and the broken stairs, fired.

"Hee hee hee," chuckled Pikel, standing again to watch the spectacle. He forgot that the spindle above him was fast unwinding, and fast dropping, and he was back to his knees when it ricocheted off his skull.

"Oooo."

"Set the rope!" he heard Ivan cry, and, shaking away his dizziness, Pikel wrapped the rope in his arms.

Ivan grasped his axe handle in his teeth (not an easy thing to do!) and started up. He noticed that the remaining assassin in the pile behind him was getting to his feet, so he jumped back down to the raised end of a plank lying between him and the man. Ivan's end snapped down and the end under the crawling assassin went up, slamming the man under the chin. He groaned and rolled away, grabbing at his shattered jawbone.

That done, Ivan leaped up again, stubby arms pulling him up the rope to the level of the other crossbowman. To the side, he noticed that Pikel was similarly climbing.

Ivan rushed on, finally getting his head high enough so that he could see the other man.

It was not a pleasant sight.

For the second time in the last few moments, Ivan Bouldershoulder stared into the wrong end of a readied crossbow.

Pikel made the ledge and let go of the rope, realizing only then that he had not secured it below him.

Ivan dropped like a stone. The crossbow fired, harmlessly high. And the stubborn assassin on the first level, his jaw grotesquely shattered, realized his folly in going to the rope under the climbing dwarf.

As he sat atop the man, atop the pile of broken stairs, Ivan, for perhaps the first time, thought it was not such a bad thing to have a scatterbrained brother.

* * * * *

Still on all fours, the young priest skittered fast and sure-footed along the edge of the adjoining building. His spindle-disks clung tightly to his hand, hanging to the end of their cord and bouncing along the building's side. Cadderly hardly noticed them, and had no time to stop and replace them in any event. Nor did the young priest note that the pain was no more in his wounded thigh.

He spotted Danica, running weakly away from him, limping, and then he spotted the two black-robed killers in pursuit, gaining on the stumbling woman with every stride.

Cadderly came up on the other side of the building, where the alley opened perpendicularly to a wide lane of craft stores called Market Square. Two merchants, up at dawn to prepare for the coming day, spotted the young priest and stared, then pointed up and called out something that Cadderly did not bother to decipher.

Too enraged to think of his movements, Cadderly slipped headfirst over the side of the building, going down hand over hand. A banner had been strung along thick ropes across the alley as a sign for one of the craftsmen's shops.

Hand over hand, foot over foot, Cadderly ran across the tightrope. He heard a shout of disbelief from the street below, didn't even realize that it was aimed his way. Back on the many-angled roof of the Dragon's Codpiece, the young priest charged off, nothing but Danica in his thoughts.

He spotted her a moment later—she had leaped across the narrow alley to the next building—stumbling over the crest of a dormer, going headlong. The two men went over right behind her.

"No!" the young priest tried to call out, but his word came out as a strange, squealing sound.

Never slowing, his eyes focused straight ahead, Cadderly flew over the short alley expanse.

One of the black-robed killers emerged from the region Danica had entered, in full flight. Cadderly feared he was too late.

* * * * *

The remaining man in the corridor darted into Cadderly's room, brushing aside the smoke and stench of charred flesh that blocked the doorway.

Pikel grabbed the rope again, and Ivan began to climb, his efforts aided by his brother's hauling movements toward Cadderly's door.

Pikel drove on, much relieved when he saw Ivan's stubby hand come over the lip of the hallway. But then four shapes emerged from Cadderly's room.

Pikel instinctively let go of the rope. He winced at Ivan's diminishing wail and the dull thump as Ivan landed again on the assassin at the bottom of the rope. Pikel couldn't worry about it, though, not with four killers just a few strides away.

But the Night Masks were no longer interested in battle. Seeing the stairs gone, they sought other avenues of escape. One grabbed the rope and, without even testing to see if it was secured, leaped over the precipice. The others ran the other way down the hall, scrambling over the railing wherever they found high spots—tables mostly—where they could get down.

Pikel thought to give chase, but he paused when he heard a door creak open, heard chanting. The next thing the green-bearded dwarf knew, he was lying several feet from where he had been standing, a sharp and burning pain in one side, and his shocked hair wildly dancing on end.

Me brudder. The words cried out in Pikel's mind over and over, a litany against the swirling dizziness, a reminder that he could not remain up here, lying helplessly on the floor.

Ivan heard the man land heavily beside him, and he felt the other one squirming slowly beneath him. The dwarf opened one heavy eyelid to see the assassin standing over him, sword in hand.

The thrust came before the dwarf could react, and Ivan thought he was dead, but the assassin struck low, beneath Ivan.

Ivan didn't question his luck. He struggled to a sitting position, trying to locate his axe, or anything else he might use against the standing killer.

Too late. The assassin's sword came up again.

"Me brudder!" Pikel cried as he flew over the precipice.

The assassin dove away, rolled to his feet, and followed his companions out the door.

Pikel hit Ivan full force.

Ivan groaned as he waited patiently (he had no choice in the matter) for Pikel to crawl off him. "If ye're looking for thanks, keep looking," Ivan grumbled.

* * * * *

Cadderly was too late in getting to the scene—for the sake of the other assassin.

The young priest relaxed as soon as he crested the steep roof. Danica was below him, in a valley between several gables. The remaining assassin was there, too, kneeling before Danica, his arms defenselessly by his sides and his head snapping to one side and the other, blood and sweat flying wide, as Danica landed blow after blow on his face.

"He is dead," Cadderly remarked when he got beside the young monk.

Danica, sobbing, slammed the man again, the shattered cartilage of his facial bones crackling under the blow.

"He is dead!" Cadderly said more emphatically, though he kept his tone calm and unaccusing.

Danica spun about, her face contorted with a mixture of rage and sorrow, and fell into his arms. Cadderly stared curiously as he wrapped his own arms about her, and Danica jumped back, staring at the young priest in disbelief.

"What—?" she stammered, backpedaling even farther, and Cadderly, noticing the change for the first time, had no answers for her.

His arms and legs, covered in white fur, had become those of a squirrel.

Seventeen
Mentor

"T urn it back," Danica pleaded, her voice edged in desperation, her hands trembling at her sides.

Cadderly stared helplessly at his squirrel-like limbs, without the slightest idea of how to begin to reverse the process. "I cannot," he admitted, as much to himself as to Danica. He looked helplessly to her, his gray eyes wide with disbelief and horror. "I cannot."

Danica moved to him, or tried to, until the pain in her side sent her lurching over. She grasped at the bloody wound in her abdomen just above her hip, and slumped to one knee.

Stubbornly, Danica got back to her feet, one hand held out in front of her to keep her concerned lover at bay.

"That must be tended," Cadderly pleaded.

"With squirrel arms?" Danica's retort stung the young priest more than she had intended. "Turn your arms and legs back to human, Cadderly. I beg you."

Cadderly stared long and hard at his limbs, feeling deceived, feeling as though his god, or the magic, had led him astray. Danica stood before him, needing him, and he, with the limbs of a rodent, could do nothing for her.

The young priest searched his memory, let page after page of the *Tome of Universal Harmony* flip through his thoughts in rapid succession. Nothing openly hinted at what he had done, at this transformation, miraculous and damning, that he had somehow brought upon himself.

But while Cadderly found no direct answers, he did begin that distant harmony, that sweet, inspiring song where all the mysteries of existence drifted past him, waiting to be grasped and deciphered. The song rang out a single word to the young priest, the name of the one person who might help him make sense of it all.

"Pertelope?" Cadderly asked blankly.

Danica, still grimacing, stared at him.

"Pertelope," he said again, more firmly. He turned his gaze to Danica, his breath coming in short gasps. "She knows."

"She knows what?" the young woman asked, wincing with every word.

"She knows," was all Cadderly could answer, for in truth, he did not really know what information the headmistress might have for him. He sensed only that the song was not lying to him, was not leading him astray.

"I must go to her."

"She is at the library," Danica argued. "It will take you three . . ."

Cadderly stopped her with an outstretched palm. He closed his mind to the stimuli around him and focused on the song again, felt it flow across the miles, calling him to step into it. Cadderly fell in with the tune, let it carry him along. The world became a dreamscape, surreal, unreal. He saw the gates of Carradoon and the western road leading into higher ground. Mountain passes zipped along beneath his consciousness, then he saw the library fast approaching, came upon the ivy-strewn walls and passed right through them . . . to Pertelope's room.

Cadderly recognized the tapestry on the back wall, to the side of the bed, the same one he had stolen so that Ivan could use it in making a replica of the drow crossbow.

"I have been waiting for you to come to me," he heard Pertelope say. The image of the room shifted and there sat the headmistress on the edge of her bed, dressed as always in her long-sleeved, high-necked black gown. Her eyes widened as she regarded the presence, and Cadderly understood that she saw him, with his rodent limbs, though he had left his corporeal form far behind.

"Help me," he pleaded.

Pertelope's comforting smile fell over him warmly.

"You have found *Affinity*," the headmistress explained, "a powerful practice, and not without its dangers."

Cadderly had no idea what Pertelope was talking about.

Affinity? He had never heard the word used in such a way.

"The song is playing for you," Pertelope remarked, "often without your bidding." Cadderly's face revealed his startlement.

"I knew it would," Pertelope continued. "When I gave you the *Tome of Universal Harmony*, I knew the song would begin to play in your mind, and I knew that you would soon find the means to decipher the mysteries hidden within its notes."

"I have not," Cadderly protested. "I mean, things are happening around me, and to me—" he looked helplessly at his own limbs, translucent replicas of his corporeal form, "—but they are not of my doing, not of my control."

"Of course they are," Pertelope replied, drawing his attention away from his polymorphed limbs. "The book is the conduit to the magical energy bestowed through the power of Deneir. You summon and guide that energy. It comes to your call and bends to your will."

Cadderly looked down helplessly, and doubtingly, at his deformed body. He knew Pertelope could see his problem, and wondered if Danica could as well, back on the rooftop in Carradoon. Those squirrel limbs flew in the face of what the headmistress was saying, for if Cadderly could control the magic, as Pertelope insisted, then why had he remained half a rodent?

"You have not learned complete control," the headmistress said to him, as though she had read his mind, "but you are still a novice, after all, untrained and with mighty powers at your fingertips."

"Powers from Deneir?" Cadderly asked.

"Of course," answered Pertelope coyly, as though Cadderly's next remark would come as no shock whatsoever to her.

"Why would Deneir grant me such powers?" the young priest asked. "What have I done to warrant such a gift?"

Pertelope laughed at him. "You are his disciple."

"I am not!" Cadderly said, and he gave a horrified expression, realizing that he had offered that admission to a headmistress of his order.

Again, Pertelope only laughed. "You are, Cadderly," she said. "You are a true disciple of our god, and of Oghma, the brother god, as well. Do not measure fealty in terms of rituals and attendance to duties. Measure it by what lies in your heart, by your morals and your love. You are a scholar, in all your inquisitive mind and in all your heart, a blessed scholar. That is the measure of fealty to Deneir."

"Not according to Avery," Cadderly argued. "How often he has threatened to throw me out of the order altogether for my indiscretions concerning those rituals you so quickly dismiss!"

"He could not throw you out of any order," Pertelope replied. "One cannot be 'thrown out' of a religious calling."

"Religious calling?" Cadderly replied. "If that is what you must label it, then I fear I was never in the order to begin with. I have no calling."

"That's absurd," replied Pertelope. "You are as attuned with the precepts of Deneir as any person I have ever mit. That, my young priest, is what constitutes a religious calling! Do you doubt the powers you have begun to unlock?"

"Not the powers," Cadderly replied with typical stubbornness, "but their source."

"It is Deneir."

"So you say," answered Cadderly, "and so you are free to believe."

"You will, too, in time. You are a priest of Deneir, a follower of a god who demands independence, the exercise of free will, and the exercise of intellect," Pertelope continued, again as though she had read Cadderly's mind. He had to wonder if Pertelope hadn't played through this scenario herself many years ago.

"You are supposed to question—to question everything, even the existence of the gods and the purpose of being alive," Pertelope continued, her hazel eyes taking on a faraway, mystical look. "If you would follow blindly from ritual to ritual, you would be no better than the cattle and sheep that dot the fields around Carradoon.

"Deneir does not want that," Pertelope went on, calmly, comfortingly, and looking directly back at the frightened young priest. "He is a god for artists and poets, free-thinkers all, else their work would be no more than replicas of what others have deemed ideal. The question, Cadderly, is stronger than the answer. It is what accomplishes growth—growth toward Deneir."

Somewhere deep inside, Cadderly prayed that Pertelope was speaking truthfully, that the apparent wisdom of her words wasn't just the feeble hope of one as confused and desperate as he.

"You have been chosen," Pertelope went on, bringing the conversation back to more concrete terms. "You hear the song and will come, over time, to decipher more and more of its notes, to better understand your place in this confusing experience that we call life."

"I am a wizard."

"No!" It was the first time the headmistress had appeared angry during the conversation, and Cadderly wisely did not immediately reply. "Your magical gifts are clerical in nature," Pertelope asserted. "Have you done anything beyond those enchantments you have witnessed other priests casting?"

Cadderly thought long and hard. In truth, everything magical he had done in some way, at least, replicated clerical spells. Even this *Affinity* was not so different from the shape-changing abilities exhibited by the woodland priests, the druids. But still, his powers were different, Cadderly knew.

"I do not pray for these spells," he argued. "I do not get out of my bed in the morning with the notion that I should be able to create light this day, or that I will find need to turn my arms into a squirrel's paws. Nor do I pray to Deneir, at any time."

"You read the book," Pertelope reasoned, stealing Cadderly's building momentum. "That is your prayer. As far as selecting spells and memorizing their particular chants and inflections, you have no need. You hear the song, Cadderly. You are one of the chosen, one of the few. I had suspected that fact for many years, and came to understand just a few weeks ago that you would take my place."

"What are you talking about?" Cadderly asked, his near panic only intensified by the fact that Pertelope, as she spoke, had begun to unbutton her long gown. Cadderly gaped in amazement as the headmistress peeled the garment off, revealing a featureless torso covered by skin that resembled the hide of a shark, covered not with skin, but with sharp pentacles.

"I was raised from childhood on the Sword Coast," the headmistress began wearily, "near the sea. My father was a fisherman, and often I would go out with him to tend the nets. You see, I found affinity with the shark, as you have with squirrels—with Percival in particular. I came to marvel at the graceful movements, at the perfection of that oft-maligned creature.

"I already explained to you that *Affinity* is a practice that is not without its dangers," Pertelope went on, giving a small, ironic chuckle. "You see, I too fell prey to the chaos curse. Under its influences, I assumed my affinity with no regard for safety, no practical restraints at all."

Cadderly winced to think that this wonderful woman, always a dear friend to him, had suffered by the curse that he had brought upon the library.

There was no malice, no blame, edging Pertelope's voice as she continued.

"The change I enacted is permanent," she said, rubbing a hand along her arm, the denticles drawing several lines of blood on her human palm. "It is painful, too, for my whole body is part human and part fish. The very air is poison to me, as would be the waters of the wide sea. I have no place left in this world, my friend. I am dying."

"No!"

"Yes," Pertelope replied easily. "I am not young, you know, and have labored long on this confusing path we call life. The curse killed me, do not doubt, and I have struggled to hang on for the very purpose that is before me this day. You, Cadderly, are my successor."

"I will not accept it."

"You cannot avoid it," answered the headmistress. "Once begun, the song never ends. Never."

The word sounded like the bang of a drum to Cadderly, suddenly terrified of what horrors he may have unlocked in the pages of that awful book.

"You will come to know the limitations of your powers," Pertelope went on. "And there are indeed limitations." She looked disconcertingly at her own destroyed arms as she spoke, making her point all too clear. "You are not invincible. You are not all-powerful. You are not a god."

"I never said—"

"Humility will be your preservation," Pertelope promptly, sharply interrupted. "Test the powers, Cadderly, but test them with respect. They will drain you and take a bit of you with them whenever you summon them. Exhaustion is your enemy, and know that enacting magic will inevitably weary the spellcaster. But know, too, that if Deneir has chosen you, he will demand of you."

Pertelope smiled warmly, revealing her confidence that Cadderly would be up to meeting the challenge.

No reciprocal smile found its way to Cadderly's face.

* * * * *

"Do you plan to go somewhere?" Ghost whispered to Bogo Rath, seeing the young wizard in the upstairs hall of the Dragon's Codpiece with a sack in hand.

The assassin stepped out of Cadderly's room and motioned for Bogo to follow him to his own room.

"The city guard has been called," the wizard explained. "They will swarm all about this place."

"And find what?" Ghost replied with a snicker, thinking it an ironic statement, given that he had just deposited Brennan's body in Cadderly's room. "Certainly nothing to implicate either one of us."

"I hit the green-bearded dwarf with a lightning bolt," Bogo admitted.

"He did not see you," Ghost retorted. "If he had, you would be dead. Both he and his brother are up and about, downstairs with Fredegar. They would have come back for you long before this if the stupid dwarf suspected you had launched that magic."

Bogo relaxed a bit. "Did Cadderly and Danica get away?"

Ghost shrugged, unable to answer. He had seen little beyond the carnage left in the wake of the violence. "Temporarily, perhaps," he answered at length, and with as much conviction as he could muster. "But the Night Masks have been set on the trail now. They will not stop until the young priest is dead."

"Then I am free to return to Castle Trinity," Bogo reasoned hopefully.

"If you try to leave now, you will invite only suspicion," Ghost replied. "And if Cadderly has managed to elude the assassins, he will likely return here. This is still the best seat at the game, for those who have the courage to play to the end."

The last words sounded clearly like a threat.

"Aid the city guard in their investigation," Ghost continued, a sudden ironic smile crossing his features. He was the artist, he privately reminded himself, already weaving new webs of intrigue. "Tell them you possess some knowledge of magic, and that you believe a bolt of lightning was set off in the upstairs corridor. When the dwarf confirms your story, you will be viewed in a favorable light."

Bogo eyed the assassin doubtfully, even more so when he remembered that Kierkan Rufo was still about, carrying information that could certainly damn him.

"What is it?" Ghost asked, seeing his mounting concern.

"Rufo."

Ghost chuckled evilly. "He can say nothing without implicating himself. And he, by all of your descriptions, is too much a coward to do that."

"True enough," Bogo admitted, "but I am still not certain of our wisdom in remaining at the inn. We have underestimated Cadderly and his friends, it would seem."

"Perhaps," Ghost said in reluctant agreement, "but do not complicate the error by overestimating the priest now. For all we know, Cadderly might lie dead in an alley."

Bogo hesitated, then nodded.

"Be gone," Ghost instructed, "back to your room, or to aid in the investigation, but say nothing to Rufo. Better that the cowardly priest be left alone to stew in his guilt and terror."

Again Bogo nodded and then was gone.

Ghost's confidence disappeared as soon as he was alone. This had been a complicated visit to Carradoon, had not been a clean kill. Even if Cadderly was dead, the toll had been horrendous, with more than half of the dedicated Night Mask band killed.

Ghost really was no longer sure that remaining at the Dragon's Codpiece would bode well for either himself or Bogo, but he feared the consequences of trying to slip away with the city guard, and two rambunctious dwarves, snooping around. He moved to his door and cracked it open an inch, curious to see what might be transpiring outside.

He watched carefully for Rufo, thinking that if the treacherous priest made any dangerous moves, he might have to kill him.

No, it had not been without complications, but that was part of the fun of it all, was it not? It was a new challenge for the artist, an intricate landscape for the fill-ing canvas.

Ghost smiled wickedly, taking comfort in the fact that he wasn't in any per-sonal danger—not while he had the *Ghearufu*, and had Vander as a waiting and helpless host on the outskirts of town.

* * * * *

Cadderly was relieved to see Danica still up and conscious when he rejoined his corporeal form on the rooftop beside the Dragon's Codpiece. The young woman's face remained contorted in pain. A crossbow quarrel protruded from her right side, hanging from skin and tunic and surrounded by a widening crim-son stain.

Cadderly did not immediately go to her. He closed his eyes and forced the song back into his thoughts. The notes drifted past until Cadderly recalled that part of the song, that page in the tome, he had been hearing back on the balcony when he had enacted the change to the squirrel form.

Danica whispered to him softly, sounding more concerned for his own safety than for her own. With some effort, Cadderly pushed her words away, concen-trated on the music. His mouth moved in silent prayer, and when he at last opened his eyes, Danica was straining to smile and his arms and legs were back to normal.

"You found your answers," the young woman remarked.

"Along with more questions," Cadderly replied. He pulled his spindle-disks from their tight hold on his finger and tucked them away, then moved beside his love.

"You were speaking," Danica said to him, "but not to me. It sounded like half of a conversation, the other half—"

"Was with Pertelope," Cadderly explained. "I, or at least my consciousness, was back in the library." He hardly noticed Danica's stare, was more interested in her sorely wounded side.

When he recalled the song this time, it sounded more distant to him, required more effort to get near it. Pertelope's warnings of exhaustion welled up in him, but he pushed his mounting fears away; Danica's health was more important.

Cadderly focused on the dangling quarrel as much as on the wound it had caused; his thoughts were as much on destruction as on healing. His chant was uttered through gritted teeth.

Danica grunted and winced. Black smoke wafted from her wound. Soon a small cloud of the stuff covered her side.

The quarrel was his enemy, was Danica's enemy, Cadderly determined. Poor Danica, dear Danica.

When the smoke dissipated, gone, too, were the crossbow quarrel and the wound.

Danica straightened and shrugged, not knowing how she could possibly thank Cadderly for what he had done.

"Are you injured?" she asked, concerned.

Cadderly shook his head and took her arm. "We must be gone," he said, his tone absent, as though he was talking more to himself than to Danica. "We must go and sit together, privately, and try to sort through the turns fate has shown us." He cocked his head, turned his attention to the growing tumult in the awakening lanes around the Dragon's Codpiece, particularly to the clip-clap of many hooves echoing from every direction.

"The city guard is about," Danica replied. "They will require information."

Cadderly continued to pull her along.

"We have nowhere to go," Danica argued as they neared the building's back edge, many soldiers coming into sight along Market Square.

Cadderly wasn't listening. His eyes were closed again and he was deep in some chant, deep in song.

Danica's eyes widened one more time as she felt herself become something less than substantial. Somehow Cadderly kept his grip on her arm and together they simply blew away, off the rooftop, riding the currents of the wind.

* * * * *

Bogo Rath slipped out of the Dragon's Codpiece a short while later, rushing briskly past the dwarves and the bereaved innkeeper in the hearth room. After brief consideration, the frightened young wizard decided that Ghost's presumptions were not worth risking his life over, and he decided, too, that departing the inn after such tragedy could not be viewed as a suspicious act.

The only thing the city guardsman asked of him as he passed through the hole where the front door had been was that he remain in town.

Bogo nodded and pointed to an inn a few doors farther up Lakeview Street, though the wizard had no intention of staying around for very long. He would go

to the inn and get a room, but would remain in Carradoon only until he had studied the spells that would allow him to leave quickly and without the possibility of
being stopped.

Eighteen
Reflections on the Water

T he morning light was still new, and the mist had not yet flown from the waters of Impresk Lake. The great three-arched stone bridge connecting the mainland to Carradoon's island section loomed ghostly. It towered above Cadderly and Danica as they drifted in a small rowboat, quiet with their thoughts and the lap of the gentle waves against the prow.

The weather was fitting to Cadderly's grim mood. He had killed a man, had burned him to a blackened ball, and had knocked another from the balcony, leaving him for dead as well. There had been no real choice, Cadderly knew, but he could not easily dismiss his guilt. Whatever the reasons, he had killed a human being.

He tried hard to not think of the man's family, children perhaps, waiting for a father that would never return.

Danica, too, sat quietly, deep in thought, at the small boat's prow. More accustomed to battle than her somewhat innocent companion, the young woman was more concerned with what had precipitated the vicious attack. What had brought the Night Masks upon her and Cadderly?

Cadderly took up the oars and gave a single stroke, reversing the drift and pushing the boat farther out from the imposing bridge. He let the oars hang in the water and turned about on the bench seat to face Danica.

"Night Masks," Danica muttered grimly.

Cadderly looked at her; the name meant little to him.

"From Westgate," Danica explained. "They are among the deadliest killers in all the Realms. We were fortunate to escape them, and I now believe I have escaped them twice."

Cadderly's expression showed that he still did not understand.

"On our journey down from the library," Danica continued, "the dwarves and I were attacked by a band of five."

"Many bandits have been reported on the roads during these troubled times," Cadderly remarked.

Danica shook her head, certain that there was a connection between the attack on the road and the one in Cadderly's room.

"Why would an assassin's guild from Westgate come after us?" Cadderly reasoned.

"Us?" echoed Danica. "No, they are after me, I fear. It was the Night Masks who killed my parents, years ago. Now they have come to finish the job."

Cadderly didn't believe a word of that explanation. He sensed that—if Danica's theories about the identity of the killer band were correct—there was more at work here than the completion of a decade-old vendetta. Cadderly contemplated his own experiences of the last few days, thought of his meeting with Rufo in the hearth room and the presence of the invisible wizard. And what had happened, he wondered, back in his own room that night?

He looked at Danica quizzically. "I found you on the floor, terrified. Tell me about your dream."

"I do not remember much," Danica admitted, and her tone revealed that she did not really see the point of it all. Cadderly was determined, though. He thought for a moment, then took out his crystal-centered spindle-disks.

He held them up before Danica's eyes and set them spinning. Even in the dim light, the crystals flickered with reflective fires. "Concentrate," Cadderly begged the woman. "Let the crystal into your mind. Please, do not use your meditative talents to block me now."

"What will this tell us?" Danica argued. "It was just a dream."

"Was it?"

Danica shrugged—it was a dream that contained references to the Night Masks, after all—and relaxed, focusing her gaze on the spindle-disks. Cadderly watched her intently, then closed his eyes and thought of the sacred tome, heard the song playing the words to a simple spell of hypnosis.

Danica sank deeper, her shoulders visibly slumping, as Cadderly quietly chanted. His words became prying questions that Danica heard only subconsciously.

Cadderly, too, allowed the hypnosis to fall over him, used it to achieve complete empathy with Danica.

The questions rolled out of his mouth, though he was barely aware of them. And Danica answered, as much with her posture and her facial expressions as with mere words.

Danica blinked her eyes open; Cadderly followed her lead. Neither of them knew how much time had passed, but Cadderly understood then, beyond any doubt, that Danica's nighttime experience had indeed been an important clue.

"It was not a dream," he announced.

Cadderly recalled what Danica had imparted to him under the hypnosis: the sense of departure from a black sphere that the young priest knew represented her identity. The image reminded the young priest vividly of his own telepathic experiences with the imp Druzil and the wizard Dorigen. Might those two be behind all this?

Cadderly dropped a hand into his pocket to feel the amulet he had taken from Rufo in Shilmista Forest, an amulet that Druzil had given Rufo to improve telepathic contact between the two. With the amulet, Cadderly had been able to sense the imp's proximity, and he took comfort that it had not signaled Druzil's presence in many weeks, not since the large battle in the forest.

But who then? he wondered.

Dorigen remained a distinct possibility.

"Possession?" he muttered, using the word as a catalyst for his thoughts.

Another image struck Cadderly then, an image of Nameless, the beggar on the road, and the horrible, shadowy shapes writhing atop his shoulders. He remembered, too, that night when Brennan had come to his room, projecting the same vile aura. Perhaps the song of Deneir had not lied to him; perhaps the attempt on Danica was not his enemy's first try at possession.

Cadderly winced, remembering Fredegar's worries that young Brennan had not been seen since that night. He tried to recall clues as he took up the oars for another single stroke against the drift.

"What is it?" Danica asked. Her tone revealed her understanding that Cadderly's mind had unlocked some of the secrets.

"They have not come for you," the young priest answered with certainty, looking over his shoulder. "They were here before you, around me, close to me." Cadderly exhaled deeply, fearing for Brennan and Nameless, and let his gaze drift across the water to the gray outline of the great bridge. "Too close."

Danica started to reply—something comforting, Cadderly knew—then she stopped and cocked her head curiously.

Cadderly began to turn his whole body about, to fully face Danica, understanding that something was wrong and fearing that the young woman had come under some mental assault.

Danica spun about, rocking the boat so suddenly that Cadderly, though he was seated near the center, almost went over the side.

"Stubborn!" Danica cried. Her hand snapped in front of her just in time to grab the wrist of the man who had tried to drive a dagger into her back. Holding tight, Danica leaped to her feet, stretched her attacker's arm to the limit, and pulled him farther over the bow.

She gave her attacker's arm a quick, violent twist and brought her free hand over the back of his fingers, jerking the man's hand back toward his wrist.

Cadderly tried to get about in the rocking boat to go to Danica's aid, but all he wound up doing was stumbling over the boat's center seat and slamming himself on the side of the head with one of the oar handles.

He realized that the stumble was a good thing, though, as a knife soared up over the side of the boat and whipped across above his head. Reacting instinctively to the threat, Cadderly forearmed the oar, freeing it from its lock to tumble into the water near the unseen attacker.

The young scholar got his spindle-disks looped onto his finger. The boat rocked, and he looked back the other way, across the boat, to see still another assassin coming up over the side.

Danica held her balance easily in the rocking craft. She continued her vicious press on the caught man's hand, finally forcing him to release his dagger.

She wasn't done with him yet.

Night Masks!

Danica's foot snapped out wide, coming back around the man's head and forcing his chin over the prow rail. Holding him tightly against the wood, Danica yanked his arm back out over the water. She locked his elbow so that he could not bend the limb and pressed straight down.

The man's eyes bulged as the bow pressed his throat up under his jaw.

Cadderly's off-balance throw soared lower than he had hoped, but while he did not get the man's head, he did get a few fingers—and the top plank of the boat. Wood splintered, the remaining oar flew off, and so did the assassin, clutching his blasted belly as he fell away into the lake.

Free of the weight, the boat rocked back so far that Cadderly feared its other side would dip under the water where the knife-thrower waited.

The young priest realized how vulnerable he was, and how vulnerable Danica was! They needed a distraction, something to allow them to get their bearings.

Water did come in over the broken side of the boat when it rocked back again, but Cadderly took no note of it, intent on the wounded man fumbling in the water with the floating oar. The shape of the oar caught the young priest's attention.

With one foot planted in the rocking boat, and with the choking man struggling frantically against her, Danica amazingly held her balance.

The struggling killer tried to come up over the side, but Danica jammed his arm down mightily, dislocating his shoulder.

The man could not even grimace at the obvious pain. His face went blank, weirdly serene. Danica understood. She brought her foot back around, released its hold on the man's head, and let him slip under the water.

Her sensibilities returned to her then, her sheer rage at the presence of the Night Masks temporarily sated by the reality of the kill. Others were about—Danica realized for the first time that others were likely about!

She turned and, to her horror, saw Cadderly disappear under the water in the grasp of a killer. Another boat, with several men in it, approached from behind; Danica did not know if they were friend or foe—until a crossbow quarrel cut the air beside her face.

Instinctively, she dove to the floor of the boat. She knew she had to get to Cadderly, but how? If she went under the water, how could she hope to stop this approaching menace?

A scream to the side turned Danica about, to peek over the broken plank. There floundered the wounded Night Mask, the one Cadderly had hit with his spindle-disks, fighting desperately to free himself from the clutches of a long, thick constrictor—a snake about the same size as one of the boat's oars.

The man somehow broke free and began swimming with all speed toward the approaching boat. The snake slithered off in pursuit, slipping under the water as it went.

Despite the peril, Danica could not help but smile. She knew that the appearance of this snake was no natural coincidence; she knew that Cadderly, and that mysterious power, had struck again.

Danica got up to her knees. The other boat was closer now; she could see a man in the prow leveling a crossbow her way. She jerked up, as though she meant to stand, then fell flat and heard the whistle of the high-flying bolt.

Now she had time to get over the side, into the water after Cadderly. Before she moved out of the boat, though, the water churned and the Night Mask appeared, his face contorted in terror and the second snake, the second oar, wrapped about his shoulder and chest. He reached for the boat, then slapped at the water and the beast.

Then he was gone.

Again the water churned, a short distance to the side. Up came Cadderly, impossibly fast, his body breaking out of the water impossibly high.

He was standing on the water! And still wearing his hat, the holy symbol set in its front glowing furiously.

Danica nearly laughed, too amazed to react any other way. Cadderly took in a few gulps of air, seeming more surprised than Danica.

He looked back toward the approaching boat—the swimming man had just about met it by then—and saw that the crossbowman was preparing another shot.

"Get in!" Danica cried, thinking Cadderly too vulnerable standing on the water out in the open. Cadderly seemed not to hear her. He was chanting, singing actually, and waving one hand slowly to and fro.

Danica looked back to the other boat, saw the man leveling the crossbow—and saw Cadderly standing in the open, vulnerable.

She scrambled to the side, grabbed at a piece of broken wood floating in the small pool at the bottom of her boat. She came up throwing, skimming the wood sidelong so that it spun and swerved . . . and plopped harmlessly into the water a dozen feet to the side of the approaching craft.

But the crossbowman had flinched, had looked her way.

A sudden swell erupted in the calm lake, near where Danica's wood had disappeared. The water reared up and rolled, as if aimed, toward the enemy boat.

The crossbowman had set his sights on Cadderly again when the wave collided against the side of his boat. Not even bracing himself at the time, the man lurched over the side and nearly lost his weapon.

At first, Danica wondered how the little piece of wood had so disrupted the stillness of the lake. She realized it was no more than coincidence, though, and she turned to the true source of the swell. Cadderly, still standing calmly, sung his soft song and waved his hand back and forth.

Another swell rose and crashed against the enemy boat, turning it about so that it was facing the bridge.

Cadderly smiled; another swell turned the boat so that it was facing the shore, directly away from him.

"Come," Cadderly said to Danica, extending his hand. "Before they get their bearings."

Danica at first misunderstood, thinking that Cadderly wanted her to help him into the boat. He resisted her pull, though, beckoning her to go to him.

The assassin who had pulled Cadderly under the water bobbed to the surface face down. The snake that had been wrapped about him became an oar again at Cadderly's command and floated benignly, a harmless piece of flotsam.

"Come," Cadderly reiterated, tugging Danica. She jumped onto him and wrapped herself about him.

Cadderly looked about, then ran for the island. Danica watched over his shoulder, taking note that his footsteps did not splash the water. Rather, the burdened young priest left depressions in the lake surface, which quickly reverted to the natural water shape, as though he was running across soft ground.

Behind them, the enemy boat finally straightened and the crossbowman pulled the swimmer up over the side. The oar that had been chasing him bobbed up over the waves.

Danica kissed Cadderly on the neck and rested her weary head on his shoulder. The world had gone crazy.

Cadderly came to the shore mumbling, thinking out loud. He kept chugging along but slowed under the weight of his burden when he hit more solid ground.

"Cadderly . . ."

"If those are professional assassins," he was saying, "we must assume they were hired by our enemies, by Dorigen perhaps."

"Cadderly . . ."

"Someone has made the connection to us," Cadderly continued, undaunted. "Someone has determined that we are, or at least that I am, a threat to be eliminated."

"Cadderly . . ."

"But how long have they been hovering about me?" the young priest muttered. "Oh, Brennan, I pray I am wrong."

"Cadderly!"

Cadderly looked right at Danica for the first time since he had left the lake.

"What?"

"You can put me down now," Danica replied.

She hit the ground running, grabbing Cadderly's wrist and tugging him along. They heard the enemy boat skid to shore through the brush behind them.

"Stubborn," Danica said, looking over her shoulder gravely.

Cadderly knew she wanted to turn and finish the fight.

"Not now," he begged. "We must get back to the inn."

"We may never get our enemies so out in the open again," Danica reasoned.

"I am weary," Cadderly replied. And indeed, the young priest was. The song no longer played in his head, but was replaced by a severe headache, the likes of which young Cadderly had never before experienced.

Danica nodded and sped on. They crashed through a hedgerow, into the back yard of one of Carradoon's finer estates. Dogs began to bark from somewhere nearby, but Danica did not veer from her path through another hedgerow and into another open yard.

Several people, older merchants and their spouses, stared at the fleeing couple incredulously.

"Get to cover and alert the city guard!" Cadderly called to them as he followed Danica past. "Thieves and murderers pursue us! Call out the city guard and send them to the bridge!"

The couple burst through another row of bushes, coming out onto a wide, flat cobblestone lane, running between lines of beautiful manor houses, between lines of staring, curious people.

Not a horse or wagon was seen on the bridge at this early hour, something Cadderly took comfort in as he and Danica started across. The young priest would have hated to place anyone directly in the path of his deadly pursuers, and he knew by the continued bark of distant, unseen dogs that the Night Masks had not given up the chase, were only a few minutes behind.

Cadderly skidded to a stop when they came to the high point in the first of the bridge's three arching supports. Danica started to question him, but was stopped by his conniving smile.

"Watch for the assassins," he said to her as he fell to his knees. He used his soaked cloak to trace a square on the stone of the wide bridge.

"The first page I ever looked at in Headmistress Pertelope's book always amazed me," he explained, not slowing in his work. "I knew it was a spell, similar to one I had seen in the book of Belisarius."

The square completed, two lines of wetness running parallel across the structure, Cadderly rose and led Danica a few dozen steps farther along.

Cadderly called up the song and began to chant, knowing the words intimately. He had to stop, though, and rub his temples to relieve the throbbing the powers caused.

They will drain you and take a bit of you with them whenever you summon them, Pertelope had warned him. *Exhaustion is your enemy . . .*

"They are on the bridge!" he heard Danica say, and he felt her tug at his arm, trying to hurry him along.

It could not be helped. Cadderly fought through the pain and weariness, forced the song into his mind and to his lips.

> *What is the bond that holds the stone?*
> *A bond that wetness breaks.*
> *What are you without the bond?*

Danica knocked him to the ground; he barely heard the crossbow quarrel pass them by.

Still he sang, his concentration complete.

> *Seep, my water, seep*
> *Through the bond, so deep.*

The leading assassin stumbled suddenly, lurched forward as though his feet had been ensnared, fell face down onto the bridge ... and sank into the mud that the section of bridge had become.

Danica and Cadderly heard splashes below as chunks of mud and stone dropped into the lake. Another assassin hit the area but managed to fall back, knee-deep in the collapsing morass.

The man who had gone in headlong screamed as he dropped out the bottom, plummeting the twenty feet or so to the churning lake.

The entire section Cadderly had marked off slipped down right behind him.

Four stunned assassins stood at the edge of the fifteen-foot gap separating them from their intended quarry, staring in disbelief.

"She said that Deneir would demand of me," Cadderly remarked to Danica, rubbing his throbbing temples. "And he will again, when we get to the inn."

"You have come into some faith?" Danica asked as they fled, leaving behind the frustrated assassins' curses and the clip-clap of many horses coming onto the bridge, bearing city guardsmen.

Cadderly looked at Danica as though she had slapped him. He calmed and shrugged, having no recourse against her logic.

They heard the shouts of guardsmen and killers as the trapped assassins, one by one, dove for the cover of the water.

The way was clear, all the way back to the Dragon's Codpiece, to dead enemies and dead friends.

Nineteen
Sorrow and Divine Joy

Shouts continued to follow Cadderly and Danica after they left the bridge and made their way onto Lakeview Street. The mist was fast flying, burned away by the steamy rays of the rising sun.

Carradoon had awakened to a travesty.

Lakeview Street was jammed with curious citizens and city guardsmen. Many heads turned to regard the young priest and his escort, Cadderly's wide-brimmed hat drooping on all sides from its soaking. Pointing fingers turned the companions' way as well, and soon a horseman, a city guard, pushed his way through the throng to stop in Cadderly's path.

"Are you a priest of the Edificant Library?" came the guardsman's blunt and gruff question.

"I am Cadderly, of the Order of Deneir," the young priest replied. He turned to Danica and shrugged, embarrassed and almost apologetic, as soon as he had spoken the last few words.

"We are making our way back to the Dragon's Codpiece, the inn of Fredegar Harriman," Danica explained, tossing Cadderly a sidelong glance, "to check on the friends we were forced to leave behind."

"Forced?" Cadderly and Danica knew the question was a test. The guardsman's eyes remained narrow and searching as he continued to scrutinize them.

"You know what occurred," Cadderly replied without hesitation.

The guardsman nodded gravely, apparently satisfied with the explanation. "Come, and quickly," he bade them, and he used his horse to nudge aside any who stood to block the couple's progress.

Neither Cadderly nor Danica enjoyed that stroll down Lakeview Street, fearful that among those many watching eyes loomed some belonging to their assassin

595

enemies. And even more fearful to the companions, considering the guard's grim tone, loomed the possibility that the victory back at the inn had not been without cost.

Their fears did not diminish when they passed the inn two doors down, where Ivan and Pikel had been staying, to find that the front rail, the window above the door, and the wall beside the door all had been smashed apart. The innkeeper, sweeping glass and wood shards from his front porch, regarded the two suspiciously, not looking away and not blinking once as they passed.

Cadderly paused and sighed deeply when the Dragon's Codpiece came into sight. He spotted the balcony of his room, the place he had used as a sanctuary from the harshness of the world for the past several weeks. The front rail lay in the street; one plank, the one that had supported Danica's ride to safety, hung out at a weird diagonal angle. There were no bodies in the street (thank the gods!), but Cadderly saw a crimson stain on the cobblestone beneath his room, and a larger one halfway across the wide street.

Danica, apparently sensing his distress at the sight, hooked her arm around his and lent him support. To her surprise, Cadderly pulled away. She looked at him, to see if she had done something wrong, but his return stare was not accusing.

He stood straight and tall, took another deep breath, and squared his shoulders.

Danica understood the significance of those simple acts, understood that, this time, Cadderly had accepted what he had been forced to do. This time, he would not run away, as he had in Shilmista; he would meet the threat head-on, strike back against those who meant to strike at him. But could he do so, Danica wondered, without ghosts like Barjin's hovering beside him for the rest of his days?

Cadderly walked past her, then smiled and waved when "Oo oi!" sounded from the door of the Dragon's Codpiece and Pikel Bouldershoulder stepped onto the front porch. The dwarf held Cadderly's lost walking stick high above his head and waved excitedly with a heavily bandaged hand.

Danica waited a moment longer and let Cadderly get far ahead of her, considering the perceived shift in the young priest's demeanor. This continuing stream of violent events was forcing Cadderly to grow up, to thicken his hide, in a hurry. Violence could be a numbing thing, Danica knew; no battle is ever harder to accept and fight than the first, no killing blow made with more reluctance than the first.

Watching her lover stride confidently to join Pikel, the young monk was afraid.

By the time Danica caught up to Cadderly, he stood silently inside the inn with both dwarves (to her relief) and with a teary-eyed Fredegar Harriman. Danica held in check her elation at Ivan and Pikel's good heath, though, for she followed Cadderly's gaze to a table in the hearth room, to Headmaster Avery's sprawling corpse. The chest was torn wide and revealed a gaping hole where the heart should have been.

"My Brennan," broken Fredegar was saying. "They killed my poor Brennan!"

Cadderly let his gaze drift about the sacked room, to the broken stairwell, the shattered chandelier atop its rubble; to the charred floor beside the long bar; to a young, unmarked body gently laid beside that bar; and to the row of six corpses, one of them still releasing wisps of smoke from under the cloth that covered it.

"Four of them, at least, got away," Ivan informed them.

"You will find another one on the roof," Danica remarked.

"Oo oi," Pikel chirped, snapping his stubby fingers and motioning for one of the guards to go and check.

"Maybe only three got away," Ivan corrected.

"Seven got away," Cadderly said absently, remembering the three men who had assaulted him and Danica from the water, and the four others in the pursuing boat.

Ivan shook his yellow-bearded face, then grumbled, "Well, there's a pack of trouble for ye."

Cadderly hardly heard the dwarf. The young priest walked slowly across the cluttered floor toward the body of the man who had served him as a father for as long as he could recall. Before he got there, though, a tall man, a city soldier, intercepted him.

"We have some questions," the man explained gruffly.

Cadderly eyed him dangerously. "They will wait."

"No," the man retorted. "They will be answered when I say. And fully! I'll brook no—"

"Leave." It was a simple word, spoken quietly and in controlled tones, but, to the city guardsman, it struck like a thunderbolt. The man stood up very straight, glanced about curiously, then headed for the front door. "Come along," he instructed his fellow soldiers, who, after exchanging surprised glances, obeyed without complaint.

Ivan started to say something to Cadderly, but Danica put a hand on the dwarf's shoulder to stop him.

Cadderly wouldn't have heard Ivan anyway. The young priest moved beside Avery's torn body and wiped a tear from his gray eyes. Avery had gotten in the way of something that really did not concern him, Cadderly suspected, and the notion brought disgust to the young man, brought yet another layer of guilt to his growing burden.

But it wasn't guilt that drove Cadderly now; it was sorrow, a grief more profound than any he had ever known. So many images of Avery's life flowed through the young priest. He saw the portly headmaster on the lane outside the Edificant Library, trying to enjoy a sunny spring day but continually hampered by Percival, the white squirrel, who dropped twigs on him from the branches above. He saw Avery at Brother Chaunticleer's midday canticle, the headmaster's face made content, serene, by the melodious song to Avery's cherished god.

How different that fatherly face seemed now, its mouth open in a final scream, an unanswered plea for help that did not come.

Most of all, Cadderly remembered the many scoldings the headmaster had given him, Avery's blotchy face turning bright red with frustration at Cadderly's apparent indifference and irresponsibility. It took the insidious chaos curse for the headmaster to finally admit his true feelings for Cadderly, to admit that he considered Cadderly a son. In truth, though, Cadderly had known it all along. He never could have upset Avery so completely and so many times if the headmaster had not cared for him.

Only now, standing beside the dead man, did Cadderly realize how much he had loved Avery, this man who had served as father.

It occurred to Cadderly that Avery should not have been down in the hearth room at such an early hour, especially not dressed so informally, so vulnerably. Cadderly digested that information almost subconsciously, filing it away with the myriad other facts he had collected and scrutinized since his flight from the assassin band.

"My Brennan, too," Fredegar blubbered, coming to Cadderly's side, draping an arm over Cadderly's shoulder to lean on the young priest.

Cadderly was more than willing to give his gentle friend the needed support, and he followed the innkeeper's lead across the floor toward the bar.

The contrast between Brennan's body and Avery's was startling. The teenager's face showed neither horror nor any signs of surprise. His body, too, seemed intact, with no obvious wounds.

It appeared that he had simply, peacefully, died.

The only thing Cadderly could think of was poison.

"They could not tell me how," Fredegar wailed. "The guardsman said he wasn't choked, and there's no blood anywhere. Not a mark on his young form." Fredegar panted desperately to find his breath.

"But he's dead," the innkeeper said, his voice rising to a wail. "My Brennan is dead!"

Cadderly shuffled to the side under the weight as Fredegar fell into him. Despite his sincere grief at the sight of Brennan, the death had raised a riddle that Cadderly could not leave unanswered. He remembered the horrible shadows he had seen dancing atop Brennan's shoulders that night at supper. He recalled Danica's story, her dream, and knew beyond doubt that someone, something, had possessed the young man, then discarded him.

Perhaps some lingering trace of what had happened remained to be seen. Perhaps telltale shadows remained on Brennan's shoulders. Cadderly opened his mind, let the song of Deneir into his consciousness again, despite the continuing, painful throb in his head.

Cadderly saw a ghost.

The spirit of Brennan sat atop the bar, looking forlorn and lost, staring with pity at his distraught father and with disbelief at his own pale body. He looked up at Cadderly, and his nearly translucent features twisted with surprise.

All the material world around the spirit became blurry as Cadderly allowed himself to fall more into Brennan's state.

Poison? his mind asked the lost soul, though he knew he had not spoken a word.

The spirit shook its head. *I have nowhere to go.*

The answer seemed so very obvious to Cadderly. *Go back to your father.*

Brennan looked at him with confusion.

The song played louder in Cadderly's throbbing head, its volume becoming ferocious. The young priest would not let it go, though, not now. He saw Brennan's spirit tentatively approach the corpse, seeming confused, hopeful yet terribly afraid. To Cadderly's eyes, the room around the spirit went dark.

Everything went dark.

"By the gods," Cadderly heard Danica whisper.

"Oooo," Pikel moaned.

A thump on the floor beside him jolted Cadderly awake. He was kneeling on the hard floor, but, beside him, Fredegar was out cold.

In front of him, young Brennan sat up, blinking incredulously.

"Cadderly," Danica breathed. Her shivering hands grasped the young priest's trembling shoulders.

"How do you . . . feel?" Cadderly stammered to Brennan.

Brennan's chuckles, as much sobs as laughter, came out on a quivering, breaking voice reflecting astonishment, as though he really didn't know how to answer the question. How did he feel? Alive!

The young man looked to his own hands, marveled that they again moved to his command. Fists clenched suddenly, and he punched them up into the air, a primal scream erupting from his lips. The effort cost the lad his newfound physical bearings, though, and he wobbled and swooned.

Ivan and Pikel rushed to catch him.

Cadderly steadied himself suddenly, his gaze snapping back across the room, to Headmaster Avery. The determined young priest rose briskly, brushed Danica aside, and stalked to the corpse.

"They took out his heart," Danica said to him meekly.

Cadderly turned on her, not understanding.

"That is their usual method," the young monk, familiar with the dark practices of the wretched Night Masks, replied. "It prevents an easy recalling of the spirit."

Cadderly growled and turned back to Avery, back to the task at which he would not fail. He called up the song, forcefully, for it would not readily come to his weary mind. Perhaps he should rest before continuing, he thought as the notes continued on a discordant path. Perhaps he had pushed the magic too far this day and should rest before delving back into the spiritual world.

"No!" Cadderly said aloud. He closed his eyes and demanded that the music play. The room blurred.

Avery's ghost was not about.

Cadderly, though his material body did not move, looked all about the room. He saw marks of blackness, supernatural shadows, on the floor beside the bodies of the dead assassins and sensed a brooding evil there.

The spirits were gone, and Cadderly got the impression their journey had been forced, that they had been torn away.

Would they receive punishment in an afterlife?

The thought did not bring compassion to Cadderly. He stared hard at the puddles of residual blackness. He thought of recalling one of those lost spirits, to question it about Avery's spirit, but dismissed the notion as absurd. The fate awaiting these souls had nothing to do with what awaited the goodly headmaster.

With sudden insight, Cadderly reached with his thoughts beyond the parameters of the room, sent out a general call to the heavens for his lost mentor's departed spirit.

The answer he received did not come in the form of words, or even images. A sensation swept over Cadderly, an emotion imparted to him by Headmaster Avery—he knew it came from Avery! It was a calmness, a contentment beyond anything Cadderly had ever experienced, divine.

A bright light gave way to nothingness. . . .

Ivan and Danica helped the young priest to his feet. Cadderly, coming fully from his trance, looked at Danica with a most sincere smile.

"He is with Deneir," Cadderly told her, and the joy in his voice prevented any reply.

Cadderly realized that his headache had flown. He, too, had found contentment.

"What do ye know?" Ivan asked him, and Cadderly understood that the dwarf was not speaking of Avery's fate. Danica also looked at the enlightened young priest curiously.

Cadderly did not immediately answer. Pieces of this puzzle seemed to be falling from the sky. Cadderly looked over to the dead assassins, then looked to Brennan and Fredegar, in the thick of an unabashed hug.

Cadderly knew where he would find more of those tumbling puzzle pieces.

* * * * *

The passing hours came as reassurance to Ghost, who sat quietly in his room, going about his day as routinely as he could. Massacres were certainly not a common thing in Carradoon, but these were troubled times and Ghost was confident that the news would grow stale soon enough. Then young Cadderly would become vulnerable to him once more.

Thoughts of abandoning the mission had crossed the assassin's mind soon after he had learned that Cadderly had escaped—and that many of his Night

Masks had not. He dismissed those thoughts, though, choosing instead to personalize this kill even more. He would get Cadderly, get him through one of his friends, and the young priest's death would be all the sweeter.

Ghost was a bit dismayed when he saw Bogo depart, more because he wanted Bogo to serve as a scapegoat if Cadderly and his friends closed in on the truth than for any practical services the wizard might provide.

The wicked man looked out his window at the afternoon sun's reflection on quiet Impresk Lake. He saw the bridge to the island clearly, saw the masons huddled out there, in boats and on the structure itself, studying the wide break.

Ghost shook his head and chuckled. He had already contacted Vander telepathically, back at the farm, and knew that Cadderly had precipitated that break. Four men had returned to the farm—four out of fourteen.

Ghost continued to stare at the gaping break in the great bridge. Cadderly had beaten them; Ghost was impressed.

But he was not worried.

* * * * *

Every detail of the battle scene—Avery's presence in the hearth room, where he should not have been; the curious, continued absence of Kierkan Rufo, who had come down from his room only long enough to identify Avery's body and answer the city guards' few questions; even the peculiar scorch mark on Pikel's tunic registered clearly in Cadderly's mind—came together in the overall picture he was forming.

He spoke with Brennan, though the young man's recollections were foggy at best, dreamlike. That fact alone confirmed Cadderly's suspicions of what had happened to Danica. The young priest made a point of telling Brennan to keep out of sight, and bade Fredegar to not tell anyone that his son was alive again.

"We must press on quickly," Cadderly explained to his three companions, gathered around him in an out-of-the-way room. "Our enemies are confused for now, but they are stubborn and will regroup."

Danica leaned back in her seat and placed her feet on the table in front of her. "You are likely the most weary among us," she replied. "If you are ready to continue, then so are we."

"Oo oi!" Ivan piped, before Pikel got the chance. The yellow-bearded dwarf offered his surprised brother an exaggerated wink, and Pikel promptly tugged hard at Ivan's beard.

Although it took him and Danica several moments to quiet the boisterous brothers, Cadderly was glad for the distraction, for the break in the exhausting tension.

"You have spoken with the guard?" Cadderly asked Danica when order was finally restored.

"Just as you suspected," the young woman replied.

Cadderly nodded; another piece fell squarely into place. "The wizard will not be there for long."

"But are ye ready to battle the likes of that one?" Ivan had to ask.

Cadderly chuckled and stood, straightening his trousers, still moist from his dip in the lake. "You make it sound as if I am going alone," he quipped.

Ivan was up in an instant, bouncing his huge axe atop one shoulder. "Can't trust that type," the dwarf explained, wanting to clarify his atypical hesitance. "Dangerous sort."

"Can't trust an angry priest, either," Cadderly retorted, taking up his walking stick and sending his spindle-disks into a few short up-and-down snaps.

"Dangerous sort," Danica finished for him, and after the sights the young woman had experienced that day, the tremendous magical powers Cadderly had revealed, the words were spoken without any hint of sarcasm.

Twenty

I Telled Ye So

Bogo Rath paced anxiously in his small room. He kicked a basket aside and watched a cockroach skitter across the floor, seeking the shadows under the bed.

"Flee, little bug," the young wizard remarked.

Bogo flipped his stringy brown hair to one side and ran his fingers through it repeatedly. He was the little bug.

He looked out the window, which was too small to get any real view, but enough to tell him that the afternoon light finally was beginning to wane. Bogo meant to leave the city at twilight, disguised among the host of beggars that departed Carradoon every evening.

Outside the gates, he could conjure a magical mount, and his ride to Castle Trinity would be swift and unhindered. The thought of getting far from Carradoon, from the young priest and his cohorts, appealed to Bogo, but the thought of facing Aballister did not. Even worse, if Ghost succeeded in finishing the task, the assassin's return to Castle Trinity would cast an unfavorable, cowardly light on Bogo.

"Boygo," he muttered. He figured he had better get used to hearing the name. Aballister and Dorigen would not soon let him forget his cowardice. The lone consolation for the young man was the fact that he had arranged the library headmaster's death.

The cockroach skittered back out for an instant, zipped across the floor and under the folds of the oversized curtain.

"That will silence them!" Bogo said to the roach. Especially Dorigen, who had been so humiliated in Shilmista Forest.

A smile found its way through the tension on Bogo's boyish face. He had killed a headmaster!

A glance at the window told him it was time to start for the western gate. He selected the components for a spell that would alter his appearance and placed them in a convenient pocket, then took up his pack.

He put it right back down when he heard chanting in the hall.

* * * * *

"Fire and water," Cadderly said in an intense, monotone voice. "Fire and water, the elements of protection. "Fire and water."

Danica and Pikel stood in front of the young priest, between Cadderly and the door. Danica flipped her hair out of her face and looked to the stairway, to the top of the crouching, nervous innkeeper's balding head. Every so often, the man peeked over the top stair, fearful for his property.

Still, Cadderly had easily convinced the man to let the three up the stairs to Bogo's room. Danica looked to Cadderly again, who chanted more forcefully now with his eyes closed and his hands waving up and down in front of him, creating a magical tapestry. The young priest had shaved his beard before they had left the Dragon's Codpiece, and now he appeared much like his old self.

And yet, he did not. Danica couldn't explain it, but somehow Cadderly appeared more confident with every move. His encounter—whatever had happened—with Avery's spirit had put a sense of calm on top of that growing confidence as well.

Danica hadn't questioned him about it, but she sensed that Cadderly now walked with the knowledge that his god was with him.

"Fire and water," Cadderly chanted, "the elements of protection." As one of his hands came up, he loosed a few drops of conjured water against the door. As the other came up right behind, Cadderly sent from it a gout of flame.

The fire hit the wet door with a hiss, the signal for Pikel.

"Oo oi," the dwarf chirped and slammed his club like a battering ram against the door. The weapon popped cleanly through the thin wood, creating a fair-sized hole but not forcing the door open. As the dwarf retracted his club, Danica realized Pikel's mistake. She reached over the dwarf, turned the handle, and easily opened the door—out.

"Oh," the deflated Pikel remarked.

Bogo's chanting from inside the room joined Cadderly's continuing prayer when the door came open. The wizard held a small metal rod in front of him, a conductive component that Danica had seen before.

Pikel had, too, and both he and the woman dove to the side, expecting a burst of lightning.

Cadderly didn't move, didn't flinch. An almost transparent, slightly shimmering field of energy appeared in the open portal.

Bogo's blast struck it with fury, the lightning driving hard against the barrier, sizzling and throwing multicolored sparks, sending a spider web of green and orange energy across the breadth of Cadderly's field to burn at the door jamb. When it had ended, a tiny pool of water lay at the base of the intact defensive field.

Wide-eyed, the frightened wizard began another spell, as did Cadderly.

Bogo pulled another component and began a fast-paced chant.

"Sneeze," Cadderly commanded.

Bogo complied, and his spell was disrupted.

The stubborn wizard growled and began again.

"Sneeze."

"Damn you!" Bogo cried, wiping the wetness from his face.

"You could not be farther from the truth," Cadderly replied calmly. "Shall we continue to play the game?

"Dispel!" Cadderly cried suddenly, his face twisting to an angry glare. The shimmering field in the doorway disappeared, and Danica and Pikel burst into the room.

Bogo realized his mistake; he should have continued to "play" as the young priest had called it, continued to force Cadderly into a defensive posture in the hopes that his spell repertoire would outlast the priest's.

Danica came straight ahead, dove, came up in a leap, and jolted forward with her landing, too fast for the surprised Bogo to react. He threw his arms out defensively, and the monk promptly wrapped them, bringing her arms up through the wizard's, then down and around, locking Bogo fast.

He did twist one wrist, though, cutting a line of blood on Danica's sleeve.

An invisible dagger!

Danica's foot shot up between her and the close wizard, crunching Bogo's nose. Dazed, Bogo offered no resistance as Danica released his other arm, cupped her free hand over the back of his clenched fingers and yanked his hand back toward his forearm, pulling his arm in the other direction at the same time.

The wizard's face contorted in agony. He tried to hold his only weapon, but Danica's foot came up again; her hand continued to pull.

Pikel joined her a moment later. "Oo," he said glumly, disappointed that the fun was already over. He heard the clang as the unseen dagger hit the floor, and he looked down for it, scratching his green-dyed hair curiously.

Cadderly walked to the bed and motioned for Danica to lead her prisoner to it. "You can let him go," the young priest offered.

Danica gave a quick, painful jerk as she released Bogo's arms, and she pushed the wizard, knocking him to a sitting position.

"We must talk, you and I," Cadderly demanded quietly.

Bogo glared up at him from the bed, an impotent threat, but Danica cuffed him anyway, on the ear.

She scowled and showed Cadderly her cut arm in answer to his surprised expression, and that seemed to satisfy the young priest's nagging conscience.

"Dorigen sent you," Cadderly said to the man.

"No."

Cadderly looked at him curiously. "I have ways of telling when you lie," he warned.

"Then you detect nothing," Bogo replied.

"You were with the Night Masks, but you are not a part of their guild," Cadderly remarked.

"You will die," Bogo promised, drawing another cuff from Danica.

"Why have they come for me?" Cadderly asked. With no answer forthcoming, he added, "I could speak with your corpse, if that would please you."

For the first time, Bogo seemed afraid. The sincere calmness of Cadderly's tone gave weight to the threat, the promise, Bogo knew and, because he wanted to grow to be an old wizard, he replied. "You got in the way," the young wizard stammered, "at the library and in the forest. You forced Abal—" Bogo stopped abruptly.

"Who?" Danica demanded, putting her face right up to Bogo's.

"Aballister," Bogo admitted, "Dorigen's mentor, my mentor."

Cadderly looked to Danica, concerned. Dorigen had been a powerful adversary. How strong might her mentor be?

"I came only to observe," Bogo went on, "as I was told."

"Oh?" Pikel cut him short, stepping past Danica, pushing her aside, and displaying the scorched hole in his leather tunic, the hole Bogo's lightning had made back at the Dragon's Codpiece.

The blood drained from Bogo's face, and his growing desperation forced him to a desperate act. He shoved his hand into a pocket, grabbed a handful of pebbles, and flung them to the floor.

A burst of minor explosions went off, blowing in rapid succession and shooting variously colored puffs of smoke into the air. The pops did nothing to the companions, other than distract them. With a quick chant, Bogo diminished to the size of a cat and slipped between Cadderly and Pikel.

Cadderly tried to call out but could not decide fast enough whether he should shout for his friends to stop Bogo or cry out a warning to the wizard. Danica finally pushed past him and Pikel, following the wizard's expected path to the door.

They heard the door close—the smoke began to clear and Bogo, outside the room and man-sized again, began a new chant.

Danica stopped, wisely not going through the portal.

From behind the door they heard Bogo cry out in terror. The friends heard a shuffle of feet, a sickening thud, then something heavy slammed against the door.

Cadderly shook his head and looked away. The tip of Ivan's double-headed axe protruded through the door, dripping crimson. As if that weren't macabre enough, Bogo's fingers, grasping helplessly and twitching, reached through the circular hole Pikel's club had made in the door. Pulled by the unbalancing weight, the door slowly creaked open.

Pikel walked past Danica and opened the door the rest of the way, peeking around it and saying, "Oo" as he regarded the hanging wizard.

"I telled ye ye couldn't trust a wizard," Ivan, standing a dozen feet down the hall with his hands on his hips, asserted. He strode up to the door and motioned for the group to come out of the room.

The young priest couldn't help but look over at the dead young wizard, a man probably not even as old as Cadderly. "We never asked his name," Cadderly remarked.

Ivan kicked the door closed, spat in his hands, and put one boot up beside Bogo for leverage. "Wondering what to put on his stone?" he asked gruffly.

Danica watched the young priest closely, looking for any signs of weakness. This time, though, Cadderly appeared to control his emotions and accept the guilt.

"Just wondering," he answered Ivan, giving a resigned shrug as though he had pushed the incident from his mind. "Get the body back in the room," Cadderly instructed the dwarves. He shook his head at the irony of one of his earlier statements, which he had made merely to scare his prisoner.

He could indeed speak with Bogo's corpse.

* * * * *

There was only the lake and the empty street. Carradoon quieted considerably as twilight neared, and the interest in the outrageous events at the Dragon's Codpiece had dissipated quickly. Only a few guests had remained at the battered inn, and with Cadderly and his companions out of the building, the place was quiet—too quiet for Kierkan Rufo.

The angular man stood in front of his room's small window, the tilt of his stance making him appear almost like a diagonal crosspiece to the glass. Many minutes passed; Rufo did not move.

He had gone too far this time, he realized, had crossed the line to the dark side of his nature. He doubted he could ever step back. He stood in reflection now, trying to follow the course that had led to this horrible position. It had begun in the library, when he had met evil Barjin and, on the priest's command, had sent Cadderly tumbling down the stairs to the hidden catacombs.

Rufo could excuse himself of that indiscretion, and all of the other members of his order, including Cadderly, had excused him as well. In the elven forest, Rufo had betrayed his companions once more, but he had redeemed himself, had come through in the end to provide his companions with the information they needed to ultimately win out. As in the library, the efforts of Cadderly and the others had averted disaster, had helped to cover Rufo's weaknesses.

Now Avery lay dead downstairs. Rufo had put the headmaster in the path of an assassin band. Rufo had stepped over, had crossed the line.

He tried to justify his actions, told himself repeatedly that he had been given no choice, that the assassins would have killed them all if he had not cooperated.

The facts did not support his excuse. Cadderly, Danica, and the dwarves (where had those two come from, anyway?) had won, had chased off the band. If Rufo had gone to them soon after his initial meeting with the young wizard, their victory would have been more swift.

Avery would be alive.

The angular man whimpered and turned from the window, suddenly feeling very vulnerable. "He deserved his fate," Rufo muttered grimly, reminding himself of the way Avery had treated him since the trouble in Shilmista. Avery would have held him back in his ascension through the Order of Deneir; the headmaster had even threatened to have him removed from the library! That was not justice, Rufo's sensibilities argued, not when the headmaster held all the power and Rufo could only stand and let Avery's whims determine his fate.

By the time Rufo had crossed the small room and collected his pack, anger had replaced his guilt. He had struck back at Avery in the only way he could, and now it was done. No one suspected him; the conspiring wizard had already fled, and Rufo had easily deflected the city guards' questions. Even more comforting, Cadderly apparently had taken the guards' conclusions for truth, for the priest hadn't asked Rufo a single question concerning the tragic events.

Rufo had to hide his smile as he paid Fredegar (from Avery's purse) for the time spent in the inn. He explained to the hospitable innkeeper that he had to return at once to the Edificant Library and report the tragic loss.

It was getting dark outside when he exited the Dragon's Codpiece, dark like the path Kierkan Rufo had stumbled down.

* * * * *

The four friends left the other inn a short while later, Cadderly tossing the fearful innkeeper a bag of coins to cover the damages and the cost of disposing of Bogo's body.

"Where do we go?" Ivan asked, impatient, now that he knew where other enemies might be, to get on with the fighting.

"Back to the Dragon's Codpiece," Cadderly replied evenly.

"What do we do when we get there?" Ivan said, not sounding happy about the choice.

"We wait," Cadderly answered, trying to calm the volatile dwarf. "We have struck hard this day and this night. All of us need some rest." Cadderly believed the words; his extensive use of magic had drained him, and he wanted nothing more than to spend the next hours in peace. After what he had learned from Bogo's spirit, though, the young priest wasn't confident he would get his wish.

The air was chill outside as the night grew dark and the first stars made their appearance.

Cadderly knew it would be a long night.

Twenty-One
Pikel Bait

Cadderly paid his friends' banter little heed. He sat by his small table, beside the *Tome of Universal Harmony*, pushing the pieces of this mental puzzle closer together, seeking information from every memory he could summon. His contemplations were not purely for reasons of information gathering, though.

Cadderly lingered on the image, the sensation, of Avery's spirit, on the divine joy he knew the dead headmaster had found. The young priest's doubts, which had followed him through all of his spiritually bereft life, could not penetrate the holy barrier of that sensation. Cadderly's logic, founded on information he could see and test with his own senses, seemed ridiculous when compared with the perceived smile of Avery's ghost.

The foundation of Cadderly's existence had been violently shaken, and yet, the young priest felt no remorse and no sense of loss. Quite the opposite—the mystery of it all gave Cadderly a sense of hope beyond anything he had known. Rather than deny what he had felt, the young priest would simply have to expand his foundation to include these wonderful new revelations.

Cadderly's unconscious chuckle turned Danica and Ivan, who sat on the bed, toward him, and their stares, in turn, awakened the young priest from his musing. Cadderly shrugged, not knowing how to begin to explain.

"Peoples," Ivan grumbled, but Danica nodded to the young priest, as though she understood the resolutions Cadderly was finding.

Dear Danica, Cadderly thought, and he did not doubt she knew, or that she approved.

* * * * *

Pikel crept along the first floor of the Dragon's Codpiece, slipping in and out of the shadows in search of the cupboards. It was late, and the dwarf was hungry, having missed three out of four meals during the course of the exhausting day.

"Hee hee hee," the dwarf tittered when he found biscuits and sweet dough. He dropped the amulet Cadderly had given him into a pocket and rubbed his plump hands together briskly, his cherubic dimples revealing his glee.

The dwarf sported an armload of food as he ascended the makeshift stairway to the second level, each step on the stairs that he and Ivan had put back together helping him to justify his filching.

His smile disappeared before he got back to Cadderly's room, though, and, as a puny human approached him a moment later, half a biscuit fell out of his mouth.

* * * * *

Danica and Ivan struggled on the bed, the young woman proving, to Ivan's disbelief, that her concentration could prevent Ivan from taking her hand down in wrist wrestling. The mighty dwarf, his bright red face framed by his yellow beard, pushed and yanked vigorously to the side, but the woman's arm, tiny compared to Ivan's gnarly and corded muscles, did not budge an inch.

"You have met your better," Cadderly remarked to Ivan, which only set the dwarf into a deeper frenzy. He hopped up on his toes and pushed with all his strength, moving the bed several inches, but Danica's position remained unchanged.

The sudden and somewhat loud scrape of the bed set off silent alarms within Cadderly. The young priest had made no secret of the fact that he and his friends were back at the inn, but he didn't want to give his potential enemies too much information.

"Quiet!" he whispered harshly, and, remembering Pikel, he closed his eyes and sent his thoughts to the missing dwarf. He expected to find the same sensations—hunger mostly—waiting for him, but when Cadderly made contact, through the power of the telepathy-enhancing amulet, his eyes popped wide open. The sensations were vague, as expected, but instead of distant thoughts of muffins and ale, Cadderly visualized hunched black shadows.

It was not Pikel on the other end! Images of dead Brennan, and of poor Nameless, filtered through Cadderly's rising sense of panic. The young priest abruptly broke contact and jumped from his seat.

"I'll get ye yet!" Ivan snarled at Danica, oblivious to Cadderly's alarm. Danica, though, facing Cadderly's way, did not miss his actions. Ivan tugged her arm to the bed as she came from her meditative state, the dwarf growling victoriously until he noticed that Danica was paying him no heed.

Danica scrambled over the bed, past Ivan. The dwarf turned about to see her and Cadderly exit the room, and realized then that the trouble likely involved his absent brother. Not pausing even long enough to locate his axe, Ivan half-crawled, half-ran out the door in pursuit.

* * * * *

Poor Pikel had never felt so weak! He stared dumbfoundedly at himself, or at his body at least, or at whatever this monster was that had stolen him.

Holding the weakling body by the throat in one hand, Ghost heard the rumble down the hall and realized that Pikel's friends would soon be on him. The thought brought an evil chuckle to his dwarven lips. He slapped aside Pikel's skinny arm and reached into one of his pockets, producing a small packet.

"Oooo," Pikel wailed, and he nearly swooned, thinking the item to be some horrible magical thing and suspecting that his life was at its end, as Ghost brought the packet up between them. But Ghost broke the packet over himself, over the dwarvish trappings, instead.

"Eh?" Pikel queried, for the imposter dwarf's face was covered in blood, blood from the packet.

With one arm Ghost lifted the puny form from the ground and hurled Pikel across the room, where he slammed into a wall and slumped to the floor.

Ghost, too, fell back, leaning heavily on the wall perpendicular to the door, and groaned.

* * * * *

Enraged Ivan grabbed both Cadderly and Danica by the backs of their tunics and hurled himself past them as soon as he discerned where Cadderly was leading them. The dwarf, without his deer-antlered helmet, hit the door head first, bursting into the room.

Staggering, Pikel lifted a shaking finger and pointed accusingly across the room, to the slender human form crawling about the base of the wall.

"Me brother!" Ivan roared, and he charged across, hands leading to throttle the weakling killer.

Danica, too, followed the imposter dwarf's trembling finger, but Cadderly came into the room more slowly, warily, paying full attention to the apparently wounded dwarf.

He had brought the song of Deneir into his thoughts. He saw the shadows crouched on Pikel's—on the imposter's!—shoulders.

"Ivan!" he cried, and, trusting in the song, he whipped his adamantite spindle-disks straight into the dwarf's face.

The dwarf flew back against the wall; real blood mingled with the fake on the green-dyed beard. "Oooo," he moaned. Across the room, Ivan let go of the weakling and came rushing back to throttle the new target.

Cadderly hadn't released the dwarf from his knowing gaze. He watched the shadows break apart, then melt down into Pikel's shoulders.

Ivan caught his brother in both hands and hoisted him off the floor, slamming him against the wall.

"Oooo," Pikel moaned again.

"Hold, Ivan," Cadderly said calmly. "Pikel is back where he belongs."

Cadderly nodded to Danica, and she turned about to face the assassin again, ready to spring at him in an instant.

"You have nowhere to run," Cadderly said to Ghost. He walked up to join Danica. "I know you."

"Shouldn't have made the damn disks so fine," Cadderly heard Ivan say behind him, to Pikel's continuing groans. The young priest looked back briefly to see Ivan tending Pikel's bloodied face.

When he turned back, the shadows were gone from the puny assassin's shoulders. Cadderly's gaze darted all about the room, fearing that the man had stolen one of his friends' identities once again. His three companions appeared the same to him, though, looking to him for direction and with confusion now, apparently recognizing the young priest's sudden distress.

"Who are you?" Cadderly muttered under his breath when he turned back to the weakling man. He let the song of Deneir sound louder in his mind, studied the aurora of this new identity.

He felt a cold wind, pictured a rocky, forlorn shore backed by towering mountains. Huge ice floes dotted the bay, waves breaking against their invulnerable sides, and a giant ship sat quiet in the calmer waters near the shore, awaiting the mighty arms that could pull its monstrous oars.

Cadderly looked into the weakling man's face and saw true fear and unexpected resignation.

Danica sensed that the puny man was about to dart for the door, and she tensed for a spring to intercept him. A whisper came into her ear, though, a magical message from Cadderly. She looked at her companion curiously.

The little man broke for the door. Danica went for him, as did Cadderly, the two getting conveniently tangled, enough for the man to get by.

Ivan dropped Pikel hard to the floor, wincing at his brother's ensuing groan.

"Halt!" Cadderly cried, looking to the fleeing man. That command was not aimed for the weakling, though, and it carried the weight of considerable magical energy.

Ivan stopped in spite of himself and the man rushed out the open door. Danica halfheartedly took up the chase, as Cadderly had instructed. She came out the front door of the Dragon's Codpiece a few moments later, saw the man turning a corner one way, and purposely went the other, to return empty-handed after an appropriate amount of time had passed.

Back in the room, Ivan stood staring in disbelief at Cadderly, tapping one heavy boot impatiently on the wooden floor.

"More waiting?" the yellow-bearded dwarf asked gruffly.

Cadderly smiled and nodded. "Not too long," he promised, and the young priest believed the claim. The puzzle was nearly complete.

Twenty-Two
Striking Back

W ell I'll be a smart goblin," Ivan whispered, peering over the back edge of
the roof of the building adjacent to the Dragon's Codpiece. Market Square
was bustling, usual for this time of the day, but the dwarf had picked out
one figure clearly, a tilting, angular man making his way through the crowd.

Danica, following the dwarf's pointing finger to spot Rufo, was over the side
in an instant, picking her way down into the alley and quickly falling into step
some distance behind the man.

"I'd have thought that one'd be long gone from here by now," Ivan remarked
to Cadderly, who sat farther from the edge, the *Tome of Universal Harmony* open
in front of him and his eyes closed. The young priest shook his head, not at all
surprised.

"Rufo would not dare the trails alone," Cadderly explained, the same argument he had used when Fredegar had told the friends Rufo intended to go back
to the library. "It is likely that he has found refuge within the city, in the temple
of Ilmater perhaps."

Ivan and Pikel shrugged at each other, neither willing to dispute Cadderly's
logic. Their young friend had been leading them through the continuing mysteries as if he knew all the answers, or knew where to find them. Pikel shrugged
again and crossed the roof to watch over Lakeview Street, while Ivan continued
his scan of Market Square. They had been on the roof for more than a day, waiting with all the patience that could be expected of dwarves.

Danica returned a few minutes later, easily scaling the back of the building.
"He is with the priests of Ilmater," she reported.

Cadderly nodded silently, not opening his eyes, not breaking the trance he
had spent hours attaining.

"He knew that," Ivan remarked dryly, the dwarf starting to feel like a pawn in somebody else's chess game. Under his breath Ivan muttered, "Damned cocky priest knows everything."

"Not yet," Cadderly replied, drawing another disbelieving shake of the head from Ivan. There was no way that Cadderly, twenty feet away, could have heard his remark.

Defeated, Ivan went back to watch for the escaped assassin, for Kierkan Rufo, or for anyone or anything else that might give the friends a clue.

Not that he believed Cadderly needed any.

* * * * *

As soon as he regained control of his giant form, Vander began to pace the barn nervously, stretching his huge arms out wide. He had nearly been caught, and, honestly, the firbolg didn't know how he had moved that weakling body fast enough to get out of the room and out of the inn.

He had spent a miserable night on the streets of Carradoon, fearful that Ghost would never give back his true form and continually looking over his shoulder, expecting to find Cadderly, the woman, or the two fierce dwarves, bearing down on him.

But now he was back, at the farm and in his familiar body. He peeked out the door at the quiet house and empty yard, not sure whether the four remaining assassins were still around.

Four remaining assassins! At least eleven of the killers were dead, with five others missing. Ghost alone walked the streets of Carradoon, except, perhaps, for the wizard, Bogo Rath. And Cadderly, now surrounded by powerful allies, remained alive and alert.

In their last spiritual passing, though, Vander had sensed clearly that Ghost remained confident, had sensed that the little man was actually enjoying the challenge of this difficult chase.

Ghost had been in trouble before, had lost entire bands of killers only to turn the tables and bring the intended victim down. He was confident, cocksure, the quality of a true warrior.

Of course, the firbolg's admiration of the little man was tempered by the knowledge that Ghost's confidence was rooted in the fact that the weakling had a quick way out of any situation. With Vander a safe distance from the fight, Ghost always had a quick and easy escape route.

How convenient.

* * * * *

"What is it?" Danica posed the question just a moment after Cadderly opened his eyes for the first time in several hours. The young priest had searched the city, had reached out with detection spells to locate the particular magical emanations of the strange item the evil little assassin carried.

"A shift in the power," Cadderly explained absently, his thoughts still firmly locked on the *Ghearufu*.

Ivan, a few feet away but overhearing the conversation, waggled his bearded face in disbelief. "If ye know where the damn thing is—" he began.

"I do not," Cadderly interrupted, "not exactly. Our enemy is in the city, somewhere south of here or, I should say, our enemy has just returned to the city."

Danica cocked her head curiously, pushed the stubborn lock of hair from her face.

"He departed the city while we had him cornered back in the room," Cadderly tried to explain, "magically. The man who physically ran away, or at least the spirit of the man occupying the killer's body, was not the same conniving person that captured Pikel."

Ivan waggled his face again, too confused to offer any remarks.

"Now he has returned to Carradoon," Cadderly went on.

"And we are to find him?" Danica stated as much as asked, and she was surprised when Cadderly shook his head.

"What would we gain?" the young priest asked. "Our enemy would only flee once more."

"What're ye thinking, then?" Ivan huffed, tired of Cadderly's cryptic clues. "Are we to sit here and wait for them killers to find us?"

Again Cadderly shook his head, and this time the action was accompanied by a wide and wicked smile. "We're going to catch our tricky friend from behind," he explained, thinking of the farmhouse that Bogo Rath's spirit had described to him. "Are you ready for a fight?"

Ivan's dark eyes popped wide at the unexpected invitation, and his response pleased his brother. "Hee hee hee."

* * * * *

"There!" Cadderly whispered harshly, pointing to a window under the spreading limbs of a wide elm tree. "Someone walked by that window, inside the house." Cadderly scanned the farmyard, wondering where Danica's stealthy progress had put her. The young monk was nowhere in sight, had disappeared into the shadows.

"Time for going," Ivan said to Pikel as he hoisted his great axe.

Pikel grabbed his brother's shoulder and cooed, pointing plaintively to the tree.

"I'm not for going up another tree," Ivan growled, but his anger couldn't hold out against Pikel's pitiful expression. "All right," the gruff dwarf conceded. "Yerself can get up the tree."

Pikel hopped at the news, and his wide smile disappeared under his helmet as the cooking pot dropped over his face. Ivan roughly adjusted it, realigned his own deer-antlered helm, and pushed his brother off.

"Ivan," Cadderly said gravely before they had gone two steps. The dwarf turned a sour expression back to the young priest.

"Do not kill anyone if it can be avoided," Cadderly said firmly, "as we agreed."

"As yerself agreed," Ivan corrected.

"Ivan." The weight of Cadderly's tone brought a frown to the dwarf.

"Damn boy's taking all the fun out of it," Ivan remarked to Pikel as the two turned and headed off once more, skittering, hopping, crawling, falling over one another, and, somehow, finally getting to the base of the wide elm.

Cadderly shook his head in disbelief that the dwarven racket hadn't alerted the whole countryside of their presence. He continued to shake his head as Pikel clambered up onto Ivan's shoulders, reaching futilely for the lowest branch. The green-bearded dwarf hopped up, dropping his club on Ivan's head, but managed to grasp the branch. Hanging by his fingers, his feet wiggling wildly, Pikel would never have gotten up, except that Ivan promptly returned the club, slamming it against Pikel's rump and nearly launching him over the thick branch.

"Oooo," Pikel moaned softly, rubbing his seat and taking the club from Ivan.

Cadderly sighed deeply; the dwarven brothers were better at defense than at stealthy attack.

* * * * *

The one guard for the four remaining Night Masks shook his head in disbelief, too, watching the dwarven escapades. He crouched in the tight and smelly chicken coop, one leg up on the wall-to-wall-perching bench, and peered through a crack in the old boards, a crack wide enough for him to level his crossbow and take aim. He figured Ivan for the tougher foe, and thought that if he could take out the dwarf on the ground, the one in the tree would be in serious trouble.

Squawk!

The startled Night Mask spun about frantically and fired, seeing a flurry of movement. The air was full of chickens—one less when the crossbow quarrel cut through—but in the dim light and close quarters, the birds seemed like one ominous, feathered foe to the man.

He got hit twice, on the face and neck, and felt the liquid oozing under his tunic. He grabbed for the wounds, hoping to stop the flow of blood.

The relieved man nearly laughed aloud when he found the blood was really eggs . . . until he realized that someone, behind the barricade of flapping chickens, must have thrown them at him. The man snarled, dropped his crossbow, and drew out a slender dagger.

The chickens quieted quickly. He saw no enemy in the small coop.

The bench, the man thought; his enemy had to be under the bench. His smile disappeared and his mouth dropped open as he started to bend.

Under the bench and, maybe, behind him.

A hand slapped across the man's mouth; another grabbed his weapon hand. His eyes opened wide, then closed tight at the searing pain as his own knife pierced his throat, under the chin, and slid unerringly to his brain.

Danica dropped the man aside and turned to regard the dwarven brothers. Ivan was under the farmhouse window by this time, with Pikel carefully picking steps in the tree right above him. It was a recipe for disaster, Danica knew, and she figured she had better get back outside and into a new position, just in case.

She paused before stepping over the dead assassin and considered the kill. Cadderly had prompted an agreement that no man would be slain if it could be avoided, and Danica, though she, like Ivan, had thought the agreement absurd, felt some pangs of guilt for not honoring the spirit of her lover's wishes. Perhaps she could have taken this guard out without killing him.

Danica felt no sympathy for the man she had killed, though. She, above all the others in her party, understood the motives and methods of the assassin band, and she reserved no mercy for anyone who would don the silver-and-black mask of the amoral guild.

* * * * *

Ivan, directly under the window, looked up in frustration as Pikel sought a secure perch in the tree branch's shaky outer reaches. Finally, when Pikel seemed on solid enough footing, Ivan placed the edge of his axe against the house and ran it slowly down the wall, scraping and bumping over each shingle.

A moment later, a curious face peered out beside the curtain. The man, sword in hand, straightened, seeing nothing there, and gradually peeked over the sill.

"Ha!" he cried, spotting Ivan. Above, a branch cracked.

"Me brother," Ivan explained, pointing up.

"Oh," the confused assassin replied.

"Ooooooo!" Pikel roared, swinging down like a pendulum, his club thick end out, like a fat lance, and securely braced. The man tried to get his sword in front of him, but got slammed in the chest and went flying away as if he had been sitting in the basket of a giant-cranked catapult.

"Come on!" Ivan cried, hopping up to the windowsill and pulling himself in beside his upside-down brother.

Pikel shrugged helplessly; things had not gone exactly as planned. The branch had snapped and Pikel's thick ankle was firmly stuck in a fork, leaving him hanging helplessly.

"Come on," Ivan, now inside the room, said again. He grabbed Pikel's free hand and tugged, dragging the dwarf halfway into the room.

"Uh-uh," Pikel tried to explain.

Thinking his brother was just being stubborn, Ivan dropped his axe, grabbed with both hands, and yanked with all his strength. Pikel came into the room, the bending, grasping branch being pulled in right behind him.

* * * * *

Vander held the barn door firmly, supporting it tightly against its hinges so that it would not creak so loudly as he gingerly cracked it open. He couldn't see the fight at the window from his angle, but he did see the trembling branches of the elm above the corner of the farmhouse roof. That, and the previous squawking of the chickens, told the giant beyond doubt that intruders were about.

Vander stopped, staring incredulously at a ball of fire hovering in the air a few feet above him, just outside the barn door. The firbolg tensed, sensing the danger, sensing that if he moved, the pausing magic would go off.

Why was the spellcaster waiting?

Slowly, Vander leaned back into the barn.

A line of flames roared down from the fireball, scorching the ground at the firbolg's feet. Vander dove to the barn floor, pulling the door closed behind him, fearing that the magic would follow him in.

Black smoke rose from the bottom of the door.

Everything went pitch black.

The stubborn firbolg rose to his feet, knowing that he had to get out the door, out of the trap.

Everything went absolutely silent.

Vander growled and eased one foot in front of the other, toward the door. He had no way of knowing if the flames remained, but he had to find out.

He heard no sound, but it seemed as if the ground rushed up in front of him, twirling dust nipping at his eyes and forcing him to fall back. He tripped over unseen crates and crashed silently to the dirt.

The disoriented firbolg's vision returned in the blink of an eye, the magical darkness dispelled. Vander heard the snap of wood as a plank broke under his hand, and he heard, too, a whirling sound above him that alerted him a moment before he tried to rise.

The firbolg stared helplessly at the air only inches above his head, at the air that had suddenly filled with magical manifestations of whirling blades.

Vander heard the door creak open and looked across his body to see a young man in a wide-brimmed blue hat.

"The blades will cut," the young man said evenly.

The trapped Vander didn't doubt it for a minute.

* * * * *

"Ooooooo!"

Danica, making her way toward the far side of the farmhouse, heard Pikel's cry as the branch holding Pikel flew out of the window.

When the pliable branch reached its end and reversed direction, Pikel's ankle slipped free and the dwarf went sailing, turning a perfect two-and-a-half back somersault to land headfirst into a pile of dust.

"I told ye not to let go!" a frustrated Ivan, holding Pikel's club, shouted from the window.

Pikel shrugged, adjusted his cooking pot, and rushed back to join his brother.

Together, the dwarves crept across the small room. It had two doors, both fortunately closed, one along the wall to their right, and the other directly across from the window, leading to one of the front rooms.

"Makes a nice rug, that one," Ivan remarked, heading for the front room and stepping over the back of the clobbered Night Mask, who was lying spread-eagle and face down on the floor, his arms flung out wide.

Instinctively, Pikel, wearing open sandals, wiggled his gnarly toes as he crossed the man's back behind Ivan, and the green-bearded dwarf nodded, surprised at just how good a rug a clobbered human might make.

"Ye know they know we're here?" Ivan asked when he reached the door.

Pikel quickly shrugged, as though that fact hardly mattered.

Ivan nodded his agreement and looked to the wooden door, his smile widening under his yellow-haired face. "Ye remember the charge at the inn?" he asked slyly.

The door burst from its hinges, crossbows clicked, and Ivan and Pikel, behind the impromptu shield, smiled wickedly to see the two darts protruding through the wood.

"These men is so predictable!" Ivan declared, and he flung the broken door aside, showing the dwarven brothers that they had entered a kitchen.

Pikel swerved left, toward a man caught between the charge and the wall who was trying to squeeze through the room's tight window. Ivan bolted right, in chase after the other assassin, heading for the growing daylight beyond the open door.

Pikel considered the struggling man's predicament for just a moment, then slammed his heavy club at the window's top frame, collapsing it to further ensnare the man.

"Hee hee hee." Thoroughly enjoying himself, the dwarf pulled the kitchen table over, unlaced the man's boots, and retied them around one of the table legs.

The remaining man stopped abruptly and swung about, thinking to catch his dwarven pursuer off guard by the sudden change in tactics.

Ivan was too crafty for that simple trick. He skidded to a halt, lifting his huge axe to easily deflect the slicing sword blade.

The assassin twirled the weapon up above his head and came in again with it, furiously, angling it left then right to poke holes through the dwarf's defenses. He scored a hit on Ivan's side, but Ivan turned with the thrust, pressing the top of his axe against the thin blade and slamming it against the wall.

The assassin fell back, holding only the hilt and first two inches of his snapped sword.

Ivan looked to the severed strap on the side of his armored suit. A single metal plate hung out an inch, but the assassin's hit had not come close to penetrating the dwarf-forged armor.

"Was it worth it?" Ivan asked in all seriousness.

The assassin snarled and flung his broken sword at the impertinent dwarf, then turned and darted out the door.

Ivan batted the missile away and broke into a charge. He dove for the man's ankles but came up short and bumped down off the front of the porch.

The Night Mask never looked back as he rushed for the stable. He leaped atop an unsaddled horse, set the beast into a dead run, and flew over the fence rail.

Ivan groaned, angered that one had escaped, and rolled to his back—and saw Danica kneeling on the farmhouse roof, crossbow loaded and level.

"Ye ever use one of them things?" the surprised dwarf asked.

Danica fired. The fleeing assassin's head snapped forward, the quarrel entering at the base of his skull. He held his seat for a few moments longer, then drifted off the horse's side, dropping to the dust as the steed ran on.

"Yup," answered Pikel, coming to the door behind Ivan.

Twenty-Three
An Offer He Couldn't Refuse

W here's the big one?" Ivan asked when he, Danica, and Pikel found Cadderly standing in the farmyard, leaning against a young tree.

Cadderly pointed to the barn. "He is occupied," the young priest explained wryly, his gray eyes turning up at their corners with his satisfied grin. "Not hurt, but not in any mood to fight back."

Danica nodded. "Then your guess was right," she remarked, her voice unmistakably revealing her distaste. "The band was led by a giant."

Cadderly recalled the images he had seen on the little assassin's shoulder back in the Dragon's Codpiece. The *aurora* change had revealed much to the observant young man, had told him the identity and, more importantly, the demeanor of the assassin band's gigantic leader.

"Dead giant." Ivan snickered hopefully.

"No," Cadderly answered him.

"Soon?" Ivan asked.

"I do not think so," Cadderly replied. The young priest looked around the yard, to the chicken coop, to the window by the tree, and to the corpse lying in the dust by the road. "I did not want these men killed," he remarked sharply.

Ivan looked to Danica. "Better to let that one get away," the dwarf whispered with obvious sarcasm.

Cadderly heard the comment and locked a deep frown on the yellow-bearded dwarf.

"It was a fight, ye . . ." Ivan began to protest, but he threw his thick hands up in disgust, snorted "Bah!" and stomped away. A few strides off, beyond the nearest corner of the house, he caught sight of the lone living Night Mask, wedged tightly in the kitchen window and no longer struggling against the pressing weight.

"There ye go, lad," the dwarf bellowed. "Me brother held out some mercy for yer foolhardy wishes." The other three moved over to join Ivan, to see what the dwarf had discovered.

"What'll ye do with him?" Ivan asked Cadderly when the young priest saw the trapped man. "Do ye have some questions ye need to ask this one? Or are ye going to give him to the city guard, ye merciful fool?"

Cadderly regarded the dwarf curiously, not understanding Ivan's anger. His ensuing question sounded clearly as an accusation. "Are you so eager to kill?"

"What do ye think the city guard'll do with him?" Ivan balked. "Ye forgetting yer fat friend, sprawled across a table with his heart cut out? And what of them that lived in this place? Do ye think the farmer and his family'll be coming back anytime soon?"

Cadderly averted his gaze, stung by the honest words. He preferred mercy, hated killing, but he could not deny Ivan's observations.

"Ye bring us out here and ask us to fight with half our hearts," Ivan blustered, spittle glistening the bottom edges of his thick mustache. "If ye're thinking that I'm one to risk me own neck to give a few more days of life to that scum, then ye're thinking wrong!"

Confusion dictated Cadderly's next move. He brought the song up in the recesses of his mind, heard the flow of Deneirian magic, and found a point where he could join in that sweet river. He had stepped fully into the spirit world several times—in Shilmista Forest, to bid farewell to Elbereth's gallant horse; in the Dragon's Codpiece, to find Brennan's wandering spirit and learn the truth of Avery's heavenly bliss—and now he found the journey short and not so difficult.

As soon as he arrived, as soon as the material world faded into indistinct grayness behind him, he heard the desperate screams of lost souls.

Leaving his corporeal body standing with his unknowing friends, Cadderly willed his spirit toward the corpse lying in the road, the man Danica had shot from the horse. The young priest ended his trek abruptly, though, terrified by the images. Huddled, shadowy things, shapes akin to those growling pools of darkness he had seen on the shoulders of evil men, encircled the doomed assassin's spirit. The dead man noticed Cadderly then and looked to him desperately.

Help me, came his silent plea.

Cadderly did not know what to do. The growling, shadowy things tightened their ring, dark claws reaching out for their victim.

Help me!

Cadderly willed his spirit toward the man, but something, his fears, perhaps, or his knowledge that it was not his place to interfere, held the young priest's spirit firmly in place.

Shadows grabbed the doomed assassin. He twisted and jerked about frantically, but the dark grip did not relent, did not release him.

Help me! The cry tore at Cadderly's heart, horrified him and filled him with sorrow all at once.

The shadows melted into the ground, taking the man's spirit with them. Only the spirit's legs remained visible, kicking futilely.

Then they, too, were gone, pulled down to eternal hell.

Cadderly found himself back in his corporeal form, his eyes open wide, sweat beaded on his forehead.

"What're ye thinking?" Ivan demanded.

"Maybe I was wrong," Cadderly admitted, looking at Danica as he spoke the words, looking for judgment in her knowing gaze.

Danica grabbed him by the arm and put her head on his shoulder. She understood the trial Cadderly had just undergone, the realization once again that war precipitated cruel actions, that their survival against this unmerciful foe demanded a resolve equally vicious.

"But he goes back to the town," Cadderly went on firmly, pointing to the man trapped in the window. "The city guard will decide his fate. He cannot harm us now, and we have no cause to kill him."

Ivan, deadly in battle but certainly no merciless killer, readily agreed. He and Pikel immediately started for the man.

"Not now," Cadderly called to them, turning them about. "Will the window hold him?"

The dwarves turned to study the broken structure.

"For a hunnerd years," Ivan decided.

"Hee hee hee," Pikel chuckled and patted his trusty club, the compliments to his mighty clubbing bringing a blush to his cherubic, fuzzy cheeks.

"Then let it hold him," Cadderly said to them. "We have other business." The young priest turned and nodded to the barn door, realizing that his spell of whirling blades would not last. If they did not get to the giant soon, they would likely wind up in yet another fight.

On Cadderly's command, Ivan and Pikel each took hold of one of the barn doors and pulled it wide. The dwarves remained behind the doors, out of sight, for Cadderly knew that most giants were not particularly fond of the bearded folk and that the sight of the brothers might send this one into a rage that would be quieted only by the monster's death.

Vander wasn't up for any fight, though. Vander wasn't up at all. He lay on his back, helpless below the magically conjured blades. The firbolg lifted his head at the sound of the opening doors and looked across his prone form to see Cadderly and Danica regarding him.

Cadderly studied the giant intently, studied the forms on Vander's shoulders. He saw again the wide mountains, the great boat in the iceberg-dotted bay, and he knew this was the same being (the same spirit at least) that the assassin had switched bodies with when Cadderly and the others had cornered the evil little man.

"I will release you," the young priest promised, "on your word that you will attack neither me nor my companions."

Vander growled at him.

"By my estimation, we have no quarrel with you, mighty giant," Cadderly went on, "and we want none. It may be that I can aid you in your struggle."

The growling stopped, replaced by an honestly perplexed expression.

"Aid it?" Ivan bellowed from behind the shielding door. "Ye didn't say nothing about aiding any stupid giant!" Before Cadderly could react, the dwarf stormed around the barn door, axe in hand, Pikel rushing in from the other side to join him.

"Ivan!" Cadderly started, but Pikel's sincere, "Oo oi!" and the look of amazement on Ivan's face stopped the young priest completely.

"Let him up," Ivan snapped at Cadderly, giving the man a push. "Ye got no cause to keep one o' his kind in the dirt!"

"Well met, good dwarves," the giant said unexpectedly.

Danica and Cadderly exchanged stunned stares and helpless shrugs, Danica blowing away a lock of her hair and blinking.

"Let him up, I say!" Ivan demanded, pushing Cadderly once more. "Can't ye see the flames of his beard?"

Cadderly mouthed the words silently as he regarded the prone giant, wondering what the red color of this one's beard had to do with Ivan's apparent approval of the monster. Cadderly had seen Ivan and Pikel go after giants with wild abandon in Shilmista Forest. What made this one so different?

"He ain't no giant," Ivan explained.

"He looks pretty big to me," the disbelieving Danica remarked.

"He's a firbolg," Ivan answered impatiently, "a friend o' the land—and a friend of the elves. We'll forgive him that, since firbolgs and dwarves get on well, too."

Ivan seemed to be winding up for a long dissertation on the subject of firbolgs, and would have continued, but Cadderly motioned for him to stop, needing nothing further. The images, the *aurora* of this strange giant, made perfect sense to Cadderly now, and he understood, too, beyond any doubts, why one of this being's honorable weal would be in league with an evil wretch.

The giant was a prisoner.

A wave of Cadderly's hand removed the magical blades. Vander growled at the indignity of it all, took up his huge sword, and got to his feet. For a moment, it seemed to Cadderly and Danica that the monster would attack, but Ivan and Pikel, nodding and smiling, walked right into the barn and struck up a conversation—in a voluminous, grumbling language that sounded like the roll of boulders down a rocky mountainside.

The giant, talking with the dwarves, kept his sword up in front of him and seemed even more nervous when Cadderly and Danica joined their companions.

"He's not to trusting us," Ivan whispered to Cadderly. Then, louder, he announced, "His name's Vander."

"If we had wanted you dead, I would have lowered the blades," Cadderly reasoned.

Vander's thick lips curled back, his giant teeth showing white through the red tresses of his beard.

"Don't ye insult the thing!" Ivan warned harshly. "Don't ye ever tell a firbolg that ye could've beaten it unless ye've already beaten it!"

"Where are my associates?" Vander demanded, his huge sword hovering in the air only a few short strides from the companions. Cadderly realized then that the firbolg could probably take one great step forward and cut him in half before he even began to form a defense—and what defense could Cadderly put up against so monstrous a beast, anyway?

"They are dead, except for one," Cadderly answered as firmly as he could, determined to show no signs of weakness, though he was less than confident of how the giant would take the news.

Vander nodded, seeming none too upset.

It was a good sign, Cadderly noted, a piece of the puzzle that fit exactly. "I came here to find you," the young priest explained, "to speak with you about our common enemy."

There, he had put things out in the open. His three friends stared at him, still not in the know about Cadderly's revelations.

"Ghost," Vander replied. "His name is Ghost." Danica and the dwarves looked to each other and shrugged.

"Together we can beat him," Cadderly promised.

Vander snickered, a curious sound indeed, coming from the giant. "You know little of him, Cadderly," he replied.

"I am still alive," Cadderly argued, not surprised at all that the giant had figured out his identity. "Can the same be said for most of Ghost's associates?"

"You know little of him," Vander said again.

"Then tell me."

Cadderly bade his friends to clean up the yard and set a watch from the house. The companions, particularly Danica, didn't seem anxious to leave their friend beside a dangerous giant, but Vander said something to the dwarves in that mountain language, and Ivan immediately took hold of Danica's arm.

"He gave me his word," Ivan explained. "A firbolg never breaks his word." Cadderly's nod further assured his concerned lover, and she left with the dwarves, looking back over her shoulder every step of the way.

"You should be wary," Vander said as soon as the others had left.

Cadderly looked at him curiously, wondering if the giant had just threatened him.

"I will not go against what I have promised," Vander assured him, "but Ghost can take my body when he chooses, and you would be an easy kill if your guard was down."

"Then we must act quickly," Cadderly replied, no tremble in his voice. "I know Ghost took your body and left you in his boots when we had cornered him in the inn. And I know, too, that the possession can be blocked."

Vander shook his head doubtfully.

"Danica, the woman you just met, blocked him," Cadderly replied. "Together, you and I can do the same. I have spells, and this." He held up the amulet he had taken from Rufo in Shilmista Forest, the imp's amulet that Cadderly had claimed as his own, that allowed the young priest to easily contact the mind of another. "The amulet will allow me to join with you in your struggle."

Vander eyed him suspiciously, but Cadderly could see he had at least intrigued the beleaguered giant.

They talked for a short while longer, then went to the farmhouse to coordinate the defenses with the others. They found the dwarves hard at work freeing the captured Night Mask from the broken window.

The man at last slipped back to the kitchen floor, shakily finding his feet. He would have offered no resistance, so obviously outnumbered, except that he spotted Vander out of the corner of his eye, standing beside the outside door. With a jerk, the man pulled free of Ivan's halfhearted hold, punched the surprised dwarf in the eye, and rushed for the door.

"Master!" he cried hopefully.

"That one's going to be trouble," Ivan muttered.

There came a great swoosh as Vander's sword cut the air and cut the man's torso cleanly in half.

"Nope," Pikel said to Ivan, both of the tough dwarves wincing at the gruesome sight.

Vander shrugged against the stunned stares that lingered on him from every direction. "If you knew him as well as I," the firbolg explained, his tone casual, "you would have killed him long before now."

"Not like that," Ivan protested, "not when me and me brother got to clean the mess up!"

Cadderly closed his eyes and fell back out of the room, back to the relative clean of the wider yard. He wondered if he would ever get as accustomed to such violence as his sturdy, battle-hardened companions.

He hoped he would not.

* * * * *

Vander took the companions to the graves of the murdered farm family, explaining grimly that he had, at least, forced the assassins to properly bury the victims.

Danica looked quizzically at Cadderly, and the young priest knew she was wondering if he meant to go straight after the spirits of the departed, to resurrect the family.

Cadderly shook his head, more a gesture for himself than to Danica. Such actions were not so simple, he knew, and he did not have time to make an attempt. Also, Cadderly, still bone-weary from his exhausting use of magic over the previous two days, was determined to save what little power remained in him.

Confident that he would soon be tested again, the young priest decided to open himself to the song only when absolutely necessary.

Besides, the horrible memories of the shadowy things pulling the assassins' doomed souls to eternal torment were too fresh in Cadderly's mind for him to want a return trip to the realm of the dead.

That afternoon, the farm was quiet once more, showing no signs that any trouble had occurred.

Watching the fast-westering sun, Cadderly led the firbolg back to the barn. If Ghost was coming for Vander, telepathically or physically, it might well happen soon.

Cadderly set his spindle-disks spinning, let their crystalline center catch the lamplight and disperse it into a myriad of dancing shapes and flickers. The willing giant slipped in to the hold of the mesmerizing crystal and let Cadderly into his thoughts. Vander put a hand into his pocket and clutched at the amulet Cadderly had given him, as though the closer contact would improve the joining of their minds.

A short while later, Cadderly sat quiet, out of sight, in one of the small stalls within the barn, enjoying the majestic images playing in his mind at the firbolg's mental recounting of his frosty, rugged homeland.

Twenty-Four

Layers of Treachery

The call drifted on the silent winds of the dimension where dwelled only the mind. It drifted inexorably toward the farm on the outskirts of Carradoon and the firbolg that had served for so long as this caller's waiting vessel.

Cadderly sensed the fear in the unseen giant, knew that Ghost had come a-calling.

Stand easy, the young priest imparted telepathically to Vander. *Do not let your fear or your anger block me from our joining.*

Cadderly knew that the profound fear, far beyond what he would have expected from a mighty and proud giant, had not diminished, but Vander mentally reached back to him, strengthening their bond.

Ghost's call meandered in; Cadderly drove it away.

Vander? the distant assassin questioned.

Like a mirror, Cadderly offered no response other than to turn the telepathic question back on the winds.

Vander!

Anger. Cadderly felt that above all else. The young priest smiled in spite of the importance of his task, pleased by the confirmation that he had somewhat unnerved the little assassin.

Then the call was no more, but Cadderly, suspecting the killer who had been so dogged in pursuing him would not give up this important link so easily, did not let his guard down.

Vander hissed; Cadderly heard it distinctly.

"Fight!" the young priest cried, aloud and mentally. Ivan and Pikel moved to the stall door, weapons ready, as Cadderly had instructed. If the assassin found

629

his way into Vander's identity, the dwarves would set upon him before he could sort out his surroundings.

But Cadderly had no intention of letting Ghost in, not while the trickster had his body as an open escape route, safely away in Carradoon. The young priest conjured an image of the spinning spindle-disks, shared it with Vander, and together they studied the hypnotic dance, remembered the specific defensive chants Cadderly had taught the giant.

Other, more evil sensations assaulted them, cluttered their space with the anger of another will. Cadderly prayed that Ghost would not understand the joining, would not realize that Vander had an ally beside him.

Cadderly watched and chanted, and the firbolg, though his anger rose dangerously, managed to keep Cadderly in his mind.

Together, they drove the would-be possessor away.

* * * * *

"You defy me?" Ghost asked in the dark alleyway. Above anything else, the assassin, vulnerable without Vander, knew this type of defiance could not be tolerated. Vander was his out, his desperate escape from any situation. He could not allow the firbolg to somehow, somewhere, find the strength to turn his distant intrusions away.

Somehow? Somewhere?

The little assassin breathed a deep sigh. What was going on at the farm? he wondered. He feared that Cadderly might be involved, but how could that be? Certainly Vander, if an attack had come, would have called out to Ghost? Might Cadderly and his friends have taken the farm so quickly that the firbolg never got the chance?

Ghost dismissed the thought. Vander was still alive; Ghost had recognized the receptacle at the other end of his telepathic call. He told himself he was being paranoid, a dangerous state of mind for a killer living on the edge of artistry and disaster. Vander had denied him before, after all, from a distance, where the *Ghearufu*'s power was not quite the same.

In a few hours, Ghost could call upon the firbolg again and get back in. Vander would not be able to keep up his mental defenses for very long. An evil grin spread across the wicked man's face as he considered the boundless possibilities for punishment.

The smile did not last long. His mind was clouded by doubts. Things were too unusual this time, and there was simply too much at stake for Ghost to readily accept that Vander had found a moment of strength to keep him out. The assassin had not located Cadderly and the young priest's friends in many hours.

"To the farm," the assassin decided quietly. He would go to the farm, punish Vander, and regroup his forces.

He slipped out of the alleyway and approached an armed man sitting comfortably on a fine horse.

"Your pardon, gentle sir," Ghost said meekly to the city guardsman. The assassin was wearing his mismatched gloves.

No need to take chances.

* * * * *

Up on the farmhouse roof, wearing the black-and-silver domino mask and nondescript clothes of a Night Mask, with the cowl of a black cloak pulled low, Danica watched the riders—two men on one horse—moving steadily down the road. The monk leveled her crossbow when the two entered the farmyard. She recognized the man on the back as the same assassin they had found at the Dragon's Codpiece. Danica's first instincts, her initial anger, prompted her to shoot the man from the horse, but Cadderly had warned her against such actions, warned her that the man might not be what he seemed.

Another factor urged Danica to hold her shot: the man in control of the horse wore the uniform of a Carradoon guardsman.

"He is a friend," the assassin on the back of the horse called out, seeing Danica atop the roof.

Danica smiled under the cowl, glad that her disguise had apparently fooled the pair.

"Friend," the guardsman said. He brought the horse into the yard, said something Danica could not hear to the other man, and dismounted, heading straight for the barn.

Danica was confused and worried. Cadderly had expected the weakling assassin to come in and confront Vander, not bring a city guardsman. She still held tight to her crossbow, still wanted to put a quarrel into the evil little man's androgynous face.

To her further surprise, the guardsman did not go into the barn; rather, he moved to the gutter along one corner and began to scale it. He was halfway up the tall structure before the man on the horse took serious note of him, and Danica thought his reaction—wide-eyed and pale—a curious thing.

"What in the Nine Hells is going on?" the young woman whispered quietly. She looked about the yard to see if Ivan or Pikel had slipped out of the barn, to try to discern if anyone inside had any idea about the strange events in the yard.

The guardsman made the edge of the roof. Danica looked up to see him, and she pulled her cowl tighter, fearing that the man had climbed only to give him a better view of her position, a better view of her.

He paid her little heed, though. He wore mismatched gloves and stood on the edge, looking down at his companion, who, by this time, was off the horse.

"You have outlived your usefulness," the guardsman explained. He laughed wildly, clapped his hands, and dove headlong off the roof.

His laughter turned to a shriek, then a groan as he hit, then silence.

Danica breathed hard, not beginning to understand what had just occurred. She looked down to the man standing beside the dead guard, saw that it was he who now wore the strange gloves. He looked up to her, shrugged his shoulders, and bolted for the barn door. By the time he got there, the gloves were gone.

* * * * *

"You resisted my call," Ghost said to Vander. "We have discussed this matter before."

"This kill is . . . ugly," Vander stammered in reply, obviously nervous in facing the man who had been his tormentor for so long. The firbolg gnawed his thick lips under his bushy red beard, wishing that his newfound allies would rush out and end this taunting nightmare.

"I am not speaking of young Cadderly!" Ghost retorted. "He will be dealt with in time, do not doubt. I have come here to speak only with you, the one who dared to resist my call!"

"I did not . . ."

"Silence!" Ghost commanded. "You know that to resist is to be punished. I cannot complete my task with an unwilling associate out here, safely from the town."

Unwilling vessel, Vander corrected, but he wisely held the thought to himself.

Ghost took a few steps across the barn floor, peering out through a crack in the side boards. "Do you remember your brother?" he teased, referring to the firbolg he had killed when Vander had run away from him, had run all the way back to the distant Spine of the World Mountains.

The wicked little assassin turned about, smiling even more widely when he noticed Vander's great hands clenched in helpless rage at the giant's side.

* * * * *

Ivan peeked through a crack in the stall's wall, then looked back, concerned, to Cadderly and Pikel.

The young priest, intent on his telepathic connection with the firbolg, did not notice the dwarf at all. He felt Vander's mounting rage, a blocking emotion that diminished their bond. Things had gone pretty much as Cadderly had expected, but he was no longer certain of how he should react. Even across the miles from Carradoon, Ghost's intrusion had been difficult to fend off. How would he and Vander fare now, with the sneaky assassin standing just a few feet in front of the firbolg?

Calm, he imparted to the firbolg. *You must remain calm.*

* * * * *

"Punishment," Ghost purred, putting one finger to his pursed lips. He fingered something in his other hand, something round and gold, though Vander could not discern exactly what it might be.

"I never told you this before," the assassin went on, smoothly, "but I did more to your son, poor boy, than take his arm."

Vander's eyes widened. His great hands twitched, trembled, and his roar shook the walls of the wooden barn.

"Time to go?" Ivan dared to ask aloud under the cover of that prolonged growl.

Cadderly's mind was filled with a wall of red, the manifestation of Vander's uncontrollable rage. The young priest was out of contact with the firbolg, he knew, and he knew, too, that by the time he managed to contact his ally once more, the disaster might well be complete. He uncoiled his legs beneath him and accepted Pikel's arm to hoist him to his feet. Neither his spindle-disks nor his enchanted walking stick offered him much hope in defeating a giant, so he clenched his hand, the hand with the enchanted ring, and reached inside his cloak for the wand.

"No!" he cried out, leading the dwarves into the main area of the barn. Cadderly calmed immediately, though, as did Ivan and Pikel behind him, when he regarded the scene, a scene that Vander apparently had well in control.

The firbolg, panting and growling, held the puny assassin in the air by the throat, shaking him hard, though the man was obviously already dead.

"Vander," Cadderly said quietly to calm the giant's rage.

The firbolg paid him no heed. With another roar of outrage, he folded the assassin in half, backward, and hurled him against the barn wall.

"He will return!" the giant wailed. "Always, he comes back for me! There can be no escape!"

"Like a damned troll," Ivan remarked from beside the firbolg, his voice reflecting sympathy for the beleaguered giant.

"Troll?" Cadderly whispered, the word inspiring an idea.

The young priest held his clenched fist out before him, barked the word, "*Fete!*" and sent a line of fire at the corpse.

He kept his concentration firm, determined to burn whatever regenerative powers he could from the wretch, determined that Vander would at last be free. He glanced sidelong at the firbolg, took note of Vander's satisfied expression, then noticed, curiously, that Vander was wearing a golden ring.

Curious indeed, Cadderly thought as he turned back to the charred body, for he was just thinking of looking for such an item on Ghost's blackened form.

Cadderly searched his memory in an instant; Vander had worn no rings.
Aurora.

"Ivan!" Cadderly cried, ending his flames and spinning about. The giant moved as well, whipping out his huge sword, with Ivan standing unsuspecting right beside it.

Cadderly proved the quicker. "*Mas illu!*" he screamed as he drew the wand. A burst of colors exploded in the firbolg's face. Blinded, the giant continued his swing, aiming for where Ivan had been.

The dwarf, warned and then blinded by the blast, fell back. He heard the tremendous rush of air as the sword passed, taking off his helmet and clipping him enough to send him into a roll.

"I knew I'd get me chance!" the stubborn dwarf growled when he at last righted himself. Never shying from a fight, Ivan took up his axe and charged back in.

Danica slipped into the barn, discerned immediately what was going on, and fired a quarrel into the firbolg's belly.

The giant howled in pain but was not deterred from parrying Pikel's power- ful charge, deflecting the overbalanced dwarf to the side, where he collided with a beam.

The giant feigned a sword thrust, then kicked out instead, sweeping Ivan aside once more.

Another quarrel caught him, this time in the shoulder, but again he seemed to hardly take note of it.

Danica was back at the door, Ivan and Pikel off to the sides, leaving Cadderly as the closest target. The young priest's first instincts told him to use his ring, to drive the beast back with a line of flame until his friends could regroup.

He realized the grim consequences for Vander, though, for the poor, proud fir- bolg who had been trapped in the weakling body and tossed aside like so much garbage. The magical ring had no power to restore burned flesh, and if this body was charred, like the assassin's corpse across the room, the firbolg would never reclaim it.

The giant lurched, popped in the back of the knee by Pikel's rebounding charge. With a grunt, the beast reached around and grabbed the green-bearded dwarf, hoisting him up into the air.

Pikel stared into the outraged giant's bloodshot eyes, then promptly stuffed his foot up the beast's flaring nostril and waggled his gnarly and smelly dwarf toes.

Half-sneezing, half-coughing, the disgusted giant hurled Pikel into the far wall and wiped his arm across his face. When he looked back at Cadderly, he found himself staring down the end of that slender wand. Thinking another attack forthcoming, Ghost snapped his eyes shut.

"*Illu*," Cadderly said calmly, and the whole barn lit up with the brightness of a midday sun in an open field. Cadderly's aim had been perfect, though, and soon the glow of his wand's magic restricted itself to the firbolg's face, particularly to the giant's eyes.

Whiteness? When Ghost opened his eyes, he saw only whiteness, glaring and blinding. The whole damned world had gone white! Or perhaps, Ghost won- dered, more curious than afraid, he had been transported to some other place.

Another stinging crossbow bolt dove into his belly, driving that notion away.

The roar shook the walls once more, and the light-blind giant charged ahead, toward the unseen bowman, flailing his sword wildly. He slammed into the edge of the open barn door, dislodged the thing, and continued out.

Danica danced quickly away, determining her role in this fight. Another quarrel sliced into the giant, lured him ahead.

Ghost felt a club slam the back of his knee again, this time slipping through his great legs and tripping him as he tried to spin and react. Down the giant sprawled, shattering a water trough with his face and arms.

Something heavy and sharp, an axe, perhaps, sliced into his ankle; a crossbow quarrel entered his shoulder, clicking off his huge collarbone.

Somehow the stubborn wretch managed to stand and stagger forward. His already wounded ankle took a hit from the heavy club.

He turned about, sword leading, but the dwarf was already out of reach and the mighty weapon smacked hard against a small tree, uprooting it. Growling with rage, Ghost heard scuffling feet as the enemy continued to flank him, to encircle him.

He tried to call for the *Ghearufu*, even though he knew his own body was inaccessible, and knew that, even if he managed to hold enough concentration to summon the thing, Cadderly would somehow follow his spirit's movements. He couldn't get to it anyway; the hits were coming too fast, from every direction.

He jerked about, one way and then another, leading with his low-cutting sword each time. Fury became his only defense, and he was confident that he was swift enough to keep his enemies at bay. Only weariness would slow him, and he hoped he could continue the blind assault until the infernal whiteness left his eyes.

Another quarrel whistled in, taking the giant in the lung this time, and Ghost heard the wheeze of his life's-breath spurting out through a bloody hole.

He swung again, and again, frantic and dizzy. He overbalanced, roaring and wheezing. He tried to step forward, but his badly gashed ankle would no longer support him, and he lurched ahead, bending low.

Right in line for the waiting Ivan.

The axe chopped into the firbolg's backbone; Ghost felt the burning flash, then felt nothing at all below his waist. His momentum carried him one more long step forward, an awkward gait on stiff, unsupporting legs, and he tumbled and turned, crashing hard into the base of the huge elm at the side of the house.

There was only whiteness, pain, numbness.

Ghost heard the three friends shuffle near him but had not the strength to lift his sword in defense. Above all else, he heard the bloody wheeze at his side.

"Got him," Ivan remarked as Cadderly rushed up to join his friends. "Ye wanting us to tie him down afore ye talk with him?"

The young priest, stone-faced, did not reply, understanding that the loss of a physical body did not end the threat of Ghost's evil. He walked to the side of the helpless giant, took his spindle-disks in hand, and hurled them with all his strength right into the firbolg's temple.

The battered monster jerked once, weirdly, then slipped to the ground at the side of the tree.

Danica, holding her crossbow low, gaped openmouthed at her lover's uncharacteristic lack of mercy.

"Take out your bolts," Cadderly instructed her, "but do not remove his ring!"

The last image the young priest saw was that of his friends exchanging confused glances, but he had no time to explain.

Spirits were waiting for him.

* * * * *

Cadderly followed the flow of Deneir's song into the netherworld without hesitation. The material world blurred to him; his friends appeared as indistinct gray blobs. As he had expected, the young priest saw the spirit of Ghost sitting near the fallen giant's body—on one of the lower limbs of the elm, actually—the spirit's head resting in its translucent palm, waiting patiently for the magical ring to open the receptacle for its return.

Cadderly knew then that he had two choices: go back and remove the giant's ring, or go and find the rightful owner of the soon-to-be-restored body. He willed himself to the barn, leaving his corporeal body standing impassively beside his friends.

Vander's spirit crouched inside the barn, terribly afraid and uncertain.

You also? came his thoughts to Cadderly.

I am not dead, Cadderly explained, and he beckoned for the firbolg to follow him, showed his lost friend what he must do.

Together, the two spirits set upon Ghost with a vengeance. They could do no real damage to the assassin's ghost, but they mentally pushed him away, combined their wills to create a spirit wind that increased the distance between the evil spirit and the recovering body.

You'll not stop me, the wretch's spirit told them, its thoughts burning into their minds.

Cadderly looked back, saw a glowing ring form beside the firbolg's massive form. *Go,* he bade Vander.

The giant's spirit rushed away; Ghost's spirit followed quickly.

Cadderly held up a hand. *No,* he commanded, and Ghost slowed almost to a stop as he passed the young priest's mental barrier. Cadderly's spirit arms wrapped about him, further delaying him, and the young priest, both his corporeal and spirit forms, smiled as Vander's spirit narrowed like a flying arrow and slipped through the glowing ring, entering the waiting giant form.

You are lost, Cadderly told the assassin, releasing his mental hold.

Ghost didn't hesitate; he rushed for the only other waiting, spiritless receptacle.

* * * * *

"Shave me if this one ain't alive again!" Ivan growled, lifting his axe dangerously above the firbolg's head. "He lifts one o' them big arms, and I'm gonna give him a headache . . ."

Danica grabbed the dwarf's arm to quiet him, explaining that the firbolg, alive or not, was in no position to threaten anyone. The reassurance sent Pikel skittering up beside the giant head, the curious dwarf bending low to watch the reawakening.

A strange mewing sound from Cadderly turned them all about. The young priest's body trembled, one eye twitched wildly, and his mouth contorted as if he were trying to say something but could not control his actions.

Ghost had gotten there first, had slipped into Cadderly's waiting shell. Cadderly rushed in right behind, felt the burning pain of rematerializing, and felt, too, that he was not alone.

"*Get out!*" he finally managed to shout, aloud and telepathically. Ghost did not respond, other than to push at Cadderly's spirit. The young priest felt the burn begin again and knew it signified that he was slipping back out of his form.

But to be pushed out then was to lose himself forever. Cadderly called on his recollections of mental battle, of his experience with the imp, Druzil, back in the forest, and called, too, upon the song of Deneir, hoping to find in its notes some clue that would give him an edge.

But Ghost, too, had experiences to call upon—three lifetimes of exchanging spirits with unwilling victims.

What it came down to was a test of willpower, a test of mental strength.

Ghost didn't have a chance.

"*Out!*" Cadderly screamed. He saw his friends, clearly for a moment, then slipped back to the spirit world and saw Ghost's stunned form, floating helplessly away.

You have not won, came the defiant assassin's promise.

Your connections are gone now, Cadderly argued. *You have no magical ring upon a corpse to give you a hold in the material world.*

I have the Ghearufu, the sinister spirit retorted. *You cannot know its strength! There will be other victims about, foolish priest, weaklings who will lose out to me. And then I will come again for you! Know that I will come again for you!*

The threat weighed heavily on Cadderly, but he didn't believe Ghost's promises were likely. A black spot appeared on the ground, accompanied by a growl, confirming Cadderly's suspicions.

Your connections to the material world are gone now, Cadderly reiterated, seeing the other spirit's confusion.

What is it? Ghost cried to Cadderly, his panic showing clearly.

A black hand shot up from the ground, grabbed the evil spirit's ankle, and held it fast. Frantic, Ghost struggled to pull away, the effort tripping him to a sitting position.

Black hands grabbed his wrists; growling shadows rose all about him.

* * * * *

Cadderly blinked his eyes open to see his concerned friends, Danica and Ivan holding him by the arms, and Pikel studying his face. He felt unsteady, thoroughly drained, and was glad for the support.

"Eh?" the green-bearded dwarf piped curiously.

"I am all right," Cadderly assured them, though his shaky voice weakened his claim considerably. He looked to Danica, and she smiled, knowing beyond doubt that it was indeed Cadderly standing before her.

"The giant's alive again," Ivan said with wonder.

"It is truly Vander," Cadderly assured them. "He returned through the power of the ring." He drew a deep breath to stop the world from swimming in front of his eyes. His head throbbed more painfully than he ever remembered.

"To the barn," he instructed, and he stepped out of Danica and Ivan's grasp and took a step forward.

He pitched sidelong to the dirt, overcome.

* * * * *

It took the young priest many minutes to orient himself when he again found consciousness. He was in the barn—the stench of burned flesh told him that more than the blurry images dancing before his half-opened eyes.

Cadderly blinked and rubbed his bleary orbs. His three friends were with him; he realized he had not been unconscious for very long.

"They just appeared," Danica explained to him, leading his gaze to the items—a small, gold-edged mirror and mismatched gloves adorning the charred and broken corpse by the wall.

"*Ghearufu,*" Cadderly said, remembering the name Ghost had given the thing. The young priest stared closely at the item, felt a sensation of brooding, hungry evil. He looked around to his friends, concerned. "Have any of you handled it?"

Danica shook her head. "Not as yet," she replied. "We have decided that the best course of action would be to bring the item to the Edificant Library for further study."

Cadderly thought differently, but he nodded, deciding it best not to argue. "Has the firbolg awakened?" he asked.

"That one'll be out for days," Ivan answered.

Again, Cadderly thought differently. He understood the regenerative powers of the magical ring and was not surprised, a moment later, when Vander, hearing the discussion, walked into the barn.

"Shave me," Ivan whispered under his breath.

"Oo oi," Pikel agreed.

"Welcome back," Cadderly greeted the giant. "You are free from Ghost—you know that—and you are free, too, to go your way. We shall escort you as far as the Snowflakes—"

"You should not make such an offer so easily," the firbolg's resonant voice interrupted, and Cadderly wondered if he had misjudged the giant, if perhaps Vander was not so innocent after all. The others were apparently thinking the same thing, for Ivan and Pikel put their hands to their weapons, preparing for another fight.

Vander smiled at them all and made no move toward his great sword, belted at his side. "I know where lies Castle Trinity, your true enemy," the firbolg explained, "and I pay my debts."

Epilogue

T he temple priests regarded Cadderly and his three companions curiously as they made their bouncing way to the guest rooms.

Rufo heard the racket and opened his door to see what was going on.

"Hello to yerself, too," Ivan growled at him, putting a hand on the angular man's chest and shoving him back into his small room. The other three came in right after the dwarf, Danica closing the door behind her.

"Are you surprised to see me . . . alive?" Cadderly asked, sweeping his blue cape dramatically from his broad shoulders.

Rufo stammered the beginnings of several words, not really knowing where to begin this unexpected conversation. Dozens of questions and fears assaulted him, stealing his voice. How much did Cadderly know or suspect? he wondered. Where was the young wizard, or the rest of the killers?

"The assassins are no more," Cadderly told him confidently, as if reading Rufo's thoughts. "And the young wizard, too, is dead."

"Got that one good," Ivan whispered to his brother, and Pikel gave the great axe, strapped to Ivan's back, a respectful pat.

"Dead," Cadderly reiterated, letting the word hang in the air ominously, "like Avery."

Rufo's chalky, sharp-featured face paled even more. Again he started to reply, to concoct some lie about the headmaster's fate, some tale that would allow him an alibi for his crimes.

"We know," Danica assured him before he got the first words past his thin, dry lips.

"I did not expect this of you," Cadderly said, hooking his walking stick into the crook of his elbow. "Even after the events at the library and in

Shilmista, I trusted that you would find a better path to tread."

Rufo ran his bony fingers through his matted black hair. His beady, dark eyes darted all about. "I do not know what you are referring to," he managed to say. "When Avery was found dead, I decided that I, too, would not be safe at the inn. I searched for you, but you were not to be found, so I came here, to be among my friends of Ilmater."

"You were afraid?" Danica asked sarcastically. "Did you fear your cohorts would cheat you?"

"I do not understand," Rufo stuttered.

Danica slapped him across the face, knocking him to a sitting position on his bed. The monk started forward, her expression an angry grimace, but Cadderly quickly intercepted her.

"Why else would you be afraid?" Cadderly asked Rufo, to clarify Danica's last statement. "If not for your cohorts, then who would threaten you?"

"He knew we'd catch him," Ivan put in, grabbing Rufo's arm with an ironlike grasp.

"You err!" Rufo stammered desperately. All the world seemed to be closing in on him. Ivan's clenching hand felt like the jaws of a wolf trap. "I did—"

"Silence!" The command from Cadderly quieted the blustering man immediately and turned his friends' incredulous stares to him. Rufo slumped in his seat and lowered his eyes, thoroughly defeated.

"You led Avery to his death," Cadderly accused him bluntly. "You betrayed me in the library, your friends in the forest, and now Avery. Do not expect forgiveness this time, Kierkan Rufo! The headmaster is dead—his blood is on your hands—and you have crossed into an area from which there is no return." Images of those awful, growling shadows assaulted Cadderly. He closed his eyes and took a few deep breaths to steady himself but found himself imagining Rufo's impending fate, of the hungry, evil things that would drag the fallen priest down to eternal torment.

Cadderly shuddered and opened his eyes. "Hold him," he instructed the dwarves.

"What are you doing?" Rufo demanded as Pikel grabbed the arm opposite the one Ivan held and the two locked him steady on the bed. "My friends will hear! They will not allow this!"

"Ilmater?" Ivan queried. "Ain't them the ones dedicated to suffering?"

"Yup," his brother answered.

"Well, with the hollering ye're about to do," Ivan snickered to Rufo, thoroughly enjoying the angular man's distress, "they're likely to build a statue to ye."

Rufo bit Pikel on the arm, but the tough dwarf just grimaced and did not let go. Danica was around the bed in an instant. She grabbed Rufo's hair and jerked his head back viciously. Between that strong hold, and the dwarves at either side of him, Rufo could only watch and listen.

Cadderly was chanting quietly, his hands moving through specific motions. He extended one finger to point toward Rufo, its end glowing white with heat.

"No!" Rufo cried. "You must let me explain!"

"No more lies," Danica hissed from behind.

Rufo screamed and twisted helplessly as Cadderly's enchanted digit branded his forehead, burned the curse of Deneir—the likeness of a single, broken candle above a closed eye—into the man's skin.

It was over in mere seconds, and Danica and the dwarves let Rufo go. He slumped forward, whimpering, not so much for the continuing pain (there was little), but for the knowledge of what Cadderly had just done to him.

Branded. He smelled the foul odor and knew it would follow him, would magically ward people away from him, for the rest of his days.

"You must never hide your mark of shame," Cadderly said to him. "You are aware of the consequences."

Indeed, Kierkan Rufo was. To hide the lawful brand of Deneir caused the lingering magic to burn deeper into one's forehead, to burn to the brain, resulting in a horrible, agonizing death.

Rufo turned an angry gaze up at Cadderly. "How dare you?" he growled with every ounce of defiance he could muster. "You are no headmaster. You have no power—"

"I could have given you over to the city guard," Cadderly interrupted, the simple logic cutting Rufo short. "Even now I could tell them of your crimes and let them hang you in the street. Would that be preferable?"

Rufo looked away.

"If you doubt my ranking in the order," Cadderly continued, "doubt that I have the power to cast such judgment over you, then simply cover the brand. We will learn soon enough if you are correct." Cadderly removed his wide-brimmed hat and held it out to Rufo. "Let us see," he prompted confidently.

Rufo shoved the hat aside and staggered to his feet.

"Highest Priest," he said hopefully when his door opened and a thick-jowled, bald-headed priest, wearing the red skullcap denoting high rank in the Ilmater order, peered in. Behind the man stood a dozen or more disciples of the temple, aroused by Rufo's agonized screams.

"They heared his yells and thinked he joined their order," Ivan whispered to Danica and Pikel, and the three, despite the gravity of the situation, could not hide their chuckles.

The Ilmater priest sniffed the air, his face twisting against the foul smell. He looked hard at Rufo, at the brand, then turned to Cadderly and asked, no anger in his tone, "What has transpired?"

"They have betrayed me!" Rufo cried desperately. "They—he—" he pointed to Cadderly, "—led Headmaster Avery Schell to his death! And now he tries to blame me, to divert attention from himself!"

Cadderly did not grow excited at the ridiculous claim.

"Would Deneir have granted me the magical brand if the tale rang at all of truth?" he asked the Ilmater priest.

"Is it authentic?" the lean priest asked, motioning to the wicked mark.

"Do you care to test it?" Cadderly asked Rufo, again extending his hat. Rufo stared at it for a very long time, at the Deneirian holy symbol set in its front center, knowing this to be the critical point in his life. He could not accept the hat and put it on—to do so would bring about his death. But refusing strengthened Cadderly's claims, showed Rufo to be an honestly branded outcast. He paused for a long moment, trying to concoct yet another excuse.

His hesitation cost him any chance of explaining.

"Kierkan Rufo, you must be gone from here," the Ilmater priest demanded. "Never again shall you be welcomed in any hall of Ilmater. Never again shall any priest of our order show you any kindness or respect."

The finality of the words sounded like a peg in Rufo's coffin. He knew there would be no point in arguing, that the decision was final. He turned, as if to move for his chest of belongings, but the Ilmater priest would brook no delays.

"Now!" the man shouted. "Your possessions will be dumped into the alley. Be gone!"

Ivan and Pikel, always ready to lend a hand, grabbed Rufo by the arms and roughly heaved him forward. Of the many witnesses, not a single one offered a word of protest.

Branded priests had no allies.

* * * * *

Cadderly had only one more task to complete before he would consider his business in Carradoon at its end, and he found assistance from a local cleric residing outside the lakeside city's tall walls. The aged priest led Cadderly and his four companions—with Vander traveling in his magically reduced state, as a red-haired and red-bearded barbarian warrior—to a small grave in the churchyard.

Cadderly fell to his knees before the grave, not at all surprised, but filled with pity and grief.

"Poor dear," the gentle old priest explained. "She went out in search of her lost husband and found him, dead, on the side of the road. Alas for Jhanine and her children." The priest waited a few moments, then nodded to the companions and took his leave.

"You knew this man?" a perplexed Danica asked, crouching beside Cadderly.

Cadderly nodded slowly, hardly hearing her.

Danica took Cadderly's arm. "Will you go for him?" she asked, a bit sourly, but with all sympathy.

Cadderly turned to her, but his eyes were looking to the past, to his exchange on the road with the unfortunate leper. *Could you cure them all?* Nameless had asked him. *Are all the world's ills to fall before this young priest of Deneir?*

"This makes no sense, and borders on irreverence," Danica remarked, misconstruing Cadderly's silence. "Where next after here? To the graves of the unfortunate farmers and the city guardsman?"

Cadderly closed his eyes and withdrew from Danica's stinging logic. He had already tried to resurrect the farmers, and the unfortunate guardsman, privately, before they had left the farm. The spirits of the farmers were not to be found, and the guardsman would not come to Cadderly's call. The effort had cost Cadderly dearly, exhausted him and taken, he knew, a little bit of his life energy forever.

"How many thousands will Cadderly recall to populate the world?" he heard Danica ask. He knew her sarcasm was not intended to be mean, only practical.

He knew Danica could not understand. This act of resurrection was not as simple as it had seemed when Cadderly had brought Brennan back from the dead. Cadderly had come to learn, painfully, that resurrection was a God-given blessing, not a magical spell. Whatever powers the young priest possessed, he could not defeat ultimate fate. Many conditions had to be met before resurrection could be granted, and many more before the spirits of the dead would heed the call and return to the world they had departed. So many conditions, and Cadderly couldn't even begin to sort through them, couldn't begin to question the divine decisions beyond his mortal understanding.

Wisely, he did not ask Deneir to grant him this act.

"My powers are for the living," he whispered, and Danica quieted, confident that he had come to understand what must be. He said a prayer for Nameless, a plea to whatever gods might be listening to judge the lost man fairly, to grant him the peace in death that had been so unfairly stolen from him in life.

Cadderly never did learn the beggar man's real name and he preferred it that way. He and his friends went back to the priest who had shown them the grave, bearing a fair amount of gold they could spare for the deserving Jhanine, but it was Vander who threw in the largest gift: Aballister's purse of gold, the advance sum given the Night Masks for Cadderly's execution.

"Do you mean to cure the ills of the world?" Danica asked Cadderly again, after the companions had left the priest's small house beside the graveyard. She looked to him pleadingly, fearful for her love, fearful that this new weight of responsibility would break him.

"I will do what I can," Cadderly replied stubbornly. "It is the most that can be asked of us, and the least that any of us should be willing to give."

A chill breeze blew in from the west, a reminder that winter was not far away. Cadderly looked into it, sought the lines of trails on the distant Snowflake Mountains, the paths that led to the Edificant Library.

Maybe it was time to go home.

The Cleric Quintet • Book Four

The Fallen Fortress

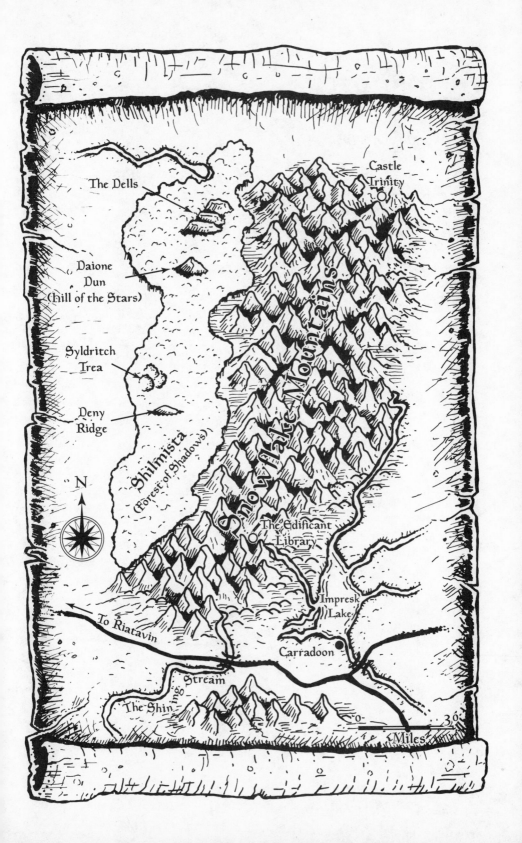

Prologue

Aballister walked along Lakeview Street in Carradoon, the wizard's black cloak wrapped tight against his skin-and-bones body to ward off the wintry blows whipping in from Impresk Lake. He had been in Carradoon less than a day, but had already learned of the wild events at the Dragon's Codpiece. Cadderly, his estranged son and nemesis, had apparently escaped the assassin band Aballister had sent to kill him.

Aballister chuckled at the thought, a wheezing sound from lips withered by decades of uttering frantic enchantments, channeling so many tingling energies into destructive purposes. Cadderly had escaped? Aballister mused, as though the thought was preposterous. Cadderly had done more than escape. With his friends, the young priest had obliterated the Night Mask contingent, more than twenty professional killers, and had also slain Bogo Rath, Aballister's second underling in the strict hierarchy of Castle Trinity.

All the common folk of Carradoon were talking about the exploits of the young priest from the Edificant Library. They were beginning to whisper that Cadderly might be their hope in these dark times.

Cadderly had become more than a minor problem for Aballister.

The wizard took no fatherly pride in his son's exploits. Aballister had designs on the region, intentions to conquer it given to him by the avatar of the evil goddess Talona. Just the previous spring, those intentions appeared easy to fulfill, with Castle Trinity's force swelling to over eight thousand warriors, wizards and Talonan priests included. But then Cadderly had unexpectedly stopped Barjin, the mighty priest who had gone after the heart of the region's goodly strength, the Edificant Library. The following season, Cadderly had led the elves of Shilmista Forest in the west to a stunning victory over the goblinoid and giantkin forces, chasing a sizable number of Castle Trinity's minions back to their mountain holes.

Even the Night Masks, possibly the most dreaded assassin band in the central Realms, had not been able to stop Cadderly. Now winter was fast approaching, the first snows had already descended over the region, and Castle Trinity's invasion of Carradoon would have to wait.

The afternoon light had grown dim when Aballister turned south on the Boulevard of the Bridge, passing through the low wooden buildings of the lakeside town. He crossed through the open gates of the city's cemetery and cast a simple spell to locate the unremarkable grave of Bogo Rath. He waited for the night to fully engulf the land, drew a few runes of protection in the snow and mud around the grave, and pulled his cloak up tighter against the deathly cold.

When the lights of the city went down and the streets grew quiet, the wizard began his incantation, his summons to the netherworld. It went on for several minutes, with Aballister attuning his mind to the shadowy region between the planes, attempting to meet the summoned spirit halfway. He ended the spell with a simple call: "Bogo Rath."

The wind seemed to focus around the withered wizard, collecting the nighttime mists in a swirling pattern, enshrouding the ground above the grave.

The mists parted suddenly, and the apparition stood before Aballister. Though less than corporeal, it appeared quite like Aballister remembered the young Bogo—straight and stringy hair flipped to one side, eyes darting inquisitively, suspiciously, one way and the other. There was one difference, though, something that made even hardy Aballister wince. A garish wound split the middle of Bogo's chest. Even in the near darkness, Aballister could see past the apparition's ribs and lungs to its spectral backbone.

"An axe," Bogo's mournful, drifting voice explained. He placed a less-than-tangible hand into the wound and flashed a gruesome smile. "Would you like to feel?"

Aballister had dealt with conjured spirits a hundred times and knew that he could not feel the wound even if he wanted to, knew that this was simply an apparition, the last physical image of Bogo's torn body. The spirit could not harm the wizard, could not even touch the wizard, and by the binding power of Aballister's magical summons, it would answer truthfully a certain number of Aballister's questions. Still, Aballister unconsciously winced again and took a cautious step backward, revolted by the thought of putting his hand in that wound.

"Cadderly and his friends killed you," Aballister began.

"Yes," Bogo answered, though Aballister's words had been a statement, not a question. The wizard silently berated himself for being so foolish. He would only be allowed a certain number of inquiries before the dweomer dissipated and the spirit was released. He reminded himself that he must take care to word his statements so that they could not be interpreted as questions.

"I know that Cadderly and his friends killed you, and I know that they eliminated the assassin band," he declared. The apparition seemed to smile, and

Aballister was not certain whether the clever thing was baiting him to waste another question or not. The wizard wanted to go on with the intended leading conversation, but he couldn't resist that bait.

"Are all . . ." he began slowly, trying to find the quickest way to discern the fate of the entire assassin band. Aballister wisely paused, deciding to be as specific as possible and end this part of the discussion efficiently. "Which of the assassins still live?"

"Only one," Bogo answered obediently. "A traitorous firbolg named Vander."

Again, the inescapable bait. "Traitorous?" Aballister repeated. "Has this Vander joined with our enemies?"

"Yes—and yes."

Damn, Aballister mused. Complications. Always there seemed to be complications where his troublesome son was concerned. "Have they gone for the library?" he asked.

"Yes."

"Will they come for Castle Trinity?"

The spirit, beginning to fade away, did not answer, and Aballister realized that he had erred, for he had asked the apparition a question which required supposition, a question which could not, at that time, be positively answered.

"You are not dismissed!" the wizard cried, trying desperately to hold onto the less than corporeal thing. He reached out with hands that slipped right through Bogo's fading image, reached out with thoughts that found nothing to grasp.

Aballister stood alone in the graveyard. He understood that Bogo's spirit would come back to him when it found the definite answer to the question. But when would that be? Aballister wondered. And what further mischief would Cadderly and his friends cause before Aballister found the information he needed to put an end to that troublesome group?

"Hey, you there!" came a call from the boulevard, followed by the sounds of boots clapping against the cobblestone. "Who's in the cemetery after nightfall? Hold where you are!"

Aballister hardly took notice of the two city guardsmen who rushed through the cemetery gate, spotting him and making all haste toward him. The wizard was thinking of Bogo, of dead Barjin, once Castle Trinity's most powerful cleric, and of dead Ragnor, Castle Trinity's principle fighter. More than that, the wizard was thinking of Cadderly, the perpetrator of all his troubles.

The guardsmen were nearly upon Aballister when he began his chant. He threw his arms out high to the sides as they closed in and started to reach for him. A cry of the final, triggering rune sent the two men flying wide, hurled through the air by the released power of the spell, as Aballister, in the blink of an eye, sent his material body cascading back to his private room in Castle Trinity.

The dazed city soldiers pulled themselves from the wet ground, looked to each other in disbelief, and fled back through the cemetery gates, convinced that they would be better off if they pretended that nothing at all had happened in the eerie graveyard.

* * * * *

Cadderly sat upon the flat roof of a jutting two-story section of the Edificant Library, watching the sun spread its shining fingers across the plains east of the mountains. Other fingers stretched down from the tall peaks all about Cadderly's position to join those snaking up from the grass. Mountain streams came alive, glittering silver, and the autumn foliage, brown and yellow, red and brilliant orange, seemed to burst into flame.

Percival, the white squirrel, hopped along the roof's gutter when he caught sight of the young priest, and Cadderly nearly laughed aloud when he regarded the squirrel's eagerness to join him—a desire emanating from Percival's always grumbling belly, Cadderly knew. He dropped his hand into a pouch on his belt and pulled out some cacasa nuts, scattering them at Percival's feet.

It all seemed so normal to the young priest, the same as it had always been. Percival skipped happily among his favorite nuts, and the sun continued to climb, defeating the chill of late autumn even this high up in the Snowflakes.

Cadderly saw through the facade, though. Things most certainly were not normal, not for the young priest and not for the Edificant Library. Cadderly had been on the road, in the elven wood of Shilmista and in the town of Carradoon, fighting battles, learning firsthand the realities of a harsh world, and learning, too, that the priests of the library, men and women he had looked up to for his entire life, were not as wise or powerful as he had once believed.

The single notion that dominated young Cadderly's thoughts as he sat up there on the sunny roof was that something had gone terribly wrong within his order of Deneir, and within the order of Oghman priests, the brother hosts of the library. It seemed to Cadderly that procedure had become more important than necessity, that the priests of the library had been paralyzed by mounds of useless parchments when decisive action was needed.

And those rotting roots had sunk even deeper, Cadderly knew. He thought of Nameless, the pitiful leper he had met on the road from Carradoon. Nameless had come to the library for help and had found that the priests of Deneir and Oghma were, for the most part, more concerned with their own failure to heal him than with the consequences of his grave affliction.

Yes, Cadderly decided, something was very wrong at his precious library. He lay back on the gray, slightly pitched roof and casually flipped another nut at the munching squirrel.

One

No Time for Guilt

The spirit heard the call from a distance, floating across the empty grayness of this reeking and forlorn plane. The mournful notes said not a discernible word, and yet, to the spirit, they seemed to speak his name.

Ghost. Clearly it called to him, beckoned him from the muck and mire of his eternal hell. *Ghost*, its melody called again. The wretch looked at the growling, huddled shadows all about him, wicked souls, the remains of wicked people. He, too, was a growling shadow, a tormented thing, suffering punishments for a life villainously lived.

But now he was being called, being carried from his torment on the notes of a familiar melody.

Familiar?

The thin thread that remained of ghost's living consciousness strained to better recall, to better remember its life before this foul, empty existence. Ghost thought of sunlight, of shadows, of killing. . . .

The *Ghearufu*! Evil Ghost understood. The *Ghearufu*, the magical item he had carried in life for so many decades, was calling to him, was leading him back from the very hellfires!

* * * * *

"Cadderly! Cadderly!" wailed Vicero Belago, the Edificant Library's resident alchemist, when he saw the young priest and Danica at his door on the huge library's third floor. "My boy, it's so good that you have returned to us!" The wiry man virtually hopped across his shop, weaving in and out of tables covered with beakers and vials, dripping coils and stacks of thick books. He hit his target as

655

Cadderly stepped into the room, throwing his arms about the sturdy young priest and slapping him hard on the back.

Cadderly looked over Belago's shoulder to Danica and gave her a helpless shrug, which she returned with a wink of an exotic brown eye and a wide, pearly smile.

"We heard that some killers came after you, my boy," Belago explained, putting Cadderly back to arm's length and studying him as though he expected to find an assassin's dagger protruding from Cadderly's chest. "I feared that you would never return." The alchemist also gave Cadderly's upper arms a squeeze, apparently amazed at how solid and strong the young priest had become in the short time he had been gone from the library. Like a concerned aunt, Belago ran a hand up over Cadderly's floppy brown hair, pushing the always unkempt locks back from the young man's face.

"I am all right," Cadderly replied calmly. "This is the house of Deneir, and I am a disciple of Deneir. Why would I not return?"

His understatement had a calming effect on the excitable alchemist, as did the serene look in Cadderly's gray eyes. Belago started to blurt out a reply, but stopped in midstutter and nodded instead.

"Ah, and lady Danica," the alchemist went on. He reached out and gently stroked Danica's thick tangle of strawberry-blond hair, his smile sincere.

Belago's grin disappeared almost immediately, though, and he dropped his arms to his sides and his gaze to the floor. "We heard about Headmaster Avery," he said softly, nodding his head up and down, his expression clouded with sad resignation.

The mention of the portly Avery Schell, Cadderly's surrogate father, stung the young priest profoundly He wanted to explain to poor Belago that Avery's spirit lived on with their god. But how could he begin? Belago would not understand; no one who had not passed into the spirit world and witnessed the divine and glorious sensation could understand. Against that ignorance, anything Cadderly might say would sound like a ridiculous cliché, typical comforting words usually spoken and heard without conviction.

"I received word that you wished to speak with me?" Cadderly said instead, raising his tone to make the statement a question and thus shift the conversation.

"Yes," Belago answered softly. His head finally stopped bouncing, and his eyes widened when he looked into the young priest's calming gray eyes. "Oh, yes!" he cried, as if he had just remembered that fact. "I did—of course I did!"

Obviously embarrassed, the wiry man hopped back across the shop to a small cabinet. He fumbled with an oversized ring of keys, muttering to himself all the while.

"You have become a hero," Danica remarked, noting the man's movements.

Cadderly couldn't disagree with Danica's observation. Vicero Belago had never been overjoyed to see the young priest before. Cadderly had always been a demanding customer, taxing Belago's talents often beyond their limits.

Because of a risky project that Cadderly had given the alchemist, Belago's shop had once been blown apart.

That had been long ago, however, before the battle in Shilmista Forest, before Cadderly's exploits in Carradoon, the city to the east on the banks of Impresk Lake.

Before Cadderly had become a hero.

Hero.

What a ridiculous title, the young priest thought. He had done no more than Danica or either of the dwarven brothers, Ivan and Pikel, in Carradoon. And he, unlike his sturdy friends, had run away from the battle in Shilmista Forest, fled because he could not endure the horrors.

He looked down at Danica again, her brown-eyed gaze comforting him as only it could. How beautiful she was, Cadderly noted, her frame as delicate as that of a newborn fawn and her hair tousled and bouncing freely about her shoulders. Beautiful and untamed, he decided, and with an inner strength clearly shining through those exotic, almond-shaped eyes.

Belago was back in front of him then, seeming nervous and holding both his hands behind his back. "You left this here when you came back from the elven wood," he explained, drawing out his left hand. He held a leather belt with a wide and shallow holster on one side that sported a hand-crossbow.

"I had no idea that I would need it in peaceful Carradoon," Cadderly replied easily, taking the belt and strapping it around his hips.

Danica eyed the young priest curiously. The crossbow had become a symbol of violence to Cadderly, and a symbol of Cadderly's abhorrence of violence to those who knew him best. To see him strap it on so easily, with an almost cavalier attitude, twisted Danica's heart.

Cadderly sensed both the woman's gaze and her confusion. He forced himself to accept it, thinking that he would probably shatter many conceptions in the days ahead. For Cadderly had come to see the dangers facing the Edificant Library in ways that others could not.

"I saw that you had nearly exhausted your supply of darts," Belago stammered. "I mean . . . there's no charge for this batch." He pulled his other hand around, producing a bandoleer filled with specially crafted bolts for the tiny crossbow. "I figured I owed it to you—we all owe it to you, Cadderly."

Cadderly nearly laughed aloud at the absurd proclamation, but he respectfully held his control and accepted the very expensive gift from the alchemist with a grave and approving nod. The darts were special indeed, hollowed out in the center and fitted with a vial that Belago had filled with volatile *Oil of Impact*.

"My thanks for the gift," the young priest said. "Be assured that you have aided the cause of the library in our continuing struggle against the evil of Castle Trinity."

Belago seemed pleased by that remark. Head bobbing once more, he accepted

Cadderly's handshake eagerly. He was still standing in the same place, smiling from ear to ear, as Cadderly and Danica walked out into the hall.

Cadderly could still sense Danica's continuing unease and could see the disappointment etched in her features. The young priest's narrowing stare attacked that disappointment. "I have dismissed the guilt because it has no place in me," was all the explanation he would offer. "Not now, not with all that is left to be done. But I have not forgotten Barjin or that fateful day in the catacombs."

Danica looked away down the hall, but hooked Cadderly's arm with her own, showing her trust in him.

Another form, shapely and obviously feminine, entered the corridor as the pair moved toward Danica's room at the southern end of the complex. Danica tightened her grip on Cadderly's arm at the scent of an exotic and overpowering perfume.

"My greetings, handsome Cadderly," purred the shapely priestess in the crimson gown. "You cannot imagine how pleased I am that you have returned."

Danica's grip nearly cut off Cadderly's blood flow; he felt his fingers tingling. He knew that his face had blushed a deep scarlet, as reddish as Priestess Histra's revealing gown. He realized, sensibly, that this was probably the most modest outfit he had ever seen the lusty priestess of Sune, the Goddess of Love, wearing, but that did not make it modest by anyone else's standards. The front was cut in a low V, so low that Cadderly felt he might glimpse Histra's navel if he got up on his toes, and though the gown was long, its front slit was incredibly high, displaying all of Histra's shapely leg when she brought one foot out in front of the other in her typically alluring stance.

Histra did not seem displeased by Cadderly's obvious discomfort or by Danica's growing scowl. She bent one leg at the knee, her thigh slipping completely free of the gown's meager folds.

Cadderly heard himself gulp, didn't realize that he was gawking at the brazen display until Danica's small fingernails dug deep lines into his upper arm.

"Do come and visit, dear young Cadderly," Histra purred. She looked disdainfully at the woman on Cadderly's arm. "When you are not so tightly leashed, of course." Histra slowly, teasingly moved into her room, the door's gentle click as she closed it lost beneath the sound of Cadderly's repeated swallowing.

"I—" he stammered, at last looking Danica in the eye.

Danica laughed and led him on down the hall. "Fear not," she said, her tone more than a little condescending. "I understand your relationship with the priestess of Sune. She is quite pitiful, actually."

Cadderly looked down at Danica, perplexed. If Danica was speaking the truth, then why had little lines of blood begun their descent on his muscled arm?

"I am not jealous of Histra, certainly," Danica went on. "I trust you, with all my heart." Just outside her room, she stopped and faced Cadderly squarely, one hand brushing the outline of his face, the other tight about his waist.

"I trust *you*," Danica said again. "Besides," added the fiery young monk in very different, stronger tones as she turned into her room, "if anything romantic ever happened between you and that single-minded, over-painted lump of too—too quivering flesh, I would put her nose somewhere in back of one of her ears."

Danica abruptly disappeared into her room to retrieve the book of notes she and Cadderly had prepared for their meeting with Dean Thobicus. The young priest remained in the hall, considering the threat and privately laughing at how true it could be. Danica was fully a foot shorter than he, and easily a hundred pounds lighter. She walked with the grace of a dancer—and fought with the tenacity of a bee-stung bear.

The young priest was far from worried, though. Histra had spent all of her life in the practice of being alluring, and she made no secret of her designs on Cadderly. But she hadn't a chance; not a woman in the world had a chance of breaking Cadderly's bond with his Danica.

* * * * *

A blackened, charred hand tore up through the newly turned earth, reaching desperately for the open air above. A second arm, similarly charred and broken at a gruesome angle halfway between the wrist and the elbow, followed, grasping at the mud, tearing at the natural prison that held the wretched body. Finally the creature found enough of a hold to pull his hairless head from the shallow grave, to look again upon the world of the living.

The blackened head swiveled on a neck that was no more than skin shriveled tight to the bone, surveying the scene. For a fleeting instant, the wretch wondered what had happened. How had he been buried?

A short distance away, down a little hill, the creature saw the glow of the evening lamps of a small farmhouse. Beside it stood another structure, a barn.

A barn!

The thin sliver of the consciousness that had once belonged to a man known as Ghost remembered that barn. Ghost had seen this body, his body, charred by that wicked Cadderly in that very barn! The evil corpse drew in some air—the action could not be called breathing where this undead thing was concerned—and dragged his blackened and shriveled body the rest of the way out of the hole. The notes of a distant, yet strangely familiar, melody continued to thrum in the back of his feeble consciousness.

Unsteadily, Ghost loped more than walked toward the structure, the memories of that horrible, fateful day coming back more fully with each stride.

Ghost had used the *Ghearufu*, a powerful device with magical energies directed toward the spirit world, to steal the body of the firbolg Vander, an unwilling associate. Disguised as Vander, with the strength of a giant, Ghost had then crushed his own body and had thrown it across the barn.

And then Cadderly had burned it.

The malignant monster looked down to his bone-skinny arms and prominent ribs, the hollow shell that somehow lived.

Cadderly had burned his body, this body!

A single-minded hatred consumed the wretched creature. Ghost wanted to kill Cadderly, to kill anybody dear to the young priest, to kill anybody at all.

Ghost was at the barn then. Thoughts of Cadderly had flitted away into nothingness, replaced by an unfocused anger. The door was over to the side, but the creature understood that he did not need the door, that he had become something more than the simple material wooden planking now blocking his way. The shriveled form wavered, became insubstantial, and Ghost walked through the wall.

He heard the horse whinnying before he came fully back to the material plane, saw the poor beast standing wild-eyed, lathered in sweat. The sight pleased the undead thing; waves of a new sensation of joy washed over Ghost as he smelled the beast's terror. The undead monster ambled over to stand before the horse, let his tongue drop out of his mouth hungrily. With all the skin burned away from the sides of the tongue, its pointy tip hung far below Ghost's blackened chin. The horse made not a sound, was too frightened to move or even to draw breath.

With a wheeze of evil anticipation, Ghost put deathly cold hands against the sides of the beast's face.

The horse fell dead.

The undead creature hissed with delight, but while Ghost felt thrilled by the kill, he did not feel sated. His hunger demanded more, could not be defeated by the death of a simple animal. Ghost moved across the barn and again walked through the wall, coming into view of the lights within the farmhouse. A shadowy shape, a human shape, moved across one of the rooms.

Ghost was at the front door, undecided as to whether to walk through the wood, tear the door apart, or simply knock and let the sheep come to the wolf. The decision was taken from the creature, though, when he looked to the side of the door, to a small pane of glass, and saw, for the first time, his own reflection.

A red glow emanated from empty eye sockets. Ghost's nose was completely gone, replaced by a blacker hole edged by ragged flaps of charred skin.

That tiny part of Ghost's consciousness that remembered the vitality of life lost all control at the sight of that hideous reflection. The monster's unearthly wail sent the barnyard animals into a frenzy and shattered the stillness of the quiet autumn night more than any violent storm ever could. There came a shuffling from inside the house, just behind the door, but the outraged monster didn't even hear it. With strength far beyond that of any mortal, he drove his bony hands through the center of the door and pulled out to the sides, splintering and tearing the wood as though it were no more than a thin sheet of parchment.

A man stood there, wearing the uniform of a Carradoon city guardsman and an expression of sheer horror, his mouth frozen wide in a silent scream, his eyes bugged out so far that they seemed as if they would fall from his face.

Ghost burst through the broken door and fell over him. The man's skin transformed, aged, under the creature's ghostly touch; his hair turned from raven black to white and fell out in large clumps. Finally the guardsman's voice returned, and he screamed and wailed, flailing his arms helplessly. Ghost ripped at him, tore at his throat until that revealing scream was no more than the gurgle of blood-filled lungs.

The creature heard a shuffle of feet, looked up from the kill to see a second man standing beyond the foyer, in a doorway at the other side of the house's small kitchen.

"By the gods," this man whispered, and he dove back into the far room and slammed the door.

With one hand, Ghost lifted the dead man and hurled him out the shattered portal, halfway across the barnyard. The undead creature floated across the floor, savoring the kill, yet hungry for more. His form wavered again, and he walked across the room and through another closed door.

The second man, also a city guardsman, stood before the wicked thing, swinging his sword frantically at the horrid monster. But the weapon never touched Ghost, slipped right through the insubstantial, ethereal mist the creature had become. The man tried to run away, but Ghost kept pace with him, walked past furniture that the man stumbled over, walked through walls to meet the terrified man on the other side of a door.

The torment went on for a long and agonizing time, the helpless man finally stumbling out into the night, losing his sword as he tumbled down the porch steps. He scrambled to his feet and ran into the dark night, ran with all speed for Carradoon, howling all the way.

Ghost could have, at any time, rematerialized and torn the man apart, but somehow the creature felt that he enjoyed this sensation, this smell of terror, even more than the actual killing. Ghost felt stronger for it, as though he had somehow fed off of the horrified man's emotions and screams.

But now it was over and the man was gone, and the other man was long dead and offered no more sport.

Ghost wailed again as the thin sliver of remaining consciousness considered what he had become, considered what wretched Cadderly had created. Ghost remembered little of his past life, only that he had been among the highest paid killers in the living realm, a professional assassin, an artist of murder.

Now the creature was an undead thing, a ghost, a hollow, animated shell of evil energies.

After more than a century of being in possession of the *Ghearufu*, Ghost had come to consider mortal forms in a much different way than others. Twice the evil man had utilized the powers of the magical device to change bodies, killing his previous form and taking the new one as his own. And now, somehow, Ghost's spirit, a piece of it at least, had come back to this plane. By some trick of fate, Ghost had risen from the dead.

But how? Ghost couldn't fully remember his place in the afterlife, but sensed that it was not pleasant, not at all.

Images of growling shadows surrounded him; black claws raked the air before his mind's eye. What had brought him back from the grave, what compelled his spirit to walk the earth once more? The creature scanned his fingers, his toes, for some sign of the regenerative ring Ghost had once worn. But he distinctly remembered that the ring had been stolen by Cadderly.

Ghost felt a call on the wind, silent but compelling. And familiar. He turned glowing eyes up toward the distant mountains and heard the call again.

The *Ghearufu*.

The malignant spirit understood, remembered hearing the melody from his place of eternal punishment. The *Ghearufu* had called him back. By the power of the *Ghearufu*, Ghost walked the earth once more. At that confused, overwhelming moment, the creature couldn't decide if that was a good thing or not. He looked again to his shriveled, gruesome arms and torso, wondered if he could withstand the light of day. What future awaited Ghost in such a state? What hopes could the undead thing hold?

The silent call came again.

The *Ghearufu*!

It wanted Ghost back—and by its power, the creature's spirit could surely steal a new form, a living form.

In Carradoon, not so far from the farmyard, the horrified guardsman stumbled to the closed gate, screaming of ghosts, crying for his slaughtered companion. If the soldiers manning the gate held any doubts about the man's sincerity, they needed only to look into his face, a face that appeared much older than the man's thirty years.

A large contingent of men, including a priest from the Temple of Ilmater, rode out from Carradoon's gate less than an hour later, hell-bent for the farmhouse, prepared to do battle with the malignant spirit. Ghost was far gone by then, sometimes walking, sometimes floating across the fields, following the call of the *Ghearufu*, his one chance for deliverance.

Only the cries of the nighttime animals, the terrified bleating of sheep, the frightened screech of a night owl, marked the ghost's passage.

Two

Step Over a Dangerous Line

The dawn had long since passed, but the room Cadderly entered was darkened still, shades drawn tight to the windows. The young priest moved to the bed quietly and knelt, not wanting to disturb Headmistress Pertelope's sleep.

If Headmaster Avery had been Cadderly's surrogate father, then wise Pertelope had been his mother. Now, with his newfound insight into the harmonious song of Deneir, Cadderly felt that he needed Pertelope more than ever. For she, too, heard the mysterious notes of that unending song; she, too, transcended the normal boundaries of the clerical order. If Pertelope had been beside Cadderly in his discussion with Thobicus, then his reasoning would have been bolstered, and the withered dean would have been forced to accept the truth of Cadderly's insights.

But Pertelope could not be with him. She lay in her bed, deathly ill, caught in the throes of a magical enchantment gone wild. Her body had been trapped in a transformation somewhere between the smooth and soft skin of a human and the sharp-edged denticles of a shark, and now neither air nor water could satisfy the headmistress's physical needs.

Cadderly stroked her hair, more gray than he remembered it, as though Pertelope had aged. He was somewhat surprised when she opened her eyes, which still held their inquisitive luster, and managed a smile in his direction.

Cadderly strained to return that look. "You must recover your strength," he whispered to her. "I need you."

Pertelope smiled again, and her eyes slowly closed.

Cadderly's sigh was one of helpless resignation. He started to turn away from the bed, not wanting to tax Pertelope's depleted strength, but the headmistress unexpectedly spoke to him.

"How went your meeting with Dean Thobicus?"

Cadderly turned back to her, surprised by the strength in that voice, and surprised also that Pertelope even knew he had met with the dean. She had not been out of her room in many days, and on the few occasions Cadderly had come to visit her, he had not mentioned his upcoming meeting.

He should have expected that she would know, though. As he considered the revelation, he reminded himself that she, too, heard the song of Deneir. She and Cadderly were intimately joined by forces far beyond what the other priests of the library could even understand, joined by a communal bathing in the river that was their god's song.

"It did not go well," Cadderly admitted.

"Dean Thobicus does not understand," Pertelope reasoned, and Cadderly suspected that the headmistress had suffered many similar meetings with Thobicus and other priests who could not comprehend her special relationship with Deneir.

"He questioned my authority in branding Kierkan Rufo," Cadderly explained. "And he ordered that I hand the *Ghearufu* . . ." Cadderly paused, wondering how he might quickly explain the dangerous device. Pertelope squeezed his hand, though, and smiled, and he knew that she understood.

"Dean Thobicus ordered me to turn it over to the library supervisor," Cadderly finished.

"You do not approve of that course?"

"I fear it," Cadderly admitted. "There is a will within the artifact, a sentient force almost, that may overcome any who handle it. I, myself, have had to struggle against the alluring calls of the *Ghearufu* since I took it from the assassin's burned body."

"You sound arrogant, young priest," Pertelope interrupted, her emphasis on the word "young."

Cadderly paused to consider the response. Perhaps his feelings could be considered arrogant, but he believed them nonetheless. He could control the force of the *Ghearufu*, had controlled it to this point, at least. Cadderly realized that he held a special insight now, a gift from Deneir, that others of his order, with the exception of Pertelope, seemed to lack.

"That is good," the headmistress said, answering her own accusation. Cadderly eyed her curiously, not quite understanding where her reasoning was leading.

"Deneir has called upon you," Pertelope explained. "You must trust in that call. When you first discovered your budding powers, you did not understand them and you feared them. It was only when you came to trust in them that you learned their uses and limitations. So it must be with your instincts and your emotions, feelings heightened by the song that ever plays in your mind. Do you believe that you know what is the best course concerning the *Ghearufu*?"

"I know," Cadderly replied firmly, not caring that he did indeed sound arrogant.

"And concerning Kierkan Rufo's brand?"

Cadderly spent a moment considering the question, for Rufo's case seemed to encompass many more edicts of proper procedure, procedures that Cadderly had obviously circumvented. "I did as the ethics of Deneir instructed me," he decided. "Still, Dean Thobicus doubts my authority with good cause."

"From his perspective," Pertelope replied. "Yours was a moral authority, while the dean's power over such situations comes from a different source."

"From a created hierarchy," Cadderly added. "A hierarchy that remains blind to the truth of Deneir." He gave a chuckle, unintentionally derisive. "A hierarchy that will hold us in check until the cost of a war with Castle Trinity multiplies tenfold, a hundredfold."

"Will it?"

It was a simple question, asked simply by a priestess who had not the strength to even rise from her bed. To Cadderly, though, the question's connotations became quite complex, implicating him and his future actions as the only possible answer. He knew in his heart that Pertelope was calling upon him to prevent what he had just predicted, was asking him to usurp the authority of his order's highest ranking priest and bring Castle Trinity's influence to a quick end.

Her coy smile confirmed his suspicions.

"Have *you* ever dared to overrule the Dean?" Cadderly asked bluntly

"I have never been in such a desperate situation," the headmistress replied. Her voice sounded weak suddenly, as though her efforts to be strong had reached their end.

"I told you when you first discovered your gift," she went on, pausing often to collect her breath, "that many things would be required of you, that your courage would often be tested. Deneir demands intelligence, but he also demands courage of spirit so that intelligent decisions can be acted upon."

"Cadderly?" The quiet call came from the door, and Cadderly looked back over his shoulder to see Danica, her face grave. Behind her stood the beautiful Shayleigh, elven maiden, elven warrior, from Shilmista Forest, her golden hair lustrous and her violet eyes shining as the dawn. She made no greeting to Cadderly, though she had not seen him in many weeks, out of respect for the obviously solemn meeting.

"Dean Thobicus is looking for you," Danica explained quietly, her tone full of trepidation. "You did not give the *Ghearufu* . . ." Her voice trailed away as Cadderly looked back to the bed, to Pertelope, who appeared very old and very tired.

"Courage," Pertelope whispered, and then, as Cadderly looked on with full understanding, the headmistress peacefully died.

* * * * *

Cadderly did not knock and wait for permission to enter the office of Dean Thobicus. The withered man was sitting back in his chair, staring out the window. Cadderly knew that the dean had just received news of Headmistress Pertelope's death.

"Have you done as you were instructed?" Thobicus snapped as soon as he noticed that Cadderly had entered, and by that time, Cadderly was already up to the man's desk.

"I have," Cadderly replied.

"Good," Thobicus said, and his anger faded, replaced by his obvious sorrow for Pertelope's passing.

"I have bid Danica and Shayleigh to assemble the dwarven brothers and Vander by the front door, with provisions for the journey," Cadderly explained, popping on his blue, wide-brimmed hat as he spoke.

"To Shilmista Forest?" Thobicus asked tentatively, as though he was afraid of what Cadderly was about to say. One of the options Thobious had offered to Cadderly was to go out and serve as emissary to the elves and Prince Elbereth, but he didn't think that was what the young priest was now hinting at.

"No," came the even answer.

Thobicus sat up very straight in his chair, a perplexed expression on his hollow, weathered face. He noticed then that Cadderly wore his hand-crossbow and the bandoleer of explosive darts. The spindle-disks, Cadderly's other unconventional weapon, were looped on the young priest's wide belt, next to a tube that Cadderly had designed to emit a concentrated beam of light.

Thobicus considered the clues for a long while. "You have turned the *Ghearufu* over to the library supervisor?" he asked directly.

"No."

Thobicus trembled with mounting rage. He started to speak several times, but wound up chewing his lips instead. "You just said that you had done as you were instructed!" he roared at last, in as furious an outburst as Cadderly had ever seen from the normally calm man.

"I have done as Deneir instructed," Cadderly explained.

"You arrogant . . . you . . . sacrilegious—" Thobicus stammered, his face shining bright red as he stood up behind the desk.

"Hardly," Cadderly corrected, his voice unshaking. "I have done as Deneir instructed, and now you, too, are to do Deneir's bidding. You will go down with me to the front hall and wish my friends and me good fortune on our all-important mission to Castle Trinity." The dean tried to interrupt but something that he did not yet understand, something intruding into his very thoughts, compelled him to silence.

"Then you will continue the preparations for a springtime assault," Cadderly explained, "a reserve plan in case my friends and I cannot accomplish what we set out to do."

"You are mad!" Thobicus growled.

Hardly.

Thobicus began to argue back—until he realized that Cadderly had not spoken the word. The dean's eyes narrowed and then popped wide as he came to realize that something was touching him—inside his mind!

"What are you about?" he demanded frantically.

You need not speak, Cadderly telepathically assured him.

"This is . . ." the Dean began.

". . . preposterous, an insult to my position," Cadderly verbally finished for him, sensing and perfectly revealing the words before Thobicus ever spoke them.

The dean fell back in his chair. *Do you realize the consequences of your actions?* he mentally asked.

Do you realize that I could shatter your mind? Cadderly responded with all confidence. *Do you further realize that my powers are bestowed by Deneir?*

The dean's faced screwed up in confusion and disbelief. What was this young upstart hinting at?

Cadderly held no love for this ugly game, but he had little time to handle things the way the proper procedures of the Edificant Library demanded. He mentally commanded the dean to stand, then to stand on the desk.

Before he knew what had happened, Thobicus found himself looking down at the young priest from a high perch.

Cadderly looked to the window, and Thobicus telepathically sensed the young priest privately musing that he could quite easily persuade the dean to jump out of it—and suddenly Thobicus believed that Cadderly could! Without warning, Cadderly released Thobicus from the mental grip, and the dean slumped down from the oaken desk and slid back into his chair.

"I take no pleasure in dominating you so," Cadderly explained sincerely, understanding that the best results might be gained by restoring the defeated man's pride. "I am allowed the power by the god that we both recognize. This is Deneir's way of explaining to you that I am correct in these matters. It is a signal to us both, nothing more. All that I ask—"

"I will have you branded!" Thobicus exploded. "I will see that you are escorted from the library in chains, tormented every step of the way as you leave this region!"

His words stung Cadderly profoundly as he continued his tirade, promising every conceivable punishment allowable by the Deneirian sect. Cadderly had been raised under those rules of order, under the precept that the dean's word was absolute rule in the library, and it was truly terrifying to the young priest to cast aside convention, even in light of the greater truth playing within the notes of the Deneirian song. Cadderly focused his thoughts on Pertelope at that terrible moment, remembering her call for courage and conviction.

He heard the harmony of the song playing in his mind, entered its alluring flow, and found again those channels of energy that would allow him into the private realm of Dean Thobicus's mind.

Cadderly and the dean exited the library a few minutes later, to find Danica and Shayleigh; the giant Vander (who was using his innate magical abilities to appear as a huge, red-bearded man); and the two dwarves—stocky, yellow-bearded Ivan and round-shouldered Pikel, his beard dyed green and pulled up over his ears, braided with his long hair halfway down his back—waiting for them. The smiling dean wished Cadderly and his five companions the best of fortunes on their most important mission, and waved a fond farewell as they walked off into the Snowflakes.

Three
Justifying the Means

Aballister leaned in close over Dorigen's shoulder, making the woman somewhat uncomfortable. Dorigen let her focus drift away from the images in the crystal ball and shook her head vigorously, purposely letting fly her long salt-and-pepper hair so that it smacked nosy Aballister in the face.

The older wizard backed up a step and pulled a strand of hair from his lips, glowering at Dorigen.

"I did not realize you were so close," Dorigen weakly apologized.

"Of course," replied Aballister in similarly feigned tones.

Dorigen clearly recognized his anger, but understood that he would accept her insult without too much complaint.

Aballister had broken his own scrying device, a magical mirror, and the experience had left him fearful of any more attempts at clairvoyance. He needed Dorigen now, for she was quite skilled at the art. "I should have announced my presence and waited for you to complete your search," Aballister said, which was as close to an apology as Dorigen had ever heard from the man.

"That would have been the appropriate course," Dorigen agreed, her amber eyes flashing with . . .

With what? Aballister wondered. Open hatred? Their relationship had been on a steady decline since Dorigen had returned from her humiliating defeat in Shilmista Forest, a defeat she had suffered at the hands of Aballister's own estranged son.

The older wizard shrugged away the personal problems. "Have you found them?" he asked evenly. He and Dorigen could settle their score after the immediate threat was eliminated, but for now, they both had greater problems. The spirit of Bogo Rath had returned to Aballister the previous night, with the information that Cadderly was indeed on his way to Castle Trinity.

The report inspired both trepidation and exhilaration in the older wizard. Aballister was obsessed with conquering the region, a goal given to him by the avatar of Talona herself, and Cadderly certainly seemed to be among the foremost obstacles to those designs. The wizard could not deny the tingle of anticipation he felt at the thought of doing battle with his formidable son. By all reports, Cadderly did not even know his relationship to Aballister, and the thought of crushing the upstart youth, both in magical battle and emotionally with the secret truth, inevitably widened a grin across cruel Aballister's angular features.

The news of Cadderly's march inspired nothing but fear in Dorigen, however. She had no desire to tangle with the young priest and his brutal friends again, especially not now, with her hands still sore from the beating Cadderly had given them. Many of her spells required precise hand movements, and with her fingers bent crooked and joints smashed, more than one spell had backfired on her since her return from the elven forest.

"I have seen no sign of Cadderly," Dorigen replied after a long pause to study again the blurry images in the crystal ball. "My guess is that he and his companions have just recently left the library, if they have left at all, and I dare not send my magical sight so near our enemy's stronghold."

"Two hours, and you have found nothing?" Aballister did not sound pleased. He paced the edge of the small room, running withered fingers across a curtain that separated this area from Dorigen's boudoir. A smile spread across the wizard's face, though, despite his trepidation, when he remembered the many games he and Dorigen had enjoyed behind this very curtain.

"I did not say that," Dorigen answered sharply, understanding the conniving grin, and she turned back again to the crystal ball.

Aballister rushed back across the room to peer over his associate's shoulder. At first, only a gray mist swirled within the confines of the crystal ball, but gradually, with Dorigen's coaxing, it began to shift and take on definite form.

The two wizards viewed the foothills of the Snowflakes, obviously the southeastern mountain region, for the road to Carradoon was plainly in sight. Something moved along that road, something hideous.

"The assassin," Aballister breathed. Dorigen regarded the older wizard curiously.

"The spirit of Bogo was cryptic on this point," Aballister explained. "This thing you have discovered was one of the leaders of the Night Mask band, the one called, appropriately it would now seem, Ghost. Apparently our dear Cadderly took from Ghost a magical device, and now the wretched creature has come back for it. Can you sense the spirit's power through your ball?"

"Of course not," Dorigen answered indignantly.

"Then go out to the mountains and watch over this one," Aballister growled at her. "We may have a powerful ally here, one that will eliminate our problems before they ever make their way to Castle Trinity."

"I will not."

Aballister straightened as though he had been slapped.

"I have not yet recovered," Dorigen explained. "My spells are not dependable. You would ask me to go near a malignant ghost, and near your dangerous son, without full use of my abilities?" Her reference to Cadderly as Aballister's son made the older wizard cringe, the obvious implication being that this entire trouble was somehow Aballister's fault.

"You have at your disposal one far more capable of estimating the strength of this undead monster," Dorigen went on, not backing down in the least. "One who can communicate with the creature if necessary and who can certainly learn more about its intentions than I."

Aballister's wrath melted away as he came to understand Dorigen's reasoning. "Druzil," he replied, referring to his familiar, a mischievous imp of the lower planes.

"Druzil," Dorigen echoed, her tone derisive.

Aballister put a crooked hand up to his sharp chin and mumbled. Still, he seemed unconvinced.

"Besides," Dorigen purred. "If I remain at Trinity, perhaps you and I . . ." She let the thought hang, her gaze directing Aballister's to the curtain across the small room.

Aballister's dark eyes widened in surprise, and his hand drooped back down by his side. "Continue your search for my s . . . for Cadderly," Aballister said to her. "Alert me at once if you discover his location. After all, I have ways of striking at the foolish boy before he ever gets near Castle Trinity."

The wizard took his abrupt leave then, seeming flustered, but with an obviously hopeful bounce in his step, and Dorigen turned back to her crystal ball. She didn't immediately return to her scrying, though, but instead considered the action she had just taken to prevent Aballister from sending her away. She held no love for the man anymore, no respect even, though he was certainly among the most powerful wizards she had ever seen. But Dorigen had made a decision—a decision forced by her will to ride this whole adventure out to a safe conclusion. She knew herself well enough to admit that Cadderly had truly unnerved her in the elven wood.

Her thoughts led her to contemplations of Aballister's intentions for his son. The wizard had allies, enchanted monsters kept in private cages in his extra-dimensional mansion. All that Aballister needed was for Dorigen to point the way.

Dorigen looked down at her still swollen and bruised hands, remembered the disaster in Shilmista, and remembered, too, that Cadderly could have killed her if he had desired.

* * * * *

They set their first camp on a high pass in the Snowflakes, sheltered from the biting, wintry wind by a small alcove in the rocky mountain wall. With Vander's gigantic bulk standing to further block the gusting breezes (the cold did not seem to bother the firbolg in the least), Ivan and Pikel soon had a fire roaring. Still, the wind inevitably found its way in to the companions, and even the dwarves were soon shivering and rubbing their hands briskly near the flames. Pikel's typical moan of "Oooo," came out more as "O—o—o—o," as his teeth chattered through the sound.

Cadderly, deep in thought, was oblivious to it all, oblivious even to the fact that his fingers were beginning to take on a delicate blue color. His head down and eyes half-closed, he sat farthest from the flames—except for Vander, who had moved out around the edge of the natural alcove to feel the full force of the refreshing wind against his ruddy cheeks.

"We're needing sleep," Ivan stuttered, aiming his comment at the distracted priest.

"O—o oi," Pikel readily agreed.

"It w—will be hard to sleep with the cold," Danica said rather loudly, practically in Cadderly's ear. The four companions looked incredulously at each other, and then back at Cadderly. Danica shrugged and moved closer to the flames, rubbing her hands all the while, but Ivan, always a bit more blunt in his tactics, took Shayleigh's longbow, reached across the fire with it, and bopped Cadderly several times atop the head.

Cadderly looked up at the dwarf. "What?"

"We was saying that it's a mite chilly for sleeping," Ivan growled at him, his claims accentuated by the puff of frosty breath accompanying each chattered word. Cadderly looked around at his shivering companions, then seemed to realize his own tingling extremities for the first time.

"Deneir will protect us," he assured them, and he let his mind's eye slip back to the pages of the Tome of Universal Harmony, the most holy book of his god. He heard again the flowing, beautiful notes of the endless song, and pulled from them a relatively simple spell, repeating it until its enchantment had touched all of his friends.

"Oo!" Pikel exclaimed, and this time his teeth did not chatter. The cold was gone; there was no better way to explain the sensation that instantly came over each of them at Cadderly's blessed touch.

"Took ye long enough," was Ivan's last muttered sentiment before he dropped back against the comfortable (to a dwarf, at least) mountain rock, clasped his hands behind his head, and closed his eyes.

The dwarves were snoring in a matter of minutes, and soon after, Shayleigh, her head against arms that grasped her propped longbow, was also resting easily. Cadderly had resumed his previous contemplative posture, and Danica, guessing that something was bothering her love terribly, fought away the temptation of sleep and kept a protective watch over him.

She would have preferred that Cadderly willingly open up to her, initiate the discussion that he obviously needed. Danica knew the man better than to really expect that, knew that Cadderly could sit and mull something over for hours, even days.

"You have done something wrong?" she asked as much as stated to him. "Or is it Avery?"

Cadderly looked up at her, and his surprised expression told Danica much, though she did not immediately elaborate on her suspicions.

"I have done nothing wrong," Cadderly said at length, a bit too defensively, and the perceptive monk understood then which of her guesses had hit the mark.

"It seems amazing how completely Dean Thobicus changed his mind concerning our quest," Danica said slyly.

Cadderly shifted uncomfortably—more evidence for Danica's perceptive eye. "The dean is a cleric of Deneir," Cadderly replied, as though that explained everything. "He seeks knowledge and harmony, and if the truth becomes known to him, he will not let pride stand in the way of changing his mind."

Danica nodded, though her expression remained doubtful.

"Our course was the proper one," Cadderly added firmly.

"The dean did not think so."

"He learned the truth," Cadderly answered immediately

"Did he?" Danica asked. "Or was the truth forced upon him?"

Cadderly looked away, saw Vander at the edge of the firelight, pacing in the blasting wind, continually sniffing at the mountain air as he walked his watch, though his eyes were more often turned toward the crystalline, star-dotted sky than to the rugged mountain landscape.

"What did you do to him?" Danica asked bluntly. Cadderly's glare fell over her in an instant, but she didn't back away in the least, trusting in her lover, trusting that the young priest could not lie to her.

"I convinced him." Cadderly spit out every word.

"Magically?"

How well you know me! the priest thought, truly amazed.

"It had to be done," he said quietly.

Danica rolled up onto her knees, shaking her head, her almond-shaped brown eyes widening.

"Was I to allow Thobicus to lead us down a path of devastation?" Cadderly asked her. "He would—"

"Thobicus?"

Cadderly's face screwed up with confusion, not understanding the significance of Danica's interruption.

"Who has let pride temper his judgment now?" Danica asked accusingly. Still Cadderly did not understand. "Thobicus?" the monk reiterated. "Are you referring to *Dean* Thobicus?" Her emphasis on the title showed Cadderly the truth. Even the headmasters of the library would rarely refer to the highest ranking priest without the proper title.

Cadderly spent many moments considering his slip. Always before, he had taken care to refer to the respected dean in the proper fashion, always the name had come to him with the title unconsciously attached, and sounded discordant if he or someone else did not identify the man as the dean. Now though, for some reason, the simple reference to Thobicus seemed more harmonious.

"You used your magic against the leader of your order," Danica stated.

"I did what needed to be done," Cadderly decided. "Do not fear, for Thobicus,"— he had honestly meant to say "Dean Thobicus" this time— "does not even remember the incident. It was a simple thing to modify his memory, and he actually believes that he sent us out on a scouting mission. He expects that we will soon return to report on our enemy's activities, so that his foolish plans for a sweeping strike might be implemented."

There could be no doubt concerning the level of horror that Cadderly's admission had instilled in Danica. She actually backed away from the young priest, shaking her head, her mouth hanging open.

"How many thousands would perish in such a war?" the young priest cried loudly, getting Vander's attention, and causing Shayleigh, too, to open one sleepy eye. Predictably, the dwarven snoring went on uninterrupted.

"I could not let Thobicus do it," Cadderly continued against Danica's silent accusations. "I could not let the man's cowardice cause the deaths of perhaps thousands of innocent men, not when I saw a better way to end the threat."

"You act on presumption," Danica replied incredulously.

"On truth!" Cadderly shot back angrily, his tone leaving no doubt that he believed his claim with all of his heart.

"The dean is your superior," Danica reminded him, her tone somewhat more mellow.

"He is my superior in the eyes of a false hierarchy," Cadderly added, similarly softening his tones. He looked around at Shayleigh and Vander, both now keenly interested in what had been a private conversation. "Headmistress Pertelope was truly the highest ranking of the Deneirian priests," Cadderly asserted.

The statement caught Danica off guard—mainly because she had held Pertelope in the highest regard and had no doubt that Pertelope was among the wisest of the Edificant Library's hosts.

"It was Pertelope who guided me along this course," Cadderly went on. He seemed vulnerable suddenly, small and uncertain, an edge of doubt finding its way through his stubborn resolve.

"I need you beside me," he said to Danica, quietly so that Shayleigh and Vander would not hear. The elven maiden grinned, though, and respectfully closed her glistening violet eyes, and Cadderly knew that her keen ears had caught every syllable.

Danica stared into the starry sky for a long moment, then moved beside Cadderly, gently taking hold of his arm and shifting in close. She looked back to the fire and closed her eyes. Nothing more needed to be said.

Cadderly knew that Danica held some doubts, though, and he did, as well. He had taken a huge gamble in mentally attacking Thobicus, and had certainly shattered the tenets of brotherhood and accepted hierarchy at the library. Now he was on the course he knew in his heart to be the proper one, but did the end justify the means?

With so many lives hanging on the decision, Cadderly had to believe that, in this instance, it did.

* * * * *

At a campsite far down the mountain trails from Cadderly's company, four adventuring travelers slept soundly. They did not notice their campfire take on a blue hue momentarily, did not notice the dog face of Druzil the imp peering out at them from within the flames.

Druzil muttered curses under his raspy breath, using the crackle of flames to cover his undeniable anger. The imp detested this scouting service, figured he would spend many hours of sheer boredom listening to the snores of inconsequential humans. He was Aballister's familiar, though, in service (if not always in willing service) to the wizard, and when Aballister had opened a planar gate in Castle Trinity and ordered him away, Druzil had been compelled to obey.

The fiery tunnel had led here, warping through the dimensions to the campfire Dorigen's scrying had targeted in the eastern foothills of the Snowflakes. Using a bag of magical blue powder, Druzil had turned the normal campfire into a gate similar to the one in Castle Trinity. Now the imp clutched a pouch of red powder, which could close the gate behind him.

Druzil held back the red powder for a few moments, wondering what fun he might find in allowing the planar gate to remain open. What excitement might a host of denizens from the lower planes cause?

The imp reconsidered immediately and poured the red powder onto the flames. If he left the gate open and the wrong creatures stepped through, then Castle Trinity's plans for conquest of the region would be lost in a swirl of chaos and destruction.

He sat in the flames for more than an hour, watching the unremarkable men. "Aballister *bene tellemara*," he muttered many times, a phrase in the language of the lower planes which basically attributed the intelligence of a slug to Druzil's wizard master.

A movement to the side, beyond the campsite, caught Druzil's attention, and for a moment he thought—he hoped—that something exciting might happen. It proved to be just another of the men, however, walking a perimeter guard, apparently as bored as the imp. The man was gone from view in a few moments, back out into the darkness.

Another long hour slipped past, and the fire burned lower, forcing Druzil to crouch down to remain concealed by the flames. The imp shook his dog-faced head, his floppy ears waggling about the sides of his canine face. "Aballister *bene tellemara*," he hissed defiantly over and over, a litany against boredom.

The wizard had sent him out with the promise that he would find the mission enjoyable, but Druzil, used to the mundane activities most often associated with familiars, such as standing guard or gathering spell components, had heard that lie before. Even Dorigen's cryptic reference to "someone that the imp might find akin to his own heart," gave Druzil little hope. Cadderly was on his way to Castle Trinity—that was the place Druzil wanted to be, watching the magical explosions as Aballister finally blasted away his troublesome son.

The imp heard a noise again from the perimeter, a sort of gasping sound followed by some shuffling. Druzil lifted his dog face clear of the flames to get a better view, and saw the guard backpedaling, scrambling, his sword out in front of him and his mouth opened impossibly wide in a silent caricature of a scream.

It was the creature stubbornly pursuing the guard that sent shivers of warped delight up the imp's lizardlike spine. It had once been human, Druzil guessed, but was now a charred and blackened corpse, hideous and hunched, and appeared as though all its bodily fluids had been sizzled away. Druzil could actually smell the permeating evil that had brought this wretched thing back to its undead state.

"Delicious," the imp rasped, his poison-tipped tail whipping about the embers behind him.

The guard continued to retreat, continued his futile attempt at a scream. The creature slapped the horrified man's sword to the side and grabbed him by the wrist, and Druzil squeaked aloud with pleasure as the skin of the doomed man's face took on a wrinkled, leathery appearance and his hair lost its youthful luster, lost all color, and began to fall out in clumps.

The ghost's hand hit the man again, in the face, and his eyes bulged and seemed as if they would pop free of their sockets. From his opened mouth came gurgling, choking sounds, and a wheeze of breath from lungs suddenly too old and hardened to properly draw breath.

The dying man tumbled backward over a log and lay very still on the ground, eyes and mouth still open impossibly wide.

A cry from the side of the camp showed that the commotion had awakened one of the others. A sturdy man, a warrior judging from his well-muscled arms and chest, charged across in front of the fire, boldly meeting the ghost. The warrior's great sword sliced across, diving at the creature's shoulder.

It seemed to connect, somewhat, but then passed right through the undead thing, as though this creature was no more than an insubstantial apparition. The ghost came on, reaching with his one working arm, seeking another victim for his insatiable hunger.

Druzil clapped his oversized hands together a hundred times in glee, thoroughly enjoying the play. The other men leaped up from their slumbers, one running off screaming into the woods, but the other two coming to the aid of their bold companion.

The creature caught one by the hair, seemingly oblivious to the frantic man's chopping axe as it turned the man's head aside and bit his throat. With hideous strength, the monster hurled the bloodied corpse away, to crash into the trees twenty feet beyond the edge of the campsite.

The remaining two men had seen enough, had seen too much. They turned and fled, one throwing his weapon aside in total, incomprehensible terror.

Ghost lunged for them once but missed, and then stood and watched their flight for just a moment before he began shuffling past the ruined campsite on his way once more, moving up into the Snowflakes as if this entire slaughter had been no more than a coincidental encounter. Druzil understood that the thing was savoring the screams of the fleeing men, though, taking perverse pleasure in their terror.

Druzil liked this creature.

The imp stepped out of the flames, looked down to the aged, dying man, laboring for breath, showing pain with every movement. Druzil heard the man's arm bone simply snap with age as he reached up for the air, heard a groan mixed in with the futile gasps.

The imp only laughed and looked away. Druzil had overheard part of Aballister's conversation with the spirit of Bogo Rath, and though that conversation had been cryptic, the imp now suspected that this horrid creature might hold a particular grudge against Cadderly. Certainly the monster seemed to be moving with purpose; it hadn't even taken the time or effort to pursue the fleeing men.

Druzil willed himself into a state of invisibility and flapped his leathery bat wings, rising up in pursuit of the ghost, thinking that perhaps he had been wrong to doubt Aballister's promises that this would be an enjoyable mission.

Four
A Taste of What's to Come

A ballister walked through a large room filled with cages, admiring his private menagerie of exotic monsters. "Dorigen has spotted the young priest and his friends," the wizard said quietly, coming to a stop between two of the largest cages, each occupied by strange-looking beasts that seemed a mixture of two or more normal animals.

"Are you hungry?" Aballister asked one winged leonine monstrosity, its tail covered with a multitude of iron-hard spikes. The creature roared in reply and butted its massive, powerful chest against the bars of its cage.

"Then fly," the wizard cooed, opening the cage door and running his skinny hands through the monster's thick mane as it ambled past. "Dorigen will guide you to my wicked son. Do teach him a lesson."

The old wizard cackled heartily. He had spent many private hours in this extra-dimensional region. He had actually created the place while studying in the Edificant Library. Aballister's biggest concerns at that time were the hovering priests always looking over his shoulder, making sure that his work was in accord with their strict rules. Little did they know that Aballister had circumvented their watchful gazes, had created this extra pocket of real space so that he could continue his most precious, if most dangerous, experiments.

That had been more than two decades before when Cadderly was a babe, and when, the wizard mused, the leonine monster and the three-headed beast behind it were also babes.

Aballister laughed aloud at the thought: he was sending two of his children out to kill the third.

The two powerful beasts followed Aballister out of the room and out another door in the extradimensional mansion that led to the rocky ridge above Castle Trinity, where Dorigen, her crystal ball in hand, waited.

* * * * *

"We are too high up," Vander protested as the party trudged along a narrow mountain trail more than halfway up a twelve-thousand-foot peak. A few scraggly branches, bare of leaves, dotted the trail, but mostly the place was wind-carved rock, ridged in some places, polished smooth in others. In this place, winter had already come in full. The snow lay deep, and the wind's bite, despite Cadderly's magical protection spells, forced the companions to continually rub their hands to keep their fingers from growing numb. The narrow trail was mostly bare to the stone, at least, perpetually windblown so that little snow had found a hold there.

"We must stay far from the lower trails," Cadderly replied, having to yell to be heard through the growling wind. "Many goblins and giantkin are about, fleeing Shilmista in search of their mountain holes."

"Better to face them than what we might find up here," Vander argued. The booming voice of the twelve-foot-tall giant, thick red beard crusted by blowing ice, had no trouble cutting through the din of the wind. "You do not know the creatures of the lands where the snow does not melt, young priest." The rugged firbolg was talking from some experience, it seemed, and the dwarves, Shayleigh, and Danica looked to Cadderly, hopeful that Vander's warning might carry some influence.

"Yeah, like that big bird I spotted, floating on the winds a mile away," Ivan put in.

"It was an eagle," Cadderly insisted, though only Ivan had actually seen the soaring creature. "Some of the eagles in the Snowflakes are quite large, and I doubt . . ."

"A mile away?" Ivan balked.

"I doubt that it was a mile," Cadderly finished, to which Ivan only shook his yellow-haired head, adjusted his helmet, which sported a pair of deer antlers, and cast a less-than-friendly glare Cadderly's way. By that time, Cadderly had found a new person to argue with, as Danica came up behind him and put a hand on his shoulder. He looked at her grim expression and recognized at once that she was in agreement with the others.

"I fear no monsters," she explained defensively, for she alone understood the pains the young priest had endured to get this quest underway. "But the land here is treacherous, and the wind uncomfortable at best. A slip on the ice could send one of us tumbling down the mountainside." Danica looked up the slope to their right and continued ominously, "And the snow hangs thick above us."

Cadderly did not have to follow her upward gaze to understand that she was referring to the very real threat of an avalanche. They had passed the remnants of a dozen such disasters, though most were old, probably from last year's spring melt.

Cadderly took a deep breath and reminded himself of his secret purpose in being up this high, and he remained adamant. "The snow here is seasonal," he replied, calling ahead to Vander. "Except for the very tops of the mountains, where we shall not go."

Vander started to protest—Cadderly expected that the firbolg would argue that these fearful snow creatures might easily come down from the mountaintops when the snow lay so deep. He had barely uttered the first syllable of protest, though, when Cadderly interrupted him with a telepathic message, a magical plea that the firbolg lead on without further argument, that standing and talking only delayed the time when they could go back down to more hospitable climes.

Vander grunted and turned about, flipping his white bearskin cloak back over one shoulder to reveal to the others that his huge hand rested uneasily on the sculpted hilt of his giant-sized sword.

"As for the wind and the ice," Cadderly said to Danica, "we shall be careful with our steps and hold fast to our resolve."

"Unless we get plucked off by a passing bird," Ivan said dryly.

"It was only an eagle," Cadderly insisted again, turning on the dwarf, his anger flaring. Ivan shrugged and walked away. Pikel, seemingly oblivious to all the arguing and quite willing to go wherever the others led him, bobbed happily at his brother's side.

"Ye ever seen an eagle with four paws?" Ivan snarled over his shoulder when he and Pikel had moved away. Pikel considered the question for a long moment before he stopped in his tracks, his smile melting away, and let out a profound, "Oooo."

Then the green-bearded dwarf skittered quickly to keep pace with the stomping Ivan. Together they walked right behind the firbolg and moved to Vander's sides when the trail was wide enough to accommodate them. The firbolg and the dwarves had become fast friends over the last days, continually trading tales of their respective homelands, places somewhat similar in rugged terrain and wicked beasts.

Cadderly came next in the procession, alone with his thoughts, still trying to reconcile his magical attack on Thobicus and contemplating the trials he knew that he would soon face, both at Castle Trinity and after Castle Trinity. Danica allowed Cadderly to get some distance away before she resumed the march, her eyes revealing a mixture of contempt and pain at the way Cadderly had just rebuked her.

"He is scared," Shayleigh said to Danica, coming to her side.

"And stubborn," Danica added.

The elf maiden's sincere smile was too infectious for Danica to hold her grim thoughts. Danica was glad that Shayleigh was beside her once more, feeling an almost sisterly bond with the spirited elf. Given Cadderly's recent mood and recent secretive actions, Danica felt as though she desperately needed a sister.

For Shayleigh, the trip was both a debt repaid and an act of sincere friendship. Cadderly, Danica, and the dwarves had come to the fighting aid of Shilmista's elves, and during their time together, Shayleigh had come to like all of them. More than one of Shilmista's haughty elves had joked at Shayleigh's expense, at the thought that an elf could so befriend a dwarf, but Shayleigh took it all in without complaint.

Less than a half hour later, on an exposed section of trail where the mountain to their right sloped up at a gentle angle, though the drop to their left remained steep, Vander pulled up short and put his great hands out to the sides to halt the dwarves. It had begun to snow again, the wind whipping the icy flakes so that the companions all had to keep their traveling cloaks tight about their faces. In that poor visibility, Vander was unsure about the unusual shape he noticed on a wide section of trail up ahead.

The giant took a tentative step forward, drawing his massive sword halfway from its sheath. Ivan and Pikel leaned backward and looked to each other from behind the firbolg. With simultaneous nods, they clutched their weapons, though they had no idea of what had put Vander on the alert.

Then Vander relaxed visibly, and the dwarves shared another shrug and tucked their hands back under their thick cloaks.

Two steps later, the shape, which Vander had identified as a snowbank, coiled up like some huge serpent and lashed out at the giant, brushing against his outstretched fingers.

Vander cried out and leaped back, grabbing at his suddenly bloody hand.

"The damn snow bit him!" Ivan yelled and rushed up, chopping with his double-headed axe. The blade passed right through the weird monster, clanging against the bare stone underneath, cutting nearly a quarter of the creature's bulk away.

But that quarter was just as alive, and just as vicious, as the main bulk, and now there were two monsters to fight.

Vander rushed in, chopping his sword with his one good hand.

Then there were three monsters.

Ivan felt an agonizing burn along one arm, but, blinded by the whipping wind and the battle frenzy, the dwarf did not realize the results of his actions. He brought his axe to bear repeatedly, unwittingly multiplying the monstrous ranks.

Cadderly had only just noticed the frenzied movements when Shayleigh's cry from behind turned him about. The young priest's eyes widened considerably when he saw the truth of Ivan's "eagle," a leonine beast taller than Cadderly and with a wingspan fully twenty-five feet across. The swooping creature did not come in close to Shayleigh and Danica, but instead abruptly broke the momentum of its dive, rearing in the air and whipping its tail over one muscled shoulder.

A volley of iron spikes shot out at the two. Danica pushed Shayleigh to the side, then contorted her own body somehow, miraculously avoiding any serious hits, though a line of blood, stark red against the white background, appeared immediately along the side of one arm.

Shayleigh was quick to ready her bow, but the leonine creature swooped away, and her shot was a long one, lost in the wind and the driving snow.

Up ahead, Vander got hit again and shrieked as Cadderly would never have believed the stoic and proud giant ever could. The young priest stumbled forward to discern the cause of the fighting, squinting and shaking his head, for he could not believe that his friends were fully surrounded by some sort of animated snow!

Their repeated blows had no effect—other than to create more monsters.

Cadderly fell into the song of Deneir, the logic that guided the harmony of his universe. He saw the spheres, not just the celestial spheres, but the magical spheres of elemental and energy-based powers. The simple and evident truths led Cadderly quickly to the conclusion that snow would best be battled with fire, and, hardly thinking about the movement, the young priest lifted his fist toward the largest section of creature between himself and his friends and uttered "*Fete!*" the Elvish word for fire.

A line of flames shot out from Cadderly's gold and onyx ring, engulfing several of the snow monsters in a sizzling blaze. Animated snow became insubstantial steam and gases, blowing away on the wind.

Then something struck hard against Cadderly's back, hurling him to the ground. Fear told him that the leonine monster must be back and he swung about, his clenched fist out in front.

He saw Danica standing protectively behind him and realized that it was she who had struck him. She now faced the newest beast that had entered the fray, a beast that had apparently been intent on the distracted young priest.

"Chimera?" Cadderly asked as much as stated when the winged, three-headed monster rushed in at Danica. Its central head and its torso were, like the other beast, those of a lion, but this one also had an orange scaled neck and head of a small dragon flanking it and a black goat's head behind.

The creature reared in midair; the dragon's head breathed forth a line of flame.

Danica jumped to the side away from Cadderly, then leaped up and caught a handhold on the stone above her, tucking her feet up high and somehow escaping the searing blast. She came back to the ledge after the fires had expired, but found no safe footing, for the flames had melted away the snow and weakened the integrity of that section of ledge. Ice reformed almost immediately in the freezing temperatures, and the young monk fell down hard onto her back. And then, dazed, Danica slipped out over the ledge.

Cadderly's world seemed to stop.

* * * * *

Farther down the trail, Shayleigh put her bow to deadly use, firing arrow after arrow at the leonine monster. Even with the powerful winds, many of her shots hit the mark, but the beast was resilient, and when its spike-throwing tail whipped about once more, Shayleigh had nowhere to run.

She grimaced at the dull thuds as several missiles blasted her to a half-sitting, half-leaning position on the mountain slope. She felt the sudden warmth of her own lifeblood flowing from several wounds. Stubbornly, the elf maiden put another arrow to her bowstring and let fly, scoring a solid hit in the monster's thick-muscled chest.

* * * * *

Cadderly dove flat to the stone, reached out desperately for Danica, who had gained a tentative handhold several feet below the ledge. She couldn't possibly climb up the ice in the driving wind and snow, and Cadderly, for all his training, couldn't reach her.

The priest sang along with the song of Deneir, again seeking out an elemental sphere, this time searching for answers in the realm of air.

Danica heard his singing and looked up plaintively, knowing that her one hand would not keep her in place for very long.

Moments later, Cadderly ended the song, looked back at Danica, and commanded her in magically enhanced tones to jump up at him. She did, trusting in her lover. Their hands brushed, just for a moment, but in that instant Danica heard Cadderly utter an arcane rune, a triggering word to a spell, and she felt a tingle as some power passed between them.

Then Danica plummeted away.

Cadderly had no time to watch her descent, had to trust fully in the revealed truths of his god. He looked all about and was relieved to see that the strong wind was working for them, forcing the two winged monsters to take long runs to get near the ledge.

Up ahead, Vander had used the break caused by Cadderly's fire to get out of the encircling monsters, and had taken Ivan with him, holding the dwarf in midair with a hand that seemed almost skinless.

Pikel had moved up a rock, but was again surrounded, beating the many vicious creatures back wildly with his tree-trunk club.

Cadderly lifted his onyx ring, but saw no clear angle. He fell into the song instead, entering the realm of fire.

"Me brother!" Ivan wailed, pulling free of Vander's grasp.

The yellow-bearded dwarf expected Vander to rush in beside him, but when he glanced at the firbolg, he realized the awful truth. The snow creatures had hit Vander several times, on both hands and forearms and once, probably when the giant had stooped to hoist up Ivan, on the side of his face. In each of these places, Vander's skin had simply dissolved, leaving garish, brutal wounds.

Now the firbolg was beyond comprehension, swaying from side to side as he barely managed to stand.

"Oo, ow!" came a cry from ahead.

Pikel needed help.

Ivan took a running stride toward his brother, then fell back in absolute shock as a ring of flames erupted around Pikel and rolled down the rock.

"Me brother!" Ivan cried again, above the sudden roar. He wanted to go forward, was willing, in spirit at least, to throw himself through the unexplained fiery curtain and die beside his dear brother. But the heat was too intense as the flames continued outward, the curtain fully twenty feet high. Steam mixed with the fires as snow and ice and the creatures were fully consumed.

Above his despair, Ivan heard a cry of hope, heard Cadderly shout out for Pikel to "Stand fast!"

A goat head butted Ivan hard on the shoulder, and a lion's paw swatted the dwarf's head, launching him backward. He cracked into Vander's knee, his deer-antlered helmet tearing firbolg skin, and his momentum knocking the stunned giant's feet out from under him. Down came Vander, on top of Ivan.

* * * * *

Blood had filled one of Shayleigh's clear violet eyes. She saw Cadderly, though, lying on the ledge, saw the chimera strike the dwarf, then swoop away, caught by the mighty wind.

Cadderly drew out something small, fumbled with the heavy belt strapped diagonally across his chest, and began to sing. From the desperate look in the young priest's eyes, Shayleigh guessed that the leonine beast had returned.

It was barely visible, perhaps thirty feet out from the ledge. Shayleigh could see that its target this time was Cadderly, and possibly the fallen dwarf and giant not far from Cadderly's flank. The monster darted in suddenly and reared, its deadly tail snapping forward.

"No!" the elf maiden cried, readying her bow. Looking back fearfully to the trail, she noticed a slight shimmer appear in the air before the priest. Shayleigh dismissed it as an optical trick of the snow and wind—until the mutant manticore's spikes entered that area and somehow reversed direction, shooting back out at the surprised beast!

Gouts of blood exploded against the leonine chest, driving the beast backward in the air. Shayleigh looked back to see Cadderly poised, hand-crossbow steadied across his free wrist. She quickly put an arrow into the monster's flank, thinking that Cadderly's tiny crossbow would be of little use.

The crossbow dart raced out at the monster. The lion roared—then roared louder as the quarrel stung its nose. For a moment, the bolt seemed a puny thing against the sheer bulk and strength of the beast, but then it collapsed on itself, crushing the vial of *Oil of Impact*. The resulting explosion sent bits of the monster's face and teeth scattering to the winds and drove the front end of the dart through the beast's thick skull.

Four paws flailing wildly, the dying monster dropped from sight.

Cadderly looked back to his ring of fire, confident that it had dispatched the snow creatures. All that remained was the chimera, floating somewhere out on the winds behind the blinding snow.

"Behind!" Shayleigh cried suddenly, spinning about and firing two quick arrows. The swooping chimera shrieked; its dragon head came in line with Cadderly, ready to loose its fiery breath once more.

Cadderly countered with a quick and simple magic, pulled from the element of water. A gusher erupted from his hands at the same time as the dragon head breathed, the fiery breath dissipating into a cloud of harmless steam.

The chimera burst through the gray veil right above the young priest, fore-claws slashing at Cadderly and knocking him to the ground.

"Ye mixed up bag o' body parts!" Ivan hooted, finally extracting himself from under the fallen giant. Two running steps put the infuriated dwarf alongside the soaring monster, and he leaped up, grabbing a horn of the black goat's head and pulling himself astride the beast.

Shayleigh followed their swooping path, ready to let fly another arrow, but she pulled up suddenly, stunned.

Danica had come back up to their level. She was walking in midair!

The chimera, all three heads looking back at those it had left behind on the ledge or at the furious dwarf scrambling about on its back, never saw the monk. Danica's spinning kick cracked the leonine jaw and nearly sent the five-hundred-pound monster tumbling headlong, and then agile Danica was up beside Ivan before the chimera could begin to react.

She drew out a silver-hilted dagger from one boot, wrapped its sculpted dragon head with her free hand, and went to vicious work on the central leonine head. Even more furious was Ivan Bouldershoulder, hands clasped about the goat horns, wrestling the thing back and forth.

The chimera banked in a steep roll, coming alongside the ledge so that Shayleigh managed another two shots before the snowstorm swallowed the beast and her friends.

The chimera came around again a moment later, and the elf prepared to fire. But Ivan suddenly popped up and regarded her incredulously, one of Shayleigh's arrows splintered and hanging from his deer-antlered helmet.

"Hey!" the dwarf bellowed, and she lowered the bow.

Ivan's distraction cost him, though, for the goat's head broke free of his grasp momentarily and butted hard against his face and forehead. Ivan spit out a tooth, grabbed the horns in both hands and butted back, and it seemed to Shayleigh that the dwarf's attack had been by far the more effective. Then they were gone again, behind the blinding sheets of snow. All was suddenly silent, save the howl of the wind.

Vander stirred and propped himself up on his elbows; Cadderly's enchanted wall of fire came down, to reveal Pikel sitting comfortably on the stone, munching a leg of mutton he had opportunistically pulled from his pack and roasted in the magical flames.

"Oo," the green-bearded dwarf said, hiding the meat behind his back when he noticed Cadderly's amazed expression.

"Do you see them?" Shayleigh asked, limping to Cadderly's side and directing his gaze back to the empty air.

Cadderly peered through the snow and shook his head.

When he looked back to Shayleigh, though, all thoughts of his monster-riding friends were replaced by the immediate needs of the wounded elf maiden. Several spikes had struck Shayleigh, one grazing the side of her head and opening a wicked gash, another deep into one thigh, a third driven into her wrist so that she could not close her hand, and a fourth sticking from her ribs. Cadderly could hardly believe that the elf was still standing, let alone firing her bow.

He listened for the song of Deneir immediately, bringing forth magics that would allow him to begin the mending of Shayleigh's wounds. Shayleigh said nothing, just grimaced stoically as Cadderly slowly drew out the spikes. All the while, the elf maiden held fast to her bow, kept her gaze out to the wide winds in search of her missing friends.

Minutes slipped past. Cadderly had the worst of the wounds closed, and Shayleigh signaled that to be enough for the time being. Cadderly didn't argue, turning his attention back to the search for Danica and Ivan.

"If the monster shakes free of them . . ." Shayleigh began ominously.

"Danica will not fall," Cadderly assured her. "Not with the enchantment I have put upon her. Nor will she allow Ivan to fall."

There was honest conviction in the priest's tone, but he sighed with some relief anyway when the chimera finally came back into view, speeding on a course that would take it directly above the ledge. Shayleigh lifted her bow, but her injured wrist would no longer allow her to pull the string back fast enough. Cadderly got a shot with his crossbow, but the chimera banked and the explosive quarrel flew harmlessly wide.

The monster roared in protest as it passed without any attacks, and the friends on the ledge could see that both its dragon and goat heads flopped lifelessly in the wind. Ivan, clutching the leonine mane, howled with enjoyment as he attempted to steer the beast by tugging one way or the other.

"Jump free!" Danica cried to the dwarf as the mountain loomed before them. The young woman stepped off the creature as it passed the ledge, skipped down across the empty air (to Pikel's amazed cry of "OO oi!" and Vander's incredulous stare) to join Cadderly and Shayleigh.

"Jump free!" Danica yelled again, this time with Shayleigh and Cadderly joining in.

The yellow-bearded dwarf didn't seem to hear them, and Danica prudently rushed back out from the ledge in case the beast headed out into the empty air once more. The chimera did bank against Ivan's stubborn pull and start back out, but this time, both Cadderly and Shayleigh were presented with perfect shots. Shayleigh's arrow dove deep into the chimera's torso, and Cadderly's quarrel got the beast on the wing, its explosive force shattering bone and sending the beast into a repeated barrel roll.

Ivan tugged and yanked frantically, looking for some place to safely land as the creature flopped about, turning back toward the towering mountain.

"Jump!" the companions pleaded with the dwarf.

"Snowbank!" Ivan yelled in high hopes, twisting the monster's head in line with a white pile jutting above the smooth slope of the mountain, just a dozen or so feet above the ledge. "Snowbank!"

Not quite—the inch of snow covering the jutting boulder did not, by any definition, constitute a snowbank

"Boom," remarked a grimacing Pikel as the chimera and Ivan crashed heavily, the dwarf bouncing back, skidding and slipping until he came to a stop, amazingly on his feet on the ledge.

The crushed chimera thrashed about near the rock until Shayleigh's next arrow sank into the leonine head, ending its agony.

Ivan turned to regard Cadderly and the others, his pupils rolling about their sockets independently of each other. Somehow, Ivan still wore his deer-antlered helmet, and somehow, Shayleigh's splintered arrow had not been dislodged.

"Who knowed?" Ivan asked innocently, giving a lame attempt at shrugging his shoulders as he fell facedown on the path.

Five

Test of Willpower

adderly and Shayleigh broke immediately for the stunned dwarf, but Danica rushed back to the ledge, grabbed Cadderly and spun him about, her lips crushing against his as she kissed him hard. She backed off suddenly, her features twisted with admiration and appreciation—and ecstasy.

Her breath came in excited gasps; her eyes darted wildly, from the open air beyond the ledge to her enchanted feet and to the man who had saved her life. "I want to do it again!" she blurted, fumbling over the words as though she couldn't help but say them.

Cadderly seemed perplexed, until he realized that his love had just walked on air. What an incredible experience that must have been! He stared at Danica for a long moment. Then, remembering Ivan's situation, he looked to Pikel, who was happily munching on his roasted mutton once more (apparently, Ivan was not too badly injured), and looked to the rock where Ivan and the chimera had abruptly ended their wild ride. All of this apparent insanity in the midst of a desperate plan, the success of which could well determine the very existence of the peoples of the region.

And Danica's sparkling brown eyes, so full of admiration, told Cadderly something more. He was coming to the forefront of it all, inevitably taking up the lead in this crusade. He had grabbed at this responsibility—fully when he had bent Dean Thobicus's mind—but now, as the true weight of that responsibility became clearer to him, he was worried.

Always before, Cadderly had depended on his powerful friends. He pointed the way, and they, through stealth and sword, facilitated the plans. Now, though, judging from the look in Danica's eyes, Cadderly's burden had increased. His mounting magical powers had become the group's primary weapon.

Cadderly would not shy away from his new role, would fight on with all his heart and all his strength. But he wondered if he could live up to his friends' expectations, if he could continue to keep Danica's eyes sparkling.

It was all too much for the burdened young priest. What began as an embarrassed chuckle ended with Cadderly sitting on the stone ledge, laughing at the very edge of hysteria.

The sight of Vander, up again and moving toward him, sobered Cadderly. Although Vander's brutal wounds had already somehow begun to mend, the giant's face showed his pain—and showed that Vander did not see anything humorous about their situation.

"I told you that we were too high up," the firbolg said in a low, firm voice.

Cadderly thought for a moment, then began to explain to the giant that, while the strange, animated snow creature might have been natural to the region, both the chimera and the other winged beast, the mutated manticore, were magical in nature and not denizens of the cold and desolate high peaks. Cadderly never finished the explanation,though, suddenly realizing the implications of his own thoughts.

Magical creatures?

What a fool I've been! Cadderly thought, and to Vander and his friends he offered only a sudden, confused expression. The young priest closed his eyes and mentally probed the region, sought out the magical eye of the scrying wizard—for someone had certainly guided the two monsters! Almost immediately, he felt the connection, felt the directed line of magical energy that could only be the probing of a scrying wizard—and promptly released a countering line to disperse it. Then Cadderly threw up magical defenses, put a veil around himself and his friends that would not be easily penetrated by distant, probing eyes.

"What is it?" Danica demanded when he had at last reopened his gray eyes.

Cadderly shook his head, then looked to Vander. "Find a sheltered area where we might set a camp and mend our wounds," he instructed the firbolg. Danica was still staring at him, waiting for an explanation, but the young priest only offered another shake of his head, feeling positively foolish for not warding them all against scrying wizards much earlier in the journey.

Again Cadderly wondered if he would disappoint those who had come to trust in him.

* * * * *

The chimera and the manticore were Aballister's creatures, his children, brought into existence and nurtured to mighty maturity by the magics of the powerful wizard. When they fell in the mountains, Aballister sensed the loss, as though a part of his own energy had been stripped from him. He left his private quarters so abruptly that he didn't even bother to close his spellbook, or to put up wards against intruders. The old wizard bounded down the hall to Dorigen's room and pounded on the door, disrupting the woman's studying.

"Find them," Aballister snarled as soon as Dorigen opened the door, pushing his way in.

"What do you know?" she asked.

"Find them!" Aballister commanded again. He spun about and grabbed Dorigen by the hand, pulling her to the seat before her crystal ball.

Dorigen tore her hand free of Aballister's grasp and eyed him dangerously.

"Find them!" the older wizard growled at her for the third time, not retreating an inch from her threatening glare.

Dorigen recognized the urgency in Aballister's wizened face, knew that he would not have come in here and treated her with such disrespect if he was not terribly afraid. She uncovered the crystal ball and stared into the item for a long while, concentrating on reestablishing the connection to Cadderly. Several moments passed with the ball showing nothing but its swirling gray mist. Dorigen pressed on, commanding the mist to form an image.

The ball went perfectly black.

Dorigen looked up to Aballister helplessly, and the older wizard pushed her aside and took her place. He went at the ball with all his magical strength, throwing his incredible willpower against the black barriers. Someone had warded against scrying. Aballister growled and threw more magical strength into the effort, almost punching through the black veil. The power of the defenses told him unmistakably who the defender might be.

"No!" Aballister growled, and he went at the barrier again, determined to force his way through those wards.

The ball remained inactive.

"Damn him!" Aballister cried, slapping the crystal from its stand. Dorigen caught the solid ball as it rolled off the table's edge. She saw Aballister wince, though the wizard stubbornly did not grab at his already swelling hand.

"Your son is more formidable . . ." Dorigen began, but Aballister cut her short with an animal-like growl. He leaped up from his seat and sent the stool bouncing away.

"My son is a troublesome insect," Aballister sneered, thinking of many ways that he might make Cadderly and his friends pay for the loss of the chimera and the manticore. "The next surprise that I will send to him will be a measure of my own powers."

A shudder coursed along Dorigen's spine. She had never heard Aballister more determined. She was Aballister's student, had witnessed many powerful displays of magic from the older man—and had known that those were just a fraction of what he was capable of launching.

"Find them!" Aballister growled again between sharp, hissing breaths, and, on as close an edge of uncontrollable rage as Dorigen had ever seen him, he swept from the room, slamming the door behind him.

Dorigen nodded as though she meant to try, but as soon as she was convinced that Aballister would not immediately return, she replaced the ball in its support and draped a cloth over it. Cadderly had countered the magic, and the scrying device would not function for at least a day, Dorigen knew. In truth, she didn't expect to find any more success the next day, either, for Cadderly was apparently on to her secret prying now and would not likely let his guard slip again.

Dorigen looked to the closed door and thought again that Aballister did not understand the power of his son. Nor the compassion, she realized as she clenched her still-mending hands and considered that, by Cadderly's mercy alone, she was still very much alive.

But neither did Cadderly understand the power of his father. Dorigen was glad that Druzil, and not she, had been sent out near the young priest, for when Aballister struck out at Cadderly the next time, it seemed to Dorigen that mountains would be leveled.

* * * * *

When Danica awakened, the glow of the fire was low, barely illuminating the nearest features of the wide cave the party had found. She heard the comforting snores of the dwarves, Ivan's grumbles complementing Pikel's whistles, and could feel that Shayleigh was soundly resting near the wall behind her.

Vander, too, was asleep, propped against a stone on the other side of the low fire. The night was dark and calm, and the snow had ceased, though the lessened wind continued a quiet, steady moan at the wide cave door. By all appearances, the campsite seemed quite serene, but the monk's keen instincts told her that something was not as it should be.

She propped herself up on her elbows and looked about. A second glow showed in the cave, far to the side and partially blocked by Cadderly's sitting form. Cadderly? Danica looked to the wide cave entrance, to where the young priest should have been standing a watch.

She heard a slight rattle, and then some soft chanting. Silently, Danica slipped out of her bedroll and eased her way across the stone floor.

Cadderly sat cross-legged before a lit candle, a parchment spread on the floor beside him, its ends anchored by small stones. Next to that was the young priest's writing kit and the *Tome of Universal Harmony*, the holy book of Deneir, both opened. Danica crept closer, heard Cadderly's low chanting, and saw the young priest drop some ivory counters to the floor in front of him.

He marked something on the parchment, then tossed a fresh quill into the air before him, watching as it spun to the stone, then making a note of its direction. Danica had been around priests long enough to understand that her love was engaged in some sort of divination spell.

Danica nearly jumped and cried aloud when she felt a hand on her back, but she kept her wits enough to take the moment to recognize Shayleigh moving up beside her. The elf looked curiously to Cadderly, then back to Danica, who only shook her head and held her hands up wide.

Cadderly read something from the book, then fumbled with his pack and produced a small, gold-edged mirror and a pair of mismatched gloves, one black and one white.

Danica's mouth dropped open. Cadderly had brought the *Ghearufu*, the evil three-piece artifact that the assassin had carried, the same powerful item that Dean Thobicus had insisted be turned over for inspection!

The significance of the *Ghearufu* sent a myriad of questions hurtling through Danica's thoughts. From what she had seen, and from what Cadderly had told her, this was an item of possession—might Cadderly's strange behavior, his hysterical laughter on the ledge, and his insistence that the group remain dangerously high in the mountains, be somehow linked to the *Ghearufu*? Was Cadderly himself fighting against some sort of possession, some evil entity that clouded his judgment while leading them all astray?

Shayleigh again put a hand on Danica's back and looked to the monk with concern, but a movement to the side distracted them both.

Vander crossed the floor in three easy strides, grabbed Cadderly by the back of his tunic, and lifted the young priest from the floor.

"What are you about?" the firbolg demanded loudly. "Do you stand your watch from inside . . . ?" The words caught in Vander's throat; the blood drained from his ruddy face. There before him lay the *Ghearufu*, the evil device that had held him as a slave for many tragic years.

Danica and Shayleigh rushed over to them, Danica fearing that Vander, in his surprise and horror, might hurl Cadderly across the cave.

"What *are* you about?" Danica agreed with Vander, but as she spoke, she crossed in front of the firbolg and strategically placed her thumb against a pressure point in Vander's forearm, quietly forcing the giant to release his grip.

Cadderly scowled and straightened his tunic, then went to gather his possessions. At first, he seemed embarrassed, but then, when he looked back to Danica's resolute stare, he steeled his gray eyes resolutely.

"You should not have brought that," Danica said to him.

Cadderly did not immediately respond, though his thoughts were screaming that the *Ghearufu* was the main reason that they were there.

The other three exchanged worried glances.

"We have come for Castle Trinity," Danica argued.

"That is but one reason," Cadderly replied cryptically. He wasn't sure whether he should tell them the truth or not, wasn't sure that he wanted to compel them to accompany him to the terrible place where the *Ghearufu* could be destroyed.

Danica felt Vander's muscles tighten, and she leaned back more firmly against the firbolg to prevent him from leaping out and throttling the young priest.

"Do you always keep such important secrets from those who travel beside you?" Shayleigh asked. "Or do you believe that trust is not an essential element of any adventuring party?"

"I would have told you!" Cadderly snapped at her.

"When?" Danica growled at him from the other side. He looked back between the two, and to Vander's outraged expression, and seemed to be losing his nerve.

"Has the *Ghearufu* found a hold on you?" Danica asked bluntly.

"No!" Cadderly shot back at once. "Though it has tried. You cannot imagine the depth of evil within this artifact."

Vander cleared his throat, a pointed reminder that the firbolg had felt the *Ghearufu*'s sting long before Cadderly even knew the item existed.

"Then what use might it be?" Shayleigh snarled.

Cadderly bit his lower lip, glancing one way and the other. He suspected that his companions would not agree with his priorities, would still consider Castle Trinity the most important of their missions. Again doubts about being in the forefront assaulted the young priest. He told himself that he owed his friends an explanation at least.

But that was just a rationalization, Cadderly knew. He wanted to tell his friends, wanted them to line up beside him on this most dangerous of duties.

"We have come out in search of Castle Trinity," he explained, his conscience gnawing over every word. "But that is only one purpose. I have done much searching and have discerned that there are few—very few—ways in which the *Ghearufu* might be truly destroyed."

"This could not have waited?" Danica asked.

"No!" Cadderly retorted angrily. At his suddenly explosive tone, the three doubters again exchanged concerned glances, and Danica virtually snarled as she regarded the *Ghearufu*.

"If I had left the *Ghearufu* at the library, we cannot even guess the extent of the disaster we would have found upon our return," Cadderly explained, his voice even once more. "And if we take it with us all the way to Castle Trinity, our enemies might find a way to use it against us." He, too, looked down at the item, his face flushed with fear.

"But it will not get to that dangerous point," the young priest insisted. "There is a way to end the threat of the *Ghearufu* forever. That is why we took the high trails," he explained, eyeing Vander directly. "There is a peak near here, somewhat legendary in the region."

"Fyrentennimar?" Danica balked, and Shayleigh, recognizing the dreaded name, gave an unintentional wheeze.

"The peak is called Nightglow," Cadderly continued, undaunted. "In decades past, it was said to burn with inner fires in the dark of night, a glow that could be seen from Carradoon and all across the Shining Plains."

"A volcano," Vander reasoned, remembering his own rugged home, tucked among many lava-spewing peaks.

"A dragon," Danica corrected. "An old red, according to the legend."

"Older still since the tales date back two centuries or more," Shayleigh added gravely. "And not just a legend," she assured them. "Galladel, who was King of Shilmista Forest, remembered the time of the dragon, remembered the devastation old Fyren brought to Carradoon and to the forest."

"The damned fool boy is thinking o' waking a dragon?" Ivan bellowed, storming up to join the circle about Cadderly. In the intrigue, no one had noticed that the rhythmic dwarven snoring had ceased.

"Uh-uhhh," Pikel said to Cadderly, waggling one finger back and forth in front of his face.

"Do you wish the *Ghearufu* destroyed?" Cadderly asked simply, aiming the thought at Vander, whom he considered his best prospect for an ally against the rising tide of protest.

The firbolg seemed truly torn.

"At what cost?" Danica demanded before Vander could sort out his thoughts. "The dragon has slept for centuries—centuries of peace. How many lives will it need to satisfy its hunger upon awakening?"

"Let a sleeping wyrm lie, me Pappy always said," Ivan piped in.

"Yup," added Pikel, nodding eagerly.

Cadderly gave a resigned sigh, scooped the *Ghearufu* into his pack, and hoisted it over one shoulder. "I have been directed to destroy the *Ghearufu*," he said, his voice full of resignation. "There is only one way."

"Then it must wait," Danica replied. "The threat to all the region . . ."

"Is a temporary danger in a temporary society," Cadderly finished philosophically. "The *Ghearufu* is not temporary. It has pained the world since its creation in the lower planes many millennia ago.

"I'll not force this upon you," Cadderly went on calmly. "I have been directed by the precepts of a god that you do not worship. Go and speak among yourselves, come to a decision together or individually. This quest is mine, and yours only by your own choice. And you are right," he said to Shayleigh, seeming sincerely apologetic. "I erred in not revealing this to you all when first we left the library. The situation was . . . difficult." He looked at Danica as he ended, knowing that she alone understood what he had gone through to "convince" Dean Thobicus.

The others moved across the cavern floor slowly, each of them glancing back at Cadderly many times.

"The boy's daft," Ivan insisted, loudly enough so that Cadderly could hear.

"He follows his heart," Danica replied quietly.

"I, too, do not doubt Cadderly's sincerity," Shayleigh added. "It is his wisdom that I question."

Pikel continued to nod his eager agreement.

"To wake a dragon," Vander said grimly, shaking his head.

"A red," Danica pointedly added, for red dragons were the wickedest and most powerful of all the evil dragons. "Perhaps an ancient red by now."

Still Pikel nodded, and Ivan slapped him on the back of his head.

"Oo," the green-bearded dwarf said, glaring at his brother.

"Ye don't go waking wyrms," Ivan put in, again loud enough for Cadderly to hear.

"There is something else I fear," Danica said. "Is Cadderly being correctly guided by his god, or is the *Ghearufu* wrongly leading him to where it might find a powerful ally?"

The thought made the others rock back on their heels, brought profound sighs from Shayleigh and Vander and a drawn-out "Ooooooo" from Pikel and Ivan, who then, apparently realizing that he was mimicking Pikel, snapped his head about to regard his brother suspiciously.

"What do we do?" Shayleigh asked.

They stood quietly for many moments before Danica dared a decision. "The threat now is Castle Trinity," she declared.

"But the *Ghearufu* does not come along with us," Vander insisted, barely able to keep his giant voice quiet. "We can bury it here, in the mountains, and return for it when the other business is completed."

"Cadderly will not agree," Shayleigh reasoned, looking at the resolute young priest.

"Then we won't ask him," Ivan replied with a sly wink. He looked Danica's way and nodded, and Danica, after a plaintive look at the man she loved, returned the nod. Alone, she moved toward Cadderly, and Ivan figured the young man would be in the bag in a moment.

"You will not go along to Nightglow," Cadderly stated, not asked, as Danica approached.

Danica said nothing. Unconsciously, she clenched and unclenched a fist at her side—a movement that Cadderly did not miss.

"The *Ghearufu* is paramount," the young priest said.

Danica still did not reply. Cadderly read her thoughts, though, saw that she was struggling with her decided course and understood that course to be one hinting at treachery. He began to sing under his breath as Danica moved in at him. Suddenly her manner became urgent; she tried to grab him, but found that he had become something insubstantial.

"Help me!" Danica called to her friends, and they rushed over, Ivan and Pikel diving for Cadderly's legs. The dwarves knocked their heads together, locked in a wrestling tumble, and it took them a few seconds to understand that they had grabbed on to nothing more than each other.

For Cadderly's corporeal form was fast fading, scattering to the wind.

Six

On the Path

D ruzil sat on a broken stump, clawed fingers tapping anxiously against his skinny legs. The imp knew the way to the Edificant Library from this point, and knew that the malignant spirit had veered off in the wrong direction and was now headed into the open and wild mountains.

Druzil was not overly disappointed—he really didn't want to go near the awful library again, and doubted that even this powerful spirit would last very long against the combined strength of the many goodly priests living there. The imp was confused, though. Was this spirit guided by any real purpose, as Druzil had initially believed, as Aballister had led him to believe? Or would the wretched thing wander aimlessly through the mountains, destroying whatever creatures it accidentally happened upon?

The thought did not sit well with the impatient imp. Logically, Druzil realized that there must be some important connection with this monster, probably a connection concerning Cadderly. If not, then why would Aballister have dispatched him to keep a watch over the uncontrollable thing?

Too many questions assaulted the imp, too many possibilities for Druzil to consider. He looked at the monster, tearing and slashing its way along a northern trail, frightening animals and ripping plants with seemingly endless savagery. Then Druzil looked inward, brought his focus into that magical area common to extraplanar creatures, and sent his thoughts careening across the mountain passes, seeking a telepathic link with his wizard master. For all the urgency of his call, he was nevertheless surprised when Aballister eagerly responded to his mental intrusions.

Where is Cadderly? the wizard's thoughts came to him. *Has the ghost caught up to him?*

Many of Druzil's questions had just been answered. Aballister's mental interrogation rolled on; the wizard prodded Druzil's thoughts with a series of questions so quickly that Druzil didn't even have time to respond. The conniving imp understood immediately that he held the upper hand in this communication, that Aballister was desperate for answers.

Druzil rubbed his clawed hands together, enjoying the superiority, confident that he could get all the information he needed by bargaining answer for answer.

Druzil opened his eyes many minutes later, having a new perspective on the situation. Aballister had been nervous—Druzil could sense that, both from the intensity of the wizard's telepathic responses and from the fact that Aballister had apparently left little unanswered this time. The wizard was a cryptic sort, always withholding information that he did not believe his lessers needed to know. Not this time, though. This time, the wizard had flooded Druzil with information about the ghost and Cadderly.

Given the imp's understanding about his master's demeanor, there could be no doubt that Aballister was teetering on a very dangerous edge. Ever since the wizard had called Druzil to his side, the imp had longed to see Aballister's power revealed in full. He had seen Aballister strike down a rival with a lightning bolt, literally frying the man; he had seen the wizard engulf a cave of upstart goblins with a ball of fire that had scored the stones and killed every one of the beasts; he had traveled to the far northland with the wizard, and had watched Aballister wipe out an entire community of taers, shaggy white beasts.

But those were just hints, Druzil knew, tantalizing tastes of what was yet to come. Even though he had never truly respected the wizard (Druzil had never respected any being from the Material Plane), he had always sensed the man's inner power. Aballister, nervous and edgy, outraged that his own son would be the one to threaten his designs on the region, was boiling like a pot about to blow.

And Druzil, malicious and chaotic in the extreme, thought the whole thing perfectly delicious.

He gave a flap of his wings and set off in pursuit of the now-distant ghost. Following the creature's trail—a wide swath of near-total destruction—was not difficult, and Druzil had the creature in sight in less than an hour.

He decided to try to contact the creature, to solidify his alliance with the ghost before it caught up to Cadderly, and before Aballister could lay claim to its destructive powers. Still invisible, the imp flew around in front of the marching ghost and perched on a low branch in a pine tree farther up its intended path.

The ghost sniffed the air as Druzil passed, even took a lazy swing that was far behind the fast-flying imp. As soon as Druzil had moved beyond its reach, it seemed to pay the unseen disturbance no more heed.

Druzil materialized as the ghost approached. "I am a friend," he announced, both in the common tongue and telepathically.

The creature snarled and came on more quickly, a blackened arm leading the way.

698 R. A. Salvatore

"Friend," Druzil reiterated, this time in the growling and hissing language common to the lower planes.

Still the advancing creature, focused on Druzil as though the imp was simply one more thing to be destroyed, did not respond. Druzil hit the ghost with a telepathic barrage, every thought signifying friendship or alliance, but the monster remained unresponsive.

"Friend, you stupid thing!" Druzil shouted, hopping to his feet and snapping his knuckles against his hips in a defiant stance. The creature was only a few yards away.

A snarl and a leap brought the monster right up to Druzil, the one unbroken arm coming about. The imp squeaked, suddenly realizing the danger, and gave a frantic flap of his wings to lift away.

Ghost ripped the branch right from the tree, hurled it aside, and smashed on viciously, and Druzil, caught within the canopy of thick evergreen boughs, scrambled for his very life, wings beating and claws tearing, trying to force some opening where he could slip through to the open air. He willed himself invisible again, but the monster seemed to sense him anyway, for the pursuit remained focused and relentless.

The creature was right behind him.

Druzil's whiplike tail, dripping lethal venom, snapped into the creature's face, blowing a wide hole in its hollowed cheek.

The creature didn't even flinch. The powerful arm came about again, tearing away a large branch, opening up the tangle enough so that the next attack would not be deflected.

Druzil clawed and kicked, fighting against the canopy wildly. And then he was through, bursting into the air where a few wingbeats brought him far from the snarling monster's reach.

The undead monster emerged from the battered tree a few moments later, stalking along the path, apparently giving no more concern to the latest creature that had fled from its terrifying power.

"*Bene tellemara*," the thoroughly shaken imp muttered, finding a perch on a jutting stone overlooking the trail and watching the uncontrollable monster's steady and undeniable progress.

"*Bene tellemara*."

* * * * *

Waist-deep in snow, Cadderly looked up the high, steep slope to the fog-enshrouded peak of Nightglow. Even using his magical spells to ward off the cold, the young priest felt the bite of the blasting wind and a general numbness creeping into his legs. He considered calling upon his most powerful magics then, as he had done to escape his misinformed friends, so he could walk along the wind up the mountainside.

Cadderly quickly reconsidered, though, realizing that he could not afford to expend any more magical energy—not with an old red dragon waiting for him. He shook his head determinedly and trudged on, step after step, hoisting one leg out of the deep, bogging snow and setting it firmly ahead of him.

One step at a time, higher and higher.

The sun had risen, the day bright and clear, and Cadderly had to squint constantly against the stinging glare of the rays reflecting off the virgin snow. Every now and then a section would shift under his weight and groan, and Cadderly would hold very still, expecting an avalanche to tumble down about him.

He thought he heard a call on the wind, Danica perhaps, shouting out his name. It was not an impossibility; he had left his friends not so far from here, and he had told them where he was headed.

That thought made Cadderly realize again how vulnerable he must now seem, a black dot on an exposed sheet of whiteness, climbing slowly, barely moving. Were any more chimeras or other winged beasts circling the area, hungry for his blood? he wondered. Right before he had begun the climb of this last slope, he had mentally searched for any signs of scrying wizards. None were apparent, but Cadderly had put up a few wards anyway.

Still, standing in the open on that slope, the young priest was not comforted. He pulled his cloak up tighter about his neck and considered again what magics he might call upon to facilitate this brutal climb.

In the end, though, he used only sheer determination. His legs ached, and he found his breathing hard to come by because of the thinner air and the exertion. He found a region of bare stone again higher up, under the foggy veil, and was somewhat surprised until he realized the reason that this area seemed much warmer. Using the warmth as a guiding beacon, Cadderly worked his way around a jutting hunk of stone and found a cave opening of good size, though certainly not large enough for the likes of an adult dragon.

The young priest understood that he had found Fyrentennimar, though, for the lair of only one type of creature could emanate enough warmth to melt the snow atop wintry Nightglow.

Cadderly unwrapped some of his outer clothing and plopped down to catch his breath and rest his weary limbs. He considered again the mighty foe he would soon face and the repertoire of spells he would need if he was to have any chance at all in this desperate quest.

"Desperate?" Cadderly whispered, pondering the sound of the grim word. Even the determined young priest had begun to wonder if "foolhardy" might be a better description.

Seven

Awe

Cadderly could not believe how warm the air grew as soon as he moved through the opening on the mountainside. He was in more of a tunnel than a cave, its walls running tight and uneven, gradually making its wormhole way down toward the heart of the mountain.

The young priest removed his traveling cloak, bundled it tight, and put it in his pack, carefully wrapping it about the *Tome of Universal Harmony*. He considered leaving the great book and some of his other most prized possessions by the entrance, fearing that even if he somehow survived his encounter with Fyrentennimar, some of his items might be burned away.

With a defiant shake of the head, Cadderly replaced the pack over his shoulder. Now was not the time for negative thinking, he decided. He took out a cylindrical metal tube and popped off the end cap, loosing a concentrated beam of light (from a magical enchantment placed on a disk inside the tube) ahead of him. Then he set off, recalling the song of Deneir as he went, knowing that he might have to call on his magical energy in an instant's notice if he was to have any chance at all against the great dragon.

Twenty minutes later he was still walking, creeping down a loose-packed slide of rocks. The heat was more intense now; even after Cadderly dispelled his cold-protecting magic, the sweat beaded on his forehead and stung his gray eyes.

He passed through several larger chambers as he moved down the tunnels, and he felt vulnerable indeed with only a small area illuminated in front of him and thick darkness looming to both sides. A twist of the outer metal shell of his device retracted the tube, somewhat widening the light beam, but still Cadderly had to fight the nervous urge to call upon his magic and brighten the entire area.

He breathed easier when he went back into a narrow tunnel, too narrow, certainly, for any dragon to squeeze through. The floor sloped downward at an easy, gradual angle for more than a hundred feet, but then suddenly turned vertical, a crawl hole dropping away into the darkness.

Sitting on the lip, Cadderly secured his gear and strapped his light tube under the bandoleer so that it aimed down below him. Then he eased himself over, picking his way carefully.

The air was stifling, the rocks pressed in on him, but Cadderly continued the descent, moving until he found the hole suddenly opening wide below him. For an instant, his feet kicked free in empty air, and he nearly fell through.

Somehow he managed to secure his position, hooking one elbow over a jag, and getting his feet back up so that he could press them against the solid wall. With his free hand, the young priest tentatively reached for his light tube, angled it down and out from him to find that he had come to the ceiling of a wide cavern.

A wide and high cavern, Cadderly feared, for the light did not reveal any floor below him. For the first time since he had entered the tunnels, he wondered if his path would actually get him anywhere near the dragon. Obviously, the small cave opening in the side of the mountain was not the huge dragon's doorway; Cadderly had not considered that perhaps the cave networks within the mound were intricate and possibly impassable.

Stubbornly, the young priest tightened the beam's focus, the sliver of light reaching far below. He then made out the subtle hue shift, the darker stone of the floor, twenty or so feet beneath him. He considered dropping—for the moment it took him to remember that he was wearing a bandoleer full of vials of volatile *Oil of Impact*!

Cadderly cursed his luck; if he had any intention of continuing along this course, he would have to call upon his magic—magic that he knew he would need in full against the likes of old Fyren. With a resigned sigh, he focused on the song of Deneir, remembering that part he had sung to Danica when she had tumbled from the mountain trail. Then he was walking down toward the cavern floor, walking in the empty air.

Cadderly understood Danica's ecstasy, understood the almost speechless excitement the young woman had felt when similarly enchanted. All logic told Cadderly that he should fall, and yet he did not. Using magic, he had completely defied the rules of nature, and, he had to admit, the sensation of air walking was incredible, better than stepping into the spirit world, better than lessening his corporeal form so that he might drift with the wind.

He could have stepped down to the stone a moment later, but he did not. He continued along through the wide chamber and into the tunnels, marching a foot off the ground, justifying his enjoyment by telling himself that he was moving more silently this way. In spite of the ever-present eeriness, in spite of the fact that he had run away from his friends and gone off into such danger alone, by the time the enchantment wore away, the young priest was smiling.

But the heat had intensified, tenfold it seemed, and what sounded like a distant growl soon reminded Cadderly that his path neared its end. He stood very still on the edge of yet another wide chamber for a few moments and listened intently, but couldn't be sure if the rhythmic breathing he thought he heard was his imagination or the sounds of the dragon.

"Only one way to find out," the brave priest muttered grimly, forcing one foot ahead of the other. He started across the floor in a crouch, light tube and crossbow held out in front of him.

He saw that the chamber was rock-filled and was curious about the fact that all of the stones seemed approximately the same size and were similarly reddish in hue. Cadderly wondered if these might be something created by the dragon, some remnant of the beast's fiery breath, perhaps. He had seen cats expel hair balls; might a dragon cough up rocks? The notion brought a nervous chuckle to Cadderly's lips, but he bit it back immediately, eyes wide with surprise.

One of the stones blinked at him!

Cadderly froze in his tracks, trying to keep the beam of light steady on the creature. To the side, another "rock" shifted, forcing Cadderly's attention. As soon as he brought the light around, he realized that these were not stones all about him, but giant toads, red-colored, with their uplifted heads higher than Cadderly's waist.

Just as Cadderly decided that he must not make any sudden moves, must try to ease his way beyond these weird creatures, a toad shuffled somewhere behind him. Despite his determination, Cadderly spun about, bringing the light to bear and startling several other monsters.

* * * * *

"I ain't going up there to fight any damned wyrm!" Ivan protested, crossing his burly arms over his chest, which put them about three inches above the level of the deep snow. The dwarf pointedly looked away from the rising slope of Nightglow.

"Uh-oh," Pikel muttered.

"Cadderly is up there," Danica reminded the stubborn, yellow-bearded dwarf.

"Then Cadderly's stupid," Ivan grumbled without missing a beat. A giant arm wrapped about him suddenly, and he was hoisted into the air, tucked in close to Vander's side.

"Hee hee hee." Pikel's mirth did little to brighten Ivan's mood.

"Why, ye thieving, dwarf-stealing son of a red-haired dragon!" Ivan roared, kicking viciously but futilely against the firbolg's powerful hold.

"We should scale straight to the opening," Danica reasoned.

"Right along Cadderly's trail," Shayleigh agreed.

"Might we hurry?" Vander asked of them. "Ivan is biting my arm."

Danica was away in a moment, scrambling with all speed up the slope, following Cadderly's obvious footprints. Shayleigh came right behind, the nimble, light-footed elf having little trouble managing the deep snow. She kept her bow out and ready, playing a watchful role while Danica tracked.

Vander plodded along behind her, trying to resist the urge to cave in the vicious Ivan's thick skull, and Pikel came last, bobbing easily in the cleared wake of the giant firbolg.

They stood in the melted region before the cave entrance a few minutes later. Shayleigh peered in, using her elven heat-sensing vision, but she poked her head back out in a moment and shrugged helplessly, explaining that the air was too warm inside for her to make out anything distinct.

"Cadderly went in," Danica said, as much to firm her own resolve as to the others. "And so must we."

"Nope," came Ivan's predictable reply.

"The enchantment that Cadderly put over you last night will not hold for long," Shayleigh reminded him. "The air is too cold this high up for even one of a dwarf's toughness."

"Better freezed than toasted," Ivan grumbled.

Danica ignored the remark and slipped into the cave. Shayleigh shook her head and followed.

Vander set Ivan on the ground, drawing curious looks from both the dwarves. "I'll not force you into a dragon's cave," the firbolg explained, and he walked by without waiting for a reply, squeezing in through the narrow entrance.

"Oo," Pikel moaned, not so filled with humor now that they had come to a critical moment.

Ivan stood resolute, his burly arms crossed over his chest and one foot tap-tapping on the wet stone. Pikel looked from his brother, to the cave, back to his brother, and back to the cave, not sure of what he should do.

"Aw, go on," Ivan growled at him a few seconds later. "I'm not for leaving the thick-headed fool to fight the dragon alone!"

Pikel's cherubic face brightened considerably as Ivan grabbed him and led the way in. When the green-bearded dwarf remembered that they were marching on their merry way to face a red dragon, that impish smile disappeared.

* * * * *

Far down the trail from the face of Nightglow, Druzil watched the black forms disappear under the high, enshrouding veil of fog. The imp had no idea of where the giant had come from—why would a giant be marching beside Cadderly?—but he was fairly confident that the other distant forms, particularly the two bobbing, short, and stout creatures, belonged to Cadderly's friends.

The undead monster seemed certain enough. Whether the creature could actually "see" the distant party, Druzil could not tell, but the monster's chosen path was straight and furious. Some beacon was guiding this otherworldlyspirit, leading it on without hesitation through the dark of night and under the light of day. The creature hadn't slowed, hadn't rested (weary Druzil was beginning to wish it would!), and it and Druzil had covered a tremendous amount of ground in a very short time.

Now, with the goal apparently in sight, the creature moved even more furiously to the base of Nightglow's treeless high slope, ripping through the snow angrily, as if the white powder's hindering depth was some deliberate conspiracy to keep the ghoulish thing away from Cadderly.

As a creature of the fiery lower planes, Druzil was not fond of the chilling snow. But as a creature of the chaotic lower planes, the imp eagerly moved along behind the undead monster, rubbing his clawed hands at the thought of the savagery that was soon to come.

* * * * *

Cadderly gently slid one foot in front of the other, inching his way toward the chamber's far exit. The giant red toads had settled again, but the young priest felt many eyes upon him, watching him with more than a passing interest.

Another few feet put him right in line with the exit; ten running strides would have gotten him through it. He stopped where he was, trying to muster the courage to break into a run, trying to discern if that would be the wisest course.

He started to lean forward anxiously, was mentally counting down to the moment when he would spring away.

A toad hopped across to block the exit.

Cadderly's eyes widened with fear and darted from side to side, looking for some other path. Behind him, toads had quietly gathered in a group, cutting off any retreat.

Was this a deliberate herding tactic? the young priest wondered with complete astonishment. Whatever it was, Cadderly knew that he had to act quickly. He considered his magic, wondered what aid he might find from the song of Deneir. He decided immediately to act more directly and began flicking his light beam at the blocking toad up ahead, trying to startle the thing out of his path.

The toad seemed to settle down more fully, grinding its considerable belly against the stone. It jerked upward suddenly. Cadderly feared for an instant that it was leaping at him—but only its head came forward, its mouth popping open and a gout of flame bursting forth.

Cadderly fell back a step as the small fireball erupted just short of him, reddening his face. He let out a cry of surprise and heard the toads shuffling rapidly behind him. Instinctively, the young priest brought his hand-crossbow up. He didn't look back, but kept his focus on the escape ahead and launched the quarrel. He ran off at once, following the dart's wake, fearing that a dozen small fireballs would incinerate him from behind before he ever got near the exit.

The toad's mouth flicked at the small missile, sticky tongue catching it in midflight and drawing it in.

The quarrel had not exploded! The tongue had apparently caught it without crushing the vial. And Cadderly, in full flight toward the toad and with nowhere else to run, had no readied alternatives, didn't even have his enchanted walking stick or spindle-disks in hand. He flicked the light tube frantically again, hoping against all reason to startle the formidable toad away. The thing just sat there, waiting.

Then the creature made a strange belching sound, its throat puffing and then retracting, and a moment later it blew apart, toad guts flying in all directions.

Cadderly threw his arms up in front of his face as he crossed through the spray and prudently ducked his head to avoid cracking it against the top rim of the low tunnel. He was many running strides out of the cavern before he dared to look back and confirm that no toads had come in pursuit. Still the frightened young priest ran, careening down the winding way, skidding to a stop and looking back, though he sensed that the tunnel had widened suddenly around him.

Cadderly stopped, frozen in place, no longer thinking about the toads but more concerned with the sound of rhythmic breathing, breathing that sounded like a tempest wind in a narrowing tunnel. Slowly, Cadderly turned his head about, and, even more slowly, he brought the light tube to bear.

"Oh, my dear Deneir," the young priest mouthed silently as the light ran along the scaly hide of the impossibly long, impossibly huge wyrm. "Oh, my dear Deneir."

The light passed the dragon's spearlike horns, crossed down the awesome beast's ridged skull, past the closed eye to the maw that could snap giant Vander in half with hardly an effort.

"Oh, my dear Deneir," the young priest muttered, and then he was kneeling, not even conscious of the fact that his knees had buckled under him.

Eight
Old Fyren

T he beast was a hundred feet long, its curled tail a hundred feet again, and armored, every inch, with large, overlapping scales that gleamed like metal—and Cadderly did not doubt for a moment that those smooth red scales were every bit as strong as tempered plates. The dragon's great leathery wings were folded now, wrapping the beast like a blanket on a babe.

But that illusion could not hold against the reality of Fyrentennimar. Had an unsettling dream inspired those six-inch-deep claw marks in the very stone near the dragon's forelegs? Cadderly wondered. And how many humans had been part of the meal that had so sated the beast's hunger that it could sleep for centuries?

In the next few moments, Cadderly thanked the gods a thousand times that he had stumbled upon Fyrentennimar while the dragon was asleep. If he had come running in here blindly and old Fyren had been awake, Cadderly would have never known what happened. His luck continued, for none of the toads were following him—the little creatures were smarter than Cadderly had expected. Still, Cadderly knew that dragon slumber was an unpredictable thing at best. He had to work fast, get his magical defenses up, and prepare himself mentally to battle the awe-inspiring beast.

He summoned the song of Deneir into his thoughts, but for many moments—interminable moments to the terrified Cadderly—could not hold the notes in any logical sequence, could not fully appreciate the harmony of the music and find his devotional *focus* within its mystical notes. It was that very harmony, the understanding of universal truths, that lent Cadderly his magical strength.

Finally Cadderly managed to enact a magical shielding sphere, an elemental inversion of the material air about him that would, he hoped, protect him from the fires of dragon breath.

The young priest took out the *Tome of Universal Harmony*, flipping to a page he had marked before leaving the Edificant Library. The origin of dragons was not known, but it was obvious to scholars that these creatures did not follow the natural and expected laws. Large as they were, there was no logical way that a dragon's wings should have been able to keep the creature aloft, and yet dragons were among the fastest fliers in all the world. Typically druidic magic, powerful against the mightiest of animals, had little power over dragons, so special protective wards had been devised to guard against these mighty beasts, by wizards and priests trying to survive in the wilder world millennia before.

The page in the *Tome of Universal Harmony* showed Cadderly these wards, guided his thoughts to the song of Deneir in a slightly different manner, altering some of the notes. Soon he had erected a barrier, called dragonbane, from wall to wall a few feet in front of him that, according to the writings, the mighty wyrm could not physically pass through.

Fyrentennimar shifted uneasily; Cadderly figured that the wyrm probably sensed the magical energies being enacted in the room. The young priest took a deep breath and told himself over and over that he had to go through with this most important quest, had to trust in his magic and trust in himself. He took the evil *Ghearufu* out of his pack, tucked his feeble weapons away (even his potent hand-crossbow would do little damage against the likes of this beast), and wiped his sweaty palms on his tunic.

He uttered a simple spell so that the clap of his hands sounded as a thunderstrike. Great wings hummed as they beat the air, uplifting the front portion of the wyrm. Old Fyren's head shot up from the ground in the span of a heartbeat, hovering a dozen feet in front of Cadderly, and the young priest had to fight the urge to fall on the stone and grovel before this magnificent creature. How could Cadderly dare to presume that anything he might do would even affect the awesome Fyrentennimar?

And those eyes! Twin beacons that scrutinized every detail, that held the young priest on trial before a word had been spoken. Surely they emanated a light of their own as intense as that coming from Cadderly's enchanted tube.

The weakness in Cadderly's legs multiplied tenfold when the dragon, tired and cranky and not at all in the mood for a parley, loosed its searing breath.

A line of flames came at Cadderly but parted as they hit his magical globe, encircling him in a fiery blaze. His translucent globe took on a greenish hue under the assault, the protective bubble seeming thick at first but fast thinning as the dragon continued to spew forth its fire.

Sweat poured from Cadderly, his tongue went dry in his mouth, and his back itched as though all the moisture in his body was being evaporated. Wafts of smoke came up from the edges of his tunic; he had a hand on the adamantite spindle-disks, but had to let go as the metal heated, and similarly had to flip his metallic light tube gingerly from hand to hand.

Still came the fires as the great dragon lungs expelled their load. Would old Fyren never end?

And then it was over. "Oh, my dear Deneir," the young priest mouthed when the green hue of his magical bubble faded and he looked at the floor just outside of his protected area. He needed no light tube to witness this spectacle. Molten stone glowed and bubbled and fast-cooled, hardening in a wavelike formation from the force of the flames.

Cadderly looked up to see the dragon's slitted lizard eyes widen with disbelief that anything could survive its searing breath. Those evil eyes went narrow again quickly, the dragon issuing a low, threatening growl that shook the floor under Cadderly's feet.

What have I gotten myself into? Cadderly asked himself, but he forced the fearful notion away immediately, thought of the evil the *Ghearufu* had spread on the land and would continue to spread if he did not destroy it.

"Mighty Fyrentennimar," he began bravely, "I am but a poor and humble priest, come to call upon you in good faith."

The sharp intake of Fyren's breath drew Cadderly's cloak around him, nearly pulled him forward beyond the line of magical dragonbane.

Cadderly knew what was coming and desperately fell back into the song, chanting at the top of his voice to reinforce his thinned fire shield. The breath came in a wicked blast, mightier than the last, if that was possible. Cadderly saw the thin green bubble diminish to nothingness, felt a blast of warmth and thought that he would sizzle where he stood.

But a blue globe replaced the green, again driving the fires harmlessly aside. Cadderly's entire body ached as though he had fallen asleep under a high summer sun; he had to stamp out small flames on the laces of his boots.

"I have come in good faith!" he cried loudly when the blast ended, old Fyren's eyes wider still with disbelief. "I need but a simple favor and then you may return to your slumber!"

Amazement turned to an unbridled rage beyond anything Cadderly would ever have believed possible. The dragon opened its mouth wide, rows of ten-inch fangs gleaming horribly, and then its head shot forward, neck snapping like a snake's coiled body. Cadderly groaned and nearly fell over, for a moment sure that he was losing consciousness and soon his life.

But the young priest nearly laughed aloud, in spite of his terror, when he peeked out to regard Fyrentennimar, the dragon's face pressed and distorted weirdly against the line of magical dragonbane. Cadderly could only think of the mischievous young boys at the Edificant Library, who would press their faces against the glass of the windows in the study chambers, startling the disciples within, then run off laughing down the solemn halls.

His unintentional lightheartedness actually aided the fortunate young priest, for the dragon backed away and looked all about, seeming unsure of itself for the first time.

"*Thief!*" Fyrentennimar bellowed, the power of the dragon voice blowing Cadderly back a step.

"No thief," Cadderly wisely assured the wyrm. "Just a humble priest . . ."

"*Thief and liar!*" Fyrentennimar roared. "Humble priests do not survive the breath of Fyrentennimar the Great! What treasures have you taken?"

"I come not for treasure," Cadderly declared firmly. "Nor to disturb the slumbers of a most magnificent wyrm."

Fyrentennimar started to retort, but seemed to reconsider, as though Cadderly's "most magnificent" compliment had given him pause.

"A simple task, as I have said," Cadderly went on, going with the momentum. "Simple for Fyrentennimar the Great, but quite beyond the abilities of any other in all the land. If you will perform . . ."

"*Perform?*" the dragon roared, and Cadderly, his hair blown back by the sheer force of the dragon's hot breath, wondered if his hearing would be permanently damaged. "Fyrentennimar does not perform! I am not interested in your simple task, foolish priest." The dragon surveyed the area right in front of Cadderly, as if trying to discern what barrier had been enacted to keep it at bay.

Cadderly considered the few options that seemed open to him. He felt that his best chance was to continue to flatter the beast. He had read many tales of heroic adventurers successfully playing to the ego of dragons, particularly of red dragons, which were reportedly the most vain of all dragonkind.

"Would that I might better see you!" he said dramatically. He snapped his fingers, as though a thought had just come to him, then whipped out his slender wand and uttered "*Domin illu.*" Instantly the wide chamber was bathed in a magical light, and all of Fyrentennimar's magnificence was revealed to him. Silently congratulating himself, Cadderly replaced the wand under his cloak and continued his survey, noting for the first time the mound of treasure across the way, beyond the bulk of the blocking dragon.

"Would that you might better see *me*," Fyrentennimar began suspiciously, "or see my *treasure*, humble thief?"

Cadderly blinked at the words and at his possible mistake. The murderous expression on Fyrentennimar's face was not hard to decipher. Then Cadderly felt his light tube growing warm, uncomfortably so, and he had to drop it to the ground. His forearm brushed against his belt buckle, and he winced in pain as bare skin contacted the fast-heating metal. It took Cadderly just a moment to understand, a moment to remember that many dragons, too, could access the realm of magical energies.

Cadderly had to act fast, had to humble the wyrm and make old Fyren desire parley. He chanted immediately, pointedly ignoring the wisps of smoke rising from his leather belt near the buckle.

A whirling ring of magical blades appeared in the air above Fyrentennimar's head.

"They will cut!" Cadderly promised, and he willed the blades lower, dangerously close to the dragon's head. He hoped to drive old Fyren down so that the beast would not be in such a position of physical superiority, hoped that his display of power would make the wyrm consider that continuing this fight might not be so wise a choice.

"Let them!" old Fyren bellowed, and his wings beat on, lifting his huge head higher, meeting the spell full force. Sparks flew as the blades chipped off of dragon armor. Tiny pieces of scales flecked away, and, to Cadderly's ultimate dismay, Fyrentennimar's roar seemed one of glee.

The dragon's tail whipped about, slamming Cadderly's magical barrier viciously, the waves of the concussion shaking the chamber and knocking Cadderly from his feet. The line of dragonbane held, though Cadderly feared that the chamber's ceiling would not. He realized then how vulnerable he truly was, how pitiful he must seem to this wyrm that had lived for centuries and had feasted on the bones of hundreds of men more powerful than he.

He had enacted protection from the fiery breath, had enacted a barrier that the beast could not physically pass through (though neither, he feared, would hold out for long), but what defense could Cadderly offer against Fyrentennimar's no doubt potent array of spells? He realized then that his defeat could be as simple a thing as Fyrentennimar tearing a hunk of stone from the wall and hurling it into him!

The dragon whipped its armored head to and fro, challenging Cadderly's enchanted blades, mocking Cadderly's spell. Foreclaws dug great ridges into the chamber's stone floor and the great tail whipped about, shattering rock and cracking apart the walls.

Cadderly could not hold out for long, was certain that he had nothing in all his arsenal that could begin to wound this monster.

He had only one alternative, and he feared it almost as much as he feared Fyrentennimar. The song of Deneir had taught him that the magical energies of the universe could be accessed from many different angles, and the way that one accessed those energies determined the grouping, the magical sphere, of the spells found within. Cadderly, for instance, had approached the universal energies differently for enacting his line of magical dragonbane than he had when entering the sphere of elemental fire to create the protective barrier against Fyrentennimar's flames.

Deneir was a deity of art, of poetry and soaring spirits, praising and accepting of a myriad of thoughtful accomplishments. Deneir's song rang out across the heavens, thrumming with the powers of many such energies, and thus a priest attuned to this god's song could find access, could find many various angles, to bend the universal energies in countless directions.

There was one particular bent of those energies, though, that ran contrary to the harmony of Deneirian thinking, where no notes rang clear and no harmony could be maintained. This was the sphere of chaos, a place of discord and illogic, and this was where young Cadderly had to go.

"It's a five-dwarf drop!" Ivan protested, holding fast to Danica's wrist. Danica could not even see the floor beneath the vertical chute and had to trust in the estimate of Ivan's heat-sensing vision. That estimate, "five-dwarf drop," twenty feet, was not so promising. But Danica had heard the thunderstrike of Cadderly's dragon-awakening clap, knew in her heart that her love was in dire need. She pulled free of Ivan's grasp, scrambled the rest of the way down the narrow chute and without hesitation dropped into the darkness.

She prayed that she could react quickly enough when at last she reached the end of the drop, hoped that the dim light of the torch Shayleigh held up in the chute would show her the floor before she slammed against it.

She saw the gray and turned her ankles to the side as she hit, launching herself into a sidelong roll, half twisting as she went. Her roll took her over backward, so that she came squarely back to her feet. Never slowing, having not absorbed enough of the fall's energy, Danica sprang into the air, turning a backward somersault. She landed on her feet and jumped again, spinning forward this time. She came up in a roll and hit the ground running, the rest of her momentum played out in long, swift strides.

"Well, I'll be a wine-drinking faerie," Ivan muttered in disbelief, watching the spectacle from above. For all his complaints, the dwarf could not let his friends endure any danger without him, and he knew that any hesitation now would force Danica to face the coming trials alone.

"Don't ye try to catch me, girl!" he warned as he let go. Ivan's landing technique was not so different than Danica's. But while Danica rolled and leaped, somersaulting gracefully and changing direction with subtle, stressless twists, Ivan just bounced.

He was up quickly, though. He adjusted his deer-antlered helmet and caught Danica by her flowing cloak as she ran back the other way, following the continuing sounds to the east.

Vander dropped down next, the tight chute posing more trouble for the firbolg than the not-so-high (for a giant) drop. Shayleigh dropped into his waiting arms, virtually springing from him in quick flight after Ivan and Danica.

Pikel came last, and Vander caught him, as well. The firbolg eyed the nestled dwarf curiously for a moment, noting that something seemed to be missing. "Your club?" Vander started to ask, and he understood a split second later, when Pikel's club, tumbling down behind the dwarf, bounced off his skull.

"Oops," the green-bearded dwarf apologized, and in looking at Vander's scowl, was glad that they had no time to stand around and discuss the matter.

Danica would have outdistanced Ivan in no time—except that the dwarf had a firm grip on her trailing cloak and would not let go. They heard the rumble of Fyrentennimar's distant voice by this point, and though they couldn't make out any words, it guided them easily. Ivan was glad when he noted that Shayleigh, still holding her torch, was gaining on them.

They passed through a few chambers, down several narrow corridors, and one wide passage. The mounting heat alone told them that they were nearing the dragon's chamber and made them both fear that Fyrentennimar had already loosed its killing breath.

Shayleigh passed Ivan, seeming as desperate as Danica, and the dwarf promptly reached out and grabbed a hold on her cloak, too. He understood their urgency, understood that both of them were fostering images of a deep-fried Cadderly, but Ivan remained pragmatic. If the dwarf had anything to say about it, they would not run helter-skelter into old Fyren's waiting maw.

Shayleigh's torch showed that they were nearing yet another wide chamber. They saw light up ahead, a residual glow, it seemed, and that led them to one inescapable conclusion.

For all of his earlier protests and stubbornness, Ivan Bouldershoulder showed his true loyalties at that point. Thinking that the dreadful Fyrentennimar waited just ahead, the tough dwarf yanked back on both cloaks, springing past Danica and Shayleigh and leading the way into the chamber before he had even had time to draw out his double-bladed battle-axe.

A flicking tongue hit him two steps inside the door—hit him, wrapped him, and pulled him sideways. Danica and Shayleigh skidded in behind, to find the chamber filled with very anxious, giant red toads. They spotted Ivan, spotted his boots at least, sticking out from the mouth of a contented-looking toad to the right. Danica started for it but was intercepted by a mini-fireball, and then another, as two more toads took up the attack.

Shayleigh hurled her torch out in front of her, had her bow up in an instant, and put it to deadly work.

Ivan didn't know what had hit him, but he understood that he was quite uncomfortable, and that he could not get his arms around to retrieve the axe strapped to his back. Never the one to listen to his own many complaints, Ivan followed the only course open to him and began thrashing about, trying to bite, trying to find something to grasp and twist. The deer rack atop his helmet snagged on something up above and again Ivan did not question his misfortune, just snapped his head up as forcefully as he could.

A toad leaped long and high at her, but Shayleigh's three arrows, fired in rapid succession, broke the thing's momentum in midflight and dropped it dead to the ground. Two more toads came flying at the elf simultaneously, and though she hit them both with perfect shots, she could not deflect their flight. One clipped her shoulder, the other crashed against her shins, and back she flew.

She would have hit the cavern floor hard, but Vander, coming in from the corridor, caught her gently in one giant hand and kept her on her feet. The firbolg was beyond her in an instant, his great sword slashing back and forth, slicing the two attacking toads in half.

A third monster came flying in from the side, but Pikel skidded in between it and Shayleigh, holding his tree-trunklike club tight over one shoulder, both his hands grasping the weapon's narrow end. With a whoop of delight, the green-bearded dwarf batted the flying toad aside. It dropped, stunned, and Pikel stood over it, squishing it with repeated strikes.

Danica fell to her back and rolled about frantically to avoid the fiery blasts. She tucked her feet in close, hoping to roll back to a standing position, and grabbed at her boots, drawing two daggers, one golden-hilted and sculpted into the image of a tiger, the other a silvery dragon.

She came up throwing, scoring two hits on the nearest toad. It closed its eyes and squatted down low to the floor, and Danica couldn't tell if she had killed it or not.

Nor could she pause to find out. Another toad was near her, flicking its sticky tongue.

Danica leaped straight up, a mongoose against a striking snake, and tucked her legs tight. She leaped again as soon as her feet touched stone, forward and high, before the toad could flick its tongue again. This time, Danica came down hard on the creature's head. One foot planted firmly, she spun fiercely, her face passing close to her ankle, her other foot flying high, straight above her. As she completed the circuit, her momentum cresting, she tightened the muscles in her sailing foot and drove it right through the toad's bulbous eye.

The weight of the blow forced Danica down from the dead thing, and she spun about, searching out the next target.

At first she thought the toad she saw to the side to be among the most curious of crossbred creatures. But then Danica realized that its antlers were not its own, but rather belonged to the indigestible dwarf it had foolishly pulled in.

The antlers jerked, this way and that, and Ivan's slime-covered head popped through. The dwarf grunted and contorted weirdly, twisting all the way about so that he was looking at his own heels, protruding from the toad's mouth, and at Danica, staring in disbelief.

"Ye think ye might be helping me outta here?" the dwarf asked, and Danica saw the now-dead toad's eyes hump up and then go back to normal as Ivan shrugged.

* * * * *

The familiar song played in Cadderly's mind, but he did not fall into its harmonic flow. He sang it backward instead, sang it sideways, randomly, forcing out whatever notes seemed to be the most discordant. Shivers ran through the marrow of his bones; he felt as if he would break apart under the magical assault. He was exactly where a priest of Deneir should not be, mocking the harmony of the universe, perverting the notes of the timeless song so that they twanged painfully in his mind, slamming doors in the pathways of the revelations the song had shown to him.

Cadderly's voice sounded guttural, croaking, and his throat was filled with phlegm. His head ached; the intensity of the shivering waves along his spine stung him repeatedly.

He thought he would go insane, had gone insane, had gone to a place where every logical course seemed to meander aimlessly, where one and one added up to three, or to ten. Cadderly's emotions similarly fluctuated. He was angry, furious at . . . what? He did not know, knew only that he was filled with despair. Then suddenly he felt invulnerable, as if he could walk past his magical barriers and snap his fingers under puny Fyrentennimar's dragon nostrils.

Still he croaked against the harmonious flow of the beautiful song, still he denied the universal truths the song had shown to him. Suddenly, Cadderly realized that he had unleashed something terrible within his own mind, that he could not stop the flashing images and the shivering pains.

His mind darted randomly, a gamesman's wheel, flitting through the accessed magical energy with no basis. He was falling, falling, dropping into an endless pit from which there could be no escape. He would eat the dragon, or the dragon would eat him, but either way, Cadderly felt that it did not matter. He had broken himself—the only logical thought he could hold onto for more than a fleeting moment was that he had overstepped his bounds, had rushed in his desperation into ultimate, unending chaos.

Still he croaked the discordant notes, played the random rantings of half-truths and untruths in his mind. One and one equaled seventeen this time.

One and one.

Whatever else assaulted Cadderly's mind, he continued to call upon the simple mathematics of adding one and one. A hundred different answers came to him in rapid succession, were generated randomly in this place, his mind, wherein no rules held true.

A thousand different answers, generated without pattern, without guidance, shot past him. And Cadderly let them go away with the rest of his fleeting thoughts, knowing them to be lies.

One and one equaled two.

Cadderly grabbed onto that thought, that hope. The simple equation, the simple, logical truth ringing as a single note of harmony in the discord.

One and one equaled two!

A thin line of Deneir's song played in Cadderly's mind simultaneously, but separately, from the discord. It came as a lifeline to the young priest, and he clutched it eagerly, not intending it to pull him from the discord, but to help him hold his mental footing within this sphere's slippery chaos.

Now Cadderly searched the dangerous sphere, found a region of emotional tumult, of inverted ethics, and hurled it with all his mental strength at Fyrentennimar.

The dragon's rage continued to play, and Cadderly understood that he had not penetrated the innate magical resistance of the beast. Cadderly realized that he was sitting then, that sometime during his mental journey, the earthquake of Fyrentennimar's thrashing had knocked him from his feet.

Again Cadderly searched out the particular region of chaos that he needed—it was in a different place this time—and again he hurled it at the wyrm. And then a third time, and a fourth. His head ached as he continued to demand the enchantment, continued to assault the stubborn dragon with false emotions and false beliefs.

The chamber was deathly quiet, except for some scrambling that Cadderly heard emanating from somewhere down the tunnel behind him, back in the toad room, perhaps.

He slowly opened his eyes, to see old Fyren sitting quietly, regarding him.

"My welcome, humble priest," the dragon said in calm, controlled tones. "Do forgive my outburst. I do not know what brought about such a tirade." The dragon blinked its reptilian eyes and glanced all about curiously. "Now, about this small task that you wish me to perform."

Cadderly, too, blinked many times in disbelief. "One and one equals two," he muttered under his breath. "I hope."

Nine
Residual Energy

D anica was the first to come to the end of the tunnel leading to the dragon's chamber. On her hands and knees, the monk quietly crept up to the lighted area and peeked in. She felt the strength drain from her as she gazed upon the magnificent wyrm, a hundred times more dreadful than the legends could begin to describe. But then Danica's delicate features twisted in confusion at the unexpected sight.

Cadderly stood right beside the dragon, talking with it easily and pointing to the *Ghearufu*, the gloves, one black, one white, and the gold-edged mirror that he had placed on the floor some distance away.

Danica nearly cried out loud when she felt a hand on her leg. She realized that it was only Shayleigh, creeping in behind her as they had planned. The elf maiden, too, seemed stunned by the spectacle in the chamber.

"Should we go in?" she whispered to Danica.

Danica considered the question for a long moment, honestly unsure of what role they should play. Cadderly seemed to have things in hand; would their unexpected presence startle the dragon, bring old Fyren into a fit of terrifying rage?

Just as Danica started to shake her head, there came an impatient call from back down the tunnel.

"What do ye see?" Ivan demanded, slime-covered from toad innards and not too happy at all.

The dragon's beaconlike gaze immediately flashed toward the tunnel, and Danica and Shayleigh again felt their limbs go weak under the awful glare.

"Who comes uninvited to the lair of . . ." the great wyrm began, but it stopped in midsentence, cocking its massive head so that it could better hear Cadderly, whispering calmly at its side.

"Do come in," the dragon bade the two in the tunnel a moment later. "Welcome, friends of the humble priest!"

It took Danica and Shayleigh some time to muster the courage to actually enter the dragon's chamber. They went straight for Cadderly, Danica hooking his arm with her own and admiring him incredulously.

Cadderly felt the weight of that trusting gaze. Again, he had been put into the forefront, had become the leader to his friends. He alone understood how tentative his hold on the dragon might be, and now that Danica and the others had arrived, their fates rested solely in his hands. They admired him, they trusted him, but Cadderly was not so sure that he trusted himself. Would he ever shed the guilt if he failed at the expense of a friend's life? He wanted to be home at the library, sitting on a sun-drenched roof, feeding cacasa nuts to Percival, the one friend who placed no demands upon him (other than the cacasa nuts!).

"The dragon likes me," the young priest explained, straining to put his smile from ear to ear. "And Fyrentennimar—the great Fyrentennimar—has agreed to help me with my problem," he added, nodding toward the *Ghearufu*.

Danica looked to the still-glowing floor near the entryway of the chamber and could guess easily enough that the dragon had utilized its deadly breath at least once already.

But Cadderly appeared unhurt—and unafraid. Danica started to ask him about the strange turn of events, but he quieted her immediately with a concerned look, and she understood that the discussion was better left until later, when they were safely away from the dragon.

Ivan and Pikel skidded into the chamber, Vander coming right behind, nearly tripping over them.

"Uh-oh!" Pikel squeaked at the sight of the wyrm, and Ivan's face went pale.

"Dwarves!" Fyrentennimar bellowed, the force of his roar driving the three beards—yellow, red, and green—out behind the friends, the heat of Fyren's breath making the three squint their eyes.

"Friends again!" Cadderly called to the dragon, and, reasoning that treasure-coveting dragons were not overly fond of treasure-coveting dwarves, the young priest motioned for the three to stay back near the tunnel.

Fyrentennimar issued a long, low growl and didn't seem convinced. The dragon could not sustain its ire, though. It blinked curiously, turned an almost plaintive look upon Cadderly, and then looked to the *Ghearufu*.

"Friends again," Fyrentennimar agreed.

Cadderly looked to the *Ghearufu*, thinking it prudent to just get things done and get out of there.

"Remain behind me," old Fyren warned Cadderly and the two women, and then came the sharp intake as the dragon's lungs expanded.

This time when Fyrentennimar breathed, there was no magical protection in place to divert his fire. The flames drove against the *Ghearufu* and against the floor. Stone bubbled, and the *Ghearufu* sizzled, angrily it seemed, as though its potent magic was fighting back against the incredible assault.

"Oooo," Ivan muttered in disbelief. Pikel put his hands on hips and growled at his brother for stealing his line. Their fight did not continue, though, as the searing heat of the dragon breath assaulted them. Vander grabbed the brothers and fell back against the wall, one huge arm up defensively in front of his eyes.

The dragon's fiery exhalation did not relent. There came a series of snapping explosions from within the flame, and a thick gray smoke arose, encircling the fiery pillar, dimming its blinding yellow light.

Cadderly nodded to Danica and Shayleigh, confident that the dragon fire was doing its work. The flaming column disappeared, and Fyrentennimar sat back, reptilian eyes scrutinizing the area and the magical item. The smoke continued to swirl, funnel-like above the *Ghearufu*. Small fires burned on both the item's gloves; the gold edges around the mirror had turned liquid and spread out in a wide flat glob. The mirror itself pulsed, bulging weirdly but remaining, it appeared, intact.

"Is it done, humble priest?" Fyrentennimar asked.

Cadderly wasn't sure. The thick smoke seemed to gain momentum in its swirl, the mirror continued to bulge and flatten.

Then it cracked apart.

Cadderly's blue hat flew away, his cape flapped up over his head and shoulders, standing out straight, snapping repeatedly, rapidly, in the sudden suction. Now the smoke whipped in circular fury, and the swirling wind became a thunderous roar.

Shayleigh's arrows left her quiver, smacked against Cadderly's back, and ricocheted past. The young priest could hardly hold his footing, leaning back at a huge angle against the vicious pull. All the small items in the area piled atop the broken mirror. The still pliable molten floor rolled up, wavelike, around the center of that tremendous pull.

Something banged hard against the back of Cadderly's legs, costing him his tentative hold. He looked down to see Shayleigh, blinded by her wild-flying golden hair, scraping her hands against the stone in a futile effort. Cadderly fell over her, and she slid away, toward the fury.

Danica stood very still a few feet back, her eyes closed in meditation, and her legs wide and firmly planted. Over by the tunnel, Vander and the dwarves had formed a chain, the firbolg holding Pikel, Pikel holding Ivan. Pikel's grip slipped suddenly, and Ivan screamed out. He resisted the pull for just a second, long enough for Pikel to dive down and grab him about the ankles.

"Humble priest!" the confused Fyrentennimar roared, and even the dragon's thunder seemed a distant thing against the tumult of the mighty wind.

Cadderly cried out for Shayleigh, found himself going along behind her as the sucking wind increased. Behind him, Danica opened her eyes, and her concern for her friends stole her meditation. She jumped forward a long stride, catching hold of Cadderly, but when she tried to stop, found her momentum too great and wound up going right over the young priest, and right over Shayleigh, and suddenly it was she who was closest to the furious vortex.

Ivan and Pikel were up in the air now, Pikel holding tight to Ivan's ankles, and Vander, behind him, had one hand tight about Pikel's ankle, the other grasping a jut in the tunnel wall.

Danica's horrified scream as she went over the vortex stole the blood from Cadderly's face. Shayleigh went in right behind her, pressed tight against her, and then Cadderly was atop the pile.

"What do I do, humble priest?" the confused dragon called, but Fyrentennimar was distracted as his own piles of treasure whipped to the call of the vortex, smacked hard against the dragon's back and widespread wings. What worth is such treasure? the dragon wondered, and in his magically confused state, Fyrentennimar decided right then that he would soon clear his cave of the worthless debris.

"Ooooooo!" Pikel wailed, blinded by his beard (as was Ivan), his muscled arms aching from the strain and his leg throbbing from Vander's giant-strong grip. Pikel feared that he would be torn right in half, but for the sake of his dear brother, he would not let go.

* * * * *

Cadderly felt an intense burning, felt as if his insides had been torn right through his skin. He was falling, spinning in a gray fog, spiraling down, out of control.

He splashed into muck, stood in the knee-deep sludge, and regarded himself and his surroundings incredulously. He was naked and filthy, apparently unhurt but standing in a vast plain of unremarkable grayness, the lake of oozing sludge stretching out in every direction as far as he could see.

Danica and Shayleigh stood near him, but they, for some reason the young priest could not understand, were still wearing their clothes.

Cadderly modestly crossed his arms in front of him, took note of the fact that both of his companions did likewise.

Danica's lips moved as though she meant to ask, "Where are we?" but there seemed no point in uttering the unanswerable question.

* * * * *

Far down Nightglow's snow-blanketed side, Druzil scratched his ugly face and watched the undead creature's shivering movements.

Ghost had not taken a step in many seconds, the first time Druzil had seen the tireless thing pause in several days. The gruesome creature made no moves at all, except for the obvious trembling.

"Why are you doing that?" the invisible imp asked under his rasping breath, hoping that the creature had not somehow detected him and was not calling upon some innate magics to locate him, or to destroy him.

The trembling intensified to a violent shaking. Druzil whined and wrapped his leathery wings defensively about him, though since they were invisible, they could not block out the terrifying sight.

Crackling noises came from the undead monster, tiny cracks appeared along its blackened skin, wisps of smoke filtered out into the brightly shining air.

"Hey?" the imp asked a moment later, when the undead thing fell into a pile of charred and shattered flakes.

* * * * *

Cadderly continued his scan of the area, of himself, and of his friends. Danica, too, seemed intent on covering up, but Cadderly didn't see the point since she was fully clothed.

Or was she?

A wail from somewhere in the unseen distance brought them all on the alert. Shayleigh went into a low crouch, slowly turning and scanning, balled fists defensively in front of her.

If she feared an attack, then why didn't she take her bow off her shoulder? Cadderly wondered. And then he understood. With a knowing nod, the young priest let go of his pointless modesty and stood straight.

Another cry, a cry of pain, sounded from somewhere distant, followed by a loud splash.

"Where are we?" Danica demanded. "And why am I the only one who has no clothes?"

Shayleigh looked at her incredulously, then looked down to her own body.

A wave rolled in at them, bringing the uncomfortable brown sludge to their waists. Cadderly grimaced at the feel of the wretched stuff, noticed for the first time the reeking stench.

"What caused so large a wave?" Shayleigh whispered, and her perceptive remark reminded Cadderly that the discomfort might be the least of his troubles.

The apparition, a puny, androgynous form with one arm bent crooked, rose from the sludge twenty feet away from them, its dangerous eyes narrowing as it regarded them.

"The assassin," Danica breathed. "But he is dead, and we . . ." She looked at Cadderly, her brown eyes wide.

"Caught by the *Ghearufu*," Cadderly replied, unwilling to offer the possibility that they, too, had died.

"Caught!" the puny form roared in a mighty, giantlike voice. "Caught that you might be properly punished!"

"Use your bow!" Danica, more afraid than she had ever been, yelled at

Shayleigh. Again, the elf gave Danica an incredulous look, then turned helplessly to her bare, as she saw it, shoulder.

Danica sneered and rushed between Shayleigh and Cadderly, taking a blocking stance between them and the approaching apparition.

Cadderly looked down, looked to the unremarkable muck to clear his head and register all that he had seen and heard. Why was he the only one who was naked? Or at least, why did he see himself that way? As did Danica, he knew, by her own words. And if Shayleigh thought that she had her bow, didn't perceive that she, too, had no clothes and no equipment, then why hadn't she taken the weapon from her back?

Danica's hands began an intricate, balancing weave in front of her. The apparition of Ghost showed no fear at all, continued to steadily glide through the muck. Danica noticed that Ghost seemed larger suddenly, and noticed that the apparition continued to grow.

"Cadderly," she breathed quietly, for now their opponent was fully ten feet tall, nearly as large as Vander. It took another step, doubling its size as it did.

"Cadderly!"

They all perceived that they were naked, but each saw the others as they had last seen the others, Cadderly mused, knowing that there must be something pertinent in that fact. He felt along his body, wondering if his equipment only appeared invisible to him, if his potent hand-crossbow might be on his hip, waiting for him to grab it. But he felt only his skin and the slimy splotches of brown, disgusting sludge.

The apparition loomed thirty feet high; its laughter mocked Danica's feeble defensive stance. With a sucking sound, one foot came up from the muck, hovered high in the air menacingly.

"Punishment!" the evil Ghost growled, stamping down.

Danica dove to the side, splashed through the muck and reappeared, her strawberry-blond locks matted to her head by the thick brown sludge.

The splash awakened Cadderly from his contemplations. His gray eyes widened as he glanced about for Danica, fearing that she had been squashed.

Shayleigh was over with the monk by then, pulling her away from the gigantic monster.

Ghost showed no more interest in Danica, though, not with Cadderly, the perpetrator of the disaster, the destroyer of his own form and of the precious *Ghearufu*, standing before him.

"Are you at peace with your god?" the giant voice teased.

Where are we? The question rifled through Cadderly's thoughts, now that the monster had threatened him, had apparently just confirmed that they were not dead. Yet this place somewhat resembled the spirit world, Cadderly knew, for he had made several ventures into that noncorporeal state.

Danica and Shayleigh rushed in front of the young priest, Danica leaping onto the leg of the giant, clawing and biting at the back of its knee. It kicked out, trying to shake her free, but if her savage thrashing was doing any real damage, the smiling Ghost did not show it.

"Perceived vulnerability," Cadderly muttered, trying to jog his thought process. His self-image, the images of his friends, and the image of their nemesis, had to be a matter of perception, since he and both his companions thought themselves naked and the other two clothed.

Shayleigh slipped free of the monster's other leg as Ghost brought it up high above Cadderly's head.

"Cadderly!" both Danica and the elf maiden cried out to their apparently distracted companion.

The huge foot slammed down; Danica nearly fainted at the thought of her lover being squashed.

Cadderly caught the foot in one hand, and absently held it steady above his head.

He, too, began to grow.

"What is happening?" the frustrated, terrified monk cried out, falling from the giant's knee and splashing away. Shayleigh caught her and held her, needing, as much as giving, the support.

Cadderly was half the creature's size, and now it was Ghost who seemed confused. The young priest heaved against the foot, hurling Ghost backward to land crashing into the muck. By the time the creature regained its stance, Cadderly was the larger.

Ghost came on anyway, snarling, wrapping his hated enemy in a tight hug.

Danica and Shayleigh moved away from the titans, not understanding, not able to help.

Cadderly's massive arms flexed and twisted. Ghost's did, too, and for a long while, neither titan seemed to gain any advantage.

Ghost bit down hard on Cadderly's neck, whipping his head about in a frenzy. It was he, not Cadderly, who then cried out in pain, though, for he was biting not vulnerable skin, but steel armor!

The wild monster lifted his arm; his fingers grew into spikes, and he smashed down at Cadderly's shoulder.

The young priest yelped in agony. Cadderly's arm became a spear, and he plunged it through Ghost's belly.

Ghost's skin parted around it, opening a hole through which the arm/spear passed without making a cut. The evil entity's skin then tightened around Cadderly's appendage, holding him fast.

Ghost's mouth opened impossibly wide, seeming the maw of a snake, complete with venom-tipped fangs.

"Cadderly," Danica breathed, thinking her love doomed, thinking that she and Shayleigh would also fall victim to this horrid apparition. She had no words to describe what ensued, could hardly remember to breathe.

Cadderly did not flinch. His head thickened, his face flattened, like the face of a hammer, and he butted straight out. This time his attack apparently caught Ghost by surprise, for the assassin's snake jaws broke apart, blood washing away the venom.

Ghost's eyes widened in shock and agony as Cadderly's impaled arm shifted shape again, angled spikes tearing out the sides of Ghost's torso.

Cadderly understood that the game was one of mental quickness, matching defense to attack, keeping perspective (yes, that word was the key!) against fearsome sights and impossible realities. He had Ghost dazed, confused, and so the momentum was his to play out.

His free arm became an axe, his razor-edged hand slicing in at the side of Ghost's neck. The evil titan reacted quickly enough for its shoulder to grow a shield, but Cadderly had simultaneously sprouted a tail like that of the manticore he had battled on the mountain trail. Even as the axe hand resounded against Ghost's shield, the tail whirled about and snapped like a whip, driving several iron spikes into Ghost's chest.

Cadderly whipped his impaled arm about viciously; Ghost somehow melded and molded his skin to match the movements, preventing Cadderly from literally tearing him in half. The tail came about again, but Ghost's chest thickened with conjured armor, somewhat deflecting the heavy blows.

Cadderly had brought Ghost to his mental limit, had taxed Ghost's formidable mind to the extreme of his thought-processing abilities. It was a game of chess, Cadderly knew, a game of simultaneous movements and anticipating defenses.

Ghost's snake maw reformed in the blink of an eye—Cadderly was actually surprised that the evil man, still holding his defenses strong, was able to enact the shift. At the same time, though, Cadderly's head became the head of a dragon, became the head of Fyrentennimar.

Ghost's snake eyes widened. He tried to shift his head into something that could deflect the attack, something that could defeat dragon breath.

He didn't think quickly enough. Cadderly breathed forth a line of fire that stole Ghost's features, sizzled his skin away to leave a skull, half human, half snake, atop the titan's skinny neck.

In the throes of agony, Ghost could not maintain his control, his mental defenses. Cadderly's manticore tail heaved a half-dozen spikes into Ghost's chest. Cadderly's axe hand drove deep into Ghost's collarbone.

With a dragon's roar of victory, Cadderly snapped his impaled arm back and forth, cutting Ghost apart at the waist. The defeated titan's top half plummeted into the muck, showering Danica and Shayleigh. Almost immediately, the slain Ghost's torso reverted to its normal size, disappearing under the brown lake. Ghost's quivering legs toppled as they shrank, slipping into the muck with hardly a splash.

Cadderly's head became human again as he turned to regard his overwhelmed companions. He caught only a fleeting image of them, though, before a wall of blackness rushed up to smash him into unconsciousness.

Ten

Soaring

"Oof!" Ivan and Pikel groaned in unison when the balancing force of the tempest abruptly ended and they dropped, flat-out, to the stone floor. Vander, too, groaned, and fell back against the wall, the huge muscles in both his arms quivering from exhaustion. The wind had simply ceased, and the smoke now dissipated, revealing Danica, Cadderly, and Shayleigh lying one on top of the other in a pile.

"Are you all right, humble priest?" Fyrentennimar asked with sincere concern.

Cadderly looked up to the great beast and nodded, very glad that the ethics reversal he had enacted upon old Fyren had not been dispelled by his spiritual absence. Danica forced herself to her feet, and Cadderly, in turn, climbed off Shayleigh, his joints aching with every step. He knew rationally that his fight with Ghost had been a mental combat, not a physical one, a belief only reinforced by the fact that neither he nor Danica and Shayleigh had any of the disgusting muck on them, and in fact appeared exactly the same as they had before the journey. Still, the young priest felt as though his body had been through a severe beating.

"What was that monster?" Danica asked. "I thought you said the assassin was already dead and gone."

"That was not Ghost," Cadderly replied. "Not really. What we found was the embodiment of the *Ghearufu*, perhaps a joined spirit, magic item and owner."

"Where?" Shayleigh wanted to know.

Now Cadderly had no definite response. "Some area of limbo between the planes of existence," he answered, shrugging his shoulders to indicate that it was only a guess. "The *Ghearufu* has been in existence for many millennia, was created by powerful denizens of chaos. That is why I had to come here, even before our vital mission to Castle Trinity."

"Ye couldn't've just left the damned thing with the priests?" Ivan grumbled, kicking stones and debris as he searched about for his windblown helmet.

Cadderly started to reiterate the importance of the quest, wanting to explain how the destruction of the *Ghearufu* was more important to the overall scheme of universal harmony than anything which might directly affect their relatively unimportant lives. He gave up, however, realizing that such profound philosophical points had no chance of getting through the pragmatic dwarf's thick head.

Danica put her hand on his shoulder, though, and nodded to him when he looked back to her. She trusted in him again—her eyes showed that clearly. He was glad for that trust, and afraid of it, all at once.

He motioned for Danica and Shayleigh to go over by the door with the other three.

"Mighty Fyrentennimar," he cried to the dragon, dipping a low, appreciative bow. "The words of the gods are proven true." Cadderly took a step to the side and lifted one of the ruined, still smoking gloves. "Nothing in all the Realms but the breath of mighty Fyrentennimar could have destroyed the *Ghearufu*; no power in all the Realms could match the fury of your fires!" The statement wasn't exactly true, but even though the dragon was apparently still thick in the hold of Cadderly's chaotic enchantment, the young priest thought it wise to be generous with the praise.

Fyrentennimar seemed to like it. The dragon puffed out his already enormous chest, honed head held proudly high.

"And now, my friends and I must leave you to your sleep," Cadderly explained. "Fear not, for we'll not again disturb your slumber."

"Must you go, humble priest?" the dragon asked, seeming sad, which prompted a curious and sympathetic "Oo" from Pikel and an assortment of incredulous curses from Ivan.

Cadderly answered with a simple "Yes," bade the dragon lay down and rest, and turned to leave, pausing at the tunnel entrance to consider his friends.

"What of the toads?" he asked, remembering them for the first time since he had gazed upon the awesome dragon.

"Splat," Pikel assured him.

"You should be more concerned for the weather," Vander remarked gravely. "You do not understand the strength of storms in the high mountains, nor the price your private venture may exact from us all."

Cadderly accepted the scolding as the firbolg continued, and Ivan, even Shayleigh, joined in. The young priest wanted to defend himself, to convince them all, as he had convinced Danica, that destroying the *Ghearufu* was the more important quest, and even if they wound up stranded until the spring, even if the delay cost them their lives against Fyrentennimar, and cost the region dearly in its battle with Castle Trinity, the destruction of the malignant magical item had been worth the price. A younger Cadderly would have lashed out at his accusers.

Now Cadderly said nothing, offered no defense against his friends' justifiable anger. He had made his choice in good conscience, had made the only choice his faith and heart could accept, and now he would accept the consequences, for himself, for his friends, and for all the region.

Loyal and trusting Danica, holding tightly to his arm, showed him that he would not suffer those consequences alone.

"We will get through the high passes," Danica said when Vander had played out his anger. "And we will prevail against the wizard Aballister and his minions in our enemies' fortress."

"Perhaps alone I could get through them," the firbolg agreed. "For I am of the cold mountains. My blood runs thick with warmth, and my legs are long and strong, able to push through towering drifts of snow."

"Me own legs ain't so long," Ivan put in sarcastically. "What do ye got for me?" he asked Cadderly sharply. "What spells, and how many? Durned fool priest. If ye meant to come here, couldn't ye have waited until the summer?"

"Yeah." Pikel's unexpected agreement stung Cadderly more than gruff Ivan's ranting ever could. But then Cadderly looked back to Danica for support and saw a mischievous look in her sparkling eyes.

"How friendly is that dragon?" she asked, leading all their gazes back to serene Fyrentennimar.

Cadderly smiled at once, though it took Ivan longer to catch on.

"Oh, no ye don't!" the yellow-bearded dwarf bellowed, but by the eager intrigue splayed on the faces of Cadderly and Danica, and by the sudden smiles of Shayleigh and the firbolg, Ivan knew he was blubbering a losing argument.

* * * * *

Shattered! Druzil imparted telepathically, emphatically, for perhaps the tenth time. *Shuttered! Gone!* From the other end of the mental connection there was no immediate response, as though Aballister could not comprehend what the imp was talking about. Twice already Aballister had ordered Druzil to find the undead monster, to discover what had transpired to destroy the evil creature's corporeal form. Both times Druzil had replied that the task was quite impossible, that he had no idea of where to start looking.

Wherever the spirit had flown, Druzil knew that it was nowhere connected to the Material Plane. The imp pointedly reminded the wizard that he had been given only one red and one blue pouch of enchanting powder, that Aballister's lack of foresight had stranded him nearly a hundred miles from Castle Trinity with no way to get through any magical gates.

A wave of anger, imparted by Aballister, washed over Druzil. The imp's mind flared with pain; he feared that the wizard's mounting rage alone might destroy him. A dozen commands filtered through, each accompanied by a vicious threat. Druzil was at a loss. He had never witnessed Aballister so enraged, had never seen such a display of sheer power from him, or even from the mighty denizens of the lower planes that he had often dealt with in his centuries there.

Druzil tried to break the connection—he had often done that in the past—but Aballister's telepathic connection remained with him, held him fast.

When Aballister finally finished and released the suddenly exhausted imp, Druzil sat back against a tree stump with his dog-faced head resting forlornly in his clawed hands. He stared at the shattered flakes of the malignant monster, let his gaze meander up the imposing side of Nightglow, to the fog and clouds wherein Cadderly and his friends had disappeared. Aballister wanted Druzil to find the young priest and dog his steps, even to try to kill Cadderly if the opportunity presented itself.

No threat Aballister could possibly impose, no display of power, would prod Druzil to make that desperate attempt. The imp knew that he was no match for Cadderly, and knew, too, that Aballister might be the only one in the region who was.

But it was obvious to Druzil that Aballister didn't want it to come to that. Whatever satisfaction the old wizard might gain in personally crushing Cadderly would not make up for the inconvenience—not at a time when larger issues loomed in the wizard's designs. Aballister had labeled the undead monster as a possible ally. Now it was gone, and Druzil sensed that Cadderly had played some part in its destruction. The imp believed, too, that his own part in this drama had come to an end. The creature had been his guide to Cadderly. Without it, Druzil doubted that he could even locate the young priest. And with the weather fast shifting to the full wintry blasts, Druzil realized that it would take him weeks to get back to Castle Trinity—probably long after Cadderly was no more than a crimson stain on a stone floor.

"*Bene tellemara,*" the imp said repeatedly, cursing foolish Aballister for not giving him more of the enchanting, gate-opening powder, cursing the foul, chill weather, cursing the undead monster for its failure, and ultimately cursing Cadderly.

Thoroughly miserable, Druzil made no move toward Nightglow, made no move at all. For many hours, the snow settling on his doggish snout and folded wings, the stubborn imp sat perfectly still on the tree stump, muttering, "*Bene tellemara.*"

* * * * *

"I do not know how long the enchantment will hold the dragon," Cadderly admitted some time later, after Fyrentennimar had eagerly led them to the lair's main entrance, a gigantic cavern on the mountain's north slope with an opening wide enough for the dragon to swoop in and out with its huge wings extended.

"It'd be a real party for old Fyren to remember old Fyren when we're a thousand feet up on the damned thing's back!" Ivan snorted loudly, drawing angry looks from four of his companions and a slap on the back of the head from Pikel.

"Ye just said . . ." the yellow-bearded dwarf started to protest to Cadderly.

"What I just admitted is not information to be given freely to Fyrentennimar!" Cadderly whispered harshly. The dragon was some distance away, peering out into the howling wind and considering their intended course, but Cadderly had read many tales describing the extraordinary senses of dragonkind, many tales where an offhand whisper had cost a parleying party dearly against an easily flattered wyrm.

"The flight will be swift," Shayleigh reasoned. "You will not have to hold Fyrentennimar for long."

Cadderly could see that the fearless elf maiden was looking forward to the ride, could see that Danica, too, held no reservations against the potential gains. Hopping up and down, clapping his chubby hands and smiling all the while, Pikel's mood likewise was not hard to discern.

"What do you say?" Cadderly asked Vander, the one member who had not made clear his feelings.

"I say that you are desperate indeed to even consider this course," the firbolg replied bluntly. "But I am indebted to you for all my life, and if you choose to ride, I will go along." He cast a sidelong glance at grumbling Ivan. "As will the dwarf, do not doubt."

"Who're ye speaking for?" Ivan growled back.

"Would you stay alone in this cave, then, and wait for the dragon's return?" the firbolg casually asked.

Ivan mulled it over for a few minutes, then huffed defiantly, "Good point."

They rushed out the front entrance soon after, into the teeth of the now raging storm. The wind did little to hinder the massive dragon's progress, though, and the heat from Fyrentennimar's inner furnace, heat that lent the power to the dragon's dreadful breath, kept the six companions warm enough.

Bent low, eyes closed, Cadderly sat closest to old Fyren's head, right at the base of the red dragon's serpentine neck. The young priest reached again into the sphere of chaotic magics, focusing all his energies into extending his vital enchantment. To his relief, the dragon seemed pleased enough to carry the riders, seemed pleased just to be out in the wide world again. That thought inspired more than a few fears in Cadderly—what had Ivan said about letting a sleeping wyrm lie?—concerning the potential implications to the people of the region, particularly the implications to Carradoon, not so far away by a flying dragon's reckoning. Cadderly had made his choice, though, and now had to trust in the wisdom of that decision and hope for the best.

Danica sat right behind her love, arms wrapped about his waist, though she took great care not to disturb the young priest's concentration.

They climbed up above the storm, into sparkling sunlight, soaring through the crisp air. When they had passed the region of clouds, Fyrentennimar dove down into a crevice between two mountains, turning sidelong within the narrow pass. His leathery wings caught the updrafts, rode them fully as he came out of his steep bank, gaining speeds beyond the imagination of his thrilled riders.

Reveling in the sensation, which was many times more exciting than air-walking, Danica let go of Cadderly, threw her arms up high and wide and let the wind whip her unkempt hair about.

The world became a blur below them; Ivan complained that he was going to be sick, but no one cared or listened.

They came up fast on a ridge, and all of them, except for the concentrating Cadderly, screamed aloud in fear that they would slam against it. But Fyrentennimar was no novice to dragonflight, and the ridge was suddenly gone, left behind in the blink of an eye.

"Son of a smart goblin!" Ivan yelled, too amazed to remember that he meant to throw up. "Do it again!" he cried in glee, and the dragon apparently heard, for another ridge, and then another, and a jutting peak after that passed below or beside them in a wild rush, to a chorus of exhilarated screams that were outdone by the applauding roars of one yellow-bearded dwarf.

None of them could begin to guess at how fast they were traveling, could even comprehend the rush of dragonflight. They crossed the bulk of the Snowflakes in mere minutes, all of them, Vander and Ivan included, now in wholehearted agreement that the choice to ride the tamed wyrm had been a good one.

But then, suddenly and unexpectedly, mighty Fyrentennimar reared, seemed to hover in the air, as his massive horned head, his great fanged maw turned back to regard Cadderly.

"Uh-oh," Pikel muttered, thinking the fun at its end.

Cadderly sat upright, fearful that he had gone past the limits of control. He could not predict the chaotic magic, for its essence was founded in illogic and was in no way described in the harmonious song of Deneir.

Cadderly looked back to Danica and Shayleigh, no longer wearing expressions of freedom and excitement, and to grim Vander, nodding as though he had expected this disaster all along. Cadderly wanted to call out to the dragon, to ask Fyrentennimar what was wrong, but, sitting atop the volatile beast, suspended a thousand feet above the ground, he couldn't find the courage.

* * * * *

Dorigen watched in amazement as her wooden door bulged and groaned. Great bubbles of wood extended into her room and then retreated. She prudently moved to the side of the small chamber, out of harm's way.

A huge bubble rolled in from the door's center, holding the wood out to its extreme for a long moment. Then the door burst apart into a thousand flying splinters, each of them glowing silver with residual energy. Silver sparks became blue almost instantly, and not a single splinter struck the floor or opposite wall, was simply consumed to nothingness in midflight.

Aballister stormed in through the open portal.

"The ghost has failed," Dorigen remarked before the fuming wizard had even said a word.

Aballister stopped in the doorway and eyed the younger wizard suspiciously. "You viewed it through your crystal ball," he hissed, considering the device on the table before Dorigen.

"I view it in your expression," Dorigen quickly replied, fearing that the wizard would handle her as he had handled the door. She tossed her long salt-and-pepper hair back from her face, ran her crooked fingers through it, and went through a myriad of other movements, all designed to deflect Aballister's mounting rage.

Truly, the older wizard seemed on the verge of an explosion. His deep-set dark eyes narrowed dangerously, bony fingers clenching and unclenching at his sides.

"Your worries are plain to see," Dorigen said bluntly, knowing that it was precisely that fact that was bothering the wizard. Aballister, Dorigen knew, was a man who prided himself on being able to sublimate his emotions, on remaining cryptic at all times so that his enemies and rivals could not find any emotional advantage to use against him. "To remain calm and distant is the secret of a wizard's strength," the coldhearted Aballister had often said in the past, but such was not the case now, not with pesty Cadderly apparently making some headway in his try for Castle Trinity.

"You viewed it with your crystal ball," Aballister accused again, his voice a low growl, and Dorigen understood that it would not be wise for her to disagree a second time.

"The chimera and manticore have been defeated?" Dorigen stated as much as asked, something she had suspected since Aballister's last visit to her room, when he had grown outraged that their scrying would no longer work.

Aballister admitted the loss with a nod. "And now the undead monster," Dorigen went on.

"I do not know that Cadderly played a part in that one's downfall," Aballister snapped. "I have Druzil looking into the matter even as we speak."

Dorigen nodded, but privately didn't agree at all. If the ghost had been destroyed, then the formidable Cadderly was surely behind it. Whether he would openly admit it or not, Aballister knew it, too.

"Have we anything else with which we might strike out at him?" Dorigen asked.

"Have you located him with your precious crystal ball?" Aballister growled back angrily.

Dorigen looked away, not wanting her superior to see the rage in her amber eyes. If he considered her scrying attempts pitiful, then why didn't Aballister take on the task himself? Aballister was no novice to scrying, after all. He had watched Barjin's movements when the priest had entered Castle Trinity, had even destroyed his valuable enchanted mirror by forcing his magic through it.

Since that time, Aballister had not attempted any scrying at all, except one failed attempt earlier in Dorigen's room.

"Well, have you?" Aballister demanded.

Dorigen snapped an angry glare over him. "Simple spells can counteract scrying," she replied. "And I assure you, your son has little trouble with simple spells!"

Aballister's eyes widened, the old wizard seeming shocked that Dorigen had spoken so bluntly to him, had emphasized once more that this danger to Castle Trinity was being perpetrated by Aballister's own son. The wizard virtually trembled with anger and briefly considered lashing out with his power to punish Dorigen.

"Prepare your defenses," Dorigen said to him.

Again, her bluntness stunned the older wizard. "Cadderly will never get close to Castle Trinity," Aballister promised, an evil grin spreading over his face and calming him visibly. "The time has come for me to personally see to that troublesome child."

"You will go out?" Dorigen's tone was incredulous.

"My magic will go out," Aballister corrected. "The mountains themselves will shudder, and the sky will cry for the death of that foolish boy Cadderly! Let us see how a priest measures up against a wizard!" He cackled gleefully and turned away, sweeping determinedly out of the room.

Dorigen rested back in her chair and stared at the blasted portal, its jamb still smoldering long after Aballister had departed. She would keep trying with the crystal ball, more out of curiosity for this young priest and his exceptional friends than for Aballister's sake. In truth, Dorigen believed that she might have made some contact just a few minutes before Aballister had disturbed her, but she couldn't be sure so she didn't mention it to the pestering wizard. It had been just a fleeting sensation of rushing air, a sensation of freedom, of flying.

She hadn't seen the dragon, couldn't even be sure that she had actually made contact with Cadderly. But if it was the young priest, then Dorigen suspected that he would beat the expected timetable and would soon be knocking on Castle Trinity's door.

Aballister didn't need to know that.

Eleven
Strafing

E nemies?" Fyrentennimar's thunderous question made the six terribly vulnerable companions hold their breath in dread.

"We are friends," Cadderly replied weakly as the dragon went into a series of short stoops and quick rises, as close to a hovering maneuver as the bulky creature could accomplish.

Fyrentennimar's serpentine neck twisted, putting his head at a half-cocked position, almost like some curious dog.

"Are *they* enemies?" the dragon roared again.

They? Cadderly noted curiously, hopefully. "Who?"

Fyrentennimar bobbed his head and erupted with laughter. "Of course, of course!" he cried, his voice no longer carrying the edge of dragon hysteria. "Your eyes are not so keen as dragon eyes! I must remember that."

"What potential enemies do you speak of?" Cadderly asked impatiently, realizing that Fyrentennimar's aimless banter might continue for some time, and aware that his enchantment might not have much time remaining.

"Back on the trail," the dragon explained. "A procession of goblins and giants."

Cadderly turned to Danica and Shayleigh. "We should continue on our way," he offered. "I can bid Fyrentennimar to let us down far from the monstrous caravan."

"How many?" Shayleigh asked grimly, one hand tightly grasping her bow and an eager sparkle in her violet eyes. Both Cadderly and Danica knew from that look that the elf maiden did not wish to simply pass the monsters by.

Cadderly looked to Danica for support. When it was not immediately forthcoming, he continued, "I do not know how long the dragon will remain calm. The risk . . ."

"All the flight is a risk," Danica replied evenly, and Shayleigh seemed to approve.

"If Shilmista was your home, you would not be so quick to allow giants and goblins to return to their holes," the elf maiden said to Cadderly. "We of the wood know well what the spring will bring upon us."

"If we destroy Castle Trinity, the monsters might not return," Cadderly reasoned.

"If you were of Shilmista, would you take that chance?"

Danica nodded at Shayleigh's logic, but her smile disappeared when she regarded Cadderly's grim expression. "Let us allow our friends to decide," the monk offered.

Not realizing how much the surly Ivan had come to enjoy dragonflight, Cadderly readily agreed.

To this point, Ivan, Pikel, and Vander, enjoying the short, fluttering airhops of the great red, had remained oblivious to the discussion.

"Ivan!" Danica called back to the dwarf. "Would you care for the chance to smash a few goblin heads?"

The yellow-bearded dwarf roared, Pikel squeaked in glee, and Danica turned a smug smile back Cadderly's way. The young priest scowled, thinking Danica's method of asking Ivan was terribly unfair—what dwarf would say no to that question?

"Let us use our new ally to our best advantage," Shayleigh said to the defeated young priest.

Cadderly relaxed against the scaly dragon neck, trying to sort out this whole situation. He knew that they should go straight on to Castle Trinity, that any fighting now could jeopardize their chance for success later, especially if the dragon escaped his enchantment.

But was he ready for Castle Trinity? After his fight to destroy the *Ghearufu* and his titanic struggle with Ghost, Cadderly wasn't so sure. Up to now, he had been primarily concerned with the *Ghearufu*, but with that task out of the way, he had begun to look ahead—to powerful wizards and a well-trained army, entrenched in a secluded mountain fortress.

Cadderly needed time to catch his breath and to better consider those dangers at the end of his intended road. He decided that an attack on the goblin band, with a dragon on his side, might actually come as a reprieve.

And he couldn't, in good conscience, deny Shayleigh's fears for Shilmista or the plaintive, determined expression on her fair elven face. The young priest had to admit, to himself at least, that there was something alluring about the idea of experiencing unleashed dragon power from this secure vantage point.

"I believe that they are enemies, mighty Fyrentennimar," Cadderly called back to the unusually patient dragon. "Is there anything we might do against them?"

In answer, the dragon dipped one wing and dropped into a stoop, plummeting at breakneck speed, then leveling out and using his momentum to begin a great rush around the mountain. From this lower point, the friends had no trouble spotting the monstrous caravan, several hundred strong and with a fair number of giants among the shuffling, hunched goblinoid ranks, trudging along a trail in a narrow valley bordered by steep, rocky walls.

Fyrentennimar kept close to the ridges, circling away from the monsters. In mere seconds, the valley and the caravan seemed far removed.

"Do tell me, humble priest," the obviously eager dragon implored Cadderly. Cadderly looked to his friends once more, to confirm the decision, and found five bobbing heads staring back at him.

"They are enemies," Cadderly confirmed. "What is our role in the battle?"

"Your role?" the great beast echoed incredulously. "Hang on to my spiked spine with all your pitiful strength!"

The dragon banked, its wings going nearly perpendicular to the ground (drawing another cry of glee from Ivan and Pikel), and then shot off around the targeted peak. The friends felt the warmth growing within the wyrm, the flaring fires of old Fyren's ire. Reptilian eyes narrowed evilly, and in realizing the wyrm's mounting intensity, Cadderly wasn't so certain that he liked this whole scenario.

They came around the base of the mountain into the entrance to the narrow valley, still in a tight bank, the rock walls rushing by the six astonished friends in a dizzying blur. The dragon leveled and dipped even lower, the tips of his wide wings only a dozen feet or so from the sheer walls. The goblins and giants at the rear of the caravan turned and let out terrified shrieks, but so swift was the dragon's flight that they had no time to even break ranks before Fyrentennimar was upon them.

A searing line of fire strafed the trailing monsters. Goblins curled up into charred balls; mighty giants toppled, slapping futilely at the deadly flames as their bodies were consumed.

Acrid smoke rose in the dragon's wake. His flames were exhausted before he had gotten very far into the long line, but Fyrentennimar proudly stayed low in his flight, let his enemies see him and fear him.

All about the valley, the monsters went into an uncontrolled frenzy. Giants squashed goblins and slammed into other giants; goblins clawed and battled with their own kin, even coming to sword blows in their desperation to get away.

"Oh, my dear Deneir," Cadderly muttered, awestruck once again by the bared power of the dragon, by the utter terror Fyrentennimar had evoked in those pitiful creatures on the ground.

No, Cadderly told himself, not pitiful. These were Shilmista's invaders, the plague that had scarred the elven wood and slaughtered many of elf prince Elbereth's people. The plague that would undoubtedly return once more in the spring to complete what had been begun.

Shayleigh, her violet eyes narrow and grim, let fly a few well-aimed bow-shots. She saw one goblin aiming a crude bow the dragon's way, but the dimwitted creature could not calculate the incredible speed, and its shot flew far behind. Shayleigh was the better archer, putting an arrow into the cursing goblin's filthy mouth.

Another bowshot followed immediately, this one knifing into a goblin's back and dropping the wretched thing dead to the ground.

Cadderly winced at that one, caught by the realization that this creature was only trying to flee and posed no threat to them. That notion assaulted the young priest's sheltered sensibilities.

Until he again remembered the elven forest, remembered the scars in Shilmista. These were enemies, he decided finally, the taste of vengeance rising in his throat. The young priest fell into the song of Deneir and suddenly wore as grim an expression as that of his elvish companion. He heard the notes loud and strong in his head, as though Deneir approved of his decision, and he readily fell into its flow.

Fyrentennimar banked upward as the valley narrowed. As soon as he had cleared the steep walls the dragon banked again, steeply, swerving around for another run at the creatures.

Those monsters at the front of the caravan might have gotten away then, slipped out the narrow end of the valley into the wide expanses where they could have broken ranks altogether.

Cadderly stopped them.

He called to the rock walls at the valley's end, concentrated his magic on one high archway. The closest monster, a fat-bellied giant, rushed through that archway, and the rocks came to life, snapping repeatedly like an enormous maw, chomping the surprised giant into a pile of bloody mush.

The second giant in line skidded to a stop, eyeing the rocks with blank amazement. Wanting to test the unbelievable trap, the behemoth plucked up a helpless goblin at its side and tossed the creature forward.

Smacking, munching sounds accompanied the goblin's screams and continued long after the cries had died away, bits and pieces of the goblin flopping through the barrier on the other side.

The grisly scene was gone from Cadderly's sight in a moment as the dragon came about. For the wyrm, the turn was tight, but still huge Fyrentennimar had to travel a great distance from the valley to manage it.

"Have him put me down," Danica implored Cadderly.

"And me!" declared Vander from farther back. The firbolg and Danica exchanged excited looks, eager to fight beside each other.

Cadderly shook his head at the outrageous idea and closed his eyes, falling back into his chanting.

"Put me down, old Fyren!" Danica called out. Cadderly's eyes popped wide, but the obedient dragon pulled up short beside a ridge, and both Danica and Vander hopped from their perches, running off before Cadderly could react.

"Hey, we're missing all the fun!" Ivan realized as the wyrm set off once more, quickly gaining altitude. The dwarf started to call out to the dragon, but Pikel grabbed him by the beard and pulled him close, whispering something into his ear. Ivan roared happily, and both dwarves scrambled from the dragon's back, one going for each wing.

"What are you doing?" Cadderly demanded.

"Just tell the damned wyrm to hold on tight!" Ivan cried back, and then he disappeared from view, crawling hand over hand down the scaly side. His head popped back up a moment later. "But not too tight!" he added, and then he was gone.

"What?" Cadderly replied incredulously, and it took him a few moments to catch on. "Fyrentennimar!" he cried desperately.

* * * * *

Danica and Vander sped off for the back and wider end of the valley, looking for any monsters that might have found their way through the stench and smoke. Only a few minutes after Fyrentennimar had put them down, with the dragon still flying wide, though now angled for his second pass, the two spotted several goblins and a single, lumbering giant coming down a barren, rocky slope, heading directly for them.

The firbolg and the monk nodded and split up, each seeking the cover of some of the many boulders in the region.

The goblins and the giant were looking back more than forward, too afraid of the dragon to even think that there might be other danger lurking ahead.

Danica came out in a rush from the side, hurling one dagger after another, dropping a pair of goblins, and then charged forward, diving into a roll before her surprised adversaries and coming up with a flurry of ferocious blows.

Facial bones were smashed apart, and knifing fingers crushed a windpipe. Before Danica had even played out her momentum, four of the nine goblins lay dead at her feet.

The evil giant, on the far side of the band, turned to meet her charge, but noticed a movement back the other way and spun about, huge club at the ready. A goblin rushed by, eyeing Danica and shrieking in fear.

Vander cleaved it in half.

"Giantkin," the club-wielding monster said to Vander in the rolling, thunderous language of the hill giants.

Vander snarled and rushed ahead, his great sword coming across in a blurring arc. The hill giant fell back, throwing its club up in a frantic defense. By sheer luck, the club fell in line with the rushing sword, Vander's blade diving many inches into the wood.

Vander tried to pull back on the sword, to retract it and slash again, but the club's hard wood held it fast.

The hill giant, much larger and several times heavier than Vander's eight hundred pounds, rushed forward, letting go of its club and spreading its huge arms out wide to engulf its foe.

Vander twisted and punched out, connecting solidly but doing little to impede his enemy's momentum. The firbolg went down heavily, under two tons of hill giant flesh.

The four remaining goblins looked as much at each other as at Danica, each waiting for one of its companions to make the first move. They circled the apparently unarmed monk, one lifting a spear.

Now that the initial surprise was gone, Danica stayed down in a defensive crouch, preferring to let her enemies come to her. The goblins wisely spread out around her, but she remained confident, turning slowly so that no creature could remain behind her.

The spear wielder pumped its arm, and Danica started to dive to the right. She stopped almost immediately, though, recognizing the goblin's move as a feint, and used the break to her advantage, coming back hard to the left, spinning low and straight-kicking one of the other goblins in the knee.

The creature jerked straight, then fell back, clutching its broken limb.

Danica was already back to circling, now eyeing the spear wielder directly, taking its measure, using its body language to discern its every thought.

* * * * *

Cadderly saw the fight off to the side, noticed Vander buried beneath the flabby folds of the monstrous hill giant. He tried to think of a way to help, but suddenly the valley walls were up around him again as Fyrentennimar began another breath-stealing approach.

Shayleigh nimbly moved about on the dragon's back, determined to play a role and firing her bow repeatedly. At first, her shots were random, nearly every one scoring a hit, but then she concentrated her fire on one hill giant. By the time Fyrentennimar's flight took her beyond range of the beast, its wide chest sported a half-dozen arrows.

"Get lower, ye damned fun-stealing wyrm!" came a cry from below, a cry informing Cadderly that Ivan and Pikel were in position. The young priest fell flat to his belly and peered over the front edge of the dragon's wing.

Hanging below him were the Bouldershoulder brothers, one in each of Fyrentennimar's clutching talons. The dragon did fly lower, and Pikel howled in glee as he put his tree-trunk club in line and used the dragon's momentum to splatter the head of a giant that was too slow in ducking.

Ivan took an axe swipe on the other side as they passed, but he mistimed the blow badly and caught nothing but air.

"Sandstone!" the frustrated dwarf bellowed.

Cadderly's orderly sensibilities could not accept the craziness about him. Helplessly shaking his head, he managed to sit back up and dropped a hand into a berry-filled pouch. He uttered the last words of the enchantment in resigned tones, then took out a handful of the berries and tossed them randomly into the air. The seeds exploded into tiny bursts of flame as they hit, startling and stinging giants, wounding and even killing a few goblins.

Fyrentennimar swerved up again, slightly, as the valley started to narrow, but the friends knew that he would not soar away, knew that he had not finished the run.

A swarm of creatures huddled about the back end of the valley, hemmed in by the sheer walls and Cadderly's biting enchantment. Their frenzy multiplied many times over as the dragon reared near them. Giants stuffed goblins through the archway (one actually passed through without being hit, to run screaming down the rocky slope on the other side), and then many giants, in sheer terror of the great dragon, jumped in themselves.

The dragon's serpentine neck shot forward, and then came the flames. Fyrentennimar's maw waved from side to side, changing the fire's angle, immolating the whole mass of creatures.

On and on it went, interminably long for the stunned Cadderly.

Agonized cries came from creatures who were soon no more than crackling bones; all the monstrous swarm seemed to flow together in a singular bubbling mass.

"Oo," Pikel muttered admiringly, the dwarf having a fine view of the catastrophe from his low perch. Ivan, shaking his head in disbelief, couldn't find the words to reply.

* * * * *

Danica saw the panic welling in the goblin, knew that it wanted to throw the spear and run off. She locked her gaze upon it fully, forced it to stare into her eyes, almost hypnotizing in their intensity.

She had to hold the goblin's shot a bit longer, until the anxious club wielder to her right made the first move.

Danica straightened and seemed to relax, though she kept her intimidating gaze steady. She dipped and turned suddenly, caught the club in both hands as it predictably came across, and slid down, hooking the surprised goblin's knees with her feet and pulling the creature around her.

The goblin jerked suddenly, its eyes popping wide, and Danica, though she couldn't see the spear sticking from the goblin's back, knew that her timing, and her understanding of her enemies, had been perfect.

She came up in a spin, tearing the club from the dying creature's grasp and hurling it straight back, into the chest of the next charging goblin. The creature fumbled with the unexpected missile for a moment, getting it tangled with its sword, then finally tossing it aside. It managed to focus its attention on Danica just as her foot snapped into its throat.

Again Danica was spinning, leaping over the dead club wielder and tearing the spear from its back. Three running strides later, she let fly the crude weapon. The spear didn't hit the mark exactly, but it did get tangled up in its original owner's legs enough to drop the goblin hard to its face.

It lay on its belly for a moment, trying to shake away its dizziness.

Then Danica was upon it, and it was dead. The monk looked back to the one remaining goblin, the first of the four she had hit. It was floundering about, half-hopping, half-crawling, as it continued to grasp at its shattered kneecap. It struggled past two of its companions, two goblins that had died grasping at daggers. Thinking to arm itself, the struggling creature ambled for the daggers, but stopped and looked up, dismayed, for Danica had gotten there first.

* * * * *

Vander slapped futilely against the giant's bulk, thrashing about with all his strength, even biting the monster on the neck. But all the savagery the powerful firbolg could muster seemed puny beneath the sheer size of the hill giant.

Vander found his breathing hard to come by and wondered how long he could hold out beneath the two-ton behemoth. His estimate lessened considerably when the hill giant began to bounce, pushing off the ground with its huge hands and free-falling back on top of poor Vander.

Vander's initial thoughts were to curl up in a ball. He realized, though, that his body could not take the pounding for long, whatever he might do—the first bounce had blasted out his breath, and he could only draw small amounts of air between each subsequent slam. Every time the hill giant came crushing back down, Vander expected his rib cage to collapse.

Without even thinking of the movement, Vander used one moment of freedom to tuck his legs up near his belly. Fortune was with the firbolg, for when the hill giant came back down, its own weight drove Vander's knees hard into its abdomen. Back up went the hill giant, higher this time, fully extending its arms that it might come back with one final slam.

Up came Vander's feet, straight out in pursuit of the monster's belly, locking the giant up high before its fall could build momentum. The desperate firbolg strained with all his might; leg muscles flexed and ripped and stood out like iron cords. The giant, its girth hanging several feet off the ground, freed up one hand and punched Vander across the face, nearly knocking him senseless.

Vander accepted the blow, but kept his focus on his legs and groaned against the strain, compelling his massive legs to straighten.

The giant rose up a few more inches; Vander knew that he could not hold the weight. He kicked out a final time, trying to buy himself precious seconds and space, then curled his legs and rolled, securing the butt of his sword against the ground and angling the blade straight up.

The giant's eyes widened in horror as it flailed its arms and thrashed about for the instant of its descent, but it could not get to the side, could not get out of line. The sword entered it at the juncture between its belly and its chest, driving upward through the monster's diaphragm. The hill giant planted its quivering arms firmly, broke its fall so that it would not further impale itself.

Vander was free, now, but he did not immediately roll out from under the giant. He grasped his blade in both arms and heaved it straight up, driving it deeper into the giant's flesh.

The quivering arms buckled altogether, and the giant slid down the blade, issuing a long, low groan as the tip of the sword came against its backbone and stopped its descent for a moment. Then the sword broke clear, and the behemoth lay very still, feeling no pain, feeling nothing at all.

Vander, pressed again under the enormous weight, jerked the sword a few times to make sure the monster was dead, then began the task of crawling out. Danica, finished with her own work, was soon crouched beside him.

* * * * *

Eventually the dragon's fire ceased, leaving the entire horde of creatures at the narrow end of the valley lying together in a bulbous, smoldering mass.

Those monsters behind the dragon could have rushed in to strike at the low-flying beast's back, but they did not, for they were too terrified to even approach the deadly wyrm.

Ivan and Pikel waved weapons at them and taunted them, trying to draw them in.

"Aw, run off then, ye cowardly bunch!" a frustrated Ivan yelled.

A moment later, when the dragon's talons let go of the dwarves, Ivan yelled a singular note of surprise. He and Pikel dropped fifteen feet to the ground, bounced right back to their feet, and hopped about, dazed.

Fifty feet behind them, the fleeing giants and goblins turned and stared curiously, not knowing which way to run.

"Humble priest, get you down!" Fyrentennimar roared, shaking Cadderly from his daze. The young priest turned back to old Fyren, wondering if the ethics enchantment had ceased, wondering if he was about to die.

"*Get you down!*" Fyrentennimar cried again, and the force of his stone-splitting voice nearly knocked Cadderly from his perch. He and Shayleigh were moving in an instant, crawling down the spiked back and tail and dropping the last few feet to the ground to stand beside Ivan and Pikel.

"Playing with dragons," Ivan remarked sarcastically under his breath.

Shayleigh lifted her bow but had to close her eyes and look away as Fyrentennimar, wings beating fiercely, pivoted in the air, whipping the smoke and dust about. The dragon dipped into a short stoop, reared again, and then fell over the remaining group of monsters, tail thrashing, spiked foreclaws slashing, great hind legs kicking, and wings beating a hurricane of wind. A swoop of the dragon's tail sent four goblins soaring, splattering them against the valley wall with force enough to shatter most of the bones in their bodies, and then the tail itself connected on the wall, opening a huge crack in the stone and leaving crimson marks where the goblins had been. A giant, horrified beyond reason, lifted its club and charged.

Fyrentennimar's maw clamped over it, hoisting it easily into the air. Squealing like some barnyard animal at the slaughterhouse, the giant freed one arm from the side of the wyrm's maw and slapped its pitiful club against its armored head.

Fyrentennimar bit the giant in half, its legs dropping free to the stone.

Even sturdy Ivan was shaken by the spectacle of the dragon's wholehearted slaughter, by the mass of bubbling corpses and the flying and broken bodies of those enemies caught in close to the enraged wyrm.

"Glad he's on our side," Ivan said, his breathless voice barely a whisper.

Cadderly grimaced at the words, remembering again the tone Fyrentennimar had used when ordering him down. He studied the dragon's lusty, hungry movements as old Fyren reveled in the blood and carnage.

"Is he?" the young priest muttered under his breath.

Twelve
Chaos

A giant's broken form came flying up over the wall of the valley, landing hard and bouncing down the rocky slope past Vander and Danica.

They heard the chaos within the valley, heard the dragon's primal roars and the horrified screams of the doomed monsters. Neither Danica nor Vander held much pity for the evil goblins and giants, but they looked to each other with honest fear, simply overwhelmed by the awakening storm within those entrapping wails.

Danica motioned for Vander to move around to the valley entrance, while she took a more direct course up the slope. Before she even got to the top, she saw monsters, and pieces of monsters, flipping into the air, tumbling about and dropping back into the frenzy. Her nerves on end, Danica could not hold back a chuckle, thinking that the scene reminded her of Pikel's work in the Edificant Library's kitchen, the druidic-minded dwarf stubbornly (and clumsily) tossing a salad of woodland flora despite Ivan's roaring protests.

The dragon's tail must have hit the stone wall then, for Danica, though she was separated from the blow by forty feet of solid stone, suddenly found herself sitting down.

* * * * *

Cadderly slipped into the dreamstate, into the song of Deneir, and reached his mental perceptions out to Fyrentennimar.

A wall of red blocked his entry

"What do you know?" Shayleigh asked, recognizing the concern, even dread, in the young priest's expression.

Cadderly did not answer. Again he fell into the song, reached out to the dragon. But Fyrentennimar's savage rage blocked him and held any real communication far away.

Cadderly knew in his heart that old Fyren would no longer consider him an ally, that in the bloodlust, the dragon had reverted to its true, wicked nature. He moved the notes of the song toward the sphere of chaos, thinking to delve there again and attempt to tame the wyrm once more.

He opened his eyes for just a minute, regarded the complete slaughter of the few remaining monsters, and sensed that no such spell could get through the outraged dragon's instinctual mental defenses.

"Get back to the far end of the valley," he said as calmly as he could to Shayleigh. "Ready your bow."

The elf maiden eyed him gravely, considering the implications of his grim tone. "The enchantment is no more?" she asked.

"Ready your bow," Cadderly repeated.

There wasn't much left of the monstrous column; Fyrentennimar would be finished in mere minutes. Cadderly called up his protective magics, drew a line of dragonbane across the valley floor, and brought a magical fire shield around him and the two confused dwarves at his side.

"What are ye doing?" Ivan demanded, always suspicious of magic and especially on edge with an enraged dragon barely a hundred yards away.

"It is a spell of the elements," Cadderly tried to quickly explain. "On me, it will stop the dragon fire."

"Uh-oh," Pikel mumbled, figuring out the implications of Cadderly's precautions.

"On you it will diminish the fire, but not completely," the young priest finished. "Get to the wall and find a rock to hide behind."

The dwarves didn't have to be asked twice. Normally, they would have remained boldly at their ally's side, ready for battle. But this was a dragon, after all.

So Cadderly stood alone in the center of the valley, surrounded by carnage, by torn reminders of the dragon's wrath. He stooped low and grabbed a handful of dirt from one of Fyrentennimar's footprints, then stood straight and resolute, reminding himself that he had done as the tenets of Deneir demanded. He had destroyed the *Ghearufu*.

Still, he thought of Danica, his love, and the new life they had begun in Carradoon, and he did not want to die.

Fyrentennimar swallowed whole the last cowering goblin and turned about. Reptilian eyes narrowed, shooting glaring beams even under the light of day. Almost immediately, those beams focused directly on Cadderly.

"Well done, mighty wyrm!" Cadderly cried out, hoping that his guess might be wrong, that the dragon might still be caught within a goodly moral code.

"*Humble priest . . .*" Fyrentennimar replied, and Cadderly thought the booming voice would surely destroy his hearing. Since he had leveled the enchantment at the dragon, Cadderly had only heard that voice twice, both times when the dragon had suspected that enemies were about. Crouched low like a hunting dog, walking on all fours with his leathery wings tucked in tight to his back, the dragon quickly halved the hundred-yard distance to Cadderly.

"You have done us a great service," Cadderly began.

"*Humble priest!*" Fyrentennimar interrupted.

The song of Deneir played in Cadderly's thoughts. He knew that he would need a diversion, something physical and powerful to gain time as he sorted through the notes of a spell he had not yet fully come to understand.

"A service both in your cave and in taking us across the mountains," Cadderly went on, hoping that he might steal some time with flattery. He remained conscious of the song as he spoke, the notes of the needed spell coming clearer with each playing. "But now, it is time for you . . ."

"*Humble priest!*"

Cadderly found no answer to the thunderous roar, the absolute indication that Fyrentennimar did not yet consider the killing to be at its end. With low growls shivering the stone beneath Cadderly's feet, the dragon stalked in.

Those eyes! Cadderly lost his concentration, caught in their hypnotizing intensity. He felt helpless, hopeless, surely doomed against this godlike creature, this terror beyond imagination. He fought for breath, fought against the welling panic that told him to run for his life.

Fyrentennimar was close. How had Fyrentennimar gotten so damned close?

The dragon's head slowly moved back, serpentine neck coiling. A foreclaw tucked up tight against the massive beast's chest, while its hind legs tamped down securely on the stone.

"Get outa there!" Ivan roared from the side, recognizing that the beast was about to spring. Cadderly heard the words and agreed wholeheartedly, but could not get his legs to move.

An arrow zipped above Cadderly's head, splintering harmlessly as it struck the dragon's impenetrable natural armor.

Intent on Cadderly the deceiver, Fyrentennimar did not seem to even notice.

Of all the things Cadderly of Carradoon would see in his life, nothing would come close to the sheer terror of seeing Fyrentennimar's ensuing spring. The dragon, so huge, shot forward with the speed of a viper, came at Cadderly with a maw opened wide enough to swallow him whole, showing rows of gleaming teeth, each as long as the young priest's forearm.

In that split second, Cadderly's vision failed him, as though his mind simply could not accept the image.

Just a dozen feet in front of him, Fyrentennimar's expression changed suddenly. His head snapped to the side and contorted weirdly, as if he was pushing against some resilient bubble.

"Dragonbane," Cadderly muttered, the success of his ward bringing him some small measure of hope.

Old Fyren twisted and struggled, bending the blocking line, refusing to relent. The great hind legs dug deep scratches into the stone, and the hungry maw snapped repeatedly, looking for something tangible to tear.

Cadderly began his chant. Another arrow whipped past him, this one grazing Fyrentennimar's eye.

The dragon's wings spread wide, lifting old Fyren upright. The dragon roared and hissed and sucked in air.

Cadderly closed his eyes and continued to chant, locking his thoughts on the notes of Deneir's song.

The flames engulfed him, scorched and melted the stone at his feet. His friends cried out, thinking him consumed, but he did not hear them. His protective globe sizzled green about him, thinning dangerously as though it would not endure, but Cadderly did not see.

All he heard was the song of Deneir; all he saw was the music of the heavenly spheres.

* * * * *

When Danica came to the lip of the valley wall and saw her love apparently immolated below her, her legs buckled and her heart fluttered—she thought it would stop altogether. Her warrior instincts told her to go to the aid of her love, but what could she do against the likes of Fyrentennimar? Her hands and feet could be deadly against orcs and goblins, even giants, but they would do little damage slamming the iron-hard scales of the wyrm. Danica could hurl her crystal-bladed daggers into the heart of an ogre ten yards away, but those blades were tiny things when measured against the sheer bulk of Fyrentennimar.

The dragon fires ended, and, looking at Cadderly, so boldly facing the wyrm in the open valley, Danica knew that she had to do something.

"Fyrentennimar the awesome?" she cried incredulously. "A puny and weak thing is he, by my own eyes. A pretender of strength who cowers when danger is near!"

The dragon's head snapped around to face her, high above on the lip of the valley wall.

"Ugly *worm*," Danica chided, emphasizing her use of "worm" instead of "wyrm," perhaps the most insulting thing one could say to a dragon. "Ugly and weak worm!"

The dragon's tail twitched dangerously, reptilian eyes narrowed to mere slits, and old Fyren's low growl reverberated through the valley stone.

Standing before the distracted dragon, Cadderly picked up the pace of his chanting. He was truly glad for the distraction, but terribly afraid that Danica was pushing the explosive dragon beyond reason.

Danica laughed at old Fyren, just crossed her hands over her belly and shook with laughter. Her thoughts were quite serious, though. She recalled the ancient writings of Penpahg D'Ahn, the Grandmaster of her sect.

You anticipate the attacks of your enemy, the Grandmaster had promised. *You do not react, you move before your enemy moves. As the bowman fires, his target is gone. As the swordsman thrusts ahead, his enemy, you, are behind him.*

And as the dragon breathes, Penpahg had said, *so its flames shall touch only empty stone.*

Danica needed those words now, with Fyrentennimar's head waving only a hundred feet below her. Penpahg D'Ahn's writings were the source of her strength, the inspiration for her life, and she had to trust them now, even in the face of an outraged red dragon.

"Ugly, ugly Fyrentennimar, who thinks he is so good," she sang. "His talons cannot tear cotton, his breath cannot light wood!" Not an impressive rhyme perhaps, but the words assaulted the overly proud Fyrentennimar more profoundly than any weapon ever could.

The dragon's wings beat suddenly, ferociously, lifting the dragon into the air—almost.

Cadderly completed his spell at that moment, and the stone beneath Fyrentennimar reshaped, animated, and grabbed at the dragon's rear claws. Old Fyren stretched to his limit, seemed almost springlike as he came crashing back down, falling tight against his haunches, but all of his subsequent thrashing could not break the valley floor's hold.

Fyrentennimar knew at once the source of his entrapment, and his great head whipped around, slamming hard against the blocking line of the dragonbane spell.

Cadderly paled—could his protective globe defeat a second searing blast of dragon breath?

"His wings cannot lift his blubber," Danica cried out. "His tail cannot swat a gnat."

The dragon's ensuing roar echoed off mountain walls a dozen miles away, sent animals and monsters rushing for the cover of their holes throughout the Snowflake Mountains. The serpentine neck stretched forward, and a gout of flames fell over Danica.

Stone melted and poured from the ledge in a red-glowing river. Pikel, hiding in an alcove beneath the region, let out a frightened squeak and rushed away.

Cadderly verged on panic, thought for sure that he had just seen his love die, and knew in his heart, despite the logical claims of his conscience, that nothing, not the destruction of the *Ghearufu* or the downfall of Castle Trinity, could be worth such a loss.

He calmed, though, when he remembered who he was thinking of, remembered the wisdom and almost magical talents of his dear Danica. He had to trust in her, as she so often trusted in him, had to believe that her decisions would be the correct decisions.

"His horns get caught in archways," Danica continued the rhyme, laughing over the words as she came back up to the ledge at a point thirty feet to the side.

"And his muscles are no more than fat!"

Fyrentennimar's eyes widened with outrage and incredulity. He thrashed his tail and legs, slammed his horned head repeatedly against the magical drag-onbane barrier, and beat his wings so fiercely that goblin corpses shifted and slid, caught up in the wind.

Like Danica, Cadderly was grinning widely, though he knew that the fight was far from won. One of Fyrentennimar's claws had torn free of the stone, and the other would soon break through. The young priest completed his next enchantment, pulled from the sphere of time, and hurled waves of magical energy at the distracted dragon.

Old Fyren felt the stone loosen about his one trapped leg, though it retight-ened immediately. The dragon, wise with years though he was, did not under-stand the significance, did not understand why the valley suddenly seemed much larger to him.

Again the wyrm sensed that Cadderly was somehow involved, and he calmed his tirade and steeled an angry glare over the supposedly "humble" priest. "What have you done?" Fyrentennimar demanded.

The dragon jerked suddenly, slammed from behind by Vander, the firbolg's huge sword smashing in hard at Fyrentennimar's trapped haunch.

"Time to go!" Ivan yelled to his brother, and the two dwarves appeared from behind their rocks, heads down in a wild charge.

To the still huge Fyrentennimar, the firbolg's hit did no real damage. A tail slap sent Vander flying away, crashing down against the base of the valley wall. Resilient, Vander came right back up, understanding that none of the band could give in to the pain and the terror, that there could be no retreat and no quarter against such a merciless and terrible foe.

The new distractions could not have come at a better moment for Cadderly. Again came the waves of his insidious magic, and to old Fyren, the valley seemed larger still.

Then the dragon understood—the "humble" priest was stealing his age! And to a dragon, age was the measure of size and strength. "Old Fyren" was more than a match for the pitiful companions, but suddenly "young Fyren" found him-self in dire straits.

"Bat-winged newt with a bumpy head, run away, run away before you're dead!" Danica cried out.

The immediate threats were the charging dwarves and the humble priest with his wicked magic. Fyrentennimar knew this rationally, knew that he should put his mouth in line with the charging dwarves and incinerate them before they got near him. But no respectable red dragon could ignore the taunt of "bat-winged newt," and Fyrentennimar's head went back up toward the ledge, his fire bursting forth in Danica's direction.

Or at least, bursting forth to where Danica had been.

By the time the fires ended with more molten stone slipping down from the ledge, Ivan and Pikel were hacking and smashing away, and while their weapons would have skipped harmlessly off the scale plating of "old Fyren," they now cracked and smashed apart the thinned and smaller scales. After only three furious swings, Ivan's axe dug deep into dragon flesh.

Similarly, Shayleigh's line of arrows chipped away at the dragon's scales. So perfect was the elf maiden's aim that the next six arrows that left her quiver hit the dragon in a concentrated pattern no larger than the brim of Cadderly's blue hat.

Cadderly was truly exhausted. His eyelids drooped heavily; his heart pounded in his chest. He went back into the song again, though, stubbornly steeled his gaze, and loosed the energies.

This time, Fyrentennimar was ready for the magical assault, and the spell was turned aside.

Cadderly came at him again, and then a third time. The young priest could barely focus his vision, could hardly remember what he was doing and why he was doing it. His head throbbed; he felt as if every ounce of magical energy he let loose was an ounce of energy stolen from his own life-force.

Yet he sang on.

Then he was lying on the stone, his head bleeding from the unexpected impact on the valley floor. He looked up and was glad to see that his enchantment had gotten through once more, that Fyrentennimar seemed not so large to him, barely taller than a hill giant. But Cadderly knew that the spells were not lasting, that Fyrentennimar's stolen centuries would soon return. They had to hit at the dragon hard right now; Cadderly had to find some offensive magic that would smash the monster while the dragon was caught in his lessened state.

But the song of Deneir would not play in the young priest's head. He could not bring to mind the name of his holy book, could not even recall his own name. The pain in his head throbbed, blocking all avenues of thought. He could hardly draw breath past the sheer physical exertion of his beating chest. He brought a hand to his pounding heart and felt his bandoleer, then, following that singular focused thought, drew out his hand-crossbow.

Ivan and Pikel went into a flurry of activity under the dragon's slashing foreclaws. Ivan got buffeted by a wing, but hooked his axe over the limb's top and would not be thrown away.

Vander's next hit on the dragon's haunch shattered several scales and drove a deep gash. Fyrentennimar roared in agony, swooped his serpentine neck about, launching his opened maw for the dangerous giant. Vander tugged his sword free, knew that he had to be quick, or be snapped in half.

It took Cadderly several moments to load and cock his weapon, and when he looked back to the fight, he found Fyrentennimar, on the stone and level with him, staring him in the eye from just a few feet away!

Cadderly cried out and fired, the quarrel blasting into the dragon's nostril and blowing pieces from his face. Cadderly, scrambling on all fours with the little strength he had left, didn't even see the hit. He calmed considerably when he at last looked back, though, when he realized that Fyrentennimar's head had only been near him, had only crossed the line of dragonbane, because Vander had lopped it off, halfway up the neck.

Pikel stood by the fallen torso, mumbling, "Oooo," over and over.

Cadderly, his senses slowly returning, did not understand the green-bearded dwarf's apparent concern, until he saw the top of Ivan's head wriggle out from under the chest of the dead wyrm. With a stream of curses to make a barkeep of Waterdeep's dock ward blush, Ivan pulled himself out, slapping Pikel's offered helping hand away. The yellow-bearded dwarf hopped to his feet, hands planted squarely on his hips, eyeing Vander dangerously.

"Riding stupid dragons!" he huffed, glancing menacingly Cadderly's way. "Well?" the dwarf roared at the confused firbolg. Vander looked to Pikel for some explanation, but the green-bearded Bouldershoulder only shrugged and put his hands behind his back.

"Move the damned thing so I can get back me axe!" Ivan howled in explanation. He shook his head in disgust, stomped over to Cadderly, and roughly pulled the man to his feet.

"And don't ye ever think o' bringing a stupid dragon along again!" Ivan roared, poking Cadderly hard in the chest. The dwarf shoved by and stormed away, looking for a quiet spot where he could brood.

Pikel followed, after patting Cadderly comfortingly on the shoulder.

Cadderly smiled, despite his pain and exhaustion, when he looked upon Pikel. As long as everything turned out all right, the easygoing dwarf cared little for any troublesome details—as was evidenced by the dwarf's not-too-well hidden "Hee hee hee" as he skipped along behind his surly brother.

Cadderly would have shaken his head in disbelief, but he feared that the effort would cost him his tentative balance.

"She is all right," Shayleigh remarked to him, coming up and following his worried gaze toward the melted ledge.

True to the elf maiden's words, Danica came running in through the valley entrance a moment later, flying with all speed for her love. She grabbed Cadderly tightly and held him close, and he needed her support, for the weariness, more complete than Cadderly had ever experienced, had come rushing back in full.

Thirteen

To Trust

S he viewed the dragon, full-sized once more, dead in the rocky vale, focused on its severed head lying a few feet from the scaly torso. All about the grisly scene, Dorigen saw the smoldering, torn remains of goblins and giants, scores of the beasts. And walking out of the valley, weary perhaps, but not one of them showing any serious wounds, went Cadderly and Danica, flanked by the two dwarves, the elf maiden, and the traitorous firbolg.

Dorigen slipped back into her chair and allowed the image to disappear from her crystal ball. At first she had been surprised to so easily get through Cadderly's magical defenses and locate the young priest, but when she gazed upon the scene, upon the carnage and the fury of Fyrentennimar, she had understood the priest's excusable defensive lapse.

Dorigen thought that she was witnessing Cadderly's end, and the end of the threat to Castle Trinity. She had almost called in Aballister, almost advised the older wizard to go out and recruit Fyrentennimar as an ally for their unhindered attack against Carradoon.

Her surprise as Cadderly literally shrank the great wyrm—by stealing its age, Dorigen presumed—could not have been more complete, and complete, too, was Dorigen's surprise as she sat back and honestly considered her own feelings during the viewing.

She had felt saddened when she thought Cadderly was surely doomed. Logically, ambitious Dorigen could tell herself that Cadderly's death would be a good thing for the designs of Castle Trinity, that the interference of the young priest could no longer be tolerated, and that in killing the young priest Fyrentennimar would have only saved Aballister the trouble. Logically, Dorigen should not have felt sympathy for Cadderly as he stood, apparently helpless, before the dreaded wyrm.

But she had, and she had silently cheered for Cadderly and his brave friends in their titanic struggle, had actually leaped up in joy when the firbolg came up from behind and lopped the dragon's head off.

Why had she done that?

"Have you sighted anything this day?" The voice startled Dorigen so badly that she nearly fell out of her chair. She quickly threw the wrap over the crystal ball, though its interior was a cloud of nothingness once more, and fumbled to straighten and compose herself as Aballister threw open the curtain now serving as her front door and whisked in beside her.

"Druzil has lost contact with the young priest," Aballister continued angrily. "It would seem that he is making fine progress through the mountains."

If only you knew, Dorigen thought, but she remained silent. Aballister could not begin to guess that the young priest was now no more than a day's march from Castle Trinity. Nor could the old wizard imagine that Cadderly and his friends would be resourceful and powerful enough to overcome the likes of old Fyren.

"What do you know?" the suspicious Aballister demanded, drawing Dorigen from her private contemplations.

"I?" Dorigen replied innocently, poking a finger against her own chest, her amber eyes wide with feigned surprise.

If Aballister had not been so self-absorbed at that moment, he would have caught Dorigen's defensive and obvious overreaction.

"Yes, you," the wizard snarled. "Have you been able to make contact with Cadderly this day?"

Dorigen looked back to the crystal ball, mulled the question over for a short moment, and then replied, "No." When she looked back, she saw that Aballister continued to eye her suspiciously.

"Why did you hesitate before answering?" he asked.

"I thought that I had made contact," Dorigen lied. "But in considering it, I have come to believe that it was only a goblin."

Aballister's scowl showed that he was not convinced.

"I fear that your son purposely misdirected my scrying attempt," Dorigen quickly added, putting the older wizard on the defensive.

"The last time Druzil saw Cadderly, he was near the mountain called Nightglow," Aballister said, and Dorigen nodded her agreement. "There is a storm brewing in that area, so it is unlikely that he will have gone very far."

"That would seem logical," Dorigen agreed, though she knew better.

The old wizard grinned evilly. "A storm brewing," he mused. "But unlike any storm my foolish son has ever encountered!"

Now it was Dorigen's turn to eye him suspiciously. "What have you done?"

"Done?" Aballister laughed. "Better to ask what I will do!" Aballister spun about in a circle, as animated as Dorigen had seen him since this whole business had begun, nearly a year before when Barjin had entered the Edificant Library.

"I grow weary of the game!" Aballister said suddenly, fiercely, stopping his spin so that his hollowed face was barely inches from Dorigen's crooked nose. "And so now, I will end it!"

With a snap of his fingers, he left the room, left Dorigen to wonder what he had in mind. The curtain now serving as her door seemed a poignant reminder of Aballister's wrath, and she couldn't contain a shudder when she thought of the magics that Aballister might soon be launching Cadderly's way.

Or at where he believed Cadderly to be.

Why hadn't she told her mentor the truth? Dorigen wondered. Aballister was planning something big, perhaps even going out personally to deal with his son, and Dorigen hadn't told him what she knew about Cadderly's position, that the young priest was many miles beyond Nightglow.

Rationally, it seemed to the woman that letting Aballister go out and deal with Cadderly would be her safest course, for if Cadderly's attempt at Castle Trinity proved successful, Dorigen, no ally of the young priest, would likely find herself in serious trouble.

Dorigen ran a finger along the length of her crooked nose, shook her long hair back from her face, and eyed the cloth covering the crystal ball. Cadderly might arrive in a day, and she had not told Aballister!

Dorigen felt strangely removed from the cascading events about her, like some distant spectator. Cadderly could have killed her in Shilmista Forest, had her unconscious at his feet. He had broken her hands and taken her magical items, putting her out of the fight.

But he had spared her life.

Perhaps it was honor that guided Dorigen now, an unspoken agreement between her and the young priest. A sense of obligation told her to let it all play out, to stand aside while they learned who was the stronger, the father or the son.

* * * * *

Back in his private chambers, Aballister held a smoking beaker aloft in trembling hands. He focused his thoughts on Nightglow, the target area, and focused his magical energies on the contents of the beaker, an elixir of great strength.

He uttered the enchanting words, spoke the arcane syllables from a nearly meditative state, losing himself in the swirling, growing energies. He continued for nearly an hour, until the vibrating power within the beaker threatened to blow apart and take Castle Trinity down with it.

The wizard hurled the beaker across the room, where it shattered at the base of the wall. A gray puff of smoke arose above it, growling, rumbling.

"*Mykos, mykos makom deignin,*" Aballister whispered. "Go out, go out, my pet."

As though it had heard the wizard's request, the gray cloud filtered through a crack in the stone wall, worked its way through all the walls and out of Castle Trinity. It rose up high on the winds, sometimes following, sometimes moving of its own accord, and all the while the wizard's magical storm cloud began to grow and darken.

Contained bursts of lightning rumbled as it soared across the mountains. Still the ominous thing thickened and darkened, and seemed as if it would explode with building energy.

It raced across the high peaks of the Snowflakes, unerringly aimed for the region around Nightglow.

* * * * *

Cadderly and his friends noticed the strange cloud, so much darker than the general overcast of the snowy day. Cadderly noticed, too, that while the more common clouds seemed to be drifting west to east, as was usual for the area's weather patterns, this strange cloud was racing almost due south.

They heard the first rumble of thunder soon after, a tremendous, though distant blast that shook the ground under their feet.

"Thunder?" Ivan balked. "Who ever heared o' thunder in the middle o' the damned winter?"

Cadderly bade Vander to lead them up higher, where they might see what was happening behind them. When they reached a higher plateau, affording them a view between several other peaks all the way back to Nightglow, the young priest wasn't so sure that he wanted to watch.

Bolt after searing bolt of lightning, crystalline clear across the miles as the already dim daylight began to wane, slammed the mountainside, splintering rocks, splitting trees, and sizzling into the snow. Huge winds bent the pines on the mountain's lower slopes nearly horizontal, and pelting ice quickly accumulated in the thick branches, bending the trees lower.

"We were wise in riding the dragon," Shayleigh remarked, quite overwhelmed, as were her companions, by the ferocity of the storm. Vander grunted, as though he had told them all, but in truth, even the firbolg, who had grown to adulthood in the harsh climate of the northern Spine of the World range, was at a loss to explain the sheer power of this distant storm.

Another tremendous bolt slammed the mountainside, brightening the deepening gloom, its rumbling wake dislodging tons of snow into a cascading avalanche down Nightglow's northern face.

"Who ever heared of it?" Ivan asked incredulously.

The worst had not yet come. More lightning, more pelting ice assaulted the region about the mountain. Other avalanches soon began, tons and tons of snow plummeting down the mountainside to resettle far below. Then came the tornado, blacker than the impending night, a twister as wide, it seemed, as the foundation of the Edificant Library. It circled Nightglow, tearing trees, burrowing huge chasms in the high-piled snow.

"We must go," the firbolg reminded them all, for he—and, he correctly guessed, his friends—had seen more than enough. Shayleigh mentioned again that they were fortunate in riding out on the dragon, and Vander put in a word that winter storms so high up were unpredictable and ultimately deadly.

Everyone readily agreed with the firbolg, but they all understood that what had happened back at Nightglow was more than a "winter storm."

Vander soon found them an uninhabited cave not too far from the valley of carnage, and truly, they were all glad to be sheltered from the suddenly frightening elements. The place was three-chambered, but snug, with a low ceiling and a lower doorway that blocked most of the wintry wind.

Vander and the dwarves set up their bedrolls in the entry cavern, the largest of the chambers. Cadderly took the smallest chamber—to the left—as his own, with Danica and Shayleigh going to the right, the monk glancing back at Cadderly with concern every step of the way.

Dusk came soon after, and then a quiet and star-filled night, so different from the storm. Soon the usual grumble-and-whistle snoring of Ivan and Pikel echoed throughout the chambers.

Danica crept back into the entry cavern, saw Vander's huge form propped in the doorway. Though he had volunteered once more to take the watch, the firbolg was asleep, and Danica didn't blame him. It seemed safe enough to her, seemed as if all the world had taken a break from the chaos, and so she slipped through to Cadderly's chamber quietly, without disturbing the others.

The young priest was sitting in the middle of the floor, hunched over a tiny candle. Deep in meditation, he did not hear Danica's approach.

"You should sleep," the monk offered, putting a hand gently on her lover's shoulder. Cadderly opened his sleepy eyes and nodded. He reached over his shoulder to grab Danica's hand, pulled her around to sit next to him, close to him.

"I have rested," he assured her. Danica had taught Cadderly several rejuvenating meditation techniques, and she did not dispute the claim.

"The road has been more difficult than you expected," Danica said quietly, a trace of trepidation evident in her normally solid voice. "And with perhaps the most difficult obstacle yet ahead of us."

The young priest understood her reasoning. He, too, believed that the fury they had witnessed battering the slopes of Nightglow had been a calling card from Aballister. And he, too, was afraid. They had survived many brutal ordeals in the last year and over the last few days on the trail, but if that storm was any indication, their greatest trials were yet ahead of them, waiting for them in Castle Trinity. Since the manticore and chimera attack, Cadderly had known that Aballister was on to them, but he had not imagined the great strength of the wizard.

An image of the landslide and the tornado assaulted his thoughts. Cadderly had enacted great magics of his own recently, but that display was far beyond his powers, he believed, far beyond his imagination!

The young priest, trying to hold fast to his resolve, closed his eyes and sighed. "I did not expect so many troubles," he admitted.

"Even a dragon," Danica remarked. "I still cannot believe . . ." Her voice trailed off into an incredulous sigh.

"I knew that dealing with old Fyren would not be an easy task," Cadderly agreed.

"Did we have to go there?" There remained no trace of anger in Danica's soft tones.

Cadderly nodded. "The world is a better place with the *Ghearufu* destroyed— and with Fyrentennimar destroyed, though I did not foresee that as a probability, even as a possibility. Of all that I have accomplished in my life, the destruction of the *Ghearufu* might be the most important."

A wistful smile crossed Danica's face as she caught the glimmer in Cadderly's barely open, but surely smiling, gray eyes.

"But not the most important of all you mean to do," the monk said coyly.

Cadderly's eyes widened, and he regarded Danica with sincere admiration. How well she knew him! He had just been thinking of the many deeds that were sorting themselves out before him, of the many demands his special relationship with his god Deneir would make on him. Danica had seen it, had looked into his eyes, and had known exactly the tone of his thoughts, if not the specifics.

"I see a course before me," he admitted to her, his voice subdued, but firm with resolve. "A dangerous and difficult course, I do not doubt." Cadderly chuckled at the irony, and Danica looked at him quizzically, not understanding.

"Even after what we witnessed before setting our camp, I fear that the most difficult of my future obstacles will be the ones brought on by friends," he explained.

Danica stiffened and shifted away.

"Not from you," Cadderly quickly assured her. "I foresee changes at the Edificant Library, drastic changes that will not be met with approval from those who have the most to lose."

"Dean Thobicus?"

Cadderly nodded, his expression grim. "And the headmasters," he added. "The hierarchy has evolved away from the spirit of Deneir, has become something perpetuated by false traditions and piles of worthless paper." He chuckled again, but there was something sad in his voice. "Do you understand what I did to Thobicus for him to allow us to come out here?" he asked.

"You tricked him," Danica replied.

"I dominated him," Cadderly corrected. "I entered his mind and bent his will. I might well have killed him in the attempt, and the effects of the assault could remain with him for the rest of his years."

An expression of confusion came over Danica, confusion fast turning to horror. "Hypnosis?"

"Far beyond hypnosis," Cadderly replied gravely. "In hypnosis, I might have convinced Thobicus to change his thoughts." Cadderly looked away, seeming ashamed. "I did not convince Thobicus. I evoked the change against his will, and then I entered his mind once more and modified his memory so that there would be no repercussions when . . . if, we return to the library."

Danica's almond eyes were wide with shock. She had known that Cadderly was uncomfortable with what he had done to Thobicus, but she had assumed that her love had exacted some charm spell over the dean. What Cadderly was talking about now, though the results had been similar to a charm, seemed somehow more sinister.

"I grabbed his will in my hand, and I crushed it," Cadderly admitted. "I stole from him the very essence of his ego. If Thobicus recalls the incident, then his pride will never, ever recover from the shock."

"Then why did you do it?" Danica demanded softly.

"Because my course was determined by powers greater than me," Cadderly said. "And greater than Thobicus."

"How many tyrants have made such a claim?" Danica asked, trying hard not to sound sarcastic.

Cadderly smiled helplessly and nodded. "That is my fear. Yet I knew what I must do," he continued. "The *Ghearufu* had to be destroyed—to study such a sentient, evil artifact would bring only disaster—and the war with Castle Trinity, if it comes to pass, will prove a travesty that cannot be tolerated, whatever side is victorious.

"I went after Thobicus in a way that left a foul taste in my mouth," Cadderly admitted. "But I would do it again, and I may have to if my fears prove true." He quieted for a moment and considered the many wrongs he had witnessed, the many things within the Edificant Library that had long ago veered from the path of Deneir, searching for some solid example he might offer to Danica. "If a young cleric in the library has an inspiration," he said at last, "divine though he believes it to be, he cannot act upon it without first receiving the approval of the dean and the permission to take time away from meaningless duties."

"Thobicus must oversee . . ." Danica began to argue, playing the pragmatic point of view.

"That process often takes as long as a year," Cadderly interrupted, no longer interested in hearing logical arguments for a course he knew in his heart to be wrong. Cadderly had heard those arguments from Headmaster Avery for all of his life, and they had fostered in him an indifference that swelled to so great a level that he had nearly deserted the order of Deneir. "You have seen how Thobicus works," he said firmly. "A wasted year will pass, and though the thoughts of the story the young cleric wished to pen, or the painting he wished to frame, might remain, the sense, the aura, that something divine might be guiding his hand will have long since flown."

"You speak from personal experience," Danica reasoned.

"Many times," Cadderly replied without hesitation. "And I know that many of the things I have become comfortable with in my life, many of the things I now know I must change, I do not want to change, for I am afraid."

He brought his finger up to Danica's lips to stem her forthcoming response. "You are not among those things," he assured her, and then he grew very quiet, and all the world, even the dwarven snoring, seemed to hush in anticipation.

"I do believe that our relationship must change, though," Cadderly went on. "What began in Carradoon must grow, or it must die."

Danica grabbed his wrist and pulled his hand away from her face, eyeing him unblinkingly, not sure of what would come next from this surprising young man.

"Marry me," Cadderly said suddenly. "Formally."

Now Danica did blink, and she closed her eyes, hearing the echoes from those words a thousand times in the next second. She had waited so long for this moment, had longed for it and feared it all at the same time. For while she loved Cadderly with all her heart, being a wife in Faerun carried expectations of servitude. And Danica, proud and capable, served no one.

"You agree with the changes," Cadderly said. "You agree with the course my life will take. I cannot do it alone, my love." He paused and nearly faltered. "I do not want to do it alone! When I have completed what Deneir has asked, when I look upon the work, there will be no satisfaction unless you are there beside me."

"When *I* have completed?" Danica echoed and asked, emphasizing Cadderly's use of the personal pronoun and trying to get some sense of what role Cadderly meant for her to play in it all.

Cadderly thought about the emphasis of her response and then nodded. "I am a disciple of Deneir," he explained. "Many of the battles he guides me to, I must fight alone. I think of it as you think of your studies. I know that, as each goal is attained, richer by far will be my satisfaction if . . ."

"What of my studies?" Danica interrupted.

Cadderly was ready for the question and understood Danica's concern. "When you broke the stone and achieved Gigel Nugel," he began, referring to an ancient test of achievement that Danica had recently completed, "what were your thoughts?"

Danica remembered the incident, and a smile spread wide across her face. "I felt your arm around me," she replied.

Cadderly nodded and pulled her close, kissing her gently on the cheek. "We have so much to show each other," he said.

"My studies might take me away," Danica said, pulling back.

Cadderly laughed aloud. "If they do, then you shall go," he said. "But you will come back to me, or I will go to you. I have faith, Danica, that our chosen paths will not take us apart. I have faith in you, and in myself."

The somber cloud seemed to fly from Danica's fair features. Her grin widened to a dimpled smile, and her brown eyes sparkled with the moisture of joyful tears. She pulled Cadderly back to her, kissing him hard and long.

"Cadderly," she said coyly, as her wistful, mischievous smile sent a stream of thoughts careening through him. A shiver rippled up his spine and then back down again as Danica added, "We are alone."

Much later that night, with the sleeping Danica cradled in his arms and the dwarven snoring continuing its relentless pace, Cadderly rested back against the wall and replayed the conversation.

"How many tyrants have made such a claim?" he whispered to the empty darkness. His considered his course once more, thought of the profound impact his intended actions would have on all the region surrounding Impresk Lake. He believed in his heart that the changes would better everyone, that the library would once again take on the true course of Deneir. He believed that he was right, that his course was inspired by a trusted god. But how many tyrants had made such a claim?

"All of them," Cadderly answered grimly after a long pause, and he hugged Danica close.

Fourteen
The Fortress

Aballister rested back in his chair, exhausted from his magical assault. He had thrown his full weight against Cadderly, had pounded the mountain region mercilessly. The wizard's smile held firm for a long while as he pondered what Cadderly, in the unlikely event that the boy was still alive, might be thinking now.

Aballister felt a tug within his mind, a gentle prodding. It was Druzil, he knew, for he had expected the imp's call. The wizard's smile became an open laugh—what might the imp, who had been so close to Nightglow, think now of him? Anxious to know, he let the imp into his mind.

Greetings, dear Druzil, Aballister said.

Bene tellemara!

Aballister cackled with glee. *My dear, dear Druzil*, he thought after a moment, *what could be the trouble?*

The imp ripped off a series of outcries, curses, and sputterings against Aballister and against wizards in general. Druzil had been caught in the edges of Aballister's storm, had been pelted by hail and nearly sizzled by a lightning blast.

Now the imp, cold and miserable, only wanted to get back to Castle Trinity. *You could come out for me*, Druzil telepathically asked.

I have not the energy, came Aballister's expected reply. *Since you allowed Cadderly to get away, I was forced to take matters into my own hands. And still I have preparations before me, for the unlikely event that Cadderly or any of his foolish friends survived.*

"Bene tellemara," the frustrated imp whispered under his breath. Now that Druzil believed he needed Aballister, he was careful to put up a blocking wall of innocuous thoughts so that the wizard would not hear the insult.

Better that I am with you if Cadderly arrives, Druzil replied, trying to find some argument to change the stubborn wizard's mind. With his magic, powerful Aballister could teleport to Druzil's side, scoop the imp up, and put them both safely back in Castle Trinity in a matter of two minutes.

I told you that I was too weary, Aballister's casual thoughts came back—and Druzil understood that Aballister was simply punishing him. *Better that you are with me?* the wizard scoffed. *I sent you on a most important mission, and you failed? Better to face Cadderly alone, I say, than with an unreliable and troublesome imp at my side. I do not yet know what happened to facilitate the destruction of the evil spirit, Druzil, but if I find that you were in any way involved, your punishment will not be pleasant.*

More likely it was your own son, Druzil's mind growled back.

The imp felt a wave of unfocused mental energy, an anger so profound that Aballister had not taken the moment to give it a clear flow of words. Druzil knew that his reference once again to Cadderly as Aballister's son had struck a sensitive nerve, even though Aballister had apparently taken care of the problem.

You will seek out the bodies of Cadderly and his friends, Aballister answered. *Then you will walk back to me, or flap those weak wings of yours when the wind permits! I'll tolerate little more from you, Druzil. 'Ware the next storm I send out to the mountains!*

With that, Aballister promptly broke off the connection, leaving Druzil cold in the snow, pondering the wizard's last words.

Truly, the imp was disgusted by the ridiculous accusation and by Aballister's continual threats. He had to admit, though, that they carried some weight. Druzil could not believe the devastation Aballister had rained on Nightglow and the surrounding region. But Druzil was cold and miserable now, deep in the wintry mountains, and constantly had to shake the fast accumulating snow off his leathery wings.

He certainly didn't like where he was, but in a way, Druzil was relieved that Aballister had refused his request to bring him home. If indeed the young priest had somehow escaped Aballister's fury—and Druzil did not think that such an impossibility—then Druzil preferred to be far away when Aballister at last faced his son. Druzil had once battled Cadderly in mental combat and had been overwhelmed. The imp had also fought against the woman, Danica, and had been defeated—even his poison had been ineffective against that one. Druzil's repertoire of tricks was fast emptying where the young priest was concerned.

The stakes were simply too high.

But these mountains! Druzil was a creature of the lower planes, a dark region mostly of black fires and thick smoke. He did not like the cold, did not like the wet feel of the wretched snow, and the glare of sunlight on the angled whitened surface of the mountain slopes pained his sensitive eyes. He had to go on, though, and would, eventually, have to return and face his wizard master.

Eventually.

Druzil liked the ring of that thought. He brushed the snow from his wings and gave a lazy flap to get him up into the air. He decided immediately that searching for Cadderly and his friends would be a foolhardy thing, and so he veered away from the settling mass of misplaced snow around Nightglow. Neither was his direction north, toward Castle Trinity. Druzil went east, the shortest route out of the Snowflakes, a course that would take him down to the farmlands surrounding Carradoon.

* * * * *

"Prepare your defenses," Dorigen said as soon as she entered Aballister's room, unexpectedly and unannounced.

"What do you know?" growled the weary wizard.

"Cadderly lives!"

"You have seen him?" Aballister snapped, coming fast out of his chair, his dark eyes coming to life with an angry sparkle.

"No," Dorigen lied. "But there are still wards blocking my scrying. The young priest is very much alive."

Reacting in quite the opposite way Dorigen had expected, Aballister erupted in laughter. He slapped a hand on the arm of his chair and seemed almost giddy. Then he looked to his associate, and her incredulous expression asked many questions.

"The boy makes it enjoyable!" the old wizard said to her. "I have not faced such a challenge in decades!"

Dorigen thought that he had gone quite insane. You have never faced such a challenge, she wanted to scream at the man, but she kept that dangerous thought private. "We must prepare," she said again, calmly. "Cadderly is alive, and it might be that he escaped your fury because he was much closer than we anticipated."

Aballister seemed to sober at once, and turned his back at Dorigen, his skinny fingertips tapping together in front of him. "It was your scrying that led me to assail Nightglow," he pointedly reminded her.

"It was Druzil's guidance, more than my own," she quickly corrected, sincerely afraid to accept blame for anything, given Aballister's unpredictable, and incredibly dangerous, mood.

She sighed, noticing Aballister subtly nod his head in agreement. "Prepare . . ." she started to say a third time, but the wizard spun about suddenly, his scowl stealing the words from her mouth.

"Oh, we shall prepare!" Aballister hissed though gritted teeth. "Better for Cadderly if he had fallen to the storm!"

"I will instruct the soldiers," Dorigen said, and she turned for the door.

"No!" The word stopped the woman short. She slowly turned her head, to look back over her shoulder at Aballister.

"This is personal," Aballister explained, and he led Dorigen's quizzical gaze across the room, to the swirling ball of mist hanging on the far wall, the entrance to Aballister's extradimensional mansion. "The soldiers will not be needed."

* * * * *

They looked down from a high perch to new battlements and a singular tower. From the outside, Castle Trinity did not seem so remarkable, or so formidable, even with the new construction that had been done. Vander, who had seen the tunnel networks beneath the rocky spur, assured them otherwise. Work on the new walls was slow now, with winter blowing thick, but guards were in abundance—humans mostly—pacing predetermined routes and continually rubbing their hands together to ward away the icy breeze.

"That is the main entrance," Vander explained, pointing to the central area of the closest wall. A huge door, oaken and ironbound, was set deep into the stone, enveloped by walkways and parapets and many soldiers. "Beyond that door is a cave entrance, barred by a portcullis, and a second, similar door. We will find guards, well-armed and well-trained, positioned every step of the way."

"Bah, we're not for going straight in the front door!" Ivan protested, and this time, the yellow-bearded dwarf found some allies for his grumbling. Danica readily agreed by reminding everyone that their only chance lay in stealth, and Shayleigh even suggested that perhaps they should have come out with Carradoon's army at their heels.

Cadderly hardly listened to the talk, trying to think of some magic that might get them in, but that would not overly tax his still-limited energies. His friends had remained optimistic, believing that he could handle the situation. Cadderly liked their confidence in him; he only wished that he shared it. That morning, leaving the cave, with the sky shining blue, Ivan had scoffed at the storm that had hit Nightglow, had called it a simple wizard's trick, and berated Aballister for not being able to aim straight

"First rule in shootin' magics!" the dwarf had bellowed. "Ye got to hit the damned target!"

"Oo oi!" Pikel had heartily agreed, and then the green-bearded dwarf, too, had made light of it all with a quiet, "Hee hee hee."

Cadderly knew better, understood the strength of the wizard's incredible display. The young priest still believed that he walked along the true path of Deneir, but images of Aballister's fury, slamming the mountain itself into surrender, stayed with him all morning.

He shook the unpleasant thoughts away and tried to focus on the situation at hand. "Is there another way in?" he heard Danica ask.

"At the base of the tower," Vander answered. "Aballister brought us . . . brought the Night Masks in that way, through a smaller, less guarded door. The wizard did not want the commoners of his force to know that he had hired the assassins."

"Too much open ground," Danica remarked. The tower was set some distance behind the two nearly finished perpendicular walls, and though the tower, too, had apparently not been completed, it stood an imposing thirty feet high, with temporary battlements ringing its top. Even if the friends managed to get past the guards on the closest walls, just a couple of archers up in that tower could make life miserable for them.

"What tricks ye got to keep them off our backs while we make the run?" Ivan asked Cadderly, gruffly slapping the young priest on the shoulder to force him from his private contemplations.

"The shortest route would be from the right, from below the spur," he reasoned. "But that would leave us running uphill, vulnerable to many defensive measures. I say that we come in from the left, down the slope of the rocky spur and around the shorter wall."

"That wall's guarded," Ivan argued.

Cadderly's wry smile ended the debate.

The friends spent the better part of the next hour in a roundabout hike to a point on the rocky spur far above Castle Trinity. With this new angle, around the side of the largest, frontal wall, they could see scores of soldiers, including large, hairy bugbears, ten-foot-tall ogres, and even a giant. Cadderly knew that this would be quite a test—for his friends' trust in him, and for his abilities. If that formidable force intercepted them before they got inside the back door, all would be lost.

The tower was fully thirty yards back from the front wall and fully forty yards away from the outermost tip of the perpendicular wall, the wall they had to run around. Ivan shook his hairy head; Pikel added an occasional "Oo," showing that even the dwarves, the most battle-hardened members of the troupe, did not think the idea feasible.

But Cadderly remained undaunted; his smile had not ebbed an inch. "The first volley will alert them—the second should get them into positions where we might get near the wall," he explained.

The others looked around to each other in confusion, their expressions incredulous. Most eyes centered on Shayleigh's quiver and the hand-crossbow at Cadderly's side.

"On my cue, when the third volley of flaming pitch soars out for the front wall, we go for the tower," Cadderly went on. "You lead the charge," he said to Danica.

Danica, though she still had no idea of what "volleys" the young priest was talking about, smiled wryly, pleased that Cadderly would not patronize her, would not try to protect her when the situation obviously called for each of them to perform specific, and dangerous, tasks. Danica knew that not many men of Faerun would allow their beloved women to rush out into danger ahead of them, and it was Cadderly's implicit trust and respect of her which made her love him so very much.

"If the archers up above catch sight of us," Cadderly continued, aiming this remark at Shayleigh, "we will need you to cut them down."

"What volley?" Shayleigh demanded, tired of the cryptic game. "What flaming pitch?"

Cadderly, already falling away, deep into his spellcasting concentration, didn't reply. In a moment, he was chanting, singing softly, and his friends hunched down and waited for the clerical magic to take effect.

"Wow," muttered Pikel at the same moment that one of the guards along the front gate cried out in surprise. Balls of flaming pitch and large spears were appearing in midair, thundering down near the wall. Soldiers scrambled and dove from the gate; the giant hoisted a slab of stone and put it in front of him defensively.

It was over in just a few instants, with no fires left burning and no apparent damage to the stonework. The soldiers remained under cover, though, calling frantic orders and pointing out many potential artillery hiding places in the ridges beyond the gates.

Cadderly nodded to Danica, and she and Shayleigh began the procession from the side, slipping from stone to stone. The diversion had apparently worked thus far, for few guards seemed concerned with the high ground to the side of the walls.

The second illusory "volley" roared in farther down the front wall, well beyond the main gates, luring the enemy's attention to the vulnerable corner where the third wall would be built. As Cadderly had predicted, those soldiers along the side wall rushed into defensive positions behind the shielding, and thicker, front wall.

Again the explosions lasted only a few seconds, but the guards were in a near-panic now, huddled tight against the battlements and the base of the wall. Not a single eye turned to the southwest, to the higher ground from which the companions approached.

Danica and Shayleigh led them up to the now-abandoned perpendicular wall without incident, light-stepped along its base away from the front wall, and peered around to the empty courtyard.

Cadderly moved in front of the group and held his hand up to keep his friends back. He concentrated on the front wall and reached out to the particles of air about him, seeing their nature revealed in the notes of Deneir's song. Slowly and subtly, using triggering words and the energy of clerical magic, the young priest altered the composition of those particles, brought them together, thickened them.

A heavy mist swelled up around the front wall, and around the front half of the uncompleted courtyard.

"Go," Cadderly whispered to Danica, and he motioned for the dwarves to follow, and for Shayleigh to come into position where she could view the tower. Without hesitation, the brave monk ran off, zigzagging across the rough, frozen ground.

On impulse, Cadderly took Shayleigh's arrow from her hand. "Get it up on top of the tower," he instructed, casting an enchantment over it and handing it back.

Danica was twenty yards out, halfway to the tower, before anyone there noticed her. Three archers took up their bows and started to call out, when Shayleigh's arrow smacked solidly into the shoulder of one. The man went down in a heap; the other two went into a frenzy, their mouths wagging wide as they tried to cry out for their companions manning the front gate.

Not a sound came from the top of the tower, the area magically silenced by the enchanted arrow.

The remaining two enemy archers opened up on Danica, but her course was too erratic and her agility too great. Arrows skipped off the frozen ground, or snapped apart as they struck, but Danica, rolling and diving, cutting sharper angles than the soldiers could anticipate, never came close to being hit.

"Hee hee hee," chuckled Pikel, running with Ivan far behind the monk and thoroughly enjoying the spectacle.

Shayleigh returned the fire with vicious accuracy, skipping arrows in between the parapet stones and forcing the guards to concentrate more on keeping their heads down than on firing at Danica. Still the men tried futilely to cry out, to warn their associates of the peril.

Vander scooped up Shayleigh, settled her atop his broad shoulders, and ran after the dwarves.

Cadderly focused once more on the front wall, loosing another illusory volley to ensure that the soldiers would remain tight in their holes. Smiling at his own cleverness, the young priest raced off after his friends.

As Danica reached the base of the tower, the door burst open and a swordsman rushed out to face her. Always alert, she rolled headlong and came up within his weapon's descending arc, the ball of her fist connecting under his chin and driving him away. Above Danica, one of the archers leaned out, angling for a killing shot. Shayleigh's arrow, loosed before he had even drawn his bow, sank deep into his collarbone.

The other archer, tight against the corner of a squared stone, responded with a shot that caught Vander in the chest, but the arrow did little to slow the giant. Howling and growling, Vander yanked out the puny bolt and hurled it away.

Her angle improved by the fact that she was ten feet above the ground, Shayleigh smiled grimly and loosed another arrow. It skipped off the squared stone and ricocheted into the enemy archer's eye. The man fell back in agony, obviously screaming—but again, not a sound came from the enchanted area.

Ivan and Pikel disappeared into the tower behind Danica; Cadderly could see that there was some fighting within. The young priest ran with all speed, slipping in on Vander's heels, but by the time he, the firbolg, and the elf maiden got there, the five goblin guards of the tower's first floor were already dead.

Danica kneeled before another doorway across the small chamber, studying its lock. She pulled the clasp off of her belt and straightened it with her teeth, then gently slipped it in and began working it, side to side.

"Hurry," bade Shayleigh, standing by the outer door. Across the courtyard, cries of "Enemies in the tower!" could be heard. The elf maiden shrugged—the deception was no more—and leaned out the door, shooting off an arrow or two to keep the enemy forces back. One quiver empty, her second growing lighter, she regretted now her decision to join in the battle in the valley.

Cadderly pulled her in by the elbow and closed the door. It was an easy thing for the priest to magically reach into the essence of the wood, to swell it and warp it so that the portal was sealed tight. Vander piled the dead goblins against the door as added security, and again all eyes focused on Danica.

"Hurry," Shayleigh reiterated, her words taking on more weight as something heavy slammed against the tower door.

With a grin to her companions, Danica slipped her makeshift lockpick behind one ear and pushed open the door, revealing a descending stairway.

Cadderly looked at the passage curiously. "Not heavily guarded and not trapped?" he mused aloud.

"It was trapped," Danica corrected. She pointed to a wire along the side of the jamb, secured in place with the other part of her belt. None of them had the time to admire the skilled monk's handiwork, though, for another, louder crash sounded on the outer door, and the tip of an axe blade poked through the wood.

Ivan and Pikel pushed ahead of Danica and rambled side by side down the stairs. Vander and Shayleigh went next, the firbolg using his innate magics to reduce himself to the size of a large man. Next came Cadderly, and then Danica, who turned back and, with a subtle twist of her pick, locked the door and rearmed the trap.

Another door blocked the way at the bottom of the stairs, but the dwarven brothers lowered their heads, locked arms, and picked up their pace.

"It may be warded!" Cadderly called out to them, understanding their intent.

The Bouldershoulders blew through the door, a series of fiery explosions erupting on their heels as they tumbled down in the midst of shattered and smoking wood. The two had been fortunate indeed to get through the portal so quickly, for tiny darts protruded from both doorjambs, dripping poison. In the underground tunnels beyond the door, the blare of horns sounded—probably magical alarms, Cadderly thought.

"What'd ye say?" Ivan yelled above the clamor, as the others came into the lower passage.

"Never mind," was all that Cadderly replied. His voice was grim, despite the sight of Pikel hopping all about, trying to put out wisps of smoke trailing from his heels and backside. The whole objective in coming to Castle Trinity with so small a force was to strike at the leaders of the enemy conspiracy, but that goal seemed unlikely now, with horns blaring and enemies beating at the closed doors behind them.

"Aw, come on and find a bit of fun!" Ivan bellowed at the obviously worried young priest. "Hold on to me cloak, boy! I'll get ye where ye want to go!"

"Oo oi!" Pikel piped in, and the brothers thundered away. They hit resistance before they even turned the first corner, and plowed through the surprised band of goblins with abandon, slaughtering and scattering the creatures.

"Which way?" Ivan called back, his words coming out at the end of a grunt as he drove his mighty axe through the backbone of one goblin that had turned to flee a split second too late. The torchlit corridor beyond the dead goblin showed several doors and at least two branching tunnels.

The friends looked to Cadderly, but the young priest shrugged helplessly, having no immediate answers amidst the sudden confusion. A series of explosions far behind them told Cadderly that their enemies had breached the second door—and had not been successful in disarming the trap.

Ivan kicked open the nearest door, revealing a huge room holding a battery of human archers and a group of giants at work leveling a ballista. "Not that way!" the gruff dwarf explained, quickly closing the door and rushing on.

In the wild run that followed, Cadderly lost all sense of direction. They passed through many portals, turned many corners, and clobbered many very surprised enemies. Soon they came to an area of better worked tunnels, with runes and bas reliefs of the teardrop symbols of Talona carved into their stone walls.

Cadderly looked to Vander, hoping that the firbolg might recognize some landmark, but Vander could not be sure.

A jolt of electricity threw Pikel back from the next door. Ivan growled and hit the portal shoulder-first, bursting through into yet another long and narrow corridor, this one lined by tapestries depicting the Lady of Poison, smiling evilly as though she clearly saw the intruders. Resilient Pikel, the hairs of his green beard dancing free of the tight braid, joined his brother in an instant.

Twenty steps in, the group was enveloped by a ball of absolute darkness.

"Keep moving!" Shayleigh bade the dwarves, for with her keen elven hearing, she had heard the approach of enemies from behind.

Cadderly felt the air beside his face move as the elf put an arrow into the air. He did not take serious note of Shayleigh's movements, though, for he was fumbling with the straps of his backpack, searching for his light tube, or for the wand, to battle the conjured darkness.

Apparently sensing that he had stopped moving, Danica grabbed the young priest's arm and pulled him along—gently, so that she would not disturb his efforts.

There came a loud click and a scrape of stone against stone, followed by a diminishing "Ooooooo . . ."

"*Domin illu!*" Cadderly cried, holding up the wand, and the darkness fled. Cadderly stood ready with his wand, Shayleigh with her bow, and Danica and Vander were into similarly defensive crouches, feeling their way along the walls.

But Ivan and Pikel were gone.

"Trapdoors!" Danica cried, spotting tiny lines in the floor ahead. "Ivan!"

There came no response, and Danica found no apparent way to open the neatly fitted portals, no cranks or handles anywhere in sight.

"Go on!" Shayleigh yelled suddenly, pulling Cadderly past her and drawing back her bowstring. Enemy soldiers were at the door behind them, barely fifty feet away.

Danica leaped the trapped region; Vander reverted to his full size and stepped across, hoisting Cadderly behind him.

"Close your eyes," the young priest whispered to his friends, and he thrust the wand back toward the door and uttered, "*Mas illu!*" A burst of brilliant lights shot forth, green and orange and popping in all colors of the spectrum in a myriad of blinding flashes.

It was over in an instant, leaving the soldiers rubbing their eyes and stumbling about the end of the corridor.

"Go on!" Shayleigh said again, firing off two more arrows into the confused throng. The other three started for the door at the corridor's other end, calling for Shayleigh to catch up.

When the elf maiden turned back around to follow her friends, they realized that she, too, had been caught in Cadderly's magical flash. Her once-clear violet eyes showed as dots of bloodshot red, and she inched down the corridor, trying to discern when to jump.

"We'll come for you!" Danica called out, but Shayleigh had already begun her leap. She landed with her heels on the edge of the trapdoor, which clicked open, and she balanced on the edge of the fall for what seemed an eternity.

Vander dove headlong, spread out wide on the floor, grabbing desperately. He caught only air as Shayleigh fell backward into the pit, the devilish door swinging tight behind her.

Danica was beside the firbolg, pulling at his sleeve, and Cadderly was beside her, his wand extended once more.

"*Mas illu,*" he said again, his voice subdued, and the brilliant burst hit the recovering soldiers once more. Many of them thought to close their eyes this time, and the charge, though slowed, would not be halted.

Vander led the rush to the far door and almost got there, but a ten-foot section of the corridor shifted suddenly, its entire perimeter turning diagonal to its original position. The surprised firbolg fell to the side, into the suddenly angled wall/floor, and disappeared from sight as that corner of the trapped area rotated on a central pivot.

Danica leaped past the angled section of corridor and snapped a kick into the door, breaking apart the locking mechanism. The door creaked open, back toward Danica, just an inch, and the monk grabbed it and pulled it fiercely, as if she were daring another trap to go off.

Cadderly, overwhelmed, came up to her, still looking back to the floor where three of his friends had disappeared, and to the wall that had taken the firbolg.

Danica grabbed his hand and pulled him in—a short passage this time, its walls bare of tapestries, that ended in another door just a dozen feet away. As soon as they crossed the threshold, a solid slab of stone dropped behind them, sealing off any possible retreat, and a portcullis fell in front of the door before them, blocking the way. They knew instantly, of course, that they were trapped, but did not appreciate the depth of their predicament until a moment later, when Danica noticed that the small passage's side-walls had begun to close together.

Fifteen

The Holy Word

D anica threw her back against the wall, pushing with all her strength while trying to plant her feet firmly on the smooth floor. She only slid forward, and the corridor narrowed relentlessly.

Cadderly's frantic gaze darted all about, from the stone slab to the portcullis, to the closing sidewalls. He tried to summon the song of Deneir, but remembered nothing immediately within its lyrical notes that might aid them now.

The walls were barely eight feet apart.

Seven feet.

Cadderly fought back his panic, closed his eyes, and told himself to concentrate and to trust in the harmonious music.

He felt Danica grab his arms roughly, but tried to ignore the disturbance. She pulled again, harder, forcing Cadderly to look at her.

"Hold your hands stiffly in front of you," she instructed, turning Cadderly's palms upward. He watched curiously as Danica turned horizontally across his palms, planting her feet against one wall and holding her arms out past her head to "catch" the other, approaching wall.

"You cannot," Cadderly started to protest, but even as he spoke, the walls closed within Danica's reach, closed and then were stopped by the meditating monk's stiffened form as surely as if a beam of metal had been placed between them.

Cadderly moved his hands away from Danica's belly—her stiffened position supported her fully—and forced himself to turn his attention away from the amazing Danica and consider the larger predicament. If the enemy detected that the walls had stopped moving, then he and Danica might soon expect some unwelcome company. Cadderly drew out his hand-crossbow and loaded an explosive dart.

He heard some mumbling from beyond the portcullis and the far door, and moved closer, straining to hear.

"Buga yarg grrr mukadig," came a deep guttural sound, and Cadderly, with his exceptional training in the various languages of Faerun, understood that an ogre outside the door had just insisted that the walls must be finished with their business by then.

Cadderly ran back, slipped under and around Danica, and placed his crossbow arm across her back for support. He also put his spindle-disks atop Danica, within easy reach, and clutched his enchanted walking stick in his free hand.

There came a cranking sound as the portcullis began to rise, and Cadderly heard a key slip into the door's lock. He steadied his crossbow and his nerves, realizing that he had to fend off the enemy long enough for Danica to dislodge herself and rush out behind him.

The door swung in, and with it came the face of an eager ogre, stupidly grinning as it looked for the squished remains of the intruders.

Cadderly's dart hit it right between the gap in its two front teeth. The young priest charged boldly, scooping up his spindle-disks.

The ogre's cheeks bulged weirdly, its eyes nearly popped free of their sockets, and then its lips flapped, spewing a stream of blood and broken teeth.

"Duh, Mogie?" its stunned companion asked as the splattered monster slid down to the floor. The second ogre bent low, trying to figure out what had happened, then looked back toward the trap-room just in time to catch Cadderly's flying adamantite spindle-disks on the side of its nose.

Cadderly flicked his wrist hard, sending the disks spinning back to him, stinging his palm, then hurled them again fiercely. The ogre's hand started up, but didn't get high enough for a block, and the beast caught the missile in the eye.

The ogre's arm, continuing its upward motion, hooked the wire, though, and Cadderly could not properly retract the disks for a third throw. Always ready to improvise, the quick-thinking young priest took up his walking stick in both hands and bashed it hard against the dazed ogre's thick forearm.

He came lower with his next strike, slamming exposed ribs, and the ogre, as Cadderly had expected, reflexively brought its arm swinging down. Cadderly's next cut came in high again, smashing the ogre on its already splattered nose. He followed through, reversed his grip, and came back around the other way, the ram's head of his walking stick connecting solidly on the base of the ogre's skull.

The monster was kneeling suddenly, its weakened arms down at its side.

Back and forth slammed Cadderly's walking stick, three times, five times, and then Danica raced past, driving a knee under the kneeling monster's chin.

The ogre's head snapped back viciously, and finally, the huge thing toppled to the floor beside its dead companion.

"Load it!" Danica instructed Cadderly, handing him back his crossbow. Behind them, they heard the crunch of wood as the closing walls bit against the opened door.

Neither one of them cared to look back

* * * * *

The chute was slick and steep, and Shayleigh, for all her frantic efforts, could hardly slow her descent. Finally, she got her back tight against the sloping floor and pushed up into the air with her longbow, searching for some hold.

There were none. The chute's ceiling, like the floor, was perfectly smooth.

A dozen unpleasant images rushed through the elf maiden's head, mostly ones of her being impaled against a wall of poison-tipped spikes beside Ivan and Pikel. Or behind Ivan and Pikel, slamming against her already stuck friends to drive them deeper onto the imagined spikes.

Still holding fast to her bow, Shayleigh angled herself to put her feet against one wall and her shoulder diagonally across the narrow chute against the other. She lifted her head and peered down into the darkness across the length of her body, hoping for some warning before she hit. With her heat-sensing eyes, she could make out traces of the dwarves' passing, residual body heat from Ivan and Pikel still showing in spots along the floor and against the curving walls.

And then there was just a blank wall, the end of the chute, and Shayleigh understood, in the split second before she collided, that since the dwarves were nowhere in sight, it must be some type of swinging trapdoor.

She hit and pushed through, but grabbed both sides of the door with widespread arms. Her bow fell below her, and she heard a dwarf grunt, followed by a small splash.

The trapdoor swung back, pinning Shayleigh's forearms between it and the stone wall. She held on stubbornly, guessing that this might be their only way out of the devious pit.

"Glad ye could make it, elf," Ivan said from below. "But ye might think of getting away from that door if any more are on their way down."

Shayleigh managed to look straight below her, to see the blurry, heated forms of Ivan and Pikel, standing waist-deep in some murky pool. She couldn't tell the exact dimensions of the room, but it was not large, and there was no other apparent door.

"Are you all right?" she asked.

"Just wet," Ivan grumbled. "And I got a bump on me head where me brother fell on me."

Pikel began to whistle and turned away. A moment later, the green-bearded dwarf spun back, frantically, and leaped onto his brother, nearly knocking Ivan under the water.

"What are ye about?" the surly dwarf demanded.

Pilel squeaked and worked hard to get his feet out of the water.

Ivan gave a sudden yell and heaved Pikel into the air. As the green-bearded dwarf hit the water, Ivan, axe in hand, began chopping wildly, his splashes even reaching Shayleigh, high on the wall.

"What is it?" Shayleigh cried. Both dwarves scrambled about, slapping at the water with their weapons.

"Something long and slimy!" Ivan bellowed back. He rushed to the wall directly below the hanging elf and began jumping up, trying futilely to reach her boots. Pikel was at his back in an instant, clambering over him, but Ivan ducked low, sending Pikel facedown into the murk, and then he leaped atop Pikel's back. All the while, Shayleigh begged for them both to calm down. And finally they did, exhausted, without coming close to reaching the elf.

"Use my longbow," Shayleigh reasoned.

"Eh?" Pikel squeaked confusedly, but Ivan understood. He splashed about, finally retrieving the dropped bow, then came to the wall and reached up with it, hooking Shayleigh's foot.

"Ye sure ye got a good enough hold?" the dwarf politely asked.

"Hurry," Shayleigh replied, and Ivan jumped and grabbed, pulled himself along the bow to get high enough to catch a handhold on the elf's boot.

"Come up over me," Shayleigh instructed. "You will have to get into the corridor first and find some way to brace yourself."

Sturdy Ivan felt guilty climbing over a slender elf maiden like that, but he understood the practicality of it, especially when his brother, still below, gave a worried, "Uh-oh."

Ivan looked down to see Pikel standing very still; a serpentine head lifted clear of the water and swayed slowly, back and forth, only a foot out from Pikel and nearly eye-level with the dwarf.

"Me brother," Ivan whispered, hardly able to find his voice. He thought of leaping back to the water and jumping between Pikel and the serpent.

"Climb," Shayleigh said to him.

Pikel began to sway with the snake, whistling as he went from side to side. They seemed somehow in harmony, dancing almost, and the snake gave no indication that it meant to strike out at the dwarf.

"Climb," Shayleigh said again to Ivan. "Pikel cannot get up until you are out of the way."

Ivan had always been protective of his brother, and a big part of him wanted to leap back atop that snake, to rush wildly to Pikel's defense. He managed to fight back the impulse, both because of his agreement with Shayleigh's logic, and because he was terribly afraid of snakes. He carefully picked handholds along Shayleigh's clothing and got up even with her, taking solace in Pikel's continued whistling, a calm song that took much of the tension from the nasty situation.

Ivan worked his way around to Shayleigh's back and squeezed through the narrow gap between her and the heavy door. When he got fully into the sloping chute, he turned sideways, bracing with his hands and feet on opposite walls.

"Pikel?" Shayleigh asked breathlessly, for the whistling had stopped.

"Oo oi!" came the hearty reply from below, and Shayleigh felt the weight on her foot as the second brother began his climb up the longbow. Pikel thoughtfully took the bow with him as he scaled Shayleigh, then slipped into the corridor and crossed over Ivan, planting his wet sandals firmly against the stretched-out Ivan's side and reaching back over his brother to help Shayleigh. This was the trickiest part of the maneuver, for Pikel and Ivan had to somehow open the doorway wide enough and long enough for Shayleigh to get through, and at the same time give the elf something solid to hold on to.

Pikel braced his club against the door, between Shayleigh's outstretched and aching arms.

"When me brother pushes, ye gotta let go with one hand and get it up to me," Ivan instructed. "Ye ready?"

"Open it," Shayleigh begged, and slowly, Pikel began to push.

As soon as the pressure lessened, Shayleigh reached back for Ivan.

She missed, and her grip with her other arm was not solid enough to support her. With a cry, the elf maiden began to fall.

Ivan caught her wrist, his stubby fingers wrapping her tightly and holding her fast against the slimy wall.

"Oooo," Pikel wailed as the whole group began to slide back dangerously toward the end of the chute.

But Ivan growled and straightened his powerful back, locking himself firmly into place. And Pikel, though his arms ached with the strain of the awkward angle, kept the pressure on the heavy door, kept it open enough for Shayleigh to scramble through. She came over Ivan, up beside Pikel, and he let the door slam shut. Then he straightened perpendicularly to his braced brother, and Shayleigh climbed above him and turned as Ivan had turned.

Ivan climbed up Pikel next, as Pikel held fast to the braced elf maiden. Ivan went across Shayleigh, standing straight up the chute. Pikel clambered up to the top, turned sidelong to Ivan, and set the next brace, and so it went, the three working as a living ladder.

"Eh?" Pikel squeaked as he set another stretching brace, around a bend and far out of sight of the chute's end.

"What ye got?" Ivan asked, climbing even with him. Then Ivan, too, saw the lines in the chute's wall—even, parallel lines, like those of a door.

The dwarf planted himself across Pikel's back, his hands fumbling about the wall. He felt a slight depression—only a dwarf would have been able to detect so minute an inconsistency in the unremarkable wall—and pushed hard. The secret door slid aside, revealing a second passageway, angling up as was this one, but with an easier grade.

Ivan looked back to Shayleigh and to Pikel.

"We know what is above us," Shayleigh reasoned.

"But can we get through the trapdoor?" Ivan replied.

"Sssh," Pikel begged them both, motioning with his chin toward the new passage. When the others quieted, they heard some scuffling from within, far away, as though some battle had been joined.

"Might be friends and might be needing us!" Ivan roared, and he went into the new passage, pulling Shayleigh, and then Pikel, in behind him. Fumbling again for the depression in the stonework, Ivan managed to close the secret door behind them, and with the lesser slope, the three made better time.

They came to a fork a short time later, the passage continuing up one way, but angling down in a narrower chute to the side. Their instincts told them to keep climbing—they had left their friends on a higher level—but the sounds of battle emanated from the lower tunnel.

"It could be Cadderly," Shayleigh reasoned.

"Giant dog!" came a familiar voice from down below.

"Traitor!" roared another powerful, and even deeper-toned, voice.

Pikel was into the chute, sliding headlong, before Ivan even cried out "Vander!"

* * * * *

Which door? Cadderly wondered, looking around at the many possible exits from the large circular room as he crossed over the bodies of the two dead ogres. He noticed, too, the many symbols carved into the walls, tridents with small vials above each point interspersed with triangular fields holding three teardrops, the more conventional design for the evil goddess, Talona.

"We must be near the chapel," Cadderly whispered to Danica. As if in confirmation, the door across the way opened and a horribly scarred man, dressed in the ragged gray and green robes of a Talonan priest, hopped into the circular room.

Danica went into a crouch; Cadderly brought his crossbow level with the man's face.

The priest only smiled, though, and a moment later all the doors of the circular room burst open. Cadderly and Danica found themselves facing a horde of orcs and goblins and evilly grinning men, including several more wearing the robes of Talonan priests. Both friends looked back to the trapped corridor, the only possible escape, but the walls were tight against each other by this point and showed no signs of opening.

For some reason, the enemy force did not immediately attack. Rather, they all stood looking from Cadderly and Danica to the first priest who had entered, apparently the leader.

"Did you think it would be so easy?" the scarred man shrieked hysterically. "Did you think to simply walk through our fortress unopposed?"

Cadderly put a hand on Danica's arm to stop her from leaping out at the foul man. She might get to him, might well kill him, but they had no chance of defeating this mob. Unless . . .

Cadderly heard the song playing in his thoughts, had a strange feeling that some powerful minion of his god was calling to him, instructing him, compelling him to hear the harmony of the music.

The evil priest cackled and clapped his hands, and the floor in front of him heaved suddenly, rose up and took a gigantic, humanoid shape.

"Elementals," Danica breathed, drawing Cadderly's attention. Indeed, two creatures from the plane of earth had arisen to the evil priest's beckoning, and Cadderly realized that this man must be formidable indeed to command such powerful allies.

But Cadderly shook the dark thought away, fell back into the song, heard the music rising to a glorious crescendo.

"He is spellcasting!" one of the other priests cried out, and the warning sent the whole of the enemy force into wild action. The foot soldiers charged, weapons waving, lips wetted with eager drool. An archer took up his bow and fired, and the clerics went into their own spellcasting, some creating defensive energy, others calling out for magical spells to assault the intruders.

Danica yelled for her love and reflexively kicked out, barely deflecting an arrow that was soaring for Cadderly's chest. She wanted to protect Cadderly, knew that they were both surely doomed, for they had no time. . . .

A single word, if it was a word, escaped the young priest's lips. A trumpet note, it seemed, so clear and so perfect that it sent shivers of sheer joy rushing along Danica's spine, invited her into its perfect resonance and held her, trance-like, in its lingering beauty.

The note created a much different effect over Cadderly's enemies, over the evil men and monsters who could not tolerate the holy harmony of Deneir's song. Goblins and orcs, and some of the men, grabbed at their bloodied ears and fell dead or unconscious to the floor, their eardrums shattered by the word. Other men swooned, their strength stolen by the bared glory of Deneirian truth, and the elementals fell back into the stone of the floor, fled back to their own plane of existence.

For many moments Danica stood trembling, her eyes closed, and then, when the last lingering echoes of the perfect note died away, she realized the folly of hesitation and expected that the horde would be upon her. But when she opened her eyes, she found only three enemies standing: the first priest who had entered the room and an associate along a side wall, both holding their ears, and a third man, a soldier not a priest, standing not so far away and glancing about in absolute confusion.

Danica leaped forward and kicked the man's sword from his hand. He looked up at her, still too perplexed to react, and the monk grabbed him by the front of his tunic and threw herself backward in a roll, planting her feet into his belly as he came over her and heaving him hard against the wall beside Cadderly, where he crumbled down in pain. Danica was upon him in a moment, fingers coiled for a deadly strike.

"Do not kill him," Cadderly said to her, for the young priest realized that if this man had escaped the pains of his most holy spell, if the man could withstand the purely harmonious note, then he was probably not of an evil nature. Cadderly glanced at him only briefly, but he noticed revealing shadows atop the man's shoulder, the man's aura personified. These were not huddled, evil things, like the ones the young priest had often witnessed when viewing wicked men in similar fashion.

Danica, trusting in Cadderly's judgment, put the man in a defensive lock, and Cadderly turned his attention back to the still-standing priests.

"Damn you!" the horribly scarred leader growled in a loud voice—and the awkward volume of that response revealed to Cadderly that his holy utterance had probably deafened the man.

"Where is Aballister?" Cadderly called out, and the man regarded him curiously, then tapped his ears, confirming Cadderly's suspicions.

Both evil priests began chanting frantically, beginning new spells, and Danica slammed the soldier to the floor and started forward.

"Get back!" Cadderly warned, and the monk was truly torn. She knew the importance of getting at the spellcasters before they could complete their enchantments, but knew, too, to trust in Cadderly's warnings.

With supreme confidence, feeling invulnerable against the priests of an evil god, Cadderly fell back into the flowing music and began his song. He felt waves of numbing energy as the priest to the side hurled a paralyzing spell at him, but within the protective river of Deneir's music, such a spell had no hold over Cadderly.

The scarred leader lifted his arm and hurled a gemstone, glowing with the mighty energies it contained. Danica leaped in front to block it, as she had blocked the arrow, while Cadderly pointed to it and cried out.

The glow in the gemstone disappeared, and on a sudden inspiration (a silent telepathic message from Cadderly), Danica caught the stone.

Cadderly grabbed the back of Danica's tunic and pulled her behind him, singing all the while. Equations and numbers flashed through his thoughts with every note. He saw the very fabric of the area about him, the relationships and densities of the different materials. Energy flowed from the torches set into sconces on the walls, and a more static energy, the very binding force which held everything in place, was clearly revealed.

The evil priests began chanting again, stubbornly, but now it was Cadderly's turn. The young priest focused on that binding force, replayed equations and changed their factors, forcing truth into untruth.

No, not untruth, Cadderly realized. Not chaos, as was the enchantment he had forced over old Fyren. In the revealing equations, Cadderly found an alternate truth, a distortion, not a perversion, of physical law. By sheer willpower and the insights the song of Deneir had offered to him, the young priest bent the binding force, turned it in on the scarred enemy leader, making him the center of gravity.

For every unsecured item near the scarred man, the floor was no longer a resting place.

Dead and downed soldiers "fell" at their leader; they did not slide along the floor, but actually toppled and plunged, as though the floor was now a vertical slope. A desk from the room behind the surprised priest crashed against his back, all its items clinging to him as though he had become a living magnet. Two of the torches within the area of warped reality leaned toward the evil priest and slowly slid along the sides of their sconces, coming to an angled rest in a precarious perch, their flames burning out to the side away from the cursed man.

The priest who had been standing at the side of the room hung straight out, his feet toward his master, his hands clutching desperately at the doorjamb.

Danica couldn't prevent a chuckle at the ridiculous sight. A ball of bodies and items had converged on the scarred leader, smashing him from every angle. The priest to the side fell last, slamming hard against a dead orc. And then everything had settled once more, everything unattached or unsupported within fifty feet of the evil priest had come to rest atop him, had pounded him and buried him.

Several groans came from within that confused pile, mostly those of the battered leader, buried somewhere far beneath the jumble.

The man's associate, lying on the outside layer of the confused pile, looked at Cadderly with sheer hatred and began again his stubborn chant.

"Do not!" Cadderly warned him. The priest did stop, but not because of Cadderly's warning. Out of the same room that had held the desk now fell an incredibly fat giant, hitting the pile with such tremendous force that those bodies on the opposite side of the pile, near Cadderly and Danica, bounced out to the side, then fell back and settled on the pile once more. The scarred leader went quiet then for the first time, and Cadderly winced, realizing that the giant had probably crushed the man.

The giant was far from dead, though. It roared and thrashed, launching bodies far to the side, then smashing them apart as they inevitably fell back into the pile.

"How long will it last?" Danica asked. Her darting eyes revealed her fear, for there was no apparent way for her and Cadderly to get out of the area. Many of the men stricken unconscious by the holy word were awakening, and that ferocious giant had not been badly wounded.

Trepidation welled up within Cadderly, dark fears for what he must do to complete this battle. He searched his spells, listened carefully to the song, seeking something that would allow him and Danica to get through without further bloodshed. But what of his friends? he wondered. If they came out behind him, and the spell was no more, they would face a formidable force.

Again the raging priest atop the pile chanted; a soldier to the side of him hurled a dagger Cadderly's way, but it was as if he were throwing up the side of a cliff, and the knife dropped back to the jumble, sticking into the back of a dead goblin. The giant climbed through next, a look of sheer hatred on its huge face.

Cadderly looked to Danica, to the gemstone, a hunk of amber, that she held. Of all the trials the young priest would ever face, none would be so agonizing as this trial of conscience. He could not fail now, though, could not allow his own weakness to threaten his mission, to threaten all the goodly peoples of the region. He waved his hand over the gemstone, uttered a few words, and it began to glow again, teeming with magical energy.

"Toss it," he instructed.

"At them?"

Cadderly thought about it and shrugged as though it did not matter. "To the side," he said, pointing to the doorjamb where the priest had been hanging.

Danica still seemed not to understand, but she tossed the enchanted stone. It followed a normal, expected course for a few feet, then crossed into the area warped by Cadderly's spell and fell in an arcing, unerring curve to strike at the pile.

With a blinding flash, all the jumble was aflame. Men cried out for a moment, then fell silent. The giant thrashed wildly, but had nowhere to run, could find nothing to roll in that was not also burning. It went on for what seemed a long and agonizing time, but was in reality merely minutes, then the only sound was the crackle of hungry flames.

* * * * *

Pikel plowed through another angled doorway and fell fifteen feet to hit the corridor floor with a resounding "Oof!"

Dazed, and unable to find his balance, the dwarf turned his gaze to the side and saw Vander—Vander's furred boots, at least—stumbling about the bodies of several dead ogres. Even larger boots moved to keep up with the dancing firbolg, a hill giant, probably, along with the dirty, naked feet of yet another ogre.

Pikel knew that Vander needed him, so he gave a determined grunt and started to pull himself off the floor.

The plummeting Ivan hit him squarely in the back. The yellow-bearded dwarf bounced up from his cushioned landing and rushed ahead, recognizing Vander's desperate situation. The hill giant had Vander wrapped in its huge arms, and the ogre, wielding a huge spiked club, was circling about them, looking for an opening.

"Traitor!" the hill giant bellowed once more.

Vander butted with his forehead, splattering the giant's nose. With a roar, the giant swung about and launched Vander into the wall with such force that it shook the whole corridor. Vander bounced back a step, trying to get his sword up, but the ogre rushed in at his side and hit him with a roundhouse that drove a spike right into the side of his head.

Down on his knees, the dying firbolg noticed Ivan rushing in and with heroic effort heaved his sword forward as though it were a spear. The blade slashed into the hill giant's shoulder, knocking the monster back, slumping, against the opposite wall, its huge hands trying to find some hold that it might pull the thing out.

The ogre's great club smashed in again, and Vander saw no more.

Tears welled in Ivan's dark eyes as he pounded down the corridor. He leaped atop the wounded giant and crunched his axe into the monster's thick skull. The ogre roared at the sight of the dwarf and rushed back across the corridor, swinging wildly.

Ivan hopped away, and the ogre's spiked club drew bloody creases down the giant's face and sent the behemoth sprawling to the floor.

"Duh," the ogre groaned stupidly, and then it jerked to the side as Ivan's axe chopped it on the leg. Like a lumberjack, the sturdy dwarf went to work, hacking with abandon, and four blows later, the ogre toppled to the floor.

Behind Ivan, the giant groaned and tried to rise. The cry of "Oooooo!" followed by the resounding smack of a tree-trunk club against flesh brought a grim smile to the yellow-bearded dwarf.

Pikel hit the stunned giant again and moved for a third strike. But the stubborn behemoth, far from finished, caught the club and pulled it aside.

Pikel let go with one hand and pointed it straight out at the giant, who seemed not to understand—not until something snapped out of Pikel's loose-fitting sleeve, snapped out with venom-dripping fangs into the surprised giant's face.

The giant let go of the club and fell back, clawing at the stinging wound, horrified. It heard Pikel's "Ooooooo!" as the dwarf, club in hand, wound up, but it never saw the killing blow coming.

Without its weapon, the ogre across the hall raised its arms defensively and called out a surrender.

But those arms, however thick, were no match for Ivan's blind fury. Vander lay dead behind him, and the dwarf was hardly in the mood to listen to anything the desperate monster might have to say. The dwarf's axe chopped down repeatedly, smashing through flesh and bone, and by the time Shayleigh joined Ivan and put a hand on his shoulder to calm him, the ogre's cries were forever silenced.

Sixteen

A Call on the Wind

The man at the base of the wall groaned, and Danica was on him in an instant, roughly pulling his arms behind his back and pushing him face-down against the hard stone. "How long will your enchantment block our way?" she snapped at Cadderly.

"Not long," the young priest replied, surprised by Danica's harsh tone.

"And what are we to do with him?" Danica gave a rough tug on the captured soldier's arms as she asked the question, drawing another groan from the battered man.

"Be easy with him," Cadderly said.

"As you were with them?" Danica asked sarcastically, waving a hand out to the smoldering pile.

Now Cadderly understood Danica's ire. The battle had been rough, as the rising stench of burning flesh reminded them.

"Why didn't you tell me what that orb would do?" Danica's question sounded as a desperate plea.

Cadderly had a hard time sorting through this seeming reversal of roles. Usually he was the one who was too softhearted, who got them into trouble by not fighting hard enough against the declared enemies. He had spared Dorigen in Shilmista Forest, had let her live when he had her helpless on the ground before him, though Danica had instructed him to finish her. And now, Cadderly had been merciless, had done as the situation demanded against his own peaceful instincts. Cadderly held little remorse—he knew that all those humans in the fiery jumble were evil-hearted men—but he was more than a little surprised by Danica's cold reaction.

She gave another tug on the prisoner's arms, as if she was using the man's pain to torment Cadderly, lashing out at the young priest by going against what he obviously desired.

"He is not an evil man," Cadderly said calmly.

Danica hesitated, her exotic eyes searching out the sincerity within Cadderly's gray orbs. She had always been able to read the young priest's thoughts and believed now that he was speaking truthfully (though where he had garnered that piece of information, Danica had no idea).

"And they were?" Danica asked somewhat sharply, again indicating the pile.

"Yes," Cadderly answered. "When I uttered the holy word, how did you feel?"

The simple memory of that wondrous moment eased much of the tension from Danica's fair face. How did she feel? She felt in love, at ease with all the world, as if nothing ugly could come near her.

"You saw how it affected them," Cadderly went on, finding his answers in Danica's serene expression.

Following the logic, Danica lessened her grip. "But it did not adversely affect this one," she said.

"He is not an evil man," Cadderly reiterated.

Danica nodded and lessened her grip. She looked back at Cadderly, though, and her expression was cold once more, a look more of disappointment than of anger.

Cadderly understood, but had no answers for his love. There had been human beings among the evil monsters in this group, men among the goblins. Danica was disappointed because Cadderly had done what was necessary, had given in to the fighting fully. She had been angry with Cadderly when he had spared Dorigen, but it was an anger founded in her fear of the wizard. In truth, Danica had loved Cadderly all the more because of his conscience, because he had tried to avoid the horrors of battle at all costs.

Cadderly looked back to the pile of corpses. He had given in, joined the fighting with all his heart.

It had to be that way, Cadderly knew. He was as horrified as Danica over what he had just done, but he would not take back the action even if he could. The friends were in desperate straits—all the region was in desperate straits—and that danger was being precipitated by the minions of this fortress. Castle Trinity, and not Cadderly, would have to take responsibility for the lives that would be lost this day.

But while that argument held solid on a logical basis, Cadderly could not deny the pain in his chest when he looked upon the pile of dead men, or the sting in his heart when he viewed Danica's disappointment.

* * * * *

"We must go!" Shayleigh said to Ivan, tugging on the dwarf's arm and looking back to the corridor behind them, where the steps of many boots could be heard.

Ivan sighed as he regarded Vander, the firbolg's head crushed and mis-shapen. A similar sigh behind him turned Ivan about to regard Pikel. He eyed his brother curiously, for something seemed out of place along the length of Pikel's tunic and undershirt.

"How'd ye get away from the snake?" Ivan asked, suddenly remembering their past predicament.

Pikel gave a short whistle, and on cue, the serpent's head streamed up from his collar and hovered in the air right beside his green-bearded cheek.

Shayleigh and Ivan fell back in shock, Ivan's axe coming up defensively between himself and his surprising brother.

"Doo-dad!" Pikel announced happily, petting the snake, which seemed to enjoy the treatment. Pikel nodded to the side, then, indicating that they should be on their way.

"Doo-dad?" Shayleigh inquired of Ivan as Pikel hopped off.

"Wants to be a druid," Ivan explained, moving to follow his brother. "He don't know that dwarves can't be druids."

Shayleigh considered the words for a long moment. "Neither does the snake," she decided, and with a final, helpless look at the dead Vander, she rushed off after her companions.

* * * * *

"My thanks to you," the soldier whispered to Cadderly, all the while eyeing the charred mass of his dead allies. The pile fell apart then, resettling upon the floor, as Cadderly's strange enchantment dissipated.

"Where is Aballister?" the young priest demanded. The man's lips seemed to tighten into thin lines.

Cadderly leaped past Danica, grabbed the man by the collar, and slammed him hard against the wall. "You are still a prisoner!" he growled in the surprised man's face. "You can be an asset to us, and we will repay you accordingly."

"Or you can be a detriment," Cadderly went on grimly. He looked back to the pile as he spoke, and the unvoiced threat drained the blood from the captured man's face.

"Lead on to the wizard," Cadderly instructed. "Along the most direct route."

The man glanced at Danica, as if pleading for some support, but the monk looked away impassively.

That gesture did not reveal the turmoil in Danica's heart. Cadderly's move and threat against the prisoner, a person he had just declared was not an evil man, had surprised her. She had never seen Cadderly so calculatingly cold, and while she could understand his determined actions, she could not deny her fears.

The prisoner took them through a door to the side, halfway around the circular room. They had only gone a dozen steps when Cadderly grabbed the man again, pushed him up against the wall and began roughly stripping off every piece of his noisy armor, even to the point of removing the man's hard-soled boots.

"Quietly," he whispered to the man. "I have but one battle left to fight, a battle against Aballister."

The man growled and pushed Cadderly away, and found Danica's silver-hilted dagger at his throat in the blink of an eye.

"The wizard is powerful," the prisoner warned, wisely keeping his voice soft.

Cadderly nodded. "And you fear the consequences of your actions should Aballister win out against us," he reasoned.

The man's lips went tight again, and he made no move to respond. Cadderly eased Danica away and again put his face close to the man's, his jaw firm and unrelenting. "Then choose," the young priest said, his voice low and threatening. "Do you take the chance that Aballister will not win out?"

The man glanced about nervously, but again said nothing.

"Aballister is not here," Cadderly reminded him. "None of your allies are here. It is just you and I, and you know what I can do."

The man started off again immediately, his bare feet making little noise as he padded along the corridor with appropriate caution. They crossed several side corridors, often hearing the sounds of other soldiers rushing about, probably in search of them. Each time some group was about, Danica looked nervously to Cadderly, as if to say that this man, who could betray them with a simple call, was his responsibility.

But the man held true to the terms of his capture, moving with all stealth as they worked their way past one guard position or patrol group after another.

When they entered one long corridor, though, a group of goblins entered it simultaneously from the other end, and they found that they had nowhere to run. The goblins, six of the beasts, advanced cautiously, weapons drawn.

The prisoner addressed them in their own croaking language, and Cadderly understood well enough to know that the man had concocted some lie about being on a mission for the priests, going to Aballister with some important information.

Still, the goblins eyed Cadderly and Danica dangerously, exchanging a few quiet remarks—doubts, Cadderly knew—amongst themselves.

Even the cooperative prisoner looked back, his expression showing sincere worry.

Danica didn't wait for events to take their obvious course. She leaped out suddenly, punching the nearest goblin in the throat, circling about, her leg flying high to connect on the next one's chest, and whipped a dagger into the face of yet another. She ducked low under a sword swipe and sprang up high from her crouch, double-kicking the sword wielder in the face and chest.

Two goblins rushed by her, more concerned with escape than with tangling against Cadderly and the soldier, but Cadderly got one with his walking stick, shattering its knee, and the soldier tackled the other.

Danica spun about and again kicked, sending one goblin flying into the wall. The creature smacked hard against the stone and bounced back, and Danica, timing her spin perfectly, promptly kicked it again. Again it bounced out; again it was launched backward by a perfectly timed kick.

The fourth time, the goblin was allowed to fall to the floor, for Danica sprang away, leaping over the prone prisoner at the back of the goblin that had slipped her grasp. One hand reached around to cup the goblin's chin while the other grabbed the hair on the back of its head.

The goblin squealed and tried to stop and turn, but Danica rushed right beside it, twisting her arms viciously, snapping the wretched thing's neck.

"Down!" Danica called, coming around behind Cadderly. The young priest fell to the floor and the goblin facing him was caught fully by surprise as Danica rushed by, connecting with a heavy punch into its ugly face. It flew backward several feet, hit the stone with a groan, and Danica ran past.

The goblin she had hit in the throat was up to its knees again, trying to find its footing. Danica leaped high into the air, coming down with her knees driving against the skinny creature's back, slamming it down fiercely. She pulled her second dagger from her boot, grabbed a clump of hair with her free hand and pulled the goblin's head back, cutting a neat line across its throat.

She did likewise to the helpless goblin that had her other dagger sticking from its face, ending its misery. And then she turned back, to see Cadderly and the prisoner staring at her incredulously.

"I do not parley with goblins," Danica said grimly, wiping her blades on the nearest monster's dirty tunic.

"You could not outrun her," Cadderly remarked to the prisoner, and the man, in turn, gave the young priest an incredulous look.

"I just thought I would mention that," Cadderly said.

They set out at once, Cadderly and Danica anxious to put some distance between themselves and the scene of the slaughter. The prisoner said nothing, just continued to lead them at a swift pace, and soon the tunnels became quieter and less filled with rushing soldiers.

Cadderly sensed that the walls in this region were not natural, though they were lined by uncut stone. The young priest could feel the residual energies of the magics that had been used to make this place, as though some powerful dweomer had pulled the natural stone from between these walls.

The sensations sent a mix of emotions through the young priest. He was glad that the captured soldier was apparently not leading them astray, glad that their search might soon come to its end. But Cadderly was worried, too, for if Aballister had created these tunnels, had magically torn the stone from these halls, then the storm at Nightglow only hinted at his powers.

Something else assaulted Cadderly's thoughts then, a fleeting, distant call, as if someone was summoning him. He paused and closed his eyes.

Cadderly.

He heard it clearly, though distantly. He felt for the amulet in his pocket which he'd acquired some time ago and with which he could communicate with the imp, Druzil. Now it was cool, indicating that Druzil was nowhere about.

Cadderly.

It was not Druzil, and Cadderly did not believe that it was Dorigen, either. Who then? the young priest wondered. Who was so attuned to him that they might make telepathic contact without his knowledge or consent?

He opened his eyes, determined not to get sidetracked. "Keep going," he instructed his comrades, taking his place beside them.

But the call remained, fleeting and distant, and what bothered Cadderly more than anything else was that it somehow sounded so very familiar.

Seventeen

Dwarven Stealth

W e must move quietly," Shayleigh pointedly instructed her dwarven companions, what seemed to her an obvious precaution. Still, Shayleigh soon came to understand that her definition of "moving quietly" was apparently very different from Ivan and Pikel's. The clomp of Ivan's boots echoed loudly off the stone walls, and Pikel's sandals double-slapped— once against the floor and once against his foot—with every pumping stride.

They rambled along several long, dark corridors, the only light coming from widely spaced torches hanging in iron sconces. Around a bend and through an archway, the three companions found the walls lined by fonts, filled with a clear, watery substance.

Ivan, needing a refreshing drink, paused and moved to scoop up some, but Pikel quickly slapped his hand away, waggling a finger in his startled brother's face.

"Uh-uhhh," the green-bearded dwarf implored, and he hopped up high and pulled a torch from its sconce. Still waggling the finger tucked under his arm, Pikel touched the fire to the liquid. The stuff hissed and sputtered, and a noxious gray cloud arose, making Ivan pinch his nose. Pikel hung his tongue out of his mouth and muttered, "Yuch."

"How did he know?" Shayleigh asked Ivan when they had cleared the stinky area.

Ivan shrugged. "Must be something to this druid stuff."

"Doo-dad!" Pikel agreed.

"Yeah, doo-dad," muttered Ivan. "Or he just knowed that this place is for Talona, and Talona's the goddess of poison."

Sly Pikel wasn't letting on. He just followed the other two, every so often chuckling, "Hee hee hee."

Around a sharp bend in the corridor, the friends found a group of enemies waiting for them.

Shayleigh fired her bow between the bobbing dwarven heads, catching the leading orc in the chest and dropping it dead.

"Frog!" Ivan called, a reference to a game he and his brother used to play. Pikel rushed in front and braced himself, squared to the next leading orc, and Ivan leaped up from behind and straddled Pikel's shoulders. Pikel fell forward, hooking Ivan's feet and his propelling his forward-flying brother into a downward arc.

The orc froze with surprise, stood there with no practical defenses, and Ivan's axe cleaved its skull, drove right down through the stupid creature's head so that it seemed as if it would literally be split in half.

The move left both dwarves sprawled on the floor, with several enemies still standing, unharmed (though after witnessing a comrade practically split down the middle, none of them seemed overly anxious to rush in). With the line of fire clear between them and Shayleigh, their hesitation was not a wise thing.

The elf maiden set her bow to furious work, hardly aiming, just firing for the mass of enemy bodies.

A few seconds, and a few arrows, later, what was left of the enemy band was in full flight.

"Now move *quietly*," Shayleigh instructed through gritted teeth.

"Quietly!" Ivan balked incredulously. "Bring the whole damned bunch of them on, I say!"

"Oo oi!" Pikel cried. The agreeing brothers turned together toward Shayleigh, to find the elf maiden back against the inner wall of the last corner, her bow up as she looked behind them.

"You may get your wish," she explained. "Goblins, led by an ogre."

Ivan and Pikel rushed up to the corner beside her and nodded to each other, as if they already had come to a silent agreement on how to approach this next fight. Ivan stooped, and this time Pikel went up on his shoulders, leaning against the wall and putting one hand up high, fingers conspicuously wrapped around the edge of the wall, in plain sight of the approaching force.

Ivan nodded for Shayleigh to fall back a few steps.

The ogre came around the corner expecting, from Pikel's high-placed hand, to find a tall foe. Pikel fell away as the monster spun around the bend, its flying club smacking harmlessly off the empty stone wall.

Ivan's axe chop gashed into the thigh of its lead leg, severing muscles and tendons.

Unable to stop its momentum, the wounded ogre continued its turn, squaring its back to Shayleigh. Still backpedaling, it jerked twice in rapid succession as arrows drove through its shoulder blades, and then it tripped altogether, falling backward. One arrow shattered under the tremendous weight, but the other, angled perfectly so that it hit the ground straight up, plunged through the massive beast, through its heart, with the arrow tip bursting out the front of the ogre's chest.

By the time the goblins, just two steps behind the ogre, came around the corner, they found their leader dead.

Not that the lead goblins even had time to register the scene. Pikel, crouched back in the corner, swiped his club across, smacking shins and sending two of the monsters sprawling—right at Ivan's feet. The yellow-bearded dwarf, his axe chopping viciously, made quick work of them.

The rest of the force, with typical goblin loyalty, turned and fled.

"They will be returning from the front," Shayleigh said grimly.

"Yeah, and the stupid goblins will hear the fighting and come back the other way, probably with a hunnerd kin!" Ivan agreed.

"You may indeed get your wish, Ivan," the elf answered grimly. "The whole force of Castle Trinity might soon squeeze us between them." Shayleigh moved to the corner and looked back, then ran up ahead and peered as far along as she could, hoping for a side tunnel, for something that could get them free of this tight area.

Pikel, already understanding their dire predicament, tuned out of the conversation. Down on his knees, he crawled along the worked wall, butting his forehead against any promising stones.

"What is he doing?" Shayleigh demanded, obviously dismayed by the dwarf's apparently ridiculous actions.

Even as she spoke, Pikel pressed his forehead back against one of the rocks. He turned to Ivan, smiling from ear to ear, and squeaked.

"There's the way!" Ivan bellowed, falling to his knees beside his brother, both of them digging with their fingers at the edges of the cut stone.

"They always put secret tunnels beside the corridor," Ivan explained to Shayleigh's doubting expression. "Drains the water in case of a flood."

Shayleigh's keen ears caught the sounds of footsteps approaching from both directions. "Hurry," she implored the dwarves, and she ran to the wall and grabbed a torch. Shayleigh rushed back around the corner, as far down as she could go, then reversed direction and ran back, dipping the torch in every font she passed, and pulling out all the other torches. All the corridor behind her was soon filled with a noxious gray cloud, leaving the passage in smoky darkness. Through it, Shayleigh could see the red dots of goblin eyes, using their heat-sensing infravision.

"Stubborn," she muttered, and she ran around the corner, down the hallway the other way, repeating the procedure. By the time she got back to the dwarves, enemies were closing from both directions. A goblin peeked around the corner, then fell back with an arrow in its eye.

"Hurry!" Shayleigh whispered harshly, coughing as the evil smoke descended over her.

"Hurry, yerself," Ivan growled back. He pulled the elf maiden down to the floor and practically stuffed her through the opening, dropping her down a muddy, descending chute. Pikel came in behind, chuckling and placing both his club and Ivan's axe in the slope behind him.

"What is he doing?" Shayleigh asked, but Pikel only put a stubby finger over his lips and whispered, "Ssssh!"

Ivan rushed across and put his back to the corner, closing his eyes so that the red glow of infravision would not give him away. Goblins shuffled around behind him.

The enemy host came moving down from the other direction.

"More than we thinks!" Ivan roared in the goblin language, a squeaking and croaking tongue. Those goblins beside the dwarf, peering ahead through the confusing veil, took up their weapons.

"Charges them! Killses them!" Ivan bellowed, and the call was repeated by many goblins as the horde rushed the approaching force. In a confusing instant, the two groups were together, hacking away, each thinking the other to be the intruders that had come to Castle Trinity.

Ivan calmly walked over to stand in front of the secret tunnel. Pikel reached out to him, but Ivan hesitated, thoroughly enjoying the battle. Finally, Pikel's patience evaporated, and he reached out with both hands, grabbed Ivan by the ankles, and jerked him from his feet, dragging him into the tunnel.

Pikel clambered over his facedown brother, out of the tunnel far enough to retrieve the block and tug it somewhat back in place. Now it was the green-bearded dwarf who hesitated, enthralled by the raging action, chuckling as one severed goblin head came bouncing by. Never one to miss an opportunity for payback, Ivan grabbed Pikel by the ankles and yanked him through the mud.

Soon after, the three friends found a way out of that crawl tunnel, into another stone-worked corridor some distance from the fighting. Ivan and Pikel led the way, their muddy faces set in a determined grimace.

Shayleigh shook her head in disbelief many times over the next few minutes as the dwarves rambled through the complex, overturning everything in their path, including a few startled goblins. Shayleigh didn't tell them to be quiet, though. She knew that their escape had been a temporary reprieve, that no matter how stealthily they might now travel, sooner or later they would meet an organized defense.

The elf smiled then, glad that she was beside the rugged Bouldershoulders. She had seen the brothers like this before, in the battles of Shilmista. Let the enemy come on, she decided. Let them face the battle-lust of the hearty dwarves!

Ivan and Pikel did slow down and become somewhat quieter when they neared a staircase, rising up out of sight just beyond a four-way intersection of wide corridors: A perfect place for an ambush. They heard singing coming from the stairs, a booming, giant voice. The corridor behind them and the two to the sides seemed empty, so they crept across.

The stairs went up, which was the way they all figured they had to go, but they could see the boots of a giant not so far up the stairs. The huge monster continued its off-key singing, apparently unaware of the intruders that had come to Castle Trinity.

"Get ye up fast," was the only explanation Ivan offered to Shayleigh, and with a wink to his brother, the two dwarves set off, using the giant's booming voice to cover their heavy steps on the wooden stairs.

Shayleigh glanced all about nervously, thinking this a bad situation. She heard the dwarves roar out in glee, though, heard the smacks as Ivan's axe and Pikel's club connected on the giant's legs. Then the whole ground shook as the behemoth tumbled down the stairs.

Shayleigh considered putting an arrow into the tumbling thing, but heard the three corridors behind her fast filling with enemy soldiers. Instead, she turned about and launched the arrow into the thickening mass behind her, not waiting to see if she had scored a hit.

The giant, though very much alive and very much enraged, lay on its back, its head toward Shayleigh and its feet still far up the staircase. It struggled to right itself, but its bulk filled the not-too-wide stairs, and in that awkward position, with both legs injured, it floundered miserably.

Shayleigh drew out her short sword and leaped ahead, skipping off the monster's face, nearly tripping on its huge nose. The giant grabbed at her with its hands, but she dodged them and stuck one when it got too near. The giant lifted a huge leg and curled it in at the knee, forming a barrier of flesh, but Shayleigh drove her sword deeply into the thick thigh and the barrier flew away. As she cleared the huge torso, the elf saw Pikel coming the other way, rushing under the one upraised leg.

Shayleigh called out, thinking that Pikel would surely be crushed, but the dwarf was already wedged tightly between the stairs and the giant's huge buttocks.

A swarm of enemies came to the bottom of the stairs, some clambering to get atop the giant, others drawing out bows and taking a bead on Shayleigh and on Ivan as the yellow-bearded dwarf rushed down to grab the elf maiden.

Pikel's pet snake bit the giant on the fleshy backside, and the monster's predictable hop gave the dwarf all the momentum he needed. Bracing his shoulder, the powerful little dwarf heaved and groaned, turning the behemoth up onto its shoulders, lifting a wall of flesh between his friends and the enemies. The giant grunted several times as it intercepted arrows, and then, with Pikel's stubby legs driving relentlessly, it went right over, wedging tightly into the low, narrow stairway entrance.

Pikel gave his snake a pat on the head and tucked it back into his sleeve, then rushed to join his friends, taking his club back from Ivan as he hopped past.

Shayleigh stood shaking her head once more.

"Stronger than ye thought, ain't he?" Ivan asked, tugging her along.

They met no foes at the top of the stairs, and Ivan and Pikel immediately lined up side by side and resumed their battle charge. Shayleigh heard no sounds about them other than the echoes of dwarven sandals and boots, and while that fact gave her some comfort, she realized that this blind rush through the complex would likely get them nowhere.

Finally Shayleigh was able to stop the brothers' wild run, reminding them that they had to sort out the maze of tunnels and try to find Cadderly and Danica.

When the dwarves had quieted, they did hear some noise, a general murmur, down a corridor to the left. Shayleigh was about to whisper that she should go ahead and stealthily check out the place, but her words were buried under Pikel's hearty "Oo oi!" and the resounding clamor of the renewed charge.

Eighteen

The Fifth Corner

T here," the prisoner said to Cadderly and Danica, pointing across a last intersection to an unremarkable door. "That is the entrance to the wizard's chambers."

Cadderly.

The call came again in the young priest's mind, from somewhere not so far away. Cadderly closed his eyes and concentrated, coming to understand that the call came from somewhere beyond the unremarkable door. When he opened his eyes once more, he found Danica eyeing him curiously.

"The man does not lie," Cadderly said to her.

The prisoner seemed to relax at that.

"Then why are there no guards?" Danica asked, more to the prisoner than to Cadderly. The man had no answer for her.

"This is a wizard," Cadderly reminded them both. "A powerful wizard by all that we have heard. There may indeed be a guardian or some protective magic."

Danica roughly pushed the prisoner forward. "You shall lead," she said coldly.

Cadderly immediately moved up beside the man, catching his arm to hold him back, and looked across him to regard Danica. "We go together?" he asked as much as stated.

Danica looked to the door, to Cadderly and the other man. She understood her love's sympathy and protectiveness toward the helpless prisoner, understood that Cadderly, convinced that this was not an evil man, would not use the prisoner as fodder.

"He and I lead," Danica decided, pulling the man from Cadderly's light grasp. "You follow."

The monk soft-stepped up to the intersection, bent low and peered both ways. She turned back to Cadderly and offered a shrug, then motioned for the prisoner to keep pace and skittered across to the door—almost.

The creature seemed to unfold from the air itself, becoming first a black line, then expanding left and right, two dimensional, then three dimensional. Five serpentine heads waved in front of the startled companions.

A hydra.

Danica skidded to a stop and hurled herself to the left, rolling from the lunging reach of three great heads.

The prisoner, not as quick as the monk, managed only a single step before a monstrous maw clamped down across his waist. He screamed and batted futilely at the scaly head as the needle-sharp teeth ripped him. A second maw descended over the man's unprotected head, stifling his scream fully. Both heads working in unison, the hydra tore the man in half.

Cadderly nearly swooned at the sight. He got his loaded crossbow up in front of him, shifting it this way and that, trying to follow the almost hypnotic motion of the weaving heads.

Where to fire?

He shot for the center of the great body, and the hydra roared in rage as the dart hit and exploded. Two heads still snapped at the dodging Danica, two continued their feast on the slaughtered man, and the fifth shot forward, far short of Cadderly, but compelling the hydra's bulky body into a short rush at the young priest.

Danica started for Cadderly, but reversed direction abruptly as the hydra shuffled by, and chose instead to work her way behind the beast. She cried out for Cadderly to run, though she could not see him around the bulk of the monster.

The lead maw came, straight as an arrow, for the young priest, testing his nerve as he struggled to get his weapon readied a second time. The serpentine maw was barely two feet away when Cadderly's arm at last came up, and he fired, the quarrel skipping off six-inch fangs, diving into the monster's mouth and blasting in a muffled explosion.

The head and neck dropped in a line on the floor, slowing the charge.

The two heads that had been after Danica, and the one finished with the dead prisoner, came swooping in, though, and the young priest wisely fell back, desperately bringing up his walking stick to fend off the nearest attack.

He knew that he had to get far enough away to reload the crossbow, had to fall into the song of Deneir and pull something, anything, from the notes. But with the maze of darting heads, the creature pacing his every retreat, Cadderly couldn't begin to hear the song, had to concentrate simply on whipping his walking stick back and forth in front of him. He did connect once, luckily, the enchanted ram's head knocking a tooth from the closest maw. That head went up to issue a roar, and Cadderly, purely on instinct, rushed under it, used the serpentine neck as a shield against the other two pursuing heads.

The fourth head, the other one to the right, spit aside the dead man's torso and would have had the young priest then, except that Danica came around from behind and snapped a kick under its jaw.

The monster's maw smacked shut; its flickering tongue fell severed to the floor.

Cadderly continued toward the door, concentrating on readying the crossbow. Danica came, too, by his side, looking back as the hydra lumbered about, dragging its one dead head along the floor as it turned.

"Get in!" she called, but Cadderly, for all his desperation, kept his wits enough to keep clear of the door. It was warded, he knew, sensing the magics upon it. Shoulder to shoulder with Danica, he brought his crossbow up again as if to shoot at the hydra. But then he turned, firing instead at the lock on the door, blowing a wide hole in the wood.

Danica hit Cadderly on the shoulder, throwing him aside. He came up against the wall, dazed, to see his love engulfed by four eagerly snapping hydra heads.

She rushed straight for the beast, ran inside its initial bites, twisting and turning, swatting blindly at anything that came near. A head turned enough to get at her, and she grabbed it by the horn, twisting with a jerk that angled the maw so that it could not wrap around her, so that the snout butted her in the ribs. Danica's other hand shot out the other way, her stiffened fingers driving through the eye of still another snapping head.

All the hydra's heads were turned completely about, facing its bulky torso. Danica grabbed the half-blinded head, threw her back against the thick serpentine neck, then dodged away as another head rushed in, its wide-opened maw biting hard into its own companion's neck Before the hydra even realized its error, the other head fell dead.

Danica was still pinned in that hellish spot, but a quarrel skipped off the side of one turned neck—off the side of one to solidly strike a second. The first head that had been struck wheeled about to view the newest attacker, while the force of the ensuing explosion drove the second head aside, opening a hole for Danica to rush out.

"The door is warded!" Cadderly cried at Danica as she darted straight for the loose-hanging portal.

It was a moot point, for Danica had no intentions of going through. She stopped and, sensing a maw rushing at her back, leaped up high, catching the top of the jamb and pulling herself straight up. The hydra's head burst through the door.

Lightning flashed several times; fire roared out from every side of the magically trapped doorjamb.

Only two heads remaining, the blasted hydra backed away. Serpentine necks crossed; reptilian eyes regarded the two companions with sudden respect.

Cadderly tried to line one up for a shot, but he hesitated, not wanting to risk a miss.

"Damn," he hissed, frustrated, after a long and unproductive moment had slipped past. He fired the bolt into the hydra's bulk, apparently doing no real damage, but driving it back another step. The hydra's living heads roared in unison. It hopped to the side, three dead necks bouncing along.

"Shoot for my back," Danica instructed and before Cadderly could ask her what she was talking about, she rushed forward, charged right between the swaying heads, drawing them in to her. "Now!" Danica ordered.

Cadderly had to trust in her. His crossbow clicked, and Danica dropped suddenly to her back, the quarrel crossing above her and splattering a very surprised serpentine face.

That wounded head did not die, though, and Danica, on her back, now had two snapping maws above her.

"No!" Cadderly cried out, and he charged ahead boldly, both hands tight on his ram's-head walking stick.

Danica kicked up, one foot and then the other, keeping the heads at bay. Cadderly saw that the head he had shot appeared fully blind, and he leaped right across Danica's prone form, smashing the head with a two-handed overhead chop.

The head recoiled, and Cadderly pursued, smacking it repeatedly.

The second head rushed in at Cadderly's back, but Danica threw her legs up and then down, snapping her back in a quick arch and hurling herself to her feet. A single stride brought her alongside the chasing head and she dipped low, drawing a dagger from her boot, then shot back up, driving the knife up to its silver dragon-sculpted hilt into the bottom jaw.

Cadderly's arms pumped relentlessly, beating the already disfigured head into a bloody pulp.

The remaining head soared up high, but Danica locked her arm over the neck and went along for the ride, holding fast to her stuck dagger. She curled up around the neck, bringing her boot to her free hand and managing to extract her second dagger.

Then she held on, stubbornly, as the monster bucked and whipped. When its frenzy finally abated, Danica plunged her second knife into its eye, pulled it back, and drove it home a second time.

Again came the monstrous frenzy. Cadderly, trying to get to Danica, got clipped on one rushing pass and was hurled ten feet down the corridor.

But Danica held on, kept both her daggers buried, working them back and forth, turning their handles around in her palms. She fell hard to her back, smacking against the stone, the monstrous neck dropping over her.

Stunned, the monk could not find her breath, could not focus her gaze, and was hardly conscious of her grip on her knives. Her instincts screamed out at her to react, to wriggle away. Her instincts screamed out at her that she was vulnerable, that the hydra head could easily shake free and snap her in half.

But the hydra was no longer moving, and a moment later, Cadderly was standing above Danica, pulling her arms free, shifting the bulky serpentine neck off her.

Shayleigh heard a murmuring up ahead, the drone of many muffled voices. She started to call out a warning to the Bouldershoulder brothers, but the dwarves had apparently heard the sound as well, for they lowered their heads and picked up the pace, Pikel's sandals slapping and Ivan's boots thumping.

Shayleigh slipped along silently right behind them, her bow ready. Around a bend in the corridor they saw a straight run past two intersections and ending at a set of double doors.

"Too many!" the elf maiden whispered harshly, slowing her pace. "Too many!"

Double doors blocked their way, then double doors hung awkwardly on broken hinges. Ivan and Pikel burst in, weapons high.

"Uh-oh," muttered the green-bearded dwarf, echoing his brother's sentiments exactly, for they had come into a huge hall, a dining area, now apparently doubling as a command post, lined with dozens of tables and more than a few enemies. Shayleigh sighed helplessly and rushed to catch up with the furious dwarves, who, in their momentum, had already charged past the first empty tables.

A group of orcs sitting closest to the door barely had the time to look up from their bowls before the dwarves fell over them, hacking and kicking, Ivan butting with his deer-antlered helmet, and Pikel a flurry of flying knees and elbows, butting forehead, and tree-trunk club.

Only one of the six orcs even managed to get out of its chair, but before the startled creature took two steps away, an arrow sliced through the side of its head, dropping it dead to the floor.

On ran the dwarves and on chased Shayleigh. Their only hope was in movement, the elf maiden knew, in rushing through too quickly for the multitude of enemies in this hall to organize against them. In full flight, she put an arrow to the side, catching a man in the shoulder as he tried to raise a bow of his own.

Tables overturned, chairs skidded aside, as the men and monsters scrambled to get out of harm's way. One unfortunate goblin got tangled up in its companion's chair. When the dwarves had passed, both the goblin and that chair lay flattened on the floor. One ogre did not run, but crossed its huge arms over its chest and stood with legs firmly planted, thinking itself an imposing barrier.

It got wounded in more than its pride when Ivan rushed right through those widespread legs, the dwarf's axe up high over his head. The ogre lurched, grabbing at its torn loins, and Pikel ran beside it, caving in the side of its knee. The ogre hadn't even hit the floor yet when Shayleigh sprang up, planting one foot on the cheek of its turned face, another on its ribs, as she ran right down the falling creature's side.

There seemed to be no method to the dwarven rush, no aim above the general chaos. Then Pikel spotted the serving area, a long counter running along the back wall.

"Oooo!" the green-bearded dwarf squeaked, his stubby finger pointing the way.

One of the three servers lifted a crossbow, but Shayleigh's arrow took him down. A second lifted a wooden tray before him like a shield, but Ivan's axe cleaved it in two and cleaved the man's face in two as well. The third man's shield, an iron pot, seemed more formidable, but Pikel's club hit it head on, and the pot snapped back to hit the man head on.

The three friends were over the counter in a flash, Shayleigh spinning about and setting her bow into frantic motion, for many enemies were now in pursuit. She scored hit after hit, but there seemed no way that she could possibly stop the closing horde.

Ivan and Pikel leaped atop the counter to either side of her, armed with stacks of metal plates. The dwarves opened up a barrage of flying metal. Dishes whizzed through the air, spinning and swerving, battering the approaching enemies.

Battering them and holding them up long enough for Shayleigh to methodically cut them down.

"Hee hee hee," chuckled Pikel, and he hopped down from the counter and grabbed up a pot of thick green soup. Over it went, splashing and spilling, setting up the obstacle of a slippery floor for those enemies that came too near.

The dwarf also scooped up a huge ladle of boiling water before he climbed back atop the counter.

An arrow skipped right past Ivan's ear, knocking into the wall behind the dwarf. Shayleigh, intent on the largest approaching monster, another ogre, noted the archer to the side, crouched beside an overturned table.

"Yerself takes the bowmen!" Ivan cried. "Me and me brother'll take on them fools that come close!"

The reasoning seemed sound, and the elf maiden forced herself to hold her nerve, forced herself to ignore the closest threats and trust in her companions. She swerved her bow to the side, saw the bowman's hip foolishly hanging out from the barrier while he reloaded, and promptly stuck an arrow into him.

The approaching ogre carried four arrows in its chest but still stubbornly came on, right for Pikel and the helpless Shayleigh.

The dwarf's eyes widened in feigned fear, and Pikel seemed to cower, causing Shayleigh to cry out. Pikel came up straight at the last moment, though, whipping out the ladle, splashing the surprised ogre's eyes and face with boiling water.

Predictably, the ogre lurched, throwing its arms up over its burned eyes. The shift cost the beast its already tentative balance in the green soup, and it skidded in to slam its knees against the sturdy stone counter. Down low, trying to recover its balance and its sight, the ogre felt a burning flash, a club-inspired explosion that caved in the top of its head.

Pikel laid his brain-stained club aside and took up more plates, sent them spinning off at enemies who were suddenly more interested in getting out of harm's way than in getting to the intruders.

"None better at kitchen fighting than a Bouldershoulder," Ivan remarked, and, looking at the chaos and carnage, Shayleigh wasn't about to disagree.

But the elf knew that more than the initial fury would be needed to win this battle. Dozens of enemies remained, for more had come into the room, over-turning tables before them, getting down under cover. She saw another archer peek up over the top rim of a table to the side, saw his bow come up.

Shayleigh was the quicker on the draw, and the better shot. While the man's arrow flew harmlessly high and wide, Shayleigh's got him between the eyes. The elf's satisfaction was short-lived as she realized that she had only five arrows remaining, and exhausted, too, was Ivan and Pikel's supply of metal plates.

* * * * *

Cadderly kneeled above what was left of his prisoner, the man's torn head and shoulders. Black shadows of guilt assaulted the young priest's sensibilities, hov-ering images judging him, telling him that this helpless man's death was his fault.

Danica was beside the young priest, urging him to his feet.

Cadderly pulled his arm free and stared hard at the gruesome sight. He thought of going into the realm of spirits, to find the dead man and . . .

And what? Cadderly realized. Might he bring the spirit back? He looked behind him, to the man's chewed lower torso. Bring the spirit back to where? Did he possess the magics to mend the torn body?

"It is not your fault," Danica whispered, his thoughts obvious to her. "You gave the man a chance. That is more than most would have offered in our situation."

Cadderly swallowed hard, swallowed Danica's wise words and let them push away his dark thoughts, his guilt.

"It could have been any one of us," Danica reminded him.

Cadderly nodded and rose from the corpse. The hydra had come at all three of them, could have snapped Danica in half, and would have if she had not been so quick. Even if Cadderly had allowed the prisoner to keep his weapon, he could have offered no defense against the hydra's brutal initial charge.

"We have to be gone from here," Danica said, and again Cadderly nodded, turning to face the loose-hanging, scorched, and blasted door. He and Danica walked through it together, side by side, coming into a small anteroom. No living enemies presented themselves immediately, but that fact did little to calm the nervous companions, for leering gargoyles stared down at them from a ledge running around the top of the room, holding needle-sharp daggers, Talona's favored weapon. Demonic bas reliefs covered the stone of supporting pillars, hordes of ghastly things dancing about the deceptively beautiful Lady of

Poison. Tapestries surrounded the room, all depicting gory scenes of battle wherein evil hordes of goblins and orcs, their weapons dripping blood and poison, overran hosts of fleeing humans and elves.

A single chair dominated the floor; it sat atop a raised dais and was flanked by tall, iron statues of fierce warriors holding gigantic swords before them—while their other hands inconspicuously clasped tiny daggers. No other doors were apparent, though a curtain covered the section of wall immediately behind the chair.

With Danica hovering protectively about him, Cadderly called up the song of Deneir, searched for clues its notes could give to him about the nature of the many things around him. He stood easier when he detected no magical influences on the gargoyle sculptures, but nearly retreated when he turned to the iron statues. Parts of them—mouth and arms, mostly—tingled with residual magical energy.

"Golems?" Danica whispered, seeing the young priest's eyes open wide.

Cadderly honestly did not know. Golems were wholly magical creatures, animated bodies of iron, stone, or other inanimate materials. They would have seemed appropriate here, for such monsters were usually created by powerful wizards or priests to serve as guardians. Certainly with everything Cadderly had heard about Aballister, the thought of the wizard possessing iron golems, the most powerful of golemkind, was not out of the question. But Cadderly would have expected to detect more magic upon such a creature.

"Where to go?" Danica asked, her tone revealing that she was growing increasingly uneasy standing vulnerable in a wizard's anteroom.

Cadderly paused for a long moment. He felt that they should go to the curtain, but if these were iron golems, and he and Danica walked up between them . . .

Cadderly shook the unpleasant image from his mind. "The curtain," he said resolutely. Danica started forward, but Cadderly caught her by the arm. If she was to trust him, when he could not be sure that he should trust himself, then he would walk beside her, not behind her.

With his walking stick, Cadderly gingerly pushed the curtain aside, revealing a door. He started to turn to Danica, to smile, but suddenly, before either of the companions could react, the iron statues swung about, swords stopping barely an inch from them, one in front and one in back

"Speak the word," the iron statues demanded in unison.

Cadderly saw Danica tense, expected her to go in a rush at her metallic adversary. A few flickering notes slipped past his consciousness, and he saw, too, the building magical energy in the iron statues' arms, particularly in the less obvious arms holding the daggers. Cadderly did not have to use magic to guess that the tips of those sneaky weapons would likely be poisoned.

"Speak the word," the statues demanded again. Cadderly focused his senses on the magical energy, saw it rising to a dangerous crescendo.

"Do not move," he whispered to Danica, sensing that if she struck out, the two daggers would do their work with deadly efficiency. Danica's hands eased down to her sides, though she hardly seemed to relax. She trusted his judgment, but Cadderly honestly wondered if that was a good thing. The magical energy appeared as if it would soon boil over, and Cadderly still had not figured out how he might begin to counter or dispel it.

It seemed to the young priest as if the golems were growing impatient.

"Speak the word!" Their unified chant rang out as a final warning. Cadderly wanted to tell Danica to dive away, hoping that she, at least, might get free before the nasty daggers struck, or those swords chopped in.

"The word is Bonaduce," came a call from beyond the door, a female voice that the two companions recognized.

"Dorigen," Danica breathed, her face scrunched with sudden anger.

Cadderly agreed, and knew that trusting in Dorigen would surely be a move wrought of desperation. But something about the word, "Bonaduce," struck a note of truth, a note of familiarity, within the young priest.

"Bonaduce!" Cadderly yelled. "The word is Bonaduce!"

Danica's incredulous stare turned even more disbelieving as the golems shifted back to their frozen, impassive stances.

Cadderly, too, did not understand any of it. Why would Dorigen aid them, especially when they were in such dire trouble? He started forward for the door and pulled the curtain fully aside.

"It must be trapped," Danica reasoned softly, taking hold of Cadderly's arm to prevent him from reaching for the pull ring.

Cadderly shook his head and grabbed the ring. Before Danica could argue, he yanked the door open.

They came into a comfortably furnished room. Soft, padded chairs were generously placed, quiet tapestries of solid color lined every wall, and a bearskin rug carpeted the floor. The only hard-edged furnishing was a wooden desk, angled in a corner opposite the door. There sat Dorigen, tapping a slender wand against the side of her crooked, oft-broken nose.

Danica was down in a defensive crouch in an instant, one hand going down to her boot to draw a dagger.

"Have I mentioned before how much you both amaze me?" the woman calmly asked them.

Cadderly sent a silent, magical message into Danica's thoughts, bidding her to hold easy and see how this might play out.

"Are we any less amazed?" the young priest replied. "You gave us the password."

"So she might kill us herself," Danica added grimly. She flipped the dagger over in her hand, grasping it by the point so that she could flick it out at Dorigen in an instant.

"That is a possibility," the wizard admitted. "I have many powers—" she tapped the wand against her cheek, "—that I might use against you, and perhaps this time, our battle would have ended differently."

"Would have?" Cadderly noted.

"Would have ended differently if I held any intention of renewing our battle," Dorigen explained.

Danica was shaking her head, obviously not convinced. Cadderly, too, had trouble believing in the woman's sudden change of heart. He fell into the notes of his song, sought out the *aurora*, the aura sight.

Shadows flickered atop Dorigen's delicate shoulders, reflections of what was in her heart and thoughts. These were not huddled, evil things, as Cadderly expected, but quiet shadows, sitting in wait.

Cadderly came back from his spell, stared at Dorigen with heightened curiosity. He noticed Danica slide a step to the side and realized that she was trying to put some ground between them, giving the wizard only a single target.

"She speaks the truth," the young priest announced.

"Why?" Danica replied sharply.

Cadderly had no answer.

"Because I grow tired of this war," Dorigen responded. "And I grow tired of playing Aballister's lackey."

"You believe the horrors of Shilmista will be so easily forgotten?" Danica asked.

"I do not wish to repeat those horrors," Dorigen replied immediately. "I am tired." She held up her hands, fingers still bent from the beating Cadderly had given them. "And broken." The words stung Cadderly, but Dorigen's soft, benign tone did not.

"You could have killed me, young priest," the wizard went on. "You could now, probably, with my own ring, which you wear, if with nothing else."

Cadderly unconsciously clenched his hand, and felt the onyx-stoned ring with his thumb.

"And I could have let the golems kill you," Dorigen went on. "Or I could have assailed you with an assortment of deadly spells as you walked through the door."

"Is this repayment?" Cadderly asked.

Dorigen shrugged. "Weariness, more than that," she said, and the woman did indeed sound tired. "I have stood beside Aballister for many years, watched him assemble a mighty force with promises of glory and rulership of the region." Dorigen laughed at the thought. "Look at us now," she lamented. "A handful of elves, a pair of silly dwarves, and two children—" she indicated Cadderly and Danica with a wave of her hand, her expression incredulous, "—have brought us to our knees."

Danica moved again to the side, and Dorigen snapped the wand down in front of her, her face suddenly twisted with a scowl.

"Do we continue?" she demanded, poking the wand ahead. "Or do we let this play out as the gods always intended?"

Another silent message came into Danica's thoughts, compelling her to relax.

"What do you mean?" Cadderly asked.

"Is it not obvious?" Dorigen replied, and then she chuckled, remembering that Cadderly still had no idea that Aballister was his father. "You against Aballister, that is what this war is all about."

Cadderly and Danica looked to each other, both wondering if Dorigen had gone insane.

"That was not Aballister's intent," Dorigen went on, chuckling still between every word. "He did not even know that you were alive when Barjin began the whole affair."

The name of the dead priest caused Cadderly to unconsciously flinch.

"And certainly it was not your intent," Dorigen continued. "You did not, do not, understand the significance, did not even know that Aballister existed."

"You babble," Cadderly said.

Dorigen's laughter heightened. "Perhaps," she admitted. "And yet I must believe that it was more than coincidence that has brought us all to this point. Aballister himself played a part in it, a part that he will possibly regret."

"By starting the war," Cadderly reasoned.

"By saving your life," Dorigen corrected. Cadderly's face screwed up even tighter.

"Inadvertently," the woman quickly added. "His hatred for Barjin, his rival, outweighed his understanding of the poisonous thorn you would become."

"She lies," Danica decided, inching a step closer to the desk, apparently preparing to spring out and throttle the cryptic wizard.

"Do you remember your final encounter with Barjin?" Dorigen asked.

Cadderly nodded grimly; he would never forget that fateful day, the day he had first killed a man.

"The dwarf, the one with the yellow beard, was held fast by Barjin's magic," Dorigen prompted, and the image came clearly to the young priest. Ivan had stopped his advance toward the evil priest, had simply frozen in place, leaving Cadderly practically helpless. Cadderly was no powerful cleric back then, could barely win against a simple goblin, and the evil priest would surely have finished him. But Ivan came out from the enchantment at the last moment, allowing Cadderly to slip from Barjin's deadly clutches.

"Aballister countered the priest's magic," Dorigen announced. "The wizard is not your friend," she quickly added. "He holds no love for you at all, young priest, as is evidenced by the assassin band he sent to kill you in Carradoon."

"Then why did he aid me?" Cadderly asked.

"Because Aballister feared Barjin more than he feared you," Dorigen answered. "He did not anticipate what the gods had in store for him where young Cadderly was concerned."

"How, then, does it play out, wise Dorigen?" Cadderly asked sarcastically, tiring of the woman's private amusement and her cryptic references to the gods.

Dorigen motioned to the far wall, spoke a word of enchantment to reveal a swirling door of misty fog. "I was instructed to strike out at you with all my powers, and then retreat. I was to try to separate you from your friends and lead you through that door," she explained. "Therein lies Aballister's private mansion, the place where he planned to finish off the young priest who has become such a problem."

Cadderly studied Dorigen closely through every word, using his aura sight to determine any traps the woman might have in store. Danica looked to him for answers, and he shrugged, convinced, against his own reason, that Dorigen had again spoken truthfully.

"And so I surrender to you," Dorigen said, and Cadderly and Danica's surprise could not have been more absolute.

The woman laid her wand on the desk and sat back comfortably. "Go and play this out to the end, young priest," she bade Cadderly, again motioning to the swirling door. "Let the destiny of the region be determined by the private battle, as fate intended it all along."

"I do not believe in fate," Cadderly replied firmly.

"Do you believe in war?" Dorigen asked.

"Do not do it," Danica whispered over her shoulder.

Dorigen's smile was wide once more. " 'Bonaduce' will get you through this portal as well."

"Do not," Danica said again, this time loudly.

Cadderly walked away from her, walked toward the wall.

"Cadderly!" Danica called after him.

The young priest wasn't listening. He had come here to defeat Aballister, to decapitate the force of Castle Trinity, so that thousands needn't die in a war. This might be a trap, might be a portal that would take him to one of the lower planes and leave him there for eternity. But Cadderly could not ignore the possibilities presented to him by Dorigen's claims, by that swirling door, and he could not ignore the truths his magic had shown to him.

He heard Danica moving behind him. "Bonaduce!" he cried, and he jumped into the swirl, and was gone.

Nineteen

Friends Lost,
Friends Found

The four-foot-high counter surrounded the three trapped companions on two sides, with a thick column, floor to ceiling, supporting it on either end of the eight-foot front section. The wall blocked their backs, leaving only a small gap to get behind the counter on one side, wide enough for two goblins or one large man. So far, only a single enemy had opted to try that route—and he was summarily blasted away by the elf maiden with her deadly bow.

Ivan and Pikel stood atop the counter as the throng advanced, throwing taunts and throwing fists, though no enemies had yet come close enough to hit. At Ivan's proclamation that orcs were "born only to clean the gooey-greens outa ogre noses," three of the pig-faced humanoids took up a wild charge. The first skidded in the spilled soup as it was about to leap for Pikel, its back leg flying out from under it and its front leg straight out and up high. It slammed hard against the counter, its ankle and lead foot up above the ledge, and Pikel promptly brought his heel around the orc's toe and bent it down flat atop the counter, bringing his full weight atop it.

The trailing orcs stumbled about, but using their fallen friend as support, managed to hold a tentative balance as they banged against the side of the counter. Ivan's axe cleaved one in the side of the head, but the other managed to deflect Pikel's first clubbing attack. That orc was soon crushed against the side, though, as many of its companions, seeing the intruders suddenly pressed, rushed in.

"We cannot hold!" Shayleigh cried out.

"Just get yerself the archers," Ivan replied, huffing and puffing with each word as he worked his axe furiously to keep the sudden mob at bay. "Me and me brother'll handle this crew!"

Shayleigh looked helplessly to her nearly empty quiver. Her hand started for her short sword as a soldier came around to the open side, but the elf realized that she did not have the time to spare for melee combat. She lamented the waste of an arrow but shot the man down anyway, hoping that his sudden death might give other enemies pause before they tried a similar route.

The counter bucked suddenly as an ogre slammed against the back of the crowd, and Shayleigh thought it would break apart, thought that she would be crushed against the wall as the irrepressible monsters pushed on.

Her actions purely wrought of terror, she turned to face the counter and put an arrow in the ogre's face. It fell back and the counter appeared to resettle on its braces. Still unsure of its solidity, the elf maiden scrambled up on a shelf against the back wall, a position that afforded her a better view of the area beyond the immediate battle.

A man braced both his hands and one foot on the counter and started to leap up, thinking the dwarves too engaged to stop him. Ivan's axe promptly broke his spine, though the dwarf took a vicious hit on the hip for the distraction. Ivan grimaced in pain, growled the wound away, and chopped furiously at a goblin attacker, the dwarf's mighty axe smashing through the creature's upraised spear, and through the creature's upturned face.

Ivan couldn't revel in the kill, though, for the press of swords and spears, cruelly tipped pole arms and slashing daggers did not relent. The dwarf skipped and hopped, dodged and parried, and every now and then managed an offensive strike.

An arrow appeared suddenly, stuck halfway through Ivan's yellow beard, and the waves of pain that assaulted the dwarf told him that it had gashed his chin as well.

"I telled ye to get yerself the archers!" he cried angrily at Shayleigh, but his bluster was lost when he looked in the direction from which the arrow had come, looked to the enemy archer lying dead on the floor, and the elven-crafted arrow sticking from his forehead.

"Never mind," the humbled dwarf finished. He hopped as a sword sliced low across and came down with one boot trapping the weapon against the counter. Ivan kicked out, shattering the man's jaw, knocking him back into the mob. Two others took his place, though, and Ivan was sorely pressed once more.

Pikel fared little better. The dwarf scored three quick kills, but was bleeding in several places, with one of the wounds fairly serious. He worked his club back and forth, tried to forget the weariness in his muscled arms, tried to forget the obvious hopelessness of it all.

He swooped left, batting aside one lunging spear, but a sword sliced in behind his club, striking against something under his sleeve and then driving through to nick at Pikel's forearm.

"Ow!" the green-bearded dwarf squeaked, bringing his arm defensively in tight to his side. Pikel's pain flew away in a moment, though, replaced by shock when the upper half of his pet snake fell out of his sleeve onto the counter.

"Ooooooo!" Pikel wailed, his little legs pumping suddenly. "Ooooooo!"

The sword wielder came in a straight thrust, but Pikel caught the blade in a free hand and flung it aside, oblivious to the lines of blood growing on his unarmored hand. The dwarf's other arm pumped straight ahead, the end of his club slamming into the attacker's face. Pikel grabbed up the club in both hands and chopped three times in rapid succession, driving the man to the floor.

Then the furious dwarf whipped a backhand cut that flung a goblin, trying to use the moment to climb atop the counter, several feet away. Back and forth came the heavy club, swatting weapons, breaking bones. Back and forth with undeniable fury; no defenses withstood the roaring dwarf's assault.

"Ooooooo!"

An ogre threw men and orcs aside to charge the counter, leaped up bravely, stupidly. Pikel smashed its knee out, spun a complete circuit and hit it again as it fell, squarely in the chest, sending it tumbling into the crowd. With the enemies directly before him knocked away by the sprawling ogre, the outraged dwarf hopped sidelong.

"Ooooooo!"

A swordsman lunged for Ivan, but Pikel smashed the man's elbow against the lip of the counter before his sword ever got close.

"Hey, he's mine!" Ivan started to protest, but Pikel, not even hearing him, continued to wail and to batter. His next swipe snapped the man's neck, but the dwarf followed through too far on his backhand, clipping Ivan and sending him flying backward from the counter.

Pikel was not even aware that he now stood alone. All that he saw was his dead snake, the serpent that had befriended him. He ran back and forth along the counter, showing no weariness in his furiously pumping limbs, feeling no pain from his many, and mounting, wounds, tasting only sweet vengeance as he continued to beat back, to overwhelm, the suddenly hesitant mob.

"We need more support up in front!" Ivan bellowed angrily as Shayleigh helped him back to his feet.

"Arrows?" Shayleigh explained, indicating her empty quiver and the single arrow she held to her bowstring.

Ivan reached up and yanked the arrow out of his face. "Here's another one for ye," the dwarf explained grimly. He jerked suddenly, weirdly, then reached over his shoulder and produced yet another long bolt.

Shayleigh's eyes widened as she looked past the dwarf, looked to a table the enemy had rolled into position so that some archers might get shots through the opening at the side of the counter. She put up her bow immediately and fired, hitting only the wood of the blocking table, but forcing the enemy bowmen to duck down behind.

"I'll get ye some arrows!" Ivan bellowed as he turned to regard the scene. Out ran the dwarf, full speed. An archer popped his head up, taking a bead. But he lost his nerve as the roaring dwarf drew near, and his shot flew harmlessly high.

Ivan narrowed his focus straight ahead, ignored the many enemies shouting and pointing his way from the side. He lowered his head and hit the heavy table full force, knocking it back over onto its legs and winding up atop it.

The three stunned archers underneath looked up in surprise. They didn't realize how vulnerable they had suddenly become with their barrier now above them until an arrow whistled in, killing one.

Two sets of eyes looked back to Shayleigh; both men were relieved to see a goblin rush across, inadvertently intercepting the elf's next shot at the cost of its own life.

Ivan came over the back side of the uprighted table, rolled in at the men head first, the flat side of his axe smacking one of the remaining archers on the side of the head. The other man scrambled to get a dagger out and readied before the dwarf could right himself and bring his axe to bear again. But Ivan had let go of his weapon, scrambled in and clamped his strong hands against the sides of the remaining enemy's head.

A dagger cut into the dwarf's shoulder, but with a growl, Ivan heaved straight upward, the man's head going flat against the bottom of the table. The dwarf continued to press, planted his feet under him and his shoulders against the table and heaved up with all his strength. Ivan ducked low as the table flew up a foot and then started to descend, but he kept his arms, and the enemy's head, up high.

"Bet that hurt," the dwarf muttered as the table slammed back down, and the man's face scrunched up.

The man was sitting awkwardly, his legs twisted beneath him, his eyes still closed tightly. Ivan punched him in the face anyway, to get him out of the way, then the dwarf scooped up his axe and the nearest quivers and charged out from under the table, back for the counter area. A crossbow quarrel drove through his calf, and he pitched headlong, but he was up in a moment, running again, gnawing his thick lips against waves of searing pain.

Shayleigh had to spin about and put her third, and last, shot into the face of an orc that had slipped over the far side of the counter, around Pikel's continuing frenzy. When the elf maiden turned back Ivan's way, she found herself faced off against another goblin. Desperate, with no time to go for her sword, Shayleigh whipped her bow across, trying to drive the creature back.

"Yous is dead," the goblin promised, but Shayleigh shook her head, even smiled, seeing a large, double-bladed axe come up high behind the creature's head.

Ivan stumbled across the goblin's back as it fell. "Here're yer arrows!" he cried, tossing Shayleigh three nearly full quivers. He had no time to hear her reply, for he spun about, axe flying wildly before him, to knock aside a thrusting spear.

Shayleigh, too, spun about, fitting an arrow as she turned and firing above the counter opposite Ivan, firing once, and then again as the press became general on all three sides.

"Dead snake!" Ivan cried repeatedly, prodding his frenzied brother on. "Dead snake!"

"Ooooooo!" Pikel wailed, and another enemy was swatted away.

But Shayleigh knew that they would need more than Pikel's frenzy to hold out, and more than the two-score arrows Ivan had just given to her. Her arms pumped repeatedly, firing to the side and out in front beside Pikel, every shot scoring a direct hit, every shot blasting an opening for yet another enemy to step in.

* * * * *

"Bonaduce!" Danica called, and she headed for the wall, leaping up into the swirling fog. She hit the stone hard, and fell back, dazed, into the room.

She rolled in a defensive somersault, feeling betrayed and vulnerable. Dorigen had gotten rid of Cadderly, and the dangerous woman still held that wand. Danica turned another somersault, coming back to her feet more than halfway across the room from the still-sitting wizard.

"The password was Bonaduce," Danica accused.

"Only those so designated by Aballister may enter his private chambers, even with the word," Dorigen explained calmly. "He wanted to see Cadderly. Apparently, you were not included."

Danica's arm jerked suddenly, and one of her daggers flew at Dorigen. It sparked as it connected with a magical shield and bounced to the floor beside the woman, who promptly put her wand in line with Danica and held her free hand up, warning the monk to stay back.

"Treachery," Danica breathed, and Dorigen was shaking her head in denial through every syllable of the word.

"Do you believe that you will kill me with that wand?" Danica asked, beginning to circle, her balance perfect, her legs ready to launch her away, with every measured step.

"I do not wish to try," Dorigen replied sincerely.

"One spell, Dorigen," Danica growled. "Or a single try with your wand. That is all you will get."

"I do not wish to try," the older woman said again, more firmly, and to accentuate her point, Dorigen dropped the wand to the desktop.

Danica stood a bit straighter, her perplexed look genuine.

"I did not lie to you," Dorigen explained. "Nor did I trick Cadderly into going somewhere he does not truly belong."

Again, the indication was that Dorigen believed a larger fate to be guiding this encounter. Danica was not so convinced as her counterpart. She believed in the power of the individual, in the choice of the individual, and not in some predestined path.

"Aballister will likely punish me for letting the young priest through," Dorigen went on, against Danica's doubting expression. "He hoped I would kill

Cadderly, or at least exhaust Cadderly's magical powers." She chuckled and looked away, and Danica realized that she could spring atop that desk and throttle Dorigen before the wizard ever reacted. But Danica did not move, held by the continued note of sincerity in the wizard's voice.

"Aballister thought the malignant spirit, the evil personification of the *Ghearufu*, would end the threat to Castle Trinity," Dorigen went on.

"The ghost that you sent after us," Danica accused.

"Not so," Dorigen replied calmly. "Originally, Aballister did send the Night Masks to Carradoon to kill Cadderly, but the return of the spirit was purely coincidence—purely a fortunate coincidence as far as Aballister was concerned.

"He did not know that Cadderly could defeat that spirit," Dorigen continued, and again came that curious chuckle. "He thought that his storm would surely destroy you all, and so it would have, except that Aballister did not know that you were far from Nightglow by that point. Fearful would he have been indeed, if he learned that Cadderly could defeat even old Fyren after he was finished manipulating the wyrm."

Danica nearly fell over backward, her almond-shaped eyes opened wide.

"Yes, I watched that battle," Dorigen explained, "but I did not tell Aballister about it. I wanted his surprise to be complete when Cadderly arrived so soon at Castle Trinity."

"Is this penitence?" Danica asked.

Dorigen looked down at her desk and slowly shook her head, running her crooked fingers through her long black-and-silver hair. "More pragmatism, I would guess," she said, looking back to Danica. "Aballister has made many mistakes. I do not know that he will defeat Cadderly, or you and your other friends. And even if we win this day, how can we hope to conquer the region with our army shattered?"

Danica found that she honestly believed the woman's words, and that made her more defensive, fearing that Dorigen had cast some charm enchantment over her. "Your reversal now does not excuse your actions over the past months," she noted grimly.

"No," Dorigen agreed without hesitation. "Nor would I call it a 'reversal.' Let us see who wins in there." She indicated the swirling mist on the wall. "Let us see where fate guides us."

Danica shook her head doubtfully.

"You still do not understand, do you?" Dorigen asked sharply, and with the change in tone, the agile monk was down immediately into her threatening crouch.

"What are you talking about?" Danica demanded.

Dorigen's answering shout stole the strength from Danica's knees, hit her so unexpectedly that she could not even babble a retort. "They are father and son!"

* * * * *

Ivan fared the best of the three trapped friends as the fighting in the dining hall raged on. In the tight opening along the side of the cubby, the stout dwarf and his mighty axe formed an impenetrable barrier. Men and monsters came against him two at a time, but they couldn't hope to get by his furious defense. And though Ivan was sorely wounded, he took up a dwarven battle chant, narrowed his focus so greatly that it did not allow him to feel the pain, did not allow his wounded limbs to weaken.

Still, the relentless press of enemies prevented Ivan from going to his brother, or to Shayleigh, both of whom needed support. The best that the yellow-bearded dwarf could do was yell out, "Dead snake!" every now and again to heighten Pikel's fury.

Shayleigh blew away the first man who tried to come over the counter, hit the next adversary, a bugbear, with four arrows in rapid succession, the hairy creature slumping dead before it ever got atop the narrow area. Shayleigh then fired one to her side, between Pikel's legs, catching an orc in the face, then turned back as another enemy, a goblin, leaped up on the counter.

She shot it in the chest, dropping it to a sitting position, then shot it again, putting out the light in its eyes.

The goblins behind this victim proved smarter than usual, though, for the dead goblin did not fall away. Using its bleeding body as a shield, the next goblin in line came up atop the counter. Shayleigh got it anyway, in the eye as it peeked over its dead comrade's shoulder, but the rush as both creatures pitched in behind the counter gave the following goblin a clear path to the elf maiden.

With no time to notch another arrow, Shayleigh instinctively grabbed for her sword. She whipped her bow across with one hand, deflecting the straight-ahead spear attack, and just managed to angle her short sword in front of her as the goblin barreled in, its own momentum impaling it.

Shayleigh jerked the dead thing to the side, throwing it down, and tore free her blade, its fine edge glowing fiercely with its elven enchantments. She had no time to take up her bow, though, and knew that she wouldn't likely get a chance to put it to use in this fight again. She dropped it to the floor and rushed ahead, meeting the next adversary before it fully cleared the counter.

The goblin was off-balance, just beginning its leap to the floor, when Shayleigh got there, her sword snapping one way, knocking the goblin's defenses aside, and then the other. Quicker than the goblin could recover, Shayleigh poked her sword straight ahead, popping a clean hole in the creature's throat. She used its shoulders as a springboard as it slumped and got up to the counter at the same time as the next enemy soldier. The man hadn't expected the rush and was pushed back, sprawling into the pressing throng, leaving Shayleigh free to smash down at the orc that was next in line.

She killed it cleanly, but a spear arced over its shoulder as she bent for the strike.

Shayleigh stood very straight, tried to keep her focus through the sudden jolt and blur of agony. She saw the spear hanging low from her hip, saw a man grab at its other end. If he managed to twist the shaft about . . .

Shayleigh hit the spear just under its embedded tip with her sword. The fine-edged elven weapon slashed through the wood, but the shocking jolt nearly sent Shayleigh falling into blackness. She held on through sheer stubbornness, forcing her sword through her most familiar attack routines to keep the pressing foes at bay until the waves of dizziness swept by.

"Ooooooo!" Pikel's club did a rotating-end dance before the stupefied expression of an ogre. The giant monster swiped across with its hand, trying to catch the curious weapon, but by then, the club was gone, brought up high above the dwarf's head.

"Duh?" the ogre stupidly asked.

The club slammed down on its skull.

The ogre shook its head, its thick lips flapping noisily. It looked up to see what had hit it, looked up and up some more, its gaze continuing for the ceiling until it over-balanced and fell backward, taking down three smaller comrades under it.

Pikel, already down at the other end of the counter, didn't even see the ogre fall. A man had come up, and the dwarf slid down low, club swiping across to blow the man's feet out from under him.

A sword gashed Pikel's hip, but down low, he saw even more clearly his poor dead snake. His club came flashing across, snapping the sword wielder's head to the side, breaking the man's neck.

"Ooooooo!" Pikel was up in an instant, fury renewed. He skidded back the other way, defeating a potential breach, then came flying back again, tripping up a climbing goblin. The creature stumbled back, its chin slamming, and hooking, against the counter's lip.

That was not a good position with Pikel's club fast descending.

But how long could Pikel last? The dwarf, for all his rage, could not deny that his movements were beginning to slow, could not deny that the press of enemies had not relented, that two soldiers had come into the back of the dining hall for every one that the companions had killed. And the friends were all hurt, all bleeding, and all weary.

Across the hall, near the door, a man flew up into the air suddenly, over the ogre that was standing before him, his arms and legs flailing helplessly. Pikel glanced back curiously that way whenever he got the chance, glanced back just in time to see a huge sword explode through the front of the ogre's chest. With power beyond anything the dwarf had ever seen, the ogre's attacker tore the impaling sword straight up, tore it through the ogre's chest and collarbone to exit at the side of the dead creature's neck. A giant arm swung around, connecting on the ogre's shoulder with enough force to send the dead thing flying head over heels away.

And Vander—Vander!—waded ahead, his fierce swipes taking down enemies two at a time.

"Oo oi!" Pikel cried, pointing his stubby finger toward the door. Shayleigh, too, noticed the firbolg, and the sight renewed her hopes and her fury. Tangled with an orc atop the counter, she punched out with her free left hand, slamming the creature's jaw. She feigned a jerk with her sword, then punched again, and a third time.

The orc swayed, balanced precariously on the counter's edge. It somehow blocked Shayleigh's darting sword, but her flying foot got it squarely on the chest, knocking it backward.

"Vander is come!" she cried, so that Ivan, too, might know, and she rushed to the forward edge, crouching low and slicing down to drive back the next would-be attacker.

"That damned ring!" Ivan bellowed into the face of the man standing before him, referring to the magical, regenerative ring that Vander wore, a ring that had once before (and now, apparently again) brought the firbolg back from the dead.

Ivan's wild laughter gave his opponent pause. The dwarf brought his axe up over one shoulder, and the startled man reacted by throwing his sword up high.

Ivan loosened his grip with his bottom hand and drove his top hand down, the butt end of the axe shooting straight out to pop the man in the face. He fell back, dazed, and Ivan tossed his axe up into the air, and in a single, fluid motion, caught it low in both hands at the bottom of its handle and whipped it diagonally across, slashing the man's shoulder.

Near the middle of the room, a spearman jabbed at the firbolg's hip, scoring a minor hit. Vander twisted about and kicked, his heavy boot connecting with the man's belly, driving up under his ribs and launching him fifteen feet into the air. Vander spun back the other way, all his weight behind an overhead chop that cleaved a goblin half.

The sight proved too much for the goblin's closest companions. Howling with terror, they rushed from the room.

Too many other enemies presented themselves for Vander to consider pursuing the goblins. An ogre rushed in at him, its club coming across to score a direct hit on Vander's breast. Vander didn't flinch, but smiled wickedly to show his attacker that he was not hurt.

"Duh?"

"Why do they keep saying that?" the firbolg wondered, and his sword took the surprised ogre's head from its shoulders.

To the companions still at the counter, Vander's walk resembled a ship rushing through choppy seas, throwing a spray of goblins and orcs and men high into the air at his sides as he passed, leaving a wake of blood and broken bodies. Vander was at the counter in a mere minute, cutting the enemy force in half. Pikel came down beside him and together they blasted an opening around to the side so that Ivan, too, might link up.

By the time the three got to Shayleigh, she was sitting atop the counter, leaning heavily on the pillar support, for her remaining enemies had gone screaming away into the halls.

Vander picked up the wounded maiden, cradling her in one arm. "We must flee this place," he said.

"They'll be back," Ivan agreed. They looked to Pikel, who was reverently extracting the bottom half of his sliced snake from his torn sleeve, muttering a quiet, "Oooo," as each inch slipped free.

Twenty

Bolt for Bolt, Fire for Fire

Cadderly did not understand where he might be; this plush, carpeted room in no way resembled the harsh stone of the underground Castle Trinity. Gold leaf ornamentation and beautifully woven tapestries hung thick on the walls, all depicting images of Talona or her symbol. The ceiling was sculpted and decorated with some exotic wood that Cadderly did not recognize. Any one of the ten chairs in the huge room, their backs and seats carved to resemble teardrops, seemed worth a dragon's hoard of treasure, with sparkling gemstones running up their legs and armrests and silk upholstering covering them from top to bottom. The whole of the image reminded Cadderly of some pasha's palace in far off-Calimport, or the private chambers of one of Waterdeep's lords.

Until he looked deeper. The song of Deneir came into Cadderly's thoughts without his conscious bidding, as though his god was reminding him that this was no ordinary room, with no ordinary host. The place was extradimensional, Cadderly realized, created by magic, woven, to the last detail, of magical energy.

Looking more closely at the nearest chair, the song playing strong in his thoughts now, Cadderly recognized the gems as variations of magical energy, saw the smooth silk as a uniform field of magic and nothing more. Cadderly remembered an experience in the tower of the wizard Belisarius, when he had battled an illusory minotaur in an illusory dungeon. On that occasion, the young priest had perverted Belisarius's handiwork, had reached down the minotaur's throat and extracted an illusory heart of his own design.

Now, in this unfamiliar and obviously dangerous setting, Cadderly needed a boost to his confidence. He focused again on the chair, grabbed at the backing's magical field, and transmuted it, elongated it, and turned it flat.

"A table would look better here," he announced, figuring that his host, Aballister, could hear his every word. And so the chair became a table of polished wood with thick, curving supports carved with eyes and candles and rolled scrolls, the symbols of Cadderly's god and the brother god, Oghma.

Cadderly looked to the only apparent exit from the grand room, a wide hallway supported by sculpted arches running directly opposite the wall he had somehow walked through. He shifted the song of Deneir slightly, searching for invisible objects or other extradimensional pockets within this pocket, but saw no sign of Aballister.

The young priest moved to the table he had created, felt its smooth polish beneath its hands. He smiled as an inspiration—a divine inspiration, he mused—swept over him, then called upon his magic and reached out to the nearest tapestry, reweaving its design. He recalled the marvelous tapestry in the great hall of the Edificant Library, pictured its every detail in his mind, and made this one a nearly exact replica. A chair beside him became a writing desk, complete with an inkwell lined with Deneirian runes. A second tapestry became the scroll of Oghma, the words of the most holy prayer of that god replacing the former image, one of evil Talona and her poisoned dagger.

Cadderly felt his strength swell from the images of his own creations, felt as if his work was moving him closer to his god, his source of power. The more he altered the room, the more this place came to resemble a shrine at the Edificant Library, and the more the young priest's confidence soared. With every image of Deneirian worship he created, more loudly did the holy song play in Cadderly's thoughts and in his heart.

Suddenly, Aballister—it had to be Aballister—stood at the opening of the ornate hall.

"I have made some . . . improvements," Cadderly announced to the cross wizard, sweeping his arms out wide. His bravado might have hid his nervousness from his enemy, but Cadderly couldn't deny the moisture that covered his palms.

In a sudden motion, Aballister smacked his hands together and cried out a word of power that Cadderly did not recognize. Immediately, the new clerical dressings disappeared, leaving the room in its former state.

Something about the wizard's motion, about the sudden flash of anger from the obviously controlled man, struck a familiar chord in Cadderly, tugged at the edges of his consciousness from a distant place.

"I do not approve of the icons of false gods decorating my private chambers," the wizard said, his voice steady.

Cadderly nodded and brought an easy smile to his face; there really was no point in arguing.

The wizard walked to the side of the entrance, his dark robes trailing out mysteriously behind him, his hollowed gaze locked fully on the young priest.

Cadderly turned to keep himself squared to the man, studied every move the dangerous wizard made, and kept the song of Deneir flowing through his thoughts. Already several defensive spells were sorted out and in line, ready for Cadderly to release them.

"You have proven a great discomfort to me," Aballister said, his voice a wheeze, his throat injured from years of compelling forth mighty magics. "But also, a great benefit."

Cadderly concentrated on the tone of the voice, not on the specific words. Something about it haunted him, again from a distant place; something about it conjured images of Carradoon, of long ago.

"I might have missed all the fun, you see," Aballister went on. "I might have sat back here in comfort and let my formidable forces bring the peoples of the region under my thumb. I shall enjoy ruling—I do so love intrigue—but the conquest, too, can be . . . delicious. Do you not agree?"

"I have no taste for food gotten at the expense of others," Cadderly said.

"But you do!" the wizard declared immediately.

"No!" the young priest was even quicker to retort.

The wizard laughed at him. "You are so proud of your accomplishments to date, of the conquests that have brought you to my door. You have killed, dear Cadderly. Killed men. Can you deny the delicious tingle of that act, the sense of power?"

The claim was absurd. The thought of killing, the act of killing, had brought nothing more than revulsion to Cadderly. Still, if the wizard had spoken to him thus a few weeks before, when the guilt of having killed Barjin hung thick around Cadderly's shoulders, the words would have been devastating. But not any more. Cadderly had come to accept what fate had placed in his path, had come to accept the role that had been thrust upon him. No longer did his soul mourn for the dead Barjin or for any of the others.

"I did as I was forced to do," he replied with sincere confidence. "This war should never have started, but if it must be played out, then I play to win."

"Good," the wizard purred. "With justice on your side?"

"Yes." Cadderly did not flinch at all with the confident reply

"Are you proud of yourself?" Aballister asked.

"I will be glad when the region is safe," Cadderly answered. "This is not a question of pride. It is a question of morality, and, as you said, of justice."

"So cocksure," the wizard said with a soft chuckle, more to himself than to Cadderly. Aballister put a skinny finger to his pursed lips and studied the young priest intently, scanning Cadderly, every inch.

It seemed a curious gesture to the young priest, as though this man expected Cadderly, for some reason, to desire his approval, as though the wizard's estimation of Cadderly's measure might be an important thing to the younger man.

"You are a proud young cock in a yard of foxes," the wizard announced at length. "A flash of confidence and brilliance that is quickly lost in a pool of blood."

"The issue is bigger than my pride," Cadderly said grimly.

"The issue *is* your pride!" Aballister snapped back. "And my own. What is there in this misery that we call life beyond our accomplishments, beyond the legacy we shall leave behind?"

Cadderly winced at the words, at the thought that any man, particularly one intelligent enough to practice the art of wizardry, could be so singularly driven and self-absorbed.

"Can you ignore the suffering you have caused?" the young priest asked incredulously. "Do you not hear the cries of the dying and of those the dead have left behind?"

"They do not matter!" Aballister growled, but the intensity of the denial led Cadderly to believe that he had struck a sensitive chord, that perhaps there was some flicker of conscience under this man's selfish hide. "*I* am all that matters!" Aballister fumed. "*My* life, *my* goals."

Cadderly nearly swooned. He had heard those exact words before, spoken in exactly the same way. Again he pictured Carradoon, but the image was a foggy one, lost in the swirl of . . . of what? Cadderly wondered. Of distance?

He looked up again to see the wizard chanting and waggling the fingers of one hand in the air before him, his other hand extended and holding a small metallic rod.

Cadderly silently berated himself for being so foolish as to let down his guard. He sang out the song with all his voice, frantic to get up his defenses before the wizard fried him.

The words stuck in Cadderly's throat as a lightning bolt thundered in, blinding him.

"Excellent!" the wizard applauded, seeing his blast absorbed into blue hues around the young priest.

Cadderly, his vision returned, took measure of his protective shield, saw that the single attack had thinned it dangerously.

A second blast roared in, grounding out at Cadderly's feet, scorching the rug about him.

"How many can you stop?" the wizard cried, suddenly enraged. He took up his chant for a third time, and Cadderly knew that his protection spell would not deflect the full force of this one.

Cadderly reached into his pouch and pulled forth a handful of enchanted seeds. He had to strike fast, to interrupt the wizard's spell. He cried out a rune of enchantment and hurled the seeds across the room, triggering a series of popping, fiery explosions.

All images were stolen in the burst of swirling flames, but Cadderly was wise enough to doubt that his simple spell had defeated his foe. As soon as the seeds left his hand, he took up a new chant.

Aballister stood trembling with rage. All the room about the wizard smoldered, several small fires sizzled and sparked along the folds of a magical tapestry behind him. He seemed uninjured, though, and the area immediately around him was unscathed.

"How *dare* you?" the wizard asked. "Do you not know who I am?"

The wild look in the wizard's eyes, purely incredulous, frightened Cadderly, brought back distant memories and distant images, and made the young priest feel small indeed. Cadderly didn't understand any of it—what unknown hold might this wizard have over him?

"Your magics fended the lightning," Aballister cackled. "How do you fare against fire?"

A small glowing globe arced through the air, and Cadderly, distracted, could not dispel its magic in time. The fireball engulfed the room, except for Aballister's protected area, and Cadderly glowed green, as the same defensive spell he had used against old Fyren's breath successfully defeated the attack

But more insidious were the aftershocks of the wizard's spell. Smoke poured from the tapestries; sparks flew from all directions at the continuing release of magical energies. Each one ignited a new green or blue spot on Cadderly's defensive shields, further wearing at them. And the young priest had no defense against the thick smoke stinging his eyes, stealing his breath.

Cadderly could hear that Aballister was casting again. Purely on reflex, the young priest threw up his clenched fist and cried out, "*Fete!*" A line of fire shot out from his ring at the same time Aballister's next lightning bolt thundered in.

This one blew away the blue globe, snaked through to slam Cadderly in the chest and hurl him backward into the burning wall. His hair danced wildly, his blue cape and the back rim of his wide hat smoldering from the hot contact.

The air cleared enough for him to see Aballister once more, standing unhurt, his hollowed face contorted in an expression of rage. What magics did he possess to get through the wizard's seemingly impenetrable globe? the young priest wondered. Cadderly had known all along that wizardry was a more potent offensive force than clerical magics, but he hadn't expected Aballister's defenses to be so formidable.

Panic welled in the young priest, but he focused on the sweet harmonies of the song and forced his fears away. He worked fast to create the same reflective field he had used against the manticore; his only chance was to turn the wizard's magic back against him.

Aballister worked faster, waggling his skinny fingers again and uttering some quick runes. Bursts of greenish energy erupted from his fingertips and hurtled across the room. The first burned painfully into Cadderly's shoulder. The young priest stubbornly held his concentration, though, enacting the shimmering field, and the second missile, and the three flying behind that, seemed to disappear for an instant and then appear again, heading back the way they had come.

Aballister's eyes widened with surprise, and he instinctively started to dodge aside. As it had with Cadderly's spells, though, the wizard's globe absorbed the energy.

"Damn you!" the frustrated Aballister cried. Out shot the metallic rod, in thundered another lightning bolt, and Cadderly, still dazed and pained from the previous hits, still trying to find his breath in the thick smoke, ducked away.

The lightning blasted into the reflective field and shot back out the other way, smashing against Aballister's globe, throwing multicolored sparks in every direction.

"Damn you!" Aballister growled again.

Cadderly noted the frustration, wondered if the wizard might be running out of attack spells or if his globe neared the end of its duration. The battered young priest tried to hold on to that hope, to use Aballister's obvious distress as a litany against the pain and the hopelessness. He tried to tell himself that Deneir was with him, that he was not over-matched.

Another lightning bolt sizzled in, this one low, cutting a wake in the carpet and slipping under Cadderly's shield. The young priest felt the burst under his feet, felt himself flying suddenly, spinning in the air.

"Not so large a shield!" Aballister cried out, his tone brimming with confidence once more. "And pray tell, how does it handle angles?"

Lying on the floor, trying to shake away the stunning effects, Cadderly realized that he was about to die. He focused his thoughts on the wizard's last question, saw the wizard chanting again, holding that metal rod, but looking to the side, to the wall.

Desperation grabbed hold of the young priest, an instinctual urge to survive that momentarily numbed him from the pain. He heard the song of Deneir, remembered the bridge he had dropped in Carradoon and the walls he had caused to bite in the mountain valley. Frantically, he searched out the elemental makeup of the bare wall behind him.

Aballister's lightning bolt hit the wall to the side and deflected at a right angle. Cadderly, reaching for the wall behind him, grabbed its stone with his magical energy and pulled a section of the slab out, reshaping it.

The lightning bolt hit the back wall, would have deflected again at the perfect angle to destroy Cadderly, except that the wall's surface had changed, was now angled differently. The bouncing blast shot out straight across the room, again slamming the wizard's globe to shower harmlessly in multicolored sparks.

Still on the floor, Cadderly closed his eyes and fell more deeply into the song. More magical missiles came in, leaping around the reflective field, diving in to scorch and slam at the young priest. The divine song compelled Cadderly to fall into its sweetest notes, the notes of healing magic, but Cadderly understood that the delay created by attending to his wounds would only invite more attacks from the wizard.

He pushed the song in a different direction, heard the croak of his pained voice, and thought he would surely suffocate from the acrid smoke. Another missile slammed his face, scorching his cheek, feeling as if it had burned right to the bone.

Cadderly sang out with all his strength, followed the song into the elemental plane of fire, and pulled from there a hovering ball of flame that shot a line of fire down on the wizard.

Cadderly couldn't see any of it, but he heard Aballister's agonized cry, heard retreating footsteps clicking on the stone of the hallway beyond the room. The smoke continued to thicken, to choke him.

He had to get out!

Cadderly tried to hold his breath, but found no breath to hold. He tried to grab at the song, but his mind was too numb, too filled with confused images of his own impending death. He kicked and crawled, grabbing at torn carpet edges and pulling himself along blindly, hoping that he could remember the exact course out of the room.

Twenty-One

Truce?

Danica spent a long while staring blankly at Dorigen. Unsure of her feelings and stunned by the news that Dorigen had just given her, the monk had no idea of where to turn or where to go. And what was Danica to do with this dangerous adversary, this woman she had battled before, this woman she had told Cadderly to kill when he had Dorigen down and helpless in Shilmista Forest?

"I have no intention of interfering with this," Dorigen said, trying to answer some of the questions etched plainly on Danica's delicate features. "Against Cadderly or against you and your other friends."

Other friends! In all the craziness of the last few minutes—the fight with the hydra, the desperate attempt to get at the wizard Aballister—Danica had almost forgotten them.

"Where are they?" the monk demanded.

Dorigen held her hands out, her expression curious.

"We were separated in a corridor," Danica explained, realizing that Dorigen probably did not know the course that had gotten her to this room. "A corridor lined with many traps. Darkness engulfed us, and the end of the corridor tilted as one tried to pass through."

"The clerical halls area," Dorigen interrupted. "They are quite adept at defending their territory."

The woman's obviously derisive tone as she mentioned the clerics gave Danica hope that the apparent rivalries within Castle Trinity might reveal a weakness.

"The dwarves and the elf fell through trapdoors," Danica went on, though she wondered if she might be giving her enemy information that could be used

821

to the detriment of her lost friends. Danica sensed that she could trust Dorigen, had to trust Dorigen, and that realization put her doubly on her guard, again bringing fears that the wizard had used some enchantment on her. Danica reached within herself, sought out her discipline and her strong will. Few charms could affect one of her rigid mental training, especially if she was aware that one might be in place.

When she focused again on Dorigen, the wizard was slowly shaking her head, her expression grim.

"The giant went through a side chute," Danica went on, wanting to finish her thought before the woman cast some evil tidings over her.

"Then the giant has probably fared better than the others," Dorigen said. "The chute would place him in a lower passage, but the trapdoors . . ." She let the thought hang ominously, slowly shaking her head.

"If they are dead . . ." Danica warned, similarly letting the words hang unfinished. She dropped into a defensive position as Dorigen stood up behind the desk.

"Let us discover their fate," the wizard replied, taking no apparent heed of the threat. "Then we might better decide our next actions."

Danica had just begun to stand straight when the room's door flew open and a contingent of several armed guardsmen, a mix of men and orcs, rushed in. Danica leaped straight for Dorigen, but the wizard uttered a quick spell and vanished, leaving the monk to grab at empty air.

Danica spun about to face the approaching soldiers, six of them, fanning out with weapons drawn.

"Hold!" came a cry as Dorigen reappeared, standing along the wall behind the soldiers. The soldiers skidded to a stop and glanced back incredulously at Dorigen.

"I have declared a truce," Dorigen explained. She looked directly at Danica as she continued, "The fighting is ended, at least until greater issues can be resolved."

None of the fighters put up their swords. They glanced from the monk to the wizard, then looked to each other for some explanation, as though they feared that they were being deceived.

"What is you about?" one burly orc demanded of the wizard. "I gots fifty dead in the dinner hall."

Danica's eyes sparkled at the news; perhaps her friends were indeed still alive. "Fifty dead, and where are the enemies?" Danica had to ask.

"Shut up!" the orc roared at her, and Danica smiled at its unbridled anger. An orc rarely cared for the deaths of companions as long as the threat to its own worthless hide had been eradicated.

"The truce stands," Dorigen declared.

The burly orc looked to the soldier standing beside it, another orc, its filthy hands wringing its sword hilt anxiously. Danica knew that they were silently deciding whether or not to attack, and it seemed as if the wizard believed the same thing, for Dorigen was chanting softly. Dorigen blinked out of sight once more; the orcs turned to Danica, roared, and came on.

Dorigen reappeared right in front of the burly orc, her hands out before her, thumbs touching and fingers wide spread. The orc threw its arms up defensively, but the sheets of flame that suddenly erupted from the wizard's fingertips rolled around the meager fleshy barriers, licked at the creature's face and chest.

The other orc came in hard at Danica. She started for the desk, hopping as though she meant to go over it. The orc swerved, heading for the side, but Danica dropped back to her feet, and kicked its sword out wide. It tried to bring the weapon back in to bear, but Danica caught its wrist, then caught its chin with her free hand. She whipped the monster's head back and forth fiercely, then snapped a quick punch to its throat that dropped it in a gasping heap.

Danica's foot was upon the side of the orc's face in an instant, ready to snap its neck if any of its companions were advancing.

They were not, and all but one of them had replaced their weapons on their belts. The single enemy still holding his sword looked at Dorigen and the smoking corpse before her, looked at the fierce Danica, and quickly decided that his remaining friends were wise in putting up their weapons.

"I declare a truce," Dorigen growled at the soldiers, and none of them made any moves to indicate that they did not agree. Dorigen turned to Danica and nodded. "To the dining hall."

* * * * *

Cadderly lay on the stone floor, sucking air into his parched throat as the fires in the room behind him died away, having consumed the magical manifestations of curtains, tapestries, carpet, and wood.

Cadderly understood that this grand hallway was purely the image of stone, magical fields too dense to be sparked apart by mere flames. The young priest felt safe from any advancing flames, and he thought it a curious thing that the properties of such extradimensional pockets followed the same physical laws that governed true materials. What might be the potential, then, if he could create something in an extradimension, through the use of magic, and bring it back to his own plane? he wondered.

Cadderly filed the notion far away in his mind, reminding himself that his present business was more pressing than any hypothetical possibilities flashing around in his always questioning thoughts. He forced himself to his knees and noted the wizard's sooty footsteps on the floor, noted by their long stride and small imprint that Aballister had left the room in full flight.

A dozen yards down, with several doors lining either side of the corridor, the wizard had apparently realized his obvious tracks, for they simply disappeared, leaving Cadderly to figure out which way Aballister had gone.

Still kneeling, Cadderly took out his crossbow and loaded an explosive dart.

He laid the weapon on the floor beside him and realized, with a quiet nod of his head, that he held one advantage over Aballister, the greatest advantage of a cleric over a wizard. By Cadderly's estimation, Aballister had not been wise to break off the combat, no matter how badly Cadderly's pillar of flame had hurt him, for now the young priest fell back into the song of Deneir, let it take him where it had compelled him previously, into the sphere of healing.

He brushed a hand over his scorched cheek, closing the wound and perfectly mending the skin. He placed his hand firmly against the mark on his chest, where the lightning bolt had thundered home. When he took up his crossbow and stood, just a few minutes later, his wounds did not seem so serious.

But where to go? the young priest wondered. And what traps and wards had the clever Aballister set for him?

He moved to the nearest door, a simple, unremarkable one to his left. He scanned for any obvious traps, then called upon his magic to scrutinize it more fully. Unremarkable, it seemed, and from what Cadderly could tell, unlocked.

He took a deep breath to steady himself, held his crossbow out in front of him, grabbed the knob in one hand, and slowly turned it. He heard a distinctive click, a hissing sound as the door's edge slipped past the jamb.

The door flew from his hand, snapped open in the blink of an eye. A fierce, sucking wind grabbed at Cadderly, pulling him to the open portal. His eyes widened in fear as he came to realize that this was a gate to yet another plane— one of the lower, evil planes judging from the growling shadows and acrid smoke filling the unbordered region in front of him. He grabbed at the doorjamb and held on with all his strength, and held on, too, to his precious crossbow.

He was stretched out fully into the new plane, feet leading the way. Fearful tingles caressed his body, a sensation that evil things were near him, touching him! The pull was too great; Cadderly knew that he could not hold on for long.

Cadderly locked his hands in place and forced himself into a state of calmness. As he had done in the previous room, he used his magic to study the magic of this area, of the door and the threshold.

All of the portal area was magical, of course, but a single spot stood out to Cadderly, its emanations of magic different and more intense than the fields about it. The young priest let go with one hand, straightened his crossbow, and drew a bead.

He couldn't be sure if this was the place of the actual gate, the specific key to the interplanar barrier, but his actions were wrought of desperation. He put the crossbow in line and let fly. His shot did not hit the mark, but struck close enough so that the resulting explosion encompassed the target spot.

The wind stopped. Cadderly's instincts and mounting knowledge of magic screamed at him to roll for the threshold, to tuck his legs in and get his hands clear of the doorjamb. He was wise enough not to question those instincts, and he dove headlong for the threshold, just ahead of the suddenly swinging door.

The door snapped shut, slamming Cadderly and pushing him on his way. He stopped rolling when he hit the corridor's opposite wall, his legs and lower back bruised and sore. He glanced back and was amazed as the door swelled and shifted shape, twisting tightly into place, seeming to meld with the surrounding jamb.

Aballister's extradimensional mansion apparently protected itself from such torn planar rifts. Cadderly managed a smile, glad that Aballister's work had been so complete and so farsighted, glad that he was not hanging in some nonspace, some formless region between the known planes.

Ten steps down the stone corridor two more doors loomed. One was unremarkable, like the one Cadderly had just encountered, but the other was iron-bound with heavy straps and showed a keyhole below the handle. Cadderly searched for traps, checked around the edges for any areas that might reveal this, too, to be a portal to another plane. Nothing dangerous became apparent, so he reached down and slowly turned the handle.

The door was locked.

It crossed Cadderly's mind more than once in the next few seconds that Aballister might be harboring yet another of his pet monsters behind this door, that blowing it open might put him into a fight with another hydra, or perhaps even something worse.

The flip side to that argument, of course, was that Aballister might be behind this door, recuperating, preparing some devilish magics.

Cadderly leveled the crossbow at the lock and fired, shielding his eyes from the expected flash. He used the moment to put another dart in place, and when he looked back, he found a scorch mark where both the lock and the handle had been, and the door hanging loose on its hinges.

Cadderly ducked to the side and pushed the door in, crossbow ready. His bow slipped down, his smile widened once more when he realized the contents of this room—an alchemy shop.

"What might bring you out of hiding, wizard?" the young priest muttered under his breath. He pushed the door closed behind him and crossed to the beaker-covered tables. Cadderly had read many texts on potions and magical ingredients, and though he was no alchemist, he knew which ingredients he could safely mix.

And, more importantly for what the young priest now had in mind, which ingredients he could not.

* * * * *

Ivan and Pikel led the charge down one corridor, cut through a room to the side, and headed out a back door into another corridor. Vander came roaring right behind them, still cradling Shayleigh, though the elf maiden was conscious and demanding to be put down. No enemies stood against the friends for this first scrambling rush. The enemy soldiers they encountered, even two ogres, fell all over themselves trying to run away. Ivan, more wounded than he cared to admit, let them go. The dwarf wanted only to find Cadderly and Danica, or to find some place where he and his three companions might hide and recover.

Through the back door of another room, the two dwarves surprised a man trying to come through the other way. He had just grabbed the door's handle when Pikel's club hit the thing, launching him across the corridor to slam against the wall. Both dwarves swarmed across the corridor and fell over him, Ivan connecting with a left hook, Pikel with a right, at the same time, on opposite sides of the unfortunate man's face.

Ivan considered finishing the unconscious soldier as his friends ambled past, but he put up his axe and ran after them. "Damned young colt," he muttered, referring to Cadderly, whose constant demands for compassion had apparently worn at the tough-skinned dwarf.

"To the side!" Shayleigh cried as Vander and Pikel dashed across the entrance to a side passage.

"Oo!" Pikel squeaked, and he and the firbolg sprinted on, a group of enemy soldiers wheeling around the corner behind them.

Ivan barreled into the midst of the force, his great axe chopping wildly.

Twenty feet ahead, Vander put down Shayleigh, who went right to work stringing an arrow. The firbolg spun about beside Pikel, determined to crash through to Ivan's rescue. The two had only taken a step or two when Shayleigh cried out, "The other way!"

Sure enough, enemies poured into the corridor from another side passage farther down, a large force led by a contingent of ogres. Shayleigh put three arrows into immediate flight, felling one of the leading ogres, but another took its place, running right over the monster's back as it fell.

Shayleigh fired again, scored another hit, and put her next arrow to her bowstring. She couldn't hold them back, though. Even if every shot were perfect, if every shot killed an enemy, she would surely be buried where she stood.

She fired again, and then the ogre was upon her, its club up high, a victorious scream erupting from its huge head.

Vander's forearm slammed it in the chin and knocked it flying into its comrades. The firbolg's great sword swiped across, disemboweling the next ogre, driving the enemies farther back.

Ivan chopped and spun, every swipe connecting. He saw an arm go flying free of one orcan torso and smiled grimly, but that smile was smacked away as he continued to turn and a goblin's club slammed him squarely in the face, taking out a tooth.

Dazed, but still swinging, the dwarf backpedaled and sidestepped, trying to keep his balance, knowing that to fall was to be overwhelmed. He heard his brother calling from not far away, heard an enemy grunt and groan as Pikel's club smacked hard against bare skin. Something slashed Ivan's forehead. Blinded by his own blood, he chopped out, connecting solidly. He heard Pikel again, to the side, and took a stumbling step in that direction.

An ogre's club caught the yellow-bearded dwarf in the lower back, launched him tumbling through the air. He crashed through several bodies, the last being Pikel's, and went down atop his brother.

Pikel heaved Ivan over behind him and hopped back to his feet, clubbing wildly at the tangled mass in front. He squeaked frantically for his brother to join him, and Ivan tried, but found that his legs would not move to his mind's call.

Ivan struggled to stand, to get beside his brother. He realized only then that he had somehow lost his axe, realized that he could not see and could not stand. Darkness engulfed his thoughts as it had his eyes, and the last thing he felt was slender but strong hands grabbing his shoulders and hauling him backward along the floor.

* * * * *

They were greeted at the dining room entrance by the groans and shrieks of the wounded. Danica started forward, her first instincts telling her to run through the carnage and seek out her friends. She stopped immediately, though, and spun about, hands crossing before her.

The sight of their dead comrades had put the soldiers who had accompanied Danica and Dorigen into a rage, and two of them stood right before the monk, their spears leveled, their faces firmly set for battle.

"The truce holds," Dorigen said calmly, acting not at all surprised by the piles of dead and mutilated Trinity soldiers.

One of the spearmen backed away, but the other stood unblinking, unmoving, trying to decide if the consequences of disobedience would outweigh the satisfaction of impaling this intruder.

Danica read his thoughts perfectly, saw the boiling hatred in his eyes. "Do it," she prodded, as eager to strike at him as he was to hit her.

Dorigen put her hand on the man's back. Flickers of electricity arced up the wizard's body, slipped down her arm and through her fingers, blowing the man to the floor several feet away. He rolled to a sitting position, the shoulder of his leather tunic smoking, metal speartip split in half, and hair dancing on end.

"The next time, you will die," Dorigen promised grimly, to him and to the other soldiers milling nervously nearby. "The truce holds."

The wizard nodded to Danica, who sped off around the room. She quickly discerned that her friends had made their valiant stand behind the small counter at the back of the hall. Finding their trail as they left the place was not difficult, since it was dotted with blood.

"M'lady Dorigen!" cried a man, rushing in behind the wizard and her soldiers. "We have them!"

Danica's almond eyes flickered at the painful news, and she ran back across the hall.

"Where?" Dorigen demanded.

"Two passages over," the man was happy to report, though his smile lessened when he noticed Danica running free. He gripped his weapon tightly, but, thoroughly confused, made no immediate moves to threaten the dangerous monk.

"Are they dead?" Danica asked, demanded.

The man looked to Dorigen plaintively, and she nodded that he should answer.

"They were alive by last reports," he replied, "but fully surrounded and sorely pressed."

Danica was again surprised by the sincerity in Dorigen's alarmed expression.

"Quickly," the wizard said to her, and Dorigen took Danica's hand and ran off, the shrugging, confused soldiers of Castle Trinity falling into ranks behind them.

*   *   *   *   *

Pikel dodged back and forth along the corridor, his club holding back the enemy line while Shayleigh picked her deadly shots around him. Pikel's club rarely came close to hitting anything other than an enemy weapon, but the corridor was fast filling with dead and wounded.

Shayleigh emptied one quiver, began working furiously on another.

"Ogre!" she heard Vander yell, and she had to spin about. An ogre had slipped past the furious firbolg and was bearing down on the elf. She put her bow up quickly and fired point-blank, her arrow disappearing into the fleshy bulk. But the ogre was not stopped, and the clubbing it gave Shayleigh sent her flying back against the wall, tumbling over Ivan. On the very edge of consciousness, she tried again to load her bow as the monster advanced.

Pikel glanced back over his shoulder—and a sword slipped over his lowered club to slash his upper arm.

"Ow," he groaned, and he turned back just in time to see another sword slip in the other way, gashing his other arm.

"Ow."

The dwarf darted forward in a feigned charge, and his enemies fell back, then he swung around, transferring the momentum of his spin into his wide-flying club. The ogre roared as its hip bone cracked loudly, and it lurched to the side.

Shayleigh's next arrow dove into its chest; Vander's heavy sword gashed into its side.

It fell headlong over Pikel as he muttered, "Uh-oh," and dove forward, trying desperately to get away. A man behind Pikel, fully intent on the dwarf, did not react quickly enough and was squashed under six hundred pounds of ogre flesh.

Pikel, laid out straight, scrambled and clawed his way from under the prostrate torso, past the ogre's hips and right out between its legs.

Other enemies had run over the creature's back and were waiting for, and stabbing at, the dwarf as he reappeared. He squeaked, "Ow! Ow!" repeatedly, taking stinging hit after stinging hit, trying to get his balance and turn about, that he might fend off the wave of weapons.

An arrow cut the air above him, and he used the distraction and the shield of a falling body to roll all the way out from under the fallen ogre. Three scrambling steps put him beside Shayleigh, the elf now holding her sword low before her, standing unsteadily.

"Together," she mumbled to Pikel, but as she spoke, a club twirled through the air and smashed her in the face, and she fell heavily to the stone.

More clubs and daggers came flying the dwarf's way. Pikel's waving club blocked a few; he looked down curiously to regard a dagger's hilt quivering from his shoulder, looked curiously to his arm that had suddenly fallen limp to his side.

Pikel tried to backtrack, stumbled and fell over Shayleigh, and had not the strength to get back up.

The side of her face against the stone, only one eye opened, Shayleigh noted the measured approach of the enemy horde, though her fleeting consciousness could not comprehend the grim consequences. The elf saw only blackness as a heavy boot slammed to the stone right before her face, its heel only an inch away from her bleeding nose.

Twenty-Two
Trump Card

Cadderly ran from the alchemy shop, pulling the ruined door closed behind him. A moment later the young priest was sprawled out on the floor, and that ironbound door was no more than a pile of burning kindling against the corridor's opposite wall. Cadderly hadn't expected the mixture to react so quickly! He put his feet under him and started running, managing to hold his balance as a second blast rocked the area, this one blowing apart the door opposite the alchemy shop and cracking the walls along the corridor.

Cadderly rounded a corner, glancing back as a fireball engulfed the area. He could only hope that the second door he had ruined was not another portal to the lower planes, could only hope that some evil, horrid denizens would not come leaping through into the corridor behind him.

He ran past another door, then skidded as he crossed by yet another, this one made of iron, not wood, and hanging open.

"What have you done?" came an angry cry from inside.

I have forced you to face me, Cadderly answered silently, a satisfied look stealing the trepidation from his face. He moved slowly to the iron door, pushing it all the way open.

Cages and glass cases of various sizes lined the huge room's walls, and a tumult of growls and squawks greeted the young priest. The wizard stood across the way, in front of another door and between the four largest cages. Three of these were empty—for the manticore, the chimera, and the hydra? Cadderly wondered—but the fourth held a creature that would grow into a fearsome beast indeed. A young dragon, its scales glossy black, narrowed its reptilian eyes evilly as it regarded Cadderly.

Cadderly noted the slight trembling of the wizard's shoulders, could tell that the exhausted man's magical energies had been greatly taxed. And the young priest's pillar of flame had hurt Aballister, for the side of the wizard's neck was red and blistered, and his fine blue robe hung in tatters.

Another explosion rocked the extradimensional complex.

Aballister gnashed his teeth and shook his head. He tried to speak, but his words came out as a singular growl.

Cadderly did not know how to respond. Should he demand the man's surrender? He, too, was weary, perhaps as weary as the older wizard. Perhaps this fight was far from over.

"Your war against Shilmista Forest was unjustified," the young priest said, as calmly as he could manage. "As was Barjin's attack on the Edificant Library."

The wizard chuckled. "And what of the attack in Carradoon?" he brazenly asked. "When I sent the Night Masks to kill you."

Cadderly believed that the man was daring him to act, was baiting him to make the first move. He looked again to that young black dragon, staring at him hungrily.

"There is still the option of surrender," Cadderly remarked, trying to equal the wizard's confidence.

"I might accept your surrender," Aballister replied sarcastically, "or I might not!" The wizard's dark eyes flashed suddenly, and his hands began a circling motion.

Cadderly had his readied crossbow up in an instant and launched the dart at Aballister without the slightest hesitation. His shot was true, but the dart skipped off the wizard's newest magical shield and struck up high on the back wall, blowing a clean hole. Sparks flared at the scorched edges, the force of the explosion threatening to unravel the binding magical energies—magical energies that were already being assaulted from the continuing bursts from the alchemy shop.

As soon as the dart skipped wide, Cadderly knew that he was vulnerable. His choice of a conventional attack prevented him from throwing up a defensive shield. Fortunately, the wizard's attack came in the form of fire, with Aballister hurling a small ball of flame across the room. The fire hit Cadderly squarely, would have burned his face and hair except that enough of his protective globe remained so that the flames were dispersed into a green glow.

The young priest recovered from the shock quickly, reaching into his pouch for some seeds to hurl back. Cadderly dropped them right back into the pouch, though, and nearly swooned, for it was neither his turn to attack, nor the wizard's.

The black dragon spit a line of acid from between the bars of its cage.

Cadderly cried out and spun, falling away to the side. He did not throw his arms up in front of him (and if he had, they surely would have been charred) as his instincts demanded. He used the training Danica had given to him, threw as much of his body as he could out of harm's way. The acid slashed across his chest, burning and biting at his skin. Rolling on the floor, Cadderly saw that his tunic was burning, that his bandoleer was burning.

His bandoleer was burning!

Screaming in terror and in pain, the young priest twirled up to his knees and pulled the bandoleer over his head. Apparently thinking that the battle had turned his way, Aballister paid Cadderly's frantic movements no heed, was deep in the throes of casting another spell.

Cadderly put the flaming bandoleer into a few quick spins over his head like a lasso and hurled it across the room, diving for cover as he threw, curling up in a fetal position with his hands tucked behind his head.

Aballister screamed in shock and fear, and the dragon roared as the first of the magical darts exploded.

One after another, the tiny bombs went off, each blast seeming louder than the one before. Metal tips and ends of the darts whipped about the room, pinging off metal bars, ricocheting off stone walls, and smashing glass.

Cadderly could not count the explosions, but he knew that he still had well over thirty darts in his bandoleer. He tightened his arms instinctively about his head, continued to scream if for no better reason than to block out the terrible tumult in the room.

And then it was over, and Cadderly dared to look out. Residual sparking fires had been lit all about the huge room. The dragon lay dead, its torso shredded by many flying darts, but the wizard was nowhere to be seen.

Cadderly had started to stand when out of the corner of his eye he noticed a giant snake slipping out of the broken side of a glass container. He put his walking stick in the constrictor's face, held it back until he could quick-step past.

A metal pole to the other side disintegrated in a flash of light. Another followed suit, and Cadderly began to understand that he had inadvertently unlocked the bindings of this entire magical pocket.

The young priest rushed across the room, through the far door, and into another, narrower corridor. The wizard stood forty feet away, one arm limp at his side, blood oozing from his shoulder, and his face blackened with soot.

"Fool!" Aballister yelled at him. "You have broken my house, but have damned yourself in its collapse!"

It was true, Cadderly realized. The magical bindings were unraveling. He started to reply, but Aballister wasn't listening. The wizard scurried through a nearby door and was gone.

Cadderly ran up and tried to follow, but the heavy wooden door would not budge. There came another explosion, and the floor bucked violently, knocking him to one knee. He glanced frantically up and down the corridor, looking for some escape; he grabbed up his crossbow, only to remember that he had no more explosive darts.

Glaring light flickered through the open door he had left behind—the light of disintegrating material, Cadderly knew. He tried to fall into his magic, to search the song for a way out.

A flash ran along the ceiling above him, leaving a wide crack in its wake, and Cadderly realized that he did not have time.

He took up his adamantite spindle-disks and looped the cord over his finger. He sent them into a few fast movements, running them down to the end of the cord, then snapping them back into his palm, to tighten the cord.

"I hope you made these good," he mumbled, speaking as if Ivan Boulder-shoulder were standing next to him. With a determined grunt, the young priest hurled the spindle-disks at the door, and they cracked off the wood, knocking a deep dent in its surface. A flick of Cadderly's wrist sent them spinning back to his hand, and he hurled them again, at the same spot.

The third throw popped a hole in the wood and a fierce wind filled with red stinging dust assaulted Cadderly. He kept his balance and his composure and whacked the door again, his spindle-disks widening the hole.

The flickering light to his side became continuous, and Cadderly glanced that way to see the very corridor dissolving, arcing fingers of electricity leading the way toward him, breaking apart the magically created stone so that it might be consumed.

Barely twenty feet away loomed nothingness.

Cadderly's weapon hit the door with all his strength behind it. He couldn't even see through the stinging dust, just flailed away desperately.

Ten feet away, the corridor was gone.

Cadderly sensed it, hurled the disks one final time, and threw all his weight against the weakened door.

* * * * *

Danica and Dorigen worked their way past scores of swarming Trinity soldiers, men and monsters alike. Many stopped to regard the fierce monk curiously, but seeing Dorigen beside Danica, they only shrugged and went on their way.

Danica knew that Dorigen could have had her overwhelmed with a single word at any time, and she spent more time looking at the wizard than at the scrambling soldiers, trying to figure out exactly what was motivating Dorigen.

They heard the firbolg's roar from beyond as they came up on one corner, heard the wind-cutting sweep of Vander's great sword and the frantic cries of dodging enemies. A goblin rushed around the bend, skidding to a stop right before Dorigen.

"Three of 'ems is down!" it shrieked, holding four crooked fingers up before it. "Three of 'ems is down!" A sickly feeling washed over Danica. "Three of 'ems is down!" The goblin's smile disappeared under the weight of Danica's fast-flying fist.

"We have a truce," Dorigen calmly reminded the volatile monk, but it seemed to Danica that Dorigen was not overly concerned, was even amused, by the wounded goblin squirming about on the floor.

Danica was up to the corner in an instant, peering around at the sight she feared to view. Ivan, Pikel, and Shayleigh lay helpless on the floor, with Vander, showing a dozen grievous wounds, straddling them, the firbolg's huge sword working back and forth furiously to keep the multitude of pressing enemies back.

An orc cried out something Danica did not understand, and the enemy troops broke ranks, rushing away from the firbolg, rushing past Danica and turning, diving, into the corridor behind her. She understood the retreat when the scene cleared, revealing a battery of crossbowmen down the hall beyond the firbolg, weapons leveled and ready.

Vander cried out in protest, apparently realizing his doom. Then a glowing apparition of a hand appeared behind him, touched him, and he swung about, his sword cutting nothing but the empty air.

Danica's first reaction was to spin and clobber the wizard, guessing that Dorigen must have been the one who had brought forth the spectral hand, and fearing what the wizard might have done to Vander. Before the monk moved, though, the crossbow battery opened up, launching a score of heavy bolts Vander's way.

They skipped and deflected harmlessly off the firbolg. Some stopped in midair, quivering before Vander, then fell, their momentum expended, to the ground.

"I am true to my word," Dorigen said dryly, walking past Danica and into the open corridor. She called for Vander to be at ease, called for her own troops to cease the fighting.

Some soldiers, orcs mostly, near Danica eyed the monk dangerously, clutching their weapons as though they did not understand and did not trust the strange events.

The soldiers who had accompanied the monk and Dorigen from the wizard's area, who had witnessed Dorigen's fury against the orc that had gone against her commands, sent a line of whispers spreading throughout the ranks, and Danica soon relaxed, the threat apparently ended. She rushed around the corner, found Vander, too, slumping against the wall, thoroughly exhausted and gravely wounded.

"It is over?" the firbolg asked breathlessly.

"No more fighting," Danica answered. Vander closed his eyes and slid slowly down to the floor, and it seemed to Danica that he would die.

Danica found the dwarves and Shayleigh alive, at least, and Shayleigh actually managed to sit up and raise one hand in greeting. Ivan was by far the worst off of the three. He had lost a lot of blood and was losing more even as Danica tried futilely to stem the flow. Even worse, his legs had gone perfectly limp and were without feeling.

"Have you any healers?" Danica asked of Dorigen, who was standing over her.

"The clerics are all dead," a nearby soldier answered for the wizard, his words sharp-edged as he, too, tended to a wounded man, a Trinity soldier fast slipping into the realm of death.

Danica winced, remembering Cadderly's brutal work against that group, thinking it terribly ironic that his necessary actions against Trinity's priests might now cost his friends their lives.

Cadderly! The word assaulted Danica as surely as would an enemy spear. Where was he? she wondered. The potentially disastrous consequences of his showdown against Aballister, his father, rang clearer to the monk now, with Ivan cradled helplessly in her arms. Shayleigh seemed stronger with every passing moment; Vander's cuts had already clotted and were somehow mysteriously on the mend; and Pikel groaned and grumbled, finally rolling over with a curious, "Huh?"

But Ivan . . . Danica knew that only his dwarven toughness was keeping him alive, doubted that even that considerable strength would support him for much longer. Ivan needed a priest who could access powerful spells of healing—Ivan needed Cadderly.

Dorigen ordered several men to assist Danica in her efforts, sent several others to the priests' private quarters to search for bandages and healing potions and salves. None of the men, standing in the blood of their own allies, seemed overly eager to aid the brutal intruders, but none dared to disobey the wizard.

Danica, pressing hard against a pumping wound in Ivan's chest, her armed soaked with blood, could only wait and pray.

* * * * *

The small sun shone red. The air was hazy with swirling dust, and the rocky, barren landscape ranged from orange hues to deep crimson. All was quiet, save for the endless, mournful call of the gusting, stinging wind.

Cadderly saw no life about him, no plants or animals, no sign even of water, and he couldn't imagine anything surviving in this desolate place. He wondered where he was and knew only that this barren region was nowhere on the surface of Toril.

"No place that has any name," Aballister answered the young priest's unspoken question. The wizard walked out from a nearby tumble of boulders and stood facing Cadderly. "At least none that I have ever heard."

Cadderly took some comfort in the fact that he could still hear Deneir's song playing in his mind. He began to sing along, quietly, his hand with the magical ring clenched at his side.

"I would be very careful before attempting any spells," Aballister warned, guessing his intent. "The properties of magic are not the same here as they are on our own world. A simple line of fire—" the wizard looked to the ring as he spoke, "—might well engulf this entire planet in a ball of flame."

"It is the dust, you see," the wizard continued, holding his hand up into the wind, then folding his long, skinny fingers to rub against the red powder in his palm. "So volatile."

Aballister's sincere calm bothered the young priest. "Your extradimensional home is no more," Cadderly said, trying to steal the wizard's bluster.

Aballister frowned. "Yes, dear Cadderly, you have become such a bother. It will take me many months to reconstruct that magnificent work. It was magnificent, don't you agree?"

"We are stranded." It was spoken as a statement, but Cadderly, fearful that his words might be true, privately intended it as a question.

Aballister's face screwed up incredulously, as though he thought the claim absurd. Cadderly took comfort in that, for if the wizard possessed some magic that would get them home, the young priest believed that Deneir would show him the way, as well.

"You are not a traveler," Aballister remarked, and he shook his head, seeming almost disappointed. "I never would have guessed that you would become so paralyzed by the comforts of that miserable library."

Now it was Cadderly who screwed up his face. What was the man saying? He never would have guessed? What revelations lay in the wizard's choice of words, his choice of tense?

"Who are you?" Cadderly asked suddenly, without thinking, without even meaning to speak the thought aloud.

Aballister's burst of laughter mocked him. "I am one who has lived many more years than you, who knows more about you than you believe, and who has defeated men and monsters much greater than you," the wizard boasted, and again his tone reflected sincere serenity.

"You may have done me a favor with your stubborn determination and your surprising resourcefulness," Aballister went on. "Both Barjin and Ragnor, my principle rivals, are dead because of you, and Dorigen as well, I would guess, since you came into my home alone."

"Dorigen showed me the way in," Cadderly corrected, more interested in deflating Aballister than in protecting the woman. "She is very much alive."

For the first time, Aballister seemed truly bothered, or at least perplexed. "She would not appreciate your telling me of her treachery," he reasoned. He started to elaborate, but stopped suddenly, feeling an intrusion in his thoughts, a presence that did not belong.

Cadderly pressed the domination spell, the same one he had used to "convince" Dean Thobicus to allow him to head out for Castle Trinity. He focused on the area of blackness he knew to be Aballister's identity, sent forth a glowing ball of energy to assault the wizard's mind.

Aballister stopped the glowing ball and pushed it back toward the young priest. *How easily you work around the limitations of our physical surroundings,* the wizard congratulated telepathically. *Though you prove yourself a fool to challenge me so!*

Cadderly ignored the message, pressed on with all his mental strength. The glowing ball of mental energy seemed to distort and flatten, moving not at all, as Aballister stubbornly pushed back.

You are strong, the wizard remarked.

Cadderly held similar feelings for his adversary. He knew his focus on the ball was absolute, and yet Aballister held him at bay. The young priest understood the synaptic movements of Aballister's thoughts, the clear flow of reasoning, the desperation of curiosity, and it seemed to Cadderly almost as if he was looking into some sort of mental mirror. They were so similar, the two opponents, and yet so different!

Cadderly's mind began to wander, began to wonder how many people of Faerun might possess similar mental powers, a similar synaptic flow. Very few, he believed, and that led him to begin calculating the probabilities of this meeting. . . .

The glowing ball, the mental manifestation of pure pain, leaped his way, and Cadderly dismissed the tangent thoughts, quickly regaining his focus. The struggle continued for many moments, with neither man gaining any advantage, neither man willing to relinquish an inch to the other.

It is of no avail, came Aballister's thoughts.

Only one will leave this place, Cadderly replied.

He pressed on, again making no headway. But then Cadderly began to hear the melody of the song of Deneir, flowing along beside him, falling into place near him and then within him. These were the notes of perfect harmony, sharpening Cadderly's focus to a point where the unbelieving wizard could not follow. Aballister's mind might have been Cadderly's equal, but the wizard lacked the harmony of spirit, lacked the company of a god figure. Aballister had no answers for the greatest questions of human existence, and therein lay his weakness, his self-doubts.

The glowing ball began to move toward the wizard, slowly, but inevitably. Cadderly felt Aballister's welling panic, and that only scattered the wizard's focus even more.

Do you not know who I am? the wizard telepathically asked. The desperation in his thoughts made Cadderly believe the words to be another pointless boast, a fervent denial that anyone could hope to defeat him in mental combat. The young priest was not distracted, maintained his focus and the pressure—until Aballister played his trump.

"I am your father!" the wizard screamed.

The words slammed into Cadderly more profoundly than any lightning bolt. The glowing ball was no more, the mental contact shattered by the overwhelming surprise. It all made sense to the young priest. Awful, undeniable sense, and after viewing the wizard's thought processes, so similar, even identical, to his own, Cadderly could not find the strength to doubt the claim.

I am your father! The words rang out in Cadderly's mind, a damning cry, a pang of loneliness and regret for those things that might have been.

"Do you not remember?" the wizard asked, and his voice sounded so very sweet to the stunned young priest. Cadderly blinked his eyes open, regarded the man and his unthreatening, resigned pose.

Aballister crooked his arms as though he were cradling a baby. "I remember holding you close," he cooed. "I would sing to you—how much more precious you were to me since your mother had died in childbirth!"

Cadderly felt the strength draining from his legs.

"Do you remember that?" the wizard asked gently. "Of course you do. There are some things ingrained deeply within our thoughts, within our hearts. You cannot forget those moments we had together, you and I, father and son."

Aballister's words wove a myriad of images in Cadderly's mind, images of his earliest days, the serenity and security he had felt in his father's arms. How wonderful things had been for him then! How filled with love and perfect harmony!

"I remember the day I was forced to give you up," Aballister purred on. His voice cracked; a tear streamed down his weary old face. "So vividly, I remember. Time has not dulled the edge of that pain."

"Why?" Cadderly managed to stammer.

Aballister shook his head. "I was afraid," he replied. "Afraid that I alone could not give you the life you deserved."

Cadderly felt only compassion for the man, had forgiven Aballister before the wizard had even asked for forgiveness.

"All of them were against me," Aballister went on, his voice taking on an unmistakable edge—and to Cadderly, the sharpness of the wizard's rising anger only seemed to validate all that Aballister had claimed. "The priests, the officials of Carradoon. 'It will be better for the boy,' they all said, and now I understand their reasoning."

Cadderly looked up and shrugged, not following the logic.

"I would have become the mayor of Carradoon," Aballister explained. "It was inevitable. And you, my legacy, my heart and soul, would have followed suit. My political rivals could not bear to see that come to pass, could not bear to see the family of Bonaduce attain such dominance. Jealousy drove them, drove them all!"

It all made perfect sense to the stunned young priest. He found himself hating the Edificant Library, hating Dean Thobicus, the old liar, and hating even Headmaster Avery Schell, the man who had served as his surrogate father for so many years. Pertelope, too! What a phony she had been! What a hypocrite!

"And so I have risen against them," Aballister proclaimed. "And I have searched you out. We are together again, my son."

Cadderly closed his eyes, put his head down, and absorbed those precious words, words he had wanted to hear from his earliest recollections. Aballister continued talking, but Cadderly's mind remained locked on those six sweet words. *We are together again, my son.*

His mother had not died in childbirth.

Cadderly did not really remember her, just in images, flashes of her smiling face. But those images certainly did not come from Cadderly's moment of childbirth.

And I have searched you out.

But what of the Night Masks? Cadderly's reasoning screamed at him.

Aballister had indeed searched him out, had sent killers to search him out, to murder him and to murder Danica.

It was only then that Cadderly suspected that the wizard had placed an enchantment over him, had sweetened his words with subtle magical energies. The young priest's heart fought back against the reasoning, against the logical protests, for he did not want to believe that he was being deceived, wanted desperately to believe in his father's sincerity.

But his mother had not died in childbirth!

Aballister's charming tapestry began to unwind. Cadderly focused on the wizard's continuing words once more—and found that the man was no longer coaxing sweet images, but was chanting.

Cadderly had let his guard down, had no practical defense against the impending spell. He looked up to see Aballister loose a sheet of sizzling blue lightning that wobbled and zigzagged through the popping red dust. The wizard apparently understood the properties of this landscape, for the blast deflected unerringly toward Cadderly.

The young priest threw his arms up, felt the jolting, burning explosion jerk his muscles every which way, felt it grab at his heart and squeeze viciously He sensed that he was flying, but felt nothing. He sensed that he had slammed hard against some rock, but was beyond the sensation of pain.

"Now you are dead," he heard Aballister say, distantly, as though he and the wizard were no longer facing each other, were no longer on the same plane of existence.

Cadderly understood the truth of that claim, felt his life-force slipping from his mortal coil, slipping into the world of the spirit, the realm of the dead. Looking down, he saw himself lying on the red ground, broken and smoldering. Then his spirit was bathed in the divine light, the same washing sensation he had felt weeks ago at the Dragon's Codpiece when he had gone in search of Headmaster Avery's spirit.

One, two, played the notes of Deneir's song.

He knew only peace and serenity, felt more at home than he had ever felt, and knew that he had come to a place where he might find some rest.

One, two.

All thoughts of the material world began to fade. Even images of Danica, his dearest love, were not tainted with regret, for Cadderly held faith that he and she would one day be rejoined. His heart lifted; he felt his spirit soar.

One, two, came the song. Like a heartbeat.

Cadderly saw his body again, far below him, saw one finger twitch slightly.

No! he protested.

One, two, compelled the song. Cadderly was not being asked, he was being told. He looked to Aballister, spellcasting once more, creating a shimmering doorway in the red air. Aballister would return to Castle Trinity, the young priest suddenly realized, and all the region would be plunged into darkness.

Cadderly understood the plea of Deneir, and no longer did his spirit protest. *One, two,* beat his heart.

When he opened his material eyes and looked upon Aballister, he was again flooded with the warm sensation of the images of childhood the wizard had conjured. Rationally, Cadderly understood that he had been under an enchantment, understood that simple logic proved Aballister's lies. But the lure of what Aballister had shown him could not be easily overcome.

Then another image came to the young priest, a memory he had blocked out, packed away in a remote corner of his mind long, long ago. He stood before the doors of the Edificant Library, a young and not so fat Headmaster Avery facing his father before him. Avery's face was blotched red from rage. He screamed at Aballister, even cursed the man, and reiterated that Aballister had been banned from ever again entering the Edificant Library.

Aballister showed no sign of remorse, even laughed at the burly priest. "Then take the brat," he cackled, and he roughly shoved Cadderly forward, tearing a handful of hair from Cadderly's head as he pulled his hand away.

The pain was intense, physically and emotionally, but Cadderly did not cry out, not then and not now. In looking back on that awful moment, Cadderly realized that he did not cry out because he was so accustomed to Aballister's commonplace abuse. He had been the outlet for the wizard's frustrations. He was the outlet as his mother had been the outlet.

His mother!

Cadderly was somehow standing, growling, and Aballister turned about, his eyes popping wide with surprise when he saw that his son still lived. Behind the wizard, the portal glowed and shimmered, sometimes showing an image of the anteroom to the wizard's mansion within its magical borders. Aballister would abandon him now, as he had abandoned him then, would go about his business and leave his son, "the brat," to fate.

More memories assaulted the young priest, as though he had opened a box that he could not close. He saw Aballister's face, twisted demonically with rage, heard his mother's pitiful cries and his own quiet sobs.

The manifestation of a huge sword appeared in the red air before him, waving menacingly. "Lie down and die," he heard the wizard say.

That sword! Aballister had used it against Cadderly's mother, had used this very same spell to kill Cadderly's mother!

"Oh, my dear Deneir," the lost young priest heard himself whimper. The song thrummed in his head of its own accord; Cadderly did not compel it to play and hardly heard the harmony of its sweet notes. He thought he heard Headmaster Avery's voice at that moment, but the notion was lost when he saw the magical sword arcing his way, slicing for his unprotected neck, too close for him to dodge.

The sword struck him and then dissolved with a sharp sizzle.

"Damn you!" the wizard, his father, cried.

Cadderly saw nothing but his mother's face, felt nothing but a primal rage focused on this murderer, this imposter. He heard a sound escaping his lips, a burst of anger and magical energy too great for him to contain. It came forth as the most discordant note of the Deneirian song Cadderly had ever heard, a purely destructive twist of the precious notes.

The very ground heaved before him, and he continued to scream. Like an ocean wave, the red soil rolled toward Aballister, a crack widening in its mighty wake.

"What are you doing?" the wizard protested, and so weak and minuscule did his voice sound beneath the roar of Cadderly's primal scream!

Aballister lurched into the air, thrown by the wave. He flailed his arms as he descended, flapping futilely, and fell into the torn crack.

The wave diminished as it rolled on, the ground becoming quiet once more.

"I am your father!" came Aballister's pleading, pained cry from somewhere not too far below the rim of the crack.

Another cry erupted from Cadderly's aching lungs, and he threw his hands up before him and clapped them together.

And following his lead, the crack in the ground, too, snapped shut. Aballister's cries were no more.

Twenty-Three
War's End

An exhausted Cadderly stepped through the door Aballister had conveniently created, stepped through the wall, which was no longer covered with a swirling mist, and into the room where he had left Danica. A dozen enemy soldiers were there, milling about and grumbling to each other, but, oh, how they scrambled when the young priest suddenly appeared in their midst! They screamed and punched each other, fighting to get away from the dangerous man. In but a few moments, only six remained in the room, and these kept their wits enough to draw their weapons and face the young priest squarely.

"Go to Dorigen!" one of them barked at another, and the man ran off.

"Stay back, I warn you!" another man growled at Cadderly, prodding forward threateningly with his spear.

Cadderly's head throbbed; he wanted no fight with this crew, or with anyone for that matter, but he could hardly ignore his precarious situation. He accessed the song of Deneir, though the effort pained him, and the next time the man prodded ahead, he found that he was holding not a spear, but a writhing, obviously unhappy serpent. The man shrieked and dropped the thing to the floor, scrambling back away from it, though it made no move to attack.

"We have your friends!" another man, the soldier who had ordered a companion to go for Dorigen, cried. "If you kill us, they, too, will be killed!"

Cadderly didn't even hear the second sentence. The proclamation that his friends were prisoners, and not dead, sent his hopes soaring. He rested back against the wall and tried hard not to think of the fact that he had just destroyed his own father.

Danica raced into the room a moment later, slammed hard into Cadderly, and threw her arms around him, crushing him in a hug.

"Aballister is dead," the young priest said to Dorigen over Danica's shoulder.

Dorigen gave him an inquisitive look, and Danica, too, backed away to arm's length and stared hard at her love.

"I know," Cadderly said quietly.

"He was your father?" Danica asked, her expression as pained as that of Cadderly.

Cadderly nodded, and his lips went thin as he tried to firm up his jaw.

"Ivan needs you," Danica said to him. She regarded the young priest carefully, then shook her head doubtfully, seeing his obvious exhaustion.

Dorigen led Cadderly and Danica back to the room they had set up for the care of the wounded. Cadderly's four friends were there—though Vander hardly seemed wounded anymore—along with a handful of Castle Trinity's human soldiers. The orcs and other goblinoid creatures had followed their own custom of slaughtering their seriously wounded companions.

Pikel and Shayleigh were both sitting up, though neither looked very steady. Their expressions brightened at Cadderly's approach, and they motioned for him to go to Ivan, lying, pale as death, on a nearby cot.

Cadderly knelt beside the yellow-bearded dwarf, amazed that Ivan still drew breath, given the sheer number of garish wounds he had suffered. The young priest realized that Ivan, for all his toughness, didn't have much time, and knew that he had to somehow find the strength to follow the song to the sphere of healing and bring forth powerful magics.

Quietly, Cadderly began to chant, and he heard the music, but it was distant, so distant. Cadderly mentally reached for it, felt the pressure in his temples, and closed his eyes as he fell into its flow, guiding it along. He swam past the notes of the minor spells of healing, knowing they would be of little use in tending the dwarf's most serious wounds. The song built to a thrumming crescendo in his thoughts, moved at Cadderly's demand into the realm of the greatest spells of healing.

The next thing the young priest knew, he was lying on the floor, looking up into Danica's concerned expression. She helped him back to a sitting position and he looked upon Ivan hopelessly.

"Cadderly?" Danica asked, and the young priest could think of several questions reflected in that one word.

"He is too tired," Dorigen answered, coming to kneel beside them both. The wizard looked into Cadderly's hollowed gray eyes and nodded, and understood.

"I must access the magic," the young priest said determinedly, and he fell right back into the song, fought hard, for now it seemed to him even more distant.

Twenty minutes passed before he woke up the next time, and Cadderly knew then that he would need several more hours of rest before he could even attempt to get into the greatest levels of healing magic again. He knew, too, in looking at the dwarf, that Ivan would not live that long.

"Why do you do this to me?" Cadderly asked aloud, asked his god, and all those about him regarded him curiously.

"Deneir," he explained privately to Danica. "He has abandoned me in my time of desperation. I cannot believe that he will let Ivan die."

"Your god does not control the minor fates of minor players," Dorigen said, again moving close to the two.

Cadderly shot her a derisive glance that plainly asked what the wizard might know of it.

"I understand the properties of magic," Dorigen replied squarely against that arrogant expression. "The magic remains to be accessed, but you have not the strength. The failing is not Deneir's."

Danica moved as if to strike out at the woman, but Cadderly grabbed the monk immediately and held her back, nodding his head in agreement with Dorigen.

"And so your magic is held," Dorigen remarked. "Is that all that you have to offer the dying dwarf?"

At first, Cadderly took her unexpected words to mean that he should bid Ivan farewell, as a friend would do, but after a moment's thinking, the young priest came to interpret the words in a different way. He motioned Danica away, spent a long minute in contemplation, searching for some possible answers.

"Your ring," he remarked to Vander suddenly.

The firbolg glanced quickly at his hand, but the initial excitement of the group died away immediately. "It will not work," Vander explained. "The ring must be worn while the wounds are received."

"Give it to me, I beg," Cadderly said, not letting down a bit in light of the grim explanation. He took the ring from the willing firbolg and slipped it over his own finger.

"There are two types of healing magic," Cadderly explained to Vander and the others. "Two types, though I have called only upon the method that begs the blessing of the gods to mend torn skin and broken bones."

Danica started to inquire further, but Cadderly had closed his eyes and was already beginning to sing once more. It took him some time to catch up to the flow of the song. Again he felt the pressure in his temples as he followed its tiring current, but he kept heart, knowing that this time, he would not have to go so far.

The four friends and Dorigen gathered around the cot, and gasped in unison as Ivan's severe throat wound simply disappeared, then gasped again as it reappeared on Cadderly's neck!

Blood bubbled from the young priest's opened throat as he continued to force the words from his mouth. Another of Ivan's wounds was erased from the dwarf's body, to appear in a similar position on Cadderly.

Danica cried out for her love and started forward, but Dorigen and Shayleigh held her back, reasoning with her to trust in the young priest.

Soon Ivan was resting peacefully, and Cadderly, showing every brutal wound the dwarf had suffered, fell to the floor.

"Oooo," groaned an unhappy Pikel.

"Cadderly!" Danica cried again, and she tore free of Shayleigh and Dorigen and ran to him. She put her head to his chest to hear his heartbeat, brushed his curly brown locks from his face, and put her face close to his, whispering for him to live.

Vander's laughter turned her angrily about.

"He wears the ring!" the firbolg roared. "Oh, clever young priest!"

"Oo oi!" Pikel squealed with glee.

When Danica turned back, Cadderly, his head uplifted, gave her a peck of a kiss. "This really hurts," he groaned, but he managed to smile as he spoke the words, his head drifting slowly back to the floor, his eyes slowly closing.

"What's wrong with *him*?" Ivan grumbled, sitting up and looking about the room with a confused expression.

By the time his friends had pushed Ivan aside and lifted Cadderly into place on the cot, the young priest was breathing much easier, and many of his wounds were unmistakably on the mend.

Later that night, the still weary priest rose from his bed and moved about the makeshift infirmary, singing softly once more, tending the wounds of his other friends, and those of Castle Trinity's soldiers.

* * * * *

"He was my father," Cadderly said bluntly. The young priest rubbed a hand across his wet eyes, trying to come to terms with the sudden explosion of memories that assaulted him, memories he had buried away many years before.

Danica shifted closer to him, locking his arm with her own. "Dorigen told me," she explained.

They sat together in the quiet darkness for many minutes.

"He killed my mother," Cadderly said suddenly.

Danica looked up at him, a horrified expression on her fair face.

"It was an accident," Cadderly continued, looking straight ahead. "But not without blame. My fath . . . Aballister was always experimenting with new magics, always pressing the energies to their very limits, and to his very limits of control. He conjured a sword one day, a magnificent glowing sword that sliced back and forth through the air, floating of its own accord."

Cadderly could not help a slight, ironic chuckle. "He was so proud," the young priest said, shaking his head, his unkempt sandy-brown locks flopping from side to side. "So proud. But he could not control the dweomer. He had overstepped his magical discipline, and before he could dispel the sword, my mother was dead."

Danica mumbled her love's name under her breath, pulled him tighter, and put her head on his shoulder. The young priest moved away, though, so that he could look Danica in the eye.

"I do not even remember her name," he said, voice trembling. "Her face is clear to me again, the first face I ever saw in this world, but I do not even remember her name!"

They sat quietly again, Danica thinking of her own dead parents, and Cadderly playing with the multitude of rushing images, trying to find some logical recollection of his earliest years. He remembered, too, one of Headmaster Avery's scoldings, when the portly man had called Cadderly a "Gondsman," referring to a particular sect of priests known for creating ingenious, and often destructive, tools and weapons without regard for the consequences of their creations. Now, knowing Aballister, remembering what had happened to his own mother, Cadderly could better understand dear Avery's fears.

But he was not like his father, he silently reminded himself. He had found Deneir, found the truth, and found the call of his conscience. And he had brought the war—the war Aballister had precipitated—to the only possible conclusion.

Cadderly sat there assaulted by a tumult of long-buried and confusing memories, assaulted by empty wishes of what might have been and by a host of more recent memories which he could now look at with a new perspective. A profound sadness that he could not deny washed over him, a sense of grief that he had never felt before, for Avery, for Pertelope, for his mother, and for Aballister.

His sadness for his father was not for the man's death, though, but for the man's life.

Cadderly repeatedly saw the red ground of that distant world closing over the fallen wizard, ending a sad chapter of wasted, misused potential.

"You had to do it," Danica said unexpectedly. Cadderly blinked at her in disbelief that soon turned to amusement. How well she knew him!

His reply was a nod and a sincere, if resigned, smile. Cadderly felt no guilt for what he had done; he had found the truth as his father never had. Aballister, not Cadderly, had forced the conclusion.

The small room lit up as Dorigen entered, bearing a candelabra. "Castle Trinity's soldiers are scattering to the four winds," she said. "All of their leaders are dead—except for myself, and I have no desire to continue what Aballister has started."

Danica nodded her approval, but Cadderly scowled.

"What is it?" the surprised monk asked him.

"Are we to let them run free, perhaps to cause more mischief?" he asked.

"There remain nearly three thousand of them," Dorigen reminded him. "You really have little choice in the matter. But take heart, young priest, for the threat to Carradoon, to the library, to all the region is surely ended. And I will return with you to your library, to face the judgment of your superiors."

My superiors? Cadderly thought incredulously. Dean Thobicus? The notion reminded him that he had many things yet to accomplish if he was to follow the course Deneir had laid out before him. One battle was ended, but another was yet to be fought.

"Their judgment will be harsh," Danica replied, and from her tone it was obvious that she did not wish any serious harm to come to the repentant wizard. "They may execute . . ." Danica's grim voice trailed off as Dorigen nodded her acceptance of that fact.

"No, they will not," Cadderly said quietly. "You will come back, Dorigen, and you will serve a penance. But with your powers and sincere desire, you have much that you can contribute. You, Dorigen, will help heal the scars of this war, and help better the region. That is the proper course, and the course the library will follow."

Danica turned a doubting look Cadderly's way, but it fell away as she considered the determination etched on the young priest's face. She knew what Cadderly had done to Dean Thobicus to get them out here in the first place; she suspected then what Cadderly meant to do to the man once they got back to the Edificant Library.

Again, Dorigen nodded, and she smiled warmly at Cadderly, the man who had spared her in Shilmista Forest, the man who apparently meant to spare her once more.

"Tell me of mercy, wise Cadderly," Dorigen remarked. "Is it strength, or weakness?"

"Strength," the young priest answered without hesitation.

* * * * *

Cadderly stood on the rocky slope above Castle Trinity, flanked by his five friends. "You have ordered them to abandon this place?" he asked Dorigen, coming up the rise to join them.

"I have told the men that they will be welcomed in Carradoon," the wizard replied. "Though I doubt that many will head that way. I have told the ogres, the orcs, and the goblins to go and find holes in the mountains, to run away and cause no more mischief."

"But many remain within the fortress?" Cadderly stated as much as asked.

Dorigen looked back to Trinity's uncompleted walls and shrugged. "Ogres, orcs, and goblins are stubborn beasts."

Cadderly eyed the fortress contemptuously. He remembered the other plane, the earthquake he had brought about to bury Aballister, and thought of doing the same thing now, of destroying Castle Trinity and cleansing the mountainside. Grinning wickedly, the young priest fell into the song of Denier, searching for the powerful magic.

He found nothing to replicate the earthquake. Confused, Cadderly pressed the notes, mentally called for guidance.

Then he understood. His release of power on the other plane had been a reaction to primal emotions, not consciously conjured, but forced by events around him.

Cadderly laughed aloud, and opened his eyes to see all six of his companions standing around him, eyeing him curiously.

"What is it?" Danica asked.

"You were thinking of destroying the fortress," Dorigen reasoned.

"Aw, do it!" bellowed Ivan. "Split the ground and drop it in!"

"Oo oi!"

Cadderly glanced around at his companions, those friends who believed him invincible, godlike. When his gaze fell over Shayleigh, though, he found the elf maiden slowly shaking her head. She understood.

As did Danica. "Split the ground and drop it in?" the monk asked Ivan incredulously. "If Cadderly can do such a feat, then why did we run about inside that cursed place?"

"We have come to expect too much," Shayleigh added.

"Oo." Pikel said it, but it aptly reflected Ivan's thoughts.

"Well, come on, then," Ivan remarked after a long pause. He put his hand on Cadderly's back and pushed the young priest along with him. "We've got a month's hiking ahead, but don't ye worry, me and me brother'll get ye all through!"

It was a good start, Cadderly decided. Ivan was taking the lead, was assuming some of the responsibility.

A good start on a long road.

Epilogue

Waves of agony rolled over Druzil when Aballister died, pains that only a familiar who had lost his wizard master could ever know. Unlike many familiars, Druzil managed to survive the assault, and when the agony had at last subsided, the imp limped his way down the trails of the eastern Snowflakes.

"*Bene tellemara*, Aballister," he grumbled under his breath, his litany against his mounting fears. It was easy enough for the intelligent imp to figure out who had brought Aballister down, and easy enough for him to figure that without the wizard, even if Castle Trinity had survived, his role in the plans of conquest had come to a sudden end. He thought briefly of going to the castle, to see if Dorigen had survived. He quickly dismissed the thought, reminding himself that Dorigen wasn't overly fond of him.

But where to go? Druzil wondered. Wizard masters were not so easy for renegade imps to find, nor were planar gates that might return Druzil to the smoky and dark lands where he truly belonged. Also, Druzil figured that his business on this plane was not quite finished, not with the precious chaos curse he'd concocted bottled up in the catacombs of the Edificant Library. Druzil wanted the bottle back, had to figure out a way to get it before that wretched Cadderly, if Cadderly was still alive, returned.

For now, though, the imp's needs were more immediate. He wanted to get out of the Snowflakes, wanted to get indoors and out of winter's chilly bite, and so he continued his course down from the high ground, down toward the town of Carradoon.

After several days, and several close calls with the wary farmers living on the edges of the wild mountains, Druzil, perched in the rafters of a barn, overheard what sounded like a promising situation. A hermit had taken up habitation in a remote shack not too far from the outer farmhouses, a solitary recluse with no friends and no family.

"No witnesses," the imp rasped, his poison-tipped tail flicking eagerly. As soon as the sun went down, Druzil flapped off for the shack, figuring to kill the hermit and take his home, and spend the cold winter feasting off the dead man's flesh.

How his plans changed when he looked upon the hermit, looked at the mark branded clearly on his forehead! Suddenly Druzil was more concerned with the possibilities of keeping this man alive. He thought again of the Edificant Library, and the powerful bottle of the chaos curse locked away in its catacombs. He thought again that he must possess it, and now, by some chance of fate, it seemed to Druzil as if his wish might come true.

Bent low under the burden of an armful of firewood, Kierkan Rufo plodded slowly, dejectedly, back to his ramshackle hut.

The Cleric Quintet · Book Five

The
Chaos Curse

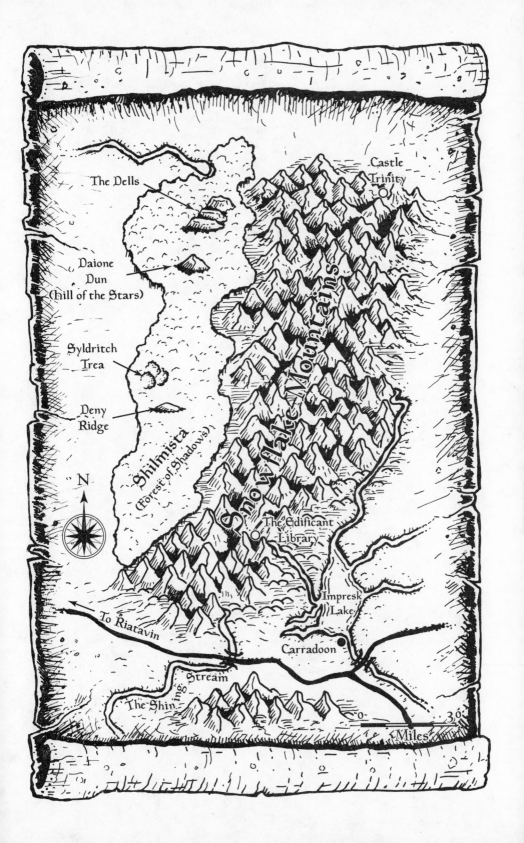

The Dells

Daione
Dun
(hill of the Stars)

Syldritch
Trea

Deny
Ridge

Shilmista
(Forest of Shadows)

N

Castle
Trinity

Snowflake Mountains

The Edificant
Library

Impresk
Lake

To Riatavin

Carradoon

The Shining Stream

0   30
Miles

Prologue

Dean Thobicus drummed his skinny fingers on the hardwood desk before him. He had turned his chair so that he faced the window, not the door, pointedly looking away as a nervous and wiry man entered his office on the library's second floor.

"You . . . you asked . . ." the man, Vicero Belago, stuttered, but Thobicus lifted a trembling leathery hand to stop him. Belago broke into a cold sweat as he stared at the back of the old dean's balding head. He looked to the side, where stood Bron Turman, one of the library's headmasters and the highest ranking of the Oghman priests, but the large, muscular man merely shrugged, having no answers for him.

"I did not ask," Dean Thobicus corrected Belago at length. "I commanded you to come." Thobicus swung about in his chair, and the nervous Belago, seeming small and insignificant indeed, shrank back near the door. "You do still heed my commands, do you not, dear Vicero?"

"Of course, Dean Thobicus," Belago replied. He dared come a step closer, out of the shadows. Belago was the Edificant Library's resident alchemist, a professed follower of both Oghma and Deneir, though he formally belonged to neither sect. He was loyal to Dean Thobicus as both an employee to an employer, and as a sheep to a shepherd. "You are the dean," he said sincerely. "I am but a servant."

"Exactly!" Thobicus snarled, his voice hissing like the warning of an angry serpent, and Bron Turman eyed the withered old dean suspiciously. Never before had the old man been so animated or agitated.

"I am the *dean*," Thobicus said, with emphasis on the final word. "*I* design the duties of the library, not *Ca*—" Thobicus bit back the rest of his words, but both Belago and Turman caught the slip and understood the implications.

The dean spoke of Cadderly.

"Of course, Dean Thobicus," Belago said again, more subdued. Suddenly the alchemist realized that he was in the middle of a much larger power struggle, one in which he might pay a price. Belago's friendship with Cadderly was no secret. Neither was the fact that the alchemist often worked on unsanctioned and privately funded projects for the young priest, often for the cost of materials alone.

"You have an inventory document for your shop?" Thobicus asked.

Belago nodded. Of course he did, and Thobicus knew it. Belago's shop had been destroyed less than a year before, when the library was in the throes of the chaos curse. The library's deep coffers had funded the repairs and the replacement ingredients, and Belago had promptly given a complete accounting.

"As do I," Thobicus remarked. Bron Turman still eyed the dean curiously, not understanding the last statement. "I know everything that belongs there," Thobicus went on imperiously. "Everything, you understand?"

Belago, finding strength in honor, straightened for the first time since he had entered the room. "Are you accusing me of thievery?" he demanded.

The dean's chuckle mocked the wiry man's firm stance. "Not yet," Thobicus answered casually, "for you are still here, and thus, anything you might wish to take would also still be here."

That set Belago back; his ample eyebrows furrowed.

"Your services are no longer required," Thobicus explained, still speaking in an awful, cold, casual tone.

"But . . . but, Dean," Belago stuttered. "I have been—"

"Leave!"

Bron Turman straightened, recognizing the inflections and the weight of magic in Thobicus's voice. The burly Oghman headmaster was not surprised when Belago stiffened suddenly and fell back out of the room. With a look to Thobicus, Turman quickly moved to close the door.

"He was a fine alchemist," Turman said quietly, turning back to the large desk. Thobicus was again staring out the window.

"I had reason to doubt his loyalty," the dean explained.

Bron Turman, pragmatic and no real ally of Cadderly, did not press the point. Thobicus was the dean, and as such, he had the authority to hire or dismiss any of the nonclerical assistants that he chose.

"Baccio has been here for more than a day," Bron Turman said to change the subject. The man he referred to, Baccio, was the commander of the Carradoon garrison, come to discuss the defense of the city and the library should Castle Trinity strike at them. "Have you spoken with him?"

"We will not need Baccio and his little army," Thobicus said with confidence. "I shall soon dismiss him."

"You have word from Cadderly?"

"No," Thobicus answered honestly. Indeed, the dean had heard nothing since Cadderly and his companions had gone into the mountains earlier that winter. But Thobicus believed that the army would not be needed, believed that Cadderly had succeeded in defeating Castle Trinity. For, as the young priest's power continued to grow, Dean Thobicus felt himself being pushed away from the light of Deneir. Once, Thobicus had commanded the most powerful clerical magic, but now even the simplest spell, like the one he had used to dispatch poor Belago, came hard to his thin lips.

He turned back to the room to see Bron Turman staring at him skeptically.

"Very well," Thobicus conceded. "Tell Baccio I will meet him this evening—but I maintain that his army should hold a defensive posture and not go traipsing through the mountains!"

Bron Turman was satisfied with that. "But you believe that Cadderly and his friends have succeeded," he said slyly.

Thobicus did not respond.

"You believe that the threat to the library is no more," Bron Turman stated. The burly Oghman headmaster smiled, a wistful look in his large gray eyes. "At least, you believe that one threat to the library is no more," he added.

Thobicus steeled his gaze, his crow's-feet coming together to form one large crease at the side of each orb. "This does not concern you," he quietly warned.

Bron Turman bowed, respecting the words. "That does not mean that I do not understand," he said. "Vicero Belago was a fine alchemist."

"Bron Turman . . ."

The headmaster held up a submissive hand. "I am no friend of Cadderly's," he said. "Neither am I a young man. I have seen the intrigue of power struggles within both our sects."

Thobicus pursed his thin lips and seemed on the verge of explosion, and Bron Turman took that as a sign that he should be leaving. He gave another quick bow and was gone from the room.

Dean Thobicus rocked back in his chair and pivoted about to face the window. He couldn't rationally call Turman on the outwardly treasonous words, for the man's reasoning was undeniably true. Thobicus had been alive for more than seven decades; Cadderly for just over two, yet, for some reason that the old bureaucrat could not understand, Cadderly had found particular favor with Deneir. But the dean had come to his power painstakingly, at great personal sacrifice and at the cost of many years of almost reclusive study. He was not about to give up his position. He would purge the library of Cadderly's open allies and strengthen his hold on the order. Headmaster Avery Schell, Cadderly's mentor and surrogate father, and Pertelope, who had been like Cadderly's mother, were both dead now, and Belago would soon be gone.

No, Thobicus would not give up his position.

Not without a fight.

One

The Promise of Salvation

K ierkan Rufo wiped the stubborn mud from his boots and breeches, and muttered quiet curses to himself, as he always did. He was an outcast, marked by an ugly blue-and-red brand of an unlit candle above a closed eye, which lay on the middle of his forehead.

"Bene tellemara," whispered Druzil. A bat-winged, dog-faced, scaly creature barely two feet tall, the imp packed more malicious evil into that tiny frame than the worst of humankind's tyrants.

"What did you say?" Rufo snapped. He glared down at his otherworldly companion. The two had been together for the last half of the winter, and neither much liked the other. Their enmity had begun in Shilmista Forest, west of the Snowflake Mountains, when Druzil had threatened and coerced Rufo into serving his wicked masters, the leaders of Castle Trinity—when Druzil had precipitated Kierkan Rufo's fall from the order of Deneir.

Druzil looked curiously at the man and squinted from the flickering light of the torch Rufo held. Rufo was over six feet tall, but bone-skinny. He always stood at an angle, tilted to the side, and that made him, or the world behind him, seem strangely incongruent. Druzil, who had spent the last few months wandering through the Snowflakes, thought Rufo resembled a tree on a steep mountainside. The imp snickered, drawing another glare from the perpetually scowling Rufo.

The imp continued to stare, trying hard to view the man in a new light. With his stringy black hair matted to his head, those penetrating eyes—black dots on a pale face—and that unusual stance, Rufo could be imposing. He kept his hair parted in the middle now, not on the side as it had always been, for Rufo could not, on pain of death, cover that horrid brand, the mark that had forced him to

860

be a recluse, the mark that made every person shun him when they saw him coming down the road.

"What are you looking at?" Rufo demanded.

"*Bene tellemara,*" Druzil rasped again in the language of the lower planes. It was a profound insult to Rufo's intelligence. To Druzil, schooled in chaos and evil, all humans seemed fumbling things, too clouded by emotions to be effective at anything. And this one, Rufo, was more bumbling than most. However, Aballister, Druzil's wizard master, was dead now, killed by Cadderly, his son, and the same priest who had branded Rufo. And Dorigen, Aballister's second, had been captured, or had gone over to Cadderly's side. That left Druzil wandering alone on the Material Plane. With his innate powers, and no wizards binding him to service, the imp might have found his way back to the lower planes, but Druzil didn't want that—not yet. For, on this plane, in the dungeons of this very building, rested *Tuanta Quiro Miancay*, the chaos curse, among the most potent and wicked concoctions ever brewed. Druzil wanted it back, and meant to get it with the help of Rufo, his stooge.

"I know what you are saying," Rufo lied, then he mimicked "*Bene tellemara*" back at Druzil.

Druzil smirked at him, showing clearly that the imp really didn't care if Rufo knew the meaning or not.

Rufo looked back at the muddy tunnel that had gotten them under the cellar of the Edificant Library.

"Well," he said impatiently, "we have come this far. Lead on and let us be out of this wretched place."

Druzil looked at him skeptically. For all the talking the imp had done over the last few weeks, Rufo still did not understand. Be out of this place? Druzil thought. Rufo had missed the whole point. They would soon have the chaos curse in their hands; why would they then want to leave?

Druzil nodded and led on, figuring that he could do little to enlighten the stupid human. Rufo simply did not understand the power of *Tuanta Quiro Miancay*. He had once been caught in its throes—all the library had, and nearly been brought down—yet, the ignorant human still did not understand.

That was the way with humans, Druzil decided. He would have to take Rufo by the hand and lead him to power, as he had led Rufo across the fields west of Carradoon and back into the mountains. Druzil had lured Rufo back to the library, where the branded man did not want to go, with false promises that the potion locked in these dungeons would remove his brand.

They went through several long, damp chambers, past rotting casks and crates from days long ago when the library was a much smaller place, and mostly underground, when these areas had been used for storage. Druzil hadn't been here in a while, not since before the battle for Castle Trinity, before the war in Shilmista Forest. Not since Barjin, the evil priest, had been killed . . . by Cadderly.

"Bene tellemara!" the imp rasped, frustrated by the thought of the powerful young cleric.

"I grow tired of your insults," Rufo began to protest.

"Shut up," Druzil snapped back at him, too consumed by thoughts of the young priest to bother with Rufo. Cadderly, young and lucky Cadderly: the bane of Druzil's ambitions, the one who always seemed to be in the way.

Druzil kept complaining, scraping and slapping his wide, clawed feet on the stone floor noisily. He pushed through a door, went down a long corridor, and pushed open another.

Then Druzil stopped, and ended, too, his muttering. They had come to a small room, the room where Barjin had fallen.

Rufo pinched his nose and turned away, for the room smelled of death and decay. Druzil took a deep breath and felt positively at home.

There could be no doubt that a fierce struggle had occurred in here. Along the wall to Rufo and Druzil's right was an overturned brazier, the remains of charcoal blocks and incense scattered among its ashes. There, too, were the burned wrappings of an undead monster, a mummy. Most of the thing had been consumed by the flames, but its wrapped skull remained, showing blackened bone with tattered pieces of rags about it.

Beyond the brazier, near the base of the wall and along the floor, was a crimson stain, all that remained as testimony to Barjin's death. Barjin had been propped against that very spot when Cadderly had accidentally hit him with an explosive dart, blasting a hole through his chest and back.

The rest of the room showed much the same carnage. Next to Barjin's bloodstain, the brick wall had been knocked open by a furious dwarf, and the crossbeam supporting the ceiling hung by a single peg perpendicular to the floor. In the middle of the room, beneath dozens of scorch marks, lay a black weapon handle, all that remained of the Screaming Maiden, Barjin's enchanted mace, and behind that were the remains of the priest's unholy altar.

Beyond that . . .

Druzil's bulbous black eyes widened when he looked past the altar to the small cabinet wrapped in white cloth emblazoned with the runes and sigils of both Deneir and Oghma, the brother gods of the library. The mere presence of the cloth told Druzil that his search was at an end.

A flap of his bat wings brought the imp to the top of the altar, and he heard Rufo shuffling to catch up. Druzil dared not approach any closer, though, knowing that the priests had warded the cabinet with powerful enchantments.

"Glyphs," Rufo agreed, recognizing Druzil's hesitation. "If we go near it, we shall be burned away!"

"No," Druzil reasoned, speaking quickly, frantically. *Tuanta Quiro Miancay* was close enough for the desperate imp to smell it, and he would not be denied. "Not you," he went on. "You are not of my weal. You were a priest of this order. Surely you can approach . . ."

"Fool!" Rufo snapped at him. It was as volatile a response as the imp had ever heard from the broken man. "I wear the brand of Deneir! The wards on that cloth and cabinet would seek my flesh hungrily."

Druzil hopped on the altar, tried to speak, but his rasping voice came out as only indecipherable sputtering. Then the imp calmed and called on his innate magic. The imp could see and measure all magic, be it the dweomer of a wizard or a priest. If the glyphs were not so powerful, Druzil would go to the cabinet himself. Any wounds he received would heal—faster still when he clutched the precious *Tuanta Quiro Miancay* in his greedy hands. The name translated into "the Most Fatal Horror," a title that sounded delicious indeed to the beleaguered imp.

The aura emanating from the cabinet nearly overwhelmed him, and at first, Druzil's heart fell in despair. But as he continued his scan, the imp came to know the truth, and a great gout of wicked laughter burst from between his pointed teeth.

Rufo, curious, looked at him.

"Go to the cabinet," Druzil instructed.

Rufo continued to stare, and made no move.

"Go," Druzil said again. "The meager wards of the foolish priests have been overwhelmed by the chaos curse! Their magic has unraveled!"

It was only partly true. *Tuanta Quiro Miancay* was more than a simple potion; it was magic driven to destroy. *Tuanta Quiro Miancay* wanted to be found, wanted to be out of the prison the priests had wrapped about it. And to that end, the concoction's magic had attacked the glyphs, had worked against them for many months, weakening their integrity.

Rufo didn't trust Druzil (and rightly so), but he could not ignore the pull on his heart. He felt his forehead's brand keenly in this place and suffered a severe headache merely from being near a structure dedicated to Deneir. He found himself wanting to believe Druzil's words; he moved inevitably toward the cabinet and reached for the cloth.

There came a blinding electric flash, then a second, then a tremendous burst of fire. Fortunately for Rufo, the first explosion had launched him across the room, clear over the altar and into an overturned bookcase near the door.

Druzil shrieked as the flames engulfed the cabinet, its wood flaring brightly—obviously it had been soaked with oil or enchanted by some incendiary magic. Druzil did not fear for *Tuanta Quiro Miancay*, for that concoction was everlasting, but if the flask holding it melted, the liquid would be lost!

Flames never bothered Druzil, a creature of the fiery lower planes. His bat wings sent him rushing into the conflagration, eager hands pulling the cabinet's contents free. Druzil shrieked from a sudden burst of pain, and nearly hurled the bowl across the room. He caught himself, though, and gingerly placed the item on the altar, then he backed away and rubbed his blistered hands together.

The bottle holding the chaos curse had been placed in a bowl and immersed in the clearest of waters, made holy by the plea of a dead druid and the symbol of Sylvanus, the god of nature, of natural order. Perhaps no god in the Realms evoked more anger from the perverse imp than Sylvan.

Druzil studied the bowl and considered his dilemma. He breathed easier a moment later, when he realized that the holy water was not as pure as it should be, that the influences of *Tuanta Quiro Miancay* were acting even upon that.

Druzil moved near the bowl and chanted softly, using one of his claws to puncture the middle finger of his left hand. Finishing his curse, he let a single drop of his blood fall into the water. There came a hissing, and the top of the bowl clouded over with vapor. Then it was gone, and gone, too, was the pure water, replaced by a blackened morass of fetid and rotting liquid.

Druzil leaped back atop the altar and plunged his hands in. A moment later, he was whimpering with joy, cradling the precious, rune-decorated bottle, itself an enchanted thing, as though it were his baby. He looked to Rufo, not really concerned if the man was alive or dead, then laughed again.

Rufo had propped himself up on his elbows. His black hair stood on end, dancing wildly; his eyes twitched and rolled of their own accord. After some time, he rolled back unsteadily to his feet and advanced in staggered steps toward the imp, thinking to throttle the creature once and for all.

Druzil's waving tail, its barbed end dripping deadly poison, brought Rufo to his senses, but did little to calm him.

"You said . . ." he began to roar.

"*Bene tellemara!*" Druzil snapped back at him, the imp's intensity more than matching Rufo's anger and startling the man to silence. "Do you not know what we have?" Smiling wickedly, Druzil handed the flask to Rufo, and the man's beady eyes widened when he took it, when he felt its inner power throb within him.

Rufo hardly heard Druzil as the imp raved about what they might accomplish with the chaos curse. The angular man stared at the swirling red liquid within the bottle and fantasized, not of power, as Druzil was spouting, but of freedom from his brand. Rufo had earned that brand, but in his twisted perception, that hardly mattered. All Rufo understood and could accept was that Cadderly had marked him, had forced him to become an outcast.

Now, all the world was his enemy.

Druzil continued to ramble excitedly. The imp talked of controlling the priests once more, of striking against all the land, of uncorking the flask and . . .

Rufo heard that last suggestion alone among the dozens of ideas the imp spewed. He heard it and believed it with all his heart. It was as if *Tuanta Quiro Miancay* was calling him, and the chaos curse, the creation of wicked, diabolical intelligence, was indeed. This was Rufo's salvation, more than Deneir had ever been. This was his deliverance from wretched Cadderly.

This potion was for him, and for him alone.

Druzil stopped talking the moment he noticed that Rufo had uncorked the bottle, the moment he smelled the red fumes wafting up from the potion.

The imp started to ask the man what he was doing, but the words stuck in

Druzil's throat as Rufo suddenly lifted the bottle to his thin lips and drank of it deeply.

Druzil stammered repeatedly, trying to find the words of protest. Rufo turned to him, the man's face screwed up curiously.

"What have you done?" Druzil asked.

Rufo started to answer, but gagged instead and clutched his throat.

"What have you done?" Druzil repeated loudly. "*Bene tellemara*! Fool!"

Rufo gagged again, clutched his throat and stomach, and vomited violently. He staggered away, coughing, wheezing, trying to get some air past the bile rising in his throat.

"What have you done?" Druzil cried after him, scuttling along the floor to keep up. The imp's tail waved ominously; if Rufo's misery ended, Druzil meant to sting and tear him, to punish him for stealing the precious and irreplaceable potion.

Rufo, his balance wavering, slammed into the doorjamb as he tried to exit the room. He stumbled along the corridor, rebounding off one wall, then the other. He vomited again, and again after that, his stomach burning with agony and swirling with nausea. Somehow he got through the rooms and corridors and half-crawled out the muddy tunnel, back into the sunlight, which knifed at his eyes and skin.

He was burning up, and yet he felt cold, deathly cold.

Druzil, wisely becoming invisible as they came into the revealing daylight, followed. Rufo stopped and vomited yet again, across the hardened remains of a late-season snowbank, and the mess showed more blood than bile. Then the angular man staggered around the building's corner, slipping and falling many times in the mud and slush. He thought to get to the door, to the priests with their curing hands.

Two young acolytes, wearing the black-and-gold vests that distinguished them as priests of Oghma, were near the door, enjoying the warmth of the late winter day, their brown cloaks opened wide to the sun. They didn't notice Rufo at first, not until the man fell heavily into the mud just a few feet away.

The two acolytes rushed to him and turned him over, then gasped and fell back when they saw the brand. Neither had been in the library long enough to know Kierkan Rufo personally, but they had heard tales of the branded priest. They looked to each other and shrugged, then one rushed back into the library while the other began to relieve the stricken man.

Druzil watched from the corner of the building, muttering "*Bene tellemara*" over and over, lamenting that the chaos curse and Kierkan Rufo had played him a wicked joke.

* * * * *

Perched high in the branches of a tree near that door, the white squirrel, Percival, looked on with more than a passing interest. Percival had come out of his winter hibernation this very week. He had been surprised to find that Cadderly, his main source of the favored cacasa nuts, was not about, and was even more surprised to see Kierkan Rufo, a human that Percival did not care for at all.

The squirrel could see that Rufo was in great distress, could smell the foulness of Rufo's illness, even from this distance.

Percival moved near his twig nest, nestled high in the branches, and continued to watch.

Two
Different Paths Taken

The three bearded members of the company, the dwarves Pikel and Ivan Bouldershoulder and the red-haired firbolg Vander, sat off to the side of the cave entrance, rolling bones, placing bets, and laughing among themselves. Ivan won a round, for the fifteenth time in a row, and Pikel swept off a blue, wide-brimmed hat, with an orange quill on one side and the eye-above-candle holy symbol of Deneir set in its front, and whacked laughing Ivan over the head.

Cadderly, seeing the move, started to protest. It was his hat, after all, simply loaned to Pikel, and Ivan's helmet was set with the antlers of a large deer. The young priest changed his mind and held the thought silent, seeing that the hat had not been damaged and realizing that Ivan deserved the blow.

The friendship between Ivan, Pikel, and Vander had blossomed after the fall of Castle Trinity. Gigantic Vander, all twelve feet and eight hundred pounds of him, had even helped Pikel, the would-be druid, re-dye his hair and beard green and braid the bushy tangle down his back. The only tense moment had come when Vander tried to put some of Pikel's dye in Ivan's bright yellow hair, something the square-shouldered, more serious Bouldershoulder did not like at all.

But the exchanges were ultimately goodnatured; the last few weeks had been goodnatured, despite the brutal weather. The seven companions, including Cadderly, Danica, Dorigen, and Shayleigh, the elf maiden, had planned to go straight from the victory at Castle Trinity to the Edificant Library. Barely a day's hike into the mountains, though, winter had come in full force, blocking the trails so that not even Cadderly, with his priestly magic, dared to press on. Even worse, Cadderly had fallen ill, though he insisted that it was simple exhaustion. As a priest, Cadderly served as a conduit for the powers of his god, and during the battle with Castle Trinity (and the weeks of fighting before that) too much of that energy had flowed through the young priest.

Danica, who knew Cadderly better than anyone, did not doubt that he was exhausted, but she knew, too, that the young priest had taken an emotional beating as well. In Castle Trinity, Cadderly had seen his past and the truth of his heritage. He had been forced to face up to what his father, Aballister, had become.

In Castle Trinity Cadderly had killed his own father.

Danica held faith that Cadderly would overcome this trauma, confident in the depth of Cadderly's character. He was devoted to his god and to his friends, and they all were beside him.

With the trails closed and Cadderly ill, the company had gone east, out of the mountains and their foothills, to the farmlands north of Carradoon. Even the lowlands were deep with a snow that the Shining Plains had not seen in decades. The friends had found a many-chambered cave for shelter, and had turned the place into a fair home over the days, using Danica's, Vander's, and the dwarves' survival skills and Dorigen's magic. Cadderly had aided whenever he could, but his role was to rest and regain his strength. He knew, and Danica knew, that when they returned to the Edificant Library, the young priest might face his toughest challenge yet.

After several weeks, the snows had begun to recede. As brutal as the winter had been, it was ending early, and the companions could begin to think about their course. That brought mixed feelings for young Cadderly, the priest who had risen so fast through the ranks of his order. He stood at the cave entrance, staring out over the fields of white, their brightness stinging his gray eyes in the morning sunlight. He felt guilty for his own weakness, for he believed that he should have returned to the library despite the snows, despite the trials he had faced, months ago, even if that meant leaving his friends behind. Cadderly's destiny waited at that library, but even now, feeling stronger once more, hearing the song of Deneir playing in the background of his thoughts again, he wasn't sure that he had the strength to meet it.

"I am ready for you," came a call from inside the cave, above Vander and the dwarves' continuing ruckus. Cadderly turned and walked past the group, and Pikel, knowing what was to come, gave a little "Hee hee hee." The green-bearded dwarf tipped the wide-brimmed hat to Cadderly, as if saluting a warrior going to battle.

Cadderly scowled at the dwarf and walked past, moving to a small stone, which crafty Ivan had fashioned into a stool. Danica stood behind the stool, waiting for Cadderly, her beautiful daggers, one golden-hilted and sculpted into the shape of a tiger, the other a silver dragon, in hand. For any who did not know Danica, those blades, or any weapons, would have looked out of place in her deceivingly delicate hands. She was barely five feet tall—if she went two days without eating, she wouldn't top a hundred pounds—with thick locks of strawberry blond hair cascading over her shoulders and unusual almond-shaped eyes a light but rich brown. On casual glance, Danica seemed more a candidate for a southern harem, a beautiful, delicate flower.

The young priest knew better, as did any who had spent time beside Danica. Those delicate hands could break stone; that beautiful face could smash a man's nose flat. Danica was a monk, a disciplined fighter, and her studies were no less intense than Cadderly's, her worship of the wisdom of ancient masters no less than Cadderly's of his god. She was as perfect a warrior as Cadderly had ever seen; she could use any weapon, and could defeat most swordsmen with her bare hands and feet. And she could put either of the enchanted daggers she now held into the eye of an enemy twenty paces away. Cadderly took his seat, pointedly facing away from the boisterous gamblers, while Danica began to softly chant.

Cadderly found a meditative focus; it was vital that he remain absolutely still. Suddenly, Danica broke into motion, her arms weaving intricate patterns in the air before her, her feet shifting from side to side, keeping perfect balance. The impossibly sharp blades began to turn in her fingers.

The first one came around in a blinding flash, but Cadderly, deep in concentration, did not flinch. He barely felt the scrape as the knife's edge brushed his cheek, barely had time to smell the oiled metal as the silver dragon whipped in under his nostrils and shot down to his upper lip.

This was a ritual that the two performed every day, one that kept Cadderly clean-shaven and Danica's finely honed muscles at their peak.

It was over in a mere minute, Cadderly's stubble swept away without a nick to his tanned skin.

"I should chop this tangle away, too," Danica teased, grabbing a handful of Cadderly's thick, curly brown hair.

Cadderly reached up and grabbed her wrist and pulled her around and down, over his shoulder so that their faces were close. The two were lovers, committed to each other for life, and the only reason they had not yet been married in open vows was that Cadderly did not consider the priests of the Edificant Library worthy of performing the ceremony.

Cadderly gave Danica a little kiss, and both jumped back as a blue spark flashed between them, stinging their lips. Immediately, both turned to the entrance to the chamber on the cave's lefthand wall, and were greeted by the joined laughter of Dorigen and Shayleigh.

"Such a bond," remarked Dorigen sarcastically. She had been the one to cause the spark—of course it had been the wizard. Once an enemy of the band, indeed one of the leaders of the army that had invaded Shilmista, Dorigen, by all appearances, had turned to a new way of life and was going back with the others to face judgment at the library.

"Never have I seen such a spark of love," added Shayleigh, shaking her head so that her long, thick mane of golden hair fell back from her face. Even in the dim light streaming in through the cave's eastern door, the elf's violet eyes sparkled like polished jewels.

"Should I add this to your list of crimes?" Cadderly asked Dorigen.

"If that was the greatest of my crimes, I would not bother to return to the library beside you, young priest," the wizard replied easily.

Danica looked from Cadderly to Dorigen, recognizing the bond that had grown between them. It wasn't hard for the monk to discern the source of that attraction. With her black hair, showing lines of gray, and her wide-set eyes, Dorigen resembled Pertelope, the headmistress at the library who had been like Cadderly's mother until her recent death. Pertelope alone seemed to understand the transformation that had come over Cadderly, the god-song that played in his thoughts and gave him access to clerical powers to rival the highest-ranking priests in all the land.

Danica could see some of the same perceptive characteristics in Dorigen. The wizard was a thinker, a person who weighed the situation carefully before acting, and a person not afraid to follow her heart. Dorigen had turned against Aballister in Castle Trinity, had all but gone over to Cadderly's side despite her knowledge that her crimes would not be forgotten. She had done it because her conscience had so dictated.

Danica had not grown to love, or even like, the woman over the weeks of forced hibernation, but she did respect the wizard, and did, to some extent, trust Dorigen.

"Well, you have been hinting at this for many days," Dorigen said to Cadderly. "Is it time for us to be on the road?"

Cadderly instinctively looked back to the door and nodded. "The passes south to Carradoon should be clear enough to travel," he replied. "And many of the passes back into the mountains will be clear as well, the snow fallen from them." Cadderly paused, and the others, not understanding why the mountain passes should be of any concern, watched him carefully, looking for clues.

"Though I fear that the melt might bring some avalanches," the young priest finished.

"I do not fear avalanches," came the firbolg's voice booming from the door. "I have lived all my life in the mountains, and know well enough when a trail is safe."

"Ye're not going back to the library," piped in Ivan, eyeing his giant friend suspiciously.

"Oo," added Pikel, apparently not too happy about it.

"I have my own home, my own family," said Vander. He, Ivan, and Pikel had discussed this matter many times over the last few weeks, but not until this moment had Vander made a decision.

Ivan obviously wasn't thrilled with it. He and Vander were friends, and saying farewell was never an easy thing. But the sturdy dwarf agreed with the firbolg's decision, and he had promised, before and now again, that he would one day travel north to the Spine of the World Mountains and seek out Vander's firbolg clan.

"But why are you talking of the mountains?" Shayleigh asked Cadderly bluntly. "Except for Vander, we'll not have to go into the mountains until we pass Carradoon, and that will entail no less than a week of walking."

"We are going in sooner," Danica answered for Cadderly, thinking that she had the man's mind read. She found that she was half right.

"Not all of us," Cadderly stated. "There would be no need."

"The dragon's treasure!" Ivan roared suddenly, referring to the cave they had left behind, where old Fyrentennimar had lived. The friends had dispatched the old red in the mountains, leaving his treasure unguarded. "Ye're thinking of the dragon's treasure!" The dwarf slapped his round-shouldered brother on the back.

"An unguarded hoard," Shayleigh agreed. "But it would take all seven of us, and many more than that, to bring that great treasure out."

"We do not even know if the treasure will be found," Cadderly reminded them. "The storm that Aballister threw at Nightglow Mountain likely sealed many caves."

"So you wish to go back to see if the treasure might be recovered," Danica reasoned.

"Recovered when the weather is more agreeable," said Cadderly. "And so we need not all make the journey to the mountain."

"What do you propose?" Danica asked, and she already knew the lines that Cadderly would draw.

"I will return to the mountain," the young priest answered, "along with Ivan and Pikel, if they are agreeable. I had hoped that you would come along as well," he said to Vander.

"Part of the way," the red-bearded giant promised. "But I am anxious . . ."

Cadderly cut him short with an upraised hand. He understood the firbolg's feelings and would not ask Vander, who had been so long from home, so long tormented by the assassin, Ghost, to delay any longer. "Any step you take beside us will be welcomed," Cadderly insisted, and Vander nodded.

Cadderly turned back to the three women. "I know you must get back to Shilmista," he said to Shayleigh. "King Elbereth will need a full report on the happenings at Castle Trinity, so that he might stand down the elven guard. The fastest route for you would be south past Carradoon, then along the more traveled trails west from the library."

Shayleigh nodded.

"And I am to accompany Dorigen back," Danica reasoned.

Cadderly nodded. "You are not of either host order," he explained, "thus, Dorigen will be your prisoner and not under the jurisdiction of the headmasters."

"Whom you do not trust," Dorigen added slyly.

Cadderly didn't bother to respond. "If all goes well at Nightglow, the dwarves and I should come to the library no more than a few days after you."

"But since I came in alone, Dorigen will remain my prisoner," Danica reasoned, and she smiled despite the fact that she did not wish to miss the adventure at Nightglow, and did not want to be apart from Cadderly at all.

"Your judgment will be more fair, I am sure," Cadderly said with a wink. "And it shall be easier for me to convince the headmasters to accept that judgment than to get them to pass a fair punishment of their own."

It was a solid plan, Danica knew, one that would likely spare Dorigen from a hangman's noose.

Dorigen's smile showed that she understood the plan's merits as well. "Again you have my gratitude," she offered. "I only wish that I believed myself worthy of it."

Cadderly and Danica exchanged a knowing look, and neither was the least bit worried about splitting the party with a prisoner in tow. Dorigen was a powerful wizard, and if she had wanted to escape, she certainly could have done so by now. Over the weeks, she had not been bound in any way, and only in the first few days had she even been guarded. Never was there a more willing prisoner, and Cadderly was confident that Dorigen would not try to escape. Even more than that, Cadderly was convinced that Dorigen would use her powers to aid Danica and Shayleigh if they got into trouble on the way to the library.

It was settled then, with no disagreements. Ivan and Pikel rubbed their hands together often and slapped each other on the back so many times that they sounded like a gallery at a fine performance. Nothing could set a dwarf to hopping like the promise of an unguarded dragon's hoard.

Danica found Cadderly alone later that morning, while the others busied themselves for the journey. The young priest hardly noticed her approach, just stood on a clear patch of stone outside the cave, staring into the towering Snowflake Mountains.

Danica moved up and hooked her arm under Cadderly's, offering him the support she thought he needed. To her thinking, Cadderly wasn't ready to return to the library. No doubt, he was still in turmoil over the last incident with Dean Thobicus, when he had forcefully bent the dean's mind to his bidding. Beyond that, with all that had happened—the deaths of Avery and Pertelope and the revelation that the evil wizard Aballister was, in truth, Cadderly's own father—the young priest's world had been turned upside down. Cadderly had questioned his faith and his home for some time, and though he had finally come to terms with his loyalty to Deneir, Danica wondered if he still had a hard time thinking of the Edificant Library as his home.

They remained silent for several minutes, Cadderly staring up into the mountains and Danica staring at Cadderly.

"Do you fear a charge of heresy?" the monk asked at length.

Cadderly turned to her, his expression curious.

"For your actions against Dean Thobicus," Danica clarified. "If he has remembered the incident and realizes what you did to him, he will not likely welcome you back."

"Thobicus will not openly oppose me," Cadderly said.

Danica did not miss the fact that he had named the man without the man's title, no small matter by the rules of the order and of the library.

"Though he most likely will have recalled much of what happened when last we talked," the young priest went on, "I expect he will solidify his alliances . . . and demote or dismiss those he suspects are loyal to me."

Despite the grim reasoning, there was little trepidation in Cadderly's tone, Danica noted, and her expression revealed her surprise.

"What allies can he make?" Cadderly asked, as though that explained everything.

"He is the head of the order," Danica replied, "and has many friends in the Oghman order as well."

Cadderly chuckled softly and scoffed at the thought. "I told you before that Thobicus is the head of a false hierarchy."

"And you will simply walk in and make that claim?"

"Yes," Cadderly answered calmly. "I have an ally that Dean Thobicus cannot resist, one who will turn the priests of my order to me."

Danica did not have to ask who that ally might be. Cadderly believed that Deneir himself was with him, that the deity had assigned him a task. Given the man's powers, Danica did not doubt the notion. Still, it bothered Danica somewhat that Cadderly had become so bold, even arrogant.

"The Oghman priests will not become involved," Cadderly went on, "for this does not concern them. The only contention I will see from them, and rightly so, will manifest itself after I unseat Thobicus as head of the Deneirian order. Bron Turman will contest me for the title of dean."

"Turman has been a leader in the library for many years," Danica said.

Cadderly nodded and seemed not at all bothered.

"His will be a powerful challenge," Danica reasoned.

"It is not important which of us ascends to the position of dean," Cadderly replied. "My first duty is to the order of Deneir. Once that is set aright, I will worry about the future of the Edificant Library."

Danica accepted that, and again the two lapsed into long minutes of silence, Cadderly staring once more at the majestic Snowflakes. Danica believed in him, and in his reasoning, but she had trouble reconciling his apparent calmness with the fact that he was out here, standing in deep contemplation, instead of at the library. Cadderly's delay revealed the true turmoil behind his cool facade.

"What are you thinking about?" she asked, and pressed her hand gently against the young priest's cheek, drawing his gaze from the mountains.

Cadderly smiled warmly, touched by her concern.

"Up there is an unguarded hoard of treasure greater than anything in all the region," Cadderly said.

"I've never known you to care much for material wealth," Danica remarked.

Again Cadderly smiled. "I was thinking of Nameless," he said, referring to a poor leper he had once met on the road outside Carradoon. "I was thinking of all the other Namelesses in Carradoon and all around Impresk Lake. The wealth of the dragon's hoard might bring great good to the land." He looked at Danica squarely. "The treasure might give all of those people names."

"It will be more complicated than that," Danica reasoned, for both of them knew well the equation of wealth and power. If Cadderly meant to share the riches with the impoverished people, he would find resistance among those. "gentlefolk" of Carradoon who equated wealth with nobility and rank and used their riches to feel superior.

"Deneir is with me," Cadderly said calmly, and Danica understood at that moment that her love was indeed ready for this fight, ready for Thobicus and all the others.

* * * * *

Several priests worked furiously over Kierkan Rufo on the cold, wet ground outside the Edificant Library's front door. They wrapped him in their own cloaks, disregarding the chill wind of early spring, but they did not miss the brand on his forehead, the unlit candle above the closed eye, and even the Oghman priests understood its significance, that they could not bring the man into the library.

Rufo continued to gag and vomit. His chest heaved and his stomach convulsed, tightening into agonizing knots. Blue-black bruises erupted under the man's sweating skin.

The Oghman priests, some of them powerful clerics, enacted spells of healing, though the Deneirians did not dare evoke the powers of their god in this man's name.

None of it seemed to work.

Dean Thobicus and Bron Turman arrived together at the door, pushing through the growing crowd of onlookers. The withered dean's eyes widened considerably when he saw that it was Rufo lying outside.

"We must bring him into the warmth!" one of the attending priests shouted to the dean.

"He cannot enter the library," Bron Turman insisted, "not with such a brand. By his own actions was Kierkan Rufo banished, and the banishment holds!"

"Bring him in," Dean Thobicus said unexpectedly, and Turman nearly fell over as he registered the words. He didn't openly protest, though. Rufo was of Thobicus's order, not his own, and Thobicus, as dean, was well within his powers in allowing the man entry.

A few moments later, after Rufo was ushered through the crowd and Thobicus had gone off with the attending priests, Bron Turman came to a disturbing conclusion, an explanation of the dean's words that did not sit well with the Oghman. Kierkan Rufo was no friend of Cadderly's; in fact, Cadderly had been the one to brand the man. Had that precipitated the dean's decision to let Rufo in?

Bron Turman hoped that was not the case.

In a side room, an empty chamber normally reserved for private prayers, the priests pulled in a bench to use as a cot and continued their heroic efforts to comfort Rufo. Nothing they did seemed to help; even Thobicus tried to summon his greatest healing powers, chanting over Rufo while the others held him steady. But, whether the spell had not been granted or Rufo's ailment had simply rejected it, the dean's words fell empty.

Blood and bile poured freely from Rufo's mouth and nose, and his chest heaved desperately, trying to pull in air through the obstruction in his throat. One strong Oghman priest grabbed Rufo and yanked him over onto his belly, pounding at his back to force everything out.

Suddenly, without warning, Rufo jerked and turned so violently that the Oghman priest went flying across the room. Then Rufo settled on the bench and calmed strangely, staring up unblinkingly at Dean Thobicus. With a weak hand, he motioned for the dean to come closer, and Thobicus, after looking around nervously, bent low, putting his ear near the man's mouth.

"You . . . you invi . . . vited me," Rufo stammered, blood and bile accompanying every word.

Thobicus stood up straight, staring at the man, not understanding.

"You invited me in," Rufo said clearly with his last bit of strength. He began to laugh then, weirdly, out of control, and the laughter became a great convulsion, and then a final scream.

None in attendance remembered ever seeing a man die more horribly.

Three

The Ultimate Perversion

T here ain't no durned cave!" Ivan roared, and a rumble from above, from the unsteady, piled snow, reminded the dwarf that a bit more care might be prudent.

If Ivan didn't get the point then, he got it a second later, when frantic Pikel ran up and slapped him on the back of the head, knocking his helm down over his eyes. The yellow-bearded dwarf grabbed a deer antler and adjusted the thing, then turned a scowl on his brother, but Pikel didn't relent, just stood there waggling a finger in Ivan's face.

"Quiet down, both of you!" Cadderly scolded.

"Oo," replied Pikel, and he seemed honestly wounded.

Cadderly, thoroughly flustered, didn't notice the look. He continued his scan of the ruined mountain, amazed that the opening—an opening large enough to admit a dragon with its wings spread wide—was no more.

"You are sure that it is not just snow?" Cadderly asked, to which Ivan stamped his boot, dislodging a chunk of snow from above that fell over him and Pikel.

Pikel popped up first, snow sliding off the edges of the flopping, wide-brimmed hat he had borrowed from Cadderly, and was ready with another slap when Ivan reappeared.

"If ye don't believe me, go in there yerself!" Ivan bellowed, pointing to the snow mass. "There's stone in there. Solid stone, I tell ye! That wizard sealed it good with his storm."

Cadderly put his hands on his hips and took a deep breath. He recalled the storm Aballister had sent to Nightglow, the wizard thinking that Cadderly and his friends were still there. Aballister had no way of knowing that Cadderly had enlisted the aid of a hostile dragon and was many miles closer to Castle Trinity.

Looking at the destruction, at the side of a mountain torn asunder by hurled magic, Cadderly was glad that Aballister's aim had been misplaced. That did little to comfort the young priest now, though. Inside this mountain waited an unguarded dragon hoard, a treasure that Cadderly would need to see his plans for the Edificant Library, and for all the region, realized. This had been the only major door, though, the one opening they could push carts through to extract the treasure before the next winter's snows.

"The whole opening?" Cadderly asked Ivan.

The yellow-bearded dwarf started to respond in his typically loud voice, but stopped and looked at his brother (who was readying yet another slap), and just growled instead. Ivan had bored through the wall of snow for more than an hour, pushing in blindly at several locations until the rock wall behind the snow curtain inevitably turned him away.

"We'll go around," Cadderly said, "to the hole on the mountain's south face that first got us into the place."

"It was a long walk between that hole and the dragon hoard," Ivan reminded him. "A long walk through tight tunnels, and even a long drop. I'm not for knowing how ye're planning to bring a treasure out that way!"

"Neither am I," Cadderly admitted. "All I know is that I need the treasure, and I'm going to find some way to get it!" With that, the young priest walked off along the trail, in search of a path that would lead him around Nightglow's wide base.

"He sounds like a dwarf," Ivan whispered to Pikel.

After Pikel's ensuing. "Hee hee hee" brought down the next mini-avalanche, it was Ivan's turn to do the head-slapping.

The trio arrived on the south face early the next morning. Climbing proved difficult in the slippery, melting snow. Ivan got almost all the way to the hole (and was able to confirm that there was indeed a hole in this side of the mountain) before he slipped and tumbled, turning into a dwarven snowball and bowling Cadderly and Pikel down the hill with him.

"Stupid priest!" the dwarf roared at Cadderly when the three sorted themselves out far down the mountainside. "Ain't ye got some magic to get us up this stupid hill?"

Cadderly nodded reluctantly. He had been trying to conserve his energies since their departure from Castle Trinity. Every day he had to cast spells on himself and his companions to ward off the cold, but he had hoped that would be the extent of his exertion until he returned to the library. Cadderly was more tired than he had ever been. His trials, especially against Aballister and Fyrentennimar, had thoroughly drained him, had forced him to delve into magical spheres that he did not understand and, by sheer willpower, bring forth dweomers that should have been far beyond his capabilities. Now young Cadderly was paying the price for those efforts. Even the weeks of relative calm, holed up in the cave, had not rejuvenated him. He could still hear Deneir's song in his head, but whenever he tried to access the greater magic, his temples throbbed, and he felt that his head would explode.

Pertelope, dear Pertelope, who alone had understood the obstacles facing Cadderly as a chosen priest of the god of the arts, had warned Cadderly about this potential side effect, but even Pertelope had admitted that it seemed as though Cadderly had little choice in the matter, that the young priest was facing enemies beyond anything she had ever seen.

Cadderly closed his eyes and listened for the notes of Deneir's song, music taught him from the *Tome of Universal Harmony*, his most holy book. At first he felt a deep serenity, as though he were returning home after a long, difficult journey. The harmonies of Deneir's song played sweetly in his thoughts, leading him down corridors of truth and understanding. Then he purposely opened a door, turned a mental page from his recollections of the most holy book and sought a spell that would get him and his friends up the mountain.

Then his temples began to hurt.

Cadderly heard Ivan calling him, distantly, and he opened his eyes just long enough to take hold of Pikel's hand and grab hold of Ivan's beard when the confused and suspicious Ivan refused Cadderly's offered grasp.

Ivan's protests intensified into desperation as the three began to melt away, becoming insubstantial, mere shadows. The wind seemed to catch them, and it carried them unerringly up the mountainside.

Pikel was cheering loudly when Cadderly came out of his trance. Ivan stood still for a long while, then began a tactile inspection, as if testing to see if all of his tangible mass had been restored.

Cadderly slumped in the snow beside the small opening in the hill, collected his wits, and rubbed the sides of his head to try to alleviate the throbbing. It wasn't as bad as the last time he had tried a major spell. Back in the cave he had tried, and failed, to make mental contact with Dean Thobicus to ensure that no invasion force was marching north toward Castle Trinity. It wasn't so bad this time, and Cadderly was glad of that. If they could get their business done quickly, and if the weather held, the three would be back at the Edificant Library within two weeks. Cadderly suspected that there waited his greatest challenge yet, one that he would need the song of Deneir to combat.

"At least there's no stupid dragon waiting in there this time," Ivan huffed, and he moved up to the entrance.

The last time Cadderly and the others had come to this spot, a fog enshrouded the area and all the snow near the hole had been melted away. The air was still warm inside the hole, but not nearly as oppressive, and ominous, as when Fyrentennimar had been alive.

Pikel tried to push Ivan aside, but the yellow-bearded dwarf held his ground stubbornly, showing that he was more intrigued by the prospects of a dragon's hoard than he let on. "I'm going in first," Ivan insisted. "Ye'll follow by twenty paces," he explained to Pikel. "So that I can call to yerself, and ye can call to Cadderly."

Pikel's head bobbed in agreement, and Ivan started for the hole. He considered it for just a moment, then removed his helmet and tossed it to Cadderly.

"Ivan," the young priest called, and when Ivan turned back, the young priest tossed him a short metallic tube.

Ivan had seen this item, one of Cadderly's many inventions, before, and he knew how to use it. He popped off the snug cap on its end, allowing a beam of light to stream forth. There was a disk inside the tube, enchanted with a powerful lightgiving dweomer, and the tube was really two pieces of metal. The outer tube, near the end cap, could be turned along a corkscrew course, lengthening or shortening the tube, thus tightening or widening the beam of light.

Ivan kept the focus narrow now, since the tunnel was so constricted that the broad-shouldered dwarf had to often turn sideways to squeeze through, so narrow that Pikel reluctantly gave Cadderly back his wide-brimmed hat before entering.

Cadderly waited patiently for many minutes, his thoughts lost in the anticipated confrontation with Dean Thobicus. He was glad when Pikel reappeared in search of rope, knowing then that Ivan had made it through the tightest of the tunnels and had come to the vertical shaft that would take him to the same level as the dragon treasure.

Twenty minutes later, both dwarves came bobbing out of the hole, Ivan shaking his head.

"It's blocked," he announced. "I can get down to the big room under the shaft, but there's nowhere to go from there. I'm thinking we might be better in trying to cut through that front door."

Cadderly blew a deep sigh.

"I'll call for me kin," Ivan went on. "Of course, it'll take 'em the bulk of the next two seasons to get down from Vaasa, and then we'll have to wait for the next winter to blow over . . . ."

Cadderly tuned out as the dwarf rambled on. By conventional means, it might take years to extract the dragon treasure, and the delay would bring about some unexpected obstacles. Word of Fyrentennimar's demise would spread fast throughout the land, and most of the peoples in the region, of races both good and evil, knew that the dragon resided in Nightglow Mountain. The fall of a dragon, especially one that had sat for centuries on a legendary treasure hoard, always brought scavengers.

Like me, Cadderly thought, and he chuckled aloud at the self-deprecating humor. He realized then that Ivan had stopped talking, and when he looked up, he found both dwarves staring at him intently.

"Fear not, Ivan," Cadderly said, "you'll not need to summon your kin."

"They would take a bit o' the treasure for their own," Ivan admitted. "By the gods, they'd probably set up a keep right inside the mountain, and then we'd be hard pressed to get a single copper outta them!"

Pikel started to laugh, but caught himself and turned a stern look on Ivan, realizing that his brother was serious, and probably correct.

"I'll get us into the mountain, and we'll have plenty of help from Carradoon when the time comes to take out the treasure," Cadderly assured them both. "But not now."

The young priest let it go at that, thinking that the dwarves need know no more. His next task, he knew, was to get to the library, to put things spiritually aright. Then he could concentrate on the treasure, could come back here rested and ready to clear the path magically for the foragers.

"This place is important to ye," Ivan remarked. Cadderly looked at the dwarf curiously, more for the tone Ivan had used than the specific words.

"More important than it should be," Ivan went on. "Ye always had money, particularly since ye penned that spellbook for the frantic wizard, but ye never seemed to care so much for money."

"That has not changed," Cadderly replied.

"Eh?" Pikel squeaked, echoing Ivan's sentiments exactly. If Cadderly had no care for money, then why were they up here in the middle of the dangerous mountains, freezing their stubby feet off?

"I care about what this treasure might bring for us all," Cadderly went on.

"Wealth," Ivan interrupted, eagerly rubbing his strong hands together.

Cadderly looked at him sourly. "Do you remember that model I kept in my room?" the young priest asked, more to Pikel than Ivan, for Pikel had been particularly enchanted with the thing. "The one of the high, windowed wall with the supporting buttress?"

"Oo oi!" Pikel roared happily in reply.

"Ye're thinking to rebuild the library," Ivan reasoned, and the dwarf blew a huff of spittle into the frosty air when Cadderly nodded. "If the durned thing ain't broke, then why're ye meaning to fix it?" Ivan demanded.

"I am thinking to improve it," Cadderly corrected. "You yourself have witnessed the strength of the model's design, and that with soaring windows. Soaring windows, Ivan, making the library a place of light, where books might truly be penned and read."

"Bah! Ye've never done any building," Ivan protested. "That much I know. Ye've no idea of the scope of the structure ye're planning. Humans don't live long enough for ye to see yer new . . . What was it ye once called that thing?"

"A cathedral," Cadderly answered.

"Humans won't live long enough to see yer new cathedral even half finished," Ivan went on. "It'll take a full clan of dwarves a hundred years . . ."

"That does not matter," Cadderly answered simply, stealing Ivan's bluster. "It does not matter if I see the completion, only that I begin the construction. That is the cost of, and the joy of, faith, Ivan, and you should understand that."

Ivan was back on his heels. He hadn't heard such talk from any human before, and he'd known many humans in his day. The dwarves and the elves were the ones who thought of the future, who had the foresight and the good sense to blaze the trail for their ancestors to walk. Humans, as far as most of the longer-living races were concerned, were an impatient folk, a group that had to see material gains almost immediately to maintain any momentum or desire for a chore.

"You have heard recently of Bruenor Battlehammer," Cadderly went on, "who has reclaimed Mithril Hall in the name of his father. Already, by all reports, the work has begun in earnest to expand on the halls, and in this generation, those halls are many times larger than the founders of that dwarven stronghold could ever have imagined when they first began cutting the great steps that would become the famed Undercity. Isn't that the way with all dwarven strongholds? They start as a hole in the ground, and end up among the greatest excavations in all the Realms, though many generations—dwarven generations!—might pass."

"Oo oi!" Pikel piped in, the wordless dwarf's way of saying, "Good point!"

"And so it shall be with my cathedral," Cadderly explained. "If I lay but the first stone, then I will have begun something grand, for it is the vision that serves the purpose."

Ivan looked helplessly to Pikel, who only shrugged. It was hard for either dwarf to fault Cadderly's thinking. In fact, as Ivan digested all that the young priest had said, he found that he respected Cadderly even more, that the man had risen above the usual limitations of his heritage and was actually planning to do something quite dwarflike.

Ivan said just that, and Cadderly was gracious enough to accept the sideways compliment without a word of argument.

* * * * *

Two Oghman priests approached the square stone mausoleum butted against the cliff behind the Edificant Library.

"Let them take care of their own, I say," muttered the muscular chap nick-named Berdole the Brutal because of his wrestling prowess and snarling demeanor. The other, Curt, nodded his agreement, for neither of them liked this detail. Kierkan Rufo had been a priest of Deneir, not Oghma, and yet, because of his brand, Dean Thobicus had determined that Oghman priests should prepare and bury the body. By custom, Rufo's body had lain in state for three days, and now it was time for the final preparations.

Berdole fumbled with his large belt ring, finally finding the long-necked key that fit the heavy door. With some effort, he opened the lock and pulled the door wide. A damp, musty smell, tinged with the scent of decay, rolled out at the two. Except to put Rufo's body inside, this structure had not been opened since the death of Pertelope in the late fall.

Curt lit and hoisted his lantern, but motioned for Berdole to lead the way in. The muscular priest obliged, his hard boots stomping noisily on the bare stone floor.

The vault was large, perhaps thirty feet square, supported at ten-foot intervals both ways by thick columns. A single window, right of the door, allowed some sunlight to trickle in, but the glass was filthy and deeply set in the thick stone, and the illumination was meager. A series of stone slabs lined the center of the room, all but one empty.

On that slab, between the two columns farthest from the door, lay Kierkan Rufo's body beneath an unremarkable shroud.

"Let us be done quickly," said Berdole, pulling the pack from his back. His obvious nervousness did not sit well with his smaller companion, who looked to Berdole the Brutal for protection.

The two did not bother to close the door as they moved in, and neither noticed the soft rush of air as an invisible creature glided in behind them.

"Maybe he threw up enough blood so this will not take so long," Berdole said with a halfhearted chuckle.

Curt snickered at the grim humor as well, knowing that jokes might be his only defense against his abhorrence of this task.

High in a corner of the mausoleum, on the opposite wall and to the right of the door, Druzil sat and scratched his doglike head, muttering curses under his breath. The imp had tried to get into this place since Rufo's body had been put here, thinking that he might somehow recover at least a portion of the chaos curse from the corpse. Too many priests had been around then, including one of the leading members of the Oghman order, and so Druzil had waited, thinking he would just break in after the others had left. He found the door locked, though, and the window blessed, so that he did not dare enter.

The imp knew enough of the human rituals to understand what the two men now meant to do. They would drain the blood from the body and replace it with a smelly, preserving liquid. Druzil had overheard that Rufo could not be given a proper Deneirian or Oghman burial, and the imp had hoped that the priests wouldn't waste their time with this pointless embalming. Druzil thought of swooping down and stinging the men with his poison-tipped tail, or of hitting them with magical spells, burning their behinds with little bolts of energy to chase them away. It simply was too risky, so all the imp could do was sit and watch and mutter silent curses.

Every drop of blood that the priests took from Rufo's body would be a little less of *Tuanta Quiro Miancay* the imp might recover.

Berdole looked at his partner and took a deep breath, holding up the large needle for Curt to see.

"I cannot watch this," Curt admitted, and he turned away and walked past a couple of the slabs, near the other set of columns.

Berdole laughed, gaining confidence from his friend's weakness, and moved beside the slab. He pushed the shroud away just enough so that he could pull out Rufo's left arm, pushing back the black robes that Rufo had been dressed in and turning the arm so that the exposed wrist was up.

"You might feel a small pinch," the muscular priest joked lightly to the corpse, drawing a disgusted groan from Curt.

From the far rafters, Druzil chewed his bottom lip in frustration as he watched the large needle go against Rufo's exposed wrist. He would have to steal the blood, he decided, every drop of it!

Berdole lined the needle's point up with the vein in Rufo's skinny wrist and angled the instrument for a good puncture. He took another deep breath, looked to Curt's back for support, then started to push.

The cold, pallid hand snapped around in a circular motion, catching the needle and Berdole's hand in a crushing grasp.

"What?" the muscular priest stammered.

Curt turned about to see Berdole hunched low at the slab, both his strong hands wrapped around Rufo's thin forearm, with Rufo's clawlike digits clasping tightly to his lower jaw. This was Berdole the Brutal, the strongest of the strong Oghmans. This was Berdole the Brutal, two hundred and fifty pounds of power, a man who could wrestle a black bear to a standstill!

Yet that skinny arm of Kierkan Rufo—of dead Kierkan Rufo!—jerked Berdole down to the slab as though his muscular frame were no more than a wet towel. Then, to Curt's disbelieving eyes, Rufo's hand pushed up and back. The muscles in Berdole's thick arms strained to their limits, but could not halt the push. Up and over went his chin—it sounded to Curt like the cracking of a large tree right before it tumbled to the ground—and suddenly, the surprised Berdole was staring at the world upside down and backwards.

The Oghman's strong hands let go of the skinny, pallid arm and twitched uncontrollably in the empty air. Rufo's fingers loosened, and Berdole fell backward to the floor, quite dead.

Curt hardly remembered to breathe. He looked from Berdole to the shrouded corpse, and his vision blurred with dizziness wrought of horror as Rufo slowly sat up.

The shroud fell away, and the gaunt, pale man turned his eyes, eyes that simmered red with inner fires, toward Curt.

Druzil clapped his clawed hands together and squealed in happiness, then flapped off for the door.

Curt screamed and fled with all speed, five long strides bringing him near the sunlight, near salvation.

Rufo waved a hand, and the heavy stone door swung shut, slamming with a bang that sounded like a drum of doom.

The Oghman threw all his weight against the door, but he might as well have tried to move a mountain. He scratched at the stone until his fingers bled. He glanced back over his shoulder and saw that Rufo was up, walking stiffly toward him.

Curt cried out repeatedly and went for the window, but realized that he had no time. He fell beyond it, backing and watching the corpse, crying for mercy and for Oghma to be with him.

Then the side wall was against his back; he had nowhere to run. Curt caught his breath finally, and remembered who he was. He presented his holy symbol, a scroll of silver on a chain about his neck, and called to Oghma.

"Be gone!" Curt cried at Rufo. "In the name of Oghma, evil undead thing, get you back!"

Rufo didn't flinch. He was ten steps away. Nine steps away. He staggered suddenly as he crossed in front of the window, as though he had been burned on the side. But the light was meager, and the monster passed beyond it.

Curt began a frantic chant of a spell. He felt strangely disconnected from his god, though, as if Rufo's mere presence had despoiled this place. Still he chanted, summoning his powers.

He felt a sting in his lower back and jerked suddenly, his spell disrupted. He turned to see the bat-winged imp, snickering wickedly as it flew away.

"What horror is this?" Curt cried. Rufo was there then, and the terrified man swung his lantern out at the monster.

Rufo caught him by the wrist and easily held the makeshift weapon at bay. Curt punched out with his other hand, connecting solidly on Rufo's chin, knocking Rufo's head to the side.

Rufo calmly turned back to him. Curt made to punch again, but Rufo hooked his arm under the man's, brought his skinny fingers around Curt's back, and grabbed the man's hair on the opposite side of his head. With terrifying strength, Rufo pulled Curt's head to the side, pressed Curt's cheek against his own shoulder, laying bare the side of the man's neck.

Curt thought that Rufo would simply snap that neck, as he had done to Berdole, but the Oghman learned better when Rufo opened his mouth, revealing a set of canine fangs, half an inch longer than the rest of his teeth.

With a look of supreme hunger, Rufo bent over and bit down on Curt's neck, opening the jugular. Curt was screaming, but Rufo, feasting on the warm blood, heard none of it.

It was ecstasy for the monster, the satiation of a hunger more powerful than anything he had ever known in life. It was impossibly sweet. It was . . . Rufo's mouth began to burn. The sweet blood became acidic.

With a roar of outrage, Rufo spun away and heaved the man away with the arm still hooked behind Curt's back. The poor man flew head over heels, his back striking the nearest column. He slid to the floor and lay very still. He felt nothing in his lower body, but his chest was on fire, burning with poison.

"What have you done?" Kierkan Rufo demanded, looking to the rafters and the perched imp.

A creature of the horrid lower planes, Druzil was not usually afraid of anything this world could present to him. The imp was afraid now, justifiably afraid of this thing that Kierkan Rufo had become. "I wanted to help you," Druzil explained. "He could not be allowed to escape."

"You tainted his blood!" Rufo roared. "His blood," the monster said more quietly, longingly. "I need . . . I need."

Rufo looked back to Curt, but the light of life had gone from the man's eyes. Rufo roared again, a horrible, unearthly sound.

"There are more," Druzil promised. "There are many more, not far away!"

A strange look came over Rufo then. He looked to his bare arms, held them up in front of his face, as though he had realized for the first time that something very unusual had happened to him.

"Blood?" he asked more than stated, and he put a plaintive look Druzil's way.

Druzil's bulbous eyes seemed to come farther out of their sockets as the imp recognized the sincere confusion on the dead Rufo's face. "Do you not understand what has happened to you?" Druzil cried excitedly.

Rufo went to take a steadying breath, but then realized that he wasn't breathing at all. Again that plaintive, questioning look fell over Druzil, who seemed to have the answers.

"You drank of *Tuanta Quiro Miancay*," the imp squealed. "The Most Fatal Horror, the ultimate chaos, and thus you have become the ultimate perversion of humanity!"

Still Rufo did not seem to understand.

"The ultimate perversion!" Druzil said again, as though that should explain everything. "The antithesis of life itself!"

"What are you talking about?" asked a horrified Rufo, Curt's blood spewing from his lips.

Druzil laughed wickedly. "You are immortal," he said, and Rufo, stunned and confused, finally began to catch on. "You are a vampire."

Four

Delusions

V ampire. The word hung in Rufo's thoughts, a dead weight on his undead shoulders. He crawled back to the stone slab and flopped down on his back, covering his eyes with his skinny, pale hands.

"*Bene tellemara*," Druzil muttered many times as the minutes passed uneventfully. "Would you have them come out and find you?"

Rufo did not look up.

"The priests are dead," the imp rasped. "Torn. Will those who come in search of them be caught so unaware?"

Rufo moved his arm from in front of his face and looked over at the imp, but did not seem to care.

"You think you can beat them," Druzil reasoned, misunderstanding Rufo's calmness. "Fool! You think you can beat them all!"

Rufo's response caught the imp off guard, made Druzil understand that despair, not confidence, was the source of the undead man's lethargy. "I do not care to try," Rufo said sincerely.

"You can beat them," the imp quickly improvised, changing his emphasis so that the statement suddenly did not seem so ridiculous. "You can beat them all!"

"I am already dead," Rufo said dryly. "I am already defeated."

"Of course, of course!" Druzil rasped happily, clapping his hands and flapping his wings to perch on the end of Rufo's slab. "Dead, yes, but that is your strength, not your weakness. You can beat them all, I say, and the library will be yours."

The last words seemed to pique Rufo's interest. He cocked his head at an angle so that he could better view the untrustworthy imp.

"You are immortal," Druzil said solemnly.

Rufo continued to stare for a long, uneasy moment. "At what price?" he asked.

886

"Price?" Druzil echoed.

"I am not alive!" Rufo roared at him, and Druzil spread his wings, ready to launch away if the vampire made a sudden move.

"You are more alive than you have ever been!" Druzil snapped back. "Now you have power. Now your will shall be done!"

"To what end?" Rufo wanted, needed, to know. "I am dead. My flesh is dead. What pleasures might I know? What dreams worth fancying?"

"Pleasures?" the imp asked. "Did not the priest's blood taste sweet? And did you not feel power as you approached the pitiful man? You could taste his fear, vampire, and the taste was as sweet as the blood that was to come."

Rufo continued to stare, but had no more complaints to offer. Druzil spoke the truth, it seemed. Rufo had tasted the man's fear, and that sensation of power, of inspiring such terror, felt wonderfully sweet to the man who had been so impotent in life.

Druzil waited a little while, until he was certain that Rufo was convinced to at least explore this vampiric existence. "You must be gone from this place," the imp explained, looking to the corpses.

Rufo glanced at the closed door, then nodded and swung about, dangling his legs over the side of the slab. "The catacombs," he remarked.

"You cannot cross," Druzil said as the vampire began stiffly walking toward the door. Rufo turned on him suspiciously, as if he thought the imp's words a threat.

"The sun is bright," Druzil explained. "It will burn you like fire."

Rufo's expression turned from curious to dour to sheer horror.

"You are a creature of the night now," Druzil went on firmly. "The light of day is not your ally."

It was a bitter pill for Rufo to swallow, but in light of all that had happened, the man accepted the news stoically and forced himself to straighten once more. "How am I to get out of here?" he asked, his tone filled with anger and sarcasm.

Druzil led Rufo's gaze to rows of marked stones lining the mausoleum's far wall. These were the crypts of the library's former headmasters, including those of Avery Schell and Pertelope, and not all of the stones were marked.

At first the thought of crawling into a crypt revolted Rufo, but as he let go of those prejudices remaining from when he had been a living, breathing man, as he allowed himself to view the world as an undead thing, a creature of the night, he found the notion of cool, dark stone strangely appealing.

Rufo met Druzil by the wall, in front of an unmarked slab set waist-high. Not knowing what the imp expected, the vampire reached out with his stiff arms and clasped at the edge of the stone.

"Not like that!" Druzil scolded, and Rufo stood straight, eyeing the imp dangerously, obviously growing tired of Druzil's superior attitude.

"If you tear it away, the priests will find you," the imp explained, and under his breath he added the expected, "*Bene tellemara.*"

Rufo did not reply, but stood staring from the imp to the wall. How was he to get inside the crypt if he did not remove the stone? These were not doors that could be opened and closed; they were sealed marker blocks, removed for burials, then mortared back into place.

"There is a crack along the bottom," Druzil remarked, and when Rufo bent low, he did see a line running along the mortar at the bottom of the slab.

The vampire shrugged his shoulders, but before he could ask Druzil how that crack might help, a strange sensation, a lightness, came over him, as though he was something less than substantial. Rufo looked to Druzil, who was smiling widely, then back to the crack, which suddenly loomed much larger. The vampire, black robes and all, melted away into a cloud of green vapor and swirled through the crack in the slab.

He came back to his corporeal form inside the tight confines of the stone crypt, hemmed in by unbroken walls. For an instant, a wave of panic, a feeling of being trapped, swept over the man. How long would his air last? he wondered. He shut his mouth, fearful that he was gulping in too much of the precious commodity.

A moment later, his mouth opened once more and from it issued a howl of laughter. "Air?" Rufo asked aloud. Rufo needed no air, and he was certainly not trapped. He would slip out through that crack as easily as he had come in, or else he could simply slide down and kick the slab free of its perch. He was strong enough to do that, he knew he was.

Suddenly the limitations of a weak and living body seemed clear to the vampire. He thought of all the times when he had been persecuted—unfairly, by his reckoning—and he thought of the two Oghman priests he had so easily dispatched.

Oghman priests! Wrestlers, warriors, yet he had tossed them about without effort!

Rufo felt as though he had been freed of those living limitations, free to fly and grab at the power that was rightfully his. He would teach his persecutors. He would . . .

The vampire stopped fantasizing and reached up to feel the brand on his forehead. An image of Cadderly, of his greatest oppressor, came clear to him.

Yes, Rufo would teach them all.

But now, here in the cool, dark confines of his chosen bed, the vampire would rest. The sun, an ally of the living—an ally of the weak—was bright outside.

Rufo would wait for the dark.

* * * * *

The highest-ranking priests of the Deneirian order gathered that afternoon at Dean Thobicus's bidding. They met in a little-used room on the library's fourth and highest floor, an obscure setting that would guarantee them their privacy.

Seclusion seemed important to the withered dean, the others realized, a point made quite clear when Thobicus shut tight the room's single door and closed the shutters over the two tiny windows.

Thobicus solemnly turned about and surveyed this most important gathering. The room was not formally set up for an audience. Some of the priests sat in chairs of various sizes; others simply stood leaning against a bare wall, or sat on the weathered carpet covering the floor. Thobicus moved near the middle of the group, near the center of the floor, and turned slowly, eyeing each of the thirty gathered priests to let them fully appreciate the gravity of this meeting. The various conversations dissipated under that scrutiny, replaced by intrigue and trepidation.

"Castle Trinity is eradicated," Thobicus said to them after more than a minute of silence.

The priests looked around at each other, stunned by the suddenness of the announcement. Then a cheer went up, quietly at first, but gaining momentum until all the gathered priests, except the dean himself, were clapping each other on the back and shaking their fists in victory.

More than one called out Cadderly's name, and Thobicus winced each time he heard it, and knew that he must proceed with caution.

As the cheering lost its momentum, Thobicus held up his hand, calling for quiet. Again the dean's intense stare fell over the priests, silencing them, filling them with curiosity.

"The word is good," remarked Fester Rumpol, the second-ranking priest of the Deneirian order. "Yet I read no cheer in your features, my dean."

"Do you know how I learned of our enemy's fall?" Thobicus asked him.

"Cadderly?" answered one voice.

"You have spoken with a higher power, an agent of Deneir?" offered another.

Dean Thobicus shook his head to both assumptions, his gaze never leaving Rumpol's. "I could not collect the information," he explained to them all. "My attempts at communion with Deneir have been blocked. I had to go to Bron Turman of Oghma to find my answers. At my bidding, he inquired of agents of his god and learned of our enemy's defeat."

That information was easily as astonishing as the report of Castle Trinity's fall. Thobicus was the dean of the Edificant Library, the father of this sect. How could he be blocked from communion with Deneir's agents? All of these priests had survived the Time of Troubles, that most awful period for persons of faith, and all of them feared that the dean was speaking of a second advent of that terrible time.

Fester Rumpol's expression shifted from fear to suspicion. "I prayed this morning," he said, commanding the attention of all. "I asked for guidance in my search for an old parchment—and my call was answered."

Whispers began all about the room.

"That is because . . ." Thobicus said loudly, sharply, stealing back the audience. He paused to make sure they were all listening. "That is because Cadderly has not yet targeted you!"

"Cadderly?" Rumpol, and several others, said together. Throughout the Edificant Library, particularly in the Deneirian order, feelings for the young priest were strong, many positive and many negative. More than a few of the older priests thought Cadderly impetuous and irreverent, lackadaisical in the routine, necessary duties of his station. And many of the younger priests viewed Cadderly as a rival that they could not compete against. Of the thirty in this room, every man was at least five years older than Cadderly, yet Cadderly had already come to outrank more than half by the library's stated hierarchy. And the persistent rumors hinted that Cadderly was already among the very strongest of the order, in Deneir's eyes.

Dean Thobicus had apparently confirmed this theory. If Cadderly could block the dean's communion with agents of Deneir, and from all the way across the Snowflake Mountains . . . !

Conversations erupted from every corner, the priests confused as to what all of this might mean. Fester Rumpol and Dean Thobicus continued to stare at each other, with Rumpol having no answers to the dean's incredible claim.

"Cadderly has overstepped his rank," Thobicus explained. "He deems the hierarchy of the Edificant Library unfit, and thus, he desires to change it."

"Preposterous!" one priest called out.

"So thought I," Dean Thobicus replied calmly. He had prepared himself well for this meeting, with answers to every question or claim. "But now I have come to know the truth. With Avery Schell and Pertelope dead, our young Cadderly has, it would seem, run a bit out of control. He deceived me in order to go to Castle Trinity." That claim was not exactly true, but Thobicus did not want to admit that Cadderly had dominated him, had bent his mind like a willow in a strong wind. "And now he blocks my attempts at communion with our god."

As far as Thobicus knew, that second statement was correct. For him to believe otherwise would indicate that he had fallen far from Deneir's favor, and that the old dean was not ready to believe.

"What would you have us do?" Fester Rumpol asked, his tone showing more suspicion than loyalty.

"Nothing," Thobicus replied quickly, recognizing the man's doubts. "I only wish to warn you all, that we will not be taken by surprise when our young friend returns."

That answer seemed to satisfy Rumpol and many others. Thobicus abruptly adjourned the meeting then and retired to his private quarters. He had planted the seeds of doubt. His honesty would be viewed favorably when Cadderly returned and the dean and the upstart young priest faced off against each other.

And they would indeed, Thobicus knew. He had neither forgotten nor forgiven the young priest for his actions. He was the dean of the library, the head of his order, and he would not be treated like a puppet by any man.

That was Dean Thobicus's greatest shortcoming. He still could not accept that Cadderly's domination had been granted by Deneir, by the true tenets of their faith. Thobicus had been tied up in the bureaucracy of the library for so long that he had forgotten the higher purpose of the library and the order. Too many procedures had dulled the goals. The dean viewed his upcoming battle with Cadderly as a political struggle, a fight that would be decided by back room alliances and gratuitous promises.

Deep in his heart, of course, Thobicus knew the truth, knew that his struggle with Cadderly would be decided by the tenets of Deneir. But that truth, like the truth of the order itself, was so buried by false information that Thobicus dared to believe otherwise, and fooled himself into thinking that others would follow his lead.

* * * * *

Kierkan Rufo's dreams were no longer those of a victim.

He saw Cadderly, but this time it was the young Deneirian, not the branded Rufo, who cowered. This time, in this dream, Rufo, the conqueror, calmly reached down and tore Cadderly's throat out.

The vampire awoke in absolute darkness. He could feel the stone walls pressing in on him, and he welcomed their sanctuary, basking in the blackness as the minutes turned into an hour.

Then another call compelled Rufo; a great hunger swept over him. He tried to ignore it, consciously wanted nothing more than to lie in the cool black emptiness.

Soon his fingers clawed at the stone and he thrashed about, overwhelmed by urges he did not understand. A low, feral growl, the call of an animal, escaped his lips.

Rufo squirmed and twisted, turning his body completely about in the crypt. At first the thrashing vampire thought to tear the blocking stone away, to shatter this barrier into a million pieces, but he kept his senses enough to realize that he might need this sanctuary again. Concentrating on the minute crack at the base of the slab, Rufo melted away into greenish vapor—it wasn't difficult— and filtered out into the mausoleum's main area.

Druzil, perched on the nearest slab, doglike chin in clawed fingers, waited for him.

Rufo hardly noticed the imp, though. When he assumed corporeal form, he felt different, less stiff and awkward.

He smelled the night air—his air—about him and felt strong. Faint moonlight leaked in through the dirty window, but unlike the light of the sun, it was cool, comfortable.

Rufo stretched his arms into the air, kicked off with one foot, and twirled around on the other, tasting the night and his freedom.

"They did not come," Druzil said to him.

Rufo started to ask what the imp might be talking about, but, as soon as he noticed the two corpses, he understood. "I am not surprised," the vampire answered.

"The library is full of duties. Always duties. The dead priests may not be missed for several days."

"Then gather them up," Druzil ordered. "Drag them from this place."

Rufo concentrated more on the imp's tone than on the actual words.

"Do it now," Druzil went on, oblivious to the fast-mounting danger. "If we are careful . . ." Only then did Druzil look up from the nearest corpse to see Rufo's face, and the vampire's icy glare sent a shiver along the normally unshakable imp's spine.

Druzil didn't even try to continue with his reasoning, didn't even try to get words past the lump that filled his throat.

"Come to me," Rufo said quietly, calmly.

Druzil had no intention of following that command. He started to shake his head, large ears flapping noisily; he even tried to utter a derogatory comment. Those thoughts were lost in the imp's sudden realization that he was indeed moving toward Rufo, that his feet and wings were heeding the vampire's command. He was at the end of the slab, then he hopped off, flapping his bat wings to remain in the air, to continue his steady progress.

Rufo's cold hand shot out and caught the imp by the throat, breaking the trance. Druzil let out a shriek and instinctively brought his tail about, waving it menacingly in Rufo's face.

Rufo laughed and began to squeeze.

Druzil's tail snapped into Rufo's face, its barbed tip boring a small hole.

Rufo continued to laugh wickedly and squeezed tighter with his horribly powerful grasp. "Who is the master?" the confident vampire asked.

Druzil thought his head would be popped off! He couldn't begin to squirm. And that gaze! Druzil had faced some of the most powerful lords of the lower planes, but at that moment, it seemed to the imp that none was more imposing.

"Who is the master?" Rufo asked again.

Druzil's tail fell limp, and he stopped struggling. "Please, master," he whined breathlessly.

"I am hungry," the vampire announced, casually tossing Druzil aside. Rufo strode for the mausoleum door with a graceful and confident gait. As he neared the door, he reached out with his will and it swung open. As he crossed through the portal, it banged closed once more, leaving Druzil alone in the mausoleum, muttering to himself.

* * * * *

Bachtolen Mossgarden, the library's cook since Ivan Bouldershoulder had gone away, was also muttering to himself that night. Bachy, as the priests called him, was fed up with his new duties. He had been hired as a groundskeeper—that was what Bachy did best—but with winter thick about the grounds, and with the dwarf gallivanting in the mountains, the priests had changed the rules.

"Slop, slop, and more stinkin' slop!" the dirty man grumbled, overturning a bucket of leftover cabbage down a slope behind the squat library. He moved to pick his nose, but changed his mind as the finger, reeking of old cabbage, neared the nostril.

"I'm even startin' to smell like the stinkin' slop!" he whined, and he banged on the metal bucket, spilling the last of its remains onto the slick, stained snow, and spun about to leave.

Bachy noticed that it had suddenly grown much colder. And quieter, he realized a moment later. It wasn't the cold that had given him pause, but the stillness. Even the wind was no more.

The hairs on the back of Bachy's neck tingled and stood on end. Something was wrong, out of place.

"Who is it?" he asked straightforwardly, for that had always been his way. He didn't wash much, he didn't shave much, and he justified it by saying that people should like him for more than appearance.

Bachy liked to think of himself as profound.

"Who is it?" he asked again, more clearly, gaining courage in the fact that no one had answered the first time. He had almost convinced himself that he was letting his imagination get the best of him, had even taken his first step back toward the Edificant Library, the back door of the kitchen only twenty yards away, when a tall, angular figure stepped in front of him, standing perfectly still and quiet.

Bachy stuttered through a series of beginnings of questions, never completing a one. Most prominent among them was Bachy's pure wonderment at where this guy had come from. It seemed to the poor, dirty cook that the man had stepped out of thin air, or out of shadows that were not deep enough to hide him!

The figure advanced a step. Overhead, the moonlight broke through a cloud, revealing Rufo's pallid face.

Bachy wavered, seemed as if he would fall over. He wanted to cry out, but found no voice. He wanted to run, but his legs would barely support him while standing still.

Rufo tasted the fear, and his eyes lit up, horrid red flames dancing where his pupils should have been. The vampire grinned evilly, his mouth gradually opening wide, baring long fangs. Bachy mumbled something that sounded like, "By the gods," then he was kneeling in the snow, his legs having buckled underneath him.

The sensation of fear, of sweet, sweet fear, multiplied tenfold, washed over Rufo. It was the purest feeling of ecstasy the wretch had ever known. He understood and appreciated his power at that moment. This pitiful slob, this man he did not even know, couldn't begin to resist him!

Rufo moved slowly, determinedly, knowing that his victim was helpless before the spectacle of the vampire.

And then he tasted blood, like the nectar he had drawn from the foolish Oghman priest inside the mausoleum before Druzil's poison had tainted it. This blood was not tainted. Bachy was a dirty thing, but his blood was pure, warm, and sweet.

The minutes slipped past, and Rufo fed. He understood then that he should stop. Somehow he knew that if he didn't kill this wretch, the man would rise up in undeath, a lesser creature, to serve him. Instinctively the vampire realized that this one would be his slave—at least until Bachy, too, had fully followed the path to becoming a vampire.

Rufo continued to feed. He meant to stop, but no level of thought could over-rule the pleasure the vampire knew. Sometime later, Bachy's husk of a corpse tumbled down the slope behind the other discarded garbage.

By the time the night began to wane, Kierkan Rufo had become comfortable with his new existence. He wandered about like a wolf scouting its domain, thinking always of the kill, of the taste of the dirty man's blood. Dried brown remnants of the macabre feast stained the vampire's face and cloak as he stood before the side wall of the Edificant Library, looking up to the gargoyles that lined its gutter system, and past the roof, to the stars of his domain.

A voice in his head (he knew it was Druzil's) told him he should return to the mausoleum, to the cool, dark crypt where he might hide from the infernal heat of the coming sun. Yet there was a danger in that plan, Rufo realized. He had taken things too far now. The revealing light of day might put the priests on their guard, and they would be formidable opponents.

They would know where to start looking.

Death had given Kierkan Rufo new insights and powers beyond anything the order of Deneir had ever promised. He could feel the chaos curse swirling within his body, which he inhabited like a partner, an adviser. Rufo could go and find a place to be safe, but *Tuanta Quiro Miancay* wanted more than safety.

Rufo was barely conscious that he had changed form, but the next thing he knew, his bat claws had found a perch on the edge of the library's roof. Bones crackled and stretched as the vampire resumed his human form, leaving Rufo sitting on the roof's edge, looking down on a window that he knew well.

He climbed head first down the wall, his strong undead fingers finding secure holds where in life he would have seen only smooth stone, past the third floor, to the second. To Rufo's surprise, an iron grate had been placed over this window. He reached through the bars and pushed in the glass, then thought of becoming vaporous and simply wafting into the room. For some reason, some instinctive, animalistic urge, as though it occurred to him that the grate had been put there only to hinder his progress, he grabbed an iron bar and, with one hand, tore the grate free and sent it spinning into the night.

The entire library was open to him, he believed, and the vampire had no intention of leaving.

Five

Well-placed Faith

Danica stared into the flames of the campfire, watching the orange and white dance and using its hypnotic effects to let her mind wander across the miles. Her thoughts were on Cadderly and the troubles. He meant to oppose Dean Thobicus, she knew, and to rip apart all the rituals and bureaucracy that the Deneirian order had been built on through the years. The opposition would be wicked and unyielding, and, though Danica did not believe that Cadderly's life would be in danger, as it had been in Castle Trinity, she knew that his pain, if he lost, would be everlasting.

Those thoughts inevitably led Danica to Dorigen, sitting wrapped in a blanket across the fire from her. What of the wizard? she wondered. What if Thobicus, expecting what was to come from Cadderly, did not respect Danica's rights as captor and ordered Dorigen executed?

Danica shook the disturbing thoughts from her mind and berated herself for letting her imagination run wild. Dean Thobicus was not an evil man, after all, and his weakness had always been a lack of decisive action. Dorigen was not likely in danger.

"The area remains clear," said Shayleigh, pulling Danica from her thoughts. She looked up as the elf maiden entered the camp, bow in hand. Shayleigh smiled and nodded to Dorigen, who appeared fast asleep.

"The mountains haven't awakened from the winter's slumber," Danica replied.

Shayleigh nodded, but her mischievous, thoroughly elven smile showed Danica that she thought the time for the spring dance was growing near. "Rest now," Shayleigh offered. "I will take my reverie later in the evening."

Danica eyed Shayleigh for a long while before agreeing, intrigued, as always, by the elf's referral to her "reverie." The elves did not sleep, not by the human definition of the word. Their reverie was a meditative state apparently as restful as true sleep. Danica had asked Shayleigh about it on several occasions, and had seen it often during her stay with the elves in Shilmista Forest, but though the elves were not secretive about the custom, it remained strange to the monk. Danica's practice involved many hours of deep meditation, and though that was indeed restful, it did not approach the elven reverie. Someday, Danica determined, she would unlock that secret and find her rest as an elf.

"Do we need to keep a watch?" she asked.

Shayleigh looked around at the dark trees. It was their first night back in the Snowflakes, after a long trek south across the open fields north of Carradoon. "Perhaps not," the elf replied. She sat at the fire's side and took a blanket from her pack. "But sleep lightly and keep your weapons close to your side."

"My weapons are my hands," Danica reminded with a grin.

Across the fire, Dorigen peeked out from under half-closed eyelids and tried to hide her smile. For perhaps the first time in all her life, the wizard felt as if she was among friends. She had secretly gone out and placed magical wards about the encampment. No need to tell Danica and Shayleigh of them, though, for Dorigen had worded the spells so that the monk and the elf could not trigger the traps.

With those comforting thoughts in mind, Dorigen allowed herself to drift off to sleep.

* * * * *

Shayleigh came out of her reverie sometime before dawn, the woods still dark about them. The elf sensed something amiss, so she rose from her bed, shrugged off the blanket, and took up her longbow. Shayleigh's keen eyes adapted quickly to the night. Towering mountains loomed as dark silhouettes all about her, and all appeared quiet and as it should be.

Still, the tiny hairs on the back of Shayleigh's neck were tingling. One of her senses was hinting at danger, not so far away.

The elf peered hard into the shadows; she tilted her head at different angles, trying to discern an out—of- –place sound. Then she sniffed the air and crinkled her nose in disgust.

Trolls. Shayleigh knew that foul odor; nearly every adventurer in the Realms had encountered a wretched troll at least once in his or her travels.

"Danica," she called softly, not wanting to warn her enemies that she knew they were about.

The wary monk came awake immediately, but made no sudden movements.

"Trolls," Shayleigh whispered, "not far away."

Danica looked to the fire, no more than glowing embers by this time, with all the wood fully consumed. Trolls hated fire, and feared it, if they feared anything at all.

Danica called quietly to Dorigen, but the wizard did not stir. A look to Shayleigh sent the elf maiden sliding gently around the side of the fire, near enough to prod Dorigen with her bow.

Dorigen grumbled and started to come awake, then popped her eyes wide when Danica yelled out. An explosion went off to one side, one of Dorigen's wards taking down a monster in flaring blue flames. But three more trolls rushed past their burning companion without regard for its terrible fate and crashed into the clearing, eyes glowing a fierce red, their stench nearly overwhelming the companions. The monsters' long, thin frames towered over the group—one had to be nearly eleven feet tall—and, as they came into the light, their rubbery skin showed as putrid grayish green.

Shayleigh's bow was up and firing in the blink of an eye, three arrows blasting into the closest troll. The monster jerked with each hit, but came stubbornly on, its skinny arms waving its hands awkwardly in wide, arcing swipes.

Shayleigh did not gain confidence from the awkward movements; the three fingers on those hands ended in long, sharp claws that could easily tear the hide from a bear. A fourth arrow hit the monster squarely in the chest, and Shayleigh hopped away, thinking it better to pummel this creature from a distance.

Two flashes, one silver, one gold, went past the elf as Danica led with her daggers. The monk leaped up and spun head over heels over the fire, following the shots (both solid hits on the next troll) at full speed. She barreled in, jumped, and spun, her trailing foot flying about to slam hard into the troll's midsection.

Danica winced at the sickly, squishy sound of that impact, but she didn't dare hesitate. She spun again for a second kick, then came up straight and landed a one-two punch on the lurching troll's jaw.

"Dorigen!" she screamed, seeing the third troll bearing down on the sitting wizard. To Danica's knowledge, Dorigen had no weapons, and few, if any, components for spellcasting—not even a proper spellbook that she might have studied. The monk, too engaged with this monster, and with Shayleigh still battling the first troll, thought her new companion doomed as the troll reached down at the blanketed woman.

There came a bright flash, and the troll fell back, holding the blanket and nothing more. That blanket flared suddenly with fire, scorching the monster's arms, causing it to scream out in pain.

Danica had no idea where Dorigen had come up with that spell, but she had no time to ponder the issue now.

The troll swiped at her repeatedly, and she did a fair, twisting dance to keep clear of its deadly arms. She came in close, inside the monster's reach, thinking to wriggle out the backside and score a few hits before the lumbering thing turned, but the troll proved faster and more resourceful than she believed, and she nearly swooned as the monster opened its wide, horrible mouth. The long, pointy teeth came within an inch of Danica's face—she could smell the thing's disgusting breath!—and the troll would have had her, except that the incredibly agile monk snapped her foot straight up before her, lifting it right in front of her face, though she had only a few inches to spare between herself and the troll.

Her kick caught the troll on its long nose and drove the proboscis up and back with a loud crackling noise. Danica was down in a crouch in an instant, dodging the flailing arms, and out she slipped, under the troll's armpit, around the back, where she exploded with fury, launching a barrage of heavy punches.

Shayleigh continued to backpedal, firing arrow after arrow into the pursuing troll. She knew that this would not do, though, for the troll's initial wounds were already on the mend. Trolls could regenerate, their rubbery skin binding of its own accord, and could take an incredible amount of punishment before falling dead.

No, not dead, Shayleigh realized to her horror, for even a dead troll, even a troll that had been cut into little bits, would come back to life, whole again, unless its wounds had been completely burned. That notion led the elf's gaze to the fire, but the embers promised little help. It would take some time to coax that glow back into any sort of flame, and Shayleigh and her companions had no time at all. The elf looked to the side of the encampment, but found that the troll that had been consumed by the explosion (which Shayleigh did not fully understand) had fallen into the snow, and already the fires that had destroyed the thing were nearly extinguished. Shayleigh muttered an elven curse.

Another arrow thudded into the troll, hitting the creature in the face. Still the stubborn thing advanced, and Shayleigh looked down to her half-empty quiver doubtfully. She thought of running into the woods then, of leading this monster away, but one look at Danica told her that she could not, that her friend would not be able to follow.

The troll that had gone unsuccessfully after Dorigen was after the monk now, it and its gruesome companion circling fast to find an exposed flank. Danica worked hard to keep up her guard against attacks from all angles, for with their long arms the trolls could simply reach around any straightforward defense.

"Where did she go?" Danica cried to Shayleigh, obviously referring to the missing wizard.

Shayleigh sighed helplessly and fired another arrow into the pursuing troll. Where indeed had Dorigen gone? she wondered, and she suspected that the wizard had determined this was a good time to escape.

Danica's powerful punch landed heavily against the side of a bending troll's head with a sickly splatting sound. When she retracted the hand, she found a bit of the monster's skin on her knuckles, along with some strands of the thing's hair. Danica groaned in revulsion when she noticed the mess, for the troll hair was writhing of its own accord.

She turned that revulsion into anger, and as the troll came about to swipe at her again, she stepped in close and pounded it repeatedly. Then she wisely fell to her knees and rolled fast to the side as the second troll came rushing at her back. Both monsters were on her as she sprang up to her feet, and up snapped her foot, knocking a lunging hand aside.

"They heal as fast as I hurt them!" the tiring monk cried in frustration.

Danica's statement wasn't quite true, as Shayleigh found out when her next arrow, her sixteenth shot, dropped the troll to the ground. She looked to her quiver, to the four arrows remaining, and sighed again.

Danica went left, was forced back to the right, and backpedaled frantically as both trolls suddenly rushed ahead. An angled log at her back, a dead tree that had toppled to lean against another tree, ended her running room.

"Damn!" she spat, and she leaped high, kicking out with both feet, scoring two hits on one of the trolls and knocking it back several steps. She realized that the other would hit her, though, and she twisted as she came down to protect her vital spots.

As the troll started its attack, an arrow slammed into the side of its head. The monster's momentum flew away in its surprise, and though the swinging arm did indeed hit Danica, there was little strength behind the blow.

Danica spun completely to regain her balance, then she quickly lashed out, her flying foot slamming the monster several times in succession.

"And when I'm finished with you," she called defiantly, though of course the beast could not understand what she said, "I'll hunt down a certain cowardly wizard and teach her about loyalty!"

At that moment, as if on cue, Danica noticed a small sphere of fire appear in the air over the closest troll's head. Before she could ask, the hovering sphere erupted, sending a shroud of hungry flames down over the troll's body.

The monster shrieked in agony and flailed wildly, but the flames would not let go and would not relent. Danica did well to slip away from the waving inferno. She kept her wits enough to concentrate on the second monster as it came around its burning companion (giving the flaming troll a wide berth), and she met the monstrous thing with another flying double-kick.

Danica had the devious notion of herding the troll into its flaming companion, but the cunning monster wanted no part of that. It staggered back from the kick, then came around again, pointedly putting Danica between it and the burning troll.

An arrow thudded into its side; it turned its ugly head to regard Shayleigh.

Danica flew into it again before it turned back, and the monster stumbled and toppled. Danica was up quickly, thinking to leap atop the monster, but she skidded to a stop, seeing another flaming sphere come to life in the air above the prone troll.

An instant later, that troll, too, was shrieking in agony, engulfed by the biting magical flames.

Shayleigh held her next shot, sensed movement to the side, and spun and fired—into the troll she had already dropped. The thing went down in a heap again, but stubbornly writhed and squirmed, trying to rise.

Danica was on it at once, pounding wildly. Shayleigh joined her, sword in hand, and with mighty hacks, cut off the troll's legs.

Those severed limbs began to wriggle immediately, trying to reattach to the torso, but Danica wisely kicked them away toward the glowing remnant of the campfire.

As soon as one of the legs touched the embers, it burst into flames, and Danica scooped it up by the other end, using it as a grotesque torch. She ran across the clearing and shoved the flaming limb into the face of the unburned troll, the amazing monster still thrashing against Shayleigh's repeated strikes. Soon, that troll, too, was ablaze, and the battle was ended.

Dorigen walked back into camp then, inspecting her work on the two flame-shrouded trolls. They were little more than crumpled black balls by that time, and their regenerative process was surely defeated by the wizard's flames.

Danica could hardly bear to look at Dorigen, ashamed of her earlier doubts. "I thought you had run off," she admitted.

Dorigen smiled at her.

"I vowed to . . ." Danica began.

"To hunt me down and teach me about loyalty," Dorigen finished for her, lightly and with no accusation in her tone. "But, dear Danica, do you not know that you and your friends have already taught me about loyalty?"

Danica stared hard at the wizard, thinking that Dorigen's bravery here, and the fact that she had bothered to stay around and aid in the fight, would weigh in her favor once they returned to the library. As she thought about it, Danica realized she was not surprised by Dorigen's heroics. The wizard had been won over, heart and soul, and, though Danica agreed that Dorigen should pay a strict penance for her actions in favor of Castle Trinity, for the war she helped direct against Shayleigh's people, the monk hoped that the penance would be positive, in which Dorigen might use her considerable magical powers for the good of the region.

"You likely saved our lives," Shayleigh remarked, drawing Danica's attention. "I am grateful."

That remark seemed to please Dorigen greatly. "It is but a pittance of the debt I owe you and your people," the wizard replied.

Shayleigh nodded her agreement. "A debt that I trust you will pay in full," she said sternly, but with apparent confidence.

Danica was glad to hear it. Shayleigh had not been cold to Dorigen in any way, but neither had the elf been friendly. Danica could appreciate the elf maiden's turmoil. Shayleigh was an intelligent and perceptive elf, one who based her judgments on an individual's actions. She, more than any of her clan, had accepted Ivan and Pikel as true friends and allies, had not allowed typically elven preconceptions concerning dwarves to cloud her judgment of them. And now she, alone among the elves of Shilmista, had seen this new side of Dorigen, had come to where she was ready to forgive, perhaps, if not to forget.

That support, as well as King Elbereth's (and Danica was confident the elf king would accept Shayleigh's judgment), might prove critical in Cadderly's forthcoming showdown with Dean Thobicus.

"It is almost dawn," Dorigen remarked. "I have no stomach for breakfast with troll stench in the air."

Danica and Shayleigh wholeheartedly agreed, so they packed up their camp and started out early. They would reach the Edificant Library in just three short days.

Six

An Invited Guest

Dean Thobicus was surprised to find a blanket draped over the lone window in his office the next morning. It ruffled as he approached, and he felt the chill morning breeze, which led his gaze to the floor, to the base of the blanket, where the window's glass lay shattered.

"What foolishness is this?" the surly dean asked as he brushed some of the glass aside with his foot. He pulled out the edge of the blanket and was surprised again, for not only was the glass broken, but the grate was gone, apparently ripped from the stonework.

Thobicus fought hard to steady his breathing, fearing that Cadderly might somehow be behind this, that the young priest had returned and used his newfound and indisputably powerful magic on the grate. The iron bars had been new, bolted in place soon after Cadderly had disappeared into the mountains. The dean had explained to the others that it was necessary to ensure that no thieves—agents of Castle Trinity, probably—broke into his office in this time of turmoil and stole off with battle plans. Actually, Thobicus had put the grate on the window not to keep anyone out, but to keep anyone from falling out. When Cadderly had mentally dominated the dean, the young priest had shown his superiority by threatening to make Thobicus leap from the window, and Thobicus knew without a doubt that he would have done exactly that if Cadderly had so instructed, that he would have been powerless to ignore the command.

Seeing that window now, broken open and with no blocking grate, sent shudders along the thin dean's spine. He eased the impromptu curtain back into place and turned about slowly, as if expecting to find his nemesis standing in the middle of the office.

He found Kierkan Rufo instead.

"What are you . . ." the dean began, then his words were lost in his throat as he recalled that Rufo had just died. Yet here the man was, standing at that curious and customary angle!

"Do not!" Rufo commanded as the dean's hand went up to grasp the blanket for support. Rufo held his own bony hand out toward Thobicus, and the dean felt Rufo's will, as tangible as a wall of stone, blocking him from grasping the blanket.

"I favor the darkness," the vampire explained cryptically.

Dean Thobicus narrowed his dark eyes to study the man more closely, not understanding. "You cannot come in here," he protested. "You wear the brand."

Rufo laughed at him. "The brand?" he echoed skeptically. He reached up and ran his nails across his forehead, tearing his own skin and scraping away the distinctive Deneirian markings.

"You cannot come in here!" Thobicus said more frantically, finally catching on that something was terribly amiss, that Kierkan Rufo had become something much more dangerous than a simple outcast. Such a brand as Rufo wore was magical, and if covered or marred, it would burn inward, tormenting then killing the outcast.

Rufo showed no pain now, though, just confidence.

"You cannot come in here," Thobicus reiterated, his voice no more than a whisper.

"Indeed I can," Rufo countered, and he smiled wide, showing bloodied fangs. "You invited me in."

Thobicus's mind whirled in confusion. He remembered those same words, spoken by Rufo at the moment of the man's death. At the moment of the man's death!

"Get out of here!" Thobicus demanded desperately. "Be gone from this holy place!" Out came the symbol of Deneir, hanging on a chain about the dean's neck, and he began a chant as he presented it before him.

Rufo felt a sting in his unbeating heart, and the glare of the pendant, seeming to flare with a life of its own, hurt his eyes. But after the initial shock, the vampire sensed something here, a weakness. This was Deneir's house, and Thobicus was supposedly the leading member of the order. Thobicus above all should have been able to drive Rufo away. Yet he could not; Rufo knew with certainty that he could not.

The dean finished his spell and hurled a wave of magical energy at the vampire, but Rufo didn't even flinch. He was staring directly at the presented holy symbol, which, to his eyes, no longer flared in the least.

"There is a blackness in your heart, Dean Thobicus," Rufo reasoned.

"Be gone from here!" Thobicus countered.

"There is no conviction in your words."

"Foul beast!" Thobicus growled, and he boldly approached, hand and holy symbol extended. "Foul dead thing, you have no purpose here!"

The vampire began to laugh.

"Deneir will smite you!" Thobicus promised. "I will . . ."

He stopped and grunted in pain as Rufo snapped a strong hand up and caught him by the forearm. "You will do what?" the vampire asked. A flick of Rufo's wrist sent the holy symbol spinning from Thobicus's weak hand. "There is no conviction in your words," Rufo said again. "And there is no strength in your heart. " Rufo let go of the arm and grasped the front of the dean's robes, easily lifting the thin man into the air.

"What have you done, fallen priest?" the confident vampire asked.

Those last two words echoed in the dean's thoughts like a damning curse. He wanted to scream out for the headmasters; he wanted to break free and rush to the window and tear the blanket aside, for certainly the light of day would do ill to this horrid, undead thing. But Rufo's claims, all of them, were true—Thobicus knew they were true!

Rufo carelessly tossed the man to the floor and paced to put himself between the dean and the window. Thobicus lay very still, his thoughts whirling with confusion and desperation, wallowing in self-pity. Indeed, what had he done? How had he fallen so far and so fast?

"Please," the vampire said, "do go and sit at your desk, that we might properly discuss what has come to pass." All through the early morning, Rufo had sat in this office, thinking that he would lie in wait for Thobicus, then simply tear the man apart. It was no longer hunger that drove the vampire—he had feasted well the previous night. No, Rufo had come after Dean Thobicus purely for revenge, had decided to strike out against all the library for the torments the Deneirians had given him in his life.

Now, unwittingly guided by the designs of the chaos curse, the vampire was thinking differently. In that moment of confrontation, Rufo had seen into the heart of Dean Thobicus, and there he had found a malignant blackness.

"Have you eaten this day?" Rufo asked pleasantly, sliding to a sitting position on the edge of the oaken desk.

Thobicus, still a bit ruffled, straightened defiantly in his chair and answered simply, "No."

"I have," Rufo explained, and laughed wickedly at the irony. "In fact, I have feasted on the one who would prepare your meal."

Thobicus looked away, his expression filled with disgust.

"You should be glad of that!" Rufo snarled at him, and slammed the desk, forcing Thobicus to jump in surprise and turn back to face the monster. "If I had not already eaten, then my hunger would have overcome me by now, and you would be dead!" Rufo said fiercely, and he bared his fangs to accentuate his point.

Dean Thobicus tried to sit still, to hide the fact that his hands were working under the desktop, fingering a loaded crossbow that he had recently come to keep there. The weapon was supported by sliding brackets so that it could be swiftly and easily pulled out in times of need. The dean's shoulders sagged a bit when he thought of the weapon, when he realized that he had put the crossbow there not for any emergency against a foe such as this, but in case Cadderly had come to him again, and had tried to dominate him.

Rufo was concerned with his own thoughts and seemed to notice neither the dean's delicate movements nor the turmoil boiling within the withered man. The vampire slid off the desk and walked to the middle of the room, one skinny finger tapping thoughtfully on his lips, still red from the blood of his meal.

Thobicus realized that he should pull out the crossbow and shoot the monster. Well versed in theology, the dean recognized Rufo for what he was, knew that he had somehow become a vampire. The crossbow bolt probably wouldn't kill Rufo, but it had been blessed and dipped in holy water, so it would at least wound him, and possibly allow the dean to flee the room. The library was waking up by now; allies would not be far away.

Thobicus held his shot, and held back his words, letting the vampire make the next move.

Rufo turned back to the desk suddenly, and Thobicus inadvertently gasped. "We should not be enemies," the vampire remarked.

Thobicus eyed him incredulously.

"What would be the gain of a fight?" Rufo asked. "For either of us?"

"Ever were you a fool, Kierkan Rufo," Thobicus dared to say.

"A fool?" Rufo mocked. "You could not begin to understand, fallen priest." Rufo threw back his head and let his laughter flow out. He spun about so that his black burial robe trailed his form like a shadow. "I have found power!"

"You have found perversion!" Thobicus declared, and he clutched the crossbow tightly, thinking that his remark would send the angry monster hurtling toward him.

Rufo stopped his spin and faced the dean. "Call it what you will! But you cannot deny my power—power gained in mere hours. You have spent all of your life in wasted study, I say, praying to Deneir."

Thobicus inadvertently glanced at his holy symbol, lying on the floor by the wall.

"Deneir," Rufo said derisively. "What has your god given you? You toil for endless years, then Cadderly . . ."

Thobicus winced, and Rufo did not miss it.

"Then Cadderly," the vampire went on, seeing the weakness for what it was, "reaches out and grasps at levels of power that will forever be beyond you!"

"You lie!" Thobicus roared, coming forward in his chair. His words sounded empty, even in his own ears.

The office door swung open then, and both Thobicus and Rufo turned to see Bron Turman stride in. The Oghman priest looked from the dean to Rufo, his eyes going wide as he, too, recognized the vampire for what it was.

Rufo hissed, showing bloody fangs, and waved his hand, his magic compelling the door to slam shut behind Turman.

Bron Turman had no intention of running back out, in any case. With a determined snarl, the Oghman grabbed at a pendant and tore the chain from his neck, presenting the silver scroll replica before him. It flashed and radiated a powerful light, and to the surprise of Dean Thobicus, the vampire backed away, ducking under his robes and hissing.

Turman recited words very similar to the ones Thobicus had used, and the holy symbol flared even more, filled the room with a glow that Rufo could not bear. The vampire fell back against the wall, started for the window, then realized that he could not go out there, under the light of the infernal sun.

Turman had him, Thobicus realized, and Rufo seemed very weak to him then, even pitiful. Without even realizing it, Thobicus had the crossbow atop the desk.

Rufo began to fight back, was struggling to stand straight. A blackness rolled out from his form, filling that section of the room.

Bron Turman growled and thrust his symbol forward, its flare attacking the vampire's darkness. Rufo hissed wickedly as he clenched his bony fists in the air.

"Shoot him!" Bron Turman implored Thobicus.

The struggle between the two was a standoff that a crossbow quarrel would break.

Thobicus took up the weapon and leveled it. He meant to pull the trigger, but hesitated as a wall of doubts came up before him. Why hadn't his presented symbol so affected the vampire? he wondered. Had Deneir deserted him, or was Cadderly somehow continuing to block his efforts to bask in the light of his god?

Mountains of doubt rolled across the dean's thoughts, black thoughts made blacker by the continuing subtle intrusions of the vampire's will. Rufo was still there, compelling, prompting doubts.

Where was Deneir? The thought haunted the withered dean. In his moment of greatest need, his god had not been there. In the one instant of his life when he had consciously called on Deneir, when he had absolutely needed Deneir, the god had deserted him!

And there stood Bron Turman, straight and confident, holding the vampire at bay with the power of Oghma in his strong hand.

Thobicus snarled and hoisted the crossbow. Evil Rufo was standing tall in his new power, standing against a man who would have easily defeated him when he had been just a disciple of Deneir, though Rufo had spent years of study.

Now, after three days of death, Rufo could match the Oghman.

Thobicus shook his head, trying to clear the mounting confusion. He pushed through one web of lies, only to find another, and to find the one he had left closing fast behind him.

Where was Deneir? Why was Cadderly so damned powerful? Where was justice, the rewards of his own long years of study? So many years . . .

Thobicus came back to the present situation, focusing his thoughts, steadying his trembling hands, and training his eye. His shot was perfect.

Bron Turman jerked from the impact and looked over at the desk in disbelief. The Oghman's grip soon weakened, and Rufo stepped forward and casually slapped the holy symbol from Turman's hand, then fell over him.

A minute later, the vampire, his face bright with fresh blood, turned to the desk. "What has Deneir ever given you?" he asked the stunned Thobicus, the old dean standing zombielike, his wrinkled face frozen with disbelief as he stared at the dead Oghman.

"He deserted you," Rufo crooned, playing on the man's obvious doubts. "Deneir has deserted you, but I will not! There is so much I can give you."

Thobicus, in his stupor, realized that the vampire was next to him. Rufo continued to whisper assurances, promising power beyond belief and eternal life, promising salvation before death. Thobicus could not resist him. The withered dean felt a pinch as the vampire's fangs jabbed into his neck.

He realized only then how very far he had fallen. He realized that Rufo had been in his mind, inciting the doubts, quietly compelling him to fire the crossbow at the powerful Oghman.

And he had complied. Doubts swirled in the air all about the dean, but no longer were they centered on the faults of Deneir. Had Deneir really deserted Thobicus when he had tried to present the holy symbol against Rufo, or had Thobicus long ago deserted Deneir? Cadderly had dominated him, and had claimed that power to be the will of Deneir.

And now Rufo . . .

Thobicus let the thought go, let the guilt go. So be it, he decided. He denied the consequences and washed in the promises of the vampire.

So be it.

Seven

Fall from Grace

Fester Rumpol watched suspiciously. He didn't understand the change that had come over Dean Thobicus. The last time he had spoken with the dean, the man was preoccupied—no, obsessed—with the notion that Cadderly was coming back to the library to tear the heart out of the Deneirian order.

Now Thobicus seemed almost jovial. He had secretly called together the four leading Deneirians, three of them headmasters, for what he termed "a most vital conference."

They were gathered in a small dining room adjacent to the main hall and kitchen, around an oaken table, bare except for huge, empty goblets set in front of the five chairs.

"Dear Banner," Thobicus chirped lightly, "do go to the cellars and fetch a particular vintage, a special red bottle on the third rack."

"A bottle of red?" Banner asked, crinkling his features. Banner favored white wines.

"A red bottle," Thobicus corrected. He turned to Rumpol and gave a wink. "Magically preserved, you know. The only way to keep Feywine."

"Feywine?" Rumpol and all the others asked together. Feywine was an elven drink, a mixture of honey and flowers and moonbeams, it was said. It was rare, even among the elves, and getting a bottle from them was nearly impossible.

"A gift from King Galladel when he ruled Shilmista," Thobicus explained. "Do go and retrieve it."

Banner looked to Rumpol, worried that the man was near an explosion. Indeed Rumpol was boiling. He feared that Thobicus had somehow learned of Cadderly's demise, and if that was the occasion of this celebration, the dean was surely out of line!

Banner waited a moment longer, then tentatively started to leave.

"Wait!" Rumpol blurted, and all the others turned to regard him. "Your mood has brightened, Dean Thobicus," Rumpol said. "Dramatically. Might we learn what has so affected you?"

"I found communion with Deneir this morning," Thobicus lied.

"Cadderly is dead," Rumpol reasoned, and the other three Deneirians immediately turned sour looks on the dean. Even the priests who despised Cadderly and his unconventional climb through the ranks would not celebrate such a tragedy—at least not publicly.

Thobicus put on an expression of horror. "He is not," he replied vehemently. "From all that I know, the fine young priest is even now on his way back to the library."

Fine young priest? Coming from Dean Thobicus, those words rang hollow indeed to Fester Rumpol.

"Then why are we celebrating?" Banner asked bluntly.

Thobicus gave a great sigh. "I had hoped we might toast the occasion with the Feywine," he groaned. "But very well, I sympathize with your impatience. Simply put, there will be no second Time of Troubles."

That brought sighs of relief and private murmurs from the group.

"And I have learned much of Cadderly as well," Thobicus went on. "The order will survive—indeed, it will be strengthened when he returns, when he and I work together to improve the ways of the library."

"You hate each other," Rumpol remarked, and looked around somewhat nervously. He hadn't meant to openly voice that opinion.

Thobicus, however, merely chuckled and seemed to take no offense. "With Deneir as moderator, our differences seem petty indeed," the dean replied.

He looked around, his bright smile infectious. "And so we have much to celebrate!" he proclaimed, and nodded to Banner, who rushed off with sincere enthusiasm for the doorway to the wine cellar.

The conversation continued, lighthearted and hopeful, with Thobicus paying particular attention to Rumpol, the man he deemed to be potentially the most troublesome. Twenty minutes later, Banner still had not returned.

"He cannot find the bottle," Thobicus remarked to quiet any trepidation. "Dear Banner. He probably dropped his torch and is stumbling around in the dark."

"Banner has the power to summon light," Rumpol said, an edge of suspicion still in his voice.

"Then where is he?" Thobicus asked. "The bottle is colorful, and should be easy enough to find on the fifth rack."

"You said the third rack," one of the others quickly put in.

Thobicus stared at him, then scratched his head. "Did I?" he whispered, then he dramatically dropped his face into his hand. "Of course," he mused. "The Feywine was in the third rack until the . . . incident." All the others knew that the

910 R. A. Salvatore

dean was referring to the dark time of the chaos curse, the time when the evil priest Barjin had invaded the library and sought to destroy the place from within.

"There was quite a bit of trouble down in that cellar," Thobicus went on. "If I remember correctly, several of the affected priests even went down there and drank to . . . shall we say, excess."

Rumpol turned away, for he had been one of those hearty drinkers.

"Fortunately, the Feywine survived, but I do recall that it was moved to the fifth rack, that being the most stable," Thobicus finished. He motioned to one of the others. "Do go and help out dear Banner," he bade, "before the man comes back here raising Cyric himself against me!"

The priest ran off for the door, and the conversation resumed, again without much concern. Fifteen minutes later, it was Rumpol who remarked that the two wine hunters were long overdue.

"If one of the lesser priests stole that bottle, my good mood will vanish," Thobicus warned.

"There was an inventory of the wine cellar," Rumpol said.

"A list I saw, though I do not recall any record of Feywine," added the other, and he gave a jovial laugh. "And I would have noted the presence of such a treasure well, I assure you!"

"Of course the bottle was mislabeled," Thobicus explained, then he nodded, as if something that should have been obvious had just come to him. "If dear Banner decided to test the wine before he returned, then likely we will find our two missing brothers sitting in a stupor in the cellar!" the dean roared. "Feywine, in its own subtle way, bites harder than dwarven ale!"

He rose to leave, and the other two were quick to join him. Their mood was light, any fears or suspicions quenched by the logical assumption offered by the dean. They got to the wine cellar door, and Thobicus took up and lit one of the small lamps set in a cabinet to one side, then led the way down the wooden staircase, into the darkness.

They heard no chatter, no drunken conversation, and grew a bit concerned when they saw that their lantern was apparently the only source of light in the damp, shadowy cellar.

"Banner?" Rumpol called softly. Thobicus stood by silently; the remaining priest began a quiet chant, thinking to bring a great magical light into the area.

That priest jerked suddenly, drawing the attention of his two companions.

"I fear a spider has bitten me," he remarked to Rumpol's questioning expression, and he began to jerk spasmodically, his eyes twitching, then rolling back into his head.

He fell facedown to the floor before Rumpol could get to him.

"What is this?" Rumpol cried, cradling the fallen priest's head. He began a frantic chant, beginning a spell that could counter any poison.

"Rumpol," Thobicus called, and though the priest did not interrupt his frantic spellcasting, he did look back to regard the dean.

His words fell away as he looked upon Kierkan Rufo, the vampire's face bright with fresh blood.

The vampire extended one pale hand toward Rumpol. "Come to me," he bade.

Rumpol felt the wave of compelling willpower roll over him. He rested the fallen priest's head back against the floor and rose without even being conscious of the movements.

"Come to me," the vampire said tantalizingly. "Join me, as has your dean. Come to me and see the truth."

Rumpol was inadvertently sliding his feet along the smooth floor, drifting toward the darkness that was Kierkan Rufo. Somewhere in the back of his mind he caught the image of an open eye above a lit candle, the symbol of Deneirian light, and it shook him from his trance.

"No!" he declared and pulled out his holy symbol, presenting it with all his heart against the undead monster. Rufo hissed and lifted his arm to shield himself from the spectacle. Dean Thobicus turned away in shame. The light from his lantern went with him as he walked around the next rack, but the light in the area near Rumpol did not diminish, bolstered by the power of his presented symbol, by the light that was in the sincere priest's heart.

"Fool!" the vampire proclaimed. "Do you think you can stand against me?"

Fester Rumpol wasn't shaken. He basked in the light of his god, used his sincere faith to blast away any horror-inspired doubts. "I deny you!" he proclaimed. "And by the power of Deneir . . ."

He stopped suddenly and nearly swooned. He glanced around to his back to see the dog-faced imp staring at him, waving its barbed, poison-tipped tail—the same tail that had dropped the other priest, and that Druzil had just poked into Rumpol's kidney.

Rumpol staggered for the stairway, stumbled to his knees as Druzil struck him a second time. Then he was up again, but the world was slipping away into blackness. The last image he saw was that of Kierkan Rufo, of Kierkan Rufo's fangs rushing for his throat.

When he was finished, the vampire found Thobicus standing by the fifth rack. There lay the priest Thobicus had sent after Banner, his chest torn apart, his heart on the floor beside him. Banner, though, surprisingly, was sitting against the rack, his head down, but very much alive.

"He heeded my call," Rufo casually explained to the confused dean. "And so I thought to keep him, for he is weak." Rufo presented a perfectly awful bloody smile to the dean. "Like you."

Dean Thobicus had not the strength to argue. He looked to the torn priest, and to living Banner, and he pitied Banner the most.

* * * * *

A few hours later, Druzil hopped and skipped into short flights about the library's hot attic, clapping his hands happily at every turn. The air was warm, he was at work in desecrating a holy place, and beneath him, Rufo, with the help of Dean Thobicus, continued dividing the priests into small groups and was summarily destroying them.

Life was suddenly very good for the malicious imp. Druzil flapped his wings and lifted himself up to one of the short peaks in the roof, so that he could survey his latest design. The imp knew all the runes of desecration and had just completed his favorite in the area directly over the library's main chapel (though that chapel was two floors down). Thobicus had provided a virtually unlimited supply of ink—reds, blues, blacks, and even a vial of a strange greenish-yellow (which Druzil favored)—and the imp knew that every stroke he ran across the floorboards put the foolish priests in the rooms below a bit farther from their respective gods.

At one point, Druzil paused, then moved away from the spot with an angry hiss. Someone was singing in a room below him—that wretched Chaunticleer, Druzil realized. Chaunticleer was singing to Deneir and to Oghma, lifting his voice against the encroaching blackness in notes pure and sweet.

It wounded Druzil's ears. He moved away from the spot, and the vibrations of Chaunticleer's voice were no more. With all that was happening in his favor, Druzil quickly forgot about the singing priest.

Happy again, Druzil clapped his hands rapidly, his toothy smile nearly swallowing his ears. When Rufo had come for him in the mausoleum the previous night, he hadn't known what to expect, had even considered using all of his magical abilities and knowledge to try to open a gate, that he might retreat to the lower planes, abandoning Rufo and *Tuanta Quiro Miancay* altogether.

Now, just half a day later, Druzil was thrilled that he had not chosen that course. Barjin had failed, but Rufo would not, the imp knew.

The Edificant Library would fall.

* * * * *

His tentative steps down into the wine cellar revealed Thobicus's continued fear of Kierkan Rufo, and his continued uneasiness with his own decisions. He still could not believe that he had killed Bron Turman, long a friend and ally. He still could not believe that he had flown so far from the teachings of Deneir, that he had thrown away the work of his entire life.

There was only one antidote to the guilt that threatened to destroy Dean Thobicus. Anger. And the focus of that anger was a young priest who would likely soon return to the library.

Cadderly had done this, Thobicus decided. Through his lust for undeserved power, Cadderly had brought all of this about.

Thobicus carried no lantern or torch as he stepped off the bottom step of the dark stairway. With each passing hour, the man grew more comfortable with the darkness. Now he could see the wine racks, even the individual bottles, though a week before he would not have been able to see his hand flapping an inch from his face in this lightless place. Rufo called it another benefit; the frightened dean wondered if it might be more a symptom.

He found Rufo in the far corner, behind the last of the racks, asleep in a wooden casket the vampire had recovered from the work shed behind the mausoleum. Thobicus moved toward Rufo, then stopped abruptly, eyes wide with fear and confusion.

Bron Turman walked toward him.

As he turned to flee, the confused dean found several others, including Fester Rumpol, blocking the way. They had come back to life! Somehow, these priests had been resurrected and had come back to destroy Thobicus!

The dean squealed and leaped for the wine rack. He climbed it like a spider, with agility the aged and withered man had not known for several decades. He neared the top and could have easily slipped over, but a command rang out within his head, an order compelling him to stop.

Slowly, Thobicus turned his head about to see Kierkan Rufo sitting up in his casket, his grotesque smile wide.

"You do not like my new playthings?" the vampire asked.

Thobicus did not understand. He looked closer at the nearest man, Fester Rumpol, and realized that Rumpol's throat was still ragged from Rufo's raking and tearing. The man could not possibly be breathing, Thobicus realized; the man was still dead.

Thobicus sprang from his perch, flying the ten feet to land with catlike grace on the stone floor. Bron Turman, near where he landed, reached out with a stiff arm and grasped him tightly.

"Tell him to let you go," Rufo said casually, but his patient facade went away immediately, replaced by a judgmental, even dangerous expression. "Take control of him!"

Without saying a word, Thobicus steeled his gaze and mentally ordered Turman to let go—and the dean was relieved indeed when the man released him and stepped back, standing quietly to the side.

"Zombies," Thobicus breathed, understanding that Rufo had animated the torn corpses into undead, unthinking servants, among the lowest forms in the hierarchy of the netherworld.

"Those who submit will know an intelligent existence, as you have come to know," Rufo declared in an imposing voice. "Those who choose to die in the favor of their god shall become unwitting servants, unthinking zombies, to their ultimate torment!"

As if on cue, Banner appeared from around the corner, smiling at Thobicus. Banner had submitted, had denied his god in the face of Kierkan Rufo.

"Greetings, Thobicus," the man said, and when Banner opened his mouth, Thobicus realized that he, like Rufo, sported a pair of fangs.

"You are a vampire," the dean whispered, stating the obvious.

"As are you," Banner replied.

Thobicus looked to Rufo skeptically, then, following another mental command, reached up to feel inside his own mouth, to feel his own set of fangs.

"We are both vampires," Banner continued, "and with Kierkan Rufo, we are three."

"Not quite," Rufo interjected. Both men regarded him curiously, Banner's eyes full of suspicion, Dean Thobicus too wrapped up in confusion.

"You are not yet fully in the realm of vampires," Rufo explained, and he knew that he was speaking the truth, though where he had gained such an understanding of this undead state, he did not know. It was the knowledge imparted by the chaos curse, he figured.

"You promised me that I would be a vampire," Banner said. "That was our deal."

Rufo held up a hand to calm him. "And so you shall be," he assured the man, "in time."

"You rose into full power soon after your death," Banner complained.

Rufo smiled and considered the chaos curse, swirling inside of him, the potion that had imparted such strength and understanding. But I had an advantage, fool Banner, Rufo thought. To Banner he only repeated his promise of, "In time."

Rufo turned to the confused Thobicus. "This very night you will suffer the blood thirst," he explained into the dean's wide-eyed stare. "And you will seek out one of the lesser priests and feed. I grant you this, but be warned. If ever you hold a thought against me, I will deny you your victims. There is no greater torment than denial of the blood thirst—this you will believe when the hunger comes to you."

Dean Thobicus's mind whirled at the unexpected news. He had become a vampire!

"This very night," Rufo said again, as if in answer to the dean's silent exclamation. "And be warned that the sun tomorrow and forever after will be your enemy. Seek a dark spot to sleep after you have fed, Thobicus."

The dean's breath came in short gasps, and when he realized that fact, he seriously wondered if this would be the last day he would ever draw breath.

"Have you done as I instructed?" Rufo asked him.

He looked up at the vampire, startled by the unexpected change in subject. He collected his wits quickly.

"The five Oghmans are on the road to Carradoon," Thobicus answered. "They wanted to wait until morning and complained that they would have only a short hour or two of light before they had to stop and set up camp."

"But you convinced them," Rufo reasoned.

"I sent them," Thobicus corrected, as defiant a tone as he had ever used against the vampire. "But I do not understand the value in allowing them out of the library. If Druzil is at work . . ."

A sharp pain in Thobicus's head cut the statement short, nearly knocking the dean from his feet.

"You question me?" Rufo asked.

Thobicus found he was on his knees, clutching his temples. He thought his head would explode, but then, as abruptly as it had started, the pain ceased. It took him a long moment to muster the courage to look up at Kierkan Rufo again, and when he did, he found the vampire at ease, Banner comfortably at his side.

Thobicus, for some reason he did not understand, hated Banner at that moment.

"The Oghmans might have sensed the desecration," Rufo explained. "Or might have soon recognized you for what you have become. They will understand the desecration fully when they return to the library, and they will welcome it."

Thobicus considered the words, and did not doubt Rufo's claim. There remained less than sixty living priests, Deneirian and Oghman, at the library, and but six visitors, none powerful enough to stand against the master vampire.

"Is the priestess of Sune in her room?" Rufo asked suddenly, startling Thobicus from his private musings. The dean nodded, and Rufo, looking to Banner, nodded as well.

Two hours later, when the sun had fallen behind the western horizon and the dark shadows had become complete, Kierkan Rufo walked out of the Edificant Library's front doors, his black robes sweeping behind him and the mischievous imp perched on his shoulder.

On a high branch in a nearby tree, a white squirrel crouched in fear, watching the vampire's progress with more than passing curiosity.

Eight
Campfires

"W hat do you see?" Danica asked Shayleigh, moving to the camp's border, where the elf stood quietly.

Shayleigh held out a delicate arm, pointing far down the mountain trails to a flickering light. Danica's heart leaped for an instant, the monk thinking she might be catching her first glimpse of the Edificant Library.

"A campfire," Shayleigh explained, seeing the monk's hopeful visage. "A group of emissaries or traders from Carradoon on their way to the library, or perhaps a band of priests heading down to the city. The spring has come, so the trails awaken to the sound of caravans."

"It is a spring you thought would be full of cries of battle," Dorigen reminded Shayleigh as she moved to join the two.

Danica eyed Dorigen curiously, wondering what the woman hoped to gain by reminding Shayleigh of the carnage in Shilmista, and of her fears that an army— an army led by Dorigen—might soon return to the wood.

"So it might," Shayleigh was quick to reply, fixing the wizard with a cool stare. "We do not know if the orckin we sent scrambling into the mountains will return to Shilmista once the trails are clear."

No gain, Danica decided. Dorigen was merely continuing her acceptance of guilt.

Dorigen did not back away from the accusing look. "If they do," she said, her chin held high, "I will demand that part of my penance be that I fight on the side of the elves in that conflict."

Well said, Danica thought. "If the elves would have her," the monk quickly put in, drawing Shayleigh's attention to her disarming smile before the suspicious elf could reply.

"We would be foolish to refuse," Shayleigh answered. She looked back to the quiet night and the distant flickers. "It is likely the orckin will enlist the aid of trolls." In her own way, the elf had, for the first time, agreed with the decision to return Dorigen to the library and argue for a positive judgment, rather than one of punishment.

Shayleigh had made no moves against Dorigen since the wizard's surrender in Castle Trinity, but neither had she befriended her. Shilmista was the elf's home, after all, and Dorigen had been instrumental in bringing ruin to the forest's northern reaches.

Behind Shayleigh's back, Danica and Dorigen exchanged hopeful nods. If King Elbereth and the elves could forgive Dorigen's crimes, then the library's claims against her would seem almost trivial.

"If it was earlier, I would suggest we go down to that light," Danica remarked. "I could do with a bit of good food, and maybe a taste of wine."

"I'd settle for ale," Dorigen said, to which Shayleigh promptly spun about and gave the wizard a sour look.

"Wine," the elf agreed, and it seemed to Dorigen and Danica as if the whole atmosphere of the encampment had suddenly changed, lightened, as if Shayleigh had come to terms with Dorigen's past and was now a true ally. The two women went to their bedrolls then, taking comfort in the knowledge that the alert elf was guarding over them.

Shayleigh remained where she was, standing quietly and watching the flicker of the distant campfire. Her second guess as to its origin had been correct; a group of priests was making its way down to Carradoon—a group of Oghman priests, sent out by Dean Thobicus.

Like Danica, Shayleigh wished the night was earlier, that they might have hiked the couple of miles down to the group.

Kierkan Rufo, approaching the flickering fire from another trail, would have been pleasantly surprised if they had.

* * * * *

He dreamed of towering spires stretching three hundred feet into the air. He dreamed of all the folk of Carradoon, and all the elves of Shilmista, congregating before the cathedral, come to worship and to find inspiration in its massive windows and walls that were, in truth, works of art.

The nave dwarfed the individual. The arching ceiling soared a hundred feet from the stone floor. Graceful walls were lined by corridors housing statues of the worthy priests of both Deneir and Oghma who had gone before. Avery Schell was there, as was Pertelope, there for all time, and at the end of the high walkway was an empty pedestal, awaiting the statue that would be most fitting in this tribute to Deneir.

The statue of Cadderly.

He dreamed of conducting a service in that cathedral, of Brother Chaunticleer's *a cappella* gift to the brother gods, Oghma and Deneir, the talented tenor's voice echoing about the graceful walls like the songs of the heavens themselves.

Then Cadderly saw himself, wearing the sash of the library's dean, leading the service, with Danica sitting proudly by his side.

He was a hundred years old, withered and worn and near death.

The shocking image shook Cadderly from his slumber, and his eyes opened wide to take in the starry sky. He closed his eyes quickly and tried to recapture that last fleeting glimpse, to learn why it might be so startling. Cadderly could only hope that the new library would be constructed before he reached his hundredth year, even if construction began in full this very summer and Ivan and Pikel delivered a thousand dwarves to help with the work.

Cadderly, so filled with divine faith, certainly did not fear his death. Then why had he awakened, and why was his forehead cold with sweat?

He looked back into the dream, forced the image to linger. Even though it was clear, it took Cadderly time to discern what might be out of place.

It was he, the old dean of the library. He looked as if he had lived a century or more, but Danica, sitting beside him, seemed no older than she was now, barely in her twenties.

Cadderly let go the surreal scene and looked up at the stars, reminding himself that it had been just a dream. The Bouldershoulders' wild snoring—Ivan snorting and Pikel whistling in response—calmed him somewhat, told him that all was as it should be.

Still, many hours passed before Cadderly found his slumber again, and that image of an old, dying priest leading a service in the cathedral went into his dreams with him.

*   *   *   *   *

Two of the five Oghmans sat awake, chatting quietly and keeping a half-hearted watch on the dark trees surrounding their encampment as the darkest hours of the night passed. None in the group was really afraid of trouble this far south in the mountains. The trails between Carradoon and the Edificant Library were well traveled, and these were powerful clerics—behind Bron Turman, the most powerful of the Oghman order at the library. They had lined the perimeter of their camp with wards that would not only alert them of the presence of monsters, but would send jolts of lightning into the creatures, probably destroying them before they ever crossed into the opening.

So these two Oghmans were awake more to enjoy the night than to guard the camp, and their eyes were more often on each other, or on the fire, than on the dark and ominous trees.

Kierkan Rufo was in those trees, along with Druzil, watching the priests' movements and listening to the rhythmic snoring of the other three, fast asleep.

Rufo nodded and began his steady approach, but Druzil, still in many ways the wiser of the two, scanned the camp's perimeter, his knowing eyes looking for the revealing emanations of magic.

He kicked off the ground and flapped his wings to land hard against Rufo's shoulder. "It is guarded," he whispered into the vampire's ear. "All the way around."

Rufo nodded again, as though he had suspected that all along. He jerked suddenly, throwing Druzil from his shoulder and lifting his black robes high into the air about him. As the material descended, Rufo's corporeal form seemed to melt away As a bat, Rufo zipped up into the treetops, Druzil following closely

"Did they think to guard from above?" the vampire bat asked the imp in a voice so high-pitched that it hurt Druzil's ears, and though Rufo had spoken loudly, the men on the ground could not even hear the sound.

The two picked their way down the branches. Rufo noticed that Druzil had turned invisible, as was the imp's way, but the vampire was surprised—pleasantly so—to learn that he could still see the imp's vague outline. Another benefit of this undead state, Rufo decided. One of many, many benefits. A few moments later, the vampire was hanging upside down from the lowest branch over the encampment, barely fifteen feet above the heads of the two seated guards. Rufo had thought to swoop right down on them, but paused, wondering if something valuable might be gained from their conversation.

"Bron Turman's going to be surprised when we walk unannounced into Carradoon," one of them was saying.

"His own fault," answered the other. "His rank does not give him the privilege of rewriting the Oghman orders without consulting the other leaders."

Rufo was impressed at how resourceful a liar Dean Thobicus could be. With all the strange goings-on, the Oghmans had been on the alert back at the library. Only the dean's hint that something was indeed amiss, instead of simply telling them that everything was all right, had brought them out here.

"If that is what Bron Turman is doing in Carradoon," the first priest remarked, his tone full of doubt.

The other nodded in agreement.

"I am not convinced of Dean Thobicus's words," the first went on. "Not even his motives. He is frightened of Cadderly's return—in that, I agree with Bron Turman's assessment."

"Do you believe Dean Thobicus wanted all the Oghmans out of the library so we would not interfere with his plans for his own order?" the other asked, to which the first only shrugged.

Rufo nearly squealed aloud at the irony of that question. If only these two knew the truth of the "order" to which they were unintentionally referring!

The ruse had worked, of that much the vampire was now certain. Almost all of the leading Deneirians were dead or undead and under his control, and now the Oghmans were divided and off their guard.

One of the priests gave a great yawn, though a moment before he had seemed perfectly alert. The other followed suit, overcome by a sudden compulsion to lie down and sleep.

"The night grows long," the first remarked, and, without even moving toward his bedroll, he slipped down to the ground and closed his eyes.

The other Oghman thought the movement somewhat silly, until it struck him as suspiciously odd that his friend should fall so quickly into slumber. He fought against that compulsion, that little suggestion in the back of his mind that sleep would be a good thing. He opened his eyes wide and vigorously shook his head. He even reached down, hoisted a waterskin, and poured the fluid over his face.

When the man tossed his head back to wet his face a second time, he was stopped by the image of a black-robed man standing on a branch fifteen feet above him.

Rufo fell down atop him with catlike grace. The vampire grabbed the man's chin and the hair on the back of his head as he opened his mouth to scream, tugging so fiercely that the man's head turned around on his shoulders with a sickening crack of bone.

The vampire stood straight, eyeing the other four, all sleeping. He would wake them one by one and give them a chance to forsake their god, a chance to kneel before him, the personification of *Tuanta Quiro Miancay*.

Nine

The Words of Romus Scaladi

Fare well," Shayleigh offered when the three women came to a fork in the trail early the next morning. One bend went south, for the library. The other continued on generally west. "King Elbereth will be pleased to hear all that I have to tell him."

"All?" Dorigen asked, and the perceptive elf maiden knew that the wizard was referring to herself, to the fact that she was still alive and well and ready to face judgment for her crimes.

Shayleigh's smile was enough of an answer for Dorigen.

"Elbereth is not a vengeful sort," Danica added hopefully.

"*King* Elbereth," Dorigen quickly corrected. "I will remain at the library," she said to Shayleigh, "whatever the decision of the priests, to await word from your king."

"A fair judgment I will be pleased to deliver," Shayleigh replied, and with a nod, she was gone, slipping down the western trail so gracefully and noiselessly that she seemed to the two women almost an illusion, an artist's tapestry, a perfect embodiment of nature. She was out of sight in mere seconds, her gray-green cloak shielding her form in the sylvan shadows, though Danica and Dorigen did not doubt that she could still see them.

"I am ever amazed by their movements," Dorigen remarked. "So supple and graceful, yet in battle, I have never known a race to match the elves' ferocity."

Danica did not disagree. During the war in Shilmista, the monk had found her first real experiences with elves, and it seemed to her that all her years of training in harmony and movement had made her somewhat akin to what came naturally to Shayleigh's people. Danica wished she had been born an elf, or had been raised among them. Then she would have been closer to the spirit of Grandmaster Penpahg D'Ahn's writings, she knew.

Still staring down the empty trail, she imagined she might return to Shilmista and work with Elbereth's people, bringing them the vision of Penpahg D'Ahn. She pictured an open meadow full of elves, practicing the graceful dance of the grandmaster's fighting style, and the sight made her heart skip excitedly.

Then Danica let go the image, shook it away as she recalled the demeanor of elvenkind, recalled what it meant emotionally to be an elf. They were a calm and casual people, easily distracted, and though fierce in battle, their way was playful. The grace of movement was their nature, not their practice, and that was very different from Danica's life. Following her mentor, the young monk was rarely casual, always focused. Even Shayleigh, whom Danica would wish at her side whenever danger was near, could not hold any course for very long. Through the weeks in the caves, waiting for winter's break, the elf had spent long hours, even days, just sitting and watching the snow, occasionally rising to dance, as though no one else had been in the room, as though nothing else in all the world mattered except the falling snowflakes and the movements that Shayleigh hardly seemed conscious she was making.

The elves could not follow the rigorous discipline of Penpahg D'Ahn. Danica didn't pretend to understand them, any of them, even Shayleigh, who had become so dear to her. The elf was fiercely loyal, she knew, but she could not begin to understand all of Shayleigh's motivations.

Shayleigh saw the world from a perspective that Danica could not comprehend, a perspective that put friendship in a different light. While Danica did not doubt the love Shayleigh felt for her, she knew that the elf maiden would likely witness the dawn of several centuries after she, Danica, had died of old age. How many new human friends would Shayleigh come to know and love in those centuries? Would the memory of Danica withstand the test of such a long time, or would she become just a fleeting moment of Shayleigh's future reveries?

Simply put, there was no way that Danica could ever be as important in Shayleigh's eyes as Shayleigh had become in hers. She would remember the elf maiden vividly until the moment of her death.

She considered that difference between them for a moment and decided that hers was the better way, the more passionate existence. Still, Danica found that she envied Shayleigh and all of her kind. The golden-haired elven maiden innately possessed what Danica sought: the peace and grace of true harmony.

"We will be there today?" Dorigen asked, and for the first time, Danica noted a slight tremor in the determined woman's voice.

"Today," Danica answered as she walked off down the southern trail.

Dorigen paused a moment, mustering her courage. She knew she was doing right, that she owed this, at least, to the library and the elves. Still, the wizard's first step along the final trail came hard, as did the second, the third, and all the rest.

Back a short distance down the western trail, Shayleigh watched Dorigen's every move. She didn't doubt Dorigen's sincerity, knew that the wizard honestly meant to follow through, but she knew the journey would be more difficult than

Dorigen implied. It was quite possible that Dorigen might be walking to her death. Somewhere along the way, Shayleigh understood, Dorigen would have to battle her survival instinct, the most basic and powerful force in any human.

Shayleigh waited a moment longer, then slipped quietly into the underbrush alongside the southern trail. If Dorigen lost that battle, she would be ready.

For the time being, Shayleigh called Dorigen a friend, but the elf maiden could not forget the scars on Shilmista. If Dorigen could not bring herself to face the rightful judgment of the victors, then Shayleigh would enact the judgment of Shilmista . . . in the form of a single, well-placed arrow.

* * * * *

"Where is Bron Turman?" one of the younger priests asked nervously. He leaned against a low railing surrounding the altar in one of the library's first-floor chapels.

"Or Dean Thobicus?" added another.

Romus Scaladi, a short, dark-complexioned Oghman whose shoulders seemed nearly as wide as the man was tall, tried to calm his five brother priests of both orders, patting his hands in the empty air and saying, "Shh," as though the men were young children.

"And surely Cadderly will return," a third priest, kneeling before the altar, said hopefully. "Cadderly will set things right."

Two of the other young priests, the only Deneirians in the group, who had listened to Thobicus's warning concerning Cadderly, looked to each other and shrugged, sharing a common fear that Cadderly might actually be the one behind all of the strange things that were going on about them. None of the leaders—of either order—had been seen all day, and both Thobicus and Bron Turman had been missing for two full days.

It was rumored, though none of this group could confirm it, that half a dozen lesser priests had been found dead in their rooms this morning, lying peacefully—under their beds! The priest who had told the group this startling news was not the best of sources, though. He was the newest member of the Oghman order, a small, weak man who had snapped his collarbone in his very first wrestling match. It was common knowledge that this man did not wish to remain in the order, and his appeals to join the Deneirian order had not been received warmly. So when they had encountered him early in the day, his belongings in a sack slung over one shoulder and his eyes squarely on the front door, the six did not panic.

Still, there was no denying that the library was strangely quiet this day—except in one corner of the second floor, where Brother Chaunticleer was holed up in his room, singing to his gods. Not a soul stirred in the headmasters' area. It was strangely quiet and strangely dark, even for the perpetually gloomy place; barriers had been constructed over nearly every window. Normally the library housed nearly eighty priests—before the disaster of the chaos curse, well over a hundred—and at any given time, five to thirty visitors. The guest list was small now, with winter just giving way, but so was the list of priests who had gone to Carradoon, or Shilmista.

So where was everybody?

Another troubling sensation that the six priests could not ignore was the subtle but definite feeling that the Edificant Library had changed somehow, as though the gloom about them was more than a physical feature. It was as if Deneir and Oghma had moved away from this place. Even the midday ritual, in which Brother Chaunticleer sang to both the gods in the presence of all the priests, had not been performed in two days. Romus himself had gone to the singing priest's room, fearing that Chaunticleer had taken ill. He found the door locked, and only after several minutes of pounding had Chaunticleer called out, telling him to go away.

"I feel as if someone has built a ceiling above me," one of the Deneirians remarked, following the suspicions of Cadderly that Dean Thobicus had implanted. "A ceiling that separates me from Deneir."

The other Deneirian nodded his agreement, while the Oghmans looked to each other, then to Romus, who was the strongest cleric among them.

"I am certain there is a simple answer," Romus said as calmly as he could, but the other five knew that he agreed with the Deneirian priest's assessment of the gods. This library had always been among the holiest of places, where priests of any goodly faith could feel the presence of their god or goddess. Even the druids who had visited had been surprised to find an aura of Sylvanus within the walls of a manmade structure.

And for the priests of Oghma and Deneir, there was, perhaps, no holier place in all of Faerûn. This was their tribute to the gods, a place of learning and art, a place of study and recital. The place of Chaunticleer's song.

"We will wrestle!" Romus Scaladi announced surprisingly. After a moment of shock, the Oghmans began to bob their heads in agreement, while the Deneirians continued to stare dumbfoundedly at the stocky Scaladi.

"Wrestle?" one of them asked.

"Tribute to our god!" Scaladi answered, pulling off his black-and-gold vest and fine white shirt, revealing a chest bulging with muscles and thick with dark hair. "We will wrestle!"

"Oooo," came a woman's purr from the back of the chapel. "I do so love to wrestle!"

The six priests swung about hopefully, every one of them thinking that Danica, the woman who not only loved to wrestle, but who could defeat any priest in the library, had at last returned.

They saw not Danica, but Histra, the alluring priestess of Sune, dressed in her customary crimson gown that was cut so low in the front that it seemed as if her navel should show, and slitted high on the thigh to show off the woman's shapely legs. Her long, lush hair, dyed so blond this week as to appear almost white, flew wildly, as usual, and her makeup was thickly applied—never had the priests seen any lips so bright red! Her perfume, also poured generously, wafted across the chapel.

Something was out of place. All six of the priests recognized that fact, though none had figured it out. Behind Histra's generous paint, her skin was deathly pale, as was the leg sticking out from under her gown. And the perfume aroma was sickly sweet, something less than alluring.

Romus Scaladi studied the woman intently. He had never much liked Histra, or her goddess, Sune, whose only tenet seemed to be the physical pleasures of love. Always, ever-hungry Histra had set the hairs on the back of Scaladi's neck to tingling, as they were now, but more than usual.

It was uncommon to see Histra on the first floor, Scaladi knew; it was uncommon for the woman to be out of her room, or out of her bed.

"Why are you here?" the wary priest started to ask, but Histra seemed not to notice.

"I do so love to wrestle," she purred again, openly lewd, and she opened her mouth and laughed wildly.

All six priests understood; all six nervous priests recognized the vampire's fangs for what they were.

Five of the six, including Scaladi and both Deneirians, went immediately for their holy symbols.

Histra continued to laugh. "Wrestle with these!" she cried, and several torn, rotting, stiff-walking men came into the room—men the priests knew.

"My dear Deneir," one of the priests muttered hopelessly.

Romus leaped forward and presented the symbol of Oghma boldly. "Be gone from this holy place, foul undead things!" he cried, and the zombies stopped their shuffling, a couple of them even turning about.

Histra hissed viciously at the monstrous group, compelling them to continue.

"I deny you!" Romus roared at Histra, and it seemed as if she nearly fell over backward. A zombie reached awkwardly for the Oghman, and he growled and punched out with his holy symbol, slamming the monster on the side of the face. Acrid smoke rose from the wound, but the monster kept on, its companions filtering around Romus to get to the others.

"I cannot turn them away!" one of the priests behind Romus cried. "Where is Deneir?"

"Where is Oghma?" cried another.

A stiff arm clubbed Romus on the shoulder. He grunted away the blow and cupped his hand under the zombie's chin, bending the head back, then slashed at the monster's throat with the edge of his holy symbol. Again came a puff of smoke from the wound, and the zombie's rotting flesh opened up easily to the strong man's blow.

But zombies needed no air, so the wound was not serious.

"Fight them!" Romus Scaladi screamed. "Beat them down!" To accentuate his point, the powerful Oghman launched a barrage of punishment on the zombie, finally lifting the corpse over his head and hurling it into a statue against the wall. The Oghman spun about to see to his friends, and found that they were not fighting, but backing away, their faces horror-stricken.

Of course, Scaladi realized. These undead monsters they now faced, these men, had been their friends!. "Do not look at their faces!" he ordered. "They are not of our order. They are mere tools, weapons!

"Weapons of Histra," Romus Scaladi finished, spinning about to face the vampiress. "Now you die," the outraged man promised, lifting his flaring holy symbol toward the monster. "By my hands."

Histra wanted nothing to do with Scaladi. Like Banner and Thobicus, she had not come into her full power yet. Even if she had, she might have thought twice about facing Scaladi, for she recognized that the man was fully in his faith, that his heart could be hers, but not his soul, for he would deny any fear—and fear was perhaps the greatest of a vampire's weapons.

Histra defiantly spat at Scaladi's presented symbol, but he saw the bluff for what it was. If he could get to her, cram his god's symbol down her wretched throat, then the zombies would be leaderless and could be more easily driven away.

Unexpectedly, Histra darted up the side toward the altar, deeper into the chapel, and Scaladi suddenly found two zombies between him and the vampiress.

The other priests were fighting now. The two Deneirians had carried weapons with them into the chapel, blessed maces, and two others had rushed to the altar table, wisely breaking off legs to use as clubs.

The remaining Oghman, the one priest who had not pulled out his holy symbol when Histra revealed herself, was off to the side of the room, trapped against the wall, shaking his head in sheer terror. And how that terror heightened when Histra pushed aside the zombies near the man and let him see her toothy smile!

Scaladi was hard pressed immediately by the zombies. He knew then, in his heart, that the library was no longer a house of Oghma, or of Deneir, that this desecration was nearly complete. The day outside was overcast, but the sun peeked through enough to be their ally.

"Fight out of the room!" Scaladi ordered. "Out of the room and out of the library!" He shifted forward, putting the two zombies' backs to the wall, trying to give his friends an avenue of escape.

On came the Deneirians, their heavy maces pounding zombies aside. Suddenly the path seemed clear for them all, and the Deneirians, and then Scaladi, bolted for the door. The club-wielding Oghmans chased after them, but one, when he tried to leap the altar rail, hooked his foot and sprawled face down on the stone floor.

Zombies swarmed over him; his companion turned back and rushed to his aid.

Scaladi was already at the chapel door when he looked back to see the disaster. His first instinct was to charge back in and die beside his comrades, and he took a step that way. But the two priests of Deneir caught him by the shoulders, and though they could not have held the powerful man back if he wanted to continue, the pause gave Scaladi a moment to see things more clearly.

"You cannot help them!" one of the Deneirians cried.

"We must survive to warn the town!" the other added.

Scaladi staggered out of the chapel.

The zombie horde tore apart the two Oghmans.

Worse still was the fate of the priest against the wall, a man who had spent many secret evenings with Histra. He was filled with too much guilt to resist the vampiress now. He shook his head in weak denial, whispered, begged, for her to go away.

She smiled and came on, and the man, despite his horror, offered her his neck.

The three fleeing priests scrambled along the corridors, meeting no resistance. The front doors were in sight, one of them open, a weak line of sun streaming into the library's foyer.

One of the Deneirians cried out and grasped at his neck, then pitched forward to the stone.

"The door!" Scaladi cried, pulling the other along. The Deneirian looked back to his brother and saw the man flailing wildly at a bat-winged imp as it hopped about his shoulder, biting at his ear and stabbing repeatedly with a poison-tipped tail.

Scaladi dived for the door—it moved away from him, seemingly of its own accord, and slammed shut with a resounding bang, and he fell headlong at its base.

"My dear Deneir," he heard his lone companion whisper. Scaladi turned himself over, to see Dean Thobicus standing in the shadows, to see Kierkan Rufo—Kierkan Rufo!—moving quietly behind the withered man.

"Deneir is gone from this place," Thobicus said calmly and unthreateningly, approaching the man with his arms open and to the side. "Come with me now, that I might show you the new way."

The young Deneirian wavered, and for a moment, Scaladi thought he would give himself over to Thobicus, who was now no more than two paces away.

The young priest exploded into action, cracking his mace across the dean's wrinkled face. Thobicus's head jerked violently to the side and he was pushed back. But only a single step—and he turned straight again, eyeing the disbelieving young Deneirian. There ensued a long pause, a long and horrible moment, the hush of a crouched predator.

Thobicus threw his arms up, fingers bent like claws, gave an unearthly roar, and sprang over the young priest, burying the man under his flailing limbs.

Scaladi scrambled about and grabbed at the door, tugging with all his considerable strength.

"It will not open," Kierkan Rufo assured him.

Scaladi tugged furiously. He heard Rufo stepping near him, right behind.

"It will not open," the confident vampire said again.

Scaladi spun about, his holy symbol thrust toward Rufo. The vampire leaned back, away from the sudden glare.

But Rufo was not Histra, was full of the swirling chaos curse and was many times more powerful. The moment of surprise passed quickly.

"Now you die!" Scaladi promised, but by the time he finished the simple statement, all conviction had flown from his voice. He felt Rufo's will inside his head, compelling him to surrender, imparting a sense of hopelessness.

Romus Scaladi had always been a fighter. He had grown up an orphan on the tough streets of Sundabar, every day a challenge. And so he fought now, with all his own will, against Rufo's intrusions.

Green bolts of searing energy burned into his hand, and his holy symbol was knocked away. Both Scaladi and Rufo looked to the side, to the smiling Druzil, still perched on the body of the Deneirian.

Scaladi looked back helplessly as Rufo grabbed his wrist and yanked him forward, the vampire's face only inches from his own.

"You are strong," Rufo said. "That is good."

Scaladi spat in his face, but Rufo did not explode with anger, as had Thobicus. The chaos curse guided this vampire, kept him focused on what was best.

"I offer you power," Rufo whispered. "I offer you immortality. You will know pleasures beyond . . ."

"You offer damnation!" Scaladi growled.

Across the foyer, the Deneirian screamed, then went silent, and Thobicus feasted.

"What do you know?" Rufo demanded. "I am alive, Romus Scaladi! I have chased Deneir and Oghma from this place!"

Scaladi held his jaw firm.

"The library is mine!" Rufo went on. He grabbed Scaladi's thick hair in one hand and with strength that horrified the Oghman, easily tugged the man's head back. "Carradoon shall be mine!"

"They are just places," Scaladi insisted, with the simple and undeniable logic that had guided the man all his life. He knew that Rufo wanted more than the conquest of places. He knew what the vampire desired.

"You can join me, Romus Scaladi," Rufo said, predictably. "You can share my strength. You like strength."

"You have no strength," Scaladi said, and his sincere calm seemed to rattle Rufo. "You have only lies and false promises."

"I can tear your heart out!" Rufo roared at him. "And hold it up, beating before your dying eyes." Histra came into the foyer then, along with a couple of her zombies.

"Would you be like them?" Rufo asked, indicating the zombies. "Either way, you will serve me!"

Scaladi looked at the wretched zombies, and to Rufo's dismay, the priest smiled. They were corporeal animations and nothing more, Scaladi knew, had to believe with all his heart. Secure in that faith, the man looked Rufo straight in the vampire's blood-red eyes, straight in the vampire's drooling, animal-like face.

"I am more than my body," Romus Scaladi proclaimed.

Rufo snapped the Oghman's head back, shattering neck bones. With one hand, the outraged vampire heaved Scaladi across the foyer, where he crashed into a wall and crumpled at its base.

Histra hissed wickedly, and Thobicus chimed in, a horrid applause as the two circled their master. Caught up in the frenzy, Rufo dismissed Scaladi's damning words and hissed and snarled with all his wicked heart.

" . . . more than my body," came a whisper from the side. The three vampires stopped their macabre dance and song and turned as one to the broken priest, propped on his elbows, his head flopping weirdly.

"You are dead!" Rufo declared, a futile denial of the priest's words.

Scaladi promptly corrected him. "I have found Oghma."

And the man died, secure in his faith.

* * * * *

Outside the library, Percival hopped excitedly from one branch to another, hearing the torment of those still alive inside. The squirrel was down to the ground, just outside the door, when Rufo slammed it shut before Scaladi.

Now Percival was high in the trees, as high as he could go, chattering frenetically and leaping from branch to branch, turning wide circles about the grove. He heard the screams, and from one window on the second floor, he heard, too, the song of Deneir, the prayer of Brother Chaunticleer.

The screams were louder.

Ten

The Nature of Evil

T he trail meandered around a wide expanse of rock, but Danica was growing impatient. She went to the stone abutment instead, looked up its
thirty-foot height, and carefully began picking her way up along a crack
in the stone.

Dorigen came to the spot beneath her. The wizard was talking, but Danica,
concentrating on hooking her strong fingers in cracks and picking rough spots
where she could set her feet, wasn't listening. Soon after, the agile monk lifted
her hand over the lip and felt about, finally grasping the thick base of a small
bush. She tested her weight, then, convinced the bush was secure, used it to pull
herself over.

From that vantage point, Danica got her first look at the Edificant Library. It
lay nestled atop a flat juncture in a climbing trail, a cliff to its northern side and
a steep drop south of the place. It seemed just a squat block of unremarkable
stone, not a particularly attractive piece of architecture, and from this distance
Danica did not notice that the small windows (there were so few) had been covered by boards and tapestries.

All seemed quiet and calm, the way things usually were at the ancient library,
and Danica, anxious to get this messy business about Dorigen's punishment
over with, was relieved to see it again. She turned about on the stone, meaning
to tell Dorigen that the library was very close, but was surprised to find the
woman scaling the cliff, slower than Danica, of course, but making progress.

Danica fell to her belly and called out directions. She was proud of Dorigen
at that moment, proud of the wizard's willingness to fight obstacles. The cliff was
small and no real challenge to one of Danica's training, but she could appreciate
how imposing it must seem to Dorigen, who had spent years with her face

930

buried in books. Yet here was Dorigen, reaching for Danica's offered hand, climbing without complaint.

A hundred yards away, concealed in a copse of evergreens, Shayleigh was equally impressed. When Danica had been so obviously exposed on the cliff face, Dorigen could have taken any number of actions to ensure her freedom. But again the wizard had proven her heart, and Shayleigh, like Danica when Dorigen had aided in the troll fight, found that she was not surprised.

Suddenly the elf maiden felt foolish for her suspicions. She reached down, unstrung her long bow, and mumbled quietly that she should have gone straight to Shilmista, as she had claimed, instead of following the two nearly all the way to the library.

They would be at the building within the hour, Shayleigh knew, and she could have been well on her way to her forest home. She waited in the trees until Danica and Dorigen had moved off again, then she, too, went to the stony rise. With a natural agility that at least matched Danica's practiced skill, the elf scampered to the top. She went down to one knee and scanned the dark line of the trail ahead as it wove in and out of hollows thick with trees and around tumbles of great boulders. Finally she spotted Danica and Dorigen, walking easily some distance ahead, and, with the patience of a being that would live for centuries, Shayleigh marked their movements along the trails, all the way to the library's front doors.

She was no longer looking for trouble from Dorigen, but rather, was saying farewell to her friends.

* * * * *

Percival greeted the two as they came onto the library's grounds, the white squirrel dancing wildly about the trees and squawking as if he had gone insane.

"I have never seen such a reaction," Dorigen remarked, for there was no missing the squirrel's frantic movements.

"That is Percival," Danica explained, "a friend of Cadderly's."

They watched curiously as the squirrel leaped down a dozen feet, ran to the end of the branch closest to them, and screamed at Danica so crazily that the woman wondered if he had contracted some disease.

"What is the matter?" Danica asked the rodent, and Percival kept hopping in circles and screeching as if he had been dropped into a kettle of boiling water.

"I have heard of a disease of the mind that affects such animals," Dorigen offered. "And once saw the result in a wolf. Look closely," she bade the monk. "If you discern foam at the creature's mouth, then you must kill the beast at once."

Danica turned a wary and knowing eye on Dorigen, and when the wizard noticed the look, she straightened and wondered what she might have said to evoke so strong a reaction.

"Percival is Cadderly's friend," Danica said again. "Perhaps Cadderly's closest friend. If you think the squirrel is mad, you would be overwhelmed by Cadderly's madness if ever he learned that we killed the animal."

That settled Dorigen. Danica eyed Percival squarely and told him to go back into the trees.

The two women turned for the door then, and Danica knocked loudly. Percival raced along the branches, higher into the boughs, following a course that allowed him to leap to the library's gutter system atop the lowest edge of the front roof. The white squirrel hopped along to a point just above the doors, meaning to leap down onto Danica and stop her progress, but by the time Percival got to the spot, Danica and Dorigen had grown tired of waiting for an answer to their knock and Danica had pushed open the unlocked doors and entered the foyer.

It was dark and quiet. Danica looked behind her and saw a heavy blanket stretched across the small windows above the doors.

"What is this?" Dorigen asked. She had never been in the library, but she surmised that this atmosphere was not normal for the place. Where were all the priests? she wondered. And why were the hairs standing up on the back of her neck?

"I have never seen the library like this before," Danica answered. The monk wasn't as suspicious or nervous as Dorigen, though. She had spent the last few years in the Edificant Library; the place had become home to her.

"Perhaps there is some ceremony going on," Danica reasoned, "one I do not understand."

Unsuspecting Danica could not begin to appreciate the truth of her statement.

* * * * *

"Phooey!"

Pikel scrunched up his little nose and waggled his head at the terrible stench. He turned suddenly and let fly a tremendous sneeze, showering his dour brother with spittle.

Not surprised (not after so many decades beside Pikel), Ivan didn't say a word.

"Troll stench," Cadderly remarked.

"Burned troll," Ivan replied, wiping his face.

Cadderly nodded and moved cautiously down the path. They were only three days from the library, moving easily along the same trail Danica and the others had used. The path went up a short rise, then around a bend and some gnarly bushes, and into a clearing that had been used as a campsite.

Cadderly's heart beat wildly as he came near that camp. He felt certain that Danica had been here, and, it would seem, had encountered some wretched trolls.

The smell nearly overwhelmed the young priest as he clambered around the bushes, skidding to a stop in front of the gruesome remains of the battle.

Three large forms, three lumps of blackened flesh, lay about the small clearing.

"Looks like they got 'em," Ivan remarked, coming in more confidently behind Cadderly.

Pikel started to chant "Oo oi!" but sneezed again instead, just as Ivan turned back to face him. Ivan answered by punching Pikel in the nose, to which Pikel responded by poking the end of his club between Ivan's knees, then diving to the side, tripping his brother. In a moment, the two were rolling about the ground.

Cadderly, on his hands and knees, searched around to determine exactly what had transpired, paying the two bouncing dwarves no heed. They had fought a dozen times over the last few weeks, and neither of them ever seemed to get hurt.

The young priest inspected the closest troll, quickly surmising that Shayleigh had hit this one with a barrage of arrows before flames had consumed it. The next troll he went to, lying across the way, far from where the campfire had been, showed no signs that it had been downed or even wounded before flames engulfed it. Cadderly searched carefully, even shifting the charred corpse to the side. He found no brand, though, no trace that any torch had been brought out to combat the troll.

He rose and turned back toward the stone circle that had held the campfire, hoping to discern how much of a fire had been burning when the trolls attacked.

Ivan and Pikel rolled right across the ashes and scattered the rocks, too absorbed in their wrestling to notice the young priest's movements. They crashed into the body of the third troll, and the blistered skin popped open, pouring forth the creature's melted fat.

"Yuck!" Pikel squealed, hopping to his feet.

Ivan hopped up, too. He grabbed his brother by the front of the tunic and heaved Pikel headlong into a bush, then coiled his muscled legs and sprang in after him, burying Pikel as he tried to stand once more.

Cadderly, worried for his absent friends and trying to confirm something important, fast grew impatient with the two, but still said nothing. He simply stormed over to the broken firepit and began his inspection.

He suspected that the fire could not have been high at the time of the attack, or the trolls, fearful of flame, would have lain in wait. He also knew that his friends would not have remained in this area after the fight—the stench would have been too great. And Danica, and particularly Shayleigh, who so revered nature, would not have left the camp with the fire burning.

As Cadderly expected, he found no charred logs of any significant size. The fire had been low. The young priest looked back to the consumed trolls and nodded, his suspicions confirmed.

"Get yer fingers outta me neck!" Ivan bellowed, drawing Cadderly's attention to the side.

Pikel stood at the clearing's edge with his back to the young priest, facing Ivan as the yellow-bearded dwarf pulled himself free of the tangling bushes.

"Get yer fingers outta me neck!" Ivan bellowed again, though he was looking straight at Pikel, who stood with his hands out wide, one empty, the other holding nothing but the dwarf's tree-trunk club.

Ivan, finally realizing the truth of it, paused and scratched at his beard. "Well, if it ain't yerself . . ." he muttered suspiciously.

Ivan leaped and spun, expecting to find an enemy standing in the bush behind him. There was indeed an enemy grabbing at Ivan's neck, but the whole of it came around with his turn.

Cadderly swallowed hard and put a hand up to shield his eyes.

"Ick," Pikel said, and gagged.

A troll arm, severed at the elbow but still alive, held on tight to Ivan, its claws clamped tightly on the back of the dwarf's neck.

"What?" Ivan asked and started to turn back. He blanched when he saw Pikel's heavy club arcing fast for him. All he could do was close his eyes and wait to be clobbered, but Pikel's aim was perfect. The green-bearded dwarf swatted the disembodied arm free of his brother and sent it flying across the way.

It collided against a tree and fell to the ground, then scrabbled away like some five-legged spider-thing, dragging the forearm behind it.

It was Ivan's turn to gag, and he grabbed desperately at his neck.

The troll arm scrambled under a bush, and Pikel started for it. The dwarf stopped abruptly when he noticed Cadderly, though, the young priest standing grim, one arm extended, his hand clenched in a fist.

"*Fete!*" the young priest cried, and from an onyx ring, which he had taken from Dorigen, there came a line of fire. It engulfed both the bush and the troll arm immediately. In mere seconds, the bush was no more than a blackened skeleton and the charred arm beneath moved no more.

To Cadderly's surprise, though, the line of fire dissipated sooner than he expected.

"Ick," Pikel said again, considering the remains.

Ivan, too, stared at the pile, his face scrunched up with disgust. Cadderly used the distraction to turn his arm to the side, and again he commanded the ring to spew forth its fire.

Nothing happened. Cadderly understood then that the enchantment in the ring was a finite thing, and now had expired. Likely, the item would still serve as a conduit, so he could probably re-empower it, or at least get Dorigen or some other wizard to do it. He wasn't too concerned, though, for he believed that his future battles would be ones of will and not physical force.

By the time he came from his contemplations and looked up to the dwarves, they were arguing again, pushing and shoving. "Can I persuade the two of you to stop your fighting and help me search?" Cadderly asked angrily.

Both dwarves stopped abruptly and bobbed their heads stupidly.

"Our friends had this camp," Cadderly explained, "and defeated the trolls."

"Got 'em good," Ivan remarked, turning to Pikel. "Smart girls to use the campfire."

"They did not," Cadderly corrected, drawing a confused look from both brothers. "The fire was low when the trolls attacked."

"Trolls look burned to me," Ivan said.

"It was Dorigen and her magic that won the day," Cadderly replied.

"Oo," Ivan and Pikel said together, and they looked at each other as they spoke.

"So ye was right," Ivan said.

Cadderly nodded. "So it would seem," he replied. "The wizard has found her heart, and it is more generous than I had dared hope." Cadderly looked to the southwest then, in the general direction of the Edificant Library. Ivan and Pikel read his thoughts in his serious expression; he was considering the nature and value of punishment.

"The ore is hid," Ivan remarked.

Cadderly, curious, looked at him.

"Dwarven saying," Ivan explained. "Ye find a lump o' stone that looks worthless, but ye can't be knowing that until ye've cracked it open. It's what's inside that counts. And it is so with Dorigen."

Cadderly smiled and nodded. "Let us be on our way," he offered, suddenly anxious to get back to the library.

To their relief, they found three sets of prints leading away from the encampment, close together.

The way friends would walk.

* * * * *

Danica and Dorigen found the first body in the small chapel to the side of the foyer. Romus Scaladi was mutilated.

"Get out," Dorigen whispered, and Danica nodded as she turned for the door, turned back toward the foyer.

The two women skidded abruptly.

Histra of Sune stood in the doorway, smiling, showing her fangs. "I am so glad you have returned," she said calmly. "There were but three women in all the library, and so many, many men. Even I could not attend to them all."

The words, and Histra's appearance—the woman was obviously dead!—brought a hundred questions to Danica's mind. She had one definite answer, though, one that concerned Histra's obvious intentions, and Danica, never one to be paralyzed by fear, was quickly in a crouch, ready to lash out. She peeked out of the corner of her eye at Dorigen, and took comfort in the mage's subtly moving lips.

Histra saw the movement, too, and opened her mouth wide in a protesting hiss, then turned as if to flee. Danica didn't want to get in the way of Dorigen's forthcoming spell, but her reactions were instinctive. She sprang ahead, quick as a hunting cat, and landed in a spin, one foot swinging wide to connect solidly against Histra's ribs.

The vampiress flew away several feet, but did not seem hurt, and came right back at Danica, arms flailing. Danica brought a foot straight up in front of her, between Histra's arms, to smack the monster in the face. Histra's head snapped back violently, but again, if the blow had hurt the vampiress, she did not show it.

Danica smelled the stench of Histra's breath and responded by jabbing a straightened and stiffened finger deep into one of the woman's blood-red eyes. That made Histra back off, but at the same moment, she snapped up her own hand and caught Danica by the forearm.

Danica could not believe the strength in that grasp; it was stronger than any grip she had felt from the huge, muscled Oghman wrestlers, stronger than any human grip could ever be. She tried to twist away, hit Histra with a rapid series of kicks and punches—all in vital areas—but the vampiress held on stubbornly. Danica felt her adversary's hot breath again, too close.

Dorigen watched the fight intently. She had been forced to dismiss her first spell, a bolt of lightning, for it would have caught Danica in its path. Now the wizard was chanting again, concentrating on a more controllable and accurate attack.

She didn't hear the slight flutter of wings behind and to the side, and her surprise was complete when the bat shifted form in midair and Kierkan Rufo caught her suddenly by the throat, jerking her head back so forcefully that Dorigen nearly lost consciousness.

Histra's lusting expression revealed her supreme confidence that this mortal woman could not really hurt her. She twisted harder on Danica's arm, taking obvious pleasure in the woman's pained face.

"You are mine," she purred, but her expression changed when a dagger, its hilt sculpted into the shape of a silver dragon, ripped deep into her elbow! Histra fell back and howled. Danica quickly retrieved her other enchanted dagger and stood facing the vampiress, not backing down an inch.

The monk's confidence slipped away considerably, though, when she peeked back over her shoulder and saw Kierkan Rufo holding Dorigen, the woman's head angled so that the man could easily snap her neck.

Danica felt a wave of nausea roll over her as she considered the implications of Rufo in the library, Rufo and Histra both vampires! She understood the coverings over the windows then, and realized, to her horror, that the place had apparently fallen fully.

"Danica," Rufo said lewdly. "My dear, dear Danica. I cannot tell you how I have longed for your return!"

Danica's knuckles whitened as she gripped her daggers tightly. She was looking for a shot, looking to put one of the enchanted knives over Dorigen's shoulder into Rufo's ugly face.

As if he read her thoughts, Rufo tightened his grip on Dorigen and jerked the mage's head back a bit more, forcing her to grimace at the pain.

"It would be a little thing to tear her head from her shoulders," Rufo taunted. "Would you like to see that?"

Danica's muscles relaxed slightly.

"Good," the perceptive vampire said. "There is no need for us to be enemies in this. Dear Danica, I will make you a queen."

"Your queen will cut your heart out," Danica replied.

She knew she shouldn't have said those words with Dorigen so obviously in peril, but the thought of what Rufo was offering filled her throat with bile. She couldn't bear to talk to the man in life. Now . . .

"I expected as much from you, stubborn Danica," Rufo retorted sharply. "But as for you, Dorigen," he purred, turning the mage's head so that she could readily view his pallid face. "We were allies once, and so we shall be allies again! Come to me, and be a queen, and know more power than Aballister could ever give you!"

For just an instant, Danica feared that Dorigen might give in. The price of refusal was obvious. Danica reconsidered her fear immediately, though, remembering all she had learned of Dorigen during their journey to the library.

"Cadderly will destroy you," Danica warned Rufo. The tall vampire relaxed his grip and turned angry eyes toward her. Nothing could get Rufo's attention more than the mention of Cadderly.

Danica locked stares with the vampire, but not before she noticed Dorigen's lips moving again.

"He should be at the library's doors by now," Danica went on, feigning confidence. "He is strong, Rufo. He crushed Aballister and all of Castle Trinity."

"I would know if he had arrived!" the vampire roared, and his tone alone told Danica that she had rattled him. "If he had, I would be eagerly . . ."

Rufo's words turned into a jumble, all his body jerking suddenly as arcs of blue lightning shot out of Dorigen's hands and pulsed about the vampire's body. Dorigen twisted, growled, and pulled away, and the final shock of the spell sent the two flying apart, wafts of smoke from Rufo's burning flesh rising in the air between them.

Dorigen was casting again, immediately, as Rufo tried to recover his senses.

"I will torture you for eternity!" the vampire promised, and Dorigen knew she was doomed, knew that she could not complete her spell before Rufo fell over her.

A spinning metallic sliver caught Rufo's attention. He threw his arm in front of his face and shrieked as the tip of Danica's dagger bored through his forearm.

Danica smelled sulphur mixed with the scent of burned flesh. She looked to Dorigen, then back to Rufo as he yanked out her dagger and tossed it to the floor.

"Run," Danica heard Dorigen say, and when she looked back to the wizard, her heart fell. Dorigen stood calmly, too calmly, a small ball of flame dancing in the air above her uplifted palm. Danica knew enough about wizardry to understand.

"No!" Rufo roared. He threw his robes tightly about him and fell within himself, seeking the source of his newfound powers.

"Run," Dorigen said again, her voice serene.

Danica had taken two steps through the doorway before she looked ahead and realized that Histra was coming for her again. She lashed out with her remaining dagger, more to throw the vampiress off balance than to score a hit, then spun to the side and down, coming around with a circling kick that caught the dodging Histra on the back of the leg. She heard Rufo command Dorigen to stop and heard the confident wizard laugh in response.

Danica kicked off, launching Histra back toward the chapel's open door and using the momentum to propel herself farther from harm's way. She stumbled for the effort, and threw herself with the flow, falling and rolling, as Rufo's form melted, as Dorigen dropped a ball of flame on the floor between herself and where the vampire had stood.

It all seemed surreal to Danica, as if all the world had gone into slow motion. Flames rolled out the chapel door; she saw Histra's hair and arms reach forward from the force of the blast. Then there was just the fireball, reaching lazily toward Danica.

She curled up, tucked her head, and became, through years of training, like stone. The flames licked at her, swirled around her, but Danica felt only the slightest heat. When it was ended, an instant later, she was unharmed, and only the fringes of her cloak had been so much as singed.

The slowmotion effect of that horrible instant was gone, reversed, it seemed, when Danica looked upon Histra, the vampiress hurling herself about the room, slamming walls and flailing against the back of her shoulders as her flesh bubbled under the hungry flames. The oaken support beams about the room smoldered; tapestries a thousand years old were fast consumed; and acrid black smoke poured from the destroyed chapel—where Dorigen had given her life.

Danica fought back tears as she scrambled for the door. She had to link up with Cadderly and the dwarves, maybe find Shayleigh. She had to . . .

The door would not open.

Danica tugged with all her might, and the handle broke off, sending her sprawling to the floor.

A green fog rolled out of a crack in the wall beside the door, swirling into a funnel cloud, then blowing away suddenly and dissipating, leaving an angry and hardly wounded Kierkan Rufo standing before the monk.

Eleven
Danica's Fall

D anica's right hook caught Rufo on the side of the jaw and snapped his head
to the side. Slowly and ominously, the vampire turned back to face the monk.
Danica hit him again with another vicious hook, then a third time, in
the same place, with the same punch.

Rufo laughed as his head turned slowly back to center, not a welt or mark on
his white cheek.

"You cannot hurt me," the vampire said in quiet, even tones.

In response, Danica drove her knee straight up between Rufo's legs, the
force of the blow lifting the vampire up on his toes.

Rufo merely smiled.

"I should have guessed you'd have nothing there to hurt," Danica said, stinging the monster with words where her fists had failed.

Rufo's face contorted, rage bubbling through his cool demeanor. A feral snarl
escaped his lips, and his arm shot forward for Danica's throat.

Danica's golden—hilted dagger, sculpted like a tiger, drove deep into Rufo's
forearm. Faster than Rufo could react, the skilled monk ripped the blade along
his arm, then tore it out and slashed Rufo across the face, mar—ring the same
cheek she had punched.

She went into a frenzy then, and so did Rufo, Danica slashing this way and
that, Rufo's grasping hands trying futilely to catch the nasty blade. Danica
scored hit after minor hit, then plunged the enchanted dagger deep into Rufo's
chest, seeking his heart.

By the way Rufo suddenly froze, his hands going wide to the side and his
expression shocked, she could tell she had hit the mark. Unblinking, eyeing the
vampire squarely and showing not a trace of fear, Danica gave a sharp, short twist.

The side of Rufo's mouth began to twitch; Danica expected he would fall.

They held that macabre pose for a long while, small growls escaping Rufo's mouth. Why didn't he fall? Danica wondered. Why didn't he just die?

Her confidence began to waver as Rufo's hand eased toward her wrist. She gave another sharp tug, and the vampire grimaced. She turned the blade again, and though Rufo's pain was obvious on his pallid face, his hand kept its steady approach.

Suddenly, his strong fingers grabbed tight to Danica's wrist. The monk's left hand went into a flurry, slamming the vampire's throat and face.

Rufo never blinked, just watched as he gradually forced Danica to retract the blade, her muscles corded with strain, no match for the physical strength of the vampire. As soon as the dagger's tip came clear of his chest, Rufo yanked Danica's arm up high.

"Fool!" he said, his smelly breath in her face.

Danica slammed her forehead into his nose.

Rufo yanked her back, and his other hand came snapping across, smacking the dagger from her hand, sending it spinning about the foyer.

"You cannot hurt me," Rufo declared again, despite his obviously painful wounds.

This time, though, both of her enchanted weapons lost to her, Danica found she believed him. And she believed Rufo would tear her apart.

"Look at me!" came a shriek from across the foyer. Both Rufo and Danica turned to see Histra kneeling by the chapel door, looking down at her hands, held out in front of her. The flesh had bubbled from fingers and arms and hung down in grotesque flaps. Histra looked plaintively at her master, and even Rufo could not disguise his disgust at the sight, for Histra, who had spent her living years primping and powdering, seemed a caricature of her former self, a cruel joke on the order of Sune, Goddess of Love. Jowls of burned flesh hung low below her chin and, though they remained intact, there was no flesh around her eyeballs, so they seemed as if they would roll from her face. Her upper lip was gone, as was the flesh on one side of her nose. Her hair, that beautiful, silky, alluring mane, was no more than short, scraggly clumps of gray.

Rufo's disgust came out as a long, low growl, and without even thinking of the movement, he clenched his hand tighter and lowered his arm, forcing Danica to her knees. The monk thought to use Rufo's distraction for her own benefit and break away, but, though she had her free hand working on only one of Rufo's grasping fingers, she could not budge the digit. She tried to twist and squirm, but without even thinking, Rufo held her steady. Soon Danica came to accept that all her efforts would get her only a dislocated elbow.

"You are a vampire," Rufo said, to comfort Histra. "Your wounds will heal." Danica didn't hear much conviction in Rufo's voice, and she understood why. Vampires healed as did trolls, knitting tears in their skin and regenerating lost blood. Histra's garish wounds, though, had been caused by fire, and they would not repair.

A smidgeon of hope crossed Histra's destroyed features.

"Find a mirror!" Danica shouted suddenly. "See what your choice has done to you!"

Rufo turned and glared down at her; she could feel his grip tightening, and that reminded her that she was taking a dangerous chance here.

"Immortality?" Danica asked boldly. She groaned as Rufo subtly shifted her arm, bent it to the side, above the elbow. "Is that what he promised you?" the monk stubbornly went on. "Then you shall be ugly for all eternity!"

Danica knew that last statement would pain Histra more than anything else in the world. Rufo knew it, too, and the look he put over Danica promised her nothing short of an agonizing death. Rufo's free hand whipped across, slapping Danica so hard on the side of her head that she nearly passed out.

She shook off the blow and could feel warm blood rolling down from her ear when Rufo hit her again.

"Your wounds will not heal!" Danica cried through clenched teeth, trying to fend off the continuing attack with her free hand.

Rufo opened his mouth wide, fangs moving near Danica's neck.

"They are of fire!" Danica yelled, then she cried out, thinking she was about to die.

Outraged beyond rational thought, Histra barreled into Rufo, slamming him back against the wall.

Danica shifted her legs and threw all her weight to one side. She heard her elbow pop out of its joint, but had to ignore the agony, had to break free.

She did so just as Rufo hurled Histra back across the foyer, where the disfigured priestess slumped to the floor, her shoulders bobbing with sobs.

Danica was up, but Rufo was ready. "Where will you run?" the vampire casually asked. Danica looked to the library's outer doors again, but Rufo laughed at that notion.

"You are mine." The vampire took a step forward, and Danica's foot came up hard, slamming his chest and knocking him back. Danica went into a spin then, her trailing foot flying wide, and Rufo, not understanding, merely laughed and stayed back, apparently out of range.

As soon as the foot whipped past, the vampire came in hard, but Danica had hit her mark perfectly, had never been aiming at Kierkan Rufo. Her foot went up high and drove through the library's outer door, splintering the wood. Rufo stepped right into a shaft of sunlight that streamed through.

The vampire recoiled, raised his arms to block the searing beam. Danica started for the door, thinking to break it wider and make her escape into daylight, but Rufo's fist shot out and clipped her shoulder, and, though Danica was quick enough to partially brace for the blow, she found herself spinning through the air.

She caught her balance and touched down in a shock-absorbing roll, then came back to her feet many yards from the door. By then Rufo had crossed the beam of sunlight and now stood blocking her way.

"Damn," Danica muttered, a fitting curse if ever there was one, and she turned and fled for the stairway.

* * * * *

Banner spent this day in sleep, a deep sleep filled with dreams of power, basking in the pleasures Kierkan Rufo had promised him. He had forsaken his god, thrown aside all that he had learned about morality in life, in exchange for that personal gain.

There was no remorse, no guilt, interrupting his slumber. Truly Banner was a damned thing.

His dream took him to Carradoon, to a brothel he had once visited, on the eve of his acceptance into the Edificant Library. How pretty the women were! How wonderful their scent!

Banner pictured them now as his queens, faces pallid, sharing his life, washing in the warmth of blood.

The warmth.

Waves of heat rolled over the sleeping vampire, and he exalted in them, picturing them as blood, a sea of warm blood.

The warmth took on a vicious edge, began to lick painfully at Banner's sides. His eyes popped open and, to his horror, he found himself immersed in a thick gray cloud. Wafts of smoke rose from the smoldering lining of his casket, tucked under a bed on the library's second floor, right above the chapel Dorigen had fireballed.

Banner's hair burst into flame.

The vampire shrieked and punched straight up, his powerful fists breaking through the wood of the casket and those splintered, burning boards fell back in atop him.

Banner scrambled wildly, kicking and thrashing apart his flaming prison. His robes flared in biting orange fires. The skin on one arm bubbled and blistered. He thought to turn gaseous, as he had seen Rufo do on occasion, but he was not enough into the realm of undeath, had not mastered vampirism to that degree.

Banner heaved the engulfed bed aside and staggered to his feet, away from the burning box. His room was ablaze; he couldn't see the door for the fiery light. Several zombies, including Fester Rumpol, stood calmly inside the conflagration, feeling no pain from the flames, though they were being consumed. They were unthinking things, and could not even comprehend that they must flee the fire, could feel neither the terror nor the pain.

Looking at Rumpol, Banner found that he envied the zombie.

Hot cinders swept into the vampire's eyes, stinging and blinding him, and he ran desperately, hoping for the door, but slamming hard into the unyielding stone wall instead.

He was down again, thrashing in agony, the hungry flames attacking from every angle as though they were a coordinated army. There was nowhere to run, nowhere . . .

Banner's eyes were gone by then, burned out, but for the first time since he had succumbed to Kierkan Rufo's temptations, the fallen priest could see the truth.

Where were Rufo's promises now? Where was the power, the warmth of blood?

In the last seconds of his existence, Banner understood his folly. He wanted to call out to Deneir, to beg forgiveness, but, like everything else in the man's existence, that intent was based on personal need. There was no charity in Banner's heart, and so he died without hope.

Across the room, the flames consumed the zombies, including the body of Fester Rumpol. The spirit, the essence, of Fester Rumpol felt none of it, for he had held true in the face of adversity, had followed his faith past mortality.

* * * * *

She came off the landing on the second floor and ran straight into Dean Thobicus. His hands clasped her upper arms, holding her steady, and, for an instant, Danica thought she had found an ally, a priest who could turn back awful Rufo.

"Fire," she stammered. "And Rufo . . ."

Danica stopped suddenly, calmed herself, and looked carefully into Thobicus's eyes. She silently mouthed, "No," over and over, slowly shaking her head.

She could not deny the truth, though, and if Dean Thobicus, too, had fallen to the darkness, then the library was doomed.

Danica took a deep, steadying breath, making no immediate move to resist, and the vampire smiled wickedly, revealing its fangs, only inches from Danica's face.

Danica's foot flashed up in front of her face, slammed Thobicus under the nose, and jerked his head back violently. The monk's arms worked in a fast circle, fists crossing in front of her chest, then going out and down over the dean's elbows. As strong as the vampire's grasp was, Danica's leverage pulled her free. Up came her foot a second time, again slamming the monster under the nose, doing no real damage, but buying Danica the moment she needed to break free.

She was back on the staircase and thought for a moment to go down, but Rufo was laughing, ascending the stairs behind her.

Up went Danica, to the third floor. A zombie stood silently in the stairway, but offered no resistance as Danica drove her fist into its bloated face, then heaved it down behind her to impede her pursuers.

She was free in the hallway of the third floor then, but where to go? She looked right, to the south, and then left, and found herself running north, toward Cadderly's room.

Rufo's feet made not a sound as he glided along the floor, but Danica heard his mocking laughter right behind her as she skidded into Cadderly's room and slammed the door in the vampire's face and dropped the locking bar into place. She found yet another zombie in the room, standing passively, and she hit it with a brutal barrage of kicks and punches that destroyed it in seconds. Its chest popped open as it fell to the floor, and Danica felt waves of nausea wash over her.

Those waves were stolen by fear when Rufo's heavy fist slammed the door. "Where will you run, sweet Danica?" the vampire chided. A second slam rattled the bar, threatened to knock the door off its hinges. Purely on instinct, Danica threw her weight against the door, bracing with all her considerable strength.

The pounding stopped, but Danica did not relax.

She saw the green vapor then, Rufo's fog, wafting in under the door, and there was no way she could stop it. She staggered across the room, mesmerized by the vampire's transformation, thinking she was doomed.

The excited chatter of a squirrel cleared her thoughts. Cadderly's room was one of the few in the library that sported a fairly large window, which the young priest often climbed through to sit on the roof and feed cacasa-nuts to Percival.

Danica leaped over the bed.

"Where will you run?" the vampire asked again, resuming his corporeal form. Rufo got his answer in the form of stinging sunlight as Danica cracked and tore apart the boards blocking the window.

"Impudence!" Rufo roared. Danica growled in reply and tore another board free of its mounting. She saw Percival then, through the glass, hopping about in circles on the roof—dear Percival, who had saved her life.

The light falling on Rufo was indirect, for the window faced east, to the Shining Plains, and the sun was on its way toward the western horizon. Still, the vampire would not approach, would not dare chase Danica out into the daylight.

"I'll be back for you, Rufo," Danica, remembering Dorigen, promised grimly. "I'll be back with Cadderly." She took a board and smashed out the glass.

Rufo snarled and took a step toward her, but was driven back by the light. He ripped the door's locking bar from its supports and tore open the portal, and Danica thought he meant to flee.

Dean Thobicus stood in the hall. He brought his hand up defensively as soon as the door went wide and the weak daylight reached him.

"Catch her!" Rufo screamed at him.

Thobicus took a step forward, despite his mind's protests. He was a creature of the dark now and could not go into the light! He looked plaintively to Rufo, but there was no compromise in the master vampire's expression.

"Catch her!" Rufo growled again.

Thobicus felt himself moving forward against the pain, against his mind's protests. Rufo compelled him, as Cadderly had once compelled him. He had given himself to the dark and could not deny Rufo's will!

Thobicus knew he was a pitiful thing then. He had been dominated in life by Cadderly, and now in death by Rufo. They were one and the same, he decided. One and the same.

Only as he approached the window did Dean Thobicus realize the truth. Cadderly had been guided by morals; Cadderly would not make him jump out the window. Cadderly, Deneir, was the light.

But Thobicus had chosen the dark, and Rufo, his master, was guided by no moral code, was compelled by nothing except his own desires.

"Catch her!" the vampire's voice, the vampire's will, demanded.

Danica had not broken enough glass to go safely through, and so she spun about and smashed the board over the approaching vampire's head.

Thobicus growled at her, and there was no joy in his apparent victory, for he knew then that he was a victim, not the victor.

Danica shoved the splintered remnants of the board at Thobicus's chest, thinking to drive the makeshift stake through his heart. He got a hand up to deflect the blow, though, and the jagged wood sank deep into his stomach.

Thobicus looked at the monk, seeming almost surprised. For a long moment, they studied each other, and Danica thought the dean seemed somehow sad and remorseful.

Rufo's will shot through Thobicus's mind again, and his thoughts were not his own.

Danica and Thobicus moved together, both breaking for the window. They went through in a clinch, glass tearing at Danica's exposed arms.

Onto the roof they rolled, Thobicus clutching tightly and Danica not daring to break the momentum, knowing that if they stopped moving, she was caught and would be dragged back in to face Rufo. Over and over they went; Thobicus tried to bite Danica, and she wedged her arm in his face, holding him at bay. For both of them the world had become a spinning blur.

Percival's chattering became a scream of protest as Danica and Thobicus plunged from the roof.

Twelve

Nowhere to Run

The vampire's fangs sought her neck, and Danica was too engaged in keeping the wild thing at bay to concentrate on landing properly. She jammed her elbow under the vampire's chin, pushing with all her strength, and twisted to put Thobicus beneath her. They flew apart under the weight of impact, to an accompanying snap that sounded like the breaking of a thick tree branch.

The vampire wasn't even dazed by the fall, but as he sprang back to his feet and rushed at Danica, compelled still by Kierkan Rufo's demands, Thobicus staggered, then looked about, as if confused.

The light of day washed over him.

Danica whimpered as she tried to stand, and found that her ankle had shattered, the bone tearing out through the skin. Pained by every movement, the stubborn monk got up on her good knee and launched herself forward, her hands grabbing tight to the vampire's ankle.

All she had wanted was to get away, but now it was Thobicus who wanted to flee, to get back into the dark comfort of the library. Danica didn't want that to happen. She could see the agony in his expression, and she knew from legends she had heard as a child that the daylight would peel the skin from his bones. Even in her intense pain, in her horrifying dilemma, the monk kept her wits enough to understand that destroying Thobicus now would be a good thing, would make the necessary trip back to purge the library that much easier.

Danica held on like a bulldog. Thobicus battered her about the head, kicked and screamed. One of Danica's eyes swelled and closed. She heard the crackle of cartilage as her nose shattered, and the pain in her ankle did not relent, even intensified to the point where she had to fight hard just to keep her senses.

Then she lay in the cold mud, in her own blood, holding nothing. Distantly she heard the retreating vampire's diminishing screams.

Thobicus ran straight for the library's front doors. Every muscle trembled from the strain, from the burn of the daylight, and he was a weakened and pitiful thing. He hurled himself against the wooden barrier and was repelled. He staggered backward and tumbled into the dirt. He could see the hole in the door where Danica had kicked, could see the cool dark beyond, beckoning to him.

A patch of skin above the vampire's right eye melted and drooped, blurring his vision. He went back for the doors, but swayed in his path and missed, falling hard against the stone wall.

"How could you do this to me?" he cried, but his voice was no more than a whisper. "How?"

The beleaguered vampire stumbled as much as ran along the wall, to the library's edge and down the side of the building. There was a tunnel somewhere to the south, he knew, a dark, cool tunnel.

He hadn't the time to find it. Thobicus realized he was doomed, cursed by his own weaknesses and by that wretch, Rufo, who had lied to him.

The sunlight was direct around the back of the building, and the vampire stopped as he began around the corner, then fell back against the stone. Where to go? Thobicus fought hard to clear his thoughts, sublimate the pain long enough to remember the mausoleum.

Cool and dark.

To get there, though, he would have to cross the sunny side of the library grounds. The fallen dean could hardly face that prospect of pain, but he understood that to stay here meant death.

With a scream of denial, Thobicus threw himself around the corner and ran with all speed for the mausoleum. The sun's fires licked at every inch of his body, burned into his very heart and pained him more than he ever believed possible. But he got there. Somehow he fell through the mausoleum's heavy door and felt the cool shade of the stone floor under his burning cheek. He crawled on his belly to the back corner, opened the crypt of headmaster Avery, and somehow found the strength to pull the fat corpse out and crawl into Avery's place.

Trembling with agony, the vampire curled into a ball and closed his eyes. Thobicus needed to sleep, to gather strength, and to consider his folly and his fate. Kierkan Rufo had lied to him.

He had lost the way to Deneir.

* * * * *

The shadows were long and slanted when Danica regained consciousness. She realized immediately that she had lost a lot of blood, and she grimaced when she mustered the strength to look down at her injury, her foot bloated and greenish, with the sharp edge of bone sticking out, caked with dried blood, a torn tendon hanging.

How could she hope to move, and yet, how could she remain in this place with the shadows growing long? Using all the concentration her years of training had given her, all the willpower that had guided her life, the monk managed to get up onto her good leg. Waves of dizziness washed over her, and she feared her change in posture would send more blood flowing from her wound.

She took a hopping step to the east, toward the main walk leading from the library. Then she was face down in the dirt once more.

Breathing hard, forcing air into her lungs so she did not pass out again—by the gods, she could not pass out again!—Danica ripped the bottom off of her shirt and bent over to reach her broken ankle. She found a stick nearby and shoved it between her teeth, biting hard as she tightly wrapped the wound, forcing the bone somewhat back into place.

She was lathered in sweat by the time she turned back to the path, but she chanted her *einto*, her mantra, and set off, first crawling, then hopping, faster and faster, away from the darkness.

Whatever comfort she took in putting the library out of sight was countered by the red sunset lining the mountains at her back. She knew that Rufo would come after her; she was a prize that wretch had craved since the moment he had seen her.

This area was familiar to Danica, and though the going was much more difficult in the thick brush, she swerved from the main path, continuing straight to the east and knowing she could pick up the trail again later on, in the morning, perhaps, after hiding from Rufo in the deep woods through the night. She found a narrow trail through the brush, a ranger's trail or a druid's, she assumed, and the going was somewhat easier. Then, with twilight descending about her, her heart fluttered with hope as three forms made their way along the trail, heading back for the library. Danica recognized the Oghman garb and nearly shouted with joy to the priests.

Her face screwed up with curiosity as she realized that one of them was walking backward, that his head had been turned around on his shoulders. Danica's breath fell away, and her hopes as well, as the stiff gait of the three men, the three dead men, became apparent, and she thought then that she was doomed, for they had to have seen her.

Danica slumped against a tree trunk, knowing she could not fight them off. They were just ten feet away.

Five feet away.

She lashed out pitifully and clipped one on the shoulder, but the zombie only staggered a foot to the side and continued walking, right past Danica!

Danica did not understand, and did not question her luck. She looked back only once at the retreating monsters, then started moving again, wondering if all the world had fallen under this darkness.

She was still moving after sunset, after twilight, when the dark grew thick and the night birds began to call out. She found a hollow and slumped, thinking she had to rest, hoping she would still be alive when the sun's first rays stretched across the Shining Plains. The hard remains of a snowdrift offered some relief as Danica packed the cold ice about her ankle. She scratched a V in the pile and secured her foot in place, then lay back, continuing her *einto*, trying to survive the night.

Sometime later, she heard music, not ominous, but gay, and she soon recognized the song as a bawdy merchant romp. After a moment of confusion, Danica remembered the season, remembered that merchants often came up from Carradoon to resupply the library after the long winter.

So all the world had not fallen, she realized, not yet, and she took hope.

Danica lay back and closed her eyes. She needed sleep.

But she could not allow herself to sleep, she understood a moment later, when she considered the larger picture. She could not remain here and let the merchant caravan roll past. She could not let these unwitting men walk into Rufo's lair, and even worse, it seemed likely to her that Rufo, in his search for her, might find the caravan this very night!

Before she was conscious of her actions, Danica was up and moving again, stumbling through the brush. She saw the campfire almost immediately and made straight for it.

She tripped before she got there and had no strength to stand up again, but crawled on, washed by dizziness and nausea.

"Here now!" cried a man at the edge of the encampment as Danica fell through the last line of brush. She saw the flash of a sword as the man leaped for her, apparently thinking her some thief, or even some wild animal.

The next thing Danica knew, she was sitting beside a canvas-topped wagon, her injured leg elevated before her and an old woman carefully tending the wound. Several men, merchants and their guards, surrounded her, all looking on worriedly, more than one biting his lip.

The old woman shifted the ankle slightly, and Danica cried out, then the woman turned to her companions and nodded her head grimly.

"You have to . . ." Danica started, fighting for the breath to speak. "You have to run."

"Easy, lass," one of the men tried to comfort. "You're safe now."

"Run," Danica said again. "Run!"

The men looked to each other, each one of them giving a confused shrug.

"To Carradoon," Danica managed to say. "Flee this—"

"Easy lass," the same man interrupted.

"A priest!" came a hopeful call from the side of the camp. "An Oghman priest!"

Hopeful smiles widened on the faces of those tending Danica, but Danica's face blanched even more.

"Run!" she screamed, and she pulled her leg free of the old woman's grasp and worked her way back along the wagon, walking her shoulders up its side until she stood once more.

The same man spoke again to comfort her.

He was the first to die, hurled clear over the high wagon to smash against the trunk of a tall tree, his neck snapped.

In a moment, the camp was in a frenzy. Two Oghman priests, who had given themselves over to the dark, and a host of zombies, now had orders to kill.

The merchants fought valiantly, realizing the price of failure, and many zombies were hacked apart. But three vampires, including the master, cut into their ranks, tearing and breaking them.

Several merchants ran off screaming into the night.

Three took up defensive stances around Danica and the old woman, who would not leave the injured monk's side.

Kierkan Rufo faced these three. Half unconscious, Danica expected a fierce battle, but for some reason, amidst all the frenzy in the encampment, this group of men stood calmly.

She realized then that Rufo was talking to them, soothing them with a web of words, intruding on their minds with his will and making them see things that were not true.

"He is lying!" Danica screamed. "Block your ears and your minds! Deny him! Oh, by the light that is your god, whatever god, see the evil for what it is!"

She never understood where that sudden power came from, where she found the strength to yell to those three doomed men, but though they soon died at the terrible hands of Kierkan Rufo, they did not succumb to the dark. They heeded Danica's words and found the strength of faith to deny the vampire.

That fight was still raging, one man scoring a vicious hit—with a silver-inlaid sword—on Rufo, when the old woman to Danica's side shrieked suddenly and fell back against the wagon.

Danica looked that way to see one of the other vampires stalking in, his fanged smile wide and his gaze set squarely on Danica.

"You leave her be!" the old woman shouted, and she produced a club from somewhere—it seemed to be the handle of a butter churn—and swatted the vampire over the head. The monster looked at the hag with curiosity, and she raised the club a second time. His hand shot out and caught her by the throat. Danica looked away but could not block the sound of cracking bone.

Then the vampire faced her, his expression wild and lewd.

Danica punched him in the mouth.

He seemed surprised, but hardly hurt.

Danica punched him again, her strength returning with her anger. She looked to the old woman who had helped her, lying dead on the ground, and her hands lashed out, one-two, scoring alternate hits on the vampire's throat. His windpipe collapsed under those hits, and no air would pass through.

But vampires did not draw breath.

Danica hit him a dozen more times before he finally caught hold of her and held her steady. He had her, and Rufo was still fighting, and there was nothing she could do.

A flash of white came in front of her face, and the vampire fell back suddenly, unexpectedly. It took Danica a moment to realize he was grappling with a clawing, biting squirrel.

Danica pushed off the wagon and hopped out, thinking only to go to Percival's aid.

The vampire extracted the rodent and tossed Percival aside, just as Danica leaped and crashed in, bowling him over. They rolled completely around, Danica bracing her good foot against the vampire's belly and kicking off with all her strength as they came around.

She heard a cracking sound, a tree branch snapping as the flying vampire crashed upside down.

When the world finally stopped spinning for poor Danica, she could appreciate the blind luck that had, for the moment, saved her, for the vampire was impaled on that broken branch, through the chest, kicking and thrashing wildly but to no avail.

She took heart, too, in seeing Percival scampering up that same tree, apparently unhurt.

Suddenly Danica was pulled to her feet, caught in the clutches of an angry Kierkan Rufo. She looked to his bare forearm and realized his wounds had healed, except for the reddened patch of skin that had crossed into the sunbeam before the broken door.

"You run no more," Rufo promised, and Danica shuddered. She was out of strength and out of breath. The fight was over.

The remaining vampire walked up beside Rufo. He looked to the tree branch, to his limply hanging friend, and an expression of evil crossed his features.

He glowered at Danica and moved steadily toward her. It struck Danica as odd at how easily Kierkan Rufo stopped the outraged vampire. Rufo merely held up his hand, and the vampire fell back a step, snarling, whining, helpless.

"This one is for me," Rufo reminded him.

The vampire looked to his companion again. "If I pull him from the branch, he will return to us," he reasoned suddenly, and by the legends, that statement was true.

"Leave him!" Rufo commanded as the vampire bounded for the impaled creature. The vampire looked back to his master.

"He went against my will," Rufo explained. "He would have killed Danica, or taken her for his own. Leave him to the fate he deserves."

Danica did note the skeptical, then wicked cloud that crossed the lesser vampire's pallid features. In that moment, the fallen Oghman hated Rufo with all his heart and soul, wanted nothing more than to rip out Rufo's throat. But that hatred fast melted into resignation, and the lesser vampire moved away.

"Our losses were great," he remarked, and it seemed curious to Danica that he should be the one to change the subject.

Rufo scoffed at the notion. "They were but zombies," he replied. "I will return tomorrow night and animate them once again, and animate those who defended this one as well." He gave Danica a shake, which sent pain flowing up from her ankle.

"What of Diatyne?" the vampire demanded, looking to the tree.

Rufo paused for a long moment. "He failed," Rufo decided. "His flesh is for the sun."

To the Oghman vampire, it seemed such a waste. But that was their way, he decided, that was the course he had chosen. So be it.

Rufo looked to Danica, his face now serene. "You need sleep," he whispered. Danica felt the words more than heard them, felt that falling into slumber would be a good thing indeed.

She shook her head vigorously, realizing she must fight Rufo to the last, on every point.

Rufo stared at her, wondering where that inner strength had come from.

Danica spat in his face.

Rufo hit her hard before he realized the movement, and Danica, battered and weak from loss of blood, fell limply to the ground. The angry vampire grabbed her by the hair and began dragging her, telling the lesser creature to gather the remaining zombies and follow him back to the library.

Rufo hadn't even cleared the encampment, though, when what was left of his heart tugged at him, reminded him of his feelings for Danica. He bent and picked her up gently in his arms, cradling her close to him, though his body had no warmth to offer. He saw the flash of her white neck in the moonlight and was tempted to feed, tempted to drink of this one's blood, and it was the strongest act Kierkan Rufo had ever taken to deny himself that pleasure, for he knew that Danica could not afford the act, would surely die and be lost to him forever if he took from her now.

High in the trees above the carnage, Percival watched the unholy procession wander away. The squirrel understood their course, so he flew off, along the branches, into the night, looking for someone who was not in league with Kierkan Rufo.

Thirteen

To Love

The vampire looked her over, and, for the first time in the years he had known Danica, she seemed so frail. A delicate flower, she was, and a strong wind could have blown her away.

Kierkan Rufo wanted to go to her, to gently stroke her pretty neck, to kiss her, softly at first, until the urgency built and he could rightly sink his fangs, the material extensions of what he had become, into that throat, and drink of Danica's blood, feel the warmth of this woman he had desired since the first moment he had seen her.

But Kierkan Rufo could not, despite the chaos curse's urging. To feed on . . . no, to join with Danica now, would kill her prematurely. Rufo did not want Danica to die, not yet, not until he could give to her enough of himself, of what he had become, that she might join him in this state of vampirism. No matter the demands of the hunger and the chaos curse, the vampire simply would not accept and would not tolerate Danica's death.

She would be his queen, Rufo decided. This existence he had chosen would be so much more fulfilling with Danica at his side.

That image of his queen was sweeter still for Rufo when he thought of how it would wound Cadderly.

As much as Kierkan Rufo desired Danica, he wanted more to hurt Cadderly. He would flaunt Danica, his Danica, before the young priest, torturing him with the knowledge that, in the end, it was Cadderly's life that was a lie.

Drool slid from the vampire's half-opened mouth as Rufo basked in the fantasy. His bottom lip trembled as he took a sliding step forward. He almost forgot his own reasoning and fell upon unconscious Danica then and there.

He caught himself and straightened, seeming almost embarrassed as he turned to Histra, poor scarred wretch that she was, standing beside him in the room.

"You will watch her," Rufo commanded.

"I am hungry," Histra remarked, and she eyed Danica as she spoke.

"No!" Rufo snarled, and the sheer force of his command knocked the lesser vampire back a step. "You will not feed on this one! And if any others come in and harbor similar thoughts, warn them well that I shall destroy them!"

A hiss of disbelief escaped Histra's bright red lips, and she looked frantically, like a starving animal, from Rufo to Danica.

"You will tend her wounds," Rufo went on. "And if she dies, your torment will be eternal!" With that, the confident master swept from the room, heading for the wine cellar to spend the daylight hours gathering his strength.

He noted the dim outline of an invisible imp perched in a corner and nodded slightly. If anything got out of line here, Druzil would warn him telepathically.

* * * * *

Danica's trip back to consciousness was a slow and painful journey. As her mind awakened, so, too, did thoughts of the carnage at the campsite, thoughts of poor Dorigen, and the realization that the Edificant Library had fallen. Tormenting dreams carried Danica to the end of her journey, and she opened her eyes with a start.

The room was dim, but not dark, and after a moment, Danica remembered she had been taken in the deep of night, and realized that the next dawn must have come. She steadied her breathing and tried to separate reality from nightmare.

She understood then that reality had become a nightmare.

Danica's hands shot up suddenly—the movement sent jolts of pain along her leg—and grasped at her neck, feeling for puncture wounds. She relaxed slightly when she was convinced that the skin remained smooth.

But where was she? She struggled to get up on her elbows, but fell back at once as Histra, carrying the stench of burned skin, leaped to her side and glared down at her.

The remaining skin on the back of Histra's head had ripped apart under the strain of support, so that her face sagged, as if she were wearing a loose and pliable mask. And those horrid eyes! They seemed as if they would fall from their destroyed sockets, land upon Danica's torso, and roll about the contours of her body.

Danica tried not to show her relief as the gruesome creature backed away. She saw then that she was in one of the bedrooms of the library, probably the private quarters of Dean Thobicus himself, for the place was handsomely furnished in dark wood. A great roll-top desk sat against the opposite wall, under a fabulous tapestry, and a leather divan was to the side of that. Even the bed showed of, and felt of, luxury. It was a huge four-posted structure with an open canopy top, and was overstuffed so as to be pillowy soft.

"So you live," Histra said, her voice full of venom. Danica could understand the source of that rage; she and Histra had been rivals in life, when Histra had tried to use her charms, to no avail, on Cadderly. Danica, with her exotic, almond-shaped eyes the color of cinnamon and unkempt strawberry blond mane, was, by all measures, a beautiful woman. Histra, despite the tenets of her religion, did not like beautiful women, not when they were rivals—and they were always rivals.

Now Histra was an ugly thing, a caricature of her former beauty, and though she obviously held every advantage in this encounter with weak and battered Danica, that fact had her on the defensive and on the verge of exploding.

Danica used her perceptions to overcome the revulsion and the fear. She could sense danger in Histra—if Histra wanted to kill her, Danica could do little to prevent it. But Histra would not kill her, Danica believed. Rufo commanded here—Danica knew that much from their encounter in the foyer—and if Rufo wanted Danica to die, he would have killed her himself, out in the forest.

"How sweet you are," Histra remarked, talking more to herself than Danica. The abruptly change in the timbre of her voice confirmed Danica's suspicions that the vampiress was walking a very fine line. Histra put a hand on Danica's face and ran it gently over her cheek and down the side of her throat.

Histra's ugly visage shot forward suddenly, mouth opened wide, drool and hot breath spitting onto Danica's face.

Danica nearly swooned, thought in that instant that her life had come to an abrupt end. She caught her control quickly, though, and looked up to find that Histra had backed off.

"I could destroy you," the vampiress said matter-of-factly. "I could rip out your heart and eat it. I could stick my fingers through your pretty almond eyes and claw at your brain."

Danica didn't know how she should react to the threats. Should she feign horror at Histra's promises, or remain aloof to it all, calling the vampiress's bluff?

She decided to call the bluff, and took it one step further. "Kierkan Rufo would not approve," she replied calmly.

Histra's open-mouthed face shot forward again, but this time, Danica did not flinch.

"He wants me," Danica said when Histra had backed off.

"I am his queen," the vampiress protested. "The master does not need you!"

"The master?" Danica whispered under her breath. It was difficult for her to associate those words with Kierkan Rufo. In life the man hadn't even mastered his own emotions. "He loves you?" she asked innocently.

"He loves me!" Histra declared. Danica began to chuckle and acted as if she were trying hard to bite it back.

"What?" Histra demanded, and she trembled visibly.

Danica realized she was taking a chance here, but she saw no other way. "Have you looked into a mirror?" Danica asked, but caught herself as she finished the question, as though something had just occurred to her. "Of course," she added softly, condescendingly. "You can no longer look into mirrors, can you?"

Danica started to say, "Rufo loves me," but decided that would push the vampiress just a bit too far. "Rufo loves no one," she corrected Histra. "He has never learned how."

"You lie."

"Neither have you," Danica continued. "In your haste to appease the goddess Sune, you never separated lust from love."

The mention of Sune brought obvious pain to Histra's twisted features. Her hand, bones showing between blackened patches of skin, went high, as if to slam down on Danica, but the room's door swung open an instant before she punched.

"Enough," said the calm voice of Kierkan Rufo.

Histra looked back over her shoulder and gradually lowered her arm.

Rufo jerked his head to the side and waved his hand across in front of him, and Histra obediently moved to the side wall and lowered her head—and the loose skin of her face hung down to almost brush her large bosom.

"Even so obviously beaten, you find the spirit to play your games," Rufo said to Danica, his tone congratulatory. He moved beside the bed and put a calm smile on his face. "Save your strength," he whispered. "Heal your wounds, and then . . ."

Danica laughed at him, stealing the fantasies, stealing the smug smile and the calm demeanor.

"And then what?" she asked sharply. "You and I shall love for eternity?" She took note that her snicker hurt the vampire profoundly. "I was just explaining to Histra that you do not know how to love."

"You and Cadderly have gathered all of that emotion for yourselves," Rufo replied sarcastically, "as though it is some finite commodity . . ."

"No," Danica retorted, "but Cadderly and I have learned to share in that emotion. We have learned what the word means."

"I have loved you . . ." Rufo started to say, but he caught himself.

"Impossible," Danica snapped back, again before Rufo could present his argument. "Impossible. You loved Histra, too. I know you did, when you first brought her to your side." Danica looked at Histra as she continued, hoping to find some clues in the vampiress's expression to aid her improvisation.

"I did not," Rufo started to argue, meaning to explain that it was not even him who brought Histra over. Danica cut him short, though, and the hanging words carried a very different meaning to Histra's ears, seemed a denial that Rufo had ever loved her.

"You did!" Danica cried with all her strength, and she had to pause for a moment just to catch her breath and beat back the ensuing waves of pain. "You loved her," she went on, sagging deep into her pillow, "when she was pretty."

That got to Histra; Danica recognized that clearly enough. The vampiress lifted her head, her already grotesque features seeming more so as they twisted with mounting rage.

"But now she is an ugly thing," Danica said, taking care that her words conveyed her disappointment with Rufo and nothing against Histra. "And no longer appealing."

Danica saw Histra take a short step forward.

"*Bene tellemara.*" Druzil, invisible and perched upon the room's desk, growled and shook his dog-faced head.

Rufo shook his head as well, wondering how this conversation had gotten so out of hand. It was difficult for him to bring things back under control while at the same time move beyond the pain that Danica's words brought him.

"If I had been scarred so," Danica pressed, "if I became ugly, as Histra has become, Cadderly would love me still. He would not seek a new queen."

Rufo's lips moved around the edges of words that did not seem sufficient. He steadied himself abruptly, straightened, and found a measure of dignity.

Then Histra barreled into him, and both flew sidelong, spinning and crashing into the wall. They bit and clawed each other, punched, kicked, anything at all to inflict pain.

Danica knew her moment of opportunity would be brief. She threw herself into a sitting position and gingerly, but as fast as she could, shifted her injured leg to the side of the bed. She stopped suddenly and went perfectly still, trying to concentrate on something minute that had caught her attention, trying to block out the continuing sounds of Rufo and Histra's struggling.

Danica's hand shot out to the side like a biting snake, fingers clenching about something she could not see, but could surely sense, an instant before the barbed tail could snap at her.

Druzil began thrashing immediately, caught fast in the woman's strong grasp. He came back to visibility, for expending the magical energy now seemed foolish; Danica obviously knew where he was.

"You are still not quick enough," Danica said coldly.

Druzil started to respond, but Danica's other hand came across furiously, pounding right between his bulbous black eyes, and suddenly, for the imp, all the room was spinning.

Druzil hit the wall hard and slumped, muttering, "*bene tellemara*" over and over. He understood what Rufo would have done to him, or would have tried to do, if his attack on Danica had been successful; in an odd way, Danica had probably saved him from banishment back to his own plane of existence. But Druzil's dedication was to the chaos curse, of which Kierkan Rufo was now the embodiment, and though Rufo would never see it, keeping this woman alive was a dangerous, dangerous thing.

Danica was off the bed by then, hopping for the door on her one good leg.

"You cannot hurt me!" Druzil rasped at her, and he came in a flurry, wings beating and tail snapping.

Danica kept her balance perfectly on her one good leg, and her hands worked to her call, spinning blocking circles in the air before her.

Druzil's tail snapped repeatedly, was parried several times, and then was caught again.

The imp growled and waggled his fingers in the air.

Greenish bolts of energy erupted from their tips and shot out, stinging Danica. "You cannot hurt me," Druzil taunted.

The imp could not keep up with the speed of Danica's next move. She jerked hard on the tail, spinning him about, then caught his wings, one in each hand, while still holding fast to the tail. Jerking and twisting, Danica tied the three ends, wing, wing, and tail, into a tight knot behind Druzil's back, and hurled the startled imp face first into the nearest wall.

"Probably knot," she agreed.

Druzil rolled about on the floor, muttering curses, not appreciating the pun, as Danica turned back for the door.

Kierkan Rufo stood before her, seeming amused at her handling of the imp. In the far corner, Histra knelt on her hands and knees, skin hanging loose to the floor, eyes downward, thoroughly beaten.

"Wonderful," Rufo congratulated, and he turned his gaze on Danica.

And Danica punched him again in the face.

Rufo turned back to her deliberately, expecting and accepting the next punch, and the third, and fourth, and the continuing barrage. Finally the vampire had enough, and with an unearthly roar that sent shivers along Danica's spine, he swept his hand across in front of him, knocking Danica off balance momentarily, and caught her by an arm.

Danica knew how to easily defeat such a tenuous hold, except that no grip she had ever witnessed was as strong as the vampire's! She was caught and feared that her elbow would shatter under the strain.

She got her free hand up to block as Rufo's wide-arcing slap raced in, but his strength blew through the defense and snapped Danica's head viciously to the side. Dazed, Danica offered no resistance as Rufo hurled her back onto the bed, and then he was atop her, his strong fingers about her throat. Danica grabbed Rufo's forearm and twisted, but again to no avail.

Then Danica simply stopped struggling, sublimated her strong survival instinct and did nothing to remove Rufo's hand from her neck, did nothing to restore the flow of air into her lungs. At that moment, Danica hoped the vampire would kill her, thought death preferable to any other option.

Then there was only blackness.

* * * * *

The trail was a winding way, sometimes looping back on itself through passable areas between towering pillars of stone. At times the view was panoramic and majestic; at others, the three companions felt almost as if they were walking along tight underground corridors.

As fate would have it, Cadderly did not see the plume of black smoke rising from the southern wing of the Edificant Library, his view blocked by the last tall mountain before the place. If he had seen the smoke, the young priest would have sought the song of his god, his magic, and walked with the wind the rest of the way to the library. For, while Cadderly was pressing anyway, anxious to aid in the battle he thought Dorigen faced, he did not listen for Deneir's song, did not want to strain his energies, which had been so sorely taxed in his battle with Aballister and Castle Trinity.

Pikel and Ivan hopped along the trail behind Cadderly, oblivious to any problems at all—except that Ivan was weary of this whole journey and badly wanted to be home again in his familiar kitchen. Pikel still delighted in wearing Cadderly's wide-brimmed blue hat, thinking it brought out the rich green in his dyed and braided hair and beard.

Ivan just thought he looked stupid.

They moved in silence for a time, and at one point, Cadderly paused, thinking he heard a song. He cocked an ear to the wind; it sounded like Brother Chaunticleer's midday offering. Cadderly looked around, gauging the distance still to go, and realized there was no way, even if the winds were perfect, that he could possibly hear Chaunticleer's song; the library was at least five miles away.

As he moved to keep up with the bouncing dwarves, Cadderly realized that the music he heard was not in his ears, but in his mind.

Chaunticleer was singing—it was definitely Chaunticleer's voice—and Cadderly was hearing it the way he heard the song of Deneir.

What could that mean?

It didn't occur to Cadderly that Chaunticleer's sweet song might be a ward against some terrible evil. He reasoned that his own mind was tuned purely to Deneir, and that Chaunticleer's offering, too, was in perfect harmony with the god.

To Cadderly, the song was a good thing. It didn't remain constant in his thoughts, but came often enough for the young priest to know that Brother Chaunticleer was going on and on, far longer than usual. Still, the young priest put no ominous connotations on that, simply figured that the man must be feeling extremely pious this day—or perhaps Chaunticleer wasn't really singing and Cadderly was just hearing the reverberations of that perfect offering.

"Are ye thinking of setting another camp?" the increasingly surly, yellow-bearded Ivan asked some time later, drawing Cadderly from the music and its unfathomable implications.

Cadderly looked at the rocky trail ahead and tried to remember exactly where he was. "Five miles left to walk, at least," he replied, "through difficult terrain."

Ivan snorted. The Snowflakes, by his estimation, were not so difficult, not even with winter still holding fast with its last fingers. Ivan was from a place far to the north, wild Vaasa and the rugged Galena Mountains, where goblinoids were thicker than pebbles and the winter wind off the Great Glacier could freeze a man solid in minutes.

The dwarf took one last disgusted glance at Pikel, who chuckled in response, then stomped past Cadderly and took up the lead. "Tonight," Ivan explained. "We'll be walking through the front doors before the stars come clear!"

Cadderly sighed and watched Ivan take a fast-paced lead. Pikel was still chuckling when he came hopping past.

"Give me that," Cadderly snapped, seeing the source of Ivan's ire. He plucked the hat from Pikel's head, brushed it off, and tapped it atop his own crown. Then he pulled from his pack the cooking pot, the impromptu helmet the green-bearded dwarf had fashioned for himself, and plopped it over Pikel's head.

Pikel's chuckle turned into a sorrowful. "Oooo."

* * * * *

Some miles from the three, to the west and north, a scrambling noise in the boughs above brought Shayleigh from her reverie. Angled in the hollow of a thick branch near the trunk of a wide elm, the elf, to an unknowing observer, would have appeared in an awkward and dangerous predicament. But a slight twist brought agile Shayleigh completely about, her back flat on the branch and her longbow somehow clear of the tangle, out and ready above her.

The elf's violet eyes narrowed as she considered the busy canopy, searching for the source of the noise. She wasn't too worried—the sun was still high above the western horizon—but she knew the sounds of the natural movements of all the area's animals, and recognized that whatever had come so noisily into the boughs of this tree had done so in wild flight.

A leaf danced suddenly, not so far above her. Back bent her bow.

Then the foliage parted, and Shayleigh eased the string back to rest, and smiled to see a familiar white squirrel staring down at her.

Percival came down in a frenzied rush, and Shayleigh's smile faded into an expression of confusion. Why would Percival, whom she'd met long ago, be so far from the library? she wondered. And what had so obviously upset the creature?

Unlike Cadderly and the dwarves, Shayleigh had seen the pillar of smoke, and, at that time, had thought to turn back and investigate. She figured it was only a ceremonial fire, though, perhaps a communal burial cairn for those priests who had died over the winter months and were now being put to their rest. So she had determined that it was not her business, that her business was, after all, to return to Shilmista with full speed, where King Elbereth, no doubt, greatly anticipated her information.

She had taken her reverie early, with the sun still high, thinking to travel through the night.

Now, seeing Percival here, hopping about and chattering frantically, Shayleigh regretted that choice to continue. She should have gone straight to the library, straight to Danica, her friend, who might have needed her help . . . and still might.

Shayleigh swung under the branch, her feet touching lightly on the next lowest. She bent her legs and fell backward, hooking the branch with her knees, and swung down so that she caught the lowest branch in one hand. She kept with the flow of her momentum to spin lightly down to the ground. Percival, following, was hard-pressed to keep up.

Shayleigh held her arm out and made a ticking noise, and Percival leaped from the lowest branch to her, accepting the ride as the elf maiden ran full speed back to the east, back to her friend.

Fourteen
Twilight

I feared I had killed you."

It was Rufo's voice, from far away, but rushing closer.

Danica opened her eyes. She was on the bed, in the same room as before, but her wrists and ankles now were securely bound to the bed's four strong posts. A throbbing, burning pain in her wounded left leg did not relent, and the monk feared the binding would cut through her skin and sever the already tattered ankle.

Worse still, there was Rufo, leaning over her, his white face softened with concern.

"My dear Danica," he whispered. He came closer, trying to soften his angular features, trying to be gentle.

Danica did not spit in his face; she was beyond any more symbolic, if ineffective, protests.

Rufo, though, recognized her disgust. "Do you not believe I can love?" he asked quietly, and a twitch on one cheek told Danica he was fighting hard to hold his calm.

Again Danica offered no response.

"I have loved you since you first came to the library," Rufo went on dramatically. "I have watched you from afar, delighting in the simple grace of your every movement."

Danica steeled her cold gaze and did not blink.

"But I am not a pretty man," Rufo went on. "Never have I been, and so it was Cadderly—" a bit of venom bubbled over at the mention of that name, "—and not I who caught your fairest eye."

The self-deprecation was pitiful, but Danica held little sympathy for Rufo. "A pretty man?" she questioned. "You still cannot comprehend how small a thing that is."

Rufo backed off, perplexed.

962

Danica just shook her head. "You would love Histra still if she was a pretty thing," she said. "But you have never been able to see beyond the skin. You have never cared for what was in someone's heart and soul because your own are empty."

"Take care with your words," Rufo said.

"They hurt because they are true."

"No!"

"Yes!" Danica lifted her head as high as the bindings would allow, her glower forcing Rufo to retreat further. "It is not Cadderly's smile I love, but the source of that smile, the warmth of his heart and the truth of his soul.

Wretched Rufo, I pity you," she decided then. "I pity that you never fathomed the difference between love and ego."

"You are wrong!" the vampire retorted.

Danica didn't blink, but she did slip back to the mattress as Rufo closed over her. She scrunched her head down on her shoulders and even whimpered a bit as he continued his advance, thinking he meant to take her against her will. For all her training and all her strength, Danica was unable to accept that possibility.

The monk, though, had touched a weakness in the vampire's heart. "You are wrong," Rufo said again, quietly. "I do love." As if to accentuate his point, Rufo brushed his hand softly down Danica's cheek, under her chin, and along her neck. Danica recoiled as much as possible, but the bindings were strong and she was weak from loss of blood.

"I do love," he said again. "Rest, my sweet. I will return when you are stronger, and I will show you pleasure, love."

Danica breathed a sincere sigh of relief as Rufo backed away, gave a final look, and swept from the room. That sigh was temporary, she knew. She tested her bindings again and, finding no luck, lifted her head to consider her wounds.

She couldn't even feel the cord holding her injured leg, only the general pain. She saw that the ankle and calf were bloated, and the exposed skin, where it was not caked with dried blood, was badly discolored. Danica felt the infection within her, adding to the weakness from the loss of blood, and she knew she could not get free of her bindings this time. Even if she could, her broken body would not give her the strength to get out of the library

Danica rested, fell back into a sense of hopelessness greater than anything she had ever known. She saw between the boards over the room's one small, west-facing window that the sun had already crested on this new day, to begin its journey to the horizon. Danica knew Rufo would return with the night.

And she would have no defense.

* * * * *

The Edificant Library came into sight late in the afternoon, a square, squat structure peeping through the more rounded and natural lines of the surrounding terrain.

That first, distant glimpse told Cadderly something was very wrong with the place. His instincts, or maybe the subtle warnings from Chaunticleer's song, screamed at him, but he didn't understand the connotations. He thought now that it was his own feelings for the library that had given him such a start.

The building was soon out of sight, blocked by high rocks as the group rounded another bend. Ivan and Pikel, after whispering together, rushed past Cadderly and set a tremendous pace, explaining that they planned to prepare a delicious supper this very night.

The sun had not yet dipped below the skyline when they came back in sight of the library, the companions cutting in at the side of the grove that lined the structure's long front walkway. All three skidded to an abrupt stop, Pikel's ensuing "Oooo" pretty much summing things up for them all.

Wisps of gray smoke still filtered from several windows on the southern wing; the smell of burned wood hung thick in the air.

"Oooo," Pikel said again.

Those inner pleas, Chaunticleer's continuing call to Deneir, erupted in Cadderly's mind, shouting for him to flee, but he ran to the doors of the place that had been his home. He should have paused there, should have taken note of the hole in the wood, the hole Danica had kicked when Rufo had cornered her.

Cadderly grabbed at the handles and tugged hard, to no avail. He turned back to Ivan and Pikel; his faced screwed up curiously. "They're locked," he said, and it was the first time Cadderly had ever known the doors to the Edificant Library to be locked.

Ivan's tremendous axe came sweeping off his shoulder; Pikel lowered his club into battering ram position and began scraping the ground with one foot, like a bull about to charge.

Both relaxed and straightened unexpectedly when they saw the doors open behind Cadderly.

"Ye're sure about that?" Ivan asked the young priest.

Cadderly turned and eyed the opening skeptically. "Swollen from the heat of the fire," he decided, and with Ivan and Pikel beside him, the young priest entered the library.

All the silent cries that he should flee flew from Cadderly the moment he crossed the threshold. He took this as a good sign, a confirmation that he had overreacted, but, in truth, Cadderly had crossed into Rufo's place, where Deneir could no longer warn him.

The foyer was not badly damaged, though the scent of soot was nearly overwhelming. To the left sat the small chapel, obviously where the fire had been most intense. The place's heavy door was apparently closed, though the friends could not see it, for a thick tapestry had been draped over it.

Cadderly eyed that tapestry for a long while. It showed elves, dark elves. Cadderly knew how valuable that tapestry was, among the finest artwork in all the library. It had belonged to Pertelope; Ivan had used its depictions to fashion the small hand-crossbow that Cadderly now wore on his belt.

What was it doing here? the young priest wondered. Who would think to use such a precious piece of irreplaceable art as a blockade against soot?

"Seems like the fire was contained," Ivan offered. Of course it had been contained, both dwarves and Cadderly realized when they took a moment to think about it. The library was more stone than wood, and there really was very little to burn in the place.

What, then, had caused so intense a fire?

Ivan started right, Pikel bobbing after, for the kitchen, but Cadderly caught him by the arm and swung him and his ducking brother about.

"I want to check the main chapel," the young priest stated, his voice detached. Ivan and Pikel looked to each other, shrugged, then turned curious gazes at Cadderly, who stood still for a long while, his eyes closed.

He couldn't hear the song of Deneir, he realized. And he could no longer hear Chauncticleer's singing, though the priest was likely closer now than when they were in the mountains. It seemed as if Deneir had flown from this place.

"What are ye thinking?" the always impatient Ivan asked.

Cadderly opened his gray eyes and looked at the dwarf.

"Well?" Ivan prompted. "What are ye thinking?"

"This place has been desecrated," Cadderly replied, and it wasn't until he had spoken the words that he understood what he was saying.

"Been burned," Ivan corrected, looking to the tapestry, not understanding what Cadderly was talking about.

"Desecrated!" Cadderly yelled, the word echoing off the stone walls and filtering up the stairway. The significance of the word, and the weight with which Cadderly had shouted it sent shivers coursing through both brothers.

"What are ye talking about?" Ivan asked quietly.

Cadderly just shook his head vigorously and spun off, making all speed for the main chapel, the holiest place in this holy place. He expected he would find priests there, brothers of both host orders, praying to their respective gods, fighting to bring Deneir and Oghma back to this library.

The chapel was empty.

Thick soot covered the intricate designs on the massive, arching pillars closest to the doors, but little else seemed out of place. The altar across the way seemed intact, all the items, the bells, the single chalice, and the twin scepters atop it exactly where they belonged.

Their footsteps resounding, the three huddled close together and made their way toward the front.

Ivan saw the body first, and pulled up to a quick stop, holding out a strong arm that bent Cadderly over at the waist and forced him to hold as well.

Pikel continued forward a step, came around when he realized that the others were not following, and used their stunned expressions to guide his own eyes.

"Oooo," the greenbearded dwarf muttered.

"Banner," Cadderly explained, recognizing the burned corpse, though its skin hung in flaps away from the bone, and its face was half skull and half blackened skin.

The eyes rotated in their sockets, settling on Cadderly, and a grotesque smile erupted, the remaining flaps of the body's lips going wide.

"Cadderly!" Banner cried excitedly, and he catapulted to a standing position, bones rattling, arms bouncing wildly, and head bobbing about. "Oh, Cadderly, how good of you to return!"

Ivan and Pikel gasped in unison and fell back. They had fought undead monsters before, alongside Cadderly in the catacombs of this very building. Now they looked to the young priest for support, for this was his place, his chapel. Cadderly, stunned, overwhelmed, fell back, too, and grabbed his hat and, more particularly, the holy symbol set in its front.

"I knew—I simply knew!—that you'd come back," the grotesque Banner rambled on. He clapped his hands, and one of his fingers, held by a mere thread of ligament, fell from the others and dangled in midair several inches from his hand.

"I keep doing that!" the exasperated thing wailed, and he began reeling in his dropped digit as though it were some empty fishhook.

Cadderly wanted to talk to Banner, to ask some questions, to get some answers. But where to begin? This was too crazy, too out of place. This was the Edificant Library, the sanctuary of Deneir and Oghma! This was a place of prayer and reverence, and yet, standing here before Cadderly was a creature that mocked that reverence, that made all the prayers sound like pretty words strung together for no particular purpose. For Banner had been a priest, a well-respected and high-ranking priest of Cadderly's own god! Where was Deneir now? Cadderly had to wonder. How had Deneir allowed this grim fate to befall one so loyal?

"Not to worry," Banner assured the three, as if they were concerned about his finger. "Not to worry. I've become quite good at putting the pieces back together since the fire, actually."

"Tell me about the fire," Cadderly interjected, seizing that one important event and holding on to it like a litany against insanity.

Banner looked at him weirdly, the bulging eyeballs rolling this way and that. "It was hot," he replied.

"What started it?" Cadderly pressed.

"How would sleeping Banner know that?" the undead thing answered brusquely. "I have heard that the wizard . . ."

Banner paused and smiled widely, and began waggling his finger in the air before him, as though Cadderly had asked a question that was out of bounds. That waggling finger, like the one before it, dropped free, this one falling all the way to the floor.

"Oh, where did it go?" Banner cried in desperation, and he whipped himself to a crouched position and began hopping about the pews.

"Are ye wanting to talk to this one?" Ivan asked, and the dwarf's tone made it obvious which answer he preferred.

Cadderly thought for a moment. Banner had stopped short of an answer—and the hint he had offered did not settle well with Cadderly! But why had the wretched thing stopped? the young priest wondered. What had compelled Banner to hold back? Cadderly did not know exactly what Banner was. He was more than an unthinking zombie, Cadderly knew, though the young priest wasn't well versed in the various versions of undeath. Zombies, and others of the lowest form of animated undeath, didn't converse, were simply unthinking instruments of their masters, so Banner apparently ranked somewhere above them. Cadderly had once battled a mummy, but Banner didn't seem to fit that mold either. He seemed benign, almost, too foolish to be a threat.

Yet, something, some impulse, had held Banner from answering.

Cadderly eyed the scrambling creature directly, presented his holy symbol, and in commanding tones said, "Banner! Spirit of Banner. I ask you again and, by the power of Deneir, demand an answer. Who started the fire?"

The undead thing stopped his frantic movements, froze perfectly still and stared at Cadderly, or, more particularly, at Cadderly's holy symbol.

Banner seemed to wince several times. "By the power of who?" he asked innocently, and then it was Cadderly who winced. What had happened to this place to push his god so very far away?

Cadderly lowered his arm, lowered the symbol of Deneir, knowing then that he would gain no useful information.

"Are ye wanting to keep talking to this thing?" Ivan asked.

"No," Cadderly said simply, and before the word had fully fallen from his lips, Ivan's axe went into a tremendous overhead arc, slicing down and taking Banner's left arm from his shoulder.

The undead thing looked curiously at that lost arm, as if wondering how he was supposed to reattach it. "Oh, I'll have to fix that," his almost lipless mouth said matter-of-factly.

Even more devastating was Pikel's attack, the tree-trunk club slamming hard atop Banner's exposed skull, dropping the undead thing into a crumpled, broken pile of flesh and bones.

Both eyes popped from their sockets and rolled about on long, thin strands. "Now that hurt," Banner said, and all three companions jumped at the unexpected response. They realized then, to their horror, that the eyeballs were not rolling randomly, but seemed to be inspecting the damage!

"So much to do!" Banner whined.

The three slowly backed away, Pikel last, whimpering a bit and shaking his head in denial. Five feet from the broken monster, they found the courage to turn away, and started off, legs pumping to gain them full speed.

"Oh, Rufo will make me fix it alone!" Banner cried.

Cadderly skidded to a stop; Ivan crashed into him, and Pikel crashed into Ivan.

"Rufo?" Cadderly asked, turning back.

"Rufo?" Ivan echoed.

"Oo oi!" Pikel agreed.

"You remember Rufo, of course," said a calm and familiar voice from behind them.

Slowly and in unison the three turned back toward the exit of the chapel to see Kierkan Rufo standing at his usual angle, not quite perpendicular to the floor.

Cadderly noticed immediately that the brand he had given Rufo had been marred, clawed away

"You do not belong in this place!" the young priest roared, finding his courage, reminding himself that this was his home, Deneir's home.

Rufo's laughter mocked him.

Cadderly moved inevitably closer, drawing the dwarves in his wake. "What are you ?" he demanded, understanding that something was terribly amiss, that something stronger than Kierkan Rufo now faced him.

Rufo smiled widely, opened his mouth in a feral hiss, proudly showing his fangs.

Cadderly nearly swooned, then caught himself. He yanked his holy symbol free of the wide-brimmed hat, and plopped the hat awkwardly on his head in the same movement. "By the name of Deneir, I banish—" he began.

"Not here!" Rufo roared back, his eyes flashing like red dots of fire. "Not here."

"Uh-oh," muttered Pikel.

"He's not a vampire, is he?" Ivan asked, and, like everything Ivan seemed to ask in here, it was obvious what answer he wanted—needed—to hear.

"If you could only understand the meaning of that word," Rufo answered. "Vampire? I am *Tuanta Quiro Miancay*, the Most Fatal Horror! I am the embodiment of the mixture, and in here, I rule!"

Cadderly's mind whirled along the terrible possibilities. He knew that name, *Tuanta Quiro Miancay*. He, above anyone else, understood the power of the chaos curse, for he had been the one to defeat it, the one who had put it in the bowl, immersed it in holy water.

But he had not destroyed it; Rufo was proof of that. The chaos curse had returned, in a new and apparently more deadly form. Cadderly felt a warmth along his leg, emanating from his pocket. It took him only a moment to remember that he had a pin in there, an amulet that Druzil had placed on Rufo in Shilmista. The amulet was tuned to the imp, so that its possessor and Druzil could be easily joined telepathically. It was warm now, and Cadderly feared what that might mean.

"Your god is gone from this place, Cadderly," Rufo chided, and Cadderly could not deny the truth of that statement. "Your order is no more, and so many have come over willingly to my side."

Cadderly wanted to argue that, wanted to not believe it. He knew of the cancer that had crept into the order of Deneir, and of Oghma, even before this newest incarnation of the chaos curse. He thought of his last encounter with Dean Thobicus. Even as he had left the Edificant Library in the early winter, Cadderly knew that he would have to return and battle the ways that had become so ingrained in this place, ways contrary to the brother gods.

Now there was Rufo, and the fall of the library seemed to make perfect sense.

The pause now, the proverbial calm before the storm, could not last long, not with two volatile and scared dwarves at Cadderly's side. Ivan shattered that calm, roared and charged forward, and hit Rufo full force with a sidelong swipe of his great axe.

The vampire lurched and flew half a dozen feet to the side, but came up straight and seemed unhurt—indeed, was even laughing!

Pikel lowered both his head and his club and charged, but Rufo casually slapped him aside, launching him end over end to crash right through two wooden pews.

Ivan charged again, and Rufo spun to the side, snapped his hand out in the air. Some force emanated from that hand, some mighty energy that slammed Ivan and sent him flying off as wildly as if he had run into the edge of a tornado. The dwarf grunted, his breath blasted from his lungs, and flew off. He hit the edge of an arch with a sharp, sickening retort, rocketed head over heels to the floor, and skidded and bounced along, leaving a trail of blood behind him.

Cadderly feared that the blow had killed Ivan. He wanted to rush to his friend's side, to call upon Deneir's healing gifts and take away Ivan's pain. Not yet, he realized. He could not go to Ivan yet. He kept his holy symbol high in the air, presented with all his faith, as he steadily approached the vampire. He was chanting, praying, demanding that Deneir hear his call and come back to this place.

Rufo winced, and seemed pained by the presented symbol, but did not back down.

"You do not belong here," Cadderly said through gritted teeth, and the symbol, flaring with a silvery flame, was barely a foot from the vampire's snarling visage. Rufo reached out and clenched his hand over the eye above candle, closed his fist upon it. There came a hiss, and wafts of smoke rose, and Rufo was obviously pained. But the vampire held on stubbornly, proving that this was his place and not Deneir's, that Cadderly's holy magic was no good, not in here.

Gradually straightening, the vampire widened a smile, his free hand, in a clawing position, rising up to his ear, ready to strike, ready to lash out for stunned Cadderly's throat.

Pikel hit the vampire from the side, and, though his club did no real damage, the jolt saved Cadderly, pushing him and Rufo far apart.

Rufo and Pikel engaged in a wrestling and slugging match, but the vampire was too strong, and Pikel was soon hurled away. Rufo turned immediately on Cadderly, the prized prey of this group, who had staggered back many feet.

A tremendous, inhuman leap brought Rufo flying up to block Cadderly's way. Perched atop a pew, the vampire raised his arms wide and leaned forward, meaning to fall over Cadderly.

Up came Cadderly's holy symbol, and this time, the quick-thinking young priest enhanced the presentation. He pulled out his light tube, popped off the end cap, and put the beam right behind the forward-thrusting symbol.

Rufo recoiled, struck and pained by the sudden glare. He spun away, his robes flying defensively as a dark barrier against the burning beam, and wailed an ungodly, unearthly wail that resounded off every wall in the library, that fell upon the ears and tugged at the heartstrings of the many minions the evil vampire had fashioned.

The building itself seemed to rise in answer to that call, responding wails and moans coming into the chapel from every direction.

Rufo melted away, transforming suddenly into a bat, and fluttered about the wide hall. Another bat came in hard through the open door, and then something bigger than a bat, but with batlike wings.

Cadderly recognized Druzil, and the imp's presence answered many questions indeed.

They heard the shuffling of stiff-legged zombies in the hall outside; they heard those of the dark rising to Rufo's side.

They had to get out—Cadderly knew they had to flee this place. Pikel, obviously thinking along the same lines, staggered to the young priest's side and together they turned for Ivan, neither of them knowing how they were supposed to carry the battered dwarf out of there.

But Ivan wasn't down. Somehow, he was standing and seemed to have shaken off the terrific hit.

The three joined and ran for the door, Rufo's laughter echoing in their ears every step. They cascaded down the hall and plowed into a jumble of zombies congregating in the foyer.

Ivan and Pikel cut through the throng like the prow of a ship through water, scattering bodies and limbs in every direction. Ivan's axe cleaved monsters in half or took limbs with every tremendous swipe, and the dwarf lowered his head and gored like a charging elk, ripping wide holes in zombie chests. Pikel flanked his brother, knocking zombies aside with his club, and Cadderly came right behind them, ready to strike, and yet, with the dwarves so efficient, the young priest had nothing to strike at!

For all their progress, though, Rufo was right behind, and a horrible, scarred vampire—Histra!—was beside him, along with that wretched imp.

Bolts of energy launched from Druzil's fingertips, scorching Cadderly's back. Rufo's mocking laughter and Histra's hungry hissing licked at the young priest's sensibilities.

"Where will you run?" Rufo cried.

Ivan's axe cut a zombie in half at the waist and the way to the open door (open to the twilight) was clear before them.

The doors swung closed with a bang that sounded like a nail in Cadderly's coffin.

"Where will you run?" Rufo cried again, and another barrage of Druzil's energy stung the running priest so badly that he nearly tumbled.

Cadderly thought to run past those doors, knowing that Rufo had closed them, that the vampire had placed a spell on them that would keep them closed.

Ivan and Pikel were never that subtle, or that quick thinking, especially on those few occasions when they were truly terrified. They cried out together, lowered their heads together, and hit the doors together, and no enchantment Rufo or anyone else could have placed on the doors would have held the portal against that charge.

The two dwarves rolled outside amidst flying splinters. Cadderly, running full out behind them, tried to jump clear of the tangle, but hooked his foot on Pikel's chin and went flying headlong to the ground.

Even that evasive, if unintentional, maneuver did not save the young priest from yet another of Druzil's volley's. Pain raced along Cadderly's razed spine. Ivan and Pikel each hooked him under one arm and ran along, dragging him with them. Ivan kept the presence of mind to scoop up the young priest's dropped light tube and holy symbol.

The slow zombies ambled out in pursuit, but the vampires did not, for the night had not fallen in full. Twenty paces down the path, Cadderly and the dwarves were running free.

But for how long? all three wondered. The sun was out of sight; the library was lost.

Fifteen
Nightfall

Shayleigh squatted atop the roof of the low structure behind the Edificant Library, eyeing the large, square building with mounting suspicion. She could tell that the fire had been fairly concentrated, as she would expect in a structure made mostly of stone, but it wasn't so much the fire that now worried the elf maiden. Two things struck her as more than a little odd. The first was the simple lack of activity around the library. Winter was on the wane and the trails were open, yet Shayleigh saw no priests milling about the place, stretching their weary limbs in the warming sunshine.

Even more curious, Shayleigh could not understand why all the windows were boarded over, especially after the fire—to her thinking, the library should have been thrown open wide to allow the smoke to filter out and fresh air to blow in. As it was, the Edificant Library was far from an airy place, but with the windows blocked, at least the ones on this side of the structure, the smoky air inside must be nearly overwhelming.

Percival, hopping along the branches of the nearest tree, did not provide much comfort. The squirrel was still obviously agitated—so wild, in fact, that Shayleigh feared he might have contracted some disease. He ran down right near her—she thought for a moment he was going to crash against her arm.

"What is it?" she said softly, trying to calm the squirrel as he hopped a circular dance on the branch.

Percival hopped down to the mausoleum roof, did that spinning dance again, chattering loudly, as if in protest, then leaped high, back to the low branch and sat facing the mausoleum squarely, still chattering.

Shayleigh ran a delicate hand through her golden hair, not beginning to understand what all of this was about.

Percival repeated the action, and this time, the squirrel's dance atop the low structure's roof was one of frenzy. He went flying back to the branch, again sitting facing the mausoleum directly, again sputtering protests.

Shayleigh realized that the squirrel was watching the low building, not watching her or the library.

"In here?" she asked, pointing straight down to the mausoleum roof. "Is something in here?"

Percival did a somersault on the branch, and his shriek sent shivers along the elf's spine.

Shayleigh stood up straight and stared down at the twig-covered slate roof. She knew enough about the customs of the humans to understand that this was a burial house, but that fact alone should not bother a squirrel, even one such as Percival, who seemed to have more understanding than a squirrel should.

"Something is in there, Percival?" she asked again. "Something bad?"

Again the white squirrel went into its frantic dance, chattering wildly.

Shayleigh crept to the front edge of the mausoleum and peeked over. There was one window, dusty and dirty, and the door was closed—but the elf maiden's keen vision showed her how clean the edges of that doorjamb were, showed that the door had been opened recently.

Shayleigh looked all around at the small field and the library's back grounds. With no one in sight, she gripped the edge of the mausoleum and gracefully rolled over, putting her feet near the ground, and hopped down.

Percival was on the roof then, near her and making more noise than the elf wanted to hear.

"Do be quiet!" Shayleigh scolded, her voice a harsh whisper. Percival sat very still and silent, his little nose twitching.

Shayleigh could see nothing moving beyond the dirty window. She fell into a deep trance and forced her eyes into the night vision of elves, where they could view things in the infrared spectrum, seeing heat and not reflected light.

From this perspective, too, the place seemed empty.

Shayleigh took little comfort in that as she let her eyes slip back into the normal spectrum of light and moved for the door. This was a crypt, after all, and any monsters inside might well be undead. Dead creatures were cold; they gave off no body heat.

Shayleigh winced at the creak of the old door as it rolled on its rusty hinges. Dim twilight filtered into the place, barely illuminating it. Shayleigh and her kin in Shilmista lived more under the stars than the sun, though, and she didn't need much light. She kept her eyes focused in the normal spectrum and silently entered, leaving Percival, who was chattering again despite her scolding, on the lip of the roof above the open door.

The mausoleum seemed empty, but the hairs on the nape of Shayleigh's neck told her otherwise. She slipped her longbow off her shoulder, as much to have something to prod about with as to have a weapon in hand, and moved in farther. She looked back to the door with nearly every step and noticed Percival perched nervously on the outside sill of the window, staring in with bulging eyes. The sight of the concerned animal almost made her laugh despite her trepidations.

She passed the first of the stone slabs, noticed then that there was more than a little blood—fairly fresh, it seemed—on the floor, along with a tattered burial shroud. The elf maiden shook her head at the continuing riddle. She slipped past the second slab, and looked at the far wall, the wall to the left of the door, lined by marked stones that she knew were grave markers.

Something—something out of place—about the far stone, the stone in the corner near the back wall of the mausoleum, caught her attention.

Shayleigh eyed it curiously for a moment, trying to discern what it was.

It was hanging crooked just a bit. Shayleigh nodded and slid a cautious step closer.

The stone flew off the wall, and the elf maiden leaped back. Out came a fat corpse, a bloated and rotting thing, to fall in a heap at the base of the wall. Shayleigh had barely registered the gruesome scene when another form leaped out of the open crypt, springing with incredible agility to stand atop the slab nearest the wall, barely a dozen feet from the startled elf.

Dean Thobicus!

Shayleigh recognized him despite the fact that half his skin had somehow melted away, and the remaining pieces were blistered and torn. She recognized the dean, and understood that he had become something terrible, something powerful.

The elf maiden continued to backpedal, thinking to cross the last slab between her and the door, use the final pillar as a block behind her, then turn and bolt. The day was long, but she knew that the light, any light, would be her ally against this one.

Thobicus crouched, animal—like, on the slab; Shayleigh, her muscles tense, expected him to spring at her. He just stared without blinking, without breathing, and she could not figure out the source of that stare. Was it hunger or fear? Was he a malicious monster or a pitiful thing?

She came beside the last slab, felt the pillar behind her shoulder. Her foot slid back and subtly turned.

The elf exploded into motion, darting behind the pillar, but the move had been anticipated and the heavy door swung closed with a tremendous crash.

Shayleigh skidded to a stop, saw Percival doing frantic somersaults on the windowsill. She felt the coldness of the dead man's approach at her back and knew then the truth, the foul demeanor of this undead monster. She spun about and went into a defensive crouch, backpedaling as Thobicus slowly stalked in.

"The door will not open," the vampire explained, and Shayleigh didn't doubt the claim. "There is no escape."

Shayleigh's violet eyes darted back and forth, searching the room. But the building was solid, with only a single window (leaded glass, which she could never get through in time) and the single door.

The vampire opened his mouth wide, proudly displaying his fangs. "Now I will have a queen," Thobicus said, "as Rufo has Danica."

The last statement hit Shayleigh hard, both for the proclamation of wretched Kierkan Rufo's return and the fact that he apparently had Danica in his clutches.

She looked to the door, and to Percival in the window, searching, searching, but she could not deny the truth of Thobicus's next statement.

"There is no escape."

* * * * *

By the time they stopped running, the library was barely visible, back along the winding trail and beyond many sheltering trees. Cadderly stood bent at the waist, gasping for breath, and not just for sheer physical exertion. What had happened to his library? his thoughts screamed at him. What had happened to the order that had guided him through all the years of his life?

Pikel, bleeding from several wounds, hopped about the small clearing frantically, several times even rebounding off the boulders lining the place on the south (which did not help his injuries), and sputtering "Oo oi!" over and over. Ivan just stood solemnly, staring back at the one visible top corner of the library, shaking his shaggy head.

Cadderly couldn't think straight, and Pikel's frenzy wasn't helping him any. On more than one occasion, the young priest's concentration narrowed on the problem at hand, seeking a solution, but then Cadderly would be brushed by Pikel, or loudly interrupted by an emphatic "Oo oi!"

Cadderly stood straight and eyed the green-bearded dwarf directly, and was about to scold Pikel, when he heard clearly the song of Deneir. It swept him away like he was a twig that had fallen into a swift stream. It didn't ask if he wanted to go along; it just took him in the current, gaining speed, gaining momentum, and all the young priest could do was hold on.

After a few moments, Cadderly found some control of his spiraling thoughts and he willingly steered himself to the middle of the stream, to the strongest notes of the song. He hadn't heard the melody this clearly since Castle Trinity, since he had destroyed his own father, Aballister, by sundering the ground beneath the evil wizard's feet. It sounded sweet, so very sweet, and relieved Cadderly of the grief for the library and his fears for the future. He was purely with Deneir now, basking in the most perfect music.

Corridors began to open wide to him, tributaries of the main river. Cadderly thought of the *Tome of Universal Harmony*, the most holy book of Deneir, the book inscribed with the very words of this song, though they were translated things. In the song, there were only notes, pure, perfect, but these notes corresponded exactly to the written text, the human translation of Deneir's music.

Cadderly knew this—Pertelope had known this—but they were the only two. Even Dean Thobicus, head of the order, had no idea of the way this music played. Thobicus could recite the words of the song, but the notes were far beyond his comprehension.

To Cadderly, it was as simple as turning pages, as following the flow of the river, and he went down one of those offered tributaries now, to the sphere of healing, and pulled spells of mending from the waters.

Minutes later, Pikel was calmed, his bleeding stopped, and Cadderly's few wounds were no more. The young priest turned to Ivan, who, by all appearances, had been hit the hardest in the brief encounter with the vampire, but to Cadderly's surprise, he found the yellow-bearded dwarf standing quietly, seeming unharmed.

Ivan returned Cadderly's dumbfounded stare, not understanding its source. "We got to hide," the dwarf reasoned.

Cadderly shook himself from his stupor; the song faded from his thoughts, but he kept faith that he could recall it if the need arose. "The open is better," the young priest reasoned. "In the light, away from the shadows."

"The light won't last!" Ivan sternly reminded him. The dwarf poked a finger to the west, where even the distant and tall mountains loomed dark now, their rim glistening in the very last rays of the day.

Without a word, or even a grunt, of explanation, Pikel rushed off quickly into the brush. Ivan and Cadderly watched him go, then turned to each other and shrugged.

"We shall find a place to hide the night," Cadderly remarked. "I'll seek the answers we need with Deneir. His blessing will protect . . ." Cadderly stopped abruptly and looked back to the library, his gray eyes wide with horror. The note of fear sounded again in his thoughts. Perhaps it was Deneir—inspired; perhaps it was just a logical conclusion by Cadderly, a moment when he considered everything in a light more clear. As mysterious as Pikel, the young priest ran back to the west, back toward the library.

"Hey!" Ivan roared as he took up the chase. Pikel came out of the bushes, then, smiling broadly and carrying his dripping waterskin.

"Huh?" he asked, seeing the others running fast back for the library. The dwarf gave a little whistle and rambled off in pursuit.

Cadderly cut to the side, a tight corner around some brambles. Ivan went right through the tangle and rammed the young priest sidelong out the other side.

"What?" the dwarf demanded. "Ye just said we'd be finding a place to hide! I'm not for going back in . . ."

Cadderly scrambled to his feet, his legs pumping before he ever got his balance, propelling him away from the grumbling dwarf. Ivan took up the chase again and paced him, and Pikel, taking similar, if painful, short cuts, was soon bobbing along on Cadderly's other side.

"What?" Ivan demanded again, trying to catch hold and stop the stubborn priest. They were at the edge of the library's entry walk then, between the lines of silent and well-groomed trees, in sight of the battered doors, closed again and apparently barricaded from behind.

"What?" Ivan growled wildly.

"She's in there!" Cadderly offered. Taking longer strides, the young priest moved ahead of the dwarves on the flat and open ground.

"Ye can't go in!" Ivan bellowed, not really understanding what Cadderly was talking about. "Night's falling full! Night's his time, the time of vampires!"

"Oo oi!" Pikel heartily agreed.

Cadderly's answer blew away any logic that Ivan could muster against going back into the library, against facing Rufo, whether or not the night had fallen.

"Danica is in there!"

Their legs were shorter, but their love for Danica was no less, and as Cadderly straightened and slowed, trying to figure out how to get through the barrier, trying to discern if the portal had been dangerously warded or trapped, Ivan and Pikel flew past him, heads down, calling out a united "Oooo!"

Rufo had bolstered the doors with both enchantments and heavy furniture and had placed half a dozen zombies behind the barrier, with orders to stand very still and simply hold the doors closed.

He shouldn't have bothered. By the time Ivan and Pikel had played out their momentum, they were face down in the foyer, with splintered wood and furniture and zombies raining down all about them.

Cadderly came in on the heels of the dwarves, his holy symbol held out strong and chanting the melodies of Deneirian music. He felt his power diminish as soon as he crossed the threshold into the desecrated place, but had enough of his momentum with him, and enough sheer anger and determination, to complete his call to his god.

The six zombies rose stubbornly and advanced on the dwarves and Cadderly. Then they froze in place, expressionless, and a golden light limned them all, head to toe. The edge where that light met either ragged clothing or skin blurred, and the glow intensified.

A moment later, the zombies were piles of dust on the floor.

Back by the entrance, Cadderly slumped against the jamb and nearly swooned, amazed at the effort it had taken him to bring Deneir into this place— amazed yet again that the Edificant Library, his library, his home, had become a place so foreign and uninviting.

* * * * *

She did not scream when Rufo leaned over her, because she did not think that anyone could hear. Neither did she struggle, for her bindings were too tight, her weakness too complete.

"Danica," she heard Rufo say softly, and the sound of her own name disgusted her, coming from that one.

The monk fell deeper into herself, tried to fall away from her corporeal body, for she knew what was to come. And for all that Danica had endured in her short life, the loss of her parents, the years of brutal and unforgiving training, the battles on the trail, she did not think she could survive this.

Rufo leaned closer; she smelled the stench of his breath. Instinctively, she opened her eyes and saw his fangs. She struggled hard against the unyielding bonds. She closed her eyes tightly, trying to deny the reality of this hellish scene, trying to will it away.

Danica felt the sting as Kierkan Rufo's fangs punctured her neck.

The vampire groaned in ecstasy, and Danica was filled with disgust. All she wanted was to get away, to flee her own battered body. She thought she would die, and she wanted to die.

To die.

The idea hung in her swirling thoughts, a flicker of salvation, the one route of escape from this horrid monster and the state of undeath that he desired for her.

Danica felt the sickness in her leg, felt the pain through all her beaten body, and she let go her defenses, accepted that sickness and pain, basked in it, called to it.

To die . . .

* * * * *

Kierkan Rufo knew true ecstasy for the first time in his life, a greater pleasure than even imbibing the chaos curse, when he felt the pulse of Danica's blood coming to his taste. Danica! This was far better than any vampiric meal he had tasted thus far. Danica! Rufo had desired her, craved her, since the moment he had first seen her, and now she would be his!

So lost was the vampire in the realization of his own fantasy, that it took Rufo a long moment to understand that the woman's blood was no longer pumping, that any sweetness he extracted from the wound on Danica's neck had to be taken forcefully. He kicked back to a kneeling position, staring down, perplexed, at this woman who would be his queen.

Danica lay perfectly still. Her breast did not rise and fall with the rhythms of breath; the dots of blood on her neck did not increase from the continuing flow of blood. Rufo could see that he had hit her artery perfectly. With other victims, the blood spurted wildly from such wounds.

But not now. Just little red dots. No force; no pulse.

"Danica?" the vampire asked, fighting hard to keep his voice steady. He knew, though. Beyond any rational doubts, the vampire knew, for Danica's face was too serene, too pale. And she was too, too perfectly still.

Rufo had wanted to bring Danica from life into undeath, into his realm to be his queen. She was tied and weak and could not escape, or so he thought.

Rufo's body trembled as he realized what had happened, what Danica had done. He fell back farther from her, to the bottom of the huge four-poster bed, brushed an arm across his bloody face, dark eyes wide with horror, and wider still with outrage. Danica had found an escape; Danica had found the one way out of Rufo's designs and desires.

Danica had died.

Sixteen
Pikel's Punch

Of all the things they had ever heard—the cries of wild animals in a mountain night, the screams of the dying on a field in Shilmista, the roar of a dragon deceived—none of them, not Cadderly or even hardy Ivan and Pikel, had felt their bones so melted as by the unearthly shriek of Kierkan Rufo, of the vampire who had lost his most precious of treasures.

Cadderly, when his wits returned, instinctively believed they should follow that sound, that it would lead to Rufo, and he, in turn, would lead to Danica. The young priest had a difficult time telling his dwarven companions that, though, and had a difficult time in his own mind in rationalizing any decision that would put him closer to the one who had loosed that wail! He looked behind him, out the door, and into the empty night. One step back, he knew, and the song of his god would sound more clearly in his thoughts. One step back . . . but Danica was ahead.

"Deneir is not with me," Cadderly whispered, to himself and not the others, "not close."

"Where are we off to?" Ivan prompted impatiently, his gnarly, hairy brow showing droplets of sweat, more from nerves than exhaustion.

"Up," Cadderly answered. "It came from the second floor, the private quarters."

They crossed the foyer and several smaller chambers, past the kitchen where Ivan and Pikel had worked as cooks for many years. They met no enemies, but the library was awakening around them. They knew that, could feel the sensation, a sudden chill in air that was not moving.

"Cadderly." The voice, the lewd, feminine voice, froze the three in their tracks, barely a dozen steps up the winding stair that led to the second floor. Cadderly, at the head of the line, his light tube in hand, turned about slowly, putting the beam over the low heads of Ivan and Pikel to shine directly on the scarred face of Histra.

The vampiress, baring her fangs, curled and hissed at the intruding light.

Pikel squeaked and launched himself, and his swinging club, smack into her, sending both of them tumbling down the stairs.

Cadderly swung about instinctively, facing up the stairs again, and threw up a defensive arm just in time to catch the charge of a ragged zombie. Back stumbled the priest, and Ivan, not really turning enough to comprehend what was happening up front, ducked and braced.

Over the low and immovable dwarf went Cadderly and the zombie, rolling in a clinch to join Pikel and Histra in the hallway below.

Pikel did a series of short hops, trying to flank the crouching vampiress. He waggled his club threateningly, then came forward in a rush, angling the club out and turning a complete spin, once and then again. He swirled out of the ineffective routine, and, dizzy, stumbled a single step.

"Eh?" the confused dwarf asked, for Histra was not in front of him, not where she had been.

Her fist connected on his shoulder, and Pikel spun again. Fortunately for the dwarf, he rotated the other way this time, and somehow the counterspin took all the dizziness from him, so that when he stopped (and luck again was with him), he found himself facing the advancing vampiress squarely.

"Hee hee hee," Pikel snickered, and he came forth in a tremendous burst, stepping somewhat to the side of his foe. Histra veered quickly to keep square, but Pikel, solid on his big dwarven feet, shifted one foot ahead of the other and threw himself at her in a purely straightforward attack. Hardened muscles corded and snapped, and the dwarf's tree-trunk club sneaked past Histra's upraised arm to smack her squarely in the face. She flew back as though launched from a crossbow, to slam the wall, but before Pikel could utter another "hee hee hee," he realized he had not, in any way, hurt her.

Pikel looked down at his club, then to the confident vampiress, then back to the club again, as though the weapon had deceived him.

"Uh-oh," the green-bearded dwarf muttered an instant before Histra's powerful slap sent him spinning. He did a perfect two-and-a-half somersault, ending up standing on his head against the wall.

Cadderly had better success against the zombie. He came up much faster than the awkward thing, and his finger was already set in the loop of the cord to his spindle-disks, two small disks joined by a short metal rod. He sent the adamantite disks spinning down to the end of their cord and recalled them to his hand, once and then again to tighten the string. As the zombie finally pulled itself to its feet, Cadderly snapped them out viciously at the thing's face.

The young priest winced at the sound of crunching bone. The zombie staggered backward several steps, but, compelled by commands it had not the intelligence to question, it came right back in, arms stupidly out wide.

The spindle-disks slammed home again, right under the chin, and when the thing began its next advance, its head lolled weirdly, with all of the supporting neck bones shattered.

It didn't rise again after the third hit, but as it fell to the floor, a tumbling dwarven missile, Pikel Bouldershoulder, went right over it, leaving the ground between Cadderly and Histra wide open.

Cadderly heard Ivan up on the stairs, engaged with some enemy. He glanced that way momentarily, then looked back to find that Histra had closed the ground, standing just a couple of feet before him, smiling that terrible, fanged smile.

Cadderly hit her solidly in the chest with the spindle-disks as she brazenly walked in, but the weapon only knocked her back a step, and she smiled again, even more widely, showing that it had not hurt her.

"Dear Cadderly," she purred. "You have no defense against me." Cadderly, like Pikel before him, looked down to the disks as if he had been deceived.

"Would you not prefer the fate I offer you?" Histra said teasingly. She seemed such a grotesque caricature to Cadderly, a mocking insult to the alluring, sensual woman she had once been. As a priestess of Sune, the Goddess of Love, Histra had primped and perfumed, had kept her curvy body in perfect physical condition, and had kept a light in her eyes that promised the purest of pleasure to any man she deemed worthy.

But now the skin of her face sagged, as did her cleavage, showing between the tatters of what had once been a beautiful crimson gown. And no perfume could overcome the burned stench that surrounded the maimed vampiress. Even worse, by Cadderly's estimation, was the look in her eyes, once a promise of pleasure, now the diabolical fires of unholiness, of evil incarnate.

"I offer you life," the ugly vampiress purred. "A better deal, for Rufo will offer only death."

Cadderly bolstered himself in the face of that awful image, and in the mere mention of Kierkan Rufo, using both to reinforce his faith, using both as a symbol, a clear reminder, of the fall to temptation. Up came his holy symbol, the light tube behind it, and never had the young priest presented the light of Deneir with so much of his heart in it.

Rufo had resisted Cadderly's symbol earlier, but Histra was not the master here, was still far from the full powers of vampirism. She stopped her advance immediately and began trembling.

"By the power of Deneir!" Cadderly cried, advancing a step, holding the symbol high and angling it down so that its flaring weight drove Histra to her knees.

"Well, we ain't going out that way!" A bruised and bloody Ivan cried as he half ran, half tumbled out of the stairway.

Cadderly growled and pushed the light lower, and Histra groveled and whimpered. Then the young priest looked to the stairs, to the host of zombies that were shuffling down behind Ivan. He looked across the hall, to Pikel, who was thankfully up again and running in circles—no, dancing, Cadderly realized. For some reason that Cadderly could not understand, Pikel was dancing around his club, gesturing with his stubby hands, his mouth moving more than Cadderly had ever seen it move.

Ivan took up the fight again at the entrance to the stairs, his mighty, wickedly sharp axe taking limbs off reaching, stubborn zombies with every swing. "There's a hunnerd o' the damned things!" the dwarf bellowed.

Something faster and more sinister than the zombies stepped through their ranks to stand before the dwarf. Ivan's axe met it head-on, and right in the chest, but as the blade connected, the vampire, not flinching, caught it by the handle and pushed it harmlessly aside.

"Hunnerd and one," the dwarf corrected dryly.

Cadderly growled and forced the symbol of his god right down on Histra's forehead, acrid smoke belching from the wound. The vampiress tried to reach up and fight off the attack, but there was no strength in her trembling arms.

"I deny you, and I damn you!" Cadderly growled, pressing with all his strength. Again, Histra was caught by the fact that she had not yet mastered her new state of undeath, that she could not quickly and easily transform into a bat or some other creature of the night, or melt into vapors and flow away.

"Hold him back!" Cadderly, knowing he had Histra defenseless, cried to Ivan. He started to call to Pikel, but just grunted, seeing that the dwarf was still weirdly dancing, worried that the dwarf's sensibilities had been knocked clear of his green-bearded head.

Ivan growled and launched a furious attack on the vampire, hitting the thing several times. But the monster, and its horde of zombies behind it, inevitably advanced. If it had been a loyal thing, a true comrade, the vampire would have rushed past the dwarf to save Histra, but as one of Rufo's two remaining vampiric minions, Baccio of Carradoon looked upon the powerful young priest and his flaring holy symbol and knew fear. Besides, Baccio realized, the demise of Histra would only strengthen his position as Rufo's second.

And so the vampire allowed this frantic and ineffective dwarf to hold him at bay.

Soon Cadderly was engulfed with black smoke. He kept up his call to Deneir, kept pressing the eye-above-candle on Histra's forehead, though he could no longer even see her through the acrid cloud. Finally, the vampiress collapsed, and Cadderly heard the thump as Histra fell hard to the floor. As the smoke wafted away, Cadderly saw that it was finished. He could only imagine—and he shuddered when he did!—the reward that awaited Histra. He thought of black, huddled shadows pouncing on her damned soul, dragging her down to hellish eternity. Still, the vampiress seemed much more peaceful in real death than she had a moment before. Her eyes reverted to their natural color, and she seemed almost at rest. Perhaps even great sins could be forgiven.

Cadderly had no more time to think about Histra. A single glance over his shoulder told him that he and his friends were being beaten back once more, that they could not, despite their fears for Danica and their determination to rescue the monk, defeat the library, Rufo's library, in the dark of night.

Baccio, too, had seen enough. With a single swipe of his hand, he sent Ivan flying away, skidding across the floor right beside Pikel. Pikel picked up his club with one hand and his battered brother with the other.

Cadderly cried out and faced the vampire squarely, presenting his symbol as he had against Histra. Baccio, an older and wiser man, and one who had more willingly gone into Rufo's service, flinched, but did not back down.

Cadderly thrust his arm forward, and Baccio winced again. Cadderly called out to Deneir and advanced a step, and Baccio found that he had to fall back. It lasted only a second, and Cadderly knew he had the upper hand, knew that if he pressed on with all his faith, he could destroy this one as he had destroyed Histra.

Baccio knew it, too, but the vampire smiled wickedly, unexpectedly, and mentally commanded his legion of zombies to swarm about him, to block him from the light of Cadderly's faith.

The first of those unthinking monsters was limned with light, as were the zombies Cadderly had met and defeated when first he and the dwarves had come back into the library. That one dissolved to dust, as did the next, but there were simply too many of the things.

Another shriek, a most terrifying wail, resounded off the walls, echoed down the stairway.

"The master is coming," Baccio mused from the back of the horde.

"To the door!" Ivan cried, and Cadderly, though his heart ached to think of Danica in this ungodly place, knew the dwarf was correct.

They rambled down the hall, easily outdistancing the slow-moving zombies. Pikel spun around the first door, slammed it closed behind them, and threw its latch.

"We will take another way up," Cadderly remarked, and he began scouring his memories, searching for the fastest route to the back stairs.

Baccio's hand smashed through the door, and the vampire's fingers casually began searching for the latch.

The three friends were running again, through the small rooms, past the kitchen, closing every door behind them. They came into the foyer, the dwarves angling for the open door, and Cadderly tried to push them straight across, toward the south wing and main chapel, where there was a balcony that led up to the second floor.

"Not out!" the young priest insisted.

"Not in!" Ivan promptly countered.

Kierkan Rufo was before them suddenly, halfway between the door to the open night and the door to the hall that would take them to the main chapel.

"Not anywhere," Ivan, skidding to a stop, remarked.

Up came Cadderly's holy symbol, the light tube shining behind it, casting its image on Rufo's face.

The vampire, trembling with rage at Danica's death, didn't shy away in the least, but began a steady approach that promised nothing short of a terrible death to the young priest.

Cadderly invoked Deneir's name a dozen futile times. They had to get out over the threshold, he realized, out of the place that Rufo had come to call home.

"Get to the door," he whispered to his companions, and he boldly stepped out in front of them. He was Cadderly, he reminded himself, chosen priest of Deneir, who had faced a dragon alone, who had sent his mind into the realm of chaos and had returned, who had destroyed the evil artifact, the *Ghearufu*, and who had overcome the terrible legacy of his heritage. Somehow none of that measured up now, not against Rufo and the fall this vampire represented, not against the ultimate perversion of life itself.

Somehow, somewhere, Cadderly found the strength to move out from the dwarves, to face Rufo squarely and protect his friends.

So did Ivan. The brave dwarf realized that Cadderly alone might be able to face off against Rufo and win. But not in here, Ivan knew. Cadderly could beat Rufo only if the young priest could get out of this desecrated place.

The yellow-bearded dwarf gave a whoop, charged past Cadderly, and skidded up before the vampire (who never took his flaming eyes off the young priest, his mortal enemy). Without fear, without hesitation, Ivan whooped again and slammed Rufo with a wicked overhead chop.

Rufo brushed the axe away and seemed to notice Ivan for the first time.

"I'm getting real tired o' this," Ivan grumbled at his ineffective axe.

The only luck poor Ivan had was that Rufo's mighty punch launched him in the general direction of the open door.

Cadderly came in hard and fast.

"You cannot hurt me!" Rufo growled, but the young priest had figured something out. He presented his symbol as best he could, holding both it and his light tube in one hand, but the real weapon was in his other hand. His finger was still fast in the loop of the spindle-disks, but they bounced along low to the floor at his side, for Cadderly now understood that they would have no real effect on a vampire. As he rushed, he had taken his second weapon off his belt, his ram's-head walking stick, which had been enchanted by a wizard friend in Carradoon.

Rufo unwittingly accepted the blow, and the enchanted weapon tore the skin from half of his face.

Cadderly's arm pumped again for a second strike, but Rufo caught his wrist and bent it over backward, forcing the young priest to his knees. Cadderly straightened his arm holding the holy symbol, used it to intercept Rufo's closing, leering face.

They held the pose for what seemed like eternity, and Cadderly knew he could not win, knew that in here even his supreme faith could not defeat Rufo.

He felt a splash against his cheek. Cadderly thought it blood, but realized in an instant that it was clean, cool water. Rufo backed off unexpectedly, and Cadderly looked up to see that a line of burned skin had creased the vampire's other cheek.

A second stream drove Rufo back, forced him to relinquish his grip on Cadderly's arm. The surprised young priest grew even more confused as Pikel stalked by, his waterskin tucked under one arm, every press sending a line of water at the vampire.

Rufo slapped at the water with smoking fingers and kept backing until his shoulders were against the foyer wall.

Pikel stalked in, his face as determined as Cadderly had ever seen it, but Rufo, too, straightened and stiffened his resolve, the moment of surprise past.

Pikel hit him again with the spray, but the snarling vampire accepted it. "I will tear out your heart!" he threatened, and came a step from the wall.

Pikel exploded into motion, turning a complete spin that dropped him to one knee and sent his club knifing across low to catch Rufo on the side of the leg. Surprisingly, there came the resounding crack of snapping bone, and the vampire's leg buckled. Down went Rufo heavily, and squealing Pikel was up and over him, club raised for a second strike.

"We got him!" unsteady Ivan bellowed from the door. Even as his brother cried out in victory, Pikel's club banged hard off the stone floor, rushed right through the mist that Rufo had become.

"Hey!" roared Ivan.

"Oooo!" agreed an angry and deceived Pikel.

"That's not fightin' fair!" Ivan spouted, and the yell seemed to take the last of his energy. He took a step toward his brother, stopped and regarded both Pikel and Cadderly curiously for an instant, then fell down flat on his face.

Cadderly glanced all around, trying to discern their next move—back in or out into the night?—while Pikel went for his brother. The young priest understood that Rufo was not defeated, knew that the other vampire and the host of zombies were not far away. Cadderly's eyes narrowed as he carefully scanned the foyer, remembering that Druzil, wretched and dangerous Druzil, was probably watching them even now. Cadderly had not forgotten the painful bite of the imp's magic, and even more so, of the imp's poisonous sting. That venom had dropped Pikel once, long ago, and while Cadderly had spells of healing to counter the poison, he suspected he would not be able to access them in here.

The night had fallen, and they were ill prepared.

But Danica was in here! Cadderly could not forget that, not for an instant. He wanted to go after her—now! To search every room in this massive structure until he found her and could hold her once more. What had awful Rufo done to her? his fears screamed at him. Spurred by that inner alarm, the young priest almost ran back toward the kitchen, back toward the zombie host and the lesser vampire.

Cadderly heard a calming voice, Pertelope's voice, in his head, reminding him of who he was, of what responsibilities his position entailed.

Reminding him to trust in Deneir, and in Danica.

It was a harder thing for the young priest than even entering this unholy place had been, but Cadderly moved to Pikel and helped support unconscious Ivan, and the three made their way back out into the open air, back out into the night.

Seventeen
One Night Free

They scrambled down the library's long front walk, between the rows of tall trees, and Cadderly, despite his urgency, could not help but think of how often he had viewed these trees as a sign that he was home. Cadderly's world had changed so dramatically in the last few years, but none of the previous turmoil, not even the deaths of Avery and Pertelope or the revelation that evil Aballister was, in truth, his father, could have prepared the young man for this ultimate change.

Cadderly and Pikel had to carry Ivan, the dwarf's head lolling back and forth, his bushy yellow hair scratching the exposed areas of Cadderly's skin. The young priest could hardly believe how much weight was packed into Ivan's muscular frame. Stooped low as he was to keep Ivan fairly level between himself and Pikel, Cadderly quickly began to tire. "We need to find a hollow," he reasoned.

The green-bearded dwarf bobbed his head in agreement.

"Yes, do," came a reply from above. Cadderly and Pikel skidded to a stop and looked up in unison, the distraction costing them their hold on poor Ivan. The unconscious dwarf pitched forward to hit the ground face first.

Rufo squatted on a branch a dozen feet above the companions. With an animal-like snarl—and it seemed so very fitting coming from him!—he leaped out, stepping lightly on the path behind the two. They spun about, crouching low, to face the vampire.

"I am already fast on the mend," Rufo chided, and Cadderly could see that the monster spoke truthfully. The wound Cadderly's walking stick had opened on Rufo's cheek was already closed, and the scar from Pikel's water had turned from an angry red to white.

The howl of a wolf cut the night air.

"Do you hear them?" Rufo said casually, and Cadderly found the vampire's confidence more than a bit unnerving. They had hit Rufo with every weapon they could muster, and yet, here he was, facing them again and apparently unafraid.

Another howl echoed through the night air.

"They are my minions, the creatures of the night," the vampire gloated. "They howl because they know I am about."

"How?" Cadderly asked bluntly. "How are you about? What have you done, Kierkan Rufo?"

"I have found the truth!" Rufo retorted angrily.

"You have fallen into a lie," the young priest was quick to correct. The vampire began to tremble; Rufo's eyes flared an angry red, and it seemed as if he would rush forth and throttle his nemesis.

"Uh-oh," muttered Pikel, expecting the charge and knowing that neither he nor Cadderly could stop it.

Rufo calmed suddenly, even smiled. "What of this might you understand?" he asked Cadderly. "You who have spent your days in worthless prayers to a god that keeps you small and insignificant. What of this might you understand? You who cannot dare to look beyond the limitations Deneir offers you."

"Do not speak his name," Cadderly warned.

Rufo laughed at him. He laughed at Deneir, and Cadderly knew it, knew that everything Kierkan Rufo had become mocked Deneir and all the goodly gods, mocked the value of, the very concept of, morality. And in Cadderly's thinking, that, in turn, mocked the very purpose of life.

The young priest, gray eyes steeled against this instrument of perversion, began a slow chant, demanding that the song of Deneir come into his head. Fire, Cadderly knew. He needed a spell of fire to hurt this one, to burn wounds that would not regenerate. How he wished Dorigen's onyx ring still held its dweomer!

Cadderly dismissed that wasted, unproductive thought and focused on his call to Deneir. He needed fire to cleanse the perversion, fire given to him, channeled through him, by his god. Cadderly's head began that familiar ache, but Cadderly did not relent, sent his thoughts sailing into the main flow of the melody's stream.

"I have her," he heard cocky Rufo say, and Cadderly's heart fluttered at that moment, and his concentration, for all his sense of purpose, wavered.

Pikel gave a squeal and rushed out in front of Cadderly, waterskin tucked under his arm. He howled and pressed, and the skin responded with a flatulent burst. Pikel looked down at the empty thing, the last drops of water dripping from its end. Then the dwarf looked to Rufo, looked into the monster's angry scowl.

"Uh-oh," Pikel whimpered, and he was diving aside before Rufo's backhand even connected. He rolled through several tight somersaults, until he collided with a tree, then hopped up, dropped his club to the ground again, and began that same curious dance he had taken up in the corridor of the library.

Cadderly did not turn aside, did not, would not, retreat from Rufo this time. The reference to Danica had disrupted his concentration, had pushed him from the flow of Deneir's song, and he had no time to fall back into it. He had his faith, though. Above everything else, young Cadderly had his convictions and would not show fear in the face of the vampire. He planted his feet firmly and presented his holy symbol, crying with all the strength he could muster, "Get you back!"

Rufo staggered to a stop and nearly retreated a step before he found, within the evil swirls of the chaos curse, the strength to resist. There was no smile on the vampire's face, though, and where his expression had once shown confidence, now there was only determination.

Cadderly advanced a step, so did Rufo, and they stood facing each other, barely three feet apart.

"Deneir," Cadderly said clearly. How the young priest wanted to fall back into the song of his god, to find a spell of fire, or a most holy word that would send waves of agonizing discord through the vampire's skinny frame! He could not, though, not with Rufo so close and so very strong. This had become a contest of will, a test of faith, and Cadderly had to hold on to the ground he had found, had to present his symbol with all his heart, and all his focus, squarely behind it.

The very air seemed to spark between them, positive and negative energy doing battle. Both men trembled with the strain.

In the distance, a wolf howled.

Every second seemed an eternity; Cadderly thought he would burst from the pressure. He could feel Rufo's evil, a tangible thing, washing over him, denying his faith. He could feel the strength of *Tuanta Quiro Miancay*, a diabolical brew he had battled before, a curse that had almost defeated him and all the library. Now it was personified, stronger still, but Cadderly was older and wiser.

Rufo tried to advance, but his feet would not come to the call of his desires. Cadderly concentrated on merely holding his ground. He didn't hope that Pikel would come rushing in, as before. He didn't hope for anything. His focus was pure. He would hold Rufo here until the dawn if necessary!

Bolts of green energy slammed into the young priest's ribs. He gasped and recoiled, and by the time he straightened and regained the edge of concentration, Kierkan Rufo was upon him, clutching his wrist, holding Cadderly's arm high to keep the symbol of Deneir out of his face.

"Allies have their places," Rufo chided.

Cadderly managed to glance to the side, to see Pikel hopping about and swinging his club desperately, chasing a teasing Druzil around the lowest branches of the nearest trees.

Rufo pressed forward, and Cadderly struggled helplessly. Ivan groaned on the ground behind him—Cadderly was surprised that the dwarf was even close to consciousness. Ivan would be of no help, though, not this time.

"I have her," Rufo said again, confident of his victory, and despite the rage that welled within Cadderly, he was caught in such a disadvantageous position that he could do nothing against the vampire's terrifying strength. Rufo was bending him backward; he thought his backbone would snap.

The vampire jerked suddenly, then again, and Rufo straightened, easing the pressure on Cadderly's spine. Rufo jerked again and groaned, his features twisted in pain.

As the fourth sting hit him, Rufo hurled Cadderly backward to the ground and wheeled about, and Cadderly saw four long arrows sticking from his shoulder blades. A fifth bolt whistled in, slamming Rufo's chest, staggering him, his red-glowing eyes wide with surprise.

Shayleigh continued a steady walking advance, calmly putting another arrow to her bowstring and sending it unerringly into the vampire. From the side, Pikel, tired of the fruitless chase, came bobbing out of the trees, club held high as he bore down on Rufo. The dwarf skidded between Cadderly and the vampire, and readied the club.

Rufo spun about suddenly, his hand thrusting in the air, sending forth a wave of energy that froze Pikel momentarily.

"Come find your lover, Cadderly," the vampire spat, taking no heed of yet another arrow that dove into his side. "I will be waiting."

Rufo's form blurred, a green mist coming up about him, engulfing him. Pikel came from his trance, shaking his head vigorously, his generous lips flapping noisily, and wound up to swing, but stopped abruptly as Shayleigh's next arrow passed right through the insubstantial vampire and thudded hard into the club.

"Oo" muttered the dwarf, considering the bolt.

"Is he going to keep doing that?" roared Ivan, and both Cadderly and Pikel swung about, surprised by the outburst.

Cadderly, back to his knees, stared hard at the tough dwarf—tough indeed, for Ivan's wounds, injuries the young priest had thought nearly fatal, did not seem so bad now!

Ivan noticed the stare and returned it with a wink, holding up his left hand to display a ring, a ring that Vander had given him at their parting. Cadderly knew the item, an instrument of healing that could even bring its wearer back from the grave, and everything then made sense to him.

Everything concerning Ivan, at least. The young priest rose to his feet and looked back the other way, to Shayleigh. What was she doing here, and how much might she know of Danica's fate?

"I have just returned," Shayleigh greeted as she neared the three, as though Cadderly's impending stream of questions were obvious to her. "I left Danica and Dorigen yesterday, in a pass high from this place, and would be halfway to Shilmista."

"Except?" Cadderly prompted.

"I saw the smoke," Shayleigh explained. "And your friend, Percival, came to me. I knew then that there was trouble at the library, but . . ."

Cadderly's face gave her pause, the young priest leaning forward, eyes wide, mouth open in anticipation.

"But I know not of Danica's fate," Shayleigh finished, and Cadderly slumped back on his heels. Rufo had told him Danica's fate, and he found that now, with Shayleigh's confirmation that Danica and Dorigen had reached the library, he could not deny the vampire's claim. Also, knowing the fate of the library, and the apparent probability that Danica and Dorigen had walked into its midst, Cadderly believed he now understood the source of the fire in the small chapel. Starting a conventional fire that would so consume a room in the stone library would not be easy, for there was little fuel to feed the flames. A wizard's fireball, though (and Dorigen was quite adept at those), would have sufficed.

"More than fire has attacked the library," Cadderly replied grimly to the elf. "Rufo has become something sinister."

"A vampire," Shayleigh said.

Cadderly nodded. "And there are others."

"One less," Shayleigh replied, to which the three friends looked at her curiously. "I found Dean Thobicus behind the library," the elf explained, "in the burial vault. He, too, was undead, but he was wounded by sunlight, I believe, and not so strong."

"And ye beat him?" Ivan asked, the dwarf neither sounding nor looking very hurt at all any more.

Shayleigh nodded. She stepped near Pikel and pulled hard on the arrow embedded in the dwarf's tree-trunk club. It came out with a pop, and Shayleigh held its tip up for the others to see. Its sharp point glistened a bright gray in the moonlight.

"Silver-tipped," Shayleigh explained. "The purest of metals, and one that the undead cannot ignore. I have few left, I fear," she explained, indicating her nearly empty quiver. "We encountered some trolls . . ."

"So we saw," said Ivan.

"I recovered some of those, and all the ones I used against Dean Thobicus," Shayleigh said. "But Kierkan Rufo just took a few with him, and I fear that my supply of arrowheads grows small." To emphasize her point, she reached down to a belt pouch and jiggled it.

"Me axe wouldn't hurt the things," Ivan huffed.

"Adamantite?" Shayleigh asked, nodding her head expectantly.

"That and iron," Ivan explained.

"Neither would my spindle-disks hurt Rufo," Cadderly added. "But my walking stick—" he held the fabulous ram's-headed baton up before him, "—is enchanted, in addition to being silver. It struck Rufo a terrible blow."

Ivan's head bobbed in agreement, then both he and Cadderly looked curiously at each other. Together they slowly turned their heads to regard Pikel, who sheepishly slipped his club behind his back.

"Just a club," Ivan remarked, sliding over to his brother and pulling the huge weapon out from behind Pikel. "I seen him take it from the trunk of a dead tree meself!"

"Just a club," Cadderly agreed. "Yet it hurt Rufo."

Pikel leaned over and whispered something into Ivan's ear, and the yellow-bearded Bouldershoulder brightened with understanding.

"He says it's not a club," Ivan explained to Cadderly. "Me brother calls it a . . ." Ivan turned a questioning glance back at Pikel, who hopped back to his toes and whispered again into Ivan's ear.

"Calls it a sha-lah-lah," Ivan explained happily.

Cadderly and Shayleigh echoed the curious word together, and then Cadderly figured it out. "A shillelagh," he said, and for a moment it made perfect sense, a shillelagh being a magical cudgel often used by druids. Such a weapon would certainly harm a vampire. A moment later, of course, it made no sense at all—where in the world did Pikel get a druid's enchanted cudgel?

"And the water?" Cadderly asked Pikel.

The proud dwarf jumped up on his tiptoes to put his lips to Ivan's ear.

Ivan's look soured as he, too, began to figure it all out, began to digest the impossibility of it all. "Druid water," he said dryly, his voice even-toned.

"Doo-dad?" Pikel squealed.

Again came the curious stares, all three wondering what in the world was happening with Pikel. Shayleigh and Ivan had seen Pikel tame a snake in Castle Trinity, but that, unlike the club and water, could be explained in other ways. But these events . . . What explanation might there be except that Pikel had found some measure of druidic magic?

With everything going on, though, this wasn't the time to press the issue, or to question their apparent good luck. Cadderly, Shayleigh, and even Ivan silently realized that if they told Pikel firmly enough that dwarves could not become druids, he might just believe them. That would do nothing except give them fewer weapons to use against Rufo.

"Then we do indeed have the means to strike Rufo," Cadderly stated firmly, ending the debate. "We have to get back into the library."

Pikel's smile went away, and Ivan was shaking his head before Cadderly ever finished the proclamation.

"On the morrow," Shayleigh put in. "If Danica and Dorigen are there, and we do not know that they are, there is nothing we can do for them this night. Trust in them. Rufo is strongest in the hours of dark."

A wolf's howl cut the night, answered by another, then a third and a fourth.

"And the vampire is mustering his forces," Shayleigh went on. "Let us be far from this place. In the night, movement is our only ally."

Cadderly looked back toward the library. Despite what Shayleigh had said, he did know, in his heart, that Danica was in there. Dorigen was in there, too, though the young priest had a terrible feeling that the wizard had met her end. Shayleigh's words about Rufo were true enough, though. This was Rufo's hour, and his allies would soon be all about them. Cadderly could not defeat Rufo, not at night, not inside the library.

He agreed and followed the elf maiden's lead as she led them off into the woods, Pikel pausing long enough to refill his skin with the clear water of a nearby stream.

Eighteen
Every Weapon

The howls erupted from every corner of shadow, from every bit of Rufo's night. Cadderly had known there were wolves in the Snowflakes, many wolves—everyone knew that—but none of the four friends suspected there were so very many so close!

Shayleigh kept the group on the move, shifting at unexpected angles through the mountain night, knifing between high lines of stone, along the very rim of deep gorges. The elf could see in the dark, and so could the dwarves, and Cadderly had his light tube, its beam kept very narrow, half concealed under his gray traveling cloak so as not to attract too much attention.

As the wolves inevitably closed in, their howls sounding like one long, mournful keen, the young priest was forced to cap the light and put the tube away. He stumbled along as best he could in a night that had grown darker still, with Pikel supporting him on one side, Ivan on the other, and Shayleigh trying hard not to get too far ahead.

At one point, it seemed as if they had been cut off, with a group of wolves howling farther along the same path they were traveling. Shayleigh looked back to the other three, her violet eyes shining clearly, even to Cadderly's poor night vision, and her expression revealing that she was fast running out of answers.

"Looks like we're fighting again," Ivan grumbled, and it was the first time Cadderly had ever seen the sturdy dwarf so obviously upset with that prospect.

Unexpectedly, the wolf pack up ahead ran on its way, across the trail and not down it at the companions. The wolves howled excitedly into the night, as if they had found some new quarry to pursue.

Shayleigh asked no questions about their good fortune. She spurred her friends ahead at full speed and came to a grove of fruit trees. Shayleigh would

995

have preferred evergreens, where dark needles might offer some cover, but the pursuing pack was not far behind and these trees were easy to climb, even for short-limbed dwarves. Up the four went, as high as the branches would allow, Shayleigh finding a secure nook and stringing her bow immediately.

The dark shapes of the large wolves came into the clear area to the side of the grove, their fur bristling silver and black in the meager light. One came to the tree right below Cadderly and Pikel, sniffing the air, then loosing yet another terrifying howl.

It was answered by all its dozen companions at the grove, and then by a larger group, the group that had been ahead of the four companions, somewhere off to the east. The cries to the east continued, heightened, and though this group had the four treed, they could not ignore the thrill of the chase. Off the pack ran, but Shayleigh and the others did not come down, the elf explaining that this might be the best defensible spot they would find for miles.

The howling continued for many minutes, frantic, as if the wolves were indeed on a fresh trail. Cadderly's heart fluttered at every cry—might it be Danica the beasts were chasing?

Then the howls lessened and became mixed with resonating snarls, and it seemed to the companions that whatever the wolves had been chasing was trapped.

"We must go help," Cadderly announced, but none of the others seemed ready to leap to the ground behind him. He looked at them, particularly at sturdy Ivan, as if he had been deceived.

"Three dozen wolves," the yellow-bearded dwarf remarked, "maybe more. All we'll be doing is giving them more to eat!"

Cadderly didn't flinch as he picked his way down to the next lowest branch.

Ivan huffed and shuffled in his own roost, moving close enough to slap Pikel and get him, too, moving. Agile Shayleigh was already on the ground, waiting for them.

Cadderly smiled secretly, glad to confirm once more that he was blessed by brave and righteous friends. The young priest's grin went away, though, and all four of the companions froze (except for Pikel, who was knocked from his perch and fell hard to the ground), when a tremendous explosion rocked the very ground under their feet and a ball of fire rose into the air in the east, accompanied by the cries of many wolves.

"Dorigen?" both Cadderly and Shayleigh asked together, but neither of them moved, not knowing what they should do.

Pikel groaned and regained his footing, shaking the twigs out of his green beard. Above, high in the tree, a small form skittered along, verily flying from branch to branch.

Ivan, in the highest perch, let out a shout and turned about, lifting his axe, but Shayleigh's call stopped him in time.

"Percival," the elf maiden explained. "It is only Percival."

Cadderly scrambled as high as he could go, meeting his squirrel friend. Percival chattered excitedly, hopping in circles on the branch, and Cadderly understood that the squirrel had been more than a casual observer in all of this, when, a moment later, he heard the frantic cries of a man, and the howls of the remaining wolves in pursuit.

Shayleigh and Pikel went back up into the tree, and all four, and the squirrel as well, fell silent, watching to the east. Shayleigh caught the movement first, and up came her bow, an arrow streaking off unerringly to take down a wolf that was nipping at the fleeing man's heels.

The man, startled and not believing he had any allies in this dark place, cried out as the bolt flew past. Cadderly recognized the voice.

"Belago," the young priest muttered.

Ivan dropped down branch by branch until he was at the lowest limb, Pikel joining him there. Both looked to the running man, figuring the angle of approach, and they shifted side by side to put themselves in line. Pikel braced Ivan's feet as the dwarf rolled under the branch, hooking his knees, his arms hanging down.

On came Belago, blindly, more wolves nipping at his heels. Another arrow sliced past him, the elf's aim perfect, but the frightened man seemed to not even register that fact. He seemed oblivious to everything except his belief that he was alone and helpless in a dark night and was about to be eaten by wolves.

He ran under the tree, only because that course was straightest, for he knew he had no time to climb.

Then he was caught, and he screamed as he went up suddenly, hoisted by powerful dwarven hands. Not knowing Ivan for an ally, he squirmed and lashed out, connecting on the dwarf's face with several solid hits. Ivan just shook his head and muttered curses against "stupid people."

Belago wasn't beginning to break free, but his squirming was preventing Ivan from getting him high out of harm's way. Finally the dwarf heaved Belago as high as he could and butted the man right in the face. Belago went limp in his arms, and Ivan, with Pikel's help, tugged him up to the branch.

Shayleigh's bow sang out several times, keeping the pack at bay as the dwarves straightened themselves out and hauled dazed Belago up a couple of branches.

"By the gods!" Vicero Belago whispered repeatedly, tears flowing freely when he at last came out of his stupor and recognized his saviors. "By the gods! And Cadderly! Dear Cadderly!" he wailed, standing on the branch to be closer to the young priest. "You have returned too late, I fear!"

Cadderly slipped over on the branch and stepped down to Belago's level, trying to calm the man. "Was Dorigen with you?" Cadderly asked at length, thinking still of the telltale explosion.

Belago didn't seem to recognize the name.

"Danica?" the young priest asked frantically. "What of Danica?"

"She was with you," the wiry alchemist replied, seeming sincerely confused.

"Danica came back to the library," Cadderly answered sharply.

"I have been out of the library for several days," Belago replied, and he quickly told his tale. As it turned out, the four friends knew more about the place than he; all the poor alchemist knew was that he had been put out, and that very dark things, it seemed, had subsequently occurred in the library. Belago had not gone to Carradoon, as Dean Thobicus had instructed. He figured to wait for Cadderly's return, or at least for the warmer weather. He had friends on the mountain and had taken refuge in a small shack with a hunter he knew, a man named Minshk, east of the library.

"Dark things were about," the alchemist remarked, referring to that time in the hunter's lodge. "Minshk and I knew that, and we were going to go to Carradoon tomorrow." He looked to the east, his eyes sad, and mournfully repeated, "Tomorrow.

"But the wolves came," the alchemist continued, his voice barely a whisper. "And something else. I got away, but Minshk . . ." Belago slumped on the branch and went quiet, and the four friends turned their attention back to the pack surrounding the grove. The wolves couldn't get to them, but those continuing howls would likely bring in something, or someone, that could.

"We should be getting outta here," Ivan offered.

For the first time, Vicero Belago's expression brightened. He reached under his heavy cloak and produced a flask, handing it toward Cadderly.

Pikel, meanwhile, had his own idea. He snapped his stubby fingers and grabbed the heavy axe from his brother's back.

Cadderly, concerned with Belago's offering, paid little heed to the dwarves' ensuing argument.

"*Oil of Impact*," the alchemist said excitedly. "I was going to make you another bandoleer of explosive darts, but I hadn't the time before Thobicus . . ." He paused, overwhelmed by the painful memory. Then his face brightened again and he pushed the flask out toward Cadderly.

"I had another flask," he explained. "Maybe you saw the blast. I was hoping to do another one, right before Ivan caught me, but I hadn't the time."

Cadderly then understood the fireball that had risen in the east, and he gingerly—so very gingerly!—accepted the gift from the alchemist.

"Hey!" Ivan cried, drawing everyone's attention. Pikel had won this round of their argument, shoving Ivan over so hard that he had to hang on to the branch by his fingertips to prevent himself from falling to the gathered wolf pack. Before the yellow-bearded dwarf could right himself or further protest, Pikel brought the axe down hard on the trunk of the tree, causing a small split. As soon as Ivan regained his balance, Pikel handed the axe back, and Ivan snatched it away, eyeing his brother curiously.

Not as curiously as Cadderly was watching. He, above all the others, even Ivan, understood what Pikel had become, what the dwarf's love of trees and flowers had given him, and the gravity of Pikel's action, the fact that the would-be druid had just brought a weapon against a living tree, did not escape the young priest. Cadderly shifted past Ivan, who was more than willing to slide away from his unpredictable brother, and came to Pikel's side, to find the green-bearded dwarf muttering—no, chanting—under his breath, a small knife in hand.

Before Cadderly could ask, for the young priest did not want to interrupt, Pikel slashed his own hand with the knife.

Cadderly grabbed the dwarf's wrist and forced Pikel to look at him directly. Pikel smiled and nodded, pointed to Cadderly, to the wound, and to the wound he had inflicted on the tree.

Cadderly came to understand as a single drop of Pikel's blood fell from his hand to land on the rough bark beside the small cut in the tree. The blood instantly rushed for the crack in the trunk and disappeared.

Pikel was chanting again, and so was Cadderly, trying to find, in Deneir's song, some energy that he could add to the dwarf's attempt.

More blood flowed from Pikel's wound, every drop finding its way unerringly to the tree's crack. A warmth rose up from that crack, the smell of springtime with it.

Cadderly found a stream of thought, of holy notes that fit the scene, and he followed it with all his heart, not knowing what would happen, not knowing what Pikel had begun.

He closed his eyes and sang on, ignoring the continuing snarls and howls of the wolves, ignoring the astonished gasps of his friends.

Cadderly opened his eyes again when the branch heaved under him, as though it had come to life. The tree had blossomed in full, large apples showing on every branch. Ivan had one in hand already, and had taken a huge bite.

The dwarf's look soured, though, and not for the taste. "Ye think I might be fattening meself up to make a better wolf meal?" he asked in all seriousness, and he pelted the apple onto the nose of the nearest wolf.

Pikel squealed with delight; Cadderly could hardly believe what he and Pikel had done. What had they done? the young priest wondered, for he hardly saw the gain of prematurely flowering the tree. The apples provided missiles they could throw at the wolves, but certainly nothing that would drive the pack away.

The tree heaved again, and then again, and then, to the amazement of everyone on the branch, except, of course, Pikel, it came alive, not alive as a plant, but as a sentient, moving thing!

Branches rolled up and snapped down, loosing showers of apples with tremendous force, pummeling the wolf pack. Even worse for the wolves, the lowest branches reached down to club them, crunching their legs under them or sending them spinning away. Belago nearly tumbled, fell right over his branch and held on desperately with wrapped arms. Ivan did fall, bouncing from branch to branch all the way to the ground. He came up at once, axe ready, expecting a dozen wolves to leap at his throat.

Shayleigh was beside him in an instant, but the dwarf needed no protection. The wolves were too busy dodging and running. A moment later, Pikel and Cadderly, and finally Belago (who came down only because he fell), were at Ivan's side. Some of the closest wolves made halfhearted attacks at the group, but the four friends were well armed and well trained, and with most of the pack scattering, they easily drove the stragglers away.

It was soon over, several wolves lying dead on the ground, the others gone from sight. The tree was just a tree again.

"Your magic bought us some time and some space," Shayleigh congratulated Cadderly. The young priest nodded, but then looked to Pikel, the green-bearded "doo-dad" smiling ear to ear. Cadderly didn't know how much of this animation had been his doing, and how much Pikel's, but now wasn't the time to explore the mystery.

"If they come back, use the flask," Belago offered, moving to Cadderly's side.

Cadderly considered the wiry man for a moment and realized that Belago was unarmed. He handed back the flask. "You use it," he explained, "but only if we absolutely need it. We've got a darker road still to travel, my friend, and I suspect we shall need every weapon we can muster."

Belago bobbed his head in agreement, though he did not know, could not know, the depth of the darkness of which Cadderly spoke.

As it turned out, they did not need Belago's flask that night, or anything else. Shayleigh put them on the move immediately, back to the west, to a grove of thick pines, and there they spent the rest of the dark hours, the five friends, and Percival, too, keeping a watchful eye from the highest boughs.

Cadderly could only assume they had hurt Rufo badly, for the vampire did not find them. That was a good thing, on the surface, but the young priest could not get it out of his mind that if Kierkan Rufo was not with him, the vampire might be with Danica.

Cadderly did not fall asleep until the night was almost at its end, until exhaustion overwhelmed him.

Nineteen
Lost Soul

Percival's chattering heralded the new dawn and brought poor Cadderly from a fitful sleep filled with nightmares. He remembered little of those horrid dreams when he opened his eyes to the glistening light of a bright new day, for they were surely the stuff of a dark night.

The young priest did know, however, that he had dreamt of Danica, and he was unnerved at that thought.

For while he was out here, in the morning light, his dear Danica was in there, in the library, in Rufo's evil hands.

The library.

Cadderly could hardly stand to think about the place. It had been his home for most of his young life, but now that time seemed so very long ago. If all the windows and doors of the Edificant Library were thrown wide now, the structure would remain a place of shadows, a place of nightmares.

Cadderly was shaken from his private thoughts by the sound of Ivan's rough voice, the dwarf taking command while sitting on a thick tangle of branches below the young priest.

"We got the weapons," Ivan was saying. "Belago there's got his bottle."

"Boom," Pikel remarked, throwing his hands up high. The force of the sudden movement nearly sent Ivan tumbling from the branch.

Ivan caught himself and started to nod, then stopped and slapped Pikel on the back of the head. "Me brother's got his club," the dwarf went on.

"Sha-lah-lah!" Pikel whooped in delight, interrupting again in an equally expressive manner. This time Ivan didn't react fast enough, and by the time he realized what had happened, he was sitting on the ground, picking clumps of sod out of his teeth.

"Uh-oh," Pikel moaned, figuring that last move would cost him another slap, as his brother began the steady climb back up to his branch.

He was right, and he accepted the punishment with a shrug. Ivan turned back to Shayleigh.

"Sha-lah-lah," Pikel said again, quietly this time, and without the expressive movement.

"Yeah," Ivan agreed, too exasperated to argue further. "And ye got yer silver arrows," he said to Shayleigh, though he was still eyeing his impetuous brother, expecting still another remark.

"My sword will prove effective as well," Shayleigh explained, holding up her fine, slender elven blade, its silver inlays gleaming bright in the morning light.

Ivan continued to scrutinize Pikel, who by this point had taken to whistling a cheery spring morning tune.

"Even better," the yellow-bearded dwarf said to Shayleigh. "And I got me axe, though it's not for hurting them vampire things. But it'll take a stiff-legged zombie in half!"

"Cadderly has his walking stick," Shayleigh offered, noticing the young priest stirring, looking for an easy route down to their level. "And more weapons than that, I would assume."

Cadderly nodded and fell heavily onto the branch tangle, sending it dipping. "I am ready for Rufo," he said groggily when the branch stopped bouncing.

"Ye should've slept more," Ivan grumbled at him.

Cadderly nodded in agreement, not wanting to get into an argument now, but in his heart he was glad he had not slept much. He would be wide awake when the trouble started, pumped full of adrenaline. His only enemy now was despair, and if he had dreamt longer of his missing love . . .

Cadderly shook his head, shook away the counterproductive thought.

"How far are we from the library?" he asked, looking to the west, where he thought the library should be.

Shayleigh motioned for him to look the other way. "Three miles," she explained, "to the east."

Cadderly didn't argue. The run through the trails been confusing at best, especially to one not blessed with elven night vision. Shayleigh knew where they were.

"Then let us be on our way," the young priest offered. "Before we lose any more daylight." He started down from the branch, but had to pause for Belago. The alchemist winked Cadderly's way and opened his weatherworn cloak, producing the volatile flask.

"Boom!" Pikel shouted from the branch above.

Ivan growled, Pikel quickly jumped to the next lowest branch, and Ivan's ensuing slap hit nothing but air, causing the dwarf to overbalance and tumble from his perch. He managed to grab Pikel's green hair during his descent, taking his brother with him.

They hit the ground together, side by side, Ivan's deer-antlered helm and Pikel's cooking pot flying away. Up they bounced to face each other squarely.

Cadderly looked to Shayleigh, who was trying to subdue a laugh and merely shook her head in disbelief.

"At least you didn't have to walk all the way back with them," the young priest offered. Belago let him pass, and Cadderly hopped down to break up the fight. In a way, the young priest was glad for the distraction. With the dangerous task and the grim possibilities staring them in the face, they could all use a bit of mirth. But Cadderly did not appreciate the dwarves' antics, and he let both the brothers know it in no uncertain terms when he finally pried them apart.

"His fault," Ivan huffed, but Cadderly, and Cadderly's accusing finger, was in his face, warning him to say no more.

"Oooo," Pikel muttered. When Belago came down a moment later, the dwarf leaned over and whispered "Boom" into his ear.

Cadderly and Ivan spun about, but Pikel was only whistling again, that cheery, innocent morning tune.

Shayleigh led them quickly, surely, and without hesitation along the myriad forks and turns in the confusing trails. The sun had barely begun its climb in the eastern sky when the Edificant Library, dark and cold, came into view, its square walls seeming to deny the warmth of the day.

They moved along the path five abreast, Ivan and Pikel on one end, Shayleigh and Cadderly anchoring the other, and poor, trembling Belago in the middle. It was only as they made the final approach, the broken doors in sight, that Cadderly took any real notice of their newest companion, the wiry man who was not a fighter. The young priest stopped the march with an upraised hand.

"You have no business going in there," he said to Belago. "Go instead to Carradoon. Warn the townsfolk of Kierkan Rufo and his creatures of the night."

Vicero Belago looked up at the young priest as though Cadderly had just slapped him across the face. "I'm not much for fighting," he admitted. "And I'm not thrilled at the prospect of seeing Kierkan Rufo, vampire or not! But Lady Danica is in there—you said it yourself."

Cadderly looked to Shayleigh, who nodded solemnly. "Determination is the only true weapon against one of Rufo's ilk," the elf put in.

Cadderly dropped a hand on Belago's shoulder, and could feel that the alchemist had drawn strength from his own words. As they resumed the march and neared the doors, though, the man trembled visibly once more.

This time it was Ivan who stopped them. "We should have our path marked out afore we go in," the dwarf reasoned.

Cadderly looked skeptical.

"We have no idea where Danica might be," Shayleigh said, "or where we might find Rufo and his most powerful allies."

"If we go wrong, we'll fight everything in the place afore we ever find Danica," Ivan argued, but then, as if he suddenly realized what he had just said, especially the part about fighting everything in the place, the fiery dwarf shrugged as if it no longer mattered and turned back to the door.

Cadderly took out his light tube and popped open its back compartment. He slid out the enchanted disk; even in the bright sunlight its glow was powerful. Then he took off his hat and set the glowing disk behind his mounted holy symbol.

The young priest looked back to the doors and sighed. At least now they would not be walking in dark places. Still, Cadderly wasn't thrilled with the prospect of wandering through the massive structure, with so many enemies to face, and with a limited amount of time. How many rooms could they search in one day? Certainly not half the number in the Edificant Library.

"We'll begin in the lower levels," Cadderly said. "The kitchen, the main chapel, even the wine cellar. Rufo probably took Danica and Dorigen to a place of darkness."

"You are assuming he has them," Shayleigh remarked, her tone reminding Cadderly that both the monk and the wizard were resourceful and cunning. "Let us keep in our thoughts that Danica might not even be in there."

Cadderly knew better. In his heart, he knew without doubt that Danica was in the library and in trouble. He started to answer the elf's doubts, but Percival answered for him, the squirrel doing a sudden, wild dance across the branches just above their heads.

"Hey, ye little rat!" Ivan bellowed, shielding his head with his burly arm.

Pikel seemed equally excited, but unlike his brother, the green-bearded dwarf wasn't protesting in the least. He pointed a stubby finger at the white squirrel and hopped up and down.

"What is it?" Cadderly and Shayleigh asked together.

Percival ran along the branch and, with a great leap, caught the edge of the library's roof, dancing along the gutter, turning a somersault and chattering excitedly.

Cadderly looked to Pikel. "Percival has found them," he stated more than asked.

"Oo oi!" the perceptive (at least where nature was concerned) dwarf agreed.

Cadderly turned back to his rodent friend. "Danica?" he asked.

Percival leaped high in the air, turning completely about.

Ivan roared in protest. "The rat found them?" he bellowed incredulously Pikel slapped him on the back of the head.

"We have nothing better," Shayleigh reminded the volatile Ivan, trying to stay yet another fight between the brothers.

Cadderly wasn't even listening. He had been with Percival for three years and knew the squirrel was not a stupid thing. Far from it. Cadderly did not doubt Percival understood they were looking for Danica.

He followed Percival, and his friends followed him, around to the south wing of the library. Much of the wing showed damage from the fire, but the wall and windows near the back of the building did not. Percival moved gracefully along the gutters, then picked his way carefully down the rough and cracked stone. With a final leap, he landed on the sill of a small second-floor window.

Cadderly was nodding before the squirrel ever stopped.

"Danica's in there?" Ivan asked doubtfully.

"The private room of Dean Thobicus," Cadderly explained, and it all made sense to him. If Rufo had Danica, a woman he had long desired, he would likely show her the most comfortable and lavish room in the library, and none was better suited than the dean's private chamber.

With Cadderly's confidence came a moment of sheer dread. If his logic was on track, and Percival was right, then Rufo did indeed have Danica!

"What's the quickest route through the building to that room?" Ivan asked, deciding not to continue his useless arguing.

"The quickest route is straight up," Cadderly remarked, drawing all their eyes skyward. Ivan grumbled for a bit, trying to figure some way to get them all up there. Finally he just shook his head, and when he looked back to the young priest to denounce the plan, the dwarf jumped in surprise. In place of his regular arms and legs, Cadderly now had the limbs of a squirrel, a white-furred squirrel!

Shayleigh, not so surprised, gave Cadderly the end of a fine cord, and up he went, easily scaling the wall to sit on the narrow ledge beside Percival.

The window was only a few inches wide, barely a squared crack in the wall. Cadderly peered in, the light from the disk on his hat casting a glow into the room. He couldn't see much of the chamber, though, for the window was more than a foot deep. He did see the bottom edge of the bed, though, and on it, under a satiny sheet, the outline of a woman's legs.

"Danica," he whispered harshly, straining to get a better angle.

"What do ye see?" Ivan called from below.

It was Danica. Cadderly knew it was Danica. He shifted back, willed his arms and legs to return to normal, and fell into the song of Deneir. He was too close now; he would not be stopped by simple stone.

"What do ye see?" Ivan demanded again, but Cadderly, lost in the song, the magic of his god, did not register the call.

He focused on the stone surrounding the window, saw it for what it was, saw its very essence. Calling to his god, he pulled his waterskin around from his back and squirted it in strategic locations, then placed his hands on the suddenly malleable stone and began to shape the material.

The window's thick glass fell out, past entranced Cadderly's working hands, and nearly clobbered Ivan as he stood, hands on hips, on the ground below.

"Hey!" the dwarf yelled, and Cadderly, even in the throes of the song, heard him. He considered his handiwork and remembered his friends, and worked a spur in the stone, that he could loop Shayleigh's cord securely about it.

Then it was done, and the window was wide, and Cadderly crawled into the room. Deneir went away from him when he entered the unholy place; he would have recognized that fact clearly if he had concentrated. Even the glow of the lighted disk, fixed on the front of his wide-brimmed hat, seemed to dim.

This, too, Cadderly did not notice. His eyes, and his thoughts, were squarely on the bed, on the figure of Danica, lying too still and too serene.

Shayleigh practically ran up the rope, rushing into the room beside Cadderly. Ivan, and then Pikel, powerful dwarven arms pumping, came up fast behind, with Pikel pausing long enough at the sill to haul poor Belago up the fifteen feet to the window.

Cadderly stood beside the bed, staring down, not finding the strength to reach out and touch Danica.

She would be cold to his touch. He knew that. He knew she was dead.

Shayleigh couldn't bear the suspense anymore; she could not bear to see Cadderly in such awful torment. She bent low over the bed and put her sensitive ear to Danica's pursed lips. A moment later, she rose, staring straight at Cadderly and slowly shaking her head. Her hand moved as well, shifting Danica's tunic to reveal the puckered wounds on the monk's neck, the twin punctures of a vampire's bite.

"Oooo," Ivan and Pikel moaned together. Vicero Belago sniffled and fought back tears.

That tangible confirmation that Danica was gone, that Rufo had taken her, sent a ball of grief spiraling through Cadderly, a spiked ball that pained the young priest in every corner of his soul, that tore at his heart and all his sensibilities. Danica dead! His love taken from him!

This Cadderly could not tolerate. By all the power of Deneir, by all the edicts of callous fate, Cadderly could not allow this to be.

He commanded the song of Deneir into his thoughts, forced its flow past the dullness of the evil veil that permeated this place. His head throbbed for the effort, but he did not relent. Not with Danica, his love, lying so pale before him.

Cadderly's thoughts careened into the flow, pushed open closed doors and rushed to the highest levels of power. He was gone from his friends, then, not physically, for his body stood very still beside the bed, but spiritually, his soul rushing free of its mortal coil into the realm of spirits, the realm of the dead.

So it was that Cadderly did not hear Shayleigh's shriek, and did not react as the strong hand shot out from under the bed to clasp the elf's ankle.

* * * * *

Cadderly could see the events in the room, but they were distant from him, somehow disconnected. Through a thick veil of smoky gray he saw his own body standing very still, saw that Shayleigh, for some reason, had apparently gone down to the floor and was being pulled under the bed.

Cadderly sensed the danger back in the room, sensed that his elven companion was in trouble. He should go to her, he knew, go to the aid of his friends. He hesitated, though, and stayed clear of his corporeal form. Shayleigh was among powerful allies—Ivan and Pikel were moving, he could see, probably rushing to her side. Cadderly had to trust in them now, for he knew that if he left this realm, he would not soon find the strength to return, not in the desecrated library. He was looking for a spirit, and spirits were fleeting things. If he hoped to get Danica back, he had to find her quickly, before she took her place in the netherworld.

But where was she? Cadderly had gone into the spirit world on several occasions, had gone after Avery Schell when he had found the headmaster lying dead, his chest torn wide, on a table in the Dragon's Codpiece tavern in Carradoon. Cadderly had gone into the spirit world after the souls of men he had killed, assassins who had been pulled down by shadowy things before the young priest could call out to them. He had gone into the spirit world after Vander, and had held back the malignant assassin Ghost while Vander found his way back to life through the enchantment of his regenerative ring.

The ring!

Cadderly saw it glowing clearly on Ivan's gnarled finger, the only distinctive thing in the room. He could use it, he believed, as a gate to get Danica back to the realm of the living. If he could somehow get Ivan to put the ring on Danica's finger, he might be able to find an easier way to usher her spirit back to her corporeal form.

But where was she? Where was his love? He called out to Danica, let the images in the room fade from his thoughts and sent his mind out in every direction. Danica's spirit should be here; she could not have been dead for long. She should be here, or at least there should be some trail of her passing that Cadderly could follow. He would pull her from the arms of a god if need be!

There was no trail. There was no spirit. No Danica.

Cadderly weakened with the realization that she was lost to him. Suddenly there seemed no purpose in his life, no reason to even bother returning to his body. Let Deneir take him now, he thought, and be done with his torment.

He saw a flicker of clarity in the dull plane he had left behind, a movement within the room. Then he saw the vampire, as clearly as he had seen Ivan's ring, coming out from under the bed.

Baccio ripped at a dull form—Shayleigh, Cadderly knew—and leaped up to his feet. He was undead, existing on both planes, as tangible to Cadderly in the spirit world as he obviously was to Ivan and the others in the material room. Yet the vampire took no note of Cadderly. Baccio's thoughts were squarely on the battle at hand, on the battle against Cadderly's friends!

Cadderly's focus became pure anger. His spirit shifted behind Baccio, his will narrowing like a spike.

* * * * *

Shayleigh was out of the fight before it ever really began. She hit the floor hard beside the bed and slid under, the vampire's strong hands slamming her shoulder as she tried to reach for her short sword.

The silver-tipped arrows had bounced free of Shayleigh's quiver with the impact, and that alone saved the wounded elf. Sheer luck brought her free hand atop one of those bolts and, without hesitation, Shayleigh whipped the thing around, sticking its silvery point deep into Baccio's eye.

The vampire went into a frenzy, battering Shayleigh, bouncing the bed up and down on its supports. Pikel lay flat on the floor by then, using his club like a billiard stick, poking it straight into Baccio's face to keep the vampire busy while Ivan yanked Shayleigh out into the clear.

Baccio came out, too, wailing and thrashing, most of his strikes landing squarely on poor Shayleigh. Pikel hit him good a couple of times, but the vampire was strong, and he accepted the blows and returned them tenfold.

Belago shrieked and cowered; Ivan rushed in with a vicious swipe, but his axe was useless against the vampire. Baccio had them on the defensive, had them dead.

The vampire lurched suddenly as if something had hit him from behind, and indeed, he had been struck, by Cadderly's spirit. He staggered forward, his trembling arms reaching behind him for some unseen wound.

What a beautiful target that presented eager Pikel. The green-bearded dwarf spat in his hands and rubbed them for a tighter grip on his shillelagh, then spun two complete circuits, building momentum, before bringing the tree-trunk club to bear against Baccio's face.

The broken monster flew away, crashing into the far wall. Still, Baccio reached around to his back, reached for the spike, the manifestation of Cadderly's will, which the young priest had driven into his back.

Cadderly's corporeal form shuddered then as the priest came back to the Material Plane. He moved deliberately, mercilessly. He reached for his hat, then changed his mind and went instead for a fold in his traveling cloak, a pocket he had sewn into the cloak during his weeks in the cave on the northern side of the Snowflakes, producing a thin, dark wand. Cadderly shook his head as he considered the instrument—over the weeks of idleness and during the excitement of the last day, he had nearly forgotten about this wand. Advancing on Baccio, the wand's tip leading the way, the young priest said calmly, "*Mas illu.*"

A myriad of bright colors exploded from the wand, every color of the spectrum.

"Ouch!" Pikel wailed, blinded by the explosion, as were all of Cadderly's friends. Cadderly, too, saw spots behind his eyelids, but he did not relent. "*Mas illu,*" he said again, and the wand complied, spewing forth another colorful burst of light.

To the friends, the bursts were optically painful but otherwise benign, but to the vampire, they were pure agony. Baccio tried to recoil from the explosions, tried to curl into a little ball and hide, to no avail. The shower of lights clung to him, attacked his undead form with the fury of hot sparks. To a living creature, the spark shower could only blind; to an undead monster, the shower could burn.

"*Mas illu*," Cadderly said a third time, and by the time the last burst ended, Baccio sat limply against the wall, staring at Cadderly with pure hatred and pure impotence.

Cadderly put away the wand and pulled the holy symbol down from his head. He walked up to stand before the wounded vampire and calmly, methodically, placed the glowing symbol on Baccio's broken face.

The vampire's trembling hand came up and clasped Cadderly's wrist, but the young priest didn't waver. He held firm his symbol and intoned a prayer to Deneir as he struck repeatedly with his ram'sheaded walking stick, thoroughly destroying the monster.

Cadderly turned about to see his four friends staring at him incredulously, amazed by the sheer, unbridled fury of the display.

Pikel moaned, and the end of his club dropped limply to the floor.

Shayleigh grimaced against the pain as she regarded Cadderly. Her right shoulder was badly torn, and the wheezing in her voice told Cadderly that Baccio's beating had probably broken a few ribs and collapsed one of her lungs. He went to her immediately, without saying a word, and sought the distant song of Deneir.

The melody's flow was not strong this time; Cadderly could not seek the higher levels of clerical power. The day was young, but he was already tired, he realized, so he accepted the weakness and found his way instead to minor spells of healing, pressing his hands gently but firmly against Shayleigh's ribs and then her shoulder.

Cadderly came back to full consciousness to find the elf resting more easily, the magic already knitting the wounds.

"You did not find Danica," Shayleigh reasoned, her voice determined but trembling from her pain and weakness. It was obvious to them all that she needed rest and could not go on.

Cadderly shook his head, confirming the elf's fears. He looked plaintively to the bed, to the serene form of his lost love. "She is not undead, though," he offered, more to bolster himself than the others.

"She escaped," Shayleigh agreed.

"Danica should not be in this place," Cadderly said. He looked determinedly to each of his friends. "We must take her from here."

"The mausoleum is clear," Shayleigh offered.

Cadderly shook his head. "Farther," he said. "We will take her to Carradoon. There, away from the darkness of Kierkan Rufo, I can better tend your wounds, and can put Danica to rest." His voice broke as he finished the thought.

"No!" Ivan said unexpectedly, drawing Cadderly's attention. "We're not for leaving!" the dwarf argued. "Not now, not while the sun's in the sky. Rufo got her, and he'll get another if we walk away. Yerself can go if ye need to, but me and me brother are staying."

"Oo oi!"

"We'll pay that one back for Danica, don't ye doubt!" Ivan finished.

Pay that one back. The sentiment bounced about Cadderly's thoughts for a while, gaining momentum and imparting strength. Pay that one back! Indeed, Cadderly would pay Rufo back. He found his heart in the thought of revenge.

"Take Danica to the mausoleum," he said to Belago and Shayleigh. "If the dwarves and I do not come to you by the time the sun has begun its descent, set out far from this place, to Shilmista or Carradoon, and do not return."

Shayleigh, as angered by the loss of Danica as any of them, wanted to argue, but as she started to reply, sharp pain racked her side. Cadderly had done all he could for her wounds; she needed rest.

"I will go with Belago to the mausoleum," she reluctantly agreed, accepting that she would only hinder her friends in her weakened state. She grabbed Cadderly's arm as he started to move away from her and locked his gray eyes with her violet orbs. "Find Rufo and destroy him," she said. "I'll not leave the mausoleum unless it is to come back into the library to your side."

Cadderly knew there was no way he would convince the valiant elf otherwise. Danica had been like a sister to Shayleigh, and the elf would never walk away from the one who had killed her sister. Understanding that sentiment, that he, too, would never walk away from this place unless Rufo was destroyed, Cadderly accepted her pledge with a knowing nod.

Twenty
Anguish

Ivan and Pikel quickly rigged the rope so that Danica's body could be lowered gently. Both the tough dwarves had tears in their eyes as they worked; Ivan reverently removed his deer-antler helm, and Pikel did likewise with his cooking pot.

When the rope was ready, Cadderly could hardly bring himself to move Danica into position. His anger could not hold against that wave of grief, the feeling of finality as he tenderly looped the elven cord under Danica's stiffened arms. He thought of going again into the spirit world to search for her, and would have gone, except that Shayleigh, as if reading his thoughts, was beside him, her hand on his shoulder.

When the young priest looked at the battered elf, her whole body quaking as she tried to hold her balance, he understood he could not expend the energy to go off again into the spirit world after Danica, that the consequences might be too high. He looked to Shayleigh and nodded, and she backed away, seeming satisfied.

It was decided that Belago should go down first, to cushion Danica's descent. The alchemist, seeming more determined than any of them had ever witnessed, took up the rope in both hands and hopped up onto the windowsill. He paused, though, then motioned for Ivan to come near.

"Ye got to do it," the dwarf said, coming close. "We need ye . . ." Ivan stopped in midsentence, realizing Belago's intentions, as the alchemist extended his arm.

"Take it," Belago offered, pushing the flask of explosive oil to Ivan. "You will need every weapon."

As soon as the dwarf had the flask in hand, Belago, without hesitation, slipped over the sill and descended quickly to the ground. Danica's body went

1011

next, and then Shayleigh, the injured elf needing nearly as much support as had Danica.

Cadderly watched forlornly from the window as the group slipped away toward the back of the library and the mausoleum. Belago had Danica's form over one shoulder, and though the load was extreme for the alchemist, he still had to pace himself so that the wounded Shayleigh could keep up.

When Cadderly turned away from the window, back to the room, he found Ivan and Pikel, helms tucked under their arms, heads bowed and cheeks streaked with tears. Ivan looked up first, his sorrow transformed into rage. "I gotta fix me axe," the dwarf said through gritted teeth.

Cadderly looked at the weapon skeptically—it seemed fine to him.

"Gotta put some silver in the damned thing!" Ivan roared.

"We haven't the time," Cadderly replied.

"I got a forge near the kitchen," Ivan retorted, and Cadderly nodded, for he had often seen the setup, which doubled as a stove.

Cadderly looked out the window. The morning light was full, sending long shadows to the west. "We have just one day," Cadderly explained. "We must finish our business before nightfall. If Rufo recognizes that we have been inside the library, as he surely will when he realizes that Baccio is destroyed, he will come after us with all his forces. I would rather face the vampire now, though only my walking stick and Pikel's club—"

"Sha-lah-lah!" the dwarf said determinedly, popping the cooking pot on top of his green hair.

Cadderly nodded, even managed a slight smile. "We must be done with Rufo this day," he said again.

"But ye'll have to kill him quick," Ivan protested, presenting his axe once more. "Kill him to death. Quick, or he'll just go into that green mist and melt away from us. I got a forge . . ." Ivan stopped in midramble and turned a wicked look toward Pikel. "A forge," he said again, slyly.

"Huh?" came Pikel's predictable reply.

"Makes the fire hot," Ivan explained.

"You will need a fire very hot to singe Rufo," Cadderly interjected, thinking he was following the dwarf's reasoning. "Magical flames that no forge could match."

"Yeah, and if we hurt him, he'll just go into a cloud," Ivan said, aiming the remark at Pikel.

Pikel considered the information, tried to connect the forge to Rufo. His face brightened suddenly, his grin ear to ear as he returned his brother's hopeful stare.

"Hee hee hee," both dwarves said together.

Cadderly didn't understand, and wasn't sure he wanted to understand. The Bouldershoulder brothers seemed secure in their secret plans, so the young priest let it go at that. He led them along the corridors of the second floor, the library quiet and brooding about them. They tore the covers from every window they crossed, but even with that, the squat stone structure was a gloomy place.

Cadderly took out his wand once more. Every time he noticed a particularly gloomy area, he pointed the wand at it and uttered the command *"Domin illu"* and, with a flash, the area became as bright as an open field under a midday sun.

"If we cannot find Rufo this day," the young priest explained, "let him come out to find his darkness stolen!"

Ivan and Pikel exchanged knowing looks. Rufo could likely counter the young priest's spells of light—Rufo had been a cleric, after all, and clerics understood such magic. Cadderly wasn't brightening the library for any practical reasons, then, but merely to challenge the vampire. The young priest was throwing down a gauntlet, doing everything he could to slap Rufo across the face. Neither Ivan nor Pikel was thrilled at facing the powerful vampire again, but as they followed their companion through the library, his anger unrelenting, the image of beaten Baccio still clear in their thoughts, they came to the conclusion that they would rather have Rufo as an enemy than Cadderly.

The three came down to the first floor, having met no resistance. Not a single zombie, vampire, or any other monster, undead or otherwise, had risen against them. Not a single answer had been offered to Cadderly's open challenge. If he had stopped to think about it, Cadderly would have realized that was a good thing, a sign that perhaps Rufo was not yet aware that they had come into his domain. But the young man was consumed with thoughts of Danica, his lost love, and he wanted something, some ally of Rufo's, or especially Rufo himself, to block his path. He wanted to strike with all his might against the darkness that had taken his love.

They came into the hallway that led to the foyer. Cadderly promptly started that way, for the main doors and the southern wing beyond them, where the fire had been. There lay the Edificant Library's main chapel, the place Rufo would have to work the hardest to desecrate. Perhaps the young priest might find sanctuary there, a base from which he and the dwarves could strike in different directions. Perhaps in that area Cadderly would find clues that would lead him to the one who had taken Danica from him.

His steps were bold and swift, but Ivan and Pikel caught him by the arms, and no amount of determination would have propelled the young priest against that strong hold.

"We got to go to the kitchen," Ivan explained.

"You have no time for silver-edging your axe," Cadderly replied sharply.

"Forget me axe," Ivan agreed. "Me and me brother still got to go to the kitchen."

Cadderly winced, not thrilled with anything that would slow the hunt. He knew he would not change Ivan's mind, though, so he nodded. "Be quick," he said to them. "I will meet you in the foyer, or in the burned-out chapel near it."

Ivan and Pikel leaned to the side to exchange concerned looks behind Cadderly's back. Neither were excited about the prospect of splitting the already small group, but Ivan was determined to go to his forge, and he knew that Cadderly would not be held back.

"Just the foyer," the dwarf said sternly. "Ye go sticking yer nose about, and ye're likely to put it somewhere it shouldn't be!"

Cadderly nodded and pulled free of the dwarves, immediately resuming his swift pace.

"Just the foyer!" Ivan shouted after him, and Cadderly didn't respond.

"Let's be quick," Ivan said to his brother as they both looked at the young priest's back. "He won't be stopping in the foyer."

"Uh-huh," Pikel agreed, and the two skittered off for the kitchen and the forge.

Cadderly was not afraid in the least. Anger consumed him, and the only other emotion nipping at its edges, fraying the wall of outrage, was grief. He cared not that Ivan and Pikel were separated from him, that he was alone. He hoped Kierkan Rufo and all his dark minions would rise to stand before him, that he might deal with them once and for all, that he might damn their undead corpses to dust, to blow on the wind.

He got to the foyer without incident and didn't even think of pausing there to wait for his companions. On he pressed, to the burned-out chapel, the room where the fire had apparently started, to search for clues. He tore down the tapestry blocking the way and kicked the charred door open.

The smoke hung heavy in the place, as did the stench of burned flesh, with nowhere to go in the library's stagnant, dead air. Cadderly knew immediately, just from that smell, that at least one person had perished here. Horribly. Thick soot lined the walls, part of the ceiling had collapsed, and only one of the many beautiful tapestries remained even partially intact on the wall, though it was so blackened as to be unidentifiable. Cadderly stared at the black cloth long and hard, trying to remember the image that had once been there, trying to remember the library when it had basked in the light of Deneir.

So deep was he in concentration that he did not see the charred corpse rise behind him and steadily approach.

He heard a crackle of dried skin, felt a touch on his shoulder, and leaped into the air, spinning so forcefully that he overbalanced and nearly fell to the floor. His eyes were wide, anger stolen by horror as he looked at the shrunken, blackened remains of a human being, a small figure of cracked skin, charred bone, and white teeth—those teeth were the worst of the terrible image!

Cadderly fumbled his walking stick and wand, finally presenting the wand before him. This creature was not a vampire, he realized, probably not nearly as strong as a vampire. He remembered his ring, its enchantment expired, and understood that the same could happen with the wand. Suddenly Cadderly felt foolish for his tirade in the upper level, for his waste of the wand's energy in stealing shadows. He tucked the wand under his arm and grabbed his hat instead. His free hand reached alternately for his walking stick and his spindle-disks, not sure of which would be the most effective, not sure if only enchanted weapons would bite into the flesh of this animated monster, whatever it might be.

Finally, Cadderly calmed and presented his hat, and his holy symbol, more forcefully. "I am the agent of Deneir!" he said loudly, with full conviction. "Come to purge the home of my god. You have no place here!"

The blackened thing continued its approach, reaching for Cadderly.

"Be gone!" Cadderly commanded.

The monster didn't hesitate, didn't slow in the least. Cadderly lifted his walking stick to strike, and reached back with his other hand, dropping the hat, to grab the wand. He growled at his failure to turn the thing away, wondering if the library was too far from Deneir now for him to invoke the god's name.

The answer was something altogether different, something Cadderly could not anticipate.

"Cadderly," the blackened corpse rasped, and though the voice was barely audible, the movement of air a strained thing from lungs that would not draw breath, Cadderly recognized the way his name had been spoken.

Dorigen!

"Cadderly," the dead wizard said again, and the young priest, too stunned, did not resist as she moved closer and brought her charred hand up to stroke his face.

The stench nearly overwhelmed him, but he stubbornly held his ground. His instincts told him to lash out with the walking stick, but he held firm his resolve, kept his nerve, and lowered the weapon to his side. If Dorigen was still a thinking creature, and apparently she was, then she must not have given in to Rufo, must not have gone over to the other side against Cadderly.

"I knew you would come," dead Dorigen said. "Now you must battle Kierkan Rufo and destroy him. I fought him here."

"You destroyed yourself with a fireball," Cadderly reasoned.

"It was the only way I could allow Danica to escape," Dorigen replied, and Cadderly did not doubt the claim.

The look that came over the young priest's face at the mention of Danica told Dorigen much.

"Danica did not escape," she whispered.

"Lie down, Dorigen," the young priest replied softly, as tenderly as he could. "You are dead. You have earned your rest."

The corpse's face crackled as Dorigen bent her tortured features into a grotesque smile. "Rufo would not permit me such rest," she explained. "He has held me here, as a present to you, no doubt."

"Do you know where he is?"

Dorigen shrugged, the movement causing flecks of skin to fall from her withered shoulders.

Cadderly stared long and hard at the gruesome thing Dorigen had become. And yet, despite her appearance, she was not gruesome, he realized, not in her heart. Dorigen had made her choices, and, to Cadderly's thinking, she had redeemed herself. He could have held her there, questioned her intensely about Kierkan Rufo and perhaps even garnered some valuable information. But that would not have been fair, he realized, not to Dorigen, who had earned her rest.

The young priest bent and retrieved his hat, then lifted his holy symbol and placed it atop the corpse's forehead. Dorigen neither retreated from it, nor was pained by it. It seemed to Cadderly as if the lighted emblem brought her peace and that, too, confirmed his hopes that she had found salvation. Cadderly lifted his voice in prayer. Dorigen relaxed; she would have closed her eyes, but she had no eyelids. She stared at the young priest, at the man who had shown her mercy, had given her a chance to redeem herself. She stared at the man who would free her from the torments of Kierkan Rufo.

"I love you," Dorigen said quietly, so as not to interrupt the prayer. "I had hoped to participate in the wedding, your wedding with Danica, as it should have been."

Cadderly choked up, but forced himself to finish. The light seemed to spread out from his holy symbol, limning the corpse, pulling at Dorigen's spirit.

As it should have been! Cadderly could not help but think. And Dorigen would indeed have been at the wedding, probably standing with Shayleigh behind Danica, while Ivan and Pikel, and King Elbereth of Shilmista stood behind Cadderly.

As it should have been! And Avery Schell and Pertelope should not be dead, should be there with Cadderly to witness his joining.

Cadderly kept his rage sublimated. He did not want that to be the last image poor Dorigen saw of him. "Farewell," he said softly to the corpse. "Go to your deserved rest."

Dorigen nodded, ever so slightly, and the blackened form crumpled at Cadderly's feet.

Cadderly considered it for a moment, was glad that Dorigen was free of Rufo. A moment later, he screamed, as loudly as he had ever screamed, the primal roar torn from his heart by the agony of the realization. "As it should have been!" he yelled. "Damn you, Kierkan Rufo! Damn you, Druzil, and your chaos curse!"

The young priest started for the chapel exit, nearly fell over in his haste. "And damn you, Aballister," he whispered, cursing his own father, the man who had abandoned him, and who had betrayed everything that was good in life, everything that gave life joy and meaning.

Ivan and Pikel thundered into the chapel, weapons held high. They skidded to a bumbling stop, falling over each other, when they saw that Cadderly was not in danger.

"What in the Nine Hells are ye yelling about?" Ivan demanded.

"Dorigen," Cadderly explained, looking to the charred corpse.

"Oo," Pikel moaned.

Cadderly continued to push for the exit, but then he noticed the large, box-like item strapped to Ivan's back and paused, his face screwed up with curiosity.

Ivan noticed the look and beamed happily. "Don't ye worry!" the dwarf assured Cadderly. "We'll get him this time!"

Despite all the pain, all the despair, the memories of Danica, and the thoughts of what should have been, Cadderly could not prevent a small, incredulous chuckle from escaping his lips.

Pikel hopped over and put his arm across his brother's shoulders, and together they nodded confidently.

It was impossible, Cadderly realized, but these were the Bouldershoulders, after all. Impossible, but Cadderly could not deny that it just might work.

"Me brother and me been thinking," Ivan began. "Them vampires don't much like the sunlight, and there's places here that never get any, windows or no windows."

Cadderly followed the reasoning perfectly—it scared him a little to think he could follow Ivan and Pikel's logic so easily!—and the notion led him to exactly the same conclusion as the dwarves had already reached.

"The wine cellar," Cadderly and Ivan said together.

"Hee hee hee," added a hopeful Pikel.

Cadderly led the charge through the kitchen and to the wooden door. It was closed and locked, barred from the inside, and that confirmed the companions' suspicions.

Ivan started to lift his heavy axe, but Cadderly beat him to it, bringing up his spindle-disks in a short, tight spin, then heaving them with all his strength at the barrier. The solid adamantite smashed through the door's wood and slammed the metal bar on the other side so forcefully that it bent and dislodged.

The door creaked open, showing the dark descent.

Cadderly did not hesitate. "I am coming for you, Rufo!" he cried, taking his first step down.

"Why don't ye just warn him!" Ivan grumbled, but Cadderly did not care.

"It does not matter," he said, and down he went.

Twenty-One
Bagged

The three had barely stepped off the rickety stairs when Rufo's zombies closed in on them. Dozens of dead priests—men who had held to their faith, Cadderly knew, and had not given in to Rufo's tempting calling—filtered around the wine racks, bothered not at all by the light shining from the young priest's wide-brimmed hat.

"Where we going?" Ivan asked, hopping out in front of the others, obviously intent on leading. A zombie reached for him, and his great axe promptly removed the thing's arm from its torso. That hardly stopped the mindless zombie, but Ivan's next chop, a downward strike on the collarbone, angled to go across the monster's chest, surely did.

Pikel immediately dropped his club to the floor and began that curious dance again.

"Where we going?" Ivan asked again, more urgently, the battle rage welling inside him.

Cadderly continued to ponder the question. Where indeed? The wine cellar was large, filled with dozens of tall racks and numerous nooks. Great shadows splayed across the floor, angled away from Cadderly and the lone source of light, making the room even more mysterious and foreboding.

Both Ivan and Pikel were into it by then, hacking and banging, Ivan ducking his head to thrash his antlers into one zombie's midsection, Pikel occasionally giving a squirt of his waterskin to keep the monstrous horde at bay.

"Close your eyes!" Cadderly cried, and the dwarves did not have to ask why. A moment later, a spark shower cut through the zombie ranks, dropping several of the monsters in their tracks. Cadderly could have wiped them all out, but he realized the dwarves were in control here and that he should use the valuable wand with restraint.

The dwarves could cut through the throng, but where should they go? Cadderly considered the cellar's layout. Using one of the lesser functions of the wand, he put a minor globe of light between the racks to his right, for he knew that at the end of those racks loomed a deep alcove. The light illuminated the cubby fully, and it was empty.

"To the back!" Cadderly called to his companions. "Straight across the cellar to the back wall."

It was only a guess, for though Cadderly was confident that Rufo would have sought the underground chambers (and the appearance of so many zombies added credence to this), where exactly he might find the vampire in this odd-shaped and uneven chamber was beyond him. He took up the rear as the dwarves plowed through the throng, cutting a wake so that Cadderly wasn't too engaged in fending off the zombies. The young priest's eyes darted back and forth, looking side to side as they crossed the racks, hoping to catch a glimpse of Rufo. Cadderly scolded himself for not keeping his light tube intact then, for the light on his hat was dispersed and could not seek the deepest crannies.

He pulled down both the lighted disk and the holy symbol, that he might better direct the illumination. Something fluttered across the shadows at the other end of the long racks, moving too quickly to be a zombie. His attention fixed on that spot, the young priest didn't notice the monster reaching for his back.

The blow nearly knocked Cadderly from his feet. He stumbled forward several steps and swung about, sensing the pursuit, his walking stick flailing across. It came up short of the mark, though, and the zombie waded in behind. Purely on instinct, Cadderly thrust out his holy symbol and cursed the thing.

The zombie stopped, held fast by the priest's magical strength. Yellow light limned its form, began to consume the edges of the zombie's material being.

Cadderly felt a wave of satisfaction in the knowledge that Deneir was with him. He pressed his attack, clenching his hand tight about the emblem of his station. The eye-above-candle flared to greater intensity; the glowing flames licking the zombie leaped and danced.

But the zombie remained, tapping the dark power of its master—its nearby master, Cadderly realized—for battle. Dark lines creased the fiery glow, breaking it apart.

Cadderly growled and stepped closer, invoking the name of Deneir, singing the melodies of the god's song.

Finally, his holy symbol made contact with the zombie, and the thing burst apart, falling into a mess of macabre chunks and puffing dust.

Cadderly fell back, drained. How powerful had Rufo become that the vampire's lesser minions could resist his holy powers so strenuously? And how far had the library gone from Deneir when Cadderly's call to the god could barely destroy such a minor creature?

"Get the durned thing off! Get the durned thing off!" Ivan yelled, drawing Cadderly's attention. The dwarf's goring horns had done their work too well, it seemed, for Ivan had a zombie stuck atop his head. It lay flat out and flailing away with its arms and legs. Pikel hopped frantically beside his brother, trying to line up a hit that would dislodge the zombie without taking Ivan's head off.

Ivan chopped the legs from another zombie that waded too near, then took a hit in the face from the one above. The dwarf tried a halfhearted swing high with his axe, but the striking angle was wrong. He went into a spin instead, the momentum forcing the zombie flat out.

Pikel braced himself and took up his heavy club. Around came the zombie's head, whipping past. Pikel was ready the next time, and he timed his strike perfectly.

The zombie was still impaled—Ivan had to carry it around for a while—but it was no longer fighting.

"Took ye long enough," was all the thanks Ivan offered his brother. A short burst launched them side by side into the next rank of zombies, which broke apart into bits in the face of dwarven fury.

Cadderly rushed to keep pace. A zombie intercepted, and it pained the young priest greatly to view his newest foe, for the dead young man had, in life, been a friend. A clubbing arm came across, and Cadderly parried. He dodged a second strike, fighting defensively, then consciously reminded himself that this was not his friend, that this animation was merely an unthinking toy of Kierkan Rufo. Still, it was not easy for Cadderly to strike out, and he winced as his walking stick obliterated his former friend's face.

The young priest pressed on to catch the dwarves. He recalled that he had seen something, something dark and quick, in the shadows.

Out it came from the side, from the wine racks. Pikel squealed and turned to meet the charge, but got bowled over and tumbled away with the monster. They rolled past Ivan, who was quick enough to chop the newest adversary's leg.

When the axe didn't bite in, both Ivan and Cadderly knew the nature of this foe.

"*Mas illu!*" the young priest cried, and the vampire howled as sparks fell over it.

"That one's yer own!" Ivan cried to his brother, and he rubbed the temporary blindness out of his eyes and went back to his zombie chopping. He paused and dipped his head, grabbing at the dead weight entangled there, and a host of monsters closed in, arms clubbing.

Cadderly started for Pikel, but saw that Ivan, with his encumbering load, was in more trouble. He rushed to join Ivan, smacked away those zombies he could reach, then took hold of the corpse and finally pulled it free of the dwarf's antlers.

Cadderly overbalanced as it fell loose, then found he was sailing backward even faster as a zombie punched him in the chest. He hit the stone floor hard, felt the breath blasted from his lungs, and his precious wand flew free of his grasp. By the time he regained his sensibilities, a zombie had its strong hands clasped firmly about his throat.

* * * * *

The vampire was agile, but none could roll better than a round-shouldered dwarf. Pikel enjoyed the ride, throwing his weight into every turn with enthusiastic abandon. Finally the living ball slammed a wine rack, and the old structure buckled, showering Pikel and the vampire with splintered wood and shards of breaking bottles.

Pikel took the worst of that, the breaking rack doing no more damage to the vampire that Ivan's axe had done. Pikel, cut in a dozen places, one eye closed by a sliver, found himself in tight quarters suddenly, the vampire against him, holding him tight in its impossibly strong arms, its sharp fangs digging at his throat.

"Oooo!" the dwarf growled, and he tried to pull free, tried to wriggle one arm out, that he might hit his adversary.

It was no use; the vampire was too strong.

* * * * *

Caddery thought to invoke Deneir's name, thought to present his holy symbol, thought to grab his walking stick and slam the zombie on the side of the head. He thought all of it and more at once, his mind whirling as the monster, its bloated face devoid of emotion, held the needed breath from his lungs.

Suddenly that bloated face rushed at Cadderly, slammed him hard, drawing blood from his lips. At first he thought the zombie had launched a new attack, then, as the thing steadily lifted from him, its grasp on his neck relaxed, and the young priest understood.

"Durned things keep getting stuck," Ivan grumbled, hoisting his axe higher and bringing the impaled zombie with it. He brought the blade close and tried to pry the zombie loose.

"Behind you!" Cadderly called.

Too late. Another of the monsters pounded Ivan hard on the shoulder.

Ivan looked at Cadderly and shook his head. "Will ye wait a minute?" he screamed into the zombie's face, and the monster promptly punched him again, raising a welt on his cheek.

Ivan's heavy boot stomped on the zombie's foot. The dwarf launched himself forward with all his weight, the sudden movement dislodging the last zombie from his axe. The two foes staggered backward, but the zombie somehow held its footing.

Ivan's hand whipped around, bringing the handle of the axe behind the zombie's shoulder, then back in front of its face. The dwarf's other hand went in a similar movement, grabbing the other end of the handle, just below the axe's huge head. With his hands behind the zombie's back and the handle crossing in front of it, tight across its shoulders and throat, Ivan had the thing off balance. It continued to club at the dwarf's back, but it was in too tight to be effective.

"I telled ye to wait," Ivan explained casually, and the muscles on his powerful arms corded and bulged as he pressed backward and down, folding the monster in half the wrong way.

Cadderly didn't see the powerful move. He was up and moving again. He searched for his wand, but saw no sign of it in the tangle and the darkness. He started for Pikel, but ran into a wall of zombies. Taking a circular route that moved him deeper into the cellar, Cadderly's attention was grabbed by something off to the side: three coffins, two open and one closed.

The young priest saw something else there, a blackness, a manifestation of evil. Huddled, shadowy images danced atop that closed coffin. Cadderly recognized the aura sight for what it was. As he had come to decipher the song of Deneir, the general weal of people he encountered was often revealed to him by shadowy images emanating from them. Normally Cadderly had to concentrate to see such things, had to call upon his god, but here the source of evil was too great for the shadows to be concealed.

Cadderly knew Pikel needed him, but he knew, too, that he had found Kierkan Rufo.

* * * * *

Pikel didn't like the feeling at all. The dwarf was a creature of natural order, who prized nature above all, and this foul, perverted thing was violating him, sinking its filthy fangs into the personal temple that was nature's gift to the dwarf.

He screamed and thrashed, to no avail. He felt his blood being drawn out, but could do nothing to stop it.

Pikel tried another tactic. Instead of pressing out with his arms, he tightened them to his sides, hoping the vampire would loosen its grip.

The monster's eyes widened in shock, and it began to tremble violently. Pikel understood when he felt the water, the "doo-dad" water being forced from his waterskin, soaking the front of his baldric and breeches.

The vampire broke the hold and leaped back, crashing into the part of the wine rack that had not collapsed, sending bottles flying. Smoke wafted from its chest, and Pikel saw that his squirting waterskin had drilled a neat hole there, right into the vampire's heart.

On came the raging dwarf, pounding with his club, crushing the perversion into the floor. He turned, sensing that zombies were converging from behind, but the undead wall parted as Ivan burrowed through to his brother's side once more.

* * * * *

Cadderly's remaining light source dimmed as he approached the coffins, his eyes set firmly on the dancing shadows, on the box that held Kierkan Rufo. He felt a warmth in his pocket then, which confused him for just a moment.

Cadderly stopped suddenly and lashed out to the side with his walking stick, smashing several bottles. A shriek and a flap of wings told him he had guessed right.

"I see you, Druzil," the young priest muttered. "Never will I lose sight of you!"

The imp became visible, crouched on the lip of one of the opened boxes.

"You desecrated the library!" Cadderly accused.

Druzil hissed at him. "There is no place here for you, foolish priest. Your god has left!"

In answer, Cadderly thrust forth his holy symbol and, for a moment, the light flared, stinging Druzil's sensitive eyes. These two had battled before, on several occasions, and each time Cadderly had proven stronger.

So it would be again, the young priest determined, but this time, Druzil, that most malicious imp, would not escape his wrath. Cadderly pulled forth the amulet, the link between him and the imp, and sent a telepathic wave at Druzil, calling loudly the name of Deneir. The image manifested itself in both combatants' thoughts as a sparking ball of light, floating toward Druzil from Cadderly.

Druzil retorted with the discordant names of every denizen of the lower planes he could think of, forming a ball of blackness that floated out to engulf the light of Cadderly's god.

The two wills battled halfway between the combatants. First Druzil's blackness dominated, but sparks of light gradually began to flash through. Suddenly the black cloud shattered and the sparking ball rolled over the imp.

Druzil shrieked in agony; his mind was nearly torn asunder, and he fled, half-crazed, looking for a corner, a place of shadows, a place far from the terrible, bared power of Cadderly.

Cadderly thought to pursue, to be rid of troublesome Druzil once and for all, but then the lid of the coffin flew away and a deeper darkness wafted out. Kierkan Rufo sat up and stared at Cadderly.

This was the way it had to be, they both knew.

Behind Cadderly, Ivan and Pikel continued to rain carnage on the unthinking minions, but neither the young priest nor Rufo noticed. Cadderly's focus was straight ahead, straight on the monster who had destroyed the library, who had taken Danica from him.

"You killed her," Cadderly said evenly, fighting hard to keep the tremor out of his voice.

"She killed herself," Rufo countered, needing no explanation as to whom Cadderly was speaking of.

"You killed her!"

"No!" Rufo countered. "You killed her! You, Cadderly, fool priest, and your ideas of love!"

Cadderly fell back on his heels, trying to sort through Rufo's cryptic words. Danica had died of her own accord? She had given up her life to escape Rufo, because she could not love Rufo, and could not accept his offer?

A tear gathered in Cadderly's gray eye. Bittersweet, it was, a mixture of pain at the loss and pride in Danica's strength.

Rufo came easily out of the coffin. He seemed to glide toward Cadderly, making not a sound.

But the room was far from quiet. Even Ivan was disgusted at the crunching sounds the zombies made when he hacked them, or when Pikel swatted them across the room. Fewer and fewer targets presented themselves.

Cadderly didn't hear it; Rufo didn't hear it. Cadderly presented his holy symbol, and the vampire promptly clamped his hand atop it. Their struggle found its apex in that small emblem, Rufo's darkness against Cadderly's light, the focus of the young priest's faith, the focus of the perversion's outrage. Acrid smoke sifted out between Rufo's bony fingers, but whether it was the vampire's flesh or Cadderly's symbol that was melting, neither could tell.

They held fast for seconds that became minutes, both trembling, neither having the strength to lift his other arm. It would end here, Cadderly believed, with these two conduits, himself for Deneir and Rufo for the chaos curse.

As the moments continued to slip by, as Cadderly forced himself to higher levels of power, remembering Danica and all that had been stolen from him, and as Rufo matched him every time, Cadderly began to understand the truth.

This was Rufo's place. For all his rage and all his power, the young priest could not hold out against the vampire, not here.

Cadderly grimaced, refusing to accept what he knew was reality. He pressed on, and Rufo matched him. His head ached to the point where he thought it would explode, but he would not let go of the song of Deneir.

Despair, black discord, found its way into the notes of that melody. Chaos. Cadderly saw red fumes in the crystalline, flowing river. The notes began to break apart.

Ivan hit Rufo hard from the side, with both his axe and his thrashing helmet. Neither weapon truly injured the vampire, but the distraction cost Rufo his moment of conquest, gave Cadderly the opportunity to break the clinch he could not win.

With a feral snarl, Rufo slapped the dwarf away, sent Ivan spinning head over heels into the nearest rack, to crash amid broken glass and splintered wood.

Cadderly's walking stick flashed across, tearing the vampire's upper arm.

Pikel came in next, pressing hard on his waterskin, forcing the last drops to spray forth.

Rufo cared nothing for the puny attack, and Pikel learned the hard way, to his dismay, that his enchantment had expired on the club. He hit the vampire full force, but Rufo didn't flinch.

"Ooooooo," Pikel wailed, following his brother's aerial course into the jumble.

Ivan's eyes were wide as he held one unbroken bottle, staring at it nervously.

Cadderly hit the vampire again, solidly in the chest, and Rufo grimaced in pain.

"I have you," the vampire promised, not backing down, and Cadderly could not disagree. The young priest went into a fury then, slapping wildly with his enchanted weapon.

Rufo matched him, and the vampire's strong fists soon gained him the advantage. In this desecrated place, in this chamber of darkness, Rufo was simply too strong.

Cadderly somehow managed to break the battle and retreat a step, but confident Rufo waded in right behind.

"Cadderly!" Ivan yelled, and both Cadderly and Rufo glanced to the side to see a curious missile heading for the vampire.

Rufo instinctively threw his arm up to block, but seemed unconcerned. Cadderly, recognizing the missile for what it was, timed his strike perfectly, hitting the flask at the same instant it bounced against Rufo's arm.

The *Oil of Impact* exploded with tremendous force, hurling Rufo against the far wall, throwing Cadderly backward to the floor.

The young priest sat up at once and considered the splintered handle of his ruined walking stick. Then he considered Kierkan Rufo.

The vampire leaned heavily against the back wall, his arm hanging loose by a single strip of skin, his eyes wide with shock and pain.

Cadderly came up with a growl, turned the remaining piece of his weapon in his hand to hold it like a stake.

"I will find you!" Rufo promised. "I will heal and I will find you!" A ghostly green light limned the vampire's form.

Cadderly cried out and charged, but slammed hard into the wall as Rufo dissolved into a cloud of vapors.

"No, ye don't!" Ivan bellowed, rising from the pile and pulling the boxlike item from his back.

"Oo oi!" Pikel agreed, rushing beside his brother, taking one of the offered handles. They skidded into the green vapor and pulled fiercely on the handles of the bellows they had stripped from their forge.

In his gaseous state, Rufo could not resist that suction, and the mist disappeared into the bellows.

"Ooooooo!" Pikel squealed and popped his fat thumb over the opening.

"Get him outside!" frantic Ivan roared, and the dwarves ran off for the stairs, yelling. "Oooooooo!" in unison.

Cadderly charged hard to keep up, holding his light ahead to show them the way. He spotted his lost wand, but had not the time to go for it.

Twenty-Two
The Highest Test

He's coming back!" Ivan yelled, and the bellows bulged weirdly as Rufo's corporeal form began to take shape once more, as the vapors began to solidify. "Ooooooo!" Pikel wailed, careening down the halls, the foyer in sight.

Cadderly skidded in first, throwing all his weight against the barricade that had been put in place to block the opening. He didn't move the material much, but he lessened its integrity, and when Ivan and Pikel hit, everything, Cadderly included, flew away. The young priest shook his head, both at the amazing power of rambling dwarves and to take the dizziness away, then he took up his wand, and followed closely.

Out into the sunlight scrambled the dwarves. Pikel's finger was no longer over the pointy opening of the bellows, but it didn't matter, for Rufo was no longer gaseous. Leather bulged and tore as a clawing hand ripped through the side of the bellows.

The dwarves ran on, dragging their load, getting Rufo as far from the gloomy library, his source of power, as possible. They cut under the shadows of the trees, out into an open, sunny field.

Rufo tore free and dug a firm hold on the turf. Both dwarves pitched headlong to the ground and came up sitting, each holding a broken handle.

With some effort, the vampire stood straight, cursing the sun, shielding his eyes from the blazing light. Cadderly stood before Kierkan Rufo, holy symbol presented with all his heart. The young priest, out from under the desecrated structure, felt his god strongly again. Rufo, too, felt Deneir keenly, Cadderly's words echoing painfully in his mind.

Rufo started for the library, but Cadderly danced around to intercept, his blazing holy symbol blocking the way.

1026

"You cannot escape," the young priest said firmly.

"You have made your choice, and you have chosen wrong!"

"What do you know?" the vampire scoffed. Rufo stood tall, defying the sun, defying Cadderly and his god. He felt the tumultuous swirl of the chaos curse within him, of *Tuanta Quiro Miancay*, that Most Fatal Horror. It was a concoction of the Abyss, of the very lowest planes.

Even in the sunlight, even battered as he had been in the fight, his arm hanging grotesquely at his side, Rufo stood strong. Cadderly could see that, could feel it.

"I deny you," the personification of *Tuanta Quiro Miancay* said evenly. The words filtered through Cadderly's thoughts, throwing up barriers, damming the river of his god's song. Rufo had spoken to Deneir, Cadderly realized, not to him. Rufo had made the claim that his choice had not been wrong, that his power was real and tangible—and he had made that claim against Deneir, against a god!

"They hold us back, Cadderly," the vampire went on, his calm tones showing strength and defiance. "They keep their secrets to themselves, cover them with pretty flowers and sunshine, petty dressings to keep us satisfied and behind which they might hide the truth."

Looking at the vampire now, standing tall and straighter than Kierkan Rufo had ever stood in life, Cadderly almost believed that Rufo had found truth. It seemed, too, as if a protective shell had formed about Rufo, a dark lining to battle the burning sunlight. How strong this one had become! The vampire continued, and Cadderly closed his eyes, the arm holding his holy symbol inevitably dropping low. The young priest didn't distinguish any of the words, just felt the hum, the alluring vibrations, deep in his soul.

"Well?" came a blunt and gruff question. Cadderly opened his eyes to see Ivan and Pikel, sitting side by side in the grass, still holding the broken handles and considering the face-off.

Well, indeed, the young priest thought. He looked squarely into his adversary's dark eyes.

"I deny Deneir," Rufo said calmly.

"You choose wrongly," Cadderly replied.

Rufo starting to hiss a response, but Cadderly froze the words in the vampire's throat, lifting again the symbol, the opened eye above a lighted candle. The sunlight brought new sparkles to the emblem, heightened its glory and strength.

In the face of that revealing glare, Rufo's dark shell melted away, and suddenly the vampire seemed not so powerful, rather a pitiful thing, a fallen man, a man who had chosen the wrong course and had spiraled down to the depths of despair.

Rufo hissed and clawed at the air. He reached for the holy symbol, meaning to engulf it as he had done inside, but this time the flesh on his skinny hand erupted into flames and curled away, leaving only whitened bone. Rufo howled in agony. He turned for the library, but Cadderly paced him, keeping that flaring symbol right in his face. And Cadderly began to sing the melodies of his god, a tune Kierkan Rufo could not withstand. Inside the library Rufo had gained the advantage, but out here, in the daylight, Deneir's song played strong in Cadderly, and the young priest opened himself up as a pure conduit for the truth of his god.

Rufo could not withstand the light of that truth.

"Oo," Pikel and Ivan muttered together, as Rufo fell back to the earth. Cadderly pressed low, singing with all his heart. Rufo rolled over and clawed at the ground to get away, like a desperate animal, but Cadderly was there in front of him, corralling him, forcing him to see the truth.

Horrible, wailing sounds escaped the vampire's throat. Somehow, Rufo managed to struggle back to his feet, to stare at the shining holy symbol in one last desperate act of defiance.

His eyes whitened, then fell back into his skull, and through the black openings wafted the red mist of the chaos curse. Rufo opened his mouth to scream, and from there, too, came the red mist, forced from his body into the open air, where it would diminish and cause no more pain.

When Rufo collapsed to the ground, he was no more than a hollow, smoking husk, an empty coil, and a lost soul.

Cadderly, too, nearly collapsed, from the effort and from the weight of the grim reality that now descended on him. He looked over his shoulder at the squat library. He considered all the losses he had witnessed, the losses to the order, the loss of his friends, of Dorigen. The loss of Danica.

Ivan and Pikel were beside him immediately, knowing he would need their support.

"She did right in choosing death," Ivan remarked, understanding that the tears rimming Cadderly's gray eyes were for Danica most of all. "Better that than fallin' in with this one," the square-shouldered dwarf added, motioning to the empty husk.

" . . . in choosing death," Cadderly echoed, those words striking a strange chord within him. She had killed herself, Rufo had said. Danica had willingly chosen death.

But why hadn't Rufo animated her? Cadderly wondered. As the vampire had animated so many of the others? And why, when he had gone into the netherworld, had Cadderly not been able to find Danica's spirit, or any trace of its passing?

"Oh, my dear Deneir," the young priest whispered, and, without a word of explanation, Cadderly ran off toward the northwestern corner of the library. The dwarves looked to each other and shrugged, then chased off after him.

Cadderly scrambled wildly, crashed through roots and bushes, clawing his way around to the back of the building. The dwarves, better at trailblazing than the taller man, nearly caught up to him, but when Cadderly got into the open field between the library and the mausoleum, he left the brothers in his dust.

He hit the mausoleum door at full speed, never considering that Shayleigh and Belago might have found a way to lock or brace it. In it swung, and in spilled Cadderly, skidding hard to the floor, scraping his elbows.

He hardly cared about the minor wounds, for when he looked to the left, to the stone slab where the two had placed Danica, he saw the. "corpse" under the shroud rising to a sitting position. He saw also that Shayleigh, with a terrified Belago beside her, was perched on the bottom of the slab, her short sword poised to plunge into Danica's heart.

"No!" Cadderly cried. "No!"

Shayleigh glanced at him, and she wondered in that instant if Cadderly, too, had been taken by the darkness, if he had come to save his lover in undeath.

"She's alive!" the young priest cried, clawing to propel himself toward the slab. Ivan and Pikel rambled in then, wideeyed and still not understanding.

"She's alive!" Cadderly repeated, and Shayleigh relaxed a bit as he arrived at the slab and pulled the shroud from fair Danica and wrapped his love in the tightest embrace they had ever shared.

Danica, back with the living again, returned it tenfold, and the day was brighter indeed!

"What of Rufo?" the elf asked the dwarves.

"Hee hee hee," Pikel replied, and both he and Ivan ran their fingers across their throats.

The four left Cadderly and Danica then, waited outside in the light that seemed brighter and warmer and more alive than any spring previous. Cadderly and Danica came out a few minutes later, the young priest supporting the injured woman. Already Cadderly had called for spells of healing to help the monk, particularly her ruined ankle, but the wound was sore and infected, and even with Cadderly's aid, it would take some time before it could support Danica's weight.

"I don't get it," Ivan stated, for all of them.

"Physical suspension," Cadderly answered for Danica. "A state of death that is not death. It is the highest mark in the teachings of Grandmaster Penpahg D'Ahn."

"You can kill yerself and come back?" Ivan balked.

Danica shook her head, smiling like she thought she would never smile again. "In suspension, one does not die," she explained. "I slowed my heart and my breathing, slowed the flow of blood through my veins, to where all who regarded my body thought I was dead."

"Thus you escaped the hunger of Kierkan Rufo," Shayleigh reasoned.

"And escaped my attention as well," Cadderly added. "That is why I could not find her when I entered the spirit realm." He looked at Danica and gave a wistful smile. "I was looking in the wrong place."

"I nearly killed you," Shayleigh said, stunned by the proclamation, her hand going to the hilt of her belted sword.

"Bah!" Ivan snorted. "It wouldn't be the first time!"

They all laughed then, these friends who had survived, forgetting for a moment the loss of the library, the loss of Dorigen, and the loss of their own innocence.

And loudest among them was Pikel's "Hee hee hee."

* * * * *

Cadderly led them back into the library the next day, seeking any lesser vampires left in dark holes, and putting to rest any zombies they encountered. When they came outside late that afternoon, the friends were certain the first two floors were clean of enemies. The next morning, Cadderly started his friends to work removing the most precious artifacts of the library, the irreplaceable artwork and ancient manuscripts. Danica was thrilled to find that all of Penpahg D'Ahn's notes had survived.

Even more thrilled was the monk, and all the others, when they found a single sanctuary within the darkness, a single spot of light that had somehow held out against the encroachment of Kierkan Rufo. Brother Chaunticleer had used his melodies as a ward against the evil, and his room had not been desecrated. Half-starved, his hair whitened from the terror he had endured, he fell into Cadderly's arms with sobs of joy and knelt upon the ground in prayer for more than an hour when the friends escorted him out.

Later that same day, a host of four-score soldiers arrived from Carradoon, having received word of the attack on the merchant caravan. Cadderly quickly put this group to work (except for a band of emissaries he sent back to the town with news of what had occurred and warnings to beware any strange happenings), and soon the library was emptied of its valuables.

Their encampment was on the lawn to the east of the library, at the back end of the field, closer to the wild trails than the gaping doors. This was too close, Cadderly informed them, so they broke down their tents, gathered up supplies, and moved down onto the trails.

"What is this all about?" Danica asked the young priest as the soldiers set up the new camp. A week had passed since the fall of Kierkan Rufo, a week in which the young priest had gathered his strength, had listened to the words of Deneir.

"The building is spoiled," Cadderly replied. "Never again will Deneir or Oghma enter it."

"You mean to abandon it?" Danica asked.

"I mean to destroy it," Cadderly replied grimly.

Danica started to ask what Cadderly was talking about, but he walked past her, back toward the field, before she could figure out where to begin. The monk paused a while before following. She remembered the scene outside Castle Trinity, Aballister's bastion of wickedness, after the wizard's fall. Cadderly had meant to destroy that dark fortress as well, but had changed his mind, or had learned that he had not the strength for such a task. What, then, was he thinking now?

Gathering black clouds atop the cliff to the north of the Edificant Library alerted all in the camp that something dramatic was going on. The soldiers wanted to secure their tents, pack their supplies tightly, fearing the storm, but Ivan, Pikel, Shayleigh, and Belago understood that this fury was well guided, and Brother Chaunticleer understood it perhaps best of all.

The group found Danica standing several feet behind Cadderly on the lawn before the squat stone structure. Silently, not wanting to disturb these obviously important happenings, they gathered about her. None but Chaunticleer dared approach the young priest. He regarded Cadderly and offered a knowing, confident smile to the others. And, though he was not a part of what was happening with Cadderly, he began to sing.

Cadderly stood tall, arms upraised to the heavens. He, too, was singing, at the top of his lungs, but his voice could hardly be heard above the roar of the wind and thunder from the black clouds, now swarming over the top of the cliff, edging their way toward the desecrated building.

A searing blast of lightning hit the library's roof. A second followed, then the wind tore in, launching shingles, then joists, to the south, across the mountainside. More lightning started several small fires. The clouds came low, seemed to hover and gather strength, then a tremendous gust of wind lifted the edge of the roof and ripped it away.

Cadderly cried out with all his strength. He was a direct conduit for the power of Deneir. Through the young priest the god sent his fury, more lightning, more wind. The roof was gone.

A solitary figure—it seemed as if one of the gargoyles lining the gutters had come to life—perched on the edge of that roof, shouting curses at Cadderly, invoking its own gods, denizens of the evil lower planes.

But here Cadderly was the stronger, Deneir the strongest by far.

A searing bolt of lightning hit the roof right beside Druzil, igniting a tremendous fire and throwing the imp far away.

"*Bene tellemara*," Druzil rasped, clawing his way toward the flames, realizing then that his time on this plane was at its end. He would leave now or be destroyed. He made it to the flames, blasts striking all about him, and uttered an incantation. Then he threw a bag of powder, which he had concocted in the library's deserted alchemy shop, into the fire.

The flames lifted and danced, blue then white-hot, and Druzil, after shouting one more curse Cadderly's way, stepped in and was gone.

The storm's fury intensified, bolt after bolt slamming the stone walls, diminishing their integrity. A darkness, funnel-shaped, reached down from the clouds. The finger of a god, it seemed, reaching down for the desecrated building.

Cadderly cried out, as if in pain, but Danica and the others resisted the urge to run to him, feared the consequences of disturbing what he had begun.

The storm crashed down in full, and the earth itself rolled to life, great waves of ground heaving at the library's foundation. The northern wall buckled first, fell inward, and, with it gone, both the front and back collapsed. Still the lightning blasted away; still the tornado grabbed at pieces of rubble and lifted them into the air, heaving them, like so much waste, far across the mountainside.

It went on unabated for many minutes, and the soldiers feared the very mountains would fall. Cadderly's friends knew better, though. They saw in their comrade a resolve and a glory beyond anything they had ever witnessed; they knew Cadderly was with Deneir fully, and that Cadderly's god would not harm him or them.

Then it was over, suddenly. The clouds broke apart so that shafts of sunlight shone down. One fell over Cadderly, outlining his form in silvery hues so that he seemed much more than a man, much more than a priest.

Danica approached him cautiously, Shayleigh and the dwarves right behind her. "Cadderly?" she whispered.

If he heard her, he did not show it.

"Cadderly?" she asked more loudly. She gave him a shake. Still there was no response. Danica thought she understood. She could appreciate the emotions that must be running through her lover, for he had just destroyed the only home he had ever known.

"Oo," Pikel and Ivan, and even Shayleigh, muttered in unison.

But their sympathy was misplaced, for Cadderly felt no remorse. He remained with his god and was seeing now a new vision, the vision that had haunted his dreams for many years. Without a word of explanation, he moved toward the scarred, rubble-strewn area, his friends in tow. Danica continued to call to him, to shake him, but he could not hear.

The vision was all-encompassing. The young priest remembered the extra-dimensional mansion that Aballister had created in Castle Trinity, remembered how he had marveled at how similar were the properties of magically created material.

A specific spot on the ground, a place flat and smooth and devoid of rubble, beckoned to him. That single spot on the ground became the only clear thing Cadderly could see outside of his mind's eye. He went to it, feeling the power of Deneir keenly, knowing what he must do. He began to sing again, and the notes were much different than those he had used to bring down the Edificant Library. These were sweet and cumulative, a building song with a crescendo that seemed very far away. He sang for minutes that became a half hour, then an hour.

The soldiers thought him insane, and Brother Chauncticleer merely shook his head, having no insight as to what his fellow Deneirian might be doing. Danica didn't know how to react, didn't know whether to try to stop Cadderly or just to stand back. In the end, she decided to trust her love, and she waited as the hour became two.

Long shadows filtered from the west, and Cadderly continued. Even Ivan and Pikel began to wonder if the storm and the earthquake had broken the man, had reduced him to a babbling idiot.

Danica held her faith, though. She would wait for Cadderly to finish—whatever he was doing—through all the next day if need be, even beyond that. She, all of them, owed the young priest at least that.

As it turned out, Danica did not have to wait through the night. With the western horizon pink with the last moments of the setting sun, Cadderly's voice lifted suddenly.

Brother Chaunticleer and many of the others ran near him, thinking that something grand was in store.

They were not disappointed. There came a sharp hissing sound, a crackle as if the sky itself were being torn asunder.

Then it appeared, on the ground before Cadderly, rising like a tree growing out of control. It was a tower, a decorated pillar of stone, an aerial buttress. It continued to grow, its tip rising into the air before Cadderly and the astonished onlookers.

Cadderly stopped his singing and fell back, exhausted, to be caught by his friends. The crowd murmured dozens of questions, most prominent among them, "What have you done?"

Danica asked that very question of Cadderly when she looked closely at his face, at the flecks of silver suddenly showing in his tousled brown hair, at the crow's-feet, the wrinkles that had not been there before, running out about his eyes.

She looked back to the buttress, a tiny portion of the cathedral of which Cadderly had oft spoken, and then back to her love, who had obviously aged with the effort. Danica grew worried, and still more with the serene look that had come over the tired and suddenly not-so-young priest.

Epilogue

Shayleigh had gone to Shilmista, and had come back in high summer to view the progress on Cadderly's new cathedral. She had expected a virtual army would be hard at work on the place, and was amazed at how few people were actually about, just Cadderly and Danica, Vicero Belago and Brother Chaunticleer, the Bouldershoulders, and a handful of sturdy men from Carradoon.

Progress had been made, though, and Shayleigh realized she should have expected no less. This was a construction of magic, not of physical toil, and it seemed as if Cadderly needed little help. Many areas were clear now of rubble, a tribute to the dwarves and the men from Carradoon, and three of the aerial buttresses were set in a line along the northern edge of what would be the new library. Twenty feet from them, to the south, Cadderly had begun construction on the wall, a delicate-looking structure.

Shayleigh gasped when she saw what the priest was now working on, a huge, arching window of multicolored glass and black iron that would fit into the wall in clear sight of the spaced buttresses. Cadderly paid attention to every detail as he worked over the rough design, flaring the tips of iron symmetrically, forming patterns with varying colors of the pieces of glass.

The elf was a creature of the forests, of the myriad beauties that nature offered and that men could not replicate, but Shayleigh found her heart lifted now, felt her spirit soaring as her imagination pictured this finished cathedral. There were too many fine details, too many intricate designs, for her to even appreciate them. It was like a wide-spreading elm, she thought, and Cadderly was painstakingly placing every individual leaf and twig.

Shayleigh found Danica along the eastern edge of the library's grounds, intently looking over a pile of parchments. Brother Chaunticleer was close by, singing to his god, calling up spells of preservation and protection as he watched over the piles of artwork and priceless manuscripts that had been brought out of the old library. Belago was close by him, inspecting the piles and singing, too. Apparently the wiry alchemist had at last found his way to a specific religion. And who could blame him? Shayleigh thought, and she smiled as she considered the man. Given the wondrous sights Belago had witnessed, most marvelous among them the construction continuing every day right in front of him, how could he not find his way to Deneir?

Danica's face brightened when she saw that her friend had returned. They exchanged warm greetings and hugs, and perceptive Shayleigh knew at once that Danica's smile hid much that was not so bright.

"He does that all day," the monk offered, pointedly looking to Brother Chaunticleer, though Shayleigh understood she was referring to Cadderly.

Shayleigh, trying to subtly change the subject, looked to the parchments on the ground before Danica.

"Lists," she explained. "Lists of men and women who will accompany me to Nightglow and the dragon's treasure. I have already sent emissaries to Shilmista."

"I passed them on the trails," Shayleigh remarked. "They probably have met with King Elbereth already, though I suspect they will tell my king nothing he does not already know."

"They will invite Shilmista to join the expedition," Danica said.

"That was expected," Shayleigh replied with a calm smile. "We understand and appreciate the friendship you and Cadderly have begun."

Danica nodded and, despite her resolve, could not help but look at her lover at the mention of his name. Cadderly was still full of energy—brimming with energy—as he worked on his vision, but he no longer appeared as a man in his early twenties. Despite the toil, his body had thickened somewhat; his muscles were broader and still strong, but not quite as sharp and hardened as they had once been.

"The construction takes a toll," Shayleigh remarked.

"The creation," Danica corrected. She sighed deeply, commanding the elf's full attention. "It was a choice," Danica began, "a choice between Deneir, this course, this purpose that Cadderly has found in his life, and . . ."

"And Danica," Shayleigh interjected softly, placing a sympathetic hand on the sitting monk's shoulder."

And Danica," the monk admitted. "A choice between Deneir's calling and the life that Cadderly, as a man, truly desired."

Shayleigh looked hard at the monk and knew that Danica truly believed her words. The generous young woman understood that Cadderly had chosen a higher love, a love that no mortal could ever match. There was no jealousy in Danica's tone, but there was indeed a sadness, a profound pain.

The two sat in silence, watching Cadderly and the dwarves. Ivan and Pikel had marked off another area, and were apparently discussing the next logical step to support the structure's already-standing towers.

"He will complete the cathedral," Danica said.

"A new Edificant Library."

"No," the monk replied, shaking her head and lifting her almond-shaped eyes to regard Shayleigh. "Cadderly never liked that name, never thought it fitting for a house of the god of literature and art and the god of knowledge. 'The Spirit Soaring' will be the name he gives this cathedral."

"How long?" Shayleigh asked.

"Cadderly and the dwarves have drawn up the plans," Danica answered, her voice trailing to a whisper. "Five years."

"Five years," Shayleigh echoed quietly, and yet, Danica had pointedly mentioned that Cadderly would live to see the completion. Only five years! "The creation takes from him," Shayleigh remarked. "It is as if he gives his own being for the cathedral's materials."

Exactly, Danica thought, but she had not the strength to answer. Cadderly had discussed it all with her, had told her this was his purpose in life. This cathedral, the Spirit Soaring, would stand for millennia, a tribute to the god he served. He had told her what the price would be, and together they had cried for the life they would not share. Soon after, Danica had bitten hard on her bottom lip and bravely added to Cadderly's point, telling him that the Spirit Soaring would be a tribute, too, to Cadderly, to the priest who had sacrificed so much.

Cadderly would hear nothing of it. The cathedral was for only the gods, and the fact that he was allowed to construct it was a gift, not a sacrifice.

"He hopes to live long enough to offer one service in the new cathedral," Danica whispered. Shayleigh rubbed her hand over Danica's shoulder, then, stricken mute, she walked away, to speak with Brother Chaunticleer and Vicero Belago. She could hardly believe the young priest's sacrifice. Humans lived a short enough time, but for one to give back perhaps three-fourths of that span was inconceivable to the long-living elf.

Danica watched Shayleigh for just a few steps, then her eyes inevitably turned back to Cadderly, back to the man she loved, and loved all the more for his determination in following the course his god had shown him. And yet, she found she hated Cadderly, too, hated that she had ever met the man and had given him her heart. When he was gone, and she was still young, how could she love another?

No, she decided, shaking her head against the pervasive pain. Better to have met and known Cadderly. Better to have loved him. That thought sent Danica's hand gently rubbing over her abdomen. She was hoping to conceive, hoping to give Cadderly another legacy, a living, breathing legacy.

Danica's smile, as she continued to watch the man, was bittersweet. She wondered if her eyes would ever again be free of tears.